PENGUIN  CLASSICS

THE ARABIAN NIGHTS
TALES OF 1001 NIGHTS
VOLUME 2

MALCOLM C. LYONS, sometime Sir Thomas Adams Professor of Arabic at Cambridge University and a life Fellow of Pembroke College, Cambridge, is a specialist in the field of classical Arabic Literature. His published works include the biography *Saladin: The Politics of the Holy War*, *The Arabian Epic: Heroic and Oral Story-telling*, *Identification and Identity in Classical Arabic Poetry* and many articles on Arabic literature.

URSULA LYONS, formerly an Affiliated Lecturer at the Faculty of Oriental Studies at Cambridge University and, since 1976, an Emeritus Fellow of Lucy Cavendish College, Cambridge, specializes in modern Arabic literature.

ROBERT IRWIN is the author of *For Lust of Knowing: The Orientalists and Their Enemies*, *The Middle East in the Middle Ages*, *The Arabian Nights: A Companion* and numerous other specialized studies of Middle Eastern politics, art and mysticism. His novels include *The Limits of Vision*, *The Arabian Nightmare*, *The Mysteries of Algiers* and *Satan Wants Me*.

The Arabian Nights
Tales of 1001 Nights

Volume 2
Nights 295 to 719

Translated by MALCOLM C. LYONS,
with URSULA LYONS
Introduced and Annotated by ROBERT IRWIN

PENGUIN BOOKS

PENGUIN CLASSICS

Published by the Penguin Group
Penguin Books Ltd, 80 Strand, London WC2R ORL, England
Penguin Group (USA) Inc., 375 Hudson Street, New York, New York 10014, USA
Penguin Group (Canada), 90 Eglinton Avenue East, Suite 700, Toronto, Ontario, Canada M4P 2Y3
(a division of Pearson Penguin Canada Inc.)
Penguin Ireland, 25 St Stephen's Green, Dublin 2, Ireland (a division of Penguin Books Ltd)
Penguin Group (Australia), 250 Camberwell Road, Camberwell, Victoria 3124, Australia
(a division of Pearson Australia Group Pty Ltd)
Penguin Books India Pvt Ltd, 11 Community Centre, Panchsheel Park, New Delhi – 110 017, India
Penguin Group (NZ), 67 Apollo Drive, Rosedale, North Shore 0632, New Zealand
(a division of Pearson New Zealand Ltd)
Penguin Books (South Africa) (Pty) Ltd, 24 Sturdee Avenue, Rosebank,
Johannesburg 2196, South Africa

Penguin Books Ltd, Registered Offices: 80 Strand, London WC2R ORL, England

www.penguin.com

This translation first published in Penguin Classics hardback 2008
Published in paperback 2010
007

Translation of Nights 295 to 719 copyright © Malcolm C. Lyons, 2008
Translation of alternative version of 'The seventh journey of Sindbad'
copyright © Ursula Lyons, 2008
Introduction and Glossary copyright © Robert Irwin, 2008
All rights reserved

The moral right of the translators and editor has been asserted

Text illustrations design by Coralie Bickford-Smith; images: Gianni Dagli Orti/Turkish and
Islamic Art Museum, Istanbul/The Art Archive

Printed in England by Clays Ltd, St Ives plc

ISBN: 978-0-140-44939-6

www.greenpenguin.co.uk

Contents

Editorial Note

This new English version of *The Arabian Nights* (also known as *The Thousand and One Nights*) is the first complete translation of the Arabic text known as the Macnaghten edition or Calcutta II since Richard Burton's famous translation of it in 1885–8. A great achievement in its time, Burton's translation nonetheless contained many errors, and even in the 1880s his English read strangely.

In this new edition, in addition to Malcolm Lyons's translation of all the stories found in the Arabic text of Calcutta II, Ursula Lyons has translated the tales of Aladdin and Ali Baba, as well as an alternative ending to 'The seventh journey of Sindbad', from Antoine Galland's eighteenth-century French. (For the Aladdin and Ali Baba stories no original Arabic text has survived and consequently these are classed as 'orphan stories'.)

The text appears in three volumes, each with an introduction, which, in Volume 1, discusses the strange nature of the *Nights*; in Volume 2, their history and provenance; and, in Volume 3, the influence the tales have exerted on writers through the centuries. Volume 1 also includes an explanatory note on the translation, a note on the text and an introduction to the 'orphan stories' ('Editing Galland'), in addition to a chronology and suggestions for further reading. Footnotes, a glossary and maps appear in all three volumes.

As often happens in popular narrative, inconsistencies and contradictions abound in the text of the *Nights*. It would be easy to emend these, and where names have been misplaced this has been done to avoid confusion. Elsewhere, however, emendations for which there is no textual authority would run counter to the fluid and uncritical spirit of the Arabic narrative. In such circumstances no changes have been made.

Introduction

The medieval Arabic story collection of *Alf Layla wa-Layla*, or the *Thousand and One Nights*, is best known in English as *The Arabian Nights*. It is reasonable to ask how old this classic work of Oriental fiction is, who wrote or compiled it and how many stories it contains. But such questions are almost impossible to answer. The collection was put together in a haphazard, unpoliced fashion over many centuries.

In the opening story which frames all the other stories in the *Nights*, the monarch Shahriyar, who has been sexually betrayed by his wife, cuts off her head and, thereafter, he takes a different virgin to bed every night and has her killed in the morning. In order to break the bloody cycle, Shahrazad, daughter of the king's vizier, volunteers to give herself to Shahriyar, but, in order to avert her execution, she starts to tell a story to her sister, Dunyazad, whom she has brought with her into Shahriyar's bedroom. Shahrazad leaves her story unfinished at the break of dawn, and Shahriyar spares her life in order to hear the rest. And so things proceed, with Shahrazad finishing one tale only to start a new one. This goes on night after night until, after a thousand and one nights, Shahriyar repents of his decision to have her killed.

This frame story of a clever bride telling stories to a jealous king in order to prolong her life goes back to a lost Sanskrit original dating from no later than the eighth century. At some point, stories from this Indian story collection were translated into Pahlavi Persian. The tenth-century Arab polymath al-Mas'udi refers to the Persian version, which was called *Hezar Afsaneh*, 'A Thousand Stories'. We do not know what was in this story collection. Although the Sasanian Persians seem to have had an extensive literature of entertainment, no examples have survived in their original Persian form. However, it seems likely that the stories of the *Hezar Afsaneh* were mostly didactic fables, often adapted from Indian originals (as was the case with the famous collection of animal stories known as the *Fables of Bidpai*). Such stories of the mirrors-for-princes kind gave guidance on good government and right conduct. The early Persian prototype of *The Arabian Nights* was probably a bit boring, and the wilder tales of marvels, monsters and mutilations were likely to have been the later inventions of Arab storytellers.

The Persian stories of *Hezar Afsaneh*, probably quite small in number, were in turn translated and adapted for an Arab audience. A ninth-century paper fragment of the opening page of the *Nights* survives (its title is *Kitab Hadith Alf Layla*, or 'The Book of the Tale of One Thousand Nights') but, though it features an early version of Shahrazad telling stories to her sister, the plot device of telling stories to prolong a life does not appear. However, Ibn Nadim's tenth-century discursive catalogue of books, the *Fihrist* (or 'Index'), mentions the story collection which he says derived from a Persian original, and he does give the frame story of Shahrazad telling stories for her life. Although he claims to have seen complete manuscripts of *The Thousand and One Nights*, he says that these comprised less than two hundred stories.

The oldest substantial surviving Arabic version of the *Nights* is a three-volume manuscript that today is in the Bibliothèque Nationale in Paris. It seems to have been put together in Syria in the late fifteenth century. It was this manuscript which formed the basis of the epoch-making translation into French by Antoine Galland (1646–1715), an antiquarian who had spent years in Istanbul studying the various pos-itions on the Eucharist taken by the Eastern Christian churches. He also collected old coins and other antiquities for the Royal Library (later to become the Bibliothèque Nationale) and the Cabinet des Médailles (a collection of coins, medals and antiquities that belonged to the French king). In the course of Galland's sojourns in the Middle East in the years 1670–75, 1675–6 and 1679–88, he had become fluent in Arabic, Persian and Turkish.

Back in France, Galland settled in Caen and published a number of scholarly works. He also assisted the Orientalist Barthélemy d'Herbelot in compiling the *Bibliothèque orientale*, a monumental work of reference mostly devoted to Islamic culture that was finally published in 1697. Around 1698, Galland translated the stories of 'Sindbad of the sea'. Then someone told him that the Sindbad stories were part of a much larger collection. This, he eventually decided, must be a longer version of the Arabic story collection known as *Alf Layla wa-Layla*, or, as he translated it, *Les Mille et une nuits*. (In fact, no early Arabic manuscripts of the *Nights* contain the Sindbad stories. They are found only in later manuscripts that were influenced by Galland's choices.) He used a Syrian manuscript of the *Nights*, though there are occasional instances of Egyptian vocabulary and turns of phrase in the text. This manuscript, which Galland bought from a friend in Paris and which ended up in the Royal Library, is, as already noted, the oldest substantial, surviving manuscript of the *Nights*. (The manuscript Galland worked from was probably in four volumes, but the fourth volume has since been lost.) There is no such thing as a canonical text of the *Nights* with a fixed number of stories in a fixed order.

The surviving three volumes of the manuscript translated by Galland contained only thirty-five and a half stories and the number of breaks within the stories into nights was well short of a thousand and one. Though he was convinced that there must be a longer manuscript of the *Nights*, Galland was unable to lay his hands on one. Therefore, in order to satisfy public demand, he added stories which had been told to him by a Syrian informant. These stories, the so-called 'orphan stories', include 'Ali Baba' and 'Aladdin'. There are no Arabic originals for them (though Arabic versions purporting to be the originals were produced by forgers in the nineteenth century). Galland also added the previously published Sindbad stories. In addition, in order to plump out his collection, he seems to have drawn on one or more Egyptian manuscripts of the *Nights*.

Galland probably intended that his translation *Les Mille et une nuits* (1704–17) should serve as a sort of sequel to d'Herbelot's *Bibliothèque orientale*. The stories offered fantasy and diversion, but edification also: 'They should also please by what they reveal of the manners and customs of Orientals, of their religious ceremonies, both pagan and Mohammedan; and these subjects are better brought out than in the authors who have written about them or in travellers' narratives.' Thus Galland claimed that he had tried to preserve the authentic way the Orientals spoke and felt – at least in so far as was compatible with *bienséance* (decorum). In fact, Galland's translation was elegant and courtly, as the conventions of eighteenth-century literature demanded. It was also heavily glossed; Galland, instead of using footnotes, sometimes explained Oriental practices within the text of his translation. Also, in cases where it seemed appropriate to him, he exaggerated the magnificence of palaces, royal robes and jewellery.

Muhsin Mahdi, the Harvard professor who in the 1980s edited the

Galland manuscript of the *Nights* in the Bibliothèque Nationale, is particularly critical of the liberties that the Frenchman took with his translation:

> Abandoning the generally lean structure and fast movement of the original in order to create a more prudish, sentimental, moralistic, romantic, or glamorous atmosphere, he was apparently willing to pay a heavy price to make his *Nuits* popular. All this, along with his frequently imperfect understanding or misunderstanding of the Arabic original and inexplicable significant omissions, reflects poorly on his knowledge of the language he was trying to translate, acquaintance with the habits and the customs of the Orientals he was trying to explain and art as a storyteller.

Be that as it may, precisely that quality of Galland's stories – 'prudish, sentimental, moralistic, romantic, or glamorous' – made them a great hit with the French reading public. More specifically, they appealed in the first instance to the ladies of the court and the salons. Galland had dedicated both the translations of the Sindbad stories and *Les Mille et une nuits* to the Marquise d'O, a lady in the service of the Duchess of Burgundy, and both these women took an interest in promoting his translations. Galland's earliest readers were mostly adult, highly cultured and female. This was an age when women presided over literary salons (an age which the cultural historian Jean Starobinski has characterized as that of 'the fictitious ascendancy of women'). Before Galland, Charles Perrault had won acclaim with the same audience when he published his *Contes* (1691–5), a collection of folk tales, including such famous stories as 'Sleeping Beauty', 'Bluebeard' and 'Cinderella', which were rewritten by him in an elegantly mock-simple style.

Earlier, Perrault had launched the fiercely debated 'Quarrel of the Ancients and Moderns', by claiming that seventeenth-century France had reached a higher level of civilization than that of ancient Greece and Rome. He attacked the ancients and, most specifically, Homer for barbarousness. Perrault's fairy stories had been collected and stylishly rewritten as a demonstration that there could be a distinctively modern French literary culture that owed little or nothing to classical precepts. Moreover, the fairy stories with his added glosses were, he claimed, more moral than most of the stories found in ancient Greek and Latin literature. Galland's collection of stories was similarly admired for the fresh repertoire of plots, settings and characters that it provided. 'Read

Sinbad and you will be sick of Aeneas,' the Gothic novelist Horace Walpole urged. Galland, like Perrault, wished to moralize and, in a prefatory note to his translation, he expressed the hope that those who read his stories would be ready to profit from the examples of the virtues and vices found in them.

Galland's French volumes were rapidly translated into English. The first English translation of the early volumes of *Les Mille et une nuits* seems to have been published London in 1708 in chapbook form. (A chapbook is a book or pamphlet of popular stories of the kind originally sold by pedlars.) For a long time, English readers were content with this translation of a translation. Only in the years 1838–41 did a three-volume translation appear, taken directly from the Arabic by Edward William Lane (1801–76). Lane, a distinguished Arabist, had spent many years in Cairo. On his return to England in 1836, he published his famous quasi-encyclopedic survey *Manners and Customs of the Modern Egyptians*. Lane seems to have intended his subsequent translation of the *Nights* to serve as a kind of supplement to this book. His translation was brought out by the same publisher, the Society for the Propagation of Useful Knowledge, and it was therefore aimed at a wide market. In his translation, the text of the *Nights* served as a pretext for lengthy and numerous footnotes explaining yet more aspects of the manners and customs of the Egyptians and Muslims more generally. The specially commissioned illustrations, executed by William Harvey, a well-known engraver who had been the favourite pupil of Thomas Bewick, and closely supervised by Lane, were almost as important to the essentially educational enterprise as were the footnotes.

Lane translated the Arabic into an antiquated, mock-biblical prose. Since he was even more prudish than Galland, his translation was heavily bowdlerized and some stories were omitted altogether on the grounds of indecency. Yet other stories were omitted because Lane claimed to find them too fantastical, vulgar or silly. But the truth seems to have been that the heavily illustrated text, which appeared in weekly instalments before being issued in three bound volumes, was losing money, and Lane was coming under pressure from his publisher to bring the unprofitable enterprise to a speedy end.

Lane translated from the Bulaq text, whereas this new Penguin translation by Malcolm Lyons has been made from Calcutta II. What do Bulaq and Calcutta II refer to? By the time Lane had begun his translation, several Arabic printed texts of the *Nights* were available. Of these the most important were first, a two-volume translation published in Calcutta by the College of Fort William for Oriental Languages in 1814 and 1818 (known to scholars as Calcutta I), and secondly the Bulaq edition (so called after the port suburb of Cairo), published in two volumes in 1835. Lane chose to work from the more recently published Bulaq text, which seems to have been based primarily on an eighteenth-century Egyptian manuscript.

Calcutta I had been commissioned by the College of Fort William in Calcutta as a textbook for teaching Arabic to East India Company officers. (Fort William had been established in 1800 to teach Oriental languages to company officials and civil servants in the colonial administration of India.) The larger, four-volume edition, known as the Macnaghten edition or Calcutta II and published in 1839–42, had a similar educational purpose. The text was based in large part on a manuscript brought to India by Major Turner Macan, a scholarly officer who, in 1829, had published an edited text of the great Persian epic the *Shahnama*. Macan had acquired the *Nights* manuscript from the estate of Henry Salt (1780–1827), British Consul in Egypt and a famous collector of its antiquities. Lane had met Salt on his first visit to Egypt in 1825 and it may have been Salt who inspired Lane's interest in the *Nights*. It seems most probable that the compilation of this manuscript was commissioned by Salt during his last years in Egypt, that is around 1824–5. The scribe or scribes made use of a late Egyptian manuscript (probably of the eighteenth century), but they supplemented it by drawing on the printed text of Calcutta I. They also seem to have drawn upon the first two volumes of an edition of the *Nights* which a German scholar, Maximilian Habicht, had started to publish in Breslau in 1824. The Salt/Macan manuscript is now lost. Very likely it was destroyed by the printers once it had served their use.

In India, Macan's manuscript had been acquired by Charles Brownlow, who offered it for scrutiny and evaluation to a panel of experts belonging to the Asiatic Society of Bengal. The results of their deliberations were published in 1837 in the *Journal of the Asiatic Society of Bengal*:

> The style of the language was declared to be singularly pure, the narrative spirited and graphic, and the collection of stories enriched with many tales either perfectly new to European readers or else given a form very different from that which they have been hitherto known, garbled and abridged by

the carelessness of translators or by the imperfections of the MSS whence they were translated.

Sir William Hay Macnaghten, the leading Arabist, having looked at volumes three and four of the manuscript, declared that it was genuine and suggested that it would be a worthwhile enterprise to translate it. In the *Journal*, he gave it as his opinion that the government should subsidize the publication, because of 'the credit which must accrue to our nation, from presenting to the Musulman population of India, in a complete and correct form and in their own classical language, these enchanting tales . . .'. In the event, the government did subscribe for fifty copies of the printed text.

As already noted, the Calcutta II text is also known as the Macnaghten edition, although the extent of his involvement in its preparation is questionable. Sir William Hay Macnaghten (1793–1841) had studied Arabic and Sanskrit at Fort William in Calcutta. He became Secretary to the Secret and Political Department in Calcutta. Emily Eden, sister of the Governor General of India and a devoted letter writer, described him as 'clever and pleasant, speaks Persian rather more fluently than English; Arabic better than Persian; but, for familiar conversation, prefers Sanskrit'. According to his wife's biography of him, Richard Burton, the future translator of the *Nights*, who was out in India in Macnaghten's time, was less flattering. 'Macnaghten was a mere Indian civilian. Like too many of them, he had fallen into the dodging ways of the natives, and he distinctly deserved his death.' It is not clear how Macnaghten had offended Burton. What is clear is that he was one of the most influential formulators of policy in British India. A committed Russophobe, he advocated a forward policy in Afghanistan, where he hoped to establish a puppet regime to block further Russian advance towards India. His promising career in the Bengal civil service was cut short when, in 1837, he moved to Simla prior to accompanying Lord Auckland on an expedition into Afghanistan. The British aim was to oust the warlord Dost Mohammed Khan from Kabul and put in their own nominee. But their troops were trapped and surprised in Kabul and Macnaghten was murdered there in December 1841. It is said that his wife first learned of her husband's death when his severed hand with his ring bearing an Arabic inscription was tossed into her tent.

Before his involvement in the ill-fated Afghan adventure, Macnaghten had volunteered to correct the Arabic of the manuscript prior to its being sent on to the printer. In this task he was to be assisted by the Maulavis of the Persian Office in Calcutta. (Maulavis were experts on Islamic law and they necessarily had to have a good knowledge of Arabic.) The chronology of Macnaghten's departure for Simla and Kabul raises doubts about his serious involvement in the production of the edition that bears his name, as planning the Afghan expedition would have left him little spare time to work on the text. Whatever the case, it is clear that the edition that was published, while based on the Macan manuscript, drew heavily on the Bulaq edition. Since Calcutta II drew on so many earlier recensions of the *Nights*, it contained more stories and usually fuller versions of those stories.

When the Calcutta II project was launched, there had been hopes that Macnaghten might translate the Arabic once it was published. In the event, it was first translated into English by John Payne (1842–1917), a poet and translator. Payne's highly literary translation was published in a single limited edition in 1882–4. Since his edition sold out and he had no intention of ever reissuing it, his friend and advisor Sir Richard Burton (1821–90) saw his opportunity. Burton was already famous for having disguised himself as a Muslim and making the *hajj* or pilgrimage to Mecca and Medina, and for his expedition undertaken with John Speke in search of the source of the Nile. He had also published a translation of the *Kama Sutra* in 1883.

Burton's translation was published in 1885–7 in sixteen volumes (six of which were supplemental volumes containing stories not found in Calcutta II) and, in order to circumvent the Obscene Publications Act of 1857, it was available to private subscribers only. While Lane's translation had been excessively prudish, Burton's was at the other end of the spectrum. He heightened the eroticism and, occasionally, the racism of what he translated. His prose was by turns pompous, slangy or tortured. However, he did provide a full translation and even supplied variant versions of some stories.

Two further translations need to be mentioned. Joseph-Charles-Victor Mardrus, a member of a Caucasian clan who grew up in Cairo, published a French translation of the *Nights* in twelve volumes between 1899 and 1904. This 'translation' is extremely inaccurate and some of the stories seem to have been invented by Mardrus. The prose was embellished in a fin-de-siècle manner. Though it is perhaps easier to read than the English of Lane or Burton, some readers may find it rather sickly. As a work of creative literature, Mardrus's version certainly has its merits, but as a rendering of an Arabic original it is almost worthless. An English translation of the French by E. Powys Mathers was published in 1923 in a private subscription edition and in a public edition in 1937.

In 1984, Muhsin Mahdi, a professor of Arabic at Harvard, published a critical edition of the oldest substantially surviving manuscript of the *Nights*, the one used by Galland that is currently in the Bibliothèque Nationale and which contains only thirty-five and a half stories extending over 282 'Nights'. Mahdi's critically edited text was subsequently well translated into English by Hussain Haddawy in 1990. Although Mahdi argued that the manuscript in question dates from the early fourteenth century, it seems clear that it in fact dates from the late fifteenth century. His view that there was a single thirteenth- or fourteenth-century core text to which, in the centuries that followed, other tales were added without any justification at all has also attracted some criticism.

In 2004, *The Arabian Nights Encyclopedia* was published in two volumes under the editorship of Ulrich Marzolph and Richard van Leeuwen. This work uses the Burton translation as 'the main point of reference' for its essays and articles, on the basis that the Burton translation provides the most comprehensive range of stories. As the article devoted to Burton puts it: 'In the present work, Burton's translation has been chosen as the major point of reference for purely pragmatic reasons . . . Burton's translation is the most complete version of texts relating to *The Arabian Nights* in English.' However, as the same article also notes: 'Some critics have criticized the translation for its archaic language and extravagant idiom, rendering it hardly digestible for the average reader.'

To quote *The Arabian Nights Encyclopedia* once more, according to Ulrich Marzolph's introduction: 'Sadly enough, no adequate complete English-language rendering of *The Arabian Nights* prepared directly from the Arabic is available.' The Penguin *Arabian Nights* aims to remedy this deficiency and this translation by Malcolm and Ursula Lyons is the first substantial translation made directly from the Arabic since Burton's in the 1880s. Like Burton's, it has been made from Calcutta II, so it includes some stories which were in the missing fourth part of the Galland manuscript and some which were added in later centuries. In addition, two of the most famous and popular 'orphan stories' have been translated from the French: 'Aladdin' and 'Ali Baba', together with an alternative version of 'The seventh journey of Sindbad'. (But this new translation does not include the other stories contained in Burton's supplementary volumes, where he drew on extra tales from the Breslau edition, an Oxford manuscript once owned by Edward Wortley-Montague, and other miscellaneous sources.) Calcutta II is a more comprehensive compilation than any of the rival printed versions of the *Nights*. But, though it has the most stories and usually the fullest version of the stories and though scholars were involved in its first printing, Calcutta II is not a scholarly text in any serious sense. It is, however, a wonderful collection of stories, many of which date from medieval times, while other tales seem to have been composed or added in the seventeenth and eighteenth centuries.

Galland, Lane and Burton produced didactic translations and used the stories as pretexts for glosses or notes. The *Nights* was treated by them as, in a sense, an ethnographic source, and in the eighteenth and nineteenth centuries the stories were often cited as a guide to the Arab way of life or the Arab mind. The Lyons translation has no such ethnographic agenda, and any annotation has been kept to a minimum. This literary translation is dedicated to the pleasure of storytelling. The book is long (approximately a million words), but its length permits a special kind of reading pleasure as it allows readers to lose themselves in a veritable sea of stories.

Robert Irwin
London

The Arabian Nights

Nights 295 to 719

  A story is also told that one night, when the caliph Harun al-Rashid was feeling restless, he summoned his vizier, Ja'far the Barmecide. When he came, the caliph said: 'Ja'far, I am very restive tonight and in a bad humour. I want you to fetch me something to cheer and relax me.' 'Commander of the Faithful,' said Ja'far, 'I have a friend, 'Ali al-'Ajami, who has a fund of entertaining stories that raise the spirits and remove sorrow from the heart.' 'Bring him to me,' said the caliph, to which Ja'far replied: 'To hear is to obey.' He left the caliph's presence to look for 'Ali, and sent a messenger to fetch him. When 'Ali had come, Ja'far told him of the caliph's summons. 'To hear is to obey,' 'Ali replied.

Night 295

Morning now dawned and Shahrazad broke off from what she had been allowed to say. Then, when it was the two hundred and ninety-fifth night, SHE CONTINUED:

  The two of them set off for the palace, and when 'Ali appeared before the caliph, he was given permission to sit, which he did. The caliph told him of his depression and went on: 'I have heard that you know many stories and tales and so I want you to tell me something that may dispel my cares and cheer me.' 'Shall I tell you of something that I have seen with my own eyes, Commander of the Faithful,' 'Ali asked, 'or something that I have heard?' 'If you have seen something, then tell me about it,' Harun replied, and 'Ali agreed. HE BEGAN:

  You must know, Commander of the Faithful, that one year I travelled from Baghdad, my home, accompanied by a servant who brought with him a small bag. I came to a certain city and while I was there, buying and selling, I was assaulted by a Kurdish ruffian, who seized the bag. 'This is mine,' he claimed, 'and all its contents are my property.' 'Muslims,' I called out, 'save me from this worst of rascals!' The bystanders told us to go to the *qadi* and to abide by his arbitration. I was happy to do this and we set off to the *qadi*. When we got there he asked why we had come, telling us to explain the case. I said: 'We have come to you as litigants with opposing claims and are content to accept your arbitration.' 'Which of you is the claimant?' the *qadi* asked. At that, the Kurd went forward and said: 'Master, this bag and its contents are mine. I lost it and then found it in the possession of this man.' 'When did you lose it?' the *qadi* asked. 'Yesterday,' replied the Kurd, 'and I spent a sleepless night because of its loss.' 'As you have recognized it, describe what is in it,' the *qadi* told him. The Kurd said: 'In it there are two silver kohl sticks, together with kohl for my eyes, a hand towel in which I placed two gilt cups and two candlesticks. There are two tents, two plates, two spoons, a pillow, two leather mats, two jugs, a china dish, two basins, a cooking pot, two clay jars, a ladle, a pack needle, two provision bags, a cat, two bitches, one large bowl and two large sacks, a gown, two furs, a cow with two calves, one goat, two sheep, a ewe with two lambs, two green pavilions, one male and two female camels, a buffalo, two bulls, a lioness and two lions, a she-bear, two foxes, a mattress, two couches, a palace, two halls, a colonnade, two chairs, a kitchen with two doors and a group of Kurds who will bear witness to the fact that this is my bag.'

'What have you to say?' the *qadi* asked me. I had been flabbergasted by what the Kurd had said and so I went forward and said: 'May God honour our master the *qadi*. There was nothing in my bag except for one little ruined house and another one with no door, a dog kennel and a boys' school, with boys playing dice. It had tents and their ropes, the cities of Basra and Baghdad, the palace of Shaddad ibn 'Ad, a blacksmith's forge, a fishing net, sticks, tent pegs, girls, boys and a thousand pimps who will testify that the bag is mine.'

When the Kurd heard what I had to say, he wept and sobbed. 'My master the *qadi*,' he said, 'this bag of mine is well known and its contents have been described. In it are fortresses and castles, cranes, beasts of prey, chess players and chessboards. There is a mare and two foals, a stallion and two horses, together with two long spears. It also has a lion, two hares, a city and two villages, a prostitute with two villainous pimps, a hermaphrodite, two good-for-nothings, one blind man and two who can see, a lame man and two who are paralysed, a priest, two deacons, a patriarch and two monks, a *qadi* and two notaries, and these will bear witness that this is my bag.'

'What have you to say, 'Ali?' asked the *qadi* and, bursting with rage, I came forward and said: 'May God aid our master the *qadi*.'

Night 296

Morning now dawned and Shahrazad broke off from what she had been allowed to say. Then, when it was the two hundred and ninety-sixth night, SHE CONTINUED:

I have heard, O fortunate king, that 'ALI SAID:

I came forward bursting with rage and said: 'May God aid our master the *qadi*. In this bag of mine is a coat of mail, a sword and stores of weapons. There are a thousand butting rams, a sheep-fold, a thousand barking dogs, orchards, vines, flowers, scented herbs, figs, apples, pictures and statues, bottles and drinking cups, beautiful slave girls, singing girls, wedding feasts with noise and tumult, wide open spaces, successful men, dawn raiders with swords, spears, bows and arrows, friends, dear ones, companions, comrades, men imprisoned and awaiting punishment, drinking companions, mandolins, flutes, banners and flags, boys, girls, unveiled brides and singing slave girls. There are five girls from Abyssinia, three from India, four from al-Medina, twenty from Rum, fifty Turkish girls and seventy Persians, eighty Kurdish girls and ninety Georgians. The Tigris and the Euphrates are there, together with a fishing net, flint and steel for striking sparks, Iram of the Columns and a thousand good-for-nothings and pimps. There are exercise grounds, stables, mosques, baths, a builder, a carpenter, a plank of wood, a nail, a black slave with a fife, a captain and a groom, cities and towns, a hundred thousand dinars, Kufa and al-Anbar, twenty chests filled with materials, fifty storehouses for food, Gaza, Ascalon, the land from Damietta to Aswan, the palace of Chosroe Anushirwan, the kingdom of Solomon and the land from Wadi Nu'man to Khurasan, as well as Balkh and Isfahan and what lies between India and the land of the Blacks. It also contains – may God prolong the life of our master the *qadi* – gowns, turban cloth and a thousand sharp razors to shave off the *qadi*'s beard, unless he fears my vengeance and rules that the bag is mine.'

The *qadi* was bewildered by what he heard the Kurd say. 'You seem to me to be two ill-omened fellows or else two atheists who are trying to ridicule *qadis* and magistrates with no fear of rebuke. No one has ever described or heard of anything stranger than what you have produced, or spoken the kind of things that you have said. By God, not all the land from China to the tree of Umm Ghailan, from Persia to the land of the Blacks or from Wadi Nu'man to Khurasan would be big enough to contain all the things that you have mentioned. Your claims are incredible. Is this bag of yours a bottomless sea, or the Day of Resurrection on which the just and the unjust will be gathered together?' He then ordered the bag to be opened and when I did this, in it were a piece of bread, lemons, cheese and olives. I threw it in front of the Kurd and went off.

When the caliph heard this story from 'Ali al-'Ajami, he laughed so much that he fell over, after which he presented him with a handsome reward.

A story is told that while Ja'far the Barmecide was drinking one night with al-Rashid, al-Rashid said to him: 'I have heard that you have bought the slave girl So-and-So. I have wanted her for a long time, as she is so very beautiful that my heart is filled with love for her. So sell her to me.' 'I shall not sell her, Commander of the Faithful,' Ja'far replied. 'Then give her to me,' said al-Rashid. 'No, I shall not,' said Ja'far. 'If you don't either sell her or give her to me,' said al-Rashid, 'I swear to divorce my wife Zubaida three times.' 'If I either sell her or give her to you, then I swear to divorce my own wife,' replied Ja'far.

After this, when they had recovered from the effects of the wine, they realized the severity of the affair into which they had fallen, and they could think of no way out. 'The only man who can deal with this,' said al-Rashid, 'is Abu Yusuf.' It was midnight when they sent for him, and when the caliph's messenger came, Abu Yusuf got up in fear, saying to himself: 'I wouldn't have been asked to come at this time had there not been a serious problem for Islam.' He left his house in a hurry, and when he mounted his mule he told his servant to take the mule's nose-bag with him as it might not have finished feeding. 'When we get to the caliph's palace,' he went on, 'give it its bag so that, if it hasn't already finished, it can eat the rest of its feed before I come out again.' 'To hear is to obey,' replied the servant.

The caliph rose to greet Abu Yusuf when he arrived, inviting him to sit beside him on his couch, he being the only man who ever shared the caliphal couch. 'We have only asked you to come because of an important matter,' the caliph said. He explained the problem, adding that he and Ja'far had been unable to think of a way out of it. 'This is a very simple affair indeed, Commander of the Faithful,' said Abu Yusuf. 'Ja'far,' he went on, 'you must sell half of the girl to the Commander of the Faithful and make him a present of the other half and in that way neither of you will have broken your oaths.' The caliph was delighted with this and both he and Ja'far followed Abu Yusuf's advice.

The caliph then ordered the girl to be fetched immediately . . .

Night 297

Morning now dawned and Shahrazad broke off from what she had been allowed to say. Then, when it was the two hundred and ninety-seventh night, SHE CONTINUED:

I have heard, O fortunate king, that the caliph then ordered the girl to be fetched immediately as he was filled with longing for her. When she was brought in, he said to Abu Yusuf: 'I want to lie with her immediately and I cannot bear to wait until the period of her ritual purification is over. How can this be managed?' Abu Yusuf replied: 'Fetch me one of the caliph's mamluks who have not been freed.' When one of them was produced, Abu Yusuf asked the caliph for permission to marry the girl to the mamluk. This man was then to divorce her before consummating the marriage, as it would then be legal for the caliph to sleep with her immediately, since there would be no need for purification. This pleased the caliph even more than the earlier solution, and when the mamluk came he gave Abu Yusuf permission to draw up the marriage contract. Abu Yusuf duly married the pair, the mamluk having agreed to this, and he then said to the man: 'Divorce her, and you shall have a hundred dinars.' 'I shall not divorce her,' the man said, and although Abu Yusuf kept increasing the offer until it had reached a thousand dinars, he still refused. 'Is it up to me to divorce her, or up to you or the Commander of the Faithful?' he asked, and when Abu Yusuf told him that it was for him to act, he insisted: 'I shall never do this.'

The caliph was furiously angry and he asked Abu Yusuf what was to be done. 'Don't worry, Commander of the Faithful,' replied Abu Yusuf, 'this is easy. Make over this mamluk to the girl as her own property.' 'I make him over to her,' said the caliph. 'Tell him that you accept,' Abu Yusuf told the girl. 'I accept,' she said. 'I then rule that they must part,' he declared, 'for, as he has become her property, the marriage is annulled.' The caliph rose to his feet and exclaimed: 'You are the kind of *qadi* whom I want in my lifetime!' He called for bowls filled with gold, which were emptied out in front of him. 'Have you anything to put this in?' he asked Abu Yusuf, who remembered the mule's nose-bag. He called for it and after it had been filled with gold he took it and went off back home. In the morning, he told his companions: 'There is no easier and shorter path to both religion and worldly affairs than knowledge, as a result of which I have been given this huge sum for answering two or three questions.'

People of culture should take note of the elegance of this affair, comprising, as it does, excellent examples, such as that of Ja'far's treatment of al-Rashid, the knowledge shown by al-Rashid and the superior knowledge of the *qadi*, Abu Yusuf – may Almighty God have mercy on all their souls.

A story is told that while Khalid ibn 'Abd Allah al-Qushairi was emir of Basra, a group of people approached him holding on to a young man of dazzling beauty, obvious culture and ample intelligence, handsomely shaped, fragrant and conveying an impression of tranquillity and gravity. When his captors brought him to Khalid, he asked them what the matter was. 'This is a thief,' they told him, 'whom we came across last night in our house.' Khalid looked at the young man and was struck by his fine and well-groomed appearance. He told the men to release him, after which he went up to him and asked him for his story. 'These people have told you the truth,' the young man said, 'and what happened was as they described it.' 'What prompted you to do that,' asked Khalid, 'an elegant and handsome man like you?' 'Greed for worldly goods,' replied the young man, 'together with the decree of God, the Sublime, the Exalted.' 'May your mother lose you!' exclaimed Khalid. 'Wasn't your handsome face, the perfection of your intellect, together with your culture enough to turn you away from theft?' 'Stop this talking, emir,' said the young man, 'and carry out the decree of Almighty God. I have brought this on myself, and God is not unjust towards His servants.'

Khalid was silent as he thought the matter over and he then brought the young man close to him and said: 'I am suspicious of this confession of yours before witnesses. I don't believe that you are a thief. There may be some story here over and above the matter of theft, and in that case tell me about it.' 'Emir,' the young man said, 'don't get the idea that

there is anything here except the crime to which I have confessed. I have
no story to tell you except that I went into the house of these people and
stole what I could. They came on me, laid hands on me and brought me
to you.'

Khalid ordered the young man to be taken to prison, and he had a
proclamation made in Basra summoning all who wanted to witness the
punishment of So-and-So the thief and the amputation of his hand to
come to such-and-such a place on the next day. When the young man
had been lodged in prison and his feet had been placed in irons, he sighed
deeply, shed tears and recited these lines:

Khalid has threatened to have my hand cut off
Unless I reveal to him her story.
I said: 'Far be it from me to reveal to him
The love for her that is lodged within my heart.
To have my hand cut off for the crime I have confessed to
Is easier for my heart to bear than her disgrace.'

The gaolers responsible for him heard this and told Khalid about it. He
ordered them to fetch him the prisoner under cover of night, and when
they brought him Khalid interrogated him and discovered him to be an
intelligent and cultured man with a delicate wit and understanding.
Khalid ordered him to be given food and after he had eaten they talked
for some time. 'I know that there is something here apart from theft,'
Khalid said. 'In the morning when the people have gathered and the *qadi*
is there, he will ask you about your crime. Deny it and say something to
save you from the punishment of amputation. The Apostle of God, may
God bless him and give him peace, said: "Where there is doubt, do not
exact the penalty."' He then had the young man returned to prison . . .

Night 298

Morning now dawned and Shahrazad broke off from what she had been
allowed to say. Then, when it was the two hundred and ninety-eighth
night, SHE CONTINUED:

I have heard, O fortunate king, that after Khalid had talked to the
young man, he had him returned to prison, where he passed the rest of
the night.

In the morning, so many came to witness the amputation that there was no one in Basra, man or woman, who was not there to see it. Khalid rode up accompanied by the leading citizens, together with others. He summoned the *qadis* and ordered the young man to be brought out. When he came, stumbling in his fetters, there was no one who did not weep for him, and women's voices were raised in lamentation. The *qadi* ordered them to be silent and then he said: 'These people claim that you entered their house and stole their goods, but perhaps you stole less than the minimum amount that entails punishment?' 'No,' said the young man, 'I stole more.' 'Perhaps you jointly owned some of this property with them?' 'No,' said the young man, 'it was all theirs and I had no right to it.' Khalid was angry and, going up to him, he struck him in the face with his whip, quoting these lines:

> Man wants to have his wishes granted,
> But it is God's own wishes that He carries out.

He now called for the butcher to cut off the young man's hand. The man brought out his knife, stretched out the victim's hand and set the knife against it. At that moment a girl rushed out from the crowd of women, wearing dirty rags. She threw herself on the young man, and then unveiled herself to show a face like a moon. The crowd raised a great clamour and a riot was close to being sparked off, when the girl cried out at the top of her voice: 'I implore you in God's Name, emir; don't have his hand cut off before you have read this note.' She passed him a note, which he opened and read. In it were these lines:

> Khalid, this is a passionate lover who is enslaved by love,
> Pierced by my glances from the bows of my eyelids.
> The arrow of my glance gave him a fatal wound.
> As an ardent lover he cannot recover.
> He has confessed to a crime that he did not commit,
> Thinking this better than to disgrace his lover.
> Go gently with this wretched man;
> His is a noble nature and he is no thief.

When Khalid had read these lines, he left the crowd, had the girl brought to him and asked her for the story. She told him that she and the young man loved each other. Wanting to visit her, he had made his way to her family's house, throwing a stone into it to alert her. Her father and her brothers, hearing the noise, had gone to look for him and, when he saw that, he had collected all the household effects, pretending that he was a thief in order to shield his beloved. She went on: 'When they saw what he was doing, they seized him, crying: "Thief!" and then they brought him to you. He confessed to theft and persisted in this so as not to bring disgrace on me. This was the action of a man who made himself out to be a thief because of his great chivalry and his nobility of soul.'

'He deserves to get his wish,' said Khalid. He then summoned the young man, kissed him between the eyes and ordered the girl's father to be brought. 'Shaikh,' he said, 'I had intended to carry out the sentence of amputation on this young man, but God, Great and Glorious, has saved me from doing that. I order that he be given ten thousand dirhams for having been willing to sacrifice his hand to preserve your honour and that of your daughter so as to save you both from shame, and I order that your daughter be given ten thousand dirhams because she told me what really happened. I now ask you to give her to him in marriage.' The shaikh agreed to this and Khalid praised and glorified God, after which he preached a fine sermon.

Night 299

Morning now dawned and Shahrazad broke off from what she had been allowed to say. Then, when it was the two hundred and ninety-ninth night, SHE CONTINUED:

I have heard, O fortunate king, that Khalid praised and glorified God, after which he preached a fine sermon. He then told the young man: 'I have married you to this girl, So-and-So, who is here present, with her consent and approval, and the consent of her father in return for this marriage portion, which amounts to ten thousand dirhams.' 'I agree to this marriage at your hands,' said the young man. On Khalid's orders the money was carried to his house and set out on trays, while the people dispersed happily.

The narrator concluded: 'I never saw a more remarkable day, beginning, as it did, with tears and disasters and ending with happiness and joy.'

When Harun al-Rashid crucified Ja'far the Barmecide, he gave orders that anyone who mourned for him or lamented him would share his fate and, as a result, the people refrained from doing this. As it happened, however, there was a Bedouin from a distant desert who used to visit

Ja'far every year, bringing him an ode, for which Ja'far would reward him with a thousand dinars, and after taking this the Bedouin would leave and would continue to use the money for his family expenses until the following year. When the Bedouin, following his usual custom, brought his ode only to find that Ja'far had been crucified, he went to the place of execution, and, making his camel kneel, he recited his ode with bitter tears and in great sorrow. He then fell asleep and in a dream he saw Ja'far, who said to him: 'You have put yourself to trouble and, on coming here, you have found me in the state that you see. Set off for Basra and ask for So-and-So, one of the merchants of the city. Tell him that Ja'far the Barmecide greets him and asks him to give you a thousand dinars by the token of the bean.'

When the Bedouin woke up he left for Basra, where he asked after the merchant, and when he met him, he passed on the message that Ja'far had given him in his dream. The man wept so bitterly that he almost died, but then he treated his visitor with honour, made him sit with him and entertained him well. For three days the Bedouin stayed there as an honoured guest, and when he was about to leave his host presented him with fifteen hundred dinars. 'One thousand of these,' he explained, 'is what Ja'far told me to give you, and the five hundred is a present from me to you. I shall also give you an annual payment of a thousand dinars.'

As he was about to leave, the Bedouin said to the merchant: 'I conjure you by God to tell me about the bean, so that I may know how this began.' THE MERCHANT SAID:

At the start of my career I was a poor man hawking hot beans around the streets of Baghdad and trying to make a living by selling them. One cold and rainy day, I went out without having anything to put on to protect me from the chill. One moment I was shivering because of the bitter cold and the next I was falling into pools of rainwater, and so bad was my condition that people would shudder to look at me. That day Ja'far was sitting with his intimates and his concubines in a palace overlooking the street. His eye fell on me, and out of pity he sent one of his followers to me. The man took me and brought me to his master, who, when he saw me, told me: 'Sell my people the beans you have with you.' I started to weigh them out, using a measure that I had with me, and in exchange for a portion of beans everyone filled up my measure with gold. This went on until I had got rid of all the beans that I had with me and there was nothing left in my basket.

I then collected together all the gold that I had been given, and Ja'far asked me if I had any beans left. 'I don't know,' I told him, and when I searched in the basket I could only find one single bean. He took it from me, split it in two, and keeping one half for himself and handing the other to one of his concubines, he asked her: 'How much will you give for this half bean?' 'Twice the amount of this gold,' she told him. I was bewildered and said to myself: 'This is impossible,' but while I was standing there in amazement, she gave instructions to one of the maids, who fetched twice as much gold as I had already got. Then Ja'far said: 'I will buy the half that I have taken for twice as much as the whole total, so take the price of your bean.' On his instructions one of his servants collected all the money and put it in my basket. I took this and left, after which I came to Basra, where I used the money to set up as a trader. God, to Whom be praise and grace, granted me prosperity and so, if I give you a thousand dinars each year as part of what Ja'far gave me so generously, it will do me no harm at all.

Look, then, at the generous nature of Ja'far, who won praise both in life and after his death, may the mercy of Almighty God be on him.

While Harun al-Rashid was seated one day on his royal throne a young eunuch came into his presence carrying a crown of red gold set with pearls and gems, sapphires and other precious stones, beyond all price. He kissed the ground before the caliph and said: 'Commander of the Faithful, the Lady Zubaida . . .'

Night 300

Morning now dawned and Shahrazad broke off from what she had been allowed to say. Her sister said: 'What a good story this is, and how pleasant, sweet and agreeable!' Shahrazad replied: 'It cannot compare with what I shall tell you this coming night, if the king spares me and lets me live.' The king then said to himself: 'By God, I shall not kill her until I have heard the rest of the tale.' When it was the three hundredth night, her sister said: 'Tell your story, Shahrazad.' 'Willingly,' Shahrazad replied, 'if the king gives his permission.' 'Go on,' said the king, and SHAHRAZAD CONTINUED:

I have heard, O fortunate king, that the eunuch said to the caliph: 'The Lady Zubaida kisses the ground before you and says that you know she has had this crown made, but it needs to be topped with a great gem. She has searched through her treasures but has not found anything large enough there to suit her purpose.' Harun told his chamberlains and deputies to look for a jewel that would do, but they failed to find anything suitable. This angered Harun, who said: 'I am the caliph, king of the kings of the earth, but I cannot find one jewel. How can this be?' He told the men to ask the merchants, and when they did, the merchants said: 'Our master the caliph will only find this jewel in the possession of a man in Basra called Abu Muhammad the sluggard.'

When the caliph was told this, he ordered his vizier, Ja'far, to send a message to the emir Muhammad al-Zubaidi, the governor of Basra, telling him to make arrangements to have this man sent to the caliph. Ja'far wrote a note to this effect and gave it to Masrur, who set off with it to Basra. The emir Muhammad was delighted by his arrival and treated him with the greatest respect, after which Masrur read him the caliph's note. He obediently despatched Masrur with an escort of his servants to Abu Muhammad. When they had come to his house and had knocked on the door, a servant came out and Masrur told him to tell his master that he was wanted by the Commander of the Faithful. After the servant had gone in and told him that, Abu Muhammad came out to find Masrur, the chamberlain of the caliph, accompanied by the servants of Muhammad al-Zubaidi. He kissed the ground before Masrur and said: 'To hear the commands of the Commander of the Faithful is to obey them.'

He invited the visitors into his house and they said: 'This can only be a quick visit if we are to follow the caliph's instructions, as he is waiting for you to come.' 'Then wait a short time for me to get ready,' said Abu Muhammad. After he had done his best to persuade them, they went in with him and in the entrance hall they found hangings of blue brocade embroidered with red gold. Abu Muhammad told a number of his servants to take Masrur to the bath in his house, and when they did this Masrur discovered remarkable walls and marble slabs adorned with gold and silver, while the water was mixed with rosewater. A crowd of servants surrounded him and his companions, attending to all their needs, and when they left the bath, they were dressed in robes of brocade embroidered with gold. When they went back into the house they found Abu Muhammad seated in his upper room underneath hangings of gold brocade set with pearls and other precious stones. The room itself was furnished with couches adorned with red gold, while he himself sat on a covering laid over a throne set with gems.

When Masrur entered, Abu Muhammad came to meet him, greeted him and sat him down beside him. He ordered a table of food to be brought, and when Masrur saw it, he exclaimed: 'By God, I have never seen anything to equal this in the caliph's palace!' There was food of every kind there, all set out on gilded china. Masrur reported that they ate, drank and enjoyed themselves until the end of the day and Abu Muhammad then presented each of them with five thousand dinars, while the next day he gave them green robes embroidered with gold and showed them the greatest deference. Masrur told him that they couldn't stay any longer for fear of the caliph, but Abu Muhammad said: 'Master, let me wait until tomorrow so that I can make my preparations to go with you.'

They stayed there that day and on the following morning Abu Muhammad's servants saddled his mule with a saddle of gold studded with all kinds of pearls and jewels. 'I wonder,' said Masrur to himself, 'if, when Abu Muhammad comes before him in all this pomp, the caliph will ask how he came to be so wealthy.' They then said goodbye to al-Zubaidi and left Basra, travelling on until they reached Baghdad. When they entered the caliph's presence and stood before him, Abu Muhammad was invited to sit, and when he had done so he addressed the caliph courteously, saying: 'Commander of the Faithful, by way of presenting my services to you, I have brought you a gift, if you will allow me to fetch it.' When the caliph agreed to this, Abu Muhammad produced a chest, and after opening it he brought out presents. Among them were trees of gold with leaves of polished emeralds and fruits of rubies, topazes and gleaming pearls, which filled the caliph with astonishment. Abu Muhammad then opened another chest and took out a tent of brocade, adorned with pearls, rubies, emeralds, chrysolites and various other gems. Its supports were made from fresh Indian aloes wood; its fringes were set with emeralds; and on it were pictures, every one representing living creatures of all sorts, both birds and beasts, and these in turn were set with rubies, emeralds, chrysolites and hyacinths, as well as precious stones of all kinds.

Al-Rashid was delighted to see all this and Abu Muhammad said: 'You should not think, Commander of the Faithful, that I have brought you this because I was influenced by fear or desire. I see myself as a common man, and this treasure is suitable for no one but the caliph. If you permit me, I shall show you some of my powers.' 'Do as you wish and let us see,' said al-Rashid. 'To hear is to obey,' replied Abu

Muhammad. He moved his lips and pointed towards the battlements of the palace, which bent down towards him and then after a second gesture went back to their place. At a wink from him, closets appeared with bolted doors, and when he spoke to them he was answered by birdsong.

All this astonished al-Rashid, who said: 'From where have you got all this, you who are known as Abu Muhammad the sluggard? I am told that your father was a barber surgeon working in the baths who left you nothing.' 'Listen to my story, Commander of the Faithful,' said Abu Muhammad . . .

Night 301

Morning now dawned and Shahrazad broke off from what she had been allowed to say. Then, when it was the three hundred and first night, SHE CONTINUED:

I have heard, O fortunate king, that Abu Muhammad said: 'Listen to my story, Commander of the Faithful, for it is so strange and wonderful that, were it written with needles on the inner corners of the eye, it would serve as a warning to those who take heed.' The caliph told him to explain and HE CONTINUED:

Commander of the Faithful, may God prolong your glory and power, when people say that I am known as 'the sluggard' and that my father left me nothing, this is true. My father, as you said, was indeed a barber surgeon, working in the baths, while I in my youth was the idlest person on the face of the earth. So ingrained was this idleness of mine that if I was sleeping on a hot day and the sun began to shine down on me, I would be too lazy to get up and move into the shade. This went on until I was fifteen years old and then my father died and was received into the mercy of Almighty God. He left me nothing, but my mother used to act as a servant and she would fetch me food and drink as I lay on my side. One day, she came to me with five silver dirhams and told me that the *shaikh* Abu'l-Muzaffar was intending to go on a journey to China, he being a good man who loved the poor. 'My son,' she said, 'take these five dirhams and come with me to ask him to use the money to buy you something from China from which, by the grace of Almighty God, you might make a profit.' I was too lazy to get up and go with her, but she swore by God that if I didn't, she would not bring me food or drink or come in to see me but would leave me to die of hunger and thirst.

When I heard that, Commander of the Faithful, I realized that she was doing this because she knew how lazy I was. So I said: 'Help me to sit up,' which she did, while I shed tears. Then I said: 'Bring me my shoes,' and when she had brought them, I asked her to put them on my feet, which she did. I told her to lift me up from the ground, and when she had done that, I told her to support me as I walked. Leaning on her and stumbling over the skirts of my robe, I walked until we got to the river bank, where we greeted the *shaikh*. 'Uncle,' I said to him, 'are you Abu'l-Muzaffar?' 'At your service,' he replied. 'Then take these dirhams,' I told him, 'and use them to buy me something from China, from which God may allow me a profit.' 'Do you recognize this young man?' he asked his companions. 'Yes,' they said. 'He is known as Abu Muhammad the sluggard, and this is the only time we have ever known him to leave his own house.' 'Hand over the dirhams, my boy,' said the *shaikh*, 'and may Almighty God add His blessing.' He took the money from me, saying: 'In the Name of God.'

After this I went back home with my mother and Abu'l-Muzaffar set off on his journey, accompanied by a number of merchants, eventually reaching China. Here he traded and then he and his companions set off for home, having finished all that they wanted to do. After he had sailed for three days, he told the others to halt, and when they asked him why, he said: 'I forgot the errand that I was supposed to run for Abu Muhammad the sluggard, so come back with me so that we can buy something for his advantage.' They said: 'For God's sake, don't make us go back. We have travelled a very long way and faced great perils and extreme hardship.' When he insisted, they offered him twice the profit that could be made on five dirhams if he would change his mind. He agreed to this and they collected a large sum of money for him.

They then sailed on until they came in sight of a populous island, where they anchored, and the merchants landed to buy up minerals, jewels, pearls and so forth. Abu'l-Muzaffar caught sight of a man sitting with a large group of monkeys in front of him, among whom was one who had had some of its hair pulled out. When their master's attention wandered, the others would lay hold of that particular monkey, strike it and throw it at their master, after which he would get up, beat them, tie them up and punish them, leading them all to become angry with the other monkey and to strike it again. When he saw it, Abu'l-Muzaffar was sorry for it and pitied it, so he asked its owner whether he would sell it to him. 'Try buying it,' the man said, and Abu'l-Muzaffar told him: 'I have five dirhams belonging to an orphan. Will you take these for it?' 'Certainly, God bless you,' the man answered, and Abu'l-Muzaffar took it and handed over the money. His servants took it to the ship and tied it up, after which they weighed anchor and sailed to another island, where they anchored.

Here there were divers who would dive for precious stones, pearls, jewels and so on. The merchants paid them a fee for this, and when the monkey saw them diving he freed himself from his bonds, jumped off the side of the ship and dived with them. 'There is no might and no power except with God, the All-Highest, the Almighty!' exclaimed Abu'l-Muzaffar. 'I've lost the monkey thanks to the ill luck of the poor fellow for whom we got it,' and he and the others despaired of ever seeing it again. At that point a number of divers broke surface and there they could see the monkey coming up with them, holding in his hands valuable jewels, which it threw down before Abu'l-Muzaffar. He was astonished and said: 'There must be some great mystery attached to this monkey.'

They again weighed anchor and sailed on to what was known as the Island of the Zanj, a race of cannibal blacks. When these people saw the ship, they sailed out to it in canoes and captured everyone on board. They tied them up and brought them to their king, who ordered that a number of the merchants be killed. Their throats were cut and their flesh was eaten, after which the remainder were left for the night tied up and in great distress. After night had fallen, however, the monkey came to Abu'l-Muzaffar and untied his bonds. When the others saw that he was free, they said: 'It may be that God will save us through Abu'l-Muzaffar.' He told them: 'Know that, by the will of Almighty God, I was freed only by this monkey . . .'

Night 302

Morning now dawned and Shahrazad broke off from what she had been allowed to say. Then, when it was the three hundred and second night, SHE CONTINUED:

I have heard, O fortunate king, that ABU MUHAMMAD WENT ON:

Abu'l-Muzaffar told the others: 'By the will of Almighty God, I have been freed by this monkey, for which I shall pay him a thousand dinars.' They said: 'We too shall each pay him a thousand dinars if he rescues us.' At that, the monkey went to them and started to free them, one after the other, until he had released them all. They then went off to their ship, which they found to be intact. Nothing had been taken from it and so they weighed anchor and sailed off. It was then that Abu'l-Muzaffar told them to pay what they had promised to the monkey and, obediently, each of them handed over a thousand dinars, while Abu'l-Muzaffar produced a thousand dinars of his own. As a result, a huge sum of money was collected for the monkey.

They now sailed on until they reached the city of Basra, where their friends met them as they disembarked. 'Where is Abu Muhammad the sluggard?' asked Abu'l-Muzaffar. My mother heard of this, and she came to me while I was sleeping to tell me that Abu'l-Muzaffar had arrived back in the city. 'Get up,' she told me. 'Go and greet him and ask him what he has brought for you, as maybe Almighty God has opened up some opportunity for you.' 'Lift me up from the ground,' I told her, 'and support me, so that I can go down to the river bank.' Then I walked off, stumbling over the skirts of my robe, until I came to the *shaikh* Abu'l-Muzaffar, and when he saw me he exclaimed: 'Welcome to the man whose dirhams saved my life and the lives of these merchants, through the will of Almighty God!' He then told me: 'Take this monkey which I have bought for you. Go off with him to your house and then wait until I come to you.'

I took the monkey off with me, saying to myself: 'By God, this is a valuable piece of merchandise.' When I got home I said to my mother: 'Whenever I sleep, you tell me to get up in order to buy and sell, so look and see for yourself this piece of merchandise.' I sat down, and while I was seated Abu'l-Muzaffar's slaves came to me and asked if I was Abu Muhammad the sluggard. When I said that I was, in came Abu'l-Muzaffar himself, following behind them. I got up to meet him, and after I had kissed his hands he told me to go with him to his house. 'To hear is to obey,' I said, and I went with him until I had got to his house. Then he told his slaves to fetch the money, which they did, and he said: 'My son, God has provided you with all this money as profit on your five dirhams.' The slaves lifted it in boxes on their heads and, after giving me the keys of the boxes, Abu'l-Muzaffar told me to lead the slaves to my house, telling me that all that wealth was mine.

When I came to my mother, she was delighted and said: 'My son, as God has provided you with all this money, give up your idle ways and go and trade in the market.' So I stopped being idle and opened a shop, in which the monkey would sit with me on my seat, eating when I ate and drinking with me. Every day, however, he would go off from early morning until noon, and then he would come back with a purse containing a thousand dinars, which he would put down beside me before taking his seat. He kept on doing this for a considerable time until I had collected a large sum of money with which I bought property and estates, planted orchards and acquired mamluks, black slaves and servant girls.

One day, I happened to be sitting with the monkey when suddenly he looked to the right and left, and while I was wondering what that might mean, through God's permission he spoke with a clear voice and said: 'Abu Muhammad.' When I heard him speak I was terrified, but he told me: 'Don't be afraid and I shall tell you about myself. I am a *marid* of the *jinn*. I came to you because you were so poor, while now you don't even know how much money you have. I now need you for something which will be to your advantage.' I asked him what that might be and he said: 'I want to marry you to a girl like a full moon.' 'How?' I asked. He said: 'Tomorrow, put on your finest robes, mount your mule with the golden saddle, go to the market of the forage sellers and ask for the shop of the *sharif*. When you sit with him, tell him that you have come to ask for his daughter's hand in marriage. If he then says that you haven't any money, reputation or good family, give him a thousand dinars, and if he asks for more, give it to him and tempt him with money.' I agreed, saying that, God Almighty willing, I would do that the next day.

The next day, I put on the most splendid of my robes and mounted the mule with the golden saddle, after which I went to the market of the forage sellers and asked for the shop of the *sharif*. I found him sitting there and so I dismounted, greeted him and sat with him . . .

Night 303

Morning now dawned and Shahrazad broke off from what she had been allowed to say. Then, when it was the three hundred and third night, SHE CONTINUED:

I have heard, O fortunate king, that ABU MUHAMMAD SAID:

I dismounted, greeted him and sat with him, having with me ten black slaves and mamluks. 'Perhaps you have some need that I may be able to fulfil,' the *sharif* said to me. 'Yes,' I said, 'I do need something,' and when he asked me what this was, I told him that I had come to ask for his daughter's hand in marriage. 'You have no money, reputation or good family,' he told me, at which I brought out a purse containing a thousand dinars of red gold and said: 'This is my reputation and my lineage. The Prophet, may God bless him and give him peace, said: "Money is an excellent reputation," and how admirable are the lines of the poet:

> If someone owns two dirhams, his lips have learned
> And can speak words of every kind.
> His companions come to listen to him and you see
> Him moving haughtily among the crowds.
> Were it not for the dirhams, in which he takes such pride,
> You would find him in the worst of states among the people.
> If a rich man says something wrong, the people say:
> "You may be right, and what you say is not impossible,"
> But if a poor man speaks the truth, they say:
> "You are a liar; what you say is wrong."
> Money invests a man with dignity and beauty in all lands.
> Money is the tongue of those who seek eloquence,
> And the weapon of whoever wants to fight.'

After the *sharif* had listened to what I had to say and had understood the point of my lines, he looked down at the ground for a while and then raised his head and said: 'If this has to be, I want another three thousand dinars from you.' 'To hear is to obey,' I answered, and I then sent one of the mamluks to my house. When this man had returned with the money that the *sharif* had demanded, and he had seen it, he left his shop, telling his servants to lock it up, and after he had invited his friends from the market to come to his house he wrote a marriage contract for me and his daughter, telling me that he would bring me in to her after ten days.

I went back home in a state of delight, and when I was alone with the monkey I told him what had happened to me and he congratulated me. Then, when the time set by the *sharif* came near, the monkey said to me: 'I want you to do something for me, and if you do, then you can have whatever you want from me.' I asked him what this was and he told me: 'At the top end of the room in which you will sleep with the *sharif*'s daughter there is a cupboard whose door is fastened with a brass ring. The keys are under the ring. Take them and open the door, and you will then find an iron chest at whose four corners are four talismanic flags. In the middle of it there is a basin full of money, while beside it there are eleven snakes. In the basin a white cock is tied up and beside the chest is a knife. Take this knife and cut the cock's throat; then cut the flags in pieces and overturn the chest. After that you can come out and deflower your bride. This is what I want you to do.' 'To hear is to obey,' I replied.

I went to the *sharif*'s house, and when I entered the room I saw the cupboard that the monkey had described. When I found myself alone with my bride, I was astonished and delighted by her indescribable beauty and grace, together with the symmetry of her form. At midnight, when she was asleep, I got up and, after taking the keys, I opened the cupboard. I took the knife, killed the cock, threw down the flags and overturned the chest. My bride woke up and when she saw that the chest had been opened and the cock killed, she exclaimed: 'There is no might and no power except with God, the Most High, the Omnipotent! The *marid* has got me.' Before she had finished speaking the *marid* had swooped on the house and carried her off. In the commotion that followed the *sharif* came in, striking his own face. 'What have you done to us, Abu Muhammad,' he exclaimed, 'and is this how you repay us? I made this talisman in the cupboard as I was afraid for my daughter because of this damned *marid*, who has been trying unsuccessfully to take her for six years. There is no place left for you here so go on your way.' I left the *sharif*'s house and, after returning to my own, I looked for the monkey but failed to find him or, indeed, any trace of him, and so I realized that he was the *marid* who had taken my bride and had tricked me into destroying the talisman and the cock which had stood in his way.

In my regret I tore my clothes and struck my own face. Nowhere could I find ease, so I left immediately, making for the desert, and walked on until evening, too preoccupied to notice where I was going. Then, suddenly, two snakes came towards me, one dark and the other white. They were fighting each other and I picked up a rock from the ground and used it to kill the dark one, which had been the aggressor. The white snake went out of sight for a while, and then came back with ten other white snakes. They approached the dead snake and tore it into bits, leaving nothing but its head, after which they went away. I was so tired that I lay down where I was, and while I was lying there, thinking over what had happened to me, I heard a voice, although I could see no one there. The voice was reciting these lines:

Leave the fates to move unchecked, and pass the night free from
    care;
In the blink of an eye God changes one state to another.

When I heard that, Commander of the Faithful, I was very worried and
concerned. Then, from behind me, I heard more lines being recited:

Muslim, guided by the Quran, be glad,
For you have reached safety.
Have no fear of the seductions of the devil;
We are a people who follow true belief.

I said: 'I conjure you, by the truth of the God whom you worship, to tell
me who you are.' The disembodied voice then took human shape and
said: 'Have no fear. We know about your good deed and we belong to
the *jinn* who believe in the Prophet. If there is anything that you need,
tell us and we will carry it out.' 'I do have a great need,' I replied, 'as I
have suffered a great misfortune whose like has probably not afflicted
anyone else.' 'Are you perhaps Abu Muhammad the sluggard?' the
newcomer asked, and when I said that I was, he said: 'Abu Muhammad,
I am the brother of the white snake whose enemy you killed. We are
four full brothers, and we all owe you a debt of gratitude for the service
you did us. You must know that it was a *marid* of the *jinn* who took the
shape of a monkey and played this trick on you, for otherwise he would
never have been able to take the girl. He had loved her for a long time
and had wanted to carry her off, but the talisman prevented him, and
had it remained he would not have been able to reach her. But don't
distress yourself over this, for we will bring you to your bride and kill
the *marid*, and the good deed you did us will not go unrewarded.' He
then gave a great and terrible cry . . .

Night 304

Morning now dawned and Shahrazad broke off from what she had been
allowed to say. Then, when it was the three hundred and fourth night,
SHE CONTINUED:
    I have heard, O fortunate king, that ABU MUHAMMAD WENT ON:
    The *'ifrit* said: 'The good deed you did us will not go unrewarded.' He
then gave a great and terrible cry after which he was joined by a group

of *jinn*, whom he asked about the monkey. 'I know where he lives,' said one of them, and on being asked where this was, he told us: 'In the City of Brass, over which the sun never rises.'

The leader told me: 'Take one of our slaves and he will carry you on his back and teach you how to recover your bride. But you must know that he is a *marid* and so while he is carrying you don't mention the Name of God, or else he will flee from you and you will fall to your death.' 'To hear is to obey,' I said, and I picked one of the slaves of the *jinn*, who bent down and told me to mount. When I had done that, he flew up into the air with me until I had lost sight of the earth. The stars appeared as firmly rooted mountains, and I could hear the heavenly angels glorifying God. All this while, the *marid* was talking to me, distracting me and diverting me from any mention of Almighty God. Then, while I was being carried, a figure wearing green robes, with flowing locks of hair and a gleaming face, approached me, carrying a lance in his hand, from which flew sparks of fire. 'Abu Muhammad,' he ordered me, 'recite: "There is no god but God, and Muhammad is the Prophet of God," or else I shall strike you with this lance.' I was already in a state of distress from having been forced to keep silent and not pronounce the Name of Almighty God, so I recited the confession of faith. The lance carrier then struck the *marid* with his lance and he dissolved into ashes, leaving me to fall from his back down again to earth. I landed in a rough sea with clashing waves, but a ship with a five-man crew saw me, came up and carried me on board.

The sailors started to talk to me in an unknown language and I had to make signs to them to show them that I couldn't understand what they were saying. They sailed on until evening, when they cast a net and caught a fish, which they grilled and with which they fed me. The voyage continued until they reached their city, where they brought me to stand before their king. After I had kissed the ground, the king, who knew Arabic, presented me with a robe of honour and told me: 'I appoint you as one of my assistants.' I asked him the name of the city and he told me that it was a Chinese city named Hanad. He then handed me over to the vizier with instructions to show me the city. In early times its inhabitants had been unbelievers, but Almighty God had transformed them into stones. I enjoyed inspecting it and I had never seen a place with more trees and fruits.

After I had been there a month, I went to a river and sat down by the bank. While I was sitting there, a rider came up and asked if I was Abu

Muhammad the sluggard. When I said that I was, he said: 'Have no fear; word of your good deed has reached us.' I asked him who he was and he said: 'I am the brother of the snake, and the girl whom you want to reach is close at hand.' He then took off his clothes and dressed me in them, repeating: 'Have no fear,' and adding: 'The *marid* who was killed while carrying you was one of our slaves.' Next he took me up behind him and rode with me to a desert, where he told me to dismount. 'Go on between these two mountains,' he said, 'until you see the City of Brass. Stop at a distance from it and don't enter until I come back to you and tell you what to do.' 'To hear is to obey,' I said.

I got down from behind the rider and walked on until I got to the city. Its wall, I could see, was of brass, and I started to walk around it in the hopes of finding a gate, but I couldn't discover one. While I was circling around it, the snake's brother suddenly came up to me; he gave me a talismanic sword that would keep people from seeing me, and then went off on his way. He had not been gone long before there was a loud cry and I saw a large number of creatures whose eyes were in their chests. On catching sight of me, they asked me who I was and what had brought me there. I explained things to them and they said: 'The girl you mentioned is with the *marid* in the city here, but we don't know what he has done with her. We ourselves are brothers of the snake.' They went on: 'Go to that spring there; see where the water enters it and go into its channel, as this will bring you into the city.' I did that and the channel took me to a subterranean vault from which I came out to find myself in the centre of the city. There I discovered my bride seated on a golden throne draped with brocade, while around the throne was a garden with golden trees, whose fruits were precious stones such as sapphires, chrysolites, pearls and corals.

When she saw me, she recognized me and was the first to greet me. 'Master,' she said, 'who has brought you here?' When I told her what had happened, she said: 'You must know that this damned *marid* is so deeply in love with me that he has told me what can hurt him and what will help him. In the city is a talisman with which, if he wanted, he could kill everyone in the city and by means of which he can force the *'ifrits* to obey any order that he gives. The talisman is on a pillar.' I asked her where the pillar was and she described the spot. Then I asked her what it was and she said: 'It is a carved eagle with writing on it that I cannot read. Take it in your hands, fetch a brazier and throw in some musk. The smoke that it gives out will attract the *'ifrits*, so that when you have done that every single one of them will present himself before you. They will obey your orders and do anything at all that you tell them. So get up and do that with the blessing of Almighty God.' 'To hear is to obey,' I said.

I then went off to that pillar and carried out all her instructions, as a result of which the *'ifrits* assembled in front of me saying: 'Here we are, master; we shall do whatever you tell us.' 'Bind the *marid* who brought this girl from her home,' I told them and obediently they went to him, tied him tightly and brought him back to me. 'We have done what you told us,' they said, and then, on my instructions, they went off, while I myself went back to my bride, told her what had happened and asked her if she would come with me. 'Yes,' she said, and so I took her out through the subterranean vault by which I had found my way in, and we made our way on until we came to the creatures who had guided me to her.

Night 305

Morning now dawned and Shahrazad broke off from what she had been allowed to say. Then, when it was the three hundred and fifth night, SHE CONTINUED:

I have heard, O fortunate king, that ABU MUHAMMAD SAID:

We made our way on until we came to the creatures who had guided me to her. I asked them to show me how to get home, which they did. They went with me to the seashore and put me on a ship, which, with favourable winds, took us to the city of Basra, and there my bride went to her father's house, where her family were overjoyed to see her. I myself burned musk as incense for the eagle talisman and the *'ifrits* came to me from all sides, saying: 'Here we are, master. What do you want us to do?' I told them to fetch all the wealth, precious stones and jewels that were in the City of Brass and to bring them to my house in Basra. When they had done that, I asked them to bring me the monkey, who was humble and dejected when they fetched him. 'Why did you deceive me, you damned creature?' I asked him, and then on my orders the *'ifrits* put him in a narrow brass bottle with a stopper of lead.

I and my wife have been living in happiness and joy and I now have treasures, wonderful jewels and quantities of wealth beyond all count or limit. If you want money or anything else, I will give my orders to the 'ifrits', who will fetch it for you immediately. All that comes about through the grace of Almighty God.

The Commander of the Faithful was filled with wonder at this and he presented Muhammad with princely gifts and appropriate benefits in exchange for what Muhammad had brought him.

A story is also told that in the days before Harun al-Rashid grew jealous of the Barmecides, he summoned one of his officers, a man named Salih. When Salih came, Harun told him to go to Mansur and to say to him: 'You owe me a million dirhams and you must bring me this sum immediately.' Harun added to Salih: 'If he does not produce it for you before sunset, cut off his head and bring it to me.' 'To hear is to obey,' said Salih, and he went to Mansur and told him what the caliph had said. 'I am a dead man,' said Mansur. 'If I sold my goods and everything that I own at the highest possible price, that would not fetch more than a hundred thousand dirhams, so where am I going to get the remaining nine hundred thousand?' Salih replied: 'Think of some way to save yourself, but be quick or else you are dead. I cannot let you have a moment more than the time that the caliph has specified, as I have to obey his orders to the letter. Hurry to find some way out of this, before time runs out.' 'Salih,' replied Mansur, 'I ask you to please take me home so that I may say goodbye to my children and my family and give my instructions to my relatives.' SALIH SAID:

I went back to his house with him, and when he started to take his leave of his family there was a great outcry throughout the house, with loud weeping, shrieks and cries for help from Almighty God. I told him: 'It has occurred to me that God might save you through the help of the Barmecides, so come with me to the house of Yahya ibn Khalid.' We went to him and when I told him about Mansur's dilemma he was filled with sorrow. He looked down at the ground for a while and then he raised his head and summoned his treasurer. 'How much is there in your treasury?' he asked, and on being told that there were five thousand dirhams, Yahya told the man to bring them to him. He then sent a messenger to his son al-Fadl with a note to say: 'I have been offered for sale some splendid estates that will never lose their value, so send me some money.' Al-Fadl sent him a million dirhams, after which he sent another man to his son Ja'far with a message to say that he was involved in some important business and needed money. Ja'far immediately sent him a million dirhams, and he continued sending requests to other members of his family until he had collected from them a huge sum of money for Mansur, although neither I nor Mansur knew of this.

Mansur said to Yahya: 'I cling to the skirts of your robe as I don't know where to get this money except from you, this being your habitual generosity. Pay off the remainder of my debt and make me your freed slave.' Yahya bent his head and wept. Then he told his page: 'The Commander of the Faithful gave my slave girl Dananir a jewel of great price. Go to her and tell her to send it to me.' The page went and brought it, after which Yahya told Mansur: 'I bought this from the merchants for the Commander of the Faithful. I paid two hundred thousand dinars for it and he then gave it to my slave girl Dananir, the lute player. When he sees it with you, he will recognize it and treat you generously and spare your life for our sake and to do us honour. You now have the full sum.'

I took the money and the jewel to al-Rashid. Mansur went with me and while we were on our way, I heard him quoting this verse:

It was not out of affection that I went to them,
But for fear of being shot with arrows.

I was amazed by his evil nature, his wickedness and depravity and the vileness of his origins and his birth. I said in answer to him: 'There are no better people on the face of the earth than the Barmecides and no one fouler or more base than you. They have ransomed you from death and saved you from destruction, conferring a favour on you by freeing you from this, and, far from showing gratitude and praising them like a man of nobility, you reward their generosity by saying this.' I then went to al-Rashid and told him the whole story . . .

Night 306

Morning now dawned and Shahrazad broke off from what she had been allowed to say. Then, when it was the three hundred and sixth night, SHE CONTINUED:

I have heard, O fortunate king, that Salih said: 'I then went to al-Rashid and told him the whole story. He was astonished by Yahya's generosity, liberality and chivalrous nature as well as by the baseness and wickedness of Mansur. He ordered the jewel to be returned to Yahya, saying: "I cannot take back any gift that I have given."'

Salih went back to Yahya and told him how badly Mansur had behaved, but he said to him: 'Salih, when a man is short of money, distressed and preoccupied, he cannot be blamed for what he says, as this does not come from his heart.' He went on trying to find an excuse for Mansur until Salih wept and said: 'The celestial sphere as it revolves cannot bring into existence another man like you. How sad it is that a man with a generous nature like yours should be buried beneath the ground.' Then he recited these lines:

Hasten to do whatever good deed occurs to you
For generosity is not always possible.
How many a man has held back from a generous action
He could have done, and then has been restrained by poverty.

A story is also told that there was a secret feud between Yahya ibn Khalid and 'Abd Allah ibn Malik al-Khuza'i, which they kept hidden. The reason for this was that Harun al-Rashid, the Commander of the Faithful, was so fond of 'Abd Allah that Yahya ibn Khalid and his sons used to say that 'Abd Allah had bewitched him. After the two men had long nursed hatred in their hearts, it happened that al-Rashid sent 'Abd Allah off to be governor of Armenia. When he had settled on the provincial throne, he was approached by an Iraqi, a cultured man of shrewd intelligence but of limited resources, whose money was gone and whose circumstances had declined. This man had travelled to visit him in Armenia with a forged letter purporting to have been sent to him by Yahya ibn Khalid. When he arrived at the palace door, he gave the letter to one of the chamberlains, who took it and passed it to 'Abd Allah. 'Abd Allah opened it, read it and studied it carefully. Realizing that it was a forgery, he sent for the Iraqi, who, on coming before him, blessed and praised him and his court. 'Abd Allah asked him: 'What prompted you to take this trouble to come to me with a forged letter? Don't be distressed, however, for I shall see that your efforts do not go unrewarded.' The Iraqi replied: 'If my arrival is unwelcome, there is no need for you to think of a pretext to keep me away. God's earth is wide and He, the Provider, lives for ever. The letter that I have brought you from Yahya ibn Khalid is genuine and not a forgery.' 'Abd Allah said: 'I shall write to my agent in Baghdad and tell him to make enquiries about it. If it is really genuine and not forged, I shall appoint you as an emir over part of my territories, or else, if you prefer a gift, I shall give you two hundred thousand dirhams, together with horses, fine camels and a robe of honour. If, on the other hand, it is a forgery, I shall condemn you to two hundred lashes and have your beard shaved off.'

On 'Abd Allah's orders, the Iraqi was taken to an apartment where he was provided with everything he needed while the affair was being investigated. 'Abd Allah then wrote to tell his agent in Baghdad that a man had come to him with a letter supposedly written by Yahya ibn Khalid. He added: 'I'm suspicious of this letter and I want you to go yourself to check on it without delay. Send me back a reply quickly to let me know whether it is genuine or false.'

When 'Abd Allah's letter reached Baghdad, his agent rode off . . .

Night 307

Morning now dawned and Shahrazad broke off from what she had been allowed to say. Then, when it was the three hundred and seventh night, SHE CONTINUED:

I have heard, O fortunate king, that when 'Abd Allah's letter reached Baghdad, his agent rode off immediately and went to the house of Yahya ibn Khalid, where he found Yahya seated with his companions and intimate friends. After greeting him, the man handed him 'Abd Allah's letter, which he read. He then told him to come back the next day so that he might have time to write a reply. When the agent had gone, Yahya turned to his companions and asked: 'How should I repay someone who forges a letter in my name and takes it to my enemy?' They each gave their opinions and every one of them proposed some form of punishment. 'What you have said is wrong,' said Yahya, 'and your advice springs from baseness and lack of magnanimity. You all know how close 'Abd Allah is to the caliph, and you know the anger and enmity that exists between 'Abd Allah and me. Almighty God has used this man as an intermediary to reconcile us, fitting him for his destined role as one who will quench the fire of hatred that has been burning ever more fiercely in our hearts for twenty years. Now, thanks to him, things will be put right, and it is up to me to fulfil his expectations and to see that his affairs are set in order. I shall write a letter to be given to 'Abd Allah asking him to show this man even more favour and to go on treating him with honour and respect.'

When Yahya's companions heard that, they called down God's blessings on him, marvelling at his generosity and the extent of his chivalry, while he called for paper and ink and wrote a letter to 'Abd Allah in his own hand. This ran: 'In the Name of God, the Compassionate, the Merciful: your letter, may God prolong your life, has reached me and, on reading it, I was glad to hear that you are well and I was delighted both by your rectitude and by the prosperity that surrounds you. I see that you thought that this noble man had forged a letter from me and had brought no message of mine. In fact, this is not true. It was I who wrote the letter and it is no forgery. I hope that your generosity, kindliness and good nature will lead you to fulfil his hopes and wishes, that you will show him the respect that is his due, allow him to achieve his aim and treat him with particular and abundant favour and kindness. Whatever you do, it is to me that you will be doing it and it is my gratitude that you will receive.'

He addressed the letter, sealed it and handed it to 'Abd Allah's agent. The agent, in his turn, sent it on to 'Abd Allah, who was delighted when he read its contents. He summoned the Iraqi and asked him which of the promised rewards he chose, so that he might confer it on him. 'The present is what I would like most,' the man told him, and so 'Abd Allah ordered him to be given two hundred thousand dirhams, ten Arab horses, five with trappings of silk and five with ornamental processional saddles, twenty chests full of clothes and ten mounted mamluks, as well as an appropriate selection of precious jewels. He then gave him robes of honour, treated him with favour and sent him off to Baghdad in great pomp.

When he had reached the city, before he went to see his family he came to the door of Yahya ibn Khalid and asked permission to come in to see him. Yahya's chamberlain went to him and said: 'Master, at the door there is a man of respectable appearance, handsome and well-turned-out, with many servants, who wants an audience with you.' Yahya gave his permission and when the Iraqi had come in and kissed the ground before him, Yahya asked him who he was. 'Sir,' replied the Iraqi, 'I am the man whom the injustice of time had killed and whom you brought back to life from the tomb of misfortunes, resurrecting me to the paradise of my desire. I was the one who forged a letter supposedly from you which I took to 'Abd Allah ibn Malik al-Khuza'i.' 'How did he treat you,' asked Yahya, 'and what did he give you?' 'What he gave me,' replied the Iraqi, 'came from your hands, your generous nature, your abundant kindness, your great generosity, your magnanimity and your graciousness. He gave me riches, gifts and other presents, all of which are here at your door. It is for you to decide and to judge.' Yahya told him: 'The service that you have done me is better than what I have done for you. I owe you a great debt of gratitude for this huge favour you have conferred on me, as you have changed the enmity that existed between me and this highly respected man to friendship and affection, and so I shall give you the same amount that you were given by 'Abd Allah.' He then ordered that the man be presented with money, horses and chests to match those given to him by 'Abd Allah, and as a result he was restored to his former prosperity, thanks to the generosity of these two noble men.

It is said that among the Abbasid caliphs there was none more learned in all branches of knowledge than al-Ma'mun. Two days each week he would sit to debate with scholars, and in his presence the *faqihs* and theologians, each seated according to his category and rank, would hold discussions. On one occasion while he was sitting with them, a stranger entered the assembly wearing tattered white robes. He took his seat at the back, behind the *faqihs*, where he could scarcely be noticed. A discussion then started which revolved around a number of thorny points. It was the custom in such debates for the question to be put to each of the participants in turn, and everyone who had some subtlety to add or an uncommon point to make would produce it. On this occasion the question came round to the stranger, and when he spoke, his answer was better than that of any of the *faqihs*. It won the approval of the caliph . . .

Night 308

Morning now dawned and Shahrazad broke off from what she had been allowed to say. Then, when it was the three hundred and eighth night, SHE CONTINUED:

I have heard, O fortunate king, that the man's reply won the approval of the caliph, who ordered the man to move to a higher place. When it was his turn to deal with the second question his answer was even better than the first and the caliph moved him up higher, and when his answer to the third problem was better and more pertinent than the first two, he was placed close to the caliph himself.

After the close of the debate, water was brought and the participants washed their hands and then ate the food that was provided. The *faqihs* left, but al-Ma'mun stopped the stranger from going out with them. He brought him near and treated him with kindness, promising him liberal favours. Preparations were made for drink to be served, and wine was circulated among the caliph's handsome drinking companions. When it came round to the stranger, he rose to his feet and said: 'Commander of the Faithful, will you permit me to have a word?' 'Say what you want,' the caliph replied. 'The caliph's august intelligence, may God exalt it, knows that today in the noble assembly this servant of yours was among the least-known and the humblest of the participants, and yet because of the small amount of intelligence he showed, the caliph brought him up to sit near him and exalted him over the others, causing him to reach a station to which he had never aspired. Now, however, the caliph wants to part his servant from that small quantity of intelligence that raised him from degradation to honour and from scarcity to plenty. Far be it from the Commander of the Faithful to envy what the servant has in the way of intelligence, renown and excellence. If the servant drinks wine, his intelligence leaves him; ignorance approaches and robs him of his decorum; he reverts to the degradation from which he came, and in people's eyes he is to be despised and ignored. I hope that in his august intelligence the caliph's grace and liberality, together with his lordly and generous nature, will not rob his servant of this jewel.'

When al-Ma'mun heard what the man had to say, he praised and thanked him, after which he made him sit down in his place and treated him with respect, ordering him to be given a hundred thousand dirhams, together with a horse on which to ride, as well as splendid clothes. In all his assemblies he gave him a place of honour over all the *faqihs* until in status and position he outranked them. God knows better.

In former times there was a merchant in the land of Khurasan named Majd al-Din, a man of wealth, with black slaves, mamluks and servants. He had been childless until he reached the age of sixty, but then Almighty God provided him with a son, whom he named 'Ali Shar. 'Ali grew up to resemble the full moon, but when he had reached manhood and was perfect in all respects his father fell fatally ill. After summoning 'Ali, he said: 'My son, the time has come for me to die and I wish to give you some injunctions.' When 'Ali asked what these were, his father told him: 'I advise you not to be over-friendly with anyone and to avoid anything that might harm or injure you. Beware of an evil companion. He is like the smith – his smoke will harm you even if his fire does not scorch you. How well the poet put it:

There is no one in this age of yours for whose affection you should
    hope,
And when Time plays you false, no friend will remain true.
Live on your own; rely on no one else.
These words hold my advice; this is enough.

Another poet said:

People are a hidden disease; do not rely on them.
Were you to study them you would find among them cunning cheats.

Another said:

To meet others brings you nothing but senseless babble.
Meet only a few, except to acquire knowledge or to better yourself.

Yet another said:

An intelligent man may have put people to the test,
But while he only tasted, I ate them.
I see their love to be deception,
While their religion is hypocrisy.'

'Father,' said 'Ali, 'I have heard and shall obey, but what am I to do then?' 'Do good when you can,' replied Majd al-Din. 'Continue to act generously and take every opportunity you can to be liberal, for you will not always succeed in your pursuits. How well the poet expressed it where he said:

It is not at every moment and every time
That generous deeds are to be done.
When the chance comes, hurry to take it
For fear it may be lost.'

'Father,' said 'Ali again, 'I have heard and shall obey . . .'

Night 309

Morning now dawned and Shahrazad broke off from what she had been allowed to say. Then, when it was the three hundred and ninth night, SHE CONTINUED:

I have heard, O fortunate king, that 'Ali said: 'I have heard and shall obey, but then what?' 'My son,' said Majd al-Din, 'remember God and He will remember you. Preserve your wealth and don't be extravagant, for if you are, you will find yourself needing help from the lowest of men. Know that a man's worth depends on what he owns. How excellent are the poet's lines:

> When I am short of funds, no friend will stay with me;
> If I am wealthy, all men are my friends.
> How many an enemy befriends me thanks to wealth;
> When money vanishes, how many friends are turned to foes.'

'What then?' asked 'Ali. 'My son,' replied his father, 'consult your elders; when you want something, never act hastily; if you show mercy to your inferiors, your superiors may have mercy on you. Treat no one unjustly, lest God put you in the power of someone who will be unjust to you. How well the poet expressed it:

> Join someone else's opinion to your own and take advice;
> Two people will not fail to see the proper course.
> Man is a mirror which shows him his own face,
> But only with two mirrors can he see the back of his own head.

Another poet said:

> Go slowly; do not rush at what you want;
> Show mercy and you will meet the Merciful.
> There is no power that God's power does not surpass,
> And no wrongdoer will escape one who does wrong.

Yet another poet said:

> Do not act unjustly when you have the power;
> For vengeance overtakes the wrongdoer.
> You may sleep but your victim is awake,
> Cursing you, and God's eye can never sleep.

Beware of drinking wine. This is the source of all evil; it does away with reason and brings the drinker into contempt. How well the poet expressed this:

> By God, I shall not fall victim to wine
> While soul is joined to body and my words are clear.
> I'll never feel a hankering for it;
> My choice companions are none but the sober.

This is my advice to you; keep it before you and God will act in my place as your mentor.' When he had said this, Majd al-Din lost consciousness, but after an interval of silence he regained his senses, asked pardon from God and recited the confession of faith. He then died and was received into the mercy of Almighty God.

'Ali Shar shed tears and bewailed the death of his father. The necessary preparations were made for the funeral and the bier was accompanied on foot by high and low alike. The Quran reciters read the Quran aloud around the coffin and no single thing that should have been done was omitted by 'Ali. Prayers were said over the grave as the body was buried, and over the grave these verses were inscribed:

> You were created from earth, becoming a live creature;
> You were taught to speak with eloquence.
> You have returned to earth, becoming a dead thing.
> It is as though you never left the earth at all.

'Ali Shar grieved deeply for his father and followed the custom of the leading men in arranging for ceremonies of mourning to be held for him. He was still in mourning when a short time later his mother died, and for her too he made similar arrangements. Then he took his seat in his shop and began the business of buying and selling, but, in accordance with his father's advice, he was not on intimate terms with anyone. This went on for a year, but after that some bastard children of fornication tricked their way into his favour and became his companions. In their company he turned to debauchery, abandoning the path of right guidance. He drank wine and frequented the company of pretty girls morning and evening. 'My father collected all this money for me,' he said to himself, 'and if I don't spend it, to whom am I going to leave it? By God, I shall follow the poet's words:

If you spend all your days acquiring and amassing wealth,
When are you to enjoy what you have got?'

As a result, he spent all his nights and days squandering his wealth until
it had all gone and he had become poor. In his straitened circumstances
and his distress he had to sell his shop, his properties and everything
else. He even had to sell his own clothes, leaving himself with a single
suit. When he was cured of his drunkenness and had begun to think
again, he was overcome by sadness. One day, when he had sat from
daybreak until afternoon without eating, he told himself that he would
make the rounds of those he had spent his money on, in the hope that
one of them might give him food for the day. He visited them all, but
when he knocked on any door, the owner would hide away from him,
pretending not to be there. Consumed by hunger, he went to the traders'
market . . .

Night 310

Morning now dawned and Shahrazad broke off from what she had been
allowed to say. Then, when it was the three hundred and tenth night,
SHE CONTINUED:

I have heard, O fortunate king, that, consumed by hunger, he went to
the traders' market, which he found crowded with people. He asked
himself what the reason for this might be, and he said: 'By God, I am
not going to move off until I have had a look at this circle of people.'
When he went up to it he found a girl, five foot tall, symmetrically
formed, with rosy cheeks and rounded breasts. She surpassed all the
people of her age in beauty, grace and perfection, being, as a poet
described her:

Created in accord with her own desires,
Perfected in beauty's mould, neither tall nor short.
Beauty itself is enamoured of her form;
Reluctance, pride and modesty prevent approach.
She appears like the full moon, slender as a bough;
She smells of musk, without match among humankind,
Formed as though from the essence of a pearl,
In each of her limbs beauty displays a moon.

The girl's name was Zumurrud, and when 'Ali Shar saw her he was astonished by her beauty and grace and he said: 'By God, I am not going to leave until I see what price she is going to fetch and until I find out who buys her.' He stood with a group of merchants who thought that he was a would-be purchaser, believing him rich because of his inherited wealth. The auctioneer stood beside the girl and called out: 'Merchants and men of wealth, who will open the bidding for this girl, the mistress of moons, the radiant pearl, Zumurrud, the curtain maker, the goal of those who seek and the delight of the desirous? Open the bidding and whoever opens it will face no blame or reproach.' 'Five hundred dinars,' said one of the merchants. 'And ten,' said another. A blue-eyed, ugly old man named Rashid al-Din said: 'And a hundred.' 'And ten,' said another, but then Rashid al-Din offered a thousand and the rest held their tongues and fell silent.

The auctioneer consulted Zumurrud's owner, who told him: 'I have sworn only to sell her to a man of her own choice, so consult her.' So the man went up to her and said: 'Mistress of moons, this merchant wants to buy you.' The girl looked at her prospective purchaser and, seeing how ugly he was, she said to the auctioneer: 'I am not to be sold to an old man whom senility has left in such decrepitude. How well the poet expressed it:

One day I asked her for a kiss;
I was wealthy and prosperous but she looked at my white hair.
Hurriedly she turned away, saying: "No,
By God, Who created man from naught,
There is nothing that I want from this white hair.
Is my mouth to be stuffed with cotton while I am still alive?"'

When the auctioneer heard what she said, he told her: 'By God, you are to be excused and you are worth ten thousand dinars.' He explained to her owner that she would not accept Rashid al-Din, and told him to ask her to look for someone else. Another buyer came forward offering the same price as Rashid al-Din, whom she had rejected. She looked at him and saw that his beard was dyed. 'What is this disgrace?' she exclaimed. 'Blackness on the face of a grey-haired man is suspicious.' With many more expressions of wonder, she recited the lines:

'I saw what I saw from So-and-So –
The back of a neck to be beaten with a slipper,

A beard which was a training ground for bugs,
The hair all askew from being tied with a headband.
You who are enthralled by my cheeks and my figure,
Why do you thoughtlessly try to fake what is impossible?
You stain your white hair with disgrace,
Hiding what has appeared, trying to cheat.
You leave with one beard and bring back another,
As though you were producing a shadow play.

How well another poet expressed it:

She said: "I see that you have now dyed your white hair."
I told her: "I have hidden it from you, who are my ears and my
   eyes."
With a loud laugh she said: "This is surprising.
Your fraudulence extends even to your hair."'

'By God, you're right,' said the auctioneer when he heard these lines,
and when the merchant asked what she had said, he repeated them to
him. The man realized that he was in the wrong and withdrew his offer.
Another merchant made a similar offer and asked the auctioneer to
consult Zumurrud. When she looked at him she discovered that he was
one-eyed. She pointed this out, quoting from the poet who said:

Never associate with a one-eyed man;
Beware of his evil and of his falseness.
Had there been any good in him at all,
God would not have blinded one of his two eyes.

The auctioneer then asked her if she would agree to be sold to another
merchant. Looking at him, however, she found that he was a small man
with a beard that hung down to his navel, and she said: 'It is to this man
that the poet's lines apply:

I have a friend with a beard that God has caused to grow
Although there is no useful purpose in its growth.
It is like a winter's night, long, dark and cold.'

At this point the auctioneer said: 'Lady, look and see whether there is
anyone here who takes your fancy and then tell me, so that I can sell
you to him.' She looked at the circle of merchants and studied them one
by one. Then her eye fell on 'Ali Shar . . .

Night 311

Morning now dawned and Shahrazad broke off from what she had been allowed to say. Then, when it was the three hundred and eleventh night, SHE CONTINUED:

I have heard, O fortunate king, that her eye fell on 'Ali Shar and this one glance was followed by a thousand sighs. Love for him entered her heart, as he was a man of remarkable beauty and more delicate than a zephyr of the north. She told the auctioneer that she was only to be sold to this man with the handsome face and the elegant figure, and she quoted the lines:

> They showed your lovely face and then blamed those whom it had
> 　　charmed.
> Had they wished to protect me, they would have veiled its beauty.

'This is the only one who will own me,' she went on. 'He has smooth cheeks; his spittle is like the fountain of Paradise; his saliva could cure the sick, and poetry and prose alike would be at a loss to describe his beauties. He is as the poet described:

> His saliva is wine, his breath musk and his teeth camphor.
> Ridwan drove him from Paradise for fear lest he enchant the houris.
> People blame him for being proud, but the full moon is pardoned for
> 　　its pride.

He has the curly hair, rosy cheeks and enchanting glance of which the poet said:

> There is a fawn who promised union;
> My eyes may look expectantly but my heart is uneasy.
> His eyelids guarantee his truth,
> But, fragile as they are, how can they keep their word?

Another poet said:

> They said: "A line of down is on his cheek;
> His beard is showing; how can he be loved?"
> I answered them: "Enough of blame; hold back.
> Even if that is really a line, it is a forgery.
> The garden of Eden is in the fruits of his cheeks,
> While his lips are shown to be the stream of Paradise."'

On hearing the verses that Zumurrud recited in praise of the handsome 'Ali Shar, the auctioneer was amazed both at her eloquence and at her resplendent beauty. Her owner told him: 'Don't be surprised either at her beauty, which puts the sun to shame, or at her knowledge of fine poetry. She can recite the Quran in all seven readings; she can relate the traditions of the Prophet in their authentic form; she can write in seven scripts; and she knows more of the sciences than the most learned scholar. Her hands are better than gold or silver in that she makes curtains of silk and sells each of them for fifty dinars, completing each one in eight days.' 'How fortunate will be the man who has her in his house as one of his choicest treasures!' exclaimed the auctioneer, and he was then instructed by her owner to sell her to the man of her choice.

He now went back and, after approaching 'Ali Shar, he kissed his hands and invited him to buy Zumurrud, describing her, telling him how much she knew, and adding: 'You are to be congratulated if you buy her, for she is a gift to you from God, Who is not niggardly with His gifts.' 'Ali Shar looked down at the ground for a time, laughing at himself and thinking: 'Up till now I have had nothing to eat, but I am embarrassed to say in front of the merchants that I have not got the money with which to buy her.' When Zumurrud saw him with his head bowed, she told the auctioneer: 'Take my hand and bring me to him, so that I may display myself to him and make him want to take me, for I am not going to be sold to anyone else.' The auctioneer took her, brought her in front of 'Ali Shar and asked him what he thought. 'Ali Shar said nothing and Zumurrud asked: 'My master and my heart's beloved, why don't you buy me? Buy me for whatever price you like and I shall bring you good fortune.' 'Ali Shar raised his head and said: 'Am I to be forced to buy? You would be dear at a thousand dinars.' 'Buy me at nine hundred then,' she said, and when he refused, she said: 'At eight hundred.' He refused again and she went on lowering the price until she came down to one hundred. 'I don't have a full hundred dinars,' he said, and she laughed and asked: 'How far short of this are you?' He then told her: 'I don't have a hundred dinars or anything else, silver or gold, dirhams or dinars. You will have to look for another purchaser.'

When Zumurrud realized that 'Ali Shar was penniless, she said: 'Take my hand and pretend that you want to examine me in private.' When he did that, she took from her pocket a purse containing a thousand dinars. 'Weigh out nine hundred of these as my price,' she told him, 'and keep the rest with you to use for us.' He did what she told him and bought her for nine hundred dinars, paying the purchase price from the purse. When he then took her home, she found this to be an empty room without furnishings or utensils. She gave him another thousand dinars and told him to go to the market and spend three hundred on these, which he did, after which she told him to buy food and drink for three dinars.

Night 312

Morning now dawned and Shahrazad broke off from what she had been allowed to say. Then, when it was the three hundred and twelfth night, SHE CONTINUED:

I have heard, O fortunate king, that Zumurrud told him to buy food and drink for three dinars, which he did. Next she wanted a piece of silk the size of a curtain, together with gold and silver thread, and silk in seven different colours. When he had bought all this, she spread out the furnishings and lit the candles. The two of them sat eating and drinking and then they went to bed and enjoyed one another, spending the night in each other's arms behind the curtains.

This was as the poet has described:

Visit your beloved with no thought for what the envious may say.
In love affairs the envious are no help.
I dreamt I saw you sleeping here with me,
As I kissed the cool tips of your lips.
In all I saw certainty and truth.
In spite of envious foes, I shall win through to it.
There is no sight more lovely to the eye
Than that of lovers lying on one bed,
Embracing each other and clothed in content,
Each pillowing the other with wrists and arms.
When their loving hearts are joined,
All others are found striking on cold iron.
You who blame them because they are in love,
Can you set right a heart that has gone astray?
One single hour of pure delight –
That is your goal; live for that single hour.

They spent the night in one another's embrace until dawn came, by which time each was filled with heartfelt love for the other.

Zumurrud then took the curtain, embroidered it with coloured silk and embellished it with gold and silver thread. She gave it a band adorned with pictures of birds, and round the border she embroidered images of all the wild animals that are to be found in the world. For eight days she worked on this, and when it was finished she trimmed it, gave it a smooth finish and then handed it to 'Ali Shar. 'Take it to the market,' she told him, 'and sell it to a merchant for fifty dinars, but take care not to let it go to a passer-by. That would lead to our being separated, as we have enemies who will not forget about us.' 'To hear is to obey,' he said and, following her instructions, he took the curtain to the market and sold it to a merchant. Then, as before, he bought another piece of silk, together with gold and silver thread, as well as the food they needed, all of which he brought to Zumurrud, giving her what was left of the money.

Every eight days she would provide him with a curtain to be sold for fifty dinars, and this went on for a whole year. When the year was up, he went to the market as usual, but after he had given the curtain to the auctioneer, a Christian came up and offered him sixty dinars. He refused, but the man kept increasing his offer until it came to one hundred dinars, with a ten-dinar commission for the auctioneer. This man came back to 'Ali Shar, and after telling him of the price offered, he tried to get him to conclude the sale. 'Master,' he said, 'don't be afraid of this Christian. He can't do you any harm.' The other merchants joined in pressing him, and so, in spite of his misgivings, he concluded the sale. He set off home with the money, only to find that the Christian was walking behind him.

'Why are you following me?' he asked, and the man replied: 'I've some business to do at the head of the lane, may God never reduce you to need.' Then, when 'Ali Shar reached his house, the man caught up with him. 'Damn you,' said 'Ali, 'why are you following me wherever I go?' 'Give me a drink of water,' said the Christian, 'for I'm thirsty, and may Almighty God reward you.' 'Ali said to himself: 'This man is a *dhimmi*. He has come to ask me for a drink and so, by God, I cannot disappoint him.'

Night 313

Morning now dawned and Shahrazad broke off from what she had been allowed to say. Then, when it was the three hundred and thirteenth night, SHE CONTINUED:

I have heard, O fortunate king, that 'Ali said to himself: 'This man is a *dhimmi*. He has come to ask me for a drink and so, by God, I cannot disappoint him.' 'Ali went into his house and fetched a jug of water. When Zumurrud saw him, she said: 'Darling, did you sell the curtain?' 'Yes,' he told her. 'To a merchant or to a passer-by?' she asked, adding: 'I feel in my heart that we are about to be separated.' 'I sold it to a merchant,' he said. 'Tell the truth,' she said, 'so that I may take my own precautions. Why have you fetched a jug of water?' 'To give a drink to the auctioneer,' he told her, at which she exclaimed: 'There is no power and no might except with God, the Exalted, the Almighty!' Then she recited the lines:

Go slowly, you who seek for parting,
And do not be deceived by an embrace.
Go slowly; Time is treacherous;
Companionship must end in parting.

When 'Ali went out with the jug, he found that the Christian was coming into the entrance hall. 'Dog,' he said, 'have you come here and how is it that you are entering my house without my leave?' 'Master,' replied the man, 'there is no difference between door and entrance hall, and I shall only move from here in order to go out. Yours is the grace, bounty, liberality and favour.' He took the jug and handed it back to 'Ali after having drunk the water. 'Ali took it and waited for him to rise. When he did not, 'Ali asked: 'Why haven't you got up and gone off on your way?' 'Master,' said the man, 'don't be one of those who act generously and then reproach those who have received their generosity, or one of those of whom the poet has written:

Those are gone who, if you came to their door with a request,
Would treat you with generosity.
If you stand at the door of those who have come after,
They will grudge you a drink of water.'

He went on: 'Master, I have had a drink, but I would like you to give me some food – whatever there is in the house, a crust of bread or a biscuit and an onion.' 'Get up without all this wrangling,' said 'Ali. 'There is nothing at all in the house.' The man replied: 'If that is true, then take these hundred dinars and fetch something from the market, even if it is only a loaf of bread, so that the two of us may share bread and salt.' 'Ali thought to himself: 'This Christian is mad. I'll take his hundred dinars, bring him two dirhams' worth of food and so have the laugh on him.' The man said: 'Master, I only want something to drive off hunger, even just a stale loaf and an onion. The best food is not something splendid but what removes hunger. How well the poet expressed it:

> When hunger can be kept at bay by a dry loaf,
> Why is it I am filled with sadness and distress?
> The most just thing is death that treats alike
> Caliphs and paupers in their wretchedness.'

'Ali told him: 'Wait here until I lock up the inner room and bring you something from the market.' The man agreed and 'Ali went and shut the room with a padlock on the door. He took the key and went to the market, where he bought toasted cheese, white honey, bananas and bread, which he brought to the Christian. When the man saw this, he exclaimed: 'Master, this is a lot – enough to feed ten men, while I am on my own. Perhaps you will eat with me?' 'Eat on your own. I am full,' 'Ali told him, but the man said: 'Master, the wise men have said that whoever does not eat with his guest is a child of fornication.' On hearing that, 'Ali sat down and ate a few mouthfuls with him. He was about to stop . . .

Night 314

Morning now dawned and Shahrazad broke off from what she had been allowed to say. Then, when it was the three hundred and fourteenth night, SHE CONTINUED:

I have heard, O fortunate king, that 'Ali sat down and ate a few mouthfuls with him. He was about to stop when the Christian took a banana, peeled it and broke it in half. In one half he put refined *banj* mixed with opium, a dirham's weight of which would knock out an elephant. He then dipped it in honey and said to 'Ali: 'Master, I swear by the truth of your religion that you must take this.' 'Ali was embarrassed at the thought of making the man break his word and so he took the banana from him and swallowed it. No sooner had it settled in his stomach than he fell head over heels, looking as though he had been sleeping for a year.

When the Christian saw that, he rose to his feet like a hairless wolf or the power of fate, and, taking the key of the inner room and leaving 'Ali lying on the floor, he ran to his brother and told him what had happened. The reason for all this was that the Christian's brother was the decrepit old man who had wanted to buy Zumurrud for a thousand dinars and whom she had been unwilling to accept, reciting satirical verses about him. Although outwardly he was a Muslim, calling himself Rashid al-Din, in secret he was an unbeliever. When Zumurrud had satirized and rejected him, he had complained to his brother, a Christian named Barsum, who later played this trick in order to take her from her master, 'Ali Shar. He had told his brother not to be sad as he would contrive to get the girl for him at no cost whatsoever, he being a wily, treacherous and corrupt soothsayer. After that, he had continued to plot and scheme until he managed to trick 'Ali, as has been described. When he had taken the key and brought word to his brother, the latter mounted his mule and, taking his servants with him, set off with Barsum to 'Ali's house. He had a purse containing a thousand dinars with him, in case he happened to meet the *wali* and had to bribe him. When he opened the room, his men fell on Zumurrud and seized her by force, threatening to kill her if she said a word. They left the house as it was, removing nothing from it, with 'Ali still lying in the entrance hall, and after shutting the door on him, they left the key of the inner room beside him.

Rashid al-Din took Zumurrud off to his mansion, where he placed her among his slave girls and concubines. 'You whore,' he said to her, 'I am the *shaikh* whom you refused to accept and whom you satirized, but now I've got you without payment.' 'God will settle your account, you evil old man,' she said, her eyes brimming with tears, 'because you have parted me from my master.' 'You lustful whore,' said Rashid al-Din, 'you are going to see how I shall punish you. I swear by the Messiah and the Virgin that, if you don't convert to my religion, I shall put you to all kinds of torture.' 'By God,' she replied, 'even if you cut my flesh into bits, I shall never forsake the religion of Islam, and it may be that Almighty God will bring me speedy relief. He is able to carry out whatever He wishes, and wise men have said that bodily suffering is preferable to what hurts religion.'

At this, Rashid al-Din called to the eunuchs and the slave girls, ordering them to throw her down, which they did. He started to beat her violently as she cried out for help, but, as no help came, she gave this up and began to say: 'God is enough for me and He will suffice.' This went on until breath failed her and her moans ceased. When Rashid al-Din had beaten her to his heart's content, he told the eunuchs to drag her out by the feet and throw her into the kitchen, where she was not to be given any food. The next morning the damned man sent for her and beat her once more, before ordering the eunuchs to throw her back again, which they did. When the pain of the beating had eased, she recited the formula: 'There is no god but God, and Muhammad is the Prophet of God,' adding: 'God is sufficient for me and how excellent a guardian is He.' She then called for help to our lord Muhammad, may God bless him and give him peace.

Night 315

Morning now dawned and Shahrazad broke off from what she had been allowed to say. Then, when it was the three hundred and fifteenth night, SHE CONTINUED:

I have heard, O fortunate king, that Zumurrud called for help to our lord Muhammad, may God bless him and give him peace.

So much for her, but as for 'Ali Shar, he stayed lying on the floor until the next day, when the effects of the drug cleared from his head. He then opened his eyes and called for Zumurrud, but there was no answer. He went into the inner room, but on finding only 'empty air and the sanctuary far removed', as the saying puts it, he realized that it must have been the Christian who was responsible for this. He wept, moaned and lamented, and through his tears he recited these lines:

Passion, do not spare me, but do not cease;
My heart finds itself between hardship and danger.
Masters, pity a slave humbled by the law of love,
A rich man among the people, who has become poor.
What can an archer do in a meeting with the foe
Whose bowstring snaps as he prepares to shoot?
When cares are multiplied for a young man,
Piled on each other, where can he escape from fate?

How many pains I took so we should not be parted,
But when fate strikes, then sight is blinded.

When he had finished this poem he sighed deeply and recited the following lines:

Those ones have left the sands of the tribe's pasturage;
The wretched lover longs for where they dwelt.
They have turned towards their own place; the spring camp
Yearns for them, whose traces are now scattered and effaced.
The beloved halted to question it and it replied,
As with an echo: 'There can be no meeting.'
This was a flash of lightning over the pasturage;
When it had gone, no gleam from it remained.

He was filled with regret when regret served no purpose; he wept and
tore his clothes, and taking a stone in each hand he went round the
city striking his breast with them, crying out: 'O Zumurrud!' He was
surrounded by children calling out: 'A madman, a madman!' and all
those who knew him wept for him and said: 'This is 'Ali Shar. What can
have happened to him?' This went on the whole day long, and when
night closed in he fell asleep in a lane, only to do the same thing again
when morning came. He spent the day wandering around the city with
his stones, but that evening he went back to spend the night in his own
house. His neighbour, a kindly old woman, saw him and said: 'My son,
may God bring you health. When did this mad fit come on?' He answered
her with these lines:

They said: 'The one you love has made you mad';
I said: 'It is only madmen who enjoy this life.'
Forget about my madness; bring me its cause.
If that cures me, then cease your blame.

The old woman realized that he was a lover parted from his beloved,
and she exclaimed: 'There is no might and no power except with God,
the Exalted, the Omnipotent! Please tell me, my son, about the misfortune that has befallen you, as maybe, if God wills it, He will enable me
to help you.' 'Ali told her everything that had happened to him in his
encounter with Barsum the Christian, brother of the soothsayer who
called himself Rashid al-Din. After hearing this, she said: 'My son, you
are to be excused,' and then she recited tearfully:

Lovers have sufficient torment in this world;
God forbid they should be tortured in hellfire.
They died of love, chastely concealing it,
A fact tradition witnesses for us.

When she had finished reciting this, she said: 'My son, get up now and buy a basket of the kind that jewellers use. Then purchase bracelets, rings, earrings and other ornaments to suit women, sparing no expense. Put them all in the basket and bring it here. I'll carry it on my head as though I was peddling the contents, and then I shall go around the houses looking for Zumurrud until, if God Almighty wills it, I shall get some news of her.' 'Ali was delighted by this and, after kissing her hands, he left in a hurry and brought her what she had asked for. She then got up and put on a patched gown, and, with a honey-coloured shawl over her head and a staff in her hand, she wandered round the alleys and the houses carrying the basket. She went from place to place, quarter to quarter and street to street until Almighty God led her to the mansion of the damned Christian, Rashid al-Din. In it she heard the sound of moaning and she knocked on the door.

Night 316

Morning now dawned and Shahrazad broke off from what she had been allowed to say. Then, when it was the three hundred and sixteenth night, SHE CONTINUED:

I have heard, O fortunate king, that the old woman heard the sound of moaning from inside the house and knocked on the door. A slave girl came down, opened it and greeted her. 'I have these things to sell,' said the old woman. 'Do you have anyone here who might like to buy something?' 'Yes,' replied the girl, and she brought the old woman into the house and sat her between the other girls. Each of them took something, and the old woman treated them with benevolence, lowering her prices for them. They were pleased with her kindness and her soft words, while, for her part, she was looking around the place trying to discover who had been moaning. She happened to turn in the right direction, and while treating the others with even more friendship and kindness, and after looking carefully, she discovered that there, lying on the ground, was Zumurrud. On recognizing her, she wept and said: 'My children, why is this girl in such a state?' The others told her the whole story and said: 'This is not of our choosing. Our master ordered us to do this, but he is now off on a journey.' 'I want you to do something for me, children,' she told them, 'and that is to free this poor creature from her bonds until you learn that your master has returned, when you can tie her up as before. In this way you will win yourselves a reward from the Lord of all creation.' 'To hear is to obey,' they said, and they untied Zumurrud and gave her food and drink. 'I wish my leg had been broken and I had never come to your house,' the old woman told them, but then she went to Zumurrud and said: 'May God bring you health, my daughter. He will fetch you relief.'

She now told Zumurrud that she had come from her master 'Ali Shar, and then instructed her to be ready on the following night and to listen for a sound. She went on: 'Your master will come for you and stand underneath the house, by the stone bench, and whistle to you. When you hear that, whistle back and lower yourself from the window on a rope. He will then take you away.' Zumurrud thanked the old woman, who went off to give 'Ali Shar the news. She told him: 'When night comes, go at midnight to such-and-such a quarter, which contains the house of the damned Rashid al-Din.' After telling him how to recognize it, she went on: 'Stand underneath it and whistle. Zumurrud will lower herself down to you, after which you can take her and go off with her wherever you want.'

'Ali thanked her and, shedding tears, he recited these lines:

Let censurers stop their chattering;
My heart is distressed; my body thin and worn.
Tears produce a chain of truthful evidence,
Both when held back and when allowed to flow.
You who are untroubled by my cares and my ambitions,
Do not take trouble to ask me how I am.
A beloved with sweet lips, soft and well shaped,
Has captured my heart with honeyed kisses and a quivering form.
Since she left me, my heart has found no rest;
Sleep has not closed my eyes and patience has not helped my hopes.
You left me prey to longing, miserable,
Tossed around between the envious and the censurers.
I do not recognize what consolation is,
And never shall I hold another in my heart.

When he had finished this poem he sighed and, with more tears, he recited:

> How excellent is the one who brought me good news of your
>   coming,
> For this was what I most wanted to hear.
> Were the messenger content with a cast-off as a gift,
> I would give him a heart torn when we took our leave.

'Ali waited until it was dark and then, when the time of the rendezvous had come, he went to the quarter that his neighbour had described for him. He saw and recognized Rashid al-Din's mansion and sat down on the bench beneath it. Here sleep overcame him – glory be to the One Who never sleeps – as passion had kept him from sleeping for some time and he had become like a drunkard. Then, while he lay asleep . . .

Night 317

Morning now dawned and Shahrazad broke off from what she had been allowed to say. Then, when it was the three hundred and seventeenth night, SHE CONTINUED:

I have heard, O fortunate king, that, while he lay asleep, a thief, who had come out that night into the outskirts of the city in order to steal something, was led by fate to pass beneath Rashid al-Din's mansion. He circled round it but could find no way to climb into it, and in his circuit he came to the bench, where he found 'Ali Shar asleep. He took his turban and after that, before he knew what was happening, Zumurrud looked out and, seeing him standing there in the darkness, thought that he was her master. She whistled and he whistled back, after which she let herself down on her rope, taking with her a pair of saddlebags filled with gold. When the thief saw this he said to himself: 'This is a wonderful thing for which there must be some remarkable cause.' He took up the saddlebags, hoisted Zumurrud over his shoulder, and set off with his booty like a flash of lightning. Zumurrud said: 'The old woman told me that my loss had made you weak, but here you are, stronger than a horse.' When he made no reply she felt his face and discovered a beard like a bath brush, as though a pig had swallowed feathers whose down had sprouted out through its throat. In her alarm she said: 'Who are you?' 'Whore,' he answered, 'I am Jawan the Kurd, the cunning, one of

Ahmad al-Danaf's gang. There are forty of us and tonight we shall all bang away at your womb from evening till morning.' When Zumurrud heard this she burst into tears and struck her face, but she realized that fate had overpowered her and that there was nothing she could do except to entrust herself to Almighty God. She submitted to the decree of God, exclaiming: 'There is no god but God! As soon as I escape from one predicament I fall into another that is greater.'

The reason why Jawan had gone there was that he had told Ahmad al-Danaf that he had been to Baghdad before and knew of a cave outside the city which was big enough to hold forty men. He added: 'I propose to go on ahead of you and bring my mother to the cave. Then I shall go back to the city and steal something there to bring you luck and keep it for you until you come. This will be your guest offering from me.' 'Do as you want,' said Ahmad, and so the Kurd went on before them and got there first. After he had installed his mother in the cave, he went out and, on finding a soldier sleeping with his horse tethered beside him, he cut the man's throat and took his clothes, his horse and his weapons, which he hid away with his mother in the cave, where he tied the horse. It was after this that he went back to Baghdad and walked through the streets until he reached Rashid al-Din's house, where, as has already been told, he took 'Ali Shar's turban and made off with Zumurrud, his slave girl.

He ran on, carrying Zumurrud, until he brought her to his mother, whom he told to watch over her until he came back in the early morning. He then left.

Night 318

Morning now dawned and Shahrazad broke off from what she had been allowed to say. Then, when it was the three hundred and eighteenth night, SHE CONTINUED:

I have heard, O fortunate king, that the Kurd told his mother to watch over Zumurrud until he came back in the early morning. He then left.

Zumurrud told herself that she had better not let slip any chance of rescuing herself by some trick, saying: 'How can I bear to wait for these forty men to come, all of whom will take their turn on me until I become like a sinking ship?' So she said to the old woman: 'Aunt, will you take me out of the cave so that I may delouse you in the sunshine?' 'Willingly, daughter,' said the old woman. 'For a long time I have not been near the baths, as these pigs keep on taking me round from one place to another.' So Zumurrud went out with her and started to delouse her, killing the lice from her head, until the delighted old woman lay down to sleep.

At this point Zumurrud got up and dressed herself in the clothes of the soldier whom Jawan had killed, strapping on his sword round her waist and putting on his turban, until she looked like a man. She then mounted his horse and took the bags of gold with her, praying: 'O kind Shelterer, shelter me for the sake of the dignity of Muhammad, may God bless him and give him peace.' She then added to herself: 'If I went to the city, I might be seen by some member of that soldier's family, which would do me no good.' So she turned away from it and rode off into the desert, taking her saddlebags with her, eating whatever was growing and drinking from streams, while her horse did the same. This went on for ten days and then on the eleventh she arrived at a pleasant and secure city, which had an air of solid prosperity. The cold of winter had left it and spring had come with its blossoms and roses. The flowers were blooming; there were running streams and the birds were singing.

When Zumurrud approached the city gate she found to her surprise that its troops, emirs and leading citizens were all gathered there and she said to herself: 'There must be some reason why the people of the city are all here at the gate.' She rode towards them and when she had got near, the soldiers hurried out to meet her before dismounting and kissing the ground in front of her, exclaiming: 'God send you victory, our lord the sultan!' The functionaries gathered in ranks before her and the soldiers arranged the people in order, repeating: 'God send you victory, and may your arrival bring blessing to the Muslims, universal sultan. May God establish you, king of the age, unique in your period and time.' When Zumurrud asked them what this was about, the chamberlain explained: 'You have been given a gift by One Who is not miserly with His gifts. He has made you king of this city and ruler over all its people. You must know that it is the custom here that when the king dies leaving no heir, the troops move out of the city and wait for three days. Whatever man comes from the direction from which you came is appointed king. Praise be to God, Who has brought us a fair-faced Turk, but even if a lesser man had come, he would still have become our king.'

Zumurrud, who showed good sense in all that she did, said: 'You must not think that I am one of the common Turks. I am highly born, but I became angry with my family and so went away and left them. Look at these saddlebags full of gold, which I have carried with me in order to allow me to give alms to poor beggars along my path.' The towns-people called down blessings on her and were as glad to have found her as she was to have found them. She said to herself: 'Now that I have got so far . . .'

Night 319

Morning now dawned and Shahrazad broke off from what she had been allowed to say. Then, when it was the three hundred and nineteenth night, SHE CONTINUED:

I have heard, O fortunate king, that Zumurrud said to herself: 'Now that I have got so far, it may be that God will reunite me with my master here, and whatever He wishes, He has the power to perform.'

She then entered the city, accompanied by the troops, who dismounted and walked in front of her until they brought her to the palace. There she too dismounted, and the emirs and grandees, with their hands under her arms, escorted her and sat her on the throne, all kissing the ground in front of her. When she had taken her seat she ordered the treasuries to be opened, and when this had been done she gave money to all the soldiers, who prayed that she be granted a long reign. Everyone, includ-ing all the people of her lands, obeyed her and things went on like this for some time. She issued orders and prohibitions, winning deep respect from the people because of her generosity and virtue. She abolished market taxes, freed prisoners and removed injustices, so that all the people loved her, but whenever she thought of her master she wept and prayed that God might reunite them.

One night, when she happened to think of him and of the days that they had passed together, she shed tears and recited these lines:

Time may have passed, but longing is still fresh;
Tears have wounded my eyes, and still more follow them.
When I weep, I weep for the sorrow of my love;
For the lover, parting is something hard to bear.

When she had finished her poem she wiped away her tears and went up to the palace. She entered the harem, where she set aside separate rooms for the slave girls and concubines, assigning them regular payments and allowances. She claimed that she wanted to have her own quarters where she could devote herself to the worship of God. She began fasting and praying to such an extent that the emirs remarked on her great piety, and the only servants whom she allowed to attend on her were two young eunuchs.

She sat on the royal throne for a year without hearing any news of her master or finding any trace of him. In her anxiety she summoned the viziers and the chamberlains and told them to fetch architects and builders who were to construct an arena for her beneath the palace walls, one *parasang* in length by one in breadth. They followed her specifications and completed this very quickly. When it was finished, she went down to it and had a huge dome placed there, in which the chairs of the emirs were arranged in ranks. She then ordered tables to be set out, laden with splendid foods of all kinds, and when her orders had been carried out, she told the state officials to eat, which they did. 'At the start of each new month,' she told the emirs, 'I want you to repeat this process and to have it proclaimed throughout the city that no one is to open his shop but that everyone is to come here and eat from the king's table, while anyone who disobeys is to be hanged over the door of his house.'

On the first day of the next month the emirs followed her orders, and the custom continued to be observed until it came to the first day of the first month of the second year. Zumurrud came down to the arena and a proclamation was made to the people that anyone who opened his shop, store or house would be hanged over his own door and that they should all come to eat from the king's table. When the announcement had been made, the tables were set out and the people came in droves, and she ordered them to sit down and to eat until they had had their fill of the various foods that were there. They did what she had told them, while she herself sat watching from her royal throne. Each of those sitting there was saying to himself: 'I am the one that the king is looking at.' When they had started on the meal, the emirs encouraged them to eat up without embarrassment, as this is what the king wanted. When they had had enough they left, calling down blessings on the king and saying to each other: 'In all our lives we have never seen a sultan who loved the poor as much as this one.'

While they were praying God to grant her a long life, she herself went back to her palace . . .

Night 320

Morning now dawned and Shahrazad broke off from what she had been allowed to say. Then, when it was the three hundred and twentieth night, SHE CONTINUED:

I have heard, O fortunate king, that Zumurrud went back to her palace, glad at what she had arranged and saying to herself: 'If it is the will of Almighty God, this may help me find out something about my master, 'Ali Shar.' On the first day of the second month, following her custom, she had the tables set out and came down herself to sit on her throne, telling the people to sit down and eat. While she was at the head of the tables, with crowds upon crowds of people taking their places, one after the other, her eye fell on Barsum the Christian, the man who had bought the curtain from her master. She recognized him and said: 'This is the first sign of a happy ending and the achievement of my wishes.'

Barsum came forward and took his place with the others in order to eat. He caught sight of a dish of rice sweetened with sprinkled sugar and, as it was at a distance from him, he pushed his way through to it before stretching out his hand, taking it and putting it down in front of him. A man sitting beside him said: 'Why don't you eat what is in front of you? This is shameful. How can you reach out to take something so far away from you? Aren't you ashamed?' Barsum insisted that he would only eat from that dish and the man said: 'Eat then, but I hope you find no enjoyment in it.' 'Let him eat from it,' said a hashish addict, 'so that I can have some myself.' 'Vilest of addicts,' the man replied, 'this is no food for you but for the emirs. Leave it alone so that it can be given back to those who are supposed to eat it.' Barsum would not listen. He seized a morsel and put it in his mouth, but as he was about to take another, Zumurrud, who had been watching him, shouted to her soldiers: 'Bring me the man who has the sweet rice dish in front of him! Don't let him eat what he is holding but throw it out of his hand.'

Four troopers went up to Barsum, threw away the food that he was clutching and dragged him face downwards until they had brought him in front of Zumurrud. People stopped eating and said to one another: 'By God, this fellow has done wrong by not eating the food that was there for him and his likes.' 'I was happy enough with the porridge in front of me,' claimed another and the hashish addict said: 'Praise be to

God, Who stopped me from taking anything from the plate of sweetened rice. After that man had put it down in front of himself I was waiting for him to enjoy it and then take some of it myself, but he was dragged off, as we saw.' 'Wait until we see what happens to him,' the others advised.

When Barsum was taken before Zumurrud, she said: 'What is your name, blue eyes, you miserable fellow, and why have you come to our country?' Barsum was wearing a white turban and he concealed his real name, saying: 'O king, my name is 'Ali. I am a weaver by profession and I am here to trade.' 'Bring me the divination table and a brass pen,' said Zumurrud. These were fetched instantly and she took them, shook the sand over the table and used the pen to draw the shape of a monkey. She then looked up and, after studying Barsum for some time, she said: 'Dog, how dare you lie to kings? Are you not a Christian named Barsum, coming here to search for something that you need? Tell me the truth or else, by the glory of God's divinity, I shall cut off your head.' Barsum stammered and the emirs and the others who were there said: 'This king is a master of geomancy. Glory be to God, Who gave him this gift!'

Zumurrud then shouted at Barsum: 'Tell me the truth or else I shall have you killed!' 'Mercy, king of the age,' Barsum pleaded. 'You have divined correctly, for this one is indeed a Christian.'

Night 321

Morning now dawned and Shahrazad broke off from what she had been allowed to say. Then, when it was the three hundred and twenty-first night, SHE CONTINUED:

I have heard, O fortunate king, that Barsum said: 'You have divined correctly, for this one is indeed a Christian.' All those present, emirs and others, were astonished at the accuracy of Zumurrud's divination. 'This king,' they exclaimed, 'is an astrologer unmatched in this world!' She then ordered Barsum to be flayed and his skin stuffed with straw and hung up over the gate to the arena. A pit was to be dug outside the city in which his flesh and bones were to be burned, with dirt and filth being thrown over them. She was obeyed and all her orders were carried out. The people said: 'The man got what he deserved, and what an unlucky mouthful it was that he took!' One of them said: 'This one will divorce his wife if ever again in his life he eats sweetened rice,' while the hashish addict exclaimed: 'Praise be to God, Who preserved me from this man's fate by keeping me from eating that rice.' They all left, thinking it taboo to take Barsum's place by the rice dish.

In the third month the tables were set out as usual and filled with dishes, with Zumurrud sitting on her throne and the soldiers, now afraid of her severity, in their customary posts. The townsfolk came in as normal and circled around the food. They looked for the plate of rice and one of them said to another: 'Hajji Khalaf.' 'Here I am, Hajji Khalid,' said the other. 'Steer clear of the sweetened rice dish,' said Khalid, 'and take care not to eat any of it, for if you do you will be hanged.' They then sat down around the table to eat, and while they were at their meal Zumurrud, who had taken her place there, turned to look at a man who was hurrying in from the arena gate. Studying him closely, she made the discovery that he was Jawan the Kurd, the killer of the soldier.

The reason why Jawan had come there was that, after leaving his mother, he had gone off to tell his companions: 'I made a good haul yesterday. I killed a soldier and took his horse, and in the night I got a pair of saddlebags filled with gold, together with a girl who is worth even more than the gold. All this I left with my mother in the cave.' His companions were delighted and, as evening came, they set off for the cave. Jawan went in ahead as they followed, intending to fetch them the money that he had talked about, but he found the place bare. He asked his mother what had happened and she told him the whole story, leaving him to bite his hands in regret. 'By God,' he swore, 'I'll hunt around for that whore and take her from wherever she may be, even if she hides in the shell of a pistachio nut, and then I shall have my revenge on her.'

He left on his search and went round place after place until he arrived at Zumurrud's city. When he entered, he found no man there and so he questioned some of the women who were looking out of their windows. They told him that on the first of each month the king would give a banquet to which the people would go to be fed, and they showed him the way to the arena, where it was laid out. He hurried there but could find no empty seat except by the dish of rice. As this was in front of him, he stretched out his hand towards it, but the people shouted at him: 'Brother, what do you mean to do?' 'I want to eat my fill from this dish,' he told them. 'If you do,' said one of them, 'you will end up hanged.' 'Shut up,' he said, 'and don't mention such a thing.' Then, stretching out his hand, he pulled the dish towards him.

The hashish addict, mentioned earlier, was sitting beside him and when he saw what he had done, he fled from his place, with the effects of the drug clearing from his head, and sat down a long way away, exclaiming: 'There is nothing I want in that dish!' The hand that Jawan put out was like a crow's foot, but after he had plunged it into the dish and drawn it out again it looked like a camel's hoof.

Night 322

Morning now dawned and Shahrazad broke off from what she had been allowed to say. Then, when it was the three hundred and twenty-second night, SHE CONTINUED:

I have heard, O fortunate king, that the hand that Jawan took out from the dish was like a camel's hoof. He turned the morsel he was holding round and round in his hand until it was like a large orange and then he quickly threw it into his mouth, from where it went down his gullet with a noise like thunder. Where it had been one could see the bottom of the plate. 'Praise be to God for not making me into food and putting me in front of you!' exclaimed a man sitting beside him. 'You've swallowed down the whole plate with a single gulp.' 'Let him eat,' said the hashish addict, 'for I seem to see in him the image of a hanged man.' Then he turned to Jawan and said: 'Eat, but may God not allow you to enjoy it.'

Jawan stretched out for a second mouthful, but as he was about to turn it round in his hand as he had done with the first, Zumurrud called out to some of her soldiers, telling them: 'Bring me that man quickly and don't let him eat what he is holding.' The men ran up to him as he was bending over the dish, seized him and took him to stand in front of Zumurrud. The others took malicious pleasure from this and told each other: 'He deserves this. We warned him, but he wouldn't listen. Whoever sits in this seat is sure to be killed, and the rice brings bad luck on everyone who eats it.'

Zumurrud asked Jawan: 'What is your name and your profession and why have you come to our city?' 'My lord the sultan,' Jawan answered, 'my name is 'Uthman. I am a gardener and the reason I have come here is that I am going round searching for something I have lost.' 'Bring me the divination table,' said Zumurrud, and she then took a pen and shook the sand on the table. After studying it for a while, she raised her head and said: 'Damn you, you foul creature. How dare you lie to kings? This sand tells me that your name is Jawan the Kurd and that you are a professional thief. You seize people's goods unlawfully and you take lives that God only allows to be taken when there is just cause.' Then she shouted at him: 'Tell me the truth about yourself, pig, or else I shall cut off your head!'

When Jawan heard what she had to say he turned pale and showed his teeth, but thinking that if he told the truth he might escape, he said: 'You are right, O king, but from now on I repent at your hands and return to Almighty God.' Zumurrud said: 'It is not lawful for me to leave an evil-doer in the path of Muslims.' Then she told her attendants: 'Take him, flay him and then deal with him as you dealt last month with his fellow liar.' They did as they were told and when the hashish addict saw Jawan being arrested by the soldiers, he turned his back on the plate of rice and said: 'I must not turn my face towards you.' The townsfolk now finished eating, dispersed and went home, while Zumurrud went to her palace and allowed her mamluks to leave.

At the start of the next month the people came to the arena as usual and when the food had been brought, they sat waiting for permission to begin. Zumurrud came in, took her seat and, as she looked at them, she found to her surprise that no one was sitting opposite the rice, although there was space enough there for four. As she was looking round, she happened to turn and see a man rushing in through the gate. He hurried on until he reached the table where he found no place free except by the dish of rice. When he sat down, Zumurrud, looking closely at him, discovered that this was the damned Christian who called himself Rashid al-Din, and she said to herself: 'What a blessed banquet this is, as this unbeliever has been caught in its toils.'

The reason for Rashid al-Din's presence was a strange one. When he had come back from his journey . . .

Night 323

Morning now dawned and Shahrazad broke off from what she had been allowed to say. Then, when it was the three hundred and twenty-third night, SHE CONTINUED:

I have heard, O fortunate king, that when the man calling himself Rashid al-Din had come back from his journey, his household had told him that Zumurrud was missing, together with the saddlebags containing the gold. On hearing the news, he tore his clothes, slapped his face and pulled hairs from his beard. He sent his brother, Barsum, to look for her throughout the lands, but when news was slow to come, he went out to search both for his brother and for the girl. Fate brought him to her city, which he entered on the first day of the month. He walked through the streets but found them empty and the shops shut. He saw women at their windows and asked about this. They told him that on the first of each month the king would give a banquet for all the townspeople and that no one was permitted to sit at home or in his shop. They directed him to the arena and when he got there he found the people crowded around the food, leaving no place free except in front of the dish of sweetened rice. He sat down there and had reached out to take some of it when Zumurrud called out to the soldiers to bring her the man who was sitting by that dish, and, as they had done before, they identified him, seized him and brought him before Zumurrud. 'Wretch,' she said, 'what is your name and your profession and why have you come to our city?' 'O king of the age,' he answered, 'my name is Rustam and I have no profession as I am a poor dervish.' 'Bring me the divination table and a brass pen,' she said, and when, as before, these had been fetched, she took the pen and drew lines on the sand table. For a time she stared at it and then she lifted her head and looked at him. 'Dog,' she said, 'how dare you lie to kings? Your name is Rashid al-Din the Christian, and your trade consists of setting traps for Muslim girls and seizing them. In outward show you are a Muslim, but secretly you are a Christian. Tell the truth, for if you do not I will cut off your head.'

Rashid al-Din stammered but then said: 'You have spoken the truth, king of the age.' She ordered him to be stretched out and beaten with a hundred strokes of the whip on each foot and a thousand strokes on his body, after which he was to be flayed and his skin stuffed with oakum. They were then to dig a pit for him outside the city in which his body was to be burned, with dirt and filth being thrown over it. After these orders had been carried out the people were given permission to eat. When they had finished, they went off on their ways, while Zumurrud went up to her palace and exclaimed: 'Praise be to God, Who has soothed my heart by allowing me revenge on those who injured me!' She returned, thanks to the Creator of earth and heaven, and recited these lines:

> They held rule and were arrogant in what they did,
> But after a time it was as though that rule had never been.
> Had they been just, they would have had a just reward,

But through their tyranny Time turned against them with disaster
   and distress.
Fate spoke to them using its silent tongue:
'This is your just reward; Time cannot be blamed.'

When she had finished this poem her thoughts turned to her master, 'Ali
Shar, and her tears flooded down, but after that she returned to her
senses and said to herself: 'God has enabled me to revenge myself on my
enemies, and it may be that He will favour me with the return of my
loved ones.' She asked His pardon, Great and Glorious as He is . . .

Night 324

Morning now dawned and Shahrazad broke off from what she had been
allowed to say. Then, when it was the three hundred and twenty-fourth
night, SHE CONTINUED:

I have heard, O fortunate king, that Zumurrud asked pardon from
the Great and Glorious God, saying: 'It may be that He will show favour
to me by reuniting me soon with my beloved 'Ali Shar, for He has the
power to do what He wants; He is kind to His servants and knows their
needs.' She praised Him, asked again for pardon and resigned herself to
the blows of fate, knowing for certain that every beginning must have
an end. She recited the lines of the poet:

Take life lightly, for all our destiny
Is held within the hands of God.
What He forbids will never come to you;
Nor will that which He orders fail to come.

She also quoted:

Let the days unfold and do not enter the house of care.
There is many an affair whose quest was hard,
But where a happy ending has granted you success.

She also quoted:

Be mild when anger affects you;
Show patience in misfortune.
Time has left the nights pregnant,
And they give birth to marvels of all kinds.

From another poet she quoted:

Endure, for if you realized what good endurance brings,
You would rejoice and pain would not distress you.
Know that if you do not bear it willingly,
You will be forced to endure Fate's decrees.

For a whole month after she had recited these lines, Zumurrud spent her days in settling disputes between her people, issuing orders and prohibitions, and her nights in tears and sobs for her lost master, 'Ali Shar. Then, at the start of the new month, she ordered the banquet to be set out in the arena as usual, where she took her seat overlooking the people, who were waiting for permission to start eating. The seat by the dish of rice was empty. From her place at the head of the tables Zumurrud watched the arena gate to see who was going to come through it, saying to herself: 'God, Who restored Joseph to Jacob and freed Job from his misfortunes, favour me by restoring my master, 'Ali Shar, through Your power and might, You Who are the all-powerful, the Lord of all creation, the Guide of those who stray, Who listens to our cries and answers our prayers. Grant my request, Lord of creation.'

Before she had finished her prayer, through the door came a young man whose figure was like the branch of a *ban* tree. In spite of his thinness and pallor, he was extremely handsome and obviously a man of great intelligence and culture. When he came in, the only empty place he could find was by the dish of rice. Zumurrud's heart fluttered as she looked at him, and when she studied him closely, she recognized that this was her master, 'Ali Shar. She wanted to cry out for joy, but managed to control herself, fearing to be disgraced publicly, and so, in spite of her churning stomach and throbbing heart, she kept her feelings concealed.

The reason why 'Ali Shar had come was this. After he had fallen asleep on the bench and Zumurrud had come down and been seized by Jawan the Kurd, he woke up to find himself bare-headed and realized that some robber must have stolen his turban while he was sleeping. He recited the formula that never brings shame on those who quote it: 'We belong to God and to Him do we return.' Then he went back to the old woman who had told him where Zumurrud was. He knocked on her door, and when she came out he burst into tears in front of her before collapsing in a faint. On coming to his senses, he told her everything that had happened to him. She blamed him harshly and told him that his disastrous misfortune was his own fault, and she went on until blood ran from his nose and he fell unconscious.

When he recovered . . .

Night 325

Morning now dawned and Shahrazad broke off from what she had been allowed to say. Then, when it was the three hundred and twenty-fifth night, SHE CONTINUED:

I have heard, O fortunate king, that when he recovered he found the old woman shedding floods of tears for him, and in his distress he recited:

> How bitter is parting for lovers!
> What pleasure is theirs in union!
> May God unite all lovers,
> And guard me, who am in agony.

The old woman grieved for him and told him: 'Sit here until I find out the news for you; I shall come back as fast as possible.' 'To hear is to obey,' he replied, and she then left him and went off. It was midday before she came back, and when she did she told him: 'I think that you are going to die of grief as you are not going to see your beloved again until you meet on the bridge to Paradise. In the morning the people in the house found that the window overlooking the garden had been pulled away. Zumurrud was missing; with her had gone a pair of saddlebags containing the Christian's gold, and when I got there I found the *wali* and a number of his men standing at the door. There is no might and no power except with God, the Exalted, the Omnipotent.'

When 'Ali Shar heard this, the light turned to darkness in his eyes; he despaired of life and was sure of death, weeping so bitterly that he fell down in a faint. Although he recovered his senses, love and parting had inflicted such damage on him that he fell gravely ill and had to stay at home. The old woman continued to fetch him doctors, provide him with drinks and make broth for him for a whole year. At last he recovered his spirit and, recalling what had passed, he recited these lines:

> Cares have gathered round me;
> I am parted from my love;
> Tears course down; my heart is burned;

Passion is increased for one who finds no rest;
Love, longing and distress wear him away.
My Lord, if there is a relief for suffering,
Grant it to me while there is still a spark of life.

At the start of the second year, the old woman said to him: 'My son, this distress and sorrow of yours is not going to bring your beloved back. Get up, pull yourself together and search through the lands for her, as you may hear some news of her.' She continued to hearten and strengthen him until she restored his energy, after which she took him to the baths and gave him wine to drink and chicken to eat. She did this every day for a month, and when he had regained his strength he set off on his travels and went on until he reached Zumurrud's city. Here he came to the arena, sat down at the banquet and reached out to take some food. The people felt sorry for him and said: 'Don't take anything from this dish, young man, as everyone who eats from it comes to grief.' 'Let me eat from it,' 'Ali replied. 'They can do what they want with me and it may be that I will find rest from this troublesome life.'

He took his first mouthful and it struck Zumurrud, who wanted to have him brought to her, that he might be hungry. She said to herself: 'The proper thing for me to do is to let him eat his fill.' As he started to eat, the people looked at him in astonishment, waiting to see what was going to happen to him. Then, when he had had enough, Zumurrud said to a number of her eunuchs: 'Go to that young man who is eating the rice and bring him to me gently, telling him that the king wants a friendly word with him.' 'To hear is to obey,' they said, and going up to 'Ali they stood before him and said: 'Master, please come to the king, but do not be worried.' 'Ali agreed to this and as he went with them . . .

Night 326

Morning now dawned and Shahrazad broke off from what she had been allowed to say. Then, when it was the three hundred and twenty-sixth night, SHE CONTINUED:

I have heard, O fortunate king, that 'Ali agreed to this and as he went with them the people said to one another: 'There is no power and no might except with God, the Exalted, the Almighty. What do you suppose the king is going to do with him?' 'He is going to treat him well,' said one of them. 'If he had wanted to harm him, he would not have left him to eat his fill.'

When 'Ali stood before Zumurrud, he greeted her and kissed the ground in front of her. She returned his greeting and, after speaking to him courteously, she asked his name, his profession and the reason that had brought him to the city. He replied: 'My name, O king, is 'Ali Shar. I belong to a merchant family and my country is Khurasan. I am here to look for a slave girl whom I have lost. She was dearer to me than my hearing and my sight and, although I have lost her, she still holds my soul. This is my story.' He then wept until he fainted. Zumurrud ordered rosewater to be sprinkled on his face and this was done until he had recovered his senses. After his recovery she ordered the divination table to be brought, together with a brass pen, and when these had been fetched she took the pen, shook the sand and studied it for some time. 'You have told the truth,' she told him, 'and God will soon unite you with her, so do not be uneasy.'

She now ordered her chamberlain to take him to the baths, to provide him with a fine set of royal robes and to mount him on one of the specially picked royal chargers. In the evening he was to be brought to the palace. 'To hear is to obey,' said the chamberlain, and he took 'Ali from her presence and went off with him. The people asked each other: 'What is the king doing, treating this young man with such kindness?' 'Didn't I tell you,' said one of them, 'that the king would not harm him as he is a good-looking fellow? I realized that when the king let him go on eating.' Each one of them had something to say and they then dispersed and went on their ways.

Zumurrud could scarcely believe that night would ever come so that she could be alone with her lover, and when it did she went into her bedchamber, pretending to be overcome by drowsiness. She was not in the habit of letting anyone sleep in her room, apart from two little eunuchs who were there to serve her, but when she had taken her place there she sent for her dear 'Ali Shar. She was sitting on a couch with candles above and below her, and golden chandeliers threw light over the room. People were surprised to hear that she had sent for 'Ali. Everyone had suspicions to voice, and one of them said: 'The king has fallen in love with this boy and tomorrow he will be made an army commander.'

When 'Ali was brought in, he kissed the ground in front of Zumurrud and called down blessings on her, while she said to herself: 'I must play a joke on him for a while and not tell him who I am.' So she asked him whether he had been to the baths and when he said that he had, she said: 'Eat some of this chicken and meat and drink some of this sweet wine, as you must be tired, and when you have done that come up here.' 'To hear is to obey,' he said and he did what she had told him. When he had finished eating and drinking, she said: 'Come up on the couch and massage me.' He started to massage her feet and her legs, which he found softer than silk. 'Go higher,' she told him. 'Forgive me, master,' he replied, 'up to the knee but no further.' 'If you disobey me this will be an unlucky night for you.'

Night 327

Morning now dawned and Shahrazad broke off from what she had been allowed to say. Then, when it was the three hundred and twenty-seventh night, SHE CONTINUED:

I have heard, O fortunate king, that Zumurrud said: 'If you disobey me this will be an unlucky night for you. You must do what I tell you and I shall then make you my beloved and appoint you as one of my emirs.' 'Ali replied: 'King of the age, what am I supposed to do to obey you?' 'Undo your trousers and lie on your face,' she said. 'This is something that I have never done in my life, and if you force me to it, I shall take my case against you to God on the Day of Resurrection. Take back everything that you have given me and let me leave your city.' He wept and sobbed, but she repeated: 'Undo your trousers and lie on your face or else I shall cut off your head.'

When he did this, she got up on his back and he felt something smoother than silk and softer than butter, so that he said to himself: 'This king is better than any woman.' She waited for a time, lying on his back, and then she turned over on the couch and 'Ali said to himself: 'Praise God, it seems as though he has not got an erection.' ' 'Ali,' she told him, 'it is a habit of mine that I cannot get an erection until my penis is stroked by hand. Come and do this until it rises, or else I'll kill you.' She lay on her back, took his hand and set it on her vagina, which he found to be smoother than silk, white, large and plump and hot as the baths or as the heart of a lover consumed by passion. 'This is an extraordinary thing,' 'Ali said to himself. 'The king has a vagina.' His own lust stirred, with his penis stretching to its fullest, and when Zumurrud saw that she burst out laughing and said: 'Master, after all this, don't you recognize me?' 'Who are you, king?' he asked, to which she replied: 'I am your slave girl, Zumurrud.'

When 'Ali learned this, he kissed and embraced her and then, realizing that she really was his slave girl, he pounced on her, like a lion on a sheep, and plunged his rod into her scabbard. He kept on playing the roles of gatekeeper at her door and imam at her prayer niche, while she joined him in bendings and prostrations, rising and falling, following her hymns of praise with lascivious wriggling and movements, so much so that the eunuchs heard her. They came and looked from behind the curtains, to find the king lying with 'Ali Shar on top of her, the one grinding and moving around and the other snorting and writhing. 'That is not how a man moves,' they said. 'It may be that this king is a woman.' But they kept the matter concealed and told no one.

The next morning, Zumurrud sent for the whole of her army and her state officials. When they had come, she told them: 'I am about to go to this man's land, so choose for yourselves someone to act in my place as your ruler until I come back to you.' They obeyed her instruction, while she began to equip herself for the journey, collecting provisions, money, supplies and treasures, together with camels and mules. Then she left the city and travelled on until she reached 'Ali Shar's land, where he returned to his own house and then distributed gifts, alms and donations. God granted him children by Zumurrud and the two of them lived in the enjoyment of perfect happiness until they were visited by the destroyer of delights and the parter of companions. Praise be to the One Who remains unchanging. Glory be to God in all things.

A story is also told that the Commander of the Faithful, Harun al-Rashid, was wakeful one night and, being unable to sleep, he kept turning from side to side, owing to his insomnia. When he became tired of it he summoned Masrur and told him to fetch someone who might relieve his condition. 'Master,' said Masrur, 'would you like to go into the palace garden and take pleasure from looking at the flowers and watching the sky inlaid with stars and the moon between them gleaming on the water?' 'That doesn't tempt me,' replied the caliph, and so Masrur went on: 'In your palace, master, there are three hundred concubines, each with her own apartment. Give instructions that each of them should be alone in her apartment, so that you can go and watch them without their knowledge.' 'Masrur,' replied the caliph, 'the palace is mine and the girls are my property, but none of this tempts me.' 'Then summon the men of learning,' proposed Masrur, 'the philosophers and the poets, so that they may conduct investigations, recite poetry and produce stories and histories.' The caliph made the same objection, and Masrur went on to suggest: 'Order your pages, your boon companions and men of wit to come and entertain you with remarkable and witty tales.' When the caliph had rejected this suggestion too, Masrur said: 'Then cut off my head . . .'

Night 328

Morning now dawned and Shahrazad broke off from what she had been allowed to say. Then, when it was the three hundred and twenty-eighth night, SHE CONTINUED:

I have heard, O fortunate king, that Masrur said: 'Then cut off my head as this may cure your sleeplessness and settle your restlessness.' The caliph laughed and told him to go and see which of his drinking companions was sitting at the door. Masrur went out and when he came back he told the caliph that 'Ali ibn Mansur, the witty Damascene, was there. 'Bring him in to me,' said the caliph.

Masrur went to fetch 'Ali, who, on his arrival, greeted the caliph; he returned his greeting and said: 'Tell me one of your stories, Ibn Mansur.' 'Shall I tell you of something that I have seen myself or something that I have heard, Commander of the Faithful?' asked 'Ali. 'If you have seen something remarkable, then tell me about it, for what has been said is not like what has been seen,' the caliph replied. 'Listen to me, then, and pay attention,' said 'Ali. 'I am listening to you with my ears, looking at you with my eyes and paying attention to you with my heart,' the caliph assured him. 'ALI SAID:

Know then, Commander of the Faithful, that I used to get an annual payment from Muhammad ibn Sulaiman al-Hashimi, the sultan of Basra. Once when I went to him as usual, I found, when I got there, that he was getting ready to ride out to hunt. We exchanged greetings and he told me to come with him. 'I'm not capable of riding,' I told him, 'so settle me in your guest house and tell your chamberlains and underlings to look after me.' This is what he did, and when he had set off to hunt, they treated me with marked respect and showed me the greatest hospitality. 'By God,' I then said to myself, 'it's strange that I have been coming for years from Baghdad to Basra and yet the only part of the place I know is what lies between the palace and the garden, and the garden and the palace. When am I ever going to get another opportunity like this to look round? I shall go off immediately on a solitary sight-seeing tour to digest my meal.'

I put on my most splendid clothes and walked through part of the city. As you know, Commander of the Faithful, there are seventy streets in Basra, each of which is seventy Iraqi *parasangs* long. I got lost among the alleyways there and began to feel thirsty. Then, while I was walking, I suddenly saw a large door with two brass rings, over which hung curtains of red brocade. It was flanked by two stone benches and from above it was overshadowed by a vine trellis. I stopped to look at the place, and while I was standing there I heard a moan that came from a sorrowful heart and a voice modulating a chant to which were set the following lines:

My body has become a place of sickness and of suffering,
Because of a gazelle who lives in a distant land.
The breezes of Zarud have stirred my sorrow.
By the Lord your Master, breezes, turn aside
To the one who should be my comfort.
Reproach him and it may be that this will move him.
Speak well, if he listens to you,
And between the two of you rehearse stories of lovers.
In your kindness do me a favour,
And when you talk to him, ask him:
'How is it you destroy a slave by your abandonment,
Although he is guilty of no fault and no transgression,
And his heart has not inclined to court another?
No firm covenant is broken, nor has any wrong been done.'
If he smiles, then gently say:
'What harm would it do were you to grant him union?
His love for you is passionate, as it should be;
His eyes are sleepless and he weeps and wails.
If he is pleased to consent, this is my object and my aim,
But if he shows an angry face,
Deceive him, saying: 'We do not know of him.'

I said to myself: 'This singer must be a person of wit, to combine elegance and eloquence with a beautiful voice.' So I went up to the door and started to raise the curtain bit by bit. There I saw a girl white as a fourteen-night-old moon, with joining eyebrows and languorous eyelids. Her breasts were like twin pomegranates; her tender lips were like camomiles; she had a mouth like the ring of Solomon; and her teeth, regularly spaced, were enough to distract the minds of all who might try to describe them in verse or prose. As the poet has said:

> Pearly teeth of the beloved, who set you in order
> And stored both wine and camomiles within your mouth?
> Who lent the dawn your smile,
> And sealed you with a lock made of carnelian?
> All those who see you are so moved with joy,
> They swagger with pride, so how of those you kiss?

Another poet said:

> Pearly teeth of the beloved, pity the carnelian;
> Do not look down on it, for has it not found you are unique?

In short, this girl possessed all possible aspects of beauty; she was a temptation for men and women alike; no one could grow tired of looking at her beauty and she fitted the description of the poet:

> If she advances, she kills, and when she turns her back,
> She fills all of mankind with love for her.
> Her beauty is that of both sun and moon;
> Harshness and aversion are not in her nature.
> Her gown opens on the garden of Eden,
> And the full moon orbits above her collar.

While I was looking at her through the curtain, she turned and saw me standing by the door. She told her maid to see who was there and the maid got up and came to me. 'Old man,' she said, 'have you no shame and do grey hairs and disgrace go together?' 'My lady,' I said, 'I admit to my grey hairs, but as for disgrace, I don't think that I have done anything disgraceful.' The lady of the house said: 'What disgrace can be greater than your invasion of a house that does not belong to you and the fact that you have been looking at women who are not yours?' 'I have an excuse for this, my lady,' I told her and when she asked me what it might be, I said: 'I am a stranger and am dying of thirst.' 'I accept your excuse,' she replied.

Night 329

Morning now dawned and Shahrazad broke off from what she had been
allowed to say. Then, when it was the three hundred and twenty-ninth
night, SHE CONTINUED:

I have heard, O fortunate king, that she said: 'I accept your excuse.'
'ALI WENT ON:

She then called to one of her slave girls and said: 'Lutf, give this man
a drink from the golden jug.' The girl fetched me a jug of red gold
studded with pearls and precious stones, filled with water that had been
mixed with pungent musk and covered with a kerchief of green silk. I
began to drink, but took my time about it, as I stole glances at the lady.
After I had been there for some time I handed the jug back to the girl,
but when I still stood there the lady said: 'Go on your way, old man.'
'My lady,' I replied, 'I am filled with anxiety.' 'About what?' she asked.
'About the changes and vicissitudes of Time,' I told her. She said: 'You
do well to be anxious, for Time is full of wonders, but which of these
have you seen that so concerns you?' 'I am thinking about the owner of
this house,' I said, 'who, while he was alive, was a friend of mine.' She
asked me the man's name and I said: 'He was Muhammad ibn 'Ali, the
jeweller, a man of great wealth.' Then I asked whether he had left any
children. 'Yes,' she replied, 'he left one girl called Budur, who inherited
all his wealth.' I asked whether perhaps she herself was his daughter.
'Yes, I am,' she said with a laugh, but then she added: 'You have been
talking for too long, old man, so go off on your way.' 'I must certainly
leave,' I told her, 'but I see that your beauty has been dimmed, so tell
me about yourself, as it may be that God will use me to bring you relief.'

'Old man,' the lady said, 'if you are someone who can keep a secret, I
will tell you mine, but tell me who you are so that I may see whether
you are worthy to hear it or not. For the poet has said:

It is only the trustworthy who keep secrets;
Only the best of people keep them hidden.
My secret is guarded in a locked room;
The key is lost and now the door is sealed.'

'My lady,' I told her, 'if you want to know who I am, I am 'Ali ibn
Mansur, the witty Damascene, the drinking companion of the Commander of the Faithful, Harun al-Rashid.' On hearing my name, she

came down from her chair and greeted me with a welcome, adding: 'Now I shall tell you my story and entrust you with my secret. I am a lover parted from my beloved.' 'My lady,' I replied, 'you are beautiful and the man whom you love must be handsome, so who is he?' 'He is Jubair ibn 'Umair al-Shaibani,' she told me, 'the emir of the Banu Shaiban,' and she went on to describe for me the most handsome young man in Basra. I asked her if they had met or corresponded. 'Yes,' she told me, 'but our love was a matter of words and did not come from the heart or the soul, for he did not keep his promises or fulfil his pledges.' I then asked her what had led them to part and she said: 'The reason for this was that one day I was sitting as a maid of mine combed my hair. When she had finished, she twisted the locks into plaits and my beauty made such an impression on her that she lent over me and kissed my cheek. At that moment Jubair came in unexpectedly. He saw the girl kissing my cheek, and at once he angrily turned on his heel and left, intending to part from me for ever, reciting these lines:

If my love is shared with someone else,
I shall leave her and live alone.
No good is to be found in the love of such a one.

From the time that he turned away from me and left until now I have had no message from him and no answer.'

I then asked her what it was that she wanted and she told me: 'I want you to take a letter to him from me. If you bring me a reply, I shall give you five hundred dinars, and if you don't, I shall pay you a hundred dinars as compensation for your journey.' 'Do as you want,' I told her and, after saying: 'To hear is to obey,' she summoned a slave girl and told her to fetch paper and an inkstand. When these were brought she wrote the following lines:

My darling, why shun me in loathing?
Where is the forbearance and sympathy we should have?
Why do you turn away and abandon me?
Your face is not the face I used to know.
Yes, the slanderers spread a false report about me.
You paid attention to their words and they said more and more.
God forbid that you believe what they have said;
Your good judgement knows better than that.
I implore you, tell me what it was that you heard;

You know what is said, and you act with fairness.
If it is true that this is because of my words,
Words can be interpreted and changed.
The Torah was revealed as the word of God,
But people altered and distorted it.
Before now, false reports were spread abroad;
In Jacob's presence, Joseph was blamed.
For all of us, me, the slanderer and you,
The Day of Judgement will be one of fear.

Budur then sealed her letter and gave it to me. I took it and went off to Jubair's house, but finding that he was out hunting, I sat down to wait for him. I was still sitting there when he came back, and when I saw him on his horse I was bewildered by his beauty and grace. He turned and saw me sitting by the door and so he dismounted and, on coming up to me, he embraced me and greeted me, leading me to think that it was the world and everything in it that I had embraced. He then took me into his house, sat me on his own couch and ordered a table to be brought in. One was fetched that was made out of Khurasanian *khalanj* wood with golden legs, and on it were dishes of all kinds of foods, with fried and roasted meats and so on. When I took my seat there, I looked hard at it and found inscribed on it the following verses . . .

Night 330

Morning now dawned and Shahrazad broke off from what she had been allowed to say. Then, when it was the three hundred and thirtieth night, SHE CONTINUED:

I have heard, O fortunate king, that 'ALI SAID:

When I sat down at the table of Jubair ibn 'Umair al-Shaibani, I looked hard at it and found inscribed on it the following verses:

Turn aside your storks* to the spring camp of the sauce bowls,
And halt at the tribe of the fries and stews.
Mourn the daughters of the sandgrouse, for whom I ceaselessly
    lament,
Along with what is roasted inside the chicken pie.

---

* 'Storks' is used as a parody for 'camels'.

My heart is sore for the two types of fish,
On pyramids of fresh bread.
By God, how fine a thing is supper,
With vegetables dipped in vinegar from little jars,
And also rice steeped here in buffalo milk,
In which women's hands have plunged up to their bracelets.
Be patient, my soul, for God is generous
And though your means be straitened, He will bring relief.

'Stretch out your hand to the food,' Jubair told me, 'and console yourself by eating what we provide.' 'By God,' I said to him, 'I shall not eat a single mouthful of your food until you do what I've come for.' 'And what is that?' he asked. So I produced Budur's letter for him, but when he had read it and grasped its contents, he tore it up and threw it down on the ground. 'Ibn Mansur,' he said to me, 'whatever other needs you have I shall fulfil, but not what has anything to do with the writer of this letter, for I shall not reply to it.' I got up to leave him angrily, but he caught hold of the skirts of my gown and said: 'Ibn Mansur, although I wasn't there with you, I can tell you what she said to you.' I asked him what this was and he said: 'Didn't the writer of the letter tell you that if you brought her a reply she would give you five hundred dinars, and if you did not, she would pay you a hundred dinars as compensation for your journey?' I agreed that this was so and he said: 'Sit with me today; eat, drink, have pleasure and enjoy yourself, after which you can take five hundred dinars for yourself.'

Accordingly, I sat with him, ate, drank and enjoyed myself pleasurably, spending the evening in conversation with him, and then I asked him if there was no music in his house. 'For a long time now we have been drinking without music,' he told me and then he called one of his slave girls, Shajarat al-Durr. She answered his summons and came to him from her apartment, bringing with her a lute of Indian manufacture wrapped up in a silken bag. She sat down, placed the lute on her lap and, after playing twenty-one different variations, she returned to the first and, accompanying herself on her lute, she recited these lines:

He who has not tasted the sweets of passion and its bitterness
Cannot distinguish union with the beloved from parting.
So it is that whoever turns from the path of love
Cannot tell which part of the road is smooth and which is rough.

I always used to find myself protesting against lovers
Until I was afflicted by love's sweetness and its bitterness.
I then gulped down its bitter cup,
And humbled myself before its slaves and its freemen.
How many a night has the beloved spent drinking with me,
Who sipped the sweet saliva from his lips!
How short-lived was the night of our union,
Where evening came at the same time as dawn.
Time vowed to part us,
And now Time has fulfilled its vow.
It passed its sentence, which cannot be revoked;
Who can oppose the orders of a master?

When the girl had finished these lines her master gave a great cry and
fell down in a faint. 'I hope that God will not punish you, old man,'
exclaimed the girl, 'but it is because we feared that he might suffer this
kind of fit that for a long time now we have not had music as we drank.
Go off now to that apartment and sleep there.' I went where she directed
me and slept until dawn, when a servant came to me carrying a purse
containing five hundred dinars. 'This is what my master promised you,'
he said, 'but don't go back to the girl who sent you here, and instead
pretend that neither you nor we have heard anything about this affair.'
'To hear is to obey,' I said and, taking the purse, I went on my way, but
I said to myself: 'The girl has been waiting for me since yesterday and,
by God, I must go back to her and tell her what happened between me
and Jubair. If I don't return, she may heap abuse on me and on all my
fellow countrymen.'

I went back and found her standing behind the door. When she saw
me she said: 'Ibn Mansur, you have not succeeded in doing what I
wanted.' 'Who told you that?' I asked. 'I can tell you something else,'
she continued: 'When you gave him my note, he tore it up and threw it
away, saying: "Ibn Mansur, whatever other needs you have I shall fulfil,
but not what has anything to do with the writer of this letter, for I shall
not reply to her." Then you got up angrily and he clutched at the edge
of your gown and asked you to sit with him for that day, adding: "You
are my guest; eat, drink, have pleasure and enjoy yourself, and then take
five hundred dinars." So you sat with him, ate, drank and enjoyed
yourself, spending the evening in conversation with him. Then a slave
girl sang such-and-such verses to such-and-such an air and he fell down

in a faint.' 'Were you there with us?' I asked her and she said: 'Ibn Mansur, have you not heard the poet's line:

Lovers' hearts have eyes that see what watchers cannot see?

But the sequence of nights and days changes everything that lies in its path.'

Night 331

Morning now dawned and Shahrazad broke off from what she had been allowed to say. Then, when it was the three hundred and thirty-first night, SHE CONTINUED:

I have heard, O fortunate king, that Budur said: 'The sequence of nights and days changes everything that lies in its path.' 'ALI WENT ON:

Budur then lifted her eyes to the sky and said: 'My God, my Lord and my Master, as you have afflicted me with love for Jubair ibn 'Umair, afflict him with love for me and transfer this love from my heart to his.' She gave me a hundred dinars by way of compensation for my journey and, after taking these, I went to the sultan of Basra, whom I found coming back from hunting. He paid me my allowance and I went back to Baghdad.

The following year I set off again for Basra to collect this allowance as usual and was again given it by the sultan. I was about to start back to Baghdad when I began to think about Budur and I said to myself: 'By God, I must go to visit her and find out what has happened between her and Jubair.' When I got there I found that the space in front of her door had been swept clean and sprinkled with water and that it was occupied by eunuchs, servants and pages. So I said: 'It may be that the girl died because of the grief that flooded her heart, and some emir or other has come to live in her house.' I left the place and went to Jubair's house, but here I found that the stone benches had been smashed and that there were no pages standing by the door as had been the custom. 'He may have died,' I told myself and I stood by the door, shedding tears and reciting these lines:

The masters have gone and my heart pursues them.
Come home, so your return may bring back my days of joy.
I stood by your house lamenting the place where you lived.
My tears poured down, while my eyelids quivered.

As the deserted ruins weep, I ask the house:
'Where is the giver of those generous gifts?'
'Go on your way,' it said, 'for those dear ones have gone,
Leaving the spring camps; they now lie buried under earth.'
May God not take from us the vision of their splendours
Throughout the land, and may their good qualities not be lost.

While I was reciting these lines in mourning for the people of the house, a black slave came out of it and, going up to me, he cursed me and told me to stop, saying: 'What are you doing reciting this lament here?' I told him that the house had belonged to a friend of mine. 'What was his name?' the man asked, and I told him: 'Jubair ibn 'Umair al-Shaibani.' 'What's supposed to have happened to him?' he asked. 'He still has his riches, fortune and possessions, but God has afflicted him with love for a girl called the Lady Budur. He is obsessed by his love for her, and because of the violence of this passion he's like a rock that's been thrown down. If he is hungry he won't ask for food, and if he thirsts he doesn't ask for drink.' I told him to get permission for me to go in to see him and he asked: 'Do you want to see him if he is in a rational mood or even if he's not?' 'Whatever the case,' I replied, 'I have to go to him.'

The slave went into the house to ask permission and then returned to say that I might go in. When I came into Jubair's presence I found him prostrate like a stone, unable to understand anything, however expressed, either allusively or in clear speech. When I spoke to him he made no reply, but one of his attendants said: 'Sir, if you know any poetry, recite it to him and raise your voice, as that will rouse him and he will speak to you.' So I recited these lines:

Have you forgotten your love for Budur or steeled yourself against
    it?
Do you spend the night awake or do your eyelids close in sleep?
Even if your tears pour down in floods,
Know you will have eternal life in Paradise.

When he heard this, he opened his eyes and said: 'Welcome, Ibn Mansur. What was a joke is now in earnest.' I asked whether there was anything that I could do for him and he said: 'Yes. I want to write her a letter and get you to take it to her. If you bring me a reply from her, I'll give you a thousand dinars, and if not, I shall pay you two hundred as compensation for your journey.' 'Do as you please,' I replied . . .

Night 332

Morning now dawned and Shahrazad broke off from what she had been allowed to say. Then, when it was the three hundred and thirty-second night, SHE CONTINUED:

I have heard, O fortunate king, that 'Ali said: 'Do as you please,' AND THEN WENT ON:

And so Jubair sent one of his slave girls for an inkstand and paper. When she had fetched him these, he wrote these lines:

> In God's Name, lady, be gentle with me,
> For love has now robbed me of all my wits.
> Love and desire for you have me within their power,
> Clothing me in sickness, leaving me a legacy of humbleness.
> My lady, before today I used to despise all love,
> Thinking it something negligible and easy.
> But when love showed the billows of its sea,
> Through God's decree I started to excuse its sufferers.
> Whether you want to pity me, to grant me union,
> Or kill me, you should not forget God's grace.

He sealed the letter, and after he had handed it to me I took it and went to Budur's house. As I had done before, I lifted the curtain bit by bit, and this time I was confronted by ten swelling-breasted virgins like moons, in the midst of whom sat the Lady Budur, like a full moon among the stars, or the sun when the clouds have cleared away, showing no sign of pain or suffering. While I was watching her in surprise, she turned in my direction and, seeing me standing at the door, she welcomed me and told me to come in. I did, and after greeting her, I handed her Jubair's note. When she saw this and grasped its contents, she laughed and said: 'The poet told no lie when he said:

> I shall endure my love for you with steadfastness,
> Until a messenger comes to me from you.

I am going to write a reply for you to take, Ibn Mansur, so that he may give you what he promised you.' 'May God reward you well,' I said, and she called to one of her girls to bring her an inkstand and paper. When these had been fetched she wrote the following lines:

How is it that I kept my word, while you were treacherous,
And while you saw I acted fairly, you wronged me?
It was you who first broke with me, treating me harshly;
It was from you that treachery first came,
While I preserved our covenant among mankind,
Guarding your honour, swearing on your behalf,
Until I saw with my own eyes what saddened me
And heard news of the foulness of your deeds.
While I exalt your worth, is mine to be held cheap?
By God, if you honoured me, I would do that for you.
I shall turn my heart from you to find solace,
Washing my hands of you in my despair.

'By God, my lady,' I told her, 'as soon as he reads this he will die,' and, tearing it up, I asked her to write something else. 'To hear is to obey,' she said and she wrote these lines:

I am consoled; my eyes now taste sweet sleep.
The censurers have told me what took place,
And my heart has agreed that it should forget you.
You have gone and my eyelids no longer shun sleep.
He lies who says distance is bitter;
To me its taste is that of sugar.
I have come to hate those who pass by with news of you,
Turning against them and thinking of this as something foul.
My whole body is free of your memory;
Let the slanderer learn this, and all who wish to know.

'When he reads this, my lady,' I told her, 'his soul will certainly leave his body.' 'Do you say this because his passion has really reached such a pitch?' she asked, and I told her: 'If I put it even more strongly, it would be true, and forgiveness is one of the qualities of the noble.' When she heard what I had to say, her eyes filled with tears and she wrote him a note the equal of which no one at your court, Commander of the Faithful, could produce. In it were these lines:

How long will this coquetry and these false accusations last?
I swear that you have brought solace to those who envy me.
It may be that I did some wrong unwittingly.
Tell me, then, what have you heard of me?
It is my desire, my darling, to set you

In the place sleep occupies in my eyes and my eyelids.
How have you come to drink the glass of love unmixed?
If then you see me drunk, do not reproach me.

When she had finished writing this . . .

Night 333

Morning now dawned and Shahrazad broke off from what she had been allowed to say. Then, when it was the three hundred and thirty-third night, SHE CONTINUED:

I have heard, O fortunate king, that 'ALI WENT ON:

When she had finished writing this, she sealed it and gave it to me. 'My lady,' I said, 'this note could cure the sick and quench raging thirst.' I took it and was setting off with it when she called me as I was leaving and said: 'Tell him: "She will be your guest tonight."' This made me very happy indeed and I took the note to Jubair, whom I found, as I came in, waiting for the answer with his eyes fixed on the door. I gave it to him and when he had opened it, read it and understood its meaning, he gave a great cry and collapsed in a faint. When he recovered he asked me whether Budur had written the note with her own hand and touched it with her fingers. I said: 'Do people write with their feet?' Then, before the two of us had finished talking, we heard the clicking of her anklets as she came into the entrance hall. When he saw her, Jubair leapt to his feet as though there had never been anything wrong with him. He embraced her as the letter *alif* embraces the letter *lam*, and his seemingly incurable disease left him.

Jubair then sat down but Budur remained standing and when I asked her why this was, she said that she would only sit in accordance with a condition agreed by the two of them. I wanted her to tell me what this was, but she said: 'No one can be allowed to learn lovers' secrets.' Then she put her mouth to Jubair's ear and secretly whispered something to him. 'To hear is to obey,' he said, and he got up and muttered something to one of his slaves, who went out for a time. When he came back he had with him a *qadi* and two notaries. Jubair rose and fetched a bag containing a hundred thousand dinars and he said to the *qadi*: 'Draw up a marriage contract between me and this girl for this amount.' The *qadi* asked Budur: 'Tell me, are you willing to accept this?' 'I am willing,' she said. The contract was then drawn up, after which Budur opened the bag, and taking a handful of coins from it she presented them to the *qadi* and the notaries. Then she gave back the bag with the rest of its contents to Jubair. The *qadi* left with the notaries, after which I sat with the two of them in pleasurable relaxation until the greater part of the night had passed.

Then I said to myself: 'These are two lovers who have long been parted, and I must get up immediately to sleep somewhere far removed from them, to allow them to be alone with each other.' So I stood up, but Budur held the skirts of my gown and said: 'What are you thinking of?' 'Such-and-such,' I told her, but she said: 'Sit down, and if we want you to go, we will send you off.' So I sat with them until it was almost dawn, when Budur told me to go to a room that had been prepared as a bedchamber for me. I slept there and in the morning a servant brought me a ewer and basin, after which I performed the ablution and performed the morning prayer. When I had sat down I saw Jubair and Budur coming out of the house baths, each wringing out their locks. I greeted them and congratulated them on their well-being and their reunion, remarking to Jubair that what had started with the insistence on conditions had ended in contentment. 'You are right,' he said, 'and you deserve generous treatment.' He then called for his treasurer and told him to fetch three thousand dinars, and when these had been brought in a bag he asked me to please accept them. 'I shall not take them,' I replied, 'until you tell me how, after you had been so strong in your rejection of Budur, this love was transferred from her to you.' 'To hear is to obey,' he said.

'You must know that we have a festival called Nauruz on which people go out in boats to enjoy themselves on the river. I and my companions went to join in the celebrations and I caught sight of a boat in which there were ten girls like moons, with Lady Budur in the middle of them, holding her lute. She played twenty-one different variations on it and then returned to the first and recited these lines:

Fire is colder than what burns in my entrails.
And rock is softer than my master's heart.
I wonder at how he has been fashioned –
A heart of stone in a body smooth as water.

I asked her to repeat the lines to the same tune but she refused . . .'

Night 334

Morning now dawned and Shahrazad broke off from what she had been allowed to say. Then, when it was the three hundred and thirty-fourth night, SHE CONTINUED:

I have heard, O fortunate king, that Jubair told 'Ali: 'I asked her to repeat the lines to the same tune but she refused, and so I told my boatmen to pelt her, which they did with oranges, until we were afraid that her boat would sink. She then went off on her way and it was because of this that love was transferred from her heart to mine.' 'ALI CONCLUDED:

After congratulating the two of them on their union, I took the bag and its contents and set off for Baghdad.

This story pleased Harun al-Rashid and his sleeplessness and ill humour left him.

A story is also told that one day al-Ma'mun, the Commander of the Faithful, was sitting in his palace to which he had summoned the state officials and the principal officers of the kingdom, as well as poets and his boon companions. Among the latter was a man called Muhammad of Basra, and it was to him that al-Ma'mun turned, telling him: 'I want you to tell me something that I have never heard before.' 'Shall I tell you of something that I have heard or something that I have seen myself?' Muhammad asked. 'Whichever is stranger,' al-Ma'mun told him. SO MUHAMMAD BEGAN:

You must know, Commander of the Faithful, that in days gone by there was a wealthy man who moved from his native Yemen to Baghdad. As he found this a pleasant place in which to live, he moved his family, his goods and his household there.

This man had six slave girls, beautiful as moons. Of these, one was white, the second dark, the third plump, the fourth thin, the fifth yellow and the sixth black. They were not only beautiful but cultured, skilled singers and musicians. One day it happened that he had all six of them with him; he sent for food and wine and they ate, drank and enjoyed themselves merrily. Their master, holding in his hand a glass which he had filled, pointed to the white girl and said: 'You, whose face is like the new moon, give us something delightful to hear.' The girl took her lute, tuned it and played airs on it until the whole place danced and then, to its accompaniment, she chanted these lines:

> I have a beloved whose image is before my eyes,
> And whose name is hidden within me.
> When I remember him, I am all heart,
> And when I look at him, I am all eyes.
> The censurer told me to forget my love for him;
> I said: 'How can what cannot happen come to be?'
> I said: 'Go, censurer; leave me;
> Do not make light of what cannot be light for me.'

The girls' master was delighted; he drained his glass and poured wine for the girls, after which he refilled his glass and, holding it in his hand, he pointed to the dark girl and said: 'Sweet-breathed light of the firebrand, let me hear your lovely voice, which bewitches all who hear it.' So she took her lute and played trilling airs on it until the whole room was filled with delight and the hearts of her audience were captivated by the looks that she turned on them. These were the lines that she recited:

> I take an oath to love no one but you
> Until I die, and never to betray your love.
> You are the full moon, veiled in loveliness,
> And all the beauties march beneath your flag.
> You have surpassed them all in grace
> And the God of all creation has shown you His favour.

Again the girls' master was delighted; he drank his glass and poured wine for the girls. He filled his glass again and, holding it in his hand, he pointed to the plump girl and told her to sing a sample of love poetry. Taking her lute she played an air that banished sorrow, reciting these lines:

> If you are truly pleased, you who are my desire,
> I do not care whether all the rest are furious.
> If I can see your handsome face,
> I do not care if all earth's kings are hid from me.
> Your pleasure is all I want in this whole world,
> You, from whom all beauty is derived.

The master was delighted; he took his glass, poured wine for the girls, filled his own glass and, holding it in his hand, he pointed to the thin girl and said: 'Houri of Paradise, let me hear your sweet words.' So she took her lute, tuned it, played airs on it and then recited these lines:

> Does what you have done to me follow the path of God?
> You have turned from me when I cannot endure without you.
> Has love no arbitrator who can judge between us,
> To ensure my rights and win me justice from you?

The master was delighted; he drained his glass, poured wine for the girls, refilled the glass and, holding it in his hand, he pointed to the yellow girl and said: 'Sun of the day, let us hear some elegant poetry.' Taking her lute, she played on it the finest of airs and recited these lines:

> When I show myself to my lover
> He draws a sword against me from his eyes.
> May God see that I get some justice from him,
> When he treats me roughly, while my heart is in his hand.
> Whenever I tell this heart to let him be,
> It still inclines to him, and to him alone.
> Among all mankind he is the one I seek,
> But Time, the mighty, envies me his love.

The master was delighted; he drank his glass, poured wine for the girls, refilled the glass and, holding it in his hand, he pointed to the black girl and said: 'O pupil of the eye, let us hear something, even if it is only two words.' She took her lute and tuned it, tightening the strings, and she played a number of airs before returning to the first and chanting these lines to its accompaniment:

> Eye, be generous with your tears;
> My ardour has lost me my being.
> I must endure passion for a beloved,
> My intimate, suffering while the envious rejoice.
> The censurers keep me far from a rosy cheek,
> Although I have a heart yearning for the rose.
> Wine cups once circulated there,
> In joy, as the lutes played,
> When the lover was still true to me and I was filled with love.
> Thanks to his faithfulness, good fortune's star shone out.
> Then, through no fault of mine, he turned away.

What is there bitterer than being shunned?
Fresh roses bloom upon his cheeks;
By God, how beautiful are rosy cheeks!
If piety allowed me to prostrate myself
To anyone but God, I would prostrate myself to him.

After this the girls got up and, after kissing the ground in front of their master, they asked him to judge between them. Looking at their beauty and gracefulness as well as the variety of their colours, he praised and extolled Almighty God and then he said: 'There is not one of you who has not studied the Quran, learned music, and acquired knowledge of our ancestors as well as of the doings of past peoples. I want each of you to get up and point to her opposite – I mean white to dark, plump to thin and yellow to black. Each is then to praise herself and find fault with her opposite, who is then to rise and do the same thing to her. In what you say you should use Quranic quotations, references to history and lines of poetry so as to display your culture and your eloquence.' 'To hear is to obey,' they said.

Night 335

Morning now dawned and Shahrazad broke off from what she had been allowed to say. Then, when it was the three hundred and thirty-fifth night, SHE CONTINUED:

I have heard, O fortunate king, that the girls told their master: 'To hear is to obey.'

The first to stand up was the white girl, who pointed at her black opposite and said: 'Woe to you, black one! Tradition has it that whiteness said: "I am the shining light; I am the rising moon." My colour is clear; my forehead is radiant and it was of my beauty that the poet said:

A white girl with polished cheeks, smooth,
Like a pearl concealed in beauty.
Her figure blooms like the letter *alif*, while her mouth
Is *mim*, with her eyebrows above it as a *nun*.
Her glances are arrows and her brows
A bow that is linked to death.
When she appears, in her cheeks, cheekbones and figure
Are roses, myrtle, sweet basil and eglantine.

By custom boughs are planted within gardens,
But how many gardens are contained within your figure's bough!

My colour is that of pleasant day, flowers in bloom and bright stars. God, in the Glorious Quran, said to His prophet Moses, on whom be peace: "Put your hand to your breast; it will come out white, without stain."* He also said, Almighty is He: "Those whose faces have been whitened will remain for ever in God's mercy."† My colour is a miracle and my beauty and grace are at the farthest point of excellence. Clothes look their best on those of my colour and it is to this that souls incline. Whiteness has many virtues. Snow is white when it falls from the sky; tradition has it that white is the best of colours and the Muslims take pride in wearing white turbans.

'It would take too long to mention all that is to be said in praise of white. The little that is sufficient is better than the long account that is incomplete, so I shall begin on your dispraise, black girl, coloured as you are like ink or soot from the smithy, whose face is like the crow that parts lovers. The poet has said, praising white and blaming black:

Do you not see that the pearl's colour makes it precious,
While one load of black coal is sold for one dirham?
Those with white faces enter Paradise,
While the black-faced will be crammed into Hell.

In one of the accounts recorded by the devout it is reported that Noah, on whom be peace, once fell asleep while Shem and Ham were sitting by his head. A gust of wind raised his clothes and uncovered his genitals. Ham looked at him and laughed without covering him, while Shem got up and did that. Their father woke and, realizing what his sons had done, he blessed Shem and cursed Ham, as a result of which Shem's face was whitened, and it is from him that the prophets, the orthodox caliphs and the kings are descended. Ham's face was blackened; he took flight to the lands of the Abyssinians and the blacks are his descendants. Everyone agrees that the blacks are stupid, as the proverbial saying has it: "How can one find an intelligent black man?"'

'Sit down,' her master told her, 'this is enough and more than enough.' He then pointed at the black girl, who got up and, pointing in turn at her white opposite, she said: 'Don't you know that among the words of Almighty God revealed to His Prophet and Apostle we find: "By the

* Quran 27.12.   † Quran 3.103.

covering night and the clear day?"* Had night not been greater than
day, God would not have sworn by it and given it precedence over day,
a point accepted by men of insight and intelligence. Don't you know
that blackness is the ornament of youth and that when white hairs come,
pleasures vanish and death is near? Were it not the most important of
things, God would not have set it in the kernel of the heart and the pupil
of the eye. How well the poet expressed it when he said:

> I love the dark ones, because they have
> Youth's colour, the heart's core, the pupil of the eye.
> I have not made a mistake if I forget the whiteness of the white,
> For I fear white hair and I fear the winding sheet.

Another said:

> The dark are to be set above the white;
> It is they who are more worthy of my love.
> The dark possess the colour of red lips,
> And the white that of the blotch of leprosy.

A third said:

> Black she may be, but still her deeds are white,
> Like eyes that shine.
> Don't be surprised if love for her has maddened me;
> For the root of madness is black bile.
> Among shadows my colour is of dark night,
> But were it not for darkness moons would not shed light.

Night is the proper time for lovers' meetings, a favour and a boon, which
should be enough to satisfy you. There is nothing like black darkness to
shelter lovers from slander and reproach, and nothing like the whiteness
of dawn to fill them with fear of disgrace. How many glories belong to
blackness and how well the poet expressed it:

> I visit while night's darkness pleads for me
> And at the incitement of the dawn I turn away.

Another said:

> How many a night have I spent in the beloved's arms,
> And it has sheltered us with its dark locks.

* Quran 9.1–2.

When dawn's light came to startle me,
I said: "Fire worshippers tell lies."

Another said:

He visited me, hidden in the robe of night,
Walking quickly thanks to fear and wariness.
I rose to lay my cheek down on his path
Submissively, sweeping away my footprints with my skirts.
The light of the new moon almost put us to shame,
Though it was as thin as the clipping of a fingernail.
I shall not tell you of what happened then;
Think only what is good and do not ask for news.

Another said:

Meet your lover only in the night.
The sun tells tales; night is a panderer.

Another said:

I cannot love a white girl bloated with fat;
My loves are dark and slender.
I am one who mounts on a lean colt
On race day, while another rides an elephant.

Yet another said:

My loved one visited me at night,
And we embraced each other.
We spent the night together,
But dawn arrived too soon.
I ask the Lord my God
To unite us once again
And make the night last as long
As the beloved lies within my arms.

Were I to go on to mention all that has been said in praise of black girls it would take too long and the little that is sufficient is better than the long account that is not complete. As for you, white girl, your colour is that of leprosy and your embraces choke your lovers. It is reported that frost and cold are to be found in hell as torment for the evil-doers, while among the merits of blackness is that the ink used to record God's word is black, and were it not for the blackness of musk and ambergris there would be no perfume to be carried to kings. So many sources of pride belong to blackness that I cannot mention them all, and how well the poet put it when he said:

Do you not see how high a price is fetched by musk,
While a load of white lime fetches one dirham?
Whiteness in the eye is ugly in a young man,
While black eyes shoot arrows.'

'Sit down,' said her master, 'for that is enough.' She took her seat and he then pointed at the plump girl, who got up . . .

Night 336

Morning now dawned and Shahrazad broke off from what she had been allowed to say. Then, when it was the three hundred and thirty-sixth night, SHE CONTINUED:

I have heard, O fortunate king, that he pointed at the plump girl, who got up and pointed in turn at the slender girl. The plump girl uncovered her legs, her wrists and her belly, revealing its folds and showing off her rounded navel. She then put on a thin shift through which her whole body could be seen and she said: 'Praise be to Him, Who has created me in this excellent form and has made me beautifully plump like the branch of a tree, adding to my grace and splendour. Praise be to Him, Who has favoured me and ennobled me by mentioning me in His glorious book, where He said, Almighty is He: "He brought a fatted calf,"* and He has made me like an orchard of peaches and pomegranates. Townspeople like to eat fat birds rather than thin ones, while everyone prefers to eat fat meat. How many sources of pride are there for fatness and how excellent are the poet's lines:

Say farewell to your beloved, for the caravan moves off,
But are you able to say farewell, O man?
When she walks to her neighbour's tent,
She walks as a plump girl, with no blemishes or weariness.

I have never seen anyone stop at the butcher's who does not ask him for fat meat, while pleasure, the wise men have said, lies in three things,

* Quran 51.26.

eating flesh, riding on flesh and inserting flesh into flesh. As for you, thin girl, your legs are those of a sparrow or the poker of an oven. You are the wood on which men are crucified; you are rancid meat, and there is nothing in you to delight the heart. The poet has said of you:

> I take refuge with God from having to make love
> When it is like rubbing the palm fibres.
> Every part of her body has a horn that butts me
> When I sleep, and so my body weakens.'

'Sit down,' said her master, 'for that is enough.' When she had taken her seat he pointed to the thin girl, who got up like the branch of a *ban* tree, a bamboo shoot or a stalk of sweet basil. She said: 'Praise be to God, Who has made me beautiful and made union with me the goal of desire, creating me like the branch to which hearts incline. If I get up, I get up lightly, and if I sit, it is with elegance. In jesting I am light-hearted, and my gaiety makes me sweet-natured. I have never found anyone describing his beloved as being "as big as an elephant", or "like a huge mountain". Rather, they say: "My beloved is slender with a slim figure." A small amount of food is enough for me, and I need only a little water to quench my thirst. I am lively when I play, and mine is a charming disposition. I am more agile than a sparrow and lighter in my movements than a starling. Union with me is what men desire and what brings pleasure to my suitors. My figure is beautiful and my smile lovely. I am like the branch of a *ban* tree, a bamboo shoot or a stalk of sweet basil. No one can match my beauty, as the poet has said:

> I have compared your figure to a twig,
> And your form is my good fortune.
> I follow after you as a distraught lover,
> Fearing the watcher may bring harm on you.

It is those like me who inspire desperate love and who drive lovers to distraction. If my beloved draws me to him, I yield, and if he tries to win my favour, I incline to him rather than turn against him. As for you, fat girl, you eat like an elephant and no amount of food, great or small, can suffice you. When lying with you, your lover can experience no relaxation nor any way of resting with you. Your huge belly stops him enjoying you and the thickness of your thighs prevents him from possessing your vagina. What beauty is there in your thick body and what smooth grace is there in your coarseness? Fat meat is fit only for the butcher and there is nothing in it that calls for praise. If anyone jokes with you, you are angry, and if a man plays with you, you become gloomy. When you try to act the coquette, you snort; you pant when you walk; when you eat, you never have enough. You weigh more than a mountain and you are worse than ruin and disaster. You cannot move and you bring no blessing. You want to do nothing but eat and sleep. When you piss it is like spurting water and when you shit you are like a bursting wine skin or an elephant changed into a woman. When you go to a lavatory you need someone to wash your private parts for you and to pluck the hairs there, and this is the height of laziness and the sign of weak-mindedness. You have nothing to boast about and it is of you that the poet has said:

> She is heavy as a bladder inflated with urine,
> With haunches like mountainous pillars.
> When she takes a walk and waddles in the west,
> She crushes the ground so that the east is shaken.'

'Sit down,' said her master, 'for that is enough.' When she had taken her seat he pointed to the yellow girl, who rose to her feet and praised and glorified Almighty God, calling down praise and blessings on His Prophet, the best of His creation. Then, pointing at the dark girl, she said . . .

Night 337

Morning now dawned and Shahrazad broke off from what she had been allowed to say. Then, when it was the three hundred and thirty-seventh night, SHE CONTINUED:

I have heard, O fortunate king, that the yellow girl rose to her feet and praised and glorified Almighty God. Then, pointing at the dark girl, she said: 'It is I whose description is to be found in the Quran. The Merciful God, when describing my colour, preferred it to all others where He referred, Almighty is He, in His clear book to "a bright yellow heifer whose colour delights those who see it".* My beauty and grace are the ultimate perfection and my colour is a wonder, being that of the dinar, the stars, the moon and the apple, while the colour of saffron surpasses all others. As my colour is remarkable, so my shape is beautiful

---

* Quran 2.64.

and exotic. My body is soft, my price is high and I encompass all beauty. In the world my colour, like pure gold, is rare. My glories are many and it was of a girl like me that the poet said:

> She is splendidly yellow like the sun,
> Or like dinars, beautiful to see.
> Saffron cannot match even part of her brightness;
> No, and her appearance does outshine the moon.

Now I shall begin on your dispraise, dark girl. Your colour is that of the buffalo, and people recoil at your sight. Whatever is your colour is blamed; if it is in food, then the food is poisoned; this is the colour of flies and of ugly dogs; it is indistinct and is one of the signs of mourning. I have never heard of dark gold, dark pearls or dark jewels. When you go to a lavatory, your colour changes, and when you come out, ugliness is added to ugliness. You cannot be recognized as black nor described as white. There are no points in your favour, as the poet has said of you:

> Her shade is that of soot; its dusty colour
> Is like earth trampled by the feet of a courier.
> Whenever my eyes fix on her,
> My distress and discomfort worsen.'

'Sit down,' said her master, 'for that is enough.' When she had taken her seat he pointed to the dark girl, who was beautiful and graceful, well formed and possessing the perfection of loveliness. Her body was soft, her hair jet-black, her figure symmetrical and her smooth cheeks rosy red. Her eyes were kohl-dark and she had an eloquent tongue. In addition to her beautiful face, her waist was slender and her buttocks heavy. She said: 'Praise be to God, Who has created me in such a way that I can neither be blamed as being fat nor humiliated as being too thin. I am not leprous white nor of a colicky yellow nor sooty black. Rather, my colour is beloved by men of intelligence. All poets in every tongue eulogize it and place it above all others, as the qualities of brown win praise. How eloquently the poet said:

> Were you to elucidate the qualities of brunettes,
> You would not look at the white or at the red.
> Their words are eloquent and their glances coquettish;
> It is they who teach sorcery and magic to Harut.

Another said:

Who will bring me a brunette whose flexible body recalls
Long, brown and graceful Samhari lances,
With quiet glances and silken cheeks,
Preaching sermons to the heart of the emaciated lover?

Another said:

I would ransom with my life a dark one, a fragment of whose colour
Leaves white behind and vies with the moon in glory.
Were he to have even as much white as this,
His beauty would be exchanged for disgrace.
It is not the wine he pours that has made me drunk;
It is his locks of hair that have intoxicated all mankind.
His beauties envied one another, but then
Each wished to be the down upon his cheek.

Another said:

Why should I not incline to the down appearing on the cheek
Of a dark one, straight as a dusky spear,
While poets have ascribed all beauty that there is
To the dark spots seen on the water lilies?
I have seen lovers, all of them, risking disgrace
Because of a mole found under a dark eye.
Are the censurers then to blame me about one,
Who is all the colour of a mole? Rid me of these fools.

I am well formed and admirably shaped; my colour is desired by kings
and loved by rich and poor alike. I am delicate, light, beautiful and
graceful, with a soft body and a high price. I represent perfect loveliness,
together with culture and eloquence. I am pretty in appearance, a fluent
speaker, light-hearted and graceful when I play. As for you, you are like
a Bab al-Luq marrow, yellow and all full of veins. Bad luck to you, pot
of watercress, rusty copper, owl face, tasting like the food of hell. Whoever sleeps with you will be brought to his grave by shortage of breath.
You have no claim to beauty and it is about those like you that the poet
has said:

Her yellowness grows worse, although she is not ill;
This constricts my chest and pains my head.
If my soul will not repent, I shall humiliate it
By kissing her face, so losing all my teeth.'

When she had finished, her master told her to sit down as she had said enough.

Night 338

Morning now dawned and Shahrazad broke off from what she had been allowed to say. Then, when it was the three hundred and thirty-eighth night, SHE CONTINUED:

I have heard, O fortunate king, that when she had finished, her master told her to sit down as she had said enough. He then saw to it that all of them were reconciled to one another, and he clothed them in splendid robes and adorned them with jewels from both land and sea. Muhammad continued: 'Never have I seen in any place or at any time more lovely girls than these, Commander of the Faithful.'

When al-Ma'mun heard his story he approached Muhammad to ask whether he knew where they and their master were to be found, adding: 'And will you be able to buy them from him for me?'

'Commander of the Faithful,' Muhammad replied, 'I hear that their master is passionately fond of them and cannot bear to be parted from them.' 'Take him ten thousand dinars for each of them, a total of sixty thousand,' said al-Ma'mun, 'carry the money with you; go off to his house and buy them from him.' Muhammad set off with the money and when he got there, he told the girls' master that the Commander of the Faithful wanted to buy them from him at that price. In order to please the caliph the man agreed to the sale and sent him the girls. When they came to him, he had an elegant salon prepared for them where he would sit with them as they all drank together, and he was filled with astonishment at their beauty and grace, as well as their contrasting colours and their eloquence.

Things went on like that for some time until their former master, who had sold them, could no longer bear to be parted from them. He sent a note to al-Ma'mun complaining of the pangs of love that he felt for his slave girls, and in it were these lines:

You robbed me of six fair and lovely girls;
Give these six beauties greetings now from me.
They were my ears, my eyes and my whole life;
They were my food, my drink and all my joy.

I shall never forget my union with their loveliness.
Now that they are gone, sweet sleep has fled from me.
Alas for the length of my distress and for my tears;
Would that I had not been created among men.
Eyelids like bows adorned the eyes that shot at me.

When this letter reached the caliph, he clothed the girls in splendid robes and presented them with sixty thousand dinars. He then sent them back to their former master, who was filled with delight at their arrival, a delight which exceeded his pleasure in the money that he received. They remained with him enjoying the most pleasant and delightful of lives until they were visited by the destroyer of delights and the parter of companions.

A story is told that one night the Commander of the Faithful, Harun al-Rashid, was very disturbed and filled with cares. He got up and walked around his palace until he came to a curtained room. He lifted the curtain and saw at the head of the room a couch on which there was something black that looked like a sleeping man, with one candle to his right and another to his left. While he was looking at this in surprise, he caught sight of a jar of old wine, on top of which was a glass. He was surprised to see this and asked himself how a black man like this could have such a thing, but on approaching the couch he discovered that what lay on it was a sleeping girl veiled by her own hair. He uncovered her face and found her to be like the moon on the night that it becomes full. He poured himself a glass of wine and drank it in honour of the roses in her cheeks, and then, feeling himself drawn to her, he kissed a mole on her face. She woke up and said: 'O loyal servant of God, what is this?' He replied: 'A guest has come to visit you by night, to be entertained until dawn.' 'Yes,' she replied, 'I swear on it by my ears and eyes.' She then brought forward the wine and the two of them drank together, after which she took her lute, tuned the strings, and, after playing twenty-one different variations, she returned to the first and, accompanying herself, she recited these lines:

In my heart it is the tongue of love that speaks to you,
Telling of me I am in love with you.
I have a witness speaking clearly of how sick I am,
As separation from you makes my wounded heart flutter.
I have not concealed the love which has worn me away;
As my passion increases, so do my tears flood down.

Before I loved you, I did not know what true love was,
But for His creation God's decrees are predestined.

When she had finished these lines she said: 'Commander of the Faithful,
I have been wronged.'

Night 339

Morning now dawned and Shahrazad broke off from what she had been
allowed to say. Then, when it was the three hundred and thirty-ninth
night, SHE CONTINUED:

I have heard, O fortunate king, that the girl told the caliph that she
had been wronged. 'How so,' he asked, 'and who has wronged you?'
'Your son bought me for ten thousand dirhams,' she told him, 'intending
to give me to you as a present, but your wife sent him another ten
thousand dirhams and told him to hide me away from you in this
apartment.' 'Ask me to grant you a wish,' said the caliph and she replied:
'I wish that you would spend tomorrow night with me.' 'If God wills,'
he replied, and then he left her and went off.

The next morning he went to his council room and sent for Abu
Nuwas, and when Abu Nuwas was not to be found he sent his chamberlain off to make enquiries about him. This man found Abu Nuwas in a
wine shop being kept as security for the payment of a thousand dirhams
that he had promised to spend on a beardless boy. When the chamberlain
asked what had happened, Abu Nuwas told him about the pretty boy
and the thousand dirhams. 'Show him to me,' said the chamberlain, 'and
if he is worth it, you are excused.' 'Wait,' Abu Nuwas told him, 'and
you will see him immediately.' While they were talking the boy came up
to them wearing a white robe on top of a red one, beneath which was a
black one. On seeing him Abu Nuwas, sighing deeply, recited these lines:

He appeared in a gown of white,
With languorous eyes and eyelids.
I said: 'You passed by, but gave me no greeting,
Although a greeting would have contented me.
Blessed be the One Who clothed your cheek with roses,
And Who creates what He wishes with none to oppose Him.'
'There is no need for argument,' he said. 'My Lord
Is marvellous in His creation, without flaw.

My robe is like my face and like my fortune,
White upon white upon white.'

When the boy heard this, he took off the white robe, and when Abu
Nuwas saw the red one that he wore beneath it, he recited even more
admiringly:

I saw in a robe, coloured like red anemones,
An enemy, though called a friend of mine.
I said in wonder: 'You are a full moon,
But you have come in a surprising guise.
Is it the redness of your cheeks that has clothed you,
Or did you dye it with the blood of lovers' hearts?'
He said: 'The sun gave me a shirt
That it had only just made when it set.
My robe, wine and the colour of my cheeks
Are red anemones, one set above the other.'

When Abu Nuwas finished these lines, the boy took off his red robe and
was left dressed in black. When Abu Nuwas saw him, after looking at
him again and again, he recited:

He came out in a robe of black,
Appearing to God's servants in the dark.
I said: 'You passed by, giving me no greeting,
Pleasing the envious and my enemies.
Your robe is like your hair and like my fortune,
Black upon black upon black.'

When the chamberlain saw the state that Abu Nuwas was in and his
infatuation for the youth, he went back and told the caliph of this. The
caliph produced a thousand dirhams and told him to take them back to
Abu Nuwas and to pay them over on his behalf in order to free him from
the debt for which he was being held. When the chamberlain had done
this, Abu Nuwas, on being freed, went to the caliph and stood in front
of him. The caliph told him to recite some poetry containing the words:
'O loyal servant of God, what is this?' 'To hear is to obey,' he said . . .

Night 340

Morning now dawned and Shahrazad broke off from what she had been allowed to say. Then, when it was the three hundred and fortieth night,
SHE CONTINUED:

I have heard, O fortunate king, that Abu Nuwas said: 'To hear is to obey,' and he then recited:

I spent a long night of misfortune and of sleeplessness,
My body worn away and filled with cares.
I rose to walk through my own quarters
And after them the women's chambers.
There I saw a black shape,
Which was a white girl veiled by her own hair,
Radiant as the full moon,
Like the branch of a *ban* tree, clothed in bashfulness.
I drank the glass she had there in one gulp;
Then I went up and kissed her mole.
She woke from sleep,
Bending like a branch when the rain falls.
Then she rose, saying:
'What is this, loyal servant of our Lord?'
I said: 'A guest has come to visit you by night,
Hoping to shelter here till dawn.'
She answered joyfully: 'My lord,
I swear by my ears and eyes to honour you.'

The caliph exclaimed in wonder: 'It is as though you were there with us.' Then he took Abu Nuwas by the hand and led him off to the girl. When Abu Nuwas caught sight of her she was wearing a blue dress with a blue veil and, being filled with admiration, he recited:

Say to the lovely girl in the blue veil:
'By God, you are my life; be kind to me.
When his beloved treats her lover roughly,
Longing stirs in him and he sighs.
By this beauty your white complexion now adorns,
I ask you, pity the lover's heart consumed by fire.
Have mercy on me; aid me in my love;
Do not accept what fools here have to say.'

When Abu Nuwas had finished these lines, the girl presented wine to the caliph and then, taking the lute in her hand, she struck up a strain and recited these lines:

Will you treat another lover fairly and wrong me,
Distancing me and favouring another?
Were there a lovers' judge, I would complain of you
To him and he might give a just ruling.
If you stop me from passing by your door,
I shall send greetings to you from afar.

The caliph then gave orders that Abu Nuwas be plied with drink until he became drunk, after which he gave him another cup, which he drank down in one gulp. While he was still clutching it, the caliph told the girl to take it from his hand and hide it, which she did between her thighs. He then drew his sword and, standing by Abu Nuwas's head, he pricked him with the point. Abu Nuwas woke up to find the caliph holding a naked sword and at once the fumes of drunkenness cleared from his head. 'Recite me a poem about your cup,' said the caliph, 'or else I will cut off your head.' So Abu Nuwas recited:

My story is most wonderful,
For the gazelle has now become a thief.
She stole my glass of wine,
When I had sipped the best of it.
And then she hid it in a place
For which my heart suffers distress.
Out of respect, I shall not give its name,
As the caliph has a share in it.

'How did you know that?' asked the caliph, adding: 'But I accept your lines.' He then ordered Abu Nuwas to be given a robe of honour and a thousand dinars, after which he went away joyfully.

A story is told that a certain man found himself in difficulties, being deeply in debt. He left his family and his household and wandered off aimlessly until at last on his travels he reached a city with high walls and lofty buildings. He entered it in a state of humiliation and wretchedness, oppressed by hunger and worn out by his journey. When he passed by one of its streets he caught sight of a number of dignitaries advancing and he went along with them until they entered what looked like a royal palace. He went in with them and they passed through it until they came to a dignified and important-looking man seated at its far end, who appeared to be from a family of viziers and was surrounded by servants and eunuchs. When this man saw his visitors he rose to receive them courteously, but the poor man, on seeing this, was filled with doubt and bewilderment . . .

Night 341

Morning now dawned and Shahrazad broke off from what she had been allowed to say. Then, when it was the three hundred and forty-first night, SHE CONTINUED:

I have heard, O fortunate king, that the poor man, on seeing this, was filled with doubt and bewilderment, owing to the splendour of the building and the servants and retainers. He hung back, bewildered, anxious and afraid for himself, until he took a seat alone and far from the others, where no one could see him.

While he was sitting there a man led in four hunting dogs in coats of various kinds of silks and brocades, with golden collars round their necks together with silver chains. He tied up each of them in a place of its own and then went off and came back bringing them each a golden bowl full of magnificent food, which he set down for them before going out and leaving them. In the extremity of his hunger the poor man, seeing the food, wanted to approach one of the dogs and share its meal, but fear held him back. Then one of them noticed him and, realizing the state that he was in, thanks to inspiration from Almighty God, it drew back from its bowl and gestured to him. He came forward and ate his fill, after which he was about to leave when the dog indicated that he should take the bowl and the food in it for himself, pushing it over to him with its paw. He took it up, left the house and went off without being followed.

After this he went to another city, where he sold the bowl, and with the money that he got for it he bought merchandise, which he took back to his own town and sold, so clearing his debts. He became rich, prosperous and fortunate, but after staying where he was for some time he told himself that he should go back to the city where the owner of the dog's bowl lived and bring him a suitably handsome present, as well as repay him for the bowl that the dog had given him. So he chose an appropriate present and, taking with him the price of the bowl, he set out on his journey.

After having travelled for a number of days and nights he reached the city and entered it to try to find the dog's owner. He walked round the streets until he got to the house, but there was nothing there but ruin and desolation, with crows cawing mournfully. Everything had changed beyond recognition, and with a palpitating heart he recited:

> The rooms are empty of their hidden treasures,
> As hearts are empty of learning and piety.
> The valley has changed; its gazelles
> And its sand hills are not those I used to know.

He added:

> Su'da's phantom came to arouse me*
> Just before dawn, in the desert, while my companions slept.
> But when I woke to look for it,
> I saw nothing but emptiness, as she herself was far away.

Looking at the ruins and seeing clearly the action of time that had left behind only traces of what had once been there to see, he did not need to be told what had happened. Then, turning away, he caught sight of a poor man whose state would cause men to shudder and move even solid rock to pity. He accosted him and asked: 'What has Time done to the owner of this place? Where are his shining moons and his gleaming stars, and what has happened to his mansion, of which only the walls are left?' The poor man replied: 'The owner is the wretched man you see before you, lamenting his fate. Don't you know that in the words of the Apostle of God there is a lesson to be heeded and a warning for whoever will heed it? He said, may God bless him and give him peace: "It is the practice of Almighty God not to raise up anything in this world without then bringing it down." The reason for this, if you ask for one, is that there is nothing strange in the reversals of fortune. This was my mansion, which I established, built and owned. I possessed shining moons and lived in luxury and splendour with slave girls of dazzling beauty, but then Time's balance turned against me. It robbed me of my servants and my wealth, reducing me to this state in which I have settled and afflicting me with calamities that it had kept concealed. But there

---

* The phantom of the beloved is a frequent visitor in Arabic love poetry.

must be a reason for your question, so stop standing here in wonder and tell me what it is.'

The visitor, who was painfully distressed, told him the whole story and added: 'I have brought you a desirable present as well as the price of the golden bowl that I took, for it was this that turned me from a poor man to a rich one, allowing me to live in prosperity rather than poverty and removing the cares that oppressed me.' The other shook his head, wept, groaned and lamented, before saying: 'Man, I think you must be mad, for this is not something that a sensible person would suggest. If one of my dogs gave you a gold bowl, how could I take it back? It would be strange indeed for me to reclaim the generous gift of a dog, even if I were in the direst of straits. By God, I shall not take as much as a fingernail's worth of anything from you, so go back where you came from, in health and safety.' The visitor then kissed his feet and left, praising him and reciting the following lines as he took his leave:

> The people and the dogs have gone;
> Peace be on both the people and the dogs.

God knows better.

The story is told that in the port of Alexandria there was a *wali* named Husam al-Din. One night, when he was sitting in his courtroom, a soldier came to him and said: 'Master, I want you to know that I entered the city tonight and went to such-and-such a *khan*, where I slept for a third of the night. When I woke I found that my saddlebag had been slit open and a purse with a thousand dinars in it stolen.' He had hardly finished speaking before the *wali* sent for his officers and told them to collect everyone in the *khan* and imprison them until morning. When morning came, he sent for the instruments of torture and brought in the prisoners in the presence of the soldier whose money had been stolen. He was about to torture them when a man made his way through the people and stood before him . . .

Night 342

Morning now dawned and Shahrazad broke off from what she had been allowed to say. Then, when it was the three hundred and forty-second night, SHE CONTINUED:

I have heard, O fortunate king, that the *wali* was about to torture them when a man made his way through the people and stood before him and the soldier.

'Emir,' said this man, 'let all these people go. They are being treated unjustly, for it was I who took the soldier's money and here is the purse that I took from his saddlebag.' He took the purse from his sleeve and put it down before the *wali* and the soldier. 'Take your money away with you,' the *wali* told the soldier, 'for you no longer have any case against these others.' Everyone there started to praise and bless the man who had confessed, who then said: 'It was not a clever trick on my part, emir, to come here myself with the purse. The cleverness would be to take it from the soldier a second time.' The *wali* asked him how he had stolen it in the first place and he said: 'I was standing in the market of the money-changers in Cairo when I saw the soldier get this gold from one of them and put it in a purse. I followed him from one alley to another but I could find no way to get the purse. He then went off on a journey, but although I followed him from town to town, and tried to play tricks on him during his travels, I still couldn't get my hands on the gold. Then, when he arrived here, I followed him into the *khan* and settled down beside him, watching him until he fell asleep. When I heard him snoring, I edged near him little by little and then I used this knife to cut open his saddlebag, after which I took the purse. This is how I did it.'

The thief then stretched out his hand and, taking the purse that was in front of the *wali* and the soldier, he went round behind them, watched by the people who thought that he was showing how he had got it from the saddlebag. Suddenly, however, he took to his heels and dived into a pool. The *wali* shouted to his retainers to go in after him and catch him, but before they had taken off their clothes and gone down the steps to the pool, the clever thief had gone off on his way. They searched for him but could not find him, for in Alexandria the lanes are interconnected, and so they had to come back empty-handed. The *wali* told the soldier that he had no claim against the other people from the *khan*, because, although he had found the culprit and had got the money back, he had failed to keep it. So the soldier got up, having lost his gold, while the others were freed, all this owing thanks to the grace of Almighty God.

A story is told that one day al-Malik al-Nasir summoned his three *walis*, the *wali* of Cairo, the *wali* of Bulaq and the *wali* of Fustat, and told each of them to tell him of the most remarkable thing that had happened to him during his period in office.

Night 343

Morning now dawned and Shahrazad broke off from what she had been allowed to say. Then, when it was the three hundred and forty-third night, SHE CONTINUED:

I have heard, O fortunate king, that al-Malik al-Nasir told each of the three *walis* to tell him of the most remarkable thing that had happened to him during his period in office. 'To hear is to obey,' they said. THE *WALI* OF CAIRO BEGAN:

My lord the sultan, the most remarkable thing that has happened to me in my time was this. In the city there were two notaries who used to act as witnesses in cases involving bloodshed and wounds. They were passionately addicted to women, drink and debauchery, but I could find no way of calling them to account for this. As I wasn't able to act, I gave instructions to all wine sellers, grocers, fruiterers, candle sellers and brothel owners to let me know when these two were drinking or indulging in debauchery, whether together or separately. If both or one of them bought anything that could be used for a drinking party, this was not to be kept secret from me. 'To hear is to obey,' they said.

It happened that one night a man came to me and told me that the two were in such-and-such a place in such-and-such a street and such-and-such a house, acting dissolutely. I got up and, after disguising myself and my page, I went to find them, with only the page for company. I walked on until I reached the door of the house, and when I knocked, a slave girl came and opened it for me. She asked me who I was, but I went in without answering, and there I saw the two notaries sitting with the owner of the house, together with a number of prostitutes and a great quantity of wine. On seeing me they got up and paid me their respects, seating me at the upper end of the room and exclaiming: 'Welcome to the honoured guest, the witty companion!', receiving me with no trace of fear.

After that the owner of the house rose and left us, coming back some time later with three hundred dinars. He, too, showed no fear. Then, addressing me as 'our master, the *wali*', they said: 'It is in your power to disgrace us or worse, and you can punish us, but this will only bring you inconvenience. You would be advised to take this money and shelter us, for Almighty God is named the Shelterer, and as He loves those of His servants who shelter others, you will receive a divine reward.' So I told myself to take the money and cover for the two of them on that one occasion, but that if I caught them again I would punish them. The money had stirred my greed and so I took it from them and left them. I left without anyone seeing me, but the next day to my surprise a messenger came to me from the *qadi*, asking me to come and see him.

I went with the messenger to his master without knowing what this was about, but when I came into his presence I saw sitting with him the two notaries and the brothel owner who had given me the three hundred dinars. This man got up and claimed that I owed him that sum, a point that I could not deny, as he produced a document, witnessed by the notaries, stating that the debt was due. The *qadi* accepted the claim on the evidence of the notaries and ordered me to pay over the money, which I had to do before I left. I was furious and determined to do them an injury, regretting the fact that I had not made an example of them, but I had to leave full of shame. This is the most remarkable thing that happened to me during my period in office.

The *wali* of Bulaq then got up and said: 'As for me, my lord the sultan, the most remarkable thing that happened to me was when I was in difficulties having accumulated a debt of three hundred thousand dinars. I sold every single thing that I could but I was able to collect no more than one hundred thousand . . .'

Night 344

Morning now dawned and Shahrazad broke off from what she had been allowed to say. Then, when it was the three hundred and forty-fourth night, SHE CONTINUED:

I have heard, O fortunate king, that THE *WALI* OF BULAQ SAID:

I sold every single thing that I could but I was able to collect no more than one hundred thousand, and this plunged me into confusion. One night, when I was sitting at home worrying about this, there came a knock on the door and I told one of my servants to see who was there. He went out but when he came back his colour had changed; he was pale-faced and trembling. When I asked what was the matter he told me that at the door there was a man naked apart from some skins, armed with a sword, and with a knife at his waist. With him were a number of others dressed in the same way, and he was asking for me.

Sword in hand, I went out to see who these might be and there they were, just as my servant had described them. I asked them their business and they said: 'We are robbers and tonight we have come by a great treasure which we have set aside for you in order to settle this problem of debt that is worrying you.' 'Where is this treasure?' I asked them, and they fetched me a large chest filled with vessels of gold and silver. I was delighted to see it, saying to myself that it would allow me to pay off my debt and leave me as much again. So I took the chest and went back into my house, but then I said to myself that it would be dishonourable to let the men go away empty-handed. So I fetched the hundred thousand dinars that I had with me and gave it to them with my thanks. They took the money and went off unnoticed under cover of night. The next morning, I looked at the contents of the chest and found them to consist of copper coated with gold and tin, worth all in all some five hundred dirhams. I found this hard to bear as I had lost my dinars and added to my woes. This is the most remarkable thing that happened to me during my period in office.

THE *WALI* OF FUSTAT THEN ROSE AND SAID:

My master the sultan, here is my most remarkable experience during my time in office. I had ten thieves hanged, each on a gibbet of his own, and I told the guards to watch to see that nobody removed any of the corpses. The next day, when I came to look at them, I found two corpses hanging from the same gibbet. 'Who has done this,' I asked the guards, 'and where is the gibbet belonging to this second corpse?' They disclaimed any knowledge of the affair, but when I was about to have them flogged, they said: 'We fell asleep last night, emir, and when we woke up we found that one of the corpses, together with its gibbet, had been stolen. We were afraid, and when we saw a passing peasant coming up towards us with his donkey, we seized him, killed him and hanged him on this gibbet in place of the corpse that had been removed.' I was taken by surprise and asked them what the peasant had had with him. They told me that he had had a saddlebag on his donkey, and when I asked what was in it they said that they didn't know. 'Bring it to me,' I told them, and when they did and I ordered them to open it, there inside it was the body of a murdered man cut into pieces. I was astonished at this sight and said to myself: 'Glory be to God. The reason that this peasant was hanged was that he was guilty of murder, and God does not treat His servants unjustly.'

A story is told that a money-changer passed some thieves while he was carrying a purse full of gold. One of these rascals boasted that he would be able to steal the purse and when the others asked him how, he told them to wait and see. He then followed the money-changer to his house, and when the money-changer went in, he threw the purse down on a shelf, after which, feeling the need to relieve himself, he went to the lavatory, telling a slave girl to bring him a jug of water. She fetched this and followed him to the lavatory, leaving the door open. The thief then entered and took the purse, after which he went back to his companions and told them what had happened . . .

Night 345

Morning now dawned and Shahrazad broke off from what she had been allowed to say. Then, when it was the three hundred and forty-fifth night, SHE CONTINUED:

I have heard, O fortunate king, that the thief took the purse and went to tell his companions what had happened to him with the money-changer and the girl. 'By God,' they said, 'this was a clever trick that not everybody could play, but now when the man comes out of the lavatory and fails to find the purse, he will punish the girl with a painful beating. There is nothing meritorious in what you have done; if you are a really clever thief, then save the girl from her punishment.' 'God willing,' the man replied, 'I shall save her and take the purse as well.'

He went back to the money-changer's house, where he found the man beating the girl because of the loss of his purse. He knocked on the door and when he was asked who he was, he said: 'I am the servant of your neighbour in the covered market.' At that, the man came out to him and asked him what he wanted. 'My master sends you his greetings,' said the thief, 'and says that you seem to have changed completely. He wants to know how you could come to throw down a purse like this at the door of your shop and then walk away and leave it. Had a stranger found it he would have taken it and gone, and if my master had not seen it and kept it safe, you would have lost it.' He then brought out the purse and showed it to its owner. 'This is mine!' exclaimed the man, and he stretched out his hand to take it, but the thief said: 'By God, I'm not going to give it to you until you write me a note for my master to confirm that you have received it from me, as otherwise he may not believe me when I tell him that you have got it. So I need a signed and sealed receipt.' The money-changer went back into his house to write this note for him to acknowledge the delivery of the purse, and at that the thief went off with the money, having saved the girl from a beating.

The story is told that 'Ala' al-Din, the *wali* of Qus, was sitting at home one night when a handsome man of fine appearance came to his door accompanied by a servant who was carrying a chest on his head. This man told one of 'Ala' al-Din's servants to go in and tell his master that he wanted to see him on a secret matter. The servant did this and was told by 'Ala' al-Din to show the visitor in. On seeing a dignified and handsome stranger, he sat the man down beside him and treated him with courtesy before asking him what he wanted. The stranger replied: 'I am a highwayman, but I want you to witness my repentance and my return to the service of Almighty God. Please help me to do this, because I have come to your district and am subject to your supervision. I have with me this chest, whose contents are worth about forty thousand dinars, to which you have a better right than I. If you give me a thousand dinars of money that is legally yours, I can use this as capital and it will help me to repent, since I shall not need to steal again, and Almighty God will reward you.'

The man then opened the chest to show 'Ala' al-Din its contents, which comprised jewellery, gems, precious metals, ring stones and pearls. 'Ala' al-Din was astonished and delighted; he called for his treasurer and told him to fetch such-and-such a purse, this being one that contained a thousand dinars.

Night 346

Morning now dawned and Shahrazad broke off from what she had been allowed to say. Then, when it was the three hundred and forty-sixth night, SHE CONTINUED:

I have heard, O fortunate king, that 'Ala' al-Din called for his treasurer and told him to fetch such-and-such a purse, this being one that contained a thousand dinars. When this was brought to him he handed it to his visitor, who took it, thanked him and left under cover of night. The next morning, 'Ala' al-Din summoned the syndic of the jewellers and, on his arrival, he showed him the chest and its contents, which turned out to be made of tin and brass, while what seemed to be gems, ring stones and pearls were all of glass. 'Ala' al-Din found this hard to stomach, but although he sent men out in pursuit of the trickster, no one was able to catch him.

The story is told that al-Ma'mun, the Commander of the Faithful, once told Ibrahim ibn al-Mahdi to tell him the most remarkable thing he had ever seen. 'To hear is to obey, Commander of the Faithful,' replied Ibrahim, AND HE WENT ON:

One day I went out to take the air and eventually I came to a place where I could smell food cooking. I was filled with a longing for this and I stood there in a state of perplexity, not being able to move on or to go into the house. Then I looked up and there, behind a window, I caught sight of the most beautiful hand and wrist that I had ever seen. My wits left me at the sight, and the hand and wrist made me forget about the smell of food and I started to think of a way to get into the house. Near it I noticed a tailor. I went up and greeted him and after he had returned my greeting I asked him to whom the house belonged. 'To a merchant,' he said, and when I asked for his name the tailor told me, adding that this man only associated with other merchants.

While we were talking, two distinguished and intelligent-looking men rode up and the tailor gave me their names, telling me that these were particular friends of the owner. I rode off to join them, and after greeting them I said: 'Abu So-and-So has been waiting for you.' I accompanied them to the door, and when they went in so did I. When the master of the house saw me, he was sure that I was a friend of theirs and so he welcomed me and sat me in the place of honour, after which the servants brought a table of food. I told myself that, as far as the food went, God had granted me my wish, but that there still remained the matter of the hand and the wrist.

We then moved to drink our wine in another room, which I could see was filled with rarities. The owner treated me with particular friendliness, addressing his conversation to me, as he thought that I was a guest of his guests, and so did the other two, as they thought that I was a friend of his. They continued to treat me like this until we had drunk a number of glasses of wine. Then out came a slave girl like the branch of a *ban* tree, elegant and beautiful. She took a lute, struck up a strain and recited these lines:

> Is it not strange that although we are in the same house,
> You neither approach nor speak to me?
> It is only our eyes that reveal our souls' secrets,
> While love's fire consumes our broken hearts.
> We gesture with our glances, and wink
> With drooping eyelids, as our hands exchange greetings.

She stirred my emotions, Commander of the Faithful, and I was moved to delight both by her beauty and by the delicacy of the lines she chanted, the elegance of whose composition I envied. In spite of that, I said to her: 'There is something that you have left out.' She threw the lute away angrily and said: 'Since when did you allow fools into your gatherings?' I saw that the others disapproved of me, and I regretted what I had done, saying to myself that my hopes were gone. As I could think of no other way in which to avoid blame I asked for a lute and said: 'I'll show you what was missing in the air that she played.' The others agreed to this and fetched me a lute. I tuned its strings and then sang these lines:

> Here is your lover, pining in distress,
> Moved with passion, his body flooded by tears.
> One hand is raised to God in hopeful prayer,
> While the other clutches at his heart.
> You see a dying lover slaughtered by his love;
> It is the beloved's eye and hand that cause his death.

The girl jumped up and threw herself down at my feet, kissing them and saying: 'Forgive me, master. I did not know how skilled you were and I have never heard artistry like this.' The delighted company began to praise and honour me and every one of them asked me to sing. I sang a joyful air, while the visitors became drunk and their wits left them so that they had to be carried to their homes. The host, together with the girl, stayed with me, and after he had drunk a number of glasses he said to me: 'Sir, I have wasted my life in that until now I have never come across a man like you. I conjure you in God's Name to tell me who you are so that I may know who is the companion whom God has granted to me tonight.' I tried to conceal this and would not tell him, but at last at his prompting I gave my name. When he heard it he jumped to his feet . . .

Night 347

Morning now dawned and Shahrazad broke off from what she had been allowed to say. Then, when it was the three hundred and forty-seventh night, SHE CONTINUED:

I have heard, O fortunate king, that IBRAHIM IBN AL-MAHDI SAID:

When the host learned my name, he jumped to his feet and said: 'I would have been astonished if excellence like this had belonged to any except a man of your distinction and I cannot thank fate sufficiently for the favour it has shown me. It may be that I am dreaming, for otherwise how could I have hoped that a member of the caliph's family would come to visit me in my house and drink with me tonight?'

I insisted that he sit down again, which he did, and he then started to ask me delicately why it was that I had come to his house. I told him the whole story from start to finish, concealing nothing. 'As for the food,' I went on, 'I had all that I wanted, but the same is not true of the hand and the wrist.' 'If God Almighty wills,' he replied, 'you will get what you want of these.' He then told one of his girls to tell one of the others to come down, and he started to summon them one after another and show them all to me, but I couldn't see the one I was looking for. 'By God, sir,' he said to me at last, 'there only remain my mother and my sister,' and these he insisted on bringing down and showing to me. I was astonished at his generosity and liberality. 'May I be your ransom,' I told him, and I then asked him to start with his sister. 'Willingly,' he answered, and when his sister came down, he showed me her hand and I could see that it was she whose hand and wrist had caught my attention.

When I told him this he ordered his servants to fetch witnesses immediately. When they had come, he produced two bags of gold and told the witnesses: 'This is our master, Ibrahim ibn al-Mahdi, the uncle of the Commander of the Faithful. He asks for the hand of my sister, and I call you to witness that I have given her to him in marriage, providing her with a bag of gold as her dowry.' Then he said to me: 'I give you my sister So-and-So in marriage for the dowry that I have stated.' 'I willingly accept that,' I replied, at which he gave one of the bags of gold to his sister and the other to the witnesses. Then he said: 'Master, I would like to prepare a room for you in which you can sleep with your wife.' His generosity put me to shame and as I felt embarrassed to sleep with his sister in his own house, I told him to send her to mine with what she needed. I swear, Commander of the Faithful, that he provided me with so much in the way of furnishings that my rooms were scarcely big enough to hold it all. Later the girl gave birth to this son of mine who is standing before you.

Al-Ma'mun was astonished by the man's generosity, and he praised him and exclaimed: 'I have never heard of anyone to equal him!' He then told Ibrahim ibn al-Mahdi to fetch him so that he could see him for himself. When the man came and was asked to speak, the caliph was so impressed by his wit and culture that he made him one of his intimates.

God is the Giver, the Bestower.

A story is told that a certain king warned his subjects that if any of them gave any alms, their hands would be cut off. As a result of this, charitable giving came to a halt and no one was able to give anything to anyone. One day, however, a starving beggar approached a woman and asked her for alms.

Night 348

Morning now dawned and Shahrazad broke off from what she had been allowed to say. Then, when it was the three hundred and forty-eighth night, SHE CONTINUED:

I have heard, O fortunate king, that the beggar asked the woman for alms. 'How can I give you anything,' she said, 'when the king cuts off the hands of everyone who gives alms?' But he repeated: 'In the Name of Almighty God, I ask you for charity.' When she heard him invoke the Name of God, her heart was softened and she gave him two loaves. News of this reached the king, who had her brought before him and then had her hands cut off, after which she went back to her house.

Sometime later the king said to his mother: 'I want to marry, so find me a beautiful wife.' His mother told him: 'Among my slave girls there is one of unsurpassed beauty, but she does have one serious defect.' 'What is that?' he asked, and his mother told him that the girl's hands had been cut off. In spite of that, he said that he wanted to look at her, and when she had been fetched he was charmed by her appearance, married her and slept with her.

This woman turned out to be the one who had lost her hands for having given two loaves to the beggar. When the king married her, her fellow wives envied her and so they wrote to him, accusing her of being an adulteress who had given birth to a son. The king sent word to his mother, telling her to take her out and abandon her in the desert, before returning. When his mother did this, the woman began to weep, bitterly lamenting her fate, and as she walked with the child on her shoulder she passed by a stream. She knelt down to drink, since the walk, together with her weariness and sorrow, had made her extremely thirsty, but as she bent her head, the baby fell into the water. While she was in floods of tears, two men passed by and asked her why she was crying. 'I was carrying my baby on my shoulder,' she told them, 'and he has fallen into the water.' 'Would you like us to fetch him out for you?' they asked, and when she said yes, they called on Almighty God and out came the child safe and sound. 'And would you like God to restore your hands as they were before?' they asked. 'Yes,' she replied, and when they had called on God, the Glorious, the Almighty, her hands were restored and were better than before. The men then asked her if she knew who they were, to which she answered: 'God knows better.' 'We are the two loaves you gave to the beggar,' they told her, 'the gift that caused you to lose your hands. So give praise to Almighty God, Who has restored them to you and given you back your son.' This she did.

A story is told that among the Israelites there was a pious man whose household used to spin cotton. Every day he would sell the spun thread, buy more cotton and use the profit left over to buy food for his family to eat that day. One day, however, when he had gone out and sold his yarn, he met a friend of his who complained to him that he was in need, and so the man gave him what he had earned and went back home with no cotton and no food. 'Where is the cotton and the food?' his household asked him, and he told them: 'So-and-So met me and complained to me of his circumstances, so I handed him the price that I had got for the yarn.' 'So what are we going to do,' they asked him, 'as we have nothing to sell?'

They did have a broken bowl and a jar, but although the man took these to the market, no one would buy them from him. As he was standing there, someone passed him carrying a fish . . .

Night 349

Morning now dawned and Shahrazad broke off from what she had been allowed to say. Then, when it was the three hundred and forty-ninth night, SHE CONTINUED:

I have heard, O fortunate king, that the man took the bowl and the jar to the market, but no one would buy them from him. As he was standing there, someone passed him carrying a fish, but as this was bloated and stinking it had found no buyer. Its owner said to the Israelite: 'Will you exchange what you cannot sell for what I cannot sell?' 'Yes,' he replied, and after handing over the bowl and the jar, he took the fish back to his household. 'What are we to do with it?' they asked. 'We shall broil it and eat it,' he told them, 'and it may be that Almighty God will make some provision for us.' They then took the fish, slit open its belly and in it they found a pearl. They told this to the Israelite and he said: 'Look to see whether it has been pierced, for if so it belongs to someone, but otherwise it is something that Almighty God has provided for us.' In fact, it turned out to be unpierced and so the next morning the Israelite took it to a friend of his who knew about jewellery. When the man asked where it had come from, the Israelite said that it was a gift from God. 'It is worth a thousand dirhams,' said his friend, 'and I will give you that, but you should go to So-and-So, who is not only wealthier than I am but also more knowledgeable.' So the man took the pearl to this expert, who told him that it was worth seventy thousand dirhams and no more. The money was paid over and porters were summoned to carry it to his house door. A beggar then came up and said: 'Give me some of what Almighty God has given to you.' The Israelite said: 'Yesterday I was like you, so take half of this,' and he then divided the money. Each of them took his half, but at that point the 'beggar' said: 'Keep the money and may God's blessing accompany it. I have been sent to you as a messenger from your Lord, to test you.' 'Glory and thanks be to God!' exclaimed the Israelite, and he and his household enjoyed the most luxurious of lives until they died.

A story is told that ABU'L-HASSAN AL-ZIYADI SAID:

There was a time when I found myself in extremely straitened circumstances, so much so that the greengrocer, the baker and the other tradesmen were pressing me for payment and in my distress I could see no way out. While I was in this state and had no idea what to do, a servant of mine came in to tell me that at the door was a pilgrim who wanted to see me. I told my man to let him in and when the visitor entered, it turned out that he came from Khurasan. We exchanged greetings, after which he asked me whether I was Abu'l-Hassan al-Ziyadi. I told him that I was and asked him what he wanted. He said: 'I am a stranger here and I want to go on the pilgrimage to Mecca, but I have with me a quantity of money which I find too heavy to carry. I want to deposit these ten thousand dirhams with you until I come back after the pilgrimage. When the pilgrim caravan returns, if you do not see me, you will know that I am dead and the money will then be a gift from me to you, whereas if I come back, it is mine.'

I told him that, God willing, I would do what he asked. He then produced a bag, and after telling my servant to fetch a pair of scales, he weighed it, handed it over to me and then went off on his way.

I fetched the tradesmen and paid off my debts . . .

Night 350

Morning now dawned and Shahrazad broke off from what she had been allowed to say. Then, when it was the three hundred and fiftieth night, SHE CONTINUED:

I have heard, O fortunate king, that ABU'L-HASSAN AL-ZIYADI SAID:

I fetched the tradesmen and paid off my debts, after which I spent the money lavishly, telling myself that, if the man were to return, God would provide me with some way out of the difficulty. A day later, however, my servant came back to tell me: 'Your Khurasanian friend is at the door.' I gave him leave to enter, and when he did, he told me: 'I had meant to go on the pilgrimage, but I then heard that my father had died and I made up my mind to go home. So give me back the money that I left with you yesterday.'

No one has ever been as worried as I was when I heard this, and I was so taken aback that I could make no reply. If I denied that he had given me the money and he made me swear to this, I would be disgraced in the next world, while if I told him that I had spent it, he would raise an outcry and expose me. So I said: 'God bless you, this house of mine is not a strong enough place in which to keep so much money. When I took your bag, I sent it off to the man who has it with him now. So come back tomorrow to fetch it, if God Almighty wills.' The Khurasanian went off, and as for me, I spent the night in a state of confusion because of his return. I could not sleep or close my eyes. I got up and told my servant to saddle my mule, but he said: 'It's still dark and the night is only just starting.' I went back to bed, but as I still couldn't sleep, I kept on waking up my servant and he kept on refusing to get up until dawn broke.

He then saddled the mule for me and I rode off with no notion of where I was going. I let the reins lie on the mule's shoulders, and while I was preoccupied with my cares and anxieties it went on eastwards from Baghdad. On my route I caught sight of a group of people and turned out of their way to avoid them, but when they saw that I was wearing a *tailasan*, they quickly followed me and then asked me: 'Do you know the house of Abu'l-Hassan al-Ziyadi?' When I told them that I was Abu'l-Hassan, they told me that the caliph wanted to see me. I went with them, and when I came into the presence of al-Ma'mun he asked me who I was and I told him that I was one of the companions of the *qadi* Abu Yusuf, a *faqih* and a student of the traditions of the Prophet. 'What is your name?' he asked, and I told him that it was Abu'l-Hassan al-Ziyadi. 'Tell me your story,' he ordered, and when I explained to him what had happened to me, he burst into tears and said: 'Damn you, it was because of you that the Prophet of God, may God bless him and give him peace, kept me awake all last night. I had fallen asleep at the start of the night, but I heard him say: "Help Abu'l-Hassan al-Ziyadi," and I woke up. I did not know who you were and so I fell asleep again, but again he came to me and said: "Damn you, help Abu'l-Hassan al-Ziyadi." As I did not know you, I fell asleep once more but again the Prophet came and repeated what he had said. After that, I did not dare to sleep and I had to spend the rest of the night awake. I roused my people and sent them out in every direction to look for you.'

Al-Ma'mun then presented me with ten thousand dirhams, telling me that these were for the Khurasanian, and then he gave me another ten thousand to use for my own purposes and to set my affairs in order. Finally, he gave me thirty thousand with which to equip myself and he told me to come to him the next day that he rode out in a state procession, when he would give me an official appointment. I left, taking the money with me, and went back home. When I had performed the morning prayer, the Khurasanian arrived. I took him into the house and brought out a bag of money, telling him that it was his. He said: 'This is not the money I left with you.' 'That is right,' I said, and when he asked the reason for this I told him the story. He burst into tears and said: 'By God, had you told me the truth to start with, I would not have asked you to return my deposit, and now I swear that I shall accept none of it . . .'

Night 351

Morning now dawned and Shahrazad broke off from what she had been allowed to say. Then, when it was the three hundred and fifty-first night, SHE CONTINUED:

I have heard, O fortunate king, that ABU'L-HASSAN AL-ZIYADI SAID:

The Khurasanian told me: 'By God, had you told me the truth to start with, I would not have asked you to return my deposit, and now I swear that I shall accept none of it and I have no further claim on you for it.' He then left me.

I set my affairs in order and on the procession day I went to al-Ma'mun's door. He was seated when I entered his presence and, after calling me to come up to him, he produced a document for me from beneath his prayer mat appointing me as *qadi* in the holy city of Medina with unlimited jurisdiction on the west side starting from Bab al-Salam and a monthly salary of such-and-such an amount. He adjured me to fear God, the Great and Glorious, and to bear in mind the concern that the Prophet of God, may God bless him and give him peace, had shown for me. The people present were astonished by what he said and, when they asked me what he meant, I told them the story from start to finish and it became widely known.

Abu'l-Hassan remained as *qadi* in the holy city of Medina until he died during the reign of al-Ma'mun, may God have mercy on him.

A story is told of a man who lost all his considerable wealth and became destitute. His wife advised him to approach one of his friends to see whether he could help to restore his fortunes. He went to the man who, on being told of his desperate position, lent him five hundred dinars with which to start trading. At the start of his career he had been a jeweller and so, taking the money, he went to the jewellers' market, where he opened a shop in which to trade.

When he took his seat in the shop three men approached him and asked him about his father. When the man told him that he was dead, they asked whether he had left children. 'The servant who sits before you,' the man replied and they said: 'Who can confirm that you are his son?' 'The market traders,' he replied. 'Collect them for us so that they may bear witness to the fact that you are his son.' When this had been done the three produced a saddlebag containing thirty thousand dinars, together with gems and precious metal, telling him that this had belonged to his father and had been left in their trust. They then left and a woman came up and wanted to buy one of the gems from the bag. It was worth five hundred dinars, but she offered three thousand and he sold it to her. He then got up and carried the five hundred dinars that he had borrowed back to his friend, telling him to take them as God had opened the road to prosperity for him. 'I gave you the money,' said his friend, 'leaving it at the disposal of God. Take it, and take this note but don't read it until you are back in your house. Then act on it.' The man went home with the money and the note, and when he opened it he found in it the following lines:

> The three who came to you were relatives of mine,
> My father, his brother and my mother's brother, Salih ibn 'Ali.
> It was to my mother that you sold the gem for cash;
> The cash and the jewels were sent by me.
> In doing this I did not want to lessen you
> But to spare you the distress of embarrassment.

A story is told that there was once a very wealthy Baghdadi who spent his money until his circumstances altered and he became reduced to penury, earning his daily bread only with the greatest of difficulty. One night he fell asleep, sad and oppressed, and in a dream a voice spoke to him saying: 'What God has provided for you is in Cairo. Follow and go to it.' So he set out for Cairo, and when he arrived there it was evening and so he went to sleep in a mosque. This happened to be near a house, and as God Almighty had decreed, a number of robbers entered the mosque and went on from it to the house. Their movements aroused the household, who raised the alarm, at which the *wali* and his men came to their rescue. The robbers fled, but when the *wali* went into the mosque they found the Baghdadi asleep. He was seized and given so severe a beating that he nearly died. He was then imprisoned and after three days the *wali* had him brought before him and asked him where he came from. On being told that he was from Baghdad the *wali* asked him what he was doing and why he had come to Cairo. The man told him what he had heard in his dream and added: 'When I got here I found that what God had provided for me was the beating that I got from you.'

The *wali* laughed so heartily that his back teeth could be seen, and then he said: 'You foolish fellow, thrice in a dream I heard a voice telling me that in such-and-such a quarter of Baghdad there is a house of such-and-such a description where at the bottom end of a garden court there is a fountain beneath which is a huge sum of money. The voice told me to go to Baghdad to fetch the money, but I did not go whereas you in your folly went from one place to another because of some foolish dream that you saw.' He then gave the Baghdadi some money to help him to get back home.

Night 352

Morning now dawned and Shahrazad broke off from what she had been allowed to say. Then, when it was the three hundred and fifty-second night, SHE CONTINUED:

I have heard, O fortunate king, that the *wali* gave the Baghdadi some money to help him to get back home. The man took this and went back. As it happened, it had been his own house that the *wali* had described, and when the man dug beneath the fountain, he found a great treasure, and God granted him fortune. This was a remarkable coincidence.

The story is told that in the palace of al-Mutawakkil 'ala'llah, the Commander of the Faithful, there were four hundred concubines, two hundred being Rumis and two hundred either half-breeds or Abyssinians. 'Ubaid ibn Tahir had given him another four hundred, half of whom were white and the other half Abyssinians and half-breeds. Among these latter was a Basran named Mahbuba, a girl of radiant beauty and grace, as well as wit and coquetry. She could play the lute, she was an excellent singer and she could compose poetry, as well as writing a calligraphic hand. Al-Mutawakkil was so infatuated by her that he could not bear to be parted from her for a single hour. When she saw how fond he was of her, she grew proud and became ungrateful for his favours, causing him to leave her in anger and to give orders that no one in the palace should speak to her.

This went on for some days, but al-Mutawakkil still felt attracted to her and one morning he told his companions that on the previous night he had dreamt of having been reconciled with her. 'We hope that God Almighty will see that this happens when you are awake,' they told him, and while he was speaking a servant girl came in and whispered something to him that made him get up and go to the harem. What the girl had told him was that the sound of someone singing to the lute had been heard from Mahbuba's room and that no one knew why this was. When al-Mutawakkil got to the room, he heard Mahbuba singing these lines to a beautiful air:

I wander through the palace but see no one;
I complain, but no one speaks to me.
It is as though I am guilty of a sin,
And no repentance now can rescue me.
Will no one intercede for me with a king
Who visited me in a dream and made his peace with me,
But then when dawn had broken,
He left me once again and broke our ties?

Al-Mutawakkil was astonished to hear these lines and wondered at the strange coincidence that had led Mahbuba to have a dream that matched his own. He entered her room, and, when she saw him, she jumped up before bending over his feet, kissing them and exclaiming: 'Master, this is what I saw in a dream last night and when I woke up I composed those lines!' Al-Mutawakkil told her that he had had the same dream, and they then embraced and made up, after which he stayed with her for seven days and nights. Mahbuba had used musk to write al-Mutawakkil's name, Ja'far, on her cheek, and when he saw this he recited:

She wrote 'Ja'far' in musk upon her cheek;
My life would ransom one who wrote this word.
Her fingers traced a single line on her cheek,
But many are the lines they have left in my heart.
Among mankind Ja'far possesses you;
May God use the wine of your kisses to help a stream flow.*

When al-Mutawakkil died, he was forgotten by all his slave girls apart from Mahbuba . . .

---

* Pun on 'Ja'far', Arabic for 'stream'.

Night 353

Morning now dawned and Shahrazad broke off from what she had been allowed to say. Then, when it was the three hundred and fifty-third night, SHE CONTINUED:

I have heard, O fortunate king, that when al-Mutawakkil died, he was forgotten by all his slave girls apart from Mahbuba, who continued to mourn for him until her death, when she was buried at his side. May God have mercy on them.

A story is told that in the days of al-Hakim bi-amri-'llah there was a butcher in Cairo named Wardan who dealt in mutton. Every day a woman used to come to him with a dinar which weighed almost as much as two and a half Egyptian dinars. With her would be a porter with a basket and she would ask Wardan for a lamb which he would give her in exchange for her dinar. She would pass the lamb to the porter and take it home, only to return next morning, and so every single day Wardan would get a dinar from her. This went on for a long time until one day Wardan, thinking the matter over, said to himself: 'There is something remarkable here in that this woman never misses a day but always buys my meat for cash.' Once, when she was not there, he asked the porter where he went with her each day. 'I don't know what to make of it,' the man replied. 'Every day she gets me to carry the lamb which she buys from you and then she spends another dinar on what else is needed for a meal, together with fruit, candles and dessert. She gets two bottles of wine from a Christian, whom she pays with another dinar, and I have to carry the whole lot to the vizier's gardens. She then blindfolds me so that I can't see where to put my feet, and she leads me by the hand, going I don't know where, until she says: "Put it down here." She has another basket there and, after giving me the empty one, she takes my hand and leads me back to the place where she blindfolded me. There she unties the blindfold and gives me ten dirhams.'

Wardan wished him well, but became even more doubtful and suspicious of the woman. He passed a disturbed night and the next morning, when she came as usual, bought the lamb for the dinar and went off after giving it to the porter, he left his boy in charge of the shop and followed her without her noticing him.

Night 354

Morning now dawned and Shahrazad broke off from what she had been allowed to say. Then, when it was the three hundred and fifty-fourth night, SHE CONTINUED:

I have heard, O fortunate king, that Wardan left his boy in charge of the shop and followed her without her noticing him. HE SAID:

I kept her in sight until she left the city, staying under cover behind her until she came to the vizier's gardens. She blindfolded the porter and I tracked her from place to place until she reached the mountain. When she got to where there was a great stone, she took the basket from the porter and I waited until she had gone off with him and then come back. She removed all the contents of the basket and disappeared for a while. I went up to the stone, which I rolled aside, and when I went down into the hole it had left, I found at the bottom a brass trapdoor lying open and a flight of steps leading downwards. I went down very slowly and reached a long and brightly lit hall, through which I went until I saw what looked like the door of a room. I explored the corner by the door and discovered a recess in which there were steps leading up on the outside of the door. I climbed these and found another small niche which had a window overlooking the room. Peering in, I saw that the woman had cut off the best bits of the lamb and put them in a cooking pot, while she threw the rest of it down for an enormous bear, who ate it all, and when she had finished cooking, she herself ate her fill. She then arranged the fruit and the dessert and, after setting out the wine, she started to drink, pouring one glass for herself and then a golden bowl for the bear. When the wine had gone to her head she stripped off her clothes and lay back. The bear mounted her and she gave him the best of what is reserved for the sons of Adam. When it had finished it sat down, but then jumped on her again and lay with her, before taking another rest. This went on ten times, before both of them collapsed unconscious and motionless.

I said to myself: 'It is time to take the opportunity,' and so I went down with a knife that would cut bones even more easily than flesh. When I reached them, I found that they were still totally motionless in their exhaustion, and so I set the knife to the bear's throat and then rested my weight on it until it came out on the other side, severing the head from the body. The bear had given a huge snort like thunder and this roused the woman in panic. When she saw the dead beast, and me standing knife in hand, she let out such a piercing shriek that I thought that her soul had left her body. Then she said: 'Wardan, is this how you repay my kindness?' 'Enemy of your own self,' I replied, 'are you so short of men that you act in this foul way?' She looked down at the ground without replying and then, staring at the bear with its severed head, she said: 'Wardan, which would you prefer to do, listen to what I tell you and so live in safety . . .'

Night 355

Morning now dawned and Shahrazad broke off from what she had been allowed to say. Then, when it was the three hundred and fifty-fifth night, SHE CONTINUED:

I have heard, O fortunate king, that WARDAN WENT ON:

The woman said: 'Wardan, which would you prefer to do, listen to what I tell you and so live in safety and luxury until the end of your days, or disobey me and so bring about your own death?' 'I choose to listen to you,' I said, 'so say what you want.' 'Cut my throat, then,' she said, 'as you have cut the throat of the bear, and then take what you want of this treasure and go off on your way.' 'I am better than the bear,' I told her, 'so turn in repentance to Almighty God and I will marry you, after which we can live on this treasure for the rest of our lives.' 'Wardan,' she said, 'there is no chance of this, for how can I live now that the bear is dead? By God, if you won't cut my throat, I shall kill you, and if you bandy words with me you will die. This is the advice that I have for you.' I said: 'I shall kill you, then, and you will go to hell, with God's curse on you.' So I seized her by the hair and cut her throat and she went to hell cursed by God, the angels and all mankind.

After that, I looked round the place and found more gold, ring stones and pearls than any king could collect. So I took the porter's basket, put in as much as I could carry and covered it with the cloak that I was wearing. I then carried it out of the treasure chamber and went off. When I reached the gate of Cairo I saw ten of al-Hakim's guards advancing, followed by al-Hakim himself. 'Wardan,' he called to me, and I said: 'At your service, your majesty.' 'Have you killed the bear and the woman?' he asked. When I told him that I had, he told me to put down the basket that I was carrying on my head, and said: 'Don't be anxious.

All the wealth that you have with you is yours and no one will try to take it from you.' When I had placed the basket in front of him, he uncovered it, and after looking at its contents, he said: 'Tell me about the woman and the bear, although I know what happened as though I had been there with you.' As I told him the story he kept saying: 'That is true,' and then he told me to come with him to the treasure chamber. I went there with him and when he found the trapdoor shut he said: 'Lift it, Wardan, for no one but you can open up this treasure chamber. An enchantment has been laid on it in your name and with your description.' I protested that I wouldn't be able to open it, but he said: 'Come on with the blessing of God.' So I moved forward, calling on the Name of Almighty God, and when I stretched out my hand to the trapdoor, it came up as though it weighed nothing at all. Al-Hakim then said: 'Go down and bring up what you find there, for since the time that the place was built, it has been decreed that only someone bearing your Name and fitting your description would be able to enter it. I have seen it written that you were destined to kill the bear and the woman, and I have been waiting for this to happen.'

Wardan went on: 'I went down, and when I had brought out all the treasure for al-Hakim, he called for pack animals and had it removed, but he gave me my basket and its contents. I took this back home and then opened a shop in the market.' This market still exists and is known as 'the market of Wardan'.

The story is told that the daughter of a certain sultan fell in love with a black slave who deflowered her, and she then developed such a passion for sexual intercourse that she could not do without it for a single hour. She complained of this to one of her ladies, who told her that nothing could copulate more frequently than an ape. As it happened, an ape-leader with a large ape passed beneath her window. The girl unveiled her face and, looking down, winked at the ape, which burst its bonds and chains and came up to her. She kept it hidden away in her room and it spent its time, night and day, in eating, drinking and copulating. Her father found out about this and was about to have her put to death . . .

Night 356

Morning now dawned and Shahrazad broke off from what she had been allowed to say. Then, when it was the three hundred and fifty-sixth night, SHE CONTINUED:

I have heard, O fortunate king, that her father found out about this and was about to have her put to death when she discovered her danger. She dressed as a mamluk, mounted a horse and took with her a mule which she loaded with huge amounts of gold, precious stones and materials. Accompanied by the ape she travelled to Cairo, where she lodged in a house by the desert. Every day she would buy meat from a young butcher, but she would only go to him in the afternoon, when she would be pale-faced and haggard, leading the young man to think that there had to be some strange reason behind this. One day, when she had come to him as usual to fetch her meat, he followed her unnoticed, staying behind her as she went from place to place until she reached her house in the desert and went in. THE YOUNG MAN SAID:

I watched her from a corner of the house and saw that, when she had settled down there, she lit a fire, cooked the meat and ate as much as she wanted, after which she gave the rest to the ape that was with her, which also ate its fill. Next, she took off the mamluk's clothes that she was wearing and dressed herself in women's finery, and I realized that this was, in fact, a woman. She brought out wine, drank it and poured some for the ape, after which it copulated with her some ten times until she fainted. The ape spread a silk sheet over her and then went off to its own quarters, but when I came down into the middle of the room, it noticed me. It was just about to attack me, when I rushed at it with a knife that I had with me, and slit open its belly. The girl woke up in fear and alarm and, on seeing the state that the ape was in, she let out so terrible a cry that she almost gave up the ghost and then fell down in a faint.

When she recovered she said to me: 'What led you to do that? For God's sake, send me after the ape.' I humoured her and told her that I would guarantee to sleep with her as often as the ape had done until eventually her fears were calmed. I then married her, but I found myself unable to satisfy her or to endure the demands she made on me. When I complained about this to an old woman and told her my wife's history, she told me what to do, saying: 'Bring me a cooking pot and fill it with pungent vinegar and then fetch a *ratl*'s weight of feverfew.' When I had done this, she put the ingredients in the pot, set the pot on the fire and got it to boil furiously. She then told me to lie with the girl, which I did until she fainted. While she was unconscious, the old woman picked her up and set the lips of her vagina to the mouth of the pot. The vapour entered her and then something came out. When I looked at this, it turned out to be a pair of worms, one black and the other yellow. The old woman explained that the black worm had been produced when she had slept with the black slave and the yellow when she had lain with the ape.

When she recovered consciousness, she stayed with me for a long time and no longer looked for sexual intercourse, as God, to my astonishment, had freed her from this appetite.

Night 357

Morning now dawned and Shahrazad broke off from what she had been allowed to say. Then, when it was the three hundred and fifty-seventh night, SHE CONTINUED:

I have heard, O fortunate king, that the young man said: 'God, to my astonishment, had freed her from this appetite. I told her what had happened and she continued to enjoy the easiest and pleasantest of lives with me, and she adopted the old woman as a mother.'

She, her husband and the old woman lived in happiness and joy until they were visited by the destroyer of delights and the parter of companions. Praise be to the living God, Who does not die and in Whose hands lie power and sovereignty.

A story is told that in the old days there was a king of great power and dignity who had three daughters, each like the shining full moon or like flowery meadows, and one son like the moon. One day, as the king was seated on his throne of state, three wise men came into his presence, one of whom had with him a golden peacock, the second a brazen trumpet and the third a horse made of ivory and ebony. 'What are these things,' asked the king, 'and what purpose do they serve?' The man with the peacock told him: 'The useful thing about this peacock is that at the end of every hour, night or day, it claps its wings and shrieks.' The man with the trumpet said: 'When this trumpet is placed over the city gate, it acts as the city's guardian, for when an enemy enters, it sounds a call so that the man can be recognized and arrested.' The man with the horse said: 'This horse is useful in that, when a man mounts it, it will take him to whatever land he wants.'

'I shall not reward you,' said the king, 'until I have tested the uses of these things.' First he tested the peacock and found that it did what its master said it would, and he followed this by testing the trumpet, with the same result. 'Ask me to grant you a wish,' he told the two wise men, to which they said: 'Our wish is that you should marry each of us to one of your daughters.' Accordingly the king gave them each a princess in marriage. The third of the trio, the man with the horse, then came forward, kissed the ground before the king and said: 'O sovereign of the age, grant me a favour in the same way that you have granted favours to my companions.' The king said that he must first test the horse, and at that the prince came forward and said: 'I shall mount it and try it out, father, to see how useful it is.' The king gave him permission to do this, and the prince came up and mounted it, but, however much he moved his legs, the horse would not budge from where it was. 'Where is this speed that you claimed for it, wise man?' the prince asked, but at that the man came up to him and showed him a screw that would make it rise in the air. 'Turn this,' he said, and when the prince turned it, the horse started to move and then flew up with him into the sky, going on and on until it was out of sight.

The prince was startled, and regretted having mounted it, telling himself that this was a trick that the man had played on him in order to get him killed. 'There is no might and no power except with God, the Exalted, the Omnipotent!' he exclaimed, and he then started to examine all the parts of the horse's body. While he was doing this, he noticed a protuberance like a cock's comb on its right shoulder and another on its left. As these were the only projections that he saw, he rubbed the one on the right shoulder of the horse, but as this made it go further up into the sky, he took his hand away. Then he looked at the knob on the left shoulder, and when he rubbed it, the horse's motion changed from a climb to a descent. It continued to come slowly down to earth, with the prince taking what care he could.

Night 358

Morning now dawned and Shahrazad broke off from what she had been allowed to say. Then, when it was the three hundred and fifty-eighth night, SHE CONTINUED:

I have heard, O fortunate king, that when the prince rubbed the left-hand knob, the horse's motion changed from a climb to a descent. It continued to come slowly down to earth, with the prince taking what care he could.

Now that he had seen how useful the horse could be, he was delighted and thanked Almighty God for the favour that He had shown him in saving him from death. His climb had taken him far above the earth and so the descent continued all day, with him turning the horse's head in whatever direction he wanted. Sometimes he would make it go down and at other times up, until, when he had got it to do all that he wanted, he took it down towards the ground. He started to look at the lands and cities there that he did not recognize, never having seen them before in his life.

Among the sights was that of a well-built city in the middle of a green and flourishing countryside with trees and rivers. He thought about this, wondering what the city's name might be and in what part of the world it lay. He started to circle around it and to reconnoitre it from right and left.

The day was coming to its end and, as the sun was about to set, he said to himself: 'I have found no better place in which to spend the night than this city. That is what I shall do and in the morning I shall go back to my family's capital and tell them all, including my father, what has happened and what I have seen.' He started to look for a place where he and the horse could stay safely out of sight, and while he was doing this he noticed in the centre of the city a palace soaring high into the sky, surrounded by extensive walls with tall battlements. 'This is a pleasant place,' he said to himself and he started to move the knob that controlled the horse's descent. It continued to take him downwards until all four of its legs rested on the flat roof of the palace.

When he had dismounted, the prince praised Almighty God and then walked round the horse, examining it and exclaiming: 'By God, the man who made you like this was wise and skilled indeed! If the Almighty extends my life and brings me back safely to my country and my family, reuniting me with my father, I shall give him the best of rewards and shower favours on him.' He remained sitting on the roof until he thought that everyone must be asleep. He was tormented by hunger and thirst, as he had eaten nothing since leaving his father, and he said to himself: 'There must be some provisions in a palace like this.' He left the horse where it was and walked away to see whether he could find something to eat, until he came across a staircase and went down. At the bottom he was impressed to find a beautifully laid-out courtyard paved with marble, but in the whole of the palace he could discover no sight nor sound of any human being. He stood in perplexity, looking right and left but having no idea where to go. 'The best thing I can do,' he told himself, 'is to go back to where I left the horse and spend the night with it. Then, in the morning, I can mount it and set off again.'

Night 359

Morning now dawned and Shahrazad broke off from what she had been allowed to say. Then, when it was the three hundred and fifty-ninth night, SHE CONTINUED:

I have heard, O fortunate king, that the prince told himself: 'The best thing I can do is to go back to where I left the horse and spend the night with it. Then, in the morning, I can mount it and set off again.' While he was telling himself this as he stood there, he suddenly noticed a light coming towards him. Looking at it more closely, he found that it came from a group of maids, among whom was a radiantly beautiful young girl like the light of the moon when full, with a slender body like the letter *alif*. She fitted the description of the poet:

She came unexpectedly in the twilight shadows,
Like the full moon on a dark horizon,
A slender girl with no match among humankind,
Most gloriously formed in the splendour of beauty.
When my eyes rested on her loveliness, I cried out:
'Glory to the One Who created man from a drop of sperm.'
I guard her from all envious eyes by the words:
'Say: I take refuge with the Lord of mankind and of the dawn.'*

* cf. Quran 113.1.

This girl was the daughter of the king of the city, who was so fond of her that he had built the palace for her. If ever she felt depressed, she and her maids would go and stay there for one or two days or more, before returning to her own quarters. As it happened, she had come that night to amuse herself and relax, and so she was walking surrounded by her maids and accompanied by a eunuch with a sword. When they got to the palace, they spread out the furnishings, released incense from the censers, played and enjoyed themselves, but while they were doing this the prince suddenly attacked the eunuch, knocked him down and took the sword from his hand. He then turned on the maids, who scattered right and left.

When the princess saw how good-looking he was, she asked him: 'Are you perhaps the man who asked my father yesterday for my hand and was rejected because my father claimed that you were ugly? By God, he told a lie when he said that, for you are indeed a handsome man.' In fact, it had been the son of the king of India who had asked her father for her hand and had been rejected because of his ugliness. Thinking the prince to be this Indian, she went up to him, embraced and kissed him and then lay down with him. Her maids then told her: 'Lady, this is not the man who asked your father for your hand. He was ugly and this one is handsome. Your rejected suitor would not even be good enough to act as this man's servant and he must clearly be someone of high rank.'

They then went over to the eunuch who had been knocked out, and when they had revived him he jumped up in a panic and looked vainly for the sword that he had been holding. The maids told him that the man who had taken it and had knocked him down was sitting with the princess. It was she whom the king had employed him to guard, fearing that the disasters of time and the blows of fate might injure her, and so he came and lifted the curtain to find her sitting in conversation with the prince. After looking at them, he asked the prince: 'Master, are you mortal or *jinn*?' 'Damn you, you vilest of slaves,' answered the prince, 'how can you confuse the children of sovereign kings with infidel devils?' Then, with the sword in his hand, he went on: 'I am the king's son-in-law. He married me to his daughter and ordered me to consummate the marriage.' When he heard this, the eunuch said: 'Master, if you are a mortal, as you claim, then she is a fitting mate for none but you and you have a better right to her than anyone else.'

He then made his way to the king, shrieking, tearing his clothes and pouring dust on his head. On hearing the noise, the king said: 'You have

alarmed me, so tell me quickly what has happened to you and be brief.'
'O king,' replied the eunuch, 'go to your daughter, for she is in the power
of a *jinn* devil in the guise of a princely-looking man. So seize him.'
When the king heard this he thought of killing the eunuch and said:
'How could you have been so careless of my daughter as to allow this
to happen to her?' Then he set off for the palace where she was, and
when he arrived and found the slave girls standing there, he asked them
what had happened to the princess. 'We were sitting with her,' they told
him, 'when suddenly this young man rushed in at us. He was like a full
moon, with the most beautiful face that we have ever seen and with a
drawn sword in his hand. When we asked who he was, he claimed that
you had married him to your daughter. This is all we know. We don't
know whether he is human or a *jinni*, but he is chaste and well mannered
and does not indulge in shameless actions.' This served to cool the king's
anger and when he slowly raised the curtain he saw the prince and his
daughter sitting and talking to each other. The prince, he could see, was
a shapely man with a face like a gleaming full moon, but such was his
jealousy for his daughter's honour that he could not restrain himself. He
lifted the curtain and with a drawn sword in his hand he rushed in at
them like a *ghul*.

'Is this your father?' the prince asked and, when she said yes . . .

Night 360

Morning now dawned and Shahrazad broke off from what she had been
allowed to say. Then, when it was the three hundred and sixtieth night,
SHE CONTINUED:

I have heard, O fortunate king, that when the prince saw the king
with a drawn sword in his hand, rushing in at them like a *ghul*, he asked
the girl whether this was her father and when she said yes, he jumped to
his feet and, grasping his sword, he gave such a terrible shout that the
king was astounded. The prince was about to attack, but the king,
realizing that the young man was the more vigorous, sheathed his sword
and stood still. When the prince came up to him, he addressed him
courteously and said: 'Young man, are you human or a *jinni*?' 'Were it
not for my respect for your authority and for your daughter's honour,'
replied the prince, 'I would shed your blood. How can you think that I
am related to devils when I am a descendant of sovereign kings who, if

they wanted to seize your kingdom, would topple you from your throne of grandeur and rob you of all that is in your lands?' These words filled the king with awe and he feared for his life, but nevertheless he protested: 'If, as you claim, you are of royal blood, how is it that you have entered my palace without my leave and dishonoured me, approaching my daughter, pretending to be her husband and claiming that I gave her to you in marriage? I have killed kings and the sons of kings who have come as her suitors, and who can save you from my power? If I call to my slaves and retainers and tell them to kill you, they will do that on the spot and who will rescue you from me?'

When the prince heard this he told the king: 'Your blindness astonishes me. Do you hope to get a more handsome husband for your daughter than me, one more steadfast, more able to repay good or evil, or one with greater power and more troops and guards?' 'No, by God,' replied the king, 'but I would like you to ask me for her hand in front of witnesses so that I can marry her to you, for if I do this in secret it will bring disgrace on me.' 'Well spoken,' said the prince, 'but if you collect your slaves, your servants and your soldiers to fight me and they kill me, as you say they will, you will disgrace yourself, and your people will not know whether to believe what you tell them or not. My advice to you is that you should do what I am going to suggest.' The king asked what this was and the prince answered: 'What I have to say is this. Either you and I can fight a duel to the death between ourselves, with the victor having the better right to the kingdom, or you can leave me here tonight and in the morning fetch for me all your troops and your servants, letting me know how many they are.' 'I have forty thousand riders,' the king told him, 'as well as my black slaves, not counting their own followers whose numbers are the same again.' The prince said: 'Bring them out to me at dawn and tell them . . .'

Night 361

Morning now dawned and Shahrazad broke off from what she had been allowed to say. Then, when it was the three hundred and sixty-first night, SHE CONTINUED:

I have heard, O fortunate king, that the prince said: 'Bring them out to me at dawn and tell them: "This man has asked me for my daughter's hand on condition that he comes out to fight you all, and he claims that

he will defeat you and that you will prove to be powerless against him."
Then leave me to fight them; if they kill me, that will keep your secret
safe and protect your honour, while if I get the upper hand, I am the
kind of son-in-law for whom you would wish.'

When the king heard this, he approved of the idea and accepted the
prince's advice, impressed by his haughty words and alarmed by his
determination to challenge the whole of the army, whose numbers had
been described to him. He and the prince then sat talking until the king
called for the eunuch and ordered him to go immediately to the vizier
with instructions to muster the troops, who were to arm themselves and
mount their horses. The eunuch carried these orders to the vizier, who,
in his turn, summoned the army officers and the state dignitaries, telling
them to mount and ride out carrying their arms.

So much for them, but as for the king, he continued talking with the
prince and was impressed by his conversation, intelligence and culture.
They were still talking when morning came, and at that point the king
got up and went to take his seat on the throne. He ordered his men to
mount and he supplied the prince with one of his finest horses, ordering
it to be provided with the best of saddles and other equipment. The
prince, however, refused to mount until he had seen the king's army for
himself, and so the two of them went together to the *maidan*, where the
prince got a view of the size of the army. The king then made a proclamation to the troops, saying: 'A young man has come to me to ask
for my daughter's hand. I have never seen anyone more handsome,
courageous or strong. He claims that he can defeat you single-handed
and that, even if you numbered a hundred thousand, to him this would
be no more than a few. When he comes out against you, meet him with
the heads of your lances and the edges of your swords, for this is an
enormous task that he has undertaken.'

The king then said to the prince: 'My son, do what you want with
them,' but the prince said: 'This is not fair treatment. How can I go out
against them on foot when they are all on horseback?' 'I told you to
mount,' replied the king, 'but you refused. However, take your pick of
the horses.' 'I don't like any of them,' the prince told him, 'and I shall
mount only the horse on which I rode here.' When the king asked him
where it was, he said: 'On top of your palace,' and when asked in what
part of the palace, he said: 'On the flat roof.' 'This is the first sign that
you are weak in the head,' the king told him. 'How the devil can a horse
be on top of the roof? But we shall see now whether you're lying or

telling the truth.' He turned to one of his officers and told him to go to the palace and fetch what he found on the roof.

The people there were amazed at what the prince had said and they asked one another: 'How can a horse come down the stairs from the roof? We have never heard anything like this,' but when the king's messenger climbed to the palace roof, he saw standing there the finest horse on which he had ever set eyes. He went up to investigate and found that it was made of ebony and ivory. Another of the king's officers had gone up there with him, and they laughed together at the sight of it and said: 'Was this the kind of horse that the young man was talking about? He must be mad, but this will soon become clear . . .'

Night 362

Morning now dawned and Shahrazad broke off from what she had been allowed to say. Then, when it was the three hundred and sixty-second night, SHE CONTINUED:

I have heard, O fortunate king, that the king's officers laughed together at the sight of it and said: 'Was this the kind of horse that the young man was talking about? He must be mad, but this will soon become clear and he may be a man of importance.'

They lifted up the horse and carried it down to set in front of the king. People crowded round to look at it, admiring the beauty of its appearance together with its splendid saddle and bridle. The king was among its admirers, being full of astonishment at it. 'Is this your horse?' he asked the prince. 'Yes it is, your majesty,' the other replied, adding: 'And you will see how wonderfully it performs.' 'Take it and mount it then,' the king told him, but the prince said: 'Only when your troops keep their distance.' The king told them to retire for one bowshot and the prince then said: 'O king, I am about to mount my horse and then I shall charge your men, scattering them right and left and breaking their hearts.' 'Do what you want,' replied the king. 'You need not spare them, for they will not spare you.'

The prince went up to mount his horse, and the king's men drew up in ranks, telling each other that, when he came between them, they would meet him with lance points and sword edges. 'By God,' said one of them, 'this is an unlucky business. How can we kill this young man with his handsome face and his fine figure?' But another said: 'By God, it will be hard to get to him. He can only be doing this because he is sure of his courage and skill.'

When the prince was settled in his saddle, he turned the knob that would make the horse climb and they stared at him to see what he was going to do. The horse stirred and moved, curvetting in the most extraordinary manner. Its interior filled with air and then it took off and rose into the sky. On seeing this, the king called to his men: 'Catch him, damn you, before he gets away,' but his viziers and officers said: 'King, can anyone catch up with a bird in flight? This has to be a great sorcerer, may God preserve you from him, so give thanks to Him for having rescued you from his clutches.'

After what he had seen, the king returned to his palace, where he went to tell his daughter what had happened during his encounter with the prince in the *maidan*. He found her full of grief for her suitor and for having been parted from him, so much so that she fell gravely ill and kept to her bed. When her father saw her in this state, he clasped her to him, kissed her between the eyes and said: 'Daughter, give praise and thanks to God for having saved us from this cunning sorcerer.' He started to tell her again what he had seen the prince do and how he had flown up into the air, but she wouldn't listen to anything he said and only wept and sobbed the more, swearing to herself that she would neither eat nor drink until God had reunited her with him. This caused her father great concern, and his distress about her condition made him sad at heart, but the more tenderly he treated her, the deeper grew her love for the prince.

Night 363

Morning now dawned and Shahrazad broke off from what she had been allowed to say. Then, when it was the three hundred and sixty-third night, SHE CONTINUED:

I have heard, O fortunate king, that the king was concerned for his daughter, but the more tenderly he treated her, the deeper grew her love for the prince.

So much for them, but as for the prince, in his solitary flight through the air he remembered the princess's beauty and grace, and as he had asked the king's companions to tell him the name of the city as well as the names of the king and his daughter, he knew that the city was San'a'. He pressed on with his journey until he came near his father's city and,

after circling around it, he made for his father's palace and landed on its
flat roof, where he left the horse. When he went down and entered his
father's presence, he found him sad and distressed at the loss of his son,
but on seeing him come in, his father rose to greet him, embraced him
and hugged him to his chest in delight.

The prince then asked his father what had happened to the wise man
who had made the horse. 'May God give him no blessing,' said the king.
'That was an unlucky hour in which I saw him, as it was he who caused
you to leave me, and since then he has been in prison.' The prince gave
orders for him to be freed, taken from prison and brought before him.
When the wise man came, the king presented him with a robe to show
his favour, but although the king showered gifts on him, he refused him
his daughter's hand. This made the man furiously angry and he regretted
what he had done, realizing that the prince had discovered the secret of
the horse and knew how to set it in motion. The king then advised his
son not to go near the horse again or ever to mount it from that day
on, adding: 'You don't know all its qualities and you have been tricked
by it.'

The prince had told his father about what had happened to him with
the princess and her father, the ruler of San'a'. 'Had the king wanted to
kill you, he would have done so,' his father told him, adding: 'But you
were not destined to die so soon.' The prince, however, filled with anxiety
because of his love for the princess, went to the horse, mounted it and
after he had turned the knob to make it climb, up it flew, high into the
sky. Next morning, when the king went to look for him, he was not to
be found and, full of concern, the king climbed up to the palace roof
only to see his son soaring into the sky. In distress at his loss the king
bitterly regretted not having hidden the horse away, and he promised
himself that, if his son returned, he would put his mind at ease by
destroying it, and he then started to weep and wail again . . .

Night 364

Morning now dawned and Shahrazad broke off from what she had been
allowed to say. Then, when it was the three hundred and sixty-fourth
night, SHE CONTINUED:

I have heard, O fortunate king, that the king started to weep and wail
again, in sorrow for him.

So much for him, but as for the prince, he flew on until he came to San'a', and then landed on the roof where he had come down the first time. Taking care to keep under cover, he went to the room of the princess, but he could find neither her, her maids or her former guard, the eunuch. In his distress he searched the palace for her until he discovered her in a different room, lying in bed and surrounded by maids and nurses. He went in and greeted them, and at the sound of his voice she got up, embraced him and started to kiss him between the eyes and to clasp him to her bosom. 'My lady,' he said, 'you have left me lonely all this time.' 'It was you who left me lonely,' she replied, 'and had you stayed away any longer, there is no doubt that I would have died.' He said: 'My lady, what do you think of my behaviour to your father and of how he acted to me? Had it not been for my love for you, who are the temptation of all mankind, I would have killed him and made an example of him for all to see, but as I love you, so I love him for your sake.' 'How could you leave me,' she asked, 'and how could there be any pleasure for me in life when you are gone?' 'Will you obey me and follow what I say?' he asked. 'Say what you want,' she replied, 'for I will agree to whatever you propose and not disobey you in anything.' 'Then come with me to my own kingdom,' he said. 'Willingly,' she told him.

The prince was overjoyed to hear this. He took her by the hand and, after getting her to swear a solemn oath that she had agreed to this, he led her to the flat roof at the top of the castle, where he mounted the horse and took her up behind him. He kept a tight grip on her, and after tying her firmly in place he moved the knob on the horse's shoulder to make it rise. When it took off with them, the maids cried out, alerting the princess's father and mother, who rushed up to the roof. Looking upwards the king saw the ebony horse flying off into the air with the eloping pair, and as he became increasingly agitated, he called out: 'Prince, for God's sake have pity on me and on my wife and do not part us from our daughter.' The prince made no reply, but, thinking to himself that the princess might regret leaving her mother and father, he asked her: 'O temptation of the age, would you like me to return you to your parents?' 'By God, my lord,' she replied, 'I don't want that, and what I do want is to be with you wherever you are, as my love for you has distracted me from everything else, even my mother and father.'

When the prince heard that, he was delighted and he made the horse travel at an easy pace so as not to alarm her. He flew on with her until he caught sight of a green meadow with a stream of running water gushing from a spring. There the two landed and after they had eaten and drunk, the prince remounted and tied the princess on behind him lest she fall. He then set off with her again and flew on until, to his great delight, he reached his father's city. He wanted to show her the seat of his father's power and to let her see that his kingdom was larger than that of her father, so he landed with her in one of the orchards where the king used to go for relaxation. He took her to a garden house that was kept ready for his father, and there at the door he left the ebony horse, telling her to look after it and saying: 'Stay here until I send a messenger to you, for I am going to my father to prepare a palace for you and to show you my kingdom.'

Hearing this, the joyful princess said: 'Do as you want,' . . .

Night 365

Morning now dawned and Shahrazad broke off from what she had been allowed to say. Then, when it was the three hundred and sixty-fifth night, SHE CONTINUED:

I have heard, O fortunate king, that hearing this, the joyful princess said: 'Do as you want,' as she realized that her entrance was to be made with the pomp and ceremony that suited one of her rank. So the prince set off, leaving her behind, and on his arrival at the city he went in to greet his father, who was delighted to see him and welcomed him warmly. The prince told him that he had brought the princess about whom he had spoken earlier. 'I have left her outside the city in an orchard,' he explained, 'and I have come to tell you so that you can prepare a procession and go out to meet her and show her your kingdom, your army and your guards.' The king willingly agreed to this and gave immediate orders for the city to be adorned with decorations. He himself, in all his pomp and splendour, rode out with all his troops, the dignitaries of his state, as well as his other officials and servants. From his own palace the prince brought out jewellery and robes and other things that are found in royal treasuries. He prepared for the princess a litter covered with green, red and yellow brocade, on which were seated Indian, Rumi and Abyssianian slave girls, together with an astonishing display of treasures. Then, leaving this with its attendants, he went on ahead to the garden house where he had deposited the princess, but although he searched through it he could not find either her or the horse. He struck himself on the face, tore his clothes and started to wander around the orchard.

At first he was bemused, but later, returning to his senses, he asked himself how she could have learned the horse's secret, when he had told her nothing at all about it. He then thought that perhaps the Persian sorcerer who had made it had come across her and had taken her in revenge for what his father had done to him. He asked the guards of the orchard whether anyone had passed them and they said: 'We have seen no one enter apart from the Persian sorcerer who went in to collect healing herbs.' When the prince heard that, he knew for certain that this was the man who had taken the girl.

Night 366

Morning now dawned and Shahrazad broke off from what she had been allowed to say. Then, when it was the three hundred and sixty-sixth night, SHE CONTINUED:

I have heard, O fortunate king, that when the prince heard that, he knew for certain that this was the man who had taken the girl.

As had been predestined, when the prince had left the princess in the garden house and had gone to his father's palace to make his preparations, the Persian had come to the orchard to collect healing herbs. He had detected a scent of musk and perfume filling the place and emanating from the princess. He went towards the source of the scent and when he came to the garden house he saw the horse that he had made with his own hands standing by the door. He was delighted by this, as its loss had been a great sorrow for him. He went up to it and found, after a thorough inspection, that it was undamaged. He was about to mount it and ride off when it occurred to him that he should look to see what the prince had brought and left there. So he went in and found the princess seated like the bright sun in a cloudless sky. When he saw her, he realized that here was a lady of high rank whom the prince had brought there on the horse, and that he must have left her while he went to the city in order to come back with a procession to escort her in with pomp and ceremony.

He then went in and kissed the ground before her. She looked up and found, on inspection, that here was a very ugly man of loathsome appearance. She asked him who he was and he said: 'My lady, I am a messenger from the prince. He sent me to you with orders to bring you to another orchard close to the city.' When she heard that, she asked where the prince himself was and he replied: 'He is with his father in the city and he is about to come now with a great procession.' 'Could he find no one to send me except you?' she asked, at which he laughed and said: 'My lady, don't be deceived by my ugly face and my unpleasant appearance. Were you to get from me what the prince has got, you would praise me. It was because of my ugliness and my frightening shape that he picked me as his messenger to you, both out of his jealousy for your reputation and because of his love for you. For otherwise he has vast quantities of mamluks, black slaves, pages, eunuchs and retainers.'

This convinced the princess and led her to believe him. So she got up . . .

Night 367

Morning now dawned and Shahrazad broke off from what she had been allowed to say. Then, when it was the three hundred and sixty-seventh night, SHE CONTINUED:

I have heard, O fortunate king, that the princess was convinced by what the Persian sorcerer had told her about the prince. So she got up, put her hand in his and asked: 'Father, what have you brought with you for me to ride?' 'Lady,' he replied, 'you can ride the horse on which you came.' 'I can't do that on my own,' she told him, at which he smiled, realizing that she was in his power, and he then told her that he would ride with her himself. He mounted and took her up behind him, keeping a tight grip on her and tying her securely in her place, ignorant as she was of his intentions. He moved the knob to make the horse rise, its interior filled with air, it stirred and moved and it then rose up into the air, flying on until it had left the city behind.

'Man,' said the princess, 'this is not what you told me about the prince when you claimed that he had sent you to me.' 'May God defile him,' answered the Persian, 'for he is a disgusting, sordid fellow.' 'Damn you,' she said, 'how dare you disobey an order given to you by your master?' 'He is not my master,' the Persian said, adding: 'Do you know who I am?' She told him that all she knew was what he had told her about himself, to which he replied: 'What I told you was a trick that I was playing on you and on the prince. I was about to spend the rest of my life grieving for this horse that you are riding. I made it myself, only to have the prince get hold of it, but now I have both it and you and I have burned his heart as he burned mine. He will never possess it again, but you can console yourself and be happy, for I shall be of more use to you than he would be.'

When the princess heard this, she slapped herself in the face and called out: 'O sorrow, I have lost my beloved and I did not stay with my father and mother.' While she wept bitterly over what had happened to her, the Persian flew on with her to the land of Rum and then landed in a green meadow with streams and trees. This was near the city of an important king, who, as it happened, had gone out that day to enjoy himself hunting. He was passing by the meadow when he saw the Persian standing there with the horse and the girl beside him. Before the Persian knew what was going on, the king's slaves took him by surprise and brought him before the king, together with the girl and the horse. The king looked at the Persian's ugliness and his unprepossessing appearance and then at the beauty and grace of the girl. He asked her: 'My lady, what is the relationship between this old man and you?' The Persian promptly replied: 'She is my wife and my cousin,' but, on hearing this, the princess gave him the lie and exclaimed: 'By God, your majesty, I don't know him and he is no husband of mine! He used trickery to seize me by force.' When the king heard this, he ordered the Persian to be beaten, and so severe was the beating that he almost died. On the king's orders he was carried to the city and thrown into prison. The king then took the princess and the horse with him, but he didn't know how to set it in motion.

So much for the Persian and the princess, but as for the prince, he put on travelling clothes, took what money he needed and set off on his travels in a state of great despondency. He moved quickly, trying to follow the trail of the princess from town to town and city to city, asking about the ebony horse, but everyone who heard him talk about it wondered at him, thinking that he was talking nonsense. He went on like this for some time, but in spite of his investigations and the number of questions that he asked, he could get no news of the missing pair. He then came to the city of the princess's father but, although he asked about her there, he heard no news and found her father grieving for her loss. He went back and set out for the land of Rum, still trying to track down his quarry and putting his questions.

Night 368

Morning now dawned and Shahrazad broke off from what she had been allowed to say. Then, when it was the three hundred and sixty-eighth night, SHE CONTINUED:

I have heard, O fortunate king, that the prince set out for the land of Rum, still trying to track down his quarry and putting his questions.

As it happened, he stopped in a *khan* where he noticed a group of merchants sitting and talking. He took a seat near them and heard one tell his companions that he had just come across something remarkable. When they asked him what this was, he said: 'I was in a certain part of such-and-such a city' – and he gave the name of the city where the princess was – 'when I heard the people there telling an extraordinary tale of how the king had gone out hunting one day with a number of his companions and state dignitaries. When they reached open country they passed by a green meadow where they found a man standing with a girl seated beside him, and with him there was a horse made of ebony. He was an ugly-looking fellow of formidable appearance, while she was a beautiful and graceful girl, radiantly perfect with an excellent figure. The ebony horse was a wonder and no one has ever seen anything more handsome or better constructed.' 'What did the king do with them?' the other merchants asked, and their companion said: 'He took the man and asked him about the girl, whom he then claimed to be his wife and cousin, but she said that this was a lie. So the king took her from him and ordered him to be beaten and thrown into prison, but I don't know what happened to the ebony horse.'

When the prince heard this he went up to the man and started to question him courteously and politely until he was told the name of the city and of the king. When he had got this information he spent a joyful night, and in the morning he set off and continued on his way until he reached the city. He was about to go in when the gatekeepers stopped him. They wanted to take him before the king so that he might be asked about his circumstances, his reason for coming to the city and what skills he had as a craftsman, these being questions that it was the king's custom to put to strangers. The prince had arrived in the evening, and as this was a time when no one could enter the king's presence or consult with him, the gatekeepers took him to the prison, intending to leave him there. The gaolers, however, seeing how handsome he was, had no wish to imprison him, and so they made him sit with them outside the prison itself, and when food was brought for them, he ate with them until he had had enough.

After they had finished eating, they started talking and, turning to the prince, they asked him where he came from. 'From Persia, the land of the Chosroes,' he told them. They laughed and one of them said: 'I have listened to stories and accounts of many peoples, Persian, and I have seen for myself their circumstances, but I have never seen or heard a bigger liar than the Persian whom we are holding in prison here at the moment,' to which another added: 'Nor have I ever seen an uglier and more loathsome-looking man.' 'What obvious lies has he told?' asked the prince, and they told him: 'He claims to be a sorcerer. The king saw him when he was out hunting. He had with him a remarkably beautiful and graceful girl, radiantly perfect and well shaped, together with a horse made of black ebony, as fine a thing as I have ever seen. The girl is with the king, who is in love with her, but she is mad. Had the man been a sorcerer, as he claims, he would have cured her, for the king is desperately looking for some remedy for her and is trying to cure her madness. The ebony horse is in the royal treasury and the ugly man who was with the girl is here with us in prison. In the dark of night he weeps and wails in self-pity and doesn't allow us to sleep.'

Night 369

Morning now dawned and Shahrazad broke off from what she had been allowed to say. Then, when it was the three hundred and sixty-ninth night, SHE CONTINUED:

I have heard, O fortunate king, that the gaolers told the prince about the Persian sorcerer whom they were holding in their prison and of how he was weeping and wailing. It occurred to the prince that he could try to arrange things so as to reach his goal, and when the gaolers wanted to sleep, they brought him into the prison and shut the door on him. He then heard the sorcerer weeping and lamenting to himself in Persian, saying as he wailed: 'Alas for the wrong that I did to myself and to the prince, and for what I did with the girl, as I neither left her behind nor got what I wanted. It was all because of my mismanagement. I tried to get what I didn't deserve and wasn't proper for a man like me, and whoever does this meets the kind of disaster into which I have fallen.'

On hearing this, the prince spoke to him in Persian and said: 'How long are you going to go on weeping and wailing? Do you think that what has happened to you has never happened to anyone else?' The sorcerer, listening to him, was glad of his company and complained to him of the miserable plight in which he found himself.

The next morning the gatekeepers took the prince to their king, explaining that he had arrived at the city the previous day too late to be presented to him. The king asked him from where he had come, his name and profession and the reason for his coming to the city, to which the prince replied: 'My name is a Persian one, Harja; my native land is Persia; and I am a man of learning, particularly in the field of medicine. I can cure the sick and the mad, and for this reason I travel through regions and cities in order to add to my knowledge, and when I see a sick person I treat him, as this is my profession.' The king was delighted to hear this and said: 'Excellent doctor, you have come to us just when you are needed.' He then went on to tell the prince about the girl, promising that if through his treatment he could cure her madness, he could have anything that he asked for. When he heard this, the prince said: 'May God ennoble you, describe the symptoms of her madness that you have seen and tell me how many days ago it was that this affected her and also how you got hold of her, together with the horse and the sorcerer.'

The king told him the whole story from beginning to end, adding that the sorcerer was in prison, and when the prince then asked him about the horse, the king said that it was in one of the palace apartments. The prince thought to himself that the prudent thing to do would be to start by inspecting the horse, for if it turned out to be sound and uninjured, then he would have all that he wanted, whereas if it no longer worked he would have to think of some other way of saving himself. He turned to the king and said: 'Your majesty, I must look at this horse you mentioned to see whether I can find anything in it that might help me cure the girl.' The king willingly gave him permission and, getting up, he took him by the hand and led him to the horse. The prince walked around inspecting it, and after checking its condition, he was delighted to discover that it was intact and undamaged. He then told the king that he would like to examine the girl, adding: 'If Almighty God wills it, I hope that I may be able to cure her by means of this horse,' and advising him to look after it carefully. The king took him to the room where the princess was, and when he went in he found her stamping and falling on the ground, as she had kept on doing, not because she was mad but to keep anyone from approaching her.

When the prince saw her in this state he said: 'O temptation of all mankind, all is well with you,' and he went on speaking to her soothingly and gently before revealing himself to her. When she recognized him, she let out a great cry before fainting from joy, while the king thought that it was through fear of him that she had collapsed. The prince then put his mouth to her ear and said: 'Temptation of all mankind, be careful not to shed my blood and your own. Wait patiently and show strength of mind, for we need patience here as well as good and subtle planning if we are to escape from this tyrant. My scheme is to go to him and tell him that what you are suffering from is something caused by an evil spirit. I shall guarantee to cure you on condition that he remove your fetters, after which the spirit will leave you. When he then comes to see you, talk to him sweetly so that he may think that I have cured you, and we can then achieve all that we want.' 'To hear is to obey,' she replied, after which he went joyfully to the king and said: 'Fortunate king, through your auspicious help I discovered what the girl's disease was and how to treat it, as a result of which I have cured her for you. Come and visit her now, but talk to her gently and treat her with kindness, promising her whatever will please her, as all that you want from her is yours.'

Night 370

Morning now dawned and Shahrazad broke off from what she had been allowed to say. Then, when it was the three hundred and seventieth night, SHE CONTINUED:

I have heard, O fortunate king, that the prince pretended to be a doctor and went to the princess to reveal himself and to tell her his plan. When she had agreed to this, he left her and went to tell the king: 'Come and visit her now, but talk to her gently and treat her with kindness, promising her whatever will please her, as all that you want from her is yours.'

The king got up and went in to visit the princess, who, on seeing him, rose, kissed the ground in front of him and welcomed him. He was delighted by this and gave orders for slave girls and eunuchs to come to attend on her, take her to the baths and provide her with jewellery and robes.

They came in to greet her and she returned their greeting gracefully and eloquently. Then they dressed her in royal robes, put a jewelled necklace round her neck and took her off to the baths, where they waited on her, and when they brought her out she was like the full moon. She went to the king, greeted him and kissed the ground before him. So great was his joy that he told the prince: 'All this is thanks to the blessings you have brought; may God grant us more of your favours.' 'Your majesty,' replied the prince, 'in order to complete and perfect her cure you should go out yourself with all your guards and your troops to the place where you found her, taking the ebony horse that was with her so that I may remove the evil spirit from her by a charm, imprison it and kill it so as to keep it from ever returning to her.'

The king agreed willingly and he had the ebony horse taken out to the meadow where he had found the princess, the horse and the Persian sorcerer. He himself rode there with his troops, taking the princess with him, but they did not know what the prince intended to do. He, for his part, acting in his role as sorcerer, gave orders, when they reached the meadow, that the king and his men should stay almost out of sight of the girl and the horse. He said: 'With your permission, your majesty, I shall release incense and recite a charm so as to imprison the evil spirit and prevent it from ever coming back to her again. Then I shall mount the ebony horse and take her up behind me. When I do that, the horse will be stirred into a walk; I shall come across to you and, as the cure will then be complete, you can do whatever you want with her.' The king was delighted to hear this and he and all his men watched as the prince mounted the horse and took the girl up behind him. He held her tightly and, after tying her firmly in place, he turned the screw to make the horse take off. It climbed into the air, watched by the soldiers until it went out of sight. For half a day the king waited, expecting the prince to return, but at last, when this did not happen, he despaired and, filled with regret and sorrow for the loss of the princess, he went back with his troops to his city.

So much for him, but as for the prince, he made joyfully for his father's city, where he landed on his palace. He left the princess there, making sure of her safety, after which he went to his father and mother, greeted them and delighted them by telling them of her arrival.

So much for the prince, the horse and the princess, but as for the king of Rum, when he got back to his city he shut himself away in sorrow and dejection. His viziers visited him and started to question him, pointing out that the man who had carried off the girl was a sorcerer and that the king should thank God for having saved him from his magical wiles. They continued to comfort the king until he was consoled for her loss.

As for the prince, he gave magnificent banquets for the townspeople . . .

Night 371

Morning now dawned and Shahrazad broke off from what she had been allowed to say. Then, when it was the three hundred and seventy-first night, SHE CONTINUED:

I have heard, O fortunate king, that the prince gave magnificent banquets for the townspeople, who spent a whole month celebrating his wedding. The marriage was then consummated and the bride and bridegroom were happy with one another. The prince's father smashed the ebony horse, destroying its workings, while the prince wrote to the bride's father, telling him about her, that he had married her and that she was in the best of states, as well as giving his messenger precious gifts and treasures to take to him. When the messenger reached his city, San'a' in Yemen, he handed them, together with the prince's letter, to the king, who was filled with joy when he read it. He accepted the gifts, treated the messenger honourably and prepared a splendid present for his son-in-law, which he sent back with the messenger. On his return the man told the prince how pleased the king of San'a' had been to receive news of his daughter, and the prince, in his turn, was delighted to hear this.

The prince wrote every year to his father-in-law and sent him presents, and they continued in this way until the prince's father died and the prince succeeded to the throne. He treated his subjects justly, conducting himself in a way that won their approval, exercising authority and commanding obedience throughout his lands and among his people. They continued like this, enjoying the most delightful and pleasant of lives in luxury and health, until they were visited by the destroyer of delights and the parter of companions. Praise be to the living God, Who does not die and in Whose hands lie power and sovereignty.

A story is also told that once, long ago in an earlier age, there was a great king, a man of power and authority, who had a vizier named Ibrahim. Ibrahim had a daughter of remarkable beauty, unrivalled in the perfection of her loveliness, outstandingly cultured and of great intelligence. She had a fondness for wine and drinking parties, as well as a liking for handsome faces, elegant poetry and witty stories, while her innate grace moved men to love her. She was as a poet described her:

I am in love with the greatest enchantress among Turks and Arabs;
She argues with me on religious law, grammar and literature.
'I am the grammatical object,' she says, 'but you put me in the
    genitive;
Why is that? This is a subject, so why is it in the accusative?'
I said to her: 'My life and my soul are your ransom;
Do you not know that time is full of changes?
If you find yourself doubting this,
See how the head of a sentence can be fitted to its tail.'

The girl's name was al-Ward fi'l-Akmam, a name that she owed to her delicacy and the perfection of her beauty,* while because of her mastery of literature she was a favourite drinking companion of the king. It was a habit of his every year to gather together the most prominent of his subjects for a game of polo, and on the day that this happened she was sitting at her window to watch the game.

While it was going on, she suddenly noticed among the players a surpassingly splendid and handsome young man, bright faced with gleaming teeth, tall and broad-shouldered. She looked at him again and again and could not see enough of him. So she asked her nurse: 'What is the name of that good-looking young man, there among the players?' 'They are all good-looking, my daughter,' said the nurse, 'so which one do you mean?' 'Wait till I point him out to you,' the girl told her, and she then took an apple and threw it at him. He looked up and saw her at the window like a moon in the dark of night, and with that one glance he fell in love. In his distraction he recited the lines:

Did an archer shoot me or was it your eyelids
That murdered the lover's heart when he looked at you?
Was the notched arrow that suddenly struck me
Shot by an army or launched from a window?

When the game was over she again asked her nurse: 'What is the name of the young man I showed you?' and the nurse told her that he was

* Al-Ward fi'l-Akmam is Arabic for 'rose in the bud'.

called Uns al-Wujud. The girl shook her head and lay down on her couch, with her thoughts on fire with love. She sighed deeply and recited these lines:

> He made no mistake who named you Uns al-Wujud,
> You who combine friendship and generosity.
> Your face is that of the full moon,
> Shedding over the world a light shared by all existing things.
> Among mankind you are unique,
> The master of beauty, and to this I call witnesses.
> Your eyebrow is an elegantly written letter *nun*;
> Your eyeball is like the letter *sad*, shaped by the loving God;
> Your figure is that of a tender branch,
> Which gives generously when the call comes.
> You have overcome all the riders of the world in might,
> But also in friendliness, beauty and liberality.

When she had finished these lines she wrote them on a sheet of paper, folded it in a scrap of gold-embroidered silk and put it under her pillow. One of her nurses had been watching her, and this woman then came to her and started talking with her until she fell asleep. Then the woman stealthily took the paper from beneath the pillow and, when she had examined it, she realized that al-Ward had conceived a passion for Uns al-Wujud. Having read it, she put it back in its place, and when her mistress woke up, she said to her: 'My lady, I would like to give you advice because of the sympathy that I have for you. You must know that love is a powerful force; if it is hidden, it can melt iron and it leaves a legacy of sickness and disease, while no one who openly proclaims it can be blamed.' 'Nurse,' asked al-Ward, 'what is the cure for passion?' 'Union,' replied the nurse. 'And how is this to be achieved?' asked al-Ward. 'My lady,' the nurse told her, 'this can be done by an exchange of messages, tender words and a multiplicity of salutations and greetings. This brings lovers together and smooths away difficulties. If you are experiencing something of this kind, I am best fitted to keep your secret, to see that you get what you want and to carry your letters.'

Although al-Ward was delighted when she heard this, she decided not to say anything until she had seen how the affair would turn out, telling herself: 'No one has learned anything about this affair from me, and I shall not give it away to this woman until I have tested her.' The nurse then said to her: 'My mistress, I had a dream in which a man came up to me and said: "Your lady and Uns al-Wujud are in love with each other. If you take a hand in the affair, carrying their letters, doing whatever they want, and keeping all this a secret, great good will come to you." Now I have told you what I saw, but it is for you to decide.' When she had heard the story of the dream, al-Ward . . .

Night 372

Morning now dawned and Shahrazad broke off from what she had been allowed to say. Then, when it was the three hundred and seventy-second night, SHE CONTINUED:

I have heard, O fortunate king, that when she had heard the story of the dream, al-Ward said: 'Can you keep a secret?' 'How could I fail to do this,' the nurse replied, 'when I am one of the noblest of the noble?' Al-Ward then brought out the paper on which she had written her poem and told the nurse to take it to Uns al-Wujud and return with his answer. She set off with it and when she reached Uns al-Wujud she kissed his hands and greeted him eloquently before giving him the paper. He read it and after grasping its meaning he wrote these lines on the back of it:

I try to divert my heart and to conceal its passion,
But my condition clearly shows I am in love.
If my tears flow, I claim my eye is injured,
Lest the censurer see my state and understand.
I was heart-whole, not knowing what love was,
But now I am a lover with a heart enslaved.
I have taken my case to you, and I complain
Of passionate love to gain your sympathy and mercy.
The letters of this message are my tears,
To make clear what I suffer at your hands.
God guard a face that is here veiled in beauty;
The full moon is its slave, the stars its servants.
In point of beauty I have never seen her like;
Her movements teach the branches how to sway.
I do not want to burden you, but still I ask
For you to visit me, as union must be prized.
If you accept it, I give you my soul;
For me union is Paradise, and rejection, hell.

He folded the letter, kissed it and gave it to the nurse, asking her to win over her mistress's heart. 'To hear is to obey,' she replied and, taking the letter, she went back to al-Ward and gave it to her.

Al-Ward kissed it and put it on top of her head before opening it, reading it and grasping its meaning. She then wrote these lines at the bottom of it:

Your heart is smitten by my loveliness;
Be patient, it may be that your love will win my favour.
When I found that this love of yours was true
And that what smote my heart had smitten yours as well,
I would have granted you the gift of union and then doubled it,
But those who keep me in seclusion held me back.
In the dark night, from the excess of love
Fires blaze within my inmost parts.
Through harshness sleep is driven from my bed,
My body is tormented by my pain.
The law of love requires love be concealed,
So do not lift the curtain that is lowered.
I am filled up with my love for a fawn;
Would that this fawn might never leave my land.

When she had finished her poem, she folded the piece of paper and gave it to her nurse, who took it and left her. On her way out she happened to meet the chamberlain, who asked where she was going. She told him that she was going to the baths, but in her agitation she dropped the paper as she went out of the door.

So much for her, but as for the paper, it was noticed by one of the eunuchs as it lay in the passage, and he picked it up. The vizier had left the harem and was sitting on his couch when this man came up to him, holding the piece of paper in his hand. He told his master where he had found it and the vizier took it from him, unfolded it and saw the lines of poetry that were written there. He read them and, after grasping their meaning, he examined the writing more carefully and recognized his daughter's hand. Weeping so bitterly that the tears dampened his beard, he went to the girl's mother, who asked him what was wrong. 'Look at what is on this paper,' he said. She took it, read it and found that it was a message from her daughter to Uns al-Wujud. She too burst out weeping, but then she regained control of herself, checked her tears and told the vizier: 'Master, there is nothing to be gained from tears and what we have to do is see whether we can find some way of protecting your honour and concealing your daughter's affair.' She continued to console him and to lighten his load of sorrow, until he told her: 'I'm afraid that this love will harm my daughter. You know how fond the king is of Uns al-Wujud and I have two reasons for fear. The first is that this is my daughter, and the second is the fact that Uns al-Wujud is a royal favourite. It may be that this affair will have serious consequences. So what do you advise?'

Night 373

Morning now dawned and Shahrazad broke off from what she had been allowed to say. Then, when it was the three hundred and seventy-third night, SHE CONTINUED:

I have heard, O fortunate king, that when the vizier had told his wife about al-Ward, he asked for her advice. 'Wait till I pray to ask for God's help,' she told him, a prayer which she then performed with two *raka's*.

When she had finished, she told her husband: 'In the middle of the Sea of Treasures there is a mountain called "the Mountain of the Mother Who Lost Her Child"' – for a reason that will be given later – 'which can only be reached with difficulty. That is where to put her.' The vizier agreed that they should build a strong castle for their daughter on that mountain, deliver supplies there year by year and give her attendants to keep her company and wait on her. He collected carpenters, builders and architects whom he sent to the mountain, and there they built a well-fortified castle whose like had never been seen. He then prepared provisions and travelling equipment, after which he went at night to visit his daughter and told her that she was to go on a journey. Her heart warned her that she was to be separated from her beloved, and when she went out and saw the preparations that had been made for travel, she wept bitterly and wrote a message on the door to tell Uns al-Wujud of the depth of her passion, a message that would make the hairs rise on his skin, melt solid rock, and cause tears to flow. These were the lines:

By God, dwelling, if the beloved passes in the morning
And gestures with a lover's salutation,
Return from me a pure and fragrant greeting.
Where I shall be in the evening I do not know.

I have no knowledge of where I am to go;
They took me off quickly and secretly,
Sheltered by night. The woodland birds,
Roosting on their branches, weep and lament for me.
The tongue of silence cries out: 'Woe
For lovers' bitter parting!'
I saw that the cups of separation had been filled,
And Time was forcing me to drink its unmixed wine.
I mixed this with the virtue of patience, excusing myself,
But patience cannot now console me for your loss.

When she had finished writing this, she mounted and rode off with her escort, crossing open country, deserts, and smooth and rough ground until they reached the Sea of Treasures, by whose shore they pitched camp. They then prepared a large boat for her, on which both she and her household embarked. Her escort's instructions were that, when they had reached the mountain and brought their passengers to the castle, they were to sail back in the boat, disembark and then break it up. They set out and did as they were ordered, but on their way back they were shedding tears over what had happened.

So much for them, but as for Uns al-Wujud, after waking up and performing the morning prayer, he mounted and set off to present his services to the king. He followed his usual route by the vizier's door, where he hoped that he might see some of the vizier's servants as he had been in the habit of doing. When he looked at the door, there written on it he saw the lines that have already been quoted. He became distraught, his entrails were consumed by fire, and although he went home, he could find no rest and no powers of endurance. He waited, a prey to distress and passion, until nightfall and then, without telling anyone, he went out in disguise at dead of night, wandering aimlessly without knowing where he was going.

He travelled all night and part of the next day until the mountains burned in the fierce heat of the sun and he was oppressed by thirst. Catching sight of a tree, beside which there was a stream of running water, he made for it and sat down in its shade by the bank of the stream. He wanted to drink, but he could not taste the water in his mouth; his colour had changed; his face was yellow and the exertion of walking had made his feet swell. He wept bitterly and through his tears he recited these lines:

Passion for the beloved makes the lover drunk;
With each increase the sweeter it becomes.
Here is a wandering lover, led astray by love;
He has no refuge or provisions for his cheer.
What pleasure does life bring for such a one
Parted from his loved ones? That would be strange indeed.
My passion for them melts me with its fire;
My cheeks are flooded by my tears.
Shall I catch sight of them or find someone
From their spring camping grounds to cure my wretched heart?

When he had finished these lines he wept until the ground was dampened by his tears, after which he got up quickly and left the place. As he was walking through the wastes, he suddenly found himself confronted by a lion. Its neck seemed smothered by its mane, its head was as big as a dome, its mouth wider than a door and it had teeth like an elephant's tusks. When he saw this beast, he felt sure that he was as good as dead and, turning towards Mecca, he recited the confession of faith and prepared for death. But he had read in books that a lion would allow itself to be deceived by flattering words and would be pleased by praise, and so he started to address it, saying: 'Lion of the forest, lord of the open lands, terrible hunter, father of fighters, sovereign of the wild beasts, I am a lover moved by longing and slain by separation from my beloved. When I parted from her, I went out of my mind, so listen to my words and pity the torments of my love.' When the lion heard this, it drew back and sat on its haunches, raising its head towards Uns al-Wujud and making playful gestures to him with its tail and its paws.

When he saw that, he recited these lines:

Lion of the desert, would you kill me now,
Before I meet the one whose love has captured me?
I am no prey for you; there is no fat on me;
And my beloved's loss has made me ill.
Parting from her has worn me down;
And I am now a shape wrapped in a shroud.
Abu Harith, lion of the fights,
Do not make censurers crow over me in my grief.
I am a lover drowned in my own tears;
Parting from my loved one has wracked me with distress.

In the dark night I only think of her,
So I forget that, for all my love, I do still live.

When Uns al-Wujud had finished reciting these lines, the lion got up and walked towards him . . .

Night 374

Morning now dawned and Shahrazad broke off from what she had been allowed to say. Then, when it was the three hundred and seventy-fourth night, SHE CONTINUED:

I have heard, O fortunate king, that when Uns al-Wujud had finished reciting these lines, the lion got up and walked towards him in a gentle manner, its eyes brimming with tears, and when it reached him, it licked him and walked in front of him, gesturing as if to say 'follow me'. Uns al-Wujud did this and for some time the lion walked on with him at its heels until it had led him up a mountain and then down it again to where he saw footprints in the desert, and these he recognized as belonging to the people who had taken al-Ward. He followed the tracks and when the lion saw this and realized that it was the trail of his beloved's escort, it went off on its way.

As for Uns al-Wujud, he walked on for several days and nights until the trail led him to the shore of a sea noisy with the sound of breaking waves, and there it broke off. He realized that those he was pursuing must have put out to sea and, as he had no hope of following them, he shed tears and recited these lines:

The loved ones are far away and I cannot endure;
How can I walk to them over the sea depths?
How can I bear it? My inmost parts have been destroyed
Through love for them; sleep turns to wakefulness.
From that day when they journeyed from their lands,
My heart has been consumed with blazing fire.
My tears flow like Saihun, Jaihun and the Euphrates,
Pouring more copiously than any flood of rain.
Because of them my eyelids fill with sores;
My heart is burned by sparks from the fires of love.
Armies of love and longing have launched their assault,
While the army of my patience is broken in retreat.

I have risked my life as a sacrifice to their love,
And this to me was the least of all my risks.
May God not hold it wrong that my eyes lighted on
That beauty which is more splendid than the moon.
I have been cast down by the wide-eyed girls
Whose arrows struck my heart, but needed no bow-string.
She deceived me with the softness of her pliancy,
As supple as the *ban* tree's branch.
I hoped for the grant of union to help me
In the sorrowful and distressing paths of love,
But I stayed there, a prey to grief,
And all I suffer is from the magic of her glance.

On finishing these lines he wept until he fainted, only recovering consciousness a long time later. He looked right and left but could see no one on the shore. As he was afraid of being attacked by wild beasts, he climbed a high hill and while he was there he heard the sound of a human voice coming from a cave. He listened and discovered that this was a hermit who had abandoned the world and devoted himself to worship. He knocked thrice at the door of the cave, but the hermit neither answered nor came out to him. So he sighed deeply and recited these lines:

How can I travel to my goal,
Leaving behind my care, distress and weariness?
Terrors of every kind have bleached my heart,
Together with my hair, young as I am.
I have found no helper in my love,
No friend to lighten passion and distress.
How long am I to struggle with this passionate love?
Fortune, it seems, has turned against me now.
Pity an ardent lover in distress,
Who drank the cup of separation and abandonment.
His entrails consumed by his heart's fire;
The pain of parting robbed him of his wits.
How terrible was the day I reached her house
And saw what there was written on the door.
I watered the earth distractedly with tears,
Hiding my plight from strangers and those near to me.
Hermit who shelters in your cave,
Perhaps you tasted love and then were carried off.

But after all this pain and difficulty,
Were I to reach my goal, care and trouble would be forgotten.

When he finished his poem, the door of the cave opened. He heard someone uttering words of sympathy and went in to greet the hermit, who returned his greeting and asked him his name. 'My name is Uns al-Wujud,' he replied, and when the hermit then asked why he had come there, he told him the whole story from beginning to end in all its details. The hermit shed tears and said: 'I have been here for twenty years and until yesterday I had never seen a single soul, but then I heard the noise of weeping and appeals for help. I looked towards the source of the sounds and I saw a large group of people, as well as tents that had been set up by the shore. The people launched a boat in which a number of them embarked and put out to sea. Later some of them brought the boat back, and after breaking it up they set off on their way. I imagine that those who made the outward journey and did not return are the ones you are looking for. If that is so, then you have great cause for distress, and your behaviour is to be excused. But there has never been a lover who has not had to endure sorrows.'

He then recited these lines:

Uns al-Wujud, you may think me free from care,
But longing and passion twist and untwist me,
As from my earliest days I have known love,
Ever since I used to be a suckling child.
I have pursued it for years, coming to know it well,
And if you ask it about me, it knows me too.
I drank the cup of passion, with its anguish and its grief,
And it has wasted me away, so thin as I am now.
Once I was strong, but my strength is no more;
The army of my endurance was destroyed,
Crushed by the swords her glances wield.
No union without harshness is found in your love;
For opposites face each other throughout Time,
And passion has forbidden all who love
To seek the seditious heresy of forgetfulness.

When the hermit finished reciting these lines, Uns al-Wujud got up and embraced him . . .

Night 375

Morning now dawned and Shahrazad broke off from what she had been allowed to say. Then, when it was the three hundred and seventy-fifth night, SHE CONTINUED:

I have heard, O fortunate king, that when the hermit finished reciting these lines, Uns al-Wujud got up and embraced him and they wept together until the hills resounded to the sound of their laments. This went on until they both fell unconscious, and when they recovered, they swore an oath of brotherhood in the sight of Almighty God. The hermit then told Uns al-Wujud that in his prayers that night he would ask for God's guidance as to what should be done, and to this Uns al-Wujud agreed.

So much for him, but as for al-Ward, when her escort brought her to the mountain and took her into the castle, she wept to see it and to see the preparations that had been made there, saying: 'By God, this is a lovely place, but it lacks the presence of the beloved in it.' On the island she noticed birds and she told one of her attendants to trap them in snares and to put every one he caught in cages inside the castle, which he did. She then sat by a window and thought over what had happened to her. This added to her passionate longing and, with tears falling, she recited these lines:

> To whom can I complain of the passion that I feel,
> Of my sorrows and of my parting from my love?
> A fire burns here between my ribs,
> But I hide it for fear of those who watch.
> I have become thin as a tooth-pick now,
> Through parting, burning love and lamentations.
> Where is my love, that he might look and see
> How I have now become a leafless tree?
> They have wronged me by hiding me away
> In a place where the beloved cannot come.
> I send a thousand greetings with the sun,
> Both when it rises and then when it sets,
> To my beloved, whose beauty shames the moon
> When he appears, more slender than a branch.
> I tell the rose that tries to match his cheek:

'You don't resemble it unless you're mine,'*
While the cool moisture of his mouth
Would chill the heat of burning fire.
How can I forget you, heart and soul of mine,
Who brings me sickness but are my doctor and my love?

Later, in the darkness of night, in the throes of passion, remembering
what she had lost, she recited:

The night is dark and lovesickness galls me;
Desire excites the pain from which I suffer.
The anguish of parting is fixed within my heart;
I am reduced to nothing by my cares.
Passion distracts me; longing consumes me,
And tears reveal the secret I would hide.
I do not know how to deal with this love,
Because of feebleness, weakness and pain.
My heart is a hell of burning flame,
Whose blazing heat tortures my inner parts.
I could not bring myself to say farewell
On the day they left. Alas for my sorrow and for my regret!
You who tell them of my plight, it is enough
That I endure what is written for me by the pen of fate.
By God, I shall never break my compact to love them;
The oaths of love are to be held sacred.
Night, greet those I love, and let them know,
As you yourself can witness, that I have not slept.

So much for al-Ward fi'l-Akmam, but as for Uns al-Wujud, the hermit
instructed him to go down into the valley and to fetch him some palm-tree
fibres, which he did, and the hermit then plaited them into the kind of
net that is used for carrying straw. Next he told Uns al-Wujud that
within the valley there were marrows which would grow up and then
wither on their roots. Uns al-Wujud was to fill the net with these marrows, tie it up, put it into the water, board it and then head out for the
open sea. 'It may be,' the hermit told him, 'that in this way you will get
what you seek, for it is only by risking your life that you can reach your
goal.' 'To hear is to obey,' said Uns al-Wujud.

He then left, with the hermit's blessing, to carry out these instructions,

---

* Pun on the name 'al-Ward', Arabic for 'rose'.

and after travelling through the valley he did what he had been told. When he had got out to sea with his net, a wind rose and carried it along until he was out of the hermit's sight. He continued to float, riding on the crest of a wave one moment and the next carried down into its trough, confronted by the wonders and perils of the sea, until after three days fate cast him up on the Mountain of the Mother Who Lost Her Child. He landed weak and giddy as a fledgling, distressed by hunger and thirst, but on the island he discovered streams of running water, birds singing on the branches and fruit trees growing either singly or in pairs. After eating some of the fruits and drinking from the streams, he started to walk, when in the distance he saw something white and carried on until he reached it. It turned out to be, as he discovered, a strongly fortified castle, whose gate, when he got to it, he found to be shut.

He sat there for three days, but then suddenly the gate opened and out came a eunuch. This man saw Uns al-Wujud sitting there and asked him where he had come from and what had brought him. Uns al-Wujud told him that he had been bringing merchandise from Isfahan when his ship had been wrecked and he had been cast up on the island by the waves. The eunuch embraced him, burst into tears and greeted him as a friend, calling down blessings on him and telling him: 'Isfahan is my own home. I had a cousin there with whom I was deeply in love when I was a young boy, but we were raided by people stronger than ourselves who took me off among their other spoils and, after castrating me, they sold me as a eunuch. This is my present state.'

Night 376

Morning now dawned and Shahrazad broke off from what she had been allowed to say. Then, when it was the three hundred and seventy-sixth night, SHE CONTINUED:

I have heard, O fortunate king, that the eunuch who had come out of the castle told Uns al-Wujud everything that had happened to him and said that his captors had castrated him and sold him as a eunuch, adding: 'This is my present state.' He then took Uns al-Wujud into the castle court, and when he entered he saw a large pool fringed with trees. On the branches were hung silver cages with golden doors in which birds were twittering and praising God, the King and Judge. He looked at the first of these that he came to and found that in it was a turtledove. When it saw him, the bird called out: 'O noble one,' causing him to faint. When he recovered consciousness he sighed deeply and recited these lines:

> Turtledove, is your love as desperate as mine?
> Pray to the Lord and coo 'O noble one';
> Is this complaint of yours a song of joy,
> Or is there passion living in your heart?
> It may be that you sing for dear ones who have gone,
> While you are left behind, wasted and ill.
> It may be that, like me, your love is lost to you;
> Rough treatment brings to light long-standing passion.
> May God guard lovers who remain sincere;
> For even as dry bones, I shall not forget my love.

After his recitation he burst into tears and fell down in a faint. Then, after he had recovered, he walked on until he came to the second cage, where he found a ringdove, which, on seeing him, chanted: 'Eternal Lord, I thank you.' With another deep sigh, Uns al-Wujud recited the lines:

> A ringdove sang: 'Eternal Lord, I thank you in my distress.'
> It may be that God in His grace will let me voyage to my love.
> Many a one with honey-sweet dark lips visited me,
> Adding fresh love to the passion that I feel.
> Fires have been kindled in my heart, burning my inmost parts;
> And tears poured out like blood, flooding my cheeks.
> I said: 'No creature lives without distress, but my distress I can endure.
> If, through God's power, I meet my love one joyful day,
> I shall give all I own as guest provision for those lost in love,
> As it is they who follow on my path,
> Freeing these birds who are imprisoned here,
> And changing all my sorrows into joy.'

Having finished these lines he walked to the third cage, from which a nightingale called out when it saw him, and, on hearing this, he recited:

> The lovely voice of this bird brings delight,
> As though it came from a lover whom love has destroyed.
> Pity the lovers in their restlessness,
> Nightly disturbed by love, longing and distress.
> This longing is so great that they seem born
> Into a world without dawn, where grief allows no sleep.

When love for my beloved maddened me,
Passion fettered me and I was held in chains;
Tears flowed down from my eyes and I exclaimed:
'My chains of tears are long and she chains me!'
Longing increased but my love was long gone;
The treasures of patience vanished; excess of passion destroyed me.
Should justice in this world unite me
With my beloved, cloaked by God's protection,
I would strip off my clothes so she might see
How rejection, absence and abandonment have emaciated me.

After finishing these lines, Uns al-Wujud walked to the fourth cage where
he found a bulbul, which, on seeing him, sang mournfully. He shed tears
and recited:

The bulbul with magic in its voice
Distracts the lover from the sounds of strings.
Uns al-Wujud, the lover, here complains
Of a passion that has left no trace of him.
How many times I listen to melodies
That melt away hard iron and stones through joy.
The morning breezes speak to me
Of meadows where flowers bloom,
And I delight to smell the breeze and listen
To the dawn chorus of the birds.
Then I remember my lost love,
And tears pour down as flooding rain.
A flame of fire burns in my inward parts,
Like sparks from burning coal.
May God permit the lover in his passion
To see his love and taste the joy of union.
Lovers possess a clear excuse,
But only those who see can recognize excuse.

After having finished these lines, he walked on for a little until he caught
sight of another cage unsurpassed for beauty by the others there. In this
was a wood-pigeon, famous among birds for its love laments, and round
its neck was a wonderfully arranged necklace of jewels. When he looked
at it he saw that it appeared pale and distracted in its cage, and, seeing
it in this condition, he shed tears and recited:

My greetings to you, wood-pigeon,
Brother of lovers, one of passion's fellowship.
I myself love a slim gazelle,
Whose gaze cuts deeper than a sword edge can.
My heart and entrails are consumed by love;
My body wastes away with love's sickness.
Pleasures of food are not allowed to me;
I cannot taste sweet sleep.
Patience has left me, as has consolation,
While love and passion stay.
How can my life be sweet now they have gone,
Who were my life, my object and my goal?

When he finished these lines . . .

Night 377

Morning now dawned and Shahrazad broke off from what she had been
allowed to say. Then, when it was the three hundred and seventy-seventh
night, SHE CONTINUED:

I have heard, O fortunate king, that when he finished these lines the
wood-pigeon appeared to be roused from its distraction, and, after
listening to his recital, it replied with cooing notes as though it was using
the universal language to recite:

Lover, you have brought back to me
A time when my youth perished,
And one I loved, the beauty of whose form
Surpassed all others, captivating me.
This love of mine sang on the hillock's trees,
Distracting me with passion from sounds of the lute.
A hunter laid a snare and then trapped him;
He pleaded for freedom and to be released.
I hoped the hunter would show clemency,
Or, noticing my love, might pity me.
May God destroy him, for, instead,
He parted me with harshness from my love.
My passion for him has increased in strength,
Consuming me with fires of separation.

May God guard any ardent lover,
Constant in love, who endures grief like mine,
And, seeing me in my cage,
Will free me in pity for my beloved's sake.

Uns al-Wujud turned to the Isfahani and asked him about the castle, its contents and its builder. The man told him: 'It was built for his daughter by the vizier of King So-and-So, who feared lest she fall victim to the blows of fate and its calamities. He installed her here with her attendants and we only open its gate once a year when provisions are brought in.' Uns al-Wujud then told himself that he had achieved his goal, although there might be a long time to wait.

So much for him, but as for al-Ward, she had found no pleasure in eating, drinking, sitting or sleeping. She got up and, as the passion and intensity of her love increased, she wandered around the castle but could find no way out. She shed tears and recited:

They have kept me by force from my beloved,
Causing me to taste anguish in my prison.
They have burned my heart with fires of love,
Preventing me from seeing him.
They have imprisoned me in a mountain castle
Set in the middle of a sea.
They wanted to ensure that I forget,
But suffering only adds to the love I feel.
And how can I forget when this love of mine
Began as I looked on the beloved's face?
All of my days are passed in grief;
My nights are spent in thoughts of him.
In my loneliness his memory is my friend,
When I despair of meeting him again.
Do you suppose that after all of this
Time will allow me to achieve my heart's desire?

When she finished these lines she went up to the castle roof, where she took some robes of Baalbaki material, tied herself to them and then lowered herself to the ground. She was wearing the most splendid of her robes, with a jewelled necklace around her throat, and she walked through the empty countryside until she came to the shore. There she saw a fisherman who had been out fishing in his boat when the wind had driven him to the island. He turned and was so alarmed by the sight of her that he put out again in order to escape. She called to him, waving her hands again and again, and reciting these lines:

Fear no harm, fisherman; like others, I am human.
Please answer when I call and listen to my tale.
If you have ever looked at a loved one,
Take pity, may God guard you, on my burning love.
I love a handsome one whose face outshines both sun and moon.
When the gazelle saw his glance, it said:
'I am his slave,' confirming its inferiority.
On his cheek, beauty wrote its elegant epitome.
Whoever sees the light of guidance follows it,
And he who strays sins as an infidel.
Whoever uses him to torment me is welcome here;
Each meeting would bring rewards and then rewards,
Rubies and the like, fresh pearls and pearls of every kind.
Perhaps my beloved will fulfil my wish;
My heart melted with longing and then broke.

On hearing this the fisherman shed tears, sorrowfully remembering the days of his lost youth when he too had been a victim of love, experiencing the force of passion and ecstasy when the fires of longing consumed him. So he recited:

How clear is my excuse for love;
For I am sick, with flooding tears,
Eyes sleepless in the dark of night,
My heart a stick that kindles fire.
From my earliest days I tested love,
And learned to distinguish in it false from true.
In love I sold my soul
For union with a distant one.
I risked my life, hoping to profit from my sale.
It is the lovers' creed that those who buy
Union with the beloved win more than mere profit.

When he finished his poem, he anchored his boat by the shore and told al-Ward to come on board, promising to take her wherever she wanted to go. She embarked and the fisherman set out with her, but when they were a little way from land an offshore breeze got up and quickly blew the boat out of sight of land, so that the fisherman could not tell where he was heading. For three days it blew violently until by God's permission it dropped and the boat, with al-Ward and the fisherman, continued on its way until it reached a city on the coast . . .

Night 378

Morning now dawned and Shahrazad broke off from what she had been allowed to say. Then, when it was the three hundred and seventy-eighth night, SHE CONTINUED:

I have heard, O fortunate king, that the boat, with al-Ward and the fisherman, continued on its way until it reached a city on the coast where the fisherman proposed to anchor.

In this city was a powerful king named Dirbas, who happened just then to be sitting with his son in the royal palace, looking out of a window. When the two of them turned towards the sea, they caught sight of the fishing boat and, looking more closely, they saw that on board was a girl like a full moon on the horizon, wearing valuable ruby earrings and a necklace of precious gems. Dirbas, realizing that she must be the daughter of some great man or of a king, went down from his palace and out of the sea gate. He saw the boat anchored by the shore, with al-Ward sleeping and the fisherman busying himself with making it fast. He roused al-Ward from her sleep, and when she woke up in tears he asked her where she was from, whose daughter she was and why she had come to his city. 'I am the daughter of Ibrahim, the vizier of King Shamikh,' she told him, 'and the reason why I have come is a strange one.'

She then told him her story in full from beginning to end, keeping nothing back, after which she sighed deeply and recited:

Tears wound my eyes and call for wonder
At the distress shown by their pouring floods,
For a beloved whose place is always in my heart,
But for whose loving union my quest has now failed.
His face is beautiful, resplendent, radiant;
In gracefulness he outdoes all Arabs and Turks,
While sun and moon bend down to him,
Like lovers following the etiquette of love.

The kohl of his eyes is a strange, magic spell
That shows a bow drawn to release its shaft.
You, to whom I have shown my plight and my excuse,
Pity a lover with whom the unmixed wine of love has played.
It is love that has thrown me into your midst,
Infirm of purpose, hoping in your honour.
If clients come to the court of a generous man,
To protect them adds to his esteem.
You, who are my hope, shelter lovers from shame,
And, sir, I beg you, bring about their union.

After finishing these lines and repeating her story, she recited tearfully:

Life has led us to see love bring a wonder;
For you may every month be Rajab, the month of peace.
Is it not strange that on the day they left
My watery tears lit fires in my entrails?
My eyelids rained down silver,
But gold was in the meadow of my cheek,
As though the bursting cloud of its saffron
Was Joseph's shirt stained with false blood.

Dirbas, on hearing this, was convinced of the depth of her love and, feeling sympathy for her, told her: 'Do not be afraid or alarmed, for you have reached your goal and I shall see to it that you get what you want and arrive at what you are seeking. Listen to my words.' He then recited:

Nobly born girl, you have achieved your end.
I bring good news that you need fear no distress.
Today I shall collect wealth to send
To Shamikh, with riders and noble horses.
I shall send sweet-smelling musk and brocades,
Together with gold and white silver.
Yes, and a letter will tell him
That I want to be linked to him by a marriage tie.
Today I shall do my best to help,
So that the man you love may be brought near.
In my time I have tasted love and know it,
So now I can excuse one who has drained its cup.*

---

* Burton notes: 'His majesty wrote sad doggerel.'

When he had finished these lines he went to his troops, and after calling for his vizier, he packed up a vast quantity of treasures for him and told him to take them to King Shamikh. 'You must fetch me one of his courtiers, the one called Uns al-Wujud,' he ordered the vizier, 'telling the king that your master wants a marriage alliance with him by marrying al-Ward fi'l-Akmam to his follower. Say: "You must send off Uns al-Wujud with me so that the marriage ceremony may be performed in the kingdom of the bride's father."' Dirbas set this out in a letter which he gave to the vizier, impressing on him that he had to fetch Uns al-Wujud on pain of being dismissed from his post. 'To hear is to obey,' replied the vizier, and he set off to take the gifts to Shamikh.

On his arrival, he presented the king with greetings from his master and handed over the letter and the gift. When Shamikh saw this and read the letter, he burst into bitter tears on seeing the name of Uns al-Wujud. 'Where can I find him?' he exclaimed to Dirbas's vizier. 'He has gone and I don't know where he is, but if you can bring him to me, I shall give you twice the value of this gift that you have brought.' He then burst into tears, groaned, lamented and recited these lines:

> Return to me my dear one; I have no need of wealth;
> I want no gifts of gems and pearls.
> To me he shone on beauty's horizon as a moon.
> Neither thought nor sense had power to capture him,
> Nor could he be compared to a gazelle.
> In shape he was a *ban* tree's branch, whose fruits were coquetry,
> But it is not in the nature of a branch to captivate men's minds.
> I reared him as a child in the bed of coquetry,
> And now I grieve for him with a troubled heart.

He then turned to the vizier who had brought him the gift and the letter and said: 'Go back to your master and tell him that Uns al-Wujud has been absent for a year and that I don't know where he has gone and have no news of him.' 'Master,' said the vizier, 'King Dirbas told me that, if I failed to bring him Uns al-Wujud, I would be dismissed from my vizierate and not be allowed to enter my city, so how can I go back without him?' King Shamikh told his own vizier, Ibrahim: 'Go with this man, taking an escort with you, and search for Uns al-Wujud throughout the lands.' 'To hear is to obey,' said Ibrahim, who then, with an escort of his own men, took Dirbas's vizier with him and set off to look for Uns al-Wujud.

Night 379

Morning now dawned and Shahrazad broke off from what she had been allowed to say. Then, when it was the three hundred and seventy-ninth night, SHE CONTINUED:

I have heard, O fortunate king, that Ibrahim, the vizier of King Shamikh, with an escort of his own men, took Dirbas's vizier with him and set off to look for Uns al-Wujud.

Whenever they met a group of Bedouin or anyone else whom they could question, they described Uns al-Wujud and asked whether anyone of this name and description had passed them. Those they questioned all said that they knew nothing about him, but the viziers went on asking after him in cities and towns, and searching for him through plains, hills and deserts until they reached the coast. There they looked for a ship on which they embarked and they sailed to the Mountain of the Mother Who Lost Her Child.

Ibrahim asked Dirbas's vizier the reason for the name and was told: 'In the old days, a Chinese *jinniya* lived there. She had fallen passionately in love with a mortal and was afraid that her family might kill her. Under the influence of her passion she looked for somewhere to hide him from them and she discovered this mountain, which was cut off from both men and *jinn* and to which they could not find their way. She then carried off her lover and placed him there, after which she would visit her own family before returning to him in secret. That went on for a long time, until she had given birth to a number of his children on that mountain, and merchants sailing past would hear them crying like a mother who had lost her child and they would ask themselves whether there was such a woman there.'

Dirbas's vizier wondered at the story, and he and his companions moved on until they reached the castle, where they knocked on the door. This was opened and out came the eunuch, who, on recognizing Ibrahim, the vizier, kissed the ground before him. Ibrahim went in and found a poor man sitting among the servants. This was Uns al-Wujud, and when Ibrahim asked where al-Wujud had come from, they told him that this was a merchant who had escaped with his life from a shipwreck in which he had lost all his goods, and that he was now a man possessed. Ibrahim left him and entered the castle, but failed to find any trace of his daughter.

He asked the slave girls and they said: 'We don't know how she left, but she only stayed with us for a short time.'

Ibrahim then shed tears and recited:

Dwelling, your birds sang and the lintels of your doors showed off
    their pride;
A lover came to you, lamenting his longing, only to find those doors
    ajar.
Would that I knew where my dear heart is lost in a house whose
    owners are now gone.
In it was every splendour, with a proud display of chamberlains.
It was hung with coverings of silk brocade; where are its people
    now?

When he finished his poem, he wept, lamented and complained, saying: 'No one can circumvent God's decree or escape the fate He has ordained.' After that he went up to the castle roof, and there he found the robes of Baalbaki material still tied to one of the battlements and reaching down to the ground. He realized that his daughter must have let herself down from here and gone off, maddened by love. Turning, he saw two birds, a crow and an owl, and, taking this as an evil omen, he heaved a deep sigh and recited:

I came to the house of the beloved in the hope
A trace of her might quench the ardour of my passion.
I failed to find her there, and only saw
Two evil omens, a crow and an owl.
The tongue of silent conscience said: 'You were unjust;
You parted two fond lovers,
So taste that pain of passion which you gave to them,
And live a life of sorrow, amidst tears and pain.'

He came down, still weeping, from the roof and ordered the servants to go out and search for their mistress on the mountain, which they did, but to no effect.

So much for them, but as for Uns al-Wujud, when he discovered that al-Ward had gone, he uttered a great cry and fell down in a faint. He remained unconscious for so long that the servants thought he must have received a summons from the Merciful and was lost in the awesome beauty of God, the Judge. The viziers despaired of finding him, and as

Ibrahim was preoccupied with the loss of his daughter, Dirbas's vizier decided to go back home, even though he had failed in his mission.

He took his leave of Ibrahim and told him that he intended to take the poor man with him in the hopes that, as he was possessed, the blessing of his presence might soften Dirbas's heart towards him and after that he could be sent to Isfahan, which was close at hand. 'Do what you want,' said Ibrahim, and the two then parted, each making for his own land.

Dirbas's vizier took Uns al-Wujud with him . . .

Night 380

Morning now dawned and Shahrazad broke off from what she had been allowed to say. Then, when it was the three hundred and eightieth night, SHE CONTINUED:

I have heard, O fortunate king, that Dirbas's vizier took Uns al-Wujud with him, still unconscious, and during a three-day journey he was carried by mule, without knowing what was happening to him. When he recovered his senses, he said: 'Where am I?' and the attendants told him that he was with the vizier of King Dirbas, after which they went to the vizier to let him know that the stranger was awake. The vizier sent him sugared rosewater and drinks which they gave him to revive him, and they continued on their way until they came close to the king's city. The king then sent a message to the vizier to say: 'If Uns al-Wujud is not with you, do not come to me,' an order that distressed the vizier. He had no idea that al-Ward was with the king, and he did not know why he had been sent to fetch Uns al-Wujud or why the king was hoping to arrange a marriage. For his part, Uns al-Wujud knew neither where they were taking him nor that the vizier had been sent to find him, while the vizier did not know that the stranger was, in fact, Uns al-Wujud.

On seeing that the stranger had recovered consciousness the vizier told him: 'The king sent me on an errand which I have not completed, and when he learned of my return he sent me a message to say that, if I had failed, I was not to enter the city.' 'What was your errand?' asked Uns al-Wujud, and the vizier then told him the whole story. 'Have no fear,' said Uns al-Wujud, 'but go to the king, taking me with you, and I guarantee that Uns al-Wujud will come.' 'Is this true?' asked the delighted vizier, and when he was told that it was, he mounted and, accompanied by Uns al-Wujud, he went to the king.

When the two of them entered the king's presence he asked where Uns al-Wujud was, and Uns al-Wujud answered: 'I know where he is, your majesty.' The king called him forward and asked: 'Where is he?' 'Very near indeed,' replied Uns al-Wujud, 'but tell me what you want from him and then I shall produce him for you.' 'Willingly,' replied the king, 'but this is a matter that requires privacy.' So he sent away his courtiers and, taking Uns al-Wujud to a private room, he told him the whole story from beginning to end. He, in his turn, then promised the king that if fine robes were given him to wear he would quickly produce Uns al-Wujud. This was done and then he said: 'I am Uns al-Wujud, on whom the envious look with sadness.'

With beguiling glances he then recited these lines:

Memory of the beloved cheers my solitude,
Though we are far from one other, it dispels my loneliness.
My eyes are all tears, and their flood
Lightens the burden of my sighs.
The violence of my longing is not to be matched;
My state as an ardent lover is remarkable indeed.
I pass my nights in wakefulness, without sleep;
Attempting to find love, I am left between hellfire and Paradise.
I have lost the virtue of patience I once had,
While the ardour of my love and my distress increase.
The pain of parting has emaciated me;
Longing has changed my appearance and my shape.
My eyelids are wounded by tears that I cannot call back.
I am helpless, and no longer have I any heart;
How many torments must I bear, one following the other?
My heart has turned grey as my hair,
In grief for the most beautiful of all.
We parted, and that was against her will,
For what she wanted was to join with me in union.
Do you suppose that after distance separated us,
Destiny will allow the joy of union with my love,
Rolling up the unfolded page of parting,
Wiping away distress with this comfort?
Will my beloved stay beside me in these lands,
And sorrow be exchanged for joy of heart?

When he had finished his poem, the king said to him: 'By God, the two of you are true lovers and shining stars in the sky of beauty. Yours is a strange and remarkable story.' He then told Uns al-Wujud the whole tale of al-Ward, and when Uns al-Wujud asked him where she was, he told him: 'She is here with me now.' He then brought in the *qadi* and the notaries to draw up a marriage contract between the two lovers, and he showered favours on Uns al-Wujud. A message was sent to King Shamikh to tell him everything that had happened in this affair, and the king, in his delight at the news, sent back word to say: 'As the marriage contract was drawn up at your court, the celebrations and the wedding night must be at mine.' He got ready camels, horses and men and sent them to fetch the bridal pair. When his message arrived, King Dirbas supplied them with large sums of money and an escort of his own men, who took them to their own city.

The day of their arrival was a red-letter one, and none more splendid had ever been seen. King Shamikh had collected all the singers with the instruments that they used for accompaniment, and he gave banquets which lasted for seven days, on each of which he distributed splendid robes and largesse to the people. Then Uns al-Wujud went to al-Ward and, after they had embraced, they sat shedding tears of joy and delight. Al-Ward recited the following lines:

Joy has come and sorrow and grief have left;
We are reunited, to the distress of envious men.
The scented breeze of union has revived hearts, souls and bodies.
Here are the perfumed joys of our companionship,
And the drums of good tidings sound in the north, south, east and
    west.
Do not think our tears are those of sorrow;
Rather, it is for joy that they rain down.
How many perils did we face which have now cleared away,
After we endured what brought us grief.
One hour of union has made me forget
All those terrors that turned us grey.

When she had finished, the two embraced again and continued to do so until they fell fainting . . .

Night 381

Morning now dawned and Shahrazad broke off from what she had been allowed to say. Then, when it was the three hundred and eighty-first night, SHE CONTINUED:

I have heard, O fortunate king, that Uns al-Wujud and al-Ward joined in an embrace which continued until they fell fainting with pleasure. When they had recovered, Uns al-Wujud recited:

> How sweet now are our nights of union
> When I receive justice from my beloved.
> Our union lasts and separation ends.
> Fate shows us favour, though once it shunned us and had turned away.
> The banners of fortune are raised over us,
> And what we drink is unmixed happiness.
> We meet, complaining of past griefs,
> And the nights' harshness that we once endured.
> But now that past is all forgotten;
> The Merciful God has blotted out what has gone.
> How pleasant and delightful now is life,
> As union only adds to the love I feel.

When he had finished, the two lovers embraced and lay together in their private chamber, continuing to entertain each other with poems, witty stories and anecdotes until they were drowning in a sea of passion. Seven days passed, but they could not tell night from day, so great was their pleasure, delight and pure joy, and it was as though this whole week was a single day. It was only when the musicians came that they realized how much time had passed, and al-Ward, taken by surprise, then recited:

> To the anger of the envious and the watchers,
> I have won what I wanted from my lover.
> For we have been united in an embrace
> With brocades and gleaming silk,
> On a leather couch filled marvellously with feathers.
> Instead of wine, we drained unmatched draughts of love.
> Through the sweetness of union, we cannot tell far from near.
> It is a marvel that seven nights have passed and we did not know.
> Felicitate me on this week and say:
> 'May God prolong your union with your love.'

When she had finished, Uns al-Wujud kissed her more than a hundred times before reciting:

> Oh, day of joy and happiness!
> The loved one came and saved me from abandonment.
> She cheered me with the sweetness of her union,
> Keeping me company with wit and grace.
> She poured for me wine of delight,
> A wine that stole away my wits.
> We lay together in our joy and happiness,
> Passing on to drink and song.
> In our excess of pleasure we could not tell
> Which day came first and which then followed it.
> Happy the lover who enjoys sweet union,
> In such delight as I have met,
> Who does not know bitter rejection's taste,
> But finds the gift that God has given me.

When he had finished, bride and groom left their chamber and distributed money and robes as gifts to the people. Al-Ward then ordered the baths to be cleared for her, and she told Uns al-Wujud: 'Delight of my eyes, I want to see you in the baths and to be alone there with you.' In the excess of her happiness, she recited:

> You won me long ago;
> The present cannot do without the past;
> Nor can I do without you, O my love.
> There is no other that I hope to meet.
> Come to the baths, you who delight my eyes,
> To find our paradise in the midst of hell.
> Which we shall fill with the aloes and with *nadd*,
> Spreading sweet scent throughout the rooms.
> We shall forgive Time for the wrongs it did,
> And give thanks to our Lord, the Merciful.
> Then, when I see you there, I shall call out:
> 'Come, my beloved, to taste happiness.'

When she had finished they went off to the baths and took their pleasure there, before returning to the palace. There they stayed enjoying the greatest of joys until they were visited by the destroyer of delights and the parter of companions. Glory be to Him, Who does not change or come to an end and to Whom all things return.

A story is told that one day, when Abu Nuwas was alone, he prepared a splendid reception room and got ready foods of all types and kinds to tempt lips and tongues. Then he went out in search of a lover who might be worthy of this, saying: 'My God, my Lord and my Master, I ask you to bring me a suitable guest for this room, a fitting companion to drink with me today.' Before he had finished speaking, he caught sight of three handsome beardless boys, who looked like the children of Paradise, of differing complexions but united in their remarkable beauty. Their pliant bodies roused hopes, as the poet said:

> I passed by two beardless boys and said:
> 'I love you.' They replied:
> 'Are you a rich man?' 'Yes,' I said, 'and generous.'
> The two boys then said: 'Done.'

Abu Nuwas was addicted to this kind of thing, taking his pleasure with pretty boys and plucking the roses of fresh cheeks, as the poet says:

> There is many an old man subject to youthful passion
> Who loves pretty boys and likes enjoyment.
> In the morning he is a Mosuli in the land of purity,
> But his memories are of the passions of Aleppo.

He went up to the boys, and when he greeted them they returned his greeting with the greatest courtesy and respect. They were then about to turn away, but he blocked their path and recited:

> Don't hurry to another;
> Within me is the mine of generosity.
> I have wine whose brilliance
> Is prepared within the monastery by monks.
> I have mutton and fowls of all types.
> Eat that and drink old wine
> That drives off every harm.
> Fornicate with one another
> And slip my penis in between you.

The boys were seduced by his verses and inclined to do what he wanted . . .

Night 382

Morning now dawned and Shahrazad broke off from what she had been allowed to say. Then, when it was the three hundred and eighty-second night, SHE CONTINUED:

I have heard, O fortunate king, that the boys were seduced by his verses and inclined to do what he wanted, so they accepted his invitation and went home with him. They found everything that he had mentioned in his poem ready and waiting in his reception room, where they sat, eating, drinking and enjoying themselves. Then they asked Abu Nuwas to judge which of them was the most handsome with the best figure. He pointed at one of them, whom he kissed twice, and then he recited:

I would give my life to ransom the mole on his cheek;
For how could money ransom such a mole?
Blessed be God, Who left the cheek hairless,
And has set all of beauty in that mole.

Then he pointed to the second, whose lips he kissed, and he recited:

There is a beloved on whose cheek is a mole,
Like musk set over pure camphor.
This sight amazed my eyes,
And the mole said: 'Bless the Prophet.'

He then pointed to the third, kissing him ten times, and recited:

Gold was melted in a silver cup
By a youth whose hands were stained with wine.
With the cupbearers he took round a glass of wine,
While his eyes brought round two more,
A handsome gazelle of Turkish stock,
Whose waist strains against the twin peaks of Hunain.
I may be settled in Baghdad the crooked,
But my heart is tugged two ways.
One love leads it to Diyar Bakr.
And another to the land of the two mosques.

Each of the boys drank two cups of wine, and when it was Abu Nuwas's turn, he took the cup and recited:

> Only take wine given by the hand of a fawn,
> Which it resembles in delicacy and he resembles it.
> No one can enjoy drinking such a wine
> Unless its pourer is a smooth-cheeked boy.

He drank the glass and, when his turn came round again, overcome by pleasure, he recited:

> Take as your companion cups of wine,
> One following the other, followed by yet more,
> From the hand of a dark-lipped beauty who, after sleep,
> Is delicate as musk or as an apple.
> Take your cup only from the hand of a fawn,
> To kiss whose cheek is sweeter than the taste of wine.

He then became too drunk to distinguish his hand from his head, and so he started to kiss and embrace the boys, wrapping legs around legs, with no concern for sin or disgrace. He recited:

> Perfect pleasure comes only when a man drinks wine
> With pretty boys as his companions.
> One of them sings to you and then another
> Raises you from the dead with a glass, greeting you.
> Every time you need a kiss
> From one, he lets you sip his lips.
> Good fortune to them; with them my day was sweet
> And marvellously pleasant.
> We take our wine both neat and mixed,
> And slake our lust on whoever falls asleep.

While they were occupied like this, there was a knock on the door and, after permission to enter had been given, in came the Commander of the Faithful, Harun al-Rashid. They all got up and kissed the ground before him, and the awe that he inspired caused Abu Nuwas to recover his senses. 'Abu Nuwas,' the caliph called to him. 'Here I am, Commander of the Faithful, may God aid you,' he answered, and when the caliph then asked: 'What is all this?', he replied: 'The matter speaks for itself.' The caliph said: 'Having asked for guidance from Almighty God, I have appointed you as *qadi* of the panders.' 'Do you want me to assume this office?' Abu Nuwas asked, and when the caliph said yes, Abu Nuwas said: 'And is there any case that you would like to bring before me?' The caliph turned away in anger, leaving Abu Nuwas and the boys, and he spent the night still full of rage against him, while Abu Nuwas himself passed the most delightful of nights in pleasure and relaxation.

The next day, when the morning star shone out, Abu Nuwas broke up his party and sent the boys away. He then dressed in his formal robes, left his house and set out for the caliph's palace. It was the caliph's habit, when he had dismissed his court, to go to his salon, where he would summon poets and musicians, together with his boon companions. Each would sit in his appointed place and nowhere else. It happened that on that day, after he had gone through this routine, Abu Nuwas arrived and was about to take his seat when the caliph summoned Masrur, the executioner, whom he ordered to strip Abu Nuwas of his clothes, tie a donkey's pack saddle on his back, fastened with a strap between his thighs, put a halter over his head and lead him round the apartments of the slave girls . . .

Night 383

Morning now dawned and Shahrazad broke off from what she had been allowed to say. Then, when it was the three hundred and eighty-third night, SHE CONTINUED:

I have heard, O fortunate king, that the caliph summoned Masrur, the executioner, whom he ordered to strip Abu Nuwas of his clothes, tie a donkey's pack saddle on his back, fastened with a strap between his thighs, put a halter over his head and lead him round the apartments of the slave girls, the harem and the other quarters, so that he might be held up to ridicule, after which Masrur was to cut off his head and bring it to him.

'To hear is to obey,' said Masrur, and he started to carry out the caliph's orders, taking Abu Nuwas around the apartments, of which there was one for every day of the year. Abu Nuwas was exercising his wit, and as everyone who saw him gave him money, he came back with his pockets full. When he was in this state, Ja'far the Barmecide, who had been absent on an important mission, arrived and entered the caliph's presence. On seeing Abu Nuwas in this state and recognizing him, he called to him. 'Here I am, master,' replied Abu Nuwas, and Ja'far asked him: 'What wrong have you done to be punished like this?' 'None at all,' said Abu Nuwas, 'except that I presented our master the caliph with the best of my poetry and he presented me with the best of his robes.' On hearing this the caliph laughed, although his heart was still full of rage, and he forgave Abu Nuwas, ordering him to be given a bag full of money.

A story is told that a Basran bought a slave girl to whom he gave the best of educations. He loved her dearly and spent all his money on pleasure and enjoyment with her until there was nothing left and he was in abject poverty. The girl then said: 'Sell me, master, as you need the money that I shall fetch. I'm sorry to see how poor you have become and it will be better for you to sell me and have money to spend, rather than for me to stay with you, and it may be that God will increase your fortune.' Because of his straitened circumstances the man agreed and he took her to the market, where the auctioneer showed her to the emir of Basra, 'Abd Allah ibn Ma'mar al-Taimi. He admired her and bought her for five hundred dinars, paying the price over to her former owner.

When her new master was about to go off with her, she burst into tears and recited these lines:

Enjoy the money you have got;
For me all that remains is care and grief.
I say to my soul, wracked as it is with woe:
'The lover has gone, however much you grieve.'

When the Basran heard her, he sighed deeply and recited:

As there is nothing that you can do here,
And death is the only way out, forgive me.
Morning and evening, my companion will be your memory;
It is of this I'll talk to my careworn heart.
Farewell. We cannot visit one another
Or enjoy union, unless Ibn Ma'mar wills it.

When Ibn Ma'mar heard their verses and saw their distress, he exclaimed: 'By God, may I never help to part you. I see that you love each other, so take the cash and the girl, man, and may God's blessing be on both of you, for the parting of lovers is hard for them to bear.' Both of them then kissed his hand and left, after which they remained together until they were separated by death. Praise be to God, Who does not die.

*

A story is told that among the Banu 'Udhra there was a graceful man who was constantly falling in love. As it happened he loved a beautiful woman from his own tribe, but although he sent messages to her day after day, she continued to treat him harshly and shun him, until the ardour of his passion had such an effect on him that he fell gravely ill and took to his bed. He could not sleep; word of his lovesickness spread through his tribe . . .

Night 384

Morning now dawned and Shahrazad broke off from what she had been allowed to say. Then, when it was the three hundred and eighty-fourth night, SHE CONTINUED:

I have heard, O fortunate king, that he took to his bed. He could not sleep; word of his lovesickness spread through his tribe, and it became so serious that he came close to death. His relatives and those of the woman kept asking her to visit him, but she refused, until he was on the point of death. When they told her, she had pity on him and came to see him. When he caught sight of her, his eyes filled with tears and he recited broken-heartedly:

> I conjure you that, when my bier passes you by,
> Carried on the shoulders of four men,
> You follow it until you give a greeting
> To the grave of a dead man buried in the earth.

When she heard this she wept bitterly and said: 'By God, I didn't think that your passion had gone so far as to threaten your life, and had I known, I would have come to your aid and enjoyed union with you.' At that, his tears fell as if from a rain cloud and he recited:

> She approached when death came between me and her,
> Granting the gift of union, when this could not help.

Then with a groan he died.

In tears the woman fell on to his corpse, kissing it and weeping, and she continued to weep until she fell down in a faint. When she recovered, she instructed her family to bury her in her lover's grave when she died. Tearfully she recited these lines:

When we lived on earth, our life was easy;
Our tribe, our dwelling and our land were proud of us.
Then Time's misfortunes broke our union
And under the earth our shrouds united us.

After she had finished her poem, she again wept bitterly and she continued weeping and wailing until she fell down in a faint. After remaining unconscious for three days, she died and was buried in her lover's grave. This was one of love's remarkable coincidences.

A story is told that al-Sahib Badr al-Din, the vizier of Yemen, had a remarkably handsome brother of whom he was very fond. He looked for a man to tutor him and found an imposing and dignified *shaikh*, a chaste and pious man, whom he installed next door to his own house. The arrangement lasted for some time, and each day the *shaikh* would come from his own house to that of Badr al-Din to teach his brother and then go back home. It happened that the man fell violently in love with the boy and was so disturbed that one day he complained to him of his plight. 'What can I do?' said the boy. 'I can't get away from my brother night or day, for he stays by me the whole time, as you see.' The *shaikh* said: 'My house is next to yours. When your brother is asleep, you can pretend to be asleep yourself. Then get up as though to relieve yourself and come to the parapet on the roof and I'll give you a hand from the other side. You can then sit with me briefly before going back without your brother noticing.' 'To hear is to obey,' said the boy. The *shaikh* then got ready gifts suitable for one of his rank.

As for the boy, he went to the latrine and after waiting until his brother had gone to bed and, some time later in the night, had fallen deeply asleep, he himself went off to the parapet, where he found the *shaikh* standing waiting for him. The *shaikh* took him by the hand and brought him to his sitting room. There they sat and drank together as the wine cups circulated and the *shaikh* began to sing. The rays of the moon, which was full that night, shone on them and they tasted such pleasure, delight and happy fortune as would dazzle mind and eye, surpassing all description. Meanwhile Badr al-Din woke, and failing to find his brother, he got up in alarm and discovered that the door was open. He went out through it and, hearing the murmur of voices, he climbed over the parapet on to the *shaikh*'s roof. He could see light streaming from the house and, looking from behind the wall, he saw the *shaikh* and his brother with the wine circulating between them. The *shaikh*, who was holding a glass in his hand, noticed him and sang the following lines:

> He poured me wine from the moisture of his mouth,
> And greeted me with down-covered cheeks.
> I spent the night in embraces, cheek to cheek,
> With a handsome youth who has no equal among mankind.
> The full moon* was looking down over us;
> Ask it not to give away its brother.

Such was the courtesy of Badr al-Din that when he heard this he said: 'By God, I shall not give them away,' and so he went off, leaving them in perfect happiness.

A story is told that a boy and a slave girl studied in the same school. The boy was in love with the girl . . .

Night 385

Morning now dawned and Shahrazad broke off from what she had been allowed to say. Then, when it was the three hundred and eighty-fifth night, SHE CONTINUED:

I have heard, O fortunate king, that the boy was in love with the girl and passionately attached to her. One day, when the other children weren't looking, he took her slate and wrote the following lines on it:

> What do you say of one emaciated by illness
> Through his great love for you, which leaves him at a loss?
> He complains of the passion and pain of his love,
> And cannot hide what lies within his heart.

When the girl took back her slate she saw this poem written on it, and on grasping its meaning, she shed tears of pity and wrote beneath the boy's lines:

> When I see a lover suffering from his love, I treat him well.
> Come what may, I will let him reach the goal of his love.

---

* A pun on the name Badr, Arabic for 'full moon'.

The teacher then happened to come in, and on finding the slate when their attention was distracted, he took it and read what was written on it. He felt sympathy for their plight and wrote the following lines beneath theirs:

Grant union to your lover; fear no punishment;
The lover is bewildered by his love.
Don't fear the awe-inspiring teacher;
He too at times suffered the pains of love.

It then happened that the girl's owner came into the school, and finding her slate, he took it and read what the three of them had written on it. He, too, then added beneath their lines:

May God not part you through the length of time,
And may your slanderers stay at a loss.
As for the teacher, I can swear by God
I never saw a greater pimp than this.

He then sent for the *qadi* and the notaries and drew up a marriage contract for the two in front of the assembled witnesses. He gave a feast for them and treated them with the greatest generosity. They lived together in pleasure and happiness until they were visited by the destroyer of delights and the parter of companions.

A story is told that al-Mutalammis fled from al-Nu'man ibn al-Mundhir and was absent for so long that it was thought he must be dead. He had a beautiful wife named Umaima, whose family advised her to remarry. She refused, but because of the number of her suitors her family continued to press her until eventually she yielded to force and reluctantly agreed to a marriage they had arranged with a man from her own tribe, although she was still deeply in love with al-Mutalammis. On her enforced wedding night, al-Mutalammis came back. He heard the noise of flutes and tambourines in the encampment and, noticing the signs of a wedding feast, he asked some boys about it. They told him: 'Umaima, the wife of al-Mutalammis, has been married to So-and-So and this is the wedding night.'

When al-Mutalammis heard this, he tricked his way in with a group of women and found the bridal pair on their dais. As the groom went up to the bride she heaved a deep sigh and recited through her tears:

Misfortunes crowd on me; would that I knew
In what land you may be, Mutalammis.

Her husband, al-Mutalammis, was a well-known poet and he answered
her:

Know I am very near at hand, Umaima,
I never ceased to long for you when the caravan halted for the night.

At that the bridegroom realized what had happened and he went out in
a hurry, reciting:

I enjoyed good fortune and then met its opposite;
May you be brought together in a spacious room.

When the bridegroom had left them, al-Mutalammis remained alone
with Umaima, and they continued to enjoy all the pleasures and delights
of a happy life until death parted them. Glory be to God, the Lord of
earth and heaven.

It is reported that the caliph Harun al-Rashid was deeply in love with
his wife, Zubaida. He laid out a pleasure garden for her, in which was a
pool fringed with trees to which water was channelled from all sides.
The trees were so thickly intertwined that if anyone went to bathe in the
pool they could not be seen because of the quantity of leaves. It happened
that one day Zubaida entered the garden and went to the pool . . .

Night 386

Morning now dawned and Shahrazad broke off from what she had been
allowed to say. Then, when it was the three hundred and eighty-sixth
night, SHE CONTINUED:

I have heard, O fortunate king, that it happened that one day Zubaida
entered the garden and went to the pool, admiring its shining beauty
and its screening trees. As it was a very hot day she took off her clothes
and went to stand in the water. It was not deep enough to cover anyone
who stood up and so she began filling a silver jug with water and pouring
it over herself. The caliph, who knew where she had gone, came down
from the palace to spy on her from behind the leaves, and he saw her
standing there naked, showing those parts that are normally kept hidden.

When she noticed him and realized what he had seen, she turned and looked at him. Modesty led her to put her hand over her private parts, but these were too plump to be entirely concealed.

The caliph, filled with delight, turned back immediately and recited:

My eyes saw the cause of my ruin,
And separation caused the fire of passion to burn up.

He did not know how to go on after that and so he sent for Abu Nuwas. When Abu Nuwas had come, the caliph told him to recite a poem for him with this as its first line. 'To hear is to obey,' said Abu Nuwas, and after the briefest of pauses he extemporized the following lines:

My eyes saw the cause of my ruin,
And separation caused the fire of passion to burn up,
Through love for a gazelle who captivated me
Beneath the shade of two lote trees.
Water poured over it from silver jugs.
She saw me and then tried to hide it,
But it was too large for her hands.
I wish that I might lie on it one hour or two.

The caliph smiled at his lines and gave him a generous present, at which he left happily.

A story is told that the Commander of the Faithful Harun al-Rashid was very restless one night and so he got up to walk in the grounds of his palace, where he found a slave girl, with whom he was deeply in love, swaying drunkenly. He fondled her and drew her close to him, so that her dress fell off and her waist-wrapper became undone, but when he asked her to lie with him, she said: 'Let me wait till tomorrow night, Commander of the Faithful. I didn't know that you were here and I am not prepared for you.' Harun left her and went off, but the next day, when the sun had risen, he sent a page to tell her that he was going to come to her room. She sent back a message to say:

The day erases what was said at night.

Harun then told his boon companions to recite a poem to him including these words. 'To hear is to obey,' they said. The first to come forward was al-Raqashi, who recited:

By God, if you experienced my passion,
Rest would turn its back on you.
You are abandoned in your hopeless love
By a girl who neither visits nor is visited.
She makes a promise, but then turns and says:
'The day erases what was said at night.'

Al-Raqashi was followed by Abu Mus'ab, who recited:

When will this agitation of yours cease?
You have not slept and cannot rest.
Is it not enough your eyes are full of tears,
While memory kindles fire within your heart?
The beloved smiled and then said in her pride:
'The day erases what was said at night.'

Abu Nuwas then advanced and recited:

Love was long, but the beloved could not be visited;
I openly revealed my love, but openness did no good.
She was drunk when she visited the palace in the night,
But dignity adorned her drunkenness.
The dress slipped from her shoulders
As I caressed her; her waist-wrapper was undone.
The breeze played over heavy buttocks,
And a branch bearing two little pomegranates.
I said: 'Make your lover a true promise';
She said: 'Tomorrow is a good time for a visit.'
I came next day and said: 'You promised.' She replied:
'The day erases what was said at night.'

The caliph ordered the first two poets to be given a purse of money each, but as for Abu Nuwas, he ordered that his head be cut off, accusing him of having been there with them in the palace on the previous night. 'By God,' said Abu Nuwas, 'I spent the night at home, and it was what you said that led me to deduce what was to be in the poem. Almighty God has said – and He is the most truthful of speakers – "the poets are followed by those who go astray. Have you not seen that they wander in every valley and that they say what they do not do?"'* So the caliph

* Quran 26.225.

forgave him and ordered him to be given two purses of money, after which they all left.

It is reported of Mus'ab ibn al-Zubair that in Medina he met 'Azza, one of the most intelligent of women, and told her that he had in mind to marry 'A'isha, the daughter of Talha, and he asked 'Azza to pay her a visit to see what she was like. When 'Azza had done this she came back to Mus'ab and said: 'I saw a face lovelier than health itself, with two large eyes, below which was an aquiline nose, two smooth cheeks, a mouth like a split pomegranate and a neck like a silver jug. Beneath was a bosom with two breasts like pomegranates, and then a slender belly with a navel like an ivory casket. Her buttocks were like sand dunes, and she had plump thighs and legs like two marble pillars, although her feet were on the large side. When you want her, you will find yourself out of this world.' On hearing this report, Mus'ab married 'A'isha and lay with her.

Night 387

Morning now dawned and Shahrazad broke off from what she had been allowed to say. Then, when it was the three hundred and eighty-seventh night, SHE CONTINUED:

I have heard, O fortunate king, that on hearing this report, Mus'ab married 'A'isha and lay with her. Later 'Azza invited 'A'isha and the ladies of Quraish to her house. Mus'ab was standing there as 'Azza sang:

How fragrant are girls' mouths,
Sweet to kiss and sweetly smiling.
Only in imagination have I tasted this,
But by these assumptions cases are decided.

On their wedding night Mus'ab stayed with 'A'isha until they had made love seven times, and in the morning a freed-woman of his met him and said: 'May I be your ransom; you are perfect in everything, even in this.'

A woman said: 'I was with 'A'isha, the daughter of Talha, when her husband came in. She leaned over towards him and, as he fell on her, she snorted and grunted with all kinds of strange movements and exotic tricks. All this was within my hearing and when Mus'ab had left, I said to her: "How can you, a woman of your distinction and noble birth, act like this while I am in your house?" She said: "A wife should provide her husband with all the stimulation and unusual movements that she can. What do you dislike about that?" "I prefer it to be done at night," I replied. "This is how I act by day," she told me, "but at night I do more, for when Mus'ab sees me he is stirred by desire and passion. He reaches out for me and I submit to him, with the result that you have seen."'

I have heard that Abu'l-Aswad bought a slave girl who had been born among the Arabs. She had a squint, but when his family criticized her to him, he expressed surprise, turned his hands palm upwards and recited these lines:

> They criticize her to me, but she has no defects,
> Except there may be some specks in her eyes.
> Although this might be thought of as a fault,
> She is slender above the waist and plump below it.

A story is told that the Commander of the Faithful Harun al-Rashid spent a night with two slave girls, one from Medina and one from Kufa. The Kufan started to massage his arms and the Medinan his legs. He had an erection, at which the Kufan said to the other: 'I see that you are trying to monopolize our capital and keep it to yourself. Give me my share.' The Medinese girl replied: 'It is reported by Malik, on the authority of Hisham ibn 'Urwa, on the authority of his father, that the Prophet said: "If someone brings uncultivated ground to life, it belongs to him and to his descendants."' The Kufan, however, taking her by surprise, pushed her aside and seized Harun's member in both her hands, saying: 'Al-A'mash reported on the authority of Khaithama, on the authority of 'Abd Allah ibn Mas'ud, that the Prophet said: "Game belongs to the hunter and not to the beater."'

A story is told that Harun al-Rashid lay with three slave girls, one from Mecca, one from Medina and one from Iraq. The Medinan stretched out her hand and stimulated his member, giving him an erection, but the Meccan jumped across and pulled it towards her. 'That is unjust,' said the Medinan. 'Malik said on the authority of al-Zuhri, on the authority of 'Abd Allah ibn Salim, on the authority of Sa'id ibn Zaid, that the Apostle of God, may God bless him and give him peace, said: "If someone brings uncultivated ground to life, it belongs to him." The Meccan girl replied: 'Sufyan said on the authority of Abu'l-Zinad, on the authority of al-A'raj, on the authority of Abu Huraira, that the Apostle of God, may God bless him and give him peace, said: "Game belongs to the hunter and not to the beater."' The Iraqi girl then pushed them both aside and said: 'Until you settle your dispute, this belongs to me.'

A story is told that there was a miller who had a donkey to do his grinding and a wicked wife whom he loved but who disliked him. She was in love with a neighbour who hated her and kept away from her. The miller had a dream in which he was told that if he dug in such-and-such a place on the donkey's track in the mill, he would find a treasure. When he woke up, he told his wife about this, saying that she must keep it a secret, but she told the neighbour . . .

Night 388

Morning now dawned and Shahrazad broke off from what she had been allowed to say. Then, when it was the three hundred and eighty-eighth night, SHE CONTINUED:

I have heard, O fortunate king, that the miller's wife told her neighbour, whom she loved, in order to ingratiate herself with him. He made an agreement with her to visit her at night, and when he had done this, he dug on the donkey's track. The two of them found the treasure and removed it, after which the neighbour asked: 'What are we going to do with it?' The woman said: 'We shall divide it into two equal parts. You must then leave your wife and I shall work out some way of leaving my husband, after which you can marry me. Then, when we are married, we can put the money together again and it will all be ours.' The man replied: 'I'm afraid that Satan will seduce you into taking another husband, for gold in the house is like the sun in the world. The proper thing is for me to keep all of it in my house in order to encourage you to free yourself from your husband and to come to me.' 'I have the same fear as you,' she told him, 'and I'm not going to hand over my share to you, for it was I who led you to it.'

When the neighbour heard what she said, his greed led him to kill her; he threw her corpse into the hole where the treasure had been, and then as day was breaking and he had no time to cover it up, he took the money and left. The miller woke up and, not finding his wife, he went into the mill and harnessed the donkey to the millwheel. He shouted at it and it started to walk round but then it stopped, and although he beat it furiously, it drew back every time he struck it, shying away from the woman's corpse, which stopped it from going on. The miller, who didn't know why it was doing that, took a knife, but although he pricked it many times, it refused to move and so in a rage he struck it in the flank and it fell down dead. When it became light the miller saw the donkey dead and his wife's corpse lying in the hole where the treasure had been. He was angry and distressed at the loss of the treasure, at his wife's death and at that of the donkey, but all this was caused by the fact that, instead of keeping his secret, he had given it away to his wife.

A story is told that a gullible man was once leading a donkey with a halter when he was seen by two clever rogues. One of this pair told the other that he proposed to take the donkey, and when his companion asked him how, he said: 'Follow me and I'll show you.' The first rogue went up to the donkey, released it from the halter and handed it over to the second, who had followed him. He then put the halter over his own head and walked behind the simpleton until the donkey had been taken out of sight. He then stopped and would not move when the simpleton tugged on the halter. The simpleton turned and, seeing the halter on a man's head, he exclaimed: 'What are you?' 'I am your donkey,' the man told him, 'and mine is a strange story. I have an elderly mother, a pious woman. I went to her one day when I was drunk and she said to me: "My son, repent to God Almighty and abandon these evil acts." I took a stick and beat her, after which she cursed me, and the Almighty transformed me into a donkey, giving me over to you. I have been with you all this time, but today my mother thought of me and, out of pity for me, she called down a blessing on me, after which God gave me back my former, human shape.' 'There is no might and no power except with God, the Exalted, the Omnipotent!' exclaimed the donkey's owner, adding: 'In His Name I implore you, brother, not to hold me responsible for what I have done to you in the way of riding you and so on.'

He then removed the halter and the man went off, while the simpleton returned home drunk with care and sorrow. 'What is the matter,' his wife asked him, 'and where is the donkey?' 'You don't know about the donkey,' he replied, 'but I shall tell you.' After he had told her the story, she was afraid that God might punish them and she exclaimed: 'How could we have spent all this time using a human being as a beast of burden?' She distributed alms and asked for God's pardon, while her husband sat for a time at home doing no work until she asked him how long he proposed to go on like that, telling him to go to the market and buy them another donkey that he could use for work. He went there and when he stood by the donkeys, he saw his own being offered for sale. When he recognized it, he went up to it and put his mouth to its ear. 'Damn you, you ill-omened fellow,' he said. 'You must have got drunk again and beaten your mother. I'm never going to buy you again.' Then he left the donkey and went on his way.

A story is told that the Commander of the Faithful Harun al-Rashid took to his bed one day at siesta time, but when he got on to it he saw fresh semen on the mattress. He was horrified and, in deep disturbance and distress, he sent for Lady Zubaida. When she came he asked her what was on the mattress and, after looking at it, she said: 'This is semen, Commander of the Faithful.' 'Tell me the truth about how this came here,' he said, 'or else I shall strike you down this very moment.' 'I know nothing about it, Commander of the Faithful,' she replied, 'and I am innocent of the crime that you suspect me of having committed.'

The caliph sent for the *qadi* Abu Yusuf and told him the story, showing him the semen. Abu Yusuf looked up at the ceiling and, seeing a crack in it, he said: 'Commander of the Faithful, the semen of bats is like that of men and this is the semen of a bat.' He then asked for a spear, which he took and thrust through the crack, at which a bat fell out. The caliph's suspicions were allayed . . .

Night 389

Morning now dawned and Shahrazad broke off from what she had been allowed to say. Then, when it was the three hundred and eighty-ninth night, SHE CONTINUED:

I have heard, O fortunate king, that the *qadi* took the spear and thrust it through the crack, at which a bat fell out. The caliph's suspicions were allayed and Zubaida's innocence proved. She gave voice to her joy at this and promised Abu Yusuf a liberal reward. She had with her precious fruits that were out of season, but she knew that in the orchard there were others, equally unseasonal. So she asked Abu Yusuf which he would prefer, the ones that were there or the ones that were not. He said: 'Our school of law does not allow us to pass judgement on the absent; this can only be done when the party in question is present.' So Zubaida had both types of fruit brought for him and, after he had tasted them both, she asked him what the difference was between them. He said: 'Every time I want to choose one, the other presents me with its evidence.' The caliph laughed when he heard this and gave Abu Yusuf a reward. Zubaida then gave him what she herself had promised and he left their presence in a happy state. Note the merit of this imam and how it was thanks to him that Zubaida's innocence was established and the cause of the stain made clear.

A story is told that, when al-Hakim bi-amri-'llah was out riding one day with his retinue, he passed by an orchard where he caught sight of a man surrounded by black slaves and eunuchs. He asked the man for a drink and the man said: 'Perhaps the Commander of the Faithful would do me the honour of dismounting to sit with me in this orchard.' Al-Hakim and his men dismounted and their host produced a hundred carpets, a hundred cloths, a hundred cushions, a hundred plates of fruit, a hundred bowls filled with sweetmeats and a hundred drinking vessels containing sugared drinks. Al-Hakim was astounded by this and told his host: 'This is amazing. Did you know that we were coming, and so prepared this for us?' 'No, by God, Commander of the Faithful,' the man replied, 'I didn't know anything of that. I am only a merchant, one of your subjects, but I have a hundred concubines and when you honoured me by dismounting here I sent to every one of them asking her to send a meal for me to the orchard. Each of them then sent some of her furnishings and what was left over of her food and drink, for they are each in the habit of providing me every day with a plate of food, another of stewed meat and another of fruit, together with sweetmeats and a bowl of wine. This is my daily lunch and I haven't produced any more for you.' Al-Hakim prostrated himself in gratitude to Almighty God, exclaiming: 'Praise be to God, Who has placed among my subjects a man wealthy enough to feed the caliph and his men without the need for preparation and using only his surplus food.' He then ordered that his host be given all the treasury dirhams that had been minted that year. These totalled three million, seven hundred thousand, and the caliph did not mount until they had been fetched and given to the man. 'Use these to help you maintain your way of life,' he said, 'for your courtesy deserves more than this.' He then got on his horse and rode off.

*

One day Chosroe Anushirwan, the just king, rode out hunting and became separated from his attendants as he pursued a gazelle. During his chase he saw a small village near at hand, and as he was very thirsty he made his way there and, going up to the door of a house that lay on his way, asked for a drink. A girl came out and looked at him, after which she went back inside and squeezed a single stalk of sugar-cane for him. She mixed the juice with water, put it in a cup and topped it with something scented that was like dust. She then passed it to Anushirwan, who looked at it and, noticing the apparent dust, drank it a little at a time until he had finished it. Then he told the girl: 'What a delicious drink that was, apart from the dirty specks floating in it.' 'Guest,' replied the girl, 'I put those in deliberately to cloud it over.' Anushirwan asked her why, and she said: 'I could see that you were very thirsty and I was afraid that you might do yourself an injury by drinking it down in a single gulp. Had it not been for the specks you would have tossed it down quickly and that would have been bad for you.' Anushirwan was filled with admiration for her words and her intelligence, realizing that what she said was prompted by a natural sharpness of wit and mental alertness. He then asked her how many stalks she had used to squeeze out that amount of juice, and he was astonished when she said that she had only used one. He asked for the tax register of the village and, on discovering that it only paid a small amount, he made up his mind to raise its tax when he returned to his capital, saying: 'How can a village where a single stalk of sugar-cane produces so much liquid pay so little tax?'

He then left the village to return to the hunt, but at the end of the day he came back and, passing by the same door on his own, he again asked for a drink. The same girl came out and when she saw and recognized him she went back in to fetch it for him. This time Anushirwan was astonished by how long she took and he asked her why this was.

Night 390

Morning now dawned and Shahrazad broke off from what she had been allowed to say. Then, when it was the three hundred and ninetieth night, SHE CONTINUED:

I have heard, O fortunate king, that Anushirwan tried to hurry the girl, asking her why she was taking so long. She told him: 'One stalk didn't produce as much as you needed, so I had to press three, and they didn't give as much as the single one had done earlier.' Anushirwan asked the reason for that and she told him: 'It was because the king's intentions had changed.' 'How did you get that idea?' he asked, and she said: 'I have heard men of intelligence saying that when a ruler's good intentions towards his people change, their blessings vanish and their advantages are diminished.'

Anushirwan laughed and gave up his idea of raising the tax. He then married the girl on the spot, being impressed by her cleverness and intelligence as well as by her eloquence.

A story is told that in the town of Bukhara there was a water carrier who for thirty years had been in the habit of delivering water to the house of a goldsmith. This goldsmith had an unusually beautiful and attractive wife, characterized by piety and chastity. One day, when the water carrier came as usual and poured his water into the cistern of the house, the woman happened to be standing in the courtyard. He went up to her and took her hand, which he rubbed and squeezed before going off and leaving her. When her husband came back from the market she said: 'I want you to tell me what it was that you did in the market today to anger Almighty God.' He denied having done anything of the kind but she insisted: 'Yes, by God, you must have done something to anger Him, and unless you tell me the truth I shall not stay in your house and neither of us will see the other again.' 'I'll do that,' he said, and he went on to explain: 'I happened to be sitting in my shop as usual when a woman came in and told me to make her a bracelet. She left and I made the bracelet for her from gold and put it up on a shelf and then, when she came back, I fetched it for her. She held out her hand and I put the bracelet on her forearm, but I was taken aback by the whiteness of her hand and the captivating beauty of her arm, remembering the poet's lines:

Arms glittering with the beauty of bracelets,
Like fire that burns over running water.
It is as though her forearm, encircled with gold,
Is water girdled amazingly with fire.

So I took her hand, squeezed it and folded it over.'

'God is greater!' exclaimed his wife. 'Why did you do that? This is surely why the water carrier who has been coming to our house for thirty years without ever betraying our trust took my hand today and squeezed it and folded it.' 'We shall ask for God's protection,' her husband said. 'I repent of my fault and you must ask God to pardon me.' 'May He pardon both you and me,' said his wife, 'and grant us well-being.'

Night 391

Morning now dawned and Shahrazad broke off from what she had been allowed to say. Then, when it was the three hundred and ninety-first night, SHE CONTINUED:

I have heard, O fortunate king, that the goldsmith's wife said: 'May God pardon both you and me and grant us well-being.'

The next day, the water carrier came and threw himself down before the woman, rubbing himself with dust. He excused himself and said: 'My lady, pardon me for what the devil prompted me to do when he led me astray and seduced me.' 'Go off on your way,' the woman said: 'The fault wasn't yours but was caused by my husband when he did what he did in his shop and God arranged for him to be punished in this world.'

It is reported that when his wife told him what the water carrier had done, the goldsmith said: 'This is tit-for-tat and had I done more, so would he.' This saying passed into common use among the people. A wife must keep to her husband both outwardly and inwardly and be content when he gives her a little, if he cannot give more. She should follow the example of 'A'isha the truthful and Fatima al-Zahra', so that she may be numbered among the virtuous company of the early Muslims.

A story is told that Chosroe, a Persian king, was fond of fish and one day while he was seated in his audience hall with his wife, Shirin, a fisherman came in with a large fish which he presented to him. Chosroe was pleased with the fish and ordered that the man be given four thousand dirhams. Shirin told him that he had done wrong and when he asked why, she said: 'After this, when you give this sum to any one of your retainers, he will be contemptuous and say: "The king only gave me what he gave the fisherman," while, if you give him less, he will say: "The king despises me and has given me less than he gave the fisherman."' Chosroe said: 'You are right, but it doesn't befit kings to take back what they have given, and the matter is over and done with.' Shirin said: 'I can find you a way to reclaim your gift,' and when Chosroe asked her how to do this, she explained: 'If you want to do that, call him back and ask him whether the fish is male or female. If he says that it is male, tell him that we want a female, and if he says it is female, tell him that we want a male.' Chosroe sent after the fisherman, who was a man of quick intelligence, and when Chosroe asked him on his return whether the fish was male or female, he kissed the ground and said: 'It is neither the one nor the other but is a hermaphrodite.' At this, Chosroe laughed and ordered him to be given another four thousand dirhams.

The fisherman now went to the treasurer for his eight thousand dirhams, which he then put in a bag that he had with him. He hoisted this on his shoulder and was about to leave when one of the coins fell out. He put down his bag and leaned down to pick it up, watched by Chosroe and Shirin. 'Your majesty,' said Shirin, 'did you see this fellow's baseness and meanness? When one dirham fell out he could not bear to leave it for one of your pages to pick up.' When Chosroe heard this, he was filled with disgust at the fisherman and said: 'You are right, Shirin.' He had the fisherman recalled and said: 'You mean-spirited fellow, you are not a proper man. Why, with all this money over your shoulder, did you bend down for the sake of a single dirham and were too miserly to leave it where it was?' The fisherman kissed the ground and said: 'May God grant long life to the king. I didn't pick it up because of its value to me but because on one side of it was an image of the king and on the other his name. I was afraid that someone might tread on it unwittingly and, as this would be a slight to the king's name and his image, I might be held responsible for it.' The king admired and approved of his answer and ordered him to be given another four thousand dirhams. He then told a herald to proclaim throughout his kingdom: 'No one should follow the advice of women, as whoever does this will lose two dirhams for each one that he would otherwise have lost.'

A story is told that Yahya ibn Khalid the Barmecide had left the palace on his way back home when at the door of his house he saw a man who got up and greeted him as he approached. 'Yahya,' the man said, 'I am in need of what you have, and God is my intermediary with you.' Yahya ordered that he be given an apartment of his own within his house and that he be brought a thousand dirhams a day by his treasurer, together with the choicest selection of his own food. This went on for a whole month, but at the end of this time the man, who had been given thirty thousand dirhams, became afraid that the sum was so large that Yahya might take it back from him and as a result he left secretly.

Night 392

Morning now dawned and Shahrazad broke off from what she had been allowed to say. Then, when it was the three hundred and ninety-second night, SHE CONTINUED:

I have heard, O fortunate king, that the man took the dirhams and left. Yahya was told of this and said: 'By God, had he stayed with me for all his days I wouldn't have stopped providing for him and treating him with the generosity due to a guest.'

The merits and virtues of the Barmecides could not be counted and this was particularly true of Yahya, in whom all glorious qualities were combined, as the poet said:

I asked generosity: 'Are you free-born?' 'No,' it replied,
'I am a slave belonging to Yahya ibn Khalid.'
'Did he purchase you?' I asked. 'Far from it,' it answered,
'He inherited me from a long line of his ancestors.'

The story is told that Ja'far ibn Musa al-Hadi had a lute girl called al-Badr al-Kabir, unrivalled in her time for beauty of face, symmetry of form, subtle wit and knowledge of singing as well as of instrumental playing. So beautiful, graceful and accomplished was she that when Muhammad al-Amin ibn Zubaida heard of her, he asked Ja'far to sell her to him. Ja'far replied: 'You know that it is not fitting for a man like me to sell slave girls and haggle over concubines. Were it not for the fact that she has been brought up in my house, I would not grudge her to you but would send her to you as a gift.'

One day, al-Amin in search of enjoyment went to Ja'far's house and Ja'far provided him with the proper entertainment for friends and told al-Badr to entertain him by singing, at which she tuned her strings and sang the sweetest of melodies. Al-Amin began to enjoy himself by drinking and he told the cupbearers to keep on plying Ja'far with drink so as to make him drunk. He then took al-Badr with him and went off to his palace, but he did not lay a hand on her. The next morning, he sent for Ja'far and on his arrival he gave him wine and told al-Badr to sing for him from behind the curtain of the harem. When Ja'far heard her voice he recognized it, but although he was angry, because of his noble spirit and magnanimity he concealed this and showed no change in his friendly behaviour.

When the drinking party was over, al-Amin told one of his followers to fill the boat on which Ja'far had come with dirhams, dinars, jewels of all types, sapphires, splendid robes and dazzling wealth. The man carried on doing this until he had placed in the boat a thousand bags of money and a thousand pearls, each worth twenty thousand dirhams. He went on adding treasures of all sorts until the boatmen had to appeal to him to stop, saying that the boat couldn't carry any more. They were then told to take all this to Ja'far's house. This is an example of the magnanimity of those great men, may God have mercy on them.

A story is told that Sa'id ibn Salim al-Bahili, in the time of Harun al-Rashid, was reduced to the direst of straits, being burdened with a quantity of debts that he could not settle. HE SAID:

I was at a loss, not knowing how to cope, as I had the greatest difficulty in paying them off; creditors were besieging my door and I was constantly harried by throngs of them. There was nothing that I could do and, faced by mounting cares and finding my circumstances so altered for the worse, I went to 'Abd Allah ibn Malik al-Khuza'i and asked him to help me with advice and to think of some plan to allow me to escape from my difficulties. He told me: 'No one can free you from the cares and worries that are distressing you, except for the Barmecides.' 'Who can put up with their haughtiness or endure their arrogance?' I asked, but he replied: 'You will have to do that if you want your affairs set to rights.'

Night 393

Morning now dawned and Shahrazad broke off from what she had been allowed to say. Then, when it was the three hundred and ninety-third night, SHE CONTINUED:

I have heard, O fortunate king, that 'Abd Allah ibn Malik al-Khuza'i told Sa'id ibn Salim al-Bahili: 'You will have to put up with that if you want your affairs set to rights.' SA'ID IBN SALIM AL-BAHILI WENT ON:

I left him and went to visit al-Fadl and Ja'far, the sons of Yahya ibn Khalid, to whom I told my tale and explained my circumstances. They said: 'May God grant you His aid so that His favour may allow you to do without that of His creatures, and may He treat you with such liberality that He alone will be enough for you, for He can do whatever

He wishes. He knows the needs of His servants and is gracious to them.'
I went off and when I returned to 'Abd Allah, distracted and disconsolate,
I repeated to him what they had said. 'Stay here with me today,' he told
me, 'to see what Almighty God decrees.' I had been sitting with him for
some time when in came my own servant, who said: 'Master, there are
large numbers of laden mules at our door and a man who says that he
is the agent of al-Fadl and Ja'far, the sons of Yahya ibn Khalid.' 'Abd
Allah said to me: 'I hope this is a happy ending for you. You'd better get
up and see what is happening.'

I left him and ran quickly back home, where I saw a man with a note
in his hand. In it was written: 'After we had heard what you had to
say when you were with us, we went to the caliph and told him that
circumstances had forced you to endure the humiliation of begging. He
told us to bring you a million dirhams from the treasury, but we said:
"He will have to pay this over to his creditors to settle his debts, so how
will he be able to meet his own expenses?" The caliph then ordered that
you be given a further three hundred thousand dirhams, while each of
us has contributed another million of our own, bringing the total to
three million, three hundred thousand, to help you put your affairs in
order.'

Note the generosity of these noble men, may Almighty God have mercy
on them.

A story is told that a woman played a trick on her husband who had
brought her a fish one Friday telling her to cook it and serve it to him
after the Friday prayer. He then went about his business, but his wife
was visited by a male friend of hers who asked her to come to a wedding
at his house. She accepted and went off with him, leaving the fish in a
jar that she had there. She stayed away from home until the following
Friday, and although her husband searched through the houses for her
and made enquiries, no one could tell him anything. When she came
back on the Friday, she took the live fish from the jar. The neighbours
gathered round and when her husband told them his story . . .

Night 394

Morning now dawned and Shahrazad broke off from what she had been allowed to say. Then, when it was the three hundred and ninety-fourth night, SHE CONTINUED:

I have heard, O fortunate king, that when she came back on the Friday, she took the live fish from the jar. The neighbours gathered round and when her husband told them his story, they disbelieved him, saying that the fish couldn't possibly have stayed alive so long. As they were convinced that he must be mad, they put him under restraint and started to laugh at him. For his part, he shed tears and recited these lines:

Here is an old woman who ranks high as an evil-doer;
The lines on her face bear witness to debauchery.
A bawd while she menstruates and a harlot when she is clean,
She divides her time between fornication and pimping.

A story is told that in the old days there was a pious woman among the children of Israel, devout and God-fearing. Every day she would go to pray in a chapel beside which was an orchard, and when she went to the chapel she would go into the orchard and perform her ritual ablution. The orchard had two elderly guards who fell in love with her and tried to seduce her. When she rejected them, they threatened that, unless she allowed them to lie with her, they would testify that she had committed fornication. 'God will protect me from your evil,' she told them, at which they opened the orchard gate and cried out. People came from all directions to ask what was the matter and the men said: 'We found this girl with a young man, who was making love to her, but he got away from us.' In those days the people would disgrace fornicators by public proclamation for three days and then stone them to death. In the case of this woman, during each of the three days of proclamation the two men came up to her and put their hands on her head, saying to her: 'Praise be to God, Who has brought punishment down upon you.'

When the people were about to stone her, they were followed by Daniel, who was then twelve years old, and this was the first of his miracles, blessing and peace be on our Prophet and on him. When he caught up with them he said: 'Don't be in a hurry to stone her until I have given my judgement.' He sat down on a chair that they had placed for him, and he then separated the two old men, he being the first to do this in the case of witnesses. Then he asked one of them what he had seen, and when the man told him what he said had happened, he asked where in the orchard this had taken place. 'In the east side, beneath a pear tree,' the man said. Daniel then put the same questions to the second man, who told his story and said that it had happened on the west side beneath an apple tree. While all this was going on, the girl was standing looking upwards with her hands raised towards the heavens, praying to Almighty God for deliverance. God then sent down a thunderbolt as punishment; the two old men were consumed by fire and God established the innocence of the girl. This was the first of the miracles of the prophet Daniel, upon whom be peace.

The story is told that the Commander of the Faithful Harun al-Rashid went out one day with Abu Ya'qub al-Nadim, Ja'far the Barmecide and Abu Nuwas. As they were going through the desert they saw an old man leaning on his donkey, and Harun told Ja'far to ask him where he came from. 'From Basra,' the man said.

Night 395

Morning now dawned and Shahrazad broke off from what she had been allowed to say. Then, when it was the three hundred and ninety-fifth night, SHE CONTINUED:

I have heard, O fortunate king, that when Ja'far asked the old man where he had come from, he said: 'From Basra.' 'Where are you going?' asked Ja'far. 'To Baghdad,' replied the man, and when Ja'far then asked him what he was going to do there, he said that he was going to look for medicine for his eyes. Harun told Ja'far to make fun of him and, although Ja'far said: 'If I do that, I shall hear something from him that I shall dislike,' Harun insisted. So Ja'far said: 'If I prescribe something to help you, how will you reward me?' The man answered: 'Almighty God will give you a better reward than I can.'

Ja'far then said: 'Listen to me and I'll prescribe you something that I shall not prescribe to anyone else.' 'What is it?' the man asked. Ja'far said: 'Take three ounces of the breath of the wind, three of the rays of the sun, three of moonshine and three of lamplight. Mix them all together and put them out in the wind for three months. After that, transfer them to a mortar with no bottom and pound them for three months. Then place them in a cracked bowl and leave this for three months in the wind. You must then use three dirhams' weight of the medicine every day before you go to sleep, and if you go on doing this for three months you will be cured, God willing.'

When the old man heard what Ja'far said, he stretched himself out over his donkey and gave vent to a disgusting fart. 'Take this in return for the medicine you have prescribed,' he said. 'If I use it and God cures me, I shall give you a slave girl whose services to you in your lifetime will end your days, and when you are dead and God has hurried away your soul to hellfire, she will smear your face with her excrement in her sorrow for you and, weeping and wailing over you, she will exclaim: "White-beard, what a fool you were!"' Harun fell over laughing and ordered the man to be given three thousand dirhams.

Al-Sharif Husain ibn Rayyan reported that the caliph 'Umar ibn al-Khattab was sitting one day to judge and arbitrate among his subjects, and with him were his senior companions, men of sound judgement. As he was seated there, a handsome and well-dressed young man was brought in by two other handsome young men, who dragged him by the collar and brought him in front of the caliph. After looking at the two of them and at their prisoner, 'Umar told them to release him and then made him come closer. He then asked the two why they had brought in the young man, and they said: 'Commander of the Faithful, we are full brothers and sincere followers of the true faith. We had an elderly father, a provident man, well respected among the tribes, free of all vices and known for his good qualities. He brought us up when we were young and treated us generously when we grew up.'

Night 396

Morning now dawned and Shahrazad broke off from what she had been allowed to say. Then, when it was the three hundred and ninety-sixth night, SHE CONTINUED:

I have heard, O fortunate king, that the two young men told the caliph: 'Our father was well respected among the tribes, free of all vices and known for his good qualities. He brought us up when we were young

and treated us generously when we grew up. In him were collected virtues
and distinctions just as the poet has put it:

They asked: "Is Abu'l-Saqr from Shaiban?" I said:
"No, by God, Shaiban derives from him."
How many a father owes fame to a noble son,
As the fame of 'Adnan rests on God's Apostle.

One day, he had gone out to an orchard of his to enjoy the sight of its
trees and to pick the ripe fruit when this young man killed him unjustly,
and we ask you to allow us to retaliate on him for his crime in accordance
with God's command.' 'Umar cast a terrifying glance at the young man
and said: 'You have listened to the account given by these two. What
have you got to say by way of an answer?'

The youth was steadfast and ready of tongue. He cast aside dismay and
apprehension, smiled and greeted the caliph in eloquent terms with courtesy, before continuing: 'Commander of the Faithful, I have listened to
their accusation; they are right in what they have told you about what took
place, and the commandment of God cannot be gainsaid, but I shall tell
you my story and it will be for you to judge. You must know I come from
the purest Arab stock, they being the noblest race under the heavens.
I was reared in Bedouin camps, but when my clan fell on hard times I
moved to the outskirts of this town with my family, together with their
possessions and their children. I was following a track leading between
the orchards with some excellent she-camels of mine, by which I set great
store. Among them was a handsome stallion of excellent breeding, which
had proved to be very prolific and which was walking with them like a
crowned king. One of the she-camels bolted across to the orchard owned
by these men's father, where trees were showing above the wall. It began
to graze on these, but I had driven it away when an old man appeared
through a gap on the wall, breathing fire in the heat of his anger. He had a
stone in his right hand and was swaying like a lion about to spring. He
struck my stallion with the stone, hitting a fatal spot so that it fell dead.
When I saw it lying there beside me, I felt coals of rage blazing in my heart
and so I took the same stone that he had used and struck him a mortal
blow, bringing him to an evil end, for killers are themselves killed. When
the stone hit him he gave a loud and distressing cry, and although I hurried
away, these two ran after me, seized me and brought me before you.'

'Umar, may God Almighty be pleased with him, said: 'You have
confessed to your crime; you cannot be allowed to go free as the law of

retaliation must be applied "and there is no time to find refuge".'* 'The imam's judgement must be obeyed,' said the young man, 'and I am content to accept the ruling of the law of Islam. I have, however, a young brother to whom his old father before his death made over a large sum of gold. He entrusted this to me, calling God to witness that it belonged to my brother and that I was to do everything I could to guard it for him. So I took it and buried it and I am the only person who knows where it is. If you condemn me to be killed here and now, the money will be lost. You will be responsible for the loss and my young brother will bring a case against you for it on the day when God will judge between his people. But if you grant me a three-day delay, I will appoint someone to take charge of my brother's affairs and I guarantee faithfully to return. I have someone who will stand surety for this.'

'Umar bent his head towards the ground and then looked up at the people standing there and asked who would stand surety for the young man's return. The young man, after studying their faces, singled out Abu Dharr and, pointing to him, he said: 'This man will be my guarantor.'

Night 397

Morning now dawned and Shahrazad broke off from what she had been allowed to say. Then, when it was the three hundred and ninety-seventh night, SHE CONTINUED:

I have heard, O fortunate king, that the young man pointed to Abu Dharr and said: 'This man will be my guarantor.' 'Did you hear that, Abu Dharr?' asked 'Umar. 'Will you give me a guarantee that he will come back?' Abu Dharr agreed to stand surety for three days and 'Umar accepted his offer and allowed the young man to leave. When the three-day period was almost up or at an end, he had still not presented himself to 'Umar, who was sitting surrounded by his companions like a moon among stars. The two accusers were waiting there, together with Abu Dharr, and they asked him: 'Where is our adversary? How can you think that he will come back, now that he has escaped? But we are not going to move from here until you produce him for us so that we can take our revenge on him.' 'I swear by the truth of God, the Omniscient,' said Abu Dharr, 'that if he fails to come at the end of the three days I shall keep

* Quran 38.2.

my word and surrender myself to the caliph.' 'Umar, may God be pleased with him, said: 'By God, if he does not come in time, then I shall deal with Abu Dharr in accordance with the dictates of Islamic law.'

There was a great clamour as those present wept and groaned. The senior companions of the Prophet suggested to the accusers that they should win praise by accepting blood money, but they refused to take anything except their revenge. Then, while the people were in a ferment, crying out in grief for Abu Dharr, up came the young man. He stood before the caliph and greeted him courteously, with his face shining and pearled with sweat, and he said: 'I have handed my young brother over to his maternal uncles and have told them all about his affairs, including where his money is buried. Then I rushed through the heat of the day in order to keep my word like a noble man.'

The people were astonished at how faithfully he had kept his promise and how courageously he had come forward to face death. One of them exclaimed to him: 'How noble you are, young man, and how faithfully you keep your word.' He replied: 'Don't you know that when death comes, no one can escape it? I kept my promise lest it be said that there is no more fidelity among mankind.' Abu Dharr then said: 'By God, Commander of the Faithful, I stood as guarantor for this young man although I didn't know from what tribe he came and had never seen him before that day, but when he turned away from the others and singled me out, saying: "This man will stand surety for me," I didn't think it proper to refuse him. Generosity did not allow me to dash his hopes where it would do me no harm to agree, lest it be said that there is no more graciousness among mankind.' At that, the two accusers said: 'Commander of the Faithful, we forgive this young man for our father's blood now that he has changed sadness into cheerfulness, lest it be said that there is no more kindliness among mankind.'

'Umar was delighted that the young man had been pardoned and at the faithfulness with which he had kept his word. He was particularly impressed by the chivalry shown by Abu Dharr, and he approved of the readiness shown by the two accusers to act with generosity. He praised and thanked them, quoting:

God repays those who do good among mankind,
And no good deed done in His Name is wasted.

He offered to pay them the blood money due for their father from the public treasury, but they said: 'We forgave the killer for the sake of God, the Generous, the Exalted, and whoever acts for this reason does not follow up his good deed with reproaches or the infliction of harm.'

A story is told that when al-Ma'mun, the son of Harun al-Rashid, came to Egypt, the guarded land, he wanted to destroy the Pyramids in order to take the treasures that they contained, but in spite of the efforts that he made in that attempt and the money he spent, he failed . . .

Night 398

Morning now dawned and Shahrazad broke off from what she had been allowed to say. Then, when it was the three hundred and ninety-eighth night, SHE CONTINUED:

I have heard, O fortunate king, that in spite of the efforts that the caliph made and the huge amounts of money that he spent in an attempt to destroy the Pyramids, he failed, and all he was able to do was to open up a small hole. It is said that in this hole he found exactly the same amount of money that he had spent, neither more nor less. This astonished him and he took the money and abandoned his intention.

There are three Pyramids, and they are among the wonders of the world. There is nothing on the face of the earth so well built, so perfectly designed or so lofty. They have been built with huge rocks, into each side of which the builders drilled holes in which they set up iron bars. They would then drill into a second stone and set it down on the first, filling the space above the bars with molten lead. This was done with engineering exactitude until the whole building was complete. Each Pyramid was a hundred cubits high, using the cubit measure employed at that time, with all four sides sloping from top to bottom over a length of three hundred cubits.

According to the ancients, the western Pyramid contains thirty treasure chambers constructed of coloured granite and filled with precious stones, heaped-up wealth, strange statues and implements, as well as magnificent weapons, all coated with a wonderful salve which will keep them from rusting until the Day of Judgement. There is glass there which can be bent but will not break, as well as types of compound drugs and various artificially produced liquids. In the second Pyramid the annals of the priests are written on granite tablets, one for each priest, containing a record of the wonders produced by his skill and of his deeds, while on the walls are pictures of people who look like idols and who are practising handicrafts of all kinds while seated on benches. Each Pyramid has a guardian who continues throughout the years to protect it from the ravages of time.

The wonders of the Pyramids have bemused men of intelligence and insight. Many poems have been written to describe them, although little advantage can be got from the descriptions. Among them are the lines:

> When kings want their ambitions mentioned
> After their deaths, the tongues of buildings tell of them.
> Do you not see that the Pyramids have remained
> Unchanged by Time's disasters?

Another poet said:

> Look at the Pyramids and listen to the tale
> They tell of Time, the treacherous,
> Could they but speak, it would be to tell us
> From start to finish all that it has done.

Another poet said:

> My two companions, is there beneath the sky a building
> To rival in its excellence the Pyramids?
> Time itself fears them, while all else
> Upon the face of earth fears Time.
> My eyes feast on the splendour of their building,
> But thoughts can take no pleasure in their purpose.

Another poet said:

> Where is the builder of the Pyramids?
> What were his people, his age and his fate?
> Monuments outlast their builders for a time,
> Then ruin overtakes them and they fall.

A story is told that a thief, who had repented sincerely to Almighty God, opened a shop in which he sold materials. It happened that, after some time had passed, one day after he had shut up his shop and gone home, a wily man came there dressed up to look like him. This was at night, and this man took some keys from his sleeve and told the market guard to light him a candle. The guard took the candle that he was given and went off to light it.

Night 399

Morning now dawned and Shahrazad broke off from what she had been allowed to say. Then, when it was the three hundred and ninety-ninth night, SHE CONTINUED:

I have heard, O fortunate king, that the guard took the candle that he was given and went off to light it. The thief then opened the shop and lit another candle that he had with him, so that when the guard came back the thief was discovered sitting in the shop studying the account book that he was holding and counting on his fingers. He stayed like that until dawn was breaking, when he told the guard to fetch him a camel driver with his camel to carry off some of his goods. When they came, the thief took four bundles of materials and gave them to the camel driver, who loaded them on his camel. The thief then shut up the shop, gave the guard two dirhams and went after the camel driver, leaving the guard believing that he was the owner.

In the light of morning, the owner of the shop arrived and the guard started to call down blessings on him because of the gift of the dirhams, while the owner was taken by surprise as he had no idea what the man was talking about. Then, when he opened his shop, he found the guttering candle and the account book thrown down on the floor, and, on further inspection, he discovered that four bales of materials were missing. He asked the guard what had happened, and the man told him of the events of the night and how a camel driver had been hired to carry the bales. 'Bring me the man who loaded these up with you at dawn,' said the owner. 'To hear is to obey,' said the guard, and he fetched the man. The owner asked him where he had taken those bales and he said: 'To such-and-such a wharf, and I put them in So-and-So's boat.' 'Come there with me,' the owner said, and when they arrived, the camel driver said: 'This is the boat and here is the boatman.' The owner then asked the boatman where he had taken 'the merchant' and his goods. 'To such-and-such a place,' the man replied, adding: 'And he then fetched a camel driver who loaded the bales on his camel and went off I don't know where.' The owner told him to fetch that particular camel driver, who, on being asked, told him that he had taken 'the merchant' and his goods from the boat to such-and-such a place. 'Come there with me and show me,' said the owner, and the camel driver took him to a place far removed from the river bank, pointing out the *khan* where the goods had been deposited and showing him 'the merchant's' storeroom. The owner went up, opened it and found the four bales intact and with nothing missing. The thief had put his cloak on top of the materials and when everything had been loaded on the camel the owner gave that to the camel driver as well. He then shut up the storeroom and went with the driver, but the thief followed them until the goods had been loaded on to the boat. Then he confronted the owner and said: 'Brother, may God preserve you, you have recovered your goods and nothing is missing. So give me back my cloak.' The owner laughed and returned the cloak without causing any trouble for the thief, after which each went on his way.

A story is told that the Commander of the Faithful Harun al-Rashid was very restless one night. He told his vizier, Ja'far ibn Yahya the Barmecide: 'I cannot sleep tonight; I am low-spirited and I don't know what to do.' Masrur, the caliph's eunuch, who was standing in front of him, laughed and the caliph said: 'What are you laughing at? Are you making fun of me or have you gone mad?' 'No, by God, Commander of the Faithful,' said Masrur.

Night 400

Morning now dawned and Shahrazad broke off from what she had been allowed to say. Then, when it was the four hundredth night, SHE CONTINUED:

I have heard, O fortunate king, that the caliph said to Masrur, the executioner: 'Are you making fun of me or have you gone mad?' 'No, by God, Commander of the Faithful,' said Masrur. 'I swear by your relationship to the Prince of the Apostles that I didn't mean to do that. The fact is that yesterday I went for a walk outside the palace, and when I got to the bank of the Tigris I saw a group of people who had collected there. I stopped and found a man called Ibn al-Qaribi, who was making them laugh. I happened to remember just now something that he said, and I was overcome by laughter. I ask your pardon, Commander of the Faithful.' 'Bring him here to me now,' said the caliph.

Masrur now hurried out and when he came to Ibn al-Qaribi, he said: 'Answer the summons of the Commander of the Faithful.' 'To hear is to obey,' said Ibn al-Qaribi, but Masrur added: 'There is one condition here. If when you enter the caliph's presence he gives you anything, you can keep a quarter of it and the rest is mine.' 'No,' replied Ibn al-Qaribi, 'half and half.' 'No,' said Masrur. 'A third for me and two-thirds for you,' offered Ibn al-Qaribi and, after much wrangling, Masrur accepted. The two went off together and when Ibn al-Qaribi came into the caliph's presence, he greeted the caliph in a manner that fitted his rank and took his place before him.

The caliph told him: 'If you fail to make me laugh, I will give you three blows with this sack.' Ibn al-Qaribi, thinking that the sack was empty, said to himself: 'What are three blows with a sack in comparison with a whipping? It can't harm me.' He then started to tell jokes that would make an angry man laugh and he produced buffoonery of all sorts, but the caliph neither laughed nor smiled. Ibn al-Qaribi, who was taken aback by this, was both worried and apprehensive as the caliph said: 'You have now earned your beating.' He took the sack and struck Ibn al-Qaribi a single blow. The sack contained four stones, each weighing two *ratls*, and when the blow fell on Ibn al-Qaribi's neck he let out a great cry. Then he remembered the agreement that he had made with Masrur and he called out: 'Excuse me, Commander of the Faithful, and let me say a couple of words.' 'Say what you want,' the caliph told him, and Ibn al-Qaribi explained: 'I have agreed to an arrangement with Masrur by which I should keep one-third of anything that the caliph gives me while two-thirds go to him, and it was only after hard bargaining that he agreed to this. Now the only thing that you have given me is a beating. This first blow is my share and the two that are still to come are his, as I have had mine. Here he is standing in front of you, Commander of the Faithful, so give him his share.' When Harun heard this he fell over laughing, and then, calling Masrur forward, he struck him once. Masrur cried out and said: 'One-third is enough for me; let him have two-thirds.'

Night 401

Morning now dawned and Shahrazad broke off from what she had been allowed to say. Then, when it was the four hundred and first night, SHE CONTINUED:

I have heard, O fortunate king, that Masrur cried out and said: 'One-third is enough for me; let him have two-thirds.' Harun laughed at them

both and ordered each of them to be given a thousand dinars, after
which they left, cheered by his generosity.

A story is told that the Commander of the Faithful Harun al-Rashid had
a sixteen-year-old son who shunned worldly things and followed the
path of asceticism and worship. He used to go out to cemeteries and say:
'You used to rule the world, but that did not save you. You have gone
to your graves, and I wish I knew what you said and what was said to
you.' He would then shed the tears of a fearful and grieving man and
recite:

> Funeral processions fill me with fear always,
> And the tears of mourners sadden me.

It happened that one day he was passed by his father in his state
procession, surrounded by his viziers, state dignitaries and officers. They
saw the son of the Commander of the Faithful wearing a woollen *jubba*
together with a headband of wool, and they said to one another: 'This
boy is putting the Commander of the Faithful to shame among the kings,
and were his father to reprove him, he might give up this behaviour.'
The caliph heard what they said and he told the prince: 'My little son,
you have put me to shame by your way of life.' The prince looked at
him without saying a word, and then he looked up to a bird that was
perched on one of the palace battlements. He said to it: 'Bird, I conjure
you by your Creator, fly down to my hand.' The bird swooped down
and the prince then told it: 'Go back where you came from,' and it flew
off again. Next he told it to settle on the caliph's hand, but it refused,
and he said to his father: 'It is you who have put me to shame among
the saints of God through your love for this world. I have made up my
mind to leave you, and it is only in the next world that I shall come back
to you.'

He then went down to Basra, where he worked as a plasterer, and he
would only accept as a day's wage one dirham and one *daniq*, using the
daniq to buy his food and giving away the dirham as alms. ABU 'AMIR
THE BASRAN SAID:

A wall had collapsed in my house, so I went to the place where the
labourers collect in order to find someone to work on it. My eye fell on
a handsome young man with a comely face and, going up to him, I
greeted him and asked: 'My friend, are you looking for work?' 'Yes,' he
replied. 'Then come with me to rebuild a wall,' I said. He agreed to do

this if I accepted his conditions, and when I asked what these were he said: 'My wage is to be one dirham and one *daniq*, and when the muezzin calls to prayer, you are to allow me to pray in the congregational mosque.' I agreed to this and took him back to my house, where he did better work than anyone I had ever seen. I offered him a morning meal but he refused it and I realized that he must be fasting. When the muezzin called to prayer, he reminded me of the condition to which I had agreed, and then undid his belt and prepared to perform the ritual ablution, which he carried out in a way that I had never seen bettered. Then he went off and prayed with the congregation in the mosque, after which he returned to his work. At the call to the afternoon prayer he again performed the ablution, went off to pray and came back to work. 'Friend,' I told him, 'this is the end of the working day, for this is as long as labourers have to work.' 'God be praised,' he exclaimed, 'you employed me until nightfall!' and he went on working until then. I gave him two dirhams, but he said: 'What is this?', and when I said: 'By God, this is only part of what you deserve because of how hard you have worked,' he threw them back at me and said: 'I want no more than what we agreed on.' I pressed him but failed to get him to agree and so I handed him one dirham and one *daniq* and off he went.

Early the next morning I went to where the labourers stood but failed to find him. So I asked about him and was told that he only came there on a Saturday. On the following Saturday I went to the place, and when I found him there I asked him to be good enough to come and work for me. 'On the conditions that you know,' he replied, and I agreed. I took him off to my house and stood watching him from where he could not see me. He would take a handful of clay and slap it on the wall, after which the stones would fit in with one another, leading me to exclaim: 'These are the actions of God's saints!' He worked all day, doing even more than before, and at nightfall I paid him his wage, which he took and then left.

On the third Saturday I went to the usual place and, as I did not find him there, I asked about him and was told that he was lying ill in the hut of So-and-So, an old woman well known for her piety, who had a reed hut in the graveyard. I went there, and when I entered I found him stretched out on the bare ground with his head on a brick and his face shining with radiance. We exchanged greetings and I sat at his head, shedding tears for his youth, his absence from his home, and his perfect obedience to God's commands. Then I asked if he needed anything and he said yes. 'What is it?' I asked. 'Come before noon tomorrow,' he said, 'and you will find me dead. Wash my corpse and dig my grave without telling anyone. Use this *jubba* I am wearing for my shroud after you have ripped it open and looked in the pocket. You are to take out what you find in it and keep it with you. When you have prayed over me and covered me with earth, go to Baghdad. Wait there for the caliph Harun al-Rashid to come out of his palace and then give him what you discovered in my pocket together with my greetings.' He then recited the confession of faith, praised God in the most eloquent of terms and recited these lines:

> Take this from a dead man to al-Rashid,
> And it will earn you a reward.
> Tell him: 'A stranger who has yearned for you,
> Long parted from you, in his love answers your call.
> It was not hate or boredom that drove him away;
> To kiss your right hand brought him near to God.
> He was parted from you, his father,
> By a soul which kept from sharing in your worldly wealth.'

When he had finished his recitation, the dying man busied himself with imploring God's pardon . . .

Night 402

Morning now dawned and Shahrazad broke off from what she had been allowed to say. Then, when it was the four hundred and second night, SHE CONTINUED:

I have heard, O fortunate king, that the dying man busied himself with imploring God's pardon, in calling down blessings and peace on the Prince of the righteous, and in repeating lines from the Quran. He then recited these lines:

> Father, do not be duped by your prosperity;
> Life ends and this prosperity will not endure.
> When you learn that your people are distressed,
> Know that responsibility for this is yours.
> When you help carry a bier to the grave,
> Know you yourself will soon be carried there.

ABU 'AMIR SAID:

When the young man had finished giving me his instructions and reciting his verses, I left him and returned home. The next morning I went back and found that he had died, may God have mercy on him. I washed the corpse, tore open his *jubba* and found in its pocket a ruby that was worth thousands of dinars, at which I exclaimed in wonder at how abstemious the young man had been. When I had buried him, I set off for Baghdad, where I went to the palace and waited for Harun to come out. When he did, I went up to him in the street and handed over the ruby. He recognized it and fell down in a faint, at which his attendants seized me. When he recovered, he told them to let me go and to bring me to the palace with all courtesy. They did that and when Harun himself got back, he sent for me and brought me to his room, where he asked me what had happened to the owner of the jewel. I told him that the man was dead and described the circumstances of his death. Harun began to weep and say: 'The son has profited, but the father's hopes are dashed.' He then called out the name of a certain woman, and she came out. When she saw me, she wanted to go back, but he told her to come forward and not to worry about me. So she entered and greeted him. He then passed her the jewel, and when she caught sight of it, she gave a great cry and fell down fainting. When she had recovered she said: 'Commander of the Faithful, what has God done with my son?' He was overcome by tears and told me to tell her what had happened, which I did. She began to weep, saying in a faint voice: 'How I long to meet you, light of my eyes; would that I could have poured drink for you when you had no one else to do this, and would that I might have cheered you when you were without a friend.'

She then recited these lines through her tears:

I weep for a stranger who met a lonely end,
Having no friend with whom to share his suffering.
After his glory and the throngs surrounding him,
He turned outcast and solitary, seeing none.
It is clear to all what our days have in store;
None of us is left untouched by death.
Absent one, it was God Who decreed your absence;
You were far removed from me, although you had been near.
My son, death has removed all hopes that we might meet,
But Judgement Day will join us once again.

I asked: 'Was this your son, Commander of the Faithful?' 'Yes,' he replied, 'and before I became caliph he used to visit men of learning and sit with the pious, but after that he began to avoid me and distance himself from me. I told his mother that, as he was devoted to the service of Almighty God, he might fall into difficulties and meet with hardship, and so I asked her to give this jewel to him to use in case of need. She passed it to him and insisted that he should take it, which he obediently did. He then left us to our worldly pursuits and stayed away until he met his God, Great and Glorious, as a pure and pious soul.'

Harun then told me to show him his son's grave. We left Baghdad together and I travelled with him until I could show him the grave, where he began to weep and wail until he fell down fainting. When he had recovered, he asked for God's pardon and repeated the formula: 'We belong to God and to Him do we return,' calling down blessings on the dead. He then asked me to become one of his companions, but I said: 'Commander of the Faithful, your son has taught me the most solemn of lessons,' and I recited these lines:

> I am a stranger, taking shelter with no man;
> I am a stranger even in my own land.
> I am a stranger without kith or kin;
> There is none here who seeks another's shelter.
> My own shelter is in the mosques and there I pass my days;
> Never throughout all time will my heart abandon them.
> Praise be to God, Lord of creation, for His bounty,
> For He preserves the soul within the body.

A story is told that AN EMINENT MAN SAID:

I happened to pass by a schoolmaster while he was teaching the children in his school, and as I could see that he was of fine appearance and well dressed, I went up to him. He rose to greet me and made me sit with him, after which I had a discussion with him about the readings of the Quran, grammar, poetry and philology. I found him perfectly equipped to deal with any question put to him; I called down a blessing on him and I told him this to his face.

After that I spent some time in his company, and every day would reveal some new excellence of his. I said to myself that this was something remarkable in a teacher, as men of intelligence agree that schoolteachers are stupid. I then left him, but every few days I would come back to visit

him to see how he was. One day, when I came to pay my usual visit,
I found the school closed and when I asked his neighbours, they told me
that he had suffered a bereavement. I thought that I should pay my
condolences to him and so I went and knocked on his door. A slave girl
came out and asked what I wanted, and I told her that I wanted a word
with her master. She said that her master was sitting alone and mourning,
so I replied: 'Tell him that his friend So-and-So wants to pay his condolences to him.' She went off and when he had been told, he said: 'Let
him come in.' She allowed me in and when I entered I found him sitting
alone with a mourning band around his head. 'May God increase your
reward,' I said, adding: 'This is a path we all have to tread, so you must
show patience.' I then asked him which of his acquaintances had died,
and he answered: 'The dearest and most beloved of all to me.' 'Do you
mean your father?' I asked, and when he replied no I said: 'Perhaps it
was your mother?' He said no to this, and no again when I asked whether
it was his brother or one of his relatives, so I asked what his relationship
was to the dead. 'This was my beloved,' he replied, and I said to myself
that this was the first sign of a lack of intelligence on his part. 'You may
find another, and one even more beautiful,' I suggested, to which he
replied: 'I never saw her, so I could not judge whether another would be
more beautiful or not.' 'This is the second sign,' I told myself, and then
I asked: 'How did you fall in love with someone whom you had never
seen?' He said: 'I was sitting at the window one day when a man passed
by on the road singing this line:

Umm ʿAmr, God reward your noble qualities,
Return my heart, wherever it may be.'

Night 403

Morning now dawned and Shahrazad broke off from what she had been
allowed to say. Then, when it was the four hundred and third night,
SHE CONTINUED:

I have heard, O fortunate king, that the man sang these lines on the
road. The schoolmaster explained: 'When I heard this I said to myself
that, were Umm ʿAmr not without an equal in the world, poets would
not write love songs about her, and so I fell in love with her. Two days
later, however, the same man passed singing this line:

The donkey left with Umm 'Amr;
She never came back, and neither did the donkey.

I realized then that she had died. I grieved for her and have spent three days in mourning.'

The narrator continued: 'I left him and went away, having established that he was a fool.'

A story told about the stupidity of schoolmasters is that one of them was visited in his school by a witty man who, in the course of a discussion with him, discovered him to have a knowledge of jurisprudence, grammar, philology and poetry, and to be cultured, sensible and refined. This surprised him as he held that teachers in schools were never wholly intelligent. When he was on the point of leaving, the teacher invited him to spend the night at his house. He accepted the invitation and they went together to the house, where his host treated him with courtesy and provided a meal for him. They ate and drank and then sat talking until the first third of the night had passed, after which the host provided a bed for his guest and went off himself to his harem.

The guest was on the point of going to sleep when suddenly there was a loud outcry in the harem. He asked what the matter was and was told that the teacher had suffered a dreadful accident and was at death's door. 'Let me see him,' the guest said and, when he was brought in, he found the man unconscious, with blood streaming from him. He poured water over the teacher's face and, when he had recovered, his guest asked what had happened, saying: 'When you left me you were in excellent form and perfectly healthy, so what went wrong?' 'My brother,' the man answered, 'after I left you I sat thinking about the works of Almighty God, and I said to myself: "Everything that God has created for man serves a useful purpose. He has made hands to apply force, feet for walking, eyes for seeing, ears for hearing, the penis for copulation and so forth and so on. These two testicles, however, serve no useful purpose for me." So I took a razor that I had by me and cut them off, and this is what happened to me.'

The guest left, saying: 'Those who say that no schoolmaster is fully intelligent are right, even if the latter know all that there is to know.'

The story is told that one of the hangers-on at a mosque could neither read nor write but used to make his living by trickery. One day, it occurred to him to open a school and teach children to read. He collected and hung up slates and sheets of paper with writing on them, put on a huge turban and sat at the school door. The passers-by, looking at the turban and at the slates and papers, thought that he must be a good teacher and so they brought him their children. He would tell one of them to read and another to write, and the children would teach one another.

One day, while he was sitting at the door of the school, he saw in the distance a woman approaching with a letter in her hand and he thought to himself that she must be coming to ask him to read it. He wondered how to deal with her, seeing that he was unable to read, and he thought of leaving to escape from her, but she caught up with him before he could get away and asked him where he was going. He told her that he was going to perform the midday prayer before coming back. 'It's a long time till midday,' she said, 'so read me this letter.' He took it from her and turned it upside down. As he stared at it, at times his turban would shake and at others his eyebrows would quiver and he appeared to be angry. The woman's husband was away from home and it was from him that the letter had come. When she saw how it had affected the teacher, she said to herself: 'My husband must be dead and this teacher is too embarrassed to tell me,' so she said: 'Sir, if he is dead, tell me.' He shook his head and said nothing, so she asked him: 'Should I tear my clothes?' 'Tear them,' he replied and when she said: 'Should I slap my face?' he told her to do that.

After taking the letter from him she went back home, where she and her children started to weep. A number of her neighbours heard this, and when they asked what was wrong they were told that the woman had just got a letter to say that her husband was dead. 'That's not true,' said one of them, 'because he sent me a letter yesterday to tell me that all was well with him; he was in good health and would be back with his wife in ten days.' This man then got up immediately and went to the woman. 'Where is the letter that came to you?' he asked, and when she fetched it he took it from her and read it. What it said was this: 'All is well with me; I am in good health and I shall be back with you after ten days. I have sent you a blanket and a brazier cover.'

The woman took the letter and went back to the teacher and said: 'What made you do what you did to me?' and she told him what her neighbour had said, that her husband was safe and well and that he had sent her a blanket and a brazier cover. 'You are right, woman,' he said, 'but you must forgive me as I was angry and preoccupied at the time . . .'

Night 404

Morning now dawned and Shahrazad broke off from what she had been allowed to say. Then, when it was the four hundred and fourth night, SHE CONTINUED:

I have heard, O fortunate king, that when the woman asked the teacher what had led him to do what he had done, he said: 'I was angry and preoccupied at the time, and when I saw the cover wrapped in the blanket I thought that your husband was dead and had been wrapped in a shroud.' The woman did not see that he was tricking her and so she accepted his excuse and went off with her letter.

A story is told that a certain king went out in disguise to investigate the affairs of his subjects. He came to a large village, which he entered alone, and as he was thirsty he stopped at the door of one of its houses to ask for a drink. A pretty woman came out with a jug of water which she gave to him and which he drank. When he looked at her, however, he was tempted and tried to seduce her. She recognized who he was and took him into her house, where she sat him down and gave him a book. 'Look at this,' she said, 'while I get myself ready, and then I'll come back to you.' The king sat down and looked at the book, which contained an admonition against fornication and an account of the tortures prepared by God for fornicators. This made his flesh creep; he repented to Almighty God and, calling out to the woman, he returned the book to her and went off.

When the woman's husband, who had been away, returned, she told him what had happened. He was taken aback, saying to himself: 'I am afraid that the king may have his eyes on her,' and he did not then dare to sleep with her. Things went on like that for some time and when the woman told her relatives what had happened to her husband, they took him up to the king. When they appeared before him, they said: 'May God ennoble the king; this man rented from us a field for tilling, but after tilling it for a time, he has left it fallow and he neither abandons it so that we can rent it to someone who will work on it, nor does it himself. This harms the land, and we are afraid that it may be spoiled if left unworked, for this is what happens to such fields.' The king asked the husband: 'What keeps you from tilling your land?' He said: 'May God ennoble the king; I heard that a lion had come there and, as I was afraid and fearful of it, I did not dare approach the field, knowing that I could not stand against the lion.' The king grasped the point and said: 'Man, the lion did not tread on your field. It is good land for tilling, so till it and may God bless it for you, as the lion will not attack it.' He then ordered the man and his wife to be given a handsome gift and he sent everyone off.

A story is told that there was a man from the Maghrib who had travelled widely, crossing deserts and seas. Fate led him to an island where he stayed for a long time, and when he went back home, he took with him the quill of a wing-feather of a young *rukh* which could hold the contents of a water skin. It is said that the wing of a young *rukh*, when it hatches, is a thousand fathoms long, and the sight of that quill used to fill people with amazement.

The man's name was 'Abd al-Rahman al-Maghribi, and he was known as 'the Chinaman' because of how long he had lived there. He used to tell marvellous stories, and among them was that he was sailing in the China seas . . .

Night 405

Morning now dawned and Shahrazad broke off from what she had been allowed to say. Then, when it was the four hundred and fifth night, SHE CONTINUED:

I have heard, O fortunate king, that he used to tell marvellous stories, and among them was that he was sailing in the China seas with a group of others when in the distance they saw an island. They anchored there and, as it was a very large place, they all disembarked, including 'Abd al-Rahman, to fetch water and wood, taking with them axes, ropes and water skins. On the island they saw a huge gleaming white dome, a hundred cubits in length. They went towards it and when they got near they found that this was a *rukh*'s egg. They started to hack at it with axes, stones and pieces of wood until it split to reveal a baby *rukh* as big as a firmly based mountain. They tried to pull a feather from its wing, but in spite of the fact that the baby's feathers were not fully formed, they all had to help each other to do this. They took as much of the flesh as they could, carrying it away with them, and they cut the root of the feather from its attachment to the quill. Then they set sail and travelled all night until sunrise, helped by a favourable wind, but as they sailed on, suddenly the *rukh* itself appeared, like a great cloud, carrying in its talons an enormous rock, larger than the ship itself. When it flew over the ship, it dropped the rock on it and its crew. The ship's speed, however, took it clear and the rock fell into the sea, causing panic as it did so, but God had decreed that the crew should be saved and He rescued them from destruction.

They cooked and ate the baby *rukh*'s flesh. Among them were some white-bearded old men and the next morning they found that their beards were black, nor did anyone who had eaten that flesh ever turn grey. Some said that the reason for the recovery of their youth and for the fact that their hair never changed colour was that they had used a spoon made of arrow wood to stir the cooking pot, while others said that it was the flesh itself. This is one of the greatest wonders.

A story is told that al-Nuʿman ibn al-Mundhir, the king of the Arabs, had a daughter named Hind. One Easter Day, this being a Christian feast day, she went out to Communion in the White Church when she was eleven years old and one of the most beautiful women of her age. It happened that on the same day ʿAdi ibn Zaid had come to al-Hira from Chosroe, bringing a gift to al-Nuʿman, and he too went to the White Church to take Communion. He was a tall man, sweet-natured, with fine eyes and smooth cheeks. With him were a number of his own clansmen, while Hind had with her a slave girl named Maria. This Maria had been in love with ʿAdi but had not been able to get to him. When she saw him in the church she said to Hind: 'Look at that young man; by God, he is the most handsome man to be seen.' 'Who is he?' asked Hind. 'ʿAdi ibn Zaid,' Maria told her. Hind then said: 'I'm afraid that he may recognize me if I go up to take a closer look at him,' but Maria said: 'How could he, when he's never seen you before?'

Hind went closer to him as he was joking with his young companions, whom he outshone in beauty and eloquence of speech, as well as in the splendour of his clothes. When she looked at him, she fell under his spell and was so taken aback that she changed colour. Maria, seeing how attracted she was to him, told her to speak to him, which she did and she then left. When ʿAdi looked at her and heard her speak, he too was fascinated and so taken aback that his heart fluttered and his colour changed, to the disapproval of his companions. He whispered to one of them to follow the girl and find out who she was, and, having done this,

this man returned to tell him that she was al-Nu'man's daughter, Hind. 'Adi left the church without knowing where he was going, such was the intensity of his love, and he recited these lines:

My two companions, do me another favour
And journey to the land of the Biqa'.
Turn me aside towards the dwelling of Hind;
Then go, and carry news of me.

After having finished his poem, he went home and spent a sleepless night in a state of agitation.

Night 406

Morning now dawned and Shahrazad broke off from what she had been allowed to say. Then, when it was the four hundred and sixth night, SHE CONTINUED:

I have heard, O fortunate king, that after having finished his poem, he went home and spent a sleepless night in a state of agitation.

The next morning he was met by Maria and, although before that he had not been in the habit of paying any attention to her, he smiled at her and asked her what she wanted. 'There is something that I need from you,' she said. 'Tell me what it is,' he replied, 'for, by God, I will give you whatever you ask.' She then told him that she loved him and wanted to be alone with him, and he agreed to that on condition that she find some way of bringing him together with Hind. He then took her into a wine seller's shop in one of the streets of al-Hira, where he lay with her. When she left she went to Hind and said: 'Don't you want to see 'Adi?' 'How can I?' asked Hind, adding: 'I am distracted by longing for him and since yesterday I've not been able to rest.' Maria told her that she would get him to come to a certain place, where Hind would be able to look at him from the palace. 'Do what you want,' Hind told her, and the two of them agreed on the place.

When 'Adi came and Hind looked down at him, she almost fell from the castle roof and she said: 'Maria, if you don't bring him in to me tonight I shall die.' She then collapsed in a faint and her maids had to carry her into the palace. Maria went to al-Nu'man and gave him a true account of the affair, telling him that Hind was desperately in love with 'Adi and saying that unless he married her to him, she would be put to shame and die of love, something that the Arabs would hold against him as a disgrace. The only solution, she told him, was to have her married to 'Adi. Al-Nu'man looked down thoughtfully for a time, and recited the formula 'We belong to God and to Him do we return' a number of times. He then asked Maria how the matter could be arranged, saying: 'I don't want to be the first to raise it with him.' She said: 'He is even more deeply and passionately in love with her, and I shall contrive things so that he doesn't find out that you know about it and you will not be put to shame.'

Maria now went to 'Adi and told him the news. 'Invite the king to a meal,' she said, 'and when he is in his cups, ask him for his daughter's hand, for he is not going to refuse you.' 'I'm afraid that that might anger him,' said 'Adi, 'and lead us to become enemies.' 'I settled the matter with him before coming to you,' Maria assured him, and she went back to al-Nu'man and told him to ask 'Adi to invite him to his house. 'There can be no harm in that,' the king replied, and three days later he asked 'Adi to invite him and his companions to a meal in his house. 'Adi agreed to this and al-Nu'man went to him. When the wine was having an effect on him, 'Adi got up and asked him for his daughter's hand, a proposal which he accepted. He arranged for the marriage and after three days he had Hind brought to her bridegroom, with whom she stayed for three years, as the two of them enjoyed the pleasantest and happiest of lives . . .

Night 407

Morning now dawned and Shahrazad broke off from what she had been allowed to say. Then, when it was the four hundred and seventh night, SHE CONTINUED:

I have heard, O fortunate king, that 'Adi stayed with Hind for three years as they enjoyed the pleasantest and happiest of lives until al-Nu'man killed 'Adi in a fit of anger. Hind mourned deeply for him and then built herself a convent outside al-Hira where she became a nun, weeping for him and lamenting until she died. Her convent is well known to this day on the outskirts of al-Hira.

It is told that DI'BIL AL-KHUZA'I SAID:

I was sitting by the gate of al-Karkh when the loveliest girl with the best figure I had ever seen went past, swaying as she walked and captivating all those who watched her doing so. When my eyes fell on her she fascinated me and my heart fluttered so wildly that I thought it must have taken flight from my breast. I went up to her reciting this line:

Tears pour from my eyes and sleep is shut away from my eyelids.

She looked at me, turned her face and quickly answered me with this line:

That is little enough for one whom languorous eyes summon with a
glance.

The speed of her reply astonished me, together with her eloquence, and so I recited a second line:

Does the heart of my lady feel sympathy for the lover whose tears
rain down?

Without pausing, she replied quickly:

If you wish for my love, know that love between us is a loan.

I had never heard sweeter speech or seen a more beautiful face, and in order to test her I changed the rhyme out of admiration for her skill with words, and I recited:

Will Time, do you think, grant us a happy meeting, uniting longing
lovers?

She smiled, showing me the loveliest and sweetest of mouths, and replied quickly and unhesitatingly:

You are Time, so gladden me with a meeting.

I got up in a hurry and started to kiss her hands, saying: 'I did not think that Time would grant me an opportunity like this. If you follow me, it will be not because you are ordered or forced to do this against your will, but as an act of grace and favour.' I then turned back, and she followed after me. At that time I had no house which I thought suitable for a girl like that, but Muslim ibn al-Walid was a friend of mine, and as he had a fine house I made my way to him. When I knocked on the door he came out and I greeted him and said: 'It is for times like these that one treasures friends.' He welcomed us graciously and invited us in, but we found that he was short of money and so he gave me a kerchief and told me to go to the market, sell it and buy food and whatever else

I needed. I went off there in a hurry, sold the kerchief and bought what we needed, but when I got back I discovered that Muslim had gone down alone with the girl into an underground room.

When he heard me come in, he jumped out to meet me and said: 'God reward and repay you, Abu 'Ali, for the favour that you have done me, and may this be added to the list of your good deeds, to be rewarded at the Day of Judgement.' He took the food and the drink and then shut the door in my face. I was annoyed by his words but I did not know what to do and he stood behind the door shaking with laughter. Seeing my annoyance, he asked me to tell him who was the author of the lines:

I spent the night within her shift while my friend spent his
Impure in heart, but undefiled in body.

I grew even angrier and I said: 'Its author was the man who said:

One within whose belt are a thousand cuckold horns,
Taller than the idol of Manaf.'*

Then I started to hurl insults at him and to abuse him for his foul act and his lack of chivalry. To start with he was silent and said nothing, but when my tirade was finished, he smiled and said: 'Damn you for a fool! You came into my house, sold my kerchief and spent my money, so with whom are you angry, you pander?' He left me and went back to the girl. I said: 'You're right to count me a fool and a pimp,' and I turned away from his door in a state of distress which has still left its effects on me today. I never had my way with the girl and I never heard of her again.

It is told that ISHAQ AL-MAUSILI SAID:

I grew tired of constantly having to be in attendance on the caliph in his palace and so early one day I mounted and rode out, intending to go on a trip through the countryside, and I had told my servants that if a messenger came from the caliph or from anyone else they were to say that I had gone off early on some important business of my own, but they did not know where. I then set out alone and went through the city, but when it got hot I stopped in a street called al-Haram . . .

* An early Arabian idol.

Night 408

Morning now dawned and Shahrazad broke off from what she had been
allowed to say. Then, when it was the four hundred and eighth night,
SHE CONTINUED:

I have heard, O fortunate king, that ISHAQ SAID:

When it got hot I stopped in a street called al-Haram to shelter from
the sun. There was a house there which had an extensive projection
jutting out over the street. Before I had been there long, a black eunuch
turned up leading a donkey which I could see was being ridden by a girl
whose saddle cloth was studded with gems and who was wearing a dress
of unsurpassable splendour. She was marked by gracefulness and had a
lovely figure and languorous eyes. I asked a passer-by about her and was
told that she was a singer.

As soon as I saw her I fell in love with her, so much so that I could
not keep my seat on my saddle. She went into the house at whose door
I had halted, and I started to think of how I could get to her. While I
was there, two handsome young men came up and asked permission to
enter the house. Its owner allowed them in and I went with them, as
they thought that he must have invited me. After we had sat for a time,
food was brought and when we had eaten, wine was placed before us. Then
the girl came out with a lute in her hand and, as we drank, she sang. I got
up to relieve myself and the owner of the house then asked the two men
about me, at which they said that they didn't know me. 'He must be a
parasite,' the owner said, 'but he is a witty fellow, so treat him well.'

I then came back and sat down in my place, after which the girl sang
these lines to a charming tune:

Say to the gazelle who is no gazelle,
And to the kohl-eyed wild calf who is no calf,
She behaves like a man in private but is no woman;
She walks like a woman but is no man.

Her performance was excellent and it impressed the guests who were
drinking. She then sang in various styles to exotic melodies, and among
these was a style of my own, in which she sang the lines:

Deserted camping grounds, abandoned by their folk,
Desolate after having been full of life, waste and erased.

Here her performance was even better than before, and she followed this with various other styles and unusual airs, old and new, among which she included another of mine, to which she sang:

> Say to the one who turns away reproachfully,
> Remaining aloof from you,
> 'You reached the goal you reached,
> Though you were only playing.'

I asked her to sing it again so that I could show her how to get it right, but one of the two guests came up to me and said: 'I have never seen a more impudent fellow than you. Not content with playing the parasite, you act brashly, confirming the proverbial saying "a parasite and brash".' I hung my head in shame making no reply, and although his friend tried to keep him away from me, he was not to be restrained. They then got up to perform the prayer, but I held back for a little until I had taken the lute and tightened and tuned it properly. Then I returned to my place and joined them in the prayer. When we had finished my opponent resumed his bitter abuse and kept on trying to pick a quarrel, while I stayed silent.

The girl then took the lute, but when she touched it she found that there was something different about it and said: 'Who has been touching my lute?' 'None of us have touched it,' they said, but she insisted: 'By God, it has certainly been touched by someone who knows about this art, as the strings have been tuned by a master.' 'It was I who tuned it,' I told her. 'For God's sake, then, take it and play on it,' she said, and I took it and played a strange and difficult air, to kill the living with delight and raise the dead. These were the lines that I sang:

> I had a heart which gave me life,
> But then it was consumed and burned with fire.
> Her love had not been granted me by God,
> And His servants have only what He grants.
> If my distress becomes the food of love,
> This, then, is what all lovers have to taste.

Night 409

Morning now dawned and Shahrazad broke off from what she had been allowed to say. Then, when it was the four hundred and ninth night, SHE CONTINUED:

I have heard, O fortunate king, that ISHAQ SAID:

When I had finished these lines they all jumped up from their places and sat in front of me, urging me to give them another song. 'Willingly,' I said, and so, accompanying myself with skill, I sang:

Who will help a heart wasted by misfortune,
The halting place of sorrows coming from all sides?
For the beloved who shot an arrow at this heart,
The blood between my entrails and my ribs was shed unlawfully.
On the day of parting it was clear that false suspicion
Had led her to leave me.
She shed my blood, which, but for love, would not have flowed,
And is there any to seek vengeance for my blood?

When the song was finished they all rose to their feet before throwing themselves to the ground in delight. I tossed the lute away, but they pleaded with me saying: 'For God's sake, don't do this to us, but give us another song, may God Almighty increase His favours to you.' I told them: 'I shall give you another song and another and another, and I shall tell you who I am, for I am Ishaq ibn Ibrahim al-Mausili. Even when the caliph summons me, I act with haughtiness, but, thanks to you, I have had to listen today to the kind of vulgar abuse that I detest, and I swear that I shall utter no single word more or sit with you any longer until you throw this quarrelsome fellow out.' The owner of the house said to him: 'I warned you of this and I was afraid for you,' after which they took him by the hand and led him off.

I then picked up the lute again and sang those of my airs that the girl had sung, after which I whispered to the owner of the house that I had fallen in love with her and could not endure without her. 'You may have her,' said the man, 'on one condition.' 'What is that?' I asked, and he said: 'That you stay with me for a month, after which the girl, with her jewellery and robes, will be yours.' I agreed to this and stayed with him for the month without anyone knowing where I was, and although the caliph looked everywhere for me he could find no news of me. At the end of the month, her master handed the girl over to me together with her treasures and he also gave me another eunuch. I took all this back home, thinking that I had won the whole world, such was my delight at having got the girl.

I rode off immediately to visit al-Ma'mun, and when I came into his presence he said: 'Damn you, Ishaq, where have you been?' When I told him the story, he gave orders that the owner of the house was to be brought to him immediately, and I told him where he lived. The caliph sent for him and asked him on his arrival about what had happened. The man told him and the caliph said: 'You are a chivalrous man and, in my opinion, you should be helped in your chivalry,' after which he gave him a hundred thousand dirhams. Next, he told me to bring the girl, which I did, and as her singing delighted him and gave him the greatest pleasure, he decreed that she was to be in attendance every Thursday at the palace and to sing from behind the curtain of the harem. I was given fifty thousand dirhams, and so not only did I gain by my excursion, but it turned out to be profitable to others as well.

It is told that AL-'UTBI SAID:

One day I was sitting with a number of literary men and while we were talking about past days, the conversation turned to tales of lovers, to which each of us contributed. One old man had remained silent, but when the others had all finished he said: 'Shall I tell you a story the like of which you have never heard?' 'Yes,' we said, and he began: 'You must know that I had a daughter who, although we didn't know it, loved a young man who for his part loved a singing girl who loved my daughter. One day I was at a gathering at which the young man was present . . .'

Night 410

Morning now dawned and Shahrazad broke off from what she had been allowed to say. Then, when it was the four hundred and tenth night, SHE CONTINUED:

I have heard, O fortunate king, that THE OLD MAN SAID:

One day I was at a gathering at which the young man was present, and the singing girl, who was also there, sang these lines:

For lovers, tears are signs of love's humiliation,
Especially for a lover finding no other who complains.

'Well done, by God, my lady,' said the young man, adding: 'Will you let me die?' 'Yes,' she replied from behind the curtain, 'if you are a true lover.' He put his head on a cushion and closed his eyes; then, when the wine cup came round to him, we shook him but he was dead.

We gathered around him with all our pleasure having turned to sadness, and immediately after that we dispersed gloomily. My family were annoyed with me because I had not come back at my usual time, but in order to astonish them I told them what had happened to the young man. My daughter heard what I said and left the room where I was and went to another. I followed her and when I entered the room, I discovered her with her head on a cushion in exactly the same way that I had described the young man as lying, and, on shaking her, I found that she too was dead. We laid out her corpse, and when we carried it on a bier the next morning we met the funeral procession of the young man. Then, on the way to the cemetery, we came across a third bier being carried, and when we asked about this, we were told that the body was that of the singing girl, who, when she heard of my daughter's death, had died in exactly the same way. All three were buried on the same day and this is the most astonishing of lovers' tales.

A story is told on the authority of al-Qasim ibn 'Adi about a man of the Banu Tamim. THIS MAN SAID:

I once went out in search of a stray beast and came to the watering places of the Banu Tayy, where I saw two groups of people standing close to each other and each group seemed to be having the same kind of argument. When I looked more closely, I saw a young man debilitated by illness and looking like a worn-out water skin. While I watched he recited these lines:

> Why does the lovely one not return?
> Is it meanness on her part or is she shunning me?
> I am ill, and all my family have visited my sickbed;
> Why are you not there among my visitors?
> Were you unwell, I would hurry to your side;
> No threats would make me leave.
> I cannot find you in the tribe and I remain alone;
> The loss of your love, you who bring me ease, is hard to bear.

A girl standing in the second group heard what he said and ran in his direction, pursued by her family. She started to strike at them, and when the young man saw this he leapt towards her, as his family rushed at him and seized hold of him. He started to pull himself away, while the girl struggled to win clear of her own pursuers. When they were both free they ran towards each other, met, embraced between the two groups and then fell to the ground dead.

Night 411

Morning now dawned and Shahrazad broke off from what she had been allowed to say. Then, when it was the four hundred and eleventh night, SHE CONTINUED:

I have heard, O fortunate king, that the young man and the girl met and embraced between the two groups, and then fell to the ground dead.

THE MAN OF THE BANU TAMIM WENT ON:

An old man came from the tents, stood over them and recited the formula: 'To God we belong and to Him do we return.' Then, shedding bitter tears, he said: 'May Almighty God have mercy on the two of you! By God, if you were not united while you were alive, I shall unite you now you are dead.' He ordered the preparations to be made, and after their bodies had been washed, they were covered by the same shroud and one grave was dug for them both. The people recited prayers over them, after which they were buried in that grave and I saw nobody, man or woman, in the two groups who was not weeping and slapping their own face. I asked the old man about the two and he told me: 'This was my daughter and the other was my brother's son. It was love that brought them to the end that you have seen.' I asked him why he had not allowed them to marry each other and he replied: 'I was afraid of shame and disgrace, into which I have now fallen.'

This is one of the remarkable stories of lovers.

It is told that ABU'L-'ABBAS AL-MUBARRAD SAID:

I was going with a company of travellers to al-Barid on business when we passed the monastery of Ezekiel. We had dismounted in the shade there when we were approached by a man who told us that in the monastery were madmen, among whom there was one who spoke words of wisdom. 'If you saw him,' the man added, 'you would be astounded by what he says.' We all got up and went into the monastery, where we

saw a man sitting bare-headed on a mat in a small room, his eyes fixed
on the wall.

We greeted him and he returned the greeting without looking at us.
'Recite him some poetry,' said our guide, 'for when he hears poetry he
speaks.' So I recited:

> You are the best of Eve's children;
> Were it not for you, there would be nothing good or pleasant in the world.
> Those to whom God has shown your face
> Win immortality, not growing old or grey.

When the man heard this, he turned towards us and recited:

> God knows that I am sorrowful,
> And I cannot express the sorrow that I feel.
> I have two souls, one that stays here,
> While the second has another place.
> I think my absent soul is like mine here,
> And that it suffers the same pain I feel.

He then asked: 'Are my lines good or bad?' 'They are certainly not bad;
on the contrary, they are very good indeed,' we told him. He reached
out for a stone that he had by him and, thinking that he was going to
throw it at us, we ran away from him, but instead he used it to strike his
own chest with violent blows. 'Don't be afraid,' he told us, 'but come
closer to hear something of mine that you can take off with you.' We
went up to him and he recited:

> When they made their camels kneel just before the dawn,
> They mounted her on the crupper; the camels took away my love.
> I looked at her through prison bars,
> And said, as my tears flowed thanks to the pangs of love:
> 'Camel driver, turn, so that I may take my leave of her;
> In separation and leave-taking lies our death.'
> I never broke my pledge of love for her;
> I wish I knew what they did with that pledge.

He then looked at me and said: 'Do you know what has happened to
them?' 'Yes,' I said, 'they are dead, may God Almighty have mercy on
them.' His expression changed and he jumped up, saying: 'How do you
know they are dead?' 'Were they alive,' I told him, 'they would not have
abandoned you in this state.' 'True, by God,' he said and added: 'Now

that they are gone, I too have no more love for life.' He quivered and then fell on his face. We rushed up and shook him, but he was dead, may Almighty God have mercy on him. Astonished and deeply saddened, we made the preparations and then buried him.

Night 412

Morning now dawned and Shahrazad broke off from what she had been allowed to say. Then, when it was the four hundred and twelfth night, SHE CONTINUED:

I have heard, O fortunate king, that ABU'L-'ABBAS AL-MUBARRAD SAID:

When the man fell dead we were saddened and, after making the preparations, we buried him. When I got back to Baghdad I went to visit the caliph al-Mutawakkil, who saw the marks of tears on my face and asked me what had happened. I then told him the story, which displeased him, and he said: 'What made you say what you did? By God, if I saw that you were not sorry for it, I would punish you.' Then he grieved for the dead lover for the rest of the day.

It is told that ABU BAKR IBN MUHAMMAD AL-ANBARI SAID:

I left al-Anbar on a journey to 'Ammuriya in Byzantine territory and on the way I halted at the monastery of Dair al-Anwar in a village close to 'Ammuriya itself. The head of the monastery, the superior of the monks, a man called 'Abd al-Masih, came to me and brought me in, and I found forty monks there who entertained me admirably that night. I left the next day after having seen a devotion to worship on the part of the monks that I had never met anywhere else. Then, after finishing my business in 'Ammuriya, I went back to Anbar.

In the following year I made the pilgrimage to Mecca, and while I was perambulating the Ka'ba I saw 'Abd al-Masih, the monk, who was also performing the perambulation together with five other monks of his. When I was sure who he was, I went up to him and said: 'Aren't you 'Abd al-Masih, the monk?' 'No,' he told me, 'I am 'Abd Allah, who seeks God's mercy.' I started to kiss his grey hairs, weeping as I did so, and then, taking him by the hand, I led him to the side to the sacred precinct, where I asked him to tell me how he had come to be converted to Islam. 'That was a great wonder,' HE REPLIED, AND WENT ON:

A group of Muslim ascetics passed by the village where our monastery stands and they sent a young man off to buy food for them. In the market he saw and was charmed by a very lovely Christian girl, who was selling bread. He fell on his face in a faint and when he had recovered he went back to his companions to tell them what had happened, adding: 'Go on your way; I am not going with you.' They reproached him and warned him, but it was no use and so they left him. He went into the village and sat by the door of the girl's shop, and when she asked what he wanted, he told her that he was in love with her. She turned away from him and he stayed there for three days without eating, staring at her face. When she saw that he was not going to leave her, she went to her family and told them about him. They turned the boys on him and the boys, for their part, threw stones at him, bruising his ribs and cutting his head. When this didn't make him leave, the villagers determined to kill him, but one of them came to me and told me of the state the Muslim was in. I went out to see him and, finding him lying on the ground, I wiped the blood from his face, carried him to the monastery and treated his wounds. He stayed with me for fourteen days and when he could walk, he left . . .

Night 413

Morning now dawned and Shahrazad broke off from what she had been allowed to say. Then, when it was the four hundred and thirteenth night, SHE CONTINUED:

I have heard, O fortunate king, that THE MONK SAID:

I carried him to the monastery and treated his wounds. He stayed with me for fourteen days and when he could walk, he left, and went back to the door of the girl's shop, where he again sat staring at her.

When she saw him there, she went up to him and said: 'By God, I am sorry for you and if you convert to my religion, I will marry you.' 'God forbid,' he replied, 'that I should shrug off monotheism and become a polytheist.' 'Then come into the house with me,' she told him. 'Do what you want with me and then go off, still following your own faith.' He said: 'I cannot sacrifice twelve years of worship for a single minute's lust.' 'Then leave me,' she said, but he replied: 'My heart will not let me go.' She turned her face away from him, and the boys, seeing him there, came up and started throwing stones at him. He fell on his face, quoting from the Quran: 'My defender is God, Who sent down the Book, and it is He Who protects the righteous.'*

I came out of the monastery and chased away the boys. Then I lifted his head from the ground and heard him say: 'My God, unite me with her in Paradise.' I carried him towards the monastery but he died before I could get him there. I then brought him out of the village, dug him a grave and buried him. Halfway through the night the girl shrieked as she lay in her bed and the villagers gathered around and asked her what had happened. She told them: 'As I was sleeping, that Muslim came to me and, taking me by the hand, he led me to Paradise, but when we reached the gate, its guardian would not let me go in and said: "This is forbidden to unbelievers." So I accepted Islam at his hands and went in with him. There I saw pavilions and trees such as I cannot describe for you, and the Muslim took me to a pavilion made of jewels and told me: "This is for you and me, but I shall not enter it until you are with me and this will be after five nights, if God Almighty wills." He then reached out to a tree growing at the door of the pavilion and picked two apples, which he gave me. He told me to eat one but to hide away the other for the monks to see. So I ate one of them and I have never experienced anything sweeter.'

Night 414

Morning now dawned and Shahrazad broke off from what she had been allowed to say. Then, when it was the four hundred and fourteenth night, SHE CONTINUED:

I have heard, O fortunate king, that 'ABD ALLAH EXPLAINED THAT THE GIRL SAID:

'He picked two apples, which he gave me. He told me to eat one but to hide away the other for the monks to see. So I ate one of them and I have never experienced anything sweeter. He then took me by the hand and led me away, bringing me back to my own house. When I woke up, I found the taste of the apple still in my mouth and the second apple was still with me. I took it out and it shone in the dark night like a bright star.'

The villagers took the girl, with her apple, to the monastery, where

* Quran 7.195.

she told us of her dream and then she produced the apple for us, which was like no other fruit that we had ever seen anywhere in the world. I took a knife and cut it into pieces, one for each of my companions, and it was the most delicious thing that we had ever tasted, with the sweetest scent, but we said: 'It may be that this was a devil who appeared to her to seduce her from her religion.' So her family took her off, and she then refused to eat or drink. On the fifth night she got up from her bed, left the house and set off for the Muslim's grave, where she threw herself down and died, without her family knowing what had happened.

The next morning, two Muslim *shaikhs*, together with two women, all wearing hair shirts, came to the village and told the inhabitants that in the village was one of God's saints who had died as a Muslim, adding: 'We shall take charge of her rather than you.' The villagers looked for the girl and found her lying dead on the Muslim's grave. 'She is one of ours,' they said. 'She died as a Christian and it is we who will look after her.' 'No, she died a Muslim and we shall do it,' they insisted. There was a violent dispute between the two sides and then one of the *shaikhs* said: 'As proof that she was a Muslim, let the forty monks of the monastery come together to try to pull her away from the grave. If they can lift her from the ground, then she was a Christian, but if they cannot, one of us will come and pull, and if he moves her corpse, then she was a Muslim.' The villagers agreed to that and the forty monks joined together, encouraging each other, but when they came to carry her off, they failed. We then tied a large rope around her waist and pulled, but the rope broke and the corpse did not move. The villagers came up and tried to move her, but still without success. When nothing that we tried would work, we told one of the *shaikhs* to come and carry her away. He came and wrapped her in his cloak, saying: 'In the Name of God, the Compassionate, the Merciful: this is in accordance with the religion of the Apostle of God, may God bless him and give him peace.' He then carried her off in his arms, and he and the other Muslims took her to a cave in which they laid her. The two women washed and shrouded the corpse, after which the *shaikhs* carried her away, prayed over her and buried her beside the grave of the young Muslim.

Having seen all this we left, and when we were alone with one another, we said to ourselves: 'It is better to follow the truth* and it is the truth that we have witnessed with our own eyes. There can be no proof of the

* Quran 10.36.

validity of Islam clearer than the one that we have seen.' I then converted to Islam, as did all the other monks of the monastery together with the people of the village. We sent to the Muslims of the Jazira asking for a teacher to instruct us in the laws of Islam and its regulations. A virtuous man came to us and showed us how to worship God and what it is that Islam decrees. Now, praise and thanks be to God, we are enjoying the greatest good fortune.

It is told that 'AMR IBN MAS'ADA SAID:

Abu 'Isa, the son of al-Rashid and the brother of al-Ma'mun, was in love with Qurrat al-'Ain, a slave girl belonging to 'Ali ibn Hisham, who was herself in love with Abu 'Isa. Abu 'Isa concealed his love, neither revealing it nor complaining of it to anyone, and letting no one into his secret as a result of his pride and his sense of manliness. He had tried by every means that he could to buy her from her master but had failed. Then, when he could no longer bear the intensity of his passion and was entirely at a loss to know what to do about her, he approached al-Ma'mun on an assembly day after the people had left him. 'Commander of the Faithful,' he said, 'were you to pay surprise visits to your officers today to test them, you would be able to distinguish the generous from the ungenerous and determine how each of them ranked in point of magnanimity.' What he intended by this speech was to get an opportunity of sitting with Qurrat al-'Ain in her master's house. Al-Ma'mun agreed that this was a good idea and ordered *The Flyer*, as the boat was called, to be prepared for him. When *The Flyer* was brought up, the caliph embarked with a number of his intimates. The first mansion he entered was that of Hamid al-Tawil of Tus, who was taken by surprise and was found seated . . .

Night 415

Morning now dawned and Shahrazad broke off from what she had been allowed to say. Then, when it was the four hundred and fifteenth night, SHE CONTINUED:

I have heard, O fortunate king, that the caliph embarked with a number of his intimates and sailed on until they reached the mansion of Hamid al-Tawil of Tus, who was taken by surprise and was found seated on a mat, surrounded by singers holding musical instruments – lutes, flutes and so forth. After the caliph had sat there for a time, Hamid produced food, but this consisted only of meat dishes with no poultry, and the caliph ignored them.

Abu 'Isa pointed out that they had arrived unexpectedly and without warning, and suggested that they move on somewhere else where more suitable preparations could be made. So the caliph with his entourage and Abu 'Isa, his brother, went to the house of 'Ali ibn Hisham. When he learned of their arrival, he greeted them with the greatest courtesy, kissing the ground in front of the caliph and leading them in, where he opened the door of the most beautiful room that they had ever seen. Its floor, pillars and walls were made of various types of marble; it was adorned with Byzantine paintings; on the floor were mats from Sind and there were Basran carpets designed to cover the length and breadth of the room. The caliph sat for a time looking round the room, its ceiling and its walls, and he then asked for something to eat. In an instant he was provided with close to a hundred types of poultry as well as other birds, together with broths, fried dishes and others pungently seasoned. He then asked for drink, and they brought him a liqueur flavoured with fruit, and sweet spices in goblets of gold, silver and crystal. Two pages, lovely as moons, brought this in, wearing gold-embroidered Alexandrian robes, carrying in front of them trays with crystal jugs of rosewater scented with musk.

Al-Ma'mun was astonished by what he saw and called for his host, who jumped up, kissed the carpet and, standing in front of him, said: 'Here I am, Commander of the Faithful.' 'Let me hear some pleasant songs,' the caliph said, and 'Ali replied: 'To hear is to obey,' after which he told one of his servants to fetch the singing girls. The man obediently left for a minute and then came back with ten eunuchs carrying ten gold chairs. When these had been arranged, in walked ten girls like gleaming moons or flowery meadows, wearing black brocade, with golden crowns on their heads. They took their seats and sang a variety of airs. One of them bewitched al-Ma'mun with her elegance and beauty. He asked her her name and she told him: 'It is Sajah, Commander of the Faithful.' He asked her to sing something and so, striking up an air, she produced these lines:

I came to the assembly, walking there in fear,
As one abashed at the sight of two lion cubs that had come.
My weapon is humility; my heart is full of passion and of dread;
I fear the eyes of enemies and those who watch.

Then I came on a tender girl,
Like a gazelle of the sand dunes which has lost her young.

'Well done, girl!' exclaimed al-Ma'mun, and he asked her who the poet was. ''Amr ibn Ma'di Karib,' she told him. 'And the air was by Ma'bid.' Al-Ma'mun drank, as did Abu 'Isa and 'Ali ibn Hisham, after which the ten girls left, to be replaced by ten others, wearing variegated Yemeni brocades, who took their seats and sang another selection of airs. The caliph looked at one of them, who was like a wild cow of the sands and who told him, when he asked, that her name was Zabya. 'Sing something, Zabya,' he said, at which full-throatedly she trilled the lines:

Freeborn dark-eyed girls, unworried by suspicion,
Like Meccan gazelles, not lawfully to be hunted;
Their smooth speech makes them seem unchaste,
But Islam turns them from obscenity.

When she had finished, the caliph praised her . . .

Night 416

Morning now dawned and Shahrazad broke off from what she had been allowed to say. Then, when it was the four hundred and sixteenth night, SHE CONTINUED:

I have heard, O fortunate king, that when she had finished, the caliph praised her, and when he asked the name of the poet, she told him that this was Jarir, while the air was by Ibn Suraij. The caliph and his companions then drank again, and the girls were replaced by another ten, like jewels, bare-headed and wearing red brocade interwoven with gold thread and studded with pearls and gems. They too took their seats and sang a number of airs. This time it was a girl radiant as the sun whose name the caliph asked. She told him that it was Fatin, and when he told her to sing she struck up an air and sang these lines:

Grant me union with you, for it is time;
I have tasted enough of separation.
Yours is a face that holds all loveliness;
I can no longer bear parting from it.
My whole life has been spent in love for you;
Would that this spending were repaid by union.

She too was praised by the caliph, and in reply to his question she told him that the poet was 'Adi ibn Zaid and that the words were set to an old air. The caliph and the others then drank again; the ten girls left and in came ten more, like gleaming stars, wearing variegated silks interwoven with red gold, while round their waists were jewelled girdles. They sat down and sang, after which the caliph asked the name of one of them, who was slender as a branch of a *ban* tree. She told him that her name was Rash', and when he told her to sing she struck up an air to which she sang these lines:

> A dark-eyed one, slender as a branch, a cure for longing,
> Like a gazelle when it passes on its way –
> I drank a toast to her cheek,
> Wresting the wine cup from her till she was bent double.
> We passed the night together, with her as my partner;
> I told myself: 'This is the goal of all desire.'

'Well done,' said the caliph, and he asked for another song. The girl kissed the ground in front of him and then sang these words:

> She came out to see the wedding at her leisure,
> In a gown perfumed with ambergris.

The caliph was delighted, and when the girl saw this she started to sing the words over and over again. At this point he ordered *The Flyer* to be brought up and was intending to embark and go off when 'Ali ibn Hisham said to him: 'Commander of the Faithful, I have a slave girl whom I bought for ten thousand dinars and who has taken over the whole of my heart. I would like to show her to you, and if she wins your approval, then she is yours, while if not, you can still hear her sing something.' 'Bring her to me,' said the caliph, and out came a girl slender as a branch of a *ban* tree, with seductive eyes and eyebrows like bows, wearing on her head a crown of red gold set with pearls and gems, beneath which was a headband inscribed in letters of chrysolite with this line:

> A *jinn* girl, taught by *jinn* to shoot at hearts using a stringless bow.

The girl walked like a straying gazelle, enchanting God's servants, until she sat down on a chair.

Night 417

Morning now dawned and Shahrazad broke off from what she had been allowed to say. Then, when it was the four hundred and seventeenth night, SHE CONTINUED:

I have heard, O fortunate king, that the girl walked like a straying gazelle, enchanting God's servants, until she sat down on a chair. Al-Ma'mun was astonished by her beauty, while Abu 'Isa was sick at heart, changing colour and turning pale. Al-Ma'mun asked him about this and he explained that it was owing to an illness that visited him periodically. 'Did you know this girl before today?' the caliph asked him, to which he answered: 'Yes, and can one hide away the moon?' When the caliph asked the girl her name, she told him that it was Qurrat al-'Ain, and when he asked her to sing, she sang the following verses:

> The loved ones left before daylight,
> Travelling with the pilgrims in the early dawn.
> Around their pavilions were pitched the tents of grandeur,
> And all were veiled with curtains of brocade.

The caliph praised her and asked who was the author of the lines, at which she told him that this was Di'bil al-Khuza'i, and that the air was by Zarzur al-Saghir. Looking at her, Abu 'Isa was choked with sobs, exciting the surprise of the others who were there. The girl turned to al-Ma'mun and asked to be allowed to sing a different set of words. He told her to do what she liked, and so she struck up an air and sang these lines:

> If you please a beloved who pleases you
> And makes this clear, make a secret of your love.
> Disappoint the tale-telling slanderers; it is rare
> That slanderers wish for anything but lovers' parting.
> They claim that, when a lover is near at hand,
> He becomes bored, and separation cures his passion.
> We have now tried both cures to no effect,
> But to be near is better than to be far away.
> To be near, however, is of no use,
> If the one you love does not, in turn, love you.

When she had finished, Abu 'Isa said: 'Commander of the Faithful . . .'

Night 418

Morning now dawned and Shahrazad broke off from what she had been
allowed to say. Then, when it was the four hundred and eighteenth night,
SHE CONTINUED:

I have heard, O fortunate king, that when she had finished, Abu 'Isa
said: 'Commander of the Faithful, it will be a relief to disclose this affair,
so would you allow me to answer her?' 'Yes,' said the caliph, 'say what
you want to her.' So Abu 'Isa, holding back his tears, recited:

> I stayed silent and did not say I was in love,
> Hiding this love from my own heart.
> If it is to be seen within my eyes,
> This is because they are close to the shining moon.

Qurrat al-'Ain then took the lute, struck up an air and sang:

> Were what you claim true,
> You would not have talked of a mere wish.
> For you could not have borne to lose a girl
> Outstanding for her beauty and her qualities.
> So all your claims are nothing more than empty words.

When she had finished, Abu 'Isa began to weep and wail, showing signs
of pain and distress. He then raised his head towards her, sighed deeply
and recited:

> My clothes cover a wasted form;
> Distraction holds my heart.
> It suffers an illness without end,
> And tears pour from my eyes.
> If ever an intelligent man makes peace with me,
> Love at that moment sends another to rebuke me.
> My Lord, I have no strength to bear all this.
> I must find either quick release or death.

When Abu 'Isa had finished, 'Ali ibn Hisham jumped up, kissed his foot
and said: 'Master, God has answered your prayer and listened to your
supplication. You can take the girl with all her rare and precious treasures, unless the Commander of the Faithful wants her.' 'Even if I did,'
said al-Ma'mun, 'I would prefer Abu 'Isa to have her rather than to take

her myself, and I shall help him to get what he wants.' He then rose and embarked on *The Flyer*, leaving Abu 'Isa behind to take Qurrat al-'Ain, which he did, going off gladly with her to his own house. Consider, then, the generosity of 'Ali ibn Hisham.

A story is told that al-Amin, the brother of al-Ma'mun, entered the house of his uncle, Ibrahim ibn al-Mahdi, where he saw a very beautiful girl playing a lute. He was attracted to her, as was immediately clear to his uncle Ibrahim, who sent her to him, along with splendid robes and precious gems. Al-Amin, however, on seeing her, imagined that his uncle must have slept with her. This made him unwilling to take her and so, while accepting the gift, he sent back the girl herself. One of the eunuchs told Ibrahim of this, and so he took an embroidered gown and wrote these lines on the bottom of it in letters of gold:

> By the One to whom men's foreheads lie prostrate in prayer,
> I swear that I know nothing of what lies beneath her skirt,
> Or of her mouth. I have not troubled myself with this.
> I only talked with her and looked at her.

He then clothed the girl in the gown, gave her a lute and sent her to al-Amin for the second time. When she came to him she kissed the ground before him, tuned her lute and sang these lines:

> You have dishonoured me by sending back my gift,
> Making it clear and plain you want to part from me.
> If you are angry about something that is past,
> Forgive for the sake of the caliphate what is over now.

When she had finished, al-Amin looked at her and, seeing what was written on the skirt of her robe, he could no longer control himself.

Night 419

Morning now dawned and Shahrazad broke off from what she had been allowed to say. Then, when it was the four hundred and nineteenth night, SHE CONTINUED:

I have heard, O fortunate king, that al-Amin looked at her and, seeing what was written on the skirt of her robe, he could no longer control himself. He drew her into an embrace, kissed her and gave her an apartment of her own. In gratitude to his uncle Ibrahim, he appointed him governor of Rayy.

A story is told that when the caliph al-Mutawakkil had been prescribed a purge, he received a large variety of rare gifts. Al-Fath ibn Khaqan sent him a slave girl, one of the most beautiful women of the age, a swelling-breasted virgin. With her he sent a crystal jar containing red wine and a red goblet on which these lines were inscribed in black letters:

> When the caliph has finished taking the cure,
> To be followed by healing and health,
> There can be no medicine better than a drink
> From this goblet of this wine,
> And the breaking of the seal given him,
> For this is good after a purge.

When the girl came to the caliph bringing the presents that had been sent with her, Yuhanna the doctor was with him, and when Yuhanna saw the lines, he smiled and said: 'By God, Commander of the Faithful, al-Fath knows more about medicine than I do, so don't disobey his prescription.' Al-Mutawakkil accepted the advice and followed the cure suggested in the lines, after which God fulfilled his hopes and returned him to health.

It is told that A CERTAIN EMINENT MAN SAID:

I never saw a quicker-witted woman with better understanding, a greater depth of learning or more natural talent or brilliance than a Baghdadi preacher known as Sayyidat al-Masha'ikh. As it happened she came to Hama in the year five hundred and sixty-one, where, seated on a chair, she would deliver salutary sermons to the people. A number of students, as well as men of learning and culture, frequented her house to debate with her on questions of Islamic law and disputed points of faith. I went to her with a cultured friend, and when we had sat down with her she set a dish of fruit before us and took her own seat behind a curtain. She had a handsome brother who stood behind us to wait on us.

When we had eaten, we started to discuss religious law. I asked her about a legal point concerning the difference between the founders of the four schools of law, to which she began to reply, but while I was listening, my companion was studying her brother's handsome face and paying no attention to her. She was looking at him from behind her curtain, and when she had finished her answer, she turned to him and said: 'You seem to me to be someone who prefers men to women.' 'Certainly,' he replied, and when she asked him why, he said: 'That is because God has made the male superior to the female . . .'

Night 420

Morning now dawned and Shahrazad broke off from what she had been allowed to say. Then, when it was the four hundred and twentieth night, SHE CONTINUED:

I have heard, O fortunate king, that he said: 'That is because God has made the male superior to the female, and I like the superior and dislike the inferior.' THE EMINENT MAN WENT ON:

She laughed and said: 'Will you debate this matter with me on equal terms?' and when he agreed, she asked what proof there was of male superiority. 'It lies both in what is recorded in tradition and what can be grasped by reason,' he replied. 'What is recorded is to be found both in the Quran and in the traditions of the Prophet. As for the Quran, God Almighty has said: "Men oversee women because of the advantage that God has given to one sex over the other."* He also said: "If there are not two male witnesses, then there should be one man and two women,"† and, in relation to inheritance: "In the case of brothers and sisters, the man should have as much as two women."‡ So Almighty God, glory be to Him, gave preference in these contexts to the male over the female, saying that the woman should have half as much as the man because he was better than her. As for the traditions of the Prophet, it is said of him, may God bless him and give him peace, that he set the blood price for a woman at half that for a man. When it comes to argument from reason, the male is active and the female passive.'

'Well done, sir,' exclaimed Sayyidat al-Masha'ikh, 'but out of your own mouth you have established the point that I want to make against you, and you have produced a proof that tells against you rather than for you. For Almighty God, glory be to Him, gave preference to the male over the female simply because of the quality of masculinity, and on this point I have no dispute with you. But as far as this quality is concerned, there is no difference between a baby, a boy, a young man, a mature

* Quran 4.38.   † Quran 2.282.   ‡ Quran 4.175.

man or an old one. If preference is to be established only because of masculinity, your nature should feel as pleasurably drawn to an old man as to a boy, as they are both males. Where we differ is in respect of the qualities to be looked for in the enjoyment of social intercourse, and here you have produced no proof that boys are better than females in this respect.'

'Lady,' my companion replied, 'do you not realize that boys have been particularized by symmetry of form, rosy cheeks, lovely smiles and sweet words? In this respect they are better than women, and the proof of that is what is recorded of the Prophet, may God bless him and give him peace, who said: "Do not look for long at beardless boys, for to glance at them is like looking at the houris of Paradise." The superior merit of boys to girls is obvious to everyone, and how well Abu Nuwas expressed it when he said:

> The least of a boy's advantages is that you need not fear
> menstruation or pregnancy.

Another poet said:

> There is a saying of the imam Abu Nuwas,
> An authority on the laws of debauchery and madness:
> "You who love downy cheeks, enjoy
> A pleasure not to be found in Paradise."

When someone wants to bestow the ultimate accolade on a girl and extol her by describing her beauties, he compares her to a boy . . .'

Night 421

Morning now dawned and Shahrazad broke off from what she had been allowed to say. Then, when it was the four hundred and twenty-first night, SHE CONTINUED:

I have heard, O fortunate king, that the man's companion said: 'When someone wants to bestow the ultimate accolade on a girl and extol her by describing her beauties, he compares her to a boy because of the latter's qualities, as the poet has said:

> Her buttocks are those of a boy, swaying in love,
> As a branch sways in the north wind.

Were it not for the fact that boys are better and more beautiful, girls would not be compared to them. Know, may God Almighty protect you, that boys are easily led. They fall in with the wishes of others; they are good company with pleasant natures, preferring agreement to disagreement. This is particularly true when streaks of down appear on their cheeks, their upper lips darken, the flush of youth is seen on their cheeks and they become like the moon when it is full. How well Abu Tammam expressed it in the lines:

> The slanderers said: "Hair is showing on his cheek";
> I said: "Don't go on about this; it is no fault
> When he can bear the burden of buttocks that tug at him,
> And above the pearl of his mouth his lip darkens.
> The rose has sworn a solemn oath
> That its wonders will never leave his cheeks.
> I spoke to him with silent eyelids,
> And his eyebrows delivered his reply.
> He has the same beauty that you used to know,
> But hair protects him from his suitors.
> How sweet and pleasant are his qualities,
> Now that his cheeks are downy and his lip is dark.
> Those who used to blame me for loving him,
> Now, talking of us both, remark: 'He is his friend.'"

Al-Hariri also expressed this admirably in his lines:

> The censurers said: "What is this love for him?
> Do you not see that hair has sprouted on his cheek?"
> I said: "If those who have found fault with me
> Study the candour in his eyes, they could not hold out."
> If you have stayed in a land where nothing grows,
> Surely you will not leave it when spring comes?

Another poet said:

> Critics have said of me: "He has forgotten," but they lie;
> He who is gripped by longing never can forget.
> I could not forget the roses of his cheek when they were there alone;
> How then can I forget when sweet basil encircles them?

Another said:

> A slender boy whose glances and whose down
> Aid one another to bring his lovers death.
> He sheds blood with a narcissus sword,
> Held by a scabbard belt of myrtle.

Yet another said:

> It is not his wine that has intoxicated me;
> Mankind are left drunk by his locks of hair.
> Although his beauties envy one another,
> All wish to be the down upon his cheeks.

This, then, is an excellence that belongs to boys and has not been granted to women, and it is sufficient for them as a distinction and a cause for pride.'

'God save you,' exclaimed Sayyidat al-Masha'ikh, 'it is you who laid down the conditions for this debate; you have talked at length and brought forward this evidence for what you have had to say. But "the truth is now clear,"* so do not turn away from it, and if you are not content with a summary of the evidence, I shall produce it for you in detail. How, I ask you, is a boy to be compared to a girl, or lambs to wild cows? The girl, with her soft voice and lovely figure, is like a shoot of sweet basil, with a mouth like a camomile flower, locks of hair as long as halters, cheeks like red anemones, a face like an apple and lips like wine. Her breasts are like pomegranates; she is supple as a branch, with her symmetrical figure and her firm flesh. She is sharp as a gleaming sword edge, with a clear forehead, joining eyebrows and dark eyes. When she speaks, moist pearls are scattered from her mouth, and she attracts hearts by her delicacy. If she smiles, you think that the full moon shines out between her lips, and swords are unsheathed from her eyes as she looks. In her is the culmination of beauty and around her all men revolve, travellers and settled folk. Her red lips are softer than butter and sweeter to taste than honey.'

* Quran 12.51.

Night 422

Morning now dawned and Shahrazad broke off from what she had been allowed to say. Then, when it was the four hundred and twenty-second night, SHE CONTINUED:

I have heard, O fortunate king, that THE MAN TOLD HOW SAYYIDAT AL-MASHA'IKH SAID:

'Her red lips are softer than butter and sweeter to taste than honey. She has a bosom like a road through a mountain pass, with twin breasts like ivory caskets. Her stomach is slender-flanked, like a fresh flower, with folded wrinkles, and her rounded thighs are like two pillars of pearl. Her buttocks undulate like a crystal sea or mountains of light. She has slender feet and hands like ingots of gold.

'You poor man, where is mankind in relation to the *jinn*? Don't you know that sovereign kings and noble rulers are always subservient to women, relying on them for their pleasure, while the women say: "It is we who hold sway and we who steal away men's wits"? How many a rich man has been impoverished by a woman? How many a great man has been abased and a noble man enslaved? Women have seduced men of culture, brought shame on the pious, taken their riches from the wealthy and brought misery on the fortunate, but that only adds to the love and respect that men of intelligence feel for them and they do not count this as an injustice or as degradation. How many a servant of God has disobeyed his Lord because of them and angered his father and mother, as love for women overpowers their hearts? Don't you know, poor man, that palaces are built for them, curtains lowered over them, maidservants bought for them and tears shed? They are given pungent musk, ornaments and ambergris. For them armies are mustered; pleasure domes are constructed for them, wealth collected, heads cut off. Whoever said "'world' means 'woman'" was right.

'As for the tradition of the Prophet that you quoted, far from helping your case, this tells against you. When he said, may God bless him and give him peace: "Do not look for long at beardless boys, for to glance at them is like looking at the houris of Paradise," he was comparing boys to the dark-eyed houris and there can be no doubt that when you compare one thing to another, the latter is superior to the former, and were women not better and more beautiful, he would not have compared boys to them. You are wrong in saying that girls are likened to boys, for it is the other way round, and one says: "This boy is like a girl." The poetry that you quote as evidence comes from what can be termed a perversion of nature. The sodomites and debauchees, transgressors who break God's law, are rebuked by Him in the Holy Quran, where He disapproves of their disgusting practices and says: "Do you approach the males among His creation and abandon your wives whom your Lord has created for you? You are transgressors."* These are the people who compare girls to boys because of their excessive depravity, their disobedience to God and the fact that they pursue their own desires as followers of Satan. This is why they talk of a catamite as "up to both tricks", so abandoning the true way and following their leader, Abu Nuwas, in his line:

A slim-waisted gamine, suited to sodomites and fornicators.

'Where you talk of the beauties of the growth of down and the darkening of the upper lip, saying that this increases a boy's beauty, by God you have missed the mark and are not telling the truth, for down exchanges beauty for its opposite.' She quoted the lines:

Hair appeared on his face and avenged
His lover for the wrongs that he had done.
I saw his face marked by what looked like smoke,
While the locks of his hair were like charcoal.
When the rest of the page of his face is black,
Where do you think the pen can write?
If any prefer him to another,
That must be because they judge like fools.

When she had finished these lines, she said to my companion . . .

Night 423

Morning now dawned and Shahrazad broke off from what she had been allowed to say. Then, when it was the four hundred and twenty-third night, SHE CONTINUED:

I have heard, O fortunate king, that THE MAN WENT ON:

When she had finished these lines, she said to my companion: 'Glory

* Quran 26.166.

be to Almighty God, how can you fail to see that it is women who provide perfect pleasure and that it is only through them that there is lasting happiness? God has promised to give dark-eyed houris to His prophets and saints in Paradise and it is these who are the reward of good deeds. If God knew that others could provide such pleasurable enjoyment, He would have promised them as a reward, but the Prophet, may God bless him and give him peace, said: "There are three things that I love in this world, women, scent and the consolation of prayer." God has given boys as servants to the prophets and saints in Paradise, as this is the domain of happiness and pleasure which requires the service of boys in order to be perfected, but to use them for any other purpose is vicious and diseased. How well the poet has put it:

For a man to need backsides is back-sliding;
Those who are attracted to noble women are themselves noble.
How many a witty and elegant man has spent his night treading
The buttocks of a boy to find himself in the morning a purveyor of
    smells,
With clothes yellowed by the dye of his anus,
Showing clearly his shame and his disgrace.
There can be no denial on a day he is defiled
By stains of excrement upon his clothes.
How different is the man who spent the night
Riding a dark-eyed girl, with magic in her glance.
For when he leaves her, she has scented him
With expensive perfume that fills all the house.
No boy can be compared to her;
And how can scented aloes wood be compared to filth?'

Then she said: 'You people have made me break the rules of modesty, putting me beyond the pale of noble women and prompting me to discuss foolish obscenities unbefitting to people of learning. But the breasts of the freeborn are the graves of secrets. These meetings are confidential and actions are judged by intentions. So I ask for pardon from the Omnipotent God for me, for you and for all the Muslims, for He is the Forgiving and the Merciful.' She then fell silent and would answer no more of our questions. So we left her pleased with what we had learned from our discussion with her, but regretful at having to part from her.

*

It is told that ABU SUWAID SAID:

One day I and a number of my friends went into an orchard to buy some fruit. By the side there we saw an old woman with a bright face but with white hair, which she was combing with an ivory comb. We stopped beside her, but she paid no attention to us and did not cover her head. I said to her: 'Were you to dye your hair black you would be prettier than a girl, so what stops you from doing that?' She looked up . . .

Night 424

Morning now dawned and Shahrazad broke off from what she had been allowed to say. Then, when it was the four hundred and twenty-fourth night, SHE CONTINUED:

I have heard, O fortunate king, that ABU SUWAID WENT ON:

When I said that to the old woman, she looked up, stared at me and recited:

I dyed what Time had dyed; mine did not last, although Time's did.
Those were the days I trailed the skirts of youth,
And was enjoyed from behind and from in front.

'How eloquent you are, old woman,' I said. 'How sincerely attached you are to what is sinful and how false in your claim to have repented of sin!'

A story is told that 'Ali ibn Muhammad ibn 'Abd Allah ibn Tahir once inspected a slave girl named Mu'nis who was being offered for sale and who was an excellent and cultured poetess. He asked her name, which he knew already, and when she told him that it was Mu'nis, he looked down at the ground for a time and then, raising his head towards her, he recited:

What have you to say to one emaciated by sickness
For love of you, and reduced to bewilderment?

'May God honour the emir,' she said, and recited:

When I see a lover injured
By the disease of love, I show him favour.

Prompted by admiration for her, he then bought her for seventy thousand dirhams and on her he fathered the distinguished 'Ubaid Allah, the author of *al-Ma'athir*.

ABU'L-'AINA' SAID:

There were two women in our street, one of whom had a man as a lover while the second had a beardless boy. They met one night on the roof of one of their houses, which was near mine, without realizing that I was there. The boy's lover said to the other: 'How can you put up with the roughness of his beard, sister, when it falls against your breast as you kiss, and his moustache rubs against your lips and your cheeks?' 'You silly creature,' said her companion, 'isn't a tree only adorned by its leaves, while a cucumber is decorated by its covering? Have you seen anything in the world uglier than a bald man whose beard has been plucked? Don't you know that a beard for a man is what locks of hair are for a woman, and what is the difference between cheeks and beards? Don't you know that Almighty God, praise be to Him, has created an angel in the heavens who cries out: "Glory be to Him, Who has adorned men with beards and women with locks of hair," and if these were not alike in attractiveness they would not have been linked together. Foolish thing, how am I going to spread myself out under a boy, who will finish before me, and abandon a man, who leans towards me and holds me tightly, enters slowly, and when he has finished comes back for more? His movements are skilful and he comes back again and again.' Her friend took her advice and said: 'By the Lord of the Ka'ba, I have forgotten about my lover.'

A story is told that there was a wealthy merchant in Cairo named Hasan al-Jauhari al-Baghdadi, a man with huge resources of money, as well as innumerable jewels, precious stones and properties. God had provided him with a handsome son, well built, rosy-cheeked, a splendid youth, the acme of beauty. His father named him 'Ali al-Misri and had him taught the Quran, scientific studies, eloquence and literature until he became outstandingly learned. It then happened that his father, under whose supervision his son had been working as a trader, fell ill and his condition worsened until he was sure that he was about to die. He summoned his son . . .

Night 425

Morning now dawned and Shahrazad broke off from what she had been allowed to say. Then, when it was the four hundred and twenty-fifth night, SHE CONTINUED:

I have heard, O fortunate king, that when he was so ill that he was sure of death, he summoned his son, 'Ali al-Misri, and said: 'My son, this world passes away but the next world remains. Every living creature must taste death, and as my own is near at hand, I want to give you some instructions. If you act on them, you will remain safe and happy until you meet Almighty God, while if you do not, you will accumulate troubles and have cause to regret not having followed them.' 'Ali said: 'How could I possibly not listen to you and act as you tell me, when it is an obligation and a duty for me to hear and obey you?'

Hasan then went on: 'My son, I have left you properties, estates, goods and huge quantities of money, so much so that were you to spend five hundred dinars a day, it would not make a hole in the total. In return, you must show piety towards God and follow His chosen Prophet, may God bless him and give him peace, by keeping to what tradition has recorded of his commands and prohibitions. Be assiduous in acting well, doing good and associating with the virtuous and the learned. You must look after the poor and needy and avoid stinginess, miserly conduct and associating with doubtful characters and evil men. Treat your servants and your family with kindness and do the same with your wife. She comes from a noble family and is pregnant with your child, and it may be that God will provide you, through her, with virtuous descendants.'

Hasan continued to exhort his son, weeping and saying: 'I pray to the generous God, Lord of the throne, the Omnipotent, to save you, my son, from any difficulty into which you may fall and provide you with a speedy release from troubles.' 'Ali for his part wept bitterly and said: 'What you say dissolves me with grief because you seem to be saying goodbye.' 'Yes,' said his father, 'for I know the state I am in. Do not forget my instructions.' Then he started to pronounce the confession of faith and to recite verses from the Quran, until, when he was at the point of death, he told his son to come near. When he did so, his father kissed him and gave a last sigh. Then his soul left his body and was received into the mercy of Almighty God.

'Ali was stricken with grief and the house was filled with noisy wailing.

Hasan's friends gathered around him and 'Ali prepared his body for burial, rendering the last honours to him. He had the bier carried out with all pomp to where prayers were said over him, and then on to the cemetery, where the appropriate passages of the Quran were recited as he was buried. The mourners then returned to his house and paid 'Ali their condolences before going on their way. 'Ali had the Friday ceremonies of mourning and the recitations of the entire Quran performed for forty days, during which he stayed at home, only going out in order to pray. On Fridays he would visit the grave and he continued praying, reciting the Quran and performing acts of devotion until his companions from among the other young merchants came to visit him. 'How long are you going to go on mourning,' they asked, 'while you neglect your own affairs and your trade, as well as abandoning your friends? This is going on too long and doing an increasing amount of harm to your health.' When they came to him, their associate was Iblis, the damned, who was whispering to them.

They began to encourage 'Ali to go off with them to the market, and again it was Iblis who tempted him to agree so that he left the house in their company . . .

Night 426

Morning now dawned and Shahrazad broke off from what she had been allowed to say. Then, when it was the four hundred and twenty-sixth night, SHE CONTINUED:

I have heard, O fortunate king, that the young merchants came to 'Ali and began to encourage him to go off with them to the market. He agreed to do that, as had been decreed by Almighty God, glory be to Him. 'Mount your mule,' they told him, 'and come with us to such-and-such an orchard, where we can enjoy ourselves and you can shed your cares and sorrows.' So 'Ali mounted his mule and, taking his slave with him, he set off with them to the orchard to which they were headed. When they arrived, one of them went to prepare a meal, which he brought there, and they ate happily and then sat talking until the end of the day, when they mounted and rode off, each to spend the night in his own house. The next morning they came back and told 'Ali to come with them. 'Where to?' he asked, and they told him that they were going to another orchard, more attractive and more pleasant than the first one. 'Ali went there with them, and on their arrival one of them went and prepared a meal, which he brought to the orchard, together with strong wine. They ate and then produced the wine, telling 'Ali: 'This is what removes care and burnishes pleasure.' They kept on encouraging him to indulge until they overcame his scruples and he joined them in drinking. They stayed talking and drinking until the end of the day and then went home. 'Ali, whose head was spinning because of what he had drunk, went to his wife's room and when she saw him in this state she asked why he was so changed. 'We were enjoying ourselves today,' he told her, 'when one of our friends brought us something to drink. I drank with the others and felt giddy.' His wife said: 'Have you forgotten your father's injunction and done what he told you not to do by associating with men of dubious reputation?' 'These aren't doubtful characters,' he told her, 'but young merchants, men with comfortable fortunes.'

He continued to go out with his friends day after day, visiting place after place, eating and drinking, until they said to him: 'We have all done our turns and now it is yours.' He agreed to this willingly and the next morning he produced the necessary food and drink in twice the quantity that the others had done and he took with him cooks, attendants and coffee-makers. They made their way to al-Rauda and the Nilometer and there they stayed for a whole month, eating, drinking, listening to music and enjoying themselves. At the end of the month 'Ali discovered that he had spent a sizeable amount of money, but Iblis, the damned, deluded him, saying: 'If you spent this much every day you would be no less wealthy.' As a result he paid no attention to his expenditure and carried on in the same way for three years in spite of the advice of his wife, who kept reminding him of what his father had said.

He paid no attention to her until he had used up all the ready cash that he had. Then he began to sell his jewels and spend what he got from them until this too was exhausted, after which he turned to his houses and property, until there was nothing of these left at all. Next came his estates and orchards, which he disposed of one after the other, and when these had gone he was left with nothing apart from the house in which he lived. He started to pull out its marble and its timbers, spending the money that these fetched until this too had gone, and then, when he was left with no source of spending money, he sold the house itself and spent what he got for it. Its purchaser told him to find somewhere else to live as he needed the house for himself. On thinking the matter over, 'Ali decided that he had no need of a house except as a place for his wife, who had presented him with a son and a daughter. He had no servants left, and as there was only himself and his family he took a large room in a courtyard, and, after having been pampered in splendour with quantities of servants and wealth, he lived there, no longer having money enough for his daily bread. 'This was what I used to warn you about,' said his wife, 'and I kept telling you to remember your father's instructions, but you wouldn't listen to me and there is no might and no power except with God, the Exalted, the Omnipotent. How are your little children going to be fed? Get up and go round your friends, the young merchants, and maybe they will give you something for today's food.'

So 'Ali got up and went to his friends, one after the other, but they refused to see him, heaping painful insults on him and refusing to give him anything. He went back and told this to his wife, who went to her neighbours to beg . . .

Night 427

Morning now dawned and Shahrazad broke off from what she had been allowed to say. Then, when it was the four hundred and twenty-seventh night, SHE CONTINUED:

I have heard, O fortunate king, that when 'Ali came back to his wife empty-handed, she went to her neighbours to beg them to give her some food for that day. She went in to see a woman whom she had known in the old days and when she entered, the woman, seeing the state that she was in, welcomed her, shed tears and asked what had happened to her. So 'Ali's wife told her everything that her husband had done and the woman repeated her welcome and insisted that she come to her for all she needed, with no question of anything being asked in return. 'Ali's wife thanked her and was then given enough to see her and her family through an entire month. Taking this, she set off home and when 'Ali saw her he wept and asked her where she had got it. 'From So-and-So,' she told him, 'for when I let her know what had happened to us, she was generosity itself and told me to ask her for anything that we needed.' 'As you have this support,' said her husband, 'I can go off somewhere in the hope that Almighty God may grant us relief.'

He took his leave of his wife, kissed his children and left without knowing where he was going, walking on until he came to Bulaq, where he saw a ship that was going to Damietta. A man who had been a friend of his father's caught sight of him and greeted him, asking where he was off to. 'Damietta,' 'Ali replied, adding: 'I want to make enquiries about some friends of mine and visit them before coming back.' The man took him home, entertained him and provided him with provisions as well as some cash before seeing him on board the ship. When it reached Damietta, 'Ali disembarked and went off, still with no idea where he was going, but as he was walking a merchant saw him and, taking pity on him, took him to his house. 'Ali stayed with this man for some time, but at last he asked himself how long he was going to continue sitting in other people's houses. He went out and found a ship that was about to sail to Syria. His host gave him provisions and brought him on board, after which 'Ali set off and eventually reached Damascus.

As he was tramping the streets of Damascus he was seen by a virtuous man who brought him to his house, where he stayed for a time. Then, when he had gone out, he came across a caravan that was leaving for Baghdad. He went back to take his leave of the merchant with whom he had been staying and he then set off with the caravan. Almighty God, glory be to Him, inspired another merchant with pity for him, and 'Ali continued to eat and drink with this man until the caravan was only a day's journey from Baghdad. It was then attacked by highwaymen, who seized everything it was carrying, and each of the few who escaped made for some place of refuge. 'Ali himself headed for Baghdad, which he reached at sunset, arriving as the gatekeepers were about to shut the gate. He called to them to let him in, which they did, and they then asked him where he was from and where he was going. 'I've come from Cairo,' he told them, 'and I had with me merchants, laden mules, slaves and servants. I went on ahead of them to look for somewhere to store my goods, but as I did so and was riding on my mule, a band of highwaymen intercepted me. They took my mule and my goods and I was at my last gasp when I managed to escape from them.'

The gatekeepers gave him a hospitable welcome and invited him to pass the night with them, saying that in the morning they would look out somewhere suitable for him. 'Ali hunted in his pocket and found a dinar left over from the ones that he had been given by the merchant in Bulaq. He gave this to one of the gatekeepers and told him to take it and spend it on something for them to eat. The man went off to the market and used the money to buy bread and cooked meat, which they all ate together, after which 'Ali spent the night with them. The next morning one of them took him off to a merchant in the city, to whom he told the story. The man believed it and, thinking 'Ali to be a trader himself, coming with merchandise, he showed him his shop and treated him with respect. He then sent to his house for a splendid robe and took him to the baths.

'ALI SAID:

When we came out he took me back home, where he provided me with a meal, and after eating we relaxed. My host then told one of his slaves to take me off and show me two houses in such-and-such a quarter and to give me the key of whichever of them I preferred. The two of us set off and came to a street in which there were three new houses standing side by side. They were locked and the slave opened the first of them, which I looked around, and when we came out we went and inspected the second. 'Which key do you want me to give you?' the slave asked, but I said: 'Whose is this big house?' 'Ours,' he said, and so I told him to open it up for me to look at. 'You don't want to have anything to do with that one,' the slave told me, and when I asked why, he told me that *jinn* lived there, adding: 'Whoever spends the night in it is found dead next morning. We don't open the door to bring out the corpse, but we have to go up to the roof of one of the other houses and fetch it out that way. This is why my master has left it empty, saying that he is not going to give it to anyone again.' I told him to open it for me to inspect, saying to myself: 'This is what I've been looking for. I shall spend the night here and by morning I shall be dead, having found relief from my present ills.' The slave unlocked the door, and when I went in, I found that it was a place of incomparable splendour. 'This is the one I choose,' I said, 'so give me the key.' 'Not before I have consulted my master,' he replied.

Night 428

Morning now dawned and Shahrazad broke off from what she had been allowed to say. Then, when it was the four hundred and twenty-eighth night, SHE CONTINUED:

I have heard, O fortunate king, that the slave refused to hand over the key before he had consulted his master. Then the slave went back to his master and told him: 'The Egyptian merchant says that he will only live in the big house.'

The owner came to 'Ali and told him that he shouldn't stay there, but 'Ali insisted, saying that he wasn't worried by the gossip. The owner told him to draw up a document stating that, were anything to happen to 'Ali, the owner himself would not have any responsibility for it. 'Ali agreed, and after a court witness had been summoned a document was written and kept by the owner, who then handed over the key to 'Ali. He took it and went into the house, to which the owner sent a slave with bedding, which he spread out over a bench behind the door before going back.

When 'Ali went in, he saw a well in the courtyard of the house and over it was suspended a bucket. He lowered this into the well, filled it and used it to perform the ritual ablution, and after the obligatory prayer he sat down for a time. A slave then brought him his evening meal from the owner's house, together with a lamp, a candle and a candlestick, as well as a bowl, a ewer and a jug, before leaving him and going home. 'Ali lit the candle and ate his meal, after which he relaxed before performing the evening prayer. He then told himself: 'Come on, take the bedding upstairs and sleep up there, as that will be better than sleeping here.' So he did this, and upstairs he found a huge room with a gilded ceiling and a floor and walls of coloured marble.

He spread out his bedding and sat reading a portion of the glorious Quran when he was taken unawares by a voice that called out to him: ''Ali, son of Hasan, shall I send you down the gold?' 'Ali asked where this gold might be, but before he had finished, gold poured down as though shot from a mangonel, and it kept on falling until it had filled the room. When this had stopped, the voice said: 'Now set me free so that I can go on my way, as my service is done and I have given you what was left in trust for you.' 'In the Name of God, the Omnipotent,' said 'Ali, 'I conjure you to tell me how this gold comes to be here.' 'Since ancient times,' the voice replied, 'it has been kept for you by a talismanic spell. I come to everyone who enters this house and say: "'Ali, son of Hasan, shall I send you down the gold?" This terrifies them and they cry out, after which I come down and break their necks, and then leave. But when you came and I called out your name and that of your father, asking you whether to send down the gold, and you asked where it was, I realized that you were its rightful owner and sent it down. There is another treasure waiting for you in Yemen, and were you to go and get it before coming back here, it would be better for you. Now I want you to set me free so that I may go on my way.' 'By God,' said 'Ali, 'I am not going to free you until you fetch me the Yemeni treasure.' 'If I do that,' said the voice, 'will you free me and free the servant of the other treasure?' 'Ali agreed and was asked to swear to this, which he did.

The servant of the treasure was then about to set off when 'Ali said: 'There's something else that I want you to do for me.' 'What is that?' asked the other, and 'Ali said: 'I have a wife and children in such-and-such a place in Cairo and I want you to fetch them to me gently and without harm.' 'God willing, I shall bring them with due pomp on a litter attended by eunuchs and servants together with the treasure from Yemen,' said the servant, who asked for three days' leave, promising that by the end of this time 'Ali would have everything delivered to him. He then left, and in the morning 'Ali went round the room to see whether he could find a safe place in which to store the gold. The room had a dais at whose edge he saw a marble slab with a screw set in it, and when he turned this the slab slid away to reveal a door. 'Ali opened it, and when he entered he discovered a large chamber containing sacks made from materials sewn together. He started to take these, fill them with gold and carry them to the chamber until he had transferred the whole pile of gold and put it there. Then he shut the door and turned the screw so that the slab went back to its place, after which he went down to sit on the bench behind the front door.

While he was sitting there, a knock came at the door and when he had got up and opened it he found the owner's slave. When the man saw him sitting there, he hurried back to his master . . .

Night 429

Morning now dawned and Shahrazad broke off from what she had been allowed to say. Then, when it was the four hundred and twenty-ninth night, SHE CONTINUED:

I have heard, O fortunate king, that the owner's slave came and knocked on the door. 'Ali opened it and when the man saw him sitting there, he hurried back to his master to give him the good news, telling him: 'The trader who stayed in the haunted house is safe and sound and is sitting on the bench behind the front door.' His master got up joyfully and set off for the house, taking with him food for breakfast. When he saw 'Ali, he embraced him, kissed him between the eyes and asked how he had got on. 'Ali told him: 'All went well and I slept upstairs in the marble chamber.' 'Did anything approach you or did you see anything?' the man asked. 'No,' replied 'Ali. 'I recited some passages from the glorious Quran and then slept until morning, when I got up, performed the ritual ablution and prayed, after which I came down and sat on this bench.' 'Praise be to God that you are safe,' he said, after which he got up and left 'Ali, and then sent him slaves, mamluks and slave girls, together with household effects. They swept out the house from top to bottom and furnished it in lavish style, after which three of the mamluks, together with three black slaves and four slave girls, stayed to serve him while the rest went back to their master's house. When the other merchants heard about him, they sent him all kinds of valuable gifts, including food, drink and clothing, and they took him to sit with them in the market. They asked him when his merchandise would arrive, and he told them that this would be after three days. At the end of the three days, the servant of the first treasure, who had poured down the gold for him, came to him and said: 'Get up and see the treasure that I have brought you from Yemen, together with your family. Part of the treasure comes in the form of precious merchandise, but everything that accompanies it in the way of mules, horses, camels, eunuchs and mamluks consists of *jinn*.'

When the servant of the treasure reached Cairo, he had found that in 'Ali's absence his wife and children had been reduced to nakedness and ever-increasing hunger. He carried them away from their lodging and out of Cairo on a litter, and provided them with magnificent clothes from the Yemeni treasure. When he returned to tell 'Ali of that, 'Ali went to invite the Baghdadi merchants to come out of the city with him to meet the caravan that was carrying his goods, adding: 'Do me the honour of bringing your wives in order to meet mine.' 'To hear is to obey,' they said, and after sending for their wives, they sat talking in one of the orchards of the city.

While they were doing this, a dust cloud was seen rising from the heart of the desert. They got up to see what had caused it, and when it cleared, under it could be seen mules, men, baggage handlers, servants and lantern bearers. They were coming forward singing and dancing, and the leader of the baggage handlers came up to 'Ali, kissed his hand and said: 'We have been delayed on the road, sir. We had intended to enter the city yesterday, but we had to wait for four days in the same place for fear of highwaymen, until Almighty God dispersed them for us.'

The Baghdadi merchants got up, mounted their mules and accompanied the caravan, while their wives waited for 'Ali's family to mount and go with them. They entered Baghdad in a great procession, with the merchants admiring the mules loaded with chests, and their wives admiring the dress of 'Ali's wife and the clothes of her children, saying to each other: 'Not even the ruler of Baghdad or any other king, noble, or merchant has clothes like these.' The procession continued on its way, the men with 'Ali and the women with his family, until they came to his house . . .

Night 430

Morning now dawned and Shahrazad broke off from what she had been allowed to say. Then, when it was the four hundred and thirtieth night, SHE CONTINUED:

I have heard, O fortunate king, that the procession continued on its way, the men with 'Ali and the women with his family, until they came to his house, where they dismounted. The laden mules were led into the centre of the courtyard, where their loads were removed and placed in the storerooms. The women went with 'Ali's family to the upper room, which they found resembled a luxuriant garden, magnificently furnished, and here they sat in happy enjoyment until noon, when a meal of the most magnificent foods and sweetmeats was brought to them. They ate and tasted the most splendid of drinks, and afterwards used rose-water and incense to perfume themselves. The company then took leave of 'Ali, and both men and women went back to their own houses. When they had got home, the men began to send the kind of presents to 'Ali that matched their own wealth, while the women sent gifts of their own to his family. As a result, he and his wife collected a large number of slave girls, slaves and mamluks, as well as accumulating stores of all kinds such as grain, sugar and other goods past all number.

The owner of the house, the Baghdadi merchant, did not leave 'Ali but stayed and said: 'Let the slaves and the servants take the mules and the other animals to another house to rest,' but 'Ali told him: 'They are going to such-and-such a place tonight.' He then gave them permission to leave the city so that when night fell they could go on their way. As soon as they were sure that they had his permission, they took their leave of him. They went out of the city and then took to the air and flew back to where they came from.

'Ali sat with the owner of the house until the end of the first third of the night, when they broke off their session, the owner returning to his own house and 'Ali going to his family. He greeted them and asked what had happened to them in the period after he had left them. His wife told him of the hunger they had had to endure, their lack of clothes and their hardship. He praised God for their safety and asked how they had come to Baghdad. His wife said: 'Last night I was sleeping with the children and then before I knew where I was, someone had lifted them and me up from the ground and we were flying through the air without suffering any harm. This went on until we landed in a place that looked like a Bedouin camp. We saw a number of laden mules and a litter carried by two large mules and surrounded by eunuchs, both boys and men. "Who are you?" I asked them. "What are these loads and where are we?" They said: "We are the servants of 'Ali ibn Hasan al-Jauhari of Cairo, and he has sent us to take you to him in the city of Baghdad." "Is it a long or a short way from here to Baghdad?" I asked. "Baghdad is not far away," they said, "and we can cover the distance while it is still dark." They then set us on the litter, and by the time that it was morning we had arrived here without having suffered any harm at all.' 'And who gave you these clothes?' 'Ali asked. His wife said: 'The leader of the caravan opened one of the chests that were being carried by the mules and took the clothes out of it. He gave me this to wear and produced others for the children, after which he locked the chest and handed me the key, telling me to keep it safe until I could give it to you. I have it here.'

She brought it out for him and he asked her if she could recognize the chest. 'Yes, certainly,' she said, and 'Ali then went down with her to the storerooms and showed her the chests. When she pointed out the one from which the clothes had been taken, he took the key from her, put it in the lock and opened it. In it he discovered a great quantity of robes, together with the keys of all the other chests. He removed these and started to open the others one by one and to investigate their contents, which consisted of jewels and precious stones the like of which no king possessed. He then locked the chests, took the keys and went with his wife to the upper room. 'All this comes through the grace of Almighty God,' he told her, and he led her to the marble slab with the screw, which he turned. He opened the door of the treasure chamber and went in with his wife to show her the gold that he had deposited there.

'Where did you get all this from?' she asked, and he told her: 'This came through God's grace. When I left you in Cairo . . .'

Night 431

Morning now dawned and Shahrazad broke off from what she had been allowed to say. Then, when it was the four hundred and thirty-first night, SHE CONTINUED:

I have heard, O fortunate king, that when 'Ali showed his wife the gold, she asked where it had come from. 'This came through God's grace,' he told her, adding: 'When I left you in Cairo I walked off without knowing where I was going, and when I got to Bulaq, I found a ship that was going to Damietta. I boarded it and when I got to Damietta, a merchant who had known my father met me and hospitably took me in. He asked where I was going and I told him I was on my way to Damascus, where I had friends.' He then went on to tell his wife everything that had happened to him from beginning to end. She said: 'All this has happened because of the prayers that your father offered for you before his death, when he used to say: "I pray to God that, if He ever brings you into difficulties, He may grant you speedy relief." Praise be to Him that He has done this for you and has returned to you more than you lost. So I implore you, my husband, in God's Name, not to return to your former association with notorious persons but show piety towards Almighty God, both openly and in secret.' She admonished him and he said: 'I accept what you say and I ask God to remove evil associates from me, helping me to serve Him obediently and to follow what has been sanctioned by His Prophet, may God bless him and give him peace.'

'Ali, his wife and his children now led the most prosperous of lives. 'Ali opened a shop in the merchants' market and stocked it with a quantity of jewels and precious stones, sitting there with his sons and his mamluks. He became one of the leading merchants of Baghdad and news of him reached the king, who sent for him. The king's messenger arrived to tell him to obey the summons and 'Ali replied: 'To hear is to obey.' He then prepared a gift for the king, taking four trays of red gold which he filled with jewels and precious stones such as no king possessed, and with these he went off to the king. On entering the king's presence he kissed the ground before him and prayed eloquently for the continuation of his glory and good fortune. 'Merchant,' said the king, 'your presence has delighted our land,' to which 'Ali replied: 'King of the age, your servant has brought you a gift which he hopes you will be generously pleased to accept.' He then produced the four trays. The king removed their coverings and when he looked at them, he saw jewels more splendid than any of his own, worth immense stores of money. 'Your gift is acceptable, merchant,' said the king, 'and, God willing, we shall repay you with one to match it,' after which 'Ali kissed his hands and left.

The king then summoned his principal officers of state and asked them: 'How many kings have asked for my daughter's hand?' 'Very many,' they replied. 'And did any of them give me a gift like this?' he went on. 'No,' they said in unison, 'for not one of them has ever had treasures like these.' The king then said: 'I have asked God for guidance as to whether I should marry my daughter to this merchant. What is your opinion?' 'You should do as you think fit,' they said, and he then ordered that the trays together with their contents be taken by the eunuchs to the women's quarters. There he went to his wife and put the trays before her. When she uncovered them, she saw gems more magnificent than any single one that she owned. 'What king has sent these?' she asked, adding: 'Perhaps it is one of the suitors for your daughter's hand.' 'No,' he told her, 'this comes from an Egyptian merchant who has arrived in our city. When I heard of this, I sent a messenger to fetch him in order to enjoy his company, thinking that he might have some jewels that I could buy for our daughter's wedding. He answered the summons, bringing these four trays, which he presented as a gift. I saw that he was a handsome young man, dignified and intelligent, with a graceful appearance, who might even be a prince. I was pleased with him and attracted to him, and I would now like to marry him to my daughter.'

The king went on to tell her how he had shown the present to his officers of state and of the questions he had asked them and of their answers, as well as how he had consulted them about the princess's marriage and what they had said. 'What have you to say yourself?' he then asked.

Night 432

Morning now dawned and Shahrazad broke off from what she had been allowed to say. Then, when it was the four hundred and thirty-second night, SHE CONTINUED:

I have heard, O fortunate king, that the king of Baghdad showed the present to his wife and told her of the qualities of 'Ali, the merchant, and that he proposed to marry his daughter to him. He then asked her what she herself had to say. 'It is for God and for you to decide, king of the age,' she replied, 'and what God wishes will happen.' 'God willing, then,' the king said, 'we shall marry her to no one but this young man.' When he went to his court the next morning, he ordered that 'Ali be brought to him together with all the merchants of Baghdad. When they were all assembled in front of him, he ordered them to sit, and when they were seated, he sent for the *qadi* of the court. The *qadi* came and was told by the king to draw up a marriage contract between his daughter and 'Ali, the Cairene merchant. 'Forgive me, lord king,' 'Ali exclaimed, 'but it is not right that a merchant like me should become your son-in-law.' 'This is a favour that I have granted to you,' the king replied, 'together with the vizierate.' He immediately followed this by investing 'Ali as vizier, after which 'Ali took his seat on the vizier's chair.

'Ali then said: 'King of the age, you have honoured me by showing me this favour, but listen to what I have to say to you.' 'Speak on,' said the king, 'and have no fear.' 'Ali said: 'Since you have proclaimed your august intention to give your daughter in marriage, this should be to my son.' 'Have you a son?' asked the king, and when 'Ali confirmed that he had, the king told him to send for him immediately. 'To hear is to obey,' said 'Ali, and he sent one of his mamluks to fetch his son, who, when he came into the king's presence, kissed the ground before him and stood there respectfully. Looking at him, the king could see that he was better-looking than his daughter and superior to her in the symmetry of his figure and the perfection of his handsomeness. 'What is your name?' the king asked him. 'Your majesty,' the fourteen-year-old youth replied, 'my name is Hasan.' The king then told the *qadi* to draw up the marriage contract between his daughter, Husn al-Wujud, and Hasan, son of the merchant 'Ali of Cairo. The *qadi* did this, and when this stage had been successfully completed, all those who were present in the king's court went off on their way.

The merchants followed 'Ali, the new vizier, back to his house and then left, after having congratulated him on his appointment. 'Ali went to his wife, who, seeing him wearing the robe of the vizierate, asked him what had happened. He told her the whole story from beginning to end and said: 'He has given his daughter in marriage to Hasan, my son.' She was overjoyed by this, and after having spent the night at home, 'Ali returned to court the next morning, where the king greeted him warmly and seated him close to his side. 'Vizier,' he said, 'our intention is to hold the wedding feast and to bring your son to my daughter.' 'Lord king,' said 'Ali, 'whatever you consider right and proper is so.' The king then gave orders for the feast; the city was adorned with decorations and the festivities lasted for thirty days, to the enjoyment and delight of the people. At the end of the thirty days, Hasan lay with the princess, enjoying her beauty and grace.

When the king's wife saw Hasan, she became very fond of him and also of his mother. On the king's orders a large palace was quickly built for him, and when he took up residence there, his mother used to stay with him for days on end before returning home. So the queen said to her husband: 'Hasan's mother cannot stay with her son and leave her husband, the vizier, nor can she stay with her husband, leaving her son.' 'That is true,' said the king, and he gave orders for a third palace to be built next to the palace of Hasan. This was done within a few days and, on the king's instructions, 'Ali's possessions were moved to the new palace, where he took up residence. The three palaces were interconnected and when the king wanted to talk with his vizier, he could walk to his palace at night or send for him, and the same was true of Hasan and his mother and father.

They continued to lead an enjoyable and pleasant life together . . .

Night 433

Morning now dawned and Shahrazad broke off from what she had been allowed to say. Then, when it was the four hundred and thirty-third night, SHE CONTINUED:

I have heard, O fortunate king, that the king, the vizier and his son continued to lead an enjoyable and pleasant life together for some time, until the king fell ill. When his condition worsened, he summoned his principal officers of state and said: 'I am gravely ill and as this illness may prove fatal, I have brought you here in order to consult you, so advise me on what you think is the proper course.' They asked: 'On what point is it that you want advice from us, your majesty?' He said: 'I am old and ill and I am afraid that after my death my kingdom may be attacked by enemies. I want you all to agree on one man for whom I can have the oath of allegiance taken as my successor, while I am still alive, so that you may feel easy about the matter.' They replied unanimously:

'We would all be content with the husband of your daughter, Hasan, the son of the vizier 'Ali. We have seen his intelligence and perfect understanding, and he knows the position of everyone, both great and small.' 'Perhaps you are saying this in my presence out of deference, but behind my back you say something else.' 'By God,' they all said, 'what we say openly and in secret is one and the same thing, and we will accept him willingly and cheerfully.' 'If that is so,' said the king, 'order the *qadi* who decides matters of religious law, together with all the chamberlains, legates and officers of state, to present themselves before me tomorrow so that we may settle the matter in the proper fashion.' 'To hear is to obey,' they said, and they then left to brief all the religious scholars and the leading emirs.

The next morning, they arrived at court and sent a message to the king asking leave to enter. When this had been granted, they went in, greeted him and said: 'We are all here in your presence.' So the king said: 'Emirs of Baghdad, who will you be content to have as your king to succeed me, so that I can confirm him as my heir before I die in the presence of you all?' They all said: 'We are agreed on Hasan, son of the vizier 'Ali, the husband of your daughter.' The king then said: 'If that is so, then go, all of you, and bring him before me.' They all rose, and after going to Hasan's palace they told him to come with them to the king. When he asked why, they told him: 'This is for something that will be good both for us and for you.' He accompanied them to the king and kissed the ground before him. 'Sit, my son,' said the king, and when he had taken his seat, the king went on: 'All the emirs have approved of you and have agreed to appoint you as their king after my death. My intention is to nominate you as my heir while I am still alive in order to have the matter settled.'

At that, Hasan got up, kissed the ground before the king and said: 'Your majesty, some of the emirs are older and senior in rank to me, so allow me to decline.' The emirs, however, insisted that they would only be satisfied with him as their king. 'My father is older than me,' said Hasan. 'He and I are one and the same thing, and it would not be right for me to be placed ahead of him.' 'Ali, however, replied: 'I approve of nothing except what my brother emirs agree on, and as they are unanimous in their choice of you, you should not disobey the king's command or go against the choice of your brothers.' Hasan looked down at the ground out of diffidence towards the king and his father. The king then asked the emirs: 'Are you content with him?' 'We are,' they said, and they all recited the opening *sura* of the Quran seven times. 'Qadi,' said the king, 'draw up a legal document confirming that these emirs have agreed to the transfer of power to Hasan, the husband of my daughter, and that he is to be their king.' This the *qadi* did, and he signed the document after they had all taken the oath of allegiance to Hasan as king, as had the old king himself, who then told Hasan to take his seat on the throne. Everyone rose and kissed the hands of King Hasan, son of the vizier, in a show of obedience to him. His judgements that day were exemplary and he distributed splendid robes of honour to the officers of state.

The court was then dismissed and Hasan went to his father-in-law and kissed his hands. 'Hasan,' said the old king, 'in the treatment of your subjects display piety towards God.'

Night 434

Morning now dawned and Shahrazad broke off from what she had been allowed to say. Then, when it was the four hundred and thirty-fourth night, SHE CONTINUED:

I have heard, O fortunate king, that when the court was dismissed, King Hasan went to his father-in-law and kissed his hands. 'Hasan,' said the old king, 'in the treatment of your subjects display piety towards God.' 'I shall achieve success through your blessing, father,' replied Hasan. He then went to his palace, where he was met by his wife and her mother, together with their servants, who all kissed his hands and congratulated him on his office, exclaiming: 'This is a blessed day!' From his own palace he then went to that of his father, where there was great rejoicing at the favour God had bestowed on him by entrusting him with the kingship. His father enjoined him to fear God and to show compassion towards his subjects, and after spending a happy and joyful night, the next morning he performed the ritual prayer, recited the specified portion of the Quran, and then went to his court. All his troops and officials were present; in delivering his judgements he ordered what was good and forbade what was evil, and he appointed some to office and deposed others. This went on until the end of the day, when the court was dismissed with due ceremony and the troops, together with everyone else, went off on their way.

Hasan then returned to the palace, where he found his father-in-law gravely ill. When Hasan wished him well, he opened his eyes and called his name. 'Here I am,' said Hasan, and the old king said: 'I am near my end. Look after your wife and her mother; fear God and be dutiful towards your parents. Live in fear and awe of God, the Judge, and know that He orders you to act with justice and charity.' 'To hear is to obey,' replied Hasan. The old king lived for three more days but was then gathered to the mercy of Almighty God. They prepared his body, covered him with a shroud, and recited the Quran, both in sections and in full, over his grave for a total of forty days. Hasan then ruled alone. His subjects were delighted with him and the days of his reign were filled with joy. His father continued to serve as principal vizier at his right hand, and he appointed a second vizier at his left. Everything was well ordered and Hasan remained as king of Baghdad for a long time. His wife, the old king's daughter, presented him with three sons, who inherited the kingdom after his death. They lived the pleasantest and happiest of lives, until they were visited by the destroyer of delights and the parter of companions – praise be to the Eternal God, Who has the power both to destroy and to establish.

The story is told that one of the Meccan pilgrims woke after a long sleep to find no trace of his companions. He got up and began to walk, but lost his way and, after a short while, he caught sight of a tent, by whose entrance an old woman was sitting, with a dog sleeping at her side. He went up to the tent, greeted the old woman and asked her for something to eat. She told him: 'Go to that wadi there and catch as many snakes as will be enough for you and I'll cook them as a meal for you.' 'I wouldn't dare to catch snakes, and I have never eaten them in my life.' 'I'll go with you and catch them,' said the old woman, 'so don't be afraid.'

She then went off with him, followed by the dog, and when she had caught as many snakes as she needed, she started to boil them. The man saw no alternative to eating them as he was afraid of becoming emaciated by hunger. After eating, he felt thirsty and so he asked the old woman for water to drink. 'There is the spring in front of you,' she said, 'so drink from it.' When he went to it he found its water was bitter, but he was so thirsty that he could see no alternative to drinking it. When he had done this, he went back to the old woman and expressed his surprise that she should stay in such a place . . .

Night 435

Morning now dawned and Shahrazad broke off from what she had been allowed to say. Then, when it was the four hundred and thirty-fifth night, SHE CONTINUED:

I have heard, O fortunate king, that the thirsty pilgrim drank from the spring of bitter water and then went back to the old woman. He expressed his surprise that she should stay in such a place, where she had to eat this kind of food and drink this kind of water. 'What is your country like?' she asked. 'We have spacious and roomy houses,' he told her, 'delicious ripe fruits, fresh water in abundance, fine food, fatty meat, many sheep and goats, together with all good things and such blessings as are only to be found in the Paradise which Almighty God describes as being reserved for his pious servants.' 'I have heard of all that,' the old woman said, 'but tell me, are you subject to a sultan who rules you unjustly and if any one of you is guilty of some fault, the sultan seizes his wealth and ruins him, while if he wants he can drive you from your house and uproot you?' 'That may well be,' the man replied, and the old woman said: 'Then, by God, that delicious food, that pleasant lifestyle and those pleasures, when combined with injustice and oppression, are deadly poison, while our food, eaten with safety, is a theriac. Haven't you heard that, next to Islam, the greatest of blessings are health and security, and these come about through the justice and good administration of the sultan, who is God's vice-regent on earth? In the old days, the rulers required only the minimum of prestige, in that when their subjects saw them, they automatically feared them, whereas nowadays rulers want all-embracing authority and total respect, as the present generation is not like its predecessors. This is the age of the ugly and puffed-up, who are characterized by stupidity and cruelty, full of hatred and hostility. If, which God forbid, they have a weak ruler, or one with no sound policy or dignity, then that is bound to lead to the destruction of his country. The proverb has it that a hundred years of injustice on the part of the sultan is better than one year's worth of injustice inflicted by the people on each other. When the people are unjust, God sets over them an unjust and tyrannical ruler.'

History has recorded that a note was once passed to al-Hajjaj ibn Yusuf on which was written: 'Fear God and do not treat His servants so oppressively.' He was an eloquent man, and when he had read the note, he went up into the pulpit and said: 'O people, Almighty God has appointed me as your ruler because of your own actions.'

Night 436

Morning now dawned and Shahrazad broke off from what she had been allowed to say. Then, when it was the four hundred and thirty-sixth night, SHE CONTINUED:

I have heard, O fortunate king, that when al-Hajjaj had read the note, he went up into the pulpit – and he was an eloquent man – and said: 'O people, Almighty God has appointed me as your ruler because of your own actions. Even if I die, you will not be freed from injustice, because of your evil deeds. Almighty God has created many people like me and if you do not have me, you will have someone who does more evil with greater injustice and harsher violence, as the poet has put it:

All power is overshadowed by the power of God;
There is no wrongdoer who will not suffer at another's hands.

Injustice is to be feared while justice is the best of all things. We pray that God may set our affairs to rights.'

A story is told that there was a man of importance in Baghdad, well off in respect of both money and property, one of the great merchants to whom God had granted worldly prosperity but not the children for whom he longed. Time passed and he had neither daughters nor sons; he grew old and frail; his back was bent and both his feebleness and his cares increased. He was afraid that his wealth and his property would be wasted if he had no son to inherit them and to preserve his name. He presented his entreaties to Almighty God, fasting by day and standing in prayer by night. He made vows to the Living and Eternal God, visited the pious and increased the number of his supplications. God then answered his prayers, taking pity on his complaint. A few days later he lay with one of his women, who conceived on that same night. After the months of her pregnancy were completed, she gave birth to a boy like a segment of the moon.

In gratitude to Almighty God, his father fulfilled his vows, gave alms and clothed widows and orphans. Seven days after his birth, the child was named Abu'l-Husn. He was suckled by wet nurses and cradled by dry nurses; mamluks and eunuchs carried him until he grew up and flourished. He studied the glorious Quran, the precepts of Islam, the tenets of true religion, calligraphy, poetry, arithmetic and archery. He was unique and unrivalled in his age, with a handsome face and an eloquent tongue. He swayed evenly as he walked, proud and haughty in his coquetry, with his red cheeks, his gleaming forehead and his darkening down. A poet, describing him, said:

> The downy spring now comes in view,
> But how can roses bloom when spring has gone?
> Do you not see what grows upon his cheek?
> Here is a violet showing through the leaves.

For a time he stayed with his father enjoying the pleasantest of lives, while for his part his father was delighted with him. Then one day, when he had grown to manhood, his father made him sit down in front of him and said: 'My son, my life is nearly at an end. Death is close at hand and it only remains for me to meet the Great and Glorious God. I have left enough for you, your children and grandchildren in the way of money, estates, properties and orchards. Fear God, my son, in respect of all I have left to you, and only follow those who can help you.'

Shortly after this he fell ill and died. His son gave him a splendid funeral and then went home, where he sat mourning for him day and night. His friends came in to see him and said: 'Whoever has left behind an heir like you has not died; what has gone has gone and mourning is only suitable for girls and women kept in seclusion.' They went on pressing him until they accompanied him to the baths and brought his mourning to an end.

Night 437

Morning now dawned and Shahrazad broke off from what she had been allowed to say. Then, when it was the four hundred and thirty-seventh night, SHE CONTINUED:

I have heard, O fortunate king, that Abu'l-Husn's friends came to the baths with him and brought his mourning to an end. He then forgot his father's injunctions, and, bemused by his wealth, he thought that his prosperity would remain unchanged and that his riches would never be exhausted. He ate, drank and enjoyed himself; he distributed costly robes and gifts; he was liberal with his gold; he was constantly eating chicken, breaking the seals on wine bottles, hearing wine gurgling out of its flasks and listening to songs.

This went on until his wealth and prosperity had gone and he found, to his dismay, that he had lost everything, the one thing remaining being a slave girl who had been part of the inheritance left him by his father. This was a girl of unparalleled beauty, grace, radiance and perfection, symmetrically formed, with a grasp of all kinds of learning and culture, who surpassed all the people of his age in her attractive qualities. Her fascination shone more brightly than a beacon; she surpassed the other beauties both in what she knew and in what she did; she swayed elegantly, and at five foot in height she was a child of good fortune. The sides of her forehead were like the new moon of Sha'ban; she had arching eyebrows, eyes like those of a gazelle, a nose like a sword edge, cheeks like red anemones, a mouth like Solomon's seal and teeth like a string of pearls. Her navel could hold an ounce of frankincense, but her waist was more slender than the body of an emaciated lover worn away by concealing his love, while her buttocks were heavier than sand hills. To sum up, in her beauty and grace she was worthy of being described in the poet's lines:

> When she comes forward,
> Her beautiful figure enchants,
> But when she turns her back,
> She kills her lovers by rejection and abandonment.
> She is a sun, a full moon or a bough;
> To be harsh or distant is not in her nature.
> The garden of Eden lies beneath the collar of her shirt,
> And the circuit of the moon is found above her necklace.

This fourteen-year-old girl was like the rising moon or a grazing gazelle, putting the sun and moon to shame, as the eloquent poet has skilfully put it:

> She is like the full moon, after the passing
> Of five days, then five and then four.
> It is not my fault that she has made me
> Look like the moon when it first appears.

Her skin was clear and her breath scented, as though she had been formed of fire and fashioned of glass. Her cheeks were rosy and her figure symmetrical, as a poet described:

She walks proudly, gleaming like gold in yellow robes,
Silver, rose red, coloured like sandalwood.
She is a garden flower or a pearl
Set in a necklace, an image in a temple.
She is slender, but if she wants to rise,
Her buttocks say: 'Stop and go slow.'
I ask for union, and her beauty says:
'Be generous,' but her coquetry says: 'No.'
Glory be to the One Who gave her beauty as her portion,
While the portion of her lover is the words of censurers.

Her beauty and her flashing smile stole away the hearts of those who looked at her and she shot at them with the arrows of her eyes. In addition, she was eloquent and an accomplished poetess.

When Abu'l-Husn's other possessions had been lost and he was clearly destitute, this slave girl was the only thing left to him. For three days he tasted no food and did not sleep, so the girl told him: 'Take me to the Commander of the Faithful, Harun al-Rashid . . .'

Night 438

Morning now dawned and Shahrazad broke off from what she had been allowed to say. Then, when it was the four hundred and thirty-eighth night, SHE CONTINUED:

I have heard, O fortunate king, that the girl told her master: 'Take me to Harun al-Rashid and ask him to pay you ten thousand dinars for me. If he thinks that this is too much, tell him: "Commander of the Faithful, the girl is worth more than that, and if you test her, her value will soar in your eyes, for she has no equal and she is only fit for one like you."' She added: 'Take care not to sell me for less than the price that I have quoted you, for this is cheap for someone like me.'

Her master did not know her true worth or that she was unrivalled in her age, but he took her and presented her to the caliph, telling him what she had said. The caliph asked her her name and when she told him that it was Tawaddud, he asked her in what branches of learning she excelled. 'Master,' she replied, 'I am familiar with grammar, poetry, jurisprudence, Quranic interpretation and philology. I know about music, the precepts of Islam, arithmetic, including division, as well as ancient legends. I know the glorious Quran and can recite it according to the seven, the ten and the fourteen readings. I know the number of its *suras* and its verses, and how it is to be divided into halves, quarters, eighths and tenths, together with the numbers of prostrations involved and the number of its letters. I know the abrogating and abrogated verses and those revealed at Medina and Mecca, with the reason for their revelation. I am familiar with the traditions of the Prophet, both as regards their content and their transmission, whether backed by complete and incomplete chains of authority. I have studied mathematics, geometry, philosophy, medicine, logic, rhetoric and exposition, much of which I know by heart. I am fond of poetry and can play the flute; I know the position of the notes and how the strings of instruments are to be moved or left at rest. If I sing and dance, I captivate, and if I adorn and perfume myself, I kill. In short, I have reached a pitch only attained by established scholars.'

When the caliph heard these claims made by so young a girl, he was astonished at her eloquence and, turning to her master, he said: 'I shall provide scholars to examine her in all the branches of knowledge to which she has laid claim, and if she can answer their questions, I shall pay the price you asked and more, but if not, then you had better keep her.' Abu'l-Husn willingly accepted and the caliph wrote to instruct the governor of Basra to send him Ibrahim ibn Sayyar, the master of prosody, the most learned expert of the age in matters of litigation, rhetoric, poetry and logic. He was to bring with him Quran reciters, men of learning, doctors and physicians, astronomers, architects and philosophers. Ibrahim himself, however, was more learned than them all.

It was not long before they arrived at the caliph's palace, with no idea of what was going on. The caliph summoned them to his audience chamber and ordered them to sit, which they did. He then ordered the slave girl Tawaddud to be brought in. She came unveiled, looking like a gleaming star, and the caliph had a golden chair set out for her. She greeted him eloquently and said: 'Commander of the Faithful, tell the learned men who are here, the Quran reciters, the doctors and physicians, the astronomers, the architects and the philosophers, to examine me.' So he told them to examine her in respect of her religion and to refute all her claims. 'To hear is to obey,' they said, 'both in respect of God and of you, Commander of the Faithful.'

Tawaddud looked down and then asked: 'Which of you is the expert in law, the readings of the Quran and the traditions of the Prophet?'

'I am the man you are looking for,' said one of them, and she then told him to put what questions he wanted. 'You have read God's glorious Quran,' he asked, 'and know the abrogating and abrogated verses, and you have studied its verses and its letters?' 'Yes,' she told him, and he said: 'Then I will ask you about the obligatory ordinances and what follows the established path. Tell me about these, girl, and tell me who is your Lord, who is your Prophet, who is your imam, in what direction do you turn to pray, who are your brothers, what is your path and what is your way.'

She answered: 'God is my Lord; Muhammad, on whom be blessing and peace, is my Prophet; my imam is the Quran; I turn towards the Ka'ba to pray; my brothers are the Muslims; good is my path, and my way is the *sunna*.' The caliph was astonished at how eloquently she spoke, young as she was. Her interrogator then asked: 'Tell me, through what do you know Almighty God?' 'Through my intellect,' she answered. 'And what is intellect?' he asked. 'There are two forms of it,' she said. 'One which is given to us and one which is acquired.'

Night 439

Morning now dawned and Shahrazad broke off from what she had been allowed to say. Then, when it was the four hundred and thirty-ninth night, SHE CONTINUED:

I have heard, O fortunate king, that Tawaddud said: 'There are two forms of intellect, one given and one acquired. The first is created by God, Great and Glorious, and given by Him to whichever of His servants He wishes, while the second is acquired by men through education and learning.' 'Well done,' said the questioner, and he then asked: 'Where is this intellect to be found?' She replied: 'God casts it into the heart and its rays rise to the brain until it becomes fixed there.' 'Well done,' said the man, before asking: 'How do you come to a knowledge of the Prophet, may God bless him and give him peace?' 'By reading God's book,' she replied, 'and by the signs, tokens, proofs and miracles.'

'Well done,' he said, 'so tell me about the obligatory ordinances.' 'There are five of them,' she said. 'The confession of faith that there is no god but God alone, Who has no partner, and that Muhammad is His servant and apostle; the performance of the prayer; the payment of the alms tax; the fast of Ramadan; and for those who can do so, the pilgrimage to God's sacred House. As for what follows God's established path, these are four things, night and day, sun and moon. They are what build life and hope, and no man knows whether at the end of things they will be destroyed.'

'Good,' he said, 'so now tell me, what are the practices of faith?' She answered: 'These comprise prayer, the alms tax, fasting, pilgrimage, the holy war and the avoidance of what is forbidden.' 'Good,' he said, 'and how should prayer be performed?' She replied: 'With the intent to worship God and to acknowledge His divinity.' 'What obligations has God imposed on you before you may perform the prayer?' he asked. 'Purification,' she said, 'the veiling of the private parts, avoidance of soiled clothes, taking one's stance in an undefiled place, turning towards the Ka'ba, standing up, having the proper intention and beginning the consecration with the formula "God is greater".' 'Good,' he said, 'so now tell me what you should take with you when you go out of your house to pray.' 'An intention to worship God,' she replied. 'And with what do you enter the mosque?' 'An intention to serve God.' 'Why do you turn to face Mecca?' 'Because of three divine precepts and the *sunna* of the Prophet.'

'Good,' he said, 'and tell me, what is the beginning of prayer, the beginning of the consecration and the conclusion?' She replied: 'Prayer begins with purification; the consecration starts with the words "God is greater"; and it ends with the word "peace".' 'What is the necessary consequence of the abandonment of prayer?' he asked. She said: 'It is recorded in the collected traditions of the Prophet that whoever abandons prayer deliberately and on purpose, without excuse, has no share in Islam.'

Night 440

Morning now dawned and Shahrazad broke off from what she had been allowed to say. Then, when it was the four hundred and fortieth night, SHE CONTINUED:

I have heard, O fortunate king, that the girl mentioned the traditions of the Prophet. 'Good,' the questioner said, 'and what is prayer itself?' 'It is what connects God's servants to their Lord, and it has ten properties: it illumines the heart; it lights up the face; it pleases the Merciful God; it angers the devil; it wards off tribulation; it protects against the evil done by enemies; it increases God's mercy and guards against His punishment;

it brings the servant close to God, his master; it prevents evil and rep-
rehensible behaviour; it is one of the necessary obligations laid down in
the Quran and it is the pillar of faith.' 'Good,' he said, 'and what is the
key to prayer?' 'The ritual ablution.' 'And what is the key to this ablution?' 'The naming of God.' 'And what is the key to this naming?' 'True
faith.' 'And what is the key to faith?' 'Reliance on God.' 'And what is
the key to this reliance?' 'Hope.' 'And what is the key to hope?' 'Obedience.' 'And what is the key to obedience?' 'The acknowledgement of
God's unity and the admission of His divinity.'

'Good,' he said. 'Now tell me of the precepts that govern ritual ablution.' 'There are six of these,' she replied, 'according to the doctrine laid
down by the imam Muhammad ibn Idris al-Shafi'i, may God be pleased
with him. These are: the intention behind the washing of the face; then
the washing of the face; the washing of the hands and forearms; the
wiping of a portion of the head; the washing of the feet and ankles; and
the order in which these are done. There are ten things established by
tradition: the invocation of God's Name; the washing of the hands before
they are dipped in the water bowl; the rinsing; the clearing of the nose;
the wiping of the whole head; cleaning the ears both outside and in with
fresh water; combing the beard if it is thick; cleaning between fingers
and toes; washing the right before the left; and doing all this thrice
without interruption. When the worshipper has finished his ablution, he
recites: "I bear witness that there is no god but God, Who is alone and
without a partner. I bear witness that Muhammad is His servant and
His apostle. O my Lord, place me among the penitent and set me with
the purified. Glory be to You, my Lord! In Your praise I bear witness
that there is no god but You. I ask You for forgiveness and I turn to You
in repentance." It is recorded in the traditions of the Prophet, may God
bless him and give him peace, that he said: "For those who recite these
words after each ablution, the eight gates of Paradise will be opened and
he can enter by whichever he wishes."'

'Well done,' said the man, 'and when someone intends to perform the
ablution, what of the angels and the devils?' She replied: 'When he gets
ready for this, the angels stand at his right hand and the devils at his left.
Then, when at the start of the ablutions he mentions the Name of
Almighty God, the devils flee from him and the angels take him under
their protection in a tent of radiance with four ropes, each attended by
an angel glorifying God and asking forgiveness for the man as long as
he stays silent or calls on God's Name. But if at the start of his ablution

the man fails to mention God, Great and Glorious, and does not stay silent, the devils take power over him, the angels leave, and the devil whispers to him until he begins to doubt and fails to perform his ablutions properly. The Prophet, may God bless him and give him peace, said: "The ritual ablution, when properly performed, drives off the devil and protects against the injustice of the ruler." He also said: "If someone who has not performed the ablution is struck by misfortune, he has no one to blame but himself." '

'Good,' the scholar said, 'and now tell me what someone should do on waking from sleep.' She replied: 'On waking from sleep, people should wash their hands three times before dipping them in the water bowl.' 'Good,' he said, 'and now tell me about the precepts that govern washing as well as what is governed by tradition.' 'The precepts,' she told him, 'comprise intention, and the use of water to wet the entire body, including hair and skin. As for tradition, this comprises a preliminary ablution, massage, the combing of the hair, and the statement that the cleansing of the feet will be postponed until the final stage of the washing.' 'Good,' he said . . .

Night 441

Morning now dawned and Shahrazad broke off from what she had been allowed to say. Then, when it was the four hundred and forty-first night, SHE CONTINUED:

I have heard, O fortunate king, that when Tawaddud told the scholar about the precepts and traditions governing ritual ablution, he said: 'Good, and now tell me about the ablutions performed with sand or dust, and the precepts and the traditions governing this.' She replied: 'There are seven reasons for this form of ablution: lack of water; fear; need for water; losing one's way on a journey; disease; bones in splints; and wounds. As for the precepts, there are four of them, covering intention, the dust, its use on the face and its use on the hands. As for tradition, this covers the pronouncing of God's Name and the cleansing of the right side before the left.'

He approved of this answer and asked her to tell him about the conditions governing prayer, its bases and its traditions. 'There are five conditions,' she told him. 'The limbs must be clean and the private parts concealed. The time must be right or thought to be so, and the worshipper must face Mecca and stand somewhere that is undefiled. As for its bases, these are: intention; the introductory formula "God is greater"; standing, when the worshipper is capable of doing so; the recitation of the first *sura* of the Quran, and, in accordance with the doctrine of the imam al-Shafi'i, the recitation of the Quranic phrase "in the Name of God, the Compassionate, the Merciful"; bowing and maintaining the position without movement; prostration and the maintenance of the position without movement; sitting down between the two prostrations and the maintaining of the position; then the final confession of faith – after which the worshipper sits, then calls down blessings on the Prophet, may God bless him and give him peace, followed by the first invocation of peace and then the expressed intention to end the prayer.

'As for what is covered by tradition, this comprises the call to prayer with the worshipper rising to his feet, the raising of his hands at the introductory "we take refuge with God", the amen, the recitation of the *sura* that follows the Fatiha, the recitation of the formula "God is greater" as the worshipper changes position, the words "may God listen to those who praise Him" and "our Lord, to You be the praise", words being spoken aloud in their proper place and under the breath in the proper place, the first confession of faith for which the worshipper sits, the prayer for the Prophet, may God bless him and give him peace, the prayer for his family, and the second confession of faith and the second invocation of peace.'

'Well done,' he said, 'so tell me about the obligations of the alms tax.' She replied: 'It is to be levied on gold, silver, camels, cattle, sheep, wheat, barley, millet, maize, beans, chickpeas, rice, raisins and dates.' 'Good,' he said, 'and now tell me at what rate it is charged on gold.' 'It cannot be levied on less than twenty *mithqals*, but the tax due on this amount of gold is half a *mithqal* and so on proportionately.' 'How much is due on silver?' he asked. 'No tax is due on less than two hundred dirhams. On this the tax is five dirhams and above this amount it rises proportionately.' 'Good,' he said, 'and now tell me what is due on camels.' 'For every five camels, one sheep is due, and for twenty-five, a female camel just entering its second year.' 'Good,' he said, 'and what about sheep?' 'For forty sheep, one is owed as tax.'

'Good,' he said, 'so now tell me about the precepts that govern fasting.' She replied: 'These comprise intention as well as abstinence from food, drink, sexual intercourse and deliberate vomiting. It is incumbent on all who are subject to the laws of Islam except for those who are menstruating or within forty days of having given birth. It must start with the appearance of the new moon or with reliable notice of its sighting which is taken as true by the one who is told of it. It is also necessary that the intention to fast must be formed on the preceding night. Tradition requires that the meal that breaks the fast should be hurried on and the last meal before daybreak delayed and that what words are spoken should be restricted to what is good, the mention of God and the recitation of the Quran.' 'Good,' he said, 'and so tell me about what does not render the fast invalid.' 'The use of ointment or kohl,' she replied, 'dust from the road; the swallowing of saliva; the emission of semen, whether this be nocturnal or caused by the sight of an unfamiliar woman; bleeding; and cupping. For none of these things invalidate the fast.'

'Good,' he said, 'and now tell me about the prayers performed at the two festivals.' 'These traditionally comprise two *rak'as* with no summons to prayer, when the worshipper does not rise. He says: "Prayer brings the people together," and in the first prayer he recites the formula "God is greater" seven times, in addition to its use as an introduction, while in the second, according to the doctrine of the imam al-Shafi'i, may God Almighty have mercy on him, it is repeated five times in addition to its use as a signal for the worshippers to rise. This is followed by the confession of faith.'

Night 442

Morning now dawned and Shahrazad broke off from what she had been allowed to say. Then, when it was the four hundred and forty-second night, SHE CONTINUED:

I have heard, O fortunate king, that the girl told the scholar about the prayers to be performed at the two festivals. 'Good,' he said, 'and now tell me about the prayers to be used during eclipses of the sun and the moon.' 'These comprise two *rak'as* without a summons to prayer or standing on the part of the worshipper. In each *rak'a*, he bends and straightens up twice, prostrates himself twice, then sits, recites the confession of faith and pronounces the formula of peace.' 'Well done,' he said, 'and now tell me about the prayer for rain.' She replied: 'It comprises two *rak'as*, with no call to prayer and no standing. The worshipper utters the confession of faith and the formula of peace and the preacher substitutes a prayer for God's mercy in place of the formula "God is greater" in the sermons of the two feasts. He turns his cloak upside down and produces prayers of intercession.'

'Well done,' he said. 'Now tell me about the *witr* prayers.' 'These must comprise a minimum of one *rak'a* and a maximum of eleven.' 'Good,' he replied, 'and now tell me about the forenoon prayer.' 'This has a minimum of two *rak'as* and a maximum of twelve.' 'Good,' he said, 'and what about the prayer of seclusion?' 'This is a matter of tradition,' she said, and when he asked about its conditions, she said: 'Intention, the fact that the worshipper must not leave the mosque except for some need, sexual abstinence, fasting and silence.' 'Good,' he said, 'and now tell me about the obligations of the pilgrimage.' 'The pilgrimage is obligatory on those who have reached maturity, who are in possession of their senses, are Muslims and are able to make the journey. It is obligatory once in a lifetime before death.' 'What are the precepts governing the pilgrimage?' he asked. 'The adoption of the pilgrim dress,' she replied, 'together with the halt at 'Arafat, the circumambulation of the Ka'ba, running the prescribed course and shaving or shortening the hair.' 'What are the precepts governing the *'umra*?' he asked, and she said: 'Adherence to what is prohibited, the circumambulation and the running.' 'And what precepts apply to what is prohibited?' he asked. She said: 'They must not wear anything that has been sewn; they must not use perfume and they must give up shaving their heads, cutting their nails, killing game and indulging in sexual intercourse.'

'What are the traditional rites of the pilgrimage?' he asked. She said: 'The use of the words "here am I", the circumambulation of the Ka'ba when the pilgrim arrives and before he leaves, passing the night at al-Muzdalifa and Mina, and the stoning.' 'Well done,' he said. 'So tell me about the holy war and its fundamentals.' She replied: 'Its fundamentals comprise an invasion by the unbelievers, the presence of the imam, preparation, and steadiness in the face of the enemy. As for what is covered by tradition, this is the encouragement to fight as is found in the Quran: "Prophet, encourage the Muslims to fight." '*

'Good,' he said, 'and now tell me about the precepts governing trade and what is laid down by tradition.' 'The precepts,' she said, 'comprise the willingness to sell and the acceptance of the offer, and that what is sold is the property of the vendor, is in usable condition and is capable of being handed over. The last precept is that interest must not be charged.

* Quran 8.66.

What is covered by tradition is the right to cancel the sale and to exercise the power of choice before the seller and the buyer part from each other, as the Prophet, may God bless him and give him peace, said: "The parties to a sale have the right of free choice while they are still together."' 'Good,' he replied, 'and now tell me what cannot be sold for what.' She said: 'On this point I know an authentic tradition reported by Nafi' of the Apostle of God, may God bless him and give him peace, according to which he forbade the sale of dry for fresh dates, fresh for dry figs, dried for fresh meat and fresh for clarified butter. So where foodstuffs are of the same kind, it is not permissible to barter one for another.'

Listening to what she had to say, her interrogator recognized that she was sharp-witted, intelligent and astute, while in addition she had a grasp of jurisprudence, the traditions of the Prophet, and Quranic interpretation. He told himself that he would have to try to manoeuvre her into a position in which he could get the upper hand over her in the presence of the caliph. So he asked her the meaning of the word *wudu'* (ritual ablution), to which she replied: 'It means cleanness and freedom from impurities.' He then asked the basic meaning of *salat* (prayer) and she said: 'It is to invoke good.' He asked about *ghusl* (the major ritual ablution) and she told him that it meant 'purification'. Then he asked the meaning of *al-sawm* (fasting) and she said that it meant 'restraint'; and when he asked about *zakat* (the alms tax), she said that it meant 'increase'. When he asked about *al-hajj* (pilgrimage), she said that it meant 'to go towards', and then when he asked about *jihad* (the holy war), she said that it meant 'to ward off'.

After this, her interrogator had nothing left to say . . .

Night 443

Morning now dawned and Shahrazad broke off from what she had been allowed to say. Then, when it was the four hundred and forty-third night, SHE CONTINUED:

I have heard, O fortunate king, that when the scholar had nothing left to say he rose to his feet and said: 'Commander of the Faithful, I testify that this girl knows more about Islamic jurisprudence than I do.' She then said: 'I will put a question to you, and if you are a man of learning, give me a quick answer.' 'Ask your question,' he said, and when she asked: 'What are the arrows of religion?' he told her: 'There are ten of these. The first is the confession of faith, which covers religious belief. The second is prayer, which is a matter of natural constitution; the third is the alms tax, a matter of purification; the fourth is fasting, which is a shield; the fifth is the pilgrimage, which is the law of Islam; the sixth is the holy war, which is a general obligation; the seventh and eighth are to command what is good and to forbid what is bad, these being matters of self-respect; the ninth is association, that is, companionship; while the tenth is the pursuit of learning, which is the commendable path.'

'That is good,' she told him, 'but there remains one question: what are the principles of Islam?' 'There are four of these,' he replied. 'Sound faith, sincerity of intent, keeping within the bounds of law and keeping one's word.' 'I have one more question,' she told him. 'If you answer it, well and good, but otherwise, I shall take your robe from you.' 'Continue,' he told her, and she asked: 'What are the branches of Islam?' He stayed silent for a time and gave no answer. 'Take off your clothes,' she told him, 'and I shall explain the branches to you.' 'Explain, then,' said the caliph, 'and I will have his robe removed for you.' 'There are twenty-two of these branches,' she said. 'They comprise adherence to the glorious Quran; following the example of the Apostle of God, may God bless him and give him peace; refraining from doing harm; eating permitted food and avoiding what is forbidden; returning what has been wrongfully seized to its owners; repentance; an understanding of religion; love for Abraham, the Friend of God, and for the followers of the divine revelation; belief in God's messengers; fear of apostasy; preparation for death; the force of certitude; forgiveness from a position of power; a show of strength from a position of weakness; endurance of misfortunes; a knowledge of God; a knowledge of what was brought by His Prophet, may God bless him and give him peace; opposing Iblis, the damned; fighting against and opposing one's own desires; and sincerity shown towards God.'

When the caliph heard this, he ordered that the robe and the shawl of the *faqih* be removed. He took them off and left the caliph's presence, defeated and ashamed. Another man then stood up and said to the girl: 'Listen to a few questions that I have to put to you.' 'Continue,' she told him, and he asked: 'On what terms can payment properly be made in advance?' She said: 'The sum must be fixed, the class of goods must be fixed and the delivery date must be fixed.' 'Good,' he said, 'and what are the principles and traditions that apply to eating?' She said: 'The principles comprise an acknowledgement that it is God Almighty Who has supplied the food and the drink, and gratitude to Him for that.'

'What is gratitude?' he asked. 'It is shown when God's servant spends all that God's generosity provides for him on the purposes for which he was created.' 'What traditions apply to eating?' he asked. She said: 'The invocation of the Name of God, washing the hands, sitting with the weight on the left hip, eating with three fingers and eating what is next to you.' 'Well done,' he said, 'so tell me about good table manners.' She replied: 'You must take small mouthfuls and not look too often at whoever is sitting with you.'

Night 444

Morning now dawned and Shahrazad broke off from what she had been allowed to say. Then, when it was the four hundred and forty-fourth night, SHE CONTINUED:

I have heard, O fortunate king, that the girl was asked about good table manners and replied. 'Good,' said the *faqih*, 'and so now tell me about heartfelt beliefs and their opposites.' 'There are three of these,' she answered. 'The first is the belief of faith, and its opposite is the avoidance of unbelief. The second is belief in the *sunna*, and its opposite is the avoidance of heresy. Third comes belief in obedience to God, and its opposite is the avoidance of disobedience.' 'Good,' he said. 'Tell me now about the conditions governing the ritual ablution.' 'It can only be performed by a Muslim,' she said, 'and one who has the power of discrimination. The water must be clean and there should be no obstacles whether physical or imposed by Islamic law.'

'Good,' he said, 'and now tell me about faith.' 'This is divided into nine parts,' she said. 'Faith in the object of worship, faith in the relationship of the worshipper to the worshipped, faith in the particularity of God, faith in the "two handfuls",* faith in destiny, faith in the abrogating verses and faith in the abrogated. It is belief in God and His angels and apostles, and belief in destined fate, whether this be good or bad, sweet or bitter.' 'Good,' he said, 'and now tell me what three things interdict three other things.' 'Certainly,' she said. 'It is reported that Sufyan al-Thauri said: "Three things remove three other things. To despise the pious removes the chance of Paradise, to despise kings leads to loss of life, and to despise what one is spending leads to loss of wealth."'

* Quran 39.67.

'Good,' he said, 'so now tell me of the keys to the heavens and how many gates they have.' She replied: 'Almighty God has said: "The heavens shall be opened and be full of gates",* while the Prophet, may God bless him and give him peace, said: "No one knows how many gates there are in the heavens apart from their Creator." Every single son of man has two gates there, one through which his daily bread is sent down to him and one through which his actions ascend. The gate of his daily bread is not closed until his life span ends, and the gate of his deeds is not closed until his soul rises to heaven.'

'Good,' he said, 'and now tell me about something, about half of something and about nothing.' She replied: ' "Something" is a Muslim, "half of something" is a hypocritical Muslim and "nothing" is an unbeliever.' 'Good,' he said, 'and now tell me about hearts.' She replied: 'There is the sound heart, the sick heart, the penitent heart, the devoted heart and the luminous heart. The sound heart was that of Abraham, the Friend of God; the sick heart is that of the unbeliever; the penitent heart is that of the pious man who fears God, and the devoted heart is that of our master Muhammad, may God bless him and grant him peace, while the luminous heart belongs to his followers. There are three types of heart belonging to scholars, one attached to this world, another to the next, and the third to the Lord. There is another triple division in which one heart is left in suspense, this being the heart of the unbeliever, another is reduced to nothing, this being the heart of the hypocrite, and the third is the steadfast heart, which is that of the Muslim. Another division lists one heart dilated by the light of faith, a heart wounded by the fear of separation, and another apprehensive of being abandoned.' 'Good,' he said.

Night 445

Morning now dawned and Shahrazad broke off from what she had been allowed to say. Then, when it was the four hundred and forty-fifth night, SHE CONTINUED:

I have heard, O fortunate king, that the second *faqih* questioned the girl and approved of her replies. At this point, Tawaddud said: 'Commander of the Faithful, this *faqih* has tired himself out asking questions and now

* Quran 78.19.

I have two for him. If he answers them, well and good, and if not, I shall take his robe and he can leave in peace.' The *faqih* told her to ask what she wanted and, in reply, she asked him about faith. 'Faith,' he replied, 'is acknowledged by the tongue, believed by the heart and acted on by the limbs of our body. The Prophet, may God bless him and give him peace, said: "No Muslim has complete faith until he possesses these five qualities in perfection: reliance on God, the entrusting of his affairs to God, surrendering to God's commands, acceptance of God's decrees and the devoting of all that he does to God. Whoever loves God, gives for the sake of God and withholds for His sake has perfect faith."'

She said: 'Tell me, what is the precept of precepts, the precept that initiates all others, the precept needed by all others, the precept that embraces all others, the traditional point that is found in every precept, and the traditional point that completes every precept?' The *faqih* stayed silent, making no reply, and so the caliph ordered Tawaddud to explain the answers, while telling the *faqih* to strip off his robe and give it to her. She said to him: 'The precept of precepts is the knowledge of Almighty God; the precept that initiates all others is the confession of faith that there is no god but God and Muhammad is the Apostle of God. The precept needed by all others is ritual ablution; the all-embracing precept is the cleansing of impurity; the traditional point found in every precept is the wiping between fingers and toes and the combing of thick beards. The traditional point that completes the precepts is circumcision.'

When it was clear that the *faqih* had failed, he got to his feet and said: 'Commander of the Faithful, I testify that this girl knows more than I do about Islamic jurisprudence together with other subjects.' He took off his robe and left as a beaten man. Tawaddud next turned to the remaining scholars present and asked which of them was the Quran reciter who knew its seven readings, together with grammar and philology. The expert got to his feet and came to sit in front of her. 'Have you read God's book,' he asked, 'and reached a sound knowledge of its verses, the abrogatory and the abrogated, the unequivocal and the ambiguous, the Meccan and the Medinan? Have you grasped their interpretation and the transmission and origins of the readings?' 'Yes,' she said, at which he went on: 'Tell me, then, how many *suras* are there in the Quran, into how many sections of ten verses can it be divided, how many letters does it contain and how many acts of prostration, how many prophets are mentioned, how many *suras* are Medinan and how many are Meccan and how many winged creatures are mentioned?' She replied: 'Sir, in the Quran there are one hundred and fourteen *suras*, of which seventy are Meccan and forty-four Medinan. As for the tenths into which it can be divided, there are six hundred and twenty-one of these; there are six thousand, two hundred and thirty-six verses, seventy-nine thousand, four hundred and thirty-nine words and three hundred and twenty-three thousand, six hundred and seventy letters, each of which brings ten blessings to the reciter. There are fourteen prostrations.'

Night 446

Morning now dawned and Shahrazad broke off from what she had been allowed to say. Then, when it was the four hundred and forty-sixth night, SHE CONTINUED:

I have heard, O fortunate king, that the girl replied to the Quran reciter's questions. She went on: 'Twenty-five prophets are named in the Quran: Adam, Noah, Abraham, Ishmael, Isaac, Jacob, Lot, Joseph, Elisha, Jonah, Salih, Hud, Shu'aib, David, Solomon, Dhu'l-Kifl, Idris, Elias, John the Baptist, Zakarias, Job, Moses, Aaron, Jesus and Muhammad (may God bless him and give him peace). As for winged creatures, there are nine of these.' When he asked what they were, she told him: 'Gnats, bees, flies, ants, the hoopoe, crows, locusts, the *ababil*,* and the bird of Jesus, on whom be peace, which is the bat.'

'Good,' he said, 'and now tell me which *sura* in the Quran is the most excellent?' 'The *sura* of the Cow,' she said. 'And which verse is the greatest?' 'The Throne verse, whose fifty words each produce fifty blessings.' 'Which verse contains nine signs?' 'God's words: "In the creation of heaven and earth, in the sequence of night and day, in the ship that sails on the sea, carrying what is useful to mankind"† – and so on to the end of the verse.' 'Good,' he said, 'and which verse is the most just?' She replied: 'God's words: "God orders justice, the doing of good, and giving to relatives, while He prohibits wickedness, evil-doing and wrong."'‡ 'Which verse is the most covetous?' 'God's words: "Does each one of you desire to enter the garden of Paradise?"'§ 'Which gives the most hope?' 'God's words: "Say: O my servants who have transgressed against your own souls, do not despair of God's mercy, as God forgives all sins,

---

* cf. Quran 105.3.   † Quran 2.159.   ‡ Quran 16.92.   § Quran 70.38.

and He is the Forgiving, the Merciful."'* 'Good,' he said, 'so tell me which reading you employ.' 'That of the inhabitants of Paradise,' she said, 'which is the reading of Nafi'.'

He then asked: 'In what verse do the prophets lie?' She said: 'In God's words: "They brought Joseph's shirt stained with false blood,"† these being Joseph's brothers.' 'In what verse do the unbelievers speak the truth?' 'In His words: "The Jews say the Christians base themselves on nothing, and the Christians say the Jews base themselves on nothing, while both read the Scriptures."‡ Here both Christians and Jews are telling the truth.' 'Where does God speak of Himself?' 'Where He says: "I created *jinn* and men only so that they should worship Me."'§ 'In what verse do the angels speak?' 'In the verse: "We praise, laud and glorify You."'¶ 'Tell me about the formula "I take refuge with God from Satan, the stoned" and what is connected with it.' 'God has decreed that this formula must be pronounced when the Quran is being recited. The proof of this is found in God's words "when you recite the Quran, take refuge with God from Satan, the stoned."'**

'Tell me,' he said, 'what words are used in the formula of refuge and what are the variants?' She replied: 'Some say: "I take refuge with God, Who hears and knows, from Satan, the stoned" while others say: "I take refuge with God, the Omnipotent." The best formula is that used in the glorious Quran and mentioned in tradition. The Prophet, may God bless him and give him peace, when starting to recite the Quran, used to say: "I take refuge with God from Satan, the stoned." It is reported by Nafi' on the authority of his father that when the Prophet, may God bless him and give him peace, got up to pray at night, he would say: "God is greater by far; abundant praise is owed to Him; glory be to God morning and evening." He would then add: "I take refuge with God from Satan, the stoned, and the evil promptings of the devils." It is reported that Ibn 'Abbas, may God be pleased with him, said: "When Gabriel first visited the Prophet, may God bless him and give him peace, he taught him the formula of refuge and went on: 'Muhammad, say: "I take refuge with God, Who hears and knows"; then say: "In the Name of God, the Compassionate, the Merciful," and then recite: "In the Name of your Lord, the Creator, Who has created man from a clot of blood."'"'

When the Quranic scholar heard what she had to say, he was astonished

---

at how eloquently she spoke and at the excellence of her knowledge. He then asked her whether God's words 'in the Name of God, the Compassionate, the Merciful' constituted a verse of the Quran. 'Yes,' she replied, 'it is a Quranic verse in the *sura* of the Ant, and also where it occurs as a division between two *suras*, although there is much dispute among the learned on this point.' 'Good,' he said . . .

Night 447

Morning now dawned and Shahrazad broke off from what she had been allowed to say. Then, when it was the four hundred and forty-seventh night, SHE CONTINUED:

I have heard, O fortunate king, that when the girl answered the scholar and told him that there was much dispute among the learned with regard to the formula 'In the Name of God, the Compassionate, the Merciful', he approved and said: 'So tell me then why these words are not written at the start of the *sura* of Immunity.' She replied: 'When this *sura* was revealed, revoking the pact between the Prophet, may God bless him and give him peace, and the polytheists, the Prophet sent 'Ali ibn Abi Talib, may God honour him, to them on a feast day taking with him this *sura*, and he recited it to them without the words "in the Name of God, the Compassionate, the Merciful".' 'Tell me then,' he said, 'of the merit of this formula and of the blessings that it brings.' She replied: 'It is reported that the Prophet of God, may God bless him and give him peace, said: "Whenever these words are recited over anything, a blessing is found in it" and also: "The Lord of glory has sworn by His glory that whenever these words are recited over a sick man, he will be cured of his sickness." It is also reported that when God created the empyrean, it became violently disturbed, but when He wrote these words on it, it came to rest. When they were revealed to the Prophet, he said: "I am safe from three things – being swallowed up in the earth, being changed into a beast and being drowned." In fact, their merits and blessings are so numerous that it would take a long time to go through them. It is reported that the Apostle of God, may God bless him and give him peace, said: "On the Day of Resurrection, a man will be brought before God and when, at His judgement, he is found to have done no good deed, he will be ordered to be thrown into hellfire. He will say: 'My God, you have not treated me justly.' God, Great and Glorious, will say: 'Why is that?' and the man will say: 'You named Yourself the Compassionate, the Merciful, and yet You want to punish me with hellfire.' The Glorious God will say: 'I did name myself the Compassionate, the Merciful, so because of My mercy, take My servant to Paradise, for I am the most merciful of the merciful.'"'

'Good,' he said, 'and now tell me when these words were first used.' She said: 'When God first revealed the Quran, the scribes wrote: "In Your Name, O my God"; then, when He revealed the verse "say: 'Call on God or call on the Compassionate; however you call on Him, His are the fairest of names,'" they wrote: "In the Name of God, the Compassionate." Then, when the revelation "Your God is one God; there is no god but God, the Compassionate, the Merciful"* came, they wrote: "In the Name of God, the Compassionate, the Merciful."'

When he heard this, the Quranic scholar silently bowed his head and said to himself: 'This is something entirely extraordinary. How can this girl talk about the first usage of these words? By God, I must try to do something to get the better of her.' So he said: 'Girl, did God reveal the Quran in one piece or section by section?' She said: 'Gabriel, the Trusted, on whom be peace, brought it down from the Lord of all to His Prophet, Muhammad, lord of the apostles and seal of the prophets, with its commands, prohibitions, promises and warnings, histories and parables, over a period of twenty years in separate verses to match each occasion.'

'Good,' he said, 'so tell me, what was the first *sura* revealed to the Apostle of God, may God bless him and grant him peace?' 'According to Ibn 'Abbas,' she told him, 'this was the *sura* of Congealed Blood† but according to Jabir ibn Abd Allah it was the *sura* of the Covered,‡ after which the other *suras* and verses were revealed.' 'Tell me,' he said, 'which was the last verse to be revealed?' 'The verse dealing with usury,' she said, 'although it is also said to be the verse "At the coming of God's aid and victory".'§

Night 448

Morning now dawned and Shahrazad broke off from what she had been allowed to say. Then, when it was the four hundred and forty-eighth night, SHE CONTINUED:

* Quran 17.110. † Quran 96. ‡ Quran 74. § Quran 110.1.

I have heard, O fortunate king, that the girl told the scholar about the last verse of the Quran to be revealed. 'Good,' he said, 'and now tell me how many of the companions of the Prophet collected the Quran in his lifetime.' 'There were four of them,' she said. ''Ubayy ibn Ka'b, Zaid ibn Thabit, Abu 'Ubaida 'Amir ibn Jarrah and 'Uthman ibn 'Affan, may God be pleased with them all.' 'Good,' he said, 'so tell me the names of the Quran reciters whose readings we follow.' 'There are four of them,' she said. ''Abd Allah ibn Mas'ud, Ubayy ibn Ka'b, Mu'adh ibn Jabal and Salim ibn 'Abd Allah.' He then asked: 'What do you have to say about God's words "What is sacrificed to idols"?'* She said: 'These are idols that are set up and worshipped in place of Almighty God, with Whom we take refuge.' He asked: 'And what do you have to say about His words "You know what is in my soul, but I do not know what is in Yours"?' She replied: 'This means "You know the truth about me and all that is mine, but I do not know what is Yours." This is shown by His words "You know what is hidden",† and it is also expressed as: "You know my essence, but I do not know Yours."'

'What have you to say about His words "Believers, do not forbid yourselves the good things that God allows you"?'‡ he asked. She said: 'My *shaikh*, may God have mercy on him, told me that al-Dahhak said that this refers to a group of Muslims who proposed to castrate themselves and wear sackcloth, as a result of which this verse was revealed. Qatada said that it was revealed after a number of the companions of the Prophet, may God bless him and give him peace, including 'Ali ibn Abi Talib, 'Uthman ibn Mus'ab and others, had thought of castrating themselves, wearing hair shirts and becoming monks.' 'What do you have to say about His words "And He took Abraham as a Friend"?'§ he asked. 'The word for "friend" (*khalil*),' she said, 'means "needy and poor", although according to another interpretation it means "a lover devoted to Almighty God, in whose devotion there is no defect".'

When the Quranic scholar saw that she spoke as easily as clouds that pass, with no hesitation, he rose to his feet and said: 'Commander of the Faithful, I bear witness before God that this girl knows more than I do about the readings of the Quran and other matters.' At that she said: 'Now I shall ask you one question; if you answer it, well and good, but if not, then take off your robe.' 'Put the question to him,' said the caliph, and she then asked: 'Which Quranic verse contains twenty-three

* Quran 5.4.   † Quran 5.116.   ‡ Quran 5.89.   § Quran 4.124.

instances of the letter *kaf*, which has sixteen *mims*, which has a hundred and forty *'ains* and which portion of the Quran does not contain the formula covering the sublimity of God?' The scholar was unable to answer and had to obey when she told him to take off his cloak. She then explained to the caliph that the verse with the sixteen *mims* is found in the *sura* of Hud, in God's words 'Noah, come down from the ark in Our peace, and blessings be upon you', and so on until the end of the verse.* The verse with the twenty-three *kafs* is the verse of Debt in the *sura* of the Cow;† while the hundred and forty *'ains* are found in the *sura* al-A'raf, in God's words 'Moses chose seventy men from his people to go at the appointed time',‡ for each man had two eyes (*'ain*).§ 'The portion that does not contain the formula of sublimity is found in the *sura* "The hour draws near and the moon has been split", the *sura* of the Merciful and the *sura* of the Happening.' At that, the scholar removed his robe and left the room abashed.

Night 449

Morning now dawned and Shahrazad broke off from what she had been allowed to say. Then, when it was the four hundred and forty-ninth night, SHE CONTINUED:

I have heard, O fortunate king, that the girl got the better of the scholar and took his robes, after which he left abashed.

At this point, the skilled doctor came forward and said to Tawaddud: 'We have finished with theology, so get ready to deal with what concerns the human body. Tell me, then, about man and how he is created; how many veins, bones and vertebrae does he have? Where is the principal vein and why was Adam called Adam?' She replied: 'Adam was called Adam because of his brown colour,¶ or an alternative suggestion is that he was created from the surface** of the earth. His breast was made from the earth of the Ka'ba, his head from that of the east and his legs from that of the west. His head was furnished with seven portals: two eyes, two ears, two nostrils and a mouth. He had two other passages, one in front and one behind. The eyes served the sense of sight, the ears that of hearing, the nostrils that of smell and the mouth that of taste,

---

* Quran 11.50.   † Quran 2.282.   ‡ Quran 7.154.   § Arabic for 'eye' is *'ain*.
¶ In Arabic, *'udma*.   ** In Arabic, *adim*.

while the tongue was created to express what was in his mind. He was compounded of four elements: water, earth, fire and air. Yellow bile is the natural constituent of fire and is hot and dry; black bile is the natural constituent of earth and is cold and dry; phlegm is the natural constituent of water and is cold and moist; while blood is the natural constituent of air and is hot and moist.

'A man has three hundred and sixty veins, two hundred and forty bones and three vital parts – the animal soul, the spiritual soul and the natural soul, each of which exercises a function of its own. God gave man a heart, spleen, lungs, six intestines, a liver, two kidneys, two buttocks, brain, bones, skin and five senses – hearing, sight, smell, taste and touch. The heart was set in the left of the breast, with the stomach in front of it. The lungs act as a fan for the heart and the liver is set opposite it on the right-hand side. God then created the diaphragm and the intestines that lie below, and He produced the bones of the chest with their grid of ribs.'

'Good,' said the doctor, 'and now tell me how many hollow chambers there are in the brain.' 'Three,' she said, 'comprising five faculties known as the inner senses, that is, the sensus communis, imagination, the controlling intellect, the power of fantasy and that of memory.' 'Good,' he said, 'and so tell me about the structure of the bones.'

Night 450

Morning now dawned and Shahrazad broke off from what she had been allowed to say. Then, when it was the four hundred and fiftieth night, SHE CONTINUED:

I have heard, O fortunate king, that the doctor asked Tawaddud to tell him about the structure of the bones. She said: 'This structure comprises two hundred and forty bones, divided into three sections – the head, the torso and the limbs. The head comprises the cranium and the face. The cranium is composed of eight bones, to which are added the four connected with the ears. The face has an upper and a lower jaw, with eleven bones in the upper and one in the lower. Added to these are the thirty-two teeth, together with the hyoid bone. As for the torso, it comprises the spinal column, the chest and the pelvis. The spinal column is made up of twenty-four bones known as vertebrae; the chest has the breastbone and twenty-four ribs, twelve on each side; and the pelvis has the two hip bones, the sacrum and the coccyx. The limbs are divided into upper and lower limbs. Each of the upper limbs is divided in its turn: firstly, into a shoulder, made up of a shoulder blade and a clavicle; secondly, into an upper arm consisting of a single bone; thirdly, into a forearm, which has two bones – the radius and the ulna; and fourthly, a hand, divided into wrist, metacarpus and fingers. The wrist is composed of eight bones set in two rows, with four in each row. The metacarpus has five bones, and the five fingers have three bones each, known as the phalanges, except for the thumb, which has only two. Each of the lower limbs is divided, firstly into the thigh, which consists of a single bone; then the shank, comprising three bones, the fibula, the shin bone and the knee bone; and thirdly, there is the foot, which is divided, like the hand, into the ankle, the instep and the toes. The ankle has seven bones set in two rows, the first with two bones and the second with five. The instep has five bones, and each of the five toes has three phalanges, except for the big toe, which has only two.'

'Good,' said the doctor, 'so tell me about the root of the veins.' She replied: 'The veins branch off from their root, the aorta, and no one knows how many there are except for their Creator, although there are claimed to be three hundred and sixty, as has already been said. God has set the tongue as an interpreter, the eyes as lamps, the nostrils as organs of smell, and the hands in place of wings. The liver is the seat of mercy, the spleen is the seat of laughter and the kidneys of guile, while the lungs are a fan, the stomach a storehouse and the heart is the body's buttress. When the heart is sound, the whole body is sound, and when it is disordered, so is the whole body.'

'Tell me, then,' said the doctor, 'of the external signs and symptoms of disease both in the external and internal organs.' 'Certainly,' she said. 'The knowledgeable doctor examines the condition of the body and by feeling the hands he draws his conclusion from their firmness, heat, dryness, coldness and dampness. He can find indications of concealed diseases in what is apparent to the senses. For instance, yellowness of the eyeball is a sign of jaundice, while a curved spine can indicate lung disease.' 'Good,' the doctor said . . .

Night 451

Morning now dawned and Shahrazad broke off from what she had been allowed to say. Then, when it was the four hundred and fifty-first night, SHE CONTINUED:

I have heard, O fortunate king, that the doctor approved of what Tawaddud said about the external signs.

'But what are the internal signs?' She replied: 'To identify diseases by internal signs, one must look at six points: the first being actions; the second, what is excreted from the body; the third, pain; the fourth, the place affected; the fifth, swellings; and the sixth, the effluvia.' Then he said: 'What harms the head?' 'Eating food on top of undigested food,' she said, 'and stuffing oneself after having already stuffed oneself, for this has destroyed whole peoples. Whoever wants a long life should take an early breakfast and not have his evening meal too late. He should not overindulge in sexual intercourse, and he must limit his use of potentially dangerous measures, that is, he should not often be bled or cupped. He should divide his stomach into three parts – one for food, one for water and one for breath. Human intestines are eighteen spans in length, of which six should be devoted to food, six to water and six for breath. It is better for him and more suitable for his body to walk at an easy pace, and this is in accordance with God's words "Do not walk proudly on the earth." '*

'Good,' he said, 'so now tell me the symptoms of yellow bile and what is to be feared from it.' She replied: 'It is to be recognized by a yellow complexion, bitterness in the mouth, dryness, a weakness of sexual appetite and a rapid pulse. Those who suffer from it are at risk of burning fevers, brain disease, carbuncles, jaundice, swellings, intestinal ulcers and extreme thirst.' 'Good,' he said, 'so tell me the symptoms of black bile and what is to be feared from it when it takes over the body.' She replied: 'It produces a delusive appetite, folly, anxiety and worries. It needs to be drained off or else it will lead to melancholy, leprosy, cancer, pains in the spleen and ulcerations in the intestines.'

'Good,' he said. 'Now tell me into how many parts medicine is divided.' 'Into two,' she answered, 'of which one concerns the treatment of sick bodies and the second the methods by which they can be restored

* Quran 17.39.

to health.' 'Tell me then,' he said, 'when is the most efficacious time in which to drink medicinal draughts?' She replied: 'It is when the sap rises in the wood, grapes form on their clusters and the stars of good omen rise, for this marks a time that is useful for the taking of draughts and the repelling of diseases.' He then said: 'Tell me, when a man drinks from a new container, at what time will his drink be pleasanter and more wholesome and a clean and sweet odour rise up for him.' She answered: 'This will happen if he waits for a time after eating. The poet has said:

> Do not be in a hurry to drink after you eat,
> As this will bring your body to harm.
> Wait for a little while when you have eaten
> And then perhaps you will get what you want.'

'Tell me,' he said, 'about the type of food which does not produce any sickness.' She replied: 'This is food that is only eaten when the eater is hungry and which does not fill the ribs. The wise Galen said that whoever wants to take food will not go wrong if he eats slowly. Let me finish by quoting from the Prophet, may God bless him and give him peace: "The stomach is the centre of disease and dieting is the principal cure. Every disease starts with indigestion, that is, what is produced by unsuitable food."'

Night 452

Morning now dawned and Shahrazad broke off from what she had been allowed to say. Then, when it was the four hundred and fifty-second night, SHE CONTINUED:

I have heard, O fortunate king, that Tawaddud said: 'The stomach is the centre of disease and dieting is the principal cure.'

The doctor then asked: 'What do you have to say about the baths?' She replied: 'No one should go to the baths in a state of repletion. The Prophet, may God bless him and give him peace, said: "What an excellent place are the baths, which clean the body and remind man of hellfire."' 'Which baths have the best water?' he asked. She replied: 'Those with sweet water, plenty of space and good air, so that the four seasons, autumn, summer, winter and spring, are represented in the atmosphere there.' He asked: 'What is the best food?' She replied: 'Food prepared by women with no great effort, which is wholesome to eat. The best type of food is broth made with meat and bread; as the Prophet, may God bless him and give him peace, said: "The superiority of this broth over the other types of food is like the superiority of 'A'isha over all other women."' 'Which food eaten with bread is best?' he asked. 'Meat,' she told him, 'as the Prophet, may God bless him and give him peace, said: "Meat is the best thing to eat with bread as it is a source of pleasure both in this world and the next."' 'Which is the best type of meat?' 'Mutton,' she said, 'but dried meat is to be avoided as there is nothing beneficial in it.'

'Tell me then about fruit,' he said. 'Eat it while it is ripe,' she said, 'but leave it when it has passed its prime.' 'What have you to say about drinking water?' he asked. 'You should not drink more than you need,' she said, 'or gulp it down, for this will give you a headache and produce various kinds of harmful disturbances. You should also not drink after you have come from the baths, after sexual intercourse or after taking food until fifteen minutes have elapsed in the case of a youth, and forty for an old man, nor should you drink after waking from sleep.' 'Good,' he said, 'and so tell me about drinking wine.' She replied: 'Are not God's words in the Quran sufficient as a deterrent where He says: "Wine, *maisir*, idols and divination arrows are filth of Satan's handiwork: avoid them and you may prosper"?* God also said: "They will ask you about wine and gambling. Say: 'These involve great sin and although they have some benefits for mankind, the sin is greater than the benefits.'" The poet has said:

> Wine drinkers, are you not ashamed to drink what God forbids?
> Leave it alone and do not go near it;
> For here is something God has censured.

Another poet said on the same point:

> I drank sinful wine until I lost my wits:
> It is an evil drink that robs a man of these.

As for its benefits, it disperses kidney stones, strengthens the intestines, dispels care, prompts generosity, preserves health, aids digestion, keeps the body sound, removes ailments from the joints and cleanses the body of putrid humours. It also causes joy and delight as well as invigorating the natural constitution. It fortifies the bladder, strengthens the liver,

* Quran 5.92.

removes blockages, reddens the cheeks, cleanses the head and the brain and slows the progress of grey hairs. Had God not forbidden it, there would have been nothing to match it on the face of the earth. As for *maisir*, it is a form of gambling.' 'Which wine is the best?' he asked. She replied: 'Wine pressed from white grapes when it is eighty days old or older. It is not like water and there is nothing on the face of the earth to match it.'

'What have you to say about cupping?' he asked. She said: 'This is used when the patient has too much blood and not when he has too little. Whoever wants to be cupped should wait for a cloudless day with no wind or rain when the moon is on the wane. This should be on the seventeenth of the month and if this happens to be a Tuesday, it will be more effective in helping the patient. Cupping is particularly useful for the brain, the eyes and for clearing the mind.'

Night 453

Morning now dawned and Shahrazad broke off from what she had been allowed to say. Then, when it was the four hundred and fifty-third night, SHE CONTINUED:

I have heard, O fortunate king, that when Tawaddud had described the advantages of cupping, the doctor asked: 'What is the best type of cupping?' and she said: 'It is best done on an empty stomach, for it adds to the powers of the mind and of memory. It is reported that the Prophet, may God bless him and give him peace, would advise cupping whenever anyone complained to him of pains in the head or the legs, adding that when the man had been cupped, he should not eat salty food on an empty stomach, as this leads to scabies, nor should he eat anything acidic.' 'What times are bad for cupping?' the doctor asked. 'Saturdays and Wednesdays,' she told him, 'and whoever is cupped on these days has only himself to blame. It should not be done either in very hot or in very cold weather, and the best time for it is the spring.'

The doctor then asked her about sexual intercourse, at which she was silent, hanging her head out of embarrassment and respect for the caliph. Then she said: 'Commander of the Faithful, it is not that I cannot reply but I am ashamed to do so, although the answer is on the tip of my tongue.' The caliph told her to speak on, and so she said: 'Intercourse has many merits and praiseworthy features, among them being that it relieves bodies filled with black bile. It calms passion, induces love, produces happiness and removes loneliness. Frequent indulgence in it is more harmful in summer and autumn than in winter and spring.'

'Tell me of its advantages,' the doctor said. 'It removes cares and evil thoughts,' she replied. 'It serves to allay both passionate love and anger, and it helps ulcers. This is the case where the constitution is predominantly cold and dry. Overindulgence weakens the eyesight and generates pains in the legs, the head and the back. You should be particularly careful not to sleep with an old woman, for old women are fatal. The imam 'Ali, may God ennoble him, said: "Four things kill the body or render it decrepit. They are: entering the baths with a full stomach; eating salty food; copulating with a full stomach; and copulating with a sick woman, for she will weaken you and make you ill, while an old woman is deadly poison." Someone else said: "Take care not to marry an old woman, even if she is richer than Qarun."'

'What is the pleasantest form of intercourse?' he asked. She replied: 'It is when the woman is young, with a good figure, beautiful cheeks and swelling breasts, as well as being well born. She will then add to your health and strength, and she fits the description:

Wherever you turn your eyes, she knows what it is you want
With no indication or explanation, but by induction.
When you look at her marvellous loveliness,
Her beauty serves for you in place of a garden.'

'Tell me, then, what is the best time for copulation?' he said. 'If you do it at night,' she said, 'the best time is when you have digested, and if by day, then after the morning meal.'

'What are the best fruits?' he asked. 'Pomegranate and citron,' she answered. 'And what are the best vegetables?' 'Endives.' 'And which are the best of the scented flowers?' 'Roses and violets.' He then asked: 'Where is a man's semen formed?' She said: 'Man has a central vein which supplies all the rest. Liquid is collected from three hundred and sixty veins and then enters the left testicle in the form of red blood. Cooked by man's natural heat it turns to a thick white substance which smells like the spadix of a palm tree.'

'Good,' he said, 'so tell me which winged creature produces semen and menstruates.' 'This is the bat,' she told him. Then he asked what it was that lived in confinement and died when it sniffed the air. 'The fish,' she answered. He asked which snake lays eggs, to which she replied:

'The *thu'ban* serpent.'* The doctor had asked so many questions that he could not go on and had to fall silent. Tawaddud then said: 'Commander of the Faithful, he has tired himself out asking me questions; now I shall put one to him and if he cannot answer it, his robe will lawfully be mine.'

Night 454

Morning now dawned and Shahrazad broke off from what she had been allowed to say. Then, when it was the four hundred and fifty-fourth night, SHE CONTINUED:

I have heard, O fortunate king, that Tawaddud said: 'He has tired himself out asking me questions; now I shall put one to him and if he cannot answer it, his robe will lawfully be mine.' 'Ask the question,' said the caliph. So she said: 'What do you have to say about something that is round as the earth and whose spine and whose resting place are hidden from sight? It is of little value; it has a narrow chest and a fetter around its throat, although it is not a runaway slave; it is in chains, although it is not a thief; it has been stabbed, but not in battle, and wounded, but not in fight. It eats away time as it passes and it drinks water in abundance. At times, it is beaten for no fault, and made to serve, although it has no competence. After being scattered, it is collected together; it is humble but not because it wants to flatter, and pregnant, although it has no child in its womb. It leans over, but does not rest on its side. It becomes dirty and then cleans itself; it endures heat and is changed; it copulates without a penis; it wrestles without anyone being wary of it; it gives rest and seeks rest; it is bitten but does not cry out; it is more generous than a boon companion but further removed than summer heat. It leaves its wife at night and embraces her by day, and it lives in the outer parts of the dwellings of the noble.'

The doctor, taken aback, stayed silent and made no reply. His colour changed and he hung his head for a while without speaking. 'Doctor,' she said, 'say something or else strip off your robe.' He got up and said: 'Commander of the Faithful, I testify that this girl knows more than I do about medicine and other subjects. There is nothing I can do to overcome her.' He then took off his robe and fled. The caliph then asked

* The reference to egg-laying is perhaps to the eel.

Tawaddud to explain her riddle to him, and she told him that the answer was a button and a buttonhole.

She then had an encounter with an astronomer, after having invited whichever of those present was an expert in this field to stand up. The astronomer came up and took his seat in front of her. When she saw him, she laughed and asked: 'Are you astronomer, mathematician and scribe?' When he said yes, she told him to ask what question he wanted, adding: 'God is Who gives success.' He then said: 'Tell me about the rising and setting of the sun.' She replied: 'It rises from sources in one region, the east, and sets in other sources in another region, the west, each of them covering one hundred and eighty degrees. Almighty God has said: "No, I swear by the Lord of the east and the west,"* and also: "It is He Who has made the sun a light and the moon a radiance, and ordained their stations that you should know how to calculate the years and to measure time."† The moon rules the night and the sun the day. They race against each other, the one trying to overtake the other, but Almighty God has said: "The sun must not overtake the moon and the night must not outstrip the day, but each moves in an orbit of its own."'‡

The astronomer then said: 'Tell me, when it is night, what happens to day and vice versa?' She quoted the Quran: '"He causes the night to enter into the day and the day into the night."'§ He then asked about the stations of the moon and she said that there were twenty-eight of them: 'Al-Sharatan, al-Butain, al-Thurayya, al-Dabaran, al-Haq'a, al-Han'a, al-Dhira', al-Nathra, al-Tarf, al-Jabha, al-Zubra, al-Sarfa, al-'Awwa', al-Samak, al-Ghafr, al-Zubanaya, al-Iklil, al-Qalb, al-Shaula, al-Na'a'im, al-Balda, Sa'd al-Dhabih, Sa'd Bal'ua, Sa'd al-Su'ud, Sa'd al-Akhbiya, al-Fargh al-Muqaddam, al-Fargh al-Mu'akhkhar and al-Risha'. These are arranged from beginning to end in accordance with the letters of the Abjad-Hawwaz alphabet and they contain an obscure secret known only to Almighty God, to Whom be the glory, and to profound scholars. They are divided among the twelve signs of the zodiac, with each of these being given two and a third stations. So al-Sharatan, al-Butain and a third of al-Thurayya are given to Aries; two-thirds of al-Thurayya together with al-Dabaran and two-thirds of al-Haq'a to Taurus; one-third of al-Haq'a, together with al-Han'a and al-Dhira' to Gemini; al-Nathra, al-Tarf and one-third of al-Jabha to Cancer; two-thirds of al-Jabha, together with al-Zubra and two-thirds

---

* Quran 70.40. † Quran 10.5. ‡ Quran 36.40. § Quran 22.60, 57.6.

of al-Sarfa to Leo; one-third of al-Sarfa, together with al-'Awwa' and al-Samak to Virgo; al-Ghafr, al-Zubanaya and a third of al-Iklil to Libra; two-thirds of al-Iklil, with al-Qalb and two-thirds of al-Shaula to Scorpio; one-third of al-Shaula with al-Na'a'im and al-Balda to Sagittarius; Sa'd al-Dhabih, Sa'd al-Bal'ua and one-third of Sa'd al-Su'ud to Capricorn; two-thirds of Sa'd al-Su'ud, Sa'd al-Akhbiya and two-thirds of al-Fargh al-Muqaddam to Aquarius; and one-third of al-Farqh al-Muqaddam together with al-Fargh al-Mu'akhkhar and al-Risha' to Pisces.'

Night 455

Morning now dawned and Shahrazad broke off from what she had been allowed to say. Then, when it was the four hundred and fifty-fifth night, SHE CONTINUED:

I have heard, O fortunate king, that Tawaddud counted off the stations and divided them among the zodiacal signs. 'Good,' said the astronomer when she had finished, 'so now tell me about their planets, their natures, how long they stay in the various houses of the zodiac, which of them are auspicious and which inauspicious, where their houses are and their ascendants and descendants.' She replied: 'This session will not be enough, but nevertheless I can tell you that there are seven planets – the sun, the moon, Mercury, Venus, Mars, Jupiter and Saturn. The sun is hot and dry, inauspicious in conjunction, auspicious in aspect. It stays in each sign of the zodiac for thirty days. The moon is cold, moist and auspicious. It stays in each sign for two and a third days. Mercury has a mixed nature in that it brings good fortune when it is in conjunction with auspicious bodies and misfortune in conjunction with the inauspicious. It stays in each sign for seventeen and a half days. Venus is temperate and auspicious, staying in each sign for twenty-five days, while Mars is inauspicious and stays for ten months in each sign. Jupiter is auspicious and stays in each sign for a year, and Saturn, which is cold and dry, is inauspicious and stays for three months in each sign.

'The sun's house is Leo, with Capricorn being its ascendant and Aquarius its descendant. The moon's house is Cancer; its ascendant is Taurus and its descendant Scorpio; it is unhealthy when it is in Capricorn. Capricorn, together with Aquarius, is the house of Saturn, whose ascendant is Libra; its descendant is Aries, and it is unhealthy when in Cancer

and Leo. Pisces and Sagittarius are the house of Jupiter. Its ascendant is
Cancer, its descendant is Capricorn and it is unhealthy when in Gemini
and Leo. The house of Venus is Leo; its ascendant is Pisces, its descendant
is Libra and it is unhealthy in Aries and Scorpio. Mercury's house is
Gemini and Virgo; Virgo is its ascendant and Pisces its descendant, while
it is unhealthy in Taurus. The house of Mars is Aries and Scorpio;
Capricorn is its ascendant and Cancer its descendant, and it is unhealthy
in Libra.'

When the astronomer saw her skill, learning, eloquence and intelligence, he looked for some way to discomfort her in the presence of the
caliph and so he asked her whether any rain would fall that month. She
bowed her head in silence and spent so long in thought that the caliph
imagined that she could find no answer. 'Why don't you say something?'
asked the astronomer. 'I shall not speak unless the Commander of the
Faithful gives me leave,' she said. The caliph laughed and said: 'And why
is that?' She replied: 'I want you to give me a sword that I may cut off
his head, for he is an atheist.' The caliph and his entourage burst out
laughing and Tawaddud said: 'Astronomer, do you not know that there
are five things known only to Almighty God?' and she recited: 'God
knows when the last hour will be, when the rain will fall, and the sex of
the child in the womb. No soul knows what it will acquire tomorrow
and no soul knows in what land it will die. God is Omniscient and
All-Knowing.'*

'Good,' said the astronomer, 'for, by God, I only wanted to test
you.' She went on: 'The almanac makers have a number of signs and
indications relating to the planets as observed at the start of the year,
and others have some empirical knowledge.' 'What signs are these?' he
asked. She replied: 'Every day is under the control of a planet. When the
first day of a year falls on a Sunday, it belongs to the sun, and this,
although God knows better, indicates injustice on the part of kings,
sultans and rulers, an unhealthy year and a lack of rain. This is combined
with popular disturbances, but cereals will be good, although lentils will
be ruined and grapes spoiled. Cotton will be dear and wheat cheap from
the start of the month Tuba to the end of Barmahat. There will be much
fighting between kings, but the year itself will be prosperous. God knows
better.'

He then asked her about a year that starts on a Monday, and she said:

* Quran 31.34.

'This is governed by the moon. It indicates that administrators and governors will act justly, rainfall will be heavy, cereals will prosper but linseed will be spoilt. Wheat will be cheap in the month of Kaihak; there will be a lot of plague and half the sheep and goats will die. There will be an abundance of grapes and a shortage of honey, while cotton will be cheap. God knows better.'

Night 456

Morning now dawned and Shahrazad broke off from what she had been allowed to say. Then, when it was the four hundred and fifty-sixth night, SHE CONTINUED:

I have heard, O fortunate king, that when Tawaddud finished telling him about Monday, the astronomer then asked her about years starting on a Tuesday. 'These are under the influence of Mars, which indicates the deaths of great men, much destruction and the spilling of blood. Cereals will be expensive and there will be a shortage of rain and a lack of fish, although numbers of the latter will increase at times and then diminish. Honey and lentils will be cheap, while linseed will be expensive. Barley will do particularly well, there will be much fighting between kings, deaths will be violent and there will be a high mortality among donkeys. God knows better.' He asked her about years that start on a Wednesday and she said: 'These are governed by Mercury, which indicates great popular disturbances, many enemies and moderate rainfall. Some crops will be spoilt and there will be a great mortality rate among riding beasts and infants. There will be many sea battles, wheat will be expensive from the month of Barmuda to Misra, while other cereals will be cheap. There will be plenty of thunder and lightning, honey will be expensive, palm trees will be fruitful, flax and cotton will be plentiful, and radishes and onions will be dear. God knows better.' He then said: 'Tell me about Thursday.' She replied: 'Thursday belongs to Jupiter, which indicates that the viziers will act with justice, the *qadis* and *faqihs* will behave well, as will the men of religion. Good things will abound; rainfall will be plentiful, and fruits, trees and cereals will flourish; flax, cotton, honey and grapes will be cheap and there will be plenty of fish. God knows better.' When he then asked about Friday, she said: 'This belongs to Venus and indicates that there will be injustice among the leaders of the *jinn*, together with perfidy and defamation. Dews will be heavy and there will be a good autumn everywhere; prices will be low in some lands but not in others. Wickedness will be found in plenty both on land and sea. Linseed will be expensive and so will wheat in the month of Hatur, although in Amshir it will be cheap.* Honey will be expensive and grapes and watermelons will rot. God knows better.' He asked her about Saturday and she said: 'This belongs to Saturn and indicates that a year starting on a Saturday will favour slaves, Rumis, and persons worthless in themselves and worthless as associates. Prices will be generally high and there will be much famine. There will be a high mortality rate, while the Egyptians and the Syrians will suffer injustice at the hands of the sultan. Crops will not flourish and cereals will decay. God knows better.'

At this, the astrologer hung his head and Tawaddud said: 'I shall put a question to you and if you don't answer, I shall take your robe.' 'Continue,' he told her, and she asked: 'Where is the seat of Saturn?' 'In the seventh heaven,' he answered. 'And of Jupiter?' 'In the sixth.' 'And of Mars?' 'In the fifth.' 'And of the sun?' 'In the fourth.' 'And of Venus?' 'In the third.' 'And of Mercury?' 'In the second.' 'And of the moon?' 'In the first.' 'Well done,' she said, 'and now I have one more question for you.' 'Continue,' he replied. 'Into how many divisions are the stars to be separated?' she asked, and at this he remained silent and made no reply. 'Take off your robe,' she said. He did this and after she had taken it, the caliph told her to explain the answer to her question. She said: 'Commander of the Faithful, there are three divisions of stars. One of these is attached to our heaven like lamps and it is these that illumine the earth. A second group of stars is thrown at the devils when they try stealthily to listen to what is said in Paradise. This is as God Almighty said: "We have adorned the heavens and the earth with lamps and have set them there so that they may be thrown at the devils."† The third group is fixed in the air and it illumines the seas and what is found in them.'

The astronomer then said: 'I have one more question, and if she answers it I will acknowledge that she has the better of me.' 'Continue,' she said.

* Tuba, Barmahat, Kaihak, Barmuda, Misra, Hatur and Amshir are months in the Coptic (solar) calendar.
† Quran 67.5.

Night 457

Morning now dawned and Shahrazad broke off from what she had been allowed to say. Then, when it was the four hundred and fifty-seventh night, SHE CONTINUED:

I have heard, O fortunate king, that the astronomer said: 'Tell me about four opposites that are consequent on four other opposites.' 'Heat, cold, moistness and dryness,' she said. 'Almighty God created fire from heat, its nature being hot and dry. He created earth from dryness, its nature being cold and dry. He created water from coldness, its nature being cold and moist, and He created air from moistness, its nature being hot and moist. He then created the twelve signs of the zodiac – Aries, Taurus, Gemini, Cancer, Leo, Virgo, Libra, Scorpio, Sagittarius, Capricorn, Aquarius and Pisces. These are based on the four humours – three on fire, three on earth, three on air and three on water. The fiery signs are Aries, Leo and Sagittarius; Taurus, Virgo and Capricorn are earthy; Gemini, Libra and Aquarius are airy; and Cancer, Scorpio and Pisces watery.'

The astronomer got up and said: 'I testify that she knows more than I do,' and he went away defeated. The caliph then asked: 'Where is the philosopher?' at which a man rose and came forward. He said to Tawaddud: 'Tell me about time, how it is determined, and its days and what it brings.' She replied: 'Time is a name applied to the hours of the night and the day, these being measurements of the courses of the sun and the moon in their orbits. This is shown by Almighty God where He says: "Night is a sign for them from which We remove the day, leaving them covered in darkness as the sun goes to its resting place. That is the decree of God, the Omnipotent, the Omniscient."'* 'Tell me then,' said the philosopher, 'how man comes to be affected by unbelief.' She replied: 'It is reported that the Apostle of God, may God bless him and give him peace, said: "Unbelief among mankind flows as the blood flows in the veins, where they rail at the world, time, night and at the Last Hour." He also said: "Let no one rail against time, for time is God, or against the world, for the world says: 'May God not aid any who revile me.' Let none of you revile the Hour, for there is no doubt that it is coming, or the earth, for this is one of God's signs, as He said: 'From it We have

* Quran 36.37–8.

created you and to it We shall return you, and We shall then bring you out from it a second time.'"*

The philosopher then said: 'Tell me about five creatures that ate and drank but were not produced from loins or wombs.' 'These are Adam, Simeon, Salih's camel, Ishmael's ram and the bird seen by Abu Bakr the Truthful in the cave.'† 'Tell me,' he said next, 'about five who are in Paradise but are neither human, *jinn* or angels.' She said: 'These are Jacob's wolf, the dog of the Seven Sleepers, Ezra's donkey, the camel of Salih, and Duldul, the mule of the Prophet,‡ may God bless him and give him peace.'

He then said: 'Tell me who it was who prayed, while he was neither on earth or in heaven.' 'This was Solomon, who prayed on his carpet when it was being carried by the wind.' He then said: 'Tell me about a man who looked at a slave girl at the time of the morning prayer. She was unlawful for him then, but at noon was lawful, only to become unlawful again by the afternoon and lawful by the sunset, but unlawful by the time of the evening prayer. Then, in the morning, she was lawful for him.' Tawaddud said: 'This man looked at someone else's slave girl in the morning, when she was unlawful for him. At noon, he bought her and she became lawful; then, in the afternoon, he freed her and she became unlawful. At sunset, he married her and she became lawful, but in the evening he divorced her, making her unlawful, while in the morning he took her back again and she became lawful for him.' 'Tell me,' he then asked, 'about a grave that moved with its occupant.' 'This was the whale of Jonah, son of Mattai, when it swallowed him.' 'Tell me then about a place on which the sun shone once but will never shine again until the

---

* Quran 22.7.

† It is not clear which Simeon Tawaddud is referring to. The camel sent by God to the early Arabian prophet Salih emerged from a rock but was killed by the wicked people of Thamud (Quran 7.73–9, 11.61–8). According to the Quran (but not to the Bible, which has Isaac as the sacrifice), at the last moment a ram was substituted for Ishmael as Abraham's sacrifice. 'The bird seen by Abu Bakr the Truthful' refers to the legend of a bird that made its nest at the mouth of a cave to protect the Prophet and Abu Bakr from discovery by hostile members of the Quraish tribe.

‡ According to legend, Jacob's wolf spoke to Jacob and told him that Joseph's brothers were not telling the truth when they claimed that Joseph had been torn to pieces by a wolf. 'The dog of the Seven Sleepers' refers to the dog (who was called Kitmir) and seven Christians who took refuge from persecution in the reign of the emperor Decius in a cave in the vicinity of Ephesus. There they fell into a miraculous sleep and awoke centuries later. It is not clear what Tawaddud had in mind when she referred to Ezra's donkey. Duldul, the grey mule of the Prophet, was famous for its longevity.

Day of Resurrection.' She said: 'This is the sea struck by Moses with his staff in which twelve passages were split, one for each of the tribes. The sun rose over it, but will not shine there again until the Resurrection.'

Night 458

Morning now dawned and Shahrazad broke off from what she had been allowed to say. Then, when it was the four hundred and fifty-eighth night, SHE CONTINUED:

I have heard, O fortunate king, that the philosopher then asked Tawaddud: 'Tell me, what was the first skirt that was trailed over the surface of the ground?' She said: 'This was the skirt of Hagar, who trailed it when Sara had put her to shame. This then became a custom among the Arabs.' He then said: 'Tell me about something that breathes although it has no life.' She replied: 'This refers to the words of Almighty God: "and the dawn when it breathes".'* 'Tell me,' he said, 'about a number of pigeons that flew to a tall tree where some of them settled on top of it and some beneath it. The ones on top of the tree said to the ones below it: "If one of you comes up, then we will be a third of the total number and if one of us flies down, then we will be the same number as you."' Tawaddud said: 'There were twelve pigeons, seven of which settled on top of the tree and five below it. If one of these latter flew up there would be twice as many above as below, while if one flew down the numbers of both groups would be equal. God knows better.' At this, the philosopher stripped off his robe and fled.

As for the story of her encounter with al-Nazzam, she turned to the scholars who were present and asked: 'Which of you can speak on all branches of knowledge?' Al-Nazzam got up and came to her, saying: 'Don't think that I am like the others.' She replied: 'I am convinced that you will be beaten because you are arrogant and God will help me to defeat you so that I may strip you of your robe. It would be better for you to send someone to fetch you something that you can put on in its place.' 'By God,' he said, 'I shall get the better of you and make you the subject of a story that people will talk about for generations to come.' 'Get ready to atone for breaking your word,' she told him.

He then said: 'Tell me about five things that God created before He

* Quran 81.18.

created mankind.' 'These are water, earth, light, darkness and fruits,' she answered. 'Tell me then about something that God created with the Hand of Power.' 'The Throne,' she said, 'as well as the tree Tuba, Adam and the Garden of Eden. These were all created by the Hand of Power, while to everything else He said: "Be," and they were.' 'Tell me,' he then asked, 'about your father in Islam.' 'This is Muhammad, may God bless him and give him peace,' she answered. 'And who is Muhammad's father in Islam?' he asked, to which she replied: 'Abraham, the Friend of God.' 'What is the religion of Islam?' he asked. 'The confession of faith that there is no god but God and that Muhammad is the Apostle of God,' she answered. 'What is your beginning and what is your end?' he asked. 'My beginning was a drop of foul sperm,' she said, 'and I shall end as a decaying corpse. I came from the earth and there I shall end. The poet puts it:

> I was created from earth and became a person
> Eloquent in question and answer.
> Then I returned to the earth and was buried there
> As it was from this that I was made.'

Al-Nazzam then asked her about something that began as wood and ended as something alive. 'This,' she said, 'was the rod of Moses when he threw it down in the valley, for then, with God's leave, it became a quick-moving serpent.' He next asked her about God's words about Moses' staff in the Quran, 'I have other uses for it.'* She said: 'Whenever Moses planted it in the ground it would blossom and produce fruit, as well as protecting him from both heat and cold. When he was tired it would carry him and it would guard his flocks from savage beasts.' 'Tell me,' he then said, 'about a female produced from a male and a male produced from a female.' She answered: 'This is Eve produced from Adam and Jesus from Mary.' His next question was about four fires, one of which eats and drinks while a second eats but does not drink, a third drinks without eating while the fourth does neither. 'The fire that eats but does not drink,' she answered, 'is the fire of this world, while the fire that eats and drinks is the fire of hell. The fire that drinks but does not eat is the sun's fire, while the fire that neither eats nor drinks is that of the moon.'

Next he asked her about the open and the shut, and she told him that 'the open' referred to the customary practices of Islam and 'the closed' to its necessary obligations. Then he said: 'Tell me about the poet's lines:

---

* Quran 20.19.

There is one who lives in the dust, whose food is by his head;
When he tastes that food, he speaks.
He rises and walks in silence while talking
And returns to the grave from which he was made to rise.
He does not deserve to be respected as a living being,
Nor is he dead and deserving compassion.'

'This is the pen,' she told him.
Next he asked about the poet's lines:

It has two closed pockets and is liable to a flow of blood;
Its ears are covered but its mouth is open.
There is something formed like a cock which pecks at its innards,
And if you put a price on it, it is worth half a dirham.

'This is the pen case,' she told him, and he then asked about the lines:

Say to the men of learning, intelligence and culture
And to every high-ranking *faqih* prominent for his discernment:
'Tell me: what did you see
From a bird in Arab lands and those of non-Arabs?
This is something without flesh or blood,
With no feathers and no down.
It is eaten cooked, it is eaten cold
And it is eaten fried when put in the fire.
It has two colours, one like that of silver
And another charming colour that does not resemble gold.
It is not seen to live, although it is not dead.
Tell me about this for it is a marvel.'

'You have taken a long time in asking about an egg worth only a *fals*,' she replied.

Al-Nazzam then asked her how many words God had spoken to Moses, and she said: 'It is reported that the Prophet of God, may God bless him and give him peace, said: "God spoke one thousand, five hundred and fifteen words to Moses."' 'Tell me then of the fourteen that spoke to the Lord of creation.' She said: 'These were the seven heavens and the seven earths when they said: "We have come in obedience to You."'*

* Quran 41.10.

Night 459

Morning now dawned and Shahrazad broke off from what she had been allowed to say. Then, when it was the four hundred and fifty-ninth night, SHE CONTINUED:

I have heard, O fortunate king, that after this he asked her to tell him about Adam and how first he was created. She told him that God created Adam from clay, the clay being made from foam, the foam from the sea and the sea from darkness. The darkness itself was created from light, which was created from a fish, with the fish being created from a rock, the rock from a ruby, the ruby from water and the water from the power of God, as He said, Almighty is He: 'When He wishes for something, He commands "Be" and it is.'*

He said: 'Tell me about the poet's lines:

One who eats without mouth or stomach,
Whose food is trees and fish;
If you feed it, it is animated and lives,
But if you give it water to drink, it dies.'

'This is fire,' she told him. So he asked about the lines:

Two lovers who are denied all pleasure
And who spend the whole night long in an embrace.
They guard people from every calamity
And at sunrise they part.

'These are the two leaves of a door,' she said. So he asked about the gates of hell and she told him: 'There are seven of these and they are named in the lines:

Jahannam, Lazan and al-Hatim,
Then count in al-Sa'ir and finish the line with Saqar.
After that comes Jahim and then Hawiya –
This is a brief account of their number.'

'Tell me then,' he said, 'about the lines:

Her long locks trail behind her
As she comes and as she goes.

* Quran 36.82.

Her eyes never taste sleep
And never shed a tear.
Never in the course of time does she wear clothing,
But she provides clothing of all kinds to mankind.'

'This is a needle,' she told him.

Next he asked her about the bridge over hell, its length and its breadth.
She said: 'It is a three-thousand-year journey in length, one thousand to
go up, one thousand to come down and one thousand on the level. It is
sharper than a sword and narrower than a hair.'

Night 460

Morning now dawned and Shahrazad broke off from what she had been
allowed to say. Then, when it was the four hundred and sixtieth night,
SHE CONTINUED:

I have heard, O fortunate king, that when she had described the bridge,
he asked: 'Tell me then, how many times does the Prophet Muhammad,
may God bless him and give him peace, intercede for each Muslim?' to
which she replied: 'Thrice.' He then asked her whether Abu Bakr was
the first convert to Islam, and when she said yes, he said that 'Ali had
preceded him. ' 'Ali,' she said, 'went to the Prophet, may God bless him
and give him peace, as a boy of seven and, in spite of his youth, God
guided him so that he never prostrated himself to an idol.' 'Tell me,' he
then said, 'which was better, 'Ali or al-'Abbas?' She realized that he was
trying to trick her, for if she said ' 'Ali', she would not be able to excuse
herself before the Abbasid caliph. She hung her head in silence for a
while, at times reddening and at times turning pale. Then she answered:
'You are asking me about two excellent men, each with his own excellence, so let us go back to where we were.' At this the caliph got to his
feet and said: 'By the Lord of the Ka'ba, that was well done, Tawaddud.'

At that, Ibrahim al-Nazzam said: 'Tell me about the poet's lines:

Its skirts are slender and its taste is sweet;
It is like a spear but has no point.
It provides advantages for mankind
And is eaten after the afternoon prayer in Ramadan.'

'This is the sugar-cane,' she replied.

He then said: 'Answer me a number of questions.' 'What are they?' she asked. He replied: 'What is sweeter than honey? What is sharper than a sword? What is swifter than poison? What is the pleasure of an hour? What is three days' happiness? What is the pleasantest day? What is the joy of a week? What is the due that even a liar will not deny? What is the prison of the tomb? What is the heart's delight? What tricks the soul? What is the death of life? What is the disease that cannot be cured? What is the disgrace that cannot be effaced? What is the beast that lives in the wild and does not approach cultivated land; it hates mankind and is created with the nature of seven powerful creatures?' She said: 'Listen to my answers and then strip off your robe so that I may explain things to you.' 'Explain,' said the caliph, 'and he will take off his robe.' So she said: 'The thing that is sweeter than honey is children who are dutiful towards their parents. What is sharper than the sword is the tongue, while what is swifter than poison is the eye of the malignant. Sexual intercourse is the pleasure of an hour, while three days' happiness is a woman's depilatory. The pleasantest day is when one makes a trading profit. The joy of a week is marriage and the due that not even a liar can deny is death. The prison of the tomb is a bad son. The heart's delight is a wife who obeys her husband, but it is also said that this is meat when it is swallowed, as this rejoices the heart. What tricks the soul is a disobedient slave, while the death of life is poverty. As for the incurable disease, this is an evil character, and the disgrace that cannot be effaced is a bad daughter. The beast that lives in the wild and does not approach cultivated land, hating mankind and created with the nature of seven powerful creatures, is the locust. Its head is like that of a horse; it has a bull's neck, an eagle's wings and the feet of a camel. Its tail is that of a snake, its belly is that of a scorpion and its horns are those of a gazelle.'

The caliph Harun al-Rashid, astonished by her skill and understanding, told al-Nazzam to take off his robe. He got up and said: 'I call all those who are present at this gathering to bear witness against me that this girl is more learned than I am and than all other scholars.' He took off his robes and told her: 'Take them, but may God give you no blessing with them.' The caliph then ordered robes to be brought for him to put on, after which he said to Tawaddud: 'There is still one thing left that you promised to do, and that is to play chess.' At his command, the masters of chess, cards and backgammon were brought to him. The chess player sat with Tawaddud, the pieces were set out and play began. Whatever move he made she very soon blocked . . .

Night 461

Morning now dawned and Shahrazad broke off from what she had been allowed to say. Then, when it was the four hundred and sixty-first night, SHE CONTINUED:

I have heard, O fortunate king, that when Tawaddud played chess with the expert, whatever move he made she soon blocked, until she got the better of him and he found himself checkmated. 'I wanted to tempt you,' he explained, 'so that you might think yourself an expert, but now set out the pieces and I'll show you.' When she had done this, he said to himself: 'Keep your eyes open or else she will beat you.' So all his moves were made with due calculation, but at the end of the game it was she who said checkmate. When he saw that, he was astonished at her skill and understanding, while she laughed and said: 'I will lay a bet with you on this third game and remove my queen for you as well as my right-side rook and my left-side knight. If you beat me, take my robes, and if I beat you, I shall take yours.' Her opponent accepted the condition, and when they had set out the pieces she removed her queen, rook and knight and then said: 'Move, master.' He said to himself: 'I must be able to beat her now that she has sacrificed these pieces.' He planned his strategy, but within a few moves she had got a new queen to face him, after which she pressed him with attacking pawns as well as other pieces. She then offered the sacrifice of a piece, which he accepted, at which she said: 'When the measure is full and the balance is equal, if you eat until you are too full, what kills you, man, is greed. Don't you see that I tempted you in order to trick you? Look and you will see that this is checkmate.' Then she told him to strip off his clothes. 'Leave me my trousers, may God reward you,' he pleaded, and then he swore by God never again to challenge anyone as long as Tawaddud remained in the kingdom of Baghdad. After that he took off his clothes, handed them to her and left.

The backgammon player came up next and Tawaddud asked: 'If I beat you today, what will you give me?' 'Ten robes of brocade from Constantinople,' he said, 'embroidered with gold, ten robes of velvet and a thousand dinars, whereas if I beat you, all I want from you is a signed note to certify that I won.' She agreed to his terms; they played and he lost, after which he got up, muttering in the language of the Franks and swearing: 'By the grace of the Commander of the Faithful, this girl has no match anywhere in the world.'

The caliph then summoned the musicians, and when they had come he asked Tawaddud whether she knew anything about musical instruments. 'Yes,' she said, and at his command a lute was produced, rubbed and worn, whose sorrowful owner had had to part from it, as a poet has described:

> God watered a land that produced a tree for a musician,
> With thriving branches and healthy roots.
> While it was green, song birds perched on it;
> Then, when it was dry, singing girls chanted over it.

The lute was brought in a bag of red satin with a cord of saffron-coloured silk. Tawaddud undid the bag and brought out the lute, on which were inscribed these lines:

> A fresh branch has become a lute for a girl
> Who sings songs of yearning for her companions in the assemblies.
> She sings to a repetitive strain,
> As though she had been taught by tuneful nightingales.

Tawaddud set the lute in her lap underneath her breasts, bending over it like a mother over her child. She played twelve airs until the whole assembly swayed with delight, and she chanted the lines:

> Cut short this parting; do not be so cruel;
> I swear to you that my heart has not forgotten you.
> Have pity on one who weeps in sadness and sorrow,
> A passionate lover enslaved by love for you.

The caliph was overjoyed and exclaimed: 'God bless you and show His mercy to your teacher!' at which Tawaddud got up and kissed the ground before him. He ordered money to be fetched, and he paid her owner a hundred thousand dinars. He then asked her to make a wish, at which she said: 'My wish is to be restored to my master who has sold me.' The caliph agreed to this and handed her back, giving her five thousand dinars for herself and taking her master as a lifelong boon companion . . .

Night 462

Morning now dawned and Shahrazad broke off from what she had been allowed to say. Then, when it was the four hundred and sixty-second night, SHE CONTINUED:

I have heard, O fortunate king, that the caliph gave the girl five thousand dinars and handed her back to her master, whom he took as a lifelong boon companion, with a monthly allowance of a thousand dinars, after which he and Tawaddud enjoyed a life of plenty.

Your majesty should admire the eloquence of this girl, together with the extent of her learning and understanding, together with her prowess in all branches of knowledge. Look, too, at the generosity of the caliph Harun al-Rashid, who, after having given all that money to her master, asked her to make a wish and when she wished to be returned to her master he gave her back, with a gift of five thousand dinars for herself, after which he made her master one of his boon companions. Where is such generosity to be found now, after the passing of the Abbasid caliphs, may Almighty God have mercy on them all?

A story is told, O fortunate king, that in the old days a certain king wanted to ride out one day with a number of his courtiers and officers of state in order to show off his splendid trappings to his people. He ordered his emirs and the great men of his state to prepare themselves to accompany him. He ordered the master of his wardrobe to bring out for him the most splendid robes that would suitably adorn him, and he had the best and finest of his pure-blood horses brought out. After this had been done, he chose the clothes that he preferred and took his pick of the horses. Then he put on the clothes, mounted the horse and rode out with his cortège, wearing a collar studded with gems, pearls of all kinds and rubies. As he rode among his men, exulting in his pride and haughtiness, Iblis approached him, put his hand on his nostril and blew arrogance and conceit into his nose. He swelled with pride, telling himself that there was no one like him in the world, and he started to manifest such a measure of haughtiness and vainglory that in his arrogance he would not look at anyone.

A man wearing shabby clothes stood in front of him and greeted him, and when the king failed to return the greeting he seized his horse's rein. 'Take your hand away,' said the king, 'for you don't know whose rein it is that you are holding.' 'There is something that I need from you,' said the man. The king replied: 'Wait until I dismount and then you can tell me what it is.' 'It is a secret,' the man said, 'and I can only whisper it into your ear.' The king bent down to listen and the man said: 'I am the angel of death and I intend to take your soul.' 'Give me time to go home to say goodbye to my family, my children, my neighbours and my wife,' the king asked, but the angel said: 'You are not going to go back and you will never see them again, for the span of your life is at an end.' He then took the king's soul and he fell dead from the back of his horse.

The angel of death went from there to a pious man, with whom Almighty God was pleased. After they had exchanged greetings, the angel said: 'Pious man, there is something that I need from you and it is a secret.' 'Whisper it in my ear,' said the man, and the angel then told him: 'I am the angel of death.' 'Welcome,' said the man. 'Praise be to God that you are here, for I have often been expecting you to arrive and you have long been absent from one who has yearned for your coming.' 'If you have any business to do, finish it,' the angel told him, but the man said: 'There is nothing I have to do that is more important than meeting my Lord, the Great and Glorious God.' 'How do you want me to take your soul,' asked the angel, 'for I have been ordered to do this in whatever way you choose?' 'Wait, then,' said the man, 'until I perform the ablution and begin to pray. When I prostrate myself in prayer, then take my soul.' The angel said: 'As I have been ordered to do whatever you want in this matter, I shall do what you say.' The man got up, performed his ablution and began to pray. While he was prostrating himself, the angel of death took his soul and Almighty God brought it to the place of mercy, approval and forgiveness.

A story is told that a certain king had collected a vast and uncountable quantity of wealth, together with quantities of every kind of thing created in this world by Almighty God, in order to make life luxurious for himself. As he wanted to give himself the opportunity to enjoy the treasures he had collected, he built for himself a lofty palace, towering into the air, such as was suitable for kings. He gave it two strong gates and posted in it as many servants, soldiers and gatekeepers as he wanted.

One day, he ordered the cook to prepare a delicious meal and he brought together his family, his retainers, his companions and his servants to enjoy his hospitality by sharing the meal with him. He took his seat on his royal throne, reclining on a cushion, and he said to himself:

'My soul, you have collected all the good things there are in this world and now you can take your ease and taste them in the enjoyment of a long life and prosperous fortune.'

Night 463

Morning now dawned and Shahrazad broke off from what she had been allowed to say. Then, when it was the four hundred and sixty-third night, SHE CONTINUED:

I have heard, O fortunate king, that the king told himself that he could taste all the good things there are in the world in the enjoyment of a long life and prosperous fortune, but before he had finished what he was saying a man arrived from outside the palace wearing tattered clothes with a bag hung round his neck, apparently a beggar asking for food. When he came, he knocked loudly with the door-ring, almost shaking the castle and rocking the throne. The servants rushed to the gate in fear and shouted: 'Damn you, what is this display of bad manners? Wait until the king has eaten and we will give you some of the leftovers.' He said: 'Tell your master to come out to me, for I have business with him that is of the greatest importance.' 'Go away, you feeble-witted fellow,' they said. 'Who are you to order our master to come out to you?' 'Tell him what I said,' he insisted, and so they went to the king and told him what had happened. 'Why didn't you scare him off,' said the king, 'drawing your swords and driving him away?' There was then an even louder knock on the door, at which the servants rushed to attack the man with clubs and weapons, but he shouted to them: 'Stay where you are. I am the angel of death.' They were frightened out of their wits, and as they trembled with terror they lost control of their limbs. 'Tell him to take someone else in my place,' said the king, but the angel said: 'I shall take no substitute for you. It is for you that I have come, to part you from the treasures that you have collected and the wealth that you have acquired and stored up.' The king then sighed deeply and, bursting into tears, he said: 'May God curse the wealth that has deceived me and harmed me by keeping me from worshipping my Lord. I used to think that it would help me, but now it is a source of grief and harm to me as I have to leave it empty-handed and it will pass to my enemies.' God then allowed his wealth to speak and it said: 'Why do you curse me? Rather, curse yourself. God created both me and you from dust, and He placed me in your hands so that through me you could make provision for your afterlife and give me as alms to the poor, the wretched and the weak, and that you could use me for the building of hospices, mosques, dykes and bridges. I would then have been a help to you in the next world, but as it is you collected me, stored me up and spent me on your own desires, showing ingratitude rather than thankfulness to me. Now you have bequeathed me to your enemies, leaving yourself remorse and regret, but what fault is it of mine and why should you abuse me?'

The angel of death then took the king's soul as he sat on his throne before he had eaten his meal, and he fell down dead. God Almighty has said: 'When they were rejoicing at what they had been given, We took them suddenly and they were in despair.'*

A story is told that a powerful king of the Israelites was sitting one day on his royal throne when he saw a man coming in through the palace door with an appearance that was both unpleasing and awesome. The king shrank back in fear at this as the man approached, but then, jumping up in front of him, he said: 'Man, who are you and who gave you permission to enter my palace and come into my presence?' 'It was the master of the house who ordered me to come,' said the man. 'No chamberlain can keep me out; I need no permission to come into the presence of kings; I fear the power of no ruler or the number of his guards. I am the one from whom no tyrant can find refuge, nor can any flee from my grasp. I am the destroyer of delights and the parter of friends.' When the king heard this, he fell on his face and his whole body trembled. At first he lost consciousness, but when he recovered he said: 'Are you the angel of death?' 'Yes,' said the angel, and the king then said: 'Allow me a single day's delay so that I may ask pardon for my sins and seek forgiveness from my Lord, returning the wealth that is in my treasuries to its owners lest I have to endure the hardship of having to account for it and the pain of punishment for it.' The angel said: 'Impossible – there is no way in which you can be granted this.'

* Quran 6.44.

Night 464

Morning now dawned and Shahrazad broke off from what she had been allowed to say. Then, when it was the four hundred and sixty-fourth night, SHE CONTINUED:

I have heard, O fortunate king, that the angel said: 'Impossible – there is no way in which you can be granted this. How can I allow you any delay when the days of your life have been counted, your breaths numbered and all your minutes set down in the book of fate?' 'Give me just one hour,' the king said, but the angel replied: 'The hour has been accounted for. It passed while you were still paying no attention and you have used up all your breaths except for one.' 'Who will be with me when I am carried to my grave?' asked the king, and the angel said: 'Nothing will be with you except for your own deeds.' 'I have no good deeds,' the king said. 'There is no doubt that your resting place will be hellfire and you will experience the anger of the Omnipotent God,' said the angel. He then took the king's soul and the king fell to the ground from his throne. There followed a great outcry among his subjects; voices were raised and there was loud wailing and weeping, but had they known what awaited the king of God's anger, their show of grief would have been even more intense and bitter.

A story is told that Alexander the Great passed by a people who were so poor that they owned no worldly goods at all. They used to bury their dead in graves dug at the doors of their houses, which they would constantly visit to clean and to sweep away the dust, and where they would worship Almighty God. Their only food was grass, together with plants that they got from the earth. Alexander sent them an envoy summoning their king to visit him, but he refused to answer the call, saying: 'I have no need of Alexander.' Alexander then visited him and asked about the condition of his people, saying: 'I don't see that any of you has any gold or silver or any worldly goods,' to which the king replied: 'No one is satisfied with the goods of this world.' 'Why do you dig graves by your house doors?' Alexander asked, and the king replied: 'This is so that we may have them before our eyes and remind ourselves of death as we look at them. In this way, as love for this world leaves our hearts, we shall not forget the world to come, and we shall not be distracted by it from our worship of Almighty God.' 'How is it that you eat grass?' asked Alexander. 'We do not want to make our bellies into graves for animals,' said the king, 'and the pleasure to be got from food goes no further than the throat.'

The king then reached out and produced a human skull, which he placed before Alexander. 'Alexander,' he said, 'do you know whose skull this is?' When Alexander said no, the king told him: 'This belonged to one of the kings of the world who used to treat his subjects unjustly and oppressively, wronging the weak and spending his days in amassing ephemeral goods. God took his soul and condemned him to hellfire. This is his skull.' He then reached out and put another skull before Alexander, again asking him whether he knew whose it was. When Alexander said no, the king said: 'This belonged to a ruler who treated his subjects justly and with compassion. When God took his soul, He placed him in Paradise and exalted him.' He then laid his hand on Alexander's head and said: 'Which of these two, do you think, will be yours?'

Alexander wept bitterly, clasped the king to his breast and said: 'If you would like to stay with me, I would hand over the vizierate to you and share my kingdom with you.' 'Never, never!' exclaimed the king. 'I have no desire for this.' 'Why is that?' asked Alexander. 'Because all mankind are your enemies, thanks to the wealth and the kingdom that you have been given,' replied the king, 'whereas for me they are all true friends because I am content with my poverty. I have no kingdom; there is nothing that I want or seek in the world. I have no ambition here and set store by nothing except contentment.'

Alexander clasped him to his breast, kissed him between the eyes and went on his way.

A story is told that King Anushirwan the Just pretended one day that he was ill and sent out some of his trusted and reliable officers with orders to go through all the regions and quarters of his realm to look for an old brick in a ruined village, telling them that the doctors had prescribed this as a cure for his ailment. They toured every part of his empire but had to come back and tell him: 'In the whole of your realm we have found no ruined place and no old brick.' This delighted Anushirwan, who gave thanks to God and said: 'I wanted to have my lands inspected and surveyed to see whether there were still any ruins there that needed restoration, but as every single place now is flourishing, then everything that needs to be done in my kingdom has been completed; it is in good order and its prosperity has reached the stage of perfection.'

Night 465

Morning now dawned and Shahrazad broke off from what she had been allowed to say. Then, when it was the four hundred and sixty-fifth night,
SHE CONTINUED:

I have heard, O fortunate king, that when his officers came back to Anushirwan and told him that they had not found a single ruined place throughout the kingdom, he gave thanks to God and said: 'Everything that needs to be done in my kingdom has been completed; it is in good order and its prosperity has reached the stage of perfection.' Your majesty should know that in the old days these kings used to concern themselves to do their best to bring prosperity to their realms, knowing that the more prosperous they were, the better off their subjects would be. They also knew that the wise men and philosophers were undeniably right in saying that religion depends on the king, the king on his troops, his troops on money, money on the prosperity of the land, and this prosperity on the justice with which the subjects are treated. As a result they would not allow anyone to act oppressively or unjustly, nor would they permit their retainers to commit acts of aggression, knowing, as they did, that their subjects would not endure injustice and that all the lands would be ruined if they fell into the hands of wrongdoers. If that happened, their inhabitants would disperse and escape to the lands of some other ruler. Their own kingdoms would thus be diminished, revenues would fall, treasuries would be emptied and the lives of their subjects would be made wretched. They would have no fondness for an unjust ruler and would constantly be cursing him; he would get no enjoyment from his kingdom and there would be no halting the process of his destruction.

A story is told that among the Israelites there was a certain judge whose wife was not only extremely beautiful but was also chaste, patient and long-suffering. The judge wanted to go on a pilgrimage to Jerusalem and he left his brother to hold his post for him, asking him to look after his wife. His brother had heard of her beauty and had fallen in love with her. When the judge had left, his brother went to the woman and tried to seduce her, but she rejected his advances, taking refuge in her piety. Although he tried again and again, she kept on refusing, until, when he had given up hope of her, he became afraid that when his brother returned, she would tell him what he had done. So he collected false witnesses to testify that she had committed adultery and took her case to the king who was ruling at the time. The king ordered her to be stoned to death and so they dug a pit, placed her in it and stoned her until she was under a heap of rocks. Then her accuser said: 'This pit will be her grave.'

In the dark of night the woman started to moan in the intensity of her pain, and a man passing on his way to a village heard her and went to her, bringing her out of the pit and carrying her back home. On his instructions his wife tended her until she was cured. As it happened, this woman had a child whom she entrusted to her patient and who was looked after by her, spending the night with her in a second room. A clever rogue caught sight of the woman and, fired by lust, he sent a message to her in an attempt to seduce her, and when she rejected him, he made up his mind to kill her. He came by night into the room where she was sleeping and attacked her with a knife, but as it happened, it was the child whose throat he cut. When he realized what he had done, he took fright and left the room, God having protected the woman from him. In the morning she found the child with its throat cut; its mother came and accused her of having killed him. His mother gave her a painful beating and was about to kill her when the husband arrived and saved her, saying: 'By God, this woman did not do that.'

The woman then ran off, not knowing where she was going. She still had some money with her and she passed a village where the inhabitants were clustered around a man who had been crucified on the trunk of a palm tree but was still alive. She asked about him and was told that the crime he had committed could only be atoned for by his death or by the payment of such-and-such a sum of money. 'Take the money,' she said, 'and set him free.' The man then repented at her hands and swore to himself that he would serve his rescuer for the sake of Almighty God until he died. He built her a cell in which he installed her, and he provided her with food by selling wood that he cut.

The woman applied herself to her devotions, and if any sick person or madman came to her, she would bless them and they would immediately be cured.

Night 466

Morning now dawned and Shahrazad broke off from what she had been allowed to say. Then, when it was the four hundred and sixty-sixth night, SHE CONTINUED:

I have heard, O fortunate king, that the woman was sought out by people, as she applied herself to her devotions in her cell.

As had been decreed by Almighty God, her husband's brother, the man who had had her stoned, became afflicted by a growth on his face, the woman who had beaten her contracted leprosy and the rogue was crippled by a painful illness. When her husband, the judge, returned from his pilgrimage to Jerusalem, he had gone to his brother and asked about his wife. His brother had told him that she was dead, and the judge had mourned her, thinking her to be in God's keeping. Rumours now started to spread among the people of a woman whose cell had become a goal for pilgrims from every part of the land, and the judge said to his brother: 'Why not go to this pious woman, as it may be that God will cure you at her hands?' 'Carry me to her,' his brother replied. Similarly, the husband of the leprous woman brought her there, as did the family of the crippled rogue when they heard of her.

All these people met at the door of her cell, where she could see everyone who approached without being seen herself. They waited for her servant to come, and when he did, they asked him to get permission for them to go in to see her. He did this and she herself, veiled and covered up, stood by the door looking at her husband and his brother, the rogue and the woman. She recognized them while they could not recognize her, and she told them that they would find no release from their sufferings until they confessed their sins, explaining: 'When the servant does this, God forgives him and grants him what he is seeking from Him.'

The judge said to his brother: 'Repent to God, brother, and do not persist in your disobedience. This will help to rescue you, as the tongue of conscience says:

On Judgement Day God brings together the wrongdoer and the
    wronged,
And He brings out those secrets that were hidden.
This is a gathering where sinners are abased,

And God will then exalt His faithful servants.
Our Lord and Master will show forth the truth
Against the wishes and desires of those who disobey.
Woe to the man who openly offends the Lord,
As though he does not know about God's punishment!
You who seek glory, glory lies
In piety, so take refuge with God.'

At this, the judge's brother said: 'Now I shall tell the truth. I did such-and-such to your wife and this is my sin.' The leprous woman said: 'I had a woman staying with me whom I accused of a crime, without knowing whether she had committed it, and I beat her. This is my sin.' The cripple said: 'I tried to seduce a woman, and after she had refused me, I went in to kill her but instead I killed a child in her arms. This is my sin.'

The woman then prayed: 'My God, as You have shown them how disobedience has brought them low, show them now the glory of obedience to You, for You have power over all things.' At this, God cured them all. The judge began to look closely at the woman and when she asked him why, he said: 'I had a wife and, if it were not for the fact that she is dead, I would swear that you were she.' His wife then revealed herself to him and together they began to praise the Great and Glorious God for the favour He had shown them in reuniting them. The judge's brother, the thief and the other woman started to ask for her forgiveness. She forgave them all and they stayed there, worshipping God constantly with her, until they were parted by death.

A story is told that ONE OF THE DESCENDANTS OF THE PROPHET SAID:
    One dark night I was circumambulating the Ka'ba when I heard the sound of a plaintive voice speaking from a sorrowful heart and saying: 'Generous God, Your grace is eternal and my heart remains faithful to the covenant.' I was so moved by listening to this that I almost died, but I followed the sound of the voice and found that the speaker was a woman. 'Peace be on you, servant of God,' I said, and she replied: 'Peace be on you, together with the mercy and blessing of God.' 'In the Name of God, the Omnipotent,' I said, 'tell me what this covenant is to which your heart is faithful.' 'Had you not invoked the Name of Almighty God,' she answered, 'I would not tell you my secret. But look at what I am holding.' I looked and saw a child sleeping heavily in her arms, and SHE CONTINUED:
    When I was pregnant, I left my home to make a pilgrimage here.

I boarded a ship, but we were met by stormy waves and contrary winds and the ship was wrecked. I escaped on a plank and it was then that I gave birth to this child. While I was holding him in my lap, with the waves buffeting me ...

Night 467

Morning now dawned and Shahrazad broke off from what she had been allowed to say. Then, when it was the four hundred and sixty-seventh night, SHE CONTINUED:

I have heard, O fortunate king, that THE WOMAN SAID:

When the ship was wrecked I escaped on a plank and then gave birth to this child. While I was holding him in my lap, with the waves buffeting me, one of the sailors from the ship reached me and joined me on the plank. 'By God,' he said, 'I wanted you when we were on the ship and now that I am here with you let me have you, or else I'll throw you into the sea.' 'Damn you,' I told him, 'has the storm you have seen not been warning enough for you?' 'I've seen this kind of thing many times and escaped, so it doesn't worry me,' he replied. 'We must hope to be saved from this misfortune by obedience to God and not by disobeying Him,' I told him, but he kept pressing me, and as I was afraid of him, I tried to trick him by saying: 'Wait until the baby goes to sleep.' At that, he took the child from my lap and threw it into the sea. When I saw the reckless way in which he had done this, in my agitation and great distress I raised my head towards heaven and said: 'You Who can come between a man and his own heart, come between me and this beast, for You are Omnipotent.' By God, I had not finished speaking when out of the sea came a creature that snatched the sailor from the plank, leaving me there alone.

As I mourned for my child, my distress and sorrow increased and I recited these lines:

The delight of my eyes, my darling child
Is lost, and passionate longing weakens me.
I see my body drowning, while my inmost parts
Are roasted by the fires of my emotion.
There can be no relief from my distress
Except through the grace of Him, on Whom I lean.

My Lord, You see what has afflicted me –
The passion that is caused by my child's loss.
Bring him to me again; be merciful,
For I have nothing stronger than my hope in You.

For a day and a night I stayed in that state, but the following morning I
caught sight of the sails of a ship in the distance. Wind and waves kept
tossing and driving me on until I got to it and was taken on board by its
crew. I looked around and there, among them, I saw my child. I threw
myself on him and exclaimed: 'This is my child! Where did you find
him?' The sailors said: 'While we were sailing along, the ship came to a
halt and we saw a monster as big as a huge city with this child on its
back, sucking his thumb, and so we took him on board.' When I heard
that, I told them my own story and gave thanks to God for what He had
given me, and I promised that I would never leave His house or quit His
service. After that, whatever I have asked from Him, He has given me.

THE PROPHET'S DESCENDANT CONTINUED:

I put my hand in the purse that I used for charity, intending to give
her something, but she said: 'Go away, you futile fellow. After telling
you of His grace and bounty, am I to take help from any other hand?' I
could not get her to accept anything from me and so I left her and went
off reciting these lines:

How many secret bounties God bestows,
Whose hidden virtues are too subtle for the wise to grasp.
How often does good fortune follow bad!
How often does He bring relief to the sad heart!
How many mornings bring distressing cares,
But in the evening joy comes on their heels.
So if one day you are in narrow straits,
Trust in the One Eternal and Exalted God.
Seek intercession from the Prophet, for God's servants
Are granted their desires when he pleads for them.

The woman continued to serve God, without leaving His house, until
she died.

A story is told that MALIK IBN DINAR, MAY GOD HAVE MERCY ON
HIM, SAID:

We had had no rain in Basra and although we went out several times to pray for it, our prayers were not answered. I then went with 'Ata al-Sulami, Thabit al-Banani, Nujaiy al-Bakka, Muhammad ibn Wasi' Ayyub al-Sakhtiyani, Habib al-Farisi, Hassan ibn Abi Sinan, 'Utba al-Ghulam and Salih al-Mazani. We arrived at the oratory when the boys were coming out of school, and although we prayed for rain we could see no signs of any answer. At midday the others went off, leaving me there with Thabit al-Banani. Then, as the night darkened, we caught sight of a black man with a pleasant face, thin shanks and a large belly, who was coming towards us. He was wearing a woollen waist-wrapper and had a price been put on them all, his clothes would not have fetched two dirhams. He brought water, performed the ablution and then went to the prayer niche and quickly performed two *rak'as*, each of whose individual movements, standing, bowing and prostration, exactly matched the others. He then looked up to the heavens and said: 'My God, my Lord and my Master, how long will You refuse to grant your servants something that does not diminish Your kingdom? Are Your resources exhausted or Your treasuries empty? I conjure You by Your love for me to send down Your rain on us now.' Before he had finished speaking, the sky clouded over and rain poured down as though from the mouths of water skins, and as soon as we left the oratory we were wading knee-deep in water.

Night 468

Morning now dawned and Shahrazad broke off from what she had been allowed to say. Then, when it was the four hundred and sixty-eighth night, SHE CONTINUED:

I have heard, O fortunate king, that MALIK IBN DINAR SAID:

Before the black man had finished speaking, the sky clouded over and rain poured down as though from the mouths of water skins, and as soon as we left the oratory we were wading knee-deep in water. We were astonished at this black man and I went up to him and said: 'Damn you, are you not ashamed of what you said?' 'What did I say?' he asked. 'You said: "By Your love for me,"' I told him, 'but how do you know that God loves you?' 'Get away from me,' he replied, 'you who are too busy to look after your own soul. Where do you suppose I was when God helped me to understand His unity and singled me out to learn about Him? Do you think that He did that for any other reason except that He loved me?'

and he then added: 'His love for me is in proportion to my love for Him.'

'Stay with me for a time,' I asked him, 'may God have mercy on you'; but he said: 'I am a slave and I have a duty to obey my junior master.' We then followed him at a distance until he entered the house of a slave dealer. Half the night had already gone and it would have taken too long to wait for the rest of it to pass, but in the morning we went to the dealer and asked him whether he had a slave to sell us. 'Yes,' he said, 'I have about a hundred slaves and they are all for sale.' He then started showing them to us one by one until he had produced seventy, but we had still not seen our man. 'These are all I have,' the dealer said, but on our way out we entered a ruined cell behind the house and standing there was the black man. 'By the Lord of the Ka'ba,' I said, 'this is the one'; and I went back to the dealer and asked him to sell him to me. 'Abu Yahya,' he told me, 'this is an unlucky and ill-starred fellow. He does nothing at night except weep, and in the daytime he is always talking of repentance.' 'That is why I want him,' I said, at which he called for the man, who came out sleepily. 'You can have him for whatever you want to give, if you don't hold me responsible for his faults,' said the dealer, and so I bought him for twenty dinars.

I asked his name and was told that it was Maimun. So I took him by the hand and we set off together on the way back to my house. He then turned to me and said: 'My junior master, why did you buy me? By God, I am not good at serving God's creatures.' I told him: 'I bought you in order to serve you myself, and this I shall do with pleasure.' 'Why is that?' he asked, and I said: 'Were you not with us last night at the oratory?' 'Did you see me?' he asked, and I told him that it was I who had gone up and spoken to him. He walked on and entered a mosque where he performed two *rak'as* and then said: 'My God, my Lord and my Master, we had a secret between ourselves, but now You have made it known to Your creatures and put me to shame among all mankind because of it. How can I enjoy life now that someone other than You knows what we shared? I call on You to take my soul this instant.'

He then prostrated himself and I waited for a time, but when he did not raise his head I shook him only to find that he was dead, may God have mercy on him. I straightened out his arms and legs and when I looked at him I saw that there was a smile on his face; his black colour was now predominantly white and his face was gleaming with radiance. While we were wondering at all this, a young man came in through the door and said: 'Peace be on you and may God grant us and you a great reward in respect of Maimun, our brother. Here is a shroud, so cover him with it.' He then gave us two garments the like of which I have never seen, which we used for his shroud. His grave is now a place where people pray for rain, as well as asking other favours from God, the Great and Glorious.

How excellent are the lines of a poet on this theme:

The hearts of the Gnostics roam in a heavenly garden
Separated from us by the veils of God.
They drink wine there that is mixed
With waters of Paradise,
And God's friendship is close at hand.
Their secret is between themselves and God, the Friend,
And is kept guarded from all other hearts.

A story is told that one of the best of the Israelites was a man who exerted himself in the worship of God and was abstemious in the things of this world, which he had removed from his heart. He had a wife who helped him and who obeyed him at all times, and the two of them got their living by making trays and fans. They would work on these all day long, and in the evening the man would go out carrying what they had made and wander round the lanes and streets looking for a buyer to whom to sell them. One day the two of them fasted, something that they did constantly, and after their day's work the man went out as usual carrying what they had produced, and while he was searching for a purchaser, he passed by the door of a worldly man who was both rich and important. The tray maker was a handsome man with a bright face, and the wife of the owner of the house, whose husband was absent at the time, caught sight of him and felt strongly attracted by him. She called for her maid and said: 'Perhaps you can find some way of bringing that man to me.' The maid went out and called the man back, pretending that she wanted to buy his goods.

Night 469

Morning now dawned and Shahrazad broke off from what she had been allowed to say. Then, when it was the four hundred and sixty-ninth night, SHE CONTINUED:

I have heard, O fortunate king, that the maid went out and called to the man. 'Come into the house,' she said, 'for my mistress wants to buy some of your goods after she has examined them and tried them out.' The man thought that she was telling the truth and, as he could see no harm in it, he went in and sat down as he was told. The maid then locked the door and her mistress came out from her room and, seizing the man by his shirt, she pulled him into it. 'How often have I longed to be alone with you!' she exclaimed. 'I can no longer bear to be without you. The room is perfumed, the food is ready, the master of the house is away tonight and I have given myself to you, although kings, leaders and rich men have sought me out and I have not listened to any of them.'

While the woman went on speaking, the tray maker kept his eyes fixed on the ground out of a sense of shame before Almighty God and in fear of His painful punishment, as the poet puts it:

There is many a grave sin that only shame has kept me from
   committing.
Shame is sin's cure, and when it goes, no cure remains.

The man wanted to escape from her but found himself powerless. So he said: 'I have something to ask from you.' 'What is it?' she asked. He replied: 'I want to take some clean water up to the highest point in your house in order to do something, and that is to wash away dirt from a place that I cannot show you.' 'This is a large house,' she told him, 'with plenty of private nooks, as well as a well-appointed privy,' but he insisted that he had to be high up. So she told her maid to take him to the top of the house. The maid did this and gave him a jug of water, after which she went back. For his part, the man performed the ritual ablution and then prayed with two *rak'as*. He looked down at the ground and thought about jumping off, but seeing how far it was he was afraid lest he be dashed to pieces. Then he thought of the penalty for disobedience to God, and to lose his life and shed his own blood seemed to him a simple thing to do. So he said: 'My God and my Lord, You see what has happened to me; my position is not hidden from You and You have power over everything. The voice of conscience repeats these lines:

Heart and conscience point towards You;
To You the heart's secrets are revealed;
If I speak, it is to You that I cry,
And when I am silent, it is to You I point –

You with Whom no partner is joined,
It is to You the poor distracted lover comes.
I have a hope, which my beliefs confirm,
But as You know my heart is fluttering.
To offer up one's life is the hardest thing to do,
But if this is Your decree, then it is easy.
If in Your bounty You allow me to escape,
You, Who are my hope, can bring this thing about.'

He then threw himself from the top of the house, but God sent an angel who carried him on his wings and brought him to the ground safe and uninjured. When he had come to rest there, he gave praise to the Great and Glorious God for the protection He had granted him and the mercy He had shown him. It was late when he returned empty-handed to his wife. When he came in carrying nothing, she asked him why he was late and what he had done with the goods that he had lost, so that he had come back without anything. He told her how he had been tempted and how God had saved him after he had thrown himself from the roof. 'Glory be to God,' she said, 'Who saved you from temptation and rescued you from this ordeal.' She then went on: 'Our neighbours are used to finding that we light our oven every night, and if they notice that we have no fire tonight they will realize that we are penniless. By way of gratitude to God, we have to conceal our poverty and so we must continue yesterday's fast through tonight, as a duty owed to Him.' She got up, filled the oven with wood and lit it in order to trick her neighbours, and she recited these lines:

I shall conceal my hardship and my sorrows,
And light my fire so as to deceive my neighbours.
I am content with what my Master has ordained;
I humble myself before Him, so that, seeing this, He may now be
    content.

Night 470

Morning now dawned and Shahrazad broke off from what she had been allowed to say. Then, when it was the four hundred and seventieth night,
SHE CONTINUED:
I have heard, O fortunate king, that the woman lit the fire in order to

trick her neighbours. After that, she and her husband performed the
ritual ablution and got up to pray. Just then, one of the neighbours came
in to ask for a light from their oven, and as she was allowed to do this,
she went to the oven and then called out: 'Come and look after your
bread before it gets burned.' 'Did you hear what she said?' the wife said
to her husband. He told her to get up and look, and so she went to the
oven and found it full of fine white bread. Taking the loaves she went to
her husband, thanking God, the Exalted and Glorious, for the great
goodness and bounty that He had bestowed on them.

They ate the bread, drank water and gave thanks to Almighty God.
Then the wife said to her husband: 'Let us pray to God that He may give
us something that may allow us to stop toiling away to earn our daily
bread and help us to apply ourselves to worshipping Him and obeying
His commands.' Her husband agreed; he prayed to God and his wife
added the amen, at which a hole opened in the roof and a jewel came
down through it, filling the whole room with its radiance. They thanked
God with even more fervent praise and were filled with delight as they
offered up their prayers to Him. Then, towards the end of the night,
when they had fallen asleep, the woman had a dream in which she
entered Paradise and saw many high seats and chairs set out in rows.
She asked what they were and was told that the high seats were for the
prophets and the chairs for the righteous and virtuous. 'Where is my
husband's chair?' she asked. 'Here it is,' she was told, but when she
looked at it she saw that there was a hole in its side. 'What is this gap?'
she asked, and she was told that it had been left by the jewel that had
fallen through the roof of their house.

She woke up tearful and sad because among the chairs of the righteous
her husband's chair was imperfect, and she said: 'Husband, pray that
God may put this jewel back in its place, for to endure hunger and
poverty for a few days is easier than your having to sit among the
virtuous on a chair with a hole in it.' The man prayed and, as they
both watched, the jewel rose through the roof. They continued to serve
God in poverty until they came into His presence, Great and Glorious
is He.

A story is told that al-Hajjaj al-Thaqafi had launched a hunt for a certain
important person and when the man was brought before him he said:
'Enemy of God, He has put you in my power.' He gave orders that the
man was to be taken to prison and chained up tightly with heavy fetters;

a cage was to be built over him which he could not leave and which no one could enter. So the man was taken off to prison and a blacksmith was fetched, together with fetters. At every blow of the smith's hammer the man raised his head towards heaven, saying: 'God is the Lord of creation and the command is His.' When the smith had finished, the gaoler built a cage over him and left him there alone. The prisoner was filled with emotion and confusion and his inner voice recited these lines:

> You Who are the goal of the seeker, You are my desire;
> My reliance is on Your universal grace.
> My state is not hidden from You;
> One glance from You is all I can wish for and seek.
> They have imprisoned me and tested me to the utmost;
> Alas for my loneliness and isolation.
> Although I am alone, the mention of Your Name befriends me,
> Keeping me company at night, when I cannot sleep.
> I care for nothing except for Your approval;
> You know what it is You see within my heart.

In the dark of night the gaoler posted a guard over the prisoner and went off to his own house. In the morning he came back and looked for the man, only to find the fetters discarded and no trace of the man himself. Filled with fear and certain of his own death, he went home and said goodbye to his family and then, carrying his shroud and the perfumes for it in his sleeve, he went to al-Hajjaj. When he stood before him, al-Hajjaj detected the scent of the perfumes and asked what it was. 'It is something that I have brought,' said the gaoler, and when al-Hajjaj asked him why he had done that, the gaoler told him about his prisoner.

Night 471

Morning now dawned and Shahrazad broke off from what she had been allowed to say. Then, when it was the four hundred and seventy-first night, SHE CONTINUED:

I have heard, O fortunate king, that the gaoler told al-Hajjaj that the prisoner had escaped. 'Damn you,' said al-Hajjaj, 'did you hear him say anything?' 'Yes,' said the gaoler. 'When the smith struck with his hammer, the prisoner looked up to the heavens, saying: "God is the Lord of creation and the command is His."' 'Don't you realize,' said al-Hajjaj, 'that the One Whom he was addressing while you were there freed him while you were absent?'

On this point, the voice of inspiration recited the lines:

Lord, from how many trials have You rescued me,
And were it not for You, I could not sit or stand.
How often and how often – I cannot count –
Have You freed me from misfortune. How often and how often!

A story is told that a virtuous man heard that in a certain town there was a smith who could put his hand into the fire and take out hot iron without suffering any harm. The man went to that town to ask for the smith and was shown where he was. When he studied the smith closely, he watched him performing this feat and so he waited until he had finished his work and then went up and greeted him, saying: 'I would like to stay as your guest tonight.' The smith welcomed him and took him home, after which they ate their evening meal and both of them went to sleep.

The visitor had seen nothing to suggest that his host was in the habit of passing the night worshipping God, but he said to himself: 'Perhaps he is hiding this from me,' and so he spent a second and then a third night there. He saw that the smith performed no more than what was traditionally added to the obligatory prayers and only seldom rose to pray at night. So he said: 'Brother, I have heard of the miraculous power that God has given you and I have seen you using it, but on looking at your devotion to worship, I have not seen any obvious source of miracles. So from where do you get this power?' THE SMITH SAID:

I will tell you about that. I was deeply in love with a girl whom I tried to seduce many times, but she was so pious that I did not succeed. Then there came a year of drought, famine and hardship. There was no food to be had and people were reduced to the extremes of hunger. While I was sitting one day, a knock came at the door; I went out and there was the girl. She said: 'Brother, I am very hungry, and I have approached you to see whether you will give me food for the sake of God.' I told her: 'You know how I love you and you know the frustration I have had to put up with because of you. I shall not give you any food until you allow me to lie with you.' She said: 'Death is better than disobedience to God.'

She went away, but two days later she came back and again made the same appeal to me, to which I gave the same answer. She came in and sat down but, although she was close to death, when I put food in front of her, her eyes filled with tears and she said: 'Feed me, for the sake of God.' 'No, by God,' I replied, 'not unless you let me lie with you.' 'Death is better than God's punishment,' she said, and she got up, leaving the food behind . . .

Night 472

Morning now dawned and Shahrazad broke off from what she had been allowed to say. Then, when it was the four hundred and seventy-second night, SHE CONTINUED:

I have heard, O fortunate king, that THE SMITH WENT ON:

The girl said: 'Feed me, for the sake of God.' 'No, by God,' I replied, 'not unless you let me lie with you.' 'Death is better than God's punishment,' she said, and she got up, leaving the food behind and going out without having eaten anything. She was reciting these lines:

> I call to the One God, Whose bounty covers all creation:
> You hear my complaint and You see my distress.
> I have met hardship and poverty,
> And my misfortunes cannot even be told in part.
> I am like a thirsty man who can see water,
> But who has no drink with which to quench his thirst.
> My soul fights me for food,
> Whose pleasure passes, while the sin of disobedience remains.

She stayed away for two days and then came knocking on my door. I went out and, although hunger made it difficult for her to speak, she said: 'Brother, I am at my wits' end and I cannot show my face to anyone but you. Will you give me food for the sake of Almighty God?' 'Not unless you let me lie with you,' I said. She came into the house and sat down. There was no food ready so I cooked something and put it in a bowl. It was then that God's grace overtook me and I blamed myself and said: 'This woman lacks both intelligence and religious knowledge but she still will not eat, although she is so hungry that she cannot do without food, and she refuses you time after time, while you, for your part, will not abandon your disobedience to Almighty God.' So I exclaimed: 'O my God, I repent before You of what I had thought of doing!' Then I took the food to her and told her to eat without

fear of harm, as I was giving it to her for the sake of the Great and
Glorious God.

She lifted her eyes to the heavens and said: 'O my God, if this man is
telling the truth, then allow no fire to harm him in this world or the
next, for You have power over all things and You are One to answer
prayer.' This was in the cold of winter, and I left her in order to get fire
from the oven. At that, a burning coal fell on my body, but thanks to
the power of the Almighty I felt no pain and I told myself that her prayer
had been answered. Even when I took the coal in my hand it did not
burn me, and so I went to her and said: 'Good news: God has answered
your prayer.'

Night 473

Morning now dawned and Shahrazad broke off from what she had been
allowed to say. Then, when it was the four hundred and seventy-third
night, SHE CONTINUED:

I have heard, O fortunate king, that THE SMITH WENT ON:

I went to the girl and said: 'Good news: God has answered your
prayer.' She threw away the morsel of food that she was holding and
said: 'My God, as You have shown me what I wanted in this man and
answered my prayer for him, take my soul, for You have power over all
things.' At that moment God took her soul, may His mercy be on her,
and the silent voice recited these lines:

> She prayed and her Master answered her,
> And forgave a sinner who had come to Him.
> He showed her that her request was granted,
> And the fate she wanted came to her.
> She had come to his door in hope of charity,
> Approaching him because distress afflicted her.
> He yielded to temptation, giving way
> To lust, which he hoped he could satisfy.
> He did not know what God intended for him,
> And, in his case, repentance came unsought.
> God in His judgement satisfies men's needs;
> Where what is destined does not come to man, he comes to it.

*

A story is told that among the Israelites there was one of the celebrated ascetics, men preserved from sin and noted for their abstinence, a man whose prayers, requests and wishes were granted by God, who wandered among the mountains and spent his nights in prayer. God had provided him with a cloud that went with him wherever he went, showering rain on him so that he could both perform his ablutions and drink. This continued until he slackened in his devotions and God removed his cloud and ceased to answer his prayers. This caused him great grief and prolonged distress and he continued to look back in longing for the time when he had been granted this miracle, sighing with grief and sadness. Then, as he slept one night, a voice spoke to him in his dream saying: 'If you want your cloud to be restored to you, go to such-and-such a king in such-and-such a place and ask him for his blessing. God Almighty will then return it to you, thanks to the blessings attendant on the king's pious prayers.' The voice then recited the lines:

> In this great need of yours, go to the pious king.
> If he prays to God, the rain cloud for which you ask will come.
> This man is of the highest rank of kings, having no match.
> With him you will discover something foretelling both good news
>   and joy.
> To find him, cross broad deserts and travel day by day.

The man then travelled to the town that had been named in his dream, where he asked for the king and was told where to find him. He went to the palace and at its gate he found a servant seated on a great chair wearing a dazzling robe. He stopped and exchanged greetings with the servant, who then asked him his business. The Israelite replied: 'I am a wronged man and I have come to take my case before the king.' 'You cannot see him today,' said the servant, 'as he has set aside one day in the week' – and he named the day – 'for petitioners, so go off, may God guide you, and wait until then.' The Israelite thought it wrong for the king to refuse to see his people and said: 'How can this man be one of the saints of the Great and Glorious God when he acts like this?'

He went to the palace to wait for the appointed day. HE SAID:

When the day came, I found a crowd of people at the gate waiting for permission to enter. I went there and stood with them until a vizier came out wearing splendid robes and accompanied by eunuchs and slaves. He told the petitioners to go in and I went with them. There the king was seated, with his officials ranged before him according to their rank and importance. The vizier brought the people forward one by one until it came to my turn. When the vizier took me to the king, he looked at me and said: 'Welcome to the man with the cloud. Sit down until I have time to deal with you.' This astonished me and I realized that he must be a saintly man, enjoying divine favour.

When he had finished with the cases brought to him, he got up, as did the vizier and the officials. He took me by the hand and brought me to his palace, at whose gate I found a splendidly dressed black slave, with weapons hanging above him and mail coats and bows to his right and left. This man got up to meet the king and was quick to do everything that was required. He opened the palace door and the king went in, still holding me by the hand, and there in front of him was a small door. The king opened this himself and he then entered, through a hall in a terrible state of dilapidation, a room which contained nothing except for a prayer mat and a bowl for ablutions, as well as some palm leaves. He took off the clothes he was wearing and put on a *jubba* of coarse white wool, as well as a woollen hood. He then sat down and, after giving me a seat, he called to his wife, and when she answered he said: 'Do you know who our guest is today?' 'Yes,' she replied, 'it is the man with the cloud.' 'Come out,' he told her, 'you need not stay hidden from him.' When she came, she was like a vision, with a face as radiant as the new moon, and she too was wearing a woollen *jubba* and a veil.

Night 474

Morning now dawned and Shahrazad broke off from what she had been allowed to say. Then, when it was the four hundred and seventy-fourth night, SHE CONTINUED:

I have heard, O fortunate king, that when the king called to his wife she came out with a face as radiant as the new moon, wearing a rough woollen *jubba* and a veil. 'My brother,' said the king, 'do you want to hear our story, or should we just give you our blessing and let you go?' 'No,' said the Israelite, 'what I most want is to hear the story.' So the king said: 'My ancestors ruled this kingdom, passing on the kingship from father to son, and when the last of them died, the throne came to me, but God led me to dislike this, and I wanted to lead a wandering life, leaving the people to look after their own affairs, but I became afraid that this would lead to civil strife, lawlessness and the fragmentation of religion. So I left things as they were; I assigned to every official an appropriate allowance; I wore the royal robes and I posted slaves at the gates to frighten evil-doers, protect the virtuous and preserve the laws. When my duties are finished, I come back here and change my clothes for those that you see me wearing. This is my cousin, who willingly shares my asceticism and helps me to worship God. By making mats out of these palm leaves by day we earn enough to have a meal at night, and we have been doing this for almost forty years. Stay with us, may God have mercy on you, until we sell our mats and then you can eat with us and spend the night here before going off with what you came for, if God Almighty wills it.' THE ISRAELITE WENT ON:

At the end of the day, a little boy came in and took the mats that the royal couple had made. He brought them to the market, where he sold them for a *qirat* and used this to buy bread and beans, which he brought back. I ate with them and then slept there. Halfway through the night they got up to pray, weeping as they did so, and then at first light the king said: 'My God, this servant of Yours begs You to send him back his cloud, and You have power over all things. My God, show him that You accept his petition and restore the cloud to him.' His wife said: 'Amen,' and at that the cloud appeared in the sky. 'Good news,' said the king to me, and as I took my leave of them and went off, the cloud followed me as before. After that, whatever request I made to God by invoking the sanctity of that pair, it was granted, and I recited these lines:

> My Lord has the choicest of servants,
> Whose hearts move through the gardens of His wisdom,
> Although their bodies remain motionless,
> Because of the pure secret in their hearts.
> You see them silently humbling themselves before their Lord,
> As though, through the unseen, they see the unseen in its clarity.

A story is told that the Commander of the Faithful 'Umar ibn al-Khattab raised a Muslim army to fight the enemy before Damascus, and they laid siege to an enemy fortress, pressing it hard. Among the Muslims were two brothers endowed by God with impetuous daring in the face of the foe. The commander of the fortress said to his leaders and champions: 'If those two could be taken by stealth or killed, I would deal with the other Muslims for you.' So they tried to trap the brothers or trick them, setting ambushes and making many sudden attacks until they managed to capture one, while the other died a martyr's death. The prisoner was taken to the commander of the fortress, who said, when he saw him: 'To have to kill this man would be a misfortune, but to return him to the Muslims would be a calamity.'

Night 475

Morning now dawned and Shahrazad broke off from what she had been allowed to say. Then, when it was the four hundred and seventy-fifth night, SHE CONTINUED:

I have heard, O fortunate king, that the prisoner was taken to the commander of the fortress, who said, when he saw him: 'To have to kill this man would be a misfortune, but to return him to the Muslims would be a calamity. I would like to see him converted to Christianity so that he could help us.' One of his officers then said: 'I can tempt him to abandon his religion. The Arabs are passionately fond of women and I have a very beautiful daughter. Were he to see her, he would fall under her spell.' The commander agreed to hand over the prisoner to this man, who took him back to his house. He then dressed his daughter in clothes that ornamented her beauty, and as the prisoner was brought in, a meal was set out for him and she stood before him like an obedient servant ready to obey her master's orders. When the Muslim saw what was happening, he took refuge with Almighty God, kept his eyes down and busied himself with the worship of God and the recitation of the Quran. He had a beautiful voice and a naturally attractive disposition, as a result of which the Christian girl fell desperately in love with him. Things went on like this for seven days and she started to express the wish that he would agree to her becoming a Muslim. The voice of her conscience recited:

Do you turn from me while my heart yearns for you?
My soul is your ransom and my heart your dwelling.
I am prepared to abandon my associates,
And leave a religion, watched over by sharp swords.
I bear witness that there is no lord but God;
This is established by proof and no doubt remains.
God may grant me union with one who turns from me,
And comfort a heart distressed by pangs of love.

Doors that are shut can once again be opened,
And wishes granted after many sorrows.

With her patience exhausted, she threw herself down in front of him
in her distress and implored him in the name of his religion to listen to
what she had to say. When he asked what this was, she said: 'Tell me
about Islam.' When he did, she was converted and purified, after which
he taught her how to pray. After she had done that, she went on to say:
'My brother, it was only because I wanted to be near you that I became
a Muslim,' but he told her: 'Islam only allows marriage in the presence
of two competent witnesses and a sponsor, together with the provision
of a dowry, and I can find no witnesses, sponsor or dowry. If you could
find some way of getting us out of this place, I would hope to return to
Islamic territory, and I give you my word that I would marry you and
only you, in accordance with the doctrines of Islam.'

The girl promised to arrange that, and she called her father and
mother and told them: 'The Muslim is weakening and wants to turn to
Christianity. I will let him have what he wants from me, but he says that
he can't do it in a place where his brother was killed. If he could go out
by way of distraction, he would do what is wanted. There could be no
harm in letting me go out with him to another town, and I guarantee
that you and the king will get what you want.' Her father then went to
the commander, who was overjoyed when he heard what her father had
to say, and the commander ordered the girl to go out with the Muslim
to the place that she had mentioned.

The two of them went to spend the day there, and then in the darkness
of night they set off on their journey, as a poet has described:

They said: 'It is almost time for us to leave.'
I said: 'How many times have I been threatened with your leaving?
My only concern is to traverse the desert,
Crossing the country, mile on mile.
If the beloved travels to some land,
With her I am again a wanderer.
My longing is my guide towards her;
And with no guide the road itself leads me.'

Night 476

Morning now dawned and Shahrazad broke off from what she had been allowed to say. Then, when it was the four hundred and seventy-sixth night, SHE CONTINUED:

I have heard, O fortunate king, that the Muslim prisoner and the girl stayed in the village for the rest of the day, and then, when it grew dark, they set off on their journey, travelling all through the night. The Muslim was mounted on a swift horse with the girl on the crupper behind him, and they rode across country all night long, until it was almost morning, when he turned off the track and set her down. They performed the ritual ablution and the morning prayer, but just then they heard the clatter of weapons, the clink of bridles, the voices of men and the sound of horses' hooves. The Muslim said to the girl: 'These must be Christians pursuing us who have caught up with us. What can we do? The horse is too tired to take another step.' 'Are you afraid?' she asked, and when he said that he was, she said: 'Where is the power of your Lord that you were telling me about, and the help that He gives to those who ask for it? Come, let us abase ourselves before Him and call on Him so that He may send us help and overtake us with His grace, Glorious and Almighty as He is.' 'Well said,' answered her companion and, as they abased themselves to God, he recited these lines:

I would need You every hour,
Even if I wore a diadem and crown.
You are my greatest need and, were this mine,
Then I would have no other needs.
You hold back nothing that is Yours;
The torrents of Your grace pour down with bounty.
Merciful God, my disobedience may hide me away,
But the radiance of Your pardon shines in its brightness.
You, Who dispel care, clear away my sorrows;
For none but You can grant us this relief.

While he was praying and the girl was saying amen to his prayers, the hoof beats were coming nearer. Suddenly the man heard the voice of his brother, who had died as a martyr, saying: 'Have no fear and don't be sad, my brother, for this is a company sent by God, together with angels who have come to witness your marriage. The angels are proud of you, and God has granted the two of you the reward of the blessed martyrs. He has folded up the earth for you so that in the morning you will be in the mountains of Medina. When you meet 'Umar ibn al-Khattab, greet him from me and say: "May God reward you richly on behalf of Islam, for you have given good counsel and exerted yourself."'

The angels raised their voices to call down blessings on the couple, saying to the man: 'God Almighty decreed your marriage to this woman two thousand years before He created your forefather Adam, on whom be peace.' Both the humans were overcome by this joyful news, rejoicing in their safety; their faith grew deeper and they were granted the steadfast guidance given to the pious. Dawn then broke and they performed the morning prayer.

'Umar ibn al-Khattab, may God be pleased with him, was in the habit of performing this prayer while it was still dark; he would enter the prayer niche, followed by two men, and he would start to recite the *suras* of Cattle or of Women until sleepers had awakened, ablutions had been performed and people coming from a distance had arrived. Before he had completed his first *rak'a* the mosque would be full, and as he performed the second, he would quickly recite a short *sura*. On that particular day he accompanied both the first and second *rak'as* with short, quickly recited *suras*, and when he had finished, he turned to his companions and said: 'Come out with me to meet the bridal pair.' They were taken by surprise as they did not understand what he meant, but they followed him as he went on ahead out of the city gate. As it was becoming light, the young Muslim, recognizing the landmarks of Medina, went towards the gate, followed by his bride. 'Umar and the Muslims met him and greeted him, after which, when they had entered the city, 'Umar, may God be pleased with him, gave orders for a feast. The Muslims came and ate, after which the young man slept with his bride, by whom God granted him children . . .

Night 477

Morning now dawned and Shahrazad broke off from what she had been allowed to say. Then, when it was the four hundred and seventy-seventh night, SHE CONTINUED:

I have heard, O fortunate king, that 'Umar, may God be pleased with him, gave orders for a feast. The Muslims came and ate, after which the young man slept with his bride, by whom God granted him children who fought on God's path and preserved the reputation of their lineage.

How well it has been said in this context:

I saw you weeping and complaining at the gates,
But you got no answer ahead of other suitors.
You may have suffered from the evil eye or some misfortune
That caused you to be shut out and turned from the beloved's door.
Awake now, wretch; call on the Name of God;
Repent as others have repented, returning, as they did, to God.
Forgiveness may rain down and clear away past sins,
As God pours out rewards on those who sin.
The fettered prisoner may at last be freed,
And captives may escape the prison of punishment.

Husband and wife continued to lead the pleasantest of lives in the most perfect joy until they were visited by the destroyer of delights and the parter of companions.

A story was told by SIDI IBRAHIM IBN AL-KHAWWAS, WHO SAID:

There was a time when I felt an urge to visit the lands of the unbelievers. I tried to restrain myself, but with no success, as although I tried to rid myself of the idea, I failed. So off I went, travelling through countries and regions, under the cover of God's care and protection, so that any Christian whom I met would look away from me and keep his distance. This went on until I came to a city at whose gate was a troop of armed black slaves carrying iron clubs in their hands. When they saw me they rose to their feet and said: 'Are you a doctor?' When I told them that I was, they said: 'Answer the king's summons.' This king, to whom they then took me, was an imposing man with a handsome face. When I entered his presence he looked at me and, after I had confirmed that I was a doctor, he said: 'Take him to her, but before he goes in, tell him of the condition.'

The servants took me out and told me: 'The king has a daughter who is gravely ill, and no doctors have been able to cure her. Each one who visits her and fails to cure her is put to death by the king. So see what you think.' I said: 'The king told me to go, so take me to her and bring me to her door.' When I got there, they knocked, and from inside a voice called out: 'Bring me the doctor who is master of the wonderful secret.' Then the princess recited:

Open the door, for the doctor has come.
Look at me, for I have a wonderful secret.
How many who seek to be close are far away,
And how many who seem distant are near at hand.
I was a stranger among you,
But the Truth has wished that I should soon find joy.
We are joined by ties of religion,
And appear as lover and beloved.
He called on me to meet him,
But censurers and watchers kept us apart.
Give up your censure and your blame;
Wretched creatures, I shall not reply.
I do not turn to the transient that disappears;
My goal is what remains and never leaves.

At that, a very old man opened the door quickly and told me to go in, which I did. I found myself in a room where scented herbs were spread, with a curtain hanging in a corner, and behind this I could hear a weak moan coming from an emaciated frame. I sat down opposite this curtain and I was about to say 'peace be on you' when I remembered the words of the Prophet, may God bless him and give him peace: 'Do not be the first to greet Jews or Christians with the words "peace be on you" and when you meet them on the road, force them to its narrowest part.' So I held back, but from behind the curtain the princess said: 'Where is the greeting of unity and sincerity, Ibrahim?' I was astonished by this and exclaimed: 'How do you know who I am?' She replied: 'When hearts and thoughts are pure, the tongue speaks of what is hidden in the mind. Yesterday I asked God to send me one of his saints through whom I might be saved, and a voice answered me from one of the corners of my room saying: "Do not grieve, for I shall send you Ibrahim al-Khawwas."'

I then asked her to tell me about herself and she said: 'It was four years ago that God's clear truth became apparent to me, and He is the truth-telling friend and the close companion. My people looked suspiciously at me and thought that I was mad. If any doctor of theirs visited me, he made me uneasy, while visitors disconcerted me.' 'What led you to your present position?' I asked her, and she replied: 'Clear proofs and obvious signs. When you see the way, both the indication and what is indicated become clear.'

While I was talking to her, the old man who was in charge of her came up and asked: 'What has your doctor done?' She said: 'He has recognized the illness and has hit on the cure . . .'

Night 478

Morning now dawned and Shahrazad broke off from what she had been allowed to say. Then, when it was the four hundred and seventy-eighth night, SHE CONTINUED:

I have heard, O fortunate king, that SIDI IBRAHIM IBN AL-KHAWWAS SAID:

The old man who was in charge of her came up and asked: 'What has your doctor done?' She said: 'He has recognized the illness and has hit on the cure, bringing me joy and happiness and doing me good, as well as pleasing me.' The old man went to the king and told him about that, and on the king's instructions he then treated me with respect. For seven days I stayed there, paying regular visits to the princess, and then she said: 'Abu Ishaq, when can we leave for the lands of Islam?' 'How can you go,' I asked, 'and who would dare such a thing?' 'The One Who brought you to me, leading you here,' she answered. 'Well said,' I replied, and so the next day we passed through the castle gate, concealed from all eyes by Him Who 'when He intends something, says "Be" and it is'.*

I never saw anyone with greater powers of endurance when it came to fasting and rising to pray than that princess. For seven years she lived beside the Ka'ba, and when she died and was buried in the territory of Mecca, God sent down blessings on her grave, and He grants His mercy to those who recite these lines:

> They fetched me a doctor when there had appeared
> Symptoms, such as flowing tears and illnesses.
> He then unveiled my face and saw beneath it
> Nothing but breath with neither soul nor body.
> He told me: 'This is something hard to cure;
> Imagination cannot grasp love's secret.'
> They said: 'When no one knows what the disease may be,
> And definition and description fail to show its nature,

* Quran 36.81.

What medicine can be effective there?'
'Leave me,' I said. 'I make no judgements based on guess.'

A story is told that a certain prophet used to worship God on a high mountain, beneath which was a spring of running water. By day he used to sit out of sight on the mountain top, reciting the Name of Almighty God, and he would look down at those who came to the spring. One day, while he was doing this, he saw a horseman ride up, dismount and drink, after which he rested. This man had put down a bag which had been fastened round his neck and which was full of dinars, but when he rode away he left it behind. Another man then came there and when he had drunk from the spring, he took the bag with the money in it and left safely. He was followed to the spring by a woodcutter, who was carrying a heavy load of firewood on his back. He sat down to drink, and at this point the rider came back anxiously and asked him where the bag was that had been there. 'I know nothing about a bag,' said the woodcutter, at which the rider drew his sword and killed him with a blow. The rider then searched through his clothes but found nothing and went off, leaving the corpse there. The prophet said: 'Lord, one man has taken a thousand dinars and another has been killed unjustly.' God then sent him a revelation, telling him: 'Concern yourself with your worship, for the ordering of the kingdom is no concern of yours. The father of this rider had forcibly plundered a thousand dinars from the father of the second man, and I allowed the son to recover his father's money, while the woodcutter had killed the rider's father, and I allowed the son to avenge his father.' The prophet said: 'There is no god but You, Glory be to You, Who are the knower of secrets.'

Night 479

Morning now dawned and Shahrazad broke off from what she had been allowed to say. Then, when it was the four hundred and seventy-ninth night, SHE CONTINUED:

I have heard, O fortunate king, that after this revelation the prophet said: 'There is no god but You, Glory be to You, Who are the knower of secrets.'

A poet has recited the following lines on this point:

The prophet saw what there was to be seen,
And he began to question the affair.
He witnessed what he could not understand;
'What is this, Lord?' he said. 'The dead man did no wrong.
This other got the wealth, for which he had not worked,
Dressed, as he was, in clothes of poverty.
The one who died had done no wrong,
O Lord of all mankind, during his life.'
God said: 'The money had belonged
To the father of the man who took it easily.
The woodcutter had killed the other's father,
And so his son successfully avenged himself.
Do not concern yourself with this, My servant;
Among men I have secrets hidden from the keenest sight.
Yield, then, to My commands, submitting to My glory,
For My decrees bring both profit and harm.'

It is reported that A PIOUS MAN SAID:

I was a boatman on the Nile at Cairo and I used to ferry people from the east bank to the west. One day, as I was sitting in my boat, an old man with a radiant face stood over me and greeted me. When I had returned his greeting, he asked me whether I would take him across for the sake of Almighty God. When I said yes, he asked whether I would also give him food, and again I agreed. He then boarded my boat and I took him across to the east bank. He was wearing a patched cloak and was carrying a water bottle and a stick, and when he was about to land he said: 'I want to entrust you with something.' When I asked what this was, he explained: 'Tomorrow God will prompt you to come to me at noon, and when you arrive, you will find me lying dead under that tree. Wash my body and wrap it in the shroud that you will find beneath my head; then pray over me and bury me in the sand there. Keep my patched cloak, my water bottle and my stick, and when someone comes to ask you for them, hand them over to him.'

I spent the night wondering at what he had said and the next morning I waited for the time that he had fixed, but when noon came I had forgotten, as he had implied that I would. Then, when it was almost time for the afternoon prayer, God prompted me and I hurried off. I found the old man lying dead under the tree, and there at his head was a new shroud, which was giving off an odour of musk. I washed his

body, dressed it in the shroud and prayed over it, after which I dug a
grave and buried him. Then I crossed the Nile and came to the west
bank at night, carrying with me the patched cloak, the water bottle and
the stick. When dawn broke and the city gate was open I saw a young
man, whom I had known in his early days as a rogue, wearing fine
clothes with marks of henna on his hands. He came up to me and said:
'Are you So-and-So?' and when I had said yes, he said: 'Hand over what
was deposited with you.' 'What is that?' I asked, and he said: 'The cloak,
the water bottle and the stick.' 'Who told you about them?' I asked, and
he replied: 'I don't know, but I spent last night at a wedding and I stayed
awake singing until morning. Then I went off to rest and I fell asleep. In
a dream I saw a man standing over me and saying: "Almighty God has
taken the soul of one of His saints, and has set you in his place. Go to
the ferryman and take from him the saint's cloak, his water bottle and
his stick, for he left these for you with this man."' I then produced those
things for him and handed them over, after which he took off his own
clothes and put on the cloak. He then went away and left me in tears at
what I had lost.

When night fell, I slept and in a dream I saw the blessed Lord of
glory. He said: 'My servant, do you find it hard to bear that I have
allowed another of My servants to return to Me? This is My favour that
I grant to any I wish, and I have power over all things.' So I recited these
lines:

> There is nothing that the lover can hope for from the beloved;
> Did you but know it, choice is forbidden you.
> Whether the Beloved wishes to grant union as a favour,
> Or turns away from you, He is not to be blamed.
> If you find no pleasure in His rejection,
> Leave, for here there is no place for you.
> If you cannot distinguish His nearness from His distance,
> You are falling behind, while love goes on ahead.
> If passion has given You mastery of my last breath,
> Or if I am led to death because of You,
> Leave me, turn from me or grant me union, it is all the same;
> Those who stand where fate places them cannot be blamed.
> In my love for You, I only want You to approve,
> And if I see that You are distant, this is just.

*

A story is told that among the best of the Israelites was a rich man who had a virtuous son, blessed by God. When the man was at the point of death, his son sat by his head and asked for his instructions. 'My dear son,' said his father, 'do not swear by God, whether truthfully or falsely.' He then died and his son took his place. This became known to the evil-doers among the Israelites, and one of them would come up to him and say: 'I had such-and-such a sum deposited with your father, as you know, so give me back what was covered by their agreement, or else swear that I am wrong.' The son would keep to his father's injunction and so give the man all that he asked.

Things went on like that until he had lost all his money and was in a state of desperate poverty. He had a pious wife, blessed by God, as well as two young children, and he told her: 'People have been making many demands on me and as long as I had anything with which to settle their claims, I handed over what they asked for, but now I am left with nothing at all, and if anyone else makes a claim you and I will be in great difficulties. The best thing for us is to escape and go to some place where no one knows us, and make our living among the people there.' So he sailed off with his wife and children without knowing where he was going, but 'no one can alter a decree made by God'.* The silent tongue recites:

You who left your home for fear of foes,
And met good fortune when you fled,
Do not be unhappy, distant as you are;
The stranger may win glory far from home.
Were the pearl to stay within the oyster shell,
It would not rest within the crown of kings.

It happened that the man's ship was wrecked. Each of his children floated off on separate planks, while he and his wife were on another two. They were separated by the waves, the wife coming ashore in one land and one of the children in another. The crew of a ship picked up the second child, while the man himself was washed up on a desert island. When he came to shore, he performed the ritual ablution using seawater, recited the call to prayer and prayed . . .

* Quran 13.41.

Night 480

Morning now dawned and Shahrazad broke off from what she had been allowed to say. Then, when it was the four hundred and eightieth night, SHE CONTINUED:

I have heard, O fortunate king, that when the man reached the island, he performed the ritual ablution using seawater, recited the call to prayer and prayed, being joined in his prayers by a number of creatures of all descriptions, who came out of the sea. When he had finished, he went to a tree on the island and relieved his hunger by eating its fruit, after which he drank from a spring that he found, and gave praise to the Great and Glorious God.

For three days he kept on praying, with the creatures coming out to join in his prayers, and when the three days had passed he heard a voice calling to him and saying: 'You pious man who has kept your word to your father and exalted the power of your Lord, do not grieve, for God, Great and Glorious, will replace for you what you have lost. On this island are treasures, hoards of wealth and things of profit, which God wishes you to inherit. They are in such-and-such a place on the island, and when you have dug them up we shall send you ships. Be generous to those on board and invite them to join you, as God will incline their hearts towards you.'

The man went to the place he had been told, and God uncovered the treasures for him, after which ships started to make frequent visits there. He treated their crews with great liberality, asking them to direct others to come to him and promising them gifts and allowances. As a result, people came from all parts, and within ten years he became the ruler of a flourishing kingdom. He was generous in his treatment of everyone who arrived and his reputation spread far and wide.

His elder son had fallen in with a man who gave him a good education, and his second son was also well brought up by a man who taught him the ways of commerce. As for his wife, she had ended up with a merchant who put her in charge of his wealth, promising not to act disloyally towards her and to help her obey the commands of the Great and Glorious God. He used to take her with him on his ship to visit whichever country he wanted.

The elder son had heard of the reputation of the island king and had set out to visit him, not knowing who he was. On his arrival, the king

entrusted him with his secrets and appointed him as his secretary. The
second son had also heard of the justice and virtue of the king and,
although he too did not know who this was, he visited him and was
appointed to oversee his affairs. The two brothers remained for some
time in the king's service without either of them knowing who the other
was. The merchant, who had with him the king's wife, then heard of
him and of his bounty and liberality. He took a selection of splendid
clothes and elegant gifts from various lands and sailed off, accompanied
by the woman, until he reached the shore of the island. He then went to
the king and presented him with his gifts, delighting him and prompting
him to produce a splendid reward.

Among the gifts were some drugs whose names and useful qualities
the king wanted to know, and so he told the merchant to stay the night
with him.

Night 481

Morning now dawned and Shahrazad broke off from what she had been
allowed to say. Then, when it was the four hundred and eighty-first
night, SHE CONTINUED:

I have heard, O fortunate king, that the king invited the merchant to
spend the night with him. The merchant replied that on his ship and in
his charge was a pious woman to whom he had guaranteed his personal
protection, adding that he had benefited by her prayers and been blessed
by her counsels. The king promised to send trustworthy servants to
spend the night protecting her and guarding her property. The merchant
agreed to this and remained with the king, who sent his secretary and
his overseer to the woman, with orders to go and stand guard that night
over the ship. The two of them went off, the one taking his post on the
stern and the other in the bow. They spent part of the night reciting the
Name of God, Great and Glorious, and then one said to the other: 'We
have been ordered to stand guard, and we must take care not to fall
asleep. So come here and let us talk about past happenings and what we
have experienced of good as well as evil.'

'My friend,' said the other, 'my misfortune was to be separated from
my father and mother, as well as from a brother whose name was the
same as yours. The reason was that my father sailed from such-and-such
a place, but shifting winds got up, the ship was wrecked and God parted

us.' 'What was your mother's name?' asked the other. 'So-and So,' was the reply. 'And the name of your father?' 'So-and-So.' The one then threw himself on the other and exclaimed: 'By God, you are really my brother!' Each of them started to tell the other what had happened to them in their childhood. Their mother was listening to what they said, but she waited rather than revealing herself, and then, when morning came, one of her sons said to the other: 'Come and talk in my house.' His brother agreed and off they went.

The merchant then arrived and found the woman in a state of great distress, and when he asked her what was wrong she said: 'Last night you sent me two men who tried to seduce me and who caused me the greatest anxiety.' The angry merchant went off to the king and told him what his agents had done. The king, who loved them because of their trustworthiness and their piety, quickly summoned them and ordered the woman to be brought to him so that she could give evidence in person of what they had done. When she came before him he asked her to tell him what had happened. She said: 'O king, I ask you in the Name of the Almighty God, Lord of the celestial throne, to tell these two to repeat what they said last night.' The king ordered them to do this and to conceal nothing. When they told him what they had said, he rose from his throne, gave a great cry and, throwing himself on them, he embraced them, exclaiming: 'By God, it is true! You are my sons.' At that the woman unveiled herself and said: 'And I, by God, am their mother.'

They were all reunited and lived the most delightful and pleasant of lives until they died. Praise be to God, Who rescues His servants when they seek Him and does not disappoint their hopes and expectations. How well it has been said on this theme:

> Everything has its appointed time, my brother.
> Things are at times erased and at other times confirmed.
> Do not grieve over a misfortune that befalls you;
> God has shown us that out of hardship there comes ease.
> Many a man suffers distress, whose outer show
> Is harmful, but within lies joy.
> There is many a one despised and hated in men's eyes,
> Concealed in whom are the miracles of God.
> Here is a man who suffered harm and sorrow,
> Visited, as he was, at one time by disasters;
> Time parted him from those he loved;

They had long been together but were then dispersed.
God favoured him and brought them back,
And in all things there are signs of our Lord.
Praise be to Him, Whose power encompasses all things;
The signs point to the fact that He is near.
He is at hand, but intellect cannot assess His qualities,
Nor can He be brought near in terms of space.

It is told that ABU'L-HASAN AL-DARRAJ SAID:

I often used to visit Mecca, may God add to its nobility, and because I knew the route and could remember where to find water, people used to follow me. It happened that one year, when I was intending to visit the Ka'ba and the tomb of the Prophet, may God bless him and give him peace, I said to myself: 'I know the way and I shall go on my own.' I walked as far as al-Qadisiya and on entering the town I went into the mosque. There in the prayer niche I saw a leper sitting, and when he caught sight of me he said: 'Abu'l-Hasan, may I go with you to Mecca?' I said to myself: 'I have avoided taking anyone with me, so why should I go with a leper?' So I told him that I was not taking anyone with me, and he said nothing more. The next morning I set out alone and went on like that until I got to al-'Aqaba, where I entered the mosque, and when I did so, there in the prayer niche I found the leper. 'Glory to God,' I said to myself, 'how did this man get here?' He raised his head, smiled at me and said: 'God does for the weak what surprises the strong.'

In the morning I went off on my own and got to 'Arafat, where I went to the mosque, only to find the leper sitting in the prayer niche. I threw myself down before him and said: 'Master, allow me to accompany you,' and I started to kiss his feet. 'You cannot do that,' he replied, at which I started to weep and wail at being deprived of his company. 'Do not take this so hard,' he said, 'for tears will do you no good . . .'

Night 482

Morning now dawned and Shahrazad broke off from what she had been allowed to say. Then, when it was the four hundred and eighty-second night, SHE CONTINUED:

I have heard, O fortunate king, that ABU'L-HASAN WENT ON:

When I found the leper sitting in the prayer niche, I threw myself

down before him and said: 'Master, allow me to accompany you,' and I
started to kiss his feet. 'You cannot do that,' he replied, at which I started
to weep and wail at being deprived of his company. 'Do not take this so
hard,' he said, 'for tears will do you no good, however many you shed.'
Then he recited:

Do you weep at being far from me when you are the cause,
And do you hope to bring back what cannot be restored?
You saw my weakness and the clear signs of my illness,
And you said: 'This is a sick man who cannot go to and fro.'
Do you not see that the Great and Glorious God
Grants us the grace His servants cannot grasp?
If to outward show I am as you can see,
My body showing the ravages of long disease,
And if I have no travel provisions to bring me
To where His servants go to wait upon their Lord,
I have a Creator Who favours me with hidden grace;
He has no equal and from Him I cannot be parted.
Go with my blessing and leave me here as a stranger,
For the lonely stranger is befriended by the One.

I left him, but to whichever pilgrimage station I came, I found that he
had got there first. Then, when I reached Medina, I lost track of him and
heard no news of him. I met Abu Zaid al-Bistami, Abu Bakr al-Shibli
and a number of other *shaikhs*, to whom I told my story, complaining
to them of what had happened to me. 'Never again will you enjoy his
company,' they said. 'That was Abu Ja'far, the leper, whose sanctity is
invoked in prayers for rain and through whose blessing prayers are
answered.'

When I heard what they said I longed even more to meet the man
again, and I prayed that God might reunite us. Then, while I was standing
at 'Arafat, I felt someone pulling me from behind, and when I turned I
saw that it was the leper. On seeing him I gave a great cry and fell down
in a faint, and when I had recovered he could not be found. That
increased my longing, and as I could find no peace of mind, I prayed to
Almighty God to allow me to see him again. A few days later I felt
another tug from behind and, turning, I saw him. This time he insisted
that I should tell him what I wanted, and so I asked him to pray on my
behalf for three things: firstly, that God should make me love poverty;
secondly, that I should never pass the night in the certain knowledge

that my daily bread was assured me; and thirdly, that He should allow me to see His glorious face. Abu Ja'far prayed for me and then left, and God Almighty answered his prayer. God has caused me to love poverty so much that I swear there is nothing in this world which I prefer. As for the second prayer, for a number of years I have never passed a night in the certain knowledge of a secure source of livelihood, and in spite of that God has never left me in need. As for my third request, I hope that God may grant me this as He has granted the first two, for He is bountiful and generous. May God have mercy on the poet who said:

> The *faqir* is dressed in self-denial and in gravity,
> While his clothes are rags and tatters.
> Pallor adorns him, as moons are adorned
> During the last night of their cycle.
> His long night prayers have made him thin,
> And tears pour from his eyelids.
> His household friend is his mention of God's Name,
> And his night companion is God in His omnipotence.
> His help is sought by those who seek refuge,
> As well as by the beasts and by the birds.
> Because of him, God sends afflictions,
> While it is through his grace rains come.
> When he prays for a misfortune to be removed,
> Wrongdoers are destroyed and tyrants fall.
> When all mankind is sick and ailing,
> He is the kindly doctor bringing help.
> His marks are clear; look at his face
> And hearts are purified as radiance shines.
> You who turn from such men and fail to see their virtue,
> It is the burden of your sins that hides them from you.
> You hope to reach them, but find yourself fettered;
> This is the burden that keeps you from your goal.
> For if you knew their worth you would respond to them,
> And rivers of tears for them would flood from you.
> A blocked nose is not quick to smell the flowers;
> The salesman knows the value of the clothes.
> Hurry towards your Master; ask for His union.
> It may be that fate will come to your aid.
> You are too far from Him and filled with hate.

Abandon this, and reach your real desire.
For all who hope are welcomed by His grace,
And He is God, the One, the Omnipotent.

A story is told that in the old days there was among the Greeks a wise man named Daniel, with pupils and followers, whom the other Greek sages acknowledged as their master and on whose learning they relied. He had no male child and one night, when he was thinking of this and weeping because he had no heir to inherit his learning, it occurred to him that God answers the prayers of those who turn to Him. The door of His grace is guarded by no gatekeeper; His sustenance is given without a reckoning to those He wishes; and He turns away no suppliant, but supplies His bounties and favours in abundance. So Daniel prayed to God to grant him this great favour and provide him with a son to succeed him. Then he went home and lay with his wife, who conceived that same night.

Night 483

Morning now dawned and Shahrazad broke off from what she had been allowed to say. Then, when it was the four hundred and eighty-third night, SHE CONTINUED:

I have heard, O fortunate king, that the wise Greek went home and lay with his wife, who conceived that same night. Some days later, Daniel set out on a voyage on which his ship was wrecked. His books were lost in the sea, but he himself climbed on to a plank holding five pages, which were all that were left of them. When he got home he put these in a chest and locked it. His wife was by now showing signs of her pregnancy and he told her: 'Know that my death is near at hand and I am soon to leave this transitory world for the world of eternity. You are pregnant and it may be that you will give birth to a son after my death. When you do, call him Hasib Karim al-Din; give him the best of upbringings and when he grows up and asks you what his father left him by way of inheritance, give him these five pages. When he reads them and grasps their contents, he will become the wisest person of his age.' He then said farewell to his wife, gave a groan and died, leaving this world and all that is in it, may Almighty God have mercy on him.

His family and his companions wept over him, and, after washing his corpse, they brought him out in great pomp, buried him and then went to their homes. A few days later his wife gave birth to a handsome boy, whom she called Hasib Karim al-Din, following her husband's instructions. After his birth she brought in astrologers, who calculated his horoscope by studying the stars. They then told his mother that he would have a long life, that he would face difficulties in his early days but that when he had escaped from these he would become a sage. After making this prediction they left.

His mother fed the boy with her milk for two years and then weaned him. When he was five years old she sent him to school to be taught, but as he learned nothing she took him away and had him taught a trade. Here too he learned nothing and would do no work at all, reducing his mother to tears. She was then advised to get him married, as, if he had a wife to look after, he might have to work at a trade. So she looked out a girl for him and married him to her, but some time later he had still not taken up any trade. Neighbours of the family, who were woodcutters, went to his mother and said: 'Buy your son a donkey, a rope and an axe. He can come to the mountain with us and we can all gather wood, sharing the money that we get for it between ourselves and him, and he can then spend his share on you.' Karim's mother was delighted when she heard this, and she bought the donkey, the rope and the axe, after which she took her son and handed him over to the woodcutters, leaving him in their charge. 'Don't worry,' they told her, 'this is the son of our master and God will provide for him.'

They took him with them to the mountain, chopped wood, loaded their donkeys and went to the city. There they sold the wood and spent the money on their families. They did this again on the next day, the day after that and so on for some time until it happened that one day, when they had gone to work, a great rainstorm burst over them, forcing them to take refuge in a large cave. Karim got up and left them, going to sit by himself in a different part of the cave. He began to strike the ground with his axe and it turned out that the place he struck sounded hollow. He spent some time digging until he discovered a rounded flagstone with a ring in it. In his joy at seeing this he called his companions . . .

Night 484

Morning now dawned and Shahrazad broke off from what she had been allowed to say. Then, when it was the four hundred and eighty-fourth night, SHE CONTINUED:

I have heard, O fortunate king, that Karim was delighted to find the flagstone with the ring. He called his companions, who gathered round him. When they saw the stone they quickly pulled it up and opened the door that they found beneath it, discovering there a pit filled with honey. They said to one another: 'Here is all this honey. What we have to do is go back to town and fetch containers in which to put it, and afterwards we can sell it and share the profit. One of us should stay here to guard it from all comers.' Karim volunteered to act as guard while the others went to get the containers, and so they left him watching over the pit for them. When they had brought containers from the town, they filled them with honey and loaded them on their donkeys. Then they returned to the town and sold their honey, before coming back again to the pit. They went on doing this for some time, selling in the town and then returning to fetch a fresh load of honey, while all the time Karim stood guard.

One day the woodcutters said to themselves: 'It was Karim who discovered the honey pit, and tomorrow he will go to the town and claim that it is he and not we who should get the money for its contents, on the grounds that he was the finder. The only way that we can get out of this is to tell him to go down into it to collect the rest of the honey, after which we can leave him there to die a miserable death, without anyone knowing about it.' They all agreed to this and went back to the pit, where they told Karim to climb down to collect the remains of the honey. When he had finished doing this, he said: 'There is nothing left, so pull me up,' but no one answered him. Instead, the others loaded their donkeys and went back to the town, leaving him there alone. He started to cry for help, weeping and exclaiming: 'There is no might and no power except with God, the Exalted, the Omnipotent! I am doomed to a wretched death.'

So much for him, but as for the woodcutters, they got back to the town where they sold their honey and they then came to Karim's mother, shedding tears as they went and saying: 'May you be granted life in exchange for Karim, your son.' 'How did he die?' she asked, and they said: 'While we were sitting on the mountain, a rainstorm burst over us and we sheltered from it in a cave. Before we noticed what was happening, your son's donkey bolted into the valley and he followed to turn it back. There was a huge wolf there and it killed him and ate the donkey.' When Karim's mother heard this she struck her face and poured dust on her head in mourning for him. The woodcutters used to bring her food and drink every day, while they themselves opened shops and set up as merchants, eating, drinking, laughing and enjoying themselves.

As for Karim, he continued his weeping and wailing, and then, as he was sitting miserably in the pit, a large scorpion fell on him. He got up and killed it, but after thinking the matter over, he asked himself: 'This pit was full of honey, so how did the scorpion get here?' He stood up to see where it had come from, and after looking right and left in the pit, he found where this must have been and noticed that light was shining through a hole. Taking out a knife that he had with him, he enlarged the hole until it was as big as a window. He made his way through it and, after he had walked on for some time, he came across a great corridor, which he went along until he came in sight of a large black iron door with a silver lock, in which was a key of gold. He went up to it and, on looking through a crack, he saw a great light shining from the other side. Taking the key, he opened the door and entered, after which he walked on until, after a time, he came to a large lake in which he saw something that glittered brightly. On approaching it, he discovered that this was a tall mound of green chrysolite on which was set a golden throne studded with gems . . .

Night 485

Morning now dawned and Shahrazad broke off from what she had been allowed to say. Then, when it was the four hundred and eighty-fifth night, SHE CONTINUED:

I have heard, O fortunate king, that when Karim got to the mound, he discovered that it was made of green chrysolite and that on it was a golden throne studded with gems of all types. Around this throne were chairs, some of gold, some of silver and some of green emerald.

Karim sighed as he came to the chairs, and when he counted he found that they were twelve thousand in number. He went up to the throne set in the middle of them and sat down on it to admire the lake and the chairs. He was still doing this when he fell asleep, but after he had slept for some time, he heard a puffing and a hissing accompanied by a great commotion. When he opened his eyes and sat up, he was terrified to discover that the chairs were now occupied by enormous snakes, each a hundred cubits long. His mouth was dry with fear and he despaired of life, as he saw the eyes of all these snakes on their chairs blazing like burning coals. Then he turned towards the lake, where he saw small snakes in numbers that only God could count. After a time a snake as big as a mule came towards him. On its back was a golden tray, and in the middle of this was another snake that glistened like crystal and had a human face.

When this snake came near Karim, it greeted him, speaking clearly, and he returned its greeting. It was then carried from its tray to a chair by one of the other snakes, after which it called out to the rest in their own language. They all came down from their chairs and called down blessings on it until it gestured to them to sit, which they did. It then spoke to Karim and said: 'Have no fear, young man. I am the queen of the snakes and their ruler.' This calmed him, and at their queen's command the others brought him food in the form of apples, grapes, pomegranates, pistachios, hazelnuts, walnuts, almonds and bananas, all of which they put down in front of him. The queen then formally welcomed him and asked his name. 'Hasib Karim al-Din,' he told her at which she said: 'Eat from these fruits, Karim, for this is our only food. Do not fear us.' On hearing this, he ate his fill, giving praise to Almighty God, and when he had had enough, the rest was removed from in front of him.

The queen now asked him where he came from, how he had got to them and what had happened to him. So he told her about his father, his birth and of how, when he was five years old, his mother had placed him in a school where he had learned nothing. He described how she had then apprenticed him to a trade, buying him a donkey, and how he had become a woodcutter. He explained how he had found the honey pit, where his fellow woodcutters had abandoned him and left, and how he had killed the scorpion that fell down on him, prompting him to widen the crack from which it had fallen. He had passed through this and found the iron door, which he had opened, and it was after this that he had reached the queen. 'This is my story from beginning to end,' he told her. 'Nothing but good shall come to you,' she said . . .

Night 486

Morning now dawned and Shahrazad broke off from what she had been allowed to say. Then, when it was the four hundred and eighty-sixth night, SHE CONTINUED:

I have heard, O fortunate king, that when the snake queen had listened to Karim's story from beginning to end, she said: 'Nothing but good shall come to you, but I want you to sit here with me for a time so that I can tell you my own story and let you know the marvellous things that have happened to me.' 'To hear your commands is to obey them,' he replied. THE QUEEN SAID:

Know then, Karim, that in the city of Cairo there was an Israelite king who had a son named Buluqiya. The king was a learned and a pious man, bent from poring over his books, and when he fell ill and was close to death, the principal officers of his state came to pay their respects to him. They greeted him and sat with him and he said: 'Know that I am soon to leave this world for the next, and the only thing that I ask you to do is to look after my son.' He then repeated the formula 'I bear witness that there is no god but God', after which he gave a groan and departed from this world, may God have mercy on him.

The courtiers laid out his corpse and washed it, after which they gave him a magnificent funeral. His son, Buluqiya, who now became ruler, treated his subjects with justice and in his time the people were at rest. One day, he happened to open his father's treasuries in order to see what was there. In one of them he came across what appeared to be a door, and when he opened this and went in he found himself in a small chamber where there was a white marble pillar with an ebony box placed on its top. Buluqiya took it and opened it, only to find inside it another box, this one made of gold. When he opened it, he discovered in it a book and, opening this, he found on reading it a description of Muhammad, may God bless him and give him peace. According to the book, Muhammad's mission would take place in the final age of the world and he was the lord of all generations, first and last.

When Buluqiya read this and acquainted himself with the characteristics of our master, Muhammad, may God bless him and give him peace, his heart became filled with love for him. He collected the leaders of the Israelites, that is, the priests, the men of learning and the monks, and showed them the book, reading it out to them. 'My people,' he said, 'I must remove my father's body from his grave and burn it.' When they asked why, he said: 'This is because he hid this book away and never showed it to me. He got its material from the Torah and the writings of Abraham, but he put it away in one of his treasuries, without letting anyone see it.' 'Your majesty,' objected the Israelites, 'your father is dead and buried. His affairs are in the hands of God, so you should not remove him from his grave.'

When Buluqiya heard what they said, he realized that they would not allow him to dig up his father and so he went to his mother and said: 'Mother, in my father's treasuries I have discovered a book containing a description of Muhammad, may God bless him and give him peace. He is God's Prophet, who will be sent by God in the last age of the world. My heart has been filled with love for him and I intend to wander through the countries of the world until I meet him, for unless I do, I shall die of love.'

He then stripped off his clothes and put on a woollen cloak and boots. 'Don't forget to pray for me, mother,' he said, and she shed tears and replied: 'What will happen to us when you have gone?' 'I cannot stay,' he told her, 'and I commit my affairs and yours to Almighty God.' He left as a wanderer, making for Syria, without any of his people knowing about this, and he travelled on until he got to the coast. There he found a ship, on which he joined other passengers, and this took them to an island on which he disembarked with the others. He then went off by himself and sat under a tree, where he fell asleep. On waking up he went back to the ship, only to find that it had already weighed anchor.

On the island he then discovered snakes as big as camels or as palm trees, who were reciting the Name of God, Great and Glorious, and calling down blessings on Muhammad, may God bless him and give him peace, repeating: 'There is no god but God,' and praising Him. Buluqiya was astonished to see this . . .

Night 487

Morning now dawned and Shahrazad broke off from what she had been allowed to say. Then, when it was the four hundred and eighty-seventh night, SHE CONTINUED:

I have heard, O fortunate king, that THE QUEEN OF THE SNAKES SAID:

Buluqiya was astonished to see the way in which the snakes were praising and worshipping God. When the snakes saw Buluqiya, they gathered round him and one of them asked him who he was, where he had come from, where he was going and what was his name. 'My name is Buluqiya,' he replied. 'I am an Israelite and I have left my country to search for Muhammad because of my passionate love for him, may God bless him and give him peace. Who are you, you noble creatures?' 'We are among the inhabitants of hell, created by Almighty God as a scourge for the unbelievers,' they told him. Buluqiya asked what brought them to the island and they said: 'Know that, because of its boiling heat, hell draws breath twice a year, once in the winter and once in the summer, and that great heat is caused by the intensity of hellfire. When it exhales, we are driven out, and then, as it breathes in, we are drawn back to it.' Buluqiya then asked if there were any larger snakes in hell, and they said: 'It is only because we are so small that we are forced out. If the largest of us crawled into the nostril of any of the other snakes in hell, they would not notice.' 'You were calling on the Name of God,' said Buluqiya, 'and invoking blessings on Muhammad, but how do you come to know about Muhammad, may God bless him and give him peace?' They told him: 'Muhammad's name is inscribed on the gate of Paradise. Were it not for him, God would not have created his creatures, Paradise or hell, the heavens or the earth. It was only for his sake that God brought into being all that exists, everywhere linking His own Name to that of Muhammad, and it is because of this that we love him.'

When he heard the snakes say this, Buluqiya's own passionate love for Muhammad increased, together with his longing for him. He took his leave of the snakes and went to the shore of the island, where he found a boat anchored. He joined the others who were on board and it took them to another island, where he landed. After walking for a time he came across snakes, big and small, in such quantities as only Almighty God could number. Among them was a white snake, brighter than crystal, sitting on a golden tray which was carried on the back of another snake as big as an elephant. This was the queen of the snakes, Karim, and I am she.

'What did you say to Buluqiya?' asked Karim. THE QUEEN REPLIED:

When I saw him, I greeted him and he returned my greeting. I asked him who he was, where he had come from, where he was going and what was his name. He told me: 'I am an Israelite named Buluqiya. I am travelling in search of Muhammad, out of love for him, may God bless him and give him peace, for I have seen his description in the revealed scriptures.' He then asked me about myself, what I was and what was my position, as well as about the snakes that surrounded me. I said: 'I am the queen of the snakes, and when you meet Muhammad, greet him from me.' He then took his leave and went back on board the ship, after which he continued on his travels until he reached Jerusalem.

In Jerusalem there was a man who had mastered all branches of knowledge and was an expert in geometry, astronomy, mathematics, natural magic and occult lore; he used to study the Torah, the New Testament, the Psalms of David and the writings of Abraham. His name was 'Affan, and he had discovered in one of his books that whoever wore the signet ring of our master Solomon would command the obedience of men and *jinn*, birds and beasts and all created creatures. He had found it recorded that when Solomon died his body was placed in a coffin and taken across seven seas with his ring still on his finger, as no man and no *jinn* could remove it, and no ship could sail to where it had been taken.

Night 488

Morning now dawned and Shahrazad broke off from what she had been allowed to say. Then, when it was the four hundred and eighty-eighth night, SHE CONTINUED:

I have heard, O fortunate king, that 'Affan had found in one of his books that no man and no *jinn* could remove the signet ring from the finger of our lord Solomon, and that no ship could sail on the seven seas across which his coffin had been taken. In another book he had found that there was a certain herb which, if squeezed, would produce a juice that could be rubbed on the feet to allow its user to walk dry-shod over any sea created by Almighty God, but no one could reach this herb unless he was accompanied by the queen of the snakes.

When Buluqiya got to Jerusalem he sat worshipping Almighty God, and while he was doing so 'Affan came up and they exchanged greetings. 'Affan saw that, as Buluqiya worshipped, he was reading from the Torah, and 'Affan asked his name, where he came from and where he was going. Buluqiya gave his name and said: 'I have come from Cairo, and I left on my travels in search of Muhammad, may God bless him and give him peace.' 'Come with me to my house,' said 'Affan, 'so that I may entertain you.' 'To hear is to obey,' said Buluqiya, and 'Affan took him home and treated him with the greatest hospitality. He then asked him for his story, saying: 'Where did you learn of Muhammad, so that you were inspired by love to set out in search of him? Who showed you the way?' Buluqiya told him the whole story from beginning to end, and when 'Affan heard this he was so amazed that he almost lost his wits. Then he said: 'Take me to the snake queen and I will take you to Muhammad. The time of his mission is still far off, but if we can get the snake queen and put her in a cage we can then go with her to the herbs on the mountains. If she is with us, through the power of Almighty God each of them will speak and tell us what use it is. For I have found in my books that there is one herb whose juice, when squeezed over the feet, will enable its user to walk dry-shod over any of God's seas. If we take the queen she will guide us to it and when we have found it, crushed it and extracted its juice, we can let her go. After that we can rub the juice on our feet, cross the seven seas to the tomb of our master, Solomon, and take the ring from his finger. Then we can reach our goal by exercising his authority; we can enter the Sea of Darkness and drink the water of life. God will allow us to live until the end of time and we shall meet Muhammad, may God bless him and give him peace.'

On hearing this, Buluqiya agreed to show 'Affan where the queen was to be found and to bring him to her. 'Affan made an iron cage and took with him two drinking bowls, one filled with wine and the other with milk. He and Buluqiya sailed for a number of days and nights until they reached the queen's island, where they landed. After they had walked some way, 'Affan put the cage down and set a trap in it in which he placed the two bowls. The two men then hid themselves for a time at some distance from the cage. The queen came up to it and when she was close to the bowls she looked at them for some time. When she smelt the milk, she left her tray and came down from the back of the snake on which she was riding. She went into the cage and came to the bowl of wine, from which she drank, but when she did so she felt dizzy and fell asleep.

'Affan saw that and went up to the cage, which he shut, trapping the queen inside it. He then went off with her, accompanied by Buluqiya. When the queen recovered her senses she found herself in an iron cage carried on the head of a man beside whom walked Buluqiya. 'Is this how you reward one who does no harm to the children of Adam?' she asked when she recognized him, and Buluqiya answered: 'Have no fear of us, queen of the snakes, for we are not going to hurt you. We want you to show us a certain herb whose juice, when squeezed and rubbed on the feet, will allow its user to walk dry-shod over any of God's seas. When we have found this we shall take it and then bring you back to your own place and let you go free.'

'Affan and Buluqiya then walked on with the queen to the mountains where the herbs grew. As they took her around them, each herb spoke by permission of Almighty God and told of its useful properties. While they were walking, with the herbs to their right and left telling them their uses, suddenly one of these spoke and said: 'Anyone who takes me, squeezes out my juice and rubs it on his feet will be able to cross any of God's seas dry-shod.' When 'Affan heard this, he put the cage down from his head and the two of them picked enough of the herb for both of them to use. They squeezed it and pressed out its juice into two glass bottles which they kept with them, and rubbed what was left over on their feet.

They then took the queen of the snakes and after they had travelled for a number of nights and days they got back to her island, where 'Affan opened the door of the cage. When she had come out, she asked them what they intended to do with the juice and they told her that they were going to smear it over their feet so that they could cross the seven seas to Solomon's grave and then take the ring from his finger. 'That is something you will never be able to do!' she exclaimed, and when they asked her why, she said: 'Almighty God gave that ring as a particular favour to Solomon, because he said: "My Lord, grant me a kingdom that cannot pass to any other after me, for You are the Generous Giver."*
As a result, it can never belong to the two of you.' Then she added: 'Had you taken one of the other herbs that were there – one which preserves the lives of all who eat it until the Last Trump – that would have done you more good than the one you picked, as this is not going to bring you what you want.' When they heard that, they were filled with bitter regret and went off on their way.

* Quran 38.34.

Night 489

Morning now dawned and Shahrazad broke off from what she had been allowed to say. Then, when it was the four hundred and eighty-ninth night, SHE CONTINUED:

I have heard, O fortunate king, that when 'Affan and Buluqiya heard what the queen said, they were filled with bitter regret and went off on their way.

So much for them, but as for the queen, when she returned to her subjects she found that their affairs were in disarray, with the strong having grown weak and the weak having died. When they saw her, they gathered around joyfully, asking what had happened to her and where she had been, and she told them of her encounter with 'Affan and Buluqiya. She then collected them all together and set off with them to Mount Qaf, where she was in the habit of spending the winter, while in the summer she would go to the place where Karim had seen her.

When she had finished telling her story to Karim, he was filled with astonishment. Then he asked her if she would be good enough to tell one of her attendants to take him back to the surface so that he could go home to his family. 'You cannot leave us until winter sets in, Karim,' she replied, 'and you will have to go with us to Mount Qaf, where you can enjoy looking at the hills, sands and trees, at the birds that sing the praises of the One Omnipotent God, and at the *marids*, *'ifrits* and *jinn*, whose numbers are known only to God.'

Karim was saddened and distressed by this, but he said to the queen: 'Tell me about 'Affan and Buluqiya and what happened to them after they left you and went off. Did they or did they not cross the seven seas and reach the grave of our master Solomon, and if they did, were they able to take his ring or not?' SHE SAID:

Know that after they left me, they rubbed the juice on their feet and walked on the surface of the sea, admiring its wonders. They went on from sea to sea until, when they had crossed all seven, they caught sight of a huge mountain towering into the sky made of green emerald; it contained a spring of running water and all its soil was musk. When they got there, they were filled with joy and they said: 'We have reached our goal.' They walked on to another high peak, on which from afar they could see a cave and over it a huge dome with radiance streaming from it. They went towards this cave, and when they reached it they entered and in it they discovered a golden throne studded with gems of all kinds, around which were set chairs in such numbers as only God could count. On this throne they saw Solomon asleep, wearing a robe of green silk embroidered with gold and studded with precious stones. His right hand lay on his breast; the ring was on his finger and its radiance outshone the light of the jewels with which the place was adorned.

'Affan taught Buluqiya a number of magical formulae and incantations, telling him to recite these without a break until he himself had taken the ring. He then advanced towards the throne, but when he had got near it, a huge snake came out from beneath it, with sparks shooting from its mouth, hissing so loudly that the whole place quivered. It spoke to 'Affan and said: 'If you do not go back, you will die,' but 'Affan was busying himself with his magic and was not to be deterred by the snake. It then blew a huge blast of air at him which almost burned the place down, and it cursed him and said: 'Unless you go back, I shall consume you with fire.' On hearing this, Buluqiya left the cave, but 'Affan, far from being alarmed, advanced towards Solomon and stretched out his hand. He had touched the ring and was about to draw it from Solomon's finger when the snake destroyed him with a blast of fire, reducing him to a pile of ashes.

So much for him, but as for Buluqiya, on seeing this he fell down in a faint . . .

Night 490

Morning now dawned and Shahrazad broke off from what she had been allowed to say. Then, when it was the four hundred and ninetieth night, SHE CONTINUED:

I have heard, O fortunate king, that when Buluqiya saw 'Affan burned and reduced to a pile of ashes, he fell down in a faint, but the Glorious God ordered Gabriel to go down to earth before the snake could blast Buluqiya. Gabriel came down quickly and found Buluqiya unconscious and 'Affan burned by the snake's breath. He approached Buluqiya, roused him from his swoon and greeted him, before asking where he had come from. Buluqiya told him the whole story from beginning to end and added: 'You must know that I only came here because of Muhammad, may God bless him and give him peace, as 'Affan told me that Muhammad's mission would come at the end of time and that only those who could live until then would meet him. This would only be possible for those who drank the water of life, which could only be done by someone who held the ring of Solomon, upon whom be peace. So I came here with 'Affan and then all this happened, leaving him burned but not me. Now I would like you to tell me where Muhammad is.' Gabriel, however, said: 'Go on your way, Buluqiya, for Muhammad's time is still distant,' and with that he rose up into the air.

Buluqiya started to weep bitterly, regretting what he had done and remembering that the queen of the snakes had told him that no one could take Solomon's ring. He was at a loss to know what to do, but after shedding more tears he went down from the mountain and walked on until he was close to the seashore. He sat there for a time, looking with wonder at the mountains, as well as at the seas and the islands, and there he spent the night. The next morning he rubbed his feet with the juice that 'Affan and he had taken from the herb, and after going down to the sea he began to walk on it.

He went on for a number of days and nights, during which he looked with wonder at the sea, its perils and its strange marvels, and he continued until he came to an island that seemed like Paradise. He went ashore and was filled with admiration for its beauty. It was, as he found, a large place, whose soil was saffron and its pebbles sapphires and other precious stones. Its hedges were of jasmine and it was planted with the finest of trees and the most splendid and sweetest of scented herbs. There were springs of running water and its wood was *qumari* and *qaqulla* aloes. In place of reeds there were sugar-canes, and everywhere there were roses, narcissi, storax, cloves, camomiles, lilies and violets, of all varieties and colours, while on the trees the birds were twittering. It was a wide island, characterized by loveliness and full of good things, encompassing every beauty and all good qualities. The singing of the birds was more graceful than the sound of lute strings, the trees towered high, the birds were vocal, the streams ran strongly and sweet water gushed from the springs. Wild calves passed by as gazelles frolicked and birds sang on the branches, so that even a distracted lover might find consolation.

Buluqiya was amazed at what he saw there, but he realized that he must have strayed from the route that he had followed on his outward journey with 'Affan. He wandered through the island, enjoying the sights until evening. Then, at nightfall, he climbed a high tree in order to sleep at the top of it and while he was thinking about the beauty of the island, there was a disturbance in the sea and out came an enormous creature which gave a great cry, frightening away all the animals on the island. From his viewpoint on the tree Buluqiya looked at it with astonishment, and after he had been watching it for some time, out of the sea emerged other creatures of all kinds, each holding a jewel that gleamed like a lantern, until in the radiance of these gems the island became as clear as day. Next from the island itself came wild beasts in quantities known only to Almighty God and, on looking at them, Buluqiya saw that these were land animals: lions, panthers, lynxes and the like. These came forward until they met the sea creatures on the shore, and they stayed talking together until morning came, at which they parted, each going on its own way.

This sight had alarmed Buluqiya, and when he came down from his tree, he went to the coast. Then, after having smeared his feet with the ointment that he had with him, he went into the Second Sea and walked over its surface for some nights and days until he came to an enormous mountain. Under the mountain was a seemingly endless valley, whose stones were magnetic and whose animals comprised lions, hares and panthers. Buluqiya climbed up to the mountain and wandered there from place to place until, when evening fell, he sat down beneath one of its peaks on the seaward side. He started to eat dried fish washed up from the sea, and while he was doing this a huge panther advanced on him with the intention of seizing him. He turned and saw the panther about to pounce, but using the liquid to anoint his feet he escaped into the Third Sea. It was a dark night with a stormy wind, and he walked on over the sea to another island. When he went on shore he discovered trees, some full of sap and others dry. From these he collected fruit, which he ate, giving praise to Almighty God, and then he wandered around inspecting the island until evening.

Night 491

Morning now dawned and Shahrazad broke off from what she had been allowed to say. Then, when it was the four hundred and ninety-first night, SHE CONTINUED:

I have heard, O fortunate king, that Buluqiya wandered around inspecting the island until evening. He slept there, and in the morning he continued his tour. Ten days later he went to the shore, anointed his feet and stepped out on to the Fourth Sea. After walking night and day he came to an island of soft white sand where there were no trees or crops. He walked there for a time and discovered that by way of wildlife it had falcons that nested in the sand. When he had seen that, he again anointed his feet and stepped on to the Fifth Sea, over which he walked night and day to a small island whose soil and whose hills were like glass. In it were veins of gold, as well as strange trees, the like of which he had not seen on his travels, together with gold-coloured flowers. He explored the island until evening, and when it became dark, the flowers started to glow throughout it like stars. Buluqiya said to himself: 'The flowers here must be those that, when dried out by the sun, fall to the ground and are blown by the winds until they are collected under the rocks and form an elixir which people take in order to make gold.'

He slept on this island until morning, and when the sun rose, he anointed his feet and went down on to the Sixth Sea. After he had walked over this for some nights and days, he came to another island, where he went on shore. He walked for a time until he came in sight of two peaks covered by quantities of trees whose fruits looked like human heads hanging by their hair. There were other trees to be seen whose fruits were like green birds suspended by their legs, others that burned like fire, with fruits like aloes, a single drop from which would consume anyone on whom it fell, and others that wept or laughed.

After having seen many marvels on that island, he walked down to the shore, where he saw a great tree, under which he sat until evening. When it grew dark, he climbed to the top of this tree and began to think about God's works. While he was doing this, the sea became disturbed and out from it came mermaids, the sea's daughters, each carrying in her hand a jewel gleaming like a lamp. They came to sit beneath the tree and started to play, to dance and to enjoy themselves, as Buluqiya watched. They kept up their games until morning, when they went back into the sea.

Buluqiya, who had looked at them with astonishment, then climbed down from his tree and, after having anointed his feet, he walked on to the Seventh Sea. For two months he carried on without seeing any mountain, island, land, valley or coast. Before he had crossed the sea, he had endured such violent hunger that he had started to snatch fish out of the water and eat them raw. On he went like this, until he reached an island full of trees and streams. He went ashore, this being in the forenoon, and began to walk, looking left and right until eventually he came to an apple tree. He stretched out his hand for an apple to eat, but at that someone shouted to him from the tree: 'If you come to this tree and eat any of its fruits, I shall cut you in half!' Buluqiya looked and saw a giant, forty cubits tall by the measurement of that period. He shrank back from the tree in terror but then asked the giant why he was keeping him from eating the tree's fruit. 'Because you are a son of Adam,' the giant answered, 'and Adam, your father, forgot his covenant with God, disobeyed Him and ate this fruit.' 'What are you?' Buluqiya asked him. 'Whose is this island and these trees, and what is your name?' 'My name is Sharahiya,' said the giant. 'The island and the trees belong to King Sakhr, one of whose servants I am, and he has entrusted the place to my care.'

Sharahiya then asked Buluqiya who he was and where he had come from, after which Buluqiya told him his story from beginning to end. 'Have no fear,' said Sharahiya, and he brought food which Buluqiya ate until he had had enough. He then took his leave and walked on for ten more days. While he was making his way through mountains and sands, he caught sight of a dust cloud suspended in the sky. He set off towards it and heard shouting together with the noise of blows and a great commotion. He walked on towards the dust and came to a huge valley, two months' journey in length. Looking to where the noise was coming from, he saw horsemen fighting one another, with rivers of blood flowing between them. Their voices were like thunder; they were armed with spears, swords and iron maces, as well as with bows and arrows, and they were engaged in a furious battle.

He was terrified . . .

Night 492

Morning now dawned and Shahrazad broke off from what she had been allowed to say. Then, when it was the four hundred and ninety-second night, SHE CONTINUED:

I have heard, O fortunate king, that when Buluqiya saw these armed men engaged in a furious battle, he was terrified, not knowing what to do. While he was in this state the horsemen caught sight of him, at which they disengaged and stopped fighting. A group of them approached him and when they drew near, his appearance took them by surprise. One of them came up to him and said: 'What are you? Where have you come from and where are you going? Who was it who showed you how to get to our country?' 'I am one of the sons of Adam,' answered Buluqiya. 'I have come because of my passionate love for Muhammad, may God bless him and give him peace, but I have lost my way.' 'We have never seen a son of Adam before,' the rider told him, 'and none of them has ever come here.'

All the horsemen were filled with astonishment at Buluqiya and at what he had told them. He himself then asked what they were and was told by the first rider that they were *jinn*. 'Why are you fighting among yourselves?' Buluqiya asked. 'Where do you live and what is the name of this valley and this land?' 'We live in the White Land,' said the rider, 'and every year Almighty God orders us to come here to fight against the unbelieving *jinn*.' Buluqiya asked where the White Land was to be found, and the rider told him: 'It is a seventy-five-year journey beyond Mount Qaf. The country here is known as the land of Shaddad ibn 'Ad and we come to fight here, our only concern being to praise and glorify God. We have a king named Sakhr and you will have to go with us to him so that he may look at you.'

They then rode off, taking Buluqiya with them to their camp. Here he saw so many enormous tents of green silk that only Almighty God could count them. Among them he was astonished to see a red silk tent, covering a thousand cubits, whose guy ropes were of blue silk and whose pegs were of gold and silver. This was the tent of King Sakhr and Buluqiya's escort took him there and brought him before the king. Buluqiya looked and saw the king seated on a great throne of red gold studded with pearls and other gems. On his right were the *jinn* kings and on his left were the wise men, emirs, officers of state and so on.

When the king caught sight of Buluqiya he ordered him to be brought in, and after this Buluqiya went forward and greeted the king, kissing the ground before him. The king returned his greeting and told him to come nearer. When Buluqiya was standing in front of him, the king ordered a chair to be brought for him, and when this had been placed beside the throne the king ordered him to sit down, which he did. 'What are you?' the king then asked him, and Buluqiya told him that he was an Israelite, one of the children of Adam. 'Tell me your story,' said the king, 'and let me know what has happened to you and how it is that you have come here.' So Buluqiya told him all the details of his wanderings from beginning to end. The king was filled with astonishment . . .

Night 493

Morning now dawned and Shahrazad broke off from what she had been allowed to say. Then, when it was the four hundred and ninety-third night, SHE CONTINUED:

I have heard, O fortunate king, that when Buluqiya had told King Sakhr the full story of his wanderings from beginning to end, the king was filled with astonishment and ordered his servants to fetch tables, which they spread with cloths. Then they brought plates of red gold, of silver and of copper. On some of them were fifty cooked camels and on others twenty, while some contained fifty sheep. In all there were one thousand, five hundred plates, and when Buluqiya saw that he was amazed.

The company then ate, as did Buluqiya, who, when he had had enough, gave thanks to Almighty God. After that, the food was removed and was replaced with fruit. When they had all finished eating, they called down praises on Almighty God and blessings on His Prophet, Muhammad, may God bless him and give him peace. Buluqiya was surprised to hear the name of Muhammad and he asked the king if he might put some questions to him. 'Ask what you want,' the king told him, and so he said: 'O king, what are you? What is your origin and how do you come to know of Muhammad, so that you call down blessings on him and love him?'

'Buluqiya,' replied the king, 'Almighty God created hellfire in seven layers, one on top of the other, each separated by the distance of a thousand years' journey. The first of these layers is called Jahannam and it has been prepared for those Muslims who disobey God's commands and die without having repented. The second layer is called Lazan and this is prepared for the unbelievers, while the third is Jahim, prepared for Gog and Magog. The name of the fourth layer is al-Sa'ir and this is for the people of Iblis; the fifth is called Saqar and is for those who abandon prayer. The sixth is al-Hutama and is for Jews and Christians, while the seventh is al-Hawiya, which has been prepared for the hypocrites. These are the seven layers.'

'I suppose,' said Buluqiya, 'that the punishments of Jahannam are easier to bear than all the others as it is the uppermost layer.' The king agreed with this, but added: 'In spite of that, Jahannam contains a thousand mountains of fire, in each of which there are seventy thousand valleys, each containing seventy thousand cities of fire. In each of these cities there are seventy thousand fiery castles, with seventy thousand fiery rooms in each, and each room contains seventy thousand couches of fire, with seventy thousand forms of torment in every one of them. None of the other layers, however, have any lighter punishments than these, as this is the first layer, while as for the other layers, only God Almighty knows the number of their torments.'

When Buluqiya heard what the king had to say he collapsed in a faint, and when he recovered he burst into tears and said: 'O king, how then will it be with us?' 'Have no fear,' said the king, 'for you must know that the fire will not burn anyone who loves Muhammad, and for his sake, may God bless him and give him peace, such a man will be freed, while hellfire will flee from all who follow his religion. As for us, Almighty God created us from fire, and the first beings that He created in Jahannam were two of his host, the first called Khalit and the second Malit. Khalit was shaped like a lion and Malit like a wolf. Malit's tail was feminine, piebald in colour, while Khalit's was masculine, in the shape of a tortoise, and was a twenty-year journey in length. God then ordered these two tails to join together and copulate, and from them were born snakes and scorpions who live in hellfire and, having reproduced and multiplied, are used by God to torture those who enter it. God then ordered the two tails to copulate a second time, and when they did this, Malit's tail was impregnated by the tail of Khalit and gave birth to seven males and seven females. These were nurtured until they grew up, and when they had done so, the females were married to the males. All but one of them were obedient to their father; the one who disobeyed became a worm and this worm is Iblis, may God Almighty curse him. He had been one of the cherubim, serving God until he was raised to heaven, where he found favour with Him and became the leader of the cherubim.'

Night 494

Morning now dawned and Shahrazad broke off from what she had been allowed to say. Then, when it was the four hundred and ninety-fourth night, SHE CONTINUED:

I have heard, O fortunate king, that Iblis had worshipped God and had become the leader of the cherubim.

'Then,' King Sakhr went on, 'when God created Adam, upon whom be peace, He ordered Iblis to prostrate himself to him and when Iblis refused, God drove him out and cursed him and it is from his seed that the devils were born. As for the other six males, his seniors, they were the believing *jinn* and we are their descendants. This is our origin, Buluqiya.'

Buluqiya, who was filled with astonishment to hear all this, then asked the king to order one of his servants to take him back to his own country. 'We cannot do that, Buluqiya,' said the king, 'unless God Almighty commands us, but if you want to leave us I can mount you on one of our mares and tell it to carry you to the edge of my dominions. When you get there you will be met by servants of a king named Barakhiya, who will recognize the mare, and after you have dismounted, they will send it back to us. This is all that we can do.' Buluqiya shed tears when he heard this, but told the king to do what he wanted, and so the king ordered the mare to be fetched. When this had been done, Buluqiya was mounted on its back and told to be careful not to dismount from it, strike it or shout in its face. 'If you do that,' they said, 'it will kill you, so stay quietly on its back until it stops, after which you can dismount and go on your way.' 'To hear is to obey,' said Buluqiya.

He mounted the mare and rode out among the tents for some time, passing by the king's kitchen before starting on his road. Here he saw cooking pots hanging up over lighted fires, each containing fifty camels. He looked with wonder at their huge size and as he was staring with more and more astonishment, the king looked out from the kitchen and noticed this. Thinking that Buluqiya must be hungry, he ordered two cooked camels to be taken to him, and when this was done they were fastened behind him on the mare's back. Buluqiya then took his leave of the *jinn* and rode on until he had reached the boundary of Sakhr's dominions. Here the mare halted and he dismounted, shaking the dust of travel from his clothes.

At this point a group of men approached him. When they saw the mare they recognized it and brought it with them as they took Buluqiya to their king, Barakhiya. On entering the king's presence, Buluqiya greeted him and was greeted by him in return. This king, Buluqiya saw, was seated in a great pavilion surrounded by his troops and his champions, with the *jinn* kings to his left and his right. He told Buluqiya to approach, and when he had done so, the king seated him by his side and ordered tables to be spread. Buluqiya saw that Barakhiya maintained the same state as did King Sakhr, and when the food had been fetched he ate his fill, as did the rest of the company, after which he gave thanks to Almighty God. When the food had been removed and the fruit that followed it had been eaten, the king asked him when it was that he had left Sakhr. 'Two days ago,' said Buluqiya. 'Do you know what distance you covered in those two days?' 'No,' replied Buluqiya. 'It was a seventy-month journey,' the king told him . . .

Night 495

Morning now dawned and Shahrazad broke off from what she had been allowed to say. Then, when it was the four hundred and ninety-fifth night, SHE CONTINUED:

I have heard, O fortunate king, that THE QUEEN OF THE SNAKES TOLD KARIM:

King Barakhiya told Buluqiya that he had covered the distance of a seventy-month journey in two days, adding: 'When you mounted the mare it was afraid of you, knowing that you were a human, and it wanted to toss you from its back. That was why they loaded it with these two camels.' Buluqiya was astonished by what the king told him and he gave thanks to Almighty God for having kept him safe. Barakhiya then asked him to tell him about his experiences and how he had come to this country. Buluqiya, in return, gave him the full story of his wanderings and of his arrival there, filling the king with amazement. He stayed there for two months.

Karim was astounded to hear the snake queen's story, and he then asked her if she would be kind enough to order one of her servants to bring him out to the surface of the earth so that he might return to his family. 'Karim,' she told him, 'I know that when you get to the surface you will first go to your family and then to the baths, where you will wash yourself. As soon as you have finished, I shall die, as that is to be the cause of my death.' 'I swear to you that I shall never enter the baths as long as I live,' Karim exclaimed, 'and when I have to wash, I shall wash at home.' She said: 'Even if you swore a hundred oaths to me, I would not believe you. This is something that cannot be, for I know that you are a son of Adam and, as such, you do not keep your word. Your father Adam made a covenant with God and then broke it. God had kneaded the clay of which he was formed for forty mornings and had made the angels bow down before him, but still he broke his covenant, forgetting about it and disobeying the command of his Lord.'

On hearing this Karim said nothing but burst into tears, and he continued to weep for ten days. After that, however, he asked the queen to tell him what had happened to Buluqiya after he had spent the two months with Barakhiya. SHE SAID:

You must know that after his stay with King Barakhiya, Buluqiya took his leave and made his way across open country, travelling by night and day, until he came to a high mountain, which he climbed. There, on top of it, he saw a great angel sitting and repeating the Name of Almighty God, as well as invoking blessings on the Prophet Muhammad. In front of the angel was a tablet inscribed with black and white letters, at which he was looking. He had two wings, one stretching out to the east and the other to the west, and when Buluqiya came up and greeted him, he returned the greeting. He then asked Buluqiya who he was, from where he had come, where he was going and what was his name. 'I am one of the sons of Adam,' replied Buluqiya, 'belonging to the children of Israel. I am a wanderer, travelling for love of Muhammad, may God bless him and give him peace, and my name is Buluqiya.' After this he astonished the angel by telling him all that had happened to him and what he had seen on his travels. He then asked the angel: 'Will you, for your part, tell me about this tablet and what is written on it? What is your task and what is your name?' 'My name is Michael,' the angel told him, 'and I am in charge of the succession of night and day, a task that is mine until the Day of Resurrection.' Hearing this, Buluqiya was filled with wonder, amazed by the angel's shape, the awe that he inspired and his enormous form.

When he had taken his leave, he travelled night and day until he reached a vast plain and when he walked on to this he discovered seven rivers and many trees. As he made his way through it he saw a giant tree under which were four angels. He approached them and found, when he studied their shapes, that one had human form, while the second was shaped like a wild beast, the third like a bird and the fourth like a bull. They were engaged in reciting the Name of Almighty God, and each of them was saying: 'My God, my Lord and my Master, I implore You by Your own truth and by the dignity of Your Prophet, Muhammad, may God bless him and give him peace, to pardon and forgive all that You have created in my own shape, for You have power over all things.'

Buluqiya, filled with amazement at this, left them and walked on night and day until he reached Mount Qaf, to whose summit he climbed. There he found another enormous angel seated, praising and glorifying God and calling down blessings on Muhammad. He saw that the angel was clenching and then unclenching his hand and folding and unfolding his fingers. While he was doing this, Buluqiya came up to him and, after they had exchanged greetings, the angel asked him: 'What are you? Where have you come from? Where are you going and what is your name?' Buluqiya told him: 'I am a son of Adam, belonging to the children of Israel. My name is Buluqiya and I am a wanderer, inspired by love for Muhammad, but I have lost my way.'

He went on to tell the angel all that had happened to him and when he had finished, he asked the angel: 'Who are you? What is this mountain and what is this task that is occupying you?' 'Know, Buluqiya,' the angel answered, 'that this is Mount Qaf, a mountain range that encircles the earth, and I hold in my hand every land that God has created in this world. When He intends to visit one of them with an earthquake, famine or fertility, war or peace, He orders me to see to it and I bring it about while still seated here. For you must know that my hand grasps the roots of the earth.'

Night 496

Morning now dawned and Shahrazad broke off from what she had been allowed to say. Then, when it was the four hundred and ninety-sixth night, SHE CONTINUED:

I have heard, O fortunate king, that the angel told Buluqiya that he held in his hand the roots of the earth. Buluqiya then asked whether God had created on Mount Qaf any land other than the one where the angel was, to which he replied: 'Yes, He has created a land white as silver whose extent is known only to Him and in which He has placed angels, whose food and drink is His praise and glorification and the invocation of blessing after blessing on Muhammad, may God bless him and give him peace. Every Friday night they come and gather on this mountain, and they spend the whole night until morning calling on Almighty God, assigning the rewards that they earn by their praise and glorification of Him, as well as their acts of worship, to sinners from among the people of Muhammad, as well as to those who perform the Friday ablution. They will continue to do this until the Day of Resurrection.'

Buluqiya next asked the angel whether God had created any mountains behind Mount Qaf. 'Yes, indeed,' the angel answered. 'Behind Qaf is a mountain range of snow and ice stretching the distance of a five-hundred-year journey, and it is this that protects the world from the fires of hell, which otherwise would burn it up. Also beyond Qaf are forty lands each forty times as large as this world of ours. Some are of gold, some of silver and some of sapphire, and each of them has its own colour. In them God has placed angels, whose only concern is to praise and glorify Him, reciting the formula of His unity and His greatness and calling on Him to bless the people of Muhammad. They know nothing of Adam and Eve or of night and day. You must know, Buluqiya, that these lands form seven layers, one on top of the other, and that God has created an angel whose qualities and power are known only to Him and who supports the seven layers on his shoulder. Beneath the angel God has set a rock, and beneath the rock he has created a bull that rests on a fish, and beneath the fish is a vast ocean. God told Jesus, upon whom be peace, about the fish, and when Jesus then asked to be allowed to look at it, He ordered an angel to take him to see it. The angel came to Jesus and took him to the ocean where the fish lived, telling him to look. Jesus did so, but did not see the fish until it passed by him like a lightning flash, at which he fell unconscious. When he had recovered, God spoke to him through the voice of inspiration and said: "Jesus, did you see the fish and did you note its dimensions?" "By Your glory and majesty, Lord," Jesus replied, "I did not see it. A huge bull, three days' journey in length, went past me, but I don't know what it was." God said: "Jesus, the thing that passed you, three days' journey in length, was merely the head of the bull (that stands on the fish), and you must know that every day I create forty such fish." When he heard that, Jesus marvelled at the power of Almighty God.'

Then Buluqiya asked the angel what God had created beneath the ocean that contains the fish, and the angel said: 'Beneath the sea is a huge region of air. Under this He has created fire, and under the fire is a giant snake called Falaq, which, were it not for its fear of Almighty God, would swallow everything on top of it, air and fire, together with the angel and what he carries, without noticing it.'

Night 497

Morning now dawned and Shahrazad broke off from what she had been allowed to say. Then, when it was the four hundred and ninety-seventh night, SHE CONTINUED:

I have heard, O fortunate king, that the angel described the fish to Buluqiya and added: 'Were it not for its fear of Almighty God, it would swallow everything on top of it, air and fire, together with the angel and what he carries, without noticing it. When God created that snake He used the voice of inspiration to tell it: "I want to leave a deposit in your charge, so guard it." "Do as You wish," the snake replied, and at God's command it opened its mouth and God put hell into its belly, saying: "Guard this until the Day of Resurrection." When that day comes, God will order his angels to come bringing chains with which they will lead hell to the place of the Last Judgement. At His command hell will open its gates, and sparks larger than mountains will fly out from it.'

On hearing the angel's words, Buluqiya wept bitterly. He then took his leave and went off towards the west until he came on two creatures seated by a great door that stood shut. When he came near, he saw that one of them was shaped like a lion and the other like a bull. He exchanged greetings with them and they asked: 'What are you? Where have you come from and where are you going?' Buluqiya told them: 'I am one of the sons of Adam and am wandering because of my love for Muhammad, may God bless him and give him peace, but I have strayed from my way.' He then asked the two what they were and what was the door by which they sat. 'We are the guardians of the door,' they told him, 'and our only concern is to praise and glorify God and to invoke blessings on Muhammad.' Buluqiya wondered at their words and asked them what was on the other side of the door. 'We do not know,' they said, at which he begged them by the truth of their mighty Lord to open it for him so that he could see for himself. 'We cannot open it,' they said, 'nor can any other created being except for Gabriel, the trusted servant, upon whom be peace.' On hearing this, Buluqiya implored God to send him Gabriel in order to open the door so that he might see what lay on the other side. God answered his prayer and ordered Gabriel to go down to earth and to open the door of the junction of the two seas so that Buluqiya might look. Gabriel came down and, after having greeted

Buluqiya, he went to the door and opened it. 'Enter,' he told Buluqiya, 'for God has commanded me to open it for you.'

When Buluqiya had gone through, Gabriel locked the door and went back up to heaven. On the inner side of the door Buluqiya found a vast sea, half of which was salty and the other half sweet. The sea was flanked by two mountains of rubies and, when he approached them, he saw there angels engaged in praising and glorifying God. He greeted them and they returned his greeting, after which he asked them about the sea and the mountains. They told him: 'This place is set beneath the empyrean and this ocean supplies water to all the seas in the world. We distribute water to the lands, sending saltwater to salty parts and fresh water to the fresh, while these two mountains were created by God to hold back the water. This is our task until the Day of Resurrection.'

The angels in their turn then asked Buluqiya where he had come from and where he was going, at which he told them his story from beginning to end. He asked them the way and they told him to go out on to the surface of the sea. So he rubbed his feet with the liquid that he had with him, took his leave and walked night and day over the sea. In the course of his journey he caught sight of a handsome young man who was also walking on the water. He approached the man but left him after they had exchanged greetings. He then saw four angels who were also walking on the sea and moving like flashes of lightning. He stood in their way, and when they came up to him he greeted them and said: 'By the truth of the Great and Glorious God, I ask you to tell me your names, where you have come from and where you are going.' The first said: 'I am Gabriel; the second angel is Israfil, the third Michael and the fourth 'Azra'il. An enormous serpent has appeared in the east, destroying a thousand cities and swallowing their inhabitants, and we have been commanded by God to go and seize it and then to throw it into hell.'

Buluqiya, astonished by the size of the angels, went on his way, travelling as usual by night and day. He reached an island and, when he had walked on it for some time . . .

Night 498

Morning now dawned and Shahrazad broke off from what she had been allowed to say. Then, when it was the four hundred and ninety-eighth night, SHE CONTINUED:

I have heard, O fortunate king, that Buluqiya reached an island and, when he had walked on it for some time, he came in sight of a handsome young man with a radiant face. When he approached, he saw that this man was seated, weeping and wailing between two tombs. Buluqiya went up to him and asked: 'What is the matter with you? What is your name? What are these two tombs between which you are sitting, and why are you shedding tears?' The young man turned towards him, weeping so bitterly that his clothes were soaked, but he then said: 'Know, my brother, that mine is a strange and wonderful story. Please sit with me and tell me everything that you have seen in your life, why you have come here and where you are going, as well as your name. Then I in my turn will tell you my own story.'

So Buluqiya sat down beside the young man and told him all that had happened to him in his wanderings from beginning to end, how his father had died, leaving him as his heir, how he had opened the chamber and found the box, how he had seen the book containing the description of Muhammad, may God bless him and give him peace, how love for Muhammad had become fixed in his heart and how because of this love he had set off as a wanderer. He then gave an account of all his experiences up to the time of his meeting. 'This is the whole of my story,' he said, adding: 'God knows better, but what will happen to me after this I do not know.' On hearing this, the young man sighed and exclaimed: 'Poor man, how little you have seen in your life! Know that I have seen King Solomon in his time, as well as innumerable other things, for mine is a strange and wonderful tale. Sit with me so that I may tell it to you and let you know why it is that I am sitting here.'

When he heard what the snake queen had to say, Karim was filled with astonishment but he said: 'I conjure you in God's Name, queen, to let me go and to order one of your servants to bring me to the surface of the earth. I swear to you that never as long as I live will I enter the baths.' 'This cannot be,' she replied, 'and I do not trust your oath.' On hearing this, Karim burst into tears, and all the snakes wept for him and began to intercede for him with their queen, saying: 'We want you to tell one of us to bring this man to the surface and he will swear to you that he will never in his life enter the baths.' The queen, whose name was Yamlikha, heard what they said; she went up to Karim and asked him to swear an oath, which he did, after which she told one of her snakes to take him to the surface. The snake came and was about to go off with him, but just then

Karim said to the queen: 'I would like you to tell me the story of the young man with whom Buluqiya was sitting between the two tombs.'

The snake queen said: 'You must know that Buluqiya sat with the young man and told him his own story from start to finish in order that the young man in his turn might reply by telling of what had happened to him in his life and why he was sitting between the tombs.'

Night 499

Morning now dawned and Shahrazad broke off from what she had been allowed to say. Then, when it was the four hundred and ninety-ninth night, SHE CONTINUED:

I have heard, O fortunate king, that when Buluqiya had told his story, THE YOUNG MAN EXCLAIMED:

Poor man, how little you have seen in your life! Know that I have seen King Solomon in his time, as well as innumerable other things. Know too, my brother, that my father was a king called Tighmus who ruled over the lands of Kabul and was lord of the Banu Shahlan, ten thousand paladins, each of whom controlled a hundred cities and a hundred walled fortresses. Under him were seven sultans, wealth was carried to him from lands that stretched from the east to the west and he was a just ruler, but although Almighty God had given him all this great empire, he had no son. It was the gift of a son that he wished from God during his lifetime so that after his death his son might succeed him to the throne. One day he summoned men of learning, astrologers, scientists and almanac experts and told them to examine his horoscope to see whether God would grant him this wish. The astrologers opened their books, calculated his horoscope and investigated its relationship to the position of the stars. Then they said: 'Know, O king, that a son will be born to you and his mother must be the daughter of the king of Khurasan.' Tighmus was overjoyed to hear this and rewarded the astrologers and the wise men with wealth beyond counting, after which they went away.

The chief vizier of King Tighmus was a great paladin, a match for a thousand riders, whose name was 'Ain Zar. Tighmus told him: 'Vizier, I want you to prepare to travel to the lands of Khurasan to ask its king, Bahrawan, to grant me his daughter's hand in marriage,' and he went on to explain what the astrologers had told him. On hearing this, the vizier went instantly to make his preparations for the journey, and he then moved out of the city with his guards, his picked champions and the rest of his troops.

So much for him, but as for Tighmus, he prepared one thousand, five hundred loads of silks, pearls and other gems, including sapphires, together with gold, silver and precious stones, as well as a vast quantity of wedding supplies. He had all this loaded on to camels and mules, which he handed over to the vizier. He also wrote a letter which ran as follows: 'Greetings to King Bahrawan. Know that I collected the astrologers, wise men and almanac experts and they told me that I would have a son only through your daughter. I am now sending you 'Ain Zar, my vizier, together with a large quantity of paraphernalia for the wedding. I have appointed him to act for me in this matter and empowered him to conclude the marriage contract. I want you to be kind enough to accommodate my wishes and settle this affair for my vizier with no neglect or delay. I shall gladly accept any favour you show me, but take care not to disobey me in this matter. You must know that God has granted me the kingdom of Kabul, making me ruler over the Banu Shahlan. This is a vast empire that He has given me; if I marry your daughter, you and I will be equal partners in it and every year I shall send you enough money to meet your needs. This, then, is what I want from you.' Having sealed the letter, Tighmus gave it to his vizier, 'Ain Zar, and ordered him to go to Khurasan.

The vizier set off and when he was near King Bahrawan's city, the king was told who was approaching. On hearing this, he told his emirs to prepare to meet 'Ain Zar and he sent them off with food, drink and so on, together with fodder for the horses. When they reached 'Ain Zar, they unloaded what they had brought and all the riders dismounted and greeted one another. For ten days they stayed there eating and drinking, and after that they mounted and set off for the city. King Bahrawan came out to meet the vizier and, after embracing him and greeting him, he took him to his citadel. The vizier presented him with all that he had brought by way of gifts, together with all the money, and he handed over Tighmus's letter. Bahrawan took this and read it, and when he had grasped its contents he was delighted and welcomed the vizier, saying: 'You will be glad to hear that I shall grant your request, and were King Tighmus to ask me for my life, I would give it to him.'

The king then went immediately to his daughter, her mother and his relatives to tell them about that and to ask for their advice. 'Do what you want,' they said . . .

Night 500

Morning now dawned and Shahrazad broke off from what she had been allowed to say. Then, when it was the five hundredth night, SHE CONTINUED:

I have heard, O fortunate king, that King Bahrawan consulted his daughter, her mother and her relatives. 'Do what you want,' they said, and so the king returned to the vizier to tell him that he had succeeded in his errand. For the next two months the vizier stayed with him and after that he said: 'I want you to give me what I have come for, so that I can go back to my own land.' 'To hear is to obey,' said the king, and he gave orders that all the wedding preparations were to be made and, when this had been done, he ordered his viziers and all the leading emirs of his state to be brought before him. When every one of them had arrived, he summoned the monks and the priests, who came and drew up a marriage contract between the princess and King Tighmus. After that, he saw to the preparations for her journey and provided her with gifts of all sorts, together with precious stones, such as would beggar description, and on his orders the city streets were carpeted and adorned with splendid decorations.

The vizier, 'Ain Zar, then escorted the princess to his own land, and when news of this reached King Tighmus he gave orders for a wedding feast and for the city to be decked out. He lay with the princess, taking her maidenhead, and after a few days she conceived. When the months of her pregnancy were completed, she gave birth to a baby boy like the moon on the night it becomes full. The news of this beautiful child filled the king with delight, and he summoned the wise men, astrologers and almanac experts, telling them that he wanted them to investigate the child's horoscope, checking it against the stars, and to tell him what fortune the boy would encounter in his life. They did this and discovered that, although the boy was destined to be fortunate in his early days, when he reached fifteen, he would fall into difficulties. It was only if he survived these that he would receive his fill of good fortune and become a greater king than his father, enjoying a successful and a pleasant life, while his enemies perished, but were he to die, what is past cannot be recalled.

Tighmus was delighted to hear this. He named his son Janshah and handed him over to nurses to be suckled and reared. This was admirably

done and when Janshah was five his father taught him to read, and he
began to study the Gospel. In less than seven years he was taught the
arts of war and how to cut and thrust; he started to ride out to hunt
and he became a champion, perfect in all branches of horsemanship,
delighting his father with the news of his prowess in all these matters.

It so happened that one day Tighmus ordered his men out to hunt and
he and his son Janshah rode with them. They went out to open country
and they busied themselves with the chase until the afternoon on the
third day. At this point Janshah's path was crossed by a strangely
coloured gazelle which took flight in front of him. He galloped after it
as he saw it fleeing, accompanied by a group of seven of his father's
mamluks, who followed behind him as fast as their swift horses would
take them when they saw him galloping after his quarry. They came to
the seashore and rushed at the gazelle, hoping to seize it, but it evaded
them and threw itself into the sea.

Night 501

Morning now dawned and Shahrazad broke off from what she had been
allowed to say. Then, when it was the five hundred and first night,
SHE CONTINUED:

I have heard, O fortunate king, that when Janshah and the mamluks
rushed at the gazelle and tried to seize it, it evaded them and threw itself
into the sea. Out at sea was a fishing boat on to which the gazelle jumped,
but Janshah and his mamluks dismounted, went on board and caught
it. They were about to return to shore when Janshah, who was looking
at a large island, told the mamluks that he wanted to visit it. 'To hear is
to obey,' they said, and they then sailed out to the island, landed and
started to look around. After that they returned to the boat, embarked
and set off back to the mainland, taking the gazelle with them. They
were still sailing when evening came and at that point a gale blew up,
driving the boat off its course and out to the open sea. They fell asleep
until morning and when they woke up, as they had no idea where to
head, they could only continue to sail along.

So much for them, but as for Janshah's father, King Tighmus, after he
had looked for his son and could not find him, he told his men to scatter
in all directions and they searched all around for the prince. One party
went to the shore, where they found the mamluk who had been left

behind with the horses. They went up and asked him about his master and the other six mamluks, and when he had told them what had happened, they took him back to the king, together with the horses, and made their report. When he heard it, the king wept bitterly, threw the crown from his head and bit his fingers in regret. He then rose quickly and wrote letters to all the islands in the sea; he collected a fleet of a hundred ships and sent his men on board with orders to scour the seas in search of his son. He then went sorrowfully back to his city with those of his guards who were left, and when Janshah's mother learned of the loss of her son, she struck her face and began to mourn for him.

As for Janshah and the mamluks who were with him, they remained adrift on the sea, and although Tighmus's scouts spent ten days looking for them, they were then forced to return to the king to tell him that they had failed. A storm wind now drove Janshah and his mamluks on to an island. They disembarked and walked on until in the middle of it they reached a spring of running water near which, while they were still at a distance, they could see a man sitting. After they had approached and greeted him, he returned their greeting and spoke to them in a tongue that sounded, to Janshah's astonishment, like the whistling of birds. The man suddenly looked right and left, and, while they were staring at him in surprise, he split into two halves, each of which went off in its own direction. At that point, crowds of people too numerous to count came down from the mountain and, when they reached the spring, they too split in halves and went towards Janshah and his mamluks with the intention of eating them. When Janshah saw this, he and the mamluks ran off, but the strangers followed in pursuit, catching and eating three of them. Janshah and the three survivors got into the boat and pushed it out to sea.

They sailed night and day with no idea where the boat was taking them, and the gazelle was killed to provide them with food. The winds then cast them ashore on another island on which they could see trees, streams, fruits and orchards. The fruits were of all kinds and the streams flowed beneath the trees, making the place into a kind of Paradise. The sight of this island delighted Janshah and he asked his mamluks: 'Which of you will land here and investigate it for us?' One of them volunteered to go and scout and then return to them, but Janshah refused his offer, saying: 'All three of you must go and reconnoitre while I stay in the boat and wait for you to come back.'

He landed them to carry out this task, and when they reached the shore . . .

Night 502

Morning now dawned and Shahrazad broke off from what she had been allowed to say. Then, when it was the five hundred and second night, SHE CONTINUED:

I have heard, O fortunate king, that when the mamluks reached the shore they went round the island from east to west without finding anyone. Then, when they penetrated into its centre, they saw in the distance a fortress of white marble with buildings of pure crystal, in the centre of which was an orchard with all kinds of fruits, both dry and fresh, such as would baffle description, together with scented plants of all sorts. There were fruit trees with birds singing on their branches, as well as a large lake. Beside this lake was a huge hall in which chairs were set out, and in the centre was placed a throne of red gold studded with all kinds of jewels and precious stones. When the mamluks saw the beauty of this fortress and its orchard they went all round it but could find no single soul. So they left and came back to tell Janshah what they had seen. When he heard their news he said: 'I must look at this place.' He disembarked and the mamluks accompanied him up to and into the fortress, whose splendour he admired, and they then walked around looking at the orchard and eating its fruits until evening. At that point they came to the chairs that had been set out, and Janshah took his seat on the throne placed in the middle, with the chairs to his right and his left. When he did so, however, he began to weep, thinking of how he had been cut off from the throne of his father, as well as of his separation from his country, his family and all his kinsfolk. The three mamluks joined in his tears, and while they were all in this state there came a sudden loud noise from the direction of the sea, and when they looked they saw apes like a horde of locusts. This was their fortress and their island, and when they caught sight of Janshah's boat, they sank it by the shore and came up to him as he was seated in the fortress.

'This was what the young man seated between the tombs told Buluqiya,' said the snake queen to Karim, and when he asked her how Janshah had dealt with the apes, SHE WENT ON:

When Janshah had gone to take his seat on the throne with the mamluks on either side of him and the apes had advanced towards them, he and his men were filled with alarm and terror. At that moment, however, a group of apes came up and, when they were near the throne on which he was sitting, they kissed the ground before him, placing their paws on their chests. They stood there in front of him for some time and then another group arrived, bringing with them two gazelles, which they slaughtered. They took the bodies to the fortress, where they skinned them, cut up their flesh, roasted it until it was thoroughly cooked, placed it on dishes of gold and silver and laid out tables. They made signs to Janshah and his companions to come and eat, and so he came down from the throne and he, the apes and his companions all ate their fill. The apes then removed the food and brought fruit, which they ate, giving thanks to Almighty God.

Janshah then, using sign language, asked the leaders of the apes to tell him about themselves and the builder of the fortress. In the same language they replied: 'Know that this place belonged to our master, Solomon, son of David, on both of whom be peace, who used to come here on pleasure once a year and then leave us.'

Night 503

Morning now dawned and Shahrazad broke off from what she had been allowed to say. Then, when it was the five hundred and third night, SHE CONTINUED:

I have heard, O fortunate king, that the apes told Janshah about the fortress, saying: 'Know that this place belonged to our master, Solomon, son of David, on both of whom be peace, who used to come here on pleasure once a year and then leave us.' They then told Janshah that he was now their king and they were his subjects, adding: 'Eat and drink, as we shall do all that you order us.' After this they rose, kissed the ground before him and left, each going off on his own way.

Janshah slept on the throne until morning, with the mamluks sleeping round him on their chairs. They were then visited by four viziers, who were the leaders of the apes, together with their followers, until the place was full of them as they lined up in rows. The viziers, using sign language, told Janshah to rule them with justice, after which the apes called out to each other and went off, leaving a few standing in front of him to act as his servants. Some time later, other apes arrived bringing with them dogs as big as horses with chains around their necks. Janshah, who had been amazed to see how large these were, was told by the viziers to mount one of them and to go with them. When he and his mamluks had mounted, the ape army, like a locust flock, went with them, some riding and some walking, adding to his astonishment. They went on until they reached the seashore, where Janshah saw that his boat had been sunk. He asked the apes where it was and they told him: 'Know, O king, that when you came to our island we knew that you were to be our ruler, but we were afraid that when we approached you, you might try to escape back to your boat and so we sank it.' On hearing this, Janshah turned to the mamluks and said: 'We have no means of getting away from these apes and so we shall have to endure what God has decreed for us.'

They all travelled on until they came to the bank of a river beside which there was a mountain, and on this mountain Janshah saw a large number of *ghuls*. He turned to the apes and when he asked about these creatures, he was told: 'These *ghuls* are our enemies and we have come to fight them.' The *ghuls*, whose huge size filled Janshah with astonishment, were mounted on horses; the heads of some of them were like cows, while others had heads like those of camels. At the sight of the apes they advanced to attack, standing on the river bank and hurling stones as huge as pillars. The battle raged violently until Janshah, seeing that the *ghuls* were getting the upper hand, shouted to his mamluks to produce their bows and arrows and to shoot at the *ghuls* so as to drive them back or kill them. The mamluks followed his orders, to the great distress of the *ghuls*, many of whom were killed, while the rest were routed and drew back in flight. When the apes saw what Janshah had done, they plunged into the river and crossed it with him, pursuing the *ghuls* until they were out of sight, having lost many dead in their defeat.

Janshah and the apes moved on until they reached a lofty mountain on which Janshah caught sight of a marble tablet with the following inscription: 'Know, you who enter this land, that you will become the ruler of the apes. You will only be able to leave them if you take the eastern pass by the mountain. It is a three-month journey and you will have to travel among wild beasts, *ghuls*, *marids* and *'ifrits*. After that you will reach the ocean that surrounds the world. If you go through the western pass, which is a four-month journey, you will find at the head of it the Valley of the Ants, and when you get there and enter it, you will have to be on your guard against these ants until you reach a high mountain which burns like fire and which takes ten days to cross.'

When Janshah saw this tablet . . .

Night 504

Morning now dawned and Shahrazad broke off from what she had been allowed to say. Then, when it was the five hundred and fourth night, SHE CONTINUED:

I have heard, O fortunate king, that when Janshah saw this tablet and read what was on it, he found that it went on to say: 'You will then come to a huge river whose current is blindingly fast but which dries up every Saturday. On its bank there is a city entirely populated by Jews who deny the religion of Muhammad and among whom there are no Muslims at all. This is the only city that there is in that land. As long as you stay with the apes, they will have the upper hand over the *ghuls*. Know that this tablet was written by Solomon, son of David, upon both of whom be peace.'

After having read the tablet Janshah wept bitterly and, turning to his mamluks, he told them what it said. He then rode off, surrounded by the apes, who were delighted by their victory over the *ghuls*. They returned to their fortress, and there for a year and a half Janshah remained as their ruler. At the end of that time, on his orders they rode out to hunt accompanied by him and his mamluks and, after having passed through wastes and deserts, they went on from place to place until he came to what he recognized from the description given on the marble tablet as the Valley of the Ants. When he saw it, he ordered his mamluks to halt. The apes halted too and for ten days they stayed there eating and drinking. Then, one night, when Janshah was alone with the mamluks, he told them that he proposed to escape through the valley to the city of the Jews, in the hope that God might rescue them from the apes and they might be able to go free. 'To hear is to obey,' they told him.

He waited until a small part of the night had passed and then he got up, as did the mamluks. They took up their arms, belting on swords, daggers and other such weapons, and then moved off together, travelling from early night until morning. When the apes woke up and could not find them, they realized that Janshah and the mamluks must have escaped. One party mounted and rode towards the eastern pass while another made for the Valley of the Ants. This group caught sight of Janshah and the mamluks as they were approaching the valley. They hurried in pursuit, but their quarry made off into the valley. Before long the apes were in a position to attack them, and they were about to kill them all when suddenly from beneath the surface of the valley out came ants like a flock of locusts, each as big as a dog. When they saw the apes, they rushed at them and ate a number of them, and although a number of ants were killed, it was they who got the upper hand. Individual ants would attack an ape and cut it in two, while it took ten apes to deal with a single ant by seizing it and tearing it apart. This furious battle lasted until evening, and at that point Janshah and the mamluks made off along the floor of the valley.

Night 505

Morning now dawned and Shahrazad broke off from what she had been allowed to say. Then, when it was the five hundred and fifth night, SHE CONTINUED:

I have heard, O fortunate king, that when evening came, Janshah and his mamluks made off along the floor of the valley. They went on until morning, but then the apes again attacked Janshah, who shouted to his mamluks to strike at them with their swords. The mamluks drew their swords and began striking out right and left. An ape with tusks like those of an elephant advanced against one of them, cutting him in half with a single blow, and then, as the apes' numbers were too great, Janshah made his escape to the far end of the valley. Here he saw a huge river, but beside this were ants in enormous numbers and when these creatures saw him coming they surrounded him. One of the mamluks used his sword against them, cutting some of them in two, but when the other ants saw that, they attacked him in numbers and managed to kill him. While this was going on, the apes came down from the mountainside and gathered in force to charge at Janshah. Seeing this, Janshah stripped off his clothes and jumped into the river, accompanied by the surviving mamluk, and the two of them swam into the centre of the stream. On the far bank Janshah could see a tree; stretching out his hand, he managed to catch one of its branches and, by holding on to it, he pulled himself on to the shore. The mamluk, however, found the current too strong for him and was carried away and dashed against the mountain, leaving Janshah standing on the bank alone. While he was squeezing the water from his clothes and drying them in the sun, the apes and the ants kept fighting fiercely, until at last the apes retired to their own land.

So much for them, but as for Janshah, he stayed weeping until evening and then, as he was very frightened and distressed by the loss of his mamluks, he went into a cave to hide. He slept there until morning, when he set out on his way and travelled for a period of nights and days, feeding on grasses, until he came to the mountain that burned like fire. After he had got there, he carried on until he reached the river that dries up once a week on Saturdays. He saw how large it was and he also saw that on its shore was a great city, the city of the Jews that he had seen mentioned on the tablet. He waited there until Saturday and when the river had dried up, he walked across it to the city. Nobody was to be seen, and so, after he had walked for a while, he opened the door of a house that he had reached and went in. The people whom he found there were silent, saying nothing at all, but when he told them that he was a stranger and hungry, they gestured to him to eat and drink but not to speak. After he had taken food and drink, he slept there that night, and in the morning the master of the house gave him a friendly welcome and asked him where he had come from and where he was going. At that, Janshah wept bitterly and told the man his story, giving the name of his father's city. His host was filled with amazement and said: 'We have never heard of your city, but we used to be told by merchants, coming with their caravans, of a country there called Yemen.' Janshah asked him how far Yemen was from the Jewish city, to which he replied that the merchants in those caravans claimed that to here from their own lands was a journey of two years and three months. 'When will the next caravan come?' Janshah asked. 'Next year,' the man answered.

Night 506

Morning now dawned and Shahrazad broke off from what she had been allowed to say. Then, when it was the five hundred and sixth night, SHE CONTINUED:

I have heard, O fortunate king, that when Janshah asked the Jew when the caravan was due, he was told that it would come next year. When Janshah heard this, he wept bitterly in grief both for himself and his mamluks, as well as for his separation from his mother and father and for what had happened to him in the course of his travels. 'Don't weep, young man,' said the Jew. 'You can stay with us until the caravan comes and then we shall send you off with it back to your own country.'

For two months after that Janshah stayed with the Jew, going out every day into the city streets to look at the sights. One day, when he was wandering around as usual, he heard a crier calling out: 'Who wants to get a thousand dinars as well as a slave girl of the rarest beauty by doing a job for me from early morning until noon?' No one answered him, and Janshah said to himself: 'This must be dangerous work for otherwise the man would not be offering a thousand dinars and a beautiful girl for a short task.' He then went up to the crier and said: 'I will do it.' On hearing this, the man took him off and brought him to a large house in which he discovered a Jewish merchant seated on an ebony chair. The crier stood before him and said: 'Merchant, for three months I have been calling out in the city and this young man is the only person who has answered me.'

When the merchant heard this, he welcomed Janshah and took him to a richly furnished room where he ordered his slaves to bring food for him. Tables were set out and when various types of foods had been brought in, the two of them ate and then, after having washed their hands, they drank from what was fetched for them. After this, the merchant got up and produced a purse containing a thousand dinars which he gave to Janshah, and he also brought in a lovely slave girl. 'Take the girl and the money,' he said, 'in exchange for the work that you are going to do.' Janshah took them, seating the girl at his side, and after reminding Janshah that he would have to work the next day, the merchant left him.

That night Janshah slept with the girl, and in the morning he went to the baths. On the orders of the merchant his slaves brought expensive clothes of silk and, after having waited for him to come out of the baths, they dressed him in these and escorted him back to the house. The merchant called for harps, lutes and wine, and he and Janshah drank, played and laughed until half the night had gone. The merchant then went off to his own harem leaving Janshah to sleep with the slave girl until morning. He went again to the baths and when he had got back the merchant came up to him and said: 'I want you to do the job that I have for you.' 'To hear is to obey,' said Janshah.

On their master's orders the servants fetched two mules, one of which the merchant mounted, telling Janshah to ride the other. He did this and he and the merchant travelled from early morning until noon, by which time they had reached a towering mountain. The merchant now dismounted and told Janshah to do the same. When he did, the merchant gave him a knife and a rope and told him to slaughter his mule. Janshah rolled up his sleeves and, going up to the mule, he tied the rope around its legs, threw it on the ground and cut its throat with the knife. He then skinned it and cut off its legs and its head until all that was left was a heap of flesh. 'Slit open its belly,' the merchant ordered, 'and then get inside. I shall sew it up and you must stay there for an hour and tell me whatever you see inside it.' Janshah did this and when he had been sewn up inside the mule, the merchant left him and went some distance off . . .

Night 507

Morning now dawned and Shahrazad broke off from what she had been allowed to say. Then, when it was the five hundred and seventh night, SHE CONTINUED:

I have heard, O fortunate king, that when the merchant had sewn up the belly of the mule with Janshah inside it, he left him and went some distance off, concealing himself in the flanks of the mountain.

Some time later an enormous bird swooped down on the mule, snatched it up and flew off to deposit it on the mountain top, intending to eat it. Janshah, sensing what the bird was doing, cut open the mule's belly and came out, and at the sight of him the bird took fright and flew away. Janshah got to his feet and started to look to the right and the left, but all he could see were human corpses dried out in the sun. 'There is no might and no power except with God, the Exalted, the Omnipotent!' he exclaimed on seeing this, and then, looking down, he caught sight of the merchant standing at the foot of the mountain and staring up at him. When the merchant saw him, he shouted to him: 'Throw me down some of the stones that are round you and I'll show you a way down.' So Janshah threw down some two hundred of these 'stones', they being sapphires, chrysolites and other precious gems. 'Now show me how to get down,' called Janshah, 'and I'll throw you some more.' But the merchant collected the gems, loaded them on to the mule that he had been riding and went off without a word, leaving Janshah alone on the summit, where he began to call for help and to weep.

For three days he stayed where he was, but after that he got up and started to walk along the mountain ridge. For two months he carried on, eating grasses, until eventually he reached the edge of the mountain. From its skirts he could see in the distance a valley with trees and fruits where birds were glorifying the One Almighty God. Janshah was delighted by this sight. He set out for this valley and walked for some time until he came to a corrie in the mountain through which rain floods drained. He climbed down this and went on until he got to the valley that he had seen. When he had made his way into this, he started to investigate, looking to his right and his left, and walking on until he came to a lofty castle towering into the sky. He approached this and went up to its gate, standing by which he saw a handsome old man whose face gleamed radiantly and who carried in his hand a sapphire staff. Janshah went up and greeted him and the man returned the greeting cordially, saying: 'Sit down, my son.'

When Janshah had taken his seat by the castle door, the old man asked him: 'Where have you come from to this land which has never yet been trodden on by the foot of man, and where are you going?' When he heard this, the extent of his sufferings caused Janshah to weep so violently that he was almost choked by tears. 'Stop crying, my son,' the old man told him, 'for you are distressing me,' and he then got up and brought some food, which he put down in front of Janshah, telling him to eat. When Janshah had done so and had given thanks to Almighty God, the old man asked him to tell him his story, with an account of his experiences. Janshah did this, describing everything that had happened to him before they met, and the old man was filled with astonishment at what he had to say.

Janshah, for his part, then asked him to whom the valley and the great castle belonged. 'Know, my son,' replied the old man, 'that the valley and everything in it, together with the castle and its surroundings, are the property of our lord Solomon, son of David, upon both of whom be peace. My name is Shaikh Nasr, king of the birds, and it was to me that Solomon entrusted this castle.'

Night 508

Morning now dawned and Shahrazad broke off from what she had been allowed to say. Then, when it was the five hundred and eighth night, SHE CONTINUED:

I have heard, O fortunate king, that Shaikh Nasr, king of the birds, told Janshah: 'Our lord Solomon entrusted this castle to me. He taught me the language of the birds, and appointed me as ruler over all the birds in the world. Every year they come to the castle, leaving again after

I have inspected them, and this is why I stay here.' On hearing this, Janshah wept again and said: 'My father, how can I find a way to get back to my own country?' 'My son,' answered the old man, 'you are close to Mount Qaf and the only way you can leave here is when the birds come, as I will then tell one of them to carry you home. Meanwhile, stay in the castle with me; eat, drink and enjoy yourself looking around its rooms until the birds arrive.'

So Janshah stayed with him and started to explore the valley, eating the fruits, taking pleasure in the sights, laughing and playing. He remained there, enjoying the pleasantest of lives, until it was almost time for the birds to come from their various regions to pay their visit to Shaikh Nasr. When the *shaikh* knew that they were about to arrive, he got to his feet and told Janshah: 'Janshah, take these keys and open the rooms in the castle. You may then look at whatever you find, but there is one room which you must take care not to open, and if you disobey me, open it and go in, no good will ever come to you.' After having reinforced this warning, he left Janshah and went off to meet the birds, who, on seeing him, flocked to him and kissed his hands, one species after another.

So much for Shaikh Nasr, but as for Janshah, he got up and started to look round the whole of the castle, opening all the rooms, until he came to the one that Shaikh Nasr had warned him not to open. He looked with admiration at its door, whose lock, he saw, was made of gold, and he said to himself: 'This room is more splendid than all the others. What can it contain that has made Shaikh Nasr forbid me to enter it? I shall have to go in and see what is there, as God's servants must bring to a finish whatever has been decreed for them by fate.' He stretched out his hand, opened the door of the room and entered. There he found a large pool, beside which was a small pavilion built of gold, silver and crystal, with windows of sapphires, paved with green chrysolite, hyacinth gems, emeralds and other jewels, set on the ground like pieces of marble. In the middle of this pavilion was a golden fountain filled with water, and around the fountain were statues of wild beasts and birds made of gold and silver, with water spouting from their bellies. When a breeze blew, wind would enter their ears and each would make its own characteristic noise. To the side of the fountain was a great hall in which was set a huge sapphire throne studded with pearls and other gems, over which was a canopy of green silk embellished with jewels and precious stones fifty cubits in width. Within this hall was an inner chamber containing the carpet that had belonged to our lord Solomon, upon whom be peace, while the pavilion itself was surrounded by a vast garden with trees, fruits and streams, as well as with beds of roses, sweet basil, eglantine and scented herbs of all kinds. When the breezes blew, the branches of the trees would bend, while the garden, as Janshah could see, contained all sorts of fruits, both fresh and dry. The whole of this was held in this one chamber.

Janshah, who was filled with astonishment, started to explore the garden and the pavilion, together with their wonderful contents. He looked at the pool and saw that its pebbles were gems, costly jewels and precious stones, while the pavilion itself was full of treasures.

Night 509

Morning now dawned and Shahrazad broke off from what she had been allowed to say. Then, when it was the five hundred and ninth night, SHE CONTINUED:

I have heard, O fortunate king, that Janshah saw the quantity of treasures in the chamber. Having looked at this with wonder, he went into the pavilion and climbed up to the throne in the hall beside the pool. He went beneath the canopy set over it, and after having slept there for some time, he got up, walked out of the pavilion door and took his seat on a chair set in front of it, from where he admired the beauty of the place.

While he was sitting there, three birds looking like doves came flying through the air to settle beside the pool. After having played around for some time, they took off their feathers and emerged as three girls, beautiful as moons, without a match in the world. They then went down to swim in the pool, playing and laughing, and filling Janshah with admiration for their beauty, grace and elegant figures, and then they came out of the water and went around looking at the garden. When Janshah saw them there, he almost went out of his mind and, getting to his feet, he walked towards them. When he got near, he greeted them and after they had returned his greeting he asked them: 'Who are you, you dazzling ladies, and where have you come from?' The youngest of them replied: 'We have come from the realm of Almighty God in order to enjoy ourselves here.' 'Pity me,' he said to her, filled with admiration for their beauty. 'Show sympathy and have compassion for my plight and for what I have had to live through.' 'Stop talking like that,' she told him,

'and go off on your way.' On hearing this, Janshah burst into tears and
with deep sighs he recited these lines:

> She appeared in the garden wearing green robes,
> With her waist-wrapper undone and her hair unloosed.
> 'What is your name?' I asked her, and she said:
> 'I am she who roasts lovers' hearts over the coals.'
> When I complained to her about my love,
> She said: 'You do not know it, but it is a rock to which you have
>   complained.'
> I told her: 'Your heart may be a rock,
> But out of rocks God has made water flow.'

The girls burst into laughter when they heard Janshah's lines, and they
then played, sang and enjoyed themselves. He brought them fruit and
they ate, drank and then slept with him that night until morning, but
when morning came they put on their feathered robes, resumed their
shapes as doves and flew away. Janshah watched them fly out of sight;
his wits almost took flight with them and after uttering a great cry
he fell down in a faint. He remained unconscious for the whole of that
day and while he was lying stretched out on the ground, Shaikh Nasr
came from his meeting with the birds to look for him so that he could
be taken back to his own country. He had told the birds: 'I have a young
son whom fate has brought here from a far land and I want you to carry
him home.' 'To hear is to obey,' they replied, but when Nasr failed
to see Janshah, he realized that he must have entered the forbidden
room. When he had searched everywhere else, he came to the door of
this room and found it standing open. He went in and discovered
Janshah lying unconscious under a tree. He fetched scented water and
sprinkled it over Janshah's face, at which he recovered and began to
look round . . .

Night 510

Morning now dawned and Shahrazad broke off from what she had been
allowed to say. Then, when it was the five hundred and tenth night,
SHE CONTINUED:

I have heard, O fortunate king, that when Shaikh Nasr saw Janshah
lying on the ground under a tree, he fetched scented water and sprinkled

it over his face, at which he recovered and began to look round from right to left. When he could see nobody but Shaikh Nasr, he sighed deeply and recited the lines:

> She appeared like a full moon on a lucky night,
> With delicate fingers and a slender figure.
> The witchery of her eyes enslaves the mind;
> Her mouth is rose red like the ruby.
> Her black hair falls down her back,
> But beware, beware of the snakes within her curls!
> Although her body may be soft; her heart
> Is harder than solid rock towards her lover.
> From the bow of her eyebrow she shoots the arrow of a glance
> That strikes home, never missing, however long the range.
> O for the beautiful one, unmatched in loveliness!
> She has no equal among all mankind.

When he had listened to these lines, Shaikh Nasr said: 'My son, did I not tell you not to open the door of this room or to go into it? But tell me what you saw there and let me know what happened to you.' So Janshah told him of how he had met the three girls while he had been sitting there, and when Shaikh Nasr heard this he said: 'These were *jinn* girls, my son. They come here every year to play and enjoy themselves, and they stay until the afternoon and then go back to their own land.' 'And where is their own land?' Janshah asked, but Shaikh Nasr replied: 'By God, my son, I do not know.' He then told Janshah: 'Take heart; come with me so that I may get the birds to take you back to your own country and abandon this love of yours.' Janshah, however, on hearing this gave a great cry and fell unconscious. When he recovered, he said: 'Father, until I meet those girls I do not want to return home, even if this means that I must die here, for I no longer have any memory of my family.' He then wept and said: 'I would be content to see the face of my beloved even once a year,' and then, with sighs, he recited:

> Would that the beloved's phantom did not visit me by night,
> And would that this love had never been created for mankind.
> For if your memory did not burn in my heart,
> Then tears would not flood down over my cheeks.
> Night and day I try to make my heart endure,
> But my body is consumed by the fire of love.

Falling at the feet of Shaikh Nasr, he kissed them and said tearfully: 'Have pity on me so that God may pity you, and help me in my affliction so that you may receive help from Him.' 'By God,' the *shaikh* replied, 'I do not know these girls and I do not know where their country may be, but as you have fallen so passionately in love with one of them, you had better stay with me until this time next year, as they will come back on the same day. When it is nearly time for them to arrive, hide beneath a tree in the garden and then, when they enter the pool and enjoy them-selves swimming there, leaving their clothes at a distance, take the clothes of the girl you want. When they see you, they will get out of the water to dress, and the girl whose clothes you have taken will say sweetly, with a lovely smile: "Brother, give me back my clothes so that I may dress and cover myself." If you do what she says and return her clothes, you will never get what you want from her. She will put them on and go off to her family, and you will never see her again. So when you get them, keep them safely under your arm and don't give them back until I return from meeting the birds. Then I shall arrange things between the two of you and send you back home with her. This is the only thing that I can do for you, my son.'

Night 511

Morning now dawned and Shahrazad broke off from what she had been allowed to say. Then, when it was the five hundred and eleventh night, SHE CONTINUED:

I have heard, O fortunate king, that Shaikh Nasr told Janshah to keep the clothes of the girl whom he wanted and not to give them back to her until he himself returned from meeting the birds. 'That is all I can do for you, my son,' he said.

Janshah calmed down when he heard this. He stayed with the *shaikh* for the next year, counting the days as they passed until the birds were due to return. When the time had come, the *shaikh* came to him and said: 'Do as I told you when you steal the girl's clothes, for I am going to meet the birds.' 'To hear is to obey, my father,' replied Janshah. When the *shaikh* had gone off to his meeting, Janshah got up, went to the garden and hid beneath a tree in a place where he could not be seen. He waited for one day and then another and then a third, but the girls did not come. Distressed and sorrowful, he began to weep and wail until he lost consciousness and then, after he had recovered, he started to look around, first at the sky, then at the earth, staring at times at the pool and at times at the dry land, with his heart throbbing because of the strength of his emotion.

He was in this state when three birds like doves came towards him through the air, each of them the size of an eagle. They alighted beside the pool and, after looking right and left and seeing no one, human or *jinn*, they took off their clothes and went into the water, where they started to play, laughing and enjoying themselves, their naked bodies gleaming like silver ingots. Then the eldest exclaimed: 'Sisters! I'm afraid that there is someone hidden in this pavilion.' The next in age said: 'Since the time of Solomon no one, human or *jinn*, has entered it,' while the youngest laughed and said: 'By God, sisters, if there is someone hiding here, I am the one whom he will take.'

The girls continued with their games and laughter, and Janshah's heart throbbed with passion as he watched them from his hiding place under the tree, where they could not see him. They then swam off to the middle of the pool, leaving their clothes at a distance. Janshah got to his feet and, moving like a lightning flash, he snatched the clothes of the youngest girl, with whom he was in love, her name being Shamsa. She turned and saw him, and in their alarm she and her companions concealed themselves in the water before approaching the bank. They looked at Janshah's face, which was as radiant as a full moon, and asked him: 'Who are you and how did you come here to steal Lady Shamsa's clothes?' 'Come here to me,' he replied, 'so that I may tell you what happened to me.' 'What is your story?' Shamsa asked. 'Why did you steal my clothes and how did you distinguish me from my sisters?' 'Light of my eyes,' Janshah answered, 'come out of the water so that I may tell you my story with an account of my experiences, and let you know how it was that I recognized you.' She said: 'My lord, the refreshment of my eyes and the fruit of my heart, let me have my clothes back so that I may put them on and cover myself, and then I shall come to you.' 'Mistress of the beautiful ones,' he replied, 'I cannot give you your clothes lest I die of love, and I shall only do this when Shaikh Nasr, king of the birds, comes back.' 'If you are not going to give them to me, then stand back a little way from us so that my sisters can come out, dress themselves and give me something with which to cover myself,' said Shamsa. 'To hear is to obey,' replied Janshah, and he then left them and went to the pavilion.

Shamsa and her sisters came out on to the bank and dressed, with the eldest giving Shamsa something of her own to wear, although she could not use it to fly. She then got up like a rising moon or a pasturing gazelle, and walked to Janshah, whom she found sitting on the throne. She greeted him and sat down near him, after which she said: 'Handsome man, it is you who have killed me and killed yourself, but tell me what has happened to you so that we may learn your story.' On hearing this, Janshah wept until his clothes were sodden with tears. Realizing that he was deeply in love with her, she got up, took him by the hand and made him sit beside her. She wiped away his tears with her sleeve and urged him to stop weeping and to tell her his story. So Janshah gave her an account of his adventures and of what he had seen.

Night 512

Morning now dawned and Shahrazad broke off from what she had been allowed to say. Then, when it was the five hundred and twelfth night, SHE CONTINUED:

I have heard, O fortunate king, that the Lady Shamsa asked Janshah to tell her all that had happened to him, which he did. When she had listened to this, she heaved a sigh and said: 'Master, if you love me, give me back my clothes so that I may put them on and return with my sisters to my family. I shall tell them what has happened to you because of your love for me and then I shall come back and carry you to your own land.' Janshah listened to this, but then burst into tears and said: 'Is it lawful in God's eyes for you to kill me unjustly?' 'How am I killing you unjustly, master?' she asked. 'Because when you put on your clothes and leave me, I shall instantly die,' he told her. When Shamsa heard this, she and her sisters burst out laughing and Shamsa said: 'Take heart and console yourself for I shall have to marry you.' Then she leaned towards him, clasped him to her breast and kissed him between the eyes and on the cheek. For a time the two of them embraced before breaking off and taking their seats on the throne. Shamsa's eldest sister then got up to walk from the pavilion to the garden, where she picked some fruits and scented herbs and brought them to the couple. They all ate, drank and enjoyed themselves delightedly, laughing and playing. Janshah was an extremely handsome man, slender and well built, and Shamsa told him: 'My darling, by God I love you very much indeed and I shall never part from you.' Janshah was delighted to hear this and smiled broadly, and they continued to laugh and play until, as they were enjoying themselves, Shaikh Nasr returned from his meeting with the birds.

They all stood up to greet him, kissing his hands, and after welcoming them, he told them to sit, which they did. Then he said to the Lady Shamsa: 'This young man is deeply in love with you and I conjure you in God's Name to treat him kindly. He comes from a great family, the descendants of kings, and his father, who rules over the lands of Kabul, has a vast kingdom.' 'To hear is to obey your orders,' she replied, and, having kissed his hand, she stood there in front of him. 'If you are sincere in what you say,' the *shaikh* told her, 'then swear to me by God that you will not play him false as long as you live.' Shamsa swore a great oath to this effect and added that she would most certainly marry him and would never leave him. When she had taken this oath to the *shaikh*, he believed her and, turning to Janshah, he said: 'Praise be to God, Who has brought the two of you to this agreement.'

The delighted Janshah together with the Lady Shamsa stayed for three months with Shaikh Nasr, eating, drinking, playing and laughing . . .

Night 513

Morning now dawned and Shahrazad broke off from what she had been allowed to say. Then, when it was the five hundred and thirteenth night, SHE CONTINUED:

I have heard, O fortunate king, that Janshah and the Lady Shamsa stayed for three months with Shaikh Nasr, eating, drinking, playing and enjoying the greatest good fortune. At the end of this period Shamsa told Janshah: 'I want to go to your own country so that you may marry me and we can stay there.' 'To hear is to obey,' said Janshah, and he let the *shaikh* know that he wanted to go home, telling him what Shamsa had said. 'Go back, then,' said the *shaikh*, 'and take good care of her.' 'To hear is to obey,' said Janshah. Shamsa then looked for her feather dress and asked the *shaikh* to tell Janshah to give it to her so that she could put it on. The *shaikh* did this and Janshah, with ready obedience, got up quickly, went to the pavilion and fetched the dress. When he had given it to her she took it, put it on and then said: 'Mount on my back, close your eyes and block your ears lest you hear the sound of the celestial sphere as it revolves. When you are on my back, use your hands to hold on to my feather dress and take care not to fall.'

When Janshah heard this, he mounted on Shamsa's back but, as she was about to fly off, Shaikh Nasr said: 'Stop; let me describe the lands of Kabul for you, as I'm afraid that the two of you may mistake the way.' Shamsa waited until he had done this, and he then told her to look after Janshah and said goodbye to the two of them. For her part, Shamsa said goodbye to her sisters, telling them to go home to their families and explain to them what had happened to her when she met Janshah. She then took to the air, flying through it like the wind's breath or like a lightning flash, and her sisters went home and told all this to their people.

Shamsa flew on from before noon until the time of the afternoon prayer, carrying Janshah on her back. She then saw a valley with trees and streams in the distance, and she told Janshah that she was going to land in it so that they might enjoy inspecting the trees and the plants and might spend the night there. 'Do what you want,' he told her, and so she flew down and alighted in the valley. Janshah dismounted and kissed her between the eyes, and then, after they had sat for a time by the bank of a stream, they got to their feet and began to roam through the valley, looking at what was there and eating its fruits. They went on like this until evening, when they came to a tree beside which they slept until morning.

Shamsa now got up and told Janshah to mount on her back. 'To hear is to obey,' he said, and as soon as he had mounted she flew off with him, continuing her flight from early morning until noon. On their way they saw the landmarks that Shaikh Nasr had described for them, and on sighting these, Shamsa flew down from the upper air to a broad stretch of meadow land where there were fine crops, pasturing gazelles, gushing springs, ripe fruits and broad streams. When she had landed, Janshah dismounted and kissed her between the eyes. 'My darling and the comfort of my eyes,' she said, 'do you know how far we have come?' When he said no, she told him that they had covered the distance of a thirty-month journey. 'Praise be to God that we have arrived safely!' exclaimed Janshah, and the two of them sat side by side eating, drinking, playing and laughing. While they were doing this two mamluks came up, one of whom being the man who had been left with the horses when Janshah had boarded the fishing boat, while the other had been with him on the hunt. When they saw him, they recognized him and asked his permission to go to give his father the good news of his return. 'Go and tell him,' said Janshah, 'and then fetch tents, as we are going to stay resting here for seven days until a ceremonial procession comes to fetch us so that we may enter in great state.'

Night 514

Morning now dawned and Shahrazad broke off from what she had been allowed to say. Then, when it was the five hundred and fourteenth night, SHE CONTINUED:

I have heard, O fortunate king, that Janshah told the two mamluks to take the news to his father, adding: 'And then fetch tents, as we are going to stay resting here for seven days until a ceremonial procession comes to fetch us so that we may enter in great state.'

The two mamluks mounted and went off to Janshah's father, calling out to him: 'Good news, king of the age!' 'What is the news?' asked King Tighmus when he heard them. 'Has my son Janshah come back?' 'Yes,' they told him, 'he is back from his travels and is nearby in the Karani meadow.' The king was so delighted by what they said that he fell to the ground in a faint. When he had recovered, he told his vizier to give each of the mamluks a splendid robe of honour and a quantity of money. 'To hear is to obey,' said the vizier, who then immediately got up and gave them these gifts, saying: 'Take the money in exchange for your good news, whether it is true or false.' 'We are no liars,' they told him, 'and only just now we were sitting with him, greeting him and kissing his hands. He told us to fetch tents as he was going to stay in the Karani meadow for seven days until the viziers, emirs and state officials go out to meet him.' The king then asked them how he was and they said: 'He has a lady with him who looks like a houri of Paradise.'

On hearing this, the king ordered the drums to be beaten and the trumpets to sound in order to spread the good news, and he sent messengers to all parts of the city to relay it to Janshah's mother as well as to the wives of the viziers, emirs and state officials. These messengers scattered throughout the city, telling the people that Janshah had returned. King Tighmus then formed up his guards and his troops and set out for the Karani meadow. Janshah was sitting with the Lady Shamsa by his side when he saw them advancing. He got to his feet and walked up to them, and when they saw him and recognized who he was, they dismounted and approached him on foot, greeting him and kissing his hands.

Janshah walked on with the troops in single file in front of him until he came to his father, who, on seeing his son, threw himself down from the back of his horse and embraced him, shedding floods of tears. He then mounted, as did Janshah, and rode off with the troops on either side. When they reached the river bank the men dismounted and set up tents and pavilions, hoisting flags, beating drums both large and small, and sounding pipes and trumpets. On the king's orders the servants brought a tent of red silk which they set up for the Lady Shamsa. For her part, she got up and, after removing her feather dress, she walked to the tent and sat down. When she was seated, King Tighmus, with his son Janshah at his side, walked towards her, and at the sight of the king she got to her feet and kissed the ground before him. He sat down with his son Janshah on his right and her on his left. After having welcomed her, he asked Janshah to tell him what had happened to him while he had been away, at which Janshah told him the story of his experiences from beginning to end, filling his father with astonishment. Turning to Shamsa, the king said: 'Praise be to God by Whose aid you have done me the greatest of favours by reuniting me with my son.'

Morning now dawned and Shahrazad broke off from what she had been allowed to say. Then, when it was the five hundred and fifteenth night, SHE CONTINUED:

I have heard, O fortunate king, that King Tighmus said to Shamsa: 'Praise be to God by Whose aid you have done me the greatest of favours by reuniting me with my son. I want you now to make a wish for whatever you want from me so that I may grant it as a favour to you.' 'What I want,' said Shamsa, 'is for you to build me a palace in the middle of a garden, with water flowing beneath it.' 'To hear is to obey,' said the king, and while the two of them were talking, Janshah's mother came forward, accompanied by all the wives of the viziers, emirs and leading citizens. On seeing her, Janshah left the tent to meet her and, after a long embrace, his mother, shedding tears of joy, recited these lines:

> I shed tears for the onslaught of delight,
> And I am overjoyed.
> Weeping is second nature to my eyes,
> Which shed tears of both joy and sorrow.

The two of them then complained to each other of the hardships inflicted on them by separation and their painful yearnings, after which the king went to his own tent and Janshah went with his mother to his. While the two of them were sitting there, messengers arrived to tell Janshah's mother that Shamsa was walking over to greet her. On hearing this, she got to her feet and welcomed her. The two ladies sat together for a time and then they both rose and went off, accompanied by the wives of the emirs and state officials until they reached Shamsa's pavilion, in which they took their seats.

King Tighmus distributed large quantities of gifts, treating his subjects with generosity in his delight at his son's return, and they all stayed there for ten days, eating, drinking and enjoying themselves. On the king's orders, his men then set off back to the city. He himself mounted, surrounded by his guards, with the viziers and chamberlains to his right and his left, and rode into the city, where Janshah's mother and the Lady Shamsa went off to their own quarters. The city itself was splendidly decorated and adorned with ornaments and draperies, while drums of all sizes were beaten in celebration. Expensive brocades were spread beneath the horses' hooves, the state officials showed their joy by producing gifts, and the spectators were dazzled. Food was provided for the poor and needy, the great wedding feast extended over ten days, and Shamsa was delighted by what she saw.

The king then sent for the builders, architects and skilled craftsmen and told them to build a palace in the garden there. 'To hear is to obey,' they replied, and the work on which they then began was completed in all its splendour. Janshah, when he learned of what was being done, ordered the craftsmen to fetch a pillar of white marble which they were to hollow out until it looked like a box. When this had been done, he took Shamsa's feather dress that enabled her to fly, put it in the pillar and buried it in the foundations of the castle, telling the builders to construct over it the arches on which the palace was supported.

When it was finished, the huge palace was furnished, set, as it was, in the middle of the garden with streams flowing beneath it. The king then arranged for the wedding to be celebrated with a great feast, the like of which had never been seen. The Lady Shamsa was escorted to the palace, and after that all the attendants left. When she entered the palace, Shamsa detected the scent of her feathered dress . . .

Night 516

Morning now dawned and Shahrazad broke off from what she had been allowed to say. Then, when it was the five hundred and sixteenth night, SHE CONTINUED:

I have heard, O fortunate king, that when Shamsa entered the palace, she detected the scent of the feathered dress that enabled her to fly. She realized where it was and wanted to recover it, but she waited until midnight, when Janshah was sunk in sleep, before going to the pillar that supported the arches. She dug a hole alongside this, leading through to where the dress had been placed, and after she had removed the lead that had been poured over it, she took out her dress, put it on and immediately flew up to the roof of the palace. There she took her seat, telling the guards to fetch Janshah to her so that she could say goodbye to him. When he was told what had happened, he went there and saw her sitting on top of the roof wearing the dress. 'Why have you done this?' he asked, and she replied: 'My darling, the refreshment of my eyes and the fruit of my heart, by God, I love you very deeply and I was filled with joy when I brought you back to your own land and met your mother and father. If you love me as much as I love you, then come to me in the jewelled castle of Takni.' After that, she immediately flew away and went back to her own people.

When Janshah heard what Shamsa said to him from the rooftop, he fell down in a faint, almost dead with grief, and the attendants went to tell his father about that. His father mounted and rode to the palace, and when he came in, it was to find his son stretched out on the ground. He burst into tears, realizing that Janshah was passionately in love with Shamsa. He poured rosewater over his face and when Janshah recovered and saw his father standing at his head, he wept in grief for the loss of his wife. When his father asked him what had happened, he said: 'You have to know, father, that the Lady Shamsa is one of the daughters of the *jinn* and her beauty led me to fall passionately in love with her. I had in my possession a dress without which she could not fly, and I took it and hid it in a pillar hollowed out to form a box. I then poured lead on this and placed it in the foundations of the palace, but she dug down there and took the dress. She put it on and flew up to the palace roof from where she told me that she loved me, reminding me how she had brought me back home and had met you and my mother, and adding that if I loved her I was to go to the jewelled castle of Takni, to find her again. She then flew from the roof and went off on her way.' 'My son,' said King Tighmus, 'do not grieve, for we shall collect the merchants and those who have travelled through far lands and ask them about that castle. Then, when we find out where it is, we can go there to visit the Lady Shamsa's family, in the hope that Almighty God will give her to you so that you may marry her.'

The king immediately went out and summoned his four viziers, whom he told to collect all the merchants and travellers in the city and to ask them about Castle Takni. He promised fifty thousand dinars to anyone who knew the place and could direct him to it. 'To hear is to obey,' said the viziers when they heard this, and they went off immediately to carry out his orders, asking the travelling merchants about Takni, but no one could tell them anything about it. They went back to tell this to the king, and when he heard the news he told them to bring beautiful concubines, slave girls who could play musical instruments and singing girls such as were only to be found in royal palaces, in order to make Janshah forget his love for Shamsa. They did as he told them, and he then sent out scouts to explore all lands, islands and climes in order to ask about Castle Takni. These men spent two months on this fruitless task, and when they returned to tell the king of their failure, he wept bitterly. He then went to see his son, and found him surrounded by concubines, slave girls, harpists and girls playing on dulcimers and other instruments, but none of this was consoling him for the loss of Shamsa. 'My son,' he said, 'I have found no one who knows about Castle Takni, so I brought you others more beautiful than her.' Janshah, on hearing his father's news, wept and recited the following lines through his tears:

Endurance has gone but love remains;
My body is sick with the strength of passion.
When will Time reunite me with Shamsa?
My bones have decayed because of the fires of separation.

There happened to be a bitter feud between King Tighmus and Kafid, the king of India, whom Tighmus had attacked, killing his men and plundering his goods. Kafid had armies and men of valour, in addition to a thousand paladins, each of whom was the leader of a thousand tribes, in every one of which were four thousand riders. He had four viziers, together with subordinate kings, nobles, emirs and numerous armies. He ruled over a thousand cities, each with a thousand castles, and he was a great and powerful king whose troops filled the whole land. He now heard that Tighmus was preoccupied by his son's love for Shamsa and had left aside the affairs of government; his armies had diminished and he himself was filled with cares and worries because of what had happened to his son. So he gathered together his viziers, emirs and state officials and said to them: 'You know that King Tighmus attacked our country, killing my father and my brothers as well as plundering our treasures. Every one of you lost a relative and had his wealth seized, his possessions plundered and his family taken captive. I now hear that he is preoccupied with the love affair of his son, Janshah, and has allowed the numbers of his troops to fall. This is the time for us to take our revenge, so prepare to set out, and get ready the equipment we need for an attack on him. There must be no slackness, as we are going to march against him, launch our assault, kill both him and his son and then take possession of his country.'

Night 517

Morning now dawned and Shahrazad broke off from what she had been allowed to say. Then, when it was the five hundred and seventeenth night, SHE CONTINUED:

I have heard, O fortunate king, that Kafid, the king of India, ordered his men to ride against the lands of King Tighmus, telling them: 'Prepare to set out, and get ready the equipment we need for an attack on him. There must be no slackness, as we are going to march against him, launch our assault, kill both him and his son and then take possession of his country.' 'To hear is to obey,' they said when they heard this, and each of them set about preparing equipment, supplies and weapons, as well as collecting men. After three months of this, when all the troops were ready, drums were beaten, trumpets blown and standards and flags set up. King Kafid led them all out and advanced to the borders of Tighmus's territory in the lands of Kabul. When they arrived there, they plundered the lands, maltreating the inhabitants, slaughtering the old and taking the young as captives. When news of this reached Tighmus, he became furiously angry. He summoned the leading men of his kingdom, together with his viziers and emirs, and said: 'You must know that Kafid has come to invade our country with the intention of meeting us in battle with armies whose numbers are known only to Almighty God. What is your advice?' 'King of the age,' they replied, 'our advice is to go out and fight so as to drive him from our lands.' 'Prepare for battle, then,' said the king, and he produced for them coats of mail, armour, helmets, swords and all the weapons needed to kill champions and destroy chiefs. The soldiers were mustered, and when they had been equipped for war, the standards were set up to the beat of drums, trumpet calls and the sound of horns.

Tighmus now led his men out to meet Kafid, and continued his march until the enemy were close by. He then camped in a valley called Wadi Zahran on the border of Kabul territory, and sent a messenger from his army with a letter to King Kafid. In it he had written: 'This is our message to King Kafid. What you have done is the action of a ruffian, and were you really a king and the son of a king you would not have acted like this and you would not have come to my lands, plundering the goods of my people and maltreating my subjects. Do you not realize that all this is an outrage on your part? Had I thought that you would dare to attack my kingdom, I would have forestalled you and driven you back from my borders, but if you retreat and abandon the feud between us, well and good. If not, then come out to meet me on the field, and have the courage to stand against me in battle.'

Tighmus sealed the letter and handed it to an aide-de-camp, whom he sent off, together with a number of spies, to scout for news. Having taken the letter, the messenger brought it to King Kafid and, as he approached, he could see tents of dark silk and blue silk flags. In between these tents there was a huge pavilion of red silk, surrounded by large numbers of guards. The messenger went up to it and, when he asked, he was told that this was the pavilion of King Kafid. He looked inside it and saw the king himself seated on a jewel-studded chair surrounded by his viziers, emirs and state officials. At this point he held out Tighmus's letter and a number of Kafid's guards came to take it from him and bring it to their king. When the latter had read it and grasped its contents, he wrote the following reply: 'This is our message to King Tighmus: we are going to take our revenge and wipe away our disgrace with pillage and rapine, killing the old and enslaving the young. Come out tomorrow to the battlefield so that I may show you how to fight.' When he had sealed the letter he handed it to the envoy, who took it and went off.

Night 518

Morning now dawned and Shahrazad broke off from what she had been allowed to say. Then, when it was the five hundred and eighteenth night, SHE CONTINUED:

I have heard, O fortunate king, that King Kafid handed the messenger the reply that he had written to the letter sent him by King Tighmus. The messenger took this and went back.

When he came to King Tighmus, he kissed the ground before him, handed over the letter and told the king what he had seen. 'O king of the age,' he said, 'I have seen more champions, together with horsemen and footmen, than can be counted, together with an endless supply of auxiliaries.'

When Tighmus had read Kafid's letter, he was furiously angry and ordered his vizier, 'Ain Zar, to ride out to attack Kafid at midnight with a thousand riders, plunging into the middle of his army and killing them. 'To hear is to obey,' answered the vizier, and he then rode out with his men to attack King Kafid. Kafid, however, had ordered a vizier of his own, named Ghatrafan, to attack Tighmus's army with five thousand horsemen and to kill them. Ghatrafan followed his orders, mounted and rode out with his men, making for Tighmus. By midnight they had covered half the distance when suddenly they came across 'Ain Zar's force. They both shouted their battle cries against one another, and a furious fight raged between them until dawn, but then Kafid's men were beaten and took flight.

Kafid was angered when he saw what had happened. 'Damn you,' he said to the fugitives, 'how did you come to lose your champions?' 'King of the age,' they told him, 'when the vizier Ghatrafan mounted, we set off to attack Tighmus and continued on our march until midnight, by which time we were halfway there, but then 'Ain Zar, Tighmus's vizier, met us with an army and champions of his own near Wadi Zahran. Before we knew what was happening we were face to face with them in the middle of their army. We fought hard against them from midnight until morning. Many were killed, but 'Ain Zar started to shout at our elephant, striking it in the face so fiercely that it took fright and started trampling down horsemen as it turned in flight. No one could see anyone else because of the dust clouds; blood was flowing in streams and had we not taken to our heels every last one of us would have been killed.'

'May the sun shine on you with anger rather than blessing!' exclaimed Kafid when he heard this.

As for the vizier 'Ain Zar, he returned to tell King Tighmus what had happened. The king congratulated him on his safety, and in his delight he ordered drums to be beaten and trumpets blown. He then inspected his men and found that they had lost two hundred strong and courageous riders. For his part, King Kafid prepared to lead out his whole force, and when he reached the battlefield he drew them up in fifteen ranks, each comprising ten thousand riders. They had with them three hundred paladins, specially picked champions, mounted on elephants. Banners and flags were raised, drums were beaten, trumpets blared and the champions came out to fight.

Tighmus had drawn up his own army in ten ranks of ten thousand riders each, and he had with him a hundred paladins riding on his right and his left. When both sides were in position, every horseman of repute rode forward and the armies clashed. Broad as it was, the ground was too narrow for the horses; drums were beaten, trumpets and bugles blown and there was a deafening noise as horses neighed and men shouted, while thick dust clouds rose over their heads. The battle raged fiercely from the start of day until the approach of darkness, at which both sides parted and retired to their own camps.

Night 519

Morning now dawned and Shahrazad broke off from what she had been allowed to say. Then, when it was the five hundred and nineteenth night, SHE CONTINUED:

I have heard, O fortunate king, that both sides parted and retired to their own camps. On inspecting his troops, King Kafid was furious to find that he had lost five thousand men, while King Tighmus was equally angry at the loss of three thousand of his bravest followers. Kafid then came out to battle a second time and drew up his men as before. Both kings looked for victory and Kafid called to his men: 'Is there any one of you who will ride out as a challenger on to the field and begin the battle for us?' At that a champion named Barkik, a formidable paladin, came forward riding on an elephant. He dismounted to kiss the ground in front of Kafid and asked his permission to ride out. He then remounted and rode off, calling: 'Will anyone dare to challenge me to a duel?' When

King Tighmus heard this, he turned to his men and said: 'Which of you will go to meet this champion?' From the ranks there then came a rider mounted on a huge horse, who, after kissing the ground before the king, asked permission to fight. He rode up to Barkik, who called to him: 'Who are you to treat me so lightly that you come out against me alone? What is your name?' 'My name is Ghadanfar ibn Kamkhil,' the rider replied. 'I have heard of you in my own country,' said Barkik, adding, 'so now prepare yourself to fight between the ranks of the heroes.'

Ghadanfar, hearing this, drew an iron mace from beneath his thigh while Barkik took his sword in his hand. They fought furiously, and although Barkik's sword struck Ghadanfar's helmet, it did him no harm, while Ghadanfar himself struck a blow with his mace that crushed his opponent's flesh against that of his elephant. At that another opponent came up, shouting: 'Who are you to kill my brother?' and, taking a throwing spear in his hand, he used it to strike Ghadanfar on the thigh with a blow that drove the mail coat into his flesh. When Ghadanfar saw that, he drew his sword and struck the man such a blow that it cut him in half, and he fell to the ground, weltering in his own blood. Ghadanfar himself then rode back to King Tighmus.

On seeing that, Kafid shouted an order to his army to advance on to the field and fight, and there they were met by King Tighmus and his men. There was a fierce battle with horses neighing and men shouting; swords were drawn and every noted horseman rode forward. While the riders charged, the cowards fled from the fight as the drums were beaten and the trumpets blown. Nothing could be heard over the din of shouts and the clash of weapons as champions died. Things went on like this until, when the sun was high in the sky, Tighmus broke off the battle and led his men back to camp, where an inspection showed that he had lost five thousand riders, while four standards had been broken. This angered him, but Kafid, for his part, found that he had lost six hundred of his bravest riders and that nine of his standards had been broken.

There was now a three-day pause in the battle, after which Kafid wrote a letter to a king called Faqun the Dog, a kinsman of his on his mother's side, which he sent off with a messenger from his camp. Faqun, on hearing what was happening, collected his men and set off to join him.

Night 520

Morning now dawned and Shahrazad broke off from what she had been allowed to say. Then, when it was the five hundred and twentieth night, SHE CONTINUED:

I have heard, O fortunate king, that King Faqun collected all his men and set off to join Kafid.

Tighmus was seated at his ease when one of his men came to tell him that he had seen a distant dust cloud rising into the sky. He ordered a squadron of his men to ride out to reconnoitre it, and they obediently left. When they came back, they said: 'O king, we saw the dust cloud and after a time the wind dispersed it and under it we could see seven standards, behind each of which were three thousand riders, and they were on their way to King Kafid.'

When King Faqun reached King Kafid, he greeted him and asked what the news was and what was the battle in which he was engaged. Kafid told him: 'You know that King Tighmus is my enemy and that it was he who killed my brothers and my father, and so now I have come to fight him and to revenge myself on him.' 'May the sun shine on you with blessing,' replied Faqun, and the delighted Kafid took him off to a tent.

So much for Tighmus and Kafid, but as for Janshah, he spent two months without seeing his father and without allowing any of the slave girls in his service to visit him. He then became very agitated and he asked one of his servants what had happened to keep his father from coming to see him. When he was told that his father was fighting King Kafid, he ordered his horse to be brought so that he might ride to join him. 'To hear is to obey,' said his servants, but when the horse had been fetched he said to himself: 'It is my own affairs that preoccupy me, and I think that what I should do is to take my horse and ride to the city of the Jews. When I get there it may be that God will allow me to meet the merchant who hired me last time to work for him. He might do the same thing with me again and, who knows, some good might come of it.' He then rode out with a thousand men, leading the people to suppose that he was on his way to fight alongside his father. When evening came, Janshah and his men camped in a large meadow, where they spent the night. When Janshah was sure that all his men were asleep, he got up secretly, tightened his belt and mounted his horse. He rode off in the direction of Baghdad because he had heard from the Jews that a Baghdadi caravan used to come to them once every two years and he thought to himself that he could go with it to their city. With this fixed resolution he set off on his way, and when his men woke up they could see no trace of him or of his horse. They rode out and searched for him in all directions, but when they failed to find any news of him they had to go back to his father to tell him what Janshah had done. Tighmus was so angry that sparks almost flew from his mouth. He dashed the crown from his head, reciting the formula 'There is no might and no power except with God' and adding: 'I have lost my son and am faced by my enemy.' His client kings and his viziers urged him to be patient, saying: 'Patience can only be followed by something good.'

Janshah himself was filled with sorrow and care both for his father's sake and because of the loss of his beloved, and it was with a wounded heart and tearful eyes that he passed sleepless nights and days. Meanwhile, Tighmus, in view of the losses that his army had suffered, broke off his battle with Kafid and, retreating from him, he retired into his city where he shut the gates and strengthened the walls. Every month Kafid would advance to the city looking for battle and he would remain there for seven nights and eight days before leading his men back to their camp, where the wounded could be treated. When they withdrew, the townspeople would busy themselves repairing their weapons and strengthening their walls, as well as preparing mangonels, and for seven years the two kings continued with this form of warfare.

Night 521

Morning now dawned and Shahrazad broke off from what she had been allowed to say. Then, when it was the five hundred and twenty-first night, SHE CONTINUED:

I have heard, O fortunate king, that Tighmus and Kafid continued with this form of warfare for seven years.

So much for them, but as for Janshah, he travelled on, crossing open country and deserts, and whenever he came to a town he would ask about Takni, the jewelled castle, but nobody could tell him anything about it, claiming that they had never heard of the name at all. When he asked about the city of the Jews, however, a merchant told him that it lay in the farthest east and he invited Janshah to go with him and his party to the Indian city of Mizrakan, from where they planned to go first to Khurasan, from there to the city of Shim'un, and then on to Khwarizm. The city of the Jews was near Khwarizm at a distance of a year and three months' journey. Janshah waited until the caravan set off and then went with it to Mizrakan. When he got there he asked about Takni, the jewelled castle, but no one could tell him anything and the same thing happened when he went with the caravan to the Indian capital, where people told him that they had never heard of the name Takni.

During the course of his journey he experienced great hardships and formidable perils, as well as hunger and thirst, but in spite of these he travelled on from India, not stopping until he reached Khurasan, ending up at the city of Shim'un. When he entered Shim'un, he asked about the city of the Jews and was told how to reach it. After journeying night and day he got to the place where he had escaped from the apes, and then he pressed on until he reached the river that flows past that city. He sat on the bank waiting patiently for Saturday to come, as then, through the power of God, the river would dry up. When he had crossed it, he went to the house of the Jew where he had stayed on his first visit, greeting him and his family. They gave him a hospitable welcome and brought him food and drink, after which they asked him about his disappearance, to which he replied that he had been in the realm of Almighty God. He spent the night with them, and the next morning, while he was looking round the city, he caught sight of a crier who was calling out: 'O people, who wants a thousand dinars and a beautiful slave girl in return for a half day's work?' 'I will do the work,' said Janshah. 'Follow me,' the crier replied, and Janshah followed him to the house of the Jewish merchant to which he had gone on his first visit. 'This boy will do the work that you want,' said the man, and the merchant welcomed him warmly and brought him to his harem. He gave him food and drink and after the meal he produced the dinars and the beautiful girl, with whom Janshah spent the night.

The next morning he took both the dinars and the girl and handed them over to the Jew who had first entertained him, after which he went back to the merchant for whom he was to work. He rode out with this man until they reached a lofty mountain, towering into the sky, and the man then produced rope and a knife and told Janshah to throw the mare he was riding down on to the ground. He did this, and, after tying it up, he cut its throat, skinned it and cut off its legs and head. Then, on the merchant's orders, he cut open its belly. 'Get inside,' said the merchant, 'and I will sew it up. Then you are to tell me whatever you see there, for this is the task for which you have been paid.' When this had been done, the merchant hid himself at some distance from the mare and after a time a huge bird swooped down on it and carried it off into the air, alighting on the summit of the mountain. It was then about to eat the mare, but, sensing this, Janshah cut himself free and, taking fright, the bird flew off. Janshah looked down and saw the merchant looking as small as a sparrow standing beneath the mountain. He shouted down to ask what he wanted, and the man replied: 'Throw me down some of the stones there and then I'll show you how to get down.' Janshah replied: 'It was you who left me stranded here five years ago when I had to suffer hunger and thirst and to endure much toil and great hardship. Now you have brought me back here in order to kill me. By God, I shall not throw anything down to you.'

Janshah now started off on his way to Shaikh Nasr, king of the birds . . .

Night 522

Morning now dawned and Shahrazad broke off from what she had been allowed to say. Then, when it was the five hundred and twenty-second night, SHE CONTINUED:

I have heard, O fortunate king, that Janshah started off on his way to Shaikh Nasr, king of the birds, and he travelled night and day with tears in his eyes and a heart filled with sorrow, eating herbs from the ground when he was hungry and drinking from streams, until at last he reached the palace of our lord Solomon and saw Shaikh Nasr sitting by the door. He went up to him and kissed his hands, and the *shaikh* returned his greeting, welcoming him warmly. 'My son,' he asked, 'what has happened to bring you here, when earlier you left happy and contented with the Lady Shamsa?' Janshah wept and told him what had taken place when Shamsa had flown away saying: 'If you love me, then come to me at the jewelled castle of Takni.'

Shaikh Nasr was taken aback by this and said: 'By God, my son, and by the truth of our lord Solomon, I know nothing about that castle and in all my life I have never heard the name.' 'What am I to do,' exclaimed Janshah, 'as the passion of my love is killing me?' 'You will have to wait until the birds come,' the *shaikh* told him, 'and we can then ask them about the castle as it may be that one of them will know about it.' This calmed Janshah, and he entered the palace and went to the chamber enclosing the pool where he had seen the three birds.

He had stayed with the *shaikh* for some time and was sitting there as usual when the *shaikh* told him that it was nearly time for the birds to arrive. The news delighted him and a few days later, when they had come, the *shaikh* came to him and said: 'Learn these magic names and then come and meet the birds.' The birds arrived to greet the *shaikh*, one species of them after another, but when he asked them about the castle of Takni, they all said that they had never heard of it. Janshah burst into tears and with a sigh he fell down unconscious. The *shaikh* then sought out a huge bird and told it to take him to the lands of Kabul, describing for it both the lands themselves and the way to get there. 'To hear is to obey,' said the bird, and when Janshah had mounted on its back the *shaikh* told him to be careful and not to lean to the side, lest he be torn in pieces. 'Block your ears against the wind,' he added, 'lest the revolving spheres and the thunder of the oceans do you an injury.'

Janshah followed the *shaikh*'s advice and the bird took off, rising high into the air and flying night and day. Then it landed in the presence of the king of the wild beasts, whose name was Shah Badri, telling him that it had lost the way that Shaikh Nasr had described for it. It then wanted to fly off again with Janshah, but he said: 'Go on your way and leave me here either to die or to find the way to Castle Takni, for I shall not return to my own country.' The bird then left him with Shah Badri and flew away. Shah Badri now asked: 'My son, who are you and where have you come from with that great bird?' In reply Janshah told him all that had happened to him from beginning to end, a tale that astonished him. He said: 'By the truth of our master Solomon, I know nothing about this castle, but I shall reward anyone who can guide us to it and then send you off there.' Janshah shed bitter tears, but he had not waited for long before Shah Badri came to him and said: 'Get up, my son. Take these tablets and learn what is written on them. Then, when the wild beasts come, we shall ask them about that castle.'

Night 523

Morning now dawned and Shahrazad broke off from what she had been allowed to say. Then, when it was the five hundred and twenty-third night, SHE CONTINUED:

I have heard, O fortunate king, that Shah Badri told Janshah to take the tablets and learn what was written on them, adding: 'Then, when the wild beasts come, we shall ask them about that castle.' It was no more than an hour before the beasts arrived, one species after another, and when they had greeted Shah Badri, he asked them about Takni, but they all said that they did not know it and had never heard of it. Janshah wept with regret that he had not gone off with Shaikh Nasr's bird, but Shah Badri told him not to be downcast, explaining: 'I have an elder brother whose name is King Shammakh and who was once held prisoner by our master Solomon against whom he had rebelled. He and Shaikh Nasr are the oldest of all the *jinn* and it may be that he knows of the castle, as he rules over all the *jinn* in these lands.' Shah Badri then mounted Janshah on the back of one of his beasts and gave him a letter to Shammakh, in which he asked that Shammakh look after him. The beast immediately set off with Janshah and carried him day and night until he had reached the king. It halted at a distance from him and stayed there by itself as Janshah dismounted from its back.

Janshah then went to King Shammakh, kissed his hands and gave him Shah Badri's letter. When he had read it and grasped its contents, he welcomed his visitor but said: 'By God, my son, never in my life have I heard of this castle, nor have I seen it.' Janshah wept in distress and Shammakh told him to explain who he was, where he had come from and where he was going. Accordingly Janshah told him all that had happened to him from beginning to end. Shammakh was astonished by his tale and said: 'My son, I do not think that our master Solomon ever heard of this castle or saw it in his life. I do, however, know a very old monk who lives in the mountains and who is obeyed by birds, beasts and *jinn* because of his many conjurations. He used to recite these against the kings of the *jinn* until they were forced to obey him because of the strength of the spells and the magic powers that he possessed, and all the birds and beasts go to present their services to him. I myself rebelled against Solomon and became his prisoner, but it was this monk who overcame me by his guile and his magical conjurations, after which I remained in his service. I know that he has travelled through every land and clime; he knows every road, every district, every place, every castle and every city, and I do not believe that there is anywhere with which he is not familiar. I shall send you to him in the hope that he may be able to guide you to your castle, for if he cannot do this, then no one can, since birds, beasts and *jinn* alike obey him and come at his call.

'Through the strength of his magic he made a staff that has three pieces. He plants it in the ground and recites a spell over the first piece, which then produces flesh and blood. When he recites another spell over the second piece it produces milk, while a spell recited over the third brings wheat and barley. When he has done that, he removes the staff from the ground and goes back to his hermitage, which is known as Dair Almas. This monkish wizard is the inventor of many strange arts and, in addition to being an adept sorcerer, he is full of guile and deceit, as well as being evil-natured. His name is Yaghmus; he is a master of incantations and spells, and I shall have to have you carried to him by an enormous bird with four wings.'

Night 524

Morning now dawned and Shahrazad broke off from what she had been allowed to say. Then, when it was the five hundred and twenty-fourth night, SHE CONTINUED:

I have heard, O fortunate king, that King Shammakh told Janshah that he would send him to the monk on an enormous bird with four wings. So Shammakh mounted Janshah on a bird of this kind, each of whose wings was thirty Hashimi cubits long; its legs were like those of an elephant and it was only able to fly twice in a year. The king had a *jinni* called Tamshun who would snatch two Bactrian camels from Iraq every day and tear them into bits for the bird to eat.

When Janshah was on the back of the bird, Shammakh instructed it to take him to Yaghmus, the monk. The bird carried him night and day until it reached the Mountain of Castles and Dair Almas. When Janshah dismounted there, he saw Yaghmus at his devotions inside his church and, going up to him, he kissed the ground and remained standing in front of him. When Yaghmus saw him, he welcomed him as a stranger from a distant land and asked him why he had come. Janshah, in tears, told him his story from beginning to end, but the astonished Yaghmus had to say: 'My son, I have never heard of this castle or come across anyone who has, and this is in spite of the fact that I was alive in the time of Noah, the prophet of God, on whom be peace, and since the time of Noah until that of our master Solomon, son of David, I have ruled over the beasts, the birds and the *jinn*. I don't believe that even Solomon had heard of the place, but if you wait patiently for the arrival of the birds, beasts and *jinn*, I'll question them and perhaps one of them may be able to give us some news of it, if Almighty God is willing to make things easy for you.'

Janshah then stayed for some time with the monk until one day, as he was sitting there, the birds, beasts and *jinn* arrived. He and Yaghmus began asking them about Castle Takni, but none of them could help as they all said that they had neither seen it nor heard of it. Janshah began weeping, wailing and entreating Almighty God, and while he was doing so the last of the birds, a huge black creature, flew down from the sky and kissed Yaghmus's hands. Yaghmus asked it about Castle Takni, and it said: 'O monk, we used to live in a vast desert behind Mount Qaf on the Crystal Mountain. When I and my brothers were little fledglings, our parents used to fly around every day to bring us food. On one occasion they flew off and stayed away for seven days, leaving us suffering from extreme hunger. When on the eighth day they came back, they were in tears and we asked what had happened to them. They said: "A *marid* snatched us away and took us to the jewelled castle of Takni, where we were brought to King Shahlan. When he saw us he was about to have us killed, but we asked him to spare us as there were little fledglings dependent on us." Were my parents still alive, they would have been able to tell you about the castle.' Janshah wept bitterly on hearing this, and he then asked the monk to tell the bird to take him to his parents' nest in the Crystal Mountain behind Mount Qaf. 'Bird,' said the monk, 'I want you to do everything that this young man says.' 'To hear is to obey,' the bird replied, and then, with Janshah mounted on its back, it left, flying night and day until it reached the Crystal Mountain, where it alighted. Then, after some time, it made Janshah remount on its back and after flying for two more days it reached the land where its parents had nested . . .

Night 525

Morning now dawned and Shahrazad broke off from what she had been allowed to say. Then, when it was the five hundred and twenty-fifth night, SHE CONTINUED:

I have heard, O fortunate king, that the bird flew on with Janshah for two more days until it reached the land where its parents had nested, and there it halted. 'This is the nest in which we were reared,' it told Janshah, who shed more tears and said to it: 'I would like you to carry me to the region where your parents used to forage for food.' 'To hear is to obey,' the bird replied, and it then flew off with Janshah for seven nights and eight days until it came to a lofty mountain on whose summit ridge it set him down, saying: 'I'm not familiar with any land on the far side of this.' Janshah was overcome by drowsiness and he now fell asleep on the peak, but when he woke, he saw in the distance a flash of light, whose radiance filled the sky. He could not think what this was, as he did not know that it was the glow from the castle for which he was searching and which was a two-month journey distant. The castle was built of red rubies, its rooms were of yellow gold, and it had a thousand towers of precious stones brought from the Sea of Darkness. This was why it was called the jewelled castle, constructed as it was of jewels and precious stones. It was a huge place and its king, Shahlan, was the father of the three girls.

So much for Janshah, but as for the Lady Shamsa, after flying away from him, she had gone back to her parents and her family and had told them about her experiences with him, explaining that he had wandered through the lands and had seen many wonders. She told them what had happened to the two of them, adding that Janshah loved her and that she loved him. When her father and mother heard this, they said: 'What you did with him was not lawful in the sight of God,' and her father then told his servants, the *marids*, about this, ordering them to bring him any man that they might see. For Shamsa had told her mother that Janshah was desperately in love with her, adding: 'He will certainly come to me, as when I flew off from the roof of his father's palace I told him: "If you love me, come to the jewelled castle of Takni."'

When Janshah saw the gleam in the sky, he set out towards it in order to discover what it was. As it happened, Shamsa had sent one of her *jinn* servants on an errand in the region of Mount Qarmus, and while this *jinni* was on his way, he caught sight of a man in the distance, went up to him and greeted him. Janshah was frightened but returned the greeting and then, when he was asked for his name, he said: 'My name is Janshah. I was captivated by the beauty of a *jinn* lady, whom I seized. I was full of love for her, but after she had visited my father's palace, she flew away from me.' Shedding tears, he went on to tell the *jinni* all that had happened between him and Shamsa, and the *jinni*, seeing his tears, was consumed by pity and said: 'Don't weep; you have reached your goal, and I can tell you that for her part she is deeply in love with you. She told her father and mother that you loved her and for her sake everyone in the castle feels affection for you, so take heart and be comforted.'

The *jinni* then carried Janshah on his shoulders and brought him to the castle, where the good news of his arrival was taken to King Shahlan as well as to the Lady Shamsa and her mother. They were overjoyed to hear this and the king ordered all his servants to come out to meet him. He himself rode out with *jinn*, *'ifrits* and *marids* . . .

Night 526

Morning now dawned and Shahrazad broke off from what she had been allowed to say. Then, when it was the five hundred and twenty-sixth night, SHE CONTINUED:

I have heard, O fortunate king, that Shahlan rode out with *jinn*, *'ifrits* and *marids* to meet Janshah, and embraced him when they met. Janshah kissed his hands, and Shahlan ordered that he be given a great robe of multi-coloured silk embroidered with gold and studded with jewels. He then presented him with a crown such as no mortal king had ever seen, together with a huge mare from the royal stables of the *jinn*. Having set Janshah on its back, he mounted himself, flanked on both sides by his servants, and together they rode in a great procession to the castle gate. When Janshah dismounted, he saw a huge palace with walls of rubies and other gems together with precious stones, while the ground was paved with crystal, chrysolite and emeralds. This filled him with wonder and he started to shed tears, which Shahlan himself and Shamsa's mother wiped away, saying: 'Less of this weeping; do not worry but know that you have reached the end of your quest.' Then, when he reached the centre of the palace, he was met by beautiful slave girls, black slaves and pages, who led him to the best seat and stood there to serve him. He was taken aback by the splendour of the place and of the walls with their precious stones and costly jewels.

Shahlan now went off to his own throne room, ordering the slave girls and the pages to bring Janshah to sit with him. When they did, Shahlan rose to greet him and then seated him at his side on his throne. Tables of food were brought and the two of them ate, drank and then washed their hands. When they had finished, Shamsa's mother came in and, after greeting Janshah warmly, she said: 'After your toil you have reached your goal, and after your sleeplessness you can now sleep. Praise be to God that you are safe.' She then went straight off to her daughter, Shamsa, and brought her to Janshah. Shamsa went up to him, greeted him, kissed his hands and then hung down her head because of the shame which she felt in front of him and her parents. She was followed by her sisters, who were with her in the palace and who came and kissed his hands after greeting him. The queen now said: 'Welcome, my son. My daughter Shamsa wronged you, but don't reproach her because of what she did to you for our sakes.' When he heard that, Janshah gave a cry and fell unconscious. The king was astonished, but when rosewater mixed with musk and fragrant perfume had been sprinkled over Janshah's face he recovered and, looking at the Lady Shamsa, he exclaimed: 'Praise be to God, Who has brought me to my goal and finally quenched the fire in my heart!' 'May you never be burned!' said Shamsa, adding: 'I want you to tell me what happened to you after we parted, and how you got here in spite of the fact that most of the *jinn* are not familiar with Castle Takni. We are not subject to any king and no one knows how to get here or has even heard of the place.'

Janshah then told her everything that had happened to him, explaining how he had got there and telling her of his father's war with King Kafid as well as of the hardships that he had suffered on his journey and the terrors and marvels that he had seen. 'All this,' he said, 'I endured for your sake, Lady Shamsa.' 'You have reached your goal,' said Shamsa's mother, 'and we give her to you as a slave.' Janshah was overjoyed and the queen told him: 'If God Almighty wills it, next month we shall have a wedding feast and arrange your marriage to her, after which you can take her back to your own country. We shall also provide you with a thousand *marids*, and, were you to give permission, the weakest of them would destroy King Kafid and his army in the twinkling of an eye. Every year we shall send you *jinn*, any one of whom will destroy all your enemies on your orders.'

Night 527

Morning now dawned and Shahrazad broke off from what she had been allowed to say. Then, when it was the five hundred and twenty-seventh night, SHE CONTINUED:

I have heard, O fortunate king, that Shamsa's mother said: 'Every year we shall send you *jinn*, any one of whom will destroy all your enemies on your orders.' Seated on his throne, the king then ordered his state officials to prepare a huge feast and to see that the city was adorned with decorations for seven days and nights. 'To hear is to obey,' they said, after which they left immediately to prepare for the wedding feast. The preparations took two months and then Shamsa's marriage was celebrated with a feast whose like had never been seen before. Janshah was brought to his bride, and he spent two years with her, eating and drinking and enjoying the most pleasant and delightful of lives. He then said to her: 'Your father has promised that we should go to my country and then spend a year there and a year here.' 'To hear is to obey,' said Shamsa, and so that evening she went to her father to tell him what Janshah had said to her. He agreed to what had been proposed, but he told her to wait till the first of the month to give him time to prepare an escort of *jinn*.

When this time had elapsed, he authorized this escort to take the married couple to Janshah's own country. He prepared for them a huge couch of red gold, inset with pearls and other gems and covered by a canopy of green silk, diversified with other colours and studded with precious stones, whose beauty dazzled the eye. Janshah and Shamsa mounted this and, as they sat there, four *jinn* servants were selected to carry it. They did this, one at each corner, and when Shamsa had said goodbye to her mother, father, sisters and relations, her father mounted and accompanied Janshah as the *jinn* carried the couch. He stayed with them until midday, when the *jinn* set it down and they all dismounted to say their farewells, with Shahlan telling Janshah to look after Shamsa, and the *jinn* to take care of both of them. He then ordered the *jinn* to take up the couch again and after a final farewell from Shamsa and Janshah he went back and they started on their way.

Shahlan had provided Shamsa with three hundred beautiful slave girls and Janshah with three hundred *jinn* servants, all of whom had mounted on to the couch before they left, and its four bearers then flew on for ten days between the heavens and the earth, covering each day the distance of a thirty-month journey. Among them there was one who knew the lands of Kabul, and when he saw them he told his companions to land there, in the great city which was the capital of King Tighmus. This they did . . .

Night 528

Morning now dawned and Shahrazad broke off from what she had been allowed to say. Then, when it was the five hundred and twenty-eighth night, SHE CONTINUED:

I have heard, O fortunate king, that the *jinn* landed at the city of King Tighmus, bringing with them Janshah and Shamsa.

Tighmus, having been defeated by his enemies, had taken refuge in the city and was in desperate straits, being hard-pressed by King Kafid. He had sued unsuccessfully for peace, and, finding no way to save himself, he was proposing to escape from his cares and sorrows by throttling himself. He got up and, after taking his leave of his viziers and emirs, he went to his own apartments to say farewell to his womenfolk. As he was doing this and while his subjects were weeping, wailing and lamenting loudly, the *jinn* servants came to the palace which was inside the fortress, where Janshah told them to set the couch down in the middle of the audience chamber. They did as they were told and Janshah stepped down together with Shamsa, accompanied by the slave girls and mamluks. They noticed that all the townspeople appeared dejected and greatly distressed, and Janshah said to Shamsa: 'My darling and the comfort of my eyes, look at how bad my father's condition seems to be.'

When Shamsa saw the distress of Tighmus and his people she ordered the *jinn* servants to strike a violent blow against the besieging army and to kill every last man of them. Janshah, for his part, instructed a particularly powerful servant named Qaratash to bring him King Kafid in fetters. The *jinn* went off, taking the couch with them, and when they had put it down on the ground they erected the canopy over it. Then, having waited until midnight, they attacked King Kafid and his army and began to kill them. One of them would snatch up eight or ten of them from the back of an elephant, fly up with them into the sky and then throw them down, tearing them to bits in the air, while others would strike with iron maces. Qaratash meanwhile went straight to the pavilion of King Kafid and, attacking him while he was seated on his throne, he seized him and soared into the air with him as he shrieked in fear. Qaratash flew on until he had deposited his captive on the couch in front of Janshah, who then ordered all four *jinn* servants to lift it and set it up in the air. Before Kafid knew what was happening, he found himself hanging between heaven and earth and in his astonishment he began to slap his face.

So much for King Kafid, but as for Tighmus, at the sight of his son he almost died with joy and with a great cry he fell down in a faint. Attendants sprinkled his face with rosewater and, when he recovered consciousness, he and Janshah embraced in floods of tears, although the king himself did not know at the time that the *jinn* were engaged in fighting Kafid. Shamsa, however, walked up to him and, after having kissed his hands, she invited him to come to the palace roof to watch the battle. He went there and sat with her, as they both looked on at what was happening. The *jinn* were raining blows on Kafid's men: one of them would take his iron mace and strike an elephant, crushing both it and its rider, until it was impossible to tell which had been elephant and which man; another would intercept a group of fugitives and shout in their faces, leaving them dead on the ground; while yet another would snatch some twenty riders up into the air before hurling them to the ground in pieces. All the while Janshah, his father and the Lady Shamsa were watching what was going on . . .

Night 529

Morning now dawned and Shahrazad broke off from what she had been allowed to say. Then, when it was the five hundred and twenty-ninth night, SHE CONTINUED:

I have heard, O fortunate king, that Tighmus, his son Janshah and Janshah's wife, Shamsa, climbed to the top of the palace and began to watch the battle between the *jinn* and Kafid's army, while King Kafid looked on in tears from his position on the couch.

The battle continued for two days until every last one of Kafid's men had been killed. Janshah then instructed the *jinn* to bring the couch down to earth in the middle of the fortress. When they had done this, Tighmus told one of them, whose name was Shimwal, to load Kafid with chains and fetters and imprison him in the Black Tower. Shimwal did this and Tighmus ordered drums to be beaten, while messengers were sent to take the good news to Janshah's mother, telling her of her son's return and of what he had accomplished. She went to him in delight, and when he saw her he clasped her to his breast. Joy caused her to faint, but after her face had been sprinkled with rosewater she recovered and embraced him, shedding tears of happiness. When Shamsa heard that she was there, she got up and went to greet her and, after a long embrace, the two sat talking. Tighmus then opened the city gates and sent messengers to spread the good news throughout the country. When this had been made public, valuable gifts and presents were sent to him and from all the lands; emirs, soldiers and kings came to greet him and to congratulate him on his victory and on the safe return of his son.

Things continued like this for some time, with rich gifts being brought to the king, who then, for the second time, arranged a splendid wedding for the Lady Shamsa and ordered that the city be adorned with decorations. Shamsa was unveiled for Janshah, decked with ornaments and wearing magnificent robes, after which the marriage was consummated. Janshah gave Shamsa a hundred beautiful slave girls to serve her, and some days later she went to King Tighmus to intercede with him for Kafid. She said: 'Let him go back to his own country, and if he then tries to harm you, I shall order one of the *jinn* to seize him and bring him back here.' 'To hear is to obey,' said Tighmus, and he then sent word to Shimwal to bring Kafid to him. When he had been fetched in chains and had kissed the ground before him, Tighmus ordered that the chains should be removed and, after this had been done, he mounted him on a lame mare and told him: 'Princess Shamsa has interceded for you, so go back to your own country and if you try to do what you did ever again, she will send one of her *jinn* servants to fetch you.' So King Kafid went home in the sorriest of states . . .

Night 530

Morning now dawned and Shahrazad broke off from what she had been allowed to say. Then, when it was the five hundred and thirtieth night, SHE CONTINUED:

I have heard, O fortunate king, that Kafid went home in the sorriest of states, while Janshah, his father and Princess Shamsa enjoyed to the full the pleasures and delights of life with the greatest and most complete joy.

All this was told to Buluqiya by the young man who was seated

between the two tombs, and he then added: 'I am Janshah, who experienced all this, Buluqiya, my brother.' Buluqiya was astonished by what
he had heard and said to Janshah: 'Brother, what are these two tombs
and why are you sitting weeping between them?' 'You must know,
Buluqiya, that we had the pleasantest and happiest of lives, staying for
one year in my own country and then going for a year to Takni, travelling
on the couch carried by our *jinn* servants, flying between the heavens
and the earth.' Buluqiya asked him how far it was between Takni and
his own land and he replied: 'We would cover a thirty-month journey
each day, and it would take us ten days to reach Takni. This went on
for some years, but it then happened that, while we were travelling as
usual, we came here and landed on our couch in order to look around
this island. We sat by the river bank, eating and drinking, until Shamsa
said that she wanted to bathe in the river. She took off her clothes and
the slave girls followed her example, after which they all went into the
water to swim. I walked along the bank, leaving the girls to enjoy
themselves with Shamsa, when suddenly a sea monster, a huge shark,
singled her out from among the others and bit her leg. She gave a cry
and died immediately. The girls came out of the water, fleeing from the
shark to the tent, and then one of them brought Shamsa's body there
and, when I saw it, I fell down in a faint. They sprinkled my face with
rosewater and when I recovered I wept over her and then told the *jinn*
servants to take the couch back to her people and to tell them what had
happened to her. They did this and it was not long before her family
arrived, washed her body, dressed it in a shroud and buried it here.
When they had finished mourning for her, they wanted to take me back
with them, but I told her father: "I want you to dig me a grave beside
hers and this I shall keep for myself so that when I die I may be buried
by her side." King Shahlan ordered one of his *jinn* servants to do that,
and when the grave had been dug they left me alone here to weep and
wail for Shamsa. This, then, is my story and the reason why I sit between
these two graves.'

He then recited these lines:

Since you left, the dwelling is no dwelling any more;
Nor is the pleasant neighbour a neighbour still.
My familiar friend is a friend no longer,
Nor do the gleaming lights still shine.

On hearing all this, Buluqiya was filled with amazement . . .

Night 531

Morning now dawned and Shahrazad broke off from what she had been allowed to say. Then, when it was the five hundred and thirty-first night, SHE CONTINUED:

I have heard, O fortunate king, that Buluqiya was filled with amazement when he heard this, and said: 'By God, I thought that I had roamed around the earth, but through listening to your story I have forgotten everything that I saw.' He went on to ask Janshah if he would kindly show him how he could leave that place safely. This Janshah did, and Buluqiya took his leave and went on his way.

All this was told by the snake queen to Karim, who asked her how she had come to know it. She said: 'Twenty-five years ago I wanted to send a large snake to Egypt to take a letter of greeting to Buluqiya. My messenger brought the letter to Bint Shumukh, who had a daughter in Egypt, and she took it there. She asked about Buluqiya, and when she had been directed to him, she greeted him and gave him my letter. When he had read it and grasped its contents, he asked the snake whether she had come from the snake queen and, when she said yes, he said: "I want to go back with you to the queen as there is something that I need from her." "To hear is to obey," Bint Shumukh said. She then took him to pay a visit to her daughter, whom she greeted. When she left, after having said goodbye, she told Buluqiya to close his eyes. He did so, and when he opened them again he found himself on the mountain where I was staying. Bint Shumukh then took him to the messenger who had brought the letter, and when this snake asked whether the letter had been delivered, Bint Shumukh said: "Yes, I delivered it to him and he came back with me. This is he."

'Buluqiya went up to greet the snake and to ask about me. The snake told him: "The queen has gone with all her armies to Mount Qaf, but when summer comes she will return here. Every time she goes to Mount Qaf she leaves me here in her place until she comes back and so, if there is anything that you need, I shall do it for you." Buluqiya said: "I want you to fetch me the herb whose juice, when it is pounded up, preserves those who drink it from sickness, age and death." The snake said: "I shall not do this until you tell me what happened to you after you left the queen and went off with 'Affan to the tomb of our master Solomon." Buluqiya recited his story from beginning to end and told what had happened to Janshah, after which he said: "And now give me what I want so that I can go home." The snake said: "I swear by the truth of our master Solomon that I don't know how to get to that herb." It then told Bint Shumukh, who had brought him, to take him back. "To hear is to obey," she said, after which she told Buluqiya to close his eyes, and when he opened them he found himself on Mount Muqattam, from where he went home. When I returned from Mount Qaf, my deputy went to me, greeted me and said: "Buluqiya sends his greetings to you," and followed this with an account of all that Buluqiya had told of what he had seen on his wanderings and how he had met Janshah.

'This is how I learned all this,' said the queen to Karim and he, in his turn, asked her about Buluqiya's experiences on his return to Egypt. She said: 'You must know, Karim, that when Buluqiya left Janshah, he travelled night and day until he reached a huge sea. He smeared the lotion he had with him on his feet and walked on the surface of this sea until he came to an island that looked like Paradise, with trees, streams and fruits. He walked around it and discovered a huge tree with leaves like ships' sails and when he came near it he saw that underneath it there was a table laid with fine foods of all kinds, while perched on the tree itself was an enormous bird with a body of pearls and emeralds, legs of silver, a ruby beak and feathers of precious stones. It was calling down praises on Almighty God and blessings on Muhammad, may God bless him and give him peace.'

Night 532

Morning now dawned and Shahrazad broke off from what she had been allowed to say. Then, when it was the five hundred and thirty-second night, SHE CONTINUED:

I have heard, O fortunate king, that when Buluqiya came to the island, he found that it looked like Paradise. He walked around it and discovered marvels, among them being a bird with a body of pearls and emeralds and feathers of precious stones. It was calling down praises on Almighty God and blessings on Muhammad, may God bless him and give him peace. When Buluqiya saw this enormous bird he asked who and what it was, and it told him: 'I am one of the birds of Paradise. You must know, brother, that when Adam was expelled from Paradise by Almighty God he was given four leaves with which to cover himself. These leaves fell on to the earth: one was eaten by worms and produced silk; another was eaten by gazelles and produced musk; bees ate the third, which then produced honey; while the fourth fell in India and produced spices. I myself wandered through all the earth until Almighty God granted me this place as a dwelling. For twenty-four hours on Friday the holy men and the leaders of the saints on earth visit it and eat the food set out here on this night and this day, this being a guest offering to them from Almighty God, after which the table and its cloth are taken back to heaven, having suffered neither diminution nor change.'

Buluqiya ate and when he had finished and given thanks to God, al-Khidr, upon whom be peace, arrived. Buluqiya stood up to greet him and was about to leave when the bird said: 'Sit down, Buluqiya, in the presence of al-Khidr.' So he took his place again and al-Khidr said: 'Tell me about yourself and give me your story.' Accordingly, Buluqiya told him everything from start to finish, up to the time when he came to where he was now sitting in front of al-Khidr.' He then asked how long a journey it was from there to Egypt, to which al-Khidr replied that it would take ninety-five years. On hearing this, Buluqiya burst into tears and, falling before al-Khidr, he kissed his hands and said: 'Rescue me from this exile, may God reward you, for I am on the point of death and there is nothing that I can do.' Al-Khidr replied: 'Pray that Almighty God may allow me to take you back to Egypt before you die.' Buluqiya presented his request in tears to God, and God accepted it, conveying to al-Khidr His divine message that Buluqiya should be brought back to his family. 'Raise your head,' al-Khidr told him, 'for God has accepted your petition and told me to take you to Egypt. Take hold of me, gripping with your hands and shutting your eyes.' Al-Khidr then took a single pace, after which he told Buluqiya to open his eyes, and when he did so he found himself at the door of his own house. He turned to take his leave of al-Khidr, but could find no trace of him.

Night 533

Morning now dawned and Shahrazad broke off from what she had been allowed to say. Then, when it was the five hundred and thirty-third night, she CONTINUED:

I have heard, O fortunate king, that when Buluqiya had been brought to the door of his own house by al-Khidr, he opened his eyes in order to take his leave of him, but could find no trace of him.

He went into his house and when his mother saw him she gave a great cry and then fell fainting for joy. Water was sprinkled on her face until she recovered, and when she did, she embraced her son in floods of tears, while he alternately wept and laughed. His family, his associates and all his friends arrived to congratulate him on his safe return; word spread through the town and gifts poured in from all quarters; drums were beaten, pipes were blown and there was great rejoicing. After this, Buluqiya told the people everything that had happened to him and how he had been brought by al-Khidr to the door of his own house. They were all amazed by that and wept until they were tired.

All this was told to Karim by the snake queen, and he too was both astonished and tearful. He then repeated to the queen that he wanted to go home, but she said: 'I am afraid that if you get back to your own country, you will not keep your word and you will break the oath that you swore not to enter the baths.' Karim took more solemn oaths that he would never do this as long as he lived, and so the queen gave orders to one of her snakes to bring him up to the surface. The snake took him from one place after another until it brought him out from the top of an abandoned well. From there he walked back to the city and went to his house, arriving in the evening at sunset. He knocked on the door, which was opened by his mother, and when she saw him standing there she gave a cry of joy and threw herself on him, bursting into tears. His wife, hearing the weeping, came out and when she saw her husband she greeted him and kissed his hands. All three were filled with delight.

They went into the house and when they were seated, with Karim in the centre of his family, he asked about the two woodcutters who had been working with him and who had left him in the well. His mother said: 'They came to me and told me that you had been eaten by a wolf in the valley. Then they became merchants in the easiest of circumstances, owning property and shops. Every day they bring me food and drink, and they have done this regularly up until now.' 'Go to them tomorrow,' Karim told her, 'and say to them: "Karim has come back from his travels, so come and meet him and greet him."'

The next morning, his mother went to the houses of the woodcutters and gave them the message that Karim had told her to bring. When they heard it the two changed colour, but they said: 'To hear is to obey,' and each of them presented her with a robe of silk embroidered with gold, telling her to give it to her son to wear and to let him know that they would come to his house the next day. She agreed to this and went back to tell Karim and to hand over the robes that they had given her.

So much for Karim, but as for the woodcutters, they collected a number of merchants and, after telling them what they had done with him, they asked what they should do now. The merchants said: 'You must each give him half of your money and of your mamluks.' All of them agreed to this and each of them brought Karim half of his money and, after they had greeted him and kissed his hands, they presented it to him and said: 'This comes from the favour that you did us, and we are at your service.' 'What is past is past,' said Karim. 'This was decreed by God, and fate overcomes caution.' They then invited him to visit the city with them and to go to the baths, but he told them that he had sworn never to enter the baths again as long as he lived. They then invited him to their homes, where they could entertain him. 'To hear is to obey,' he said, and he went home with them and was entertained by each one for a night at a time during the course of a week.

Karim was now a man of wealth with properties and shops; the other merchants gathered around him, listening to the story of his adventures, and he became one of their leaders. Things went on like this for some time until one day, when he happened to be walking in the city, he came across a friend of his, a bath keeper, who saw him as he was passing the door of the baths. Catching his eye, the bath keeper greeted him, embraced him and said: 'Do please come in for a bath so that I may entertain you.' Karim told him about his oath but the man swore that he would divorce his three wives thrice if he did not come in and wash. Karim was at a loss to know what to do and said: 'Do you want to orphan my children, destroy my house and hang the burden of sin on my neck?' The man, however, threw himself at Karim's feet, kissed them and entreated him to enter, saying that the burden of sin would be his. The bath attendants and everyone there gathered around Karim, took him into the baths and stripped him of his clothes, but as soon as he had entered, taken his seat by the wall and poured water over his head, in came twenty men who told him to get up and go with them as he was required by the king.

The men sent one of their number to the king's vizier, who, when the news was brought to him, mounted with sixty mamluks and rode to the baths, to meet Karim. The vizier greeted him warmly, gave the bath keeper a hundred dinars and told him to produce a horse for Karim to ride. He and Karim rode off with the escort until they had reached the royal palace, where they all dismounted. They took their seats in the palace, and when food had been brought they ate and drank and then washed their hands. The vizier presented him with two robes of honour, each worth five thousand dinars, and told him: 'It is by the favour of God and His mercy to us that you have come, for the king, who suffers from leprosy, is on the point of death and we have learned from our books that his life is in your hands.' Karim was astonished by this, but he went with the vizier and the leading officers of state through the seven doors of the palace until they came into the presence of King Karazdan. Karazdan was king of Persia and lord of the seven climes. In his service were a hundred sultans who sat on chairs of red gold, together with ten thousand paladins, each of whom had a hundred lieutenants, together with a hundred executioners carrying swords and axes. They found the king lying with his face wrapped in a kerchief, groaning with pain. On seeing this, Karim was taken aback by the awe inspired by the king and, after kissing the ground before him, he called down blessings on him. Then the principal vizier, a man named Shamhur, came up to him, greeted him warmly and seated him on a lofty chair at King Karazdan's right hand.

Night 534

Morning now dawned and Shahrazad broke off from what she had been allowed to say. Then, when it was the five hundred and thirty-fourth night, SHE CONTINUED:

I have heard, O fortunate king, that the vizier Shamhur came up to Karim and seated him on a chair at the right hand of King Karazdan. Food was brought in, and after they had eaten, drunk and washed their hands, Shamhur got up and everyone else in the assembly rose out of respect for him. Walking over to Karim, he said: 'We are at your service. Whatever you wish for, even if this is half the kingdom, we shall give it to you, for the king's cure is in your hands.' He took Karim by the hand and led him to the king. Karim uncovered his face and, on looking, he was taken aback to see that the king was in the final stage of his illness. Shamhur then bent over his hand, kissed it and repeated: 'We want you to cure this king, and you can have whatever you ask for. This is what we are looking for from you.' 'Yes,' said Karin, 'I am certainly the son of Daniel, the prophet of God, but I know nothing of the science of medicine. I was made to study it for thirty days, but, although I wish that I knew enough to cure the king, I learned nothing at all.' 'Don't go on about this,' Shamhur told him: 'Were we to gather together all the doctors of the east and the west, no one would be able to cure him but you'. 'How can I possibly do that,' asked Karim, 'when I know nothing about his disease or its cure?' 'You can cure him,' insisted the vizier, and when Karim said: 'If I knew how, I would do that,' the vizier explained: 'You know its cure well enough, for it is the snake queen, and you know where she is, and have seen her and stayed with her.'

When Karim heard this, he realized that all this had happened because he had gone into the baths and he was full of regret when regret was no longer any use. He said: 'How can this queen have anything to do with me? I don't know her and I have never heard this name in all my life.' 'Don't deny that you know her,' said Shamhur. 'I have proof that you do and that you stayed with her for two years.' 'No, I don't know her,' Karim insisted. 'I have never seen her and the only time that I have heard of her is now, from you.' Shamhur then produced a book, which he opened and studied before saying: 'The snake queen will meet a man who will stay with her for two years. Then he will leave her and come back to the surface of the earth and when he goes into the baths his belly will turn black.' He then told Karim: 'Look at your belly,' and when Karim did, he saw that it was black. 'It has been black from the day of my birth,' he said, but Shamhur told him: 'I assigned three mamluks to every bath house with orders to watch everyone who entered, to look at their bellies and to report to me. When you went in, they looked and found that your belly was black and so they sent me word. I had not believed that I would meet you today, but the only thing that I want from you is for you to show me the place from where you came out, after which you can go about your business. We shall be able to seize the snake queen, and we have someone who will bring her to us.'

Karim heard all this and was filled with bitter but futile regret at having entered the bath house. The emirs and viziers kept coming to press him to tell them about the queen, but without success, as he kept insisting that he had neither seen nor heard anything. Shamhur then summoned the executioner and, on his arrival, Shamhur ordered him to strip off Karim's clothes and give him a severe beating.

The executioner did this and the severity of the flogging brought Karim to the point of death. Shamhur told him: 'We have evidence that you know where the snake queen is, so why deny it? Show us the place where you came out, for we have someone who can seize her, and you can then leave unharmed.' He spoke with friendliness, allowed Karim to stand up and presented him with a robe of honour embellished with red gold and precious stones. Karim then said obediently: 'I'll show you the place,' and when Shamhur heard this he was overjoyed and rode out at the head of his men, together with all his emirs, led by Karim.

They rode on to the mountain, where Karim entered the cave, weeping in his distress. The emirs and viziers dismounted and walked behind him until they got to the well from which he had emerged. Shamhur came there and then sat down to release a cloud of incense, as he recited conjurations and spells, exhaling and muttering, for he was a skilled magician and diviner, with a knowledge of the spiritual world and other such matters. When he had finished his first spell he recited a second and then a third, and whenever the incense was used up he put more of it on the fire. Finally he called: 'Snake queen, come out!' At that, the water in the well sank out of sight, a great door opened and there was a loud cry like a thunderclap so that it seemed as though the well had collapsed. Everyone who was there fell to the ground unconscious, or, in some cases, dead. From the well emerged an enormous snake as big as an elephant with sparks like coals flashing from its eyes. On its back was a dish of red gold studded with pearls and other gems, and in the centre of the dish was a snake whose radiance illumined the place. It had a human face and clear speech. This was the snake queen. She looked to right and left before her glance fell on Karim, and she said to him: 'Where is your covenant now and the oath that you swore for me that you would not enter the baths? But there is no way in which to avoid fate, nor can what is written on the forehead be avoided. God has arranged that my life should be ended by you, and this is His decree, as He intends that I should die and that King Karazdan should be cured of his disease.' Then she wept bitterly and this moved Karim to shed tears of his own.

When the damned vizier Shamhur saw the snake queen, he stretched out his hand to lay hold of her, but she said: 'Draw back your hand, damn you, or otherwise I shall breathe on you and turn you into a heap of black ashes.' She then called out to Karim and said: 'Come and take me in your hand. Then put me on this plate that you have brought with you and carry it on your head, for it has been ordained from past eternity that I should die at your hands, and nothing can ward off this fate.' So he took her and carried her on his head, at which the well resumed its former appearance. The whole party set off, with Karim carrying on his head the plate on which the queen had been placed. In the course of their journey, she said secretly to him: 'Karim, listen to my advice, even though by acting as you have done you have broken your covenant and forsworn yourself, as was decreed by fate from before Time began.' 'To hear is to obey,' Karim replied, adding: 'What is it that you tell me to do?' She said: 'When you get to the vizier's house, he will tell you to kill me and to cut me into three pieces. Refuse and don't do it, saying that you know nothing of butchery, so that he will have to kill me himself and do what he wants with me. When he has killed me and cut me up, a messenger will come from King Karazdan asking the vizier to come to him. He will place my flesh in a copper cooking pot which he will put on the stove before he goes to the king. He will tell you to light the fire beneath it and wait until froth comes from the flesh, when you are to take the froth, put it in a bottle and wait until it cools. You are then to drink it, he will say, after which you will never again suffer from any bodily pain. When it froths up a second time, he will tell you to keep this froth in another bottle, for him to take when he returns from the king in order to cure a disease in his loins. He will give you the two bottles before going to the king. When he has left, light the fire and take the first lot of froth that appears, put it in a bottle, but keep the bottle with you, taking care not to drink it, for if you do, it will do you no good. Put the second lot in the other bottle, wait until it is cold and keep it with you until you can drink it. When Shamhur comes back from the king and asks for the second bottle, give him the first and see what happens to him.'

Night 535

Morning now dawned and Shahrazad broke off from what she had been allowed to say. Then, when it was the five hundred and thirty-fifth night, SHE CONTINUED:

I have heard, O fortunate king, that the snake queen told Karim not to drink from the first lot of froth and to keep the second. The snake queen went on: 'When the vizier comes back from the king and asks for the second bottle, give him the first and see what happens to him. You can then drink the second bottle, after which your heart will become a home of wisdom. Then take the flesh, put it on a copper plate and give it to the king to eat. When he does and it settles in his stomach, cover his face with a kerchief and wait until noon so that his stomach may cool down. Then give him something to drink and he will be cured of his illness and go back to being as healthy as ever he was, through the power of Almighty God. Listen to my advice and pay it the closest attention.'

The party rode on to Shamhur's house, where Shamhur told Karim to go in with him, and when they had done so the escort dispersed and went their own ways. Karim took the plate with the queen on it from his head, and Shamhur told him to kill her. 'I know nothing of butchery,' he replied, 'and never in my life have I slaughtered anything. If you have some reason for doing this, do it yourself.' So Shamhur took the queen from the plate and killed her. On seeing that, Karim wept bitterly and Shamhur laughed at him and said: 'You silly fellow, why are you weeping for the death of a snake?' After that, he cut the body into three pieces and put them in a copper pot, which he set over the fire. He sat there watching the flesh cooking, but while he was doing that a mamluk came to him to say that he was urgently wanted by the king. 'To hear is to obey,' said Shamhur, and he then got up and brought two bottles to Karim, telling him: 'See to the fire under this pot. Wait until the first lot of froth appears as the flesh cooks, and when it does, scoop it off and put it in one of these bottles. Wait until it cools and then drink it, for this will make you healthy and never again will you suffer bodily pain or sickness. When it froths a second time, put that froth in the other bottle and keep it by you until I get back from the king. I shall then drink it, as I suffer from a pain in my loins which it may cure.'

Shamhur then went off to visit the king, having repeated his instructions to Karim, who for his part tended the fire beneath the pot until he was able to remove the first lot of froth, which he put in one of the two bottles. He kept this with him and continued to stoke the fire until the flesh frothed again. He scooped off this froth and put it in the second bottle, which he also kept. Then, when the meat was cooked, he took the pot off the fire and sat waiting for Shamhur to come back. When he did, he asked Karim what he had done and Karim told him that he had carried out his instructions. 'What did you do with the first bottle?' Shamhur asked him. 'I have just drunk it,' Karim said. 'I can't see that it has changed your body at all,' said Shamhur, but Karim told him: 'I feel that my whole body from head to foot is burning like fire.' The wily Shamhur had, in fact, tried to trick him by hiding the truth from him, and he now said: 'Give me the other bottle to drink, as it may cure the pain in my loins.' It was, in fact, the contents of the first bottle that he drank, thinking that this was the second, and no sooner had he drunk than the bottle fell from his hand. His body immediately swelled up, showing the truth of the proverb 'Whoever digs a pit for his brother will fall into it.'

Karim, looking at this with astonishment, became afraid of drinking from the second bottle, but then he thought about the snake queen's instructions and told himself: 'If what is in the second bottle was noxious, the vizier wouldn't have chosen it for himself.' So, putting his trust in God, he drank, and God then flooded his heart with springs of wisdom, opening up for him the fountainhead of knowledge, so that he was filled with joy and delight. He took the flesh from the pot, put it on a copper dish and left Shamhur's house. Looking up, he could see the seven heavens and all they contained as far as the lote tree at the furthest point of Paradise; he could see how the celestial sphere revolved, as God revealed all this for him; he saw the fixed stars and the orbits of the planets, and he saw the shape of both land and sea. From this he deduced the sciences of geometry, astrology, astronomy and the lore of the celestial sphere, as well as arithmetic and everything connected with it. He understood the ordering of the eclipses of the sun and the moon and other such matters. Then he looked down at the ground, noting stones, plants and trees and grasping all their characteristics and their uses. From this he deduced the science of medicine, natural magic and chemistry, as well as the art of manufacturing gold and silver.

He walked on, carrying the flesh, until he came to King Karazdan's palace. On entering it, he kissed the ground and wished the king health to compensate for the loss of his vizier Shamhur. The king was very angry at this and burst into tears, as did the other viziers, together with the emirs and ministers of state. Then he said: 'Shamhur was with me just now and he was in the best of health. He left to fetch me the snake's flesh, when it had been properly cooked. How did he come to die and what happened to him?' Karim told him the whole story of how Shamhur had drunk from the bottle and how his stomach had then swelled uncontrollably until he died. The king was filled with grief and said to Karim: 'What will become of me now that Shamhur is dead?' 'Do not concern yourself,' replied Karim, 'for I shall cure you within three days, leaving your body entirely free of disease.' The delighted king told him: 'All I want is to be cured of this leprosy, even if it takes years.'

Karim rose and fetched the pot, which he put down in front of the king. Then he took some of the snake queen's flesh and fed it to him, afterwards covering him up and spreading a kerchief over his face. He sat beside him and told him to sleep, which he did from noon until sunset, by which time the piece of flesh had made its way round his stomach. After that, Karim woke him, gave him something to drink and then told him to go to sleep again. He slept all night long until morning, and when it was light Karim repeated his treatment of the day before. Over a period of three days he gave the king three pieces of flesh, after which the king's skin dried up and then peeled off. He began to sweat, with the sweat running from his head down to his feet, after which he was cured, with no trace of illness left in his body. 'You must now go to the baths,' Karim told him, and when he had been taken there and brought out again, his body was like a silver rod and he recovered his health, becoming fitter than he had ever been. He put on his finest clothes, took his seat on his throne and gave permission to Karim to sit beside him. A table was spread at his command, and after the two of them had eaten and washed their hands he had wine brought in, and when this was done they both drank.

The king now collected all the emirs, viziers and troops, together with the grandees of his state and his principal subjects, all of whom congratulated him on his successful cure, and drums were beaten as the city was adorned with decorations in honour of his recovery. When they were all collected he said: 'Viziers, emirs and officials of state, know that I have appointed this man, Hasib Karim al-Din, who has cured me of leprosy, as my grand vizier in place of the vizier Shamhur.'

Night 536

Morning now dawned and Shahrazad broke off from what she had been allowed to say. Then, when it was the five hundred and thirty-sixth night, SHE CONTINUED:

I have heard, O fortunate king, that the king told his viziers and the grandees of his state that he had been cured of his disease by Hasib Karim al-Din, and had appointed him as his grand vizier in place of Shamhur. The king went on: 'Whoever loves him loves me; whoever honours him shows honour to me and whoever obeys him obeys me.' 'To hear is to obey,' they all said, and they rose, kissed Karim's hand,

greeted him and congratulated him on his new office. The king presented
him with a splendid robe of honour embroidered with red gold and
studded with pearls and other gems, the least of which was worth five
thousand dinars, together with three hundred mamluks, three hundred
concubines shining like moons, three hundred Abyssinian slave girls and
five hundred mules laden with money, together with cattle, sheep and
goats, buffaloes and cows such as would be tedious to describe. After
this, the king told his officers of state, his principal officials, mamluks
and all his other subjects to present Karim with gifts.

Karim, followed by the viziers, emirs and state officials, rode to the
palace that the king had cleared for him and took his seat on a chair.
His escort came to kiss his hand again, offering their congratulations on
his appointment and presenting their services. His delighted mother
added her congratulations, as did his family, and they were all filled with
joy. His former companions, the woodcutters, then arrived with their
felicitations and after that he mounted and rode to the palace of Shamhur, which he sealed up, taking possession of all its contents and having
them moved to his own palace.

The total ignoramus, who had not been able to read or write, was
now, through the power of Almighty God, a master of all branches of
learning, the fame of whose knowledge and wisdom spread through all
the lands. He won renown for the depth of his knowledge of medicine,
astronomy, geometry, astrology, chemistry, natural magic and the
spiritual sciences, as well as others.

One day, he said to his mother: 'Mother, Daniel, my father, was a
wise and excellent man, so tell me, what books and other things did he
leave behind?' When she heard this, his mother produced the chest in
which Daniel had placed the five pages that were all that was left of the
books that had been lost at sea, and she told Karim that there was
nothing more than what was in the chest. Karim opened it, took out the
five pages and, when he had read them, he told his mother that they
were part of a book and asked her where the rest of it was. She said that
Daniel had taken all his books to sea with him and when his ship
had been wrecked they had been lost. 'Almighty God saved him from
drowning,' she told him, 'but these five pages were all that was left of
his books. When he came back from his voyage I was pregnant with you
and he said: "You may give birth to a boy, so take these pages and keep
them with you and when he grows up and asks what I left him, give
them to him and tell him that these are his only legacy." Here they are

for you.' Karim then mastered all the sciences and remained there, eating and drinking and enjoying the pleasantest of lives until he was visited by the destroyer of delights and the parter of companions.

This is the end of the story of Hasib, son of Daniel, may God have mercy on him, and God knows better what is the truth.

Shahrazad said: 'The story of Hasib Karim al-Din is not more remarkable than that of Sindbad.' 'How is that?' said the king, and she continued: 'In the time of the caliph Harun al-Rashid, the Commander of the Faithful, there was in the city of Baghdad a man called Sindbad the porter, a poor fellow who earned his living by carrying goods on his head. On one particularly hot day he was tired, sweating and feeling the heat with a heavy load, when he passed by the door of a merchant's house. The ground in front of it had been swept and sprinkled with water and a temperate breeze was blowing. As there was a wide bench at the side of the house, he set down his bundle in order to rest there and to sniff the breeze.'

Night 537

Morning now dawned and Shahrazad broke off from what she had been allowed to say. Then, when it was the five hundred and thirty-seventh night, SHE CONTINUED:

I have heard, O fortunate king, that Sindbad set down his bundle on the bench in order to rest and to sniff the breeze. From the door came a refreshing breath of air and a pleasant scent which attracted him, and as he sat he heard coming from within the house the sound of stringed instruments and lutes, together with singing and clearly chanted songs. In addition, he could hear birds twittering and praising God Almighty in all their varied tongues – turtledoves, nightingales, thrushes, bulbuls, ringdoves and curlews. He wondered at this and, filled as he was with pleasure, he moved forward and discovered within the grounds of the house a vast orchard in which he could see pages, black slaves, eunuchs, retainers and so forth, such as are only to be found in the palaces of kings and sultans. When he smelt the scent of all kinds of appetizing foods, together with fine wines, he looked up to heaven and said: 'Praise be to You, my Lord, Creator and Provider, Who sustains those whom You wish beyond all reckoning. I ask You to forgive all my sins, and I repent of my faults to You. My Lord, none can oppose Your judgement or power, or question Your acts, for You are omnipotent, praise be to You. You make one man rich and another poor, as You choose; You exalt some and humble others in accordance with Your will and there is no other god but You. How great You are! How strong is Your power and how excellent is Your governance! You show favour to those of Your servants whom You choose, for here is the owner of this house living in the greatest prosperity, enjoying pleasant scents, delicious food and all kinds of splendid wines. You have decreed what You wish with regard to your servants in accordance with Your power. Some are worn out and others live at ease; some are fortunate while others, like me, live laborious and humble lives.'

He then recited these lines:

How many an unfortunate, who has no rest,
Comes later to enjoy the pleasant shade.
But as for me, my drudgery grows worse,
And so, remarkably, my burdens now increase.
Others are fortunate, living without hardship,
And never once enduring what I must endure.
They live in comfort all their days,
With ease and honour, food and drink.
All are created from a drop of sperm;
I'm like the next man and he is like me,
But oh how different are the lives we lead!
How different is wine from vinegar.
I do not say this as a calumny;
God is All-Wise and His decrees are just.

When Sindbad the porter had finished these lines, he was about to pick up his load and carry it off when a splendidly dressed young boy, well proportioned and with a handsome face, came through the door, took his hand and said: 'Come and have a word with my master, for he invites you in.' Sindbad wanted to refuse, but finding that impossible, he left his load with the gatekeeper in the entrance hall and entered. He found an elegant house with an atmosphere of friendliness and dignity, and there he saw a large room filled with men of rank and importance. It was decked out with all kinds of flowers and scented herbs; there were fruits both dried and fresh, together with expensive foods of all kinds as well as wines of rare vintages; and there were musical instruments played by beautiful slave girls of various races. Everyone was seated in his appointed place and at their head was a large and venerable man whose facial hair was touched with grey. He was handsome and well shaped, with an imposing air of dignity, grandeur and pride. Sindbad the porter was taken aback, saying to himself: 'By God, this is one of the regions of Paradise, or perhaps the palace of a king or a sultan.' Then, remembering his manners, he greeted the company, invoking blessings on them and kissing the ground before them.

He stood there with his head bowed . . .

Night 538

Morning now dawned and Shahrazad broke off from what she had been allowed to say. Then, when it was the five hundred and thirty-eighth night, SHE CONTINUED:

I have heard, O fortunate king, that after Sindbad the porter had kissed the ground before the company, he stood there with his head bowed in an attitude of humility until the master of the house gave him permission to sit and placed him on a chair near his own, welcoming him and talking to him in a friendly way before offering him some of the splendid, delicious and expensive foods that were there. The porter, after invoking the Name of God, ate his fill and then exclaimed: 'Praise be to God in all things!' before washing his hands and thanking the company. The master of the house, after again welcoming him and wishing him good fortune, asked his name and his profession. 'My name is Sindbad the porter,' his guest replied, 'and in return for a fee I carry people's goods on my head.' The master smiled and said: 'You must know, porter, that your name is the same as mine, and I am Sindbad the sailor. I would like you to let me hear the verses which you were reciting as you stood at the door.' Sindbad the porter was embarrassed and said: 'For the sake of God, don't hold this against me, for toil and hardship together with a lack of means teach a man bad manners and stupidity.' 'Don't be ashamed,' said his host. 'You have become a brother to me, so repeat the verses that I admired when I heard you recite them at the door.' Sindbad the porter did this, moving Sindbad the sailor to delighted appreciation, after which THIS SECOND SINDBAD SAID:

I have a remarkable story to tell you covering all that happened to me before I acquired my present fortune and found myself sitting where you see me now. For it was only after great labour and hardship that I achieved this, having had to face perils upon perils and to endure difficulties and discomforts in my early days. I made seven voyages, and a surprising and astonishing story is attached to each; all this happened through the decree of fate, from whose rulings there is no escape.

Know, my noble masters, that my father was one of the leading citizens and merchants of Baghdad, a man of riches and ample means. He died when I was a small boy, leaving me money, possessions and estates. When I grew up and took all this over, I ate well, drank well, associated with other young men, wore fine clothes and went out with my friends and comrades. I was quite sure that these benefits would continue to be mine, until after a time I came to my senses and recovered from my heedlessness only to discover that the money was all gone, that my situation had changed and that all I had once owned was lost. I was frightened and bewildered, but then I thought of something I had once heard from my father about Solomon, the son of David, on both of whom be peace. Solomon is reported to have said: 'Three things are better than three other things. The day of one's death is better than the day of one's birth, a live dog is better than a dead lion and the grave is better than poverty.' So I got up and collected what I had in the way of furnishings and clothes and sold them. I went on to sell my property and everything else that I owned, all of which brought me three thousand dirhams. It then occurred to me to travel in foreign parts, as I remembered these lines of poetry:

> It is through toil that eminence is won;
> Whoever seeks the heights must pass nights without sleep.
> The pearl fisher must brave the depth of ocean
> If he is to win power and wealth.
> Whoever hopes to rise without effort
> Will waste his life in search of the impossible.

After I had thought all this over I made up my mind to go to sea and so I went off to buy a variety of trade goods, as well as things that I would need for the journey. I boarded a ship and sailed downriver to Basra with a number of other merchants. We then put out to sea and sailed for a number of days and nights, passing island after island and going from sea to sea and from one land to another. Whenever we passed land, we bought, sold and bartered, and we sailed on like this until we reached an island which looked like one of the meadows of Paradise.

The ship's master put in there, dropping the anchors and running out the gangway. After everyone on board had disembarked they lit fires under stoves and busied themselves in various ways, some cooking, some washing and some, including me, looking around the island and exploring the various districts. Afterwards we gathered again to eat, drink, play and enjoy ourselves, but while we were doing this, the master, standing at the side of the ship, shouted out to all of us at the top of his voice: 'Save yourselves! Hurry, board the ship as fast as you can; if you want to escape destruction, leave all your things and save your lives. This island is not a real one. It is a giant fish that has stayed motionless here in the middle of the sea until it has become silted up with sand on which trees have grown over time so that it looks like an island. When you lit your fire, it felt the heat and has started to move. It is just about to dive into the sea and you will all be drowned. Save yourselves before death overtakes you . . .'

Night 539

Morning now dawned and Shahrazad broke off from what she had been allowed to say. Then, when it was the five hundred and thirty-ninth night, SHE CONTINUED:

I have heard, O fortunate king, that SINDBAD SAID:

The master called out to the passengers: 'Save yourselves before death overtakes you, and abandon your things!' On hearing this, everyone left all their belongings, including pots and stoves. Some but not all reached the ship before the 'island' moved, plunging into the depths of the sea with everything that was on it, and the sea with its boisterous waves closed over it.

I was one of those who had been left on the 'island', and, together with the others, I found myself underwater, but Almighty God rescued me and saved me from drowning by providing me with a large wooden tub that had been used for washing. I held on to this for dear life, straddling it and using my legs like oars in order to paddle as the waves tossed me to and fro. The master had hoisted sail and he went off with those who had managed to get on board, showing no concern for the rest of us, who were drowning. I followed the ship with my eyes until it was out of sight, and I was quite sure that I was going to die. Night fell while I was still struggling in the water and my struggles lasted for a day and a night until, with the help of wind and wave, I came to rest under the high shore of an island where trees were growing out over the water. I had been on the point of drowning, but now I clutched at the branch of a lofty tree and clung on to it until I had managed to pull myself up on to the island itself. I discovered that my legs were numb and the soles of my feet showed traces of having been nibbled by fish, something I hadn't noticed earlier because of my distress and exhaustion. I was, in fact, the nearest thing to a corpse when I was thrown up there, having lost my senses and being plunged into dismay.

I stayed in this state until the sun roused me next day. My feet, I discovered, had swollen up but I moved as best I could, at times crawling and at others shuffling on my knees. There were many fruits there, which I started to eat, as well as freshwater springs, and I stayed like this for some days and nights until I had recovered my spirits and could move freely again. I started to think about my position as I walked around the island looking among the trees at what God had created there, and I made myself a crutch from the wood of the trees with which to support myself. Things went on like this for some time until one day, when I was walking along the shore, I saw in the distance something that I took to be a wild beast or some sea creature. I went towards it with my eyes fixed on it and discovered that it was a fine mare that had been tethered there on the shore. When I got near, it frightened me by giving a great scream and I was about to retrace my steps when from somewhere underground a man appeared. He shouted to me, coming after me and calling out: 'Who are you? Where have you come from and why are you here?' I told him: 'You must know, sir, that I am a stranger. I was on a ship but I and some others found ourselves washed into the sea, where God provided me with a wooden tub on which to ride. It floated off with me until the waves cast me up on this island.'

When the man heard my story, he took me by the hand and said: 'Come with me,' and when I did, he took me to an underground chamber with a large hall, at the head of which he made me sit. Then he brought me food, and, as I was hungry, I ate my fill before relaxing. He asked me about my circumstances and what had happened to me, and I told him my whole story from beginning to end, to his great astonishment. When I had finished, I implored him not to be hard on me, assuring him that what I had told him was the truth, and adding: 'I would like you to tell me who you are, why you are sitting here in this underground room and why you have tethered that mare by the shore.' He replied: 'There are a number of us scattered around the shores of this island, and we are the grooms of King Mihrjan, in charge of a number of his horses. Every month at the time of the new moon we bring thoroughbred mares that have never been covered and tether them on the island, after which we hide ourselves here underground so that no one can see us. Then a stallion, one of the sea horses, scents the mare and comes out of the sea. It looks around and when it sees nobody, it mounts her and after having covered her it gets down and wants to take her with him. Because of the tether she cannot go, and he screams at her, butting her with his head and kicking her, and when we hear the noise we know that he has got down from her, and so we come out and yell at him. This alarms him and he goes back into the sea, leaving the mare pregnant. The colt or filly to which she gives birth is worth a huge sum of money, and has no match on the face of the earth. This is the time for the stallion to come out and after it does, God willing, I shall take you with me to King Mihrjan . . .'

Night 540

Morning now dawned and Shahrazad broke off from what she had been allowed to say. Then, when it was the five hundred and fortieth night, SHE CONTINUED:

I have heard, O fortunate king, that SINDBAD SAID:

The groom told me: 'I shall take you with me to King Mihrjan and show you our country. You must know that, had you not met us, you would have found nobody else here and you would have died a miserable death, with no one knowing anything about you. I have saved your life and I shall see that you get back to your own country.'

I blessed the man and thanked him for having been so exceedingly good to me, and while we were talking a stallion came out of the sea and jumped on the mare with a loud snort. When it had finished its business it got off her, wanting to take her with it, and when it failed, she kicked and screamed at him. At that, the groom took sword and shield and went out of the door of the room, shouting to his companions to help him and striking his sword against his shield. A number of others arrived brandishing spears and shouting, at which the stallion took fright and made off into the sea like a water buffalo, disappearing under the surface. My man sat down briefly and was then joined by his companions, each of whom was leading a mare. When they saw me with him, they asked me about myself and I repeated what I had told him. They then came up to me, spread out a cloth, and invited me to share their meal, which I did. Then they got up and mounted, taking me with them on the back of one of the mares.

We went on until we reached the city of King Mihrjan, and when the others had gone in and told him my story, he asked for me. They took me and placed me before him, after which we exchanged greetings. He gave me a courteous welcome and then asked me about myself, at which I told him all that had happened to me and all that I had seen, from beginning to end. He was amazed by my experiences and said: 'My son, you have had a remarkable measure of good luck, and had fate not allotted you a long life, you would never have escaped from these dangers, but, thanks be to God, you are safe.' He then treated me with kindness and generosity, taking me as one of his intimates and talking to me in the friendliest of terms. He appointed me as his port agent to keep a register of all ships coming to land, and I stayed with him, carrying out his business and receiving all manner of kindnesses and benefits from him. He supplied me with the most splendid of robes and I took a principal role in presenting intercessions to him and settling the people's affairs.

I stayed with him for a long time, but whenever I found myself by the shore, I would ask the visiting merchants and the sailors where Baghdad lay in the hope that someone would be able to tell me, so that I might leave with him and go back to my own country. Not one of them, however, knew anything about Baghdad or about anyone who went there, and so I remained helpless and tired out by my long exile.

After things had gone on like that for some time, I went one day into the presence of the king and found that he had a number of Indians with him. After we had exchanged greetings they welcomed me, and when they had asked me about my country . . .

Night 541

Morning now dawned and Shahrazad broke off from what she had been allowed to say. Then, when it was the five hundred and forty-first night, SHE CONTINUED:

I have heard, O fortunate king, that SINDBAD SAID:

In return I asked about theirs. They told me that their people were made up of a number of different castes, and among these were the

Shakiris, the noblest of them all, who would never wrong or oppress anyone, and the so-called Brahmins, who drank no wine but lived happily, enjoying entertainment and pleasure and owning camels, horses and cattle. There were, in fact, seventy-two castes into which the Indians were divided, something that completely astonished me.

In Mihrjan's kingdom I noticed that there was an island named Kasil, from which there were to be heard the sounds of tambourines and drums being beaten all night long, although the other islanders and travellers who visited it told me that its inhabitants were serious-minded and intelligent people. In the sea there I saw a fish that was two hundred cubits in length and another with a face like that of an owl. All in all, I saw so many strange wonders on that voyage that it would take too long to tell you them all.

I continued to look around the island and note what was there until one day, as I was standing by the shore, staff, as usual, in my hand, up sailed a large ship with many merchants on board. It put in to the port and, on the orders of its master, the sails were furled, the anchors dropped and the gangways run out. The crew took a long time in unloading the cargo, while I stood there noting it all down. Then I asked the master whether there was anything left and he said: 'Yes, sir; there are some goods in the hold, but these belong to one of our company who was drowned off one of the islands on our outward voyage. We have kept them as a deposit and we intend to sell them, keep a note of the price and then pass on what they fetch to his family in Baghdad, the City of Peace.' I asked him the name of the owner and he said: 'He was Sindbad the sailor, and we lost him at sea.' When I heard what he said, I looked at him closely and recognized him. I gave a loud cry and said: 'Captain, those goods are mine and I am Sindbad the sailor. I joined the other merchants who disembarked on the "island", and when you shouted to us as the fish started to move, some got off while others, myself included, were submerged in the waves. God Almighty rescued me from drowning by providing me with a large tub which had been used on board for washing. I got on to it and paddled with my feet until the winds and waves helped me to reach this island, where I came ashore. Through God's help I met the grooms of King Mihrjan, who took me with them to this city and introduced me to him. When I told him my story he showed me favour and appointed me as clerk of this port, an office from which I have profited, and I have gained his approval. So these goods that you have are mine and they are my means of livelihood.'

Night 542

Morning now dawned and Shahrazad broke off from what she had been allowed to say. Then, when it was the five hundred and forty-second night, SHE CONTINUED:

I have heard, O fortunate king, that SINDBAD SAID:

I told the captain that the goods were mine and represented my means of livelihood. The captain quoted the formula: 'There is no might and no power except with God, the Exalted, the Omnipotent,' adding: 'No one has any integrity or conscience left.' I asked him why he had said that after having listened to my story, and he said: 'You heard me say that I had with me goods whose owner had been drowned, and now you want to take them without having any right to them. This is a crime on your part, and as for the owner, we saw him sink, and of the many others with him, not one escaped. So how can you claim that the goods are yours?' 'Captain,' I told him, 'if you listen to my story and follow what I am telling you, you will see that what I say is true, for lying is a characteristic of hypocrites.' I then went over for him everything that had happened to me from the time that I left Baghdad with him until I got to the 'island', where I was plunged into the sea. When I had told him some details of what had passed between us, both he and the other merchants realized that I was telling the truth. They recognized me and congratulated me on my safety, saying: 'By God, none of us believed that you could have escaped drowning, but God has given you a new life.' Then they handed over my goods, marked with my name, from which nothing at all was missing. I opened the packages and took out something precious and expensive, which the crew helped me to carry as a gift to the king. I explained to him that this was the ship on which I had sailed and that every single one of my goods had been returned to me. It was from them, I added, that I had chosen the present.

The king was filled with amazement when he heard this, and he realized that everything I had told him was true. He showed me great affection and treated me with even greater generosity, showering me with gifts in return for mine. I then disposed of all the goods I had with me at a great profit, after which I bought more goods of all kinds in the city. When the other merchants wanted to put to sea, I loaded all that I had on to the ship and then went to the king to thank him for his goodness and kindness and then to ask him to allow me to return to my own country and my family. He said goodbye to me and presented me as I left with many goods from the city. When I had taken my leave of him, I boarded the ship and with the permission of Almighty God we sailed off. Good fortune attended us and fate helped us as we travelled night and day until we reached Basra in safety. I was delighted at my safe return, and after we had landed and stayed for a short time, I set off for Baghdad, the City of Peace, taking with me many valuable loads of all kinds of goods. When I got to my own district of the city, I went to my house and was met by all my family and friends. I bought large numbers of eunuchs, retainers, mamluks, concubines and black slaves, as well as houses, properties and estates, until I had more of these than ever before. I enjoyed the company of my friends and companions, and was more prosperous than ever, forgetting the time that I had spent abroad, together with the toils and distress that I had suffered and the terrors of the voyage. I occupied myself with pleasures and enjoyment, good food and expensive wine, and continued to do so. This, then, is the story of my first voyage and tomorrow, God willing, I shall tell you the story of the second of my seven.

Sindbad the sailor then entertained Sindbad the landsman to supper, after which he ordered him to be presented with a hundred *mithqals* of gold, telling him: 'I have enjoyed your company today.' The other Sindbad thanked him, took the gift and went on his way, thinking with wonder about the experiences people have. He slept at home that night but the next morning he went back to the house of Sindbad the sailor, who welcomed him on his arrival and treated him with courtesy, giving him a seat in his salon. When his other companions came, he provided them with food and drink and when they were cheerful and happy he began to tell them the story of the second voyage.

'You must know, my brothers,' he said, 'that, as I told you yesterday, I was enjoying a life of the greatest pleasure and happiness . . .'

Night 543

Morning now dawned and Shahrazad broke off from what she had been allowed to say. Then, when it was the five hundred and forty-third night, SHE CONTINUED:

I have heard, O fortunate king, that when Sindbad's companions came, HE TOLD THEM:

I was enjoying a life of the greatest pleasure until one day I got the idea of travelling to foreign parts, as I wanted to trade, to look at other countries and islands and to earn my living. After I had thought this over, I took out a large sum of money and bought trade goods and other things that would be useful on a voyage. I packed these up and when I went down to the coast I found a fine new ship with a good set of sails, fully manned and well equipped. A number of other merchants were there and they and I loaded our goods on board. We put to sea that day and had a pleasant voyage, moving from one sea and one island to another, and wherever we anchored we were met by the local traders and dignitaries as well as by buyers and sellers, with whom we bought, sold and bartered our goods.

Things went on like this until fate brought us to a pleasant island, full of trees with ripe fruits, scented flowers, singing birds and limpid streams, but without any houses or inhabitants. The captain anchored there and the merchants, together with the crew, disembarked to enjoy its trees and its birds, giving praise to the One Omnipotent God, and wondering at His great power. I had gone with this landing party and I sat down by a spring of clear water among the trees. I had some food with me and I sat there eating what God had provided for me; there was a pleasant breeze; I had no worries and, as I felt drowsy, I stretched out at my ease, enjoying the breeze and the delightful scents, until I fell fast asleep. When I woke up, there was no one to be found there, human or *jinn*. The ship had sailed off leaving me, as not a single one on board, merchants or crew, had remembered me. I turned right and left, and when I failed to find anyone at all, I fell into so deep a depression that my gall bladder almost exploded through the force of my cares, sorrow and distress. I had no possessions, no food and no drink; I was alone, and in my distress I despaired of life. I said to myself: 'The pitcher does not always remain unbroken. I escaped the first time by meeting someone who took me with him from the island to an inhabited part, but this time how very, very unlikely it is that I shall meet anyone to bring me to civilization!'

I started to weep and wail, blaming myself in my grief for what I had done, for the voyage on which I had embarked, and for the hardships I had inflicted on myself after I had been sitting at home in my own land at my ease, enjoying myself and taking pleasure in eating well, drinking good wine and wearing fine clothes, in no need of more money or goods.

I regretted having left Baghdad to go to sea after what I had had to endure on my first voyage, which had brought me close to death. I recited the formula: 'We belong to God and to Him do we return,' and I was close to losing my reason. Then I got up and began to wander around, not being able to sit still in any one place. I climbed a high tree and from the top of it I started to look right and left, but all I could see was sky, water, trees, birds, islands and sand. Then, when I stared more closely, I caught sight of something white and huge on the island. I climbed down from my tree and set out to walk towards it. On I went until, when I reached it, I found it to be a white dome, very tall and with a large circumference. I went nearer and walked around it but I could find no door and the dome itself was so smoothly polished that I had neither the strength nor the agility to climb it. I marked my starting point and made a circuit of it to measure its circumference, which came to fifty full paces, and then I started to think of some way to get inside it.

It was coming on towards evening. I could no longer see the sun, and the sky had grown dark; I thought that the sun must have been hidden by a cloud, but since it was summer I found this surprising and I raised my head to look again. There, flying in the sky, I caught sight of an enormous bird with a huge body and broad wings. It was this that had covered the face of the sun, screening its rays from the island. I was even more amazed, but I remembered an old travellers' tale . . .

Night 544

Morning now dawned and Shahrazad broke off from what she had been allowed to say. Then, when it was the five hundred and forty-fourth night, SHE CONTINUED:

I have heard, O fortunate king, that SINDBAD SAID:

I was filled with amazement at the bird I saw on the island, and I remembered an old travellers' tale of a giant bird called the *rukh* that lived on an island and fed its chicks on elephants, and I became sure that my 'dome' was simply a *rukh*'s egg. While I was wondering at what Almighty God had created, the parent bird flew down and settled on the egg, covering it with its wings and stretching its legs behind it on the ground. It fell asleep – glory be to God, Who does not sleep – and I got up and undid my turban, which I folded and twisted until it was like a rope. I tied this tightly round my waist and attached myself as firmly as

I could to the bird's legs in the hope that it might take me to a civilized region, which would be better for me than staying on the island.

I spent the night awake, fearful that if I slept, the bird might fly off before I realized what was happening. When daylight came, it rose from the egg and with a loud cry it carried me up into the sky, soaring higher and higher until I thought that it must have reached the empyrean. It then began its descent and brought me back to earth, settling on a high peak. As soon as it had landed I quickly cut myself free from its legs, as I was afraid of it, although it hadn't noticed that I was there. I was trembling as I undid my turban, freeing it from the bird's legs, and I then walked off, while, for its part, the bird took something in its talons from the surface of the ground and then flew back up into the sky. When I looked to see what it had taken, I discovered that this was a huge snake with an enormous body. I watched in wonder as it left with its prey, and I then walked on further, to find myself on a high ridge under which there was a broad and deep valley, flanked by a vast and unscalable mountain that towered so high into the sky that its summit was invisible. I blamed myself for what I had done and wished that I had stayed on the island, saying to myself: 'That was better than this barren place, as there were various kinds of fruits to eat and streams from which to drink, whereas here there are no trees, fruits or streams.' I recited the formula: 'There is no power and no might except with God, the Exalted, the Almighty,' adding: 'Every time I escape from one disaster, I fall into another that is even worse.'

I got up and, plucking up my courage, I walked down into the valley, where I discovered that its soil was composed of diamonds, the hard and compact stone that is used for boring holes in metals, gems, porcelain and onyx. Neither iron nor rock has any effect on it; no part of it can be cut off and the only way in which it can be broken is by the use of lead. The valley was full of snakes and serpents as big as palm trees, so huge that they could have swallowed any elephant that met them, but these only came out at night and hid away by day for fear of *rukhs* and eagles, lest they be carried away and torn in bits, although I don't know why that should be. I stayed there filled with regret at what I had done, saying to myself: 'By God, you have hastened your own death.' As evening drew on, I walked around looking for a place where I could spend the night, and I was so afraid of the snakes that in my concern for my safety I forgot about eating and drinking. Nearby I spotted a cave and when I approached it, I found that its entrance was narrow. I went into it and then pushed a large stone that I found nearby in order to block it behind me. 'I'm safe in here,' I told myself, 'and when day breaks I shall go out and see what fate brings me.'

At that point I looked inside my cave only to see a huge snake asleep over its eggs at the far end. All the hairs rose on my body and, raising my head, I entrusted myself to fate. I spent a wakeful night, and when dawn broke I removed the stone that I had used to block the entrance and came out, staggering like a drunken man through the effects of sleeplessness, hunger and fear. Then, as I was walking, suddenly, to my astonishment, a large carcass fell in front of me although there was no one in sight. I thought of a travellers' tale that I had heard long ago of the dangers of the diamond mountains and of how the only way the diamond traders can reach these is to take and kill a sheep, which they skin and cut up. They then throw it down from the mountain into the valley and, as it is fresh when it falls, some of the stones there stick to it. The traders leave it until midday, at which point eagles and vultures swoop down on it and carry it up to the mountain in their talons. Then the traders come and scare them away from the flesh by shouting at them, after which they go up and remove the stones that are sticking to it. The flesh is left for the birds and beasts and the stones are taken back home by the traders. This is the only way in which they can get hold of the diamonds.

Night 545

Morning now dawned and Shahrazad broke off from what she had been allowed to say. Then, when it was the five hundred and forty-fifth night, SHE CONTINUED:

I have heard, O fortunate king, that Sindbad started to tell his companions everything that had happened to him on the diamond mountain and how the merchants could only collect diamonds by the kind of trick that he described. SINDBAD CONTINUED:

I looked at the carcass and remembered the story. So I went up to it and cleared away a large number of diamonds which I put in my purse and among my clothes, while I stored others in my pockets, my belt, my turban and elsewhere among my belongings. While I was doing this, another large carcass fell down and, lying on my back, I set it on my breast and tied myself to it with my turban, holding on to it and lifting it up from the ground. At that point an eagle came down and carried it off into the air in its talons, with me fastened to it. The eagle flew up to the mountain top where it deposited the carcass, and it was about to tear at it when there came a loud shout from behind it, together with the noise of sticks striking against rocks. The eagle took fright and flew off, and, having freed myself from the carcass, I stood there beside it, with my clothes all smeared with blood. At that point the trader who had shouted at the eagle came up, but when he saw me standing there he trembled and was too afraid of me to speak. He went to the carcass and turned it over, giving a great cry of disappointment and reciting the formula: 'There is no might and no power except with God. We take refuge with God from Satan, the accursed.' In his regret he struck the palms of his hands together, exclaiming: 'Alas, alas, what is this?'

I went up to him, and when he asked me who I was and why I had come there, I told him: 'Don't be afraid. I am a mortal man, of good stock, a former merchant. My story is very remarkable indeed, and there is a strange tale attached to my arrival at this mountain and this valley. There is no need for you to be frightened, for I have enough to make you happy – a large number of diamonds, of which I will give what will satisfy you, and each of my stones is better than anything else that you can get. So don't be unhappy or alarmed.'

The man thanked me, calling down blessings on me, and as we talked the other traders, each of whom had thrown down a carcass, heard the sound of our voices and came up to us. They congratulated me on my escape and, when they had taken me away with them, I told them my whole story, explaining the perils that I had endured on my voyage as well as the reason why I had got to the valley. After that, I presented many of the diamonds that I had with me to the man who had thrown down the carcass that I had used, and in his delight he renewed his blessings. The others exclaimed: 'By God, fate has granted you a second life, for you are the first man ever to come here and escape from the valley. God be praised that you are safe.'

I passed the night with them in a spot that was both pleasant and safe, delighted that I had escaped unhurt from the valley of the snakes and had got back to inhabited parts. At dawn we got up, and as we moved across the great mountain we could see huge numbers of snakes in the valley, but we kept on our way until we reached an orchard on a large and beautiful island, where there were camphor trees, each one of which could provide shade for a hundred people. Whoever wants to get some camphor must use a long tool to bore a hole at the top of the tree and then collect what comes out. The liquid camphor flows down and then solidifies like gum, as this is the sap of the tree, and when it dries up, it can be used for firewood. On the island is a type of wild beast known as the rhinoceros, which grazes there just as cows and buffaloes do in our own parts. It is a huge beast with a body larger than that of a camel, a herbivore with a single horn some ten cubits long in the centre of its head containing what looks like the image of a man. There is also a species of cattle there. According to seafarers and travellers who have visited the mountain and its districts there, this rhinoceros can carry a large elephant on its horn and go on pasturing in the island and on the shore without paying any attention to it. The elephant, impaled on its horn, will then die, and in the heat of the sun grease from its corpse will trickle on to the head of the rhinoceros. When this gets into its eyes, it will go blind, and as it then lies down by the coast, a *rukh* will swoop on it and carry it off in its talons in order to feed its chicks both with the beast itself and with what is on its horn. On the island I saw many buffaloes of a type unlike any that we have at home.

I exchanged a number of the stones that I had brought with me in my pocket from the diamond valley with the traders in return for a cash payment and some of the goods that they had brought with them, which they carried for me. I travelled on in their company, inspecting different lands and God's creations, from one valley and one city to another, buying and selling as we went, until we arrived at Basra. We stayed there for a few days and then I returned to Baghdad.

Night 546

Morning now dawned and Shahrazad broke off from what she had been allowed to say. Then, when it was the five hundred and forty-sixth night, SHE CONTINUED:

I have heard, O fortunate king, that when Sindbad returned from foreign parts, he went to Baghdad.

When Sindbad reached Baghdad, the City of Peace, he went to his own district and entered his house. He had with him a large number of diamonds, as well as cash and a splendid display of all kinds of goods. After he had met his family and his relatives, he dispensed alms and gave gifts to every one of his relations and companions. He began to enjoy good food and wine, to dress in fine clothes and to frequent the company of his friends. He forgot all his past sufferings, and he continued to enjoy a pleasant, relaxed and contented life, with entertainments of all sorts. All those who had heard of his return would come and ask him about his voyage and about the lands that he had visited. He would tell them of his experiences and amaze them by recounting the difficulties with which he had had to contend, after which they would congratulate him on his safe return.

This is the end of the story of all that happened to him on his second voyage, and when he had finished his account he said: 'Tomorrow, God willing, I shall tell you about my third voyage.' When he had told all this to Sindbad the landsman, those present were filled with astonishment. They all dined with him that evening and he gave orders that the second Sindbad be given a hundred *mithqals* of gold. Sindbad the landsman took these and went on his way, marvelling at what his host had endured, and, filled with gratitude, when he reached his own house, he called down blessings on him.

The next morning, when it was light, he got up and, having performed the morning prayer, he went back to the house of Sindbad the sailor as he had been told to do. On his arrival he said good morning to his host, who welcomed him, and the two sat together until the rest of the company arrived. When they had eaten and drunk and were pleasantly and cheerfully relaxed, SINDBAD THE SAILOR SAID:

Listen with attention to this tale of mine, my brothers, for it is more wonderful than what I told you before, and it is God Whose knowledge and decree regulate the unknown. When I got back from my second voyage I was happy, relaxed and glad to be safe, and, as I told you yesterday, I had made a large amount of money, since God had replaced for me all that I had lost. So I stayed in Baghdad for a time, enjoying my good fortune with happiness and contentment, but then I began to feel an urge to travel again and to see the world, as well as to make a profit by trading, for as the proverb says: 'The soul instructs us to do evil.' After thinking the matter over, I bought a large quantity of goods suitable for a trading voyage, packed them up and took them from Baghdad to Basra. I went to the shore, where I saw a large ship on which were many virtuous merchants and passengers, as well as a pious crew of devout and godly sailors. I embarked with them and we set sail with the blessing of Almighty God and His beneficent aid, confident of success and safety.

On we sailed from sea to sea, island to island and city to city, enjoying the sights that we saw, and happy with our trading, until one day, when we were in the middle of a boisterous sea with buffeting waves, the captain, who was keeping a lookout from the gunwale, gave a great cry, slapped his face, plucked at his beard and tore his clothes. He ordered the sails to be furled and the anchors dropped. 'What is it, captain?' we asked him, and he told us to pray for safety, explaining: 'The wind got the better of us, forcing us out to sea, and ill fortune has driven us to the mountain of the hairy ones, an ape-like folk. No one who has come there has ever escaped, and I feel in my heart that we shall all die.' Before he had finished speaking we were surrounded on all sides by apes who were like a flock of locusts, approaching our ship and spreading out on the shore. We were afraid to kill any of them or to strike them and drive them off, as we thought that if we did, they would be certain to kill us because of their numbers, since 'numbers defeat courage', as the proverb has it. We could only wait in fear lest they plunder our stores and our goods.

These apes are the ugliest of creatures, with hair like black felt and a horrifying appearance; no one can understand anything they say and they have an aversion to men. They have yellow eyes and black faces and are small, each being four spans in height. They climbed on to the anchor cables and gnawed through them with their teeth before proceeding to cut all the other ropes throughout the ship. As we could not keep head to wind, the ship came to rest by the mountain of the ape men and grounded there. The apes seized all the merchants and the others, bringing them to shore, after which they took the ship and everything in it, carrying off their spoils and going on their way. We were left on the island, unable to see the ship and without any idea where they had taken it.

We stayed there eating fruits and herbs and drinking from the streams until we caught sight of some form of habitation in the centre of the island. We walked towards this and found that it was a strongly built castle with high walls and an ebony gate whose twin leaves were standing open. We went through the gate and discovered a wide space like an extensive courtyard around which were a number of lofty doors, while at the top of it was a large and high stone bench. Cooking pots hung there on stoves surrounded by great quantities of bones, but there was nobody to be seen. We were astonished by all this and we sat down there for a while, after which we fell asleep and stayed sleeping from the forenoon until sunset. It was then that the earth shook beneath us, there was a thunderous sound, and from the top of the castle down came an enormous creature shaped like a man, black, tall as a lofty palm tree, with eyes like sparks of fire. He had tusks like those of a boar, a huge mouth like the top of a well, lips like those of a camel, which hung down over his chest, ears like large boats resting on his shoulders, and fingernails like the claws of a lion. When we saw what he looked like, we were so terrified that we almost lost our senses and were half-dead from fear and terror.

Night 547

Morning now dawned and Shahrazad broke off from what she had been allowed to say. Then, when it was the five hundred and forty-seventh night, SHE CONTINUED:

I have heard, O fortunate king, that when Sindbad and his companions caught sight of this formidable creature, they were terrified. SINDBAD SAID:

When he had reached the ground, he sat for a short while on the bench before getting up and coming over to us. He singled me out from among the other traders who were with me, grasping my hand and lifting me from the ground. Then he felt me and turned me over, but in his hands I was no more than a small mouthful, and when he had examined me as a butcher examines a sheep for slaughter, he found that I had been weakened by my sufferings and emaciated by the discomforts of the voyage, which had left me skinny. So he let go of me and picked another of my companions in my place. After turning him over and feeling him as he had felt me, he let him go too and he kept on doing this with us, one after the other, until he came to the captain, a powerful man, stout and thickset with broad shoulders. He was pleased with what he had found and, after laying hold of the man as a butcher holds his victim, he threw him down on the ground and set his foot on his neck, which he broke. Then he took a long spit, which he thrust up from the captain's backside to the crown of his head, after which the creature lit a large fire and over this he placed the spit on which the captain was skewered. He turned this round and round over the coals until, when the flesh was cooked, he took it off the fire, put it down in front of him and dismembered it, as a man dismembers a chicken. He started to tear the flesh with his fingernails and then to eat it. When he had finished it all, he gnawed the bones, leaving none of them untouched, before throwing away what was left of them at the side of the castle. He then sat for a while before stretching himself out on the bench and falling asleep, snorting like a sheep or a beast with its throat cut. He slept until morning and then got up and went off about his business.

When we were sure that he had gone we began to talk to one another, weeping over our plight and exclaiming: 'Would that we had been drowned or eaten by the ape men, for this would have been better than being roasted over the coals! That is a terrible death, but God's will be done, for there is no might and no power except with Him, the Exalted, the Omnipotent. We shall die miserably without anyone knowing about us, as there is no way left to us to escape from this place.' Then we went off into the island to look for a hiding place or a means of escape, as we didn't mind dying provided we were not roasted over the fire. But we found nowhere to hide and when evening came we were so afraid that we went back to the castle.

We had only been sitting there for a short while before the ground beneath us began to shake again and the black giant came up to us. He started turning us over and inspecting us one by one as he had done the first time, until he found one to his liking. He seized this man and treated him as he had treated the captain the day before, roasting and eating him. He then went to sleep on the bench and slept the night through, snorting like a slaughtered beast. When day broke he got up and went away, leaving us, as he had done before. We gathered together to talk, telling one another: 'By God, it would be better to throw ourselves into the sea and drown rather than be roasted, for that is an abominable death.' At that point one of our number said: 'Listen to me. We must find some way of killing the giant so as to free ourselves from the distress that he has caused us, and also to free our fellow Muslims from his hostility and tyranny.' I said: 'Brothers, listen. If we have to kill him, we must move some of these timbers and this wood and make ourselves a species of ship. If we then think of a way of killing him, we can embark on it and put out to sea, going wherever God wills, or else we could stay here until a ship sails by on which we might take passage. If we fail to kill him, we can come down and put out to sea, for even if we drown we would still escape being slaughtered and roasted over the fire. If we escape, we escape, and if we drown, we die as martyrs.' 'This is sound advice,' they all agreed, and we then set to work moving timbers out of the castle and building a boat which we moored by the shore, loading it with some provisions. Afterwards we went back to the castle.

When evening came, the earth shook and the black giant arrived like a ravening dog. He turned us over and felt us one by one before picking out one of us, whom he treated as he had done the others. Having eaten him he fell asleep on the bench, with thunderous snorts. We got up and took two iron spits from those that were standing there. We put them in the fierce fire until they were red hot, like burning coals, and then, gripping them firmly, we carried them to the sleeping, snoring giant, placed them on his eyes and then bore down on them with our combined strength as firmly as we could. The spits entered his eyes and blinded him, at which he terrified us by uttering a great cry. He sprang up from the bench and began to hunt for us as we fled right and left. In his blinded state he could not see us, but we were still terrified of him, thinking that our last hour had come and despairing of escape. He felt his way to the door and went out bellowing, leaving us quaking with fear as the earth shook beneath our feet because of the violence of his cries. We followed him out as he went off in search of us, but then he came back with two others, larger and more ferocious-looking than himself. When we saw him and his even more hideous companions, we panicked, and as they caught sight of us and hurried towards us, we boarded our boat, cast off its moorings and drove it out to sea. Each of the giants had a huge rock in his hands, which they threw at us, killing most of us and leaving only me and two others.

Night 548

Morning now dawned and Shahrazad broke off from what she had been allowed to say, Then, when it was the five hundred and forty-eighth night, SHE CONTINUED:

I have heard, O fortunate king, that when Sindbad and his companions boarded their boat the black giant and his companions threw stones at them, leaving only three survivors. SINDBAD SAID:

The boat took us to another island and there we walked until nightfall, when, in our wretched state, we fell asleep for a little while, but when we woke, it was only to see that a huge snake with an enormous body and a wide belly had coiled around us. It made for one of us and swallowed his body as far as the shoulders, after which it gulped down the rest of him and we could hear his ribs cracking in its belly. Then it went off, leaving us astonished, filled with grief for our companion and fearful for our own safety. We exclaimed: 'By God, it is amazing that each death should be more hideous than the one before! We were glad to have got away from the black giant but our joy has been short-lived, and there is no might and no power except with God. By God, we managed to escape from the giant and from death by drowning, but how are we to escape from this sinister monster?'

We walked around the island until evening, eating its fruits and drinking from its streams, until we discovered a huge and lofty tree which we climbed in order to sleep there. I was up on the top-most branch, and when night fell the snake came through the darkness and, having looked right and left, it made for our tree and swarmed up until it had reached my companion. It swallowed his body as far as the shoulders, and then coiled round the tree with him until I heard his bones cracking in its belly, after which it swallowed the rest of him before my eyes. It then slid down the tree and went away. I stayed on my branch for the rest of the night and when daylight came, I climbed down again, half-dead with fear and terror. I thought of throwing myself into the sea to find rest from the troubles of the world, but I could not bring myself to commit suicide as life is dear. So I fastened a broad wooden beam across my feet with two other similar beams on my right and my left sides, another over my stomach, and a very large one laterally over my head, to match the one beneath my feet. I was in the middle of these beams, which encased me on all sides, and after I had fastened them securely, I threw myself, with all of them, on to the ground. I lay between them as though I was in a cupboard, and when night fell and the snake arrived as usual, it saw me and made for me but could not swallow me up as I was protected on all sides by the beams and, although it circled round, it could find no way to reach me. I watched it, nearly dead with fear, as it went off and then came back, constantly trying to get to me in order to swallow me, but the beams that I had fastened all around me prevented it. This continued from sunset until dawn, and when the sun rose the snake went off, frustrated and angry, and I then stretched out my hand and freed myself from the beams, still half-dead because of the terror that it had inflicted on me.

After I had got up, I walked to the end of the island, and when I looked out from the shore, there far out at sea was a ship. I took a large branch and waved it in its direction, calling out to the sailors. They saw me and told each other: 'We must look to see what this is, as it might be a man.' When they had sailed near enough to hear my shouts, they came in and brought me on board. They asked for my story, and I told them everything that had happened to me from beginning to end, and they were amazed at the hardships I had endured. They gave me some of their own clothes to hide my nakedness and then brought me some food, allowing me to eat my fill, as well as providing me with cold, fresh water. This revived and refreshed me, and such was my relief that it was as though God had brought me back from the dead. I praised and thanked Him for His abundant grace, and although I had been sure that I was doomed, I regained my composure to such an extent that it seemed as if all my perils had been a dream.

My rescuers sailed on with a fair wind granted by Almighty God until we came in sight of an island called al-Salahita, where the captain dropped anchor.

Night 549

Morning now dawned and Shahrazad broke off from what she had been allowed to say. Then, when it was the five hundred and forty-ninth night, SHE CONTINUED:

I have heard, O fortunate king, that SINDBAD SAID:

When the ship anchored off the island, everyone disembarked, merchants and passengers alike, unloading their wares in order to trade. The master of the ship then turned to me and said: 'Listen to me. You are a poor stranger who has gone through a terrifying ordeal, as you have told us, and so I want to do something for you that may help you get back to your own land and cause you to bless me for the rest of your life.' When I had thanked him for this he went on to say: 'We lost one of our passengers, and we don't know whether he is alive or dead, as we have heard no news of him. I propose to hand over his goods to you so that you may sell them here in return for payment that we shall give you for your trouble. Anything left over we shall keep until we get back to Baghdad, where we can make enquiries about his family, and we shall then hand over the rest of the goods to them, as well as the price of what has been sold. Are you prepared to take charge of these things, land them on the island and trade with them?' 'To hear is to obey, sir,' I said, adding my blessings and thanks for his generous conduct. So he ordered the porters and members of the crew to unload the goods on the shore and then to hand them over to me. The ship's clerk asked him whose goods these were so that he could enter the name of the merchant who owned them. 'Write on them the name of Sindbad the sailor,' the master told him, 'the man who came out with us but was lost on an island. We never heard of him again, and I want this stranger to sell them and give us what they fetch in return for a fee for his trouble in selling them. Whatever is unsold we can take back to Baghdad, and if we find Sindbad, we can give it back to him, but if not, we can hand it over to his family in the city.' 'Well said!' exclaimed the clerk. 'That is a good plan.'

When I heard the master say that the bales were to be entered under my name, I told myself: 'By God, I am Sindbad the sailor, who was one of those lost on the island,' but I waited in patience until the merchants had left the ship and were all there together talking about trade. It was then that I went up to the master and said: 'Sir, do you know anything about the owner of these bales that you have entrusted to me to sell for him?' 'I know nothing about his circumstances,' the master replied, 'only that he was a Baghdadi called Sindbad the sailor. We anchored off an island, where a large number of our people were lost in the sea, including Sindbad, and until this day we have heard nothing more about him.' At that I gave a great cry and said: 'Master, may God keep you safe. Know that I am Sindbad the sailor and that I was not drowned. When you anchored there, I landed with the other merchants and passengers and went off to a corner of the island, taking some food with me. I so enjoyed sitting there that I became drowsy and fell into the soundest of sleeps, and when I woke up I found the ship gone and no one else there with me. So these are my belongings and my goods. All the merchants who fetch diamonds saw me when I was on the diamond mountain and they will confirm that I am, in fact, Sindbad. For I told them the story of what had happened to me on your ship and how you forgot about me and left me lying asleep on the island and what happened to me after I woke up and found no one there.'

When the merchants and the passengers heard what I had to say, they gathered around me, some believing me and some convinced that I was lying. While things were still undecided, one of the merchants who heard me mention the diamond valley got up and came to me. He asked the company to listen to him and said: 'I told you of the most remarkable thing that I saw on my travels, which happened when my companions and I were throwing down carcasses into the diamond valley. I threw mine down as usual and when it was brought up by an eagle there was a man attached to it. You didn't believe me and thought that I was lying.'

'Yes,' said the others, 'you certainly told us this and we didn't believe you.' 'Here is the man who was clinging to it,' said the merchant. 'He presented me with valuable diamonds whose like is nowhere to be found, giving me more than I had ever got from a carcass, and he then stayed with me until we reached Basra, after which he went off to his own city. My companions and I said goodbye to him and went back to our own lands. This is the man. He told us that his name was Sindbad the sailor and that his ship had gone off leaving him on the island. He has come here as proof to you that I was telling the truth. All these goods are his; he told us about them when we met and what he has said has been shown to be true.'

When the master heard this he came up to me and looked carefully at me for some time. Then he asked: 'What mark is on your goods?' I told him what it was and then I mentioned some dealings that we had had together on our voyage from Basra. He was then convinced that I really was Sindbad and embraced me, saluting me and congratulating me on my safe return. 'By God, sir,' he said, 'yours is a remarkable story and a strange affair. Praise be to God, Who has reunited us and returned your goods and possessions to you.'

Night 550

Morning now dawned and Shahrazad broke off from what she had been allowed to say. Then, when it was the five hundred and fiftieth night, SHE CONTINUED:

I have heard, O fortunate king, that when it was clear to the master and the merchants that this was really Sindbad, the master said: 'Praise be to God, Who has restored your goods and possessions to you.' SINDBAD WENT ON:

After that I used my expertise to dispose of my goods, making a great profit on the trip. I was delighted by this, congratulating myself on my safety and on the return of my possessions.

We continued to trade among the islands until we came to Sind, where we bought and sold, and in the sea there I came across innumerable wonders. Among them was a fish that looked like a cow and another resembling a donkey, together with a bird that came out of a mollusc shell, laying its eggs and rearing its chicks on the surface of the sea and never coming out on to dry land at all. On we sailed, with the permission of Almighty God, enjoying a fair wind and a pleasant voyage until we got back to Basra. I stayed there for a few days before going to Baghdad, where I went to my own district and entered my house, greeting my family as well as my friends and companions. Feeling joyful at my safe return to my country, my family, my city and my properties, I distributed alms, made gifts, clothed widows and orphans and gathered together my companions and friends. I went on like this, eating, drinking and enjoying myself with good food, good wine and friends, having made a vast profit from my voyage and having forgotten all that had happened to me and the hardships and terrors that I had endured. I have told you the most marvellous things that I saw on it and, God willing, if you come to me tomorrow I shall tell you the story of my fourth voyage, which is even more remarkable than those of the first three.

Sindbad the sailor then gave orders that Sindbad the porter should be given his usual hundred *mithqals* of gold and that tables should be laid with food. The whole company ate with him, still filled with amazement at the tale of their host's experiences, and then after supper they went on their ways. As for Sindbad the porter, he took his gold and went off astonished by what he had heard. He spent the night at home and the next morning, when it was light, he got up, performed the morning prayer and walked to the house of Sindbad the sailor, greeting him as he went in. His host welcomed him with gladness and delight, making him sit with him until the rest of his companions arrived. Food was produced and they ate, drank and enjoyed themselves, until SINDBAD BEGAN TO TELL THE STORY OF THE FOURTH VOYAGE:

Know, my brothers, that when I got back to Baghdad and met my companions, my family and my friends I enjoyed a life of the greatest happiness, contentment and relaxation, forgetting everything in my well-being, and drowning in pleasure and delight in the company of my friends and companions. It was while my life was at its most pleasant that I felt a pernicious urge to travel to foreign parts, to associate with different races and to trade and make a profit. Having thought this over, I bought more valuable goods, suitable for a voyage, than I had ever taken before, packing them into bales. When I had gone down from Baghdad to Basra I loaded them on a ship, taking with me a number of the leading Basran merchants. We put out, with the blessing of Almighty God, on to the turbulent and boisterous sea and for a number of nights and days we had a good voyage, passing from island to island and sea to sea until one day we met a contrary wind. The master used the anchors to bring us to a halt in mid-ocean lest we founder there, but while we were addressing our supplications to Almighty God a violent gale blew up, which tore our sails to shreds, plunging all on board into the sea, together with all their bales, goods and belongings.

I was with the others in the sea. I swam for half a day, but I had given up all hope when Almighty God sent me part of one of the ship's timbers on to which I climbed, together with some of the other merchants.

Night 551

Morning now dawned and Shahrazad broke off from what she had been allowed to say. Then, when it was the five hundred and fifty-first night, SHE CONTINUED:

I have heard, O fortunate king, that SINDBAD SAID:

The ship sank and I climbed on a beam, together with a number of the other merchants. We huddled together as we rode on it, paddling with our legs, and being helped by the waves and the wind. This went on for a day and a night, but in the forenoon of the second day the wind rose and the sea became stormy, with powerful waves. The current then cast us up on an island, half-dead through lack of sleep, fatigue and cold, hunger, thirst and fear. Later, when we walked around the place, we found many plants, some of which we ate to allay our hunger and sustain us, and we spent the night by the shore. The next day, when it was light, we got up and continued to explore the various parts of the island. In the distance we caught sight of a building and kept on walking towards it until we stood at its door. While we were there, out came a crowd of naked men, who took hold of us without a word and brought us to their king. We sat down at his command and food was brought which we did not recognize and whose like we had never seen in our lives. I could not bring myself to take it and so I ate nothing, unlike my companions, and this abstemiousness on my part was thanks to the grace of Almighty God as it was this that has allowed me to live until now.

When my companions tasted the food, their wits went wandering; they fell on it like madmen and were no longer the same men. The king's servants then fetched them coconut oil, some of which was poured out as drink and some of which was smeared over them. When my companions drank the oil their eyes swivelled in their heads and they started to eat the food in an unnatural way. I felt sorry for them, but I did not know what to do about it and I was filled with great uneasiness, fearing for my own life at the hands of the naked men. For when I looked at them closely I could see that they were Magians and that the king of their city was a *ghul*. They would bring him everyone who came to their country or whom they saw or met in their valley or its roads. The newcomer would then be given that food and anointed with that oil; his belly would swell so that he could eat more and more; he would lose his mind and his powers of thought until he became like an imbecile. The Magians would continue to stuff him with food and coconut oil drink until, when he was fat enough, they would cut his throat and feed him to the king. They themselves would eat human flesh unroasted and raw.

When I saw this I was filled with distress both for myself and for my comrades, who, in their bewildered state, did not realize what was being done to them. They were put in charge of a man who would herd them around the island like cattle; as for me, fear and hunger made me weak and sickly, and my flesh clung to my bones. The Magians, seeing my condition, left me alone and forgot about me. Not one of them remembered me or thought about me, and so one day I contrived to move from the place where they were, and walked away, leaving it far behind me. I then saw a herdsman sitting on a high promontory, and when I looked more closely I could see that he was the man who had been given the job of pasturing not only my companions but many others as well, who were in the same state. When he saw me he realized that I was still in possession of my wits and was not suffering from what had affected the others. So he gestured to me from far off, indicating that I should turn back and then take the road to the right, which would lead to the main highway. I followed his instructions and went back, and when I saw a road on my right I followed it, at times running in terror and then walking more slowly until I was rested. I went on like this until I was out of sight of the man who had shown me the way and I could no longer see him nor could he see me.

The sun then set and as darkness fell I sat down to rest, intending to go to sleep, but I was too afraid, too hungry and too tired to sleep that night. At midnight I got up and walked further into the island, carrying on until daybreak, when the sun rose over the hilltops and the valleys. I was exhausted, hungry and thirsty and so I started to eat grass and some of the island plants, going on until I had satisfied my hunger and was satiated. Then I got up and walked on, and I continued like this for the whole of the day and the night, eating plants whenever I was hungry. This went on for seven days and seven nights until, on the morning of the eighth day, I caught sight of something in the distance and set off towards it. I got to my destination after sunset and looked carefully at it from far off, as my heart was still fluttering because of my earlier sufferings, but it turned out to be a group of men gathering peppercorns. They saw me as I approached and quickly came and surrounded me on all sides, asking me who I was and where I had come from. I told them that I was a poor unfortunate and then went on to give them my whole story, explaining my perils, hardships and sufferings.

Night 552

Morning now dawned and Shahrazad broke off from what she had been allowed to say. Then, when it was the five hundred and fifty-second night, SHE CONTINUED:

I have heard, O fortunate king, that when Sindbad saw the men who were collecting peppercorns on the island, they asked him about himself and he told them what had happened to him and what hardships he had endured. HE WENT ON:

'By God,' they exclaimed, 'this is an amazing story, but how did you escape from the blacks and get away from them on the island? There are vast numbers of them and as they are cannibals no one can pass them in safety.' So I told them what had happened to me and how they had taken my companions by feeding them on some food which I did not eat. They were astonished by my experiences and, after congratulating me on my safety, they made me sit with them until they had finished their work, after which they brought me some tasty food, which I ate because I was starving. I stayed with them for some time and then they took me with them on a ship, which brought me to the island where they lived. There they presented me to their king, whom I greeted and who welcomed me courteously and asked me about myself. I told him of my circumstances and of all my experiences from the day that I left Baghdad until I came to him. He and those with him were filled with astonishment at this tale. He told me to sit by him and he then ordered food to be brought, from which I ate my fill. Then I washed my hands and thanked, praised and extolled Almighty God for His grace.

When I left the king's court I looked around the city, which was a thriving place, populous and wealthy, well stocked with provisions and full of markets and trade goods, as well as with both buyers and sellers. I was pleased and happy to have got there, and I made friends with the people, and their king, who treated me with more honour and respect than he showed to his own leading citizens. I observed that all of them, high and low alike, rode good horses but without saddles. I was surprised at that and I asked the king why it was, pointing out that a saddle made things more comfortable for the rider and allowed him to exert more force. 'What is a saddle?' he asked, adding: 'I have never seen one or ridden on one in my life.' 'Would you allow me to make you one so that you could ride on it and see its advantages?' I asked, and when he told me to carry on, I asked him to provide me with some wood. He ordered everything I needed to be fetched, after which I looked for a clever carpenter and sat teaching him how saddles should be made. Then I got wool, carded it and made it into felt, after which I covered the saddle in leather and polished it before attaching bands and fastening the girth. Next I fetched a smith and explained to him how to make stirrups. When he had made a large pair, I filed them down and then covered them with tin, giving them fringes of silk. I fetched one of the best of the king's horses, a stallion, which I then saddled and bridled, and when I had attached the stirrups I brought him to the king. What I had done took the fancy of the king, who was filled with admiration, and, having thanked me, he mounted the horse and was delighted by the saddle. In return for my work he gave me a huge reward, and when his vizier saw what I had made, he asked for another saddle like it. I made him one and after that all the principal officers of state and the state officials began to ask me to make them saddles. I taught the carpenter how to produce them and showed the smith how to make stirrups, after which we started to manufacture them and to sell them to great men and the employers of labour. This brought me a great deal of money and I became a man of importance in the city, commanding ever greater affection and enjoying high status both with the king and with his court, and also with the leading citizens and state officials.

One day, while I was sitting with the king enjoying my dignity to the full, he said to me: 'You have become a respected and honoured companion of ours; you are one of us and we cannot bear to be parted from you or that you should leave our city. I have something to ask of you, and I want you to obey me and not to reject my request.' 'What is it that you want of me, your majesty?' I asked, adding: 'I cannot refuse you, because you have treated me with such kindness, favour and generosity, and I thank God that I have become one of your servants.' The king said: 'I want you to take a wife here, a beautiful, graceful and witty lady, as wealthy as she is lovely, so that you may become one of our citizens and I can lodge you with me in my palace. Do not disobey me or reject my proposal.' When I heard what he said, I was too embarrassed to speak and stayed silent. Then, when he asked why I did not answer, I said: 'My master, king of the age, your commands must be obeyed.' He sent at once for the *qadi* and the notaries, and he married me on the spot to a noble lady of high birth and great wealth, who combined beauty and grace with her distinguished ancestry, and who was the owner of houses, properties and estates.

Night 553

Morning now dawned and Shahrazad broke off from what she had been allowed to say. Then, when it was the five hundred and fifty-third night, SHE CONTINUED:

I have heard, O fortunate king, that SINDBAD SAID:

After the king had married me to a great lady, he presented me with a fine, large detached house, providing me with eunuchs and retainers and assigning me pay and allowances. I lived a life of ease, happy and relaxed, forgetting all the toils, difficulties and hardships that I had experienced. I told myself that when I went back to my own country, I would take my wife with me, but there is no avoiding fate and no one knows what will happen to him. My wife and I were deeply in love; we lived in harmony, enjoying a life of pleasure and plenty over a period of time. Almighty God then widowed a neighbour of mine, and, as he was a friend of mine, I went to his house to offer my condolences on his loss. I found him in the worst of states, full of care and sick at heart. I tried to console him by saying: 'Don't grieve for your wife. Almighty God will see that you are well recompensed by providing you with another, more beautiful one, and, if it is His will, you will live a long life.' He wept bitterly and said: 'My friend, how can I marry another wife and how can God compensate me with a better one when I have only one day left to live?' 'Come back to your senses, brother,' I told him, 'and don't forecast your own death, for you are sound and healthy.' 'My friend,' he said, 'I swear by your life that tomorrow you will lose me and never see me again.' 'How can that be?' I asked him, and he told me: 'Today my wife will be buried and I shall be buried with her in the same grave. It is the custom here that, when a wife dies, her husband is buried alive with her, while if the husband dies it is the wife who suffers this fate, so that neither partner may enjoy life after the death of the other.' 'By God,' I exclaimed, 'what a dreadful custom! This is unbearable!'

While we were talking, a group comprising the bulk of the citizens of the town arrived and started to pay condolences to my friend on the loss of his wife and on his own fate. They began to lay out the corpse in their usual way, fetching a coffin in which they carried it, accompanied by the husband. They took it out of the city to a place on the side of a mountain overlooking the sea. When they got there, they lifted up a huge stone, under which could be seen a rocky cleft like the shaft of a well.

They threw the woman's body down this, into what I could see was a great underground pit. Then they brought my friend, tied a rope round his waist and lowered him into the pit, providing him with a large jug of fresh water and seven loaves by way of provisions. When he had been lowered down, he freed himself from the rope, which they pulled up before putting the stone back in its place and going away, leaving my friend with his wife in the pit.

I said to myself: 'By God, this death is even more frightful than the previous one,' and I went to the king and asked him how it was that in his country they buried the living with the dead. He said: 'This is our custom here. When the husband dies we bury his wife with him, and when the wife dies we bury her husband alive so that they may not be parted either in life or in death. This is a tradition handed down from our ancestors.' I asked him: 'O king of the age, in the case of a foreigner like me, if his wife dies here, would you treat him as you treated my friend?' 'Yes,' he replied, 'we would bury him with her just as you have seen.'

When I heard this, I was so concerned and distressed for myself that my gall bladder almost split and in my dismay I began to fear that my wife might die before me and that I would be buried alive with her. Then I tried to console myself, telling myself that it might be I who died first, for no one knows who will be first and who second. I tried to amuse myself in various ways, but within a short time my wife fell ill and a few days later she was dead. Most of the townsfolk came to pay their condolences to me and her family, and among those who came in accordance with their custom was the king. They fetched professionals who washed her corpse and dressed her in the most splendid of her clothes together with the best of her jewellery, necklaces and precious gems before placing her in her coffin. They then carried her off to the mountain, removed the stone from the mouth of the pit and threw her into it. My friends and my wife's family came up to take a last farewell of me. I was calling out: 'I'm a foreigner! I don't have to put up with your customs,' but they did not listen or pay any attention to me. Instead they seized me and used force to tie me up, attaching the seven loaves and the jug of fresh water that their custom required, before lowering me into the pit, which turned out to be a vast cavern under the mountain. 'Loose yourself from the rope!' they shouted, but I wasn't willing to do that and so they threw the rest of it down on top of me before replacing the huge stone that covered the entrance and going away.

Night 554

Morning now dawned and Shahrazad broke off from what she had been allowed to say. Then, when it was the five hundred and fifty-fourth night, SHE CONTINUED:

I have heard, O fortunate king, that when Sindbad was put into the pit with his dead wife they closed up its entrance and went off. SINDBAD SAID:

In the pit I came across very many corpses together with a foul stink of putrefaction and I blamed myself for my own actions, telling myself that I deserved everything that had happened to me. While I was there I could not distinguish night from day and I began by putting myself on short rations, not eating until I was half-dead with hunger and drinking only when I was violently thirsty, because I was afraid of exhausting my food and my water. I recited the formula: 'There is no might and no power except with God, the Exalted, the Omnipotent,' adding: 'Why did I have the misfortune to marry in this city? Every time I say to myself that I have escaped from one disaster, I fall into another that is worse. By God, this is a terrible death. I wish that I had been drowned at sea or had died on the mountains, for that would have been better than this miserable end.'

I went on like this, blaming myself, sleeping on the bones of the dead and calling on Almighty God to aid me. I longed for death, but, in spite of my plight, death would not come and this continued until I was consumed by hunger and parched by thirst. I sat down and felt for my bread, after which I ate a little and drank a little before getting up and walking round the cavern. This was wide with some empty hollows, but the surface was covered with bodies as well as old dry bones. I made a place for myself at the side of it, far away from the recent corpses, and there I slept. I now had very little food left and I would only take one mouthful and one sip of water each day or at even longer intervals for fear of using up both food and water before my death. Things went on like this until one day, as I was sitting thinking about what I would do when my provisions were exhausted, the stone was suddenly moved and light shone down on me. While I was wondering what was happening, I saw people standing at the head of the shaft. They lowered a dead man and a live woman, who was weeping and screaming, and with her they sent down a large quantity of food and water. I watched her but she didn't see me, and when the stone had been replaced and the people had gone, I stood up with the shin bone of a dead man in my hand and, going up to her, I struck her on the middle of her head. She fell unconscious on the ground and I struck her a second and a third time, so killing her. I took her bread and what else she had, for I noticed she had with her a large quantity of ornaments, robes, necklaces, jewels and precious stones. When I had removed her food and water, I sat down to sleep in my place by the side of the cavern. Later I began to eat as little of the food as was needed to keep me alive lest it be used up too soon, leaving me to die of hunger and thirst.

I stayed down there for some time, killing all those who were buried alive with the dead and taking their food and water in order to survive. Then, one day, I woke from sleep to hear something making a noise at the side of the cavern. I asked myself what it could be, and so I got up and went towards whatever it was, carrying with me a dead man's shin bone. When the thing that was making the noise heard me, it fled away and I could see that it was an animal. I followed it to the upper part of the cave and there coming through a little hole I could see a ray of light like a star, appearing and then disappearing. At the sight of this, I made my way towards it, and the nearer I got, the broader the beam of light became, leaving me certain that there was an opening in the cave leading to the outer world. 'There must be some reason for this,' I said to myself. 'Either it is another opening, like the one through which I was lowered, or it is a crack leading out of here.' I thought the matter over for a while and then went towards the light. Here I discovered that there was a tunnel dug by wild beasts from the surface of the mountain to allow them to get in, eat their fill of the corpses and then get out again. On seeing this I calmed down, regained my composure and relaxed, being certain that, after my brush with death, I would manage to stay alive.

Like a man in a dream, I struggled through the tunnel to find myself overlooking the sea coast on a high and impassable mountain promontory that cut off the island and its city from the seas that met there. In my delight, I gave praise and thanks to God, and then, taking heart, I went back through the tunnel to the cave and removed all the food and water that I had saved. I took some clothes from the dead to put on in place of my own, and I also collected a quantity of what they were wearing in the way of necklaces, gems, strings of pearls and jewellery of silver and gold, studded with precious stones of all kinds, together with other rare items. I fastened the clothes of the dead to my own and went through the tunnel to stand by the seashore. Every day I would go back down to inspect the cave, and whenever there was a burial I would kill the survivor, whether it was a man or a woman, and take the food and the water. Then I would go out of the tunnel and sit by the shore, waiting for Almighty God to send me relief in the form of a passing ship. I started to remove all the jewellery that I could see from the cave, tying it up in dead men's clothes.

Things went on like this for some time . . .

Night 555

Morning now dawned and Shahrazad broke off from what she had been allowed to say. Then, when it was the five hundred and fifty-fifth night, SHE CONTINUED:

I have heard, O fortunate king, that SINDBAD SAID:

I started to remove from the cave whatever jewellery and other such things as I came across, until one day, while I was sitting by the shore, I saw a passing ship out at sea in the middle of the waves. I took something white from the clothes of the dead, fastened it to a stick and ran along with it, parallel to the shore, waving it towards the ship, until the crew turned and caught sight of me as I stood on a high point. They put in towards me until they could hear my voice, and then they sent me a boat manned by some of their crew. As they came close they said: 'Who are you and why are you sitting there? How did you get to this mountain? Never in our lives have we seen anyone who managed to reach it.' I told them: 'I'm a merchant whose ship was sunk. I got on a plank together with my belongings, and by God's aid I was able to come up on shore here, bringing them with me, but only after I had exerted myself and used all my skill in a hard struggle.'

The sailors took me with them in the boat, carrying what I had fetched from the cave tied up in clothes and shrouds. They brought me to the ship, together with all of these things, and took me to the master, who asked: 'Man, how did you get here? This is a huge mountain with a great city on the other side of it, but although I have spent my life sailing this sea and passing by it, I have never seen anything on it except beasts and birds.' 'I'm a merchant,' I told him, 'but the large ship on which I was sailing broke up and sank. All these goods of mine, and the clothes that you see, were plunged into the water, but I managed to load them on to a large beam from the ship and fate helped me to come to shore by this mountain, after which I waited for someone to pass by and take me off.' I said nothing about what had happened to me in the city or in the cave, for fear that someone on board might be from the city. Then I took a quantity of my goods to the master of the ship and said: 'Sir, it is thanks to you that I have escaped from this mountain, so please take these things in return for the kindness you have shown me.' The master did not accept, insisting: 'We take no gifts from anyone, and if we see a shipwrecked man on the coast or on an island we take him with us and give him food and water. If he is naked we clothe him, and when we reach a safe haven we give him a present from what we have with us as an act of generosity for the sake of Almighty God.' On hearing that, I prayed God to grant him a long life.

We then sailed on from island to island and from sea to sea. I was hopeful that I would escape my difficulties, but although I was full of joy that I had been saved, whenever I thought of how I had sat in the cave with my wife I would almost go out of my mind. Through the power of God we came safely to Basra, where I landed and spent a few days before going on to Baghdad. There I went to my own district and, when I had entered my house, I met my family and friends and asked them how they were. They were delighted by my safe return and congratulated me. I then stored all the goods that I had with me in my warehouses and distributed alms and gifts, providing clothes for the widows and orphans. I was filled with joy and delight and renewed old ties with friends and companions, enjoying amusements and entertainments.

These, then, were the most remarkable things that happened to me on my fourth voyage, but, my brother, dine with me this evening, take your usual present of gold, come back tomorrow and I shall tell you of my experiences on my fifth voyage, as these were stranger and more wonderful than anything that happened before.

Sindbad the sailor then ordered that Sindbad the porter be given a hundred *mithqals* of gold. Tables were set and the company dined, before dispersing in a state of astonishment, as each story was more surprising than the last. Sindbad the porter went home and spent the night filled with happiness and contentedness as well as with amazement. The next day, when dawn broke, he got up, performed the morning prayer and walked to the house of Sindbad the sailor, whom he greeted. His host welcomed him and told him to sit with him until the rest of his companions arrived, after which they ate, drank and enjoyed themselves, chatting to one another. Then Sindbad the sailor began to speak.

Night 556

Morning now dawned and Shahrazad broke off from what she had been allowed to say. Then, when it was the five hundred and fifty-sixth night, SHE CONTINUED:

I have heard, O fortunate king, that Sindbad began to tell of his adventures and experiences. HE SAID:

Know, my friends, that when I had returned from my fourth voyage I immersed myself in pleasure, enjoyment and relaxation, forgetting all my past experiences and sufferings because I was so delighted by what I had gained in the way of profit. I then again felt the urge to travel and to see foreign lands and islands and so, after thinking things over, I bought valuable goods suitable for a voyage, packed them in bales and travelled from Baghdad, heading for Basra. When I got to the coast I saw a tall ship, large and with good lines and new fittings, which so took my fancy that I bought it. I hired a captain and a crew under the supervision of my own slaves and servants, and then loaded it with my merchandise. A number of merchants arrived and paid me to take them and their goods on board, after which we set out cheerfully and happily, looking forward to a safe and profitable voyage.

We travelled from island to island and from sea to sea, inspecting islands and lands, and disembarking to trade. Things went on like this until one day we came to a large, uninhabited island. This was a barren waste, but on it was a huge white dome which, on investigation, turned out to be a gigantic *rukh*'s egg. The merchants who came up to look at it did not recognize what it was and so they broke into it by striking at it with stones. A large amount of fluid came out and then they could see the *rukh* chick. They dragged this out of the egg, killed it and cut off large quantities of its flesh. I was on board at the time and they did not tell me what they had done until one of the passengers said to me: 'Sir, get up and look at this egg which we thought was a dome.' When I got up to look and saw the merchants striking at the egg, I shouted: 'Don't do that or the *rukh* will come, sink our ship and destroy us!' They did not listen to me, but while they were busy with the egg the sun was hidden away from us; the day was obscured and a cloud darkened the sky. We looked up to find what was between us and the sun, and there we could see the wings of a *rukh*, which were blocking the sunlight from us and shadowing the sky.

When the *rukh* found its egg cracked, it shrieked at us until it was joined by its mate, and the two of them started to circle around our ship, screaming at us with a noise louder than thunder. I cried to the captain and the crew to put out to sea for safety before we could be destroyed. The merchants came on board and the captain cast off the ship's lines as fast as he could, and we left the island heading out to sea. The *rukh* saw us and left us for a while as we sailed with all the speed we could in order to escape and win clear of its territory. Suddenly, however, we caught sight of the two of them following our course. They caught up with us, each carrying in its talons an enormous rock that it had picked up in the mountains. One of them dropped its rock on us, but as the captain hauled round the rudder, the falling rock narrowly missed us, although when it fell into the sea beneath the ship, its huge impact tossed us up and down and gave us a view of the seabed. Then its mate dropped the one that it was carrying, which was smaller than the other, but, as fate had decreed, it fell on our stern, smashing it, breaking the rudder into twenty pieces and plunging all on board into the sea. As I tried my best to save myself for dear life's sake, Almighty God sent me one of the ship's timbers and, after clinging to this, I managed to get astride it and started to use my feet as paddles, helped on my way by wind and wave.

It happened that the ship had gone down near an island in the middle of the sea and divine providence cast me ashore. I was at my last gasp when I came to land, half-dead with what I had experienced in the way of hardship, distress, hunger and thirst. For some time I lay sprawled on the shore, but when I had rested and regained my composure I penetrated into the island and discovered it to be like one of the gardens of Paradise, with flourishing trees, gushing waters and birds that chanted the praises of the Glorious and Eternal God. There were many trees and fruits, as well as flowers of all kinds, and so I ate my fill of the fruits and satisfied my thirst by drinking from the streams, giving thanks to Almighty God and praising Him.

Night 557

Morning now dawned and Shahrazad broke off from what she had been allowed to say. Then, when it was the five hundred and fifty-seventh night, SHE CONTINUED:

I have heard, O fortunate king, that when Sindbad escaped drowning and reached the island, he ate from its fruits and drank from its streams, giving thanks and praise to Almighty God. HE SAID:

I stayed there like that until evening came and night fell, when, thanks to the combination of hardship and fear that I experienced, I slept like the dead, having heard no sound on the island or seen anyone. I stayed asleep until morning, and then I got to my feet and was walking among the trees when I came across a stream flowing from a spring of water beside which was seated a fine-looking old man with a waist-wrapper made of leaves. I thought to myself that he might have come to the island as a survivor from a wrecked ship and so I went up to him and greeted him. He returned my greeting with a gesture but said nothing. I then asked him why he was sitting there, but he shook his head sadly and gestured with his hand as if to say: 'Carry me from here on your shoulders to the other side of the stream.' I said to myself: 'If I do him this service and carry him where he wants, God may reward me for the good deed.' So I went up to him and when I had lifted him on my shoulders I carried him to where he had been pointing before, telling him to take his time in getting down. But, far from doing that, he wrapped his legs around my neck, and when I looked at them I could see that they were black and rough as buffalo hide. I took fright and tried to throw him off, but he squeezed my neck with his legs, nearly throttling me. Everything turned black and I lost consciousness, falling to the ground in a dead faint. Then he raised his legs and beat me painfully on the back and shoulders until I got up again with him still on my shoulders. I was tired of carrying him, but he gestured to me with his hand to take him through the trees to the best fruits. When I tried to disobey him, he used his legs to strike me more violently than if he had whipped me.

He kept on pointing where he wanted to go, and I would take him there. If I faltered or was slow he would beat me, and I was like his prisoner. We went through the trees to the centre of the island with him urinating and defecating on my shoulders. This went on night and day, for when he wanted to sleep he would wind his legs around my neck, have a brief nap and then get up and beat me to make me rise in a hurry. So severe were my sufferings that I had no power to disobey him, and I blamed myself for having lifted him up in the first place out of pity. Things went on like this until I reached the point of complete exhaustion and I said to myself: 'I did him a good turn but it has turned out badly for me and, by God, I shall never do anyone else a service as long as I live.' Such were my hardships and distress that every minute and every hour I wished that Almighty God would let me die.

When this had lasted for some time, a day came when I carried my incubus to a place on the island where there were great quantities of gourds, many of which were dry. I took a large one of these, removed its top and cleaned it out, after which I took it to a vine and squeezed grapes into it until it was full. Then I closed it up again and put it out in the sun, where I left it a number of days until its contents had turned to pure wine. I started to drink some of this each day to help me fight off exhaustion in my dealings with that devil, as every sip that I took strengthened my resolution. One day, when he saw me drinking, he gestured with his hand as if to say: 'What is that?' 'Something pleasant,' I told him, 'that brings encouragement and enjoyment,' and I began to run with him, dancing between the trees, stimulated by the wine, clapping my hands and singing with joy. On seeing this, he gestured to me to hand him the gourd so that he could drink from it, and in my fear I handed it over to him. He gulped down all that was left in it, threw it on the ground and became merry and unsteady on my shoulders, until, when he had become even more sodden in his drunkenness, his whole body relaxed and he started to sway from side to side on my shoulders. When I saw that he was drunk and unconscious, I took hold of his legs and unwrapped them from my neck, after which I lowered myself to the ground with him, and sat down, throwing him off.

Night 558

Morning now dawned and Shahrazad broke off from what she had been allowed to say. Then, when it was the five hundred and fifty-eighth night, SHE CONTINUED:

I have heard, O fortunate king, that Sindbad threw the devil from his shoulders. HE SAID:

I could scarcely believe that I had managed to free myself and escape from my miserable state, but I then began to fear that, when he recovered from his drunkenness, he might do me some harm and so I picked up a large rock, went up to him as he slept and struck him a blow on the head that left him a lifeless mass of mixed flesh and blood, may God show him no mercy.

In my relief I walked to where I had first come ashore on the coast of the island, and there I stayed for some time, eating fruit, drinking from the streams and keeping a lookout for any passing ship. One day, I was sitting thinking over what had happened to me and the plight that I was in, wondering whether God would allow me to return safely to my own country to rejoin my family and friends, when suddenly a ship came sailing through the boisterous sea waves without a check until it anchored by the island. Those on board disembarked and I went up to them. When they caught sight of me, they hurried up and gathered around me, asking me about myself and why I had come to the island. They were astonished when I told them about my experiences, and they said: 'The man who rode on your shoulders is called the Old Man of the Sea, and you are the only one on whom he mounted who has ever escaped. God be praised that you are safe!' They fetched me food, and I ate until I had had enough, after which they gave me some clothes to wear in order to cover my nakedness and they then took me with them to their ship.

We sailed for some days and nights until fate brought us to a lofty city, all of whose houses overlooked the sea. The place is known as the City of the Apes, and at nightfall all its inhabitants leave by the sea gates and embark on skiffs and boats, spending the night at sea lest the apes come down from the mountains and attack them. I went ashore in order to look around, but before I knew it, my ship had sailed off, leaving me to regret having landed there. I remembered my companions and my first and second adventures with the apes and so I sat there weeping sorrowfully. One of the townsfolk approached me and said: 'Sir, it seems that you are a stranger here.' 'Yes,' I told him, 'I am a poor stranger. I was on board a ship that anchored here and I disembarked to look at the city, but when I got back no ship was to be seen.' 'Come with us,' he said, 'and get into this skiff, for if you stay here at night the apes will kill you.' 'To hear is to obey,' I replied, and so I got up immediately and went on board with the man and his companions. They pushed the boat out from land, sailing on until they were a mile off shore, and there I spent the night with them. The next morning they sailed back to the city, where they disembarked, and each of them went about his business. They did this every night, and any of them who stayed behind in the city at night was set upon by the apes and killed. In the day the apes would leave the city, eat fruit in the orchards and sleep in the mountains until evening, when they would come back to the city, which is in the furthest part of the lands of the Blacks.

The most remarkable thing that happened to me there was when one of the group with whom I had spent the night on the boat asked me whether I, being a stranger in those parts, had any trade that I could practise. 'No, by God, brother,' I told him. 'I am a merchant and a man of means. I owned a ship which was laden with wealth and goods, but it was wrecked at sea with the loss of everything on it and it was only by God's leave that I escaped drowning. He sent me a piece of timber on to which I clambered, and it was to this that I owed my safety.' The man then brought me a cotton bag and told me to take it and fill it with pebbles from the city. He went on: 'Go out with a group of townspeople to whom I will introduce you as a companion, telling them to look after you. Do what they do, and this may bring you something to help you get back to your own land.' He took me out of the city, where I selected a number of small pebbles to fill my bag. We then saw a group of men coming out to whom my mentor introduced me, commending me to their care and telling them: 'This man is a stranger, so take him with you and teach him the gatherers' trade so that he may be able to earn his daily bread, and God may reward you.' 'To hear is to obey,' they answered, and they welcomed me and took me with them on their expedition.

Each one of these men carried with him a bag like mine, filled with pebbles, and they walked on until they reached a broad valley with many high trees that no one could climb. In the valley were large numbers of apes who were alarmed by the sight of us and swarmed up the trees. My companions started to pelt them with the stones that they had in their bags, to which the apes replied by breaking off from the trees and throwing down what turned out to be coconuts. When I saw what the others were doing, I picked out an enormous tree with many apes on it, went up to it and started to throw stones at them. The apes tore off coconuts and when they threw them down at me, I gathered them, as the others were doing, and by the time that I had used up all the stones in my bag, I had got a large number of nuts. When everyone had finished what they were doing, they put together all they had collected and we went back to the city in what was left of the day, each of us carrying as much as he could.

I went to my friend who had introduced me to the others and gave him what I had gathered, thanking him for his kindness, but he told me to keep the nuts and sell them so as to profit from the sale price. He then gave me the key to a room in his house, telling me: 'Store the surplus coconuts here; go out with the gatherers every day just as you did today; then pick out the bad nuts and sell them, using what you get for them for your own purposes, while storing the good ones here. It may be that you can save enough to help you with your voyage home.' 'Almighty God will reward you,' I told him.

I then did what he told me, filling my bag with stones every day, going out with the gatherers and doing what they did, as they helped me with advice, showing me trees that had plenty of nuts. This went on until I had collected a large store of good coconuts and had made a lot of money from what I had sold. I started to buy whatever took my fancy and found myself enjoying life as my status increased throughout the city. Things continued like this until one day, as I was standing by the shore, I saw a ship that steered for the city and anchored off the shore. On board were merchants with their goods, and they started to trade, buying up coconuts as well as other things. I went to my friend and, after I had told him of the arrival of the ship, I said that I wanted to go back home. 'It is for you to decide,' he told me, and so I took my leave of him, having thanked him for his kindness to me. Then I went to the ship, met the captain and paid him to take me with him, after which I stowed my coconuts and what else I had on board.

Night 559

Morning now dawned and Shahrazad broke off from what she had been allowed to say. Then, when it was the five hundred and fifty-ninth night, SHE CONTINUED:

I have heard, O fortunate king, that Sindbad left the City of the Apes and went on board the ship, taking with him his coconuts and his other belongings, and paying the captain for a passage. HE SAID:

The ship sailed that same day, and we went from island to island and sea to sea. Whenever we stopped at an island, I would use my coconuts for trade and barter, and God gave me in exchange more than I had had with me at the start and had lost. One island that we passed produced cinnamon and pepper, and some people told me they had seen that every bunch of pepper had a large leaf to shade it and to keep off raindrops in wet weather. When the rain stopped, the leaf would turn away and hang down at the side of the bunch. In exchange for coconuts I took away with me a large quantity of cinnamon and pepper from there. Later we passed the island of al-Asirat, which produces Qumari aloes wood, and after that another island, five days' journey in length, which has Chinese aloes wood that is superior in quality to the Qumari. The inhabitants of this latter island are more degraded and irreligious than those of the former: they are fond of depravity, they drink wine and know nothing about the call to prayer or how to pray.

Later we came to the pearl beds, and here I gave the divers some of my coconuts and told them to go down and see what my luck would bring them. They dived there and came up with a great quantity of large and valuable pearls. 'By God, master,' they told me, 'your luck was in!' I put all that they had brought me on board and we sailed off with the blessing of Almighty God, carrying on until we reached Basra.

I landed at Basra and, having stayed there for a short time, I left for Baghdad, where I went to my own district and came to my house. When I greeted my family and my friends, they congratulated me on my safe return and, after having put all the goods that I had with me in store, I clothed widows and orphans, gave away alms and gifts and made presents to my family, my companions and my friends. God had recompensed me with four times more than I had lost, and thanks to this profit I forgot all the hardships that I had suffered and I reverted to the friendly social life that I had enjoyed before. These were my most remarkable experiences on my fifth voyage, but it is now time for supper.

When the company had finished eating, Sindbad the sailor ordered Sindbad the porter to be given a hundred *mithqals* of gold, which he took before leaving, filled with wonder at what had happened. The next morning he got up, performed the morning prayer and returned to Sindbad the sailor's house, where, on entering, he greeted his host. He was told to take a seat and the two Sindbads sat talking together until the rest of the company arrived. They chatted to one another, and when tables had been laid with food, they ate, drank and enjoyed themselves, after which SINDBAD THE SAILOR BEGAN TO TELL THEM THE STORY OF HIS SIXTH VOYAGE:

Know, my dear friends and companions, that after my return from my fifth voyage, in my pleasures, enjoyments and happy contentment I forgot all my past hardships. I remained in this state of joy and gladness until, while I was sitting relaxed and satisfied, a number of merchants came to me having obviously just returned from a voyage. I remembered my own return and how delighted I had been to rejoin my family, my companions and my friends, together with the pleasure I had experienced at returning to my own land. I felt a longing for travel and trade and so I made up my mind to set out once again. I bought splendid and valuable goods suitable for a voyage, and, having loaded my bales, I travelled from Baghdad to Basra. There I found a large ship, on board which were traders and men of importance who had with them costly goods. I stowed my own with theirs on the ship, and we left Basra in safety.

Night 560

Morning now dawned and Shahrazad broke off from what she had been allowed to say. Then, when it was the five hundred and sixtieth night, SHE CONTINUED:

I have heard, O fortunate king, that Sindbad prepared his bales and loaded them on a ship at Basra before setting out on his voyage. SINDBAD SAID:

We sailed on from place to place and city to city, trading and looking at foreign lands. Fortune was with us; our voyage went well and we made profits until one day, as we were sailing on our way, the captain suddenly gave a great cry, threw down his turban, struck his face and plucked at his beard before collapsing in the centre of the ship, overcome by distress. Merchants and passengers gathered around him to ask what was the matter. 'You must know,' he told us all, 'that we have strayed from our course. We have left the sea on which we were sailing and entered one whose ways I do not know. Unless God sends us some means of escape we are all dead, so pray to Him to save us from this.' He then got up and climbed the mast with the intention of lowering the sail, but the wind was too strong and the ship was driven back. While we were near a lofty mountain the rudder was smashed and the captain climbed down from the mast reciting the formula: 'There is no might and no power except with God, the Exalted, the Omnipotent,' and adding: 'No one can ward off fate. By God, we are in mortal peril and there is no possible escape for us.'

Everyone on the ship wept for themselves and said their farewells, convinced that their lives were at an end and there was no hope left. The ship struck the mountain and was dashed to pieces, its timbers being scattered and everything in it being submerged in the waves. The merchants fell into the sea; some were drowned while others, including me, came to land by clinging on to the mountainside. The island on which we found ourselves turned out to be a big one and was the site of a large number of wrecks; the beach was full of goods thrown up by the sea from sunken ships whose crews had been lost, the extent of this jetsam being enough to bewilder and confuse the mind.

I climbed to the highest point there, and as I walked I caught sight of a freshwater spring gushing out at the base of the mountain and flowing to a point opposite it. All the survivors from the ship who had come ashore scattered throughout the island and, dazed by the quantity of goods and effects that they saw on the beach, they started to act like madmen. For my part, I saw in the middle of the spring great numbers of gems of all sorts, precious stones, sapphires and huge pearls fit for kings. They were lying like pebbles in the bed of the stream as it flowed through the low ground, and the land surrounding the spring sparkled because of the precious stones and other such things that it contained. We also discovered there a quantity of the finest quality Chinese aloes wood together with Qumari aloes, as well as a spring that produces a type of raw ambergris which oozes out like wax over its sides, thanks to the sun's heat, and extends along the shore. Sea creatures then come out and swallow it before returning to the sea, and when it becomes heated in their bellies they vomit it out and it solidifies on the surface of the water. Both its colour and its condition change and the waves drive it on shore where travellers and traders, who can recognize it, collect it and then sell it. Pure raw ambergris that has not gone through this process overflows the side of that spring and solidifies on the ground. When the sun rises, it melts again, producing a scent which makes the whole valley smell of musk, and when the sun leaves it, it solidifies. The place where this raw ambergris is to be found is completely inaccessible, for the mountain range that rings the island is unscalable.

We continued to wander around the island looking at the resources that Almighty God had provided there, but bewildered by what we could see of our own situation and full of fear. We collected some provisions by the shore and started to ration them out, eating a mouthful every day or every second day to avoid using up our food and then dying miserably of starvation and fear. We would wash the corpses of all those who died and shroud them in what clothes and materials were washed up on the beach. Many did die, leaving only a few behind, as we had been weakened by stomach pains caused by our exposure to the sea. Within a short time every one of my friends and companions had died, one after the other, and had been buried, leaving me alone on the island. Of our large store of food, only a little was left, and I wept over my plight, saying: 'I wish that I had died before my companions so that they could have washed my body and buried me, but there is no might and no power except with God, the Exalted, the Omnipotent.'

Night 561

Morning now dawned and Shahrazad broke off from what she had been allowed to say. Then, when it was the five hundred and sixty-first night, SHE CONTINUED:

I have heard, O fortunate king, that Sindbad buried all his companions and was left alone on the island. HE WENT ON:

Soon after this I got up and dug myself a deep grave beside the shore, saying to myself: 'When I sicken and know that death is at hand, I shall lie down in this grave and die there. The wind will keep blowing sand over me until it covers me and so I shall be buried.' I started to blame myself for the folly that had made me leave my country and my city in order to travel to foreign parts, in spite of what I had suffered on my first, second, third, fourth and fifth voyages. On every single one of them I had been faced with terrors and hardships that grew worse and worse each time. I did not believe that I could escape to safety and I regretted having set out to sea again, telling myself that I had been in no need of money for I had plenty, so much, in fact, that I could not have spent it all, or even half of it, in my lifetime. That was enough and more than enough.

Then, however, I started to think the matter over and I told myself: 'The stream fed by the spring must have an end as well as a beginning, and there has to be a place where it flows into inhabited country. The right thing to do is for me to make myself a small raft, big enough for me to sit on, which I can take down and launch on the stream. I can set off on it, and if I find a way out, then God willing I shall escape, and if I don't, then it will be better to die there than here.'

Having sighed over my fate, I got up and worked hard at collecting timber from the island, both Chinese and Qumari aloes wood. What I got I lashed together on the shore with ropes from wrecked ships, and then I took matching planks from them and set them on top of the timbers. I made the raft just about as broad as the stream, or a little bit less, tying it together as firmly as I could. I took with me a store of precious stones, gems, cash and pearls as big as pebbles, together with other treasures from the island, as well as some good, pure, raw ambergris. This I loaded on to the raft together with everything else I had collected from the island, and I took all the food that was left. I then launched the raft on the stream, adding two pieces of wood, one on either side, to serve as oars, following the advice of the poet who said:

> Leave a place where there is injustice;
> Abandon the house to lament its builder.
> You can find another land in place of that one,
> But you will never find another life.
> Do not let the blows of fate concern you;
> Every misfortune will reach its end.
> Whoever is fated to die in a certain land
> Will die in no other place than that.
> Send out no messenger on a grave matter;
> The soul's one sincere advisor is itself.

I set out downstream on the raft, wondering what was going to happen to me. I reached the place where the stream entered an underground channel in the mountain, and as the raft came to this passage I found myself plunging into thick darkness. The raft was swept on by the current until it got to a place so narrow that its sides rubbed against the edges of the channel, while my head scraped the roof. I had no way of going back and I started to reproach myself for having put my life in danger, telling myself: 'If this is too narrow for the raft, there can be little chance that it will get out, and as I cannot go back, there can be no doubt that I will die a miserable death here.' I lay face down on the raft because of the lack of space and drifted on with no means of telling whether it was night or day because of the darkness under the mountain. I was terrified and in fear of my life the further I went along the stream, which widened at times only to narrow again. The darkness made me feel extremely tired; I couldn't resist falling into a doze and so I went to sleep, face downwards, and how far it travelled while I slept I could not tell.

When I woke, I found myself out in the light and, opening my eyes, I discovered that I was on a broad stretch of shore with the raft moored to an island. There was a crowd of Indians and Abyssinians around me, and when they saw me get up they came up to me and spoke to me in their own tongue. I couldn't understand what they were saying and I kept thinking that it was all a dream, as I was still suffering from the effects of the hardships that had overwhelmed me. Since I couldn't follow their language and could make no reply, one of them approached me and said in Arabic: 'Peace be on you, brother. What are you? Where have you come from and why are you here? How did you get into this stream and what land is there behind the mountain, as we have never known of anyone coming to us from there?' 'Who are you?' I asked in my turn, 'and what land is this?' 'Brother,' he answered, 'we are farmers and we had come to water the crops and fields that we cultivate when we discovered you asleep on this raft. We took hold of it and tied it up here so that you could get up at your leisure. But now tell us why you have come here.' 'For God's sake, sir,' I said, 'bring me some food for I am starving, and after that ask me any questions you want.' The man hurried off to fetch food, and when I had eaten my fill, I relaxed, regained my composure and recovered my spirits. I gave thanks to Almighty God for all His mercies and was filled with joy to have emerged from the river and to have reached these people. I then told them everything that had happened to me from start to finish, including my experiences in the narrow stream.

Night 562

Morning now dawned and Shahrazad broke off from what she had been allowed to say. Then, when it was the five hundred and sixty-second night, SHE CONTINUED:

I have heard, O fortunate king, that when the raft beached on the island and Sindbad saw a group of Indians and Abyssinians there, he relaxed. They asked him to tell them his story. SINDBAD WENT ON:

After talking among themselves, they told me that they would have to bring me with them in order to show me to their king so that I might tell him what had happened to me. So they took me, together with the raft and all the cash, goods, gems, precious stones and jewellery that was on it, and when they brought me into the king's presence, they told him about me. He welcomed me warmly and asked me about myself and what had happened to me, after which I told him the full story of my adventures from beginning to end. The tale filled him with astonishment and he congratulated me on my escape. I then went to the raft and took a large quantity of precious stones, gems, aloes wood and raw ambergris, which I presented to him and which he accepted, showing me even greater honour and lodging me in his palace. I associated with the leading citizens, who treated me with the greatest respect, and I did not leave the palace.

Visitors to the island would ask me about my own land and in return for what I told them I would ask and receive information about theirs. One day, the king questioned me about my country and about the rule of the caliph in the lands of Baghdad, at which I told him about the justice with which he controlled his state. He was impressed by this and said: 'By God, the caliph acts in a rational and an attractive way. You have endeared him to me and I intend to prepare a present for him and to get you to take it to him.' 'To hear is to obey, master,' I said. 'I shall bring it to him and tell him that you are an affectionate friend.'

For some time I continued to stay with the king, enjoying the greatest honour and respect and leading a pleasant life, until one day, when I was sitting in the palace, I got news that a number of the townspeople had prepared a ship with the intention of sailing to the region of Basra. I told myself that I should go with them as I would never have a better opportunity than this, and so I immediately hurried off, kissed the king's hand and told him that I wanted to leave with this group on the ship that they had fitted out, as I felt a longing for my own people and my own land. 'Do what you like,' he told me, adding, 'but if you want to stay with us, you will be welcome, as we have become fond of you.' 'You have overwhelmed me with your kindness and generosity,' I replied, 'but I feel a longing for my people, my country and my family.' When he heard this, he called for the merchants who had fitted out the ship and instructed them to look after me. He made me many presents, as well as paying for my passage on the ship, and he entrusted me with a splendid gift for the caliph Harun al-Rashid in Baghdad. I took my leave of him and of all the friends whose company I had frequented, and then embarked with the merchants. We set sail, relying on God, and had a pleasant voyage with fair winds, passing from sea to sea and island to island, until, through our reliance on God, we arrived safely at Basra.

After I had disembarked, I stayed at Basra for some days and nights until I made my preparations, loaded my goods and set off for Baghdad, the City of Peace. There I had an audience with the caliph, to whom I presented the king's gift together with a full account of what had happened to me. When I had placed all my wealth and goods in store, I went to my own district, where I was met by my family and friends, and I made gifts to all my family, distributing alms and giving presents. Some time later, the caliph sent to ask me the reason behind the gift that had been given to him and details about its source. I told him: 'By God, Commander of the Faithful, I don't know the name of the city from which it came nor how to get there, but when the ship on which I was travelling was sunk, I came ashore on an island with a river in the middle of it on which I launched a raft that I had made for myself.' I went on to repeat what had happened to me on my voyage, how I had got clear of the river and reached the city, what had happened when I had got there and why I had been sent back with the gift.

The caliph was astonished by my tale, and he ordered the recorders to write it down and store the account in his treasury so as to provide a lesson for all who might read it. He then showed me the greatest favour and I stayed in Baghdad, living as well as I had done before and forgetting all my sufferings from beginning to end, while I enjoyed the pleasantest of lives in pleasure and delight. This, then, my brothers, is what happened to me on my sixth voyage and, God willing, I shall tell you of my seventh, which was even more strange and remarkable than the others.

*

Sindbad the sailor then ordered tables to be set with food, and when his guests had dined with him he ordered that Sindbad the porter be given a hundred *mithqals* of gold. The porter took the gift and went off as the other guests dispersed, astonished by what they had heard.

Night 563

Morning now dawned and Shahrazad broke off from what she had been allowed to say. Then, when it was the five hundred and sixty-third night, SHE CONTINUED:

I have heard, O fortunate king, that when Sindbad had told the story of his sixth voyage, all the company went off. As for Sindbad the porter, he spent the night at home and then, after having performed the morning prayer, he went to the house of Sindbad the sailor, who, when all the rest of the company had assembled, began to tell them the story of the seventh voyage. HE SAID:

You must know that when I returned from my sixth voyage, I resumed my former lifestyle of pleasure, relaxation and delight, and for a time I enjoyed continuous happiness and gaiety night and day, my gains and profits having been enormous. However, I then felt a longing to travel in foreign lands, to sail, to associate with merchants and to listen to their stories. When I had thought the matter over, I packed a quantity of splendid goods suitable for a voyage and transported them from Baghdad to Basra. There I found a ship ready to put to sea, on board of which were a number of leading merchants. I embarked and made friends with them, and we set out on our voyage in good health and safety and with a fair wind we reached a city called Madinat al-Sin. We were very cheerful as we talked with one another about our journey and about matters of trade, but while we were doing this, a headwind blew up into a gale. Both we and our goods were drenched by torrential rain, and we had to cover the goods with felt and canvas lest they be ruined. We addressed our prayers and supplications to Almighty God, imploring him to rescue us from the storm, and as we were doing so the captain tightened his belt, tucked up his sleeves and climbed the mast. After looking right and left, he turned to us, slapped his face and plucked at his beard. 'What is the news, captain?' we asked him. 'Ask Almighty God to rescue us from our plight,' he answered. 'Weep for yourselves and take leave of one another, for the wind has driven us to the ultimate sea in the world.'

He then climbed down from the mast and opened a box from which he took a cotton bag. He undid its fastening and took from it soil that looked like ashes, which he moistened with water. After waiting a short while, he sniffed at it and then took a little book from the box, from which he read. He then told us that it contained an astonishing revelation, the gist of which was that no one who came to this part of the world would escape from it with his life. 'This,' he told us, 'is the Region of the Kings, which contains the grave of our master Solomon, the son of David, on both of whom be peace. In it there are enormous and hideous serpents which attack and swallow every ship that comes here together with all its contents.' We were dumbfounded on hearing what he had to say, but before he had finished speaking the ship was lifted up from the sea and then crashed down again and we were terrified to hear a roar like a peal of thunder, which left us half-dead and sure that we were about to perish. Then we saw a fish as big as a huge mountain making for the ship. In our fear we wept bitterly for ourselves and prepared to die, but as we watched it coming towards us, wondering at its formidable size, suddenly another one approached that was bigger than anything we had yet seen. We had said our farewells, shedding tears for ourselves, when we caught sight of a third monster, even larger than the first two. We lost all our senses, being stunned by fear and terror as these three creatures started to circle around the ship. The third of them had just opened its mouth to swallow it and everything in it, when suddenly the ship was lifted up by a violent gust and brought down on a huge reef, where it was smashed. All its timbers were scattered and its cargo, together with the merchants and passengers, was plunged into the sea.

I stripped down to a single garment and swam for a short time before I found one of the ship's timbers, to which I clung. I managed to get astride it and, as I held on to it, the winds and waves tossed me around on the surface of the sea. One moment I would be carried up on a wave and the next hurled down again, so that in my fear I had to face the most extreme hardships as well as sufferings caused by hunger and thirst. I started to blame myself for what I had done and for abandoning a life of ease in order to court difficulty. I told myself: 'Sindbad, you have not turned away from your folly. Time after time you face these hardships and difficulties but still you go to sea, and if you say that you have given this up, you lie. So you have to endure whatever misfortune you meet, as you deserve everything that happens to you . . .'

Night 564

Morning now dawned and Shahrazad broke off from what she had been allowed to say. Then, when it was the five hundred and sixty-fourth night, SHE CONTINUED:

I have heard, O fortunate king, that when Sindbad was thrown into the sea, he mounted on a wooden plank, telling himself: 'I deserve everything that has happened to me, and all this is decreed for you by Almighty God to turn you from your greed, which is the cause of your sufferings, in spite of the fact that you have riches in plenty.' HE WENT ON:

Then I came to my senses and said: 'This time I make a sincere promise to Almighty God that I will renounce travelling and never again talk of it or think about it.'

I continued to address tearful supplications to Almighty God, remembering the ease, joy, pleasure and relaxation that I had enjoyed, and things went on like this through the first day and the second day, but then I came to land on a large island with many trees and streams. I began to eat the fruits of the trees and drink from the streams until I had revived. My spirits came back; my resolution strengthened and I relaxed, after which I walked through the island and found on the other side of it a large freshwater river flowing with a strong current. I remembered my earlier adventure with the raft and I said to myself that I would have to construct another one like it in the hope that I might find a way out of my predicament. If I managed to escape, I would have got all that I wanted and I would swear to Almighty God never to set out on another voyage, while if I perished, I would be at rest and no longer have to face trouble and hardship. So I started to collect wood from the trees, and this, although I did not know it, was fine sandalwood, whose like was nowhere else to be found, and when I had done that, I managed to twist boughs and creepers from the island into what could serve as ropes, with which I lashed my raft together.

'If I come off safely,' I told myself, 'it will be God's doing,' and after that I boarded the raft and launched it on the river. It took me to the end of the island but then went even further, and for three whole days I floated on. For most of the time I slept; I ate nothing at all, but when I was thirsty I drank from the river. Weariness, hunger and thirst had reduced me to little more than a sick chicken by the time the raft brought me to a high mountain, under which the river entered. When I saw that, I feared for my life, remembering the straits in which I had found myself on my last river journey. I tried to stop the raft and to get off it on to the mountainside, but the current was too strong and it dragged the raft, with me on it, under the mountain. When I saw what was happening I was sure that I was going to die, and I recited the formula: 'There is no might and no power except with God, the Exalted, the Omnipotent.'

The raft floated on for a short distance, but then it reached a broad stretch where I could see a large valley into which the water fell with a roar like thunder and a rush like that of wind. I clutched my raft with both hands, fearful I might fall off. The waves were tossing me right and left as the current carried the raft down into the valley, and I could neither stop it nor bring it in towards the shore. This went on until it brought me alongside a large and well-built city, full of people, and when they saw the current carrying me downstream on my raft in the middle of the river, they threw me nets and ropes. They managed to bring the raft in to land and there I collapsed half-dead of hunger, sleeplessness and terror.

One of the crowd of spectators, a dignified-looking old man, welcomed me and passed me a number of fine clothes with which I covered my nakedness. He then took me with him and brought me to the baths, before providing me with revivifying drinks and fragrant perfumes. When we left the baths he took me into his house, where his family showed pleasure at meeting me. I was made to sit in an elegant room and my host prepared some splendid food for me, which I ate until I was full, and I then gave thanks to Almighty God for having rescued me. Servants brought me hot water with which I washed my hands, and slave girls fetched silk towels, which I used to dry my hands and wipe my mouth. As soon as I had finished, the old man got up and provided me with a chamber of my own, standing by itself at the side of his house, and he gave instructions to his servants and slave girls to serve me and to do anything I might want. I remained being waited on in the guest chamber for three days, eating well, with plenty to drink and surrounded by pleasant scents, until, as my fears subsided, I recovered my spirits and became calm and relaxed.

On the fourth day, the old man came to me and said: 'We have enjoyed your company, my son, and we thank God that you are safe. Would you like to come down with me to the market by the shore where you can sell your goods? With the price that you get for them you may be able to buy some things that you can use for trade.' I stayed silent for a while, saying to myself: 'Where am I to get any goods and why is he talking like this?' But he said: 'Don't be concerned or worried, my son; come with me to the market and if you find someone who will give you an acceptable price for what you have, I shall take it for you, and if not, I shall put your goods in my warehouses and keep them until a better time comes for trading.' I thought this over and decided that I had better accept his offer in order to find out what these 'goods' might be. So I said: 'To hear is to obey, uncle, for whatever you do brings blessings, and I cannot disobey you in anything.' So I went with him to the market and found that he had taken my raft to pieces, it being of sandalwood, and had told the auctioneer to call for bids.

Night 565

Morning now dawned and Shahrazad broke off from what she had been allowed to say. Then, when it was the five hundred and sixty-fifth night, SHE CONTINUED:

I have heard, O fortunate king, that Sindbad went with the old man to the shore, where he found that his raft of sandalwood had been dismantled and the auctioneer was calling for bids. SINDBAD SAID:

The merchants gathered and when the bidding opened, it went up and up until it ended at a thousand dinars. The old man then turned to me and said: 'That is the price of your goods at times like these, my son. Do you want to sell at this price or would you prefer to wait? I can store the wood for you in my warehouses until the price rises and then sell it for you.' 'It is for you to decide, sir,' I told him, 'so do what you want.' 'My son,' he said, 'will you sell it to me for a hundred dinars more than the price offered by the merchants?' 'Certainly,' I told him. 'I agree to the sale and accept the price.' At that, he told his servants to remove the wood to his warehouses and I went back with him to his house. We sat down and he counted out the entire purchase price for me, after which he brought me bags in which the money was placed, and these were secured with an iron lock, whose key he handed over to me.

Some time later he said to me: 'My son, I have a proposal to make to you and I hope that you will follow my wishes in the matter.' I asked what this was, and he explained: 'I am now an old man. I have no son, but I do have a pretty young daughter, as rich as she is beautiful, whom

I would like to marry to you. You could then stay with her here in this country and I would pass over to you all my wealth and my possessions. For I am old and you can take my place.' I stayed silent for a time without speaking, and he went on: 'Obey me in this, my son. I want to help you and, if you do what I ask, I will marry you to my daughter; you will be like a son to me and every single thing that I own will pass to you. If you want to go trading and to travel to your own country, no one will stop you. This wealth is at your disposal, so do what you want with it and make your own choice.' 'By God, uncle,' I told him, 'you have become like a father to me. I have experienced so many terrors that I no longer have any powers of judgement or know what to do, and as a result it is up to you to do whatever you want.' At this point the old man told his servants to fetch the *qadi* and the notaries, which they did, and he then gave his daughter to me in marriage and provided a grand feast by way of celebration. When I was taken to my bride, I found her to be very lovely indeed, well shaped and wearing ornaments, robes, valuable stones, jewellery, necklaces and precious gems which, although no one could have valued them exactly, were worth thousands upon thousands of dinars. I was filled with delight when I lay with her, and we fell in love with each other.

I stayed with my wife for some time, enjoying the greatest happiness and contentment. Her father was then gathered to the merciful presence of Almighty God. We prepared him for the funeral and then buried him, after which I took over all his possessions while all his attendants were transferred to my service. He had been the leader of the merchants, none of whom, thanks to his status, had done any dealings without his knowledge and consent, and they now put me in his place as his successor.

On further association with the townsfolk, I discovered that once a month a change came over them. They could be seen to sprout wings, with which they would fly off into the upper air, leaving no one in the city apart from children and women. I told myself that on the first of the month I would ask one of them to take me with them to wherever they were going. When the first of the month arrived, their complexions changed as their appearance altered, and so I went to one of them and begged him for God's sake to take me with him as a spectator and then bring me back. He told me that this was impossible, but I kept pressing him until he consented, and when I had got the agreement of the others, without telling any of my household, my servants or my companions,

I clung on to him as he soared with me up into the sky. He flew so high with me on his shoulders that to my astonishment I heard the angels in the dome of heaven glorifying God. I said: 'Glory and praise be to God,' but before I had finished, fire came out of heaven, which almost consumed the townsfolk. They dived down and, as they were furiously angry with me, they put me down on a lofty mountain and then flew away and left me.

Alone on the mountain I blamed myself for what I had done, and I recited the formula: 'There is no might and no power except with God, the Exalted, the Omnipotent,' adding: 'Every time I escape from one disaster, I fall into another that is even worse.' I stayed on the mountain not knowing where to go when suddenly I caught sight of two young men walking there, resplendent as moons, each holding a golden staff on which he leaned. I went up to them and, after we had exchanged greetings, I conjured them in God's Name to tell me who and what they were. 'We are servants of Almighty God,' they told me, after which they gave me a staff of red gold that they had with them, before going on their way. I walked along the summit of the mountain, supporting myself on the staff and thinking about the two young men, when from beneath the mountain there emerged a snake with a man in its mouth whom it had swallowed up to his navel. He was shrieking and calling out: 'Whoever saves me will be saved by God from every calamity,' and so I advanced on the snake and struck it on the head with my golden staff, at which it spat the man out of its mouth.

Night 566

Morning now dawned and Shahrazad broke off from what she had been allowed to say. Then, when it was the five hundred and sixty-sixth night, SHE CONTINUED:

I have heard, O fortunate king, that when Sindbad struck the snake with the golden staff that he was holding, it spat the man out of its mouth. SINDBAD WENT ON:

He came up to me and said: 'As it was you who rescued me from that snake, I shall not leave you and you will be my companion on this mountain.' I welcomed him and we were making our way over the mountain when we were approached by a group of men. When I looked at them, I noticed that among them was the one who had flown with me on his shoulders. I went up to him and excused myself politely, adding: 'My friend, this is not the way in which friends should treat each other.' He said: 'It was you who almost had us killed by glorifying God while you were on my back.' 'Don't hold it against me,' I replied. 'I didn't know about this, but I shall not speak another word.' He agreed to take me back with him, but on condition that I would not mention the Name of God or glorify Him while he was carrying me, after which he took me up and flew off with me as he had done before, bringing me to my own house. My wife met me and greeted me, but after congratulating me on my safe return, she warned me: 'Take care not to go out with these people again and have no dealings with them. They are brothers of the devils and don't know how to call on the Name of Almighty God.' 'How did your father deal with them, then?' I asked her. 'My father was not one of them and did not do what they do. My advice, now that he is dead, is that you should sell everything that we have, use the purchase price to buy goods, and then sail back to your own country and your own family. I shall go with you as there is nothing to keep me here now that both my parents are dead.'

After that, I began to sell my father-in-law's possessions bit by bit, while waiting for someone to sail from the city whom I could accompany. I was still doing this when a group of city merchants made up their minds to embark on a voyage, and as they could not find a ship, they bought timber and built a large one for themselves. I hired myself a passage with them and, after having paid the price in full, I embarked with my wife and all that we could take with us, abandoning our properties and estates. We put out to sea and sailed on from island to island and sea to sea, enjoying fair winds, until we came safely to land at Basra. I did not stay there but hired a passage on another ship, on which I loaded everything that I had brought with me, and set off for Baghdad. There I went to my own district and, on coming to my house, I met my family, my companions and my friends, and then I stored all my goods in my warehouses. My family calculated that on this seventh voyage I had been absent for twenty-seven years and this had made them despair of ever seeing me again. When I arrived and told them of all my adventures, they were filled with astonishment and congratulated me on my safe return.

I now vowed to Almighty God that after this, my seventh and last, voyage I would never again travel either by land or sea, for I no longer felt any desire for this, and I gave thanks to Almighty God, glory be to

Him, with grateful praise, for having brought me back to my family, my land and my country. So consider, Sindbad the landsman, what happened to me during my experiences and adventures.

'Don't hold against me what I said about you,' said the other Sindbad, and the two of them continued to enjoy an increasingly happy, cheerful and contented life as friends until they were visited by the destroyer of delights, the parter of companions, the wrecker of palaces and the filler of graves, the bearer of the cup of death. Praise be to the living God, Who does not die.

Alternative version of Sindbad's seventh voyage (from Galland): 'Sindbad and the elephant graveyard'

SINDBAD CONTINUED:

After returning from my sixth voyage, I completely abandoned any thought of ever making another. Apart from being of an age which only asked for rest, I had firmly promised myself I would no longer expose myself to the kind of dangers I had so often encountered. All I thought of was to spend the rest of my life in peace and quiet. However, one day, when I was entertaining some friends, a servant came to tell me that one of the caliph's officials was asking for me. I left the table and went up to the man. 'The caliph,' he said to me, 'has charged me to come and tell you that he wants to speak to you.' I followed him to the palace, where he presented me to this prince, whom I greeted, prostrating myself at his feet.

'Sindbad,' he said, 'I need you to do me a service: I want you to bear my reply and my presents to the king of Serendib, as it is only right that I should return him the courtesies he has shown me.'

The caliph's command came upon me as a bolt from the blue. 'Commander of the Faithful,' I said to him, 'I am ready to carry out all that your majesty orders me to do, but I most humbly beseech you to reflect that I am wearied by the unbelievable hardships I have suffered, and have even made a vow never to leave Baghdad.' I then took the opportunity of giving him a long and detailed account of all my adventures, which he patiently listened to right to the end.

'I admit,' he said, 'that these are indeed the most extraordinary events, but they should not prevent you from undertaking for my sake the voyage I am going to propose to you. To carry out the commission I am giving you, all you have to do is go to the island of Serendib. After that, you will be free to return. But you must go there, for you can see that it would not be proper for me or for my dignity to be indebted to the king of that island.' Seeing that the caliph's demand was absolute, I indicated to him that I was ready to obey. He was very pleased at this and gave me a thousand dinars to cover the expenses of my voyage.

I took only a few days to prepare for my departure, and as soon as the caliph's presents were delivered to me together with a letter in his own hand, I set out and took the route to Basra, where I embarked. My voyage was very successful, and I arrived at the island of Serendib. There I explained to the ministers the commission with which I had been charged, and begged them to get me an audience without delay, which they duly did. I was led with honour to the palace, where I greeted the king by prostrating myself before him, as was the custom.

This king immediately recognized me and showed particular pleasure at seeing me again. 'Ah! Sindbad!' he exclaimed. 'Welcome. Since you left, I swear I have often thought of you. I bless this day, since we meet again.' I paid him my compliments and, after thanking him for the kindness he showed me, I presented him with the caliph's letter and his gifts, which he received with great satisfaction. The caliph had sent him a bed covered with golden cloth, valued at a thousand dinars; fifty robes of a very rich material; a hundred others of the finest white cloth from Cairo, Suez, Kufa and Alexandria; a second bed covered with crimson cloth and yet another of a different kind; a large but shallow agate vase, the thickness of a finger and half a foot wide, the base of which represented in bas-relief a man with one knee on the ground holding a bow with an arrow, ready to shoot at a lion; and finally a splendid table which tradition had it came from the great Solomon. The caliph's letter ran as follows: 'Greetings, in the Name of the Sovereign Guide of the Right Way, to the mighty and fortunate king, from 'Abdallah Harun al-Rashid, whom God has set in the place of honour, after his ancestors of happy memory. We received your letter with joy and send you this from the council of our Porte, the garden of superior minds. We hope that as you look on it, you will recognize our good intentions and will be pleased with it. Farewell.'

The king of Serendib was very pleased to see that the caliph returned the friendship which he had shown him. A little after this audience, I asked leave to depart, which I had great difficulty in obtaining. As he dismissed me, the king gave me a substantial present. I immediately re-embarked, with the intention of returning to Baghdad; but I had not the fortune to arrive there as I hoped, as God ordered otherwise.

Three or four days after our departure we were attacked by pirates, who had very little difficulty in seizing our vessel as we were in no state to defend ourselves. Some members of the crew wanted to put up a resistance, but it cost them their lives; as for myself and all those who were prudent enough not to oppose the pirates' intentions, we were made slaves.

After the pirates had stripped us of our clothes, giving us in exchange some tattered rags, they took us far off to a large island where they sold us. I fell into the hands of a rich merchant, who, no sooner had he bought me, took me to his house, where he fed me well and dressed me in the clothes appropriate to a slave. A few days later, as he had not yet discovered who I was, he asked me whether I knew some trade. Without revealing much, I replied that I was not an artisan but a merchant by profession and that the pirates who had sold me had stripped me of all I had. 'But tell me,' he went on, 'can you not use a bow and arrow?' I replied that this was something I had practised in my youth and that I had not forgotten it since. He then gave me a bow and some arrows and, making me mount behind him on an elephant, he led me to a vast and extensive forest some hours' journey from the town. We went some way into it, and when he decided we should stop, he made me get down. Then, showing me a large tree, he said: 'Climb up this tree and shoot at the elephants you will see pass, for there are a vast number of them in this forest. If any of them falls, come and tell me.' On saying this, he left me some provisions and followed the path back to the town, while I lay in wait on the tree for the whole of the night.

All that time I did not see a single elephant; but the next morning, as soon as the sun had risen, I saw a large number appear. I shot several arrows at them, and at last one of them fell to the ground. The others immediately withdrew, leaving me free to go and tell my master what I had just killed. In return for this news, he rewarded me with a good meal, praising my skill and embracing me warmly. We then went together to the forest, where we dug a trench in which we buried the elephant. My master proposed to return when the animal had decayed and extract its tusks and sell them.

I continued hunting like this for two months, and not a day passed when I did not kill an elephant. I did not always hide in the same tree, but sometimes hid in another. One morning, when I was waiting for the elephants to arrive, I was very astonished to see that instead of passing in front of me as they usually did as they traversed the forest, they stopped and came towards me with a horrible noise and in such great numbers that the ground was covered with them and trembled under their steps. They approached my tree and surrounded it, their trunks raised and their eyes fixed on me. At this astonishing sight, I remained motionless and was seized with such terror that my bow and arrows fell from my hands.

My fears were not unfounded. After the elephants had stared at me for some time, one of the largest of them encircled the bottom of the tree with his trunk and, with an almighty effort, he uprooted it and threw it on the ground. I fell with the tree; but the animal took me up with its trunk and set me on its back, where I sat more dead than alive, with the quiver strapped to my shoulders. It then put itself at the head of all the other elephants, who followed it in a herd, carrying me off to a spot where it put me down before going off with all those that had accompanied it. Imagine, if you can, the state I was in: I thought I was dreaming rather than awake. At last, after remaining stretched out on the ground there for some time, I got up, seeing no more elephants around. I discovered that I was on quite a broad and long hill which was covered with the bones and tusks of elephants. I must admit that this sight filled me with unquantifiable thoughts. I admired the instinct of these animals and was quite sure this was their cemetery and that they had purposely brought me there as a lesson so that I should stop persecuting them, since I did it for the sole purpose of getting their tusks. I did not stop on the hill but directed my steps in the direction of the town, where I arrived at my master's, after walking for a day and a night. I met no elephant on my way, which made me realize that they had gone off deeper into the forest so as to allow me to proceed without obstacle to the hill.

As soon as my master saw me, he cried: 'Ah, poor Sindbad! I was very worried to know what had become of you. I went to the forest, where I found a newly uprooted tree, and a bow and arrows lying on the ground, and after having looked for you in vain, I despaired of ever seeing you again. Tell me, I beg you, what happened to you and by what good fortune are you still alive?' I satisfied his curiosity, and the next morning the two of us went to the hill, where he was highly delighted to discover that what I had told him was true. We loaded the elephant on which we had come with as many tusks as it could carry, and when we got back, he said to me: 'Brother – for I can't treat you as a slave any longer after

the pleasure you have given me by a discovery which will make me rich
– may God bless you with all happiness and prosperity! I declare before
Him that I now give you your liberty! I kept from you what you are now
going to hear: every year the elephants of our forest make us lose a vast
number of slaves whom we send in to look for ivory. Despite the advice
we give them, sooner or later they lose their lives thanks to the wiles of
these animals. God has delivered you from their fury and has given this
favour to you alone. It is a sign that He cherishes you and needs you in
this world for the good you may do there. You are giving me an unbelievable advantage; up till now we have only been able to get ivory by
endangering the lives of our slaves, and now an entire town is enriched
thanks to you. Don't think that I believe that I have sufficiently rewarded
you just now by giving you your liberty; I want to add to this gift a large
quantity of riches. I could get the whole town to make you your fortune:
but this is a glory I want to keep for myself.'

To this kind speech, I replied: 'May God preserve you, master! The
liberty you have granted me is quite enough to acquit yourself of any
obligation you have towards me; and the only reward I ask for the
services that I have had the good fortune to give you, and to your town,
is for permission to return to my own country.' 'Well, then,' he replied,
'the monsoon will soon bring back ships to load up with ivory. I will
then send you home and will give you the means of getting you there.' I
thanked him once more for giving me my liberty and for his favours,
and I stayed with him while waiting for the monsoon. During that time,
we made so many trips to the hill that we filled his storehouses with
ivory. All the merchants of the town who engaged in the same trade did
likewise, for it could not be kept a secret from them for very long.

The ships finally arrived and my master, having himself chosen the
ship on which I was to embark, loaded half of it with ivory for me.
Nor did he forget to load it with abundant provisions for my voyage,
and furthermore he obliged me to accept costly gifts, curiosities of
the country. After I had thanked him as much as I could for all the kindnesses I had received from him, I embarked. We set sail, and as the
adventure which had procured me my liberty was so extraordinary,
I had it continually in my thoughts.

We stopped at a few islands to take in refreshments. As our vessel had
come from a port on the continent of India, we landed there, to avoid
the dangers of the sea passage to Basra, and I had my ivory offloaded
there, having resolved to continue the journey by land. I obtained a vast

sum of money for my ivory, out of which I bought several rarities to give as presents, and when my retinue was ready, I attached myself to a large caravan of merchants. I journeyed for a long while and suffered much; but I endured all with patience, reflecting that I need no longer fear tempests, pirates, serpents, nor all the other perils I had encountered.

All these fatigues finally came to an end and I arrived happily at Baghdad. I immediately went to present myself to the caliph, to give him an account of my embassy. The caliph told me that the length of my voyage had caused him some disquiet but that he had always hoped that God would not abandon me. When I told him about the adventure of the elephants, he appeared to be very surprised and would have refused to believe it had he not known that I told the truth. He found this story and the others that I told him so curious that he charged one of his secretaries to write them down in letters of gold to be preserved in his treasury. I withdrew very content with the honour and the presents he gave me; then I devoted myself entirely to my family, my parents and my friends.

This was how Sindbad finished the narration of his seventh and last voyage. Addressing himself to Hindbad,* he added: 'Well, then, my friend, have you ever heard of anyone suffering as much as I have, or of any mortal finding himself in such pressing difficulties? Isn't it right that after such travails I should enjoy a quiet and pleasant life?' As he finished these words, Hindbad went up to him, kissed his hands and said: 'One must admit, sir, that you have experienced terrible perils; my troubles are nothing compared to yours. If they afflict me for a time, I console myself with the thought that I get some profit from them. You not only deserve a quiet life, but are worthy of all the riches you possess, since you make such good use of them and are so generous. May you then continue to live happily till the hour of your death.'

Sindbad gave another hundred dinars to him, received him among his friends and told him to quit his profession as porter and continue to come and eat with him; so that he had cause to remember Sindbad the sailor for the rest of his life.

I have also heard that in the old days in Damascus there was a caliph named 'Abd al-Malik ibn Marwan. One day while he was sitting with

---

* The name given by Galland to Sindbad the porter/landsman.

the kings and sultans of his empire, they began to discuss tales of past peoples and came to the stories of our master Solomon, son of David, on both of whom be peace, which contained accounts of what Almighty God had granted to him by way of rule and authority over mankind, *jinn*, birds, beasts and so on. The caliph was told: 'We have heard from our predecessors that Almighty God gave to our master Solomon what He gave to no one else, and Solomon advanced to a stage that no one else has reached, in that he would imprison *jinn*, *marids* and devils in brass bottles, which he would close up with lead, adding his seal.'

Night 567

Morning now dawned and Shahrazad broke off from what she had been allowed to say. Then, when it was the five hundred and sixty-seventh night, SHE CONTINUED:

I have heard, O fortunate king, that the caliph 'Abd al-Malik ibn Marwan held a discussion with his officers and the dignitaries of his empire during which they mentioned our master Solomon, and the authority that God had granted him. He was said to have advanced to a stage that no one had reached before, so much so that he would imprison *marids* and devils in brass bottles, which he would close up with lead, adding his seal.

Talib ibn Sahl then told the story of a man who had sailed to the lands of India with a number of others. During the course of their voyage the wind drove them to an unknown land, which they reached in the dark of night. At daybreak black people, naked like wild beasts, emerged from caves. They could not understand what was said to them, but they had a king of their own race who alone among them knew Arabic. When he saw the ship and its crew, he came out with a number of his people and gave a friendly welcome to his visitors. He then asked them about their religion and, when they told him, he said: 'No harm will come to you.' They themselves then asked about the local religion, and were told that the inhabitants followed one of those faiths that had preceded Islam and the mission of Muhammad, may God bless him and give him peace, at which the sailors admitted that they didn't understand what he was talking about and knew nothing about that religion.

The king then told them that they were the first visitors ever to come to his country, and by way of guest provisions he gave them the flesh of birds and wild beasts, as well as fish, these being the only kinds of foods that were to be had. The ship's company then landed to look around the city. They found a fisherman casting his net into the sea for fish, and when he pulled it out, it contained a brass bottle with a lead seal stamped with the seal of Solomon, son of David. The fisherman took it out and broke it, and from it came blue smoke that rose high into the sky. They heard a terrible voice crying: 'Prophet of God, I repent, I repent,' and the smoke formed into an awesome shape of terrifying appearance, whose head reached the mountain tops. It then disappeared, leaving the visitors with their hearts almost leaping out of their throats, whereas the blacks appeared to think nothing of it. Talib's informant went back to the king to ask him about it, and the king told him: 'This was one of the *jinn* whom Solomon, son of David, in his anger, imprisoned in bottles like these, before sealing them with lead and throwing them into the sea here. Very often, when the fishermen cast their nets, they bring up the bottles, and when they are broken, a *jinni* comes out. He thinks that Solomon is still alive and so repents and calls out: "I repent, prophet of God."'

'Abd al-Malik was astonished when he heard this, and exclaimed: 'God be praised! What great power was granted to Solomon!' Among those who were at his assembly was al-Nabigha al-Dhubyani,* who said: 'What Talib told you is true, as is proved by the lines of the first of the wise poets:

An example is found in Solomon, when God said to him:
"Become my regent; rule with diligence.
Reward those who obey you for their obedience,
But imprison those who disobey for all eternity."

He used to put these disobedient ones in brass bottles, which he threw into the sea.'

The caliph approved of al-Nabigha's speech and said: 'I should like to see one of these bottles myself.' Talib replied: 'You don't have to leave your own lands to do that, Commander of the Faithful, if you tell your brother, 'Abd al-'Aziz ibn Marwan, to fetch you one from the Maghrib. Your brother should send a message to Musa ibn Nusair† telling him to go from the Maghrib to the mountain that I mentioned and fetch the

---

* Real name Ziyad ibn Mu'awiya, a celebrated pre-Islamic poet.
† (AD 640–717) governor of north Africa at the time of the Arab invasion of Spain.

bottles that you want, since the farthest part of his province adjoins that mountain.' The caliph approved and said: 'This is sound advice and I want you to go to Musa to act as my messenger in this affair. You will take with you my white flag together with whatever money, emblems of rank and so on that you want, while I shall look after your family in your absence.' Talib agreed willingly and the caliph said: 'Set off, then, with the blessing and help of God.' He had a letter written to his brother, 'Abd al-'Aziz, who was his lieutenant in Egypt, and another to Musa, the governor of the Maghrib, ordering him to go himself to search for Solomon's bottles, leaving his son in charge of the country. He was to take guides with him, spend money freely, recruit numbers of men, and show no slackness in his quest or take refuge in excuses. He put his seal on the letters and handed them to Talib, urging him to travel as fast as he could underneath the caliphal banners, and providing him with money as well as with an escort of horse and foot to help him on his way. He also ordered that all his household expenses be paid.

Talib set off on his way to Egypt . . .

Night 568

Morning now dawned and Shahrazad broke off from what she had been allowed to say. Then, when it was the five hundred and sixty-eighth night, SHE CONTINUED:

I have heard, O fortunate king, that Talib set out together with his companions, and when he reached Cairo he was met by the governor, who lodged him in his palace and treated him with all possible honour during his stay. He was then provided with a guide to lead him to Upper Egypt, where he and his party came to the emir Musa ibn Nusair. As soon as Musa learned of his arrival, he came out gladly to meet him, and when the caliph's letter was handed to him he took it, read it, grasped its contents and put it on his head, exclaiming: 'To hear is to obey, Commander of the Faithful.'

He then decided to summon the principal officers of state and, when they came, he asked them about the problem posed by the letter. They told him that if he wanted someone to guide him to the place that the caliph had mentioned, the man he needed was the *shaikh* 'Abd al-Samad ibn 'Abd al-Qaddus al-Samudi, a knowledgeable man and an experienced traveller who was familiar with the wastes, the deserts and the seas, together with the lands and regions, their inhabitants and wonders. 'You should make an approach to him,' they said, 'for he will lead you to where you want to go.' Musa sent for 'Abd al-Samad, and when he came he turned out to be a very old man, made decrepit by the passage of time. Musa greeted him and said: 'Shaikh 'Abd al-Samad, 'Abd al-Malik ibn Marwan, the Commander of the Faithful, has given me such-and-such instructions, but I know very little about this country and I have been told that you are an expert who knows all its tracks. Would you be willing to do what the caliph wants?' In reply, the *shaikh* told Musa and Talib: 'This is a long and rough journey with few tracks,' and when Musa asked how long it would take, the *shaikh* said: 'Two years and some months on the outward half and the same on the way back,' adding, 'and you will meet many difficulties and perils, as well as coming across strange wonders. You are a champion of the holy war; enemies are close to our lands and, if you are absent, the Christians may come out against us. You will have to appoint a deputy to govern the country in your place.' Musa agreed and appointed Harun, his son, to act as deputy, getting an oath of allegiance sworn to him and ordering the troops to follow all his instructions without disobedience. They agreed to this, Harun being an energetic and intrepid man and a great fighter.

'Abd al-Samad then told Harun that their goal was only four months' distance away on the seashore, and that there was grass and water at all the linking stages. 'God will make this easy for us through your blessing,' he said, 'as you stand in place of the Commander of the Faithful.' Musa then asked 'Abd al-Samad if he knew whether any king had crossed this land before, and was told that it had been done by the king of Alexandria, Daran the Rumi.

The expedition then set off and travelled on until they reached a palace, which 'Abd al-Samad told Musa to enter, as there was a lesson to be learned there. Musa, together with his intimates, accompanied him and when they got to the door they found it open. They saw lofty columns and flights of steps, among these latter being two extended staircases of coloured marble, whose like had never been seen. The roofs and walls were inlaid with gold, silver and precious stones, and over the door was a tablet with an inscription in Greek. 'Shall I read it for you, emir?' 'Abd al-Samad asked. 'Do so, God bless you,' said Musa, 'for all that has happened on this journey has happened because of the blessing that you have brought.' 'Abd al-Samad then read out the inscription, which contained the following lines of poetry:

This people and their works lament the empire they have lost.
The palace brings the last news of its lords, who all lie buried here.
Death parted and destroyed them, throwing to the ground what they
    had gathered in.
It is as though they halted here to rest, but then set off again in
    haste.

Musa was overcome by tears, but then said: 'There is no god but
the Living and Everlasting God, Who does not pass away.' He entered
the palace and was lost in wonder at the beauty of its construction as he
looked at its pictures and statues. He caught sight of lines inscribed over
a second doorway and asked 'Abd al-Samad to come and read them out.
These were the lines:

How many once alighted in these halls, only to leave,
And Time's disasters struck others as well!
What they had hoarded was divided up;
They left it for others to enjoy and went on their way.
What blessings they once had! How much they ate!
But they themselves are eaten in the earth.

Musa wept bitterly and the world lost its colour for him, but he
exclaimed: 'We have been created for some great purpose!' When he and
his companions examined the palace further, they discovered that it was
entirely empty of inhabitants, its rooms and courts desolate and deserted.
In its centre was a lofty dome towering into the sky, which was surrounded by four hundred graves. When Musa approached them, he
noticed that among them was a marble tomb on which the following
lines were inscribed:

How often have I stood in battle and brought death!
How many things have I been witness to!
How much I ate and how much wine I drank!
How often have I heard the singing girls!
How often have I ordered and forbade!
How many stubborn fortresses you see
That I besieged and sacked,
Taking their lovely women as my spoils!
But in my folly I was led to sin,
To satisfy desire with transient things.
So hold a reckoning with yourself, young man,

Before you have to drink the cup of death,
For soon earth will be sprinkled over you,
As you lie lifeless in your grave.

After shedding tears with his companions, Musa approached the tomb
and discovered that it had eight doors of sandalwood with golden nails,
ornamented with silver stars and studded with all kinds of precious
stones. Over the first door these lines were inscribed:

What I left, I did not leave from generosity;
This was decreed by fate, which governs us.
For long I lived in happiness; men envied me;
I was a savage lion in my den, never at rest.
I would not give away a single mustard seed,
Such was my greed, even were I burned alive,
Until I fell victim to the fate
Decreed for me by God, the Omnipotent.
When He decreed that I was soon to die,
However much I spent, it would not ward off death.
The troops that I had mustered could not help,
Nor did a friend or neighbour rescue me.
In life's long journey I had tired myself,
In good fortune and bad, shadowed by death.
Another will have your goods before day breaks,
And men will come to bear your corpse and dig your grave.
On Judgement Day you will face God, alone,
Laden and burdened with your guilt and sin.
Do not be tricked by this world's finery.
Look at family and at neighbours, how it treated them.

On hearing this, Musa wept so bitterly that he lost consciousness, but
when he had recovered he went inside the dome and there he found a
long grave of formidable proportions, above which was a tablet of
Chinese iron. The *shaikh* 'Abd al-Samad came up and read out the
following message that was inscribed on it: 'In the Name of God, the
Everlasting, Who exists for all eternity; in the Name of God, Who neither
begets nor was begotten and Who has no peer; in the Name of God, the
Glorious, the Omnipotent; in the Name of the Living and Immortal
God . . .'

Night 569

Morning now dawned and Shahrazad broke off from what she had been allowed to say. Then, when it was the five hundred and sixty-ninth night, SHE CONTINUED:

I have heard, O fortunate king, that when 'Abd al-Samad had read out the message that I have quoted, he saw written after it on the tablet: 'You who have reached this place, take note from what you see of the changes and chances of Time. Do not be deceived by this world and its finery, its falseness, its calumnies and its delusive ornaments. It is a guileful and treacherous flatterer, whose goods are borrowed and which takes back what is lent from the borrower. It is like the elusive dream of a sleeper, or a desert mirage which the thirsty man takes to be water, and Satan embellishes it for man until the hour of his death. Since this is what the world is like, neither trust it nor turn towards it, for it betrays all who rely on it and depend on it in their affairs. Do not fall into its snare or clutch at its skirts. I owned four thousand bay stallions and a palace; I married a thousand princesses, swelling-breasted virgins like moons, and I had a thousand sons like grim lions; for a thousand years I lived a life of happiness and pleasure; no other king on earth was able to match the wealth that I collected and I thought that my good fortune would last and never wane. Then the destroyer of delights and the parter of companions came upon me unawares, this being death, which turns habitations to desolation and destroys old and young, babies, children and their mothers. We lived at ease here in this palace until we were visited by the fate decreed for us by the Lord of creation, the Master of earth and sky, and the punishment of God, the clear Truth, came upon us. Two of us died every day until very many had perished, and when I saw that destruction had made its way into our lands and had visited us, drowning us in the ocean of death, I summoned a scribe and ordered him to write down these lines with their admonitions, and to inscribe them in exact series on these doors, tablets and tombs. I had an army of a million hardy riders with lances, chain mail, swords of iron and strong arms. I ordered them to put on their long coats of mail, gird on their sharp swords, hold their formidable lances firmly raised and mount their horses. Then, when the judgement of God, the Lord of creation, the Lord of heaven and earth, came upon us, I asked them if they could ward off the fate sent us by the Omnipotent King. They said that they could not, and added: "How can we fight against One to Whom no chamberlain denies access, the Lord of the door that has no door-keeper?" So I told them to bring out my wealth, which was stored in a thousand pits, each holding a thousand *qintars* of red gold, and the same amount of white silver, together with pearls and other jewels and treasures, such as no other king in the world possessed. When they had done that and had placed it all before me, I asked: "Can you save me by using all this to buy me one single extra day of life?" They could not and they resigned themselves to the decree of fate, while I myself had to endure the misfortune that God had decreed for me. My life was taken from me and I was left in my grave. If you ask my name, I was Kush ibn Shaddad, son of 'Ad the great.'

On the tablet were also inscribed these lines:

If you remember me after so long,
After Time's changes and its happenings,
I am the son of Shaddad, who ruled mankind,
The king of every quarter of the earth.
All the recalcitrant bowed down to me,
From Syria to Egypt to Adnan.
For in my glory I subdued all kings;
The people of the earth feared my authority.
The tribes and serried armies were in my power,
While all the lands and peoples lived in fear.
When I was mounted, I saw that my hosts,
On neighing horses, were a million men.
No one could count the riches that I had;
I stored them up to ward off fate's assault,
And I had planned to use the whole of this
As ransom for my life and to postpone my death,
But God decreed that His will should be done,
And I was left alone without a friend,
For death that parts us all visited me,
And I was moved from power to lowliness.
I was confronted by all those past deeds
For which I had to answer as a sinner.
You who are on the edge of death, take care
And guard against fate's blows, may God guide you.

When he saw how that people had been destroyed, Musa wept until he fainted. Later, as he and his companions were walking around in the palace and examining its rooms and its pleasure grounds, they came across a table standing on four marble legs which was inscribed with the words: 'At this table ate a thousand one-eyed kings and a thousand kings whose eyes were sound. All of them have departed this life and lie buried in their graves.' Musa noted down all these inscriptions before leaving the palace, from which he took nothing but that table.

He and his men then rode off with 'Abd al-Samad in front, guiding them. They had travelled all that day, then a second day and then a third, when they came in sight of a high hill, on whose crest, as they looked, they could see a rider made of brass carrying a broad-headed spear which gleamed almost blindingly. On this statue there was an inscription that read: 'You who come to me, if you do not know the road to the City of Brass, rub the rider's hand. It will turn and you must take whichever direction it points to when it stops; go freely and without fear, for it will lead you to the city.'

Night 570

Morning now dawned and Shahrazad broke off from what she had been allowed to say. Then, when it was the five hundred and seventieth night, SHE CONTINUED:

I have heard, O fortunate king, that accordingly the emir rubbed the statue's hand, which turned like lightning and pointed to a different direction from the one that he and his party were taking. So they set off on what turned out to be the right way, and they followed it night and day until they had covered a long distance. Then one day, in the course of their journey, they caught sight of a pillar of black stone in which stood a figure sunk up to its armpits. This had two huge wings and four hands, one pair like those of a man and a second pair with claws like a lion's paws. The hair on its head was like horses' tails; it had two eyes like burning coals and in the middle of its forehead a third eye like that of a lynx, from which flashed sparks of fire. The figure itself was black and tall and it was crying out: 'Praise be to God, Who has decreed that I must endure the great affliction of this painful punishment until the Day of Resurrection.' Musa's men were scared out of their wits by this sight and turned back in flight. Musa himself asked 'Abd al-Samad what the figure was, and when he said that he didn't know, Musa told him to go up to it and investigate in the hope of finding out more about it. 'Abd al-Samad said that he was afraid, but Musa told him: 'There is no need to fear as he cannot reach you or anyone else, placed as he is.' So 'Abd al-Samad approached and asked the figure: 'What is your name and what are you? What placed you here like this?' It replied: 'I am an *'ifrit* of the *jinn*. My name is Dahish, son of al-A'mash, and I am kept confined here by the might and power of God to undergo torment for such time as He pleases.'

Musa then told the *shaikh* to ask him why he was imprisoned in the pillar, and when he did, THE *'IFRIT* SAID:

My story is a strange one. One of the children of Iblis had an idol made of red carnelian, which was entrusted to my care and which was worshipped by a great and important sea king, the leader of an army of a million *jinn*, whose swords were at his disposal and who would answer his summons however difficult matters might be. These *jinn*, his servants, were under my command and obedient to my orders, and they all rebelled against the authority of Solomon, son of David. As for me, I would enter into the middle of the statue and from it give my commands and prohibitions, and, as it happened, the king's daughter loved it, frequently prostrating herself before it and worshipping it wholeheartedly. She was the loveliest lady of her time, beautiful and graceful, and radiantly perfect. Solomon heard about her and sent a message to her father saying: 'Give me your daughter in marriage; smash your idol of carnelian and bear witness that there is no god but God and that Solomon is His prophet. If you do that, we shall share alike in both profits and obligations, but if you refuse, I shall bring against you armies you cannot resist. You will have to prepare to answer to God when you have donned your shroud, for my armies will fill every open space and leave you as a figure of the dead past.'

When Solomon's messenger arrived, the king showed excessive insolence in his self-esteem and pride. He asked his viziers what they had to say about the message, Solomon's request for the hand of the princess and his demand that the king destroy the carnelian idol and adopt his religion. They answered: 'Great king, how can Solomon attack you when you are in the middle of this great sea? Even if he moves against you, he will not be able to defeat you, as the *marids* will fight for you. If you ask for help from the idol that you worship, it will aid you and bring you victory. The best thing to do is to consult your lord' – by which they meant the idol – 'and listen to its reply. If it advises you to fight Solomon, then do so, but otherwise, do not fight.' On hearing that, the king went immediately to the idol, offering sacrifices and killing sacrificial victims. He prostrated himself before it, shed tears and recited these lines:

> My Lord, I know your power, but here is Solomon, who wants you
>   smashed.
> My Lord, I seek your aid. Command me and I shall obey.

The *'ifrit*, half buried in the pillar, then told 'Abd al-Samad and his listening companions: 'In my ignorance and folly, caring nothing for Solomon, I entered the idol and began to recite:

> I have no fear of him, I the omniscient.
> If he wants to fight me I shall march on him and snatch away his
>   soul.

When the king heard my answer his confidence was strengthened and he decided to give battle. Solomon's envoy was met with a painful beating when he arrived, and repulsed ignominiously with a threatening message: "You are guilty of wishful thinking. Are you threatening me with vain words? Either come to me or I shall come to you."

'When Solomon's messenger returned to tell him everything that had happened, Solomon became furiously angry and even more determined. He collected armies of *jinn*, men, beasts, birds and venomous reptiles. He ordered his vizier al-Dimriyat, the king of the *jinn*, to gather together *marids*, and al-Dimriyat mustered six hundred thousand devils, while at his command Asaf ibn Barkhiya collected a force of a million or more men. He provided equipment and arms, after which he and the *jinn* and men mounted on his flying carpet with the birds flying overhead and the beasts following below. When he reached his destination he encircled the sea king's island, filling the ground with his forces.'

Night 571

Morning now dawned and Shahrazad broke off from what she had been allowed to say. Then, when it was the five hundred and seventy-first night, SHE CONTINUED:

I have heard, O fortunate king, that THE *'IFRIT* SAID:

When Solomon surrounded the island with his armies, he sent a message to the king saying: 'I have now come, so either defend yourself against my attack or enter my service, acknowledging that I am God's messenger, breaking your idol, worshipping the One God, the object of all worship, and giving me your daughter in lawful wedlock. Then you and your people must recite the formula: "I confess that there is no god but God and that Solomon is the prophet of God." If you say that, then you are assured of safety, while if you refuse it will not help you to try to shelter yourself from my attack in this island. God, the Blessed and Exalted, has commanded the wind to obey me and to carry me to you on this carpet. I shall make an example of you and your punishment will be a lesson to others.'

When Solomon's messenger brought his master's message to the king, the king replied: 'This demand cannot be met, so tell him that I am coming out against him.' The messenger went back to Solomon and gave him this reply, after which the king summoned the people of his land and collected a million *jinn* from among those who were subject to him, to whom he added the *marids* and devils from the islands and mountain tops. He equipped his armies, opening his armouries and distributing weapons. As for God's prophet Solomon, he drew up his armies, ordering the wild beasts to divide in two, with one half taking up their station on the right of the men and the other on their left. The birds were to patrol the islands, and when the attack was launched they were to peck out the eyes of their enemies with their beaks and strike at their faces with their wings, while the wild beasts were to savage their horses. 'To hear is to obey,' they all replied, 'for we owe obedience to God and to you, prophet of God.'

Solomon then set up for himself a marble throne studded with gems and plated with red gold, seating his vizier Asaf ibn Barkhiya on his right, together with the human kings, and his other vizier al-Dimriyat, with the kings of the *jinn*, on his left. In front of him were the beasts, together with the vipers and the other snakes. They then launched a concerted attack on us and fought against us for two days over a wide battlefield. On the third day, disaster overtook us and God's judgement came upon us. I was the first to come out against Solomon with my troops, and I told them to hold their positions while I went out to challenge al-Dimriyat. He came to meet me like a huge mountain with blazing flames and billowing smoke, and as he came, he shot at me with a fiery meteor, and this bolt of his proved stronger than my fire. So loudly did he bellow that it seemed to me that the sky had fallen in on me, and the mountains shook at the sound of his voice. At his command, his force then launched a single charge against us; each side shouted against the other; fire and smoke rose high; hearts were almost splitting and the fight became furious. The birds were attacking us from the air and the beasts were fighting on the ground. I continued my duel with al-Dimriyat until we had tired each other out, but then I weakened and my companions and my troops deserted me as the tribes of my *marids* were routed. At that, Solomon, God's prophet, called out: 'Seize this great tyrant, ill-omened and miserable as he is!' Men attacked men and *jinn* fought *jinn*; our king was defeated, while the spoils fell to Solomon as his troops charged ours, with the wild beasts spreading around us to right and left and the birds overhead tearing out eyes, sometimes with their talons and sometimes with their beaks, using their wings to strike at men's faces. The beasts savaged the horses and tore at the men until most of us were stretched on the ground like fallen palm trunks. I myself flew away from al-Dimriyat, but he pursued me over the distance of a three-month journey until I fell into the plight in which you see me.

Night 572

Morning now dawned and Shahrazad broke off from what she had been allowed to say. Then, when it was the five hundred and seventy-second night, SHE CONTINUED:

I have heard, O fortunate king, that when the *'ifrit* imprisoned in the column had told Musa and his companions his story from beginning to end, they asked him the way to the City of Brass and he pointed it out to them. Although the city was said to have twenty-five gates, there was no trace of any of them, while the walls were like a mountain ridge, or iron poured into a mould. Musa and his men dismounted, as did the *shaikh* 'Abd al-Samad, but although they did their best to discover either a gate or some other way in, they could not find one. Musa then asked Talib: 'Talib, how are we going to get into the city? We have to discover a gate through which we can go.' 'God preserve the emir,' answered Talib. 'Rest here for two or three days until, God willing, we think of some way of doing this.' At that, Musa told one of his servants to take a camel and ride round the city to see whether he could discover any trace of a gate or any place where the wall was lower than it was by their camp. The man mounted and rode at a fast pace for two days and nights without resting. On the third day he came back to the others, filled with astonishment at what he had seen of the extent and height of the walls, which he told Musa were at their lowest where he was.

Musa then took Talib and 'Abd al-Samad and climbed a mountain opposite the city, which overlooked it. When the three of them reached the summit, before them was a city as large as any that eye had ever seen, with lofty palaces, splendid domes, well-maintained houses, flowing streams, trees and gardens with ripe fruits. It had strong gates but lay empty and desolate, with no trace of human life. Throughout it, owls were hooting; birds circled around its courts and crows were croaking in its quarters and streets, lamenting those who had once lived there. As Musa stood on the mountain, he was filled with sorrow for the emptiness and desolation of the place now that its people had gone. 'Praise be to God,' he exclaimed, 'Who remains unaltered by the passing ages, and Whose power called all creation into being!'

As he was praising God, the Great and Glorious, he happened to turn towards a place where he could see seven tablets of white marble gleaming in the distance. He approached them and found that on them were inscriptions, which he ordered to be read for him. 'Abd al-Samad came up and, after studying what was written, he read out what it contained in the way of admonitions, warnings and exhortations for those who had eyes to see. The first inscription, in Greek script, ran as follows: 'Son of man, how little heed you pay to what lies before you, distracted as you are by your age and your years. Do you not know that the cup of death has been filled for you and that soon you must drain it? Look to yourself before you go to your grave. Where are those who ruled the lands, subdued mankind and commanded armies? By God, they were visited by the destroyer of delights and the parter of companions, death that destroys flourishing dwellings and which brought them from their spacious palaces to the narrow tomb.'

At the foot of the tablet, these lines were inscribed:

Where are the kings who flourished on the earth?
They left behind what they had built and made to prosper.
In their graves they will be held to account for what they did;
Once they were wealthy, but now they are dried bones.
Where are their armies, which could not help to ward off death?
Where is the wealth they hoarded and stored up?
The Lord of the throne's decree visited them suddenly;
No wealth could save them, nor was there any aid.

Musa was stunned, and tears ran down over his cheeks as he said: 'By God, asceticism in this world is the best way to ensure a happy outcome.' He had an inkstand and paper fetched and copied down this inscription, after which he went up to the second tablet. On this was written: 'Son of man, why are you deceived by what has existed from past eternity, and what has caused you to neglect the fate that must befall you? Do you not know that this world is the house of perdition, in which no one can find a resting place, however fixedly you look at it and devote yourself to it? Where are the kings who brought prosperity to Iraq and ruled the corners of the world, or those under whom Isfahan and Khurasan flourished? The herald of death summoned them and they obeyed the summons, answering the call of extinction. The buildings they had raised were of no service to them, and what they had gathered and prepared did not protect them.'

At the foot of the tablet were inscribed these lines:

Where are the builders of these lofty towers,
With their chambers that have no match?
They gathered armies, fearing to be abased
By God's decree, but still they were brought low.
Where are the Chosroes with their strong fortresses?
They left the lands and it is as though they had never been.

Musa wept and exclaimed: 'We have been created for some great purpose!' Then, when he had transcribed this inscription, he moved on to the third . . .

Night 573

Morning now dawned and Shahrazad broke off from what she had been allowed to say. Then, when it was the five hundred and seventy-third night, SHE CONTINUED:

I have heard, O fortunate king, that the emir Musa went up to the third tablet and found written on it: 'Son of man, love for this world distracts you and causes you to forget your Lord's commands. Day after day your life passes, leaving you happy and content, but you should make provision for the Day of Resurrection and prepare to answer in the presence of the Lord of mankind.'

At the bottom of the tablet were inscribed these lines:

Where is he who brought prosperity to the lands
Sind and Hind, as a proud tyrant?
Zanj and Abyssinians obeyed him,
And Nubians, in his overweening haughtiness.
Expect no news of what lies in the grave;
You will find none who can tell you of that;
He was overtaken by the disasters of fate,
And the palaces he built could not save him.

Having shed bitter tears, Musa went up to the fourth tablet, on which
he found written: 'Son of man, how long a delay will you be granted by
your Lord, while you are plunged in the sea of your pleasures, getting
the best from each day as though you need never die? Son of man, do
not be deceived by the enjoyment that is given you by your days, nights
and hours, as they pass unheeded. Know that death is lying in wait for
you and mounting on your shoulder. No day passes on which he is not
with you morning and evening; beware of his assault and be on guard
against it. I shall be with you in the grave when you have been robbed
of length of life and all your temporal delights have gone to waste. Listen
to my words! Put your trust in the Lord of lords! Nothing in this world
endures, for this is no more than a spider's web.'

At the foot of the tablet were inscribed these lines:

Where is the man who laid foundations for these lofty towers,
And saw to it that they were built so high?
Where is the garrison of the strong fortresses?
They have all gone, like those who are no more.
They lie in their graves, to be held to account
On a day when all hearts shall be put to the test.
Nothing remains except Almighty God,
To Whom honour is always due.

This inscription was noted down tearfully by Musa, who then came
down from the summit of the hill with a clear picture of the vanity of
this world in his mind. After he had rejoined his men, he and they spent
the rest of the day thinking about ways in which to enter the city. He
asked Talib, his vizier, and his leading companions: 'How are we going
to get into this city to look at its marvels, and perhaps to find something
that may win us favour with the Commander of the Faithful?' Talib
replied: 'May God continue to show His favour to the emir. We must

construct a ladder and climb up to see whether we can get to the gate from the inside.' 'That is what had struck me,' Musa told him, 'and it is a good idea.' So he summoned carpenters and smiths and told them to prepare timbers and make a ladder with iron rungs. They did this carefully, spending an entire month on the work, after which the men gathered around the completed ladder and set it upright against the wall, whose height it matched so exactly that it looked as though it had always been there. Musa was astonished by this and exclaimed: 'God bless you! You have done this so skilfully that it looks as though you had measured it against the wall.' He then asked who would be the first to go up to the top of the wall and then walk along it to try to find a way down into the city. When the scout had investigated the position, he was to tell the rest of them how to open the gate.

A volunteer was found, and after Musa had wished him good fortune, he climbed up to the top of the ladder. He stood on the wall, gazed down at the city and then clapped his hands and called out at the top of his voice: 'How beautiful you are!' after which he threw himself down into the city, so that flesh and bone were crushed. Musa exclaimed: 'If this is how a sensible man acts, what would a madman do? Were this to happen to all of us here, there would be nobody left and our quest and that of the Commander of the Faithful would fail. Let us go, for there is nothing in the city that we need.' Someone else disagreed and said: 'Perhaps another man will be steadier than he was,' and so a second volunteer, followed by a third, a fourth and then a fifth, went up, until a total of twelve had gone. Each one of them acted like the first, and at that point 'Abd al-Samad said: 'No one should go except me, for an experienced man is not the same as a tyro.' 'You mustn't do that,' Musa told him. 'I am not going to allow you to climb on to that wall, as if you die, you will be the death of all of us. None of us will be able to survive, since you are our guide.' 'It may be that I shall be allowed to succeed in this by the will of Almighty God,' 'Abd al-Samad replied, and everyone there agreed that he should climb the ladder. So he got to his feet, summoned up his energy, and exclaimed: 'In the Name of God, the Compassionate, the Merciful!' He then started up the ladder, calling as he did so on the Name of Almighty God and reciting the Verses of Deliverance from the Quran.

When he got to the top of the wall, he clapped his hands and stared down. 'Don't do it!' everyone shouted. 'Don't throw yourself down,' and they recited the formula: 'We belong to God and to Him do we return,' telling themselves: 'If he falls, we are all dead.' Then he gave a loud laugh and sat there for a long time, calling on the Name of Almighty God and reciting the Verses of Deliverance, after which he got up and called out at the top of his voice: 'You're in no danger, emir, for the Great and Glorious God has protected me from Satan and his deceitful wiles through the blessing brought by the words: "In the Name of God, the Compassionate, the Merciful".' 'What have you seen?' asked Musa. 'When I got to the top of the wall,' 'Abd al-Samad told him, 'I saw ten girls as lovely as moons, who were calling to me and . . .'

Night 574

Morning now dawned and Shahrazad broke off from what she had been allowed to say. Then, when it was the five hundred and seventy-fourth night, SHE CONTINUED:

I have heard, O fortunate king, that 'Abd al-Samad said: 'When I got to the top of the wall I saw ten girls, lovely as moons, who were gesturing with their hands, inviting me to come down and join them. It seemed to me that what lay beneath me was water and I wanted to dive down into it, as the others had done, but then I saw them lying there dead and I stopped myself from following them. I recited verses from the Holy Quran, and God protected me from the wiles of the girls. They left and I did not jump down, as God had saved me from their magical arts. There is no doubt that this was a spell produced by the people of the city to keep away anyone who wanted to look at it or get into it, and as a result our companions are lying there dead.'

'Abd al-Samad then walked along the wall until he came to two brazen towers which he could see had two golden gates, but these had no bolts and there was nothing to show how they could be opened. For a time he stood there looking until he noticed that in the middle of the gate was a brass image of a rider with his hand outstretched as though he was pointing, and inscribed there was a line of writing. When 'Abd al-Samad read it, he found that it said: 'Rub the nail in the rider's navel twelve times and the gate will open.' When he looked more closely he found a nail carefully and firmly set in the navel, and as soon as he had rubbed it twelve times, the gate opened with a sound like thunder.

'Abd al-Samad went through it, excellent man that he was, with a knowledge of every language and every script. He walked on until he came into a long hall and down some steps into a room with a number of fine benches on which corpses were lying with splendid shields, sharp swords, strung bows and notched arrows hung up above their heads. Behind the gate was an iron bar together with wooden poles and delicate latches, set in well-constructed locks. 'It may be that these people have the keys,' said 'Abd al-Samad to himself, and, as he looked, he noticed one of them, who appeared to be the oldest, lying on a high bench in the middle of the dead, and he told himself that it was probably he who held the keys. He might have been the gatekeeper of the city, the others being under his command. So he approached the corpse and when he lifted up its clothes, there were the keys attached to its waist. He was almost ecstatically joyful when he saw this and, taking the keys, he went up to the gate. He opened the locks and tugged at the bolts and fastenings of the gate; when these had been undone the gate itself opened, giving out a sound like thunder, because of its formidable size and its huge fastenings. At that, 'Abd al-Samad glorified God, his cry being echoed by his companions in their joy and happiness.

Musa was delighted that 'Abd al-Samad was safe and that the city gate had been opened, while the rest of the company thanked the *shaikh* for what he had done. They were all in a hurry to get through the gate, but Musa warned them that something might go wrong after they had entered, and so he ordered that only half of them should go in while the other half were to stay behind. He went in himself with half of his men, fully armed. They saw the dead bodies of their companions and buried them, and they also saw the gatekeepers, servants, chamberlains and officers all lying dead on silken couches. When they reached the city market, they found that it covered a huge area with high buildings, no one of which overtopped the others. The shops were open, with their scales hanging up and the copper pots arranged in orderly rows; the *khans* were filled with goods of all sorts, but the traders could be seen dead in their booths with their flesh desiccated and their bones crumbled away, a lesson for those who could learn. There were four separate markets to be seen, with shops filled with merchandise.

Musa's men went from these to the silk market, where, in addition to silk, there was brocade woven with threads of red gold and white silver in colours of all kinds, with the owners lying dead on leather mats but looking as though they were just about to speak. They moved on to the jewellers' market with its pearls and sapphires, and from there to that of the money-changers, who were lying dead on carpets of silks of various kinds, with their booths filled with gold and silver. Next they came to the market of the druggists with its perfumes, pungent musk, ambergris, aloes, *nadd*, camphor and so on. Here too all the people were dead and nothing in the way of food was to be found there. When they left, they discovered nearby a splendidly built and embellished palace, where, on entering, they found unfurled banners, unsheathed swords, strung bows, shields suspended with chains of gold and silver and helmets gilded with red gold. In the palace halls were ivory benches overlaid with glistening gold and silks on which lay men whose flesh had dried on their bones. They might have seemed to the ignorant to be sleeping, but they were dead, having met their fate through famine.

Musa halted, praising and glorifying God, while studying the beauty of that admirably built and excellently constructed palace, with its splendour and fine design, plentifully embellished, as it was, with green lapis lazuli. Engraved around it were these lines:

Man, look here at what you see;
Be on your guard before you have to leave.
Send on to help you provisions of good deeds,
For all who live in a house will have to leave.
Look at those who once adorned their homes,
But then went to their graves to account for what they did.
They built, to no avail; they stored up wealth,
But this wealth did not save them when their time had come.
How many hopes they placed on what could not be theirs;
But hopes were not to help them in the grave.
From highest rank they were brought down
To the lowliness of a narrow grave – a wretched fall!
When they were buried, a voice was heard to cry:
'Where are your thrones, your crowns and all your robes?
Where are the faces that were veiled away,
Protected by the curtains and the drapes?'
The grave has a clear answer for the questioners:
'The roses are no longer on their cheeks.
For many days they ate and drank their wine,
But after their fine foods, they too were eaten.'

Musa wept until he fainted and he then ordered the lines to be written down. After that, he entered the palace . . .

Night 575

Morning now dawned and Shahrazad broke off from what she had been allowed to say. Then, when it was the five hundred and seventy-fifth night, SHE CONTINUED:

I have heard, O fortunate king, that the emir Musa entered the palace, where he saw a large chamber with four large rooms, lofty and wide, each facing the other, multi-coloured and adorned with gold and silver. In the centre was a large marble fountain covered with a canopy of brocade, while the rooms had alcoves, in each of which was an ornamental fountain with a marble basin and a stream of water coming from below them, the four streams flowing together into a large pool of variegated marble. Musa told 'Abd al-Samad to go in there with him, and when they entered the first room they found it filled with gold, white silver, pearls and other gems, sapphires and precious stones. They also discovered chests filled with brocades, red, yellow and white, while when they went to the second room they found a store of weapons and military equipment such as gilded helmets, mail shirts made by Da'ud, Indian swords, Khatti spears and locked coffers over which hung curtains embroidered in various patterns, and when they opened one of the latter they found it full of weapons embellished with gold, silver and gems. There were more of these coffers in the fourth room, and when they opened one of them they found it filled with plates and drinking vessels of gold and silver, together with glass bowls, drinking cups studded with brilliant pearls, carnelian goblets and so on.

Musa's men began to take what suited them, each one carrying off as much as he could, but as they were about to leave, in the middle of the palace they caught sight of a teak door inlaid with ivory and ebony and plated with gleaming gold. An embroidered silk curtain hung over it, and it had locks of white silver which had to be opened by a trick, as there was no key. 'Abd al-Samad came forward and, thanks to his knowledge and proficiency, together with his courage, he managed to open them. The others then entered a marble hall whose sides were covered with hangings on which were pictured birds and beasts that astonished everyone who looked at them, as they were worked in gold and white silver, with eyes of pearls and sapphires. Next they came to a court, the artistry of whose construction won the admiration of Musa and 'Abd al-Samad, and when they passed through it, they found another made of polished marble set with gems. Its floor looked like flowing water, and as it gave the impression that whoever tried to pass through it would slip, Musa told 'Abd al-Samad to scatter something on it that would allow them to walk over it.

When he had contrived to do this, the others went through and discovered a great dome built of stones coated with red gold, more beautiful than anything any of them had ever seen. In the middle of this was a large marble shrine around whose sides were ornamented windows with a grating of emeralds, more precious than any king could afford. Within was a canopy of brocade set over pillars of red gold, and inside this were birds whose feet were green emeralds and under each of them was a net of brilliant pearls spread above a fountain. Placed at the side of this fountain was a couch adorned with pearls, gems and sapphires, and on this lay a girl like a radiant sun, lovelier than anyone they had ever seen. She was wearing a dress decked with fine pearls; on her head was a crown of red gold and a jewelled band, while a jewelled necklace, with gems sparkling from its centre, encircled her throat, and on her forehead were two jewels that shone like the sun. She seemed to be watching the newcomers, and looking from right to left.

Night 576

Morning now dawned and Shahrazad broke off from what she had been allowed to say. Then, when it was the five hundred and seventy-sixth night, SHE CONTINUED:

I have heard, O fortunate king, that when Musa saw her he was amazed and taken aback by her beauty, the redness of her cheeks and the blackness of her hair, while those who looked at her thought that she could not be a corpse but must be alive. They greeted her, but Talib called down a blessing on the emir and said: 'Please understand that she is dead and lifeless, so is unable to return your greeting.' He went on to point out: 'She is no more than an artfully preserved shell. Her eyes were removed after death and given a backing of quicksilver before being put back in place. As they gleam, it seems as though the eyelashes are moving them and so they appear to be twinkling to those who look at her, while, in fact, she is dead.' 'Glory to God,' exclaimed Musa, 'Who has subjected his servants to death!'

The couch on which the girl lay had steps leading up to it and on these were two slaves, one white and the other black, one holding a steel mace and the other a jewelled sword that was blindingly bright. Between them was a golden tablet on which could be read the words: 'In the Name of God, the Compassionate, the Merciful: praise be to God, Who created man, the Lord of lords, the Cause of causes. In the Name of God, the Everlasting, the Eternal; in the Name of God, the Master of destiny and fate: son of man, how long will you continue to hope in your ignorance, forgetting that you must come to your end? Do you not know that death has summoned you and is coming quickly to take your life? Be prepared to leave and take provisions from this world, which you are soon to abandon. Where is Adam, the father of mankind? Where is Noah and where are his descendants? Where are the kings, the Chosroes and the Caesars? Where are the lords of India and Iraq? Where are those who ruled all the regions of the world? Where are the Amalekites and where are the mighty monarchs? Their palaces stand empty and they have left their families and their lands. Where are the kings of the Persians and the Arabs? They all died and are now dried bones, and all the lords of rank are gone. Where are Qarun and Haman? Where is Shaddad, son of 'Ad? Where are Kanan and Dhu'l-Autad? He who cuts off lives has cut off theirs and left their places desolate. Did they make provision for the Day of Resurrection and prepare to answer to the Lord of mankind? O man, if you do not know me, I shall tell you my name and my lineage, for I am Tarmazayan, daughter of the Amalekite kings, who acted with justice in the lands. My own kingdom was greater than any other ruler had ever possessed. I was just in my judgements, treating my subjects with fairness, and was generous with my gifts, freeing slaves, both male and female. I long enjoyed a life of pleasure and ease until fate struck and I was overwhelmed by disasters. For seven consecutive years, no drop of rain fell and no grass grew on the surface of the land. We ate the provisions that we had, and then we turned to our beasts and ate them until there was nothing left. I had all our money brought to me, and, having weighed it out, I sent it off with reliable men who toured the regions, visiting every single town in their search for food, but without success. After a long absence, they returned to us, bringing back the money. We then brought out all our goods and treasures, closed the gates of the city's forts and surrendered ourselves to our Lord's decree, entrusting our affairs to Him. Then, as you see, we all died, leaving behind our buildings and our treasures. This is our story, and of the reality of our power only the traces remain.'

At the bottom of the tablet, Musa and his men saw the following lines written:

Sons of Adam, do not be mocked by hope;
Whatever you store up, you will have to leave.
I see you covet this world and its finery,
And it was for this that generations before you strove.
They gathered wealth lawfully and unlawfully,
But when their time had come, fate could not be turned back.
They led huge armies and they gathered wealth,
But on their last journey, wealth and buildings were left behind.
They were laid down in narrow graves,
Where they stay to account for what they did.
They are like a caravan that unsaddled
One dark night where there were no guest provisions.
The caravan master called out to them:
'You cannot stay here, so load up again.'
They were all afraid and terrified,
And neither halting nor moving on could they find cheer.
Send on provisions of good deeds to cheer you in the world to come;
It is only in the fear of God that we should act.

As Musa wept, 'Abd al-Samad continued to read: 'By God, piety is our chief duty; through it we achieve our goals and it is our firm support. Death is the clearest truth, the certain promise and the end to which we must return. Learn your lesson from those who have preceded you to the grave and outstripped you on their way to the next world. Do you not see that your grey hairs have summoned you to the grave, bringing you news of your death? Be alert, since you must be judged, but you are hard of heart and misled regarding your Lord. Where are the peoples that have gone before and serve as a lesson for those who can learn? Where are the kings of China, the masters of might and power? Where is 'Ad, son of Shaddad, and the buildings he raised up? Where is Nimrod, the mighty tyrant? Where is Pharaoh, who refused to believe his God? They were overwhelmed by death, which spared neither young nor old, female nor male. They were cut off by fate, which severs lives and causes night to succeed day. You who come to this place and see us should learn not to be deceived by this world and its vanities, for it is treacherous and full of wiles, a place of perdition and deception. Blessed is the man who is mindful of his sins, fears his Lord, is just in his dealings and

makes provision in advance for the Day of Judgement. You whom God
has enabled to enter our city, take what you can of our wealth, but do
not touch anything that has been placed on my body to cover my
nakedness and to equip me on my journey from this world. Fear God
and do not remove any of this lest it bring about your death. This is my
advice and the charge that I lay on you. Farewell, and I pray that God
may save you from misfortunes and from sickness.'

Night 577

Morning now dawned and Shahrazad broke off from what she had been
allowed to say. Then, when it was the five hundred and seventy-seventh
night, SHE CONTINUED:

I have heard, O fortunate king, that when Musa heard this he wept
so bitterly that he fainted, and later, when he had recovered, he wrote
an account of it all in order to learn from what he had seen. He then
told his men to fetch their saddlebags and to fill them with the money,
the utensils, the treasures and the jewels that were there. Talib said to
him: 'Are we going to leave this girl with what is covering her? There is not
and has never been anything like it; it is worth more than all the money
you can take and will be the best gift with which to win the favour of the
Commander of the Faithful.' 'Didn't you listen to the instructions on her
tablet?' asked Musa. 'She charged us to leave this, and we are not a
people who break faith.' Talib repeated: 'Are we to leave this treasure
and these jewels just because of these words? What can she do with
them, now that she is dead? These are worldly decorations to adorn the
living, while a cotton robe will do to cover the girl, and we have a better
right to the rest.' He then approached the stair and walked up the steps
until he had reached a point between the two pillars and the two guards.
At that, one of them struck him in the back while the other cut off his
head with a blow from his sword, and he fell dead. 'May God not pity
your fall!' exclaimed Musa. 'There is wealth in plenty here, but avarice
exposes the greedy to reproach.'

He ordered the soldiers to come in and they then loaded their camels
with riches and precious stones, after which they were told to shut the
gate, leaving it as it had been when they came. Their route then took
them along the coast until they came to a high mountain overlooking
the sea in which there were many caves inhabited by a black race who

wore leather loincloths, with leather burnouses covering their heads, speaking an incomprehensible language. When they saw Musa's men they ran off to the caves, their women and children standing at the entrances. Musa asked 'Abd al-Samad who they were and was told by him that these were the ones for whom the caliph was looking. So the Arabs dismounted and pitched their camp, unloading their treasure. Before they had settled there, the king of the blacks came down from the mountain and approached them. He knew Arabic, and when he reached Musa they exchanged greetings and Musa treated him with respect. The king then asked him whether he and his men were humans or *jinn*, to which Musa replied: 'We are humans, but because you live alone here on this mountain cut off from mankind and because of your huge size, you must be *jinn*.' 'No,' the king corrected him, 'we are human, descendants of Ham, the son of Noah, on whom be peace, and the name of the sea here is al-Karkar.' 'How do you know about religion,' asked Musa, 'when no prophet has brought you the divine revelation in a land like this?' 'You must know, emir,' answered the king, 'that from the sea here a figure appears to us whose radiance illumines the horizons and who calls out in a voice that all can hear, near and far alike: "Children of Ham, humble yourselves before the One Who sees but is not seen, and recite: 'There is no god but God, and Muhammad is the Prophet of God.' I am Abu'l-'Abbas al-Khidr." Before that we used to worship one of our own number, but al-Khidr summoned us to the worship of the Lord of mankind, and he taught us words which we repeat.' When Musa asked him what these were, he said: 'They are these: "There is no god but God alone, Who has no partner. His is the kingdom and the praise; He gives life and death and His power extends over all things." These are the words that we use in our worship, and they are the only ones we know. Every Friday night we see a radiance that extends over the surface of the land and we hear a voice that calls out: "Glorious and holy God, Lord of the angels and the spirit! His will is done and what He does not will does not come about. Every good thing comes through His favour and there is no might and no power except with Him, the Exalted, the Omnipotent."'

Musa told him: 'We are companions of the ruler of Islam, 'Abd al-Malik ibn Marwan, and we have come because of the brass bottles that you have in your sea in which *marids* were imprisoned by Solomon, son of David. He has told us to fetch him some of these so that he may look at them and inspect them.' The king willingly agreed to help and, while he entertained Musa with a meal of fish, he ordered his divers to bring some of Solomon's bottles from the sea. They fetched twelve of these to the delight of Musa, 'Abd al-Samad and their men, as their mission for the caliph was now accomplished. Musa presented the king with a great many splendid gifts, while for his part he gave Musa some extraordinary sea creatures that looked like humans, telling him that the guest provision for the three days of his stay would consist of their flesh. 'We must take some of them back with us to show to the Commander of the Faithful,' Musa told him, 'as this will appeal to him even more than Solomon's bottles.'

He and his men then took their leave and travelled on until they got to Damascus, where they entered the caliph's presence. Musa told him everything that they had seen, and described the poems, information and admonitions that they had collected, as well as reporting Talib's death. 'I wish that I had been with you,' said the caliph, 'so as to have seen what you saw.' He then took the bottles, opening them one after the other, marvelling at the *marids* who came out, each repeating: 'I repent, prophet of God, and I shall never be disobedient again.' As for the mermaids, on whose flesh the king of the blacks had entertained them, wooden troughs were made for them which were filled with water and into which they were put, but the heat was too much for them and they died. The caliph then collected the treasure and distributed it among the Muslims . . .

Night 578

Morning now dawned and Shahrazad broke off from what she had been allowed to say. Then, when it was the five hundred and seventy-eighth night, SHE CONTINUED:

I have heard, O fortunate king, that when 'Abd al-Malik ibn Marwan, the Commander of the Faithful, saw the bottles and their contents, he was filled with astonishment. He then ordered the treasure to be collected and distributed among the Muslims, remarking that God had never given to anyone else the like of what he had given to Solomon, son of David. Musa then asked that his son be allowed to take over his governorship, while he himself went to Jerusalem the Noble in order to worship God. The caliph duly appointed his son, and Musa set off for Jerusalem, where he later died.

This is the end of the complete account of the City of Brass as it reached us. God knows better.

We have also heard that in former times there was a king who had a large army and many auxiliaries, a man of importance and wealth, but one who throughout his long life had never fathered a son. This disturbed him and so he prayed to God in the name of the Prophet, may God bless him and give him peace, invoking the glory of the prophets, saints and martyrs among His servants who were near to Him, and asking that he be given a son to console him and to inherit the kingdom after his death. He then got up immediately, went to his private chamber and sent for his wife, with whom he lay. By the permission of Almighty God, she conceived, and when the time of her pregnancy had been completed, she gave birth to a boy whose face was like the full moon on its fourteenth night. When this boy was five years old he was entrusted to one of the king's servants, a wise and skilled philosopher by the name of Sindbad, and when he was ten Sindbad instructed him in philosophy and philology until no one then living could match him in debate on matters of learning, philology and understanding. On hearing that, his father provided him with a number of Arab champions to teach him horsemanship. The boy excelled in this, exercising himself in the arts of war on the practice ground until he surpassed his peers and all others living at that time.

One day, when Sindbad the wise was studying the stars, he saw that, according to the prince's horoscope, if in the next seven days he spoke a single word, this would bring about his death. He went to the king and told him about this, and when the king asked him what should be done, he suggested that the prince be put in a room where he could be entertained by listening to musical instruments, and there he should stay until the seven days were up. The king sent to one of his favourite singing girls, the most beautiful of them all, and told her to take the prince to her quarters and to keep him there with her, not letting him come to the palace for seven days. She took him by the hand and sat him down in her pavilion, where there were forty rooms, in each of which were ten slave girls. Every one of these had with her a musical instrument and when any one of them began to play, the whole pavilion would dance with delight to the notes. Around it was a running stream whose banks were planted with fruit trees and scented herbs.

The prince was an indescribably handsome and graceful boy, and when he had spent a single night there, his father's favourite concubine fell in love at the sight of him. She could not restrain herself and threw herself on him, but he said: 'God willing, when I leave here and see my father I shall tell him what you did and he will kill you.' So the girl went to the king and fell down before him, weeping and wailing. He asked her: 'What is the matter? How is your master? Is he not well?' 'Sir,' she said, 'the prince tried to seduce me and then wanted to kill me, but I kept him off and then ran away from him, and I am never going to go back to him or to the pavilion.'

When the king heard that, in his rage he summoned the viziers and ordered them to kill the prince. They told each other that, although the king had made up his mind to have the prince killed, he would be sorry for it afterwards. 'The boy is dear to him,' they said, 'as he was born after his father had been in despair. He will then blame us and ask why we did nothing to stop him from killing his son.' At that, the first vizier came forward and promised that, for twenty-four hours, he would keep the king from doing what would be harmful for them. He got up, went into the king's presence and stood before him, asking permission to speak. When this had been granted, he said: 'Your majesty, had fate provided you with a thousand sons, you would not have brought yourself to have one of them killed on the word of a slave girl, who may be telling the truth but may be lying. This may be a trick on her part directed against your son.' 'Do you know anything about the wiles of women, vizier?' asked the king. 'Yes,' said the vizier, and HE TOLD THE FOLLOWING TALE:

I have heard that once there was a king who was enamoured of women. One day, when he was alone in his palace, his eye fell on a lovely and graceful girl on the flat roof of a house. When he saw her, he could not stop himself from falling in love and so he asked about the house. He was told that it belonged to a certain vizier, and so he got up immediately and summoned the vizier, who, on his arrival, was sent off with orders not to return before he had inspected a number of districts in the kingdom. When the man had gone the king contrived to enter his house, and the girl, recognizing him, jumped up and welcomed him, kissing his hands and feet. She then stood at a distance, being anxious to serve him, and she said: 'Master, what is the reason for this fortunate arrival of yours? For people like me are not worthy of such an honour.' 'It is love and desire for you that has brought me here,' the king replied, at which she again kissed the ground before him and said: 'Master, I am not fit to be the slave of one of your servants, so how should I enjoy such great

favour with you and occupy such a position?' The king reached out for
her but she said: 'There will be time enough for this. Wait, your majesty,
and stay all day with me so that I may get you something to eat.'

The king sat down in the vizier's place, and the girl brought him a
book containing admonitions and moral stories to read while the meal
was being prepared. The king took it and started to go through it, and
the warnings and maxims he found in it were enough to deter him from
committing adultery, making him unwilling to act in disobedience to
God. Then, when the food was ready, the girl brought it to him on ninety
dishes. The king took a spoonful from each, but although the types of
food varied, their taste was the same. In his surprise he pointed this out
to the girl, and she told him that she had produced this as a parable for
his instruction. 'What is the idea behind it?' he asked, and she told him:
'May God preserve the king. In your palace you have ninety concubines
of various colours, but they all taste the same.' When the king heard
that, he was ashamed and got up immediately and went out of the house,
without harming her in any way. In his embarrassment, as he left for his
palace, he forgot his signet ring, which was under the cushion on which
he had been sitting. When he was seated in the palace the vizier arrived
and, after having presented himself and kissed the ground before the
king, he reported on what he had been sent to inspect. He then went
back home and, taking his usual seat, he put his hand under the cushion,
where he discovered and picked up the king's ring. He took the matter
to heart and kept away from his wife for a whole year, not even speaking
to her. She did not know why he was angry . . .

Night 579

Morning now dawned and Shahrazad broke off from what she had been
allowed to say. Then, when it was the five hundred and seventy-ninth
night, SHE CONTINUED:

I have heard, O fortunate king, that the vizier kept away from his wife
for a whole year, not even speaking to her. She did not know why he
was angry, and after a long delay, during which she had still not found
out the reason, she sent a message to her father telling him that her
husband had left her on her own for a whole year. Her father promised
to lodge a complaint against him while he was in the presence of the
king.

One day, when the father went to court, he discovered the vizier with the king, and with him was the *qadi* of the army. He made his complaint, saying: 'May Almighty God preserve the king. I had a beautiful garden that I planted with my own hands and on which I spent my money until its harvest of fruit was ripe. Then I gave it to this vizier of yours and he ate what he wanted from it but then abandoned it. He gave it no water and so the flowers withered; its beauty vanished and its condition changed.' 'What he has said is true,' acknowledged the vizier. 'I used to look after this garden and eat its fruit, but when I went to it one day I saw traces left there by a lion, and I abandoned it, fearing for my own life.' The king realized that the 'trace' which the vizier had found was his signet ring which he had forgotten and left behind. He said to the vizier: 'Let me assure you that you can go back to your garden safely. Although the lion went there, it did not go too close, and I swear by the honour of my ancestors that it did no harm.' 'To hear is to obey,' said the vizier, and he went back to his house, where he sent word to his wife and made his peace with her, being assured of her chastity.

'I have also heard, O king, that there was a merchant who was often on his travels,' the first vizier said, AND HE WENT ON:

He had a beautiful wife whom he guarded jealously because of his love for her and for whom he bought a parrot which used to tell him what had happened in his absence. While he was away on one of his journeys his wife fell in love with a young man, who used to visit her and to whom she granted her favours during the course of her husband's absence. On his return, the parrot told him what had happened and said: 'While you were away, master, a young Turk used to come to visit your wife and she received him with the greatest favour.' He thought of killing the woman, but when she learned of this she said: 'Husband, fear God and come back to your senses. Does a bird have intelligence or understanding? If you want me to show you how to tell when it is lying and when it is telling the truth, go off tonight and sleep in a friend's house. Then come back tomorrow morning and question it, in order to see if it is telling the truth or not.'

The husband went off to one of his friends and spent the night there, and at nightfall his wife took a piece of leather matting with which she covered the parrot's cage; she then sprinkled water over the mat and fanned it with a fan, while bringing the lamp close to it so that it shone like a lightning flash. She went on fanning the cage until morning. Then, when her husband came, she told him to go and question the parrot. He went to the bird and asked it what had happened on the previous night. 'Master,' it said, 'who could see or hear anything last night?' 'Why was that?' he asked. 'Because of the rain and wind, as well as the thunder and lightning,' the parrot replied. The man said: 'That is not true. Nothing like that happened last night,' but the parrot insisted: 'I have only told you what I saw with my own eyes and what I heard.' The man then assumed that everything the parrot had told him about his wife was false, and he wanted to make his peace with her. 'By God,' she said, 'I am not going to be reconciled until you kill this parrot who told lies about me,' and so he went and killed it. After he had stayed for a few days with his wife, he caught sight of the young Turk coming out of his house. This made him realize that the parrot had told the truth while his wife had lied, and he regretted having killed it. He immediately went to his wife and cut her throat, swearing to himself that as long as he lived he would never marry again.

'I have only told you this, your majesty,' the vizier concluded, 'to show you the extent of women's wiles and to point out that haste leads to regret.' The king then changed his mind about having his son executed, but the next day the girl came to him, kissed the ground in front of him and said: 'O king, how is it that you have neglected what is due to me? The other kings will hear that you gave an order and that it was countermanded by your vizier, although to obey a king is to carry out his commands. Everyone knows of your justice and fairness, so give me justice in respect of your son.'

She went on: 'I have heard that there was a fuller who used to go out every day to the bank of the Tigris to bleach cloth. His son would go with him and pass the time by swimming in the river. His father did not stop him, but one day while the boy was swimming his arms grew tired and he sank. Seeing this, his father jumped in and swam towards him, but when he had managed to get hold of him, the boy clung to him, with the result that both of them were drowned. In the same way, your majesty, if you do not stop your son and revenge me on him, I am afraid that both of you will drown.'

Night 580

Morning now dawned and Shahrazad broke off from what she had been allowed to say. Then, when it was the five hundred and eightieth night, SHE CONTINUED:

I have heard, O fortunate king, that when the girl had told the king the story of the fuller and his son, she said: 'I am afraid that both you and your son will drown.' THE GIRL WENT ON:

I have heard a story of the wiles of men that a man loved a beautiful woman who had a husband who loved her as much as she loved him. She was virtuous and chaste and the man could find no way in which to approach her until, after a time, he thought of a trick. Her husband had a young page whom he had brought up in his house and whom he trusted. The would-be lover went to this page and continued to flatter him with gifts and favours until he was willing to agree to anything that was asked of him. One day, the man suggested that he invite him to the house while his mistress was out. The page agreed and when his mistress had gone to the baths and his master was in his shop, the page went to his friend and, taking him by the hand, brought him into the house, where he showed him everything that was there. The man, who was intent on ensnaring the woman, had brought with him the white of an egg in a container, and this he managed to pour over the husband's bed without the page noticing. He then left the house and went on his way.

After a while the husband came back, and when he went to his bed to rest he found it damp and, after picking up what he found there, he inspected it and thought to himself that it was human sperm. He looked angrily at the page and asked him where his mistress was. 'She has gone to the baths,' the page said, 'but she will be back straight away.' The husband's suspicions were confirmed and, as he was sure that this was sperm, he told the page to go at once and fetch her. When she came he jumped up and, after giving her a painful beating, he tied her hands and was about to cut her throat. She shrieked to the neighbours, and when they came she told them: 'This man wants to kill me, and I don't know what I have done wrong.' They went up to the husband and told him: 'You cannot touch her. Either you have to divorce her or, if not, you have to treat her well. We know she is chaste; she has been a neighbour of ours for a long time and we have never known her to do anything wrong.' He told them: 'I have found semen like that of a man's in my bed,

and I don't know the reason behind it.' One of the men there asked to be
shown this 'semen', and after seeing it he said: 'Fetch me fire and a pan.'
When he got these, he took the egg white, heated it over the fire, tasted it
and then gave it to the others to try. They confirmed that this was egg
white, and the husband realized that he had wronged his wife and that
she was innocent. He had been ready to divorce her, but thanks to the
intervention of the neighbours the pair were reconciled and the plot that
the would-be lover had laid against the unsuspecting woman failed.

'Know, your majesty,' the girl went on, 'that this is one of the wiles of
men.' The king then renewed his order that his son be executed, but at
that point the second vizier came forward, kissed the ground before him
and said: 'Do not be in a hurry to kill your son, your majesty, for it was
only after you had been reduced to despair that his mother gave birth to
him. It is our hope that he will prove a treasure for your kingdom and a
guardian of your wealth. Wait in patience, for he may have something
to say in his own defence and if you have him killed prematurely you
will regret it, just as the merchant did.' 'How was that,' asked the king,
'and what is the story?' THE SECOND VIZIER SAID:

There was a merchant who was frugal in what he ate and drank. One
day, he went off to a certain town and while he was walking in the markets
he came across an old woman who was carrying two loaves of bread. 'Are
these for sale?' he asked, and when she said yes, he haggled until he bought
them from her at a very cheap price, after which he took them back home
and ate them that same day. The next day he went back to the same place,
where he found the old woman with another two loaves, which he also
bought. Things went on like this for twenty days, but after that the old
woman disappeared, and although he asked about her, he could find no
news. Then, one day, he came across her in a street, and after stopping to
greet her he asked her why she had gone away and was no longer selling
loaves. She was reluctant to answer his question, but when he pressed
her to tell him, she said: 'Sir, the answer is that I used to look after a
man who had a gangrenous sore on his spine. His doctor used to take
flour, mix it with fat and apply it all night long to the sore. Then, in the
morning, I would take the mixture, make two loaves out of it and sell
them either to you or to someone else, but the man died and I could not
make the loaves any more.' When the man heard that, he recited the
formula: 'We belong to God and to Him do we return. There is no might
and no power except with God, the Exalted, the Omnipotent!'

Night 581

Morning now dawned and Shahrazad broke off from what she had been allowed to say. Then, when it was the five hundred and eighty-first night,

SHE CONTINUED:

I have heard, O fortunate king, that when the old woman told the merchant about the two loaves, he exclaimed: 'There is no might and no power except with God, the Exalted, the Omnipotent!'

After that he could not stop vomiting until he fell ill, regretting what he had done when regret was of no use.

THE SECOND VIZIER WENT ON:

I heard another story about women's wiles: there was once a man who used to stand with a drawn sword as a king's guard. He was in love with a girl to whom he was in the habit of sending his page with messages. One day, while the page was with her, he began to fondle her and she leaned over and embraced him. He asked her to lie with him and she agreed, but while they were making love, the page's master knocked on the door. The girl put her lover in a cellar and then opened the door, at which the man came in with his sword. He sat down on her bed and she began to joke with him and fondle him, clasping him to her breast and kissing him. He had started to make love to her when suddenly her husband knocked at the door. 'Who is that?' the man asked, and when she told him that it was her husband he said: 'What are we to do now?' 'Get up,' she told him, 'draw your sword and stand in the hall. Then shout insults and abuse at me, and when my husband comes in, go on your way.' The man did as he was told, and when the husband came in, he saw the man standing with a drawn sword in his hand, shouting abuse and threatening his wife. At the sight of her husband her lover felt ashamed and, sheathing his sword, he left the house.

The husband then asked his wife: 'What was the reason for all that?' 'It was lucky that you came when you did,' she told him, 'for you have rescued a Muslim from death. I was up on the roof spinning, when in came a page who was being pursued. He was out of his mind and panting in fear of death as that man came running up as fast as he could behind him, holding a drawn sword. The page fell in front of me, kissed my hands and my feet and said: "Lady, save me from someone who wants to kill me unjustly." So I hid him in our cellar, and when the man came in with his naked sword and asked me where he was, I refused to tell him anything and then, as you saw, he began to abuse me and threaten me. Praise be to God, Who brought you to me, for I didn't know what to do and there was nobody here to rescue me.' 'You did well, woman,' her husband told her, 'and God will reward you well for what you did.' He then went to the cellar and called to the page: 'Come out! No harm will come to you.' The page came out timidly and the man kept saying sympathetically: 'Calm down; no harm will come to you,' while the page, for his part, called down blessings on him. Both of them then left without knowing what it was that the woman had contrived.

'Know, O king,' the vizier continued, 'that this is one example of the wiles of women, so beware of relying on what they say.' At that the king changed his mind about having his son killed, but on the third day the girl came back and, after having kissed the ground before him, she again insisted that he right the wrong that his son had done her and not listen to his viziers. 'There is no good to be had from evil viziers,' she said, adding: 'Do not be like the king who relied on the word of one of them.' 'How was that?' asked the king, and SHE TOLD HIM:

I have heard, O fortunate and judicious king, that a certain ruler had a son whom he loved and treated with the greatest honour, preferring him to all his other sons. One day, this prince told his father that he wanted to go out hunting and accordingly his father ordered everything to be got ready for him, telling one of his viziers to attend on him and to see that all his wants were satisfied while he was away. The vizier collected everything the prince might need and the two of them were accompanied by eunuchs, officers and pages. They set out on their hunt and came to a green region with grass, pasture and water, where there were great quantities of game. The prince told the vizier that he found the place attractive and so the hunting party halted there for a number of days. Then, after the prince had enjoyed himself thoroughly, he gave the order to move on, but at that point his path was crossed by a gazelle which had become separated from its herd. The prince felt an urge to hunt it down and he told the vizier that he was going to give chase. 'Do as you like,' the vizier told him, and so he rode off after it alone, pursuing it for the whole day until nightfall.

At that point the gazelle went up into a tract of rocky ground and, as the night was getting dark, the prince wanted to go back, but he did not know which direction to take. He rode on until morning in a state of perplexity, finding no way out of his difficulties and being forced to carry on, hungry, thirsty and afraid, with no idea where he was going. At midday, in the burning heat, he found himself looking down on a solidly built city with tall buildings, but it was desolate, with owls and crows as its only inhabitants. Then, as he stopped there to look in wonder at what could be seen of it, he caught sight of a lovely, graceful girl who was weeping beneath a wall. He asked her who she was and she told him: 'I am Bint al-Tamima, daughter of al-Tayyakh, king of the Grey Land. One day I went out to relieve myself and was snatched up by an *'ifrit* who flew off with me, but as he was flying in mid-air a fiery meteor struck him and he was consumed by fire. I fell on this spot and I have been here for three days, suffering from hunger and thirst, but when I saw you I began to have fresh hopes that I might survive.'

Night 582

Morning now dawned and Shahrazad broke off from what she had been allowed to say. Then, when it was the five hundred and eighty-second night, SHE CONTINUED:

I have heard, O fortunate king, that when the princess spoke to the prince, telling him that when she saw him she had begun to hope that she might survive, the prince, moved by pity, took her up behind him on his horse, comforted and consoled her and said: 'If God, the Glorious and Almighty, restores me to my people and my family, I will send you back home.' He rode off, asking God for deliverance, until the girl asked him to put her down so that she might relieve herself under the cover of a wall. He halted and helped her to dismount and then waited for her as she went off behind the wall, but when she came out her appearance was so frightful that his whole body trembled; he was frightened out of his wits and his colour changed. She jumped up behind him in all her ugliness and asked: 'Prince, why have you lost colour?' 'I was thinking over something that worries me,' he told her. 'Then look for help from your father's armies and his champions,' she told him, but he replied: 'The person who concerns me won't be frightened off by armies or troubled by champions.' So she said: 'Use your father's wealth and his treasures to help you,' but he objected: 'The person who concerns me will not be satisfied with money or treasures.' She said: 'You think that you have in the heavens a god who sees but is not seen and who has power over all things.' 'Yes,' he answered, 'we have none but Him.' 'Call on Him then,' she said, 'and perhaps He will allow you to escape from me.' So the prince raised his eyes to heaven and called on God with all sincerity: 'My God, I seek Your help in my present trouble,' gesturing with his hand at his companion, and at this she fell to the ground like a lump of burned coal. The prince gave praise and thanks to God and pressed onwards with God's help and guidance until he reached his own land and returned to the king, his father, after having despaired of life. All of that happened because the vizier, who had gone with him, had planned that he should die on his journey, but Almighty God rescued him.

The girl went on: 'I have told you this, your majesty, so that you may realize that evil viziers are not sincere and have no good intentions with regard to their kings. You have to be on your guard against them.' The king accepted what she had to say and renewed his order that his son be executed. At this point the third vizier came forward and promised his colleagues that for this day he would stop the king from doing what would harm them. When he came into the king's presence, he kissed the ground before him and said: 'Your majesty, I will give you good advice, as I have at heart your interests and those of your dynasty. I tell you that the right thing to do is not to be hasty in killing your son, your darling and the fruit of your heart. It may be that what he did was something minor which this girl has exaggerated to you, and I have heard that the inhabitants of two villages killed each other because of a single drop of honey.' 'How was that?' asked the king and THE THIRD VIZIER SAID:

I was told, O king, that there was a man who used to hunt wild beasts in desert country. One day, he came to a mountain cave in which he found a hollow full of honey. He put some of this into a water skin which he had with him and, with the skin on his shoulder, he went to the city, accompanied by his hunting dog, of which he was very fond. He stopped by the shop of an oil seller and showed him the honey, which the man was willing to buy. The hunter opened up his water skin and extracted the honey to show him, but a drop fell on to the ground. Flies collected over it and birds then swooped down. The shopkeeper had a cat, which pounced at the birds, but the hunter's dog then leapt at it and killed it. The shopkeeper killed the dog and in his turn was killed by the hunter. These men came from different villages, and when the two sets of villagers heard what had happened, they took their arms and their gear and confronted each other angrily, continuing to fight until many of them lay dead – how many God alone knows.

'I have also heard concerning the wiles of women that a certain woman was given a dirham by her husband in order to buy rice,' the third vizier said, AND HE WENT ON:

When she went to the rice seller, he gave her the rice but then started fondling and squeezing her, saying: 'Rice is only nice with sugar, and if you want the sugar then come into my shop for an hour.' She went in and he told his slave: 'Weigh out a dirham's worth of sugar for this woman,' giving him a secret sign as he did so. The slave took the woman's kerchief, emptied out the rice that was in it and filled it instead with soil, while in place of sugar he put stones. He then tied the kerchief up and left it for her. On her way out she took it and went back home, thinking that it contained rice and sugar. When she got home, she gave the kerchief to her husband, who discovered the soil and stones in it. She had fetched the cooking pot, but he said: 'Did I tell you that we wanted to build something, so that you brought me soil and stones?' When she looked she realized that the servant of the rice seller had tricked her, but, standing there with the pot in her hand, she said: 'I went to get a sieve but absent-mindedly fetched the cooking pot instead.' 'What were you thinking of?' her husband asked, and she told him: 'I dropped the dirham that I had with me in the market and I was too ashamed to hunt around for it with people watching, but as I didn't want to lose it, I gathered up the soil from the place where it fell, intending to sieve it. I had gone to fetch the sieve but brought the pot instead.' She then went off and fetched the sieve, which she gave to her husband, saying: 'You sieve it, for your eyes are better than mine.' So he sat down and sieved the soil until his face and his beard were full of dust, not realizing how she had tricked him or what she had done.

This, your majesty, is one example of women's wiles. You should also note the saying of Almighty God in the Quran: 'Great are the wiles of women,'* where He also says: 'Satan's wiles are weak.'†

The king was pleased and convinced by what the vizier had said in order to restrain him from acting in a fit of emotion. As he thought over the

* Quran 12.28.   † Quran 4.78.

Quranic verses that had been quoted to him, the light of good counsel shone in the sky of his understanding and in his soul, and he gave up his intention to have his son put to death. On the fourth day, however, the girl came to him, kissed the ground before him and said: 'O fortunate and judicious king, I have shown you clearly what is rightfully owed me, but you have treated me unjustly and put off avenging me on the one who wronged me because he is your son and your heart's darling. The Glorious and Almighty God will help me against him as He helped the prince against his father's vizier.' 'How was that?' asked the king and SHE SAID:

I have heard, O king, how one of the kings in past times had an only son who, on reaching manhood, was married by his father to the lovely and graceful daughter of another king. Her cousin had earlier asked her father for her hand, but he had not been willing to give her to him. When she married someone else, in a fit of jealous rage the disappointed suitor decided to send gifts to the vizier of the king, her father-in-law. He forwarded presents of great value, together with large sums of money, to the vizier, asking him to devise a scheme to get the prince killed or else to trick him into withdrawing from the marriage, explaining that he was moved by jealousy, as the girl was his cousin. When the gifts reached the vizier, he accepted them and sent back a consoling and heartening message to the man, promising to do what he wanted.

The princess's father summoned the prince to his capital for the wedding and, when this message came, the king gave permission to his son to leave, sending with him the vizier who had been bribed, together with an escort of a thousand men, as well as gifts, litters, pavilions and tents. The vizier, who secretly harboured evil thoughts against the prince, intended to trick him. So, when they reached a stretch of desert, he remembered that there in the mountains was a spring of running water known as al-Zahra, which would turn any man who drank from it into a woman. With that in his mind, the vizier halted his men nearby and then mounted his horse, asking the prince: 'Would you like to ride out with me to look at a spring of water here?' There was no one else with them as the prince rode off with him, not knowing what the future held in store, and they went on until they came to the spring. The prince dismounted, washed his hands, drank from it and was transformed into a woman. When he realized what had happened, he gave a cry and then wept until he fainted. The vizier went up to him, commiserating with him and asking what had happened to him. The prince told him and the vizier continued his commiserations, shedding tears at his misfortune and exclaiming: 'May Almighty God protect you against this! How is it that so disastrous a misfortune should strike you when we were going on our way so happily to your wedding with the princess? I have no idea now whether we should go to her or not. It is for you to decide, so what do you want to do?' 'Go back to my father,' the prince said, 'and tell him what has happened to me, for I am not going to leave here until this change is reversed or until I die of grief.'

The prince then wrote a letter to his father telling him what had happened, and the vizier, who was secretly delighted with what he had done, took it and left for the king's capital, abandoning the prince together with his escort. When he reached the king, he told him about what had happened and gave him his son's letter. The king was deeply saddened and sent to the wise men and the masters of mysteries, telling them to throw light for him on his son's misfortune, but he got no answer. The vizier then sent the good news of this to the princess's cousin, who was overjoyed to hear it, hoping that he could now marry her. He sent valuable presents and large stores of money to the vizier, thanking him profusely.

As for the prince, he stayed by the spring for three days and nights without eating or drinking, relying in his misfortune on God, the Glorious, the Exalted, Who never disappoints the hopes of those who put their trust in Him. Then, on the fourth night, a rider appeared wearing a crown on his head and looking like one of the sons of kings. 'Young man,' the rider asked, 'who brought you here?' The prince told him what had happened to him, explaining that he was on his way to his wedding and that the vizier had brought him to the spring from which he had drunk, with the result that he had changed sex. As he spoke he was overcome by tears and, hearing what he had to say, the rider was moved by pity and said: 'It was your father's vizier who brought this disaster on you, for there is only one man who knows about this spring.' He then told the prince to mount and go with him to his house, where he would be his guest that night. 'Before I ride with you,' said the prince, 'tell me who you are.' 'I am the son of the king of the *jinn* and you are the son of a human king, so take heart and console yourself that your cares and sorrows will be at an end, as this is a simple matter for me.'

The prince accompanied him, without concerning himself about his escort, and they rode from daybreak until midnight. The *jinn* prince then asked whether he realized what distance they had covered in that time, and when he said: 'I have no idea,' the other told him that this was a year's journey for a fast traveller. The astonished prince asked: 'How am I to get back to my people?' but his guide said: 'That is not your concern but mine, and when you have been cured of your affliction, it will be easy for me to see that you return to them faster than the blink of an eye.' The prince was overjoyed to hear this and thought that the whole thing had been a dream. 'Praise be to God, Who has the power to return the wretched man to happiness!' he exclaimed in his delight.

Night 583

Morning now dawned and Shahrazad broke off from what she had been allowed to say. Then, when it was the five hundred and eighty-third night, SHE CONTINUED:

I have heard, O fortunate king, that the *jinni* delighted the prince by telling him that when he had been cured he would return to his people faster than the blink of an eye. THE GIRL WENT ON:

The two of them continued on their way until morning, by which time they had reached a green and fertile land with tall trees, tuneful birds, splendid meadows and lofty palaces. The *jinn* prince dismounted and, after telling his companion to follow his example, he took him by the hand and led him into one of the palaces, where he found a dignified and imposing ruler, with whom he stayed all day, eating and drinking. At nightfall the *jinn* prince remounted his horse, and he and the human prince rode out under cover of darkness, pressing on until morning. By then they were in a dark and uncultivated land of rocks and black stones, like a district of hell. 'What is this place called?' asked the human prince and the other told him: 'It is the Black Land, and it belongs to a *jinn* king called the Two Winged, whom no other king can subdue and whose land cannot be entered by anyone without his leave. So stay where you are until I ask his permission.'

The prince halted and his companion left him for a while. When he came back, the two continued on their way until they came at last to a spring of water flowing from dark mountains. The *jinn* prince told the human to dismount and drink from it, and when he had done that he instantly became a man again, just as he had been before, through the power of Almighty God. He was overjoyed and asked: 'Brother, what is the name of this spring?' 'It is known as the Women's Spring,' said the other, 'and no woman can drink from it without becoming a man. So give praise and thanks to God for your cure and then mount your horse.' The prince did this, and they both rode off at a fast pace for the rest of the day until they had returned to the *jinni*'s land. The prince remained there, being lavishly entertained, and the two of them ate and drank until nightfall. 'Do you want to go back to your family tonight?' asked his host, and when the other said: 'Yes, as I need to see them again,' the *jinni* called for one of his father's slaves, named Rajiz, and told him: 'Take this young man from here on your shoulder and see to it that he is with his father-in-law and his wife before daybreak.' 'To hear is to obey,' said Rajiz, 'I shall do this most gladly.' He left for a time, and when he returned it was in the form of an *'ifrit*. The startled prince panicked, but his *jinn* companion told him: 'No harm will come to you. Mount your horse and ride it up on to Rajiz's shoulder.' 'No,' said the prince, 'I shall climb up myself and leave the horse with you,' and so he dismounted and climbed on the *'ifrit*'s shoulder. 'Close your eyes,' said the *jinni*, and when the young man did so the *'ifrit* flew off with him between the heavens and the earth. He had no idea what was happening to him, but by the time that the third and last watch of the night had come, he was on the roof of his father-in-law's palace. He was told to dismount and when he had, the *'ifrit* said: 'Open your eyes, for this is the palace of your father-in-law and of his daughter,' after which he left him and flew away.

When day broke and the young prince had recovered from his alarm, he came down from the roof, and on seeing him his father-in-law rose to greet him, filled with amazement at finding him there. 'Other people can be seen coming through doors,' he exclaimed, 'but you come down from the sky!' 'What happened was the will of God, the Glorious and Exalted,' the prince said, and the astonished king expressed delight at his safe return. When the sun had risen he ordered his vizier to have great feasts prepared, and when this had been done the marriage was celebrated and consummated. The prince stayed there for two months, after which he set out for his father's city. As for the bride's cousin, he died of jealous passion when the prince slept with her, and in this way God, the Glorious and Almighty, allowed the prince to triumph both over his rival and over his father's vizier. All was well and when he brought his bride to his father in a state of perfect happiness, his father came out to meet him with his troops and his viziers.

I hope, your majesty, that Almighty God will allow you to get the better of your own viziers, and I ask you to right the wrong your son did me.

On hearing this, the king gave orders that his son be executed.

Night 584

Morning now dawned and Shahrazad broke off from what she had been allowed to say. Then, when it was the five hundred and eighty-fourth night, SHE CONTINUED:

I have heard, O fortunate king, that when the girl had told the king her story and asked him to right the wrong done to her by his son, his father ordered his execution. This was on the fourth day, and it was the fourth vizier who came in, kissed the ground before the king and said: 'May God strengthen the king and aid him. O king, take your time with regard to this sentence that you are determined to carry out. No intelligent man acts until he has looked at the consequences of his action and the proverb has it that Time does not befriend whoever does not consider these consequences. Those who fail to proceed carefully suffer what happened to the bath keeper at the hands of his wife.' The king asked what this was, and THE FOURTH VIZIER SAID:

I have heard that there was a bath keeper whose baths were patronized by the leading men and persons of importance in his city. One day, in came a handsome young man, the son of a vizier, who was stout and thickset. The bath keeper waited on him, and when his customer had taken off his clothes, the bath keeper could not see his penis, which was hidden between his thighs because he was so fat; all that could be seen of it was something that looked like a hazelnut. The bath keeper felt sorry for him and clapped his hands together in regret. When the young man saw this he asked the reason for it and the bath keeper replied: 'It is because you are in such a difficult position. You live a life of ease and are handsome and good-looking, but you lack what would give you a man's enjoyment.' 'That is true,' said the young man, 'and you have reminded me of something that I was forgetting.' The bath keeper asked what this was, and the youth said: 'Take this dinar and fetch me a pretty woman with whom I can try myself out.'

The bath keeper went to his wife with the dinar and told her: 'The son of one of the viziers has come into my baths and, although he is as handsome as the moon on the night it becomes full, he does not have a man-sized penis but only a little thing that looks like a hazelnut. I was sorry for him, young as he is, and he gave me this dinar to fetch him a woman on whom he could test himself. You have a better right to the dinar; this will do us no harm as I shall protect you and you can sit laughing at him for an hour. So take the money.' His wife, who was an exceedingly beautiful woman, took the coin and got up to put on her ornaments and her finest clothes, after which she went out with her husband, who brought her to the vizier's son in a private room. When she got there and looked at him, she saw to her astonishment how handsome and good-looking he was, like a full moon, while he, for his part, immediately lost control of his senses at the sight of her.

The two of them stayed in the room and locked the door, after which the young man took her and clasped her to him. As they embraced, he had an erection like that of a donkey and he mounted her and stayed for a long time as she sobbed and shrieked, twisting and turning beneath him. Her husband started to call to her, saying: 'That's enough. Come out. It has been a long day for the child that you are suckling.' 'Go to your baby and then come back,' the young man kept saying, but she insisted: 'If I leave you, I shall die, and as for my son, he can cry himself to death or be brought up as an orphan without a mother.' So she stayed with the young man until he had made love ten times, with her husband on the other side of the door calling to her, shouting, shedding tears and praying for help which did not come. He kept on doing this and threatening to kill himself, and when he could find no way to get to his wife, in an excess of wretchedness and jealousy, he climbed to the top of the baths and threw himself down to his death.

'I have also heard another story of the wiles of women,' the fourth vizier continued, and when the king asked what this was, HE SAID:

O king, I was told that there was a lovely, graceful and beautiful girl, perfectly formed and without any equal. She was seen by a young libertine who fell deeply in love with her, but she was too chaste to think of adultery and had no wish for him. As it happened, however, her husband left to visit another land and the young man began sending her message after message every day. When she did not reply to him, he went to an old woman living nearby, and after having greeted her he sat complaining to her of his sufferings as a lover and of his passion for the lady whom he wanted to possess. 'There is no need to worry,' said the old woman. 'I can guarantee you success and, God willing, get you what you want.' At this, he gave her a dinar and went on his way.

The next morning the old woman went to renew her acquaintanceship with the girl, and she then started to visit her daily, sharing her morning and evening meals and taking away some food from her house for her own children. She used to joke laughingly with her hostess until she had succeeded in corrupting her to the extent that she could not bear to be parted from her visitor for a single hour. On leaving the house, the old woman used to take a piece of bread, smear it with fat, add some pepper and feed it to a bitch. This went on for some days, and the bitch would follow her because of her kindness in providing this treat. One day, she added a large quantity of pepper to the fat that she gave to the bitch, whose eyes watered when it had eaten it because of the heat of the pepper. It followed the old woman apparently shedding tears, to the great astonishment of the girl, who asked: 'Mother, why is this bitch crying?' 'My daughter,' answered the old woman, 'there is a strange story here. This bitch was once a lovely girl, perfect in her beauty, a companion and friend of mine. A young man in the same quarter fell so passionately in love with her that he had to take to his bed. He sent her a number of messages in the hope that she might have pity on him, but she refused, and although I advised her to do what he asked out of compassion and mercy, she would not take my advice. The young man lost patience and complained to some of his friends, after which they produced a magic charm which changed her human shape to that of a dog. When she saw what had happened to her and how she had been metamorphosed, she found that I was the only one in the world to feel sorry for her and she came to my house looking for sympathy, kissing my hands and my feet and weeping. I recognized her and said: "How many times did I give you advice, but it did you no good?"'

Night 585

Morning now dawned and Shahrazad broke off from what she had been allowed to say. Then, when it was the five hundred and eighty-fifth night, SHE CONTINUED:

I have heard, O fortunate king, that THE FOURTH VIZIER SAID:

This story of the bitch was all a trick to deceive the lady and get her to fall in with the old woman's purpose, and the old woman continued: 'When I saw my friend in that state I was sorry for her and kept her with me. This is how she is now, and whenever she thinks about what she was once like she weeps for herself.'

On hearing this story, the girl became very frightened and said: 'By God, mother, this story of yours has frightened me.' The old woman asked why this was, and the girl said: 'There is a handsome young man who is in love with me and has sent me many messages but I have refused to have anything to do with him and now I am afraid lest the same thing happen to me as happened to this bitch.' 'Take care not to reject my advice, daughter,' said the old woman, 'for I am very afraid for you. If you don't know where he lives, tell me what he looks like and I'll bring him to you, but don't let anyone's heart turn against you.' When the girl described the young man to her, the old woman pretended ignorance, giving the impression that she did not know him, but saying that she would go and ask about him. Then, when she left, she went straight to the man and said: 'Cheer up, for I have duped the girl. At noon tomorrow, come and wait for me at the top end of the quarter, and I shall come and take you with me to her house, where you can enjoy yourself with her for the rest of the day and all the night.' The young man was delighted and gave her two dinars, promising her another ten when he had got what he wanted.

The old woman went back to the girl and said: 'I recognized the man and talked over the matter with him. I found him very angry with you and determined to do you an injury, but I went on trying to win him over and I have persuaded him to come to you at the time of the noon prayer tomorrow.' The girl was delighted and said: 'Mother, if he is happy to come to me, then I shall give you ten dinars.' 'I am the only one who can see to it that he comes,' the old woman replied, and then, the next morning, she told the girl: 'Get a meal ready, put on your finery and wear your best clothes, while I go off and bring him to you.' So the girl got up to adorn herself and to prepare food, while the old woman went out to wait for the young man, but he did not come. She went round looking for him but could find no news of him. 'What am I going to do?' she asked herself. 'Will the food that the girl has prepared go to waste, as well as the promise of money that she made me? I will not let this scheme go for nothing, and so I shall have to look for someone else and bring him to her instead.' While she was going round the street, she caught sight of a handsome young man whose face showed signs that he had been on a journey. She went up to him and said: 'Would you like food, drink and a girl who is ready and waiting for you?' 'Where is that?' the young man asked, and she said: 'With me, in my house.' So he went off with her, but what she did not know was that this man was the girl's husband.

When she came to the house, she knocked on the door and went in after it had been opened by the girl herself, who then ran off to finish dressing and perfuming herself. Congratulating herself on her masterly plot, the old woman brought the young man into the sitting room. In then came the girl, only to discover her husband, with the old woman sitting beside him. On the spur of the moment she had to improvise a trick, and what she did was to pull off her slipper and say to her husband: 'This was not the pledge that we had between us. How can you betray me and behave like this to me? When I heard that you had come back, I decided to use this old woman to test you and she has made you fall into the temptation against which I warned you. I used to think that you were chaste, but now that I have seen you with her I know for certain that you must have broken our agreement and that you frequent dissolute women.' She started to hit him on the head with her slipper, while, for his part, he protested his innocence, swearing that never in his life had he played her false or done what she had accused him of doing. He continued to swear by Almighty God and she continued to strike him, weeping, shrieking and calling: 'Help me, Muslims!' He put his hand over her mouth, but she bit it and he then began to cringe before her, kissing her hands and feet. She was not prepared to accept this, and went on slapping him until she winked to make the old woman stop her. The old woman then went up to her, kissed her hands and feet, and got the two of them to sit down. When they were seated, the husband began to kiss the old woman's hand, exclaiming: 'May God Almighty give you the best of rewards for having saved me from her,' while, for her part, the old woman was filled with admiration for the girl's trick. This, O king, is an example of the wiles and trickery of women.

When the king heard the story, he accepted its lesson and changed his mind about having his son executed . . .

Night 586

Morning now dawned and Shahrazad broke off from what she had been allowed to say. Then, when it was the five hundred and eighty-sixth night, SHE CONTINUED:

I have heard, O fortunate king, that when the fourth vizier had told the king his story, he changed his mind about having his son executed, but then on the fifth day the girl came to him holding a cup of poison in her hand, calling for help and slapping her cheeks and her face. 'O king,' she cried, 'either grant me justice and avenge me on your son, or else I shall drain this poisoned cup and die. Then the wrong you have done me will cling to you until the Day of Judgement. These viziers of yours are trying to associate me with wiles and cunning, but nowhere in the world are there any wilier than they. Have you not heard the story of the goldsmith and the singing girl?' 'What happened to them?' asked the king and SHE SAID:

There was once a goldsmith who was inordinately fond of women and of drinking wine. One day, when he was in a friend's house, he looked around and saw on a wall a picture of the loveliest and most charming girl whom anyone had ever seen. He looked at it again and again, admiring the beauty of the painting, until he had fallen so deeply in love with it that he fell ill and was on the point of death. One of his friends came to visit him and sat by his head, asking him how he was and what his complaint might be. 'My brother,' replied the goldsmith, 'all my sickness and all my sufferings are caused by heartache, for I have fallen in love with a picture painted on the wall of a friend of mine.' His visitor said reproachfully: 'This shows a lack of intelligence on your part. How can you fall in love with a picture on a wall, something that can do neither harm nor good; it cannot look, see, take or withhold?' 'The painter must have painted it using a beautiful model,' said the goldsmith, and when his friend pointed out that it might have been a work of imagination, the goldsmith replied: 'At all events, I am dying of love, and if the painting has a subject to be found in this world, I hope that Almighty God will let me live long enough to see her.'

Those who were at his sickbed went off and asked about the painter, only to find that he had gone to another town. They sent him a letter describing their friend's miserable state and asking him how he had come to paint that picture, whether it was an imaginary portait or whether he had seen the model for it in this world. In his reply he wrote: 'I painted it using as a model a singing girl belonging to a vizier in the city of Kashmir in India.' When the goldsmith heard the news, he made his preparations and set out from his native Persia on his way to India. After much toil, he reached Kashmir and entered the city, where he took up residence. Then, one day, he went to a perfume seller, a native of the place, who was a shrewd, intelligent and sensible man, and asked him about the king and his way of life. 'Our king is an upright man,' the perfume seller replied, 'who conducts himself well, is good to those who are in his service and treats his subjects with justice. The only people whom he dislikes in the world are magicians, and when he comes across one of them, male or female, he has them thrown into a pit outside the city, where he leaves them to starve to death.' The goldsmith next asked about the viziers, each of whose conduct and character the Kashmiri described for him, until the conversation came round to the singing girl, and the goldsmith was told to which of the viziers she belonged.

For some time after that he waited until he had worked out a scheme. On a night of rain and thunder with a stormy wind, he took with him the tools of a thief and set out for the palace of the girl's owner. He managed to fasten his rope ladder with grappling hooks and climbed to the roof, from where he made his way down into the courtyard. He saw all the slave girls asleep on their couches, and there on a couch of marble was a girl as glorious as the full moon on its fourteenth night. He went up to her, sat by her head and lifted the covering. This was embroidered with gold, and there was a candle at her head and another at her feet, each of ambergris and each in a candlestick of gleaming gold, while beneath her pillow under her head was a silver casket containing all her jewellery. He took out a knife and gave her a superficial wound on the buttocks, at which she woke up in alarm. When she saw him she kept quiet, being too frightened to cry out, but then, thinking that he wanted her treasures, she said: 'Take the casket and everything in it. It will do you no good to kill me and I appeal to your honour to protect me.' So the goldsmith took the casket and went off.

Night 587

Morning now dawned and Shahrazad broke off from what she had been allowed to say. Then, when it was the five hundred and eighty-seventh night, SHE CONTINUED:

I have heard, O fortunate king, that the goldsmith went to the vizier's palace, where he wounded the girl on the buttocks and went off with the casket that contained her jewellery. THE GIRL WENT ON:

The next morning, taking it with him, he went to the king and, after having kissed the ground before him, he said: 'O king, I am a sincere friend of yours. I left Khurasan, my own country, to travel to you because of your reputation for fair and just dealing with your subjects, which made me want to serve under your banner. I arrived at your city at the end of the day to find the gate shut, and so I had to sleep outside it. While I was still half-awake I caught sight of four women, one of whom was riding on a broomstick and another on a fan, and I realized that they must be witches who were on their way into the city. One of them came up to me and, after kicking me, she struck me with a fox's brush which she was holding in her hand. The sharpness of the blow caused me pain and so I struck back with a knife that I had with me and wounded her on the backside as she turned away. When I did so, she fled off before me, dropping this casket and its contents. I took it and on opening it I discovered this valuable jewellery. Please take it, for I have no need of it, as I am a wanderer in the mountains who has cleansed his heart of worldly things and all worldly desires.' He then left the casket with the king and went on his way.

When he had gone, the king opened the casket, took out all the ornaments and started turning them over in his hand. Among them he discovered a necklace that he had presented as a gift to the vizier who owned the singing girl. He summoned the man and asked him, on his arrival: 'Is this the necklace that I gave you?' When the vizier saw it, he recognized it and said yes, adding: 'And I gave it to a singing girl of mine.' The king told him to fetch the girl immediately, and when she had been brought into his presence he told the vizier to inspect her buttocks to see whether or not there was the mark of a wound. When the vizier looked, he found the scar left by the knife and said to the king: 'Yes, master, she has been wounded.' 'There can be absolutely no doubt that she is a witch, as the pious man said,' the king told him, and he then ordered her to be put into the witches' pit. She was sent there that day, and when night fell the goldsmith, finding that his trick had worked, went to the guard posted by the pit with a purse containing a thousand dinars in his hand. The two of them sat talking for the first third of the night, after which the goldsmith came to the point and said: 'Brother, you have to know that this girl is innocent of what she has been charged with and it was I who got her into this position.' After having told the man his story from beginning to end, he went on: 'Take this purse of a thousand dinars, my brother, and let me have the girl, so that I can take her off with me to my own country. You will find it more useful to have the money than to keep the girl here, and you will be rewarded by God on our behalf, as the two of us will call down blessings on you and pray for your safety.' The guard was astonished when he heard how the trick had been worked and, taking the purse and its contents, he left the girl to the goldsmith on condition that he would not stay with her in the city for a single hour. The goldsmith went off with her immediately and travelled as fast as he could until he returned to his own land, having done what he had set out to do.

Look, then, O king, at the cunning wiles of men. Your viziers are trying to stop you from avenging me, but a time will come when you and I shall stand before a just Judge, Who will take vengeance for me from you.

When the king heard what she said, he again ordered his son to be executed, but at that point his fifth vizier came in, kissed the ground before him and said: 'Great king, take your time and be in no hurry to have your son killed. Many a hasty act is followed by repentance, and I am afraid that you may have to repent like the man who never laughed again for the rest of his life.' 'How was that?' asked the king.

The vizier said: 'I have heard a story, O king, that at his death a certain man, one of those who owned houses and cattle, wealth, eunuchs, slaves and properties, left a young son. When the boy grew up, he began to pass his time eating and drinking, listening to music and songs and making generous gifts, until he had spent what his father had bequeathed him and all his wealth was gone.'

Night 588

Morning now dawned and Shahrazad broke off from what she had been allowed to say. Then, when it was the five hundred and eighty-eighth night, SHE CONTINUED:

I have heard, O fortunate king, that THE FIFTH VIZIER SAID:

When the son had lost the money that his father had bequeathed him and it was all gone, he resorted to selling his slaves, male and female, together with his properties, but when he had spent everything that he had, both his father's money and everything else, he became so poor that he was forced to work as a labourer. Things went on like this for a year until one day, when he was sitting under a wall waiting for someone to hire him, a handsome and well-dressed *shaikh* came up and greeted him. 'Uncle,' said the young man, 'have you met me before?' 'I don't know you at all, my son,' the man replied, 'but although you are reduced to this state, I see that you have been well brought up.' 'The decree of fate has been fulfilled,' the young man said, and he went on to ask whether there was any job that he could do for the man. 'Yes, my son,' the *shaikh* replied, 'there is a small job on which I should like to employ you,' and when he was asked what this was, he said: 'I have ten other *shaikhs* living with me in the same house, with nobody to run our errands. We can supply you with food and clothes and, if you are prepared to act as our servant, we will give you, in cash and kind, enough to restore you to your former prosperity.' 'To hear is to obey,' said the young man, at which the *shaikh* told him: 'This is on one condition,' and he went on to explain: 'The condition is that, whatever you see us doing, you must keep our secret, and if you see us shedding tears you must not ask us why.' The young man agreed to this and the *shaikh* said: 'Come with me, my boy, with the blessing of Almighty God.'

The young man then walked behind the *shaikh*, who took him to the baths, and after his body had been cleansed of dirt the *shaikh* sent out a man who brought in a fine linen robe. This was given to the young man to wear, and after that the *shaikh* took him to his house where his companions were assembled. When he entered he found himself in a lofty, spacious and solidly built house with facing rooms and halls, in each of which was a fountain, with twittering birds and windows on all sides, overlooking an attractive garden around which the house was built. The *shaikh* took him to one of the rooms, which was adorned with coloured marble, its roof ornamented with lapis lazuli and gleaming gold and its floor spread with carpets of silk. Here he found ten *shaikhs* seated facing each other, dressed in mourning, weeping and wailing. This astonished the newcomer, and he was about to question his guide when he remembered the condition and held his tongue. His guide then handed over to him a chest containing thirty thousand dinars and said: 'Spend this in an appropriate way on our needs and on your own. You are to be trusted, so look after what I have handed over to you.' 'To hear is to obey,' the young man replied.

For a number of days and nights he spent the money for the *shaikhs*, and then one of them died. His companions took the body, washed it, dressed it in a shroud and buried it in a garden behind the house. They continued to die one by one, until the young man's original employer was the only one left and the two of them were alone in the house. Things went on like that for a period of years until the *shaikh* himself fell ill. The young man despaired of his life and went up to commiserate with him. 'Uncle,' he said, 'I have given you unstinting service for twelve years and I have acted in good faith, serving you to the best of my ability.' 'Yes, my son,' the *shaikh* replied, 'you served us until my companions were gathered into the keeping of the Great and Glorious God, and it is now my turn to die.' 'You are in danger,' the young man said, 'and so I would like you to tell me the reason for your weeping and why you went on lamenting and grieving so sorrowfully.' 'My son,' replied the *skaikh*, 'there is no need for you to know this, so don't press me to do what I cannot. I have prayed to Almighty God not to afflict anyone else with my misfortune, and if you want to escape from what has happened to us, do not open that door.' He pointed to it, and warned his companion against approaching it, adding: 'But if you do want to share our fate, open it and you will find the reason for what you have seen of our grief. Then you will repent when repentance will do you no good.'

Night 589

Morning now dawned and Shahrazad broke off from what she had been allowed to say. Then, when it was the five hundred and eighty-ninth night, SHE CONTINUED:

I have heard, O fortunate king, that the surviving *shaikh* warned the young man against opening the door lest he repent when repentance would do him no good. THE FIFTH VIZIER WENT ON:

The *shaikh*'s illness worsened and, when he had died, the young man washed him with his own hands, wrapped him in a shroud and buried him beside his companions. He himself continued to live in the house, in possession of all its contents, but he was disturbed and worried about the fate of the others. One day, when he was thinking over what the *shaikh* had said and how he had told him not to open the door, it crossed his mind to go and look at it. He went towards where the *shaikh* had pointed and searched until he discovered a small door covered in spiders' webs with four steel locks. When he looked at it he remembered the warning and turned away, but he kept on being tempted to open it and although he resisted the urge for seven days, on the eighth he yielded, telling himself that he had to do this in order to see what would happen to him. 'What God has fated and decreed cannot be held back and nothing happens except by His will,' he told himself. So he got up, broke the locks and opened the door.

When he had done this, he saw a narrow passage and began to walk along it, coming out after three hours on the bank of a great river. He was looking right and left when a huge eagle swooped down from the sky and carried him off in its talons, flying between earth and heaven, until it had brought him to an island in the middle of the sea, where it let him fall, and left him. He was in a state of bewilderment, not knowing where to go, but, as he was sitting there one day, a ship's sail appeared at sea like a star in the sky. He pinned his hopes of rescue on this ship and kept his eyes fixed on it as it drew near. When it arrived, he found that it was a skiff of ivory and ebony with oars of sandalwood and aloes wood and plates of gleaming gold. It was crewed by ten virgins, as beautiful as moons, who, when they saw him, came from the boat and kissed his hands, saying: 'You are the bridegroom king.' One of them, like the sun shining in a clear sky, approached him holding a silken bag containing royal robes and a golden crown studded with all kinds of precious stones. She dressed him in the robes and put the crown on his head, after which she and the others carried him to the skiff, where he found carpets of coloured silk. Then they set sail and put out to sea.

The young man said: 'When I went off with them I was sure that this must be a dream and I had no idea where they were going. Then, when they came near to land, I saw that the shore was crowded with mail-clad troops in such numbers that only the Glorious and Almighty God could count. They brought up five excellent horses for me, with golden saddles set with all kinds of pearls and precious stones. I chose one and rode off on it, accompanied by the other four, and when I did so, they raised flags and banners above my head, beating drums, large and small, with the troops formed up on my right and left. As we went, I continued to wonder whether I was asleep or awake; I could not believe that I was riding in a procession but thought that this must all be a dream.

'We came to a green plain with palaces, gardens, trees, streams, flowers and birds that were praising God, the One, the Omnipotent, and then troops of men poured out like a rushing stream from between the palaces and the gardens until they had filled the plain. When they got near me they halted, and from them a king came out riding alone, preceded by some of his principal officers on foot.'

When the king came close to the young man he dismounted, and when the young man saw this, he did so too. They exchanged courteous greetings and remounted, and the king said: 'Come with me, for you are my guest.' They rode off together, exchanging conversation as the troops in their formations rode before them to the royal palace, where they all halted before entering.

Night 590

Morning now dawned and Shahrazad broke off from what she had been allowed to say. Then, when it was the five hundred and ninetieth night, SHE CONTINUED:

I have heard, O fortunate king, that the king took the young man with him in a procession to the palace. THE FIFTH VIZIER SAID:

The king entered, holding his guest by the hand, and then seated him on a golden throne, taking his own seat beside him, but when the king's mouth-veil had been removed, 'he' turned out to be a girl like the sun shining in a clear sky, beautiful, graceful and perfect, both proud and bold. The young man, looking at the acme of delight and felicity, was filled with wonder at her loveliness. She told him: 'Know, O king, that I am the queen of this land and that among all the troops that you have seen, both horse and foot, there are no men but only women, for here the men till the ground, and sow and reap, occupying themselves with agriculture, building and other useful crafts, while women are the judges, administrators and army leaders.'

While the young man was sitting there filled with astonishment, the vizier came in, who turned out to be a venerable and dignified grey-haired old lady. 'Bring me the *qadi* and the notaries,' the queen told her, and when she had gone to do that, the queen leaned towards the young man, talking with him, amusing him and removing the sense of strangeness that he felt with her courteous words. Finally she went up to him and said: 'Are you willing to take me as your wife?' He rose to his feet and was kissing the ground in front of her when she stopped him. 'I am the least of your servants,' he protested, but she said: 'Do you not see all these servants and troops, together with the wealth, stores and treasures?' 'Yes,' he told her, and she went on: 'All this is at your disposal to grant and bestow,' but then she pointed to a closed door and added: 'You can do what you want with everything else except for this door, which is not to be opened, and if you do open it you will regret it when regret will no longer help you.'

She had hardly finished speaking when the vizier came back with the *qadi* and the notaries, all of whom were grave and dignified old ladies whose hair flowed over their shoulders. When they took their places before the queen, she ordered them to draw up a marriage contract and they married her to the young man. A feast was held, attended by all her troops, and when they had eaten and drunk, the young man lay with her and, finding her to be a virgin, he took her maidenhead.

He stayed with her for seven years in the happy enjoyment of the most delightful, carefree and pleasant of lives until one day he remembered about the door which he was not to open. He said to himself: 'She would not have told me to do this unless within it were great treasures, more splendid than any I have seen.' So he got up and opened it, but there on the other side of it was the bird that had carried him from the shore and left him on the island. When the bird saw him it said: 'I give no welcome to one who will never see happiness again.' When he saw and heard the bird he tried to run from it, but it followed him and snatched him up, flying off with him between earth and heaven until, after a time, it put him down in the place from which it had taken him, and then went off and left him.

He stayed where he was until he had recovered his senses, but then he remembered the prosperity, grandeur and honour that he had enjoyed, with his mounted escorts and his powers of command and prohibition. He began to weep and wail and for two months he sat by the shore where the bird had left him, filled with longing to return to his wife.

Then one night, while he was sitting there sleepless, sad and careworn, he heard the sound of a voice although he could see no one. The voice called out: 'Great though your pleasure was, never, never shall what is past return to you.' When he heard this, he gave up hope of seeing his queen again and regaining his lost happiness. He went back to the *shaikh*'s house, realizing that they had suffered the same fate and that this was the reason for their sorrowful tears, for which he now found an excuse. Grief and sorrow took hold of him and he went into the room where they had sat, and he continued to weep and wail, shunning food, drink, pleasant perfumes and laughter until he died and was buried at their side.

Haste, you must realize, your majesty, is not to be commended, for it leaves a legacy of regret, and this is the advice that I give you.

When the king heard that, he accepted the warning and advice, and changed his mind about having his son executed.

Night 591

Morning now dawned and Shahrazad broke off from what she had been allowed to say. Then, when it was the five hundred and ninety-first night, SHE CONTINUED:

I have heard, O fortunate king, that when the king had heard the vizier's story, he changed his mind about having his son executed.

On the sixth day, the girl came to the king with the naked blade of a knife in her hand. 'My lord,' she said, 'it seems that you are not prepared to listen to my complaint and to consult what you owe to your honour in respect of my enemies, your viziers, who maintain that women are guileful and treacherous. They want to ensure that I do not get my rights and to make you disregard what is due to me, but I shall prove to you that men are wilier than women by telling you the story of a certain prince who found himself alone with a merchant's wife.' 'What is the story?' asked the king, and THE GIRL SAID:

I have heard that there was once a particularly jealous merchant with a very beautiful wife. So great was his jealous fear that he would never settle with her in any city, but instead he built an isolated villa for her, standing by itself in the countryside. It was tall and strongly built, with reinforced doors and solid locks, and whenever he wanted to visit the city he would lock the doors and take the keys with him hung around his neck.

One day, while he was staying in the city, the prince rode out on an excursion to enjoy the open spaces. He had looked for a long time, examining the empty country, until he caught sight of the villa, from one of whose windows a noble lady was gazing. Her beauty so astounded him that he wanted to get to her, but found that he could not. On his orders one of his pages brought him an inkwell and paper, on which he wrote a note to say how deeply he was in love. He fixed the note to the head of an arrow and shot it into the grounds of the villa, in whose garden the lady was then walking. She told one of her slave girls to hurry and fetch it for her and, as she could read, she discovered when she looked at it that the prince claimed to be deeply and passionately in love with her. In reply she wrote that her own love for him was greater than his for her, and when she looked from her window and caught sight of him, she threw her note down to him, feeling an even stronger surge of longing. He for his part, on seeing her, came underneath the villa wall and called to her: 'Lower me a thread to which I can tie this key for you to keep by you.' She did this, and he tied the key to the thread before going back to his viziers, to whom he complained of his love for the lady, telling them that he could not bear to be without her. One of them asked what it was that he wanted done, and the prince explained: 'I want you to put me in a chest which you are to deposit with this merchant in his villa, telling him that it is yours. Leave it there until I have had my way with the lady for some days, and then fetch it back.'

The vizier willingly agreed to this and, after going to his own palace, the prince entered a chest of his, which the vizier then locked. He took it to the merchant's villa and when the merchant had come to meet him, kissed his hands and asked whether there was any service or anything else that he could do for him, the vizier said: 'I want you to put this chest in the most secure place that you have.' On the merchant's instructions the porters carried it into the villa and left it there in a closet. He himself then went off on some errand and his wife went to the chest, which she opened with the key that she had with her, letting out the young prince, who was glorious as the moon. When she saw him, she put on her finest clothes and took him to the sitting room, where she sat eating and drinking with him for seven days, shutting him up in the chest and locking it whenever her husband was there.

Then, one day, the king asked for his son, and the vizier went quickly
to the merchant's villa to ask for his chest.

Night 592

Morning now dawned and Shahrazad broke off from what she had been
allowed to say. Then, when it was the five hundred and ninety-second
night, SHE CONTINUED:

I have heard, O fortunate king, that the vizier came to the merchant's
villa to ask for his chest. THE GIRL WENT ON:

The merchant hurried home at what was for him an unusual time and
knocked at the door. On hearing his knock, his wife took the prince
and put him in the chest, but she forgot to lock it, and when her husband
came in with the porters and they tried to lift it by the lid, it flew open,
revealing the prince. The merchant recognized him when he saw him.
He went to the vizier and told him to come in and take the prince as no
one else could lay hold of him. The vizier did this and when he and his
men had left, the merchant divorced his wife, swearing that he would
never marry again.

'I have also heard, O king,' the girl continued, 'that a witty man once
went to the market and bought a boy who was being offered for sale,
and whom he then took home, telling his wife to look after him,' AND
SHE WENT ON:

One day, after the boy had been living there for some time, the man
told his wife to go out the next day to enjoy herself and relax in the
garden, which she gladly agreed to do. The boy heard that, and that
night he prepared food as well as collecting drink, dessert and fruit. He
went off to the garden and put the food under one tree, the drink under
another and the fruit and nuts under a third on the path that his master's
wife would take. The next morning, his master told him to accompany
his mistress to the garden and gave orders that what food, drink and
fruit they might need should be provided.

The lady came out and, after mounting her horse, she went to the
garden escorted by the boy. When they got there, a crow cawed and the
page said: 'That is right.' 'Do you understand what the crow says?' asked
the lady, and when he said that he did and she asked what it was, he
told her that it was telling them: 'There is food under this tree. Come

and eat it.' 'I see that you do understand the language of birds,' she said. 'Yes,' he replied, and she went to the tree where she found food prepared, which they proceeded to eat. This made a great impression on her because she believed that he really did know what the crow had been saying, and when, after their meal, it cawed again as they were looking round the garden and the page again said: 'That is right,' she asked what it was saying. This time he told her: 'My lady, it says that under such-and-such a tree there is a jug of water flavoured with musk as well as some old wine.' The two of them went there, and when they found this, it increased her astonishment and added to her admiration for the boy. She sat there drinking with him and when they walked further into the garden and the crow cawed a third time, she asked him what it meant this time, as again he had said: 'That is right.' 'It is saying that under such-and-such a tree are fruits and dessert,' he told her, and when they went to the tree, that was what they found. When they had eaten and walked further on, the crow cawed again and the boy picked up a stone, which he threw at it. 'Why are you trying to hit the crow and what did it say?' she asked. 'My lady,' he replied, 'it was something I cannot repeat to you.' 'Say it and don't be shy,' she told him, 'for there are no obstacles to hinder us.' He kept on refusing and she continued to insist, until eventually she swore that he must tell her. Then he said: 'The crow was telling me: "Do with your mistress what her husband does with her."' On hearing this, she laughed so much that she fell over and said: 'This is an easy matter and I can't refuse you.' She went towards a tree, spread a rug beneath it and called the page to come and satisfy her.

Suddenly the page noticed his master looking at him from behind and calling to ask why his mistress was lying there crying. 'She had what was almost a fatal fall from a tree,' the boy told him, 'and it was only the Glorious and Exalted God Who restored her to you. She has been lying here for some time to recover.' When the lady saw her husband standing over her, she got up pretending to be injured and in pain, exclaiming: 'Oh my back, oh my ribs! Come to me, my friends, for there is no life left in me!' Her startled husband told the boy to fetch the horse for his mistress and help her to mount, after which he held one of the stirrups while the boy held the other, saying all the while: 'May God cure you and restore you to health.'

'This, O king, is an example of the treacherous wiles of men,' the girl said, 'so do not let your viziers stop you from coming to my aid and avenging me.' She then burst into tears, and when the king saw this, she being his favourite slave girl, he renewed the order for his son's execution. It was then that the sixth vizier came in and, after having kissed the ground before him, he said: 'May God grant glory to the king; I am here to advise you in all sincerity to delay in the matter of your son . . .'

Night 593

Morning now dawned and Shahrazad broke off from what she had been allowed to say. Then, when it was the five hundred and ninety-third night, SHE CONTINUED:

I have heard, O fortunate king, that the sixth vizier advised the king: 'Delay the execution of your son, for falsehood is like smoke, while truth is firmly buttressed, and the light of truth dispels the darkness of lies. You must realize how great is the deceitfulness of women, for Almighty God says in His glorious book: "The guile of women is great."* I have heard a story of how a woman played a trick on a number of state officials that had never been known before.' 'How was that?' asked the king, and THE VIZIER SAID:

There was once a merchant's daughter with a husband who was often away on his travels. Once her husband went to a distant land and was away so long that, finding it hard to bear, she fell in love with an elegant young man of merchant stock, who loved her as she loved him. Her lover had a dispute with a man who brought a complaint against him to the *wali* of the city, who put him in prison. When the merchant's wife heard of this she was distraught, and so, putting on her finest clothes, she went to the *wali*'s house. She greeted him and passed him a note in which she had written: 'The man whom you are holding in prison is my brother, who had a dispute with So-and-So. The people who bore witness against him were lying and he is being held unjustly. There is no one else who can intervene for me or take my part except for him, and I ask you in your kindness to release him.'

The *wali* read the note, and when he looked at the woman he fell in love with her. 'Go into the house,' he told her, 'and I shall have him brought before me and then send for you to take him away.' 'Master,' she said, 'I have no helper apart from Almighty God. I am a stranger

---

* Quran 12.28.

here and I cannot go into anyone's house.' 'I shall not release him for you until you do that, so that I can have my way with you.' 'If that is what you want,' she told him, 'you must come to my house, stay there, and sleep and rest for the whole day.' He asked where her house was, and when she had told him, she went out, leaving him in a state of distraction. She then went to the *qadi* of the city. 'My lord, the *qadi*,' she addressed him, and when he had answered, she went on: 'Please look into my affair, and Almighty God will reward you.' 'Who has wronged you?' he asked, and she told him: 'Sir, I have a brother, my one and only relative, and it is because of him that I have had to come to you. The *wali* has put him in prison and people have given false evidence against him to say that he is a wrongdoer. I am asking to you intercede for me with the *wali*.' The *qadi*, for his part, fell in love at the sight of her and told her to go into his house with his slave girls to rest there for a while with him. He promised to send a message to tell the *wali* to release her brother, and added that, if he knew how much her brother owed, he would pay it himself in order to have his way with her, so impressed was he by how well she had spoken. 'If you do things like this, then how can we blame others?' she asked. 'If you won't go in, then go about your business,' he told her, and she replied: 'If that is what you want, master, then it would be less conspicuous and better for you to come to me in my own house. In yours there are slave girls and eunuchs, as well as people coming and going. I am a woman who knows nothing about that kind of thing, but necessity compels.' He asked where she lived and, after telling him, she fixed a rendezvous with him on the day that she had promised to meet the *wali*.

After she had left the *qadi*, she approached the vizier and presented him with a complaint about the desperate situation of her brother in the *wali*'s prison. The vizier tried to seduce her, promising that if he could have his way with her, he would have her brother freed. 'If that is what you want,' she told him, 'then come to me, for this will give us better shelter. It is not far away and you know that we women need to be clean and tidy.' When he asked, she told him where she lived and fixed an appointment for him on the same day as the others. She then left him and approached the king of the city, to whom she presented the same petition, asking him to have her brother freed. 'Who has imprisoned him?' asked the king. She told him that it was the *wali*, and when he heard her speaking, the arrows of love pierced his heart and he told her to go into the palace with him so that he might send a message to the *wali* to have her brother released. 'Your majesty,' she said, 'it is easy for you to do this whether I want it or not. If you do want me, that is my good fortune, but were you to condescend to come to my house, that would be an honour for me, as the poet has said:

> My companions, have you seen or heard
> That I was visited by one of such nobility?'

The king agreed to her suggestion and was told to come to her house, which she described for him, on the same day as the others.

Night 594

Morning now dawned and Shahrazad broke off from what she had been allowed to say. Then, when it was the five hundred and ninety-fourth night, SHE CONTINUED:

I have heard, O fortunate king, that the woman agreed to the king's proposal, told him where her house was, and arranged for him to come on the same day as the *wali*, the *qadi* and the vizier. THE SIXTH VIZIER WENT ON:

Her next visit was to a carpenter, to whom she said: 'I want you to make me a cupboard with four compartments, one above the other, each of which must have a door that can be locked. Tell me how much you will charge and I shall pay you.' 'My fee is four dinars, but what I would like is for you to allow me to sleep with you, chaste as you are, and I would then charge you nothing.' 'If that is what must be,' she replied, 'then make five compartments, each with its own lock.' The carpenter agreed willingly and she arranged for him to bring her the cupboard on the same day that she had fixed for the others to come to her house. He suggested that she should sit and wait so that she could take the cupboard away there and then and afterwards he could visit her at his leisure. So she sat there until it was finished, and when she got home she had it placed in her sitting room. Next she took four sets of clothes to the dyer and had each of them dyed a different colour, after which she prepared food and drink, together with scented herbs, fruits and perfumes.

When the appointed day arrived she put on her finest clothes, adorning and perfuming herself, and then spreading all kinds of splendid carpets in her room before sitting down to wait for her visitors. It was the *qadi* who arrived first, and when she saw him she got to her feet and kissed the ground in front of him before taking him by the hand and seating him on the couch. She lay back, fondling him, but when he wanted to take her, she said: 'Master, remove your clothes and your turban and put on this yellow gown together with this covering for your head so that I can bring the food and the drink and you can then make love to me.' She took away his clothes and his turban, and he put on what she had provided for him, but just at that point there came a knock at the door. 'Who is it knocking?' the *qadi* asked. 'It must be my husband,' she told him, and he said: 'What can we do? Where can I go?' 'Don't be afraid,' she answered, 'for I can put you in this cupboard.' 'Do what you want,' he told her, and at that she took him by the hand and put him in the bottom compartment, locking its door on him.

She then went to the house door and opened it to find the *wali* there. She kissed the ground before him and, after having led him by the hand to the couch, she said: 'This whole house is yours; I am your slave and one of your servants; you can stay all day with me, but take off what you are wearing and put on this red robe, which serves as a nightgown.' She put on his head a shabby piece of cloth that she had with her and then removed his clothes. After that she joined him on the couch and the two of them fondled each other, but when he reached out for her she told him: 'Master, this day is yours and no one will share it with you, but please, in your kindness, write a note for me ordering the release of my brother from prison so that I may be easy in my mind.' 'To hear is to obey,' he said. 'I am at your service.' He then wrote a note to the official concerned, telling him: 'As soon as you get this, release So-and-So without delay or procrastination and do not send the bearer back with any query.' When he had sealed the note, she took it from him and then returned and had started to fondle him on the couch when a sudden knock came at the door. The *wali* asked who it could be, and she told him that it must be her husband. He asked what was to be done, and she said: 'Go into this cupboard until I get rid of him, and then I'll come back to you.' So she took him and put him into the second compartment, locking the door on him. While all this was going on, the *qadi* was listening to what they were saying.

The lady then went off and opened the house door, where she found the vizier. On seeing him she kissed the ground in front of him, greeted him with respect and said: 'Master, you have honoured my house by coming here; may God not deprive us of this sight.' She got him to sit down on the couch and told him to take off his robe and turban and put on a light gown that she provided for him. He did this and she gave him a blue gown and a conical cap of red. 'What you were wearing,' she said, 'were the robes of your office, which you should leave until the proper time comes to put them on again, but these are suitable for a pleasant drinking party and for sleeping.' When the vizier had put them on, she fondled him on the couch, but when he wanted her, she held him off, saying: 'There will be time enough for that.' A knock then came at the door and, when he asked, she again said that it must be her husband, and again, when the vizier asked what to do, she told him not to be afraid but to go into the cupboard so that she could send her husband away and come back to him.

When she had shut him in the third compartment she opened the house door and, finding the king standing there, she kissed the ground before him, led him by the hand to the dais and sat him down on the couch. 'You have honoured me, your majesty,' she told him, 'and if I could give you the world and all its contents, it would not be equal in value to a single one of the steps that you have taken on your way to me.'

Night 595

Morning now dawned and Shahrazad broke off from what she had been allowed to say. Then, when it was the five hundred and ninety-fifth night, SHE CONTINUED:

I have heard, O fortunate king, that when the king entered the woman's house, she told him: 'If I could give you the world and all its contents, it would not be equal in value to a single one of the steps that you have taken on your way to me.' THE SIXTH VIZIER WENT ON:

Then, when he was seated, she said: 'I ask your permission to say one thing.' 'Say whatever you want,' he told her, and she continued: 'Master, take your ease and remove your robes and your turban.' What he was wearing then was worth a thousand dinars, and when he took it off she gave him in exchange a patched mantle worth no more than ten dirhams. She then started to fondle him in a familiar way, and all the while the others in the cupboard were listening to what was going on but none of them could say a word. The king stretched out a hand to her neck and wanted to take her, but she said: 'There will be time for this later; I promised earlier to entertain you here, and you will be delighted by what I have for you.' While they were talking there was a knock on the door and when the king asked who it was she told him that it must be her husband. 'Get him to go away of his own free will,' he said, 'or else I shall go out to him and force him to leave.' 'Don't do that, your majesty,' she said, 'but wait for me to get rid of him by using my skills.' 'What am I to do meanwhile?' he asked and, taking him by the hand, she put him into the fourth compartment, which she locked, before going to open the house door.

This time it was the carpenter who stood there. He came in and greeted her, after which she said: 'What about those compartments that you made?' 'What's wrong with them?' he asked. 'This one is too narrow,' she said, and when he insisted that it was wide enough, she told him to go into it and see for himself, as it was not big enough to hold him. 'It would hold four people,' he insisted, after which he went into the fifth compartment, only to have her lock him in. She then took the *wali*'s note to the official in charge and when he had taken it and read it, he duly released her lover from prison. When she explained what she had done, her lover asked her what they should do next, to which she answered: 'We have to leave this city and go somewhere else, for after this we cannot stay here.' So they packed up their possessions, loaded them on camels and set off straight away for another city.

As for the would-be lovers, they stayed for three days in the compartments of the cupboard with nothing to eat. They suffered from retention of urine, as for all this time they had not relieved themselves. Eventually the carpenter urinated over the head of the king, the king over that of the vizier, the vizier over that of the *wali* and the *wali* over that of the *qadi*. 'What foulness is this?' exclaimed the *qadi*. 'Aren't we in a bad enough state without you doing this?' The *wali* then raised his voice and said: 'May God reward you well, *qadi*,' and, on hearing his voice, the *qadi* recognized who this was. It was the *wali* who then complained loudly, and the vizier was next to raise his voice and say: 'May God reward you well, *wali*,' and, in his turn, the *wali* recognized that this was the vizier. The process was repeated with the vizier and the king, but when the king recognized the voice of the vizier, he stayed silent and did not give himself away. Then the vizier said: 'God damn that woman for what she has done to us. She has got all the officers of state to come to her apart from the king.' The king, however, having listened to them, said: 'Be silent, for I was the first to fall into the net of that shameless harlot.' 'As for me,' said the carpenter, 'what did I do wrong? I made her a cupboard for four gold dinars and when I came to get my money she played a trick on me and locked me in here.' They then started to talk to each other, consoling the king with their conversation and relieving his gloom.

The neighbours noticed that the house appeared empty and told each other: 'Yesterday the wife of So-and-So was living there next door to us, but now we can't hear the sound of anyone speaking in the house or see anyone there. We must break down the doors and find out what has happened, lest the *wali* or the king come to hear of it and put us in prison, making us regret not having acted earlier.' They then broke in, and there they found a wooden cupboard from which could be heard the moans of men suffering from hunger and thirst. They told one another that there might be a *jinni* inside it, and one of them suggested collecting firewood and burning it. At that, the *qadi* called out: 'Don't do that' . . .

Night 596

Morning now dawned and Shahrazad broke off from what she had been allowed to say. Then, when it was the five hundred and ninety-sixth night, SHE CONTINUED:

I have heard, O fortunate king, that THE SIXTH VIZIER SAID:

When the neighbours were about to fetch firewood and burn the cupboard, the *qadi* called out to them: 'Don't do that,' but they told each other that the *jinn* can take human shape and speak with human voices. The *qadi*, hearing this, recited some verses from the Glorious Quran and then told the neighbours to come close to the cupboard. When they had done that, he told them who he was and added: 'I am the *qadi*; you are So-and-So and So-and-So, and there are a number of us in here.' 'How did you get there? Tell us,' they said, and he told them the story from beginning to end. They then fetched a carpenter, who opened the *qadi*'s compartment and then those of the *wali*, the vizier, the king and the other carpenter. They were all wearing the clothes they had been given, and when they came out they each burst into laughter at the sight of the others. As the lady had removed their own clothes they sent to their own people for replacements, and when these were brought they went off, trying to keep out of sight. See then, your majesty, that this is what the woman did with these men.

*

'I have also heard,' the sixth vizier continued, 'that a certain man used to wish that in his lifetime he might witness the Night of Power,' AND HE WENT ON:

One night, while he was gazing up at the sky, he caught sight of the angels, and there were the doors of heaven standing open, as all things, wherever they were, prostrated themselves in worship. On seeing that, he told his wife: 'God has shown me the Night of Power and I have been promised that three wishes of mine will be granted, so I need your advice.' His wife told him to pray to God to enlarge his penis, but when he had uttered the prayer, his penis became as big as the stalk of a gourd and he was hardly able to stand up with it; if he wanted to make love to his wife, she would run from place to place to avoid him. 'What am I to do?' he asked, adding: 'This was your wish because of your lasciviousness.' 'I don't want it to stay as big as this,' she told him, and so he raised his head towards the heavens and said: 'O my God, rescue me from this affair and free me from it.' He then found himself with a smooth surface and no penis at all. When she saw him, his wife exclaimed: 'As that's what you are like now, I've no need of you!' 'This was all thanks to your disastrous advice and your mismanagement,' he replied. 'God granted me three wishes, through which I could have had everything that is good for me in this world and the next, but now I have wasted two and there is only one left.' She said: 'I pray that Almighty God may restore your penis to the size that it was before.' He prayed, and this is what then happened.

This, your majesty, was caused by the woman's bungling, and I have mentioned it to convince you that this is a characteristic of women, coupled with foolishness and feeble-mindedness. Pay no attention to what the girl has said to you, and don't kill your son, your heart's blood, for that would ensure that your fame will not live on after you.

The king rescinded the order for his son's execution, but on the seventh day the girl arrived shrieking, having kindled a large fire, and the attendants brought her into his presence, holding her by the arms. 'Why have you done this?' he asked, and she said: 'Unless you avenge me on your son, I shall throw myself into this fire. I have no wish to live, and before coming here I wrote my will and gave away all my wealth as alms, for I am determined to die and then you will be as sorry as the king who tortured the female bath attendant.' 'How was that?' asked the king, and SHE SAID:

I have heard, O king, that there was once a pious, devout and ascetic woman who used to go to the palace of a certain king where her reputation was such that people would ask for her blessing. One day, when she entered as usual and sat beside the queen, the queen handed her a necklace worth a thousand dinars, telling her to take it and look after it until she herself had come out of the baths, when she would take it back again. The baths were in the palace itself, and when the woman had taken the necklace she sat in the royal apartment waiting for the queen to go to them and return. She put the necklace under her prayer mat before getting up to pray, but just then a bird flew in and carried it off, putting it in a crack in one of the corners of the palace. The woman had gone out to relieve herself, and when she came back she didn't realize what had happened. On her return, the queen asked her for the necklace, but the woman for her part couldn't find it and, although she hunted, she could discover no trace nor any news of it. 'By God, my daughter,' she said, 'nobody came to visit me. After I took the necklace, I put it under the prayer mat, but I don't know whether one of the servants saw it and took it without my noticing while I was praying. The truth about this is known to Almighty God.'

When the king heard of that, he ordered his wife to torture the woman with fire and to give her a severe beating . . .

Night 597

Morning now dawned and Shahrazad broke off from what she had been allowed to say. Then, when it was the five hundred and ninety-seventh night, SHE CONTINUED:

I have heard, O fortunate king, that THE GIRL SAID:

The king ordered his wife to torture the attendant with fire and to give her a severe beating, but in spite of the various tortures that were applied to her, she neither confessed nor accused anyone else. On the king's orders she was imprisoned and placed in fetters. It then happened one day that as he was seated on an island in a pool in the middle of the palace grounds, with his wife at his side, he noticed a bird that was pulling the necklace from a crack in the corner of the palace. He called out to a slave girl who was there, and she caught up with the bird and took the necklace away from it. Realizing that the accused woman had been wronged, the king was filled with regret, and when she was brought before him on his orders, he started to kiss her head, weeping and asking her forgiveness, repenting what he had done to her. He ordered her to be given a large sum of money, but, although she forgave him, she refused to accept the money and when she left the palace she swore to herself that she would never again enter anyone's house. Instead, she wandered in mountains and valleys worshipping Almighty God until she died.

As another example of masculine wiles, I have heard, O king, that a pair of doves, one male and one female, had collected a store of wheat and barley in their nest as provision for winter. In the summer the grains shrivelled and diminished and the male dove accused his mate of having eaten them. She kept protesting: 'No, I swear by God that I didn't eat any of them,' but he refused to believe her and beat her with his wings as well as pecking her with his beak until he had killed her. Then, when the weather turned cold, the grains expanded to their former size and the male dove realized that he had killed his mate unjustly, regretting this when regret was of no use. So he lay down beside her, weeping and wailing over her in sorrow and neither eating nor drinking until he fell ill and later died.

'A further example of men's trickery towards women is found in a story that is more wonderful than all of these.' 'Tell it to me,' the king ordered, and SHE BEGAN:

I have heard, O king, that there was once a princess named al-Datma, unequalled in her age for beauty and grace, symmetrically formed, radiant and charming. She stole men's hearts away, but in her pride at having no rivals, although all the princes asked for her hand, she would not take any of them, saying that she would only marry someone who could defeat her in the cut and thrust of single combat. 'If anyone can do this,' she would say, 'I shall gladly marry him, but if I win, I shall take his horse, his weapons and his clothes and write on his forehead: "This is a slave freed by al-Datma."'

Princes used to come from far and near, but she would defeat them and then put them to shame, taking their weapons and branding them. News of her reached a Persian prince named Bahram, who made the long journey to her court, taking with him horse and foot, as well as wealth and royal treasures. When he got there, he sent a splendid gift to the king, her father, who came to meet him and received him with the greatest courtesy. The prince then despatched his viziers with a message for him, telling him that he wanted to ask for the princess's hand. In reply, the king replied: 'My son, I have no authority over my daughter al-Datma, as she has sworn only to marry someone who can defeat her in single combat.' 'It is to fulfil this condition that I have come from my city,' said the prince, at which the king arranged for the two of them to meet on the next day.

When the time came, her father sent a message to al-Datma asking her to accept Bahram's challenge, and when she heard this, she made her preparations, equipped herself for the fight and rode out to the tournament ground, as did Bahram, who was determined to face her. News of the duel had spread, and people had come from all parts to be there when al-Datma came out, fully armed and wearing a sword belt, with her face veiled. For his part, Bahram rode out to meet her, splendidly equipped and fully armed. Each charged the other, and then they spent a long time circling each other and fighting furiously. In Bahram, al-Datma found a braver and more skilful opponent than any she had met earlier. She began to be afraid that she might be put to shame before the spectators, and when she realized that he was certain to defeat her, she decided to fall back on a trick. She unveiled her face, which shone more brightly than the moon, and the prince was so astonished when he looked at her that his strength failed him and his resolution weakened. On seeing this, the princess charged him and plucked him from his saddle, holding him in her hand like a little bird in the talons of an eagle, while for his part he was so distracted by her beauty that he did not realize what was happening to him.

She took his horse and his arms, after which she branded him and let him go. When he had recovered his senses, he spent some days neither eating, drinking nor sleeping, both because of his defeat and because love for the girl was now firmly rooted in his heart. He sent slaves back to his father with a letter in which he said that he could not come home until he had got what he wanted or died in his quest. This message distressed his father, who wanted to send an army to help him, but was dissuaded by his viziers, who urged patience. For his part, the prince decided to use guile in order to reach his goal. He disguised himself as a feeble old man and went to the princess's garden, which she used to visit most days. There he met the gardener and told him: 'I am a stranger from a distant land and from my youth I have had more skill in husbandry and in the tending of plants and scented herbs than anyone else.' The gardener was delighted to hear this and took him into the garden, where he

entrusted him to the care of his assistants. The prince started on his
duties, looking after the trees and tending the fruits, until one day, while
he was going about his work, a party of slaves came into the garden with
mules laden with carpets and various utensils. When he asked about
that, they told him that the princess wanted to come and look at the
garden. At that, he went off and fetched the jewellery and robes that he
had brought with him from home. He took them to the garden and sat
down with some of them set out in front of him, and he then started to
tremble, giving the impression that this was a symptom of senility . . .

Night 598

Morning now dawned and Shahrazad broke off from what she had been
allowed to say. Then, when it was the five hundred and ninety-eighth
night, SHE CONTINUED:

I have heard, O fortunate king, that the prince, in the guise of a very
old man, sat in the garden with jewellery and robes set out before
him, pretending to be trembling as a symptom of age and senility and
weakness. THE GIRL WENT ON:

An hour later, slave girls and eunuchs arrived, with the princess in the
middle of them, like the moon among stars, and they began to walk
around, picking fruits and looking at the sights. Underneath one of the
trees they saw Bahram sitting, and when they went up and looked at
him, he appeared to be a very old man with tremors in his hands and feet,
while in front of him were treasures fit for kings. They were astonished at
this and they asked him what he proposed to do with the jewellery,
laughing at him when he told them: 'I want to use it to marry one of
you.' 'And when you marry, what will you do with your bride?' they
asked. 'I shall give her a single kiss and then divorce her.' 'I hereby marry
you to this girl,' the princess said, and Bahram went up to his bride,
leaning on his staff, shaking and stumbling. He then kissed her and gave
her the jewellery and the robes. She was delighted and the others laughed
and went back home.

The next day they came back, and when they approached Bahram
they found him sitting in the same place with even more treasures set
out in front of him. They sat down with him and again asked what he
was going to do with all this, to which he answered: 'I shall use it to
marry one of you, as I did yesterday.' The princess produced another

bride for him and when he had gone up to her and kissed her, he gave her the jewellery and the robes, after which they all went home.

When the princess saw the treasures that he had given to her slave girls, she said to herself: 'I have a better right to these and no harm will come to me.' So the next morning she went out of her palace alone, disguised as a slave girl and going by hidden paths in order to meet 'the old man'. When she came to him, she said: 'Old man, I am the king's daughter. Would you like to marry me?' 'Very willingly,' he replied, and he produced yet more valuable and costly treasures, which he handed over to her. He then got up to kiss her. She was feeling safe and assured, but when he came to her he seized her roughly, threw her to the ground and deflowered her. 'Don't you know me?' he asked. 'Who are you?' she said, and he then told her: 'I am Bahram, son of the king of Persia. It was for your sake that I disguised myself and left my family and my kingdom.' She got up from under him in silence, neither answering him nor saying anything else, because of the shock of what had happened to her. She said to herself: 'If I kill him, it will do me no good,' and then, after thinking it over, she decided that the only thing she could do would be to flee with him to his own country. She collected her wealth and her treasures and then sent word of this to him, so that he could get ready and collect what money he had himself. They agreed on a night on which to leave and then, mounted on excellent horses, they set off under cover of darkness, and when dawn broke they were far away.

They continued on their way until they reached Persia and approached the city of Bahram's father, who rode out delightedly to meet them with all his men when he heard of their coming. Some days later, he sent a splendid gift to al-Datma's father together with a letter in which he said that al-Datma herself was with him and asked for her wedding furnishings. When the gift arrived and was received by her father, he was filled with happiness and treated the envoys who had brought it with the greatest honour. He had a banquet prepared and summoned the *qadi* and the notaries to have a marriage contract drawn up between Bahram and his daughter. He then distributed robes of honour to the Persian envoys and sent off all that his daughter would need. Bahram stayed with her until they were parted by death.

'Look and see, O king, what wiles men employ against women, and as for me, I shall never give up my just claim until I die.' The king then renewed the order for his son's execution, but the seventh vizier now presented himself and, after having kissed the ground before him, he said: 'Wait until I can advise you, your majesty, for to act patiently and slowly is the way to achieve your hopes and gain your wishes, while haste leads to regret. I have seen the shameless way in which this girl has been inciting you to commit terrible acts, and, as your servant, I, who have been overwhelmed by your gracious favours, have advice to offer since I know what no one else knows of the wiles of women. I have heard, for instance, the story of the old woman and the merchant's son.' 'What was that?' the king asked, and THE VIZIER SAID:

I have heard that there was once a wealthy merchant with a dearly loved son. One day, the son said to his father: 'Father, I have a wish that I would ask you to fulfil for me.' 'What is it, my son,' his father asked, 'so that I may grant it to help you get what you want, even if you ask for the light of my eyes?' 'I would like you to give me enough money to let me go with the merchants to Baghdad, in order to look at the palaces of the caliphs. Other merchants' sons have described the places to me, and I would like to see for myself.' 'Little son,' his father objected, 'how could I bear to be parted from you?' 'I have said what I have to say,' the boy replied, 'and I must go to Baghdad whether you approve or not, for I feel a longing in my soul that can only be cured if I do this.'

Night 599

Morning now dawned and Shahrazad broke off from what she had been allowed to say. Then, when it was the five hundred and ninety-ninth night, SHE CONTINUED:

I have heard, O fortunate king, that the boy told his father that he insisted on going to Baghdad. THE SEVENTH VIZIER WENT ON:

When his father was sure that he meant what he said, he provided him with thirty thousand dinars' worth of trade goods and put him in the care of some merchants, whom he trusted, after which he said goodbye and returned home. His son went on with his companions until, when they reached Baghdad, the City of Peace, he went to the market and hired for himself a pleasant and attractive house whose appearance had filled him with astonishment and amazement. In it birds twittered; its rooms faced one another; its floor was paved with coloured marble and its ceilings were gilded with lapis lazuli. He asked the doorkeeper what its monthly rent would be, and when the man said: 'Ten dinars,' he asked whether he was telling the truth or joking. 'By God,' said the man, 'I am serious, for no one who moves in here stays for more than one or two weeks.' The young man asked why this was, and the doorkeeper told him: 'All the tenants leave either as sick men or as corpses, and so the house has a bad reputation with everyone, and as no one dares live here, the rent has fallen this low.'

The young man was astonished to hear this and said: 'There must be something here that is responsible for this,' but then he thought the matter over and recited the formula: 'I take refuge with God from Satan, the accursed.' Dismissing the matter from his mind, he moved in and set about his business, buying and selling. He stayed there for some days without being affected by any of the disasters that the doorkeeper had mentioned, but then one day, as he was seated by the house door, a grey-haired old woman like a spotted snake passed by. She kept on praising and glorifying God, and clearing away stones and obstacles from the road. She seemed surprised to see him sitting there, and he asked her: 'Do you know me or do I remind you of someone?' When she heard him speak she hurried up to him and, having greeted him, she asked how long he had been living there. He told her that he had been there for two months, and she said: 'It was this that surprised me. We don't know each other, my son, nor do you remind me of anyone. What is remarkable, however, is that everyone else who has lived in this house has either fallen sick or died, and I am certain that you are putting your young life in danger. But perhaps you have not gone up to the top and looked from the belvedere there?'

She then went on her way, and after she had left him he started to think over what she had said, telling himself that, in fact, he had not gone up to the roof and that he did not know that there was a belvedere. He went back inside straight away and started to search in every corner until in one of them he discovered a small door between whose posts a spider had woven its web. When he saw that, he told himself: 'It may be that the spider wove this web because inside lies death,' but he comforted himself with the words of Almighty God: 'Say: nothing shall come upon us except what has been decreed for us by God.'* So he opened the door, climbed a small flight of stairs and came out on the roof, where he saw the belvedere and sat down to rest and to admire the view. From there he could see an elegant and well-kept house at the top of which was a

* Quran 9.51.

lofty terrace looking out over the whole of Baghdad. On the terrace was a girl like a houri of Paradise, and love for her immediately occupied his whole heart, robbing him of his wits and bequeathing him the misfortunes of Job and the sorrows of Jacob. When he looked at her more closely, he said to himself: 'When people say that whoever lives in this house sickens or dies, it may be because of this girl. I wish I knew how to rescue myself, as I am out of my mind.'

He went down from the roof thinking over his problem and sat down in the house, but finding himself unable to rest he went out and took his seat by the door, not knowing what to do. At that moment the old woman came walking by, calling on the Name of God and glorifying Him as she went. When he saw her, the young man got to his feet and, having first greeted her with good wishes, he went on: 'Mother, I was well and healthy until you advised me to open the door. I saw the belvedere, opened it up and when I looked from the top of it I saw a sight that stunned me. I think that my death has come on me and I know that no one else can cure me but you.' When she heard this, she laughed and told him: 'God willing, no harm will come to you.' At these words the young man went into the house, and when he came out he was carrying a hundred dinars in his sleeve. 'Take these, mother,' he said. 'Treat me as a master does his slaves and come quickly to my help, for if I die yours will be the blood guilt on the Day of Resurrection.'

The old woman agreed willingly but said: 'I want you to help me in a small matter through which you will be able to get what you want.' When he asked what this was, she told him: 'The help that I want is for you to go to the silk market and ask for the shop of Abu'l-Fath ibn Qaidam. After they have shown you how to get there, sit down, greet him and ask him for the gold embroidered head-veil, the most beautiful thing that he has there. Then buy it from him, however high the price may be, and keep it with you until, God willing, I come back to you tomorrow.' After she had left, the young man spent the night twisting and turning as though he was sleeping on burning coals, but then in the morning he put a thousand dinars in his sleeve and went to the silk market. When he asked for the shop of Abu'l-Fath ibn Qaidam, one of the merchants told him where it was, and on his arrival he saw Abu'l-Fath himself, a dignified and wealthy man surrounded by pages, eunuchs and attendants. The crown of his good fortune was his wife, who was the girl on the terrace and who had no equal among the children of kings.

After an exchange of greetings Abu'l-Fath told his visitor to sit down,

and when the merchant's son had taken his seat he asked to be shown
the veil, which he described. Abu'l-Fath told a servant to fetch a silk
package from the upper end of the shop, which he then opened and from
which he took out a number of veils whose beauty was enough to
bewilder his visitor. Then the merchant's son caught sight of the one
that the old woman had described, and bought it for fifty dinars, after
which he went happily back to his house.

Night 600

Morning now dawned and Shahrazad broke off from what she had
been allowed to say. Then, when it was the six hundredth night, SHE
CONTINUED:

I have heard, O fortunate king, that the young man bought the veil
from the merchant and went home. THE SEVENTH VIZIER SAID:

There he noticed the old woman coming towards him, and at the sight
of her he got to his feet and handed over the veil. She then told him to
fetch a live coal, and when he had done this she brought the edge of the
veil close to the coal and singed it, before folding it up as it had been
before. She then took it off with her to Abu'l-Fath's house, where she
knocked on the door. When the girl heard her voice she got up and
opened the door, for she knew the old woman, who was one of her
mother's friends and companions. The girl asked what the old woman
wanted, adding that her mother had left and gone back home. 'I knew
that she wasn't here, my daughter,' the old woman answered. 'I have
just been with her in her house and the only reason that I have come to
you is that I was afraid of missing the time of prayer. I know that you
are cleanly and that your house is ritually pure, and so I wanted to
perform the necessary ablution here.' The girl let her come in, and when
she did, the old woman greeted her and called down blessings on her.
The old woman took a jug of water and went into the lavatory, where
she performed her ablution before going to pray, but afterwards she told
the girl: 'I think that the eunuchs have been walking in the place where
I prayed and so it is unclean. Please find me somewhere else to pray, for
my first prayer was invalid.' The girl then took her by the hand and said:
'Mother, come and perform your prayer by the couch on which my
husband sits.' When the old woman was brought there she stood up to
pray, calling on God and bowing, but then, without the girl noticing,

she slipped the gilded veil under a cushion. When she had finished she left, after calling down a blessing on her hostess.

At the end of the day, Abu'l-Fath came back to his wife and took his seat on the couch. She fetched him food and when he had eaten his fill and washed his hands, he was leaning back on the cushion when his eye happened to fall on the edge of the veil, which was sticking out from under it. He pulled it out and when he looked at it he recognized it and thought that his wife must have been unfaithful to him. He called to her and asked where the veil had come from. She swore that no one apart from him had visited her, and he stayed silent for fear of disgrace, being himself a companion of the caliph. He told himself: 'If I open up this door, I'll be shamed throughout Baghdad.' He couldn't say anything publicly and he did not speak one word about the matter to his wife, whose name was Mahziya. Instead, he called her and told her that he had heard that her mother was ill with heart pains, and that, as all her women friends were at her mother's house weeping over her, she should go there too. When she there, she found her mother in good health, and after she had been sitting there for some time, porters arrived carrying all her belongings from Abu'l-Fath's house. 'What has happened to you, daughter?' her mother asked, to which she had to say that she didn't know. Her mother then burst into tears of grief for Mahziya's separation from her husband.

Some days later, the old woman came to her while she was in her mother's house and greeted her fondly, saying: 'My darling daughter, you have disturbed me.' Then she went to Mahziya's mother and asked: 'What is the news? What has happened between your daughter and her husband? I hear that he has divorced her, but what did she do to cause all this?' 'It may be that thanks to your blessing her husband will go back to her,' her mother said, 'so pray for her, sister, for you are one who fasts and stands in prayer all night long.' The three of them, Mahziya, her mother and the old woman, stayed talking in the house until the old woman said: 'Don't worry, my daughter. God willing, I shall soon bring you and your husband together again.'

She then went to the young man and told him to make preparations for a splendid party as she was going to bring the girl to him that night. He, for his part, set about getting all that was needed in the way of food and drink and then sat waiting for the two of them to arrive. The old woman approached Mahziya's mother and said: 'Sister, we are holding a wedding feast and I want you to send your daughter off with me to enjoy herself and forget her cares and worries, after which I shall return her to you just as I found her.' Mahziya's mother got up and dressed her daughter in her most splendid clothes, decking her out in the best of her jewellery and finery, after which, when the girl was ready to leave, she went with the old woman to the door and started to give her advice. 'Take care that no one sets eyes on her,' she said, 'for you know the position that her husband holds with the caliph. Don't delay, but bring her back as quickly as possible.'

The old woman then went off to the young man's house, taking with her the girl, who was under the impression that this was the house where the wedding was to be held, but when she went to the sitting room . . .

Night 601

Morning now dawned and Shahrazad broke off from what she had been allowed to say. Then, when it was the six hundred and first night, SHE CONTINUED:

I have heard, O fortunate king, that THE SEVENTH VIZIER SAID:

When the girl entered the house and went to the sitting room, the young man jumped up to meet her, embraced her and kissed her hands and feet. She was bewildered by his beauty and it seemed to her that the room, with its scented flowers, food and drink, was all part of a dream. When the old woman saw the impression that all this had made on her, she told her to have no fear as she herself would remain there and not leave her for a minute, adding: 'You are a fitting mate for him and her for you.' The girl sat there covered in confusion, but the young man kept on joking with her, making her laugh and entertaining her with poems and stories until she relaxed and began to enjoy herself. She ate and drank and, being pleasantly affected by the wine and emotionally moved by the young man's handsomeness, she took a lute and sang. On seeing that, the young man became drunk but not with wine, and set no store by his own life.

The old woman left them, and when she came back in the morning she greeted them and asked the girl what kind of a night she had had. 'A pleasant one,' Mahziya replied, 'thanks to your help and your good offices.' 'Get up,' the old woman told her, 'for we must go back to your mother.' On hearing this, the young man produced a hundred dinars for her and said: 'Leave her with me tonight.' So the old woman went off to

Mahziya's mother and said: 'Your daughter sends you her greetings, but the bride's mother has insisted that she stay with her this coming night.' 'Give my greetings to both of them, sister,' said the other, 'and if the girl is happy with that, then there is no harm in her spending the night there so that she may enjoy herself and come back at her leisure. The only thing that I am afraid of is that her husband may offer her some violence.'

The old woman played trick after trick on Mahziya's mother until the girl had stayed away for seven days, on each of which the young man had given her a hundred dinars. At the end of this time, however, the mother said: 'Bring me my daughter this instant, for she has been away for so long that I am becoming concerned and suspicious.' The old woman was annoyed by this but left and made her way to the girl. Taking her by the hand she went away with her, leaving the young man lying on his couch in a drunken sleep. When they got home, Mahziya's mother was delighted and filled with joy to see her daughter and said: 'I was so concerned about you, my daughter, that I said something that pained my sister here.' 'Go and kiss her hands and feet,' said Mahziya, 'for she attended to my needs like a servant, and if you don't do what I tell you then I am no longer your daughter and you are not my mother.' So her mother immediately got up and made her peace with the old woman.

When the young man woke from his drunken sleep, although he could not find the girl, he was happy with what he had got, having achieved what he wanted. He was then approached by the old woman, who greeted him and said: 'What did you think of my performance?' 'Very well planned and executed,' he told her, and she then said: 'Come on, we have to put right the wrong that we did and restore the girl to her husband, for it was we who got them to part.' He asked her what he was supposed to do, and she said: 'Go to Abu'l-Fath's shop, greet him and sit with him. I shall pass by and when you see me, get up quickly and take hold of me, dragging me by my clothes, abusing me and threatening me. Then demand that I give you the veil and tell Abu'l-Fath: "Don't you recognize the veil that I bought from you for fifty dinars? What happened was that my slave girl put it on and part of its edge got scorched so she passed it to this old woman to give to someone to repair it for her. The old woman took it and went away, and I haven't seen her from that day on."' 'I'll do that willingly,' the young man promised, and he set off at once to walk to Abu'l-Fath's shop. After he had been sitting there for some time, the old woman passed by, holding a string of prayer beads in her hands, which she was counting. At the sight of her, he jumped to his feet, pulled at her clothes and started abusing and reviling her, while she spoke gently to him, saying: 'My son, you are to be excused.'

The market traders gathered round the two of them and asked what the matter was. The young man said to them: 'I bought from this merchant a veil for which I paid fifty dinars. My slave girl put it on briefly, and as she sat in front of a perfumed fire to fumigate it, a spark jumped out and burned a hole on its edge. We passed it over to this old woman, who was to give it to a repairer and then return it to us, but from that time on we have had no sight of her.' 'What this young man says is true,' the old woman said. 'Yes, I did take it, but then I went to a certain house which I was in the habit of visiting, and I put it somewhere there and forgot about it. I don't know where it is and, poor woman that I am, I was afraid of its owner and did not dare confront him.'

While all this was going on, Abu'l-Fath was listening . . .

Night 602

Morning now dawned and Shahrazad broke off from what she had been allowed to say. Then, when it was the six hundred and second night, SHE CONTINUED:

I have heard, O fortunate king, that THE SEVENTH VIZIER SAID:

When the young man had laid hold of the old woman and spoken to her about the veil, as she had coached him, Abu'l-Fath was listening to everything that was said, and when he had followed the account that the wily old woman had concocted with the young man, he got to his feet and exclaimed: 'God is greater than all! I ask His pardon, Omnipotent as He is, for the sins I have committed and for the suspicions that I have had. Praise be to God, Who has revealed the truth.' He went up to the old woman and asked whether she was in the habit of calling on his wife. 'Yes,' she told him, 'I do go to your house and to other houses as well for virtuous purposes, but from the day that I lost the veil no one had told me anything about it.' 'Did you ask anyone in my house?' asked Abu'l-Fath. 'Sir,' she said, 'I did go there to ask, but they told me that you had divorced your wife and so I came back and from that day on I have not asked anyone else.' Abu'l-Fath turned to the young man and said: 'Let this old woman go, for I have the veil.' He fetched it from his shop and then, in the presence of all the market traders, he handed it over to be mended before going to his wife. He paid her a sum of money and took her back with profuse apologies, imploring God to pardon him – all this without knowing what the old woman had done.

This, your majesty, is an example of the wiles of women.

'I have also heard that once a certain prince went out alone on a pleasure trip,' said the seventh vizier, AND HE CONTINUED:

He passed by a green meadow with trees, fruits, birds and flowing streams and, being attracted by its beauty, he sat down there and took out some dried fruits that he had with him and started to eat. While he was eating, he noticed that a huge column of smoke was towering into the sky from the meadow and, alarmed by that, he got up and climbed a tree, where he hid himself. From the top of the tree he could see an *'ifrit* coming out of the stream and carrying on his head a locked chest of marble. He put this down in the meadow and when he had unlocked it, out came a human girl like the sun shining in a clear sky. The *'ifrit* sat her down in front of him and looked at her, after which he put his head on her lap and fell asleep. She took hold of his head and propped it against the chest, after which she got up and began to walk to and fro. Happening to look up at the tree, she caught sight of the prince and gestured to him to come down. He refused and she said: 'If you don't come down and do with me what I tell you, I shall waken the *'ifrit* and tell him about you, at which he will kill you on the spot.'

The frightened prince climbed down and she then kissed his hands and feet and enticed him to make love to her. He agreed to this and when he had done what she wanted, she told him to give her the signet ring that was on his hand. He handed it over and she wrapped it in a silk kerchief that she had with her, adding it to more than eighty other rings that were already there. 'What do you do with these rings?' the prince asked her, and she told him: 'This *'ifrit* snatched me from my father's palace and locked me in this chest, whose key he keeps with him. He carries the chest on his head with me inside it wherever he goes, as he is so jealous that he can scarcely bear to be away from me for a single hour, and he keeps me from what I long to do. When I realized this, I swore that I would never refuse anyone who wanted to lie with me, and the number of rings that I have equals the number of my lovers, for I take the signet ring of each man who makes love to me and put it in this kerchief. Now, go on your way so that I may look for someone else, as the *'ifrit* will not wake up just yet.'

The prince, who could not believe what had happened, went back to his father's palace. His father knew nothing of how the reckless girl, with no thought for the consequences, had seduced his son, and when he heard that the signet ring was missing, he ordered his son to be put to death. He then left his throne room and entered his palace. His viziers persuaded him to spare the prince's life, and later the king summoned them one night; when they were all present, he rose to greet them and thanked them for what they had done to make him change his mind. They were also thanked by the prince, who complimented them on how they had got his father to spare him, promising that, God willing, he would reward them most generously. He then told them how it was that he had come to lose the ring, after which they wished him a long life and high fame before leaving.

'Look then, O king,' the vizier went on, 'at the wiles of women and what they do to men.' The king again withdrew his decision to have his son executed, and the next morning, while he was seated on his throne, his son entered, holding the hand of his mentor, Sindbad. He made a most eloquent speech, praising his father, the viziers and state officials, thanking them and eulogizing them. The men of learning, emirs, soldiers and nobles were present in the throne room and all were filled with admiration for his eloquence, rhetorical skill and masterly delivery. His father was overjoyed and, having called him forward, he kissed him between the eyes before summoning Sindbad and asking him why his son had stayed silent for seven days. 'Master,' Sindbad answered, 'his safety lay in his saying nothing. During those seven days I feared for his life, as I have known about this affair since the day that he was born, and all this was shown in his horoscope. But now the evil has passed thanks to your majesty's good fortune.' This delighted the king, who then asked his viziers: 'If I had had my son put to death, would the reponsibility for the wrong have rested with me or with the slave girl or with Sindbad, his tutor?' No one there was prepared to answer, and so Sindbad said to the prince: 'It is for you to reply to this, my son.'

Night 603

Morning now dawned and Shahrazad broke off from what she had been allowed to say. Then, when it was the six hundred and third night, SHE CONTINUED:

I have heard, O fortunate king, that when Sindbad told the prince to reply, the prince said: 'I have heard that a certain merchant was entertaining guests in his house and he sent out his slave girl to buy a jug of milk in the market. She got the jug and was on her way home when a kite flew overhead with a snake in its talons, which it was squeezing, and, unbeknown to the girl, a drop of the snake's venom fell into the jug. When she got back, her master took the milk from her and he and his guests drank it up, but no sooner had it settled in their stomachs than they all died. Can you see, your majesty, who was at fault in this?' One of those who were present suggested that everyone who drank was responsible, while another pointed to the girl who had left the jug uncovered. As for Sindbad, he asked the prince what he thought himself, to which he replied: 'I say that these people are wrong. Neither the girl nor the company were at fault. Their life spans and what God had allotted to them by way of provision had come to an end, and because of that it was fated that they should die.' This astonished all who were there, and they raised their voices, invoking blessings on the prince and saying: 'Master, there was never so good an answer as this, and you are now the most learned of the people of your age.' 'No,' said the prince, 'I am not learned. The blind old man, the three-year-old child and the five-year-old child knew more than I do.' 'Tell us the story of these three,' they asked, and THE PRINCE SAID:

I have heard that there was once a wealthy merchant who made frequent journeys to foreign parts. When he was proposing to go on one of his trips, he asked people who came from the place that he wanted to visit which trade goods would produce the best profit. 'Sandalwood,' they told him, 'for it fetches a high price.' So that was what he bought, using up all his capital in the process, and he then set off on his journey. He reached his destination at the end of the day and there he came across an old woman who was driving a flock of sheep. When she saw him, she asked him who he was and he told her that he was a foreign merchant. 'Be on your guard against the people here,' she warned him, 'for they are a bunch of scheming thieves who swindle foreigners to get the better of them and then gobble up all that they have. This is my advice to you.' Having said this, she left him.

The next morning, one of the townsfolk met him, greeted him and asked where he had come from, and when the merchant told him, the man went on to ask: 'What goods have you brought with you?' 'Sandalwood,' the merchant told him, 'for I have heard that it fetches a good price with your people.' 'Whoever gave you that advice was wrong,' the man said, and added: 'We use nothing but sandalwood for heating our cooking pots, and its price here is exactly the same as that of firewood.' When he heard this the merchant was sad and regretful, and he didn't know whether or not to believe what he had been told. He lodged in one of the *khans* of the city and lit a fire of sandalwood under his cooking pot. On seeing this, the man who had accosted him earlier asked if he would sell him the wood at whatever price he wanted for each measure. The merchant agreed and the man moved all the wood to his own house, in return for which the merchant wanted gold.

In the morning, when he walked into the city, a blue-eyed man, one of whose eyes was missing, caught hold of him and said: 'It was you who destroyed my eye and I shall never let go of you.' The merchant denied it, insisting that that could never have happened, but the people gathered around and, although they asked the one-eyed man to wait until the next day for his compensation, the merchant had to find a guarantor for the payment before they would let him go. As he went off, he discovered that the strap of his sandal had been broken when the one-eyed man had pulled him. He stopped at a shoemaker's shop, gave him the sandal and asked him to repair it, promising to pay him what he wanted. Next on his way he came across a party of gamblers; he sat down with them to relieve his cares and worries and, when they invited him, he joined in their game. They got the better of him and then gave him the choice either of drinking up the sea or of handing over all his money. The merchant asked them to wait until the next day and he then went off, sunk in gloom because of what he had done and not knowing how things would turn out.

As he sat careworn and worried, the old shepherdess passed by and looked at him. 'It seems that the city folk have got the better of you,' she said, 'for I can see that something has happened to distress you.' He then told her the whole story of his experiences from beginning to end. 'As for the man who told you about the sandalwood,' she said, 'the price of sandalwood here is ten dinars a *ratl*, but I can suggest a way that may free you from your difficulties. You must go to such-and-such a gate, where you will find an old blind man seated. He is wise, very knowledgeable and experienced; everybody goes to him to ask about what they want and he tells them what will be to their advantage. He knows about tricks, magic and swindles and, as he is a sharp fellow, all the rogues gather round him each night. Go to him but keep yourself hidden from your opponents, so that you can listen to what they say without them seeing you. He will tell them which schemes will succeed and which will fail, and you may hear something that will allow you to free yourself from your creditors.'

Night 604

Morning now dawned and Shahrazad broke off from what she had been allowed to say. Then, when it was the six hundred and fourth night, SHE CONTINUED:

I have heard, O fortunate king, that the old woman told the merchant to go to the expert around whom the townsfolk gathered, but to keep under cover in the hope of hearing what would free him from his creditors. THE PRINCE WENT ON:

When the merchant left her, he followed her directions, keeping under cover, and when he saw the *shaikh* he sat down near him. It was not long before the man's followers arrived to bring their problems to him, and when they came they greeted him and exchanged salutations with one another before sitting in a circle around him. Among them the merchant recognized his four creditors. When they had eaten the food that the *shaikh* produced for them, each began to give an account of what he had done that day. The man who had bought the sandalwood told of how he had bought it at less than its proper price, the bargain being that he should return a full measure of whatever the vendor wanted. The *shaikh* told him: 'Your man got the better of you,' and when he asked how that could be, the *shaikh* said: 'If he wants a full measure of gold or silver, are you going to give it to him?' 'Yes,' the man replied, 'and I shall still be in profit.' 'And if he says: "I shall take a measure full of fleas, half of them male and half female," what will you do?' the *shaikh* asked, and the man had to acknowledge defeat. Next came the one-eyed man, who told him: 'I saw a blue-eyed stranger today and I pretended to quarrel with him, hanging on to him and shouting out that he had knocked out my eye. I didn't let him go until others who were there guaranteed that he would come back and compensate me for it.' 'If he wants to get the better of you, he can do it,' the *shaikh* said and, when the man asked him how, he explained: 'He would tell you: "Pluck out your eye and I will pluck out mine. Then we can weigh them, and if mine is equal to yours then what you say is true." He would have to pay you compensation, but you would be blind while he would be able to see with his remaining eye.' The one-eyed man realized that his victim could in fact get the better of him in this way.

The next to come was the shoemaker, who told the *shaikh*: 'I came across a man today who gave me his sandal to repair and when I asked about payment he said that he would give me enough to satisfy me after I had done the repair; but I am not going to be satisfied with anything less than all his money.' 'But if he wants to take his sandal and not give you anything, he can do it,' the *shaikh* pointed out. The man asked how that could be, and the *shaikh* said: 'He can say to you: "The sultan's enemies have been routed and his adversaries weakened, while the numbers of his children and his helpers have increased. Are you content or not?" If you say that you are, he can take his sandal and go, and if you say that you are not, he will take it and strike you on the face and the back of the neck.' The man had to acknowledge that he was beaten.

Then came the gambler, who said: 'I met a man and won a bet with him. Then I told him that if he drank up the sea I would hand over all my wealth to him, but if he did not, then he was to give me all his.' 'If he wanted,' the *shaikh* said, 'he could get the better of you,' and when the man asked how, the *shaikh* explained: 'He could tell you to hold the mouth of the sea for him and pour it out for him to drink. As you couldn't do that, this would allow him to defeat you.'

The merchant, who had been listening to all that, realized what he had to say in order to get the better of his opponents, and when they left the *shaikh* the merchant went back to his lodgings. The next morning the gambler who had challenged him to drink the sea arrived and the merchant said: 'Pass me the mouth of the sea and I shall drink it.' As the man could not do this, the merchant won and the other had to ransom himself for a hundred dinars. When he had left, the shoemaker arrived and asked for what would satisfy him. The merchant said: 'The sultan has defeated his enemies and destroyed his opponents, while the numbers of his children have increased. Are you satisfied or not?' 'Yes, I am satisfied,' the shoemaker said, at which the merchant took his sandal and went off without paying anything. Then the one-eyed man came to ask for compensation for his eye. The merchant said: 'Pluck out your eye and I shall pluck out mine. Then we can weigh them both and if they are equal, this will show that you are telling the truth and you can then be recompensed.' 'Wait a while,' said the man, and he then made his peace with the merchant by paying him a hundred dinars. When he had gone he was succeeded by the man who had bought the sandalwood. 'Take the price for your wood,' he told the merchant. 'What are you going to give me?' the merchant asked, and the man replied: 'We agreed on one measure of wood for one of something else, so, if you want, you can have gold or silver.' The merchant told him: 'I shall take my measure in fleas, half male and half female,' and when the man admitted that he could not produce that, he, as the defeated party, had to hand back the sandalwood and pay a hundred dinars by way of indemnity. The merchant then sold the wood at his own price, took the money and returned home.

Night 605

Morning now dawned and Shahrazad broke off from what she had been allowed to say. Then, when it was the six hundred and fifth night, SHE CONTINUED:

I have heard, O fortunate king, that when the merchant had sold his sandalwood and received the price, he left the city and went home. THE PRINCE THEN WENT ON:

As for the three-year-old child, there was once a licentious man with a passion for women who heard of a beautiful woman living in another city. He went there, taking a gift with him, and then wrote her a note describing the longing and passion from which he was suffering and how his love had caused him to abandon his own city and come to her. She gave him permission to visit her and, when he got to her house and went in, she rose to meet him and received him with honour and respect, kissing his hands and providing him with the best possible guest provision of food and drink. She had a young three-year-old child whom she left as she busied herself with doing the cooking, but when her visitor suggested that they should sleep together, she objected that the boy was sitting there watching. 'He is a little child who doesn't understand and cannot even speak,' said the man. 'You wouldn't say that if you knew how intelligent he is,' she told him. The boy then realized that the rice his mother was preparing was cooked, and he cried loudly. When his mother asked him why, he said: 'Spoon me out some rice and put some butter in it.' She did this and he ate, but he then burst into tears again and she asked: 'What are you crying for, my son?' 'Mother,' he said, 'pour me some sugar on top of it.' 'You are an unlucky child!' the man exclaimed angrily, but the child replied: 'It is you who are the unlucky one, you who put yourself to the trouble of travelling from place to place in order to fornicate. I cried because there was something in my eye, which the tears then removed, and then I ate rice, butter and sugar until I had had enough. So which of us is unlucky?' The man was ashamed to hear what the child had to say and, remembering the lessons of religion, he mended his ways on the spot and went back home, leaving the woman untouched, and remained in a state of penitence for the rest of his life.

THE PRINCE CONTINUED:

As for the five-year-old, I have heard, O king, that four merchants shared a fund of a thousand dinars which were all put together in a single purse. They took this off with them to buy goods and on their way they came across a beautiful garden, which they entered, leaving the purse with the woman who was employed to look after it. After looking around the garden, they ate, drank and relaxed, and then one of them said: 'I have some perfume with me, so let us wash our heads in this stream and then perfume ourselves.' 'We would need a comb,' said another, while a third suggested: 'Let's ask the woman in charge, as she may have one.' One of them got up and went to her, but then told her to give him the purse. 'Not until you are all here or your companions tell me to hand it over to you,' she replied. The others were in a place where she could see and hear them and so, when the man said: 'She won't give me anything,' they called to her: 'Give it to him.' On hearing this, she handed over the purse and the man took it and ran off. His companions, finding that he was slow to come back to them, went to the woman and asked her why she had not given him the comb, to which she replied: 'What he asked me for was the purse, and I only gave him that with your permission. Then he went away.' When they heard what she had to say, they struck their faces and laid hold of her, insisting that they had only allowed her to give him the comb. 'He never said anything to me about a comb,' she told them, but they took her before the *qadi* and told him the whole story. He then made her responsible for the return of the purse, and some of her creditors were made to stand surety for her.

Night 606

Morning now dawned and Shahrazad broke off from what she had been allowed to say. Then, when it was the six hundred and sixth night, SHE CONTINUED:

I have heard, O fortunate king, that the *qadi* made the woman responsible for the return of the purse, and some of her creditors were made to stand surety for her. THE PRINCE WENT ON:

The woman left his court in a state of bewilderment, not knowing where to go. She was met by a five-year-old child who, seeing the state that she was in, asked her what the matter was. She ignored him as he was so young, but, after he had repeated the question three times, she said: 'A group of people came into my garden and left with me a purse containing a thousand dinars, telling me not to hand it over to any one of them unless all the others were present. They then went in to enjoy themselves looking round the garden, after which one of them came to me and asked me to give him the purse. "Not until your friends are here," I told him. "But I have their permission," he said and, when I still wouldn't give it to him, he shouted to the others: "She won't give it to me." They were close by and they called back to me: "Give it to him." So I gave him the purse and he took it and went off. Then, when they found that he was slow in returning, they came out and asked me why I hadn't given him the comb. "He didn't say anything about a comb," I told them. "It was only the purse that he talked about." Then they laid hold of me and took me before the *qadi*, who made me responsible for the return of the purse.' 'Give me a dirham to buy sweets with,' said the child, 'and I'll tell you how to get out of this.' She gave him the dirham and asked him what he had to say. 'Go back to the *qadi*,' he told her, 'and say to him: "It was agreed between the five of us that I should only give back the purse when all four of them were there."' So back she went to the *qadi* and repeated what the child had said to her. 'Was this your agreement?' the *qadi* asked the three, and when they confirmed that it was, he said: 'Produce your companion for me and then you can have the purse.' So the woman left and went away safe and without having suffered any loss.

*

When the king, the viziers and the courtiers heard what the prince had to say, they exclaimed: 'Your majesty, your son is the most outstanding of the people of this age!' They called down blessings on him and on his father, who clasped the prince to his breast and kissed him between the eyes. He then asked him about the slave girl and the prince swore by the Omnipotent God and His noble Prophet that it was she who had tried to seduce him. His father believed him and said: 'It is for you to decide her case. If you wish, I shall have her executed, or else do what you want with her.' 'Banish her from the city,' said the prince, after which he lived with his father enjoying the most pleasant and luxurious of lives until they were visited by the destroyer of delights and the parter of companions. This is the end of the story of the king, his son, the slave girl and the seven viziers.

I have also heard that there once was a merchant called 'Umar who left three children, the eldest Salim, the youngest Judar and the middle one Saliim. He brought them up until they reached manhood, but his favourite was Judar. When this was clear to his brothers, they became jealous of Judar and started to dislike him. Realizing this, their father, who was then an old man, was afraid that, if he were to die, they might cause trouble for their brother, and so he summoned a number of his relations, together with judicial administrators and men of learning. He told them to bring out the money and the materials that he owned, and when they had done this he told them to divide all this into four parts according to the principles laid down by Islamic law. When they had made the division, he gave one portion to each of his sons and kept one for himself. Then he said: 'This was all my wealth. Now that I have distributed it, there's no more for them to have either from me or from each other and so, when I die, there is no need for them to quarrel. I have given them their inheritance during my lifetime and the portion that I have kept for myself will go to my wife, their mother, to help with her living expenses.'

Night 607

Morning now dawned and Shahrazad broke off from what she had been allowed to say. Then, when it was the six hundred and seventh night, SHE CONTINUED:

I have heard, O fortunate king, that when the merchant had made a fourfold division of his money and the materials he owned, he gave each of his sons one share and kept the fourth for himself, telling them that this would go to their mother, to help with her living expenses. Soon after this 'Umar died and, far from being content with what he had done, his other sons wanted to get more from Judar, claiming that it was he who had their father's money. The case was taken to court and the Muslims who had been present at the division of the inheritance gave evidence as to what they knew of it. The judge then kept them from encroaching on each other's share, but the dispute had been costly both for Judar and for his brothers. The latter abandoned their claim for a while, but then schemed against Judar for a second time, and again the case was taken to court, losing them all money. In spite of that they kept on trying to damage Judar, taking the case from one unjust judge to another, losing their own money and wasting his, until all their father's inheritance had been spent on bribery. Judar's brothers then went to their mother and, after jeering at her, they took her money, beat her and drove her away. She went to tell Judar what they had done and began to curse them. 'Don't curse them, mother,' Judar said, 'for God will repay both of them for this. But both they and I are poor, and this wrangling costs money. We have often taken the case before judges, but, far from doing us any good, we have lost all that our father left us and have been disgraced by those who have been called as witnesses. Am I then to have another quarrel with them because of you and take the case to court? This cannot be, so stay here with me and I shall share what food I have with you. Pray for me and God will give both of us our daily bread. Leave them to face God's punishment for what they have done and console yourself with the lines:

If the fool wrongs you, let him be,
And wait awhile for his punishment.
Avoid unhealthy wrongdoing;
A mountain that wrongs another will be ground to dust.'

Judar continued to console his mother until she accepted the situation and stayed with him. He then equipped himself with a fishing net and went out every day in a different direction, to the river or the pools or anywhere else where there was water. Some days he would earn ten *nusfs* and on others twenty or thirty. He spent the money on his mother, while at the same time having enough to eat and drink well. His brothers, meanwhile, practised no craft and were unable to trade; they were crushed by poverty and distress, having squandered all that they had taken from their mother, and they became wretched and naked beggars. At times they would approach their mother in all humility, complaining of hunger, and in her tenderness of heart she would give them any food that had gone bad, or if there was anything that had been cooked the day before she would tell them to eat it up quickly and leave before their brother came. 'He wouldn't find this easy to accept,' she would tell them, 'and were he to harden his heart against me, you would disgrace me in his eyes.' They would then wolf down the food and go off.

One day when they came she put out a cooked dish for them, together with some bread, and they began to eat. At that moment, to their mother's shame and confusion, in came their brother, Judar. She hung her head before him, afraid that he might be angry with her, but he smiled at his visitors and welcomed them, exclaiming: 'This is a blessed day! How is it that you have come on such a day to visit me?' He embraced them lovingly and went on: 'I never wanted you to keep away from me and not come here to see me or your mother.' 'By God, brother,' they told him, 'we have been longing for you and we only kept away because we were ashamed of what happened between us, which we bitterly regret. That was the work of the devil, may Almighty God curse him, and you and our mother are our only blessing.'

Night 608

Morning now dawned and Shahrazad broke off from what she had been allowed to say. Then, when it was the six hundred and eighth night, SHE CONTINUED:

I have heard, O fortunate king, that when Judar came home and found his brothers, he welcomed them and said: 'You are my only blessing.' His mother called down blessings on him and praised his generosity, after which he again welcomed his brothers and invited them to stay, saying: 'God is generous and I bring in plenty to live on.' The three were reconciled and Judar's brothers spent the night there sharing his supper and eating breakfast the next day.

He then took his net and left, relying on God, the Provider. His brothers went off and when they came back at noon their mother produced a meal for them, while he himself returned in the evening bringing with him meat and vegetables. Things went on like this for a month, with Judar catching fish, selling them and spending the money he earned on his mother and his brothers, the two of whom doing nothing but eating and amusing themselves. It then happened that one day Judar took his net to the river and made a cast, only to find when he drew it out that it was empty. He made a second cast but again it was empty, and he told himself: 'There are no fish here.' So he went and cast his net somewhere else, but again without success and, although he continued to wander round from one place to another from dawn to dusk, he failed to catch even one single small fish. 'This is strange,' he told himself. 'Are there not any fish in the river any longer and, if so, why?'

With the net over his shoulder he went back sorrowfully and full of care, worried about his brothers and his mother since he had no idea what to give them to eat. He came to a baker's oven around which was a crowd of people with money in their hands wanting to buy bread, while the baker himself was paying no attention to them. He stood there sighing and the baker called out a welcome to him and asked him if he was wanting bread. When he made no reply, the baker said: 'If you don't have the money, take what you need and you can pay me later.' So Judar asked for ten *nusfs*' worth of bread, and the baker gave him an extra ten in cash, telling him to bring him twenty *nusfs*' worth of fish the next day. Judar swore to do that, and he took the bread as well as the money, with which he bought a piece of meat and some vegetables, saying: 'Tomorrow God will help me out of my difficulties.'

When he had gone back home and his mother had cooked the food, he ate his evening meal and went to sleep. The next day he took his net and, when his mother told him to sit down and have his breakfast, he refused, telling her to eat with his brothers. He then went to the river, but after three casts he had to try somewhere else and this went on until the afternoon, by which time he had caught nothing at all. He walked away dispiritedly on a route on which he couldn't avoid passing the baker, and when the baker saw him there, he weighed out the bread and produced the coins, saying: 'Come on, take this and go. If you caught nothing today, you will tomorrow.' Judar wanted to present his excuses, but the baker said: 'Go off; there is no need to explain. If you had caught anything you would have been carrying it with you, and when I saw you empty-handed I realized that you had got nothing. If this happens again tomorrow, don't be ashamed to come for bread, as you can pay me later.'

On the third day he visited the pools until the afternoon, but he found

nothing at all there and so he had to return to the baker to fetch the
bread and the coins. This went on for seven days, after which he became
depressed and made up his mind to go to Lake Qarun. He was on the
point of making a cast there when, before he knew it, up rode a Maghribi
on a mule. The rider was wearing a splendid robe, and the mule, all of
whose trappings were embroidered, carried over its back embroidered
saddlebags. The man dismounted and said: 'Peace be on you, Judar, son
of 'Umar,' to which Judar replied: 'And peace be on you, pilgrim.'
'Judar,' said the man, 'there is something I want you to do, and if you
do it, it will bring you a great deal of good. You will be my companion
and manage my affairs.' Judar asked him what he had in mind, promising
to do what he wanted without fail. 'Recite the Fatiha,' the man told him,
and when they had both done this, the man brought out a silk cord and
told him to tie his hands behind his back as firmly as possible. 'Then
throw me into the lake,' he went on, 'and wait a little. If you see my
hand raised from the water before the rest of me appears, then throw
your net at me and pull me in quickly, but if you see my foot, then leave
me, for you will know that I am dead. In that case take the mule and the
saddlebags and go to the traders' market, where you will find a Jew
called Shumai'a. Give him the mule and he will hand you a hundred
dinars. Take them and go on your way, but keep the matter secret.'

Judar tied the man's arms tightly as the man kept telling him to tie the
cord tighter, and Judar then did as he was told, throwing him into the
lake, where he sank from sight. For a time Judar stayed watching, but
then he saw the man's legs coming out of the water. Realizing that he
must be dead, he took the mule and went off to the traders' market,
where he saw the Jew sitting on a chair in the doorway of his storehouse.
At the sight of the mule, the Jew exclaimed: 'He must be dead!', adding:
'And it was his greed that killed him.' He then took the mule from Judar,
gave him a hundred dinars and told him to keep the affair secret. Judar
went off with the money, after which he got what bread he needed from
the baker and gave him a dinar in return. The baker calculated his debt
and told him: 'I now owe you two days' worth of bread.'

Night 609

Morning now dawned and Shahrazad broke off from what she had been allowed to say. Then, when it was the six hundred and ninth night, SHE CONTINUED:

I have heard, O fortunate king, that the baker calculated what Judar owed him for the bread and told him: 'I now owe you two days' worth of bread.' Judar went from the baker to the butcher, to whom he gave another dinar. He took his meat and told the man to credit what was left over from the dinar to his account. Then he fetched vegetables and went home, where he found his brothers pestering his mother for something to eat. She was saying: 'Wait for your brother to come, as I haven't anything here at all.' So he went in and told them to take the food and eat it, at which they fell on the bread like *ghuls*. He gave the rest of the gold to his mother, telling her: 'When my brothers come, give them some money to buy food with while I am away.'

He then spent the night at home, and the next morning, taking his net with him, he went back to Lake Qarun. He was about to make a cast when another Maghribi, even more splendidly equipped than the first, rode up on a mule with a pair of saddlebags and two small boxes, one in each bag. He addressed Judar by name, and when they had exchanged greetings the newcomer asked whether another Maghribi had come on the day before riding a mule like his. Judar was nervous and denied having seen anyone lest he be asked where the man had gone, as if he then said that he had drowned in the lake, the newcomer might accuse him of having been responsible. The man was not taken in by his denial and said: 'Poor fellow, that was my brother, who got here before me.' Judar repeated: 'I don't know anything about this,' but the man went on: 'Didn't you tie him up and throw him into the lake, after he had told you that if his hands appeared you were to throw your net and pull him out quickly but that if his feet came up he would be dead? In that case you were to take his mule to the Jew, Shumai'a, who would give you a hundred dinars. It was his feet that appeared and you did take the mule to the Jew, who did give you the money.' 'If you know all that, why do you ask?' said Judar, and the man replied: 'Because I want you to do the same thing to me as you did to my brother.' He then produced a silk cord and said: 'Tie me up and throw me in. If what happened to my brother happens to me, take the mule to the Jew and get a hundred

dinars from him. Come on now.' Judar went forward and, having tied
him up, he gave him a push so that he fell into the lake and sank. When
Judar had waited for some time, he saw the man's feet emerging from
the water and he exclaimed: 'He has died miserably! God willing, Maghribis will come to me every day to be tied up and die, and if I get a
hundred dinars for each dead man, that will be enough for me.'

He then went off with the mule, and on seeing him the Jew said: 'The
other one must be dead.' 'Long life to you,' replied Judar, and the Jew
repeated: 'This is the reward of the greedy,' after which he took the mule
and gave Judar a hundred dinars. Judar went off with the money to give
to his mother, who asked where he had got it. When he told her, she
said: 'You shouldn't go to Lake Qarun again, as I'm afraid that you may
come to some harm at the hands of these Maghribis.' 'Mother,' he told
her, 'I only throw them into the water because they want me to. What
am I supposed to do? This business brings me in a hundred dinars a day
and I come home quickly. By God, I'm not going to stop going to the
lake until there are no more Maghribis to be seen.'

On the third day he went off and, as he was standing there, another
Maghribi appeared riding on a mule with saddlebags, even more splendidly equipped than the first two. He greeted Judar by name, causing
him to wonder to himself how they all came to know him, and when he
had returned the greeting, the man asked him whether any Maghribis
had passed by that spot. 'Yes, two,' he said, and the man then asked
where they had gone. 'I tied them up and threw them into this lake,
where they drowned,' Judar told him, adding: 'And this is what will
happen to you too.' The man laughed and said: 'Poor fellow, every living
creature meets its destined fate,' after which he dismounted from his
mule and, producing the silken cord, he told Judar to do the same thing
with him as he had done with the others. 'Put your hands behind your
back so that I can tie them, for I am in a hurry and time is passing,' said
Judar. The man did this and Judar tied him up and gave him a push so
that he fell into the lake. He then stood waiting and this time the
Maghribi raised his hands out of the water and called to him to throw
his net. Judar did this and when he had pulled the man in, he discovered
that he was clutching two fish coloured like red coral, one in each hand.
'Open the boxes,' the man told him, and when this had been done, he
put one fish in each of them and then closed them up. He then embraced
Judar and kissed him on both cheeks, saying: 'May God rescue you from
every hardship. Had you not thrown me the net and pulled me out,

I would have gone on holding these fish and stayed submerged until I died, for I should not have been able to get out of the water.' 'For God's sake, pilgrim,' Judar said, 'tell me about the two who drowned earlier and about these two fish as well as about the Jew.'

Night 610

Morning now dawned and Shahrazad broke off from what she had been allowed to say. Then, when it was the six hundred and tenth night, SHE CONTINUED:

I have heard, O fortunate king, that Judar asked the Maghribi to tell him about the two who had drowned earlier. THE MAGHRIBI REPLIED:

You must know, Judar, that both of them were my brothers; one of them was called 'Abd al-Salam and the other 'Abd al-Ahad, while my name is 'Abd al-Samad. The 'Jew' is another of our brothers; his name is 'Abd al-Rahim and far from being a Jew, he is a Maliki Muslim.* Our father taught us magic, as well as how to solve riddles and to uncover hidden treasures. We four brothers practised our magic craft until the *marids* and the *'ifrits* became our servants. Then when our father, whose name was 'Abd al-Wadud, died he left us a great inheritance and we divided up the treasures, the wealth and the talismans until we came to the books. We began to share them out but we could not agree on one of them, a book called *Legends of the Ancients*, a unique and invaluable work, worth more than its weight in jewels, as it contained an account of all hidden treasures together with the solutions to riddles. Our father had used it in his work; we ourselves knew a small section of it by heart and each of us wanted to own it in order to discover what else was there.

When we began to argue about it, we were joined by our father's teacher, who had instructed him and taught him magic and divination, a man called al-Abtan the seer. He told us to fetch him the book, and when we had given it to him he said: 'You are the sons of my son and I cannot wrong any one of you. Whichever of you wants to get this book must go on a quest for the treasure of al-Shamardal and fetch me his celestial globe, his kohl case, the signet ring and the sword. A *marid* named al-Ra'd al-Qasif serves the ring, and no king or sultan has any power over its owner, so that if he wants to rule the whole wide world,

---

* Reference to Malik ibn Anas, founder of one of the principal schools of Islamic law.

that will be within his power. As for the sword, if its bearer draws it in the face of an army and brandishes it, the army will be routed, while if, as he is brandishing it, he says: "Kill this army," a bolt of fire will come from the sword and destroy it all. Whoever has the globe can, if he wants, sit inspecting all lands from east to west and whatever part he wants to see, he can do so by turning the globe where he wants and looking into it. He will then have a view of the land and its people as though they were all there in front of him. If he is angry with any city and turns the globe towards the sun with the intention of burning the city to the ground, this is what will happen. As for the kohl case, whoever uses its contents on his eyelids will see all the treasures of the earth.'

Al-Abtan continued: 'I lay down one condition on you: whoever proves unable to open up this treasure will have no right to the book, while whoever succeeds in bringing me the four treasures will be its rightful owner.' When we had agreed to the condition, he went on: 'Know, my children, that the treasure of al-Shamardal is under the control of the sons of the Red King. Your father told me that he had tried to uncover it but had failed, and the Red King's sons had fled from him to an Egyptian lake, known as the lake of Qarun, where they defied him. He followed them to Egypt but was unable to overcome them because the lake into which they had entered was guarded by a talisman, and . . .'

Night 611

Morning now dawned and Shahrazad broke off from what she had been allowed to say. Then, when it was the six hundred and eleventh night, SHE CONTINUED:

I have heard, O fortunate king, that when al-Abtan had told this to the brothers, he added that their father had come back defeated, having been unable to take al-Shamardal's treasure from the sons of the Red King. THE MAGHRIBI WENT ON:

'After this failure,' al-Abtan said, 'your father came and complained to me, and I cast a horoscope for him which showed me that the only person who could take the treasure was a young Cairene by the name of Judar, son of 'Umar, through whom the sons of the Red King could be captured. This Judar was a fisherman, and the place to meet him was by Lake Qarun. The talismanic spell could only be broken if Judar were to

tie the hands of whoever was destined to succeed and then throw him
into the lake. There the treasure seeker would have to fight with the Red
King's sons; if he was the lucky one, he would manage to seize them, but
if not, he would die and his feet would emerge, while in the case of the
successful man it would be his hands. Judar would then need to throw
him the net and bring him out of the water.' My brothers said: 'We will
go even if this means our death.' I said that I would go too, but our
brother, the 'Jew', told us that he wanted no part of this, and we arranged
that he would go to Cairo disguised as a Jewish merchant. If any one of
us drowned in the lake, he was to take the mule and the saddlebags from
Judar and give him a hundred dinars. The first of us to come to you was
killed by the sons of the Red King and they went on to kill my second
brother, but they could not get the better of me and so I seized them.

'Where are they, then?' Judar asked. 'You saw them, didn't you?' the
man said. 'I shut them up in the two boxes.' 'But those were fish,'
objected Judar. 'No, they weren't,' replied the man. 'They were *'ifrits* in
the shape of fish. But you must know,' he went on, 'that it is you and
you alone who can open up the treasure. Are you willing to follow my
instructions and to go with me to Fes and Meknes, where we can do
this? I will give you whatever you want and I swear that you will be a
brother to me in the sight of God. Afterwards you will be able to go
back to your family with a happy heart.' 'Pilgrim,' replied Judar, 'I am
responsible for my mother and my two brothers . . .'

Night 612

Morning now dawned and Shahrazad broke off from what she had been
allowed to say. Then, when it was the six hundred and twelfth night,
SHE CONTINUED:

I have heard, O fortunate king, that Judar told the Maghribi that he
was responsible for his mother and his two brothers. 'It is I who provides
for them,' he went on, 'and if I go off with you, who will give them their
daily bread?' 'That is a feeble excuse,' the man replied, 'for, if it is a
matter of expense, we'll give you a thousand dinars to pass on to your
mother to spend until you get back home, and if you go, you will be back
within four months.' When Judar heard him say 'a thousand dinars', he
told him: 'Produce the money, pilgrim, and I will leave it with my mother

and go off with you.' So the man brought it out for him, and on taking it off to his mother, Judar told her of his encounter with the Maghribi. 'Take these dinars,' he said, 'and spend them on yourself and on my brothers, for I am going to the west with the Maghribi. I shall be away for four months and I shall do very well for myself, so pray for me, mother.' 'You will make me lonely, my son,' she told him, 'and I am afraid for you.' 'No harm can come to one whom God protects, and the Maghribi is a good man,' he told her, and he went on to tell her how lucky he was. She said: 'May God soften his heart towards you. Go with the man, my son, and perhaps he will give you something.' So he said goodbye to her and left.

When he got back, 'Abd al-Samad, the Maghribi, asked him whether he had consulted his mother. 'Yes,' he replied, 'and she blessed me.' 'Get up behind me,' 'Abd al-Samad told him, and when he had mounted on the mule's back the two of them travelled on from noon until the time of the afternoon prayer. By then Judar was hungry, but he could not see that 'Abd al-Samad had anything to eat with him and so he said: 'I wonder, pilgrim, whether you have forgotten to bring any food with you to eat on the way.' 'Are you hungry?' the man asked, and when Judar said that he was, he dismounted together with Judar and said: 'Bring down the saddlebags.' When Judar had done this, 'Abd al-Samad asked him: 'What would you like, my brother?' 'Whatever there is,' replied Judar, but 'Abd al-Samad insisted that he say what he wanted. 'Bread and cheese,' Judar told him. 'Poor fellow,' replied 'Abd al-Samad, 'that's not for the likes of you. Ask for something good.' 'Just at the moment anything would be good,' said Judar. 'Do you like roast chicken?' he was asked, and when he had said yes, 'Abd al-Samad asked whether he liked rice with honey. After he had again said yes, 'Abd al-Samad went on to ask about a string of different dishes, until he had named twenty-four of them. Judar said to himself: 'He must be mad. How can he produce these for me when he has neither kitchen nor cook? I'd better tell him that that's enough.' So he said: 'Enough of that. Are you trying to make me long for all these dishes when I can't see anything at all?' 'You are welcome, Judar,' replied 'Abd al-Samad, and he then put his hand in the saddlebag and brought out a gold plate on which were two hot roast chickens. He put his hand in again and this time he took out another gold plate with a kebab on it, and went on drawing plates from the saddlebag until, to Judar's astonishment, he had produced every single one of the twenty-four types of food that he had mentioned. 'Eat, you poor fellow,' said 'Abd al-Samad. 'Sir,' answered Judar, 'have you put a kitchen and people to cook for you in the saddlebag?' 'Abd al-Samad laughed and said: 'It has a talismanic charm whose servant, if asked, would immediately produce a thousand different types of food every hour.' 'What a good bag it is!' exclaimed Judar.

The two companions then ate their fill, after which 'Abd al-Samad threw away the leftovers and put the empty dishes back in the saddlebag. He reached into it again and drew out a jug from which they drank and which they used for their ablutions before performing the afternoon prayer. 'Abd al-Samad then returned it to the bag, into which he also put the two boxes. He loaded the saddlebags on to the mule, mounted and told Judar to get up as well, so that they could set off. He asked Judar if he knew how far they had come from Cairo and when Judar said: 'By God, I don't,' he told him: 'We have covered the distance of a month's journey.' 'How can that be?' Judar asked, and 'Abd al-Samad explained: 'The mule that we are riding is a *marid* of the *jinn*, which can cover a year's journey in a single day, but for your sake it is going slowly.'

When the two had mounted, they set off westwards. In the evening 'Abd al-Samad brought out supper from the saddlebags, and in the morning, breakfast. For four days they went on like this, riding until midnight and then dismounting to sleep, before setting off again in the morning, with Judar asking 'Abd al-Samad for anything he wanted and 'Abd al-Samad producing it for him from the saddlebags. On the fifth day they arrived at Fes and Meknes, and when they entered the city everyone who met 'Abd al-Samad greeted him and kissed his hand. That went on until they came to a door on which he knocked. It opened to show a girl radiant as the moon, to whom he said: 'Rahma, my daughter, open up the pavilion for us.' 'Willingly, father,' she replied, and she went back in, swaying her hips in a way that robbed Judar of his wits, making him say to himself that she must be a king's daughter. She opened the door of the pavilion and 'Abd al-Samad took the saddlebags from the mule's back and said to it: 'Go off now, God bless you.' At that a chasm opened into which the mule went down before the earth closed up again. 'Sheltering God,' exclaimed Judar, 'praise be to You for allowing us to escape from the back of that mule!' 'Don't be surprised, Judar,' 'Abd al-Samad said. 'I told you that this was an *'ifrit*. Now, come into the pavilion with me.'

They both went in and Judar was astonished at the quantity of splendid furnishings, the rarities, the strings of jewels and the precious stones that he saw there. When they were seated, 'Abd al-Samad said to his daughter: 'Rahma, fetch such-and-such a package.' She got up and brought a package which she put down in front of her father and, when he had opened it, he drew out of it a robe worth a thousand dinars. 'Put this on, Judar, for you are welcome here,' he said. Judar did so and it made him look as though he was one of the kings of the west. 'Abd al-Samad then put his hand into the saddlebags, which he had placed in front of him, and took out plates containing foods of various sorts until he had produced a meal with forty different dishes. 'Come up and eat,' he told Judar, 'and don't blame me . . .'

Night 613

Morning now dawned and Shahrazad broke off from what she had been allowed to say. Then, when it was the six hundred and thirteenth night, SHE CONTINUED:

I have heard, O fortunate king, that when the Maghribi took Judar into the pavilion, he spread a cloth for him on which were forty different types of food. 'Come and eat,' he said, 'and don't blame me, for I don't know what food you would like, but if you tell me, I shall get it for you without delay.' 'By God, sir pilgrim,' Judar replied, 'I am fond of all kinds of foods and there is nothing that I dislike. You don't need to ask me questions; just bring everything that you can think of and I shall do nothing but eat.'

Judar stayed with 'Abd al-Samad for twenty days, on each of which he was given a robe, and food was produced from the saddlebags. 'Abd al-Samad never bought any meat or bread and never cooked, as he took all that he needed from the saddlebags, including various kinds of fruits. Then, on the twenty-first day, he told Judar to come with him, saying that this was the day on which the treasure of al-Shamardal was destined to be opened. Judar left with him and the two of them walked through the city and then out of it, where they each mounted a mule and travelled on until noon. They came to a river where 'Abd al-Samad dismounted, and Judar followed his instructions to do the same. 'Abd al-Samad called to two slaves and gestured to them with his hand, at which they took the mules, each going off on his way, but after a brief absence one of them came back with a tent which he set up, while the other brought a mattress which he laid down in the tent, surrounding it with pillows and cushions. One of them then fetched the two boxes containing the fish, while the other brought the saddlebags. 'Come here, Judar,' said 'Abd al-Samad, and when Judar had come and sat down beside him, 'Abd al-Samad brought out plates of food from the saddlebags and they ate their morning meal. Then 'Abd al-Samad took the boxes and recited a spell over them. 'Here we are, sorcerer of the world, have mercy on us,' came two voices from within, and while they were calling for help and 'Abd al-Samad was reciting his spell, the two boxes burst into pieces. As the pieces flew apart, two bound figures appeared, saying: 'Spare us, sorcerer of the world. What are you going to do with us?' 'I am going to burn you to death unless you pledge to help me open the treasure of al-Shamardal,' 'Abd al-Samad replied. 'We give you our pledge and we shall do this for you, but on condition that you fetch Judar, the fisherman, as it is only he who can succeed in opening it, and he alone can enter the treasure chamber.' 'I have already brought him, and he is here, listening to you and looking at you.'

When the two had given 'Abd al-Samad their word to perform the task, he set them free. Then he brought out a wand and some tablets of red carnelian which he placed on top of the wand. He took a brazier in which he placed charcoal, and with a single puff he lit it, before fetching incense. 'Judar,' he said, 'I am going to recite a spell and put the incense on the fire. When I start my spell, I shall not be able to say anything else lest it be broken, so I want to tell you what you must do in order to reach your goal.' 'Tell me, then,' said Judar, and 'Abd al-Samad continued: 'You have to know that when I recite my spell and put the incense on the fire, the water in the river will dry up and you will see a golden door, as big as the gate of a city, with two metal rings. Go down to it, knock on it gently and then wait for a while before knocking again more loudly. Wait again, and then give three knocks, one after the other. You will hear a voice saying: "Who is knocking on the door of the treasure house without knowing how to unravel its mysteries?" You are then to say: "I am Judar, the fisherman, son of 'Umar." The door will open and out will come someone with a sword in his hand and he will say: "If you are that man, stretch out your neck and I shall cut off your head." Do that without fear, for when he lifts the sword up in his hand and strikes you, he will collapse in front of you; you will see him as a lifeless figure and his blow will neither hurt you nor do you any harm, whereas if you disobey him, he will kill you. When by obeying him you have destroyed his talismanic power, go in and knock on another door that you will see there. This time a rider will come out mounted on a horse with a spear carried over his shoulder. He will say: "What has brought you to this place which neither man nor *jinn* can enter?" When he then brandishes his spear at you, expose your breast to him and he will strike you before collapsing on the spot as a lifeless body. If you don't do this, he will kill you. Enter the third door and a man will come out to meet you holding a bow and arrows. He will shoot at you and you must expose your breast to him, so that he falls lifeless before you; if you do not, you will be killed. Then go in through the fourth door . . .'

Night 614

Morning now dawned and Shahrazad broke off from what she had been allowed to say. Then, when it was the six hundred and fourteenth night, SHE CONTINUED:

I have heard, O fortunate king, that the Maghribi told Judar: 'Go and knock on the fourth door. It will be opened for you and an enormous lion will come out and attack you, opening its mouth to show that it wants to eat you. Don't be afraid and don't run away, but when it reaches you, hold out your hand to it and it will instantly fall down, having done you no harm. On entering the fifth door, you will be met by a black slave who will ask you who you are. When you tell him that you are Judar, he will say: "If that is so, then open the sixth door." Go up to it and say: "'Isa, tell Musa to open the door," at which it will open. Go through and you will find two snakes, one on the left and the other on the right. Both of them will open their mouths and attack you instantly. You are to hold out your hands to them and each of them will bite a hand, but if you don't do that, they will kill you. When you go in to knock on the seventh door, your mother will come out and say: "Welcome, my son. Come forward so that I may greet you." Say to her: "Stay away from me and take off your clothes." "My son," she will answer, "I am your mother to whom you owe a debt for having suckled and raised you. How can you make me strip?" You must threaten to kill her if she refuses, and if you look to your right you will find a sword hanging on the wall. Take it and draw it against her, ordering her to take off her clothes. She will try to delude you, humbling herself before you, but have no pity on her and every time that she takes something off, tell her to remove the rest. Keep on threatening to kill her until she has taken off all her clothes, after which she will collapse.

'You will then have unravelled all the mysteries and broken the talismanic spells, so saving your own life. When you enter the treasure chamber, you will find gold lying in heaps, but pay no attention to any of it. At the upper end of the chamber, you will see a recessed room screened by a curtain. Pull aside the curtain and there you will find al-Shamardal, the magician, lying on a golden couch, with, by his head, something round that gleams like the moon. This is the celestial globe; he himself is girt with a sword, and on his finger is a ring and round his neck a chain to which is attached a kohl case. Fetch these four treasures and take care not to forget anything that I have told you or to disobey the instructions, for if you do you will have cause for regret and find yourself in fearful danger.'

'Abd al-Samad repeated these instructions a second time and then a third and a fourth, until Judar said: 'I know them by heart, but how can anyone face these talismans that you have mentioned or endure such fearful horrors?' 'Don't be afraid, Judar,' 'Abd al-Samad replied, 'these are nothing but lifeless figures,' and he set about calming Judar's fears until Judar exclaimed: 'I rely on God!' After that, 'Abd al-Samad threw the incense on the fire and started to recite a spell. This went on for some time until the water disappeared and the bed of the river could be seen, showing the door of the treasure chamber. Judar went down and knocked, after which he heard a voice saying: 'Who is knocking on the door of the treasure house without knowing how to unravel its mysteries?' When Judar gave his name, the door opened and out to meet him came a figure with a drawn sword, who told him to stretch out his neck. When he did so, the figure struck him and then collapsed. The same thing happened at the second door and this went on until he had put the talismans of all seven doors out of action.

Then his mother came out and greeted him, but he replied: 'What are you?' She said: 'I am your mother, to whom you owe a debt because I suckled and raised you, and I carried you for nine months, my son.' He told her to take off her clothes, but she protested: 'You are my son. How can you strip me?' 'Take them off,' he repeated, 'or else I shall behead you with this sword,' and, stretching out his hand, he unsheathed it against her, saying: 'Unless you strip off your clothes, I shall kill you.' After a long wrangle she yielded to his repeated threats and took off some, but he insisted that she take off the rest, and after another wrangle she took off something else. This went on and she kept exclaiming: 'My son, your upbringing has been wasted!' until only her drawers were left. 'Have you a heart of stone, my son,' she protested, 'that you would shame me by uncovering my private parts? This is unlawful.' 'That is true,' he said, 'so don't take off your drawers.' At that she gave a cry and called out: 'He has made a mistake, so beat him!' and the servants of the treasure gathered together and rained blows like raindrops on him, giving him a beating which he was never to forget in his life. Then they pushed him away and threw him outside the gate of the treasure chamber, whose doors closed shut as they had been before.

'Abd al-Samad picked him up immediately as the river started to flow again . . .

Night 615

Morning now dawned and Shahrazad broke off from what she had been allowed to say. Then, when it was the six hundred and fifteenth night, SHE CONTINUED:

I have heard, O fortunate king, that when the servants of the treasure had beaten Judar and thrown him out, the doors closed and the river started to flow again. 'Abd al-Samad got up and recited a spell over Judar until he came back to his senses and recovered from his stupor. 'What have you done, poor fellow?' 'Abd al-Samad asked, and Judar told him: 'I overcame all the obstacles until I came to my mother. We had a long wrangle and she started taking off her clothes, until, when only her drawers were left, she said: "Don't put me to shame, for it would be unlawful to uncover my private parts." So out of pity for her I let her keep them on, at which she shouted out: "He has made a mistake; beat him!" Then people came from I don't know where and beat me almost to death, after which they pushed me out. I don't know what happened to me after that.' 'Did I not forbid you to disobey the instructions?' asked 'Abd al-Samad, adding: 'You have injured me and injured yourself, for had she stripped off her drawers, we should have got what we wanted. As it is, you will have to stay with me until this same day next year.'

He immediately summoned his two slaves, who took down the tent and carried it off, coming back after a short absence with the two mules. 'Abd al-Samad and Judar each mounted one of them and then returned to Fes. Judar stayed with 'Abd al-Samad enjoying good food and drink, with splendid clothes being given to him every day, until the year had passed and the appointed day had come again. 'Abd al-Samad told him of this and said: 'Come with me.' Judar agreed and was then taken outside the city, where the two of them saw the two slaves with the two mules. They mounted and rode to the river, where the slaves pitched the tent and equipped it with its furnishings. When 'Abd al-Samad had brought out the saddlebags, they ate their morning meal and then, as before, he produced the wand and the tablets, lit the fire and fetched the incense. 'Judar,' he said, 'I want to give you your instructions.' 'Sir pilgrim,' Judar replied, 'if I had forgotten the beating that I got, then I would have forgotten the instructions too.' 'You remember them, then?' 'Abd al-Samad asked, and when Judar said that he did, 'Abd al-Samad went on: 'Look after yourself and don't think that the woman is your mother. She is only a talismanic figure shaped like your mother, whose purpose is to get you to make a mistake. You may have escaped alive the first time, but if you get it wrong this time, what they throw out will be your dead body.' 'If I do get it wrong,' said Judar, 'then I shall deserve to be burned.'

So 'Abd al-Samad put the incense on the fire and recited his spell, at which the river dried up. Judar went and knocked on the door and, after it had opened, he disabled the seven talismans before reaching his 'mother', who greeted him as her son. 'How can I be your son, you damned creature? Take off your clothes,' he said. She began to try to trick him, removing one garment after another until only her drawers were left. 'Take them off, damn you,' he said, and when she had done so she was only a lifeless form.

He entered the treasure chamber but paid no attention to the gold that he saw lying in heaps. Instead, he went to the recess where he saw al-Shamardal, the magician, lying girt with his sword and with a ring on his finger, the kohl case on his breast and above his head the celestial globe. Judar went up to him, unfastened the sword and took the ring, the globe and the kohl case. As he went out, a fanfare sounded as the servants of the treasure called out to congratulate him on the gift that he had been given. This fanfare continued until he had left the chamber and returned to 'Abd al-Samad, who, for his part, stopped reciting his spell and burning the incense, and got up to greet him and embrace him, before taking the four treasures that were now handed to him. He then called to the slaves, who took the tent away and came back with the mules, on which 'Abd al-Samad and Judar rode back to Fes. 'Abd al-Samad then brought out the saddlebags and began taking plates laid with various types of food from them, until a whole meal was set out before him. 'Eat, Judar, my brother,' he said, and when Judar had eaten his fill, the leftovers were emptied out on to other plates and the empty ones were put back in the saddlebag.

'Abd al-Samad now said: 'Judar, you have left your land and your own country for my sake and you have done what I wanted you to do for me. I now owe you a wish, so wish for whatever you want. It is Almighty God Who grants it and I am merely the means towards this. Do not be ashamed to ask for what you want, for you deserve it.' 'Sir,' replied Judar, 'the wish that I would make to God and then to you is that you would give me this pair of saddlebags.' 'Fetch them,' said 'Abd al-Samad, and when they had been brought, he said: 'Take them, for you have a right to them and if you had asked for something different I would have given it to you. But, poor man, they will only help you when it comes to food. You have faced hardships with me, and I promised to send you home with a happy heart, so in addition to these bags from which you can get your food, I will give you another pair filled with gold and jewels. I shall see that you get back to your own country, where you can become a merchant and clothe yourself and your family without concerning yourself about expense, taking your food and that of your family from the saddlebags. The way to use them is to put your hand in one with the words: "I conjure you by the great names to whom you owe obedience, servant of the saddlebag, to produce me such-and-such a dish." Even if you asked for a thousand different ones each day, they would be brought for you.'

'Abd al-Samad then summoned a slave with a mule, and filled one saddlebag with gold and another with jewels and precious stones. 'Mount on this mule,' he said to Judar, 'and the slave will walk on before you until he brings you to the door of your own house, because he knows the way. When you get there, take the saddlebags but hand the mule over to the slave, who will bring it back. Do not let anyone know your secret, and now I entrust you to God.' 'May He reward you amply,' replied Judar, and he then put the saddlebags on the mule's back and mounted, as the slave walked on in front of him. The mule followed the slave that day and all through the night until morning on the second day, when Judar entered by the Bab al-Nasr, only to discover his mother sitting there as a beggar. In consternation he dismounted and threw himself on her. She burst into tears at the sight of him, and he mounted her on the mule and walked by her stirrup until he got home. There he helped her to dismount and, taking the saddlebags, he left the mule in the charge of the slave, who took it and went back to his master, for both slave and mule were devils.

As for Judar himself, he found it hard to bear that his mother had been reduced to begging and when he had got to the house he asked her whether his brothers were well. When she told him that they were, he asked her why she had been begging on the street. 'Because I was hungry,' she replied. 'Before I left I gave you a hundred dinars one day, a hundred on the next and a thousand on the day I went,' he said. 'My son,' she replied, 'your two brothers cheated me and took the money, saying that they wanted to buy goods with it, but when they got it they drove me away and I have been so hungry that I had to start begging in the streets.' 'Mother,' he told her, 'now that I am back, no harm will come to you and you need never have any worries, for this pair of saddlebags is full of gold and jewels, as well as many other good things.' 'You are a lucky man, my son,' she told him. 'May God be pleased with you and grant you more of His favours. But go and bring me some bread, because I had nothing to eat yesterday evening and am perishing of hunger.' 'You are very welcome to this, mother,' Judar said, laughing. 'Ask for whatever you want to eat and I shall bring it for you immediately, for I've no need to buy anything from the market or to find a cook.' 'You don't seem to have anything with you, my son,' she objected, but he said: 'In these saddlebags are all kinds of foods.' 'Anything that one has is enough to satisfy hunger,' she said. 'That is right,' he replied, 'and when there are no provisions, a man can be satisfied with the minimum, but when that's not the case, he will want to eat well. I now have the means, so ask for what you want.' She asked for hot bread and a bit of cheese, but he objected: 'This does not suit your status.' 'You know my status, so give me what fits it,' she said, and he told her: 'What is suitable is roast meat, roast chicken, rice with pepper, sausages, stuffed gourds, stuffed lamb, stuffed ribs and sugared vermicelli with broken nuts and honey, together with fried doughnuts and almond pastry.' She thought that he was laughing at her and making fun of her, and so she called out in disgust: 'What's happened to you? Are you dreaming or mad?' 'What makes you think that I am mad?' he asked, and she replied: 'Because you mention all these splendid dishes, and who could afford to pay for them or know how to cook them?' 'I swear by my life,' he said, 'that

I will certainly give you every one of them to eat this very minute.' 'I don't see anything,' she objected. On his instructions she brought the saddlebags, but when she felt them, she found them empty. However, she passed them to him and after he had stretched out his hand, he produced dishes laden with food until every single thing that he had mentioned was there. 'The bags are small,' his mother said, 'and there was nothing in them and yet you have taken all this out of them. Where were these dishes?' He told her: 'You must know, mother, that the Maghribi gave these bags to me. They have a talismanic spell and the talisman has a servant. Whoever wants something must recite the magic names and say: "Servant of the saddlebag, bring me such-and-such a type of food," and he will then fetch it.' 'May I reach in and ask for something?' she asked, and when he had agreed to this, she stretched out her hand and said: 'I conjure you, servant of the saddlebag, by the duty you owe to these names, to bring me stuffed ribs.' She then saw that there was a plate in the bag and, when she reached in and took it, she found that on it were expensive stuffed ribs. So she went on to ask for bread and for every type of food that she wanted, after which Judar told her: 'When you have finished eating, mother, put what is left of the food on to other plates and put the empty ones back in the bag, for this is how the talisman works. Look after the bag.'

Judar's mother then took the bag into her own keeping, and he told her to keep the secret and to carry the bag with her. 'Whenever you need something,' he went on, 'take it from the bag. Use it for alms-giving and for feeding my brothers whether I am there or not.' He and she then began to eat and at that point in came the two brothers, who had heard the news from one of the locals. This man had said: 'Your brother has come back, riding on a mule, with a slave going ahead of him, wearing a most magnificent robe.' They each said to the other: 'I wish that we had not mistreated our mother, for she is bound to tell him what we did and we shall be put to shame.' But then one of them said: 'She has a soft heart, and even if she does tell him, his heart is even softer than hers and he will accept our excuses.' So they went in to meet him and he rose to his feet and greeted them warmly before telling them to sit down and eat, which they did as they were weak with hunger. They went on until they were full, and Judar then told them to take what was left of the food and distribute it to the poor and needy. 'Brother,' they said, 'leave it for our supper.' 'When it is time for supper, you can have even more than this,' promised Judar, and so they took out the leftovers and told every poor man that passed them: 'Take and eat,' until there was nothing left. They then took back the plates, and Judar told his mother to put them into the saddlebag.

Night 616

Morning now dawned and Shahrazad broke off from what she had been allowed to say. Then, when it was the six hundred and sixteenth night, SHE CONTINUED:

I have heard, O fortunate king, that when Judar's brothers had finished their meal, he told his mother to put the plates in the saddlebag. That evening, Judar entered the courtyard and produced a meal with forty different dishes from the bag, after which he went out and sat between his brothers, telling his mother to bring in the supper. She came and when she saw the plates filled with food, she set the table and brought in the plates one after the other until all forty were there. They all had their supper and Judar again told his brothers to take what was left of the food and to distribute it among the poor and needy, which they did. After supper he brought them sweetmeats, which they ate, with the leftovers, on his instructions, being given to the neighbours. The same thing happened the next day at breakfast, and things went on like this for ten days. Then one of the brothers said to the other: 'How does this come about? Our brother produces a guest meal for us in the morning, another at noon, a third in the evening, and sweetmeats late at night, and he distributes what is left over to the poor. This is the kind of thing that sultans do, and how has he become so prosperous? Should you not ask about all these different kinds of foods and the sweetmeats, as well as about the leftovers he distributes to the poor? We never see him buying anything or lighting a fire, and he has neither kitchen nor cook.' 'By God, I don't know the answer to that,' replied his brother, 'but do you know anyone who will tell us the real secret behind it?' 'The only one who could do that is our mother,' said the other.

So they made a plan and went to her while Judar was absent, telling her that they were hungry. She said that she had good news for them and then went to the courtyard, where she made her request to the servant of the saddlebags and produced a hot meal. 'This food is hot,' they said, 'but you neither cooked nor lit a fire.' 'The dishes came from the saddlebags,' she told them, and when they asked what the bags really were, she told them that they were covered by a talismanic spell and had to be asked for from the servant of the talisman. She then told them the story of the bags, but warned them to keep it a secret. 'The secret is safe with us, mother,' they assured her, 'but tell us how it works.' So she taught them, and they started to stretch out their hands and bring out whatever they wanted, without Judar knowing anything about it.

When they had learned how to use the saddlebags, Salim said to Saliim: 'Brother, how long are we going to be like Judar's slaves, living off his bounty? Why shouldn't we play some trick on him and get the saddlebags for ourselves?' 'How can we do that?' asked Saliim, and his brother said: 'We can sell him to the captain of the Suez fleet.' 'But how can we arrange to sell him?' the other asked. 'You and I will go to the captain and invite him to a meal, together with two of his men. Whatever I tell Judar you are to confirm it, and at the end of the evening I'll show you what I shall do.' After they had agreed on this, the two of them went to the captain's house and told him: 'Captain, we have come on an errand which will please you.' 'Good,' replied the captain, and they went on: 'We two are brothers and we have a third one, a debauched good-for-nothing. When our father died he left us some money, which we divided up, and our brother took his share of the inheritance, only to spend it on depravity and evil living. When he had been reduced to poverty, he got the better of us, complaining to the police that we had taken his money and the money of our father. We took the affair up to the courts but lost money, and then, after he had left us alone for a time, he lodged a second complaint. This went on until we had been impoverished, but he has not stopped persecuting us, so causing us great distress, and what we want is for you to buy him from us.' The captain said: 'If you can bring him here to me by some means or other, I shall quickly send him off to sea.' 'We cannot bring him,' they replied, 'but you can come as our guest and bring with you two of your men and no more. Then, when he falls asleep, all five of us, working together, can seize him and gag him and you can take him off from the house under cover of night and do what you want with him.' 'To hear is to obey,' the captain said, adding: 'Will you sell him for forty dinars?' They agreed to this and told him to come to such-and-such a quarter after the evening prayer, where he would find one of them waiting for him.

He told them to go off, and they went to look for Judar. After having waited for some time, Salim went up to him and kissed his hand. Then, when Judar asked him what he wanted, Salim said: 'You must know, brother, that I have a friend who often invited me to his house while you were away. He showed me innumerable kindnesses and always treated me hospitably, as my brother knows. I greeted him today and he invited me to a meal, but I told him that I couldn't leave my brother, at which he said: "Bring him, too." I told him: "He won't agree to that, but perhaps you and your brothers" – who were sitting with him – "would come to us as guests?" I gave the invitation thinking that they would refuse, but in fact they accepted it and my friend told me to wait for him at the door of the small mosque, where he would come with his brothers. I'm afraid that he will arrive, and although I'm ashamed to press you, would you set my mind at ease by entertaining them tonight, for you are so generous a person? If you don't want to do this, let me take them to a neighbour's house.' 'Why should you do that?' asked Judar. 'Is our own house too small or have we no food to give them? Shame on you for having consulted me. All you need is enough good food and more for them, as well as sweetmeats, and if you bring in guests while I am away, then ask our mother to produce extra food for you. So off you go and fetch them, for this will bring us blessings.'

Salim now kissed Judar's hand and went to sit down by the mosque door where he waited until after the evening prayer, when he saw the captain and his men approaching. He took them into the house, where Judar greeted them, sat them down and chatted with them, not knowing what their secret purpose was. He then told his mother to serve supper, and she fetched whatever he asked for from the saddlebag, until forty different dishes had been set before the visitors. They ate until they had had enough and the meal was then cleared away, a meal which the sailors thought they owed to Salim's generosity. When the first third of the night had passed, Judar produced sweetmeats for them, which were served by Salim, while Judar and Saliim stayed seated. The conspirators then said that they wanted to sleep, so Judar got up and went off to sleep himself, while the others dozed until they could take him unawares. Then they got up and made a concerted attack on him, and before he knew what was happening, he was gagged and bound. They carried him out of the house under cover of night . . .

Night 617

Morning now dawned and Shahrazad broke off from what she had been allowed to say. Then, when it was the six hundred and seventeenth night, SHE CONTINUED:

I have heard, O fortunate king, that the men seized Judar and carried him out of the house under cover of night, and then sent him off to Suez, where his feet were chained. He remained silent and stayed there toiling like a prisoner or a slave for a whole year.

So much for him, but as for his brothers, when morning came they went to their mother and told her that he was not yet awake. 'Wake him up, then,' their mother said to them. 'Where was he sleeping?' they asked. 'With the guests,' she told them, and they said: 'Perhaps he went off with them, while we were asleep. He has tasted the pleasures of life in foreign parts and has a wish to make his way into treasure chambers. We heard him talking with the Maghribis, and they were telling him that they would take him with them and uncover a treasure for him.' 'Did he meet with Maghribis?' their mother asked, and when they told her that that was who their guests had been, she agreed that he might have gone with them, adding: 'But God will guide him on his way, for he is a lucky man and will meet with great good fortune.' Then she burst into tears, as she found it hard to part from him, but the brothers said: 'You damned woman, are you so fond of Judar, while as for us, you would be neither glad nor sorry if we were here or not? Aren't we your sons, just as Judar is your son?' 'You are,' she told them, 'but you are a pair of wretches who have never helped me in any way or done any good to me since the day of your father's death, while as for Judar, he has been more than good to me, comforting me and being generous to me. It is only right that I should weep for him because of the help that he has given both to me and to the two of you.'

When the brothers heard what their mother had to say, they showered abuse on her and beat her, after which they went in and searched through the saddlebags, removing the jewels from one and gold from the other, as well as taking the pair covered by the talismanic spell. 'This was our father's money,' they told their mother. 'No, by God,' she replied. 'It belongs to your brother, Judar, and he brought it from the Maghrib.' 'That's a lie,' they insisted. 'It belonged to our father and we have a right to dispose of it.' So they divided it between themselves, but they then quarrelled over the talismanic saddlebags, each saying that it was he who should take them. Neither of them would yield and their mother said: 'My sons, you have divided the pair that contained the jewels and the gold, but no price can be put on this pair and if you cut them in two, the talisman will no longer work. So leave them with me and I'll fetch you food whenever you want and content myself with a mouthful. If you give me any clothes, this will be an act of generosity on your part, and each of you will be able to set up a business in the city. You are my sons and I am your mother, so let us stay as we are for fear of disgrace if your brother happens to return.' They refused to accept this and spent the night quarrelling. One of the king's guards happened to be a guest in a neighbouring house, and when he leaned out of an open window there he heard the whole quarrel and what the two were saying about dividing what they had taken. The next morning this man went to Shams al-Daula, who was king of Egypt at the time, and told him what he had heard. The king sent for the brothers and when they had been brought to him, he had them tortured until they confessed, after which he confiscated the saddlebags and imprisoned them, while making their mother a daily allowance that was sufficient for her needs.

So much for them, but as for Judar, he spent a whole year's service at Suez. Then, when he was at sea, a wind got up which dashed the ship on which he and his companions were sailing against a mountain. The ship broke up, throwing the whole crew into the water, and Judar was the only one to reach land, while all the others died. After he had got ashore, he walked on until he came to a Bedouin camp, and when they asked him about himself, he said that he had been one of the crew of a ship and then told them his story. In their camp was a merchant from Jedda who took pity on him and said: 'Would you like to enter my service, Egyptian, and I'll supply you with clothes and take you with me to Jedda?' Judar agreed to this and went there with the merchant. He was very well treated, and when the merchant then decided to make the pilgrimage he took him with him to Mecca. Once they were there, Judar went off to the sanctuary in order to circumambulate the Ka'ba, and there he came across his friend 'Abd al-Samad, the Maghribi, who was doing the same thing.

Night 618

Morning now dawned and Shahrazad broke off from what she had been
allowed to say. Then, when it was the six hundred and eighteenth night,
SHE CONTINUED:

I have heard, O fortunate king, that when Judar was circumambulating
the Ka'ba, he met his friend 'Abd al-Samad, the Maghribi, who was
doing the same thing. On seeing Judar, 'Abd al-Samad greeted him and
asked him how he was, at which Judar burst into tears and told him
what had happened. 'Abd al-Samad took him back to his house, where
he gave him a robe of unparalleled splendour and told him: 'Your evil
times are over.' He then read Judar's fortune in the sand and told him
what had happened to his brothers and how they were imprisoned by
the king of Egypt, adding: 'You will be welcome to stay with me until
you have finished the pilgrimage ceremonies, and you will meet nothing
but good.' 'Sir,' said Judar, 'let me go back to the merchant with whom
I came in order to take my leave of him before coming back to you.' 'Do
you owe him money?' asked 'Abd al-Samad, and when Judar said no, he
told him to go and do this and then come back straight away, adding:
'Decent people recognize their obligation to those who have given them
bread.'

So Judar went and took his leave, telling the merchant that he had
met his brother. 'Go and fetch him,' said the man, 'and I shall treat him
as a guest.' 'There is no need for that,' Judar replied, 'as he is a man of
wealth with many servants.' So the merchant gave him twenty dinars,
saying: 'This settles my obligations,' and then said goodbye to him. After
leaving him, Judar came across a poor man, to whom he gave the
dinars, before going on to 'Abd al-Samad, with whom he stayed until
the ceremonies were over. 'Abd al-Samad then gave him the ring that he
had removed from the treasure of al-Shamardal, telling him to take it,
as it would bring him what he wanted. 'It has a servant named al-Ra'd
al-Qasif,' he explained, 'and if you need anything in the world and rub
the ring, al-Ra'd will appear to you and do whatever you tell him.' He
himself then rubbed the ring in front of Judar and al-Ra'd appeared,
saying: 'Here I am, master. I shall give you whatever you want. Would
you like me to restore a ruined city, ruin one that is flourishing, kill a
king or rout an army?' 'Abd al-Samad said: 'Ra'd, this man is now your
master, so look after his interests.' He then dismissed him and told Judar:

'When you rub the ring, he will come to you and you can order him to do what you want, as he will never disobey you. So go back to your own country and look after the ring, for you can use it to outwit your enemies, and you should never forget how powerful it is.' 'Sir,' said Judar, 'with your permission I shall go home.' 'Rub the ring, then,' said 'Abd al-Samad, 'and when Ra'd appears, mount on his back, and if you say: "Take me to my own land this very day," that is exactly what he will do.'

After saying goodbye to 'Abd al-Samad, Judar rubbed the ring. Ra'd appeared and said: 'Here I am, master, and I shall give you whatever you want.' 'Take me to Cairo today,' Judar told him. 'That shall be done,' said Ra'd, and he flew off carrying Judar from noon until midnight before setting him down in the courtyard of his mother's house and then leaving. Judar went in to see his mother and when she saw him, she got up and greeted him tearfully, telling him what the king had done to his brothers and how he had had them beaten and had taken the talismanic saddlebags, as well as the bags with gold and jewels. On hearing this, Judar was concerned by his brothers' misfortune, and he told his mother: 'Don't grieve for what has passed, for I shall show you this minute what I can do and I shall fetch my brothers.' He then rubbed the ring and when Ra'd appeared, saying: 'Here I am, master, and I shall give you whatever you want,' Judar said: 'My orders are that you should bring me my two brothers from the king's prison.' Ra'd disappeared into the earth and appeared in the middle of the prison. Both brothers were in great distress and wretchedness because of their sufferings there. They had reached the stage of wishing for death, and one was saying to the other: 'By God, brother, this hardship has lasted too long. How much longer are we going to be imprisoned? Death would come as a relief.' At that moment, the earth opened up and Ra'd came out. He picked them up and descended again into the earth, as they fainted in terror. Then, when they had recovered their senses, they found themselves in their own house with their brother Judar sitting there with their mother beside him. Judar gave them a friendly greeting, but they hung down their heads and began to weep. 'Don't shed tears,' he told them, 'for it was greed and the devil that prompted you to do it. How it was that you came to sell me I do not know, but I console myself with the thought of Joseph, whose brothers, by throwing him into the pit, did more to him than you did to me.'

Night 619

Morning now dawned and Shahrazad broke off from what she had been
allowed to say. Then, when it was the six hundred and nineteenth night,
SHE CONTINUED:

I have heard, O fortunate king, that Judar said to his brothers: 'How
did you come to do this to me? Turn to God in repentance and, if you
ask His forgiveness, He will forgive you, for He is forgiving and merciful.
As for me, I have forgiven you; I welcome you and no harm shall come
to you.'

So Judar began to put them at their ease, until they regained their
spirits, and he then told them of everything that he had had to endure in
Suez until he met the *shaikh* 'Abd al-Samad and of how he had got the
ring. 'Don't blame us on this occasion, brother,' they said, 'but if we do
the same kind of thing again, then do what you want with us.' 'No harm
shall come to you,' Judar repeated, 'but tell me what the king did with
you.' 'He had us beaten, threatened us and took the saddlebags,' they
told him. 'He will have cause to regret that,' said Judar, who then
rubbed the ring. Ra'd appeared, to the consternation of the brothers,
who thought that Judar would tell him to kill them. They went to their
mother and began to say: 'Mother, we are under your protection; mother,
intercede for us.' She told them not to be afraid, and meanwhile Judar
told Ra'd to fetch all the jewels that were in the king's treasury, together
with whatever else was there, leaving behind nothing at all. He was also
to bring the talismanic bags and the pair of bags filled with jewels which
the king had taken from his brothers. 'To hear is to obey,' said Ra'd,
and he left immediately, collected everything that was in the treasury, as
well as the saddlebags together with their contents, and placed all this
in front of Judar. 'Master,' he told him, 'I left nothing behind there.'

Judar told his mother to keep the bag of jewels, but left the talismanic
bag in front of him. He then ordered Ra'd to build a high palace that
night, gilding it by way of adornment, and supplying it with magnificent
furnishings. 'Don't let the sun rise before you have completed it,' he
added, and Ra'd promised to have it done. He then disappeared into the
earth, after which Judar produced food and they all ate contentedly
before falling asleep. As for Ra'd, he collected his *jinn* and told them to
build the palace. Some of them cut stones, others did the building,
others whitewashed it, others painted it and another group provided the

furnishings. By the time day broke, it was ready to the last detail and Ra'd went to Judar and said: 'Master, the palace is finished and complete. Would you like to come and look at it?' Judar, his mother and his brothers all went to look and what they saw was a palace of unmatched splendour, the beauty of whose construction caused the mind to boggle. Judar, who had spent no money on it, was delighted with it, even while he was still outside on the road. He asked his mother whether she was prepared to live in it and she said yes, calling down blessings on him. He then rubbed the ring and Ra'd appeared, saying: 'Here I am.' 'I command you to fetch me forty beautiful white slave girls and forty black ones, together with forty mamluks and forty black slaves.' 'You shall have them,' said Ra'd, and he then went with forty *jinn* to the lands of India, Sind and Persia, carrying off beautiful girls and youths whenever they saw them. He sent another forty, who fetched pretty black girls, and forty who brought black slaves, all of whom were then taken to fill up Judar's palace. He showed them to Judar, who admired them and who told him to fetch robes of the greatest splendour for everyone. 'At your service,' said Ra'd, and Judar went on: 'Bring a robe for my mother to wear and another for me.' Ra'd brought all the robes and Judar distributed them to the slave girls and told them: 'This is your mistress; kiss her hand and do not disobey her, for all of you, white and black alike, are to serve her.' He then gave robes to the mamluks, who kissed his hand, as well as to his brothers. He himself was now like a king with his brothers like viziers, and as his own house was large enough he lodged one of his brothers, with his slave girls, in one part of it, and the other, with his, in another, while he and his mother lived in the new palace, each of them living in his own quarters like a sultan.

As for the king's treasurer, he wanted to take some things out from the treasury, but when he went there he found that it was empty, as in the poet's line:

> The hives were full of honey, but when the bees left, they were
> empty.

He gave a loud cry and fell unconscious, and then, when he had recovered his senses, he went out, leaving the door open, and came to King Shams al-Daula to tell him that the treasury had been emptied that night. 'What have you done with the wealth that I had there?' the king demanded. 'By God,' the treasurer told him, 'I didn't do anything to it at all and I don't know how the treasury became empty. Yesterday, when I went in, it was full, but today there was nothing there, although the doors were locked. No one had bored through the wall or broken the lock, so no thief could have got in.' 'Have the saddlebags gone?' the king asked, and when the treasurer said that they had, he nearly went out of his mind.

Night 620

Morning now dawned and Shahrazad broke off from what she had been allowed to say. Then, when it was the six hundred and twentieth night, SHE CONTINUED:

I have heard, O fortunate king, that when the king's treasurer told him that the contents of the treasury, together with the saddlebags, had gone, he nearly went out of his mind. Rising to his feet, he ordered the treasurer to lead the way and then followed him to the treasury, where he found nothing. 'Who has plundered this, showing no fear of my power?' he asked, and overcome with rage and fury he summoned his court. The army leaders came, each thinking that the king was angry with him, but he told them: 'Know that last night my treasury was plundered and I have no idea who could have so little fear of me that he broke in and did this.' 'How could that be?' they asked. 'Ask the treasurer,' the king said, and when they did he told them: 'It was full yesterday, but when I went in today I found it empty, although there was no hole in the wall and the door had not been forced.' They were all astonished to hear that, and none of them had anything to say except for the guard who had earlier informed on Judar's brothers. He went to the king and said: 'King of the age, all last night I watched builders at work and at daybreak I saw a palace of matchless splendour. When I asked about this, I was told that Judar had come back and that it was he who had had the palace built, having brought in mamluks and slaves, as well as providing great sums of money. He freed his brothers from prison and is there in his palace like a sultan.' 'Look in the prison,' ordered the king, but when his men had done this, they brought back word that they had found no trace of the brothers. 'It is clear who is guilty,' the king said, 'for whoever freed them is the man who took my money.' The vizier asked who that was, and the king told him: 'It was Judar, their brother, and he must have taken the saddlebags. So send an emir with fifty men to arrest him and his two brothers; they are to set a seal on all his possessions and to fetch me the brothers to be hanged.

Hurry,' he added, for he was still furious, 'send out an emir to bring them to me so that I may have them killed.' 'Be patient,' said the vizier, 'for God is patient and is not quick to punish His servants when they disobey Him. Someone who can have a palace built in a single night, as these people report, can have no match in this world and I'm afraid that the emir may find himself in difficulties because of him. So wait until I can make a plan and we can discover what really happened, so as to ensure that you get what you want, king of the age.' The king agreed to this, and the vizier went on: 'Send the emir to him and invite him here. I shall look after him for you and pretend to be fond of him, asking him about himself. We can then see whether he is strong-willed, in which case we can think of some scheme against him, but if he seems weak-willed, then arrest him and do what you want with him.' 'Send him an invitation,' said the king.

The vizier instructed an emir named 'Uthman to go and invite Judar on behalf of the king to come as his guest, and the king added that 'Uthman was not to fail in this mission. 'Uthman was both stupid and conceited, and when he arrived at Judar's palace he saw a eunuch seated on a chair in front of the door. This man did not get up on his arrival, and in spite of the fact that there were fifty men with 'Uthman, it was as though no one had come. 'Uthman went up to him and said: 'Slave, where is your master?' 'In the house,' the eunuch replied, and as he spoke he continued to lounge on his chair. 'Uthman became angry and said: 'You ill-omened slave, aren't you ashamed to lie there like a good-for-nothing while I'm speaking to you?' 'Be off,' replied the eunuch, 'and don't talk so much.' On hearing this, 'Uthman drew his mace in a rage and was about to strike the 'eunuch', not knowing that, in fact, he was a devil. When this devil saw him draw out his mace, he got up, rushed at him, seized it from him and gave him four blows. His fifty-man escort took this amiss and drew their swords with the intention of killing him. 'Are you drawing your swords, dogs?' the latter cried, and he attacked them, and whoever struck him found himself crushed with blows from the mace and spattered with blood. They were all put to flight and they kept on running as he struck them, until they had fled far away from the door of the palace, after which their attacker went back and sat down on his chair, paying no attention to anyone.

Night 621

Morning now dawned and Shahrazad broke off from what she had been allowed to say. Then, when it was the six hundred and twenty-first night, SHE CONTINUED:

I have heard, O fortunate king, that when the 'eunuch' had put 'Uthman, the king's officer, and his escort to flight, and driven them from Judar's door, he went back to sit on his chair by the palace door, paying no attention to anyone. 'Uthman and his escort returned, routed and beaten, and stood in front of the king, to whom they explained what had happened to them. 'King of the age,' 'Uthman said, 'when I got to the door of the palace, I saw a eunuch sitting proudly there on a golden chair. He had been sitting up, but when he saw me he lay back contemptuously and did not rise, and when I began to speak to him, he answered me while still sprawling there. I grew angry and drew out my mace with the intention of striking him, but he took it from me and used it to knock me down, after which he struck my escort and threw them to the ground. We were powerless against him and so we fled.' The king was angry and ordered a hundred men to go to the 'eunuch', but when they did and advanced on him, he got up with his mace and went on striking them until they ran away from him, after which he went back and sat down again on his chair. The hundred men returned to the king and told him what had happened, explaining that they had run off in fear. The king then sent two hundred, who suffered the same fate, and after that he said to the vizier: 'Vizier, I order you to take five hundred men and bring me this eunuch quickly, together with his master, Judar, and Judar's two brothers.' 'King of the age,' replied the vizier, 'I need no soldiers; I shall go to him alone and unarmed.' 'Go then,' the king told him, 'and do whatever you think appropriate.'

The vizier threw aside his weapons, put on a white robe and took a string of prayer beads in his hand. He walked alone and unaccompanied until he reached Judar's palace, where he saw the 'eunuch' sitting. Unarmed as he was, he then went up to him and sat down beside him with all courtesy, saying: 'Peace be upon you.' 'And upon you, human,' replied the other, adding: 'What is it that you want?' When the vizier heard him say 'human', he realized that this must be a *jinni* and he said, quaking with fear: 'Is your master, Judar, here?' 'Yes,' said the other, 'he is in the palace.' 'Go to him, sir,' said the vizier, 'and tell him that the king Shams al-Daula invites him as a guest, sending him greetings and asking him to honour his house and eat his food.' The doorman said: 'Stay here until I ask him.' The vizier stood there politely as the doorman went into the palace and said to Judar: 'Master, the king sent an emir to you with fifty men, but I beat him and routed them. Then he sent a hundred men, whom I struck, and they were followed by two hundred, whom I drove off. Now it is his unarmed vizier who has come to invite you to a reception. So what do you say?' 'Go and bring the vizier here,' Judar told him, and so the doorman went down and told the vizier to come and speak to his master. 'Willingly,' said the vizier, who then went up to the palace and came into Judar's presence, to find him seated in greater state than the king on a carpet more splendid than any that the king himself could produce. He was bewildered by the beauty of the palace, its decorations and its furnishings, in comparison with which he himself looked like a pauper. When he had kissed the ground before Judar and called down blessings on him, Judar asked him what his mission was. 'Sir,' replied the vizier, 'your friend the king Shams al-Daula greets you and longs to see you. He has prepared a reception for you, so will you set his mind at rest by accepting his invitation?' 'As he is my friend,' replied Judar, 'take him greetings from me and ask him to come to me.' When the vizier had agreed to this, Judar brought out the ring, rubbed it and told Ra'd, when he appeared, to fetch one of the most splendid robes. When this had been brought, he told the vizier to put it on, which he did, and Judar then told him to go and take his message to the king.

The vizier went off, wearing a more splendid robe than any he had ever worn before, and when he came into the presence of the king, he told him about Judar, extolling the splendour of the castle and its contents. When the vizier gave him Judar's invitation, the king alerted his guards, all of whom rose to their feet, and he then ordered them to mount and to bring him his horse, so that they might go to Judar. When he himself had mounted, they all set off for Judar's palace.

Judar himself had told Ra'd: 'I want you to fetch 'ifrits in the shape of men from among your jinn to stand as guards in the courtyard of the palace so that the king may see them. They are to fill him with fear and alarm so as to make him tremble and realize that my power is greater than his.' Ra'd produced two hundred jinn dressed as guards, splendidly equipped, powerful and burly. When the king saw them he was afraid of them, and then, when he came into Judar's presence, he saw him seated in more splendour than any king or sultan. He greeted and saluted him, but Judar did not rise or show him any respect or tell him to be seated, but left him standing.

Night 622

Morning now dawned and Shahrazad broke off from what she had been allowed to say. Then, when it was the six hundred and twenty-second night, SHE CONTINUED:

I have heard, O fortunate king, that when the king came in, Judar did not rise or pay any attention to him or tell him to sit, but left him standing there. The king became afraid and could neither sit down nor leave. He started to tell himself: 'If this man were afraid of me, he would not ignore me, and it may be that he is going to punish me because of what I did to his brothers.' At this point, Judar said: 'King of the age, it does not befit someone like you to treat people unjustly and to seize their wealth.' 'Sir,' the king replied, 'do not blame me, for it was greed that forced me to do that, as fate had decreed, but were it not for misdeeds there would be no forgiveness.' He started to apologize for what he had done and to ask for pardon and indulgence, quoting these lines in his appeal:

Generous son of a noble race, do not blame me for what I did.
If you wrong me, I forgive you, and if I am in the wrong, please
forgive me.

He went on abasing himself before Judar until Judar said: 'May God forgive you,' and told him to sit, which he did. He then produced for him robes as a token of forgiveness, and ordered his brothers to bring out food. After they had eaten, he gave robes to all the king's entourage and treated them honourably, before telling the king to go. He left, but every day he would come back to Judar's palace and it was only there that he would hold his court, as their familiarity and friendship increased.

When this had been going on for some time, the king told his vizier in private that he was afraid that Judar might kill him and seize his kingdom. 'King of the age,' the vizier replied, 'you need have no fear about the kingdom, for what he already has is greater than it and to take it would lessen his authority. If you are afraid that he might kill you, you have a daughter whom you can marry to him so that the two of you will

be as one.' The king then asked him to act as a go-between, and the
vizier said: 'Invite him here and then we shall spend the evening in one
of the rooms. Tell your daughter to put on all her finery and to walk
past its door, as when he sees her he will fall in love with her. When we
know that he has, I shall go up to him and tell him that she is your
daughter, after which I shall lead the conversation on until, before you
know anything about it, he will ask you for her hand. When you have
given her in marriage to him, you and he will be at one; you will be safe
from him and if he should die, you will get a great inheritance from him.'
'That is true, vizier,' said the king, and he arranged for a reception to
which he invited Judar.

Judar came to the palace and they all sat until evening in a room there,
becoming increasingly friendly with one another. The king had sent to
tell his wife to deck the princess out in all her finery and to walk with
her past the door of the room. She did what he had told her, and as she
went past with her daughter, a girl of matchless beauty and grace, Judar
caught sight of her. 'Ah!' he exclaimed as he gazed at her; he became
unstrung, being overcome by passionate love and, seized by a rapturous
ardour, he turned pale. The vizier said: 'I hope there is nothing wrong,
master, but why is it that you seem to have changed and to be in pain?'
'Vizier,' answered Judar, 'whose daughter was that, for she has robbed
me of my wits?' 'She is the daughter of your friend the king,' the vizier
told him, 'and if you admire her, I shall speak to him and get him to give
her to you in marriage.' 'If you do that, I swear by my life that I shall
reward you with whatever you want,' promised Judar, adding: 'I shall
pay the king whatever he wants by way of a bride price, and we shall be
friends and relatives.' 'You are certain to get your wish,' the vizier told
him, after which he said in private to the king: 'Judar, your friend, wants
a closer link with you, and he has asked me to approach you on his
behalf to request the hand of your daughter, the Lady Asiya. Do not
disappoint my hopes, but accept my intercession and he will pay whatever bride price you want.' 'As for the bride price,' the king replied, 'it
has already been paid to me and the girl is one of his servants. I shall
give her to him in marriage and he will do me a favour if he accepts.'

Night 623

Morning now dawned and Shahrazad broke off from what she had been allowed to say. Then, when it was the six hundred and twenty-third night, SHE CONTINUED:

I have heard, O fortunate king, that when the vizier told the king that Judar wanted a closer link with him by marrying his daughter, the king told the vizier that the bride price had already been paid, that the girl was one of his servants and that he would be doing him a favour by accepting her hand.

The next morning the king summoned a meeting of his court, which was attended by both high and low. The *shaikh* al-Islam was there, and Judar asked for the hand of the princess. The king repeated that the bride price had already been paid, but when the marriage contract had been drawn up, Judar sent for the saddlebag that contained the jewels, which he then presented to the king in return for this. Drums were beaten, pipes sounded and wedding garlands set out, after which Judar slept with his bride. He and the king were then on an equal footing, but after the two of them had stayed together for some time, the king died. The army wanted Judar to take power and, after he had resisted much pressure, he eventually agreed and was installed as ruler. He gave orders for a mosque to be built over the king's tomb, and provided it with endowments. This was in the Bundaqaniyin, while his own palace was in the Yamaniya quarter. After he came to power he built houses and a mosque, as a result of which the district was named after him and became the Judariya quarter.

He ruled for some time with his two brothers as viziers, Salim being vizier of the right and Saliim vizier of the left, but after no more than a year one of them said to the other: 'How long is this going to go on? Are we going to spend all our lives as Judar's servants, without being able to enjoy power or fortune while he is alive? The question is, how can we kill him and take his ring and the saddlebags?' 'You are more knowledgeable than I am,' said Saliim, 'so think of some way of disposing of him.' 'If I do that,' Salim replied, 'do you agree that I should be the sultan and you the vizier of the right, with the ring and the saddlebags being mine?' 'I do,' his brother answered, and so they agreed to murder Judar because of their love of worldly power. To carry out their plot they told Judar that they wanted to be able to boast that he had come to their house and had been kind enough to accept their hospitality.

They kept on treacherously pressing him to do this until he agreed, and when he asked to whose house he should go, Salim said: 'To mine, and after I have entertained you, it will be Saliim's turn.' Judar raised no objection and went with Saliim to Salim's house, where he was offered food in which poison had been put. When he ate it, his flesh decomposed, and Salim got up to remove the ring from his finger. It would not come off and so Salim took his knife and cut away the finger. Then he rubbed the ring and Ra'd appeared, saying: 'Here I am. Ask what you want.' 'Seize my brother and kill him,' Salim told him, 'and then take the two corpses, the one poisoned and the other slain, and throw them down in front of my soldiers.' So Ra'd seized and killed Saliim and then removed the corpses and threw them in front of the army officers, who were sitting eating at a table in the palace. When they saw that Judar and Saliim were dead, they were afraid and stopped eating and asked Ra'd who was responsible for this. 'It was Salim,' Ra'd told them and at that moment Salim came in and said: 'Eat and enjoy yourselves. I have taken the ring from my brother Judar, and this *marid* who is standing before you is the servant of the ring. I ordered him to kill Saliim lest he should attempt to take the kingdom from me as he was a treacherous man and I was afraid that he might play me false. Now that Judar is dead, I am your sultan. Are you going to accept me or shall I rub the ring and have Ra'd kill you, great and small alike?'

Night 624

Morning now dawned and Shahrazad broke off from what she had been allowed to say. Then, when it was the six hundred and twenty-fourth night, SHE CONTINUED:

I have heard, O fortunate king, that Salim told his soldiers that if they did not accept him as their sultan, he would rub the ring and have them all killed, great and small alike. 'We shall take you as our ruler,' they said. He then ordered that his brothers be buried, and after he had summoned a meeting of his court, some people accompanied the biers and others went in procession ahead. When they returned to the court, Salim took his seat on the throne and they swore allegiance to him. He then told them to draw up a marriage contract between him and Judar's widow. They pointed out that she would have to wait for the legally prescribed period, but he said: 'I know nothing about this period or anything else, and I swear by my life that I shall lie with her tonight.' So they drew up the marriage document and sent to inform the widow of this. 'Invite him to come in,' she said, and when he did, she pretended to be glad and welcomed him warmly, but put poison in the water and so killed him. She took the ring and broke it so that no one should ever own it again and she cut up the saddlebags. Then she sent word to the *shaikh* al-Islam and told the people to make their choice of a king to rule them.

This is the complete story of Judar as it has come down to us.

I have also heard that in the old days among the great kings there was a brave leader called Kundamir. He was a very old man, but in his old age Almighty God provided him with a son, whom, because of his beauty, he named 'Ajib. 'Ajib was entrusted to midwives and wet nurses, as well as to the king's slave girls and concubines, until he grew older and then, on his seventh birthday, his father handed him over to a priest of his own religion, who for three full years taught him the law and tenets of the infidels and whatever else he needed to know, until he became skilled. He turned out to be strong-minded and a sound thinker who, in addition to his learning, was eloquent and distinguished as a philosopher, arguing with men of learning, consorting with the wise and so filling his father with pride. His father then had him taught how to ride and how to manage both lance and sword until he became a bold rider. Before the end of his twentieth year he had surpassed all his contemporaries in every skill, and with his mastery of all the techniques of warfare he became a refractory devil, headstrong and tyrannical. On his hunting trips he would ride out with a thousand horsemen, attacking riders, robbing passers-by and capturing the daughters of kings as well as other ladies.

After frequent complaints had been made about him, his father called to five of his slaves and, when they had come, he told them: 'Seize this dog.' They set on 'Ajib and tied him up, after which the king told them to beat him, and this they did until he lost consciousness. He was then imprisoned in a room where he could not tell the difference between earth and sky or length and breadth. He stayed there as a prisoner for two days and a night, after which the emirs approached his father, kissed the ground before him and interceded for 'Ajib. His father released him and 'Ajib waited for ten days before going into his father's room at night while he was asleep and striking off his head. The next day he mounted his father's throne and ordered his men to put on their mail and stand in front of him, ranged on his right and his left, with drawn swords. When the emirs and officers came in, they were bewildered to find their king dead and his son seated on the royal throne. 'Men,' said 'Ajib, 'you have seen what happened to your king. I shall be generous to whoever obeys me, but any who disobey me will meet the same fate as the king.' When they heard this they were afraid of being attacked and so they kissed the ground before him and said: 'You are our king and the son of our king.' He thanked them and, as a token of his pleasure, he ordered money and materials to be brought out, and he conferred splendid robes of honour on them, deluging them with money, and so winning their affection and their obedience. He also gave robes of honour to the governors and to the *shaikhs* of the Bedouin tribes, whether independent or tributary.

Every region was subject to him, all his subjects obeyed him, and so for five months he gave judgements, commands and prohibitions, until one night he saw a dream which left him startled and afraid. He could not go back to sleep and in the morning when he sat on his throne, with his guards to his right and his left, he summoned the interpreters of dreams and the astrologers and told them to explain what he had seen. When they asked what this was, he said: 'I seemed to see my father standing in front of me uncovering his penis. Something the size of a bee came out of it, but it grew bigger until it was like a huge lion with claws like daggers. I was frightened of it and before I could think what to do it sprang at me and struck me with its claws, tearing open my belly and causing me to wake up in terror.' The interpreters looked at one another, wondering how to answer. 'Great king,' they said, 'this dream shows that your father had a son who will prove to be your enemy and who will overcome you. So be on your guard against him because of this dream.' When he heard this, 'Ajib said: 'I have no brother to fear and what you say is a lie.' 'We have only told you what we know,' they replied, after which in his anger he had them beaten.

He then got up and went into his father's palace, where he discovered on investigation that one of his father's concubines was seven months pregnant. He ordered two of his slaves to take her to the sea and drown her. They took her by the hand and brought her to the shore, but when they were about to drown her they saw how lovely she was and said to each other: 'Why should we drown her? We can take her to the forest and have a marvellous life with her there, enjoying her favours.' So they took her and travelled for some days and nights until they were a long way from any habitation, and there they brought her to a thick forest with fruits and streams. They decided to lie with her, but each of them said: 'I'll have her before you.' As they were quarrelling, a group of blacks came on them. They drew their swords and both sides attacked each other, which led to a furious fight, and in the twinkling of an eye the two slaves were killed.

As for the girl, she wandered off alone into the forest, eating fruit and drinking from the streams, and continued to do this until she gave birth to a brown-skinned boy, healthy and well formed. She named him Gharib* because she herself was in exile and, after cutting the umbilical cord, she wrapped him in some of her own clothes and began to suckle him, sad at heart because of her fall from pampered luxury.

Night 625

Morning now dawned and Shahrazad broke off from what she had been allowed to say. Then, when it was the six hundred and twenty-fifth night, SHE CONTINUED:

I have heard, O fortunate king, that the girl stayed in the forest, sad at heart. In spite of her great sorrow and the fear caused by her solitude, she began to suckle the baby. Then one day, while she was still in that state, she was suddenly met by riders and men on foot with hawks and hunting dogs, their horses laden with storks, herons, cranes, diving birds and water fowl, together with wild beasts, hares, gazelles, wild cows, young ostriches, lynxes, wolves and lions. On reaching the forest, these Bedouin found the girl suckling her baby on her lap and, going up to her, they asked if she was human or *jinn*. She told them that she was human and they alerted their emir, Mirdas, chief of the Banu Qahtan, who was out hunting with five hundred emirs from his cousins and his clan. The hunters carried on with their hunt until they came in sight of the girl, and when she had told them her story from beginning to end, Mirdas cried out to them in astonishment. When they ended their hunt, they returned to their clan, where Mirdas took the girl to a place of her own and assigned five slave girls to attend on her. He fell deeply in love with her and lay with her, as a result of which she immediately conceived,

---

* Arabic for 'stranger'.

and at the end of her pregnancy she gave birth to a boy whom she named Sahim al-Lail.

The baby was entrusted to the midwives with his brother until he grew up and acquired skill under the protection of Mirdas, who then entrusted both boys to a *faqih* to be given religious instruction, and later to Arab champions who were to teach them how to use lance and sword as well as bows and arrows. By the time that they had reached the age of fifteen, they had learned everything they needed and had surpassed all the other brave clansmen, each of them on his own being able to face a thousand riders.

Mirdas had many enemies, but his men were the bravest of the Arabs, heroic horsemen and unapproachable in battle. Among his neighbours was a friend of his, an emir named Hassan ibn Thabit, who had asked for the hand of a noble lady of his own tribe and who then invited all his companions, including Mirdas, the Qahtanid chief, to the wedding. Mirdas accepted and took with him three hundred riders, leaving behind another four hundred to guard the womenfolk. He made the journey to Hassan, who met him and placed him in the seat of honour. At the wedding celebration all the riders who had come to attend it were provided with a feast, after which they dispersed to go home, but what confronted Mirdas on his return to camp was the sight of dead bodies lying on the ground, with birds hovering over them to the right and the left. Trembling with fear, he went into the camp and there he was met by Gharib wearing mail and congratulating him on his safe return. Mirdas asked what had happened and Gharib told him that they had been attacked by al-Hamal ibn Majid with five hundred riders from his tribe.

The reason behind this was that Mirdas had a daughter named Mahdiya, a girl of unsurpassed beauty. Al-Hamal, the chief of the Banu Nabhan, had heard of her, but when he had come to Mirdas with five hundred men to ask for her hand, Mirdas had rejected him and sent him away disappointed. From then on he had been watching Mirdas, and when Mirdas left for Hassan's wedding, al-Hamal rode out with his fighting men and attacked the Qahtanids, killing some of their riders and driving the others in flight to the mountains. Gharib and his brother had been away hunting with a hundred others, and when they got back at midday it was to find Hassan and his Nabhanis in possession of the camp and all its contents. The raiders had taken the girls, including Mirdas's daughter, Mahdiya, who was being led off with the captives.

Gharib saw this and became demented with anger, shouting curses to his brother Sahim and calling out: 'They have plundered our camp and seized our women. Come on, charge them and rescue the prisoners and the women.' The two brothers with their hundred men attacked their enemies, and Gharib, growing angrier and angrier, started to harvest heads and pour out cups of death until he fought his way to al-Hamal and saw Mahdiya as a captive. He attacked al-Hamal, unhorsing him with a thrust, and by afternoon he had killed most of the enemy and routed the remainder. He freed the prisoners and rode back to camp with al-Hamal's head on his spear, reciting these lines:

I am the hero distinguished on the day of battle;
The *jinn* of the earth fear the sight of my shadow.
When I brandish my sword in my right hand,
Death rushes from the left.
When men look at my spear,
They see a spearhead like a crescent moon.
My name is Gharib, the hero of my clan;
Few though my men may be, I have no fear.

Before he had finished his poem, Mirdas arrived and was dismayed and frightened to find sprawling corpses and birds circling on either side. Gharib, after congratulating Mirdas on his safe return, told him all that had happened in his absence, and Mirdas thanked him for what he had done, saying: 'Your upbringing was not wasted.' He then went to his pavilion and his clansmen began to praise Gharib, saying: 'Had it not been for him, emir, no one in the camp would have escaped.' Mirdas renewed his thanks.

Night 626

Morning now dawned and Shahrazad broke off from what she had been allowed to say. Then, when it was the six hundred and twenty-sixth night, SHE CONTINUED:

I have heard, O fortunate king, that when Mirdas returned to camp and his men came to meet him, they praised Gharib, and Mirdas thanked him for what he had done. When Gharib had killed al-Hamal and rescued Mahdiya, she had shot him with an arrow from her eyes and he had fallen into the toils of love. He could not forget her and, drowning in passion, he could no longer taste the sweetness of sleep or enjoy food or drink. He would ride out on his horse, climb mountains, recite poetry and not come home until evening, showing the signs of passionate love. He told his secret to one of his friends and it then spread through the camp until it reached the ears of Mirdas, who stormed in a tempestuous fit of uncontrollable rage, snarling and snorting, and cursing the sun and moon. 'This is the reward of those who rear the children of fornication!' he exclaimed, adding: 'If I don't kill him, I shall be put to shame.' He consulted one of the wise men of his tribe, telling him the secret and asking his advice about killing Gharib. The wise man said: 'Earlier he rescued your daughter from captivity and so, if you have to kill him, you must get someone else to do it, lest people begin to have doubts about you.' 'Think of some plan for me,' Mirdas told him, 'for you are the only one who can show me how to do this.' The wise man said: 'Wait till he goes out hunting and then take a hundred riders with you and hide in a cave. When he gets there, take him by surprise and cut him in pieces, as in that way you will not be shamed.' 'That is a good plan,' replied Mirdas.

Mirdas chose a hundred and fifty riders from his tribe, huge and powerful men, whom he induced to help him. He watched until Gharib had left on a hunting trip in distant valleys and mountains and he then rode out with his filthy band and laid an ambush, so as to attack and kill Gharib on his way home from his hunt. As they were lying in wait among the trees, suddenly they themselves were attacked by five hundred gigantic riders, who killed sixty of them and captured the remaining ninety, tying up Mirdas himself. The reason for this was that when al-Hamal was killed and the survivors of his force were routed, in their flight they went to his brother, who was furiously angry when he heard what had happened. He collected his giant champions and after having selected five hundred of them, each fifty cubits tall, he set out to avenge his brother. He and his men then fell in with Mirdas, as was reported, and after having captured him and his force, he and his riders dismounted. He told them to rest, saying: 'Our idols have given us an easy revenge. Guard Mirdas and his men until I can take them off and put them to death in the most horrible of ways.' Mirdas, finding himself tied up, regretted what he had done, and said: 'This is the reward for injustice.' His captors, happy with their victory, fell asleep while he and his men, in their bonds, despaired of life in the certainty that they would be put to death.

So much for them, but as for Sahim, who had earlier been wounded, he went to see his sister, Mahdiya, who got up and kissed his hands, exclaiming: 'May these hands never be withered, and may your enemies never have cause to gloat over you! For had it not been for you and Gharib, we would still be held captive by our enemies. I have to tell you, however, my brother, that your father has gone out with a hundred and fifty riders intending to kill Gharib, and you know how damaging this would be, as he protected your honour and rescued your goods.' When Sahim heard this, the light in his face became dark. He armed himself, mounted his horse and rode out to where his brother was hunting. Gharib had killed a large quantity of game and, having found him, Sahim went up to him and greeted him. 'Why did you go off without telling me?' he asked, and Gharib replied: 'That was only because I saw that you were wounded and I wanted to let you rest.' Sahim then warned him to be on his guard against Mirdas, telling him what had happened and how Mirdas had gone out with a hundred and fifty riders, intending to kill him. 'God will see that his scheme recoils on him!' exclaimed Gharib, and he and his brother then set off back to the camp. Evening fell, but they rode on until they reached the valley where their enemies were resting. They heard horses neighing in the darkness, and Sahim said: 'My father and his men must be lying in ambush here, so come away,' but Gharib dismounted and, passing his bridle to Sahim, he said: 'Wait here until I come back.'

He went on until he could see who was there, only to find that the men were not from his clan. He heard them talking about Mirdas and saying: 'We shall not kill him until we are back in our own land.' Gharib then realized that they must be holding Mirdas, his uncle, as a prisoner and he said to himself: 'I swear by Mahdiya's life that I shall not leave before I have freed her father and saved her from distress.' He went on searching for Mirdas until he found him tied up with ropes and then, sitting down beside him, he said: 'Uncle, may you be saved from this shameful bondage.' Mirdas was bewildered to see him and exclaimed: 'My son, I ask for your protection! Repay the debt you owe for your upbringing and set me free.' 'If I do, will you give me Mahdiya?' Gharib asked. 'My son,' Mirdas replied, 'I swear by the truth of my faith that she will be yours for all time.'

Gharib untied him and said: 'Go towards the horses, for your son Sahim is there.' Mirdas slipped away and came to Sahim, who was delighted to see him and congratulated him on his safety, while in the meantime Gharib was releasing the other prisoners one after the other, until all ninety had been freed. They gathered at some distance from the enemy and Gharib supplied them with equipment and horses, telling them to mount and spread out around the enemy, raising their slogan, 'Sons of Qahtan!', and then, when the enemy were awake, drawing back, while still keeping them encircled. He himself waited until the last third of the night, and then raised the Qahtanid war cry. His men replied with a single shout: 'Sons of Qahtan!', a cry which echoed around the mountains until the enemy thought that the whole Qahtanid tribe had attacked them. They all snatched up their weapons and fell on each other.

Night 627

Morning now dawned and Shahrazad broke off from what she had been allowed to say. Then, when it was the six hundred and twenty-seventh night, SHE CONTINUED:

I have heard, O fortunate king, that when they were roused from sleep and heard Gharib and his men shouting 'Sons of Qahtan!', they thought that the whole Qahtanid tribe had attacked them and so they picked up their weapons and fell on each other. While this was going on, Gharib and his men held back, and the slaughter continued among their enemies until daybreak, when Gharib, Mirdas and the ninety rescued prisoners attacked the survivors, killing a number and routing the rest. The Qahtanids rounded up the stray horses and set off back to their camp with the arms and armour they had taken. Mirdas could hardly believe that he was safe, and when they got to their camp they were given a joyful reception before entering their tents by those who had stayed behind. When Gharib went to his tent, the young men crowded around him and he was saluted by old and young alike, and Mirdas, on seeing the young men flocking around Gharib, hated him even more than before. He turned to his kinsmen and told them this, adding: 'What distresses me is to see these people gathering around him, and tomorrow he will ask me for Mahdiya's hand.' His advisor suggested that he should ask Gharib for something beyond his powers, a suggestion that Mirdas accepted with delight.

The next morning, as he sat on his couch surrounded by his clansmen, Gharib arrived with his own men and a following of youths. He approached Mirdas and when he kissed the ground before him Mirdas showed pleasure and rose to meet him before seating him at his side. 'Uncle,' said Gharib, 'you made me a promise, so fulfil it.' 'My son,' Mirdas replied, 'Mahdiya is yours for all time, but you are short of money.' 'Ask what you want, uncle,' Gharib said, 'and I will raid the emirs of the Arabs in their own parts and the kings in their cities so as to bring you enough wealth to fill up the lands from east to west.' 'My son,' Mirdas told him, 'I swore by all the idols that I would only give Mahdiya to someone who would avenge me and clear away my shame.' 'Tell me on which king you want vengeance, so that I may go to him and smash his throne over his head!' Gharib exclaimed. Mirdas replied: 'I had a valiant son who went out hunting with a hundred heroes. They passed from valley to valley until, when they had gone far into the mountains, they reached the Valley of Flowers and the castle of Ham ibn Shith ibn Shaddad ibn Khald, the home of a black giant seventy cubits tall, who fights using trees that he tears out of the ground. When my son got there, this giant came out and killed him together with a hundred of his men. Only three escaped to bring the news back to me, and when I then collected my champions and went out to fight him we could not get the better of him. I was distressed that I could not avenge my son, and I swore that I would only give my daughter in marriage to someone who could do this for me.'

When Gharib heard this, he said: 'Uncle, I shall go to this giant and, with the help of Almighty God, I shall avenge your son.' 'If you do defeat him,' said Mirdas, 'you will win from him such treasures and wealth as no fire could consume.' Gharib then said: 'In order to hearten me in my quest, confirm for me publicly that you will give me your daughter's hand.' When Mirdas had done this, calling on the tribal elders to witness it, Gharib left full of joy that he had got what he hoped for and went to tell his mother what had happened. 'My son,' she said, 'you have to realize that Mirdas hates you. He is only sending you off to that mountain in order to rob me of the sight of you, so take me with you and leave this tyrant's lands.' 'Mother,' he replied, 'I shall not do that until I have got what I want and have overcome my enemy.'

The next morning, in the light of dawn, he was about to mount his horse when two hundred of his young companions, powerful riders and fully armed, arrived and called out to him: 'Take us with you to help you and to cheer you on your way.' He welcomed them gladly, calling down blessings on them and saying: 'Ride on, my friends.' He and they travelled for two days, and at evening on the second day they dismounted beneath a towering mountain and fed their horses. Gharib himself went off to walk on the mountain, and he came to a cave from which light was shining. He went to its top end and there he discovered a three-hundred-and-forty-year-old *shaikh*, his eyes screened by bushy eyebrows and his mouth covered by a moustache, his whole appearance filling his visitor with reverential awe. 'My son,' the *shaikh* said, 'it seems to me that you are one of the unbelievers who worship stones in place of the Omnipotent God, Who created night and day and the revolving sphere of heaven.' On hearing this, Gharib shuddered and replied: '*Shaikh*, where is this Lord so that I may worship him and look my fill on Him?' The *shaikh* told him: 'No one in this world can look on this great Lord, my son. He sees but is not seen; He is seated on high but is present in every place through the signs left by His works; it is He who brings into being everything that is; He is the controller of Time and the creator of men and *jinn*; He has sent the prophets to guide His creation along the true path. Those who obey Him are brought into Paradise, but the disobedient are consigned to hell.'

Gharib then asked what the formula of worship might be for the followers of this great Lord, Who has power over all things. The *shaikh* said: 'I am one of the people of 'Ad, the unbelievers who acted tyrannically in the lands. God sent them a prophet named Hud, but they disbelieved him and God destroyed them with a blasting wind, but I and some others believed and were saved from punishment. Then I was with the people of Thamud and I saw what happened to them with their prophet, Salih. After Salih, the Almighty sent another prophet, named Abraham, the Friend, to Nimrod, the son of Kan'an, and what happened to him is well known. When my own people who had believed in God died, I came to this cave to worship Him, and He supplies me with food for which I do not have to take thought.' Gharib then asked: 'What do I have to say in order to join the ranks of those who worship this mighty Lord?' and the *shaikh* told him: 'Say: "There is no god but the God of Abraham, the Friend of God."' So Gharib accepted the faith of Islam with both his heart and his tongue, and the *shaikh* told him that the sweetness of the true faith was firmly lodged in his heart, after which he taught him some of the ordinances of Islam as well as some things from the sacred books.

After all this, the *shaikh* asked Gharib for his name, and when Gharib had told him, he asked where he was going. Gharib told him his story from beginning to end until he got as far as mentioning the *ghul* of the mountain, in search of whom he had come.

Night 628

Morning now dawned and Shahrazad broke off from what she had been allowed to say. Then, when it was the six hundred and twenty-eighth night, SHE CONTINUED:

I have heard, O fortunate king, that when Gharib became a Muslim, he told his story to the *shaikh* from beginning to end until he got as far as mentioning the *ghul* of the mountain, in search of whom he had come. 'Are you mad,' the *shaikh* asked him, 'that you come alone on this quest?' Gharib told him that he had two hundred men with him, but the *shaikh* said: 'Even if you had ten thousand, you could not defeat him. He is known as the *ghul* who eats men, God preserve us from him. He is one of the descendants of Ham, and is the son of Hindi, who colonized India, which is named after him. Hindi left this son, whom he called Sa'dan the *ghul*, a headstrong tyrant and a rebellious devil. He eats nothing but human flesh and although his father, before his death, forbade him to do this, he was not to be stopped and became even more oppressive. With great difficulty and after a series of wars his father drove him out of India and he came here and built himself a castle in this valley, where he lives and to which he comes back after robbing travellers on the roads. He has five hulking and violent sons, any one of whom can attack a thousand champions, and he has collected enough wealth, spoils, horses, camels, cattle and sheep to fill the valley. I am afraid that he will harm you, but I shall ask Almighty God to grant you victory over him through the power of the declaration of His unity. When you attack unbelievers, call out: "God is greater," for this will leave them helpless.'

The *shaikh* then gave Gharib a steel mace weighing a hundred *ratls*, on which were ten rings which clashed like thunder when it was brandished, together with a jewelled sword made from a thunderbolt, which was three cubits long and three spans in width and which could cut a rock in two. He also presented him with a coat of mail, a shield and a volume of scripture, telling him to return to his men and to expound Islam to them. Gharib left, happy to have become a Muslim, and when he came to his men they greeted him and asked what had kept him away so long.

He told them everything that had happened to him from start to finish, and when he had explained Islam to them they were all converted. The next morning he rode off to take leave of the *shaikh*, and, having done that, he went back to his men only to be confronted by a rider in full armour which allowed only the corners of his eyes to be seen. 'Strip off your clothes, you Arab scum,' the newcomer called to Gharib, 'or else I shall destroy you.' Gharib charged at him and the terrors of the battle that followed were enough to turn a child's hair grey and to melt the solid rocks that were around them, but when the man took off his face-veil he turned out to be Gharib's own half-brother Sahim.

The reason why he had come there was that he himself had been away when Gharib had set out to find the *ghul*. On Sahim's return, as he could not find Gharib, he had gone to his mother, whom he discovered in tears, and when he asked her why she was weeping she told him that Gharib had left. Sahim allowed himself no rest but armed himself, mounted his horse and rode off until he reached his brother, after which they started to fight. When Sahim uncovered his face, Gharib recognized him and, having greeted him, he asked: 'What led you to do this?' 'I wanted to see how I compared with you on the field and to test the strength of my cuts and thrusts,' Sahim replied, and after Gharib had expounded Islam to him, he became a Muslim.

They then rode on to the Valley of Flowers. The *ghul* caught sight of their dust and told his sons to ride out and fetch him this prey, at which all five mounted and set off towards the Arabs. Gharib, seeing that they were intent on attacking, set spurs to his horse and called out: 'Who are you? What is your race and what do you want?' By way of reply, Falhun, the eldest son of the *ghul*, said: 'Dismount and tie each other up so that we may drive you to our father. He can then roast some of you and cook others, as it is a long time since he last ate human flesh.' On hearing this, Gharib charged at Falhun, brandishing his mace so that its rings clashed with the sound of thunder, filling Falhun with dismay. Gharib struck him a light blow between his shoulder blades and he fell like a lofty palm tree, at which Sahim dismounted with some of his men and tied him up before putting a rope around his neck and dragging him along like a cow. When his brothers saw that he had been taken prisoner, they charged Gharib, but all but one were captured. The fifth fled back to his father, who said: 'What is behind you and where are your brothers?' His son told him: 'They were captured by a boy with no hair on his cheeks and only forty cubits tall.' 'May the sun shed no blessing on you!'

exclaimed his father on hearing this, and then, coming down from the castle, he uprooted a huge tree and made for Gharib on foot, as he was too large to be carried by a horse. His son followed him, and when they came within sight of Gharib, the *ghul* attacked the Arabs without a word, crushing five of them with a blow of his tree. He then made for Sahim and aimed a blow at him with his tree, but Sahim swerved aside and the blow was wasted. In his fury the *ghul* threw away the tree and swooped on Sahim, snatching him up as a hawk snatches a sparrow. Gharib, seeing this, called out: 'God is greater!' and invoked the glory of Abraham, the Friend of God, as well as calling on Muhammad, may God bless him and give him peace.

Night 629

Morning now dawned and Shahrazad broke off from what she had been allowed to say. Then, when it was the six hundred and twenty-ninth night, SHE CONTINUED:

I have heard, O fortunate king, that when Gharib saw his brother was a prisoner in the hands of the *ghul*, he called out: 'God is greater!' and invoked the glory of Abraham, the Friend of God, as well as calling on Muhammad, may God bless him and give him peace. Turning his horse's head towards the *ghul*, he shook his mace, crying out, as its rings clashed: 'God is greater!' He then struck the *ghul* on the ribs, laying him out unconscious on the ground and enabling Sahim to escape from his clutches. When the *ghul* recovered his senses he found himself tied up and fettered, while his son, seeing his father captured, turned in flight. Gharib, however, rode after him and unhorsed him with a blow of his mace that landed between his shoulder blades, so that he too was securely tied up with his brothers and his father, who were then dragged off like camels.

The Arabs went to the castle, which they found filled with goods, money and treasures, and they also discovered twelve hundred Persians bound and fettered. Gharib took his seat on the *ghul*'s throne, which had once belonged to Sas, son of Shith, son of Shaddad, the son of 'Ad, with his brother Sahim on his right and his men flanking him on the right and the left. He then ordered the *ghul* to be brought before him. 'How do you find yourself now, you damned creature?' he asked, and the *ghul* replied: 'In the most miserable state of humiliation and confusion,

master, seeing that I and my sons are roped like camels.' Gharib told
him: 'I want you to adopt my religion, that is, the religion of Islam, and
acknowledge the unity of God, the Omniscient, the Creator of light
and darkness, Who made all things, the only God, the King and Judge,
and to acknowledge that Abraham, the Friend of God, on whom be
peace, was His prophet.' The *ghul* and his sons were converted, and as
they were sincere in their conversion, Gharib had them released. Sa'dan
the *ghul* then came forward to kiss Gharib's feet, as did his sons, but
Gharib stopped them and they stood with the others.

Gharib now asked Sa'dan about the Persians. 'Master,' replied Sa'dan,
'they are captives whom I took from Persia, and they are not alone.'
'Who is with them, then?' Gharib asked, and Sa'dan told him: 'The
daughter of Sabur, king of Persia, whose name is Fakhr Taj, and who
has with her a hundred slave girls, radiant as moons.' Gharib was astonished to hear this and asked Sa'dan how he had come across them. 'My
sons and I went out with five of my slaves,' Sa'dan told him, 'and as we
found no booty on our way, we spread out through the open country
and the deserts, but it seemed that only in Persia would we find what we
wanted. We were still going around looking for spoil, so as not to go
back empty-handed, when we caught sight of a dust cloud and sent out
one of our slaves to investigate. He was away for some time and on his
return he told us that this was Princess Fakhr Taj, daughter of Sabur,
king of the Persians, Turks and Dailamis, travelling with an escort of
two thousand riders. "That is good news you have brought," I told the
slave, "for there can be no greater spoils." I and my sons then attacked
the Persians, killing three hundred of them and capturing twelve hundred, as well as taking the princess together with the treasures and wealth
that she had with her. We then brought them to this castle.' On hearing
this, Gharib asked: 'Did you violate her?' 'No, by your life and by the
truth of my new religion,' Sa'dan assured him. 'That was well done,'
said Gharib, 'for her father rules the world and will certainly send armies
after her and ravage the lands of her captors. Whoever does not look to
the consequences of his actions, as the proverb says, will not find that
Time is his friend. So where is the princess?' 'I gave her and her maids a
pavilion of their own,' Sa'dan told him, and when Gharib asked to be
shown this, he said: 'To hear is to obey.'

Gharib then rose and walked to the pavilion with the *ghul*, where they
found the princess, who, after having been cosseted in luxury, was sad,
humiliated and in tears. At the sight of her, Gharib thought that the

moon was close at hand and he glorified God, the Omniscient Hearer, while, for her part, on looking at Gharib, she recognized him as a valiant hero with the marks of courage showing in his face, testifying for him rather than against him. She got up and kissed his hands, before falling down at his feet and saying: 'Champion of the age, I am under your protection. Save me from this *ghul*, as I'm afraid that he may deflower me and then eat me. Take me as a servant for your servants.' 'I promise to guard you safely until you are returned to your father and regain your imperial splendour,' replied Gharib. The princess called down on him the blessings of long life and advancement, after which he gave orders that her men were to be set free. He then looked at her and asked what had made her leave her palace to travel through the deserts and so fall prey to highway robbers. 'Master,' she replied, 'my father and his Persian subjects, together with the Turks, Dailamis and Magians, worship fire in place of the Omnipotent God. In our country there is what is known as the Monastery of Fire, where the daughters of the Magian fire worshippers come every year at the time of the feast and stay for a month before returning to their own lands. I and my maids went out as usual, and my father sent an escort of two thousand men to guard me, but we were attacked by this *ghul*, who killed some of us and captured the rest, before imprisoning us in this castle. This is what happened to us, champion of the age, may God guard you against the misfortunes of Time.' 'Don't be afraid,' Gharib repeated, 'for I will return you to your imperial palace,' at which she kissed his hands and feet.

After leaving her, he gave orders that she should be treated with honour, and then the next morning he got up, performed the ritual ablution and prayed with two *rak'as*, following the custom of our father Abraham, the Friend of God, upon whom be peace, as did Sa'dan the *ghul*, and his sons, while all the Arabs joined in prayer behind him. He then asked Sa'dan to show him the Valley of Flowers. Sa'dan agreed and he and his sons, together with Gharib and his Arabs and the princess and her maids, all went out. There were a hundred and fifty girls, together with a thousand slaves who acted as herds for Sa'dan's camels, cattle and sheep, and Sa'dan told them to slaughter some of these, cook their morning meal, and serve it among the trees. Gharib went with the others, and when he saw the valley, he discovered that it was wonderfully beautiful, with trees standing in groups or in isolation. The nightingale was trilling its song and the turtledove was filling with its song the whole valley that God had made.

Night 630

Morning now dawned and Shahrazad broke off from what she had been allowed to say. Then, when it was the six hundred and thirtieth night, SHE CONTINUED:

I have heard, O fortunate king, that when Gharib and his men, together with the *ghul* and his followers, went to the Valley of Flowers, he found birds, among whom the turtledove was filling with its song the whole valley that God had made. The beautiful chant of the bulbul sounded almost human; no one could describe the lovely song of the blackbird; the pigeon's voice could drive men mad with love; while parrots eloquently answered ringdoves. There were fruit trees with two types of every fruit, pomegranates sweet and sour on the branches, almond-apricots, camphor-apricots and Khurasanian almonds, plums intertwined in the branches of *ban* trees, oranges gleaming like fiery torches, citrons weighing down the branches, lemons, the remedy for loss of appetite, sorrel, which cures jaundice, and dates, red and yellow, on their parent trees, the creation of the Lord on high. It was about a place like this that the lovesick poet said:

> When the birds sing at daybreak by their pool,
> The distracted lover is consumed with longing.
> In its fragrance it is like a paradise,
> With shade and fruit and flowing streams.

Gharib was delighted by this, and on his orders a pavilion was set up for Fakhr Taj among the trees and spread with magnificent furnishings. When he had taken his seat, food was brought and the company ate until they had had enough. He then asked Sa'dan whether he had any wine, to which he answered that he had a cistern full of an old vintage. 'Bring me some of it,' Gharib told him, at which Sa'dan sent ten slaves who fetched a large quantity of it, and everyone there ate, drank and enjoyed themselves. Moved by joy, Gharib remembered Mahdiya and recited these lines:

> I thought of the days when we were closely joined,
> And a fire of love stirred in my heart.
> By God, it was not willingly that I left you,
> But the changes fortune brings are strange.

Peace, greetings and a thousand salutations
From a lover sad and heartbroken.

For three days they continued to eat, drink and enjoy themselves before going back to the castle. Gharib then sent for his brother Sahim and, when he had come, he said: 'Take a hundred riders with you and go back to fetch your father and mother and your tribe, the Qahtanids, so that they may live here for all time. I myself shall go to Persia in order to return Princess Fakhr Taj to her father, and meanwhile you, Sa'dan, are to stay in this castle with your sons until we come back to you.' 'Why don't you take me to Persia with you?' Sa'dan asked, and Gharib replied: 'Because it was you who captured the princess, and if her father, King Sabur, sets eyes on you he will eat your flesh and drink your blood.' On hearing that, Sa'dan gave a bellow of laughter like a clap of thunder and said: 'By your life, master, if the Persians and the Dailamis all combined against me, I would give them death to drink.' 'You are certainly able to do that,' Gharib replied, 'but I want you to stay in your castle until I return.' 'To hear is to obey,' Sa'dan replied. Sahim and his Qahtanids then left for home while Gharib set out for Persia, taking with him Princess Fakhr Taj and her people and making for Sabur's capital.

So much for them, but as for King Sabur, he had been expecting his daughter to return from the Monastery of Fire, and when she was overdue he was consumed with anxiety. He had forty viziers, of whom the oldest, most knowledgeable and learned was called Didan, and it was to him that Sabur said: 'Vizier, my daughter is slow in coming back. I have heard no news of her and it is past the time that she was due to return, so send a courier to the Monastery of Fire to find out what has happened.' 'To hear is to obey,' replied Didan, and after he had left the king's presence, he sent for the principal courier and told him to start out at once for the monastery. The man set off, and when he got there he asked the monks about the princess, only to be told that they had not seen her that year. He then went back to the city of Isbanir, where he came to Didan and told him this, after which Didan went to Sabur to pass on the news. Sabur was beside himself with agitation. He dashed his crown on to the ground, plucked at his beard and fell down senseless.

When water was sprinkled on him he recovered, and then, tearfully and sorrowfully, he recited:

When you had gone, I called on patience and on tears;
Although tears answered me, patience did not.

If the passing days have parted us,
This is their custom, marked, as they are, by treachery.

He then summoned ten commanders and ordered them to ride out with
ten thousand horsemen, each to a different region in search of the
princess, which they proceeded to do, while her mother and her slave
girls wore black, scattered ashes and sat weeping and mourning.

So much for them . . .

Night 631

Morning now dawned and Shahrazad broke off from what she had been
allowed to say. Then, when it was the six hundred and thirty-first night,
SHE CONTINUED:

I have heard, O fortunate king, that King Sabur sent out his troops to
search for his daughter, while her mother and her slave girls wore black.
But as for Gharib and the remarkable things that happened to him on
his journey, after he had travelled for ten days, on the eleventh he saw a
dust cloud rising into the sky. He called for the leader of Fakhr Taj's
Persians and told him to investigate what this was. Obediently the Persian
rode off and questioned the riders whom he found beneath the cloud,
one of whom told him that they were five thousand of the Banu Hattal,
led by Samsam ibn al-Jarrah, coming in search of booty. The Persian
hurried back to Gharib and passed on the news, at which Gharib called
to his Qahtanids and to the Persians to arm themselves, which they did.
As they rode on, they were met by the Arabs, who were calling out:
'Plunder, plunder!' to which Gharib shouted in reply: 'May God disgrace
you, Arab dogs!' He then charged them, turning them back like the brave
hero he was, calling out: 'God is greater! Oh for the religion of Abraham,
the Friend of God, upon whom be peace!' There was a fierce battle with
sword blows and confused cries, which lasted until darkness fell in the
evening, when the two sides withdrew from each other. On inspecting
his men, Gharib found that five Qahtanids and seventy-three Persians
had been killed, while Samsam had lost more than five hundred dead.

When Samsam dismounted, he wanted neither to eat nor to sleep,
telling his men: 'Never in my life have I seen anyone fight like this
boy, who would sometimes use his sword and at other times his mace.
Tomorrow, however, I shall go out to meet him in the field of battle and

challenge him to a duel, after which I shall cut those Arabs in pieces.'
Gharib, for his part, went back to his men and was met by Fakhr Taj,
who was weeping and frightened by the terror of what she had seen. She
kissed his foot in the stirrup and said: 'May your hand not wither and
may your enemy never have cause to gloat over you, champion of the
age! Praise be to God, Who has preserved you today, for I was frightened
for you as you fought those Arabs.' When he heard this, Gharib laughed
at her and said, encouragingly and soothingly: 'Don't be afraid, princess,
for even if there were enemies enough to fill this whole plain, I could
destroy them through the strength of the Exalted and Supreme God.'
After thanking him and praying for his victory, she went off to her
maids, while he dismounted, washed his hands and cleaned away the
blood of the infidels.

The two sides remained on guard until morning, when they mounted
and rode to the field of battle. Gharib was the first to arrive, and he came
up to the unbelievers and cried out: 'Which of you is not too lazy or weak
to come here to fight?' A huge and powerful giant of the descendants of
'Ad rode out to challenge him, calling out: 'Scum of the Arabs, take what
is coming to you, for I have good news for you of your death!' He carried
an iron club weighing twenty *ratls*, but Gharib avoided the blow that he
aimed at him and the club buried itself a cubit's depth into the ground.
As the giant bent over because of the force of his blow, Gharib struck
him with his iron mace, smashing his forehead so that he fell, as God
hurried his soul on its way to hellfire. Gharib rode to and fro, challenging
his foes; a second rider came out and was killed and the same thing
happened to the third, and this went on until ten had died. The unbelievers, seeing the strength of his blows, avoided him and held back,
until their chief called out: 'May God grant you no blessing! I shall go
out to meet him myself.' He armed himself and rode out until he had
come up to Gharib. 'Arab dog,' he cried, 'have you become strong
enough to challenge me on the field and to kill my men?' 'Come out and
fight,' Gharib told him, 'and avenge your riders.'

Samsam did not spare himself but met Gharib courageously, and
the two exchanged such blows with their maces that both sides were
bewildered, and every eye was fixed on them as they circled round the
field. Of the two blows that were struck, Gharib succeeded in avoiding
that of Samsam's, while his own, as it fell, smashed into Samsam's chest,
felling him to the ground as a lifeless corpse. His men then made a
concerted charge against Gharib, but Gharib met it, calling out: 'God is

greater! Victory and triumph are ours while those who reject the religion of Abraham, the Friend of God, will find no help.'

Night 632

Morning now dawned and Shahrazad broke off from what she had been allowed to say. Then, when it was the six hundred and thirty-second night, SHE CONTINUED:

I have heard, O fortunate king, that when Samsam's men launched a concerted charge against Gharib, he attacked them, calling out: 'God is greater! Victory and triumph are ours and the unbelievers will be disappointed.' When the unbelievers heard him mention the One Omnipotent and Almighty God, Who sees but cannot be seen,* they stared at each other and asked: 'What are these words that make us tremble, weaken our resolve and cut short our lives? They are sweeter than anything we have ever heard.' They agreed to stop fighting until they had had a chance to ask about the meaning of this, and so they drew back and dismounted. Their elders held a meeting and, after consulting each other, they decided that ten of them should go to Gharib, and so ten of their best men, whom they selected, set off for his camp. As for Gharib and his men, they had gone back to their tents, surprised by the withdrawal of their enemies, and it was then that the ten came up and asked for a meeting. When they had kissed the ground and prayed that Gharib be granted glory and a long life, he asked them why they had stopped fighting. 'Master,' they told him, 'you terrified us by the words that you shouted at us.' He then asked: 'What bringers of calamity do you worship?' and they told him that their gods were Wadd, Suwa' and Yaghuth, the gods of the people of Noah. Gharib replied: 'We worship only Almighty God, the Creator of all things, Who sustains all life. It is He Who created the heavens and the earth, establishing the mountains and causing water to flow out of rock. He causes the trees to grow and He supplies food for the animals in the wastes. He is the One All-Powerful God.' When they heard that, they were delighted by the declaration of His unity and exclaimed: 'This is a mighty Lord, Compassionate and Merciful.' Then they asked: 'What do we have to say to become Muslims?' and Gharib told them: 'Say: "There is no god but the God of

* Quran 6.103.

Abraham, the Friend of God,"' after which the ten sincerely accepted
the faith of Islam. 'If the sweetness of the faith of Islam is truly lodged
in your hearts,' Gharib said, 'then go to your people and present it to
them. If they accept it, then they will be safe, but if not, we will burn
them with fire.'

The ten then went back to the others and set out the Islamic faith for
them, explaining the way of true belief. Their companions accepted this
with hearts and tongues, and then hurried on foot to Gharib's camp,
where they kissed the ground before him and prayed for his glory and
advancement. 'Master,' they said to him, 'we have become your slaves,
so give us whatever orders you wish, as we shall listen, obey and never
leave you, since it has been through you that God has guided us.' He
prayed that they might be well rewarded and told them to go back home
and then to leave with their goods and their children, going on ahead of
him to the Valley of Flowers and the castle of the *ghul*. He told them
that he himself planned to escort Princess Fakhr Taj, the daughter of
Sabur, king of the Persians, and then come back. 'To hear is to obey,'
they said, and they then left immediately and returned to their tribe,
filled with joy at their conversion, after which they explained Islam to
their wives and children, all of whom were converted. They then struck
camp and set off with their goods and their flocks to the Valley of
Flowers. Sa'dan the *ghul* came out to meet them with his sons, but
Gharib had instructed them that when this happened and Sa'dan was
about to attack them, they were to call on the Name of God, the Creator
of all things, as on hearing this, he would welcome them instead of
fighting them. So when he and his sons had emerged and were about to
charge, they called aloud the Name of Almighty God, after which Sa'dan
greeted them with the greatest courtesy and asked them about themselves. When they told him about their meeting with Gharib he was
delighted and allowed them to settle there, deluging them with favours.

So much for them, but as for Gharib, he travelled for five days with
Princess Fakhr Taj on the road to Isbanir and then on the sixth day he
caught sight of a dust cloud and sent out one of the Persians to investigate. The man rode off and then came back quicker than a bird in flight,
to say: 'Master, this is the dust of a thousand of our riders sent out by
the king to look for the princess.' On hearing that, Gharib ordered his
men to dismount and pitch camp, which they did. When the Persians
came up to them, they were met by the princess's escort, who told
Tuman, the commander of the newcomers, what had happened to her.

When he heard about Gharib, he went to him, kissed the ground before him and asked him how the princess was. Gharib sent him to her tent and, on entering into her presence, he kissed her hands and feet and told her about the distress of her father and mother, and she, in her turn, told him what had happened to her and how Gharib had rescued her from the *ghul* . . .

Night 633

Morning now dawned and Shahrazad broke off from what she had been allowed to say. Then, when it was the six hundred and thirty-third night, SHE CONTINUED:

I have heard, O fortunate king, that the princess told Tuman every-thing that had happened in her encounter with the *ghul* of the mountain, how he had captured her, how she had been rescued by Gharib, and how the *ghul* would otherwise have eaten her, adding: 'My father must give Gharib half of his kingdom.' Tuman then went to kiss Gharib's hands and feet, thanking him for the service that he had done and asking his permission to return to Isbanir to give the good news to the king. When this had been granted, he started off and Gharib followed him.

Tuman pressed on with his journey until he was within sight of Isbanir, and he then went up to the palace and kissed the ground before King Sabur. 'What is the news, bringer of good tidings?' asked the king. 'I shall not tell you until you reward me for it,' Tuman replied. 'Tell me, and I shall satisfy you,' said the king, and Tuman told him: 'It is welcome news of the Princess Fakhr Taj that I bring, king of the age.' When Sabur heard Fakhr Taj's name he fell down in a faint and had to be sprinkled with rosewater until he revived. He then called to Tuman, telling him to come nearer and to describe what had happened. Tuman came up and recounted the story, at which the king struck his hands together, exclaim-ing: 'Oh, poor Fakhr Taj!' He then ordered that Tuman be given ten thousand dinars and appointed as governor of Isfahan and its lands. He sent all his emirs to ride out to meet the princess, while the chief eunuch went in to delight the princess's mother and all the ladies of the harem by giving them the news, and he was rewarded by the queen with a robe of honour and the gift of a thousand dinars. When the townspeople heard about this, they adorned the markets and the houses with decor-ations, while the king himself, accompanied by Tuman, rode off until they came in sight of Gharib. At this point Sabur dismounted and walked forward some steps to greet him, while Gharib followed his example. They then embraced and greeted each other, and Sabur bent over to kiss Gharib's hands and to thank him for the good deed that he had done him.

Both parties pitched their tents and Sabur went in to see his daughter, who rose and embraced him, telling him all that had happened to her and how Gharib had rescued her from the clutches of the *ghul*. 'By your life, queen of beauties,' her father said, 'I shall overwhelm him with gifts.' 'Take him as a son-in-law, father,' she told him, 'to help you against your enemies, for he is a man of courage.' She only said this because she had lost her heart to Gharib, but her father objected: 'You know, don't you, that Khirad Shah, the king of Shiraz and its lands, a strong ruler with powerful armies, has asked for your hand with a hundred thousand dinars as a bride price?' 'Father,' she replied, 'I don't want that marriage, and if you force me against my will, I shall kill myself.'

Sabur left her tent and went to Gharib, and as Sabur sat there looking at him, he found that he wanted to look still more, saying to himself: 'By God, my daughter may be excused for loving this Bedouin.' Food was brought and, when they had eaten, they passed the night there before setting off in the morning for the city, which they entered riding side by side. This was a day of great celebrations. Fakhr Taj went to her royal palace, where she was met by her mother and her maids, who raised cries of joy, while Sabur took his seat on his throne, with Gharib on his right and the other kings, chamberlains, emirs, deputies and viziers standing on his right and his left. They congratulated him on his daughter's safe return and he told them: 'Let all who love me give robes of honour to Gharib,' after which robes were showered on Gharib like rain.

He stayed enjoying Sabur's hospitality for ten days, after which he wanted to leave, but Sabur presented him with another robe and swore by his faith that he should not go until a month was up. 'Your majesty,' Gharib told him, 'I have asked for the hand of an Arab girl and I want to consummate the marriage.' 'Which of the two is more beautiful, your Arab girl or Fakhr Taj?' Sabur asked him, to which Gharib replied: 'King of the age, how can the slave be compared to the master?' Sabur then went on: 'Fakhr Taj became your slave when you rescued her from the clutches of the *ghul* and there is no other husband for her but you.' Gharib got up, kissed the ground and said: 'King of the age, you are a king while I am a poor man and it may be that you will ask for a heavy bride price.' 'Know, my son,' the king told him, 'that King Khirad Shah, the lord of Shiraz and its lands, has asked for Fakhr Taj's hand in return for a hundred thousand dinars, but I have chosen you before all others and I have appointed you as the sword of my state and my shield against vengeance.' Then, turning to his nobles, he said: 'Bear witness, my subjects, that I have given my daughter in marriage to my "son" Gharib.'

Night 634

Morning now dawned and Shahrazad broke off from what she had been allowed to say. Then, when it was the six hundred and thirty-fourth night, SHE CONTINUED:

I have heard, O fortunate king, that Sabur, king of the Persians, told his nobles to bear witness to the fact that he had given his daughter, Fakhr al-Taj, in marriage to his 'son' Gharib. He then shook Gharib by the hand and the princess became his wife.

Gharib now said: 'Set a bride price for me to bring you, for in the castle of Sasa I have more wealth and treasures than can be counted.' 'My son,' Sabur replied, 'I want neither money nor treasures from you, and the only bride price that I shall accept is the head of al-Jamraqan, the king of al-Dasht and ruler of al-Ahwaz.' Gharib replied: 'I shall go to fetch my men and then I shall march against this enemy and ravage his lands.' 'May you receive a good reward,' said Sabur, after which the people dispersed, high and low alike, while Sabur thought that if Gharib set out against al-Jamraqan he would never come back again.

In the morning both he and Gharib rode out and the troops were ordered to mount and ride to the exercise ground, where they were ordered to entertain the king by jousting. When the Persian champions had ridden against one another, Gharib told the king that he wanted to join in with them on one condition. When Sabur asked what this was, he said: 'That I wear a thin shirt and use a lance with no point on whose tip I shall place a rag soaked with saffron. All your champions can attack me using lances with points and if they get the better of me, then my life is theirs as a gift, but if I win, then they must carry my mark from the field.' Sabur ordered the army commander to bring forward the Persian champions from whom he picked out twelve hundred kings and men of valour, telling them in Persian that whichever of them killed the Bedouin would be welcome to have whatever he wanted. They vied with each other to be first in riding against Gharib, but when they attacked him, truth was clearly separated from falsehood and the serious from the frivolous, as Gharib called out: 'My trust is in the Lord, the God of Abraham His Friend, the Omnipotent from Whom nothing is hidden, the One, the All-Powerful, Whom no eye can see.'

A giant Persian champion rode out against him, but Gharib allowed him no time to resist before he had marked his whole chest with saffron. Then, when he turned back, Gharib struck him on the nape of his neck with his lance and laid him out on the ground. His servants carried him off, after which he was followed by a second, a third, a fourth and a fifth. One after the other the champions came out until Gharib had put his mark on all of them, and when Almighty God had given him victory over them, they left the field. Food was then brought, followed by wine, and they ate and drank. Gharib drank until he was befuddled and then, after he had gone out to relieve himself, he could not find his way back and went into the palace of Fakhr Taj. She was overjoyed to see him and called to her maids to go to their own rooms. When they had gone off on their separate ways, she kissed Gharib's hand and said: 'Welcome to my lord, who freed me from the *ghul*. I am for ever your servant.' She then pulled him to her bed and embraced him, inflaming his passion so that he deflowered her and then stayed with her until morning.

So much for them, but as for Sabur, he had thought that Gharib must have left, and when he came into his presence in the morning, he rose to greet him and seated him at his side. The other kings then entered and, after kissing the ground, they ranged themselves on the right and the left and started to talk of Gharib's bravery, praising God, Who had granted him such courage in spite of his youth. While they were talking, they caught sight of the dust of approaching horses through the palace windows and the king ordered his couriers to let him know what this was. One of them rode out to investigate and on his return he said: 'Your majesty, under the dust I found a hundred riders with an emir called Sahim al-Lail.' When Gharib heard this, he said: 'Master, this is my brother, whom I had sent off on an errand, and I shall go to meet him.' He then rode off with his hundred Qahtanids, together with a thousand Persians in a great procession, though true greatness belongs only to God, until he reached Sahim. The two dismounted to embrace each other before remounting, and Gharib then asked his brother whether he had brought his clan to the castle of Sasa and the Valley of Flowers. Sahim told him: 'When that treacherous dog, Mirdas, heard that you had taken the castle of the *ghul* he became more and more angry and said: "Unless I leave these parts, Gharib will come and take my daughter Mahdiya without any bride price." He then removed his daughter, his clan, his family and his possessions, made for Iraq and entered Kufa, where he asked protection from King 'Ajib, who is asking for Mahdiya's hand.'

When Gharib heard what Sahim had to say, he almost expired of grief and exclaimed: 'By the truth of the religion of Abraham, the Friend of God, and by the truth of the Almighty God Himself, I shall go to the land of Iraq and make war there.' He went back to the city, where he and his brother entered the palace and kissed the ground. Sabur rose for Gharib and greeted Sahim, after which Gharib told him what had happened. Sabur gave orders that he was to be reinforced by ten commanders, each with ten thousand men chosen from the bravest of the Arabs and the Persians. They took three days to make their preparations, after which Gharib set out for the castle of Sasa. Sa'dan the *ghul* came out with his sons to meet him and kissed his feet in his stirrups. Then, when he had been told what had happened, Sa'dan said: 'Master, sit here in your castle and I shall go to Iraq with my sons and my men and lay waste to the city, bringing back all its defenders tightly bound before you.' Gharib thanked him but told him that they would all go together. On Gharib's orders Sa'dan made his preparations and they all set off for Iraq, leaving a garrison of a thousand riders to guard the castle.

So much for Gharib, but as for Mirdas, when he took his people to Iraq, he had with him a splendid gift, which he brought to Kufa and presented to 'Ajib. He kissed the ground and called down blessings suitable for kings on 'Ajib before asking for his protection.

Night 635

Morning now dawned and Shahrazad broke off from what she had been allowed to say. Then, when it was the six hundred and thirty-fifth night, SHE CONTINUED:

I have heard, O fortunate king, that when Mirdas appeared before King 'Ajib, he asked him for his protection.

'Tell me who has wronged you so that I may protect you against him, even if he is Sabur, king of the Persians, the Turks and the Dailamis,' said 'Ajib. Mirdas complained: 'King of the age, it is a youth whom I brought up in my own household who has wronged me. I found him in a valley, held in his mother's lap, and I then married his mother, from whom I had a child. I named my son Sahim al-Lail, while his half-brother was called Gharib. He grew up in my household and turned out to be a fiery thunderbolt and a terrible calamity. He killed al-Hamal, chief of the Banu Nabhan, and he is a man-slayer who has overthrown champions. I have a daughter who would suit no husband other than you, but he asked me for her hand, in return for which I told him to fetch me the head of the *ghul* of the mountain. Gharib went to challenge him and captured him, after which he took him into his own service. I hear that he has become a Muslim and is calling on people to convert to his religion. He freed Sabur's daughter from the *ghul* and has taken possession of the castle of Sasa, son of Shith, which contains the treasure hoards of the ancients and the moderns alike. He left to escort Sabur's daughter, and is sure to bring with him the wealth of Persia when he comes back.'

When 'Ajib heard what Mirdas had to say, his appearance altered and he turned pale, as he was sure that he was facing death. He asked Mirdas: 'Is Gharib's mother with him or with you?' to which he replied that she was with him in his tents. 'What is her name?' 'Ajib asked, and when 'Ajib told him that it was Nusra, he exclaimed: 'That is the woman! Send for her.' When he looked at her, he recognized her and said: 'You damned woman, where are the two slaves whom I sent off with you?' She told him that they had killed each other because of her, and he then drew his sword and cut her in two. Her body was dragged off and thrown out, but 'Ajib was filled with uneasiness and said to Mirdas: 'Marry me to your daughter.' 'She is one of your servants and I have given her to you in marriage as I am your slave,' Mirdas replied. 'Ajib then said: 'I would like to set eyes on that son of a whore, Gharib, and kill him after having inflicted tortures of all kinds on him.' He then ordered Mirdas to be given thirty thousand dinars as a bride price, together with a hundred pieces of silk brocade embroidered with gold, a hundred others with ornamented borders, as well as kerchiefs and golden necklaces. Mirdas went off with this huge bride price and exerted himself to make preparations for Mahdiya's wedding.

So much for them, but as for Gharib, he travelled to the strong and well-fortified city of al-Jazira, which marks the start of Iraqi territory. He ordered his men to prepare to attack it, and when its inhabitants saw what was happening, they closed their gates, strengthened their walls and alerted their king. He looked out from his palace battlements and saw a large Persian army. 'What do these Persians want?' he asked his people, but they could only say: 'We don't know.' This king was called al-Damigh because he used to brain his opponents in battle, and among his servants was a wily fellow like a spark of fire, called Sabuʻ al-Qifar. It was this man whom the king summoned and told to go to investigate the Persians and find out what they wanted, before coming back as fast as he could. He went off like the wind, and when he approached Gharib's tents a number of Arabs got up and asked him who he was and what he wanted. He told them: 'I am a messenger from the king of the city to your leader.' They took him and led him between tents, pavilions and banners, until they brought him to the pavilion of Gharib, and after entering they told Gharib that a messenger had arrived. 'Bring him to me,' Gharib said, and when the messenger came in he kissed the ground and called down on him the blessings of a long life and continued glory. Gharib asked him what his errand was and he said: 'I am a messenger from the king of the city of al-Jazira, al-Damigh, the brother of Kundamir, lord of Kufa and of the land of Iraq.' When he heard this, tears streamed from Gharib's eyes and, looking at the messenger, he asked him his name. 'Sabuʻ al-Qifar,' the man replied, and Gharib then told him: 'Go to your master and tell him that the leader of this force is Gharib, the son of Kundamir, lord of Kufa, who was killed by his son, ʻAjib, and that I am here to take vengeance on him, treacherous dog that he is.'

Sabuʻ al-Qifar went off and returned joyfully to al-Damigh. He kissed the ground and when al-Damigh asked him what he had discovered, he told him that the leader of the force was his nephew and then explained the whole story to him. Al-Damigh thought that he must be dreaming, and he asked Sabuʻ al-Qifar whether he was telling the truth. 'Yes, your majesty,' the other replied, 'I swear it by your life.' Al-Damigh then ordered the leaders of his people to mount, and he rode out with them to Gharib's camp. Gharib, on hearing that the king had come, went out to meet him and the two of them greeted each other and embraced, before Gharib took his uncle into the camp and sat with him in the place of honour. Al-Damigh was delighted to have met his nephew, and turning to him he said: 'I am sad at heart that I did not avenge your father, but I had not the power to face that dog, your brother, for he has a large army while mine is small.' 'It is this that I have come to do, uncle,' Gharib told him, 'and I shall remove this shame and rid the lands of him.' 'There is a double vengeance for you to take,' al-Damigh told him, 'one for your father and another for your mother.' 'What has happened to my mother?' Gharib asked, and al-Damigh told him: 'Your brother 'Ajib killed her.'

Night 636

Morning now dawned and Shahrazad broke off from what she had been allowed to say. Then, when it was the six hundred and thirty-sixth night, SHE CONTINUED:

I have heard, O fortunate king, that when Gharib heard his uncle tell him that his brother 'Ajib had killed his mother, Gharib asked why and al-Damigh told him what happened and how Mirdas had given 'Ajib his daughter in marriage, which he was about to consummate.

When Gharib heard this, he went out of his mind and he lay fainting until he was almost dead, but when he had recovered, he shouted an order to his army to mount and ride. Al-Damigh asked him to wait until he could get ready to bring his men to go with him, but he said: 'I cannot bear to wait, uncle, so make your preparations and meet me in Kufa.' He then rode off to Babel, whose inhabitants were filled with alarm. They had a king named Jamak, who had a force of twenty thousand riders, and this was joined by another fifty thousand from the nearby towns, who camped in front of the city. Gharib wrote a letter to Jamak, and when his messenger reached the city he called out: 'I am an envoy.' The gatekeeper went to the king, who, when he had been told that a messenger had come, gave orders that he should be brought to him. The gatekeeper went out and fetched the man, who kissed the ground and handed Jamak the letter. Jamak opened it and read the following message: 'Praise be to the Lord of creation, the Master of all things, Who sustains all life, the Omnipotent. This letter is sent from Gharib, the son of Kundamir, king of Iraq and the lands of Kufa, to Jamak. As soon as you receive it, you are to break your idols and acknowledge the unity of the Omniscient God, Who created light and darkness and all other things and Who has power over everything. If you fail to do what I say, I shall see to it that this will be the most disastrous of days for you. Peace be on those who follow right guidance and fear the destruction that is to come, obeying the Most High God, Lord of the latter and the former things, Who says to something "be" and it is.'

When Jamak read this, he showed the whites of his eyes; his face turned pale and he shouted at the messenger: 'Go to your master and tell him to come out to fight tomorrow morning, when it will be seen who is the true chief.' The messenger returned to give the news to Gharib, who ordered his men to arm themselves for battle. Meanwhile Jamak had his tents pitched in front of those of Gharib, and his men poured out like a flood tide, spending the night with the intention of fighting next day. Then, in the morning, both sides rode out and formed up in ranks, with drums beating and spears raised, as horses pawed the ground, and the wide plain was filled with men as the champions advanced.

The first to come out to challenge was Sa'dan, the *ghul* of the mountain, carrying a huge tree on his shoulder. He advanced between the armies and shouted: 'I am Sa'dan the *ghul*! Does anyone dare to come out to fight? Let him be no idle weakling.' Then he called to his sons: 'Bring me wood and make a fire, for I am hungry,' and they, in turn, summoned the slaves, who collected firewood and lit a fire in the middle of the battlefield. There then came out to meet him a haughty giant from among the unbelievers, who was carrying on his shoulder a mace as big as a ship's mast. He advanced on the *ghul*, calling out: 'Woe to you, Sa'dan,' and when Sa'dan heard this, his mood darkened and he whirled his tree around until it whistled through the air. His opponent met the blow with his mace, but the weight of the tree drove the mace back, crushing his skull so that he fell to the ground like a lofty palm tree. Sa'dan called to his slaves: 'Drag off this fatted calf and roast him quickly.' They hurried to skin and roast the man, before presenting him to Sa'dan, who ate him, crunching his bones. When the infidels saw this, shudders ran right through their bodies. They lost heart, changed colour and told one another that whoever went out to face the *ghul* would never feel the wind's breath again, as he would be eaten and his bones gnawed through. In their fear of him and his sons, they stopped fighting and fled back to the city.

Gharib now shouted to his men to attack the fugitives, and his Arabs and Persians attacked Jamak and his people, putting them to the sword until twenty thousand or more of them had been killed. Many fell among the crowd jamming the city gate, which could not be closed, and during the assault Sa'dan seized a mace from a dead man and, brandishing it in the face of his foes, he made his way to the city square. He then attacked Jamak's palace, confronted him and struck him down unconscious with a mace blow, before annihilating the palace guards. At that, the rest of Jamak's men shouted for quarter.

Night 637

Morning now dawned and Shahrazad broke off from what she had been allowed to say. Then, when it was the six hundred and thirty-seventh night, SHE CONTINUED:

I have heard, O fortunate king, that when Sa'dan the *ghul* attacked the palace and annihilated its defenders, they asked for quarter. 'Tie up your king,' Sa'dan told them, and when they had done this and picked him up, Sa'dan drove them ahead of him like sheep and brought them before Gharib, after most of the other citizens had been killed by his men. When Jamak recovered consciousness, he found himself in bonds, with Sa'dan saying: 'Tonight I shall have this king for my supper.' On hearing this, Jamak looked towards Gharib and said: 'I am under your protection.' 'If you accept Islam,' Gharib told him, 'you will be safe from the *ghul* and from the punishment of the Living and Eternal God.' At that, Jamak accepted Islam with both his heart and his tongue, and when he had been released on Gharib's orders, he offered conversion to his people, who all accepted it and entered Gharib's service. Jamak went back to the city and sent out food and drink to Gharib's men, who spent the night at Babel before being ordered by Gharib to move off in the morning.

They next came to Mayyafariqin, which they found to be deserted, as its inhabitants, hearing what had happened to Babel, had left it and gone to Kufa, where they told 'Ajib what had happened. 'Ajib was violently disturbed; he collected his paladins, told them of Gharib's advance and ordered them to prepare for battle. He held a muster of his army, which numbered thirty thousand horse and ten thousand foot. He sent for more men and collected another fifty thousand horse and foot, after which he rode out with this huge force. After five days, he found Gharib's army camped at Mosul and had his tents pitched in front of theirs.

Gharib wrote a letter, and turning to his men he said: 'Which of you will take this to 'Ajib?' Sahim sprang to his feet and promised to do that and to bring back a reply, at which Gharib handed it to him. Sahim went to 'Ajib's pavilion, and when the guards told 'Ajib that he was there, he said: 'Bring him to me.' They had brought him into his presence and

'Ajib asked: 'Where have you come from?' 'I have come to you from the king of the Persians and the Arabs, the son-in-law of Sabur, the ruler of the world,' Sahim replied. 'He has sent you a letter and wants a reply.' 'Ajib asked for the letter and when it had been passed to him, he opened it and read it. In it was written: 'In the Name of God, the Compassionate, the Merciful; peace be upon Abraham, the Friend of God: to continue, as soon as this letter reaches you, you are to acknowledge the unity of God, the Giver, the Causer of causes, Who drives the clouds, and you are to abandon the worship of idols. If you accept Islam, you will be my brother with authority over me, and I shall not take vengeance on you for what you did to my father and my mother, but if not, I shall move quickly against you, ravage your lands and cut off your head. I have given you good advice. Peace be on those who follow right guidance and obey the Most High God.'

When 'Ajib had read the letter and taken note of its threats, his eyes sank into their sockets and he gnashed his teeth in fury before tearing up the letter and throwing it away. Sahim found this hard to bear and so shouted at 'Ajib: 'May God wither your hand because of what you have done.' 'Seize this dog and cut him to pieces with your swords,' 'Ajib called to his men. They attacked Sahim, but he drew his sword and fought so fiercely that he had killed more than fifty of them before breaking free and returning, covered in blood, to Gharib. 'What is this, Sahim?' Gharib asked, and when Sahim told him what had happened, in his rage Gharib cried out: 'God is greater!' and had his war drums beaten. The paladins mounted; the ranks were drawn up, heroes joined together and horses curvetted on the battlefield, with their riders wearing armour and close-meshed coats of mail, carrying swords, with long lances supported on their thighs. 'Ajib rode out with his men and each side charged the other.

Night 638

Morning now dawned and Shahrazad broke off from what she had been allowed to say. Then, when it was the six hundred and thirty-eighth night, SHE CONTINUED:

I have heard, O fortunate king, that both Gharib and 'Ajib rode out with their men. Each side charged the other. The arbiter of war gave his judgements in which there is no injustice, as his mouth is sealed and he cannot speak. Streams of blood poured out; clearly marked patterns appeared on the ground and men's hair turned white in the fury and heat of battle. Feet slipped, and while the brave stood firm in defiance, cowards turned back in flight.

The battle continued until the end of the day when darkness fell and drums were beaten as a signal to disengage. Each side broke away, retiring to spend the night in their own camp. The next morning the signal for battle was given again; both sides armed, with their good swords slung from their shoulders and their brown lances tucked against their thighs. They mounted their short-haired horses, which struck sparks from their hooves, and drew up in ranks like a flooding sea, shouting out that there would be no pause in the day's fighting. Sahim was the first to open the battle, riding out between the ranks, brandishing two swords and two lances and demonstrating feats that left even skilled fighters bewildered. He then called out: 'Which of you is not too lazy or too weak to come out to fight?' An unbeliever like a spark of fire came out against him, but before he had time to resist, Sahim struck him down. A second followed and was killed and the same fate befell the third and the fourth and so on, until by midday Sahim had killed all his challengers, amounting to two hundred men. At this point 'Ajib ordered his men to charge; heroes met heroes amidst the confused shouts of a furious battle; polished swords clashed; men were killed agonizingly, and as the blood flowed the skulls of corpses served as horseshoes.

Furious fighting continued until darkness fell at the end of the day, when both sides broke off and retired to spend the night in their tents. They then remounted and came out again to fight. The Muslims were waiting for Gharib to ride in his usual place under the banners, and when he did not come, one of Sahim's slaves went to his pavilion but failed to find him, and when he asked the servants, they said that they knew nothing about him. In a state of great distress he took the news to the army, who held back, saying: 'If Gharib is not here, the enemy will destroy us.'

The story behind Gharib's absence is a strange one which we shall relate in its proper sequence. When 'Ajib had returned from his battle against Gharib, he called for one of his servants, a man named Sayyar, and said: 'Sayyar, I have kept you in reserve for a day like this, and now my orders are that you should go through Gharib's camp until you reach his pavilion and then you can demonstrate your cleverness by bringing him to me.' 'To hear is to obey,' Sayyar replied. He managed to get to the pavilion in the dark of night when everyone had gone off to bed, and he stood there as though he was in attendance on Gharib. Gharib felt thirsty and asked him for water, but the jug of water that Sayyar brought had been drugged, and no sooner had Gharib drunk it than he fell down head over heels. Sayyar wrapped him in his cloak and carried him off to 'Ajib's camp, where he stopped and threw him before his master. 'What is this, Sayyar?' 'Ajib asked him, to which he replied: 'This is your brother Gharib.' 'Ajib was delighted and said: 'May the idols bless you. Now free him and wake him up.'

Sayyar made him inhale vinegar, and when he had recovered his senses and opened his eyes he found himself tied up and in a tent that was not his own. 'There is no might and no power except with God, the Exalted, the Omnipotent!' he exclaimed, and 'Ajib shouted at him: 'Do you dare draw your sword against me, you dog, and seek to kill me in revenge for your father and mother? I shall send you off to meet them today and rid the world of you.' 'Infidel hound,' Gharib answered, 'you are going to see against whom fortune's wheel turns and who will be crushed by the Omnipotent King. He knows the secrets of men's hearts and He will leave you helpless and tormented in the fires of hell. Take pity on yourself and recite with me: "There is no god but the God of Abraham, the Friend of God."' When 'Ajib heard this he snorted and roared, cursing his own stone idol and calling for his executioner and the execution mat. His vizier, however, who though outwardly an infidel was a secret Muslim, got up, kissed the ground and said: 'Don't act in haste, your majesty, until we can tell who will win and who will lose. If we turn out to be the victors, then we can kill this man, but if we lose, then it will help us to have him in our power.' 'The vizier is right,' said the emirs.

Night 639

Morning now dawned and Shahrazad broke off from what she had been allowed to say. Then, when it was the six hundred and thirty-ninth night, SHE CONTINUED:

I have heard, O fortunate king, that when 'Ajib was on the point of killing Gharib, his vizier told him not to be in a hurry, for Gharib was in his power, and so 'Ajib ordered that his brother be fettered and manacled, leaving him in his tent with a thousand strong men to guard him.

Gharib's army had looked in vain for their king, and that morning they were like sheep without a shepherd, but Sa'dan the *ghul* shouted to them to arm themselves and to rely on the protection of God. So the Arabs and the Persians put on their armour and their close-meshed coats of mail and mounted their horses. When the chiefs and the leaders had ridden out under their banners, Sa'dan himself advanced, wheeling and turning, with a mace weighing two hundred *ratls* over his shoulder. 'Idolaters,' he shouted, 'come out, for this is the day of battle. Whoever knows me knows enough of the damage that I can wreak, and to any who don't know me, I say that I am Sa'dan, the servant of King Gharib. Which of you is not too lazy or too weak to come out to fight?' An infidel like a spark of fire rode out and charged at him, but Sa'dan met him with a stroke from his mace which broke his ribs and laid him out as a lifeless corpse on the ground. 'Light the fire,' he shouted to his sons and his slaves, 'and roast every infidel who falls, and when they have been properly cooked bring them to me to eat.' Following his orders, they lit a fire in the middle of the battlefield and threw the corpse on it, after which, when it was cooked, they took it to Sa'dan, who tore at its flesh and gnawed at its bones.

The infidels were terrified by what they saw, but 'Ajib shouted to them: 'Charge, damn you, and cut the *ghul* to pieces with your swords.' Twenty thousand of them charged, encircling Sa'dan and shooting at him with bolts and arrows, until he had twenty-four wounds, from which blood flowed on to the ground. He had been left isolated, but at that the Muslim champions charged the infidels, calling for help from the Lord of creation, and fighting went on until nightfall. Sa'dan, who was like a drunk man because of the blood that he had lost, had been captured, bound and put in the tent with Gharib. 'There is no might and no power except with God, the Exalted, the Omnipotent!' exclaimed Gharib when he saw him, and when he asked Sa'dan what had happened, the *ghul* replied: 'Master, Almighty God, praise be to Him, decrees both suffering and relief, and both must be experienced.' 'That is true,' agreed Gharib.

'Ajib passed a happy night and told his men to ride out and attack the Muslims the next day until not one of them remained. 'To hear is to obey,' they replied. As for the defeated Muslims, they spent the night weeping both for their king and for Sa'dan, but Sahim said: 'Don't concern yourselves, for Almighty God will soon send you relief.' He waited until midnight, and then he went to 'Ajib's camp, threading his way through the pavilions and tents until he found 'Ajib seated on his royal throne, surrounded by his kings. He himself, disguised as a servant, went up to the candles burning there, snuffed them out and relit them using the volatile form of *banj*. He waited for a time outside the pavilion until the smoke from the drug had affected 'Ajib and the kings and they had collapsed like dead men. He left them and went to the prison tent, where he discovered Gharib, Sa'dan and their thousand guards, who had been overcome by sleep. 'Damn you,' he shouted to them, 'don't sleep but watch over your prisoners and light the cressets.' He took one of these, kindled it with firewood, filled it with *banj* and carried it around the tent. When those inside inhaled the drugged smoke they all fell asleep, but Sahim, who had brought a sponge impregnated with vinegar, held this under the nostrils of Gharib and Sa'dan until they recovered their senses, after which he released them from their bonds. They were delighted to see him and called down blessings on him before leaving with all the guards' weapons.

Sahim told them to go back to camp, which they did, while he himself entered 'Ajib's pavilion, wrapped him in a mantle and carried him off to the Muslim camp, veiled from the infidels by the Merciful God. When he got to Gharib's pavilion he unwrapped the mantle so that Gharib could see what was in it, and on discovering that this was his brother 'Ajib, who had been tied up, he shouted out: 'God is greater! Victory and triumph!' After blessing Sahim, he told him to rouse 'Ajib, and when Sahim had given 'Ajib vinegar and frankincense, he recovered from the drug and, on finding himself fettered and chained, he hung his head.

Night 640

Morning now dawned and Shahrazad broke off from what she had been allowed to say. Then, when it was the six hundred and fortieth night, SHE CONTINUED:

I have heard, O fortunate king, that when Sahim seized and drugged 'Ajib, he brought him to his brother, Gharib, and then roused him. He opened his eyes to find himself fettered and chained, and hung his head. 'Look up, damn you,' said Sahim, and when 'Ajib raised his head he found himself surrounded by Arabs and Persians, with his brother seated on his royal throne. He said nothing, but Gharib shouted: 'Strip the dog!' He was stripped and whipped until he was weakened to the point of unconsciousness, when he was left in the charge of a hundred guards.

When Gharib had finished punishing him, he and his men heard shouts of 'There is no god but God!' and 'God is greater!' coming from the tents of the infidels. The reason for this was that, when Gharib had left al-Jazira, his uncle, al-Damigh, had stayed behind for ten days before setting out with twenty thousand riders. When he was close to the battlefield, he sent a scout to reconnoitre it. A day later the man came back and told him what had happened to Gharib at the hands of his brother. Al-Damigh waited until nightfall and then raised the battle cry 'God is greater!' and attacked the infidels, putting them to the sword. When Gharib and his men heard the cry, Gharib told his brother Sahim to go and discover what was happening. Sahim went close to the fight and asked the camp servants, who told him of the arrival of al-Damigh with twenty thousand men, explaining that he had said: 'By the truth of Abraham, the Friend of God, I shall not abandon my nephew but play a hero's part, drive back the unbelievers and win the favour of the Omnipotent King.' He had then launched a night attack on the infidels.

Sahim returned, and when he told Gharib what his uncle had done, Gharib ordered his own men to arm and mount and then to go to his uncle's aid. So they rode out and charged the infidels, putting them to the sword, and by the time morning came, they had killed some fifty thousand of them, captured another thirty thousand and scattered the rest throughout the length and breadth of the land. When the Muslims then drew back, having been granted aid and victory by God, Gharib rode up to meet his uncle and, after greeting him, thanked him for what he had done. 'Do you suppose that the dog 'Ajib fell in the fight?' asked al-Damigh, and Gharib replied: 'You will be pleased to hear that he is tied up in my tent.' Al-Damigh was delighted by the news, and when they had got back to the camp the two kings dismounted to enter Gharib's pavilion, but there was no 'Ajib to be found. Gharib cried out: 'By the glory of Abraham, the Friend of God, what a disastrous and ill-omened day this is!' and then, calling to the servants, he said: 'Damn you, where is my prisoner?' They replied: 'When you rode out we went with you, as you hadn't told us to guard him.' 'There is no might and no power except with God, the Exalted, the Omnipotent!' exclaimed Gharib, but his uncle told him not to be hasty or to take the matter to heart, adding: 'Wherever he goes, we shall pursue him.'

The reason for 'Ajib's escape was that his servant Sayyar had concealed himself among the Muslims, waiting until he was sure that Gharib had ridden out leaving no one to guard his prisoner. He had then taken 'Ajib and set off into the countryside, carrying him on his back, overwhelmed as 'Ajib was by the pain of his beating. Sayyar hurried on from the start of the night until the next day, when he came to a spring of water by an apple tree. There he put 'Ajib down and washed his face. 'Ajib opened his eyes and, recognizing Sayyar, he said: 'Sayyar, take me to Kufa so that I may recover, collect my troops and crush my enemy.' He added that he was hungry, and Sayyar then went to a wood where he caught a young ostrich which he killed and cut up before bringing it back to his master. When he had collected firewood, he struck a light, kindled a fire and roasted it before feeding it to 'Ajib and bringing him water from the spring, so revivifying him. He then went to a Bedouin camp and stole a horse, and after mounting 'Ajib on this, he set off with him towards Kufa. The two of them travelled for some days until, as they approached the city, its governor came out to meet and greet his king, whom he found still weak from the beating given to him by his brother. After 'Ajib had entered the city, he summoned the doctors and, when they had come, he told them to cure him within ten days. 'To hear is to obey,' they said, and they started to apply soothing treatments until he had fully recovered from the effects of his injuries. He now ordered his vizier to send letters to all his twenty-one governors, who collected their troops and hurried to meet him in Kufa.

Night 641

Morning now dawned and Shahrazad broke off from what she had been allowed to say. Then, when it was the six hundred and forty-first night, SHE CONTINUED:

I have heard, O fortunate king, that 'Ajib sent to summon his troops, who then came to Kufa.

As for Gharib, chagrined by 'Ajib's escape, he sent a thousand men in pursuit but, although they spread out in all directions, travelling for a day and a night, they found no news of him and had to go back and tell this to Gharib. Gharib then sent for his brother Sahim, and was distressed that he was not to be found, as he feared that some disaster might have happened. At that moment, however, Sahim himself came in and kissed the ground before him. On seeing him, Gharib got up and asked where he had been. 'Your majesty,' Sahim told him, 'I went to Kufa and found that the dog 'Ajib had returned to his palace where on his instructions doctors had successfully treated him for his injuries, after which he wrote to his governors, who have brought him troops.' Gharib ordered his own men to march and they struck camp and set off for Kufa, which they found surrounded by armies like an endless flooding sea. He and his force camped in front of them, pitched their tents and raised their banners. Then, as night fell, they lit fires and both sides stood on guard until daybreak.

Gharib got up and, after having performed his ablution, he prayed with two *rak'as*, following the practice of our father Abraham, the Friend of God, upon whom be peace. He then ordered the drums to be beaten; standards fluttered and riders put on their coats of mail and mounted their horses, calling out their own names by way of challenge and making for the battlefield. The first to start the fight was Gharib's uncle, al-Damigh, who rode between the ranks so that all could see him, brandishing two swords and two lances and demonstrating feats that left the riders bewildered, astonishing both sides, while calling out: 'Which of you is not too lazy or too weak to come out to fight? I am al-Damigh the king, the brother of King Kundamir.' An infidel like a spark of fire rode out and charged him without a word, but al-Damigh met him and thrust at his chest with his lance, whose point came out on the other side of his shoulder, as God hurried his soul to hellfire, an evil resting place. A second challenger came out and was killed, as was the third, and things went on like that until seventy-six infidel champions had fallen. At that point they were no longer prepared to risk single combat, and so 'Ajib shouted to them: 'Damn you, if you all go out against him one after the other, he will leave no single one of you alive. Make a concerted charge against the enemy so as to wipe them from the face of the earth, their skulls trampled by your horses' hooves.'

At that they waved their fearsome banner and both sides clashed; blood flowed on to the ground in streams; the arbiter of war gave his judgements in which there is no injustice; the brave stood firm-footed on the battlefield; while the cowards were routed and fled, not believing that the day would ever end or that night would bring its darkness. The battle continued until evening, when the light faded, but although the infidels then sounded their drums to break off the fight, Gharib was not prepared to stop and charged them, followed by the Muslim monotheists. How many heads were severed and throats cut; how many hands and spines were slashed through; how many knees and sinews were crushed; and how many men, old and young alike, were slaughtered!

By the time morning had come, the infidels had made up their minds to turn and flee and, as the light spread, they were routed. The Muslims pursued them until noon, capturing more than twenty thousand of them, and these were brought back with their hands tied. Gharib himself halted at the gate of Kufa and ordered a herald to proclaim throughout the city that he would give quarter to all who were willing to abandon idolatry and acknowledge the unity of the Omniscient God, the Creator of mankind and of light and darkness. When this proclamation was made, everyone, young and old alike, accepted Islam, before going out to renew their professions of faith in front of Gharib, who was filled with happiness and delight.

After that, Gharib asked about Mirdas and his daughter Mahdiya, and was told that Mirdas had camped behind the Red Mountain. He sent for his brother Sahim and, when he had come, he despatched him to find news of his father. Without delay Sahim mounted and, armed with a brown lance, he pressed on towards the Red Mountain, but his investigation brought him no news of Mirdas and no trace of his people. Instead of them he came across an old Bedouin, broken by the burden of years, whom he asked about them and where they had gone. 'My son,' the old man replied, 'when Mirdas heard that Gharib had attacked Kufa, he was terrified and he took his daughter and his clan, together with all his slaves, both male and female, and set off across the desert, but where he was making for, I don't know.' After hearing this, Sahim went back to tell his brother the news. Gharib was distressed by it, but he took his seat on the royal throne of his father, opened his treasuries and distributed money to all his paladins, sending out scouts to track down Mirdas while he himself stayed in Kufa. There he summoned his ministers of state, who came obediently, followed by the citizens, and he distributed splendid robes of honour among them, instructing them to look after the interests of his subjects.

Night 642

Morning now dawned and Shahrazad broke off from what she had been allowed to say. Then, when it was the six hundred and forty-second night, SHE CONTINUED:

I have heard, O fortunate king, that Gharib distributed robes of honour to the Kufans and instructed them to look after the interests of his subjects. One day, he went out to hunt with a hundred riders. He rode on until he reached a wooded valley, with many fruits and streams as well as birds, a grazing ground for antelopes and gazelles, a restful place with scents to revive the flagging spirit. It was a bright day and he and his party halted there and stayed until the following morning. Gharib then carried out the ritual ablution and performed two *rak'as*, giving praise and thanks to Almighty God. All of a sudden there came a sound of noise and shouting from the neighbouring countryside and Gharib sent Sahim to investigate. Sahim set off at once and rode on until he could hear cries and see plundered goods, spare horses being led and captured women and children. He asked a shepherd there what had happened and was told: 'This is the harem of Mirdas, the Qahtanid chief, and his goods, together with those of his clan. Mirdas was killed yesterday by al-Jamraqan, who plundered his goods, took his women and children as captives, and seized the property of his whole clan. He is a headstrong tyrant who is in the habit of coming out to raid and rob on the roads, and neither the Bedouin nor the kings can do anything about him, for he is a plague.'

When Sahim heard that his father had been killed, the women captured and the goods plundered, he went back to his brother to tell him what had happened. This inflamed Gharib's anger and excited his indignation, making him eager to remove this disgrace and to take his revenge. He rode out with his men, looking for an opportunity to attack, until he came up with the raiders. Then he shouted: 'God is greater! Have at the infidel robbers!' In a single charge he killed twenty-one champions and then halted on the battlefield, calling out boldly: 'Where is al-Jamraqan? Let him come out to meet me, so that I may pour him a cup of humiliation and free the lands of him.' Before he had finished speaking, out came al-Jamraqan like a cannonball or a rock falling from a mountain, mail-clad and huge, dashing against Gharib like the headstrong giant he was, with no word of greeting, while Gharib for his part came to meet him like a ravening lion.

Al-Jamraqan was carrying in his hand a heavy mace of Chinese iron, one blow from which would have crushed a mountain. He struck at Gharib's head, but Gharib swerved aside and the mace struck the ground, burying itself half a cubit deep. Gharib then took his own club and crushed al-Jamraqan's fingers with a blow on his hand. As al-Jamraqan dropped the mace, Gharib leaned from his saddle and snatched it faster than a bolt of lightning, before using it to strike him on the ribcage so that he fell to the ground like a lofty palm tree. Sahim seized him, tied him up and dragged him away at the end of a rope. Gharib's riders then attacked al-Jamraqan's men and killed fifty of them before the rest turned in flight and continued to ride off until they had got back to their tribe, alerting them with their shouts. The garrison of their castle rode out to meet them and asked them what had happened. When they were told by the fugitives that their chieftain had been captured, they hurried out to rescue him, making for the valley.

After having captured al-Jamraqan and routed his men, Gharib dismounted and ordered al-Jamraqan to be brought before him. When he came, he said humbly to Gharib: 'I am under your protection, champion of the age.' 'Arab dog,' Gharib replied, 'do you dare to intercept the servants of Almighty God on the roads with no fear of the Lord of creation?' 'Master,' said al-Jamraqan, 'what is this Lord of creation?' 'What ill-omened thing do you worship?' asked Gharib. 'I worship a date pastry made with butter and honey,' al-Jamraqan told him. 'Sometimes I eat it and then I make another.' Gharib collapsed with laughter, but then said: 'Miserable man, the only object of worship is Almighty God, Who created you and Who sustains all life. Nothing is hidden from Him and He has power over all things.' 'Where then is this mighty God so that I may worship him?' asked al-Jamraqan, and Gharib told him: 'You must know that the name of this god is God and it is He Who created the heavens and the earth; He caused the trees to grow and the streams to flow; He made the beasts and the birds, Paradise and hellfire, but He is veiled from our sight and sees but cannot be seen. He sits looking out from on high; it is He Who created us and Who gives us our daily bread; praise be to Him, for there is no god but He!' When al-Jamraqan heard what Gharib had to say, his inner ear was opened and he said, trembling: 'Master, what do I have to say to become one of you and to win the favour of this mighty Lord?' 'Say: "There is no god but the God of Abraham, the Friend, the messenger of God,"' Gharib told him, and al-Jamraqan recited this confession of faith and was numbered among God's elect. 'Have you tasted the sweetness of Islam?' Gharib asked him, and when he answered yes, Gharib ordered him to be set free. When this had been done, he kissed Gharib's foot and the ground before him.

While this was happening, a dust cloud suddenly began to fill the whole sky . . .

Night 643

Morning now dawned and Shahrazad broke off from what she had been allowed to say. Then, when it was the six hundred and forty-third night, SHE CONTINUED:

I have heard, O fortunate king, that when al-Jamraqan accepted Islam, he kissed the ground before Gharib, but while this was happening, a dust cloud suddenly began to fill the whole sky, and Gharib sent Sahim out to investigate. He left like a bird in flight, and after an hour's absence he came back and told Gharib that this was the dust of the Banu 'Amir, the companions of al-Jamraqan. Gharib said to al-Jamraqan: 'Ride out to meet your people and to offer them conversion to Islam. If they obey you, they will be safe, but if not we shall put them to the sword.' At this al-Jamraqan rode off, and when he approached with his men and called out to them, they recognized him and dismounted, coming to meet him on foot and saying: 'Master, we are glad that you are safe.' He replied: 'My people, whoever obeys me will be safe, but if anyone disobeys me I shall cut him down with this sword.' 'Give us what orders you want,' they told him, 'for we shall not disobey them.' He then told them to recite: 'There is no god but the God of Abraham, the Friend of God.' They asked him where he had heard this and he told them of his encounter with Gharib, adding: 'You know that I am your leader on the battlefield and in the thick of the fight, and yet one single man captured me and made me taste humiliation and degradation.' When they heard what he had to say, they all repeated the proclamation of God's unity, after which al-Jamraqan led them to Gharib. They renewed their profession of faith in front of him, calling down on him the blessings of victory and glory, and kissing the ground before him. He received them gladly and told them to go back to their tribe and to offer them conversion to Islam. Al-Jamraqan and his men said: 'Master, we shall never leave you but we shall go and fetch our children and bring them to you,' at which Gharib told them to go off and then to join him in Kufa.

Al-Jamraqan rode off with his men, and when they came to their tribe they invited their wives and children to accept Islam, which they all did, and after that they dismantled their houses and tents and drove off their horses, camels, sheep and goats, making for Kufa. When Gharib himself reached Kufa, his riders came out to meet him in a procession. He entered his palace and took his seat on his father's throne, with his paladins

standing on his right and his left. Then his scouts came in and told him
that his brother 'Ajib had gone to al-Jaland ibn Karkar, ruler of the city
of Oman and the land of Yemen. When Gharib heard this news, he told
his men to prepare to move out in three days' time and he offered the
thirty thousand whom he had captured in the first battle conversion to
Islam and the chance of accompanying him. Twenty thousand accepted,
and the ten thousand who refused were put to death. Al-Jamraqan
arrived with his men, and after they had kissed the ground before Gharib,
he presented them with splendid robes of honour. Al-Jamraqan himself
was appointed army commander and told to ride out ahead of the army
with the chiefs of his clan and twenty thousand horses, making for
al-Jaland's lands. 'To hear is to obey,' he said, and he and his force left
their women and children in Kufa and set off.

Gharib now inspected Mirdas's harem and his eye fell on Mahdiya,
who was among the women there, as a result of which he fell down
unconscious and had rosewater sprinkled on his face. When he had
recovered his senses, he embraced her and took her to his sitting room
where he sat with her, and the two later slept together without committing fornication. The next morning he went out and took his seat on his
royal throne, after which he presented his uncle, al-Damigh, with a robe
of honour and appointed him as his regent over the whole of Iraq,
instructing him to take care of Mahdiya until he returned from his
expedition against his brother 'Ajib. Al-Damigh agreed to this and Gharib
left with twenty thousand horse and ten thousand foot on his way to
Oman and Yemen.

When 'Ajib had reached Oman with his beaten army, its inhabitants,
together with their king, al-Jaland, had seen their dust and scouts had
been ordered to find out what it meant. After some time they came back
to tell him that under the dust cloud was a king named 'Ajib, the lord of
Iraq. Al-Jaland was surprised that he had come to Oman, but told his
people to go out and meet him. They did this and pitched tents for him
by the gate of the city, after which 'Ajib went sorrowfully and in tears
to al-Jaland, the husband of his cousin, who had borne him sons. When
the king saw the state that 'Ajib was in, he said: 'Tell me your news,' and
'Ajib then told him from beginning to end everything that had happened
to him in his dealings with Gharib. 'O king,' he explained, 'this man
orders people to worship the Lord of heaven and forbids them to serve
idols and other gods.' This aroused al-Jaland's worst passions and he
exclaimed: 'I swear by the truth of the radiant sun that I shall leave no

single place for your brother's people to hold. Where did you leave them and how many of them are there?' 'When I left them they were in Kufa,' answered 'Ajib, 'and there were fifty thousand of them.' Al-Jaland then summoned his men and ordered his vizier, Juwamard, to take seventy thousand riders to meet the Muslims in Kufa and bring them back alive so that he might torture them.

Juwamard set out for Kufa with his army, and after a week on the march they came to a wooded valley with streams and fruits, where he ordered a halt . . .

Night 644

Morning now dawned and Shahrazad broke off from what she had been allowed to say. Then, when it was the six hundred and forty-fourth night, SHE CONTINUED:

I have heard, O fortunate king, that when al-Jaland sent Juwamard with his army to Kufa, they came to a wooded valley with streams and fruits, where Juwamard ordered a halt and where they rested until midnight. At that point he told them to move on and he himself mounted his horse and rode ahead of them until daybreak. He then went down into another tree-lined valley, filled with the scent of flowers, where birds were singing and branches bending. Satan puffed him up with pride, and he recited these lines:

> I plunge with my army into seas of battle dust,
> Leading off those I capture through my strength and my exertions.
> Throughout the lands the riders know
> That I am the man they fear, the defender of my clan.
> I shall put Gharib in chains and fetters,
> And ride back joyfully, my happiness complete.
> I shall put on my mail and take up arms,
> Riding into the thick of every fight.

He had scarcely finished his poem before a haughty mail-clad rider came out from among the trees, shouting at him: 'Halt, you Arab robber! Strip off your clothes, your arms and armour and dismount in order to save your life.' The rider was al-Jamraqan, and when Juwamard heard what he said, light turned to darkness in his face and, drawing his sword, he attacked, crying out: 'Arab thief, do you dare try to hold me up? I am the commander of the army of al-Jaland ibn Karkar coming to fetch Gharib and his men in chains.'

When al-Jamraqan heard this, he exclaimed: 'What pleasant news this is for me,' and he charged at Juwamard, reciting these lines:

I am the rider famed in the press of battle,
Whose sword and spear the foeman fears.
I am al-Jamraqan, whose help is sought in war,
And whose thrusts are known to every rider.
Gharib is my emir, my imam and my lord –
A hero in battle on the day that two sides meet,
An imam of piety, asceticism and power,
Annihilating foes upon the battlefield.
He summons us to the religion of God's Friend,
Reciting divine verses in despite of false idols.

Al-Jamraqan had marched with his men for ten days from Kufa and then, on the eleventh, they had halted and stayed until midnight before he had ordered them to set off again. He had ridden ahead on their line of march and had gone down into the valley, where he heard Juwamard reciting the lines that have been quoted, and then attacked him like a savage lion, cutting him in two with a blow from his sword. He waited for his commanders to come up and, after telling them what had happened, he ordered them to split up into groups of five, with each five taking five thousand men and encircling the valley, while he himself stayed there with the Banu 'Amir. 'When the enemy's vanguard arrives,' he went on, 'I shall charge them, calling out: "God is greater!" and when you hear this shout, launch your own charge, raising the same cry and striking with your swords.' 'To hear is to obey,' they said, and when they had made the rounds of their men, passing on Gharib's orders, everyone dispersed around the valley as dawn was breaking.

The enemy arrived like a flock of sheep, filling the high ground and the low, and at that moment al-Jamraqan and the Banu 'Amir charged with a shout of 'God is greater!' which was heard by both Muslims and infidels alike. On all sides the Muslims cried: 'God is greater! Victory and triumph! May God abandon the infidels!' The mountains and hills, and all the surrounding countryside echoed the cry and, as the dismayed infidels struck at each other with their sharp swords, the pious Muslims attacked like fiery sparks. All that could be seen were heads severed and struck off, streams of blood and distracted cowards. By the time that faces could be made out again through the dust, two-thirds of the infidels had been killed and God had hurried their souls to hellfire, an evil resting place. The survivors turned in flight, scattering through the deserts and pursued by the Muslims, who went on capturing and killing them until midday. By the time the Muslims returned, they had taken seven thousand prisoners, while only twenty-six thousand of the infidels, most of them wounded, got back home. The Muslims, aided to victory by God, retired, having collected the horses, the arms and armour, the baggage and the tents, which they sent off to Kufa escorted by a thousand riders.

Night 645

Morning now dawned and Shahrazad broke off from what she had been allowed to say. Then, when it was the six hundred and forty-fifth night, SHE CONTINUED:

I have heard, O fortunate king, that al-Jamraqan killed Juwamard when they fought, and then killed or captured a large number of his men, taking their wealth, their horses and their baggage. These were sent to Kufa with an escort of a thousand riders.

As for al-Jamraqan and his Muslims, they dismounted and invited their prisoners to embrace Islam, which they accepted with both hearts and tongues. They were then released from their bonds and were joyfully embraced by al-Jamraqan's men. He himself allowed what was now a huge force to rest for a day and a night before setting off in the morning for the lands of al-Jaland, while a thousand of his riders escorted the booty back to Kufa. There, to his delight, they gave Gharib the good news of what had happened. He turned to Sa'dan the *ghul* and told him to follow al-Jamraqan with twenty thousand men and, when this force had been collected, Sa'dan and his sons mounted and set out for Oman.

The defeated remnants of the infidels returned to their city weeping and lamenting. Al-Jaland was taken aback and asked them what had happened, and when they told him the story he swore at them and asked how many Muslims there had been. 'O king,' they told him, 'there were twenty banners and under each of these there were a thousand riders.' On hearing this, al-Jaland exclaimed: 'May the sun shed no blessing on you! Damn you, were you beaten by twenty thousand men, when there were seventy thousand of you with Juwamard, who could hold his own against three thousand on the field of battle?' In a paroxysm of rage he drew his sword and shouted an order to his attendants to attack the fugitives. The guards drew their swords and the survivors were cut down to the last man, their bodies being thrown to the dogs. Al-Jaland then called out to his son, ordering him to move against Iraq with a hundred thousand men and lay it to waste.

There was no better rider to be found in his father's army than this prince, al-Qurajan, who used to charge alone against three thousand foes. He now pitched his tents outside the city, while all his champions came out, equipped and armed themselves and followed their leader, squadron after squadron. Al-Qurajan, swollen with pride, recited the lines:

> I am al-Qurajan, the famous,
> The conqueror of nomads and settled folk.
> How many a rider have I killed,
> Felling him like a cow!
> How many an army have I scattered,
> Rolling their skulls like balls!
> I shall attack Iraq,
> Shedding enemy blood like rain.
> I shall capture Gharib and his paladins,
> And their punishment will be a lesson to all those who can see.

When his army had been on the move for twelve days, they saw a dust cloud rising to cover the horizon, and at the sight of it he sent out his scouts to discover what it meant. They went off, and after they had passed beneath the banners of the advancing force, they returned to tell al-Qurajan that these were the Muslims. He was glad to hear that and he asked the scouts whether they had counted the numbers, to which they replied that they had made out twenty standards. 'By the truth of my religion,' he said, 'I shall not send out anyone else against them, but I alone shall attack them, leaving their skulls to be trampled by our horses.'

The dust was that of al-Jamraqan's men, and when he looked at the infidels and saw that their army was like the swelling sea, he halted his force and ordered his tents to be pitched. His men dismounted and raised their banners, calling on the Name of the Omniscient King, the Creator of light and darkness, the Lord of all things, Who looks out from on high and sees but is not seen, praise be to Him, Almighty as He is, for there is no god but He. The infidels also dismounted and pitched camp, but al-Qurajan told them not to sleep until they were armed and ready, adding: 'When it comes to the last third of the night, mount and ride down this small band.' His orders were heard by one of al-Jamraqan's spies, who was standing there to listen to the infidels' plans. When al-Jamraqan had been told of this, he turned to his paladins and said: 'Arm yourselves and at nightfall bring me the mules and the camels, as well as all the kinds of bells that you can find, and hang these around their necks.' There were more than twenty thousand camels and mules, and the Muslims waited until the infidels were asleep, after which al-Jamraqan ordered them to mount and ride, trusting in God and seeking help from the Lord of creation. He told them to drive the animals towards the infidels, pricking the beasts with their lance points, and, having done this, they launched an attack on the tents of the infidels. All the bells sounded as the Muslims, following the animals, raised the shout of 'God is greater!' and the mountains and hills rang with the Name of the Almighty King, the Omnipotent and Great. When they heard the noise, the horses charged, trampling the tents, as the infidels lay sleeping.

Night 646

Morning now dawned and Shahrazad broke off from what she had been allowed to say. Then, when it was the six hundred and forty-sixth night, SHE CONTINUED:

I have heard, O fortunate king, that al-Jamraqan launched a night attack against the infidels with his men, his horses and his camels as they lay asleep. Al-Qurajan's men woke in dismay and, snatching up their weapons, they attacked each other until most of them had been killed. Then, when they looked and found no single Muslim corpse but only armed Muslims on horseback, they realized that they had been tricked. Al-Qurajan called out to the survivors: 'You bastards, they have done to us what we wanted to do to them, and their scheme has worked better!' They were about to charge when a huge dust cloud rose up, blocking the horizons, and was carried high into the air by the wind, while underneath it could be seen gleaming helmets and glittering mail worn by none but famous heroes carrying Indian swords and flexible lances. When the infidels saw the dust they stopped fighting, and both sides sent out scouting parties, which rode there, looked and came back with the news that this was a Muslim force.

The newcomers were the troops sent out by Gharib with Sa'dan the *ghul*, and it was he who was riding at their head. He joined his pious co-religionists and at that point al-Jamraqan and his men charged the infidels like sparks of fire, striking at them with sharp swords and quivering Rudaini lances. So thick was the dust that the day was darkened and men were blinded; the courageous fighters stood firm while the cowards took flight, making for the open spaces of the deserts, while blood flowed in streams on to the ground. Fighting continued until evening came and darkness fell. The Muslims then broke off the battle and went to their tents, where they ate their food and passed the night until darkness had cleared away and the next day's dawn had broken, when, after the morning prayer, they rode out again to battle.

At the close of the fighting, al-Qurajan found that two-thirds of his men had fallen to the swords and lances of the Muslims, while most of the rest were wounded. So he told them that the next day he himself would go to the battlefield to challenge the Muslim heroes. When it was light the next morning both sides rode out, and while shouts rose, swords flashed, brown lances were levelled and the battle ranks formed up, it was he who came out to begin the fight, calling out: 'Let no idle weakling come out to face me today!' Both al-Jamraqan and Sa'dan the *ghul* were standing under the Muslim banners, but it was the chief of the Banu 'Amir who rode out to answer the challenge. The two opponents charged at each other like butting rams, but after a while al-Qurajan took hold of his opponent's coat of mail and used it to drag him from the saddle, dashing him to the ground. While he was distracted by his fall, the infidels tied him up and took him to their camp. Al-Qurajan wheeled and turned, repeating his challenge. He captured a second leader, and went on to capture a series of others, one after the other, until he had taken seven before midday.

At that point al-Jamraqan bellowed so loudly that the battlefield resounded and both armies heard it. Then, full of fury, he charged at al-Qurajan, reciting these lines:

I am al-Jamraqan the bold,
All riders fear to face me, the ravager of fortresses
That are left to mourn the loss of their defenders.
Al-Qurajan, follow the path of right guidance,
Quitting the way of error.
Acknowledge the unity of God, Who raised the heavens,

Who causes the waters to run and sets fast the hills.
The Muslim will be sheltered in Paradise,
And spared the painful punishment.

When al-Qurajan heard this, he snorted and roared, cursing the sun and the moon, and he then charged at al-Jamraqan, reciting:

I am al-Qurajan, Time's greatest hero;
The lion in his covert trembles at my shadow.
I conquer castles and hunt down wild beasts;
All riders fear me in the fight.
Al-Jamraqan, if you do not believe me,
Then come out now and challenge me.

At this, al-Jamraqan charged with a stout heart; such were the sword blows of both champions that the ranks cried out. They thrust with their lances, shouting at each other, and they continued to fight until the afternoon had passed and the day was drawing to its close. It was then that al-Jamraqan rushed at al-Qurajan and struck him to the ground with a mace blow on his chest. He fell like the trunk of a palm tree and the Muslims tied him up, dragging him off with a rope, like a camel. When the infidels saw their chief a prisoner, they were filled with pagan fanaticism and charged at the Muslims in the hope of setting him free, but the Muslim champions met them and left them cast down on the ground, while the survivors took flight, looking for safety as the sword strokes whistled through the air behind them. The Muslims pursued until the infidels had been dispersed through the mountains and deserts, after which the Muslims came back to collect spoils in plenty, horses, tents and so on, amounting to enormous booty. Al-Jamraqan invited al-Qurajan to accept Islam, but in spite of threats he refused and as a result his head was cut off and carried on a lance point as the Muslims resumed their march on Oman.

When the infidels told their king, al-Jaland, that his son had been killed and his army destroyed, he dashed his crown to the ground and struck his face until blood flowed from his nostrils and he fell to the ground unconscious. Rosewater was sprinkled on him and when he had recovered, he called for his vizier and instructed him to write to all his governors with orders to fetch every man who could wield a sword, thrust with a lance or carry a bow. The letters were written and sent off with couriers, after which the governors made their preparations and left with a huge army numbering a hundred and eighty thousand men. The tents, the camels and the horses were ready and they were about to march when al-Jamraqan and Sa'dan the *ghul* arrived with seventy thousand mail-clad riders like grim lions. At the sight of them, al-Jaland exclaimed joyfully: 'By the truth of the radiant sun, I shall leave them no lands nor any to carry back news, for I shall ravage Iraq and revenge my heroic son before the fire of my anger cools.' He then turned to 'Ajib and said: 'Iraqi dog, it is you who have brought this on us, and I swear by my God that if I fail to avenge myself on my foes I shall see that you die the worst of deaths.'

On hearing this, 'Ajib was filled with distress and began to blame himself, but he waited until the Muslims had halted and pitched their tents. Then, under cover of darkness, he took the survivors of his clan away from the tents and told them: 'Cousins, when the Muslims advanced, both I and al-Jaland were filled with fear, and I realized that he didn't have the power to protect me from my brother, or from anyone else. What I think we should do is to set off when everyone is asleep and make for King Ya'rub ibn Qahtan, who has more troops and greater power.' When his clan heard this they agreed with him, and so he told them to light fires at the entrances of their tents and leave under cover of darkness. They did what he told them and by the time morning broke they were already far away.

As for al-Jaland, he rode out in the morning with two hundred and sixty thousand armoured men wearing closely woven coats of mail. The war drums were beaten and the battle ranks drawn up, while, on the other side, al-Jamraqan and Sa'dan came with forty thousand fierce and excellent fighters, prompt in pursuit, one thousand of whom were grouped beneath each standard. When both sides had formed up, they came out to fight, drawing their swords and levelling their flexible lances in order to pour cups of death.

The first to begin the battle was Sa'dan, like a granite mountain or a *marid* of the *jinn*, and when he had killed his first opponent and thrown him down on the battlefield, he shouted to his sons and his servants to light a fire and roast the corpse. When this had been done, they brought it to him, and he proceeded to eat it, crunching the bones as the infidels stood looking on from a distance, calling on the radiant sun. As they were flinching from him, al-Jaland shouted out: 'Kill this foul creature!' but the first leader to challenge him fell and he continued to kill one rider after another until, after he had left thirty dead, the base infidels held back, saying: 'Who can fight against *jinn* and *ghuls*?' Al-Jaland then ordered a hundred of them to attack and to bring him Sa'dan alive or dead. They made at him with swords and lances, but he met them with a heart stronger than flint, proclaiming the unity of God, the Judge, Whose attention nothing can distract, and shouting: 'God is greater!' He struck at their heads with his sword, cutting them off, and in a single charge he killed seventy-four of them, routing the remainder. At this point al-Jaland ordered ten leaders, each commanding a thousand men, to shoot at Sa'dan's horse so that when it fell under him they could seize him. Ten thousand charged and were met by Sa'dan with a stout heart, and when al-Jamraqan and the Muslims saw this, they shouted 'God is greater!' They charged in their turn, but before they could reach Sa'dan, his horse had been killed and he himself had been captured.

The Muslims continued to fight until darkness fell and they could no longer see. Sharp swords were clashing as bold riders stood firm while cowards were discomfited, but in relation to the unbelievers the Muslims were like a white blaze on the body of a black bull.

Night 647

Morning now dawned and Shahrazad broke off from what she had been allowed to say. Then, when it was the six hundred and forty-seventh night, SHE CONTINUED:

I have heard, O fortunate king, that the battle continued to rage between Muslims and unbelievers, and that in relation to the latter the Muslims were like a white blaze on the body of a black bull. The battle had continued until nightfall, when both sides broke off, the infidels having suffered innumerable casualties. Al-Jamraqan and his men were filled with such sadness for the loss of Sa'dan that they could enjoy neither food nor sleep, but on inspecting their ranks they found that fewer than a thousand were dead. Al-Jamraqan promised that the next day he himself would take the field, killing the infidel champions and capturing their families to use as ransom for Sa'dan, with the permission of God, the Judge, Whose attention nothing can distract. This consoled and cheered the Muslims, who dispersed to their tents.

As for al-Jaland, when he had entered his pavilion and taken his seat on the royal throne, surrounded by his guards, he called for Sa'dan, and when he had been brought before him, al-Jaland said: 'You mad dog, least of the Arabs, wood carrier, who was it who killed my son, al-Qurajan, the hero of the age, the slayer of his foes, the overthrower of champions?' Sa'dan told him: 'He was killed by al-Jamraqan, the leader of the army of King Gharib, the prince of champions, and I roasted him and ate him because I was hungry.' When al-Jaland heard this, his eyes sank back into his head and he ordered that Sa'dan's head be cut off. The executioner advanced eagerly, but Sa'dan strained against the ropes that bound him and broke them, after which he attacked the executioner, snatched the sword from him and struck off his head. He then made for al-Jaland, but al-Jaland threw himself down from his throne and took flight, so Sa'dan fell on the bystanders and killed twenty of the king's intimates while the rest of the commanders fled. Shouts were raised throughout the infidel army as Sa'dan attacked, striking right and left, and as he continued to cut at them with his sword, they dispersed, leaving him a clear path out of their camp as he fought his way to the Muslim tents. The Muslims had heard the infidels shouting and had wondered whether they had received reinforcements, but while they were in a state of uncertainty, they were cheered by Sa'dan's arrival. The most delighted of them was al-Jamraqan, who joined the others in greeting him and congratulating him on his escape.

So much for them, but as for the infidels, they and al-Jaland returned to their tents after Sa'dan had gone, and al-Jaland exclaimed: 'I swear by the truth of the radiant sun, the dark night, the light of day and the planets, I didn't think that I would escape death today, for had I fallen into the hands of the *ghul* he would have eaten me and he would have thought no more of me than of an ear of wheat or barley or a grain of corn.' His men confirmed that they had never seen anyone do what the *ghul* had done, and al-Jaland then told them that the next day they were to arm themselves, mount and crush the Muslims beneath their horses' hooves.

The Muslims, for their part, were all delighted by their victory and by Sa'dan's escape. Al-Jamraqan promised: 'Tomorrow I shall display my prowess on the battlefield and show you what befits a man like me. I swear by the truth of Abraham, the Friend of God, that I shall savagely slay the infidels, bemusing all men of understanding with my sword blows. I intend to charge against the right wing and then the left, and when you see me attack the king underneath the banners, then do your best to charge behind me, so that God may bring about what is due to be accomplished.'

Both sides spent the night on guard until the sun rose the next day, when they mounted faster than the blink of an eye, facing each other to the ominous croaking of the crows as the battle ranks were drawn up. Al-Jamraqan was the first to start the battle, wheeling, advancing and challenging his enemies. Al-Jaland was about to charge with his men when a dust cloud was seen, filling the horizons and darkening the day. When it was scattered by the winds, under it could be seen mail-clad champions, with sharp swords, piercing lances and men like lions, fearless and dauntless. At the sight of it, both sides held back from the battle and sent out scouts to discover who was stirring up the dust. The scouts vanished from sight underneath it, and when they came back later in the day the infidel reported that this was a Muslim army under King Gharib, while when the Muslim scout brought back the same news, it was received with joy by al-Jamraqan's men, who rode out to meet their king, dismounting and kissing the ground before him in greeting . . .

Night 648

Morning now dawned and Shahrazad broke off from what she had been allowed to say. Then, when it was the six hundred and forty-eighth night, SHE CONTINUED:

I have heard, O fortunate king, that the Muslims were delighted by the arrival of King Gharib, and they kissed the ground before him in greeting as they circled around him. He returned their greeting cheerfully, delighted at their safety, and when they had returned to their camp and set up pavilions and standards for him, he took his seat on his royal throne, surrounded by his ministers of state. They then told him all that had happened to Sa'dan.

As for the infidels, they came together to look for 'Ajib, but when they failed to find him either in their own ranks or in their camp, they reported to al-Jaland that he must have fled. In a fit of rage al-Jaland bit his fingers and said: 'By the truth of the radiant sun, the treacherous dog must have escaped into the deserts with his worthless clansmen. It is only by hard fighting that we can drive back these enemies, so take heart, strengthen your resolve and be on your guard against the Muslims.' Gharib for his part exhorted his men in the same terms, adding: 'Seek help from your Lord and ask Him to give you victory over your enemies,' to which they replied: 'O king, you will see what we shall do on the field of battle.'

Both sides waited until dawn broke on the following day, and as the sun rose over hilltops and valleys Gharib performed two *rak'as*, in accordance with the practice of Abraham, the Friend of God, upon whom be peace. He then wrote a letter which he sent with his brother Sahim to the infidels. 'What do you want?' al-Jaland's men asked him when he arrived, and he told them: 'I'm looking for your leader.' 'Stay where you are until we consult him,' they said, and when they had gone to tell al-Jaland of his arrival, al-Jaland said: 'Bring him before me.' So they fetched Sahim and al-Jaland asked: 'Who sent you?' 'King Gharib,' he replied, 'to whom God has given rule over the Arabs and the Persians. Take his letter and give him a reply.' Al-Jaland took the letter, opened it and read what Gharib had written, which was: 'In the Name of God, the Compassionate, the Merciful, the One, Eternal, Omnipotent and Omniscient Lord, the God of Noah, Salih, Hud and Abraham, the Master of all things. Peace be on those who follow right guidance and fear the consequences of evil, in obedience to the Exalted King and in pursuit of the right path, preferring the next world to this. To continue: al-Jaland, there is no object of worship apart from God, the One, the Omnipotent, the Creator of night and day and of the celestial sphere. It is He Who sent out the righteous prophets; it is He Who caused rivers to run, Who has raised up the heavens, spread out the earth and caused trees to grow. It is He Who gives food to the birds in their nests and to the beasts in the deserts, for He is the Great God, Forgiving and Compassionate, the Veiler, Whom no eye can see, Who makes night alternate with day. It is He Who sent out the messengers and Who revealed the holy books. You must know that the religion of Abraham, the Friend of God, is the one true religion and if you accept it you will save yourself from the cutting swords and, in the world to come, from the torment of hellfire. If you refuse, you will be destroyed, your lands ravaged and all traces of you wiped away. Send me the dog 'Ajib so that I may avenge my father and mother.'

When al-Jaland had read the letter he said to Sahim: 'Tell your master that 'Ajib has fled with his people and we don't know where he has gone, but as for me, I shall not abandon my religion; tomorrow we shall meet in battle and the sun will grant us victory.' Sahim went back to his brother and told him what had happened. Both sides stayed where they were throughout the night, and the next morning the Muslims armed themselves and mounted, calling on God, the Giver of victory, the Creator of bodies and souls, and raising the cry: 'God is greater!' The earth shook as the drums were beaten; every chief and daring champion rode out to the field of battle as the ground trembled. The first to start the fight was al-Jamraqan, who rode out, bewildering all who saw him as he juggled with his sword and javelin, and calling: 'Who will come out to fight? Let no idle weakling challenge me. It was I who killed al-Qurajan, the son of al-Jaland, so who will come to avenge him?' As soon as al-Jaland heard his son's name, he shouted to his men: 'You bastards, bring me the slayer of my son so that I may eat his flesh and drink his blood.' A hundred champions charged, but al-Jamraqan killed most of them and forced their leader to flee. Seeing what al-Jamraqan had done, al-Jaland called for a concerted attack. The dreadful banners were shaken, the two armies confronted each other and, as Gharib and Jamraqan charged with the Muslims, enemies met and both sides clashed like the meeting of two seas. Yemeni swords and spears set to work shredding breasts and torsos; the angel of death appeared before the eyes of both sides; dust rose into the sky; ears were deafened; tongues were dumb and death was all around; while brave men stood firm and cowards fled.

The fighting continued until the end of the day, when drums sounded the recall and both sides disengaged and returned to their tents.

Night 649

Morning now dawned and Shahrazad broke off from what she had been allowed to say. Then, when it was the six hundred and forty-ninth night, SHE CONTINUED:

I have heard, O fortunate king, that when the battle ended and both sides dispersed, each to their own tents, Gharib took his seat on his royal throne and, as his companions lined up around him, he told them: 'I am distressed and grieved by the flight of the dog 'Ajib. I don't know where he has gone, but if I fail to catch up with him and take my revenge on him, I shall die of sorrow.' At this point Sahim, his brother, came forward, kissed the ground and promised to go to the infidel camp in order to find news of the treacherous dog. 'Go and find out about the pig,' Gharib told him, and so Sahim disguised himself in the clothes of an infidel and set off for the enemy tents, looking just like one of them. He found them sleeping, drunk with the effects of battle, the sentries the only people still awake. He passed on until he reached al-Jaland's pavilion and, finding him sleeping with no one to guard him, he managed to drug him with volatile *banj* until he was like a dead man. He then went out and fetched a mule on which he placed the king wrapped in a sheet taken from his bed and, after covering this with a mat, he set off again.

When he came to Gharib's pavilion, the Muslims there did not know him and asked him who he was. He laughed and uncovered his face, at which point they recognized him and Gharib asked what he was carrying. 'This is al-Jaland, son of Karkar,' Sahim told him, and when the bundle had been undone, Gharib recognized him and told Sahim to bring him back to consciousness. Sahim gave him a mixture of vinegar and helle-bore which caused the *banj* to be expelled from his nose and he opened his eyes to find himself among the Muslims. 'What nightmare is this?' he asked, before closing his eyes and falling asleep again. Sahim kicked him and said: 'Open your eyes, damn you.' When al-Jaland did, he said: 'Where am I?' and Sahim told him: 'You are in the presence of King Gharib, son of Kundamir, the lord of Iraq.' On hearing this, al-Jaland exclaimed: 'O king, I am under your protection. I have done nothing wrong. It was your brother who brought us out to fight, and after stirring up this feud between us, he ran away.' 'Do you know which way he went?' Gharib asked, but al-Jaland replied: 'No, by the truth of the radiant sun, I don't know that.'

Gharib then ordered that al-Jaland be fettered and guarded, after which the leaders dispersed, each to his own tent. Al-Jamraqan went back with his own clansmen and told them: 'Cousins, I intend to do something tonight to win honour from King Gharib.' 'Do what you want,' they replied, 'for we shall obey your commands.' 'Arm yourselves,' he said, 'and I shall go with you. Tread softly so that not even an ant knows you're there, and spread out around the tents of the infidels. When you hear me raise the cry "God is greater!", shout this out in your turn, and then draw back, heading for the city gate, and we shall ask for help from Almighty God.'

His men armed themselves fully and waited until midnight before dispersing around the infidels, where they kept in position for some time until al-Jamraqan clashed his sword against his shield and shouted 'God is greater!' so loudly that the valley resounded. His men followed his example and the valley, the mountains, the sands, the hills and the de-serted camping grounds echoed to the cry. The infidels started up in alarm and began to attack each other with their swords, but meanwhile the Muslims had drawn off and made for the city gates where they killed

the gate guards, and making their way into the city itself, they captured
it, together with all its wealth and women.

So much for al-Jamraqan, but as for Gharib, when he heard the cry
'God is greater!' he mounted and rode out with his entire force. Sahim
went forward to the scene of the fighting and discovered that al-Jamraqan
had attacked with the Banu 'Amir, spreading destruction among the
infidels. He returned to tell Gharib what had happened, and Gharib
called down blessings on al-Jamraqan. In the meantime the infidels were
still fighting as hard as they could and turning their swords on one
another, and this went on until dawn broke, at which point Gharib
called out: 'Charge, noble Muslims, and win the favour of the Omniscient
King!' The pious then attacked the impious, wielding keen swords and
plunging supple spears into the breasts of the unbelieving hypocrites.
When these latter tried to enter their city, al-Jamraqan and his clan came
out against them and they were caught as if between two encircling
mountain ranges. Their dead were too many to be counted and the
survivors scattered through the open deserts . . .

Night 650

Morning now dawned and Shahrazad broke off from what she had been
allowed to say. Then, when it was the six hundred and fiftieth night,
SHE CONTINUED:

I have heard, O fortunate king, that when the Muslims charged the
unbelievers, they cut through them with sharp swords until the unbelievers scattered through the open deserts, pursued by the Muslims until
they had been dispersed among the flat lands and the hills.

When the Muslims returned to the city, Gharib entered al-Jaland's
palace and sat on his throne, surrounded to the right and the left by his
companions. He summoned al-Jaland, who was quickly brought before
him, and when he refused the offer of conversion to Islam Gharib had
him crucified on the city gate, after which he was shot full of arrows
until he looked like a hedgehog. Gharib then presented al-Jamraqan with
a robe of honour and said: 'You are now the ruler of this place, with full
authority to govern it, for it was by your own sword and with the help
of your men that you conquered it.' At this, al-Jamraqan kissed Gharib's
foot, thanked him and prayed that victory, glory and fortune would
long favour him. Gharib opened al-Jaland's treasuries and inspected the

wealth that they contained, which he then distributed to the leaders and the banner-carrying fighting men and then to the girls and boys.

He did this for ten days, but then one night as he lay asleep he saw a terrifying dream and woke up frightened and alarmed. He roused his brother Sahim and told him: 'I saw in my dream that we were in a broad valley when two predatory birds swooped down on us, bigger than any I had ever seen in my life, with legs as long as lances. They attacked us and we shrank from them in fear. This was what I saw.' When Sahim heard this, he said: 'O king, this shows that you have a great enemy against whom you must guard yourself.' Gharib did not sleep for the rest of the night and in the morning he called for his horse and mounted it. When Sahim asked where he was going, he said: 'I am feeling depressed this morning and I intend to go off for ten days until I recover my spirits.' Sahim advised him to take an escort of a thousand riders, but Gharib said: 'I shall go only with you and no one else.'

At that the two of them mounted their horses and rode off, making for the valleys and the plains, and they went on from one valley to the next and one plain to another until they passed a valley full of trees, fruits and streams, scented by flowers, with birds singing on the branches, the nightingale chanting its melodies, the turtledove filling it all with song, the tuneful bulbul rousing the sleepers, and the blackbird producing its human-sounding notes, while the pigeon and the ringdove were eloquently answered by the parrot, and the trees bore two species of every edible fruit. The brothers were delighted by the valley and they ate its fruits, drank from its streams and sat down in the shade of its trees, where drowsiness overcame them and they fell asleep – praise be to Him, Who does not sleep.

While they were both asleep, two powerful *marids* swooped down on them, each of whom put one of them over his shoulder and flew up with them above the clouds into the upper air, so that when the brothers woke up they found themselves between heaven and earth. When they looked, they discovered that one of the *marids* had the head of a dog, while the other, who was like a tall palm tree, had the head of an ape, with hair like horse tails and claws like those of lions. On seeing this, the brothers exclaimed: 'There is no might and no power except with God!'

The reason behind this was that a certain *jinn* king called Mar'ash had a son named Sa'iq who was in love with a *jinn* girl whose name was Najma. Sa'iq and Najma had met in that valley, having taken the shape of birds. They had been seen by Gharib and Sahim, who, thinking that they were real birds, had shot at them with arrows. Only Sa'iq had been hit, and as his blood flowed, Najma, in her grief, had snatched him up and flown off with him, fearing that she too might be shot. She had brought him to the gate of his father's palace, where the gatekeepers carried him in and put him down before his father. When Mar'ash saw his son with an arrow in his ribs, he cried out: 'Alas, my son, tell me who did this so that I may ravage his lands and hasten his destruction, even if he is the greatest of the kings of the *jinn*.' Sa'iq opened his eyes and said: 'Father, it was a human who killed me in the Valley of the Springs,' and as soon as he had said this, he gave up the ghost. Mar'ash struck himself on the face until blood poured from his mouth, and he then summoned two *marids* and ordered them to go to that valley and to bring him anyone whom they found there. When they arrived they saw Gharib and Sahim asleep, and so they snatched them up and took them to Mar'ash.

On waking up and finding themselves in mid-air, the brothers had recited the formula: 'There is no might and no power except with God, the Exalted, the Omnipotent.'

Night 651

Morning now dawned and Shahrazad broke off from what she had been allowed to say. Then, when it was the six hundred and fifty-first night, SHE CONTINUED:

I have heard, O fortunate king, that when the *marids* had snatched Gharib and Sahim, they brought them to Mar'ash, king of the *jinn*. The king, in front of whom they had been placed, was seated on his royal throne. He was as large as a huge mountain and had four heads, one of a lion, another of an elephant, the third of a panther and the fourth of a lynx. 'O king,' said their captors, 'these are the two whom we found in the Valley of the Springs.' The king looked at them furiously, snorting, roaring and breathing out sparks of fire from his nose, so that all present were terrified. 'Human dogs,' he said, 'you killed my son and have lit a fire in my heart.' 'Who was this son of yours whom we killed, and who saw him?' asked Gharib, to which the king replied: 'Were not the two of you in the Valley of the Springs when you saw my son in the shape of a bird and shot an arrow at him, which brought about his death?'

'I don't know who killed him,' said Gharib, 'but I swear by the truth of the One Omnipotent and Eternal God, Who knows all things, and by the truth of Abraham, the Friend of God, that we saw no bird and killed neither bird nor beast.' When Mar'ash heard Gharib swearing by the greatness of God and by Abraham, His Friend, he realized that here was a Muslim, while he himself worshipped fire rather than the Omnipotent God. He shouted to his people: 'Fetch me my Lady!', at which they brought him a golden oven. They set this before him, lit its fire and threw aromatic drugs on to it, so that it produced green, blue and yellow flames, and the king and his attendants bowed down in worship before it. Meanwhile Gharib and Sahim were proclaiming the unity and greatness of God and testifying to His omnipotence. When Mar'ash looked up and saw that they were standing there and not prostrating themselves, he said to them: 'Dogs, why don't you bow down?' Gharib cursed them all and said: 'Prostration is only owed to the Worshipful King, Who brought all things from non-existence into existence. It is He Who brings water out of solid rock and Who fills the father's heart with tenderness towards his children. He is not to be described as either sitting or standing. He is the Lord of Noah, Salih, Hud and of Abraham, His Friend, the Creator of Paradise and the fire of hell, as well as of trees and fruits. He is the One God, the Omnipotent.'

When Mar'ash heard this, his eyes sank back into his head and he called to his attendants: 'Tie up these dogs and sacrifice them to my Lady.' Sahim and Gharib were bound and were about to be thrown into the fire when part of the cornice of the palace suddenly fell on to the oven, shattering it and putting out the fire, leaving nothing of it but ashes floating in the air. 'God is greater!' exclaimed Gharib. 'He brings aid and victory, while the unbelievers are abandoned. God is greater, and those who worship fire rather than Him in His omnipotence are forsaken.' 'You are a magician,' Mar'ash said. 'You have bewitched my Lady and caused this misfortune.' 'Madman,' Gharib told him, 'if the fire had an inner soul and the power of reason it would have protected itself from harm.' Hearing this, Mar'ash roared and raged, cursing the fire and saying: 'By the truth of my religion, it is in the fire and only in the fire that I shall have you killed.' So he ordered Gharib and Sahim to be held while a hundred *marids* were ordered to collect a huge quantity of firewood and to set light to it. They did this and a great fire blazed until dawn, when Mar'ash rode out, mounted on an elephant and seated on a golden throne studded with gems, surrounded by the various tribes of the *jinn*. Sahim and Gharib were now brought and, when they saw the blaze of the fire, they prayed for help from the One Omnipotent God, the Creator of night and day, the Mighty One, Who sees but is not seen, the Kind, the Omniscient. As they continued to call on Him, a cloud suddenly came up from the west, moving to the east, and from it came rain like a flooding sea, which put out the fire.

Mar'ash and his army were full of fear and went back to the palace, where the king turned to his vizier and his ministers of state and asked them what they thought about the two humans. 'Your majesty,' they told him, 'had they not been in the right, this would not have happened to the fire, and so we have to say that they are telling the truth.' Mar'ash agreed: 'The clear path of truth has been shown to me. Fire worship must be a false religion as, had the fire been a goddess, it would have protected itself from the rain that quenched it and the stone that smashed its oven, turning it into ashes. I myself now believe in the God Who created fire and light, shade and heat. What do you say?' 'We follow you and listen obediently,' they replied. The king then summoned Gharib and, when he was brought before him, the king embraced him and kissed him between the eyes, before welcoming Sahim in the same way. His guards crowded around the two men, kissing their hands and their heads.

Night 652

Morning now dawned and Shahrazad broke off from what she had been allowed to say. Then, when it was the six hundred and fifty-second night, SHE CONTINUED:

I have heard, O fortunate king, that when Mar'ash, king of the *jinn*, and his people were guided to Islam, he summoned Gharib and his brother Sahim and kissed them between the eyes. His men crowded around the two men, kissing their hands and their heads. The king took his seat on the royal throne, seating Gharib on his right and Sahim on his left, and he then asked Gharib what he had to say in order to become a Muslim. 'Say: "There is no god but the God of Abraham, the Friend of God,"' Gharib told him, and at that Mar'ash and his people accepted Islam with both hearts and tongues. Gharib stayed with them for some time teaching them how to pray, but then, remembering his own people, he heaved a sigh. 'Sorrow is over and joy and delight have come,' Mar'ash told him, but Gharib said: 'O king, I have many enemies and I am afraid that they will harm my people,' and he told the story of his dealings with his brother 'Ajib from beginning to end. Mar'ash promised to send someone to find out what was happening to the Muslims, adding that he would not allow Gharib to leave until he had seen him for long enough to satisfy him. He summoned two powerful *marids*, one named al-Kailajan and the other al-Qurajan, and when they had come and kissed the ground, he ordered them to go to Yemen to discover what was happening to the armies of Gharib and Sahim. 'To hear is to obey,' they said, before setting off to fly there.

So much for Gharib and Sahim, but as for the Muslims, they had mounted and ridden out with their leaders to pay their respects to Gharib in his palace, but the servants told them that the king and his brother had ridden away at dawn. So the leaders remounted and set off for the valleys and mountains, following the trail until they came to the Valley of the Springs, and there they found the equipment belonging to Gharib and Sahim lying on the ground and their horses grazing. 'By the glory of Abraham, the Friend of God!' they exclaimed. 'It was from here that the king went missing.' Then they scattered and spent three days investigating the valley and its mountains, but without finding any news. They began a period of mourning, but they also summoned scouts and told them to disperse through cities, fortresses and castles to look for news of Gharib. 'To hear is to obey,' the scouts replied, and so they split up, each making for a different region.

Word reached 'Ajib through his spies that his brother was lost and that nothing had been heard of him. He welcomed the news delightedly, and went to King Ya'rub ibn Qahtan, with whom he had taken refuge. This king now provided him with a force of two hundred thousand giant riders, with whom he marched off against the city of Oman. Al-Jamraqan and Sa'dan came out to fight, but after the Muslims had lost many men, they retreated into the city, shut the gates and strengthened the walls. It was at this point that al-Kailajan and al-Qurajan, the two *marids*, arrived to find the Muslims besieged. They waited until nightfall when they attacked the unbelievers with their two sharp *jinn* swords, each twelve cubits long, which would shatter any rock that they struck. As they charged, they cried: 'God is greater! Victory and triumph; may God abandon those who do not believe in the religion of Abraham, the Friend of God!' In the fury of their attack, with fire coming from their mouths and their nostrils, they killed great numbers of the unbelievers, who came out of their tents and, on seeing the astonishing things that were happening, shuddered and were driven out of their minds in their con-fusion. Then they caught up their weapons and began to attack one another, as the *marids* scythed through their necks, calling out: 'God is greater! We are the servants of King Gharib, the friend of Mar'ash, king of the *jinn*!' and they continued to strike with their swords until midnight. To the unbelievers it seemed as though all the mountains were full of *'ifrits*, and so they loaded their tents, baggage and possessions on camels in order to leave, the first to flee being 'Ajib.

Night 653

Morning now dawned and Shahrazad broke off from what she had been allowed to say. Then, when it was the six hundred and fifty-third night, SHE CONTINUED:

I have heard, O fortunate king, that the infidels tried to leave, with 'Ajib being the first to flee. The Muslims were astonished by what had happened and gathered together in fear of being attacked by the tribes of the *jinn*, while the two *marids* continued to pursue the fugitives until they had been scattered throughout the deserts. Only fifty thousand of the original two hundred thousand escaped to make their way home, defeated and wounded. Meanwhile the *marids* had told the Muslims: 'King Gharib, your lord, and his brother send you greetings. They are being entertained by Mar'ash, king of the *jinn*, but they will soon be with you.' The Muslims were overjoyed to hear that Gharib was well and they exclaimed: 'May God reward you for your good news, you noble spirits!' The *marids* returned and, on entering the palace, they found Gharib and Mar'ash sitting together and told them what had happened and what they had done. 'May God reward you,' they both replied, and Gharib was relieved of his anxiety.

Mar'ash then said: 'Brother, I want to show you our country and to let you see the city of Japheth, the son of Noah, upon whom be peace.' 'Do as you want,' replied Gharib, and Mar'ash called for horses. He mounted with Gharib and Sahim and, escorted by a thousand *marids*, they moved off like a segment cut lengthways from a mountain, travelling on, enjoying a view over valleys and mountains, until they came to Japheth's city, where the inhabitants, great and small, came out to meet Mar'ash. He entered in a great procession and then went up to Japheth's palace, where he took his seat on the royal throne of marble latticed with gold bars set at the top of ten steps and spread with all sorts of coloured silks. He addressed the townspeople as they stood before him and asked: 'Children of Japheth, son of Noah, what did your fathers and your fathers' fathers worship?' They told him: 'We found them worshipping fire and so we followed their example, but you know better about that.' 'O people,' he said, 'I have found that fire is merely one of the creations of Almighty God, Who created all things. When I realized that, I surrendered myself to the One Omnipotent God, the Creator of night and day and of the celestial sphere, Who sees but cannot be seen, the Kind and Omniscient. Accept Islam so that you may be saved from the anger of the Omnipotent and from the punishment of hellfire in the world to come.'

When they had all accepted this with hearts and tongues, Mar'ash took Gharib by the hand and showed him round Japheth's palace, with all its marvels. He went to the armoury to let him see Japheth's weapons, and Gharib, looking at a sword that hung on a golden peg, asked him to whom it belonged. Mar'ash told him: 'This was the sword of Japheth, Noah's son, which he used to fight against both men and *jinn*. It was forged by Jardum the wise, who inscribed on its back Great Names of God, and were it to strike a mountain, the mountain would be destroyed. Its name is al-Mahiq, and it kills anyone, man or *jinn*, on whom it falls.' When Gharib heard of its excellences, he said that he wanted to inspect it, and when Mar'ash told him to do what he wanted, he reached out and drew it from its sheath, as it gleamed and sparkled, with death creeping along its edge. It was twelve spans in length and three in breadth. Gharib wanted to take it, and Mar'ash said that, if he could deliver a blow with it, he could have it. Gharib agreed to this and took it in his hand, in which, to the astonishment of everyone present, both men and *jinn*, it became as light as a stick. 'Well done, prince of riders!' they exclaimed. 'Keep your hand on this treasure for which the kings of the earth long in vain,' Mar'ash told him, 'and mount so that I may show you more.'

Gharib and Mar'ash both mounted, and men and *jinn* alike walked in their train . . .

Night 654

Morning now dawned and Shahrazad broke off from what she had been
allowed to say. Then, when it was the six hundred and fifty-fourth night,
SHE CONTINUED:

I have heard, O fortunate king, that when Gharib and Mar'ash rode
out of the city of Japheth, men and *jinn* walked in their train between
empty palaces and houses and gilded streets and gates. When they had
gone out of the city gates, they looked around gardens with fruit trees
and running streams, where birds were singing to the glory of the
Almighty and Eternal God. They continued their tour until evening,
when they went back to spend the night in Japheth's palace. On their
arrival food was brought to them, and when they had eaten, Gharib
turned to Mar'ash and said: 'O king, I wish to go back to my people and
my troops as I don't know how they are doing without me.' 'Brother,'
said Mar'ash when he heard this, 'I don't want to lose you and I shall
not let you go for an entire month, so that I may enjoy your company
to the full.' Gharib could not disobey him and so stayed for a month in
Japheth's city. Then, at the end of a meal, Mar'ash presented him with
rare gifts, precious stones, jewels, emeralds, hyacinth gems, diamonds
and ingots of gold and silver, as well as musk, ambergris and pieces of silk
interwoven with gold. He gave two robes of ornamented gold brocade to
Gharib and Sahim, and for Gharib a crown had been made of inestimable
value, set with pearls and gems. All of this was packed into bags and
Mar'ash summoned five hundred *marids* and told them to be ready to
leave the next day in order to escort Gharib and Sahim back to their
own lands. 'To hear is to obey,' they said, and they all passed the night
with the intention of setting out on this journey. At dawn, however, the
land was filled with the noise of horses, drums and trumpets.

The newcomers were seventy thousand *marids* who could both fly and
dive under water. They were commanded by a king named Barqan and
there was a great and strange reason for his arrival which I shall tell in
due course by way of entertainment. This Barqan was the lord of the
Carnelian City and the Golden Palace, and he ruled over five towers,
each containing five hundred thousand *marids*. He and his people
worshipped fire rather than the Omnipotent King, and he himself was
Mar'ash's cousin. Among Mar'ash's people there was an infidel *marid*
who had falsely pretended to accept Islam and had then slipped away

from the rest and had gone to the Carnelian Valley, where he went to Barqan's palace. He kissed the ground before the king and prayed for the continuance of his glory and good fortune before telling him that Mar'ash had been converted to Islam. When Barqan heard the full account of this he snorted, roared and cursed the sun and moon, as well as the fire with its sparks. 'By the truth of my religion,' he swore, 'I shall kill my cousin and his people, together with this human, leaving no single one of them alive.' He summoned the *jinn* clans and chose seventy thousand *marids*, and travelled with them to the city of Jabarsa, which he surrounded, as we have already told. He himself dismounted in front of the city gate, where he pitched his tent.

Mar'ash called a *marid* and told him to go out and discover what the newcomers wanted before coming back quickly. This scout went to Barqan's camp, where the *marids* hurried up to him and asked him who he was and then, when he told them that he was a messenger from Mar'ash, they brought him before Barqan. He prostrated himself and said: 'My master has sent me to you to find out why you have come.' 'Go back to him,' Barqan said, 'and tell him that his cousin Barqan has come to greet him.'

Night 655

Morning now dawned and Shahrazad broke off from what she had been allowed to say. Then, when it was the six hundred and fifty-fifth night, SHE CONTINUED:

I have heard, O fortunate king, that Mar'ash's messenger came to Barqan and said: 'My master has sent me to you to find out why you have come.' 'Go back to him,' said Barqan, 'and tell him that his cousin Barqan has come to greet him.' The message was taken back to Mar'ash, who said to Gharib: 'Sit where you are until I greet my cousin and then come back to you.' He mounted and rode out to Barqan's camp, but this was a trick on Barqan's part in order to seize him when he came, for he had stationed his *marids* all around and told them: 'When you see me embrace him, take hold of him and bind him.' 'To hear is to obey,' they replied. When Mar'ash came and entered Barqan's pavilion, Barqan rose to meet him, but as they embraced, the *marids* rushed at him and tied him up. 'What is this?' Mar'ash said, looking at Barqan, and Barqan replied: '*Jinn* dog, are you abandoning your faith and the faith of your fathers and your forefathers to adopt a religion that you do not know?' 'Cousin,' Mar'ash replied, 'I have found that the religion of Abraham, the Friend of God, is the true faith and every other one is false.' 'Who told you that?' Barqan asked. 'Gharib, the king of Iraq,' Mar'ash told him, 'whom I have with me as a most honoured guest.' At this, Barqan swore: 'By the truth of fire, light, shade and heat, I shall kill you both,' after which he imprisoned Mar'ash.

When Mar'ash's servant saw what had happened to his master, he fled back to the city and brought the news to Mar'ash's clan. They cried out and mounted their horses. Gharib asked what was happening, and when they told him, he shouted to Sahim: 'Saddle me one of the two horses that Mar'ash gave me.' 'Are you going to fight against the *jinn*, brother?' Sahim asked, and Gharib replied: 'Yes, with the sword of Japheth, and I shall ask for help from the Lord of Abraham, the Friend of God, for He is Master and Creator of all things.' When Sahim had saddled him one of the *jinn* horses, a roan as big as a castle, he armed himself and rode out with the mail-clad clans of the *jinn*, while Barqan came out with his own followers. The battle ranks formed up and the first to challenge was Gharib, who rode to the battlefield drawing Japheth's sword. Its brilliant light dazzled the eyes of all the *jinn*, filling their hearts with fear, and Gharib astonished them as he brandished it, calling out: 'God is greater! I am Gharib, king of Iraq, and there is no religion but that of Abraham, the Friend of God.' When Barqan heard this, he exclaimed: 'This is the man who led my cousin to abandon and change his religion! I swear by the truth of my own faith that I shall never again sit on my throne until I have cut off his head and ended his life, after which I shall return my cousin and his people to their old beliefs, killing anyone who disobeys me.'

He mounted on an elephant, white as paper, like a lofty tower. He shouted at the beast and plunged an iron goad into its flesh, at which it trumpeted and carried him to the battlefield, where he rode up to Gharib. 'Human dog,' he cried, 'what took you to our land to corrupt my cousin and his people and cause them to change their religion? Know that this is your last day in this world.' When Gharib heard this, he said: 'Be off with you, least of the *jinn*,' and at that Barqan drew out a javelin, shook it and aimed it at Gharib. When the blow missed he threw a second javelin, but Gharib snatched it out of the air, shook it and then hurled it at the elephant. It pierced the beast from one side to the other and it fell down dead, while Barqan was flung off and lay like a lofty palm tree.

Gharib gave him no chance to move but struck him on the neck with
the flat of Japheth's sword, and as he lay unconscious the *marids* rushed
up and bound him. When his people saw this, they charged in an attempt
to free him, but Gharib and the Muslim *jinn* attacked in their turn.
Gharib's feats with his talismanic sword were enough to cure the sick
and to win the approval of God, Who answers prayer. Every blow he
struck cut through his enemy, whose soul was instantly reduced to ashes
in hellfire. The Muslim *jinn* shot fiery arrows at the infidels and as the
smoke spread, Gharib wheeled right and left, scattering them in front of
him. Flanked by al-Kailajan and al-Qurajan, he made his way to Barqan's
pavilion, where he shouted to the two of them to release their master,
which they did, breaking his fetters.

Night 656

Morning now dawned and Shahrazad broke off from what she had been
allowed to say. Then, when it was the six hundred and fifty-sixth night,
SHE CONTINUED:

I have heard, O fortunate king, that when Gharib called to al-Kailajan
and al-Qurajan to release their master, they did so, breaking his fetters.
Mar'ash then told the *marids* to fetch him his arms and armour as well
as his flying horse. He had two of these, one of which he had given to
Gharib, while the other he kept for himself. They brought the horse to
him, and after he had armed himself, he charged with Gharib, both their
horses soaring through the air, with their troops behind them. The two
of them were calling out: 'God is greater!' until the earth, the mountains,
the valleys and the hills re-echoed the cry. They killed huge numbers of
the infidel devils, more than thirty thousand of them, before they turned
back to Japheth's city, where they took their seats on their royal thrones.

They then ordered Barqan to be fetched, but he was nowhere to be
found. The reason for this was that, after having captured him, Gharib
and Mar'ash had been too busy fighting to think about him and as a
result one of his *'ifrit* servants got to him first, freed him and set off back
with him to his people, but when this *'ifrit* discovered that some of these
were dead and others in flight, he flew off with the king and set him
down in the Golden Palace of the Carnelian City. Here the king sat down
on his royal throne and the survivors of the slaughter came to him and
congratulated him on his safe return, but he said: 'Where is there safety?

My army has been slaughtered; I was captured and they have destroyed the respect in which I was held among the tribes of the *jinn*.' 'Your majesty,' they told him, 'kings are always both inflicting and suffering disasters,' but he said: 'I have to avenge myself and clear away my shame, or else I shall be an object of contempt among the *jinn*.' So he wrote letters and sent them to the *jinn* of the fortresses, who came in obedience to his summons. When he inspected them, he discovered that they totalled three hundred and twenty thousand giant *marids* and devils. They asked what he wanted and he told them to prepare for a journey in three days' time. 'To hear is to obey,' they replied.

So much for King Barqan, but as for Mar'ash, when he returned and failed to find Barqan, he was upset and said: 'Had we left a hundred *marids* to guard him, he would not have got away, but where can he go to escape us?' He then said to Gharib: 'Brother, Barqan is treacherous and will not fail to look for vengeance. He will certainly collect his clans and come against us, and so I propose to attack him while he is still weakened by his defeat.' Gharib agreed that there was no fault to be found in this sound plan, and Mar'ash went on to say: 'Allow the *marids* to take you to your own country and leave me to fight against the unbelievers so that my burden of sin may be lightened.' 'No!' exclaimed Gharib. 'I swear by the truth of the Merciful and Generous God, the Shelterer, I will not leave these lands until I have destroyed all the infidel *jinn*, whose souls God will hurry to hellfire, an evil resting place, and the only ones to escape will be those who worship the One Omnipotent God. Sahim, however, should be sent back to Oman to be cured' – for he had fallen ill.

Mar'ash summoned the *marids* and told them to carry Sahim, together with the wealth and gifts, to Oman. 'To hear is to obey,' they replied, and they then took up Sahim, together with the gifts, and set out for the lands of men. Mar'ash for his part sent letters to his fortresses and to all his governors, who answered his summons with a force of a hundred and sixty thousand *jinn*. When they had made their preparations, they set off for the Carnelian City and the Golden Palace, covering in a single day the distance of a year's journey. They halted to rest in a valley, where they spent the night, but then in the morning when they were about to set off again, the advance guard of Barqan's army appeared. The *jinn* shouted and the armies met in the valley, charging each other, killing and struggling furiously as the earth shook. Things went from bad to worse; seriousness replaced absurdity; there were no empty words; and as long lives were cut short, the infidels found themselves humiliated and in disorder. Gharib charged, proclaiming the unity of the One God, the Venerated and Exalted, cutting through necks and leaving heads rolling on the ground, so that before evening seventy thousand infidels had fallen. At that, drums sounded the recall and the two sides separated.

Night 657

Morning now dawned and Shahrazad broke off from what she had been allowed to say. Then, when it was the six hundred and fifty-seventh night, SHE CONTINUED:

I have heard, O fortunate king, that when the two sides drew away and separated, Mar'ash and Gharib, who had lost more than ten thousand *marids*, wiped their weapons clean and went to their tents, where food was brought and they ate, congratulating each other on their safety. For his part, Barqan went to his tent full of regret for his own losses and he said: 'My people, if we stay here and fight like this for three days, every last one of us will be killed.' 'What shall we do then, your majesty?' they asked him, and he replied: 'We shall attack them under cover of night while they are asleep, and we shall leave no single one to take back the news. So arm yourselves and attack your enemies in one concerted charge.' 'To hear is to obey,' they told him, and they made their preparations for an attack.

Among the unbelievers was a *marid* named Jandal, who was secretly inclined to accept Islam. When he saw what the others were intending to do, he slipped out and went to Mar'ash and Gharib to tell them of their plan. Mar'ash turned to Gharib for advice and Gharib told him that they themselves should launch a night attack of their own and scatter their enemies throughout the deserts, by the power of God, the Omnipotent. Mar'ash summoned the *jinn* leaders and said: 'You and your people must arm yourselves, and when night falls, file out on foot in companies of a hundred, one after the other, leaving the camp empty. Take cover among the hills and when you see that our enemies have penetrated among the tents, charge them resolutely from all sides, relying on your Lord. You will be victorious and I myself shall charge with you.'

When night fell the infidels attacked the Muslims' tents, calling on fire and light for help, but at that point the Muslims launched their own attack, calling for aid from the Lord of creation and shouting: 'Most

Merciful God, Creator of all things!' They mowed down their enemies and before morning came the infidels were lifeless corpses, with the survivors making for the deserts and torrent beds. Mar'ash and Gharib returned victorious thanks to God's aid, and, after the spoils of the unbelievers had been collected, they spent the rest of the night in camp before setting out in the morning for the Carnelian City and the Golden Palace.

As for Barqan, when the tide of battle turned against him and most of his army had fallen in the night, he turned in flight with those who were left. He reached the city and when he had entered the palace he gathered his clans and told them to take whatever they had there and meet him on Mount Qaf at the court of the Blue King, the Lord of the Piebald Castle, who would avenge them. So they took their womenfolk, their children and their wealth and made for the mountain. When Mar'ash and Gharib reached the city, they found the gates open with no one there to give them any news. Mar'ash then took Gharib to show him around. The foundations of the city walls were made of emeralds; the gate was of red carnelian with silver nails; while the roofs of the houses and the palaces were of aloes wood and sandalwood. They walked around the streets and lanes until they reached the Golden Palace and passed from hall to hall, finding them made of royal hyacinth gems, with emeralds and rubies instead of marble. When they went in, the two kings were struck with amazement at its beauty, and they went on from place to place until they had passed through seven halls. Then, when they got to the palace itself, they found four recessed rooms, no one of which resembled another, and in the middle of the palace was a fountain of red gold, above which stood statues of lions with water flowing from their mouths, as well as other astounding sights. The central room was furnished with carpets of coloured silk and in it were two thrones of red gold studded with pearls and gems, and here Mar'ash and Gharib took their seats on Barqan's throne, while their followers entered the Golden Palace in a great procession.

Night 658

Morning now dawned and Shahrazad broke off from what she had been allowed to say. Then, when it was the six hundred and fifty-eighth night, SHE CONTINUED:

I have heard, O fortunate king, that Mar'ash and Gharib took their seats on Barqan's throne and organized a great procession. Gharib now asked Mar'ash what his plans were, and Mar'ash told him that he had sent out a hundred riders to discover where Barqan had gone so that he might follow him. They waited in the Golden Palace for three days, after which the scouts returned with news that Barqan had gone to Mount Qaf and had asked for and received protection from the Blue King. 'What do you think, brother?' Mar'ash asked Gharib, and Gharib replied: 'If we don't attack them, they will attack us.' So the two of them ordered their troops to prepare to leave after three days. They had got ready and were about to go when the *marids* who had taken Sahim and the king's presents to Oman arrived and came to Gharib, kissing the ground in front of him. Gharib asked them about his people, and they said: 'After your brother 'Ajib fled from the battle, he went to Ya'rub ibn Qahtan and then made for India and approached its king, to whom he told his story and from whom he asked for and received protection. The king wrote to all his governors and collected an army like a flooding sea with no beginning and no end, and he intends to ravage Iraq.'

When Gharib heard this, he exclaimed: 'May the infidels perish! Almighty God will give victory to Islam, and I shall show them how to fight.' 'King of men,' said Mar'ash, 'I swear by the truth of the Greatest Name of God that I shall go with you to your kingdom, destroy your enemies and see that you get what you desire.' Gharib thanked him, after which they passed the night with the intention of moving out, and so when morning came they left on their way to Mount Qaf. A day's march later, they headed for the Piebald Castle and the Marble City, built of rock and marble and founded by Bariq ibn Faqi', the father of the *jinn*. It was he who had built the Piebald Castle, so called because it was constructed with alternate bricks of silver and gold, and it had no match in any other land.

When they were within half a day's march of the city, they halted to rest and Mar'ash sent out a scout to reconnoitre it. He went off and on his return he said: 'The city is full of *jinn*, as many as the leaves on the trees or the drops of rain.' Mar'ash asked Gharib for his advice, and Gharib said: 'O king, split your army into four divisions to surround the enemy and then let them shout: "God is greater!" before drawing back. This should be done at midnight, and then you will see what will happen among the tribes of the *jinn*.' So Mar'ash brought up his army and divided them as Gharib had advised. They armed themselves and waited until midnight, when they took up position around the enemy and raised the cry: 'God is greater! Oh for the religion of Abraham, the Friend of God, on whom be peace!' The infidels were roused up and startled by this and, grasping their weapons, they fell on one another and by daybreak most had been killed, with only a few surviving. Gharib then shouted to the Muslim *jinn* to charge those who were left, calling out: 'I am with you and God will give you the victory!' Mar'ash attacked together with Gharib, who unsheathed his *jinn* sword, al-Mahiq, cutting off noses, severing heads and routing the battle ranks. He got the better of Barqan and killed him with a blow, and when Barqan had fallen as a bloodstained corpse, he did the same to the Blue King. By morning, the infidels had been wiped out and not one of them was left to take back the news.

Mar'ash and Gharib entered the Piebald Castle, whose bricks were of silver and gold, with lintels of crystal and arches held in place by green emeralds. There was a fountain with tinkling bells, around which were spread silks embroidered with gold thread and set with jewels, and the kings found wealth that could neither be counted nor described. Next they entered the courtyard of the king's harem, which they found to be elegant and clean, and when Gharib looked at the women there he caught sight of a girl as lovely as any that he had ever seen, wearing a robe worth a thousand dinars. She was surrounded by a hundred slave girls who were holding up the skirts of her dress with hooks of gold, and she was like the moon among the stars. Gharib was astonished and bewildered at the sight of her, and he asked some of the slave girls who she was. They told him: 'This is Kaukab al-Sabah, the daughter of the Blue King.'

Night 659

Morning now dawned and Shahrazad broke off from what she had been allowed to say. Then, when it was the six hundred and fifty-ninth night, SHE CONTINUED:

I have heard, O fortunate king, that when Gharib asked some of the slave girls who the girl was, they told him: 'This is Kaukab al-Sabah, the daughter of the Blue King.' Gharib turned to Mar'ash and said: 'King of the *jinn*, I wish to marry this girl.' Mar'ash replied: 'This castle and all the wealth and people it contains are your spoils, for had it not been for

your scheme to destroy Barqan together with the Blue King and their
armies, they would have annihilated us. So the wealth is yours and the
people are your slaves.' Gharib thanked him for his courteous speech,
after which he went up to the girl, and the more carefully he looked at
her, the stronger became his love until he forgot Fakhr Taj, the daughter
of King Sabur, lord of the Persians, Turks and Dailamis, as well as
Mahdiya. The girl's mother had been the daughter of the king of China,
and the Blue King had snatched her from her castle and then deflowered
her. She had become pregnant and then given birth to the girl, whom,
because of her beauty and grace, she had named Kaukab al-Sabah,* the
mistress of beauties. Her mother had died when she was forty days old,
and she had been brought up by nurses and midwives until, when she
had reached the age of seventeen, the events took place that led to the
killing of her father, whom she had hated and whose death delighted
her. Gharib, filled with love, put his hand in hers and when he lay with
her that night he found her to be a virgin.

Gharib now ordered that the Piebald Castle be demolished and he
divided the spoils among the *jinn*, receiving as his own share twenty-one
thousand tiles of gold and silver, together with an untold quantity of
money and precious stones. Mar'ash then took him to inspect the marvels
of Mount Qaf before they returned to complete the demolition of the
Piebald Castle and the distribution of its wealth. They then returned to
Mar'ash's palace and after five days Gharib asked leave to return to his
own country. Mar'ash offered to accompany him, but Gharib said: 'No,
by the truth of Abraham, the Friend of God, I shall not put you to the
trouble and I shall not take any of your people except for al-Kailajan
and al-Qurajan.' Mar'ash pressed him to take ten thousand *jinn* riders
to serve him, and although Gharib repeated that he would only take the
two whom he had named, Mar'ash ordered a thousand *marids* to carry
Gharib's share of the spoils and to go back with him to his kingdom. At
the same time he told al-Kailajan and al-Qurajan to stay with him and
to follow his orders. 'To hear is to obey,' they replied.

At this point Gharib told the *marids* to carry Kaukab al-Sabah as well
as the treasure, while he himself was about to set off on his flying horse,
but Mar'ash told him: 'Brother, this horse can only live in our country
and if it goes to the lands of men, it will die.' He added: 'I have here a
sea horse, the like of which is not to be found in Iraq or throughout the

* Arabic for 'morning star'.

world.' He ordered it to be brought forward and when Gharib saw it in front of him, it took his breath away. They then hobbled it and al-Kailajan carried it while al-Qurajan brought what he could. Mar'ash embraced Gharib, shedding tears at having to part and saying: 'Brother, if anything happens to you that you cannot deal with, send for me and I shall come to you with an army that will lay waste to the earth and everything on it.' Gharib thanked him for his kindness and congratulated him on his conversion to Islam, after which the *marids* set off with him and the horse.

In the space of two days and one night they covered the distance of a fifty-year journey before approaching the city of Oman, close to which they halted in order to rest. Gharib then turned to al-Kailajan and told him to go and find news of his people. When he returned, he said: 'O king, your city is being attacked by an army of unbelievers like a flooding sea and your men are fighting them. They have sounded the war drums and al-Jamraqan has gone out to challenge the battlefield.' When he heard this, Gharib cried out: 'God is greater!' and he told al-Kailajan to saddle his horse and to fetch him his armour and his lance, adding: 'This is a day on which the true hero will overcome the coward on the field of battle.' Al-Kailajan did what he was told and Gharib armed himself, hanging Japheth's sword from his shoulder before mounting the sea horse and riding towards the armies. Al-Kailajan and al-Qurajan said: 'Do not disturb yourself, but let us go to the unbelievers and scatter them throughout the deserts, destroying all their settlements, so that no single one of them remains, with the help of God, the Exalted, the Almighty.' 'By the truth of Abraham, the Friend of God,' replied Gharib, 'I shall not let you fight until I am on horseback.'

There was a remarkable reason behind the arrival of the infidel army.

Night 660

Morning now dawned and Shahrazad broke off from what she had been allowed to say. Then, when it was the six hundred and sixtieth night, SHE CONTINUED:

I have heard, O fortunate king, that when Gharib had told al-Kailajan to go and find out what was happening to his people, he came back to say that his city was being attacked by a large army. When 'Ajib had gone with the troops of Ya'rub ibn Qahtan to besiege the Muslims, al-Jamraqan and Sa'dan had made a sally in which they were joined by al-Kailajan and al-Qurajan, and the unbelievers had been routed and 'Ajib had fled. He had then told his clansmen: 'If we go back to Ya'rub after his men have been killed, together with his own son, he will tell us that had it not been for us, this would not have happened, and he will kill every last one of us. I think that we should move to India and go to King Tarkanan, who will avenge us.' 'Take us there, may the fire bless you,' they said, and so they marched night and day until they reached the capital of India, where they asked for an audience with King Tarkanan. 'Ajib was allowed to enter and, after kissing the ground, he repeated the blessings that are customarily called down on kings, before saying: 'Your majesty, give me protection and may the fire with its sparks and the darkness with its gloom protect and guard you.' Tarkanan looked at him and asked: 'Who are you and what do you want?', to which he replied: 'I am 'Ajib, king of Iraq. My brother wronged me; he and his subjects have adopted the religion of Islam and he has won control over the lands, driving me from place to place. So now I have come to you, hoping that in your magnanimity you will grant me protection.'

When he heard what 'Ajib had to say, Tarkanan's anger was roused and he swore by the truth of the fire that he would both avenge 'Ajib and allow no one to worship anything but his goddess, the fire. He called for his son and told him: 'Prepare to go to Iraq to destroy everyone there. You are to tie up all those who do not worship fire, and torture them as an example to others. Instead of killing them, however, you are to bring them to me and I shall torment them in various ways, giving them the cup of humiliation to drain, before making an example of them to teach a lesson to all the people of this age.' To accompany the prince his father picked a force of eighty thousand horse, eighty thousand giraffe riders and ten thousand elephants, each with howdahs of sandalwood latticed with gold, whose plates and nails were made of silver and gold and which were covered with canopies of gold and emeralds. There were also war litters, each carrying eight men armed with various weapons. The prince himself was the champion of his age, unequalled in his bravery, his name being Ra'd Shah.

Ra'd Shah spent ten days in making his preparations and his army then set off like a storm cloud, arriving at Oman after a two-month march and surrounding the city, to the delight of 'Ajib, who was certain of victory. Al-Jamraqan, Sa'dan and all the Muslim champions came out to the battlefield as drums were beaten and horses neighed. Al-Kailajan looked down over this scene before going back to tell Gharib. Gharib, as we have said, mounted and rode among the infidels, waiting for a challenger to come out to begin the fight. Sa'dan the *ghul* came out to challenge and was met by an Indian champion, whom he instantly struck down with his mace, crushing his bones and leaving him stretched out on the ground. A second opponent was killed and a third overthrown, and Sa'dan continued to fight until he had killed thirty warriors. At this point he was faced by an Indian champion named Battash al-Aqran, the uncle of Tarkanan and the hero of the age, who was worth five thousand riders on the battlefield. 'Arab thief,' Battash cried, 'are you so proud of yourself that you dare kill the kings and champions of India and capture its riders? This is your last day on earth.' On hearing this, Sa'dan's eyes reddened; he charged at Battash and struck at him with his club, but the blow missed and, unbalanced by its force, Sa'dan fell to the ground. Before he could recover, he had been tied up and the Indians dragged him off to their camp.

Al-Jamraqan, seeing his comrade captured, cried out: 'Oh for the religion of Abraham, the Friend of God!' and, urging on his horse, he made for Battash. The two circled round each other for a while, but Battash then attacked, seized hold of al-Jamraqan's mail coat, pulled him from his saddle and threw him to the ground, after which the Indians tied him up and dragged him to their camp. Champion after champion came out to face Battash, until he had taken twenty-four leaders captive, to the great distress of the Muslims. On seeing this, Gharib drew from beneath his knee the golden mace of Barqan, king of the *jinn*, weighing a hundred and twenty *ratls*.

Night 661

Morning now dawned and Shahrazad broke off from what she had been allowed to say. Then, when it was the six hundred and sixty-first night, SHE CONTINUED:

I have heard, O fortunate king, that when Gharib saw what had happened to his champions, he drew the golden mace of Barqan, king of the *jinn*. At his prompting, the sea horse carrying him bounded on like a gust of wind, and when he had reached the centre of the field he shouted: 'God is greater! Victory and triumph; may God abandon those who reject the religion of Abraham, the Friend of God!' He charged against Battash and struck him to the ground with a blow from his mace. He then turned towards the Muslims and, seeing his brother Sahim there, he said: 'Tie up this dog.' Sahim rushed forward and after tying Battash tightly he took him off, leaving the Muslims to wonder at this display of prowess, while the unbelievers said to each other: 'Who is this rider who has come out from their ranks and captured our comrade?' While this was going on, Gharib was repeating his challenge and when another Indian leader came out to face him he struck him with his mace, stretching him out on the ground. Al-Kailajan and al-Qurajan tied him up and handed him over to Sahim, after which Gharib went on capturing champion after champion until by the end of the day he had taken fifty-two of the Indian leaders prisoner.

The drums then sounded the recall and Gharib left the field, making for the Muslim camp. The first to meet him was Sahim, who kissed his foot in his stirrup and exclaimed: 'May your hand never wither, champion of the age! Tell us who you are.' At that, Gharib lifted up the chain mail that screened his face and, on recognizing him, Sahim shouted out: 'Muslims, this is your lord and king, Gharib, who has come from the land of the *jinn*!' On hearing that, they jumped down from their horses and came up to him, kissing his feet in his stirrups and greeting him in delight at his safe return, before going back with him into the city. There he took his seat on the royal throne as his overjoyed people flocked around him. Food was produced and they ate, after which Gharib told them of all his experiences on Mount Qaf with the tribes of the *jinn*. They were filled with astonishment and gave thanks to God for his safety.

He then ordered them to go off to their beds, and when they had gone, only the *marids*, al-Kailajan and al-Qurajan, who had never left his side, remained with him. He asked them: 'Can you take me to Kufa so that I may enjoy the company of my womenfolk and then bring me back at the end of the night?' 'Master,' they told him, 'this is the easiest of requests.' The distance from Kufa to Oman is a sixty-day journey for a fast rider and al-Kailajan said to al-Qurajan: 'I shall carry him there and you can bring him back.' Al-Kailajan then carried Gharib with al-Qurajan flying beside him, and it was only an hour before they had reached Kufa and deposited Gharib by the palace door. He went in to see his uncle, al-Damigh, who rose at the sight of him and greeted him. 'How are my wives, Kaukab al-Sabah and Mahdiya?' Gharib asked, and al-Damigh assured him that they were both in good health. A eunuch went to tell the ladies of his arrival, at which they raised a cry of joy and rewarded the eunuch for his good news. When Gharib came in they rose to greet him and then, after some conversation, al-Damigh entered and Gharib astonished the three of them by telling of his experiences with the *jinn*.

For the rest of the night until nearly dawn Gharib slept with Kaukab al-Sabah. He then went out to the *marids* and, after saying goodbye to his family, his wives and his uncle, al-Damigh, he mounted on the back of al-Qurajan, with al-Kailajan flying alongside him. Before the darkness had cleared away he was back in the city of Oman, where he and his men armed themselves. He had ordered the city gates to be opened when a horseman rode up from the infidel army bringing with him al-Jamraqan, Sa'dan the *ghul* and the other captured Muslim leaders whom he had set free, and whom he now handed over to Gharib. The Muslims were delighted at their safe return and having armed themselves, they mounted and prepared for the fight as the war drums were beaten. For their part, the infidels rode out and formed up in their ranks.

Night 662

Morning now dawned and Shahrazad broke off from what she had been allowed to say. Then, when it was the six hundred and sixty-second night, SHE CONTINUED:

I have heard, O fortunate king, that when the Muslims had ridden out to the battlefield, the battle was opened by Gharib, who drew al-Mahiq, the sword of Japheth, and rode out between the ranks shouting: 'Those who recognize me know enough of the damage that I can do, and I tell those who do not know me that I am Gharib, king of Iraq and Yemen. I am Gharib, the brother of 'Ajib.' When Ra'd Shah, the son of the Indian king, heard this, he called to his commanders telling them to bring him 'Ajib, which they did. He then said: 'You know that this is your quarrel and you are responsible for it. It is your brother who is here on the field of battle; go out to meet him and bring him to me as a prisoner so that I may make an example of him by hanging him upside-down on a camel and taking him to India.' 'O king,' said 'Ajib, 'send someone else to fight him, as I am unwell this morning.' At this, Ra'd Shah snorted and roared and then said: 'I swear by the truth of the fire with its sparks, and by light, dark and heat, if you don't go out to meet your brother and fetch him to me quickly, I shall end your life by cutting off your head.'

'Ajib plucked up his courage and rode out, and when he approached Gharib he called out: 'Arab dog, vilest of all those who knock in tent pegs, do you dare to vie with kings? Take what is coming to you, for here is good news of your death.' 'What king are you?' said Gharib when he heard this, and 'Ajib replied: 'I am your brother, and this is your last day on earth.' When Gharib was certain that this was indeed 'Ajib, he shouted: 'Revenge for my father and mother!' He gave his sword to al-Kailajan before charging at 'Ajib and striking him so terrible a blow with his mace that he almost knocked out 'Ajib's ribs. He then seized him by the collar of his coat of mail and dragged him from his saddle, hurling him on to the ground. The *marids* then pounced on him, tied him tightly and led him away, abased and humiliated.

Gharib, in his delight at having captured his enemy, recited these lines:

I have achieved my goal; my distress is at an end;
To You, my Lord, be praise and thanks.
I grew up humble, poor and lowly,
But God has granted me my every wish.
I have taken the lands and overcome their peoples,
But were it not for You, my Lord, I would be nothing.

When Ra'd Shah saw the result of the duel between 'Ajib and his brother, he called for his horse, took up his weapons and armed himself, after which he rode out on to the field. When he came near Gharib he shouted: 'Wood carrier, vilest of the Arabs, have you become so mighty that you capture kings and champions? Dismount, allow your hands to be tied, kiss my foot and set free my champions. Then come with me in chains to my own kingdom, where I shall pardon you and appoint you as *shaikh* of our lands so that you can have a mouthful of bread to eat.' On hearing this, Gharib almost fell over laughing and then said: 'Mad dog, mangy wolf, you are about to see against whom fortune's wheel will turn.' He then called to Sahim to fetch him the prisoners, and when they had been brought he cut off their heads, at which Ra'd Shah set upon him with force and fury and the two of them continued to attack, retire and clash until as night fell the drums sounded the recall.

Night 663

Morning now dawned and Shahrazad broke off from what she had been allowed to say. Then, when it was the six hundred and sixty-third night, SHE CONTINUED:

I have heard, O fortunate king, that when the drums sounded the recall, both adversaries broke away from each other and retired to their own camps, where their men congratulated them on their safety. 'It is not like you to have to fight for so long,' the Muslims told Gharib, to which he replied: 'I have fought with many champions and chiefs, but I have never seen anyone who could strike better blows than this prince. I considered drawing Japheth's sword and killing him with a blow that would shatter his bones, but I delayed because I thought that I would take him prisoner and allow him to share in the faith of Islam.' So much for Gharib, but as for Ra'd Shah, when he went to his pavilion and took his seat on his throne, the Indian leaders came and asked him about his opponent. He said: 'I swear by the truth of the fire with its sparks that never in all my life have I seen a champion like this man, but tomorrow I shall capture him and lead him away humiliated and abased.' Next morning the war drums sounded and the armies prepared for battle; they hung their swords from their shoulders, raised their war cries, mounted their fine horses and rode out from their tents, until the whole land, with its hills, valleys and open plains, was filled with men.

The first to start the fight was King Gharib, the bold rider, the great lion, who rode to and fro challenging his enemies to come out to face him and calling: 'Let no idle weakling come out to face me today.' Before the words were out of his mouth, Ra'd Shah appeared, mounted on an elephant that looked like a huge dome, on whose back was a howdah secured by bands of silk, with its mahout perched between its ears. This man carried a prong in his hand with which he would strike the elephant to make it swing to the right or the left. When it came close to Gharib's horse, the horse shied away at the sight of a creature that it had never seen before and Gharib dismounted; leaving his horse in the care of al-Kailajan, Gharib drew his sword al-Mahiq and advanced on foot towards Ra'd Shah until he was in front of the elephant. It had been Ra'd Shah's custom when he found himself overmatched by any champion to take with him on his howdah something called a lasso, this being a species of net, wide at the bottom and narrow at the top, with rings fastened to its lower end through which passed a silken cord. He would make for his opponent and his horse, cover them with the net and then pull the cord. The rider would be unseated and Ra'd Shah, who had won many victories in this way, would take him prisoner. When Gharib approached, Ra'd Shah lifted up the net he was holding and threw it so that it spread out over him and then pulled him up on to the elephant's back. He then shouted to the elephant to take him back to his army. Al-Kailajan and al-Qurajan had not left Gharib, and when they saw what had happened to him they seized hold of the elephant while Gharib himself struggled in the net until he had torn through it. The *marids* then attacked Ra'd Shah, tied him up with a fibre rope and led him off. The two armies then charged each other like the meeting of twin seas or two mountains clashing, while the dust rose up into the sky. The fighters were blinded in the fury of the fight; blood flowed and the battle continued to rage with no shortage of cuts and thrusts until, when night fell, drums sounded the recall and both sides separated.

Of the Muslims who were present that day, many were killed and most were wounded, thanks to those of the enemy who were riding on elephants and giraffes. Gharib found this hard to bear and after he had given orders for the wounded to be treated, he turned to his commanders and asked them for their advice. 'O king,' they told him, 'the elephants and the giraffes are the cause of the trouble, and if we could be safe from them we would have the upper hand.' Al-Kailajan and al-Qurajan said: 'We shall draw our swords, attack the enemy and kill most of them,' but at that point one of al-Jaland's Omani counsellors came forward and guaranteed to deal with the Indian army if Gharib obediently followed his advice. Gharib turned to his commanders and told them to follow whatever instructions this expert gave them. 'To hear is to obey,' they replied.

Night 664

Morning now dawned and Shahrazad broke off from what she had been allowed to say. Then, when it was the six hundred and sixty-fourth night, SHE CONTINUED:

I have heard, O fortunate king, that Gharib told his commanders that they were to follow whatever instructions this expert gave them. The man picked out ten of them and asked them what force they had, to which they replied that they had ten thousand men. He then took them to the treasury, where he armed five thousand of them with muskets and taught them how to shoot. When dawn broke, the infidels made their preparations; their fully armed infantry were preceded by the beasts, elephants and giraffes, carrying their own fighting men. Gharib came out with his champions; the ranks were drawn up and, to the sound of the drums, the commanders advanced as the beasts moved forwards. At this point the Omani shouted to the marksmen, who busied themselves with their arrows and their leaden bullets before loosing off a volley. The shot penetrated the ribs of the beasts, who screamed and turned on the Indian champions and their infantry, crushing them underfoot. The Muslims then charged, encircling the Indians from left to right as the elephants trampled them, scattering them throughout the open plains. The Muslims pursued them with their Indian swords and only a few of the elephants and giraffes escaped.

Gharib and his men went back delighted by their victory, and the next morning the spoils were distributed. After a pause of five days Gharib took his seat on his royal throne and sent for his brother 'Ajib. 'Dog,' he said to him, 'why do you collect kings to oppose me, when it is the Omnipotent God Who aids me against you? If you accept Islam, you will be saved, and because of that I shall not avenge my father and mother on you but will restore you to your throne and subordinate myself to you.' 'Ajib, however, when he heard what his brother had to say, insisted that he would never abandon his religion and was put in irons with a hundred strong slaves to guard him. Gharib then turned to Ra'd Shah and asked him what he had to say about Islam, to which he replied: 'Master, I will accept your religion, for were it not fine and true, you would never have defeated us. If you stretch out your hand, I shall bear witness that there is no god but God and that Abraham, His Friend, is the apostle of God.' Gharib was pleased by his conversion and asked him whether the sweetness of faith was firmly fixed in his heart. When Ra'd Shah replied that it was, Gharib asked whether he would go back to his own lands. 'O king,' Ra'd Shah answered, 'my father will kill me for having abandoned his religion.' 'I shall come with you,' Gharib told him, 'and with the help of God, the Generous, the Bountiful, I shall establish you as king so that the lands and the people obey you,' at which Ra'd Shah kissed his hands and feet.

The Omani whose advice had led to the rout of the Indians now received great quantities of wealth as a reward, and Gharib then sum-

moned al-Kailajan and al-Qurajan, telling them, when they had answered
the summons, to carry him to India. 'To hear is to obey,' they said.
Gharib took with him al-Jamraqan and Sa'dan, who were carried by
al-Qurajan, while al-Kailajan carried Gharib himself together with Ra'd
Shah. The *marids* then set off for India . . .

Night 665

Morning now dawned and Shahrazad broke off from what she had been
allowed to say. Then, when it was the six hundred and sixty-fifth night,
SHE CONTINUED:

I have heard, O fortunate king, that Gharib, al-Jamraqan, Sa'dan the
ghul and Ra'd Shah were carried by the *marids*, who set off for India,
leaving at sunset and arriving in Kashmir before the night had ended.
Gharib and his party were landed in the palace and set off down the
stairs. King Tarkanan had heard from fugitives of the fate of his son and
of his army; he had been told that they were in great distress and that
his son could neither sleep nor find enjoyment in anything. Tarkanan
was brooding about this when suddenly in came a group of people
among whom he was astonished to see his son. He was alarmed by the
marids and Ra'd Shah turned to him and said: 'Where can you go, you
treacherous fire worshipper? Damn you, abandon this religion of yours
and worship the Omnipotent King, the Creator of night and day, the
Invisible Lord.' Tarkanan had with him an iron mace, which he now
hurled at his son, but it missed and struck a pillar, demolishing three
stones. 'Dog,' he then said, 'you have destroyed my armies, abandoned
your faith and now come to make me abandon mine.' At that Gharib
went up to him and struck his neck, knocking him down. Al-Kailajan
and al-Qurajan tied him up securely, as all his women fled.

Gharib took his seat on the royal throne and told Ra'd Shah to deal
with his father's case. 'Misguided old man,' said Ra'd Shah to Tarkanan,
'accept Islam and you will be saved from hellfire and from the anger of
the Omnipotent God.' 'I shall die as a fire worshipper and nothing else,'
his father replied, and at that Gharib drew his sword, al-Mahiq, and
struck him a blow that cut him in two, as God hastened his soul to the
fire, an evil resting place. On Gharib's orders his corpse was fastened to
the palace gate, half on the right and half on the left, and then at the end
of the day Gharib told Ra'd Shah to put on the royal robes. When he

had done this he sat down on his father's throne with Gharib on his right, while al-Kailajan and al-Qurajan, together with al-Jamraqan and Sa'dan the *ghul*, stood on his right and his left. Gharib instructed them to bind every king who entered and to allow no leader to escape. 'To hear is to obey,' they replied.

After this, when the leaders arrived, they came to the palace to present their respects. The first to come was the commander-in-chief, who was amazed and astonished to see the two halves of Tarkanan's body fastened to the gate. Al-Kailajan attacked him, and pulled him to the ground by his collar before tying him up and dragging him into the palace, where he was kept in chains. By the time the sun rose, a total of three hundred and fifty had been tied up by al-Kailajan, who then brought them before Gharib. Gharib asked them whether they had seen the body of their king fastened to the gate, and when they asked who had done that he told them: 'It was I who did this with the help of Almighty God and I shall do the same to anyone who disobeys me.' 'What do you want from us?' they said, to which he replied: 'I am Gharib, the king of Iraq, who destroyed your champions. Ra'd Shah has adopted the religion of Islam and has become a great king with authority over you. Accept Islam and you will be safe, whereas if you disobey me you will regret it.' At this they recited the confession of faith and were inscribed in the roll of the blessed. 'Has the sweetness of faith truly entered into your hearts?' Gharib asked, and when they said that it had, he ordered them to be released. He then presented them with robes of honour and told them to go to their people and offer them conversion to Islam, sparing those who accepted and killing those who refused.

Night 666

Morning now dawned and Shahrazad broke off from what she had been allowed to say. Then, when it was the six hundred and sixty-sixth night, SHE CONTINUED:

I have heard, O fortunate king, that Gharib told Ra'd Shah's men to go to their people and offer them conversion to Islam. If they accepted, they were to be spared, while if they refused they were to be killed. They left and, after having collected all those over whom they had authority, they told them what had happened, before offering them conversion to Islam. Only a few refused and these were killed, after which the news was given to Gharib. He, for his part, praised Almighty God, exclaiming: 'Praise be to God, Who has allowed us to bring this about easily and without fighting!' He then stayed in Kashmir for forty days until he had smoothed out difficulties and destroyed the fire temples and other places of worship, building mosques in their place. In the meanwhile Ra'd Shah had packed up for him an indescribable quantity of rare gifts, which he sent off by sea, and then Gharib mounted on the back of al-Kailajan and Sa'dan, with al-Jamraqan, on that of al-Qurajan. When they had said goodbye, they set off and travelled through the night, reaching Oman by dawn, where they were met by the Muslims, who greeted them joyfully. Gharib then went on to Kufa and when he reached the gate he ordered his brother 'Ajib to be brought out and sentenced him to be crucified. Sahim fetched iron hooks, which were attached to the tendons of 'Ajib's heels, and he was hung up on the gate before being shot full of arrows on Gharib's orders until he had become like a hedgehog.

Gharib then entered Kufa and entered his palace, where he took his seat on his royal throne and dealt with affairs of state until nightfall, when he went to his harem, where the slave girls congratulated him on his safe return and Kaukab al-Sabah rose to embrace him. He spent the night with her and in the morning, after rising to perform the morning prayer after the ritual ablution, he again took his seat on the throne. Preparations were now begun for his marriage to Mahdiya, involving the slaughter of three thousand sheep, two thousand cattle, a thousand goats and five hundred camels, together with four thousand chickens, a large number of ducks and five hundred horses. No such an Islamic wedding had ever been seen before, and at the end of it Gharib lay with Mahdiya and took her maidenhead. He stayed for ten days in Kufa, after which he recommended to his uncle that he treat his subjects justly and left, taking with him his womenfolk and his champions. He went to meet the Indian treasure ships, all of whose contents were distributed to the army, enriching its champions, and the march continued until they arrived at the city of Babel. Here Gharib gave a robe of honour to his brother Sahim and appointed him as its ruler.

Night 667

Morning now dawned and Shahrazad broke off from what she had been allowed to say. Then, when it was the six hundred and sixty-seventh night, SHE CONTINUED:

I have heard, O fortunate king, that Gharib gave a robe of honour to his brother Sahim and appointed him as governor of Babel. After another ten-day pause, Gharib moved on with his men to the castle of Sa'dan the *ghul*, where they rested for five days. He then told al-Kailajan and al-Qurajan to go to Isbanir and enter the royal palace to find news of Fakhr Taj and to fetch him one of the king's relatives to tell him what had been happening. 'To hear is to obey,' they said, after which they set off for Isbanir, but as they were flying between heaven and earth they caught sight of an enormous army like a flooding sea. Al-Kailajan suggested to al-Qurajan that they go down to investigate, and when they did and walked among the soldiers they discovered that these were Persians. They asked some of them what the army was and where it was going and were told: 'We are going to kill Gharib and everyone who is with him.' On hearing this the *marids* went to the pavilion of the army commander, whose name was Rustam, where they waited until the Persians were asleep on their couches and Rustam was sleeping on his throne. They then carried him off, throne and all, leaving the Persian fortifications and arriving before midnight at Gharib's camp.

They went to the entrance of his pavilion and asked permission to enter. When Gharib heard, he sat up and told them to come in, at which they brought in the throne with Rustam asleep on it. 'Who is this?' Gharib asked, and they told him: 'He is a Persian king who has brought a huge army with the intention of killing you and your people. We carried him here so that he might tell you whatever you want to know.' On Gharib's instructions they then fetched a hundred champions who were told to draw their swords and to stand by Rustam's head. When that had been done they roused Rustam, who, on opening his eyes, found a dome of swords above his head. He closed them again, exclaiming: 'What is this nightmare?' but when al-Kailajan pricked him with his sword point, he sat up and asked: 'Where am I?' Al-Kailajan replied: 'You are in the presence of King Gharib, the son-in-law of the king of the Persians. What is your name and where are you going?' When Rustam heard Gharib's name, he wondered to himself whether he was awake or sleeping, but Sahim struck him and said: 'Why don't you answer?'

Rustam raised his head and said: 'Who brought me from my tent, where I was among my own men?' 'These two *marids* brought you,' Gharib told him, and when he looked at them he soiled his trousers as they advanced on him, baring their teeth and drawing their swords. 'Come and kiss the ground in front of King Gharib,' they told him, and in his terror, realizing that he was not asleep, he stood up and kissed the ground, exclaiming: 'May the fire bless you and may your life be long!' 'Persian dog,' replied Gharib, 'fire is not to be worshipped, as it does no harm and no good except to food.' 'Who, then, is to be worshipped?' Rustam asked, and Gharib replied: 'The object of worship is the God Who created you and formed you and created the heavens and the earth.' 'What do I have to say in order to become one of the followers of that God and to enter into your religion?' asked Rustam. Gharib told him: 'Say: "There is no god but the God of Abraham, the Friend of God."' Rustam then recited the confession of faith and was inscribed in the roll of the blessed.

Rustam now told Gharib: 'Master, your father-in-law, King Sabur, wants to have you killed and he has sent me with an army of a hundred thousand men to destroy you and your followers to the last man.' 'Is this the way that he repays me for having saved his daughter from captivity or death?' Gharib exclaimed, adding: 'God will requite him for harbouring such malice.' He then asked Rustam his name, and when Rustam told him, saying that he was Sabur's commander-in-chief, Gharib told him that he would put him in command of his own force. He then asked after Princess Fakhr Taj, to which Rustam replied with a prayer for Gharib's life. Gharib, understanding this, asked how she had come to die and Rustam said: 'When you went off to your brother, a slave girl went to your father-in-law and asked whether he had told you to sleep with her mistress, Fakhr Taj. "No, by the truth of the fire," he replied and, drawing his sword, he went to her and said: "You wicked woman, how did you come to let this Bedouin sleep with you with no bride price or any proper wedding?" "It was you who allowed him to do that, father," she replied. "Was he intimate with you?" Sabur asked, and when she said nothing but bowed her head towards the ground, he shouted to the midwives and the slave girls: "Tie up this whore and inspect her vagina." They did this and they reported that she had lost her maidenhead. He then rushed at her and was about to kill her, but her mother got up and stopped him, saying: "Don't kill her lest this bring dishonour on you but shut her up in a cell until she dies." He did this but then, when night fell, he sent two of his close companions, telling them to take her away and throw her into the river Jaihun without telling anyone about what they had done. They followed his orders and no one heard any more of her, as her time was past.'

Night 668

Morning now dawned and Shahrazad broke off from what she had been allowed to say. Then, when it was the six hundred and sixty-eighth night, SHE CONTINUED:

I have heard, O fortunate king, that when Gharib asked about Fakhr Taj, Rustam told him that her father had had her drowned. When Gharib heard this story, everything went black for him; his mood darkened and he said: 'I swear by the truth of the Friend of God that I shall march on this dog, destroy him and ravage his lands.' He sent messages to al-Jamraqan and to the lords of Mayyafariqin and of Mosul, before turning to Rustam and asking him how many men he had. 'A hundred thousand Persian riders,' Rustam replied, at which Gharib told him to take ten thousand Muslims and go to occupy the attention of the Persians by attacking them, saying that he himself would follow on his heels. Rustam mounted and moved off towards the Persian army with his ten thousand, saying to himself: 'I shall do something that will establish my reputation with King Gharib.' After a seven-day march, he had come to within half a day's journey of the Persians. He divided his men into four divisions and told them to circle round the Persians and then attack. 'To hear is to obey,' they said. They rode from evening and by midnight they were in position. Since the loss of Rustam the Persians had been staying peacefully in their camp, and when the Muslims attacked, with their cry of 'God is greater!' they started from their sleep as the swords played among them and they slipped and stumbled. They faced the anger of the Omniscient God, and Rustam raged among them like fire in dry wood so that by the end of the night they were all either killed, wounded or in flight, while the Muslims took their baggage, tents, pay chests, horses and camels as plunder.

The Muslims then rested in the Persian tents until Gharib arrived. When he saw how Rustam had planned the destruction of the Persians and the defeat of their army, he presented him with a robe of honour and said: 'As it was you who broke the Persians, all the spoils are yours.' Rustam kissed his hand and thanked him, after which the army rested that day before setting off to march against King Sabur.

The defeated survivors came into Sabur's presence complaining of the huge catastrophe that they had suffered. Sabur asked how this had happened and who was responsible for it. They told him that they had been attacked by night, and when he asked who had attacked them they told him that this had been his own commander-in-chief, who had converted to Islam, and that Gharib himself had not got there. When Sabur heard his, he hurled his crown to the ground, exclaiming: 'We are now worthless!' Then he turned to his son, Ward Shah, and said: 'My son, there is no one who can deal with this affair except you.' 'Father,' replied the prince, 'I swear by your life that I shall bring you Gharib and the leaders of his people in chains and I shall destroy all his followers.'

The prince then mustered his army and found that he had two hundred and twenty thousand men. They spent the night with the intention of setting off the next day, but when dawn broke and they were about to leave, they were confronted by a dust cloud that spread throughout the sky, blocking sight. King Sabur had ridden out to say goodbye to his son, but when he saw the size of the cloud he ordered a scout to find out what it meant. The scout left and on his return he said: 'Master, Gharib and his champions have come.' At that, the baggage was unloaded and the battle ranks drawn up.

When Gharib arrived at Isbanir and saw that the Persians were intent on fighting, he urged his men to charge, calling down God's blessing on them. Standards were waved, Persians and Arabs clashed in a general mêlée and blood flowed in streams. As men looked death in the face, the brave advanced while cowards turned in flight, and the fighting continued throughout the day, until drums sounded the recall and both sides disengaged. Sabur ordered his camp to be pitched by the city gate, while Gharib set up his own camp opposite that of the Persians. Every man then retired to his tent.

Night 669

Morning now dawned and Shahrazad broke off from what she had been allowed to say. Then, when it was the six hundred and sixty-ninth night, SHE CONTINUED:

I have heard, O fortunate king, that when the armies of Sabur and Gharib disengaged, every man retired to his tent. The next morning they mounted their splendid horses, and after having armed themselves and taken up their lances they raised their battle cries and the lordly champions advanced like bold lions.

The first to start the battle was Rustam, who rode to the middle of the field calling out: 'I am Rustam, leader of the champions of the Arabs and the Persians. Who will come out to fight? Let no idle weakling challenge me today.' Tuman came out from the Persian side, and the two charged each other attacking ferociously, but Rustam, dashing at his opponent, struck him a blow with his mace, which weighed seventy *ratls*, driving his head down into his chest and leaving him dead on the ground, weltering in his blood. This distressed Sabur, who ordered his troops to charge the Muslims, which they did, calling on the bright sun for help, while the Muslims called on the Omnipotent King. The Persians outnumbered them and were inflicting losses on them when Gharib shouted and advanced resolutely, drawing Japheth's sword, al-Mahiq, and charging with al-Kailajan and al-Qurajan at his stirrups. He fought his way on with his sword until he reached Sabur's standard-bearer, whom he struck on the head with the flat of his sword, knocking him to the ground unconscious, and the *marids* then carried him off to the Muslim camp. When the Persians saw the fall of the standard, they turned in flight to the city gates, pursued all the way by the Muslims with their swords. In the crush at the gates many died, and the gates themselves could not be closed. The Persians who tried to pass through were attacked by Rustam together with al-Jamraqan, Sa'dan, Sahim, al-Damigh, al-Kailajan, al-Qurajan and all the Muslim champions and their riders. They called out: 'Quarter! quarter!' and when the Muslims stopped fighting, they threw down their arms and equipment and were led like sheep to Gharib's camp.

Gharib himself had returned to his pavilion, where he removed his weapons and put on his state robes after having washed off the blood of the infidels. When he had taken his seat on his throne, he called for

Sabur, who was brought before him. 'Persian dog,' he cried, 'what led you to do what you did with your daughter? Why did you think that I would not make her a suitable husband?' 'O king,' said Sabur, 'don't blame me for what I did, as I have repented and I only came out to fight you because I was afraid of you.' When Gharib heard that, he ordered Sabur to be laid on his back and beaten, and the beating continued until he could groan no more, after which he was put with the prisoners. The Persians were then summoned and offered conversion to Islam, at which a hundred and twenty thousand were converted and the rest put to the sword. All the inhabitants of the city accepted Islam and Gharib entered in a great procession to take his seat on Sabur's throne, after which he conferred robes of honour, gave gifts and distributed the spoils and the gold, winning the affection of the Persians by including them in the distribution, so that they prayed for his victory, glory and long life.

The mother of Fakhr Taj then began to mourn her daughter's memory and the palace was filled with shrieks and cries. On hearing this, Gharib went to see what the matter was and Fakhr Taj's mother came up to him and said: 'Sir, when you came, I thought of my daughter and said to myself that, had she been alive, your coming would have made her happy.' This moved Gharib to tears and after taking his seat he called for Sabur, who was brought shuffling in chains. 'Persian dog,' said Gharib, 'what did you do to your daughter?' 'I gave her to two of my men,' Sabur replied, 'and told them to drown her in the Jaihun.' The two were called before Gharib and asked whether this was true. 'Yes,' they said, adding, 'but we didn't drown her, your majesty, as we had pity on her and so we set her free on the bank of the Jaihun, telling her: "Save yourself but don't come back to the city or else your father will kill you and kill us as well." This is what we did.'

Night 670

Morning now dawned and Shahrazad broke off from what she had been allowed to say. Then, when it was the six hundred and seventieth night, SHE CONTINUED:

I have heard, O fortunate king, that the two men told Gharib about Fakhr Taj, telling him that they had left her on the bank of the Jaihun. When Gharib heard this, he summoned the astrologers and, when they had come, he told them to use the divination table to discover whether

Fakhr Taj was alive or dead. After investigating, they reported: 'King of the age, we have seen that the princess is still alive and has given birth to a son. Both of them are with a band of *jinn*, but her absence from you will last for twenty years.' They then asked for how long he had been on his travels and, when he counted this up, he found that he had been away for eight years. 'There is no might and no power except with God, the Exalted, the Omnipotent!' he exclaimed.

Messengers were now sent to all the castles and fortresses in Sabur's realm and the governors obediently answered the summons. Then, when Gharib was sitting in his castle, he saw a dust cloud rising to darken the skies and after summoning al-Kailajan and al-Qurajan, he told them to find out what it meant. They went off and, after penetrating the cloud, they snatched up a rider and brought him before Gharib, saying: 'Ask this man, as he is from the army that is coming.' Gharib asked whose army it was and the man told him: 'Your majesty, this is Khirad Shah, king of Shiraz, who has come to fight you.' The reason for this was that after the outcome of the battle between Sabur and Gharib, Sabur's son had fled to the city of Shiraz with the remnant of his father's army, where he entered into the presence of its king, Khirad Shah, kissing the ground before him with tears running down his cheeks. 'Raise your head, young man, and tell me what makes you weep,' the king said. The prince replied: 'Your majesty, an Arab king called Gharib has appeared and has seized my father's realm, killing and bringing destruction on the Persians.'

When Khirad Shah had been told the whole story of Gharib's attack from beginning to end, he asked: 'Is all well with my promised wife, Fakhr Taj?' 'Gharib has taken her,' the prince said, and at that Khirad Shah exclaimed: 'I swear by my life that I shall leave no Bedouin or Muslim alive on the face of the earth!' He wrote messages and sent them to his lieutenants, who mustered an army numbering eighty-five thousand men. He opened his armouries and distributed coats of mail and weapons to them, before setting out with them for Isbanir, where they all halted before the city gate. Al-Kailajan and al-Qurajan came forward, kissed Gharib's stirrup, and said: 'Master, to satisfy us, leave this army to us.' 'Do what you want with them,' replied Gharib, and at that the *marids* flew to Khirad Shah's pavilion, where they found him seated on his throne, with Sabur's son sitting at his right hand and his leaders surrounding him in two ranks, discussing how to kill the Muslims. Al-Kailajan snatched up the son of Sabur while Khirad Shah was seized by al-Qurajan and they were brought to Gharib, who had them beaten until they lost consciousness. The *marids* returned and after having drawn their swords, which no man could carry, they set about the unbelievers, whose souls God hastened to hellfire, an evil resting place. All that could be seen were two gleaming blades scything down men like corn, with no swordsmen visible. The unbelievers abandoned their tents and rode off without waiting to saddle their horses, pursued for two days by the *marids*, who killed them in huge numbers before returning to Gharib, whose hand they kissed. He thanked them for what they had done and told them that the spoils were theirs alone and were not to be shared by anyone else. They left, calling down blessings on him, and after having collected the plunder they went back to their own lands to rest. So much for Gharib and his Muslims.

Night 671

Morning now dawned and Shahrazad broke off from what she had been allowed to say. Then, when it was the six hundred and seventy-first night, SHE CONTINUED:

I have heard, O fortunate king, that after the rout of Khirad Shah's army, Gharib told al-Kailajan and al-Qurajan to take the spoils, in which no one else was to share. They collected these and retired to their own lands.

As for the unbelievers, they did not halt in their flight until they reached Shiraz, where they held a period of mourning for their dead. King Khirad Shah had a brother called Siran the sorcerer, who was unsurpassed in his age as a magician. He lived apart from his brother in a castle surrounded by woods and streams, with birds and flowers, half a day's journey from Shiraz. The fugitives went there and came into his presence, weeping and wailing. When he asked why this was, they told him what had happened and how Khirad Shah and Sabur's son had been snatched away by the *marids*. When Siran heard this, light turned to darkness in his eyes and he exclaimed: 'I swear by the truth of my religion that I shall kill Gharib and his men, ravage their lands and leave no one behind to tell the tale.' He then recited a spell to summon the Red King, and when he had come, he ordered him to go to Isbanir and attack Gharib as he sat on his throne. 'To hear is to obey,' the Red King replied. He went to Isbanir, but when Gharib caught sight of him, he drew his sword, al-Mahiq, and attacked him, supported by al-Kailajan and al-Qurajan, who charged at his army killing five hundred and thirty of them and seriously wounding the Red King himself. He turned back in flight and his wounded followers fled back to Siran's castle, which was known as the Castle of the Fruits. They entered Siran's presence wailing and lamenting and said: 'Wise magician, Gharib has with him the talismanic sword of Japheth, son of Noah, which destroys all whom it strikes, and he has also got two *marids* from Mount Qaf, given to him by King Mar'ash. It was he who killed Barqan when he went to Mount Qaf, and he also killed the Blue King, as well as many other *jinn*.'

When Siran heard this he dismissed the Red King, who went off on his way, while he himself cast a spell and summoned a *marid* named Zu'azi', to whom he gave a dirham's weight of volatile *banj*. 'Go to Isbanir,' he told him, 'and make for Gharib's palace in the shape of a sparrow. Wait until he falls asleep and there is no one else there; then take the *banj* and put it into his nostrils, after which you are to bring him to me.' 'To hear is to obey,' said the *marid*, who then went off to Isbanir and came to the palace in the shape of a sparrow. He perched on one of the windows and waited until nightfall, when the other kings retired to their beds and Gharib fell asleep. At that point he came down, and bringing out the powdered *banj* he sprinkled it in Gharib's nostrils. Then he wrapped the unconscious king in a sheet from his bed and flew off with him like a storm wind. It was not yet midnight when he reached the Castle of the Fruits, where he brought Gharib to Siran. Siran thanked him for what he had done and was about to kill Gharib while he still lay drugged, when one of his men restrained him and said: 'Wise magician, if you kill him, the *jinn* will destroy our lands, for his friend, King Mar'ash, will attack us with all the '*ifrits* that he has.' 'What should we do with him, then?' asked Siran, and the man replied: 'Throw him into the Jaihun while he is still drugged. He will not know who did it, and he will drown without anyone being any the wiser.' So Siran instructed the *marid* to carry Gharib away and throw him into the river.

Night 672

Morning now dawned and Shahrazad broke off from what she had been allowed to say. Then, when it was the six hundred and seventy-second night, SHE CONTINUED:

I have heard, O fortunate king, that the *marid* carried Gharib to the Jaihun. When the *marid* got to the river, he found himself reluctant to do what he had been told and so he constructed a wooden raft tied together with ropes, and on this he placed Gharib before pushing it out into the current, which caught it and swept it away.

So much for Gharib, but as for his people, when they came next morning to present their services to him, he was not to be found, although his prayer beads were lying on his throne. They waited for him to emerge, and when he did not they asked the chamberlain to go to the harem to see whether he was there, although he was not in the habit of staying away so long. The chamberlain went in and asked those there, but they had not seen him since the day before, something which caused consternation when he told the others. They decided to see whether he had gone to take a stroll in the gardens, but when they asked the gardeners whether he had passed them, they said that they had not seen him. All the gardens were searched by the worried courtiers, and at the end of the day they returned in tears. Al-Kailajan and al-Qurajan scoured the city but came back after three days having found no news, and the people put on black robes and raised their complaints to the Lord of mankind, Who does whatever He wishes.

So much for them, but as for Gharib, he drifted down the river for five days lying on his raft, which the current then swept out into the open sea, where it was tossed to and fro by the waves. This so disturbed his stomach that the *banj* was expelled from it, and he opened his eyes to find himself out at sea at the mercy of the waves. 'There is no might and no power except with God, the Exalted, the Almighty!' he exclaimed, adding: 'Who can have done this to me?' Then, while he was at a loss to know what to do, he caught sight of a passing ship and signalled to the sailors with his sleeve. They came and picked him up and then asked him who he was and from which country he had come. 'Give me something to eat and drink to help me recover, and then I shall tell you who I am,' he said, and they fetched him food and water, and after he had eaten and drunk, he recovered his wits. He then asked the crew their race and their religion, and they said: 'We are from al-Karaj and we worship an idol called Minqash.' 'Woe betide you and the idol you worship!' Gharib exclaimed. 'You dogs, nothing may be worshipped except God, Who created all things and Who says to something "be" and it is.' At that, they attacked him in a mad rage, trying to seize him, but although he had no weapons he knocked down and killed all those whom he struck with his fists. After he had accounted for forty of them, they got the better of him by weight of numbers and tied him tightly. 'We shall not kill him,' they said, 'until we get to our own country and can show him to our king.'

They sailed on to al-Karaj . . .

Night 673

Morning now dawned and Shahrazad broke off from what she had been allowed to say. Then, when it was the six hundred and seventy-third night, SHE CONTINUED:

I have heard, O fortunate king, that when the sailors had seized Gharib and tied him up, they said: 'We shall not kill him until we get to our own country.' They sailed on to al-Karaj, a city built by a tyrannical giant who had used sorcery to set at each of its gates a brass statue which would blow on a trumpet if any stranger entered the city. When it sounded, all the inhabitants would come out to seize the newcomer and kill him if he refused to accept their religion. When Gharib was brought in, the statue blew a loud blast, and the king in alarm got up and went to visit his idol, to find fire and smoke coming out of its mouth, its nose and its eyes. Satan had entered its belly and spoke with its tongue, saying: 'O king, a man called Gharib has come to you. He is the king of Iraq who is telling people to abandon their religion and to worship his lord, and so when he is brought before you, do not let him live.'

The king left and had taken his seat on his throne when Gharib was brought before him. 'O king,' his captors said, 'we discovered this young man, who does not believe in our gods, when he was about to drown,' and they told him what had happened. 'Take him to the temple of the great idol,' the king ordered, 'and cut his throat in front of it so that it may be pleased with us.' The vizier pointed out that this would not be the right way to kill him, as he would die in a minute. 'Let us keep him in prison,' he suggested, 'collect firewood and then set it alight.' Accordingly, wood was collected and a fire lit that burned until morning. At that point the king and the townspeople went out to it, and the order was given to bring Gharib. The guards went to fetch him, but he was not to be found and they had to come back and tell the king that he had escaped. When the king asked how this had happened, they told him: 'We found the chains and the fetters thrown aside, although the doors were locked.' 'Did he fly up into the sky or burrow down into the earth?' asked the king in his astonishment, to which they replied: 'We do not know.' The king then said: 'I shall go to my god and ask him, for he will tell me where the man has gone.' The king then approached the idol to prostrate himself before it, but it was no longer there and he began to rub his eyes, saying to himself: 'Are you asleep or awake?' Then he turned to his vizier and said: 'Dog of a vizier, where is my god and where is the prisoner? If you had not advised me to have him burned, I would have had his throat cut. It is he who has stolen my god and made his escape, and for this I must have vengeance.' So he drew his sword and struck off the vizier's head.

There is a strange explanation for the disappearance of Gharib and the idol. He had been shut in a cell at the side of the dome, where it stood, and he got up to call on the Name of Almighty God, asking Him, Great and Glorious as He is, for relief in his distress. His prayer was heard by the *marid* who was in charge of the idol and whose mouthpiece it was. 'I am disgraced,' the *marid* exclaimed, 'before One Who sees me although I cannot see Him!' He went to Gharib, threw himself at his feet and said: 'Sir, what do I have to say to become one of your party and to join your religion?' Gharib told him to say: 'There is no god but the God of Abraham, the Friend of God.' The *marid* repeated this and was inscribed in the roll of the blessed. His name was Zilzal, son of al-Muzalzil, and his father was one of the great kings of the *jinn*. He now released Gharib from his fetters and carried both him and the idol into the upper air.

Night 674

Morning now dawned and Shahrazad broke off from what she had been allowed to say. Then, when it was the six hundred and seventy-fourth night, SHE CONTINUED:

I have heard, O fortunate king, that the *marid* carried both Gharib and the idol into the upper air. So much for him, but as for the king, having failed to find the idol when he went in to ask about Gharib, he killed the vizier, as has been recorded, but his troops, seeing what had happened, renounced idolatry, drew their swords and killed him. Then they started to fight one another and after three days of mutual slaughter only two of them were left. One of these overcame the other and killed him but was then himself killed by boys. The boys then struck out at each other until every last one of them was dead. Following on this, the women and girls rushed out and made for the villages and fortified towns, leaving the city empty except for its owls. So much for them.

When Zilzal carried off Gharib, he made for his own lands, the Camphor Islands and the Crystal Palace with the enchanted calf. King al-Muzalzil had a piebald calf which he ornamented and dressed in robes of gold brocade with ornaments, taking it as a god. One day, when he and his people went to visit it, they found it in a state of distress. 'My god,' asked the king, 'what has disturbed you?' 'Al-Muzalzil,' replied the devil in the belly of the calf, 'your son has been converted to the religion of Abraham, the Friend of God, by Gharib, the lord of Iraq,' and he then told the king what had happened from beginning to end. Having heard this, al-Muzalzil left in a state of perplexity and took his seat on his royal throne, where he summoned the officials of his state and told them what he had heard from the calf. They were filled with astonishment and asked what they were to do. 'When my son comes,' al-Muzalzil told them, 'and you see me embrace him, then lay hold of him.' 'To hear is to obey,' they replied.

Two days later, Zilzal came to his father with Gharib and the king of al-Karaj's idol, but when he entered the palace door the guards rushed him and Gharib and brought them before al-Muzalzil, who looked angrily at his son and said: 'Dog of a *jinn*, have you abandoned your religion and the religion of your fathers and forefathers?' 'I have embraced the true religion, and if you accept Islam you will be saved from the wrath of the Omnipotent King, the Creator of night and day,' Zilzal replied. Al-Muzalzil, angered by this, exclaimed: 'Bastard, do you dare say this to my face?', after which Zilzal was imprisoned on al-Muzalzil's orders. He then turned to Gharib and said: 'You miserable mortal, how did you delude my son into abandoning his faith?' Gharib replied: 'I brought him from error into true guidance and from hellfire to Paradise.' Al-Muzalzil called to a *marid* named Sayyar and told him: 'Take this dog and put him in the Valley of Fire, so that he may die' – this being a valley whose burning heat was instantly fatal to everyone who entered it. It was surrounded by a lofty, smooth and impassable mountain chain.

The damned Sayyar came forward and flew off with Gharib, making for the desolate region of the earth, until, when he was within an hour's journey of the valley, he grew tired of carrying Gharib and put him down in another valley with trees, streams and fruits. When the tired *marid* alighted, Gharib, shackled as he was, got down from Sayyar's back and waited until he had fallen asleep, snoring in his weariness. Gharib then worked on his bonds until he had freed himself, after which he took up a heavy stone and hurled it down on the *marid*'s head, crushing his bones so that he died instantly. Gharib then went into the valley . . .

Night 675

Morning now dawned and Shahrazad broke off from what she had been allowed to say. Then, when it was the six hundred and seventy-fifth night, SHE CONTINUED:

I have heard, O fortunate king, that when Gharib had killed the *marid*, he went off into that valley and discovered that it was in a large island in the middle of the sea with all the kinds of fruits that lips and tongues could wish for. For a period of years he stayed there drinking from the streams and eating the fruits as well as fish that he caught. After seven years of this lonely existence, one day while he was sitting there, two *marids* came down to him from the sky, each carrying a man. When they saw him they asked him: 'What are you and to which tribe do you belong?', thinking that he must be a *jinn* because his hair had grown so long. He answered their question by saying that he was not a *jinn*, and telling them his story from beginning to end. They were sorry for him, and one of them said: 'Stay where you are until we have delivered these two lambs to our king, one for him to eat in the morning and the other in the evening. Then we shall come back and take you to your own country.' Gharib thanked them but asked where their two lambs were, to which they replied: 'These two mortals are the lambs.' 'I take refuge with the God of Abraham, the Friend of God, the Lord of all things, the Omnipotent!' exclaimed Gharib, and the *marids* then flew off. Gharib sat there waiting and after two days one of them came back, bringing clothes for him to put on, after which he took Gharib up and flew off with him into the upper air, far away from the earth, where he could hear the sound of the angels glorifying God in heaven.

The angels aimed a fiery dart at the *marid*, who tried to escape by diving towards the earth, but when he was within a spear's throw of the surface the dart caught up with him. Gharib had jumped down from his shoulder before the dart struck him, reducing him to ashes, while Gharib himself fell into the sea, sinking to a depth of two fathoms. He then rose to the surface and swam all that day, the following night and the next day, until he had become so weak that he was sure he was going to die. When the third day came he had despaired of life, but at that point he caught sight of a tall mountain, to which he swam. He came to shore there and walked on the mountain, getting food from plants and then resting for a day and a night. He climbed to the summit and went down the other side, after which he walked on for two more days before reaching a city with walls and towers, together with trees and streams. When he got to the gates, the gate guards seized him and brought him to their queen.

The name of this queen was Jan Shah. She was five hundred years old and every man who came into the city was brought before her, after which she would take him and lie with him, killing him when he had finished her business. In this way she had slaughtered great numbers of men. When Gharib was brought to her, she was impressed by him and she asked him his name, his religion and his country. 'My name is Gharib,' he told her. 'I am king of Iraq and my religion is Islam.' 'Abandon your religion and adopt mine,' she told him, 'and then I shall marry you and make you a king.' Gharib looked angrily at her and cursed both her and her religion. 'Do you insult my idol, which is made of red carnelian studded with pearls and gems?' she cried, and then she told her men: 'Shut him in the idol's dome as it may soften his heart.' They did this and locked the doors on him . . .

Night 676

Morning now dawned and Shahrazad broke off from what she had been allowed to say. Then, when it was the six hundred and seventy-sixth night, SHE CONTINUED:

I have heard, O fortunate king, that the guards took Gharib and shut him in the dome of the idol, locking the doors on him before going on their way. Gharib looked at the red carnelian statue with necklaces of pearls and gems around its neck and, advancing on it, he lifted it up before dashing it to pieces on the ground, after which he slept until daybreak.

The next morning the queen took her seat on her throne and told her guards to bring in the prisoner. They went to fetch him and when they opened the dome and went in, they found the idol smashed. They beat their faces so violently that blood flowed from the corners of their eyes, and then they advanced on Gharib to lay hands on him, but he struck one of them and then another, killing them both, and he went on striking one after the other until, when he had killed twenty-five, the rest took flight. They went shrieking to the queen, and when she asked them what was wrong they said: 'The prisoner has broken your idol and killed your men.' They told her the whole story, at which she dashed her crown to the ground and exclaimed: 'Idols have no more value!' She then rode out towards the idol's temple with a thousand champions and found Gharib, who had come out from it. He took a sword and began to kill opponents and throw others to the ground. At the sight of his bravery Jan Shah fell deeply in love with him and said: 'I have no need of the idol, and what I want is for Gharib to lie in my arms for the rest of my life.' She ordered her men to withdraw and stay away from him, after which she went up and muttered a spell which paralysed his arm, relaxing the forearm muscles so that the sword fell from his hand, and the queen's men then seized and pinioned him, leaving him humiliated and helpless.

The queen went back to sit on her royal throne, ordering her guards to go off and leave her alone. Then she said: 'Arab dog, do you break my idol and kill my men?' 'You damned woman,' he answered, 'had that idol been a god, it would have defended itself.' 'Sleep with me,' she told him, 'and I shall pass over what you have done.' He refused and she threatened him with the most painful of tortures, after which she took some water, recited a spell over it and sprinkled it on him, so turning him into a monkey. She kept him in a cell, providing him with food and water and assigning keepers to look after him. After two years had passed, one day she called for him to be brought to her, and said: 'Will you listen to me?' He made a sign with his head to indicate yes, and, pleased by this, she released him from her spell. She had food brought and when he had eaten he toyed with her and kissed her, so winning her confidence. Then, when night fell, she lay back and said: 'Come and do your business.' 'Yes,' he said, but after mounting on her breast he broke her neck and did not get up until she was dead.

He now caught sight of an open closet, and when he entered it, he discovered a jewelled sword and a shield of Chinese iron. He put on full armour and waited until morning, when he went out and took his stand by the palace gate. The emirs arrived intending to go in to present their services to the queen, only to find him standing there wearing his armour. He told them: 'You people, abandon your idolatry and worship the

Omniscient King, the Creator of night and day, the Lord of all mankind, Who brings life to dry bones. He is the Creator of all things and has power over all things.' On hearing this the infidels attacked him, but he charged at them in his turn, moving among them like a ravening lion and killing them in large numbers . . .

Night 677

Morning now dawned and Shahrazad broke off from what she had been allowed to say. Then, when it was the six hundred and seventy-seventh night, SHE CONTINUED:

I have heard, O fortunate king, that Gharib charged at the infidels and killed a large number of them, but by the time night fell their numbers were having an effect and all of them were exerting themselves to capture him. Just then, however, a thousand *marids* armed with swords attacked the infidels, with Zilzal, son of al-Muzalzil, at their head, putting them to the sword and causing them to drain the cup of death, as Almighty God hastened their souls to hellfire, leaving none of them to tell the tale. The rest called for quarter and believed in God, the Judge, Who is not distracted by one thing from another, the Destroyer of the Chosroes, the Overthrower of tyrants, the Lord of this world and the next.

Zilzal greeted Gharib and congratulated him on his safety, at which Gharib asked who had told him of his plight. Zilzal replied: 'When my father imprisoned me and sent you to the Valley of Fire, I was in prison for two years, after which he released me. I stayed with him for a further year until I was restored to his favour, and then I killed him and won the support of the army. After I had ruled for a year I fell asleep thinking of you, and in a dream I saw you fighting against the people of Jan Shah. So I took these thousand *marids* and came to you.' Gharib was astonished by this coincidence, and he then took the wealth of the queen and of her people, appointing a governor over the city. The *marids* carried off the booty together with Gharib himself, and by nightfall they were back in Zilzal's city, where he stayed as Zilzal's guest for six months.

He then wanted to leave, and Zilzal, having prepared gifts, sent three thousand *marids* to carry all the treasure from the city of al-Karaj, adding it to the wealth of Jan Shah. On his orders they brought all this to Isbanir, while Zilzal himself carried Gharib. They arrived before midnight and when Gharib looked, he saw that the city was surrounded by a huge army like a flooding sea. 'What is the reason for this siege, brother, and where have these troops come from?' he said to Zilzal, before alighting on the castle roof and calling out to Kaukab al-Sabah and Mahdiya. The two ladies started up from sleep in astonishment and said: 'Who is calling us at this hour?' 'It is I, Gharib, your master, the hero of wonderful deeds,' he replied. They were filled with delight when they heard this, as were the slave girls and the eunuchs, and when he came down they threw themselves on him with cries of joy that resounded throughout the palace. The officers, roused from their beds, came up to the palace to discover what was happening, and they asked the eunuchs whether one of the slave girls had given birth. 'No,' they replied, 'but the good news is that King Gharib has arrived.'

The emirs were delighted, and after Gharib had greeted his harem he came out and they threw themselves on him, kissing his hands and feet, praising and extolling Almighty God. Gharib took his seat on his throne and at his summons his companions came and sat around him. In reply to his question about the army encamped outside, they said: 'They have been here for three days; there are both *jinn* and men with them, but we don't know what they want and there has been no fighting and no parleys.' Gharib promised to send a letter to them on the following day to discover their purpose, and they then told him that the name of the army's leader was Murad Shah and that he had with him a hundred thousand horse, three thousand foot and two hundred *jinn*.

This army had come to Isbanir on an important matter.

Night 678

Morning now dawned and Shahrazad broke off from what she had been allowed to say. Then, when it was the six hundred and seventy-eighth night, SHE CONTINUED:

I have heard, O fortunate king, that this army had come to Isbanir on an important matter. When Sabur had sent off his daughter, Fakhr Taj, with two of his men, he had instructed them to drown her in the Jaihun. They had taken her out of the city but had then told her to go off where she wanted provided she didn't let her father see her, as in that case he would kill all three of them. She wandered off helplessly, not knowing where to go and wishing that Gharib were there to see her plight. On she went from land to land and from valley to valley until she passed by a valley full of trees and streams, in the middle of which was a high castle, strongly built, as though it belonged to the garden of Paradise. Fakhr Taj made for it, and when she entered she found it carpeted with silks and full of vessels of gold and silver. In it there were a hundred beautiful girls who, when they saw her, rose to greet her, thinking that she must be one of the daughters of the *jinn*. They asked her about herself and she told them her story, explaining that she was the daughter of the king of Persia. When they heard what she had to say, they sympathized with her and consoled her, telling her to take heart and be cheerful, adding: 'You can have whatever you want to eat or drink or wear, and we are all at your service.' She blessed them and, when they then brought her food, she ate her fill before asking them who was their master, the lord of the castle. 'His name is Salsal, son of Dal,' they told her, 'and he comes here for one night in each month, leaving in the morning to exercise his rule over the tribes of the *jinn*.'

Fakhr Taj had stayed for five days with these girls when she gave birth to a son as beautiful as the moon. They cut the umbilical cord, putting kohl on his eyes and naming him Murad Shah, while his mother tended to him. Soon afterwards, King Salsal arrived mounted on a paper-white elephant as big as a lofty tower, surrounded by troops of *jinn*. When he entered the castle the hundred girls came to meet him and kissed the ground. With them was Fakhr Taj, and when Salsal saw her he asked the others who she was. 'She is the daughter of Sabur, king of the Persians, the Turks and the Dailamis,' they told him, and when he then asked who had brought her there, they told him her story. He was sorry for her and said: 'Don't grieve, but wait until your son has grown to manhood. Then I shall go to Persia, strike your father's head from his shoulders and place your son on his throne for you.' She rose, kissed his hand and called down blessings on him.

She stayed there and brought up her son with those of Salsal. They began to ride horses and to go hunting, so that Murad Shah learned how to pursue wild beasts and hunt down savage lions whose flesh he would eat, until his heart became harder than stone, and by the time that he had reached the age of fifteen he had a haughty spirit. At that point he asked his mother who his father was, and she told him: 'My son, your father is Gharib, the king of Iraq, and I am the daughter of the king of Persia.' When he had heard what she had to tell him, he asked: 'Did my grandfather order you and my father to be killed?' When she said yes, he pleased her by saying: 'I swear by the debt that I owe you for having raised me that I shall go to your father's city, cut off his head and bring it to you.'

Night 679

Morning now dawned and Shahrazad broke off from what she had been allowed to say. Then, when it was the six hundred and seventy-ninth night, SHE CONTINUED:

I have heard, O fortunate king, that Murad Shah had been in the habit of riding out with two hundred *marids* with whom he had been brought up, and together they started launching raids and cutting roads. They penetrated as far as Shiraz, which they attacked, and during an assault on the royal palace Murad Shah cut off the head of the king as he sat on his throne and killed large numbers of his men, while the rest called for quarter and kissed his stirrup. When he counted them, he discovered that they numbered ten thousand riders, who then took service with him on an expedition to Balkh. There they killed the king, destroyed his army and took control of his people, after which they went on to Nurain, by which time Murad Shah's army numbered thirty thousand riders. The ruler of Nurain came out to offer his submission, with money and gifts, and the thirty thousand moved on first to Samarkand and then to Akhlat, both of which they took. From there on they captured every city that they reached until the army had swollen to a huge size. The wealth and the treasures they had taken were divided among them by Murad Shah, who won their affection both by his bravery and by his generosity. It was after this that he came to Isbanir, and here he told his followers: 'Wait until the rest of my army arrives, and then I shall seize my grandfather, bring him before my mother and cure her sorrow by cutting off his head.' He sent an escort to fetch her, and it was because of this that there had been no fighting for three days.

In the meanwhile Gharib came together with Zilzal and forty thousand *marids*, who were carrying wealth and gifts. When Gharib asked about the attacking force, his men told him that they did not know where they had come from and that for three days there had been no fighting on either side. It was after this that Fakhr Taj arrived. She embraced her son, who told her to sit in her tent until he brought her her father, and she prayed that the Lord of mankind, the Ruler of heaven and earth, might give him victory. The next morning Murad Shah rode out to the sound of the war drums, flanked on the right by his two hundred *marids*, and on the left by his mortal kings. Gharib heard the drums, mounted and rode forward, summoning his army to battle, with the *jinn* on his right and his men on the left. Murad Shah himself advanced in full armour, riding from right to left of the line and calling out: 'Let no one come out against me except your king! If he defeats me, he will be the leader of both these armies, and if I defeat him, I shall kill him as I have killed others.'

When Gharib heard this, he said: 'Off with you, Arab dog,' and each charged at the other, thrusting with their lances until they broke and then striking with their swords until they were blunted. They continued to charge and retreat, advance and retire, until midday when their horses collapsed beneath them. They then seized hold of one another, and Murad Shah, attacking Gharib, caught him up with the intention of dashing him to the ground, but Gharib seized hold of his ears and tugged with all his might. It seemed to Murad Shah that the sky had fallen in on the earth, and he called out at the top of his voice: 'I am under your protection, champion of the age.' Gharib tied him up . . .

Night 680

Morning now dawned and Shahrazad broke off from what she had been allowed to say. Then, when it was the six hundred and eightieth night, SHE CONTINUED:

I have heard, O fortunate king, that when Gharib seized hold of Murad's ears and tugged at them, Murad called out: 'I am under your protection, champion of the age.' Gharib tied him up, and at that Murad's *marids* were about to charge to his rescue when Gharib attacked them with a thousand *marids* of his own, who were about to fall on them when they called for quarter and threw down their arms.

Gharib now took his seat in his pavilion, which was of green silk, embroidered with red gold and studded with pearls and jewels. At his summons, Murad Shah was brought before him hobbling in his fetters, and at the sight of Gharib he hung his head in shame. 'Arab dog,' Gharib said, 'what kind of a man are you to ride out and measure yourself against kings?' 'Master,' Murad Shah replied, 'don't hold this against me, for I have an excuse.' 'What kind of excuse is this?' asked Gharib, and Murad Shah replied: 'I came to take vengeance for my father and mother on Sabur, king of the Persians. He wanted to have them killed, but my mother escaped and whether or not he killed my father I don't know.' 'By God, you are to be excused!' exclaimed Gharib, and he then went on to ask who his parents were and what were their names. Murad Shah replied: 'My father was Gharib, king of Iraq, and my mother's name is Fakhr Taj, the daughter of Sabur, the Persian king.'

When Gharib heard this he gave a great cry and fell down in a faint, but after he had been sprinkled with rosewater he recovered and asked: 'Are you the son of Gharib by Fakhr Taj?' 'Yes,' he replied, and Gharib said: 'You are a champion and the son of a champion. Release my son from his fetters.' At that, Sahim and al-Kailajan came forward and freed him, after which his father embraced him and gave him a seat at his side. 'Where is your mother?' he asked, and when Murad Shah told him that she was in his tent, Gharib told him to bring her to him. Murad Shah mounted and rode back to his camp, where his companions met him, full of joy at his safe return, but when they asked him how he was he replied: 'This is not the time for questions,' and he went to his mother and told her what had happened. She was overjoyed, and when he brought her to his father the two of them embraced in happiness at their reunion. Both Fakhr Taj and Murad Shah accepted Islam and, when it was expounded to them, their army embraced it with hearts and tongues, to Gharib's delight. He then sent for Sabur and his son and reproached them for what they had done. He offered them conversion, and when they refused it he had them crucified on the city gate.

Isbanir was adorned with decorations by its joyful citizens, who crowned Murad Shah with the crown of the Chosroes, accepting him as king of the Persians, the Turks and the Dailamis. Gharib sent off his uncle al-Damigh as king of Iraq, while he himself was obeyed by all lands and peoples. He remained in his kingdom, treating his subjects with justice and winning the love of all. They continued to lead the pleasantest of lives until they were visited by the destroyer of delights and the parter of companions. Praise be to the Eternal God, Whose glory remains and Whose great gifts are showered on His creatures.

This is what we have heard of the story of Gharib and 'Ajib.

A story is also told that 'ABDALLAH IBN MA'MAR AL-QAISI SAID: 'One year I went on pilgrimage to the Haram of Mecca. When I had completed my pilgrimage, I went back to visit the tomb of the Prophet of God, may God bless him and give him peace, and one night when I was sitting in the Rawda, between the tomb and the pulpit, I heard a low voice moaning softly and when I listened I could distinguish the following lines:

Has the lament of the doves in the lote tree prompted your sorrow,
Rousing unease within your heart,
Or are you distressed by the memory of a lovely girl,
Who has brought thoughts to trouble you?
Night is long for the sick at heart
Who complain of passion and the loss of patience.
My beloved allows no sleep to the lover who burns with love,
Flaming like lighted coals.
The full moon bears witness for me that I am in love,
And full of longing for one who is like it.
I never thought that love would cause me pain,
Until, unwittingly, I felt its power.

The voice then broke off and, as I did not know where it came from, I stayed there in perplexity until suddenly it started again, reciting sorrowfully:

Has a visit from Rayya's phantom stirred your sorrow,
A phantom coming in the dark depths of night?
Love has accustomed your eyes to sleeplessness,
But when this phantom came, your inmost heart was roused.
I called out to the night, when in its darkness,
It was like a sea in flood with tossing waves:
'Night, how long you are for a lover
Whom none can help or aid, apart from dawn.
For it is love that comes to bring you low.'

When the reciter began on these lines I moved towards the sound of his voice, and by the time that he had finished them I had reached him. He turned out to be a most handsome youth whose cheeks did not yet show traces of down, and on which tears had worn twin channels.

Night 681

Morning now dawned and Shahrazad broke off from what she had been allowed to say. Then, when it was the six hundred and eighty-first night,
SHE CONTINUED:

I have heard, O fortunate king, that 'ABDALLAH SAID:

When the reciter began on these lines I moved towards the sound of his voice, and by the time that he had finished them I had reached him. He turned out to be a most handsome youth whose cheeks did not yet show traces of down, and on which tears had worn twin channels. I wished him well and he returned my greeting before asking who I was, to which I replied that I was 'Abdallah ibn Ma'mar al-Qaisi. He then asked whether there was anything that I wanted, and I said: 'I was sitting in the Rawda tonight when I was stirred by the sound of your voice. I would like to help you, so tell me what disturbs you.' He told me to sit down and when I had he said: 'I am 'Utba ibn al-Hubab ibn al-Mundhir ibn al-Jammuh al-Ansari. I went this morning to the Mosque of al-Ahzab, where I stayed to perform my *rak'as* and prostrations, after which I went off on my own to continue my devotions. Suddenly a band of women appeared, radiant as moons and swaying as they walked. They were surrounding a girl of extraordinary beauty and perfect loveliness, who stood over me and asked: "'Utba, what would you say to union with one who wants union with you?" She then went off and left me, and I have heard nothing more or come across any trace of her, and so I am wandering to and fro not knowing what to do.'

He gave a cry, collapsing on the ground in a faint, and when he recovered, it was as though the delicate complexion of his cheeks had been dyed with saffron. He then recited these lines:

My heart can see you from a distant land,
But can yours, far off as it is, see me?
My heart and my eyes grieve for you;
My soul is with you; your memory stays with me.
My life would have no pleasure without you,
Even in Paradise, the garden of immortality.

''Utba, my nephew,' I said, 'repent to God and ask His forgiveness for your sin, since before you lies the terror of the Day of Judgement.' 'Far be that from me,' he answered, 'for I shall never forget this until the two acacia gatherers return.'*

I stayed with him until dawn broke, and then I told him to go with me to the mosque. We stayed there until we had performed the noon prayer

---

* 'Until the two acacia gatherers return' is a proverbial expression for 'never'.

and although the women arrived at that point, the girl was not with them. ''Utba,' they said, 'what do you think has happened to the one who wanted union with you?' 'What has happened to her?' he asked, and they told him that her father had taken her off on a journey to al-Samawa. I asked them the girl's name and they told me that she was Rayya, the daughter of al-Ghitrif al-Sulami. 'Utba then raised his head and recited these lines:

My two companions, Rayya left at dawn,
And her caravan is on its way to al-Samawa.
My two companions, I am overwhelmed by tears;
Does anyone have tears for me to borrow?

I said: ''Utba, I have come here with ample funds, intending to use them to help satisfy the needs of honourable men, and I swear by God that I shall use them for you so as to get you what you want and more. Come with me to the assembly of the Ansar.'* We got up and went there, after which I greeted those present and they returned a courteous greeting. 'Men of the Ansar,' I said, 'what have you to say about 'Utba and his father?' 'They are among the chiefs of the Arabs,' was the reply, and so I went on: 'You must know that 'Utba has been struck down by the calamity of love, and I would like your help on a visit to al-Samawa.' 'To hear is to obey,' they replied, and we rode out in their company until we came near the Sulami camp. When al-Ghitrif learned that we were there, he quickly came out to meet us and greeted us courteously. In return we wished him a long life and told him that we had come as his guests. 'You have come to the most generous and liberal of camps,' he answered, and he then called to his slaves, who spread out mats and cushions and slaughtered camels and sheep. We said: 'We shall not eat your food until you grant us our request.' 'And what is that?' he asked, and we told him: 'We ask you to give your noble daughter in marriage to 'Utba ibn al-Hubab ibn al-Mundhir, a well-born man of high repute.' He replied: 'My brothers, my daughter, for whose hand you ask, is her own mistress, but I shall go in and tell her.'

He got up angrily and went to Rayya, who asked him the reason for this show of rage, and he told her: 'Some of the Ansar have come to ask me to give you away in marriage.' 'They are noble chiefs,' she pointed out, 'and the Prophet, on whom be the best of blessings, intercedes for them with God. To whom do they want to marry me?' 'A young man

* The Ansar were the Medinese who helped Muhammad after his flight from Mecca.

named 'Utba ibn al-Hubab,' her father replied, and she said: 'I have heard that he keeps his promises and gets what he wants.' Her father said: 'I have sworn that I shall never marry you to him, for I have heard tales of your talk with him.' 'What was that?' she asked, and then she added: 'I swear that the Ansar must not be given an uncivil refusal, so turn them away politely.' When he asked how that was to be done, she said: 'Ask them for a high bride price and they will go away.' He approved of this and went out quickly and said: 'My daughter accepts, but wants a bride price worthy of her. Who will provide it?' 'I will,' I said, and he then told me: 'I want a thousand bracelets of red gold, five thousand dirhams minted in Hajar, a hundred robes, plain and striped, and five bladders full of ambergris.' 'I promise you that,' I said, 'so do you consent to the marriage?' 'I consent,' he replied.

I sent a number of the Ansar to Medina who fetched all I had promised, and after this camels and sheep were slaughtered, as the people assembled for a feast. We stayed there for forty days, after which the Sulamis said: 'Take your bride.' We mounted her on a howdah and thirty camels carried her wedding gifts. We took our leave and set off, but when we were within one stage of Medina we were attacked by a raiding party who were, I think, Sulamis. 'Utba charged them and killed a number of them, but came back wounded and collapsed on the ground. The local inhabitants came to help us and drove off the attackers, but by that time 'Utba was dead. We cried out in sorrow, and when Rayya heard the news she threw herself down from her camel and leaned over him with an agonized cry, reciting these lines:

> I showed patience, but how could I be patient,
> Consoling my soul that it was on its way to you?
> Had it acted fairly, it would have forestalled all others
> By going before you on the road to death.
> When you and I have gone, no one will treat a friend fairly;
> No soul will be in harmony with another.

She then sighed once and gave up the ghost. We dug a single grave for the two of them and buried them in the earth. I went back to the lands of my own people and stayed for seven years before returning to visit the shrines of Medina. I had made up my mind to go to 'Utba's grave, and when I got there I found a tall tree growing on which were hung strips of red, yellow and green cloth. I asked the local people what it was called and they said: 'The tree of the bride and groom.' I stayed there for a day and a night before leaving, and this was the end of my dealings with 'Utba, may God Almighty have mercy on him.

A story is also told that al-Nu'man's daughter Hind was the most beautiful of all the women of her time. When al-Hajjaj was told how lovely she was, he asked for her hand in marriage and offered a huge sum of money for her, as well as promising two hundred thousand dirhams as a wedding gift. The marriage was arranged and when it had been consummated, he stayed with her for a long time. Then, one day, he went to her room while she was looking at herself in a mirror. She was reciting these lines:

Hind is a pure-bred Arab mare, covered by a mule.
If she produces a filly, the praise will all be hers,
But if it is a mule, the mule has fathered it.

When he heard that he went back and never came to visit her again, while for her part she knew nothing about what had happened. He then wanted to divorce her and sent 'Abd Allah ibn Tahir to do this for him. 'Abd Allah went to her and said: 'Al-Hajjaj Abu Muhammad has delayed the payment of the two hundred thousand dirhams that were your wedding gift. I have brought them with me and he has entrusted me as his agent to divorce you.' She said: 'Let me tell you, Ibn Tahir, that I never enjoyed a single day when we were together. If we part, by God, I shall never regret him and you can keep the two hundred thousand dirhams as a reward for bringing me the good news that I am free from the dog of Thaqif.' 'Abd al-Malik ibn Marwan heard about her. Her beauty, the symmetry of her form, the sweetness of her diction and her flirtatious glances were described to him, and he sent to ask for her hand in marriage.

Night 682

Morning now dawned and Shahrazad broke off from what she had been allowed to say. Then, when it was the six hundred and eighty-second night, SHE CONTINUED:

I have heard, O fortunate king, that when the caliph 'Abd al-Malik heard of Hind's beauty and grace, he sent to ask for her hand. In reply she sent a letter saying: 'Praise be to God and blessings be on His Prophet,

Muhammad, may God bless him and give him peace. To continue: you must know, Commander of the Faithful, that the dog has licked the bowl.' The caliph laughed when he read this and in his reply he quoted a saying of the Prophet: 'When the dog licks the bowl, wash it out seven times, once using earth.' He added: 'So wash off the dirt from where the bowl was used.' After she had read his letter she could not refuse, but she wrote back starting her letter with the praise of God and continuing: 'I shall only marry you on one condition, and if you ask what this is, I shall tell you. The camel carrying my litter is to be led to wherever you are by al-Hajjaj, who is to be barefooted but dressed in his usual clothes.'

When the caliph read this, he roared with laughter and sent an order to al-Hajjaj to tell him to do this. After reading the message, al-Hajjaj sent word to Hind to tell her to make her preparations, and when her litter was ready, he came with his retinue to her door. When she got on to the litter, her slave girls and eunuchs mounted around her, while al-Hajjaj walked barefoot holding the reins of the camel. As he led it she began to jeer at him, mocking and laughing at him, as did her attendants and slave girls. On her instructions, the attendants drew back the curtain of the litter so that she was face to face with him. When she laughed at him, he recited:

> You may laugh, Hind, but on many a night
> I left you awake and weeping.

She answered him with these two lines:

> If our lives are safe, what do we care for the loss of money and goods?
> Money can be won and glory restored, when a destructive disease is
>   cured.

She continued to laugh and make fun of him until she was nearly at the caliph's city. When she got there she dropped a dinar on the ground and called out: 'Camel driver, I have dropped a dirham; look for it and give it back to me.' Al-Hajjaj looked down but could only see a dinar. When he told her this, she said: 'No, it is a dirham.' When she insisted that it must be a dirham and he repeated that it was a dinar, she embarrassed him by saying: 'Praise be to God, Who has given me a dinar in exchange for a worthless dirham. Give it to me.' He then brought her to the caliph's palace where she went in to meet him, subsequently becoming a favourite of his.

Night 683

Morning now dawned and Shahrazad broke off from what she had been allowed to say. Then, when it was the six hundred and eighty-third night, SHE CONTINUED:

I have heard, O fortunate king, that in the days of the caliph Sulaiman ibn 'Abd al-Malik* there was a man of the Banu Asad named Khuzaima ibn Bishr. He showed generosity and great liberality, and treated his companions well. He continued to follow this path until fortune brought him down and he found himself in need of help from those to whom he had been so generous. They did help him for a time, but they grew tired of it, and when he noticed this he went to his wife, who was his cousin, and said: 'Cousin, I see that my companions have changed, and so I have made up my mind not to leave my house until I die.' He bolted the door and stayed there eating what food there was in the house until this was exhausted and he was at his wits' end.

'Ikrima ibn al-Fayyad al-Raba'i, governor of al-Jazira, was an acquaintance of his, and one day, when 'Ikrima was in his assembly room, Khuzaima's name was mentioned and 'Ikrima asked how he was, only to be told that he was at home in the direst of straits, having locked himself in. 'This has happened because he had been so generous,' said 'Ikrima, adding, 'but how is it that he has not found anyone to help and support him?' 'He received nothing of that kind,' people told him, and so, when night came, 'Ikrima took four thousand dinars and put them in a single bag. He then ordered his riding beast to be saddled and, without his family's knowledge, he rode out secretly, accompanied by one of his servants, who was carrying the money. When he got to Khuzaima's door he took the bag from the servant and sent him off, after which he went up and knocked on the door himself. When Khuzaima came out, 'Ikrima gave him the bag and said: 'Use this to put your affairs in order.' Khuzaima took it and, finding it heavy, he put it down and took hold of 'Ikrima's bridle, saying: 'Who are you, may my life be your ransom?' 'I have not come at a time like this because I wanted you to recognize me,' 'Ikrima said, but Khuzaima insisted: 'I shall not let you go until you tell me who you are.' 'I am Jabir Atharat al-Kiram,'†

---

* Reigned AD 715–17.
† i.e. 'the curer of the afflictions of the generous'.

'Ikrima told him, and when Khuzaima said: 'Tell me more,' he refused.

When 'Ikrima had gone, Khuzaima took the bag to his wife and said: 'Good news! God has brought us prompt relief and good fortune. If these are dirhams in this bag, there are a lot of them, so get up and light the lamp.' 'There is nothing to light it with,' she told him, and he started to finger the coins in the darkness. He discovered that they felt rough, like dinars, but he refused to believe that this could be true. As for 'Ikrima, when he got home he discovered that his wife had missed him, and that when she had asked about him, she had been told that he had ridden off. She disapproved of this and said suspiciously: 'The governor of al-Jazira does not ride out at the dead of night unaccompanied by servants and without letting his family know, except to call on a wife or a concubine.' 'God knows that it was neither of these that I went to visit,' he told her, but she pressed him to tell her why he had gone. 'I only went at that time so that no one should know,' he said, but then, when she continued to insist, he said: 'Will you keep it secret?' 'Yes,' she replied, and he told her how things were and what he had done. 'Would you like me to swear to this?' he asked, to which she replied: 'No, no. You have set my heart at rest and I can rely on what you told me.'

The next morning Khuzaima settled with his creditors and put his affairs in order, before setting out to visit Sulaiman ibn 'Abd al-Malik, who was then in Palestine. When he reached the gate of the palace and asked the chamberlains for permission to enter, one of them went to tell the caliph that he was there. The caliph knew of his great reputation for generosity and so gave his permission. When Khuzaima entered, he greeted the caliph in a manner suited to his position, and the caliph asked him what had kept him away for so long. 'My circumstances,' Khuzaima replied. 'And what stopped you coming to me?' the caliph went on, and Khuzaima said that he had been sick. 'Why have you come now?' asked the caliph, and Khuzaima told him: 'One night, when I was sitting at home, a man knocked at my door' – and he went on to explain what had happened and to tell him the story from start to finish. The caliph asked him whether he knew the man and Khuzaima said: 'No, Commander of the Faithful, for he was concealing his face and the only thing I heard him say was that he was Jabir Atharat al-Kiram.' The caliph was deeply moved by this act of generosity and said: 'If only I knew who he was, I would repay him for this.'

Khuzaima was now presented with an imperial standard and appointed to replace 'Ikrima as governor of al-Jazira, after which he started for home. When he was nearly there, 'Ikrima and the people of al-Jazira came out to meet him. 'Ikrima and Khuzaima exchanged greetings before entering the city together. Khuzaima took up his residence in the governor's palace and told 'Ikrima to provide a surety and for an audit to be conducted. The audit showed that 'Ikrima owed a large sum of money, and Khuzaima asked for the money to be paid. When 'Ikrima said that he had no means of doing that, Khuzaima insisted that it must be done. 'I have no money,' repeated 'Ikrima, 'so do what you have to do,' at which Khuzaima ordered him to be imprisoned.

Night 684

Morning now dawned and Shahrazad broke off from what she had been allowed to say. Then, when it was the six hundred and eighty-fourth night, SHE CONTINUED:

I have heard, O fortunate king, that Khuzaima ordered 'Ikrima to be imprisoned. While he was in prison, Khuzaima again sent to demand what was due and in reply 'Ikrima said: 'I am not one of those who protect their wealth at the expense of their honour, so do what you want.' Khuzaima ordered that he be chained up in prison, and 'Ikrima stayed there for a month or more until this confinement weakened and emaciated him. News of this distressed his wife, who sent for an intelligent and knowledgeable freed-woman of hers and said: 'Go at once to the door of the emir Khuzaima ibn Bishr and say that you have some advice for him. When one of his people asks you what this is, say that you will only tell the emir himself. Then, when you get to him, ask him to speak to you in private, and afterwards, when you are alone with him, say: "What is this that you have done? Could you only repay Jabir Atharat al-Kiram by punishing him with harsh confinement in fetters?" '

The woman did as she was told, and when Khuzaima heard what she said, he cried out at the top of his voice: 'Oh, how terrible! Is that he?' 'Yes,' she told him, and at once he called for his riding beast to be saddled. He then summoned the leading citizens and when they came he took them to the prison gate. He opened it and, when he and the others went in, they saw 'Ikrima sitting in a sadly altered state, worn out by painful beatings. 'Ikrima hung his head in embarrassment at the sight of Khuzaima, but Khuzaima went up to him and bent over to kiss his head. 'Ikrima asked why he was doing this now, and Khuzaima replied:

'Because of how badly I repaid you for your generous action.' 'May God forgive both you and me,' 'Ikrima told him, at which Khuzaima ordered that his fetters be taken off and put on his own legs. 'Ikrima asked what he wished to do, to which Khuzaima replied: 'I want to suffer what you have suffered,' but 'Ikrima conjured him in God's Name not to do that. They left the prison together and went to Khuzaima's house, where 'Ikrima was about to take leave of him, but Khuzaima stopped him. When 'Ikrima asked what he wanted, Khuzaima said: 'I want to change your appearance as I would be even more ashamed in front of your wife than I am in front of you.' On his orders the baths were cleared, and when the two of them went in Khuzaima ministered to 'Ikrima in person. After they had left, Khuzaima presented him with an expensive robe, mounted him on a riding beast and gave him a large sum of money. Having accompanied him home, he asked permission to present his excuses to 'Ikrima's wife, and when he had done this he asked 'Ikrima to go with him to Sulaiman ibn 'Abd al-Malik, who was at that time in Ramla. 'Ikrima agreed and the two of them set off together.

When they reached Ramla, the chamberlain went in to tell the caliph that Khuzaima ibn Bishr had arrived. This alarmed the caliph, who said: 'There must be something seriously wrong if the governor of al-Jazira comes here without having been summoned.' He gave permission for Khuzaima to enter, and when he had come in, the caliph said, before even greeting him: 'What is behind all this?' 'Something good,' Khuzaima replied, and the caliph asked what had brought him. 'I have got hold of Jabir Atharat al-Kiram,' Khuzaima told him, 'and I wanted to give you the pleasure of meeting him, as I saw how eager you were to find out about him and how you longed to see him.' 'Who is he, then?' the caliph asked, and Khuzaima told him that this was 'Ikrima al-Fayyad. The caliph told him to approach, and when he had come up and pronounced the ceremonial greeting, the caliph welcomed him and brought him close to where he was sitting. Then he said: ''Ikrima, the good that you did proved unwholesome for you,' and he added: 'Now note down a list of every single one of your needs and wants.' When 'Ikrima had done that, the caliph ordered that all that he had asked for should be provided instantly, and that in addition to the things that he had listed, he should be given ten thousand dinars and twenty chests full of robes. The caliph then presented him with an imperial standard and appointed him as ruler of al-Jazira, Armenia and Azerbaijan. 'Khuzaima's case is in your hands,' he told him. 'If you want, leave him in his office or, if you'd rather, dismiss him.' 'I shall restore him to his office, Commander of the Faithful,' 'Ikrima told him, and he and Khuzaima left the caliph's presence together and continued to serve him for the rest of his caliphate.

A story is also told that during the caliphate of Hisham ibn 'Abd al-Malik* there was a well-known man known as Yunus al-Katib. Yunus set out on a journey to Damascus, taking with him an extremely beautiful slave girl who possessed all the attributes that she could ever need, her price being a hundred thousand dirhams. Not far from Damascus, the caravan halted at a pool and Yunus dismounted beside it and took out some food that he had with him, together with a flask of wine. At that point, a handsome and dignified young man mounted on a roan horse and accompanied by two servants came up and, after greeting him, said: 'Will you accept me as a guest?' 'Yes,' replied Yunus and the man dismounted and then asked for some wine, which Yunus gave him. He then said: 'Would you please sing something,' and Yunus sang:

> She has more loveliness than any mortal has possessed;
> In my love for her, both tears and wakefulness bring me delight.

The young man was transported with joy, and as Yunus poured him more and more wine, drunkenness took hold of him and he said: 'Tell your slave girl to sing.' So the girl sang:

> She is a houri whose beauties cause my heart bewilderment;
> Neither bough nor sun nor moon can rival her.

The young man was delighted, and he stayed, with Yunus pouring him yet more wine until they had both performed the evening prayer. Then he asked Yunus what had brought him to Damascus, to which Yunus replied: 'To settle my debts and put my affairs in order.' 'Will you sell me this slave girl of yours for thirty thousand dirhams?' the man asked. 'I need more than that,' said Yunus, 'together with God's grace.' 'Would you be content with forty thousand?' the other asked, and Yunus replied: 'That would cover my debts, but it would then leave me empty-handed.' 'I shall take her for fifty thousand and give you a set of clothes as well as money for your journey, and you shall share in my fortune as long as I live.' At that, Yunus agreed to the sale and the man asked: 'Will you trust me to bring you the money tomorrow and let me take the girl off

---

* Reigned AD 724–43.

now, or would you prefer to keep her until I fetch it for you tomorrow?'
A mixture of wine, shame and fear of the stranger led Yunus to say:
'Yes, I trust you, so take her off and may God give you a blessing with
her.' The man then told one of his servants: 'Take her up on your beast,
mount behind her and ride off with her.' He himself mounted his horse,
said goodbye to Yunus and rode away.

He had not been gone for long before Yunus, thinking the matter
over, realized that he had made a mistake, and he said to himself: 'What
have I done, handing over my slave girl to an unknown man? I don't
know who he is, and even if I knew, how can I reach him?' He sat
worrying about this until the time came for morning prayer, and when
his companions went into Damascus, he was still sitting there, at a loss
to know what to do. He stayed until the sun became too hot for him
and he had become tired of the place. He thought of going into the city,
but said to himself: 'If I do, I can't be sure that a messenger won't come
and then fail to find me, in which case this will be a second injury that I
have done myself.' So he sat in the shade of a wall that he found there
until in the afternoon he was approached by one of the two servants
who had accompanied the young man. Yunus was delighted at the sight
of the man, saying to himself that he could think of nothing in his life
that had ever given him more pleasure. 'I am afraid that we have been
slow,' said the servant when he came up, but Yunus said nothing to him
about the distress he had suffered. The servant asked him: 'Do you know
who it was who took the slave girl?' and when Yunus said no, the servant
told him: 'That was Walid ibn Sahl, the heir to the caliphate.' Yunus
stayed silent, and the man then told him to get up and mount, for he
had a horse with him on which he set Yunus, and the two of them rode
up to a house and went in.

When the slave girl caught sight of her former master, she rushed to
greet him and he asked her how she had got on with the man who had
bought her. She said: 'He put me into this room and ordered that I be
given everything that I needed.' Yunus sat with her for a while until one
of the servants of the master of the house arrived and told him to come.
The servant brought him to his master, and Yunus discovered Walid, his
guest of the day before, seated on his couch. 'Who are you?' Walid
asked, and Yunus replied: 'I am Yunus al-Katib.' 'Welcome,' said Walid.
'By God, I have been longing to see you, for I have heard of your
reputation. What kind of a night did you have?' 'A good one, may
Almighty God grant you glory,' Yunus replied. 'Didn't you perhaps

regret what you did yesterday and say to yourself: "I have handed over
my slave girl to a stranger without knowing his name or where he comes
from"?' Walid asked, and Yunus replied: 'God forbid that I should feel
regret for her, emir, as even had I made a present of her to you, this
would have been the least of gifts . . .'

Night 685

Morning now dawned and Shahrazad broke off from what she had been
allowed to say. Then, when it was the six hundred and eighty-fifth night,
SHE CONTINUED:

I have heard, O fortunate king, that Yunus replied: 'God forbid that I
should feel regret for her, emir, as even had I made a present of her to
you, this would have been the least of gifts, for what is she in comparison
with your rank?' 'By God,' Walid told him, 'I regretted taking her from
you and I said to myself: "Here is a stranger who doesn't know me, and
I have pressed him and importuned him in my hurry to take the girl."
Do you remember our conversation?' 'Yes,' replied Yunus, and Walid
went on: 'Will you sell me the girl for fifty thousand dirhams?' Yunus
agreed and Walid told a servant to fetch the money. When it had been
brought, Walid told the man to bring fifteen hundred dinars, which he
did. Walid then told Yunus to take the first sum, which was the girl's
price and then said: 'The thousand dinars are for your good opinion of
me, while the five hundred are for your travel expenses and to cover the
presents you buy for your family. Are you content with this?' 'Indeed I
am,' Yunus replied, and he kissed Walid's hands, exclaiming: 'By God,
you have filled my eyes, my hands and my heart!'

'I have not yet been alone with her or heard enough of her singing,'
Walid now said, and he sent to fetch her. When she came he told her to be
seated, and after she had sat down he told her to sing. She sang these lines:

> You who possess the sum of all beauty,
> Sweet in your nature and your coquetry,
> All loveliness lies with Arabs and with Turks,
> But nowhere in the world have you your match, gazelle.
> Fair one, show pity to a lover,
> Even if all you promise is the visit of a phantom.
> My rightful due from you must be disgrace and shame,

While wakefulness at night is sweetness to my eye.
I'm not the first maddened by love for you.
How many men before me have you killed?
Were you my one possession in the world, that would content me,
For you are dearer to me than wealth or life itself.

Walid was delighted and thanked Yunus for having brought her up and
trained her so well. Then he told a servant to fetch a horse with its saddle
and trappings, together with a pack mule, and he said: 'Yunus, when
you hear that the caliphate has passed to me, join me and I swear that I
shall load you with gifts, give you a high position and enrich you for all
the days of your life.' Yunus took the money and left, returning after
Walid had become caliph. Walid then kept his promise and showed him
even greater kindness. Yunus said: 'I stayed with him in the greatest
happiness and splendour, enjoying the easiest of circumstances and great
wealth with enough estates and wealth to last me all my life and to
provide for my heirs.' Yunus remained there until Walid was killed, may
Almighty God have mercy on him.

A story is also told that one day Harun al-Rashid, the Commander of the
Faithful, was walking with Ja'far the Barmecide when he came across a
number of girls drawing water and went over to them to get a drink. As he
did so, one of them turned to the others and recited the following lines:

Tell your phantom to turn away from my bed while I sleep,
So that I may have rest and the raging fire be quenched within my
    bones.
Ill with love, I twist to and fro on my sickbed.
This, as you know, is my state, but can any union with you last?

The caliph admired both her beauty and her eloquence . . .

Night 686

Morning now dawned and Shahrazad broke off from what she had been
allowed to say. Then, when it was the six hundred and eighty-sixth night,
SHE CONTINUED:
  I have heard, O fortunate king, that when the caliph heard these lines
he admired both the girl's beauty and her eloquence and said: 'Daughter

of noble parents, are these your own words or are you quoting?' She told him that they were her own, and he said: 'If that is so then keep the sense but change the rhyme at the end.' So she recited:

Tell your phantom to turn away from my bed while I lie asleep,
So that I may have rest and my body's raging fire be quenched.
Ill with love, I turn to and fro on my bed of sorrow.
This, as you know, is my state, but has union with you a price?

'You have taken this from another,' the caliph said, and when she insisted that the words were her own, he told her to keep the meaning and change the rhyme again. She recited:

Tell your phantom to turn away from my bed at the time of sleep,
That I may have rest and the raging fire be quenched within my
        heart.
Ill with love, I turn to and fro on my sleepless bed.
This, as you know, is my state, but what way is there to your union?

The caliph again dismissed the lines as having been borrowed, and again the girl insisted that they were her own. So he told her once again to keep the meaning and change the rhyme, at which she recited:

Tell your phantom to turn away from my bed while I lie asleep,
So that I may rest and the raging fire be quenched within my ribs.
Ill with love, I turn to and fro on my bed of tears.
This, as you know, is my state, but can union with you return?

'From what part of the tribe do you come?' the caliph asked her, and when she said: 'From the middlemost tent with the highest tent pole,' he realized then that she was the daughter of a tribal chief. 'And to what horse herds do you belong?' she asked him, and he answered: 'From those with the highest tree and the ripest fruit.' She then kissed the ground and called down blessings on him, saying: 'May God aid you, Commander of the Faithful,' before leaving with the other Bedouin girls. 'I must marry this girl,' said the caliph to Ja'far, and so Ja'far went to her father and told him that the Commander of the Faithful wanted his daughter. He agreed willingly and promised that she would be given to him, after which he provided her with what she needed and took her to the caliph. He married her, and when the marriage had been consummated she became one of his favourites and his generous gifts served to maintain her father's position among the Bedouin.

Some time later her father died and news of this was brought to the caliph. He went dejectedly to the girl, and when she saw his gloom she got up, went to her room and stripped off her finery, exchanging it for mourning clothes. She raised a lament and when she was asked the reason for this, she said: 'My father is dead.' Her attendants went to tell this to the caliph, and he got up and went to ask her who had told her. 'Your face, Commander of the Faithful,' she replied, and when he asked how that was, she said: 'Since I have been with you, this is the only time that I have seen you looking like this. Because of my father's age he was the only one for whom I was afraid, but may you be granted life, Commander of the Faithful.' His eyes filled with tears and he tried to console her for her loss. She stayed grieving for her father for some time, and then she joined him, may God have mercy on them both.

A story is also told that Harun al-Rashid, the Commander of the Faithful, being unable to sleep one night, got out of bed and began to walk from room to room but only became more and more restless. In the morning he ordered al-Asma'i to be fetched. A eunuch went to the gatekeepers to pass on the caliph's orders, and when al-Asma'i came, the caliph was told. He ordered al-Asma'i to be admitted, and welcomed him, telling him to be seated. Then he said: 'I want you to tell me the best stories that you have heard about women's poetry.' 'To hear is to obey,' al-Asma'i replied, and he went on: 'I have heard a great deal, but there are only three verses, recited by three girls, that I admire.'

Night 687

Morning now dawned and Shahrazad broke off from what she had been allowed to say. Then, when it was the six hundred and eighty-seventh night, SHE CONTINUED:

I have heard, O fortunate king, that al-Asma'i said: 'Commander of the Faithful, I have heard a great deal of this poetry but there are only three verses, which were recited by three girls, that I admire.' 'Tell me about them,' ordered the caliph. AL-ASMA'I REPLIED:

You must know, Commander of the Faithful, that while I was spending a year in Basra, one day when it was too hot for me, I searched for a place in which to have a nap but without success. I looked right and left and then I caught sight of a vaulted passage that had been swept out and sprinkled with water. In it was a wooden bench under an open window from which came a scent of musk. I entered the passage and sat down on the bench, intending to sleep, when I heard the sweet voice of a girl saying: 'Sisters, we are here today to enjoy each other's company, so come, let us put down three hundred dinars and each of us will recite a couplet of poetry, with the dinars going to whoever produces the most attractive and beautiful couplet.'

They willingly agreed to this and the senior recited:

It would delight me if the beloved visited me in my sleep,
But were this while I was awake, it would be more delightful still.

Then the second recited:

It was the beloved's phantom that came to me in my sleep,
And I welcomed it with the warmest of greetings.

The youngest then recited:

I would ransom with my family and my life the one who, every night,
Is my bedfellow, whose fragrance is more sweet than musk.

I said: 'If her beauty matches that of this couplet, then this is perfection.' I got down from the bench and was about to leave when a girl came out and told me to sit down. I went back again and she gave me a sheet of paper written in the most beautiful of hands, with straight *alifs*, hollowed *has* and rounded *was*. It ran as follows: 'We write to tell the *shaikh*, may God prolong his days, that we are three sisters who have sat to enjoy each other's company. We have put down three hundred dinars to be taken by whichever of us produces the most attractive and beautiful couplet. We have appointed you to judge the contest, so give your decision, peace be on you.' I asked her to bring me paper and an inkstand and in a short time she brought me out a silver inkstand and gilt pens. So I wrote these lines:

I tell of three girls who once spoke together,
And my words are those of a tried and tested man.
The three of them are like the early dawn,
And in their power is the lover's tortured heart.
As eyes slept, they were hidden away from sight,
Turning from one who kept his distance.
Then they revealed what they were hiding in their hearts,

Yes, and they took poetry as a playful game.
A loving girl, proud and high-born, smiled,
Showing a sweet mouth with well-spaced teeth,
And said: 'It would delight me if the beloved visited me in my
    sleep,
But were this while I was awake, it would be more delightful still.'
Her ornate line had finished with a smile.
Then her successor took a breath and, with emotion, said:
'It was the beloved's phantom that came to me in my sleep,
And I welcomed it with the warmest of greetings.'
The youngest made the best reply.
In the most pleasant and delightful words:
'I would ransom with my family and my life the one who, every
    night,
Is my bedfellow, whose fragrance is more sweet than musk.'
I thought over what they said, to give my judgement,
Leaving no grounds for mockery to the wise,
And gave my verdict to the youngest one,
As what she said was nearest to the mark.

I gave the sheet of paper to the girl, who went back up into the house,
and this was followed by a hubbub of dancing and clapping. I told myself
that this was no place for me and so I got down from the bench and was
about to leave when the girl called to me, saying: 'Sit down, al-Asma'i.'
'Who told you that I was al-Asma'i?' I asked her, and she replied: '*Shaikh*,
even if we did not know your name, we would recognize your verses.'
So I sat down again and the door opened as the first girl came out
carrying a bowl of fruit and another of sweetmeats. I helped myself to
both and expressed my thanks, after which I was about to leave when
again the girl called to tell me to sit down. I looked up and saw a pink
hand in a yellow sleeve, which looked to me like the full moon showing
through clouds. She threw me a purse containing three hundred dinars
and said: 'These are mine, but I pass them to you as a gift because of the
verdict that you gave.'

'Why did you prefer the youngest?' asked the caliph, and al-Asma'i
replied: 'May God grant you long life, Commander of the Faithful. The
eldest said: "It would delight me if the beloved visited me in my sleep,"
which is a restricted condition that may or may not be fulfilled. The next

greeted a phantom which visited her in her sleep, but the youngest recalled that she had really slept with her lover, whose scent she had found sweeter than that of musk and for whom she was prepared to ransom her family and her life. No one is prepared to offer their life except for those whom they find dearer than themselves.' 'Well done, al-Asma'i!' exclaimed the caliph, and he handed him another three hundred dinars in exchange for his tale.

A story is also told that Ishaq al-Mausili once asked al-Rashid to give him leave for a day so that he might be alone with his family and his friends, and al-Rashid allowed him to take Saturday off. ISHAQ SAID:

I went home and began to prepare what I needed in the way of food and drink, telling the doorkeepers to shut the doors and to allow no one in to see me. When I was in my sitting room surrounded by my womenfolk, a handsome and venerable-looking old man entered, wearing white robes and a soft shirt with a shawl over his head and a silver-handled stick in his hand. He diffused a sweet scent that filled the house and the portico. I was very angry that he had been allowed in and I thought of dismissing the doorkeepers, but the newcomer greeted me with the greatest courtesy, and after I had returned his greeting I told him to sit down. When he was seated he started to tell me stories about the Arabs and their poetry until my anger cooled, and I thought that my servants must have tried to please me by letting in a man of such culture and wit. I asked him if he would like some food and he said that he did not need any, but when I asked if he wanted wine, he replied: 'That is up to you.' I then drank a *ratl* and poured the same for him, after which he said: 'Abu Ishaq, will you sing something so that I may listen to this artistry of yours in which you outdo high and low alike?' This annoyed me, but I composed myself and struck up a tune on my lute to which I sang. He said: 'Well done, Abu Ishaq,' and this made me even more angry, as I said to myself: 'This fellow is not content with what he has done already, coming in without leave and making brash requests, but now he uses my name without knowing how to address me properly.'

The man now said: 'If you will sing some more, I will repay you.' So I decided to take the trouble and, picking up the lute, I sang, trying to do my very best because he had mentioned repayment.

Night 688

Morning now dawned and Shahrazad broke off from what she had been allowed to say. Then, when it was the six hundred and eighty-eighth night, SHE CONTINUED:

I have heard, O fortunate king, that the man now said: 'If you will sing some more, I will repay you.' ISHAQ WENT ON:

So I decided to take the trouble and, picking up the lute, I sang, trying to do my very best because he had mentioned repayment. He was delighted and said again: 'Well done, sir.' He then asked my permission to sing himself and, although I said: 'Do what you want,' I thought that he must be feeble-witted to sing in my presence after he had listened to my own singing. But he took the lute and fingered it and I swear that it seemed to me to be speaking the purest Arabic in a beautiful, melodious tone. He then began to sing the following lines:

My heart is wounded. Who will give me for it
Another heart that has no wound?
No one was ready to do such a deal,
For who would buy the unsound with the sound?
The longing in my heart has made me groan,
Like a drunken man, wounded by wine.

By God, I thought that the door, the walls and everything in the house were answering him and singing with him, so beautiful was his voice, and it seemed to me that I could hear my own limbs and my clothes responding to him. I was so stupefied that because of my emotion I could neither speak nor move.

He then sang these lines:

Doves of the winding valley, return again;
I am sad as I wait to hear your voices.
I nearly died as they flew back to the thicket,
And I almost gave away my secrets when they came.
As they call loudly to one who is not there,
It is as though they had drunk wine or had gone mad.
I have never seen the like of these;
They weep but their eyes pour down no tears.

Then he produced more lines:

> Breeze of Nejd, when you move from Nejd,
> Your passing adds to the passion that I feel.
> In the shining light of morning a dove calls.
> Perched on branches of the *ban* tree and the myrtle,
> Lamenting as a boy who weeps for love,
> Showing such longing as I have never shown.
> Men say that when the lover is near his love,
> He grows bored, and that distance is a cure for passion.
> I have tried both, and neither one cured me,
> But to be near is better than to be far,
> Though how can nearness be of help
> When the beloved feels no love?

The stranger then said: 'Ibrahim, sing this song that you have heard and follow the same technique in your singing. Then teach it to your slave girls.' 'Sing it again to me,' I told him, but he replied: 'You don't need to have it repeated, for you have already grasped it all.' Then, to my astonishment, he vanished in front of my eyes. I got up to fetch a sword and, having drawn it, I went to the door leading to the women's quarters, which I found locked. 'What did you hear?' I asked the slave girls, and they said: 'We heard the most delightful and beautiful singing.' In my bewilderment I went to the house door, but this too was locked and, when I asked the doorkeepers about the *shaikh*, they said: 'What *shaikh*? By God, no one has come in today.' I had gone back to think the matter over when a voice came to me from the side of the house, saying: 'There is nothing to fear, Abu Ishaq. It was I, Abu Murra,* who was with you today, but there is no need to be frightened.' So I went to al-Rashid and told him what had happened, and he said: 'Sing over to me the songs that you learned from him.' So I struck the lute and discovered that these songs were firmly fixed in my heart. They delighted al-Rashid and he started drinking as he listened, although he was not given to indulging himself in wine, and he said: 'I wish that Abu Murra would give me the pleasure of his company for one day as he gave it to you.' He then ordered me to be presented with a gift, which I took and left.

---

* The devil.

SHAHRAZAD CONTINUED:

A story is also told on the authority of Masrur the eunuch that one night the Commander of the Faithful, Harun al-Rashid, was very wakeful and told him to see which poets were waiting at his door. MASRUR SAID:

I went out to the anteroom and found Jamil ibn Ma'mar al-'Udhri, whom I told to obey the caliph's summons. 'To hear is to obey,' he said. He then went in with me, and when he came into the caliph's presence, he greeted him ceremoniously and the caliph returned his greeting, telling him to be seated. 'Jamil,' he then said, 'have you any remarkable stories?' 'Yes indeed, Commander of the Faithful,' replied Jamil. 'Which would you prefer – things that I have seen with my own eyes or others that I have heard?' 'Tell me about something that you have seen yourself,' the caliph said. 'Certainly, Commander of the Faithful,' answered Jamil, 'but pay me your full attention as you listen.' At that, al-Rashid took a pillow of red brocade embroidered with gold and stuffed with ostrich feathers which he placed under his thighs and on which he rested his elbows, before telling Jamil to start his tale.

Jamil began: 'You must know, Commander of the Faithful, that I was once deeply in love with a girl, whom I would visit time after time . . .'

Night 689

Morning now dawned and Shahrazad broke off from what she had been allowed to say. Then, when it was the six hundred and eighty-ninth night, SHE CONTINUED:

I have heard, O fortunate king, that when Harun reclined on a brocaded pillow, he told Jamil to begin his story. JAMIL BEGAN:

You must know, Commander of the Faithful, that I was once deeply in love with a girl, whom I would visit time after time, as she was all that I could ask for and desire in this world. Then lack of pasturage forced her family to move and I did not see her for a while. I was drawn towards her and my longing for her so disturbed me that I told myself that I should go to her. One night, spurred on by this emotion, I got up, saddled my she-camel, put on my turban and dressed myself in old clothes, taking with me my sword and my spear. I mounted and rode off on my quest, travelling fast. It was a very dark night when I started, but in spite of that I made myself ride down into valleys and up hills, listening to the roars of lions, the howling of wolves and the cries of wild beasts on every side. I was distracted and my wits were wandering, but I did not stop calling on the Name of Almighty God.

While I was riding like this I was overcome by sleep, and while I was drowsing my camel led me out of my way. Then suddenly something struck me on the head and I was startled awake to find myself surrounded by trees, with streams nearby and birds singing their various songs on the branches. The trees were so tightly packed together that I had to dismount and lead my camel with my hand on its reins, but I used all my skill to win free of them and eventually I came out on to open ground. There I straightened the saddle and remounted without knowing where I was going or where fate would lead me. As I looked out over the desert, I caught sight of a fire at the upper end of it and so, urging on the camel, I set off in its direction. When I looked from closer at hand I could see that a tent was pitched there and a spear stuck in the ground with a pennon fixed to it, while horses were standing beside it and camels were pasturing freely.

As there were no others tents in sight, I said to myself that there must be something of great significance in this one, and so I went up to it and called: 'People of the tent, peace be on you together with God's mercy and His blessing.' From the tent there then emerged a nineteen-year-old youth, like a shining full moon, with a look of high courage in his eyes. He returned my greeting and added: 'I think that you must have lost your way.' 'That is so,' I confirmed, and I asked him to direct me. 'My Arab brother,' he said, 'our country is a haunt of lions and this is a dark, gloomy and cold night. I'm afraid that you might fall prey to wild beasts, so stay and relax with me and tomorrow I will set you on your way.' I dismounted from my camel and hobbled it with the end of its rein before taking off the outer clothes that I was wearing. When I had been sitting there for some time, the young man went and slaughtered a sheep before lighting a bright fire. From the tent he then produced fine spices and good salt, and he began to carve pieces of meat, roast them on the fire and pass them to me. While he did so he was mixing sighs with tears, and then with a loud groan he wept bitterly and recited these lines:

Nothing remains to him but failing breath,
And a eye whose pupil has faded.
In every joint throughout his limbs,
Disease has taken a firm hold.

Tears flow and his entrails burn,
But still he stays without a word.
Enemies weep in pity for him;
Alas for one pitied by those who should gloat.

I realized then, Commander of the Faithful, that here was a distracted lover, for love can only be recognized by those who have tasted it. I wondered whether to ask him about this, but then I had second thoughts and said to myself: 'How can I intrude on him by asking him questions when I am his guest?' So I stopped myself and ate my fill of the meat. When we had both eaten, he got up and went into the tent, from which he brought out a clean washbowl, a handsome jug, a silk towel whose edges were embroidered with red gold and a flask filled with musk-scented rose-water. I was astounded by this elegance and courtesy, saying to myself that I was not used to such refinement in the desert. When we had washed our hands and talked for a while, he got to his feet and entered the tent, where he put up a partition of red brocade between us before saying: 'Come in, chief of the Arabs. Here is your bed, for you must have been tired out tonight, as this journey of yours has been a hard one.' I went in to find a couch of red brocade, and when I had taken off my clothes I passed the most comfortable night that I had ever spent . . .

Night 690

Morning now dawned and Shahrazad broke off from what she had been allowed to say. Then, when it was the six hundred and ninetieth night, SHE CONTINUED:

I have heard, O fortunate king, that JAMIL SAID:

I passed the most comfortable night that I had ever spent, but I could not stop thinking about the young man.

Then, at dead of night when all should be asleep, I caught the sound of a soft voice, more delicate and gentle than any I had ever heard. I raised the curtain that separated us and saw the loveliest of girls sitting by the young man's side. They were weeping and complaining of the pain of love and passion, and of their great longing to be together. I wondered to myself how a second person could be there, for when I had entered the tent there had been only the young man on his own. Then I told myself: 'This must be one of the daughters of the *jinn* who is in love with him, and they come here to be alone together,' but then, when I looked at her more closely, I could see that she was an Arab girl, whose unveiled face would put the bright sun to shame and whose radiance illumined the tent. As soon as I was sure that he was in love with her, I lowered the curtain again, remembering how jealous lovers are, and after covering my face I went to sleep.

The next morning I dressed and performed the ritual ablution before the obligatory prayer. Then I thanked my host for his kindness and asked him to show me my way. He looked at me and said: 'Don't be in a hurry, chieftain. Hospitality extends for three days and I am not the man to let you go until after that.' So I stayed with him for three days, and on the fourth, as we sat talking, I asked him his name and lineage. He said that he was of the Banu 'Udhra and he gave me his name together with that of his father and his paternal uncle. It turned out that he was a cousin of mine and he belonged to the noblest family of his clan. So I asked him: 'Cousin, what brought you to isolate yourself here in this desert, abandoning the luxury that you and your family enjoy, leaving your slaves, male and female, in order to live here on your own?'

When he heard my question, Commander of the Faithful, his eyes brimmed over with tears and he explained: 'I fell passionately and madly in love with a cousin of mine, and as my love increased I could not bear to be parted from her. I asked my uncle for her hand but he refused me and married her to another of our clansmen who, after consummating the marriage, took her to where she has been for this last year. When she had been removed from my sight, the pangs of love and the strength of my passionate longing led me to abandon kith and kin, together with my friends and my possessions, in order to live here by myself in this desert, where I have grown used to being on my own.' 'Where is the camp of your beloved's people?' I asked him. 'Nearby,' he told me, 'on the top of this hill, and every night when people are asleep and all is still she steals away secretly from her camp, without being noticed, and she and I talk. I stay like this, enjoying her company for an hour each night, so that God may bring to pass what is decreed by fate. It may be that I shall succeed in spite of the envious, or God may settle the matter for me, and He is the best of judges.'

When the young man told me his story, Commander of the Faithful, I felt sorry for him, but in spite of being anxious to help him, at first I was perplexed, as I did not want him to be dishonoured. Then I said: 'Cousin, shall I tell you of a scheme through which, God willing, you may find a successful way to resolve your problem and by means of it God may allay your fear?' 'Speak on, cousin,' he told me, and so I said: 'At night, when the girl comes, mount her on my camel, which is a fast one, while you ride your horse. I shall take one of these other camels and ride with you throughout the night so that, by morning, we shall have covered a large tract of desert and you will have reached your goal and won your heart's darling. God's lands are broad and I swear to help you as long as I live, with my life, my wealth and my sword.'

Night 691

Morning now dawned and Shahrazad broke off from what she had been allowed to say. Then, when it was the six hundred and ninety-first night, SHE CONTINUED:

I have heard, O fortunate king, that Jamil suggested to his cousin that he should take the girl and they should both ride off at night. He promised to help him as long as he lived. JAMIL WENT ON:

After hearing this, the young man told me that he would wait until he had consulted his cousin as she was an intelligent and sensible girl with an insight into affairs. When night had fallen he was waiting for her to come at her usual time, but she was late. I saw him go out of the entrance of the tent, open his mouth and breathe in the air that was coming from the direction where she was, as though to catch her scent. He was reciting these lines:

> Breeze that blows to me from where my beloved is,
> You bring a token from her, but do you know when she will come?

He went back into the tent and waited there for a time in tears and then he told me: 'Something must have happened to her tonight. There may have been an accident or something else may have prevented her.' He told me to stay where I was until he brought back news, and he went off into the night with his sword and shield. Some time later he came back holding something in his hand. He called to me and I hurried up to him. 'Do you know what has happened?' he asked, and when I said no he told me: 'By God, I have lost my cousin tonight. She set out to come here but met a lion on the way; it killed her and this is all that remains.' He then threw down what he had been carrying and this turned out to be a mixture of cartilage and such bones as had been left.

He now tossed aside his bow, took a bag and told me: 'Don't go until

I come back to you, if God Almighty wills it.' After some time he came back holding the head of a lion, which he tossed on to the ground. He asked for water, which I fetched for him, and then he washed out the lion's mouth and started to kiss it, shedding tears as his sorrow for his lost love grew more acute. He began to recite:

Lion, you brought yourself into danger;
You are dead, but through her loss you have brought me grief.
I was one of a pair, but you have left me solitary,
While she lies buried deep within the earth.
I say to Time, who has wronged me by this separation:
'God forbid that you show me another friend in her stead.'

He then said to me: 'Cousin, I ask you in God's Name, and through the obligations of the relationship that we share, to remember my instructions. You will soon find me lying dead in front of you and when that happens, wash me and place these bones, which are all that is left of my cousin, in my shroud. Bury us together in the same grave and inscribe these lines over it:

We once lived a life of ease on earth,
United in our dwelling and our land.
Changes of time then parted us,
But the shroud united us again within our grave.

He re-entered the tent, weeping bitterly, and came out again after a time, sighing and crying out, until he gave a groan and died. I was so distressed at seeing this that my grief almost led me to join him. I went up to him and laid him out, before carrying out his instructions and placing both the lovers in a single shroud and burying them in the same grave. I stayed by their grave for three days before leaving, and for two years I came back a number of times to visit them. This is their story, Commander of the Faithful.

Al-Rashid approved of what he had heard and he presented Jamil with a robe of honour and a substantial reward.

A story is also told, O fortunate king, that Mu'awiya, the Commander of the Faithful, sat one day in his audience chamber in Damascus, with the windows open on all four sides so that the breeze could enter. It was a very hot and windless day, and as he was sitting there at noon in the midday heat, he noticed a man stumbling along barefooted, scorched by the heat of the ground. Looking at him, the caliph said to his companions: 'Has Almighty God, praise be to Him, created anyone more wretched than one who has to go out at this time of day like this man?' 'He may be coming to see the caliph,' said one of them, and Mu'awiya replied: 'By God, if he does come to me, I shall give him a gift, and if he has been wronged, I shall help him.' He then told a servant to stand at the door and if the Bedouin asked to see the caliph, not to stop him. The servant went out, and when the Bedouin came up to him, he asked what he wanted. 'I want to see the Commander of the Faithful,' the man said. 'Go in,' the servant told him, and when he had entered, he greeted Mu'awiya . . .

Night 692

Morning now dawned and Shahrazad broke off from what she had been allowed to say. Then, when it was the six hundred and ninety-second night, SHE CONTINUED:

I have heard, O fortunate king, that when the servant gave permission to the Bedouin to enter, he greeted the caliph, who asked him to what clan he belonged. 'To the Banu Tamim,' the man replied, and when Mu'awiya asked him what had brought him at such a time, he said: 'I have come to make a complaint to you and to ask for your help.' 'Against whom?' Mu'awiya asked. 'Against Marwan ibn al-Hakam, your agent,' the man replied, and he recited these lines:

> Mu'awiya, generous, forbearing, excellent,
> Liberal, learned, rightly guided, the giver of favours,
> I have come to you because my means are straitened:
> I look for help; do not disappoint my hopes of justice.
> Grant me justice against an oppressor,
> Whose ill-treatment was harder for me to bear than death.
> In his hostility he robbed me of Su'ad,
> Wrongfully and with no justice taking away my wife.
> He thought of killing me, but my death
> Was not yet due, nor was God's provision for me yet complete.

As he recited this, the Bedouin breathed fire and Mu'awiya, having listened to the lines, spoke words of welcome and asked him to tell his story. THE MAN THEN SAID:

Commander of the Faithful, I had a wife with whom I was deeply in love and I lived contentedly and happily, maintaining myself thanks to a herd of camels that I owned. Then, in a drought, all my beasts died, camels and horses alike, and I was left with nothing. I had few resources; my wealth was gone and, as I was in a sorry state, those who had been eager to visit me despised me and found me burdensome. When my father-in-law learned how badly off I was, he took my wife back from me, disowned me and drove me away roughly.

I approached your governor, Marwan ibn al-Hakam, hoping that he would help me. He had my father-in-law brought before him and asked him about the case, to which he replied that he did not know me. I said: 'May God grant the emir prosperity; it would be wise to summon the woman and ask her about what her father has said, so that the truth may become clear.' Marwan sent to fetch her, and when she came and stood in front of him he was struck with admiration for her and became hostile to me. He angrily dismissed my case and sent me to prison, so that it was as though I had fallen from the sky and been blown away by the wind into a distant land. He then asked her father to marry her to him for a bride price of a thousand dinars and ten thousand dirhams, guaranteeing to free her from 'that Bedouin'. Her father was attracted by the offer and agreed, after which Marwan sent for me, and, glaring at me like an angry lion, he said: 'Bedouin, divorce Su'ad.' 'I shall not,' I told him, at which he handed me over to a group of his servants, who began to inflict a variety of tortures on me. Eventually I found nothing for it but to divorce her, after which he sent me back to prison, until the compulsory period of waiting before remarriage was over and he married her. I was then released and I have come to take refuge with you and to ask for your help.

He then recited these lines:

My heart burns and fire blazes up.
I am sick, and the doctor is at a loss.
In my heart is a coal that shoots out sparks.
My eyes shed tears that fall in showers.
No one can help except my Lord and the emir.

His body then shook and his teeth chattered until he collapsed in a faint, writhing like a newly killed snake. When Mu'awiya heard his story and his lines, he exclaimed: 'Marwan has overstepped the bounds of religion in his wrongful and wicked dealings with a Muslim wife,' . . .

Night 693

Morning now dawned and Shahrazad broke off from what she had been allowed to say. Then, when it was the six hundred and ninety-third night, SHE CONTINUED:

I have heard, O fortunate king, that when Mu'awiya heard the Bedouin's story, he exclaimed: 'Marwan has overstepped the bounds of religion in his wrongful and wicked dealings with a Muslim wife,' and he told the Bedouin: 'I have never before heard a story like this.'

He called for an inkwell and paper and wrote to Marwan: 'I have heard that you have overstepped the bounds of religion in your dealings with your subjects. Those who are in positions of authority must not be seduced by lust and must restrain themselves from its pleasures.'

I have cut short the lengthy passage that he added here, but it contained these lines:

> Damn you, you have failed in the duties of your office;
> Ask God's pardon for playing the fornicator's part.
> A poor wretch has come to me in tears,
> Complaining to me of the sorrows of being parted from his wife.
> I swear an oath to God that I shall not break;
> Yes, and I shall be true to my religion and my oath.
> If you should disobey the order I send you,
> I will leave you as vulture food.
> Divorce Su'ad, equip her and send her quickly,
> With al-Kumait and Nasr ibn Dhiban.

He folded the letter, sealed it and sent for al-Kumait and Nasr ibn Dhiban, whom he used to employ on matters of importance because of their reliability.

These two took the letter and, after making the journey to Medina, where they came into the presence of Marwan, they greeted him and handed it to him, telling him how the matter stood. Marwan shed tears as he read it, and he then went to Su'ad and told her that he could not disobey the Commander of the Faithful. He divorced her in the presence

of al-Kumait and Nasr ibn Dhiban, and equipped them for their return
journey with Su'ad. He then wrote these lines to Mu'awiya:

> Commander of the Faithful, do not be hasty;
> I am fulfilling your vow with friendship and goodwill.
> I committed no sin by falling in love,
> So how can I be called traitor and fornicator?
> You will be visited by a sun which has no match
> Among all God's creation, men or *jinn*.

He sealed the letter and passed it to the two envoys.

Al-Kumait and Nasr set off, and when they came to Mu'awiya they
gave him the letter, which he read. 'Marwan has done well to obey me,'
he said. 'But he has gone on at length in talking about the girl.' He then
ordered her to be brought before him. When he looked at her, he was
convinced that he had never seen anyone more lovely or perfectly formed
and, when he talked to her, he discovered that she combined eloquence
with clarity of exposition. He then ordered the Bedouin to be brought
in, and he for his part was still unsettled by the way that fortune had
turned against him. Mu'awiya asked him if he would be consoled for
the loss of Su'ad if he were to be given in exchange three swelling-breasted
virgins, lovely as moons, with a thousand dinars for each and a yearly
allowance from the treasury to suffice his needs and enrich him. On
hearing this, the Bedouin groaned and Mu'awiya thought that he had
died, and when he then recovered, he asked him what was wrong. The
man replied: 'In distress and suffering I called for your help against the
injustice of Marwan, but from whom can I get help if you too treat
me unjustly?'

He then recited:

> May God preserve your rule! Do not leave me
> Like one seeking help from heat by entering the fire.
> Return Su'ad to a distraught wretch,
> Whose mornings and evenings are spent with cares and memories.
> Set me free and do not grudge her to me.
> If you are generous, I shall not be ungrateful.

He added: 'Commander of the Faithful, if you gave me the caliphate that
has been conferred on you, I would not take it without Su'ad,' and he
recited:

My heart will accept no love but that for Su'ad;
My love for her is both my food and drink.

Mu'awiya told him: 'You admit that you divorced her, and Marwan
makes the same admission. I shall leave the choice to her. If she chooses
someone else, I shall marry her to him, and if she chooses you, I shall
hand her over to you.' The Bedouin agreed, and Mu'awiya asked: 'What
do you say, Su'ad? Who is dearer to you, the noble and glorious Commander of the Faithful with his palaces, his power, his wealth and the
luxury in which you see he lives, the unjust and tyrannical Marwan ibn
al-Hakam, or this hungry and impoverished Bedouin?' In reply she
recited these lines:

This man, hungry and wretched as he is,
Is dearer to me than neighbours and family,
Than the caliph with his crown and Marwan, his governor,
And all the rich with their silver and their gold.

She added: 'Commander of the Faithful, I shall not forsake this man
because of the turns of fortune or the treachery of Time. Ours is a
relationship of long standing that cannot be forgotten and a love that
does not wither away. As I enjoyed the good days with him, so it is right
that I should endure misfortune at his side.'

Mu'awiya was struck with wonder at her intelligence, her love and
her fidelity. He ordered her to be given ten thousand dirhams and handed
her over to the Bedouin, who took her and left.

A story is also told, O fortunate king, that Harun al-Rashid was sleepless
one night and sent for al-Asma'i and Husain al-Khali'. When they came
he ordered them to tell him stories, starting with Husain. HUSAIN
AGREED TO THIS AND BEGAN:

One year, Commander of the Faithful, I went down to Basra in order
to present an ode in praise of Muhammad ibn Sulaiman al-Rabi'i. He
accepted it and told me to stay with him. One day, I went out by way of
al-Mahaliyya to al-Mirbad and, as it was very hot indeed, I came up to
a large door to ask for a drink. There I was met by a girl like a supple
branch, with slumberous eyes, arching eyebrows and smooth cheeks.
She was wearing a mantle of San'a' work and her dress was the colour
of pomegranate blossom, but its colour was dimmed by the whiteness of
her body. Beneath her dress shimmered two breasts like pomegranates

and a belly like folded Egyptian linen, with wrinkles like white paper folded and filled with musk. Around her neck was suspended an amulet of red gold that dangled between her breasts, and over her forehead hung a lock of hair black as jet. Her eyebrows joined above her large eyes and, in addition to her smooth cheeks, she had a curved nose beneath which was a jewel-like mouth with teeth like pearls. She was drenched in perfume, but she appeared distracted and confused as she paced to and fro in the hallway, as though trampling on the hearts of her lovers with legs that filled her anklets so that they made no sound. She was as the poet describes:

> Every separate portion of her beauties
> Gives an example of the lovely whole.

I was filled with awe at the sight of her, Commander of the Faithful, and when I went up to greet her, I found that the house, the hallway and the whole street were filled with the scent of musk. She replied to my greeting in a low voice, as though her heart was sorrowful and burning with the fire of passion. I said: 'My lady, I am an old man and a stranger, suffering from thirst. Were you to order a glass of water to be brought to me, God would reward you.' 'Go away, old man,' she replied, 'for I am too distracted to think of water or food.'

Night 694

Morning now dawned and Shahrazad broke off from what she had been allowed to say. Then, when it was the six hundred and ninety-fourth night, SHE CONTINUED:

I have heard, O fortunate king, that the girl said: 'Old man, I am too distracted to think of water or food.' HUSAIN WENT ON:

'Why is that, lady?' I asked her, and she said: 'Because I love someone who does not treat me fairly, and I want one who does not want me. As a result I suffer the sleeplessness of those who have to count the stars.' 'Can there be on the face of the earth anyone whom you want who does not want you?' I asked, and she said: 'Yes indeed, and that is thanks to the excess of beauty, perfection and grace that he enjoys.' I then asked why she was standing in the hall and she told me: 'This is the route that he takes and this is the time that he passes.' 'Has this passion been produced by any meeting or conversation that you have had?' I asked.

She gave a deep sigh and tears rolled down her cheeks like dew falling on a rose. Then she recited:

We were like two branches of a *ban* tree in a garden,
Scenting the fruits of pleasure in a life of ease.
But then the two of us were split apart;
Sad is the sight of one longing for the other.

I then asked her how deeply love had affected her, and she said: 'I see the sun shining on the walls of his family's house and I think that the sun is him. If I catch sight of him suddenly, I turn pale: my life's blood takes flight from my body, and for a week or two I don't regain my wits.' 'Excuse me,' I told her, 'for I suffer from a passion like yours: I am preoccupied with love and am emaciated and weakened. I can see that you are pale and thin, which shows clearly that you are suffering from the pangs of love. But how could you have failed to fall in love, you who are an inhabitant of the lands of Basra?'

She said: 'Before I fell in love with this young man, I was graceful and supremely beautiful so that all the leading men of Basra fell under my spell and then I myself was ensnared by this young man.' 'And what parted you?' I asked. 'The misfortunes of Time,' she replied, adding: 'Ours is a strange tale. At the New Year's festival I had invited a number of girls from Basra, among them being a slave girl belonging to Siran, who had been brought from Oman at a cost of eighty thousand dirhams. She was passionately fond of me, and when she came in she threw herself on me and almost tore me to bits with her pinches and bites. We sat by ourselves enjoying our wine and waiting for our food to be ready. We were completely happy and she started to play with me and I played with her. Sometimes I was on top of her and then she was on top of me, until, flushed by wine, she put her hand on the fastening of my drawers. We had no evil intentions but the fastening came undone and, as we played, my drawers came down. At that moment the young man took me by surprise by coming in and, angered by what he saw, he made off and away like an Arab colt that has heard the bells of its bridle jingling.'

Night 695

Morning now dawned and Shahrazad broke off from what she had been allowed to say. Then, when it was the six hundred and ninety-fifth night, SHE CONTINUED:

I have heard, O fortunate king, that the girl said: 'When my beloved saw me playing with Siran's slave girl, as I have told you, he left in anger. I have spent three years excusing myself to him and trying to win him over and conciliate him, but he will not spare me a glance, write me a word, speak to any messenger of mine or listen to anything that I say.' HUSAIN WENT ON:

I asked her whether he was Arab or Persian and she told me angrily that he was one of the leading men of Basra. When I asked whether he was old or young, she looked at me askance, called me a fool and said: 'He is like the moon on the night it becomes full, smooth and beardless, his only defect being that he has turned away from me.' 'What is his name?' I asked, and when she asked what I was proposing to do, I told her that I would try my best to meet him in order to reunite them. 'I will tell you on condition that you take a note to him,' she said, and when I had agreed, she told me that he was Damra ibn al-Mughira, known as Abu'l-Sakha, and that he had a mansion in al-Mirbad.

She then called to her servants in the house to bring her an inkstand and paper, and, after rolling up her sleeves to show forearms like silver ingots, she started her letter with the formula of God's praise and went on: 'Master, the fact that I have left out the blessing from the beginning of this note is a sign of my inadequacy. Had my prayers been answered, you would never have left me, but leave me you did in spite of the number of my prayers. Were it not that I can no longer hold back because of my sufferings, the trouble that I have taken to write this letter would be a source of shame to me, as I have despaired of you and know that you will not answer. The most that I wish for, master, is that you should glance into my hallway as you pass by on the street, and so bring back a dead soul to life. Even better than that would be for you to write me a note in your own hand – may God endow it with every blessing – in return for all those private meetings that we held alone on nights long gone, as you must remember. Am I not wasting away out of love for you? If you answer my request I shall be grateful to you and thankful to God. Farewell.'

I took the letter and went off. Then, next morning, I came to the door of Muhammad ibn Sulaiman and found his salon packed with men of importance. I caught sight of a young man who was an adornment to the assembly, surpassing all the others there in the splendour of his beauty, and to whom the emir had given a place higher than his own. When I asked about him I was told that this was Damra ibn al-Mughira, and I said to myself that it was not surprising that the poor girl had been distracted by love for him. I then left and went to al-Mirbad, where I waited by the door of his house, and when he arrived with his entourage I jumped up and, after having greeted him effusively, I handed him the girl's letter. When he had read it and noted its contents, he told me that he had taken another in her place and asked me if I would like to see her. When I said that I would, he called and out came a swelling-breasted girl who put to shame the sun and the moon, walking quickly but not through fear. He passed her the letter and told her to reply to it. When she read it, its contents made her turn pale and she said to me: 'Old man, ask God's pardon for what you have done.' So I left, dragging my feet, until I came back and, after asking permission, I went in to see the girl. She asked me what I had brought, and I said: 'Misery and despair.' She replied: 'Don't concern yourself about Damra, as this is a matter for the power of God,' and she then ordered me to be given five hundred dinars, after which I left.

Some days later, as I passed by, I noticed a party of servants and riders and went in. It turned out that they were companions of Damra who were asking the girl to go back to him, while she was saying: 'No, by God. I shall never look him in the face again.' Then she prostrated herself in thanks to God, gloating over Damra's disappointment. I went up to her and she produced a letter for me which read, after the invocation of God: 'My lady, if I did not wish to spare your feelings, I would describe some of the sufferings that you have inflicted on me and I would excuse myself, although it was you who injured me and it was you who wronged both yourself and me. You clearly broke your word and were unfaithful in preferring someone else to me and rejecting my love. That was your choice and I can only ask for God's help.' She showed me the rare gifts he had sent to her, whose value came to thirty thousand dinars. When I next saw her, she had married him.

Al-Rashid said: 'Had Damra not forestalled me, I would have made an approach to her.'

*

A story is also told, O king, that ISHAQ IBN IBRAHIM AL-MAUSILI
SAID:

I was at home one winter's night when clouds had spread across the
sky and rain was pouring down in floods as though from the mouths of
water skins. No one was abroad on the streets, coming or going, because
of the rain and the mud; I was depressed because none of my friends had
come to visit me and it was too muddy for me to go to them. So I told
my servant to bring me something to distract me, but although he fetched
food and drink, I could not enjoy the meal as there was nobody to keep
me company, and I kept on looking out of the windows and watching
the roads until night fell. Then I remembered a slave girl who belonged
to one of the sons of al-Mahdi, with whom I had been in love and
who was an accomplished singer and musician. 'Were she here with me
tonight,' I said to myself, 'I would be completely happy and no longer
have to spend the time worried and uneasy.'

Just at that moment there was a knock on the door and a voice called:
'May a beloved come in who is standing at the door?' 'It may be that
the tree of my wishes has born fruit,' I said to myself, and when I went
to the door I found my mistress wrapped in a green cloak with a covering
of brocade on her head to protect her from the rain. She was in a sad
state, covered in mud up to her knees, her clothes drenched by water
from the gutters. 'My lady,' I exclaimed, 'what has brought you here
through all this mud?' She said: 'When your messenger came to me and
told me how full you were of love and longing, there was no help for it
but to answer the summons and hurry here to you.'

I was taken aback by this.

Night 696

Morning now dawned and Shahrazad broke off from what she had been
allowed to say. Then, when it was the six hundred and ninety-sixth
night, SHE CONTINUED:

I have heard, O fortunate king, that when the girl came and knocked
on the door, Ishaq went out and said: 'My lady, what has brought you
here in conditions like these?' She replied: 'When your messenger came
to me and told me how full you were of love and longing, there was no
help for it but to answer the summons and hurry here to you.' ISHAQ
WENT ON:

I was taken aback by this, but as I didn't want to tell her that I had not sent anyone, what I said was: 'Praise be to God, Who has reunited us after the sufferings that I have had to endure. If you had been any slower in coming, I would have had to go to you because of the extent of my longing and love.' On my instructions, my servant now fetched a container filled with hot water to help her tidy herself, and as he poured the water over her feet, I myself took charge of washing them. Then I called for one of the most splendid of my robes, which I gave her to wear after she had taken off her own. We sat down and I called for food, but she refused to eat. I asked if she wanted wine, and when she said yes, I fetched wine cups. 'Who will sing?' she asked, but when I volunteered, she said that she did not want that, nor did she agree when I suggested that one of my slave girls should sing. 'Sing yourself, then,' I said, but she refused, and when I asked who was going to do it then, she replied: 'Go out and find someone to sing for me.'

I went out obediently but unhopefully, certain that in weather like that I was not going to find anyone. I walked on until I got to the main street, and there I caught sight of a blind man tapping on the ground with his stick. He was muttering: 'May God give no good reward to my hosts. If I sang, they would not listen and, if I stayed silent, they made fun of me.' 'Are you a singer?' I enquired, and when he said that he was, I asked: 'Would you give us the pleasure of your company for the rest of this night?' 'If you want that, then take hold of my hand,' he replied, and so I led him by the hand back to my house and said to the girl: 'My lady, I have brought a singer to entertain us. He is blind and so he will not be able to see us.' 'Bring him to me,' she said, and when I had done this I invited him to eat, which he did sparingly and then washed his hands. I then fetched him wine and he drank three glasses before asking me who I was. When I told him that I was Ishaq ibn Ibrahim al-Mausili, he said: 'I have heard of you and I am pleased to be drinking with you now.' 'I am glad that you are pleased,' I told him, and he then asked me to sing for him. As a joke I took the lute and said: 'To hear is to obey.'

When I had finished the song, he told me: 'Ishaq, you are not far from being a singer.' This was a blow to my self-esteem and so I threw the lute away. 'Do you have no one here who can sing well?' he asked. When I told him that I had a girl with me, he said: 'Tell her to sing,' and I asked: 'Will you sing yourself when you have satisfied yourself about her performance?' 'Yes,' he replied, but when she had sung, he said: 'She has no skill,' and she threw away the lute in anger saying: 'I have done

my best and if there is anything you can do, then produce it for us.'
'Fetch me a lute that has not been touched by any hand,' the blind man
said, and on my orders my servant produced a new one. After fingering
it, he struck up a strain that I did not recognize and then set about
singing these lines:

> Through the gloom of a dark night there came
> A devoted lover, knowing the times of rendezvous.
> What roused me was a greeting and the words:
> 'May a loved one enter, who is standing by the door?'

The girl looked at me askance and said: 'Could you not keep our secret
for a single hour before entrusting it to this man?' I swore that I had not
told him anything and excused myself to her before starting to kiss her
hands, tickle her breasts and bite her cheeks until she laughed. Then I
turned to the blind man and asked him to sing again. He took the lute
and sang these lines:

> How often have I visited lovely girls,
> Touching their dyed fingers with my hands,
> Tickling the pomegranate breasts
> And nibbling at the ruddy apple cheeks.

'Who told him what we were doing?' I asked her. 'That's right,' she said,
and we moved away from him. He then said that he needed to relieve
himself and so I told my servant to take a candle and go ahead of him.
He went out, and then, as he was taking a long time, we went to look
for him, but without success. The doors were locked and the keys were
in their cupboard, leaving us to wonder whether he had been snatched
up into the sky or had sunk into the earth.

I then realized that this was Iblis, who had played the pimp for me,
and I remembered the lines of Abu Nuwas:

> I wondered at Iblis in his pride and evil intent;
> He was too haughty to prostrate himself to Adam,
> But then became a pimp for Adam's seed.

A story is also told that IBRAHIM IBN ISHAQ SAID:

I was a particular friend of the Barmecides. One day, while I was at
home, a knock came at my door and my servant went out and then came

back to tell me that a handsome youth was asking leave to enter. I gave permission and in came a young man who was showing signs of illness. 'I have been trying to meet you for a long time,' he said, 'as there is something that I need from you.' When I asked him what that was, he brought out three hundred dinars, set them before me and said: 'Please accept these and, in exchange, let me have an air to which to set verses that I shall recite.' I told him to produce the verses . . .

Night 697

Morning now dawned and Shahrazad broke off from what she had been allowed to say. Then, when it was the six hundred and ninety-seventh night, SHE CONTINUED:

I have heard, O fortunate king, that when the young man came to Ishaq, he set three hundred dinars before him and said: 'Please accept these and, in exchange, let me have an air to which I can set verses that I shall recite.' IBRAHIM WENT ON: I told him to produce the verses and he recited:

> By God, my eye has wronged my heart;
> Let it quench the grief of love with tears.
> Time is among those who blame me for my love.
> But, wrapped within my shroud, I shall not see her face.

I composed an air for him like a lament and sang it, after which he fainted until I thought that he was dead. When he recovered he asked me to sing it again, but I said: 'God forbid,' telling him I was afraid lest it kill him. 'I wish it would,' he said, and he continued to entreat me humbly until I took pity on him and sang it again. This led to an even more violent reaction, but in spite of the fact that I was quite certain that he was dead, I went on sprinkling him with rosewater until he recovered and sat up. I thanked God for his recovery before returning him his dinars and saying: 'Take your money and leave me.' 'I don't need it,' he said, 'and you can have as much again if you sing the air once more.' I was attracted by the thought of the money, and I told him that I would do this but only on three conditions, the first being that he should stay and eat with me so as to strengthen himself, the second being that he should hearten himself by drinking wine and the third that he should tell me his story. HE DID AS I ASKED AND SAID:

I come from Medina. One day, I went out on an excursion and took the road to al-'Aqiq with some companions. It was then that, among a group of girls, I caught sight of one like a branch decked with dewdrops, whose glances slew all those at whom she looked. She and her friends sheltered in the shade until evening and, when they left, I discovered that my heart was suffering from wounds that were slow to heal. When I went back, I tried to find out about the girl, but without any success, and when I attempted to follow up her trail in the markets, no one could tell me anything and I fell sick with grief. I then told my story to a relative of mine, who said that I should not worry, explaining: 'It's still spring and we can expect rain. Then the girl will go out and I shall come with you, after which you can do what you want.'

This comforted me and I waited until the water course at al-'Aqiq ran full and became a popular spot to visit. I went there with my brothers and some other relatives, and we sat in the same place that I had been before. Before we had been waiting for long, the women came hurrying up like horses running in a race and I asked one of my female relatives to tell the girl: 'This man says: "How well the poet expressed it when he said:

She shot an arrow at my heart and turned away,
Leaving me with new wounds and scars."'

When my messenger has gone to her and told her that, she said: 'Tell him how well this was answered in the lines:

I have the same complaint as you. Patience!
It may be that our hearts will soon be cured.'

I said nothing more for fear of a scandal and got up to leave. She rose at the same time and I followed her until she saw that I had discovered where she lived. After that she started to come to me, while I would go to meet her, and this happened so often that it became widely known and word reached her father. I kept on trying to meet her and complained to my father, who collected my relatives and went to her father to ask for her hand in marriage. He said: 'Had this request come to me before my daughter had been put to open shame, I would have accepted, but as it is now notorious, I'm not going to prove that the gossip was right.'

Ibrahim continued: 'I sang the air to him again, and he left after telling me where he lived, and we then became friends. Ja'far ibn Yahya held an assembly, which I attended as usual, and I sang the young man's lines for him, to his great delight. He drank some wine and asked me whose lines they were, at which I told him the young man's story. Ja'far instructed me to ride over and to assure him that he would get what he wanted, and after I had gone to him, I brought him to Ja'far, who asked him to repeat the story. He did that and Ja'far then delighted him by saying that he would guarantee to marry him to the girl. He stayed there with us, and in the morning Ja'far rode to al-Rashid, who was charmed when he heard the story. He ordered us both to come and told me to sing the air, to which he drank. He then sent a letter to his governor in the Hijaz telling him to make liberal provision for the girl's father and her family and to send them to him with all honour. They were not long in coming and al-Rashid summoned the father and told him to marry his daughter to the young man. He was then given a hundred thousand dinars and returned to his family.

'The young man stayed as one of Ja'far's boon companions until the fall of the Barmecides, after which he returned with his family to Medina. May Almighty God have mercy on all their souls.'

A story is also told, O fortunate king, that the vizier Abu 'Amir ibn Marwan had been given an exceedingly handsome Christian boy. Al-Malik al-Nasir noticed him and asked the boy's master where he had come from. 'From God' was the reply, at which the king exclaimed: 'Are you trying to terrify me with stars and imprison me with moons?' The vizier apologized and took care to prepare a present which he sent to the king along with the boy, to whom he said: 'You must be part of the present, but had I not been forced to do this I would never have let you go.' He wrote these lines:

Master, this moon has risen on your horizon,
And the horizon is a fitter place for moons than earth.
I seek to please you with the gift of this precious soul. Never before
Have I seen one who sought to please you with his own heart's
    blood.

Al-Nasir approved of this and rewarded the vizier with a large quantity of money and an assured position. Some time later, the vizier was presented with one of the loveliest of women as a slave girl. He was afraid that al-Nasir might hear of this and might ask for her, as had happened in the case of the boy. So he prepared an even more lavish gift and sent it to him with her.

Night 698

Morning now dawned and Shahrazad broke off from what she had been allowed to say. Then, when it was the six hundred and ninety-eighth night, SHE CONTINUED:

I have heard, O fortunate king, that when the vizier had been given this slave girl, he was afraid that al-Nasir might hear of her and the same thing would happen as had done with the boy. So he prepared an even more lavish gift and sent it to him with her. He wrote the following lines:

Master, here is the sun, following the moon,
Sent to you so that sun and moon may meet,
A conjunction promising felicity.
So enjoy through them the river of Paradise.
They have no match in beauty,
Just as you have no match as king of all mankind.

As a result he enjoyed even greater favour with al-Nasir, but then his enemies spread a report that he still had a passion for the boy and continued to talk about him while under the influence of wine, gnashing his teeth at the thought that he had given him away. So al-Nasir threatened that if he kept talking about the boy he would cut off his head, and then wrote him a letter, purporting to come from the boy, in which he said: 'Master, you know that you used to be mine alone and I was always happy with you. Although I am with the king, I would prefer to be alone with you, but I am afraid of his power. Can you think of some way of asking me back from him?' Al-Nasir sent this note with a youngster, who was to tell the vizier that it came from the boy and that al-Nasir himself had not said anything to him.

When Abu 'Amir understood the dangerous deception in this message brought by al-Nasir's servant, he wrote these lines on the back of the paper:

Should a man of experience and discretion
Do his best to go into the lion's den?
I am not a man whose intelligence is overcome by love,
Nor am I ignorant of what the envious claim.
I have willingly presented you with my life;
But how can life be brought back once it leaves?

When al-Nasir read this, he was struck with wonder at the intelligence of the vizier and after that he would never listen to anything said by his detractors. Al-Nasir later asked him how he had escaped from the snare that had been laid for him, and the vizier told him: 'It was because my intelligence was not trapped by love.'

A story is also told, O fortunate king, that in the time of the caliph Harun al-Rashid there was a man called Ahmad al-Danaf and another called Hasan Shuman, both of whom were wily and resourceful men who had performed remarkable feats. Because of this the caliph presented them both with robes of honour and appointed them as joint commanders of the city watch, each with a monthly allowance of a thousand dinars and each with forty men under their command. Ahmad was responsible for the district lying outside the city wall. He and Hasan rode out with their men accompanied by the emir Khalid, the *wali*, together with a herald who proclaimed that, in accordance with the orders of the caliph, Ahmad al-Danaf was to be the sole commander of the right-flank company of the city watch of Baghdad while Hasan Shuman was to command the left flank. Their orders were to be obeyed and they were to be treated with respect.

In the city there was an old woman known as Dalila the wily, with a daughter who was known as Zainab the trickster. When they heard the proclamation, Zainab said to Dalila: 'Look at this man, Ahmad al-Danaf, mother. He came here when he was thrown out of Cairo and he played his tricks in Baghdad until he ingratiated himself with the caliph and became commander of the right wing of the watch, while that scabby fellow, Hasan Shuman, commands the left. They are given two meals a day and each of them has a thousand dinars a month, while we sit at home with no jobs, no status, no respect and no one to ask after us.'

Dalila's husband had commanded the city watch of Baghdad with a monthly allowance of a thousand dinars from the caliph, but he had died, leaving two daughters. One of these was married, with a son called Ahmad al-Laqit, while Zainab the trickster was unmarried. Dalila herself was a mistress of wiles, deception and subterfuge. She could trick a snake out of its hole and tutor Iblis in double-dealing. Her husband had been in charge of the caliph's pigeons, with a monthly salary of a thousand dinars, and it was he who had reared the carrier pigeons which took letters and messages, with the result that in emergencies each bird was dearer to the caliph than one of his own sons.

Zainab now told her mother to play some trick to win them a reputation in Baghdad and get them the salary that her father had been paid.

Night 699

Morning now dawned and Shahrazad broke off from what she had been allowed to say. Then, when it was the six hundred and ninety-ninth night, SHE CONTINUED:

I have heard, O fortunate king, that Zainab told her mother to play some trick to win them a reputation in Baghdad and get them the salary that her father had been paid. Dalila swore that she would outdo both Ahmad al-Danaf and Hasan Shuman and so, getting up, she veiled her face and clothed herself in wool like a poor woman with a dress that went down to her ankles, a woollen *jubba* and a broad belt. She took a jug which she filled up to its neck with water, and she then put three dinars in its mouth, which she covered with a tuft of palm fibre. Around her neck she wore a rosary the size of a load of firewood and in her hand she carried a flag made of red and yellow patches. She went out calling on the Name of God, but while her tongue was praising Him, her heart was galloping on the racetrack of evil, as she looked out for some trick to play in the city.

She went from one lane to another until she came to one that was paved with marble and had been swept and sprinkled with water, and there she saw an arched doorway with a marble threshold where a Maghribi gatekeeper was standing. The house belonged to the chief of the caliph's officers, a landed proprietor who enjoyed a large income. He was called Hasan Sharr al-Tariq,* because his blow came before his word, and he was married to a beautiful girl whom he loved. On their wedding night she had made him swear to take no other wife and to spend no single night away from home.

One day, when her husband went to the caliph's court, he noticed that each of the emirs was accompanied by one son or two, and then, when he went into the baths and looked at his face in the mirror, he saw that there were more white than black hairs in his beard. He said to himself: 'God took away your father and will He not provide you with a son?' He was in an angry mood when he went back to his wife and, when she

---

* Literally 'Evil of the Road'.

wished him a good evening, he said: 'Get away from me. From the day that I first saw you nothing has gone right for me.' 'Why is this?' she asked, and he said: 'On our wedding night you made me swear to take no other wife. Today I saw that every single emir had one or two sons. I thought about dying without issue, and a man who leaves no heir will not be remembered, and I am angry because you are barren and cannot conceive by me.' His wife invoked God's Name against him and said: 'I have worn away mortars by pounding powders and medicines, and the fault is not mine but yours. You are a flat-nosed mule with watery and infertile sperm that cannot inseminate and produce children.' 'I am going on a journey,' he told her, 'and when I come back I shall take another wife.' 'It is God Who determines my fortune,' she told him. He then left her and each of them was sorry for having blamed the other.

Later, as the girl looked out of the window like a fairy princess in all her jewels, Dalila, who was standing outside, saw her in her finery and her rich clothes and said to herself: 'It would be a true test of cunning to take this girl from her husband's house, strip her of her jewellery and clothes and take the lot.' So she stood beneath the window of the house calling repeatedly on the Name of God, and what the girl saw was an old woman dressed as a Sufi whose white clothes were like a dome of light and who was saying: 'Come, you saints of God.' The women of the quarter looked out of their windows and exclaimed: 'God has sent us aid! Radiance is spreading from the face of this *shaikha*.' Khatun, the wife of the emir Hasan, burst into tears and told her slave girl: 'Go down and kiss the hand of Abu 'Ali, the gatekeeper, and tell him to let the *shaikha* come in so that we may be blessed by her presence.' The girl went down and did what she was told, passing on her mistress's message to the gatekeeper . . .

Night 700

Morning now dawned and Shahrazad broke off from what she had been allowed to say. Then, when it was the seven hundredth night, SHE CONTINUED:

I have heard, O fortunate king, that the girl went down to tell the gatekeeper that her mistress's instructions were that he should let the *shaikha* come in to see her so that both she and everyone else there might be blessed by her presence, and he in his turn went to kiss Dalila's hand, but she would not let him and said: 'Keep away from me lest you spoil my state of purity. But you too are drawn to God and have won the attention of His saints. May He free you from this servile state, Abu 'Ali.'

Abu 'Ali was in difficulties, as he was owed three months' wages which he did not know how to get from the emir. He said: 'Give me a drink from your jug, mother, so that I may get a blessing from you.' She took the jug from her shoulder and twirled it through the air with a flick of her hand so that the fibre covering fell from its mouth and the three dinars dropped on the ground. Abu 'Ali saw them, picked them up and said to himself: 'By God, this *shaikha* is a lady of power. She discovered my secret, found that I needed spending money and conjured up three dinars for me from the air.' He took them in his hand and said: 'Aunt, take these three dinars which have fallen on the ground from your jug.' 'Keep them away from me,' Dalila said, 'for I am one of those who are unconcerned about worldly things. Take them yourself and use them for your own purposes in place of what you are owed by the emir.' Abu 'Ali took this as a matter of divine inspiration and heavenly aid.

The slave girl now kissed Dalila's hand and took her to her mistress, whom she found, on entering, to be like a treasure freed from talismanic spells. Dalila greeted her, kissed her hand and said: 'Daughter, it is divine providence that has brought me to you.' Khatun produced food for her, but she said: 'I only eat the food of Paradise and break my fast on no more than five days in the year. But I can see that you are worried and I want you to tell me why.' 'Mother,' replied Khatun, 'on my wedding night I made my husband swear that he would take no other wife. Then he looked at other men's sons and, in his longing for them, he accused me of being barren, while I told him that he was an infertile mule. He went off in a fit of anger, promising to take another wife when he came back from his journey. I am afraid that he will divorce me and marry another, as he is a man of property with a large income, and if he has sons by another wife it is they who will take the wealth and the property instead of me.' 'Daughter,' said Dalila, 'don't you know about my master, Abu'l-Hamalat? If any debtor goes to him as a pilgrim, God will free him of his debt, and any barren woman who visits him will conceive.' When Khatun told her that since the day of her wedding she had not left her house either to offer condolences or congratulations, Dalila said: 'I shall take you with me on a visit to Abu'l-Hamalat. If you cast your burden on him and make a vow to him, it may be that when your husband comes back from his journey and lies with you, you will conceive either a daughter or a son, and the child, of whichever sex it may be, will become a dervish in the service of the *shaikh* Abu'l-Hamalat.'

Khatun got up and put on the most splendid of her clothes as well as all her jewellery, telling her maid to keep an eye on the house. 'To hear is to obey, my lady,' the girl replied, and Khatun then went down and was met by the gatekeeper, who asked where she was going. When she told him that she was going to visit the *shaikh* Abu'l-Hamalat, he said: 'I swear to fast for a year if this *shaikha* is not a holy saint. She has mystical powers and she gave me three dinars of red gold, having found out my secrets and knowing that I was in need, without my having to ask her.' So Dalila set off with Khatun, telling her as she went: 'When you visit the *shaikh* Abu'l-Hamalat, you will find comfort: through the permission of Almighty God you will conceive and, thanks to the blessing brought by the *shaikh*, you will regain your husband's love and never again hear any hurtful words from him.' Khatun agreed to visit the *shaikh*, and Dalila said to herself: 'Where can I strip her of her clothes while the people are going to and fro?' She then told Khatun to walk behind her while still keeping her in sight, explaining that she had many burdens which people would lay upon her and that all those who had votive offerings to make would present them to her and kiss her hand. So Khatun followed at a distance, with her anklets tinkling and the tassels in her hair sounding, as Dalila led her to the merchants' market.

Dalila now passed the booth of a very handsome young merchant, Sayyid Hasan, whose cheeks had not yet sprouted down. When he saw Khatun approaching, he started to look at her out of the corner of his eye and, on noticing this, Dalila made a sign to her and told her: 'Sit by this booth until I come for you.' Khatun did as she was told, and when she had sat down in front of Hasan's booth he cast her a glance that was followed by a thousand sighs. Dalila then went up to him, greeted him and asked him if he was Hasan, the son of Muhsin, the merchant. 'Yes,' he said, 'but who told you my name?' 'Good people directed me to you,' she replied, and added: 'Know that the girl over there is my daughter. Her father was a merchant who died, leaving her a great deal of money. She is of marriageable age, and "Try to find a husband for your daughter but not a wife for your son" is a saying of the wise. This is the first day that she has ever been out, and my inner heart has been prompted to make me marry her to you. If you are poor, I shall provide you with capital and in place of your one shop, I shall open two for you.' Hasan said to himself: 'I asked God to send me a bride and He has granted me three gifts: wealth, a woman and fine clothes.' 'Well spoken, mother,' he said to Dalila. 'My own mother has long been saying that she wanted to find me a wife, but I would never agree, telling her that I would only marry a girl whom I had seen for myself.' 'Get on your feet and follow me,' Dalila told him, 'and I shall let you see her naked.'

Hasan got up to accompany her, taking with him a thousand dinars in case he needed to buy something . . .

Night 701

Morning now dawned and Shahrazad broke off from what she had been allowed to say. Then, when it was the seven hundred and first night, SHE CONTINUED:

I have heard, O fortunate king, that Dalila told Hasan: 'Get up and follow me and I shall let you see naked.' Hasan got up to accompany her, taking with him a thousand dinars in case he needed to buy something or to pay the fees for the marriage contract. Dalila instructed him to walk at a distance from Khatun while still keeping her in sight, and she wondered to herself where she could take him and strip the two of them while Hasan's shop was shut, and she walked further on followed by Khatun, who in turn was followed by Hasan, until she came to a dyer's shop. The master dyer was called al-Hajj Muhammad, a man like a taro knife, splitting both males and females alike, who was fond of eating both figs and pomegranates. This man heard the tinkling of anklets and, on raising his head, he caught sight of the girl and the young man. Dalila sat down by his booth, greeted him and asked: 'Are you al-Hajj Muhammad, the dyer?' 'Yes, I am,' the man replied. 'What do you want?' 'Good people directed me to you,' she replied. 'Look at this pretty girl, who is my daughter, and that handsome beardless boy, who is my son. I brought them up at great expense, but mine is a large rickety house, and although I have propped it up with wood I have been told by the builder to move out and not return to live in it until he has repaired it, lest it collapse on me. I came out to look for a lodging and, as I have been directed to you by honest folk, I would like to leave my daughter and my son with you.' 'Here is ready-buttered bread,' Muhammad said to himself, and he told Dalila: 'It is true that I have a house with a hall and an upper floor, but I need it all for guests and for the peasants who supply me with indigo.' 'My son,' Dalila said, 'at the most it will be one or two months before my house is repaired. We are strangers here, so please share your guest rooms with us and I swear by my life that, if you want, we shall welcome your guests as our own, eating and sleeping with them.'

Muhammad then handed her a bunch of keys, one big, one small and one crooked, telling her that the first was for the house itself, the crooked one for the hall and the little one for the upper floor. She took them and went to the lane, followed by Khatun, who was herself still followed by Hasan. When she saw the house door, she opened it and went in, as did Khatun. 'Daughter,' Dalila told her, 'this is the house of the *shaikh* Abu'l-Hamalat,' and, after having shown her the hall, she told her to go upstairs, undo her veil and wait for her. Khatun went up and sat down to wait, after which Hasan came into the house and was met by Dalila, who told him: 'Sit in the hall until I bring my daughter for you to look at.' When he went in and sat down, she went to Khatun, who told her that she would like to visit the *shaikh* before other people arrived. 'Daughter,' Dalila said, 'I am afraid for you,' and when Khatun asked why this was, she explained: 'My son is here and, although he is the *shaikh*'s lieutenant, he is an idiot who cannot tell the difference between summer and winter and always goes about naked. If a girl like you comes in to visit the *shaikh*, he pulls off her earrings, tearing her ears, and then cuts up her silk dress. So take off your jewellery and your clothes so that I can keep them for you until you have made your visit.' Khatun did this and handed over the jewels and clothes to Dalila, who said that she would hang them for her on the *shaikh*'s curtain, so as to win a blessing.

Dalila took what she had been given and hid them somewhere on the stairs, leaving Khatun in her shift and drawers. She then went to Hasan, whom she found waiting expectantly for Khatun, but when he asked where she was, Dalila beat her breast. 'What is wrong?' he asked, and she replied by cursing evil and envious neighbours. 'They saw you coming in with me,' she explained, 'and when they asked me about you, I said that I had chosen you as a husband for my daughter. That made them envy me and they said to my daughter: "Is your mother so tired of providing for you that she wants to marry you to a leper?" I then swore to her that I would only let her see you when you were naked.' 'I take refuge in God from the envious!' exclaimed Hasan, and he uncovered his arms, which Dalila could see were white as silver. 'Have no fear,' Dalila told him. 'I shall let you see her naked as she will see you.' 'Let her come to look at me,' he said, and he then removed his sable fur, his belt and his knife, before taking off his clothes and leaving himself in his shirt and drawers. He put his thousand dinars among his things, and Dalila said: 'Give all your things to me to keep for you.' She took them and, after putting them together with those of Khatun, she carried them all off, locking the door on the two of them before going off on her way.

Night 702

Morning now dawned and Shahrazad broke off from what she had been allowed to say. Then, when it was the seven hundred and second night, SHE CONTINUED:

I have heard, O fortunate king, that when Dalila had taken Hasan's things and those of Khatun, she locked the door on them and went off on her way. She left what she was carrying with a perfume seller, and then went to the dyer, whom she found sitting waiting for her. 'I hope that you were pleased with the house,' he said, to which she replied: 'It is a fortunate place and I am on my way to fetch porters to carry our belongings and furnishings, but my children want me to bring them bread and meat. Would you take this dinar and provide this for them, and then go and eat with them?' 'But who will stand guard over my shop and the things that people have left here?' he asked. 'Your boy,' she said, and after he had agreed to this, he took a bowl and a lid to cover it and went off to get the food.

So much for him – and the sequel will come later – but as for Dalila, she took back from the perfume seller what she had taken from Khatun and Hasan and then returned to the dyer's shop and told his boy: 'Go to your master, and I shan't leave until both of you come back.' 'To hear is to obey,' the boy said, and Dalila then took everything that was in the shop and called to a hashish-eating donkey man who had had no work for a week. 'Do you know my son, the dyer?' she asked him, and when he said that he did, she went on: 'The poor man is penniless and in debt. Whenever he is put in prison, I have to free him, and so I want to have him declared bankrupt. I'm going off to return their goods to his customers, and to get this done I want to hire your donkey for a dinar. When I'm away I want you to take the scoop and use it to empty out the vats before breaking them, together with the jars, so that when the *qadi* sends someone to investigate, he will find nothing here.'

'The dyer has been good to me,' said the man, 'and so I'll do him a favour.'

Dalila took everything and loaded it on the donkey, after which, under God's protection, she set off home. There she went to Zainab, her daughter, who asked what she had been up to. She boasted that she had played four tricks on four people, a young merchant, the wife of an emir, a dyer and a donkey man, and she added: 'I have brought you all their belongings on the man's donkey.' Zainab pointed out that she would never be able to go through the town again for fear of the emir whose wife she had robbed of her belongings, of the young merchant whom she had stripped, of the dyer whose customers' goods she had taken from his shop and of the owner of the donkey. 'Bah!' Dalila replied. 'The only one who concerns me is the donkey man, because he knows me.'

As for the dyer, he got the meat and bread, which his servant carried on his head, and when he passed his shop he saw the donkey man breaking his vats. There were no goods of any description left there and the place had been wrecked. 'Stop!' he called to the donkey man, who did so, exclaiming: 'Praise be to God that you are safe, master! I felt for you.' 'Why?' asked the dyer. 'What happened to me?' 'You lost your money,' replied the man, 'and you were to be made bankrupt.' 'Who told you that?' the dyer asked, and the man said: 'Your mother, and she told me to break the vats and empty out the jars lest when the inspector comes he might find something in your shop.' The dyer cursed, beat his breast and said: 'My mother is long since dead.' He lamented the loss of his goods and those of his customers, while the donkey man mourned the loss of his donkey. He then said to the dyer: 'Get my donkey back from your mother,' at which the dyer laid hold of him and started to pummel him, saying: 'Bring me the old woman,' while the donkey man said: 'Bring me my donkey.'

A crowd gathered around . . .

Night 703

Morning now dawned and Shahrazad broke off from what she had been allowed to say. Then, when it was the seven hundred and third night, SHE CONTINUED:

I have heard, O fortunate king, that the dyer and the donkey man laid hold of one another and started to exchange blows, each accusing the other. A crowd gathered a round them and one man said: 'What's the story, master Muhammad?' 'I'll tell you,' said the donkey man, and he told them what had happened to him, adding: 'I thought that the dyer was going to thank me, but when he caught sight of me, he beat his breast and said that his mother was dead. For my part, I want my donkey back from him, as he has played this trick on me in order to take it from me.' The bystanders asked Muhammad whether he had entrusted his shop and its contents to the old woman because he knew her. 'No, I don't know her,' he replied, 'but she lodged with me today, together with her son and daughter.' 'In my judgement,' said one of those present, 'the dyer is responsible for the donkey,' and when he was asked why, he explained: 'The only reason why the donkey man was happy to give his donkey to the old woman was that he had seen that the dyer had entrusted her with his shop and its contents.' Someone else said: 'Master Muhammad, as you have taken the woman as a lodger, it is up to you to bring this man his donkey.' They all then set off for his house, and what happened will be told later.

As for Hasan, the young merchant, he waited for Dalila to come, but she did not bring her 'daughter', while Khatun, on her part, waited for her to bring permission from her lunatic son, the lieutenant of Shaikh Abu'l-Hamalat. When Dalila failed to arrive, she got up to visit the *shaikh* herself, but when she went into the hall she was met by Hasan. He asked her where her mother was, who had brought him in order to marry him to her. 'My mother is dead,' Khatun told him and went on to ask whether he was her lunatic son, the lieutenant of Shaikh Abu'l-Hamalat. 'She is no mother of mine,' Hasan told her, 'but rather a scheming old woman who has tricked me out my clothes and taken my thousand dinars.' 'She tricked me too,' said Khatun, 'by bringing me here to visit Abu'l-Hamalat and making me strip.' 'I hold you responsible for the return of my clothes and my money,' Hasan told her, and she replied: 'And for my part I hold you responsible for the return of my clothes and my jewellery, so fetch me your mother.'

At this point, in came the dyer and saw the two of them half-naked. 'Tell me, where is your mother?' he said, and each of them in turn explained everything that had happened to them. The dyer lamented the loss of his goods and of his customers' possessions, while the donkey man again mourned the loss of his donkey and insisted that the dyer return it to him. 'This old woman is a trickster,' the dyer said, and he then told Hasan and Khatun to leave so that he could lock the door. 'It will bring disgrace on you if we come into your house with our clothes and leave without them,' Hasan pointed out, and so the dyer supplied both of them with clothes and sent Khatun back to her house. What happened to her after her husband came back from his journey will be told later.

As for the dyer himself, he locked up his shop and told Hasan to come with him to look for the old woman in order to hand her over to the *wali*. Hasan went with him and they were accompanied to the *wali*'s house by the donkey man. They told the *wali* that they had a complaint, and when he asked them about it, they explained what had happened. 'How many old women are there in the town?' he asked. 'Go and look for her, and when you get hold of her, I'll force a confession out of her for you.' So they went around looking for Dalila and what happened to them will be told later.

As for the wily Dalila herself, she told Zainab, her daughter, that she wanted to play another trick, and when Zainab said that she was afraid for her, she said: 'I am like an old bean which can't be harmed by water or fire.' Then she got up and dressed herself as the servant of some important person and went out to look for a trick to play. She passed by a lane that had been spread with carpets, where lamps were hanging and singing could be heard together with the beating of tambourines. There she saw a slave girl carrying a little boy splendidly dressed in a silver-embroidered robe, with a tarboosh studded with pearls on his head. Round his neck was a jewelled collar of gold, and he was wearing a velvet cloak.

The house belonged to the doyen of the merchants of Baghdad, and the child was his son. He also had a virgin daughter whose betrothal was being celebrated that day. Her mother had with her a number of women and singing girls and, as the little boy would cling on to her wherever she went, she called the slave girl and told her to take him and play with him until the party was over. Dalila went into the house and saw the child being carried on the slave girl's shoulder. She asked her what it was they were celebrating, and when the girl told her that the singers were there for the betrothal of the daughter of the house, Dalila said to herself that it was up to her to take the child from her by a trick.

Night 704

Morning now dawned and Shahrazad broke off from what she had been allowed to say. Then, when it was the seven hundred and fourth night, SHE CONTINUED:

I have heard, O fortunate king, that Dalila said to herself that it was up to her to take the child from the slave girl by a trick. After praying to avert bad luck, she produced from her pocket a small brass token that looked like a dinar and said to the girl, who was a foolish creature: 'Take this dinar. Go to your mistress and tell her that Umm al-Khair, to whom she has been generous, is delighted for her and will come with her daughters on the day of the wedding reception and will give presents to the bride's attendants.' The slave girl said: 'My young master here clings on to his mother whenever he catches sight of her,' but Dalila told her: 'Give him to me while you go off on this errand.' So the girl took the token and entered the house, while Dalila carried the boy into the lane, where she stripped him of his ornaments and his clothes. She then said to herself: 'Dalila, it would be a true mark of cunning if in the same way that you deceived the slave girl and took the child from her, you were to play another trick and leave him as surety for something worth a thousand dinars.'

She went to the jewellers' market, where she saw a Jewish goldsmith sitting behind a crate full of jewellery, and she told herself that the clever thing to do would be to cheat the Jew into giving her a piece worth a thousand dinars while she left the child with him as surety. When the Jew looked at this child, he recognized him as the son of the doyen of the merchants. He was himself a wealthy man, but he felt envy every time his neighbour sold something and he did not.

So he asked Dalila what she was looking for and she said: 'Are you master 'Adhra, the Jew?' – for she had already found out his name. When he said that he was, Dalila explained: 'The sister of this child, the daughter of the doyen of the merchants, is engaged to be married. Her betrothal is being celebrated today and she needs some jewellery. Let me have two pairs of gold anklets, a pair of gold bracelets, pearl earrings, a belt, a dagger and a signet ring.' She took goods worth a thousand dinars from him and said: 'I am taking these on approval. The family will take what they want, and I'll bring you back the money for them. Meanwhile, keep this child with you.' 'As you wish,' said the goldsmith, and Dalila took the jewellery and went back home. When her daughter, Zainab, asked what tricks she had played, she told her how she had made off with the child, stripping him of his clothes, and then had left him as a pledge for a thousand dinars' worth of jewellery which she had taken from the Jew. 'You'll never be able to walk through the city again,' Zainab told her.

Meanwhile the slave girl had gone to her mistress and said: 'My lady, Umm al-Khair greets you and is happy for you. On the day of the wedding reception she and her daughters will come with wedding presents.' Her mistress asked where the child was, and the girl explained that she had left him with Umm al-Khair lest he cling on to his mother and that she had been given money for the singing girls. When she gave this to the girls' leader, it was found to be a brass token, and her mistress then said: 'You whore, go down and look for your master.' When she went down, she found neither the child nor the old woman, and she fell on her face with a loud cry. Joy turned to sorrow in the house. The boy's father arrived and, when he had been told the whole story by his wife, he set out to look for his son, with all the other merchants searching in different directions. He himself went on looking until he came across his son, naked, in the goldsmith's shop. 'This is my son!' he exclaimed. 'I know,' said the goldsmith, and his father took the child, forgetting in his delight to ask about his clothes.

When the goldsmith saw the man take the child, he held on to him, exclaiming: 'God help the caliph against you!'* 'What's the matter with you?' the merchant asked, and the Jew said: 'The old woman took jewellery worth a thousand dinars from me for your daughter and left this child as surety, for otherwise I wouldn't have handed over the things to her. The only reason that I trusted her was that I knew that the boy was yours.' 'My daughter doesn't need any jewellery,' protested the merchant, 'so hand over my son's clothes.' The Jew called out: 'Muslims, help me!' and at that the donkey man, the dyer and Hasan, the young merchant, who had been going round searching for Dalila, came up and asked the two why they were quarrelling. When they were told the story, they said: 'This old woman is a trickster and she cheated us before cheating you,' and they went on to tell their own tales. The merchant said: 'Now that I have found my son, I shall treat his clothes as his ransom, but if I get hold of the old woman I shall demand that she hand

* i.e. 'You wicked fellow!'

them back.' He then took his son back to his mother, who was delighted by his safe return.

As for the Jew, he asked the other three where they were going and when they told him that they intended to continue their search, he said: 'Take me with you.' He then asked if any of them knew the old woman, to which the donkey man replied: 'I do.' The Jew said: 'If we all go together, we shan't be able to find her, as she will escape from us. Each one must go by a different way and we can meet at the shop of Mas'ud the Maghribi barber.' When they had gone off on their several ways, Dalila came out to play another trick and was seen and recognized by the donkey man, who caught hold of her and said: 'Damn you, have you been at this trade for long?' 'What is the matter with you?' she asked, and he said: 'Give me back my donkey.' 'Conceal what God conceals, my son,' she told him and then asked: 'Is it your donkey you want or the other people's belongings?' He told her that it was his donkey, and she said: 'I saw that you were a poor man and so I left it for you with the Maghribi barber. Stay away from me so that I can go to him and ask him politely to give it to you.'

She now went up to the barber, kissed his hand and burst into tears. When he asked her what was wrong, she said: 'Look at my son standing there. He fell ill and exposed himself to the fresh air, as a result of which he has gone out of his mind. He used to be a donkey dealer and now, sitting, standing or walking, he keeps saying: "My donkey!" A doctor has told me that his mind is deranged and that the only cure is for two of his teeth to be pulled out and for his temples to be cauterized twice. Take this dinar and call out to him that you have his donkey.' The barber said: 'May I fast for a year if I don't let him have his donkey right enough,' and he then told one of his two craftsmen to go and heat two nails. As Dalila went off on her way, he called to the donkey man and told him when he came up: 'Your donkey is with me. Come on, poor fellow, and take it, for I swear by my life that I'll give it to you right enough.' He took the man and brought him into a dark room where he proceeded to knock him down, after which his men dragged him off and tied his hands and feet. The barber then pulled out two of his teeth and cauterized his temples twice before leaving him.

The man got to his feet and asked the barber: 'Why have you done this?', to which he replied: 'Your mother told me that you became deranged because you exposed yourself to the fresh air while you were ill, and that whatever you did you kept saying: "Where is my donkey?", so I have now let you have a donkey.' 'May God punish you for having pulled out my teeth,' the man said, but the barber replied: 'This was what your mother told me,' and he went on to repeat what Dalila had said. 'May God bring her misery!' exclaimed the man, and he and the barber left the shop and went off quarrelling. When the barber got back he discovered the place empty, as after he and the donkey man had gone, Dalila had returned and removed all its contents before going to tell her daughter everything that had happened to her and what she had done.

When the barber saw his shop empty, he laid hold of the donkey man and said: 'Bring me your mother.' 'That wasn't my mother,' the man told him. 'She is a trickster who has worked her wiles on many people and she has taken my donkey.' At this point, up came the dyer, the Jew and Hasan, the young merchant. They saw the barber holding on to the donkey man, who had burn marks on his temples. When they asked him what had happened, he told them the full story, and the barber added his own version. 'This old woman is a trickster and we too are victims of hers,' they said, and when they had explained to the barber what had happened to them, he locked up his shop and went off with them to the house of the *wali*. 'It is only through you that we can settle this matter and recover our goods,' they told him. 'And how many old women are there in the town?' the *wali* repeated, before asking whether any of them knew her. 'I do,' said the donkey man, adding: 'Give us ten of your men.' He then went out with the *wali*'s men, followed by the others, and as he was going round with them he caught sight of Dalila coming towards him. He and the *wali*'s servants laid hands on her and took her back to the *wali*'s house, where they waited under the window for him to come out.

The men had been awake so long in their attendance on their master that they now fell asleep. Dalila pretended to be sleeping herself, and when the donkey man and his companions also dozed off, she slipped away from them and entered the *wali*'s harem, where she kissed the hand of its mistress and asked her where the *wali* was. 'He is sleeping,' the lady told her, and went on to ask what she wanted. Dalila said: 'My husband is a slave dealer and he gave me five mamluks to sell while he went off on a journey. The *wali* met me and bought them for a thousand dinars, with a two-hundred-dinar commission for me. He told me to take them to his house and here they are with me.'

Night 705

Morning now dawned and Shahrazad broke off from what she had been allowed to say. Then, when it was the seven hundred and fifth night, SHE CONTINUED:

I have heard, O fortunate king, that Dalila went to the *wali*'s harem and told his wife that the *wali* had bought the mamluks from her for a thousand dinars, with a two-hundred-dinar commission to be given to her, and had told her to bring them to his house. It happened that the *wali* had given his wife a thousand dinars to look after, saying that they would use the money to buy mamluks, and so, when she heard what Dalila said, she was sure that this was what he had done. So she asked where the mamluks were, and Dalila told her that they were asleep under the window of her mansion. The lady looked out and saw the barber, who was dressed like a mamluk, Hasan, who looked like a mamluk, and the dyer, the donkey man and the Jew, who were all clean-shaven like mamluks. 'Each one of these,' she said, 'is worth more than a thousand dinars,' and so she opened her money-box and gave Dalila the thousand dinars, telling her to go off for the moment, and that, when her husband woke up, she would get the extra two hundred for her. 'A hundred of them will be for you to put under your drinking jar,' said Dalila, 'and the other hundred you can keep for me until I come back.' She then asked to be let out through the postern door, after which she went back to her daughter, sheltered by God, the Shelterer. Zainab asked her what she had done, to which she replied: 'I played a trick on the *wali*'s wife and got these thousand dinars from her by selling her the donkey man, the Jew, the dyer, the barber and the young merchant, making them out to be mamluks. But my greatest danger comes from the donkey man, for he knows me.' 'You've done enough, mother,' Zainab said, 'so sit back, as the pitcher cannot always avoid being cracked.'

As for the *wali*, when he woke up, his wife said: 'I am glad for you about the five mamluks you bought from the old woman.' 'What mamluks?' he asked. 'Why try to hide it from me?' she said. 'God willing, they may become holders of offices like you.' The *wali* swore that he had bought no mamluks, and asked who had told her that. 'The old broker,' she said, 'from whom you bought them and to whom you promised a thousand dinars in payment, with two hundred as her commission.' 'Did you give her the money?' he asked, and she said: 'Yes, and I saw them with my own eyes. They were each wearing clothes worth a thousand dinars, so I sent out your officers to keep an eye on them.' The *wali* went down and saw the Jew, the donkey man, the barber, the dyer and Hasan, the young merchant. He asked his men: 'Where are the five mamluks whom we bought for a thousand dinars from the old woman?' 'There are no mamluks here,' the men said, 'but only these five who took hold of the old woman and arrested her. She must have slipped away into the harem while we were all asleep, as a slave girl came out and asked us if the five people whom the old woman had brought were with us, and we said yes.' 'By God,' the *wali* swore, 'this is the greatest swindle.' The five were demanding that he get them back their property, but he said: 'The old woman was your mistress and she sold you to me for a thousand dinars.' 'God's law does not permit this,' they objected, 'for we are free men and cannot be sold. We shall take you before the caliph,' but the *wali* insisted: 'It was only thanks to you that she found her way here, and I shall sell you to the galleys for two hundred dinars each.'

While they were quarrelling, the emir Hasan returned from his journey to discover his wife stripped of her clothes. When she told him what had happened, he said: 'It is the *wali* whom I blame,' and, going to him, he said: 'Do you allow old women to go round the town tricking people and taking their goods? This is your responsibility and it is from you that I shall look for the return of my wife's belongings.' He then asked the five victims for their stories, and when they had told him everything that had happened, he said: 'You have been wronged,' and he went on to ask the *wali* why he was holding them. 'It was thanks to the five of them that the old woman found her way to my house, took my thousand dinars and sold them to my wife,' the *wali* replied. 'Emir Hasan,' the five told him, 'you are our representative in this case.' At that, the *wali* said to the emir: 'I shall take responsibility for your wife's belongings, and I guarantee to deal with the old woman, but which of you can recognize her?' They all said that they could and told him: 'Send out ten of your men with us and we will arrest her.'

So the *wali* gave them ten men and the donkey man said: 'Follow me, for I can recognize her by her blue eyes.' Just then Dalila appeared, coming out of a lane, and they seized hold of her and took her to the *wali*'s house. When he saw her, he said: 'Where are the goods of these people?' to which she replied: 'I didn't take them, nor did I see them.'

The *wali* told the gaoler to keep her in his gaol until the next day, but he replied: 'I shall not take her or lock her up lest she play some trick on me and I be held responsible for her.' So the *wali* mounted and took Dalila with an escort out to the bank of the Tigris, where he ordered his executioner to hang her up by her hair. She was hoisted up by a pulley and ten men were left to guard her, after which the *wali* returned home.

It now became dark and the guards fell asleep. As it happened, there was a Bedouin who had heard someone saying to a friend: 'Praise be to God for your safe return. Where have you been?' The other told him: 'I have been in Baghdad, where I breakfasted on honey doughnuts.' 'I shall have to go there and eat that,' the Bedouin said to himself, for he had never seen honey doughnuts in his life and had never been to Baghdad. He mounted his horse and rode off, saying to himself: 'Doughnuts are good to eat, and on my word as an Arab I am going to eat them with honey.'

Night 706

Morning now dawned and Shahrazad broke off from what she had been allowed to say. Then, when it was the seven hundred and sixth night, SHE CONTINUED:

I have heard, O fortunate king, that the Bedouin mounted his horse and set off for Baghdad saying to himself: 'Doughnuts are good to eat, and on my word as an Arab I am going to eat them with honey.' As he came to where Dalila was hanging he was repeating this, and she heard what he was saying. He went up to her and said: 'What are you?' She said: 'I am under your protection, *shaikh* of the Arabs.' 'May God protect you,' he replied, and he went on to ask why she was being punished. 'I have an enemy, an oil seller,' she told him. 'He fries doughnuts, but when I stopped to buy something from him, I happened to spit and my spittle fell on a doughnut. He brought a complaint against me to the governor, who ordered me to be hung up here and that, while I hang, I must be made to eat ten *ratls*' weight of honey doughnuts. "If she eats them, release her," he said, "and if not, leave her there" – but I cannot eat sweet things.' 'On my word as an Arab,' the Bedouin said, 'the only reason I have left my camping ground is to eat honey doughnuts, and I'll eat them instead of you.' 'But no one can do that,' she told him, 'unless he is hung here in my place.' She tricked him into releasing her and then hung him up where she had been, after first having taken off the clothes he was wearing. She put these on and rode off on his horse, with his turban on her head, to her daughter, Zainab. Zainab asked her about this and she said: 'They hung me up,' before telling her of her encounter with the Bedouin.

So much for her, but as for the guards, when one of them woke up, he roused the others and they found that day had broken. Then one of them looked up and called: 'Dalila.' The Bedouin replied: 'By God, I don't eat *balila*, so have you brought the honey doughnuts?' 'This is a Bedouin!' the guards exclaimed, and one of them asked him: 'Where is Dalila and who released her?' He said: 'I did it, since she shouldn't be forced to eat honey doughnuts as she can't digest them.' They then realized that the Bedouin knew nothing about her and had been tricked by her. They discussed whether to flee or to meet whatever fate God had decreed for them, and while they were talking this over, up came the *wali* accompanied by Dalila's victims. 'Get up and release Dalila,' he told the guards, and the Bedouin repeated: 'I don't eat *balila*, so have you brought the honey doughnuts?' The *wali* looked up at the cross, where he saw the Bedouin hanging in place of Dalila. 'What's this?' he asked the guards, and they replied: 'Pardon, master.' 'Tell me what happened,' he said, and they explained: 'We had spent a sleepless time with you on the night watch and we said to ourselves: "Dalila is fixed to the cross," so we dozed off. Then, when we woke, we found this Bedouin hanging there. We are at your mercy.' 'This was a trick,' the *wali* said, 'so may God pardon you.'

They released the Bedouin, who laid hold of the *wali* and told him that he would appeal to the caliph against him and that he would hold him responsible for the return of his horse and his clothes. On being asked, he told his story and the astonished *wali* said: 'Why did you release her?' 'Because I didn't know that she was a trickster,' the Bedouin told him. The others then repeated that they held the *wali* responsible for their belongings, adding: 'We handed her over to you and she was in your charge,' and insisting that they would take their case against him to the caliph's court.

The emir Hasan had gone to the court when the *wali*, the Bedouin and the other five arrived, saying: 'We have been wronged.' 'Who has wronged you?' asked the caliph, and each of them came forward and told his story, ending with the *wali*, who said: 'Commander of the Faithful, the woman tricked me and sold these five men to me for a thousand dinars, although they were freeborn.' 'I shall ensure the return of all that you have lost,' said the caliph, before going on to tell the *wali*: 'I give you the task of producing the old woman.' The *wali*, however, shook his head and said: 'I can't undertake to do that. I had suspended her on a cross, but she tricked this Bedouin into freeing her, hung him up in her place and went off with his horse and his clothes.' 'Should I give the job to someone else?' the caliph asked, and the *wali* replied: 'Give it to Ahmad al-Danaf. He gets a thousand dinars a month and has forty-one followers, each of whom draws a hundred dinars a month.' So the caliph summoned Ahmad, and when he answered the summons the caliph told him to produce Dalila. 'I guarantee to do that,' Ahmad replied, and the caliph kept the five victims and the Bedouin in his palace.

Night 707

Morning now dawned and Shahrazad broke off from what she had been allowed to say. Then, when it was the seven hundred and seventh night, SHE CONTINUED:

I have heard, O fortunate king, that when Ahmad was told to produce Dalila, he told the caliph that he guaranteed to do so.

Ahmad and his men went down to the hall saying to each other: 'How are we to arrest her? How many old women are there in the town?' One of them, 'Ali Kitf al-Jamal, said to Ahmad: 'Why should you consult Hasan Shuman? Is he so very good?'* Hasan said: 'Why do you try to belittle me, 'Ali? I swear by the Greatest Name of God that I am not going to help you in this business,' after which he left in anger. Ahmad then said: 'Boys, let each officer take ten men and go off, every one to a different quarter, to search for Dalila.' Accordingly, 'Ali took ten men and left, as did the other officers, and each band went in a different direction, having previously settled on the quarter and the lane in which they were to meet.

Word spread throughout the city that Ahmad al-Danaf had undertaken to arrest Dalila, the mistress of wiles. 'If you're really sharp,' Zainab told her mother, 'you will play a trick on Ahmad and his men.' 'The only one whom I fear,' said Dalila, 'is Hasan Shuman,' to which

* A reference to a sentence omitted in the text.

Zainab replied: 'I swear by my lovelock that I will get the clothes of all forty-one of them.' She then got up, put on a dress and a veil and went to a perfume seller, who had a large room with two doors. She greeted him and gave him a dinar, telling him to take it in exchange for letting her use his room until evening. He gave her the keys and she went off and loaded carpets on the donkey her mother had taken from its owner. She spread these throughout the room and in every alcove she put a table with food and wine. She then stood at the door unveiled just as 'Ali Kitf al-Jamal and his men happened to be coming along. She kissed his hand and, seeing that she was a pretty girl, he fell in love with her and asked her what she wanted. 'Are you Ahmad al-Danaf?' she asked. 'No,' he told her, 'but I am one of his company and my name is 'Ali Kitf al-Jamal.' 'Where are you going?' she asked, and he told her: 'We are going around looking for an old woman, a trickster, who has taken people's goods and whom we want to arrest. But who are you and what is your business?' Zainab said: 'My father was a wine merchant in Mosul. He died, leaving me a large sum of money, and I have come here out of fear of the authorities. I asked people who would protect me, and they told me that only Ahmad al-Danaf could do that.' 'Ali promised that from then on she would be under the protection of Ahmad's troop, and she said: 'To set my mind at ease, take a bite to eat and a drink of water.' When 'Ali and his men agreed she took them into the room, where they ate and drank, but she drugged them with *banj* and stripped them of their clothes.

She played the same trick on the rest of Ahmad's men, and when he came in his unsuccessful search for Dalila he could not find any of them but instead he saw the girl, who kissed his hand and at the sight of whom he fell in love. 'Are you Captain Ahmad al-Danaf?' she asked. 'Yes,' he replied, 'and who are you?' 'I am a stranger from Mosul,' she told him. 'My father was a wine merchant there. He died, leaving me a large sum of money, and I have come here out of fear of the authorities. I have opened this wine shop and the *wali* has levied a tax on me, but I want to be under your protection, as you have a better right to the money that the *wali* takes.' 'Don't give him anything,' replied Ahmad, 'and I shall make you welcome.' She said: 'In order to set my mind at ease, eat some of my food.' Ahmad went in, ate and drank wine until he fell down drunk, when she drugged him and took his clothes. She then loaded everything on to the Bedouin's horse and the stolen donkey, and left after reviving 'Ali Kitf al-Jamal. When 'Ali recovered consciousness, he found himself naked and he saw Ahmad al-Danaf and all his company lying there drugged. He used an antidote to revive them, and when this had taken effect and they had seen the state that they were in, Ahmad said: 'What is this, boys? We were going around looking to catch the old woman, and this whore has caught us. How Hasan Shuman will crow over us! But we have to wait until darkness comes before we can go off.'

Hasan Shuman was asking the officer of the watch where the men were, when in they came without their clothes and he recited these lines:

What people get may be the same;
What they produce is different.
Some are learned; some are fools;
Some stars are dim and others bright.

He looked at them and asked who had tricked them and stripped them. They told him: 'We were supposed to be looking for an old woman, but it was a pretty girl who took our clothes.' 'That was a good trick she played on you,' he said, and when they asked whether he knew her, he said: 'Yes, and I know the old woman too.' 'What are you going to say to the caliph?' they asked, and he then told Ahmad to shake his head in the caliph's presence. 'He will ask who is responsible for producing the old woman, and if he goes on to say: "Why haven't you arrested her?" tell him: "I don't know her, so put Hasan Shuman in charge of the case," and if he does, I shall arrest her.'

They spent the night there, and the next morning they went to the caliph's court and kissed the ground. 'Where is the old woman, Captain Ahmad?' the caliph asked, and when Ahmad shook his head the caliph asked why he was doing that. Ahmad said: 'I don't know her, so leave her to Hasan Shuman, who knows both her and her daughter.' Hasan then said: 'The old woman has not played these tricks because she wanted other people's property but to show off her cleverness and that of her daughter so as to get you to pay the two of them the same allowance that you gave her husband.' He asked that she should not be put to death and promised to bring her to the caliph, who, for his part, promised to accept his intercession and spare her on condition that she return the stolen goods. 'Give me an assurance of pardon,' said Hasan. 'She is covered by your intercession,' the caliph told him, giving him the kerchief which served as a token of clemency.

Hasan now went to Dalila's house and called to her. He was answered by her daughter, Zainab, and when he asked where her mother was, she said: 'Upstairs.' 'Tell her to fetch the things that she took and to come with me to meet the caliph, for I've brought her the kerchief of pardon, and if she doesn't come willingly she will only have herself to blame.' Dalila came down and tied the kerchief round her neck, after which she gave Hasan the things that she had taken to be loaded on to the donkey man's donkey and the Bedouin's horse. 'Where are the clothes of my captain and his men?' he asked, and Dalila told him: 'I swear by the Greatest Name of God that it wasn't I who stripped them.' 'That's right,' said Hasan, 'but this was a trick played by your daughter, Zainab, who was doing you a favour.'

He set off, accompanied by Zainab, for the caliph's court, where he presented the stolen goods to the caliph and brought Dalila before him. When he saw her, he ordered that she be thrown on to the execution mat. She appealed to Hasan for protection, and he kissed the caliph's hands, exclaiming: 'Spare her, for you promised to pardon her!' 'I shall do this for your sake,' the caliph told him, and he then asked Dalila her name. When she told him, he said: 'You are nothing but a scheming and wily woman,' this being how she got the title of 'Dalila the wily'. Next he asked: 'Why did you disturb us by playing these tricks?' 'It was not because I wanted these people's goods,' she said, 'but I had heard of those other tricks played in Baghdad by Ahmad al-Danaf and Hasan Shuman and I said to myself that I too could do that kind of thing. Now I have given back what I took.' The donkey man, however, said: 'I invoke Islamic law. It was not enough for her to take my donkey, but she put me in the power of the Maghribi barber, who pulled out my teeth and twice cauterized my temples.'

Night 708

Morning now dawned and Shahrazad broke off from what she had been allowed to say. Then, when it was the seven hundred and eighth night, SHE CONTINUED:

I have heard, O fortunate king, that the donkey man said: 'I invoke Islamic law. It was not enough for her to take my donkey, but she put me in the power of the Maghribi barber, who pulled out my teeth and twice cauterized my temples.' The caliph ordered him to be given a hundred dinars and he gave another hundred to the dyer to refurbish his

shop. They called down blessings on him and went off, while the Bedouin
took his belongings and his horse, exclaiming: 'I must never enter Baghdad
or eat honey doughnuts!' Everyone else took what was theirs and they
all then dispersed. The caliph then allowed Dalila a wish and she said:
'My father served you as postmaster, while I reared the carrier pigeons
and my husband was city captain. What I want is to take over my
husband's post, while my daughter wants that of my father.' The caliph
authorized this, and Dalila then told him: 'I would like to be doorkeeper
of the *khan*.' The caliph had built a *khan*, three storyes high, as a hostel
for merchants, and he assigned to it forty slaves and forty dogs that he
had taken from the ruler of Sulaimaniya when he deposed him, providing
them with collars. There was also a slave who did the cooking for the
others and who fed the dogs their meat. The caliph agreed to entrust the
position to Dalila, but said that if anything went missing from the place,
she would be responsible for it. She accepted this condition and went on
to ask that her daughter be allowed to live in the loft on top of the gate,
as it had a roof terrace and pigeons could only he reared where there was
plenty of space. This too was agreed by the caliph.

Zainab moved all her possessions there, hanging up the robes of Ahmad
al-Danaf's forty men and those of Ahmad himself, and she took charge of
the forty carrier pigeons. The caliph had put Dalila in charge of the forty
slaves, telling them to follow her orders. She used to sit behind the *khan*
door, but every day she would go to court in case the caliph needed to send
a message somewhere, staying there until evening while the slaves looked
after the *khan*, and at night the dogs would be let loose to guard it.

This is what happened to Dalila the wily in Baghdad.

'Ali al-Zaibaq the Cairene was a trickster living in Cairo when the chief
of police there was a man called Salah al-Misri, who had a force of forty
men. These men used to set traps for 'Ali, expecting that he would fall
into one of them, but when they looked, they would find that he had
slipped away like mercury and this was why he was called 'Ali al-Zaibag.*
One day, when he was sitting in his hall with his men, he felt depressed
and gloomy, and when his lieutenant saw him there with a frown on his
face, he asked: 'What's wrong, chief? If you're out of sorts, take a stroll
through the city, as a walk in the markets will cure your cares.' So
'Ali got up to walk through Cairo, but he only became more and more

---

* Zaibaq means mercury in Arabic.

depressed. He passed a wine shop and thought of going there to get drunk, but when he went in he found seven rows of people sitting there. He told the proprietor that he would only sit alone, and so the man put him in a room by himself and brought him wine. When he had drunk himself silly, he left the place and set out through the city.

He walked on and on through the streets until he reached al-Darb al-Ahmar and, thanks to the awe in which he was held, the road emptied before him. He turned to see a water carrier, with his jug, calling out on the road: 'Take and give! The only drink comes from raisins; the only union is with the beloved and only the intelligent sit at the top table.' 'Come here and pour me a drink,' 'Ali called, and the man gave him the jug, but after staring at it 'Ali upset it and poured the contents on to the ground. 'Aren't you going to drink?' the man asked, and 'Ali again said: 'Pour it for me,' but again he upset the jug and poured away the water. He went on to do this a third time, and the man said: 'If you're not going to drink, I'm off.' 'Pour me a drink,' 'Ali told him, and this time, when the man filled the jug and passed it to him, 'Ali took it from him, drank and gave him a dinar. The man looked at him contemptuously and said: 'Good luck, good luck to you, young man! Little men are great in some people's eyes.'

Night 709

Morning now dawned and Shahrazad broke off from what she had been allowed to say. Then, when it was the seven hundred and ninth night, SHE CONTINUED:

I have heard, O fortunate king, that when 'Ali gave the water carrier a dinar, the man looked at him contemptuously and said: 'Good luck, good luck to you, young man! Little men are great in some people's eyes.' 'Ali went up to him and seized him by his shirt, drawing a costly dagger such as the one described in the lines:

Strike the stubborn enemy with your dagger,
Fearing nothing but the Creator's power.
Avoid those who are to be blamed,
And never abandon generous qualities.

'*Shaikh*,' he said, 'talk sense. Your water skin would fetch three dirhams at the most and I only emptied out one *ratl* of water from the jug.' The water carrier agreed, and 'Ali went on: 'I gave you a gold dinar, so why do you despise me? Have you ever seen a braver or a more generous man than me?' 'Yes, I have,' the water carrier replied, 'for while women have been bearing children, there has never been a brave man in this world who was not generous.' 'Who was it whom you found to outdo me?' 'Ali asked, and THE MAN SAID:

I had a remarkable adventure. My father was the chief of the water carriers in Cairo. When he died he left me five camels, a mule, a booth and a house, but a poor man is never satisfied until he dies. I said to myself that I would go to the Hijaz, so I took my string of camels and kept on borrowing money until I had collected five hundred dinars, but I lost all this on the pilgrimage. I told myself that, were I to go back to Cairo, my creditors would imprison me for debt and so I set off with the Syrian pilgrims, and after reaching Aleppo I went on to Baghdad. There I asked for the chief of the water carriers, and after I had been directed to him I went in and recited the first *sura* of the Quran for him. He asked me about my circumstances and, when I had told him all that had happened to me, he let me have an empty booth and gave me a water skin and other equipment. The next morning I set out to walk around the city, trusting in God, but when I passed the jug to a man so that he could take a drink, he told me: 'I don't need a drink as I've not eaten. A miser invited me to his house and produced two pitchers of water. I said: "You miserable fellow, are you offering me a drink after having given me nothing at all to eat?"' So he told me to go away, adding: 'When I have had some food, then you can pour me some water.' I went up to someone else, but all he did was to say: 'May God provide for you,' and things went on like this until noon. Up till then nobody had given me anything at all and I said to myself that I wished I had never come to Baghdad.

Just then I saw a number of people running. I followed them and saw a long file of men riding two by two, with scarfs around their tarbooshes, wearing burnouses and protected with felt and steel. I asked a man who they were and he told me that this was the retinue of Captain Ahmad al-Danaf. 'What is his post?' I asked, and I was told that he was responsible for order at court and in Baghdad itself, as well as for policing the suburbs. He was paid a monthly salary of a thousand dinars by the caliph, while each of his men got a hundred and Hasan Shuman got the same pay as Ahmad. The men were now on their way from the court to their barracks. At that point, Ahmad caught sight of me and asked me for a drink. I filled the jug and passed it to him, but he upset it and poured out the water. He did this again, but the third time he took a sip, like you. Then he asked me where I came from and when I said: 'Cairo,' he exclaimed: 'God bless Cairo and the Cairenes!' before going on to ask why I had come to Baghdad. I told him my story, explaining that I owed money and had come to escape debt and poverty. He welcomed me and gave me five dinars, after which he said to his men: 'Be generous to this man for the sake of God.' They each gave me a dinar and Ahmad said: '*Shaikh*, as long as you stay in Baghdad, you can have this every time you pour water for us.' I kept on going to these people and receiving their generosity so that when, after some days, I counted up what I had got from them, I found that it came to a thousand dinars.

I said to myself that the proper thing to do would be to go back to Egypt, and so I went to Ahmad's headquarters and kissed his hands. When he asked me what I wanted, I said: 'I want to go home,' and I recited these lines for him:

Wherever a stranger stays,
It is like a castle built on winds.
A breath of air destroys what he has made,
And so this stranger has made up his mind to leave.

I added that a caravan was setting out for Cairo and that I wanted to go back to my family. He gave me a mule and a hundred dinars, before saying: '*Shaikh*, I want to entrust you with something. Do you know the people in Cairo?' 'Yes,' I said . . .

Night 710

Morning now dawned and Shahrazad broke off from what she had been allowed to say. Then, when it was the seven hundred and tenth night, SHE CONTINUED:

I have heard, O fortunate king, that THE MAN WENT ON:

Ahmad gave me a mule and a hundred dinars, before saying: '*Shaikh*, I want to entrust you with something. Do you know the people in Cairo?' 'Yes,' I said, and he told me: 'Take this letter and deliver it to 'Ali al-Zaibaq of Cairo. Tell him: "Your chief sends you his greetings, and he is now with the caliph."' So I took the letter from him and came back to Cairo, and when my creditors saw me I settled my debts. I started to work again as a water carrier, but I haven't delivered Ahmad's letter as I don't know where the man is based.'

'You can relax happily,' said 'Ali, 'for I'm the man you want and I was the first of Captain Ahmad's young men. So hand over the letter.' The water carrier gave it to him, and he opened it and read it. In it he found these lines:

> Ornament of the handsome, I have written to you
> On paper that will travel with the winds.
> Could I fly, I would do so out of longing,
> But how can a bird fly whose wings are clipped?

It went on: 'Greetings from Captain Ahmad al-Danaf to the senior of his children, 'Ali al-Zaibaq of Cairo. I have to tell you that I targeted Salah al-Din al-Misri and buried him alive with the tricks that I played on him, so that I won over his men, among them being 'Ali Kitf al-Jamal. I was then attached to the court and put in charge of policing Baghdad as well as the suburbs. If you want to keep to the agreement that we made, then come to me. You may be able to bring off some coup here that will ingratiate you with the caliph and get him to give you a salary and allowances, as well as providing you with a base, which is what I would like. Goodbye.'

When 'Ali had read the letter, he kissed it and put it on his head before handing the water carrier ten dinars as a reward for the good news. He then went back to his headquarters, where he passed this on to his followers and told them to look after each other. Next he removed the clothes that he was wearing and put on a long cloak and a tarboosh, taking a case containing a spear twenty-four cubits long made of bamboo whose sections fitted into one another. His lieutenant said: 'Are you going off when our coffers are empty?' but 'Ali said: 'When I get to Damascus, I'll send you enough to keep you going.'

He then went on his way and joined up with a caravan in which the chief of the merchants was travelling with forty of his colleagues. All their goods had been loaded except for those of their chief, which were still on the ground, and 'Ali heard the caravan leader, a Syrian, telling the muleteers to come and help him, only to be answered with insults and abuse. 'Ali told himself that the best thing for him would be to travel with this man. He himself was a handsome, beardless boy, and so he went up and greeted the Syrian, who welcomed him and asked what he wanted. 'Uncle,' 'Ali said, 'I see that you are single-handed with forty mule-loads of goods. Why didn't you bring people to help you?' 'My son,' the Syrian replied, 'I hired two lads, provided them with clothes and put two hundred dinars in the pockets of each of them, but after they had helped me as far as al-Khanika, they ran off.' 'Where are you making for?' asked 'Ali, and when the Syrian told him: 'Aleppo,' he said: 'I shall help you.'

They loaded the goods and set out, together with the chief of the merchants on his mule. The Syrian was glad to have 'Ali with him, and fell in love with him. At nightfall the caravan halted and they ate and drank, after which, when it was time for sleep, 'Ali lay down on his side on the ground and pretended to be asleep. The Syrian slept near him, but 'Ali got up and sat down at the entrance to the chief's pavilion. The Syrian turned over, meaning to take 'Ali in his arms, and when he could not find him he said to himself: 'He may have been taken by someone else to whom he made a promise, but I have a better right to him, and another night I shall keep him with me.'

As for 'Ali, he stayed where he was by the merchant's pavilion until it was nearly dawn, after which he came and lay down near the Syrian. When the man woke up to find him there, he said to himself: 'If I ask him where he has been, he will leave me and go off.' 'Ali continued to outwit him until they came to a wood with a cave which served as a den for a fierce lion; every caravan that passed would draw lots, the loser being thrown to the lion. This time it was the chief of the merchants who drew the short straw, and the lion appeared, blocking the path and waiting for its victim. In great distress the merchant went to the caravan leader and cursed him and his journey, before telling him to give the goods that he had with him to his children after his death. The cunning 'Ali asked what this was all about, and when they told him, he said: 'Why do you run away from a desert cat? I'll undertake to kill it for you.' The caravan leader went to the merchant and told him about this, after which he promised to give 'Ali a thousand dinars if he killed the lion, while the others also promised to reward him.

'Ali then discarded his cloak, uncovering his steel coat, and then, taking a steel sword, he tightened the screw that fastened its blade to its hilt before going out alone and shouting at the lion. For its part, the lion leapt at him, but he struck it between the eyes with his sword, cutting it in half as the caravan leader and the merchants looked on. 'Have no fear, uncle,' he called to the leader, who replied: 'My son, I shall for ever be your servant,' while the chief of the merchants put his arms around him, kissed him between the eyes and presented him with a thousand dinars. Each of the other merchants gave him twenty dinars, and he deposited the whole sum with the chief.

The next morning, they started off towards Baghdad and came to the Forest of Lions and the Valley of Dogs. Here there lurked the tribe of a recalcitrant Bedouin highwayman, who came out against them, causing them to run away. The chief of the merchants exclaimed: 'My money is lost!' but just then 'Ali appeared, wearing a leather jacket hung with bells. He fitted together the sections of his spear, and mounted a horse that he had snatched from those the Bedouin had with him. He then challenged the man to a duel with spears and caused the mare he was riding to bolt as 'Ali jingled his bells. He cut through the man's spear and then struck off his head with a blow to the neck. When his followers saw this they closed in on 'Ali, but with a shout of 'God is greater!' he charged at them and put them to flight, after which he fastened the Bedouin's head on his spear point. The merchants rewarded him and the caravan went on to Baghdad. There he asked the chief of the merchants for the money that he had entrusted to him and this he gave to the caravan leader, saying: 'When you get to Cairo, ask for my headquarters and give this money to my lieutenant there.'

He entered Baghdad the next morning and went through the streets asking for the headquarters of Ahmad al-Danaf, but no one would direct him there. When he came to the square of al-Nafd he found children playing, among them a boy called Ahmad al-Laqit, and 'Ali told himself that he would only find what he wanted by asking the children. He looked round and saw a sweet seller, some of whose wares he bought. Then he called to the children, but Ahmad al-Laqit drove them away before going up to 'Ali himself and asking him what he wanted. 'Ali told him: 'I had a son who died and I saw him in a dream asking for sweetmeats, which is why I have bought some to give to every child.' He presented Ahmad al-Laqit with a piece, and when the boy looked at it he saw a dinar sticking to it. 'Go away,' he said. 'If you ask about me, you will find that I am no catamite.' 'Boy,' said 'Ali, 'a clever fellow takes the pay and a clever fellow offers it. I've been going round the town asking for the headquarters of Ahmad al-Danaf, but no one will show me the way. This dinar is for you if you direct me.' The boy said: 'Follow me as I go on ahead until I get there, and then I shall catch up a pebble with my toes and throw it against the door so that you can see which it

is.' They went off, one after the other, until the boy caught up the pebble
and threw it at the door, which 'Ali then marked.

Night 711

Morning now dawned and Shahrazad broke off from what she had been
allowed to say. Then, when it was the seven hundred and eleventh night,
SHE CONTINUED:

I have heard, O fortunate king, that when Ahmad al-Laqit had gone
ahead of 'Ali and shown him the place, 'Ali now laid hold of the boy and
tried unsuccessfully to get the dinar back from him, before telling him
to go off, adding: 'You deserve a gift because you are sharp, intelligent
and brave. If God wills that the caliph appoint me as a captain, I'll make
you one of my band.'

When the boy had left, 'Ali went up to the house and knocked on the
door. Ahmad al-Danaf told his lieutenant to open it, saying: 'This is the
knock of 'Ali al-Zaibaq the Cairene.' When it had been opened, 'Ali went
in and greeted Ahmad, who embraced him, while his forty men added
their own greetings. Ahmad gave him a robe and told him: 'When the
caliph appointed me captain, he gave me clothes for my followers and I
kept this for you.' 'Ali was seated in the place of honour, and when food
and drink had been provided they all ate and drank until they were
drunk, keeping it up until morning. Ahmad then told 'Ali not to go
wandering through the streets of Baghdad but to stay in the house.
'Why?' 'Ali asked, adding: 'I've not come to be shut up, but to see the
sights.' 'My son,' Ahmad told him, 'don't imagine that Baghdad is like
Cairo. This is the seat of the caliphate and there are vast numbers of
tricksters, as roguery sprouts here like vegetables in the countryside.' For
three days 'Ali stayed in the house, and Ahmad then said that he wanted
to present him to the caliph so that he could be given an allowance.
'Wait for the right moment,' 'Ali told him, after which Ahmad left him
alone.

Later, while 'Ali was sitting in the house and feeling depressed and ill
at ease, he decided to cheer himself up by going out and walking through
the city. So he went off and walked from street to street until in the
middle of the market he came across a cookshop and went in to eat.
When he got up to wash his hands he came across forty slaves wearing
felt-padded tunics with steel swords marching two by two. Bringing up

the rear and mounted on a mule was Dalila the wily, wearing a helmet covered with gold leaf and plated with iron, a mail coat and equipment to match. She was on her way back from the court to her *khan*, and, when her eye fell on 'Ali, she looked at him closely and noted that he was of the same height and breadth as Ahmad al-Danaf. He was wearing a loose robe as well as a hooded cloak and carrying a steel blade among other things, and it was quite clear that here was a man of unimpeachable courage.

On her return to the *khan*, Dalila went to her daughter, Zainab, and got out the divination table, and when she shook the sand over it she discovered that the young man was 'Ali the Cairene and that his good fortune would eclipse hers and that of her daughter. Zainab asked her: 'What did you see, mother, that made you turn to divination?' to which she answered: 'Today I saw a young man who looks like Ahmad al-Danaf, and I'm afraid that if he hears that you stripped Ahmad and his men of their clothes, he may come here in order to play a trick on us to avenge his chief and the forty men. I think he must be staying in Ahmad's headquarters.' 'What are you worried about?' Zainab asked, adding: 'I think that you have taken his measure.'

Zainab now put on her most splendid dress and went out to walk through the streets, captivating all who saw her, making promises, swearing oaths, listening to what they said and flaunting herself brazenly. She went from market to market until she saw 'Ali al-Zaibaq coming towards her. She rubbed against him with her shoulder and then turned and exclaimed: 'God preserve people of taste!' 'What a beautiful figure you have!' he told her, and asked: 'Who do you belong to?' 'To a fine fellow like you,' she said, and when he went on to ask whether she was married or single, she said that she was married. 'My place or yours?' he asked. 'I'm the daughter of a merchant,' she told him, 'and my husband is a merchant. This is the first day in my life that I have ever been outside, and that is because I had prepared food and was about to eat when I found that I had no appetite for it. Then, when I saw you, I fell in love with you. Can you bring yourself to console me and join me in a bite?' 'Whoever is invited must accept,' 'Ali replied, and as she walked on he followed her from street to street.

As he walked behind her, 'Ali said to himself: 'How can you do this in a strange city? The proverb has it that those who fornicate while abroad will have their hopes dashed by God. I shall politely put her off.' So he said: 'Take this dinar and fix another time for me,' but she swore by the

Greatest Name of God: 'You must come home with me now so that I can show how I love you.' He followed her until she came to the locked door of a house with a high portal. 'Open the lock,' Zainab told him, but when he asked where the key was, she told him that it was lost. 'Whoever opens a lock without a key is a robber who should be punished by the magistrate,' he said, adding, 'and as for me, I've no idea how to do it.' She drew the veil from her face and he gave her a glance which was followed by a thousand sighs. She then let the veil hang down over the lock and recited the names of the mother of Moses over it, at which it opened without a key. She went in, and 'Ali followed and saw swords and weapons of steel.

Zainab removed her veil and sat down with him. Saying to himself: 'Finish off what God has decreed for you,' he leaned towards her to kiss her cheek, but she covered it with the palm of her hand, exclaiming: 'Pure pleasure only comes at night!' She then produced food and drink and they ate and drank, after which she got up and filled the water jug from the well and poured it over his hands, which he washed. All of a sudden, while they were doing this, she began to beat her breast and said: 'My husband had a ruby ring which was pledged for five hundred dinars. I put it on but it was too big and so I used wax to fix it more tightly, but when I let down the water bucket it must have fallen into the well. Turn to look at the door while I take my clothes off before going down there to recover it.' 'It would be a disgrace if you were to go down while I'm here,' 'Ali objected and added: 'No one is going down except me.' He stripped off his clothes and tied himself to the well rope, after which Zainab let him down into the well. The water was deep and after a time she told him: 'I haven't got enough rope left. Untie yourself and drop down.' He did this, but, far as he sank into the water, he still didn't reach the bottom. Zainab meanwhile veiled herself and, taking his clothes, she went back to her mother . . .

Night 712

Morning now dawned and Shahrazad broke off from what she had been allowed to say. Then, when it was the seven hundred and twelfth night, SHE CONTINUED:

I have heard, O fortunate king, that after 'Ali had gone down into the well, Zainab veiled herself and, taking his clothes, she went back to her mother and told her: 'I have taken the clothes of 'Ali the Cairene and left him in the well of the house of the emir Hasan, from which he's not likely to escape.'

This emir was away at court at the time. When he came back, he found the door open and said to his groom: 'Why didn't you lock up?' 'I did, with my own hand,' the man protested, and Hasan then swore that a robber must have entered. He went in and looked around but found no one there. So he told the groom to fill the water jug so that he could wash, and the groom took the bucket and lowered it into the well. When he tried to draw it up again, he found it heavy, and when he looked down, he saw something sitting in it. He let it down again and called out: 'Master, an *'ifrit* has come out from the well.' 'Go and fetch four Quranic scholars to recite the Quran at it so it may go away,' Hasan told him. When the four had come, Hasan told them to stand around the well and recite. His servant and his groom came to let down the bucket, and this time when 'Ali took hold of it he hid himself inside it and waited until he was nearly on a level with Hasan and the others. He then jumped among the reciters, who started to hit out at each other, shouting: "*Ifrit*, *'ifrit*!" Hasan could see that this was a young man and asked: 'Are you a robber?' 'No,' said 'Ali, and Hasan went on: 'Why did you go down into the well?' 'Ali replied: 'I polluted myself in my sleep and went down to wash in the Tigris, but when I plunged into the water the current pulled me under the surface and eventually I came out in this well.' 'Tell the truth,' Hasan said, and when 'Ali had told him the whole story, Hasan sent him away dressed in some old clothes.

When he got back to Ahmad al-Danaf's base and told him what had happened, Ahmad said: 'Didn't I tell you that in Baghdad there are women who play tricks on men?', while 'Ali Kitf al-Jamal exclaimed: 'By the Greatest Name of God, tell me how you can be the leader of the Cairo youngsters and still have your clothes taken by a girl.' 'Ali found this hard to stomach and regretted what he had done, but Ahmad gave him another robe and Hasan Shuman asked if he knew the girl. When he said no, Hasan said: 'It must have been Zainab, the daughter of Dalila the wily, the gatekeeper of the caliph's *khan*. Have you fallen into her toils?' 'Yes,' said 'Ali, and Hasan went on to tell him that it was this girl who had taken the clothes of Ahmad, their chief, and of all his company. 'This is a disgrace for you!' exclaimed 'Ali, and when Hasan asked what he proposed to do, he said that he wanted to marry her. 'You'll never be able to do that, so forget about her,' Hasan told him, but when 'Ali went on to ask how to manage it, Hasan then encouraged him and said: 'If you drink out of my hand and march under my banner, I'll see that you get what you want from her.'

'Ali agreed to this, and Hasan told him to take off his clothes. When he had done that, Hasan took a cauldron and boiled up in it something that looked like pitch, which he smeared on 'Ali's body, as well as on his lips and cheeks, until he looked like a black slave. He used red kohl on his eyes and dressed him in the clothes of a servant, before giving him a tray on which were kebabs and wine. He said: 'In the *khan* there is a black cook and you now look like him. The only things that this man needs from the market are meat and vegetables, so approach him politely, address him in the argot of the blacks, greet him and say: "It has been a long time since I met you in the pub." He will tell you: "I've been busy. I've forty black slaves to look after, cooking them one meal in the morning and another in the evening, as well as feeding forty dogs and preparing food for both Dalila and her daughter, Zainab." Say to him: "Come on. Let's eat kebabs and drink some beer," after which go into the house with him and make him drunk. When you've done that, ask him how many different dishes he has to cook, what the dogs eat and where the keys of the kitchen and the pantry are kept, as a drunk man will tell you everything that he would conceal if he were sober. After that, drug him and put on his clothes, take the knives from his belt and the vegetable basket, and go to the market and buy meat and vegetables. After that you can enter both the kitchen and the pantry of the *khan* and cook the meal. Put it in a bowl and then take it to Dalila after you've added *banj* to it so as to drug the dogs, the slaves, and Dalila and Zainab as well. Go upstairs and fetch all the clothes you find, and if you want to marry Zainab, bring the forty carrier pigeons with you.'

'Ali went off, and when he saw the cook he greeted him and repeated what Hasan had told him to say. The cook told him he was busy looking after the slaves and the dogs in the *khan*, after which 'Ali took him off and made him drunk before asking how many dishes he had to cook. The man told him that he cooked five different dishes in the morning and five in the evening, adding: 'And yesterday they asked me for a sixth, rice and honey, as well as a seventh, which was cooked pomegranate seeds.' 'How do you serve this?' 'Ali asked, and the cook said: 'First I take up Zainab's tray and then that of Dalila, after which I give the slaves their evening meal. Then I feed the dogs, giving each one its fill of meat, and it takes at least one *ratl*'s weight of this to satisfy them.'

As fate would have it, 'Ali forgot to ask about the keys, but he managed to get the cook's clothes, which he put on, and he took the basket and went to the market, where he bought the meat and the vegetables.

Night 713

Morning now dawned and Shahrazad broke off from what she had been allowed to say. Then, when it was the seven hundred and thirteenth night, SHE CONTINUED:

I have heard, O fortunate king, that 'Ali drugged the cook and took his knives, which he put in his waistband. He took the basket and went to the market to buy meat and vegetables. He then went back, and when he entered the door of the *khan* he saw Dalila sitting there looking at everyone who came in or went out, and he saw the forty armed slaves, but this did not daunt him. When Dalila caught sight of him, she recognized him and said: 'Go back, you robber chief. Are you thinking of playing a trick on me in this *khan*?' 'Ali, in his disguise as a black slave, turned to her and asked: 'What are you saying, doorkeeper?' 'What have you done with the cook?' she asked. 'Have you killed him or drugged him?' 'What cook are you talking about?' said 'Ali. 'I'm the only cook here.' 'You're lying,' she told him. 'You are 'Ali al-Zaibaq from Cairo.' Using the argot of the blacks, 'Ali replied: 'Doorkeeper, are Cairenes white or black? I am not going to serve here any longer.' At that, the black slaves asked: 'What's wrong, cousin?' and Dalila said: 'He's no cousin of yours. This is 'Ali al-Zaibaq from Cairo and I think that he has drugged your cousin or killed him.' They insisted that he was Sa'dullah the cook, one of theirs, but she denied it again and insisted that he was 'Ali the Cairene, who had dyed his skin. 'Who is this 'Ali?' 'Ali said. 'I am Sa'dullah.' 'I have some ointment that can test this,' Dalila said, but when she fetched it and rubbed it on his arm, the black dye didn't come off and the slaves said: 'Let him cook our meal for us.' 'If he is really one of yours,' Dalila told them, 'he'll know what you asked for yesterday and how many dishes he cooks each day.' They asked 'Ali about this, and he said: 'I gave you lentils, rice, soup, ragout and rose sherbet, with rice and honey as a sixth dish, while a seventh was cooked pomegranate seeds, with the same in the evening.' 'True enough,' they said, and Dalila then told them: 'Go in with him, and if he knows where the kitchen and the pantry are, then he is indeed your cousin, but if not, kill him.'

As it happened the cook had brought up a cat, and whenever he came to the kitchen, this cat would stand by the door and then jump up on his shoulder as he went in. When it saw 'Ali coming, it jumped up, and when he put it down again, it walked in front of him to the kitchen. He realized that where it stopped must be the kitchen door, and so he took the keys, noticing that some feathers were still sticking to one of them. He understood that this must be the kitchen key and so he opened the door, put the vegetables inside and went out again. The cat ran on in front of him, making for another door, which he could tell must be that of the pantry, and when he took the keys he saw that one had traces of grease on it and, recognizing that this must be the right one, he used it to open the pantry door. The slaves told Dalila that, had he been a stranger, he would neither have known where the two rooms were nor have been able to pick out the right keys from the bunch. 'This is our cousin, Sa'dullah,' they insisted, but she said: 'It was the cat who showed him where the rooms were, and he picked out the keys by inference. This does not take me in.'

'Ali then went to the kitchen and cooked the meal. He took a tray up to Zainab, in whose room he saw all the clothes of his companions, and after that he went down again and prepared Dalila's tray, before feeding the slaves and giving meat to the dogs. In the evening he repeated the process. The door of the *khan* was only to be opened and shut, both morning and evening, while it was light, and so he then got up and called out to those in the *khan*: 'The slaves are on watch and the dogs have been released. Anyone who comes out has no one to blame but themselves.' He had delayed feeding the dogs and had poisoned their meat, so that when he put it down for them, they died after eating it, while he had used *banj* to drug all the slaves as well as Dalila and Zainab. He then went up and took all the clothes, together with the carrier pigeons, opened the door of the *khan* and left. When he got to Ahmad's headquarters, Hasan Shuman saw him and asked what he had done. 'Ali told him the whole story and Hasan thanked him, before getting him to strip and then restoring his natural colour by boiling up some herbs with which he washed him. 'Ali went back to the cook, returned his clothes to him and brought him back to consciousness. The cook went to the vegetable seller, collected vegetables and returned to the *khan*.

So much for 'Ali, but as for Dalila the wily, one of the merchants living in the *khan* went down at dawn from the floor on which he was living to find the door open, the slaves drugged and the dogs dead. When he came to Dalila, he discovered that she too had been drugged and that on her throat was a sheet of paper. By her head was a sponge steeped in the antidote to *banj*, and when he applied this to her nostrils she regained consciousness. 'Where am I?' she asked, and the merchant told her: 'When I came down, I found the door open; both you and the slaves were drugged and the dogs were dead.' Dalila took the note and read: ''Ali the Cairene did this.' She then applied the antidote to the slaves and to Zainab, saying: 'Didn't I tell you that this was 'Ali?' She told the slaves to keep the matter quiet and she said to Zainab: 'How many times did I tell you that 'Ali would not fail to take his revenge, and he has done this in return for what you did to him. He could have acted differently with you, but he stopped at this as a mark of goodwill in the hope of winning our affection.'

She changed her masculine clothes for those of a woman, tied a kerchief round her neck as a mark of peace and set out for the headquarters of Ahmad al-Danaf. When 'Ali had come there bringing the clothes and the carrier pigeons, Hasan Shuman had given Ahmad's lieutenant money to buy forty pigeons, which he did, before cooking them and serving them to the men. It was at this point that Dalila knocked at the door, and Ahmad, who recognized her knock, told his lieutenant to get up and open the door. When he did this, Dalila came in . . .

Night 714

Morning now dawned and Shahrazad broke off from what she had been allowed to say. Then, when it was the seven hundred and fourteenth night, SHE CONTINUED:

I have heard, O fortunate king, that when the door was opened for Dalila, she came in and Hasan Shuman said: 'What has brought you here, you ill-omened old woman? You and your brother, Zuraiq the fishmonger, are two of a kind.' 'Captain,' said Dalila, 'I was in the wrong and here am I at your mercy, but tell me which of you was it who played this trick on me.' 'He is the foremost of my company,' Ahmad told her, and she said: 'For God's sake, ask him on my behalf to do me the favour of handing back the carrier pigeons and what else belongs to them.' 'God reward you, 'Ali!' exclaimed Hasan Shuman. 'Why did you cook those pigeons?' 'I didn't know that they were carrier pigeons,' 'Ali told

him, and Ahmad sent his lieutenant to fetch them. He handed the dish
to Dalila, who took a piece and chewed it before saying: 'This isn't the
flesh of a carrier pigeon, for I fed them on musk grains and the musk
gives their flesh its own taste.' Hasan Shuman said: 'If you want to get
your own pigeons back, then do what 'Ali wants.' 'What is that?' asked
Dalila, and Hasan replied: 'He wants you to marry him to your daughter,
Zainab.' 'I've no power over her except through her own goodwill,'
Dalila replied, and Hasan then told 'Ali to return the pigeons, which he
did to her delight. 'You owe us a full reply,' Hasan said to her, and she
told him: 'If 'Ali wants to marry Zainab, this trick that he has played is
not a real piece of cleverness. What would be a really sharp piece of
work would be for him to ask for her hand from my brother, Captain
Zuraiq, who is her guardian. It is he who calls out: "A pound of fish for
twopence," and who has hanging up in his shop a purse containing two
thousand gold dinars.' When Ahmad and his men heard what she said,
they exclaimed: 'What are you saying, you whore? You want to rob us
of our brother 'Ali.'

Dalila then went back to the *khan* and told Zainab that 'Ali had asked
for her hand. Zainab was delighted, as the fact that 'Ali had not raped
her had made her love him, and so she asked her mother what had
happened next. Dalila told her that she had made a condition that 'Ali
ask her uncle Zuraiq for her hand, thus guaranteeing 'Ali's death.

'Ali himself turned to the others and asked what kind of a man Zuraiq
was. They said: 'He is the leader of the gangs of Iraq. He can almost
bore through mountains, grasp the stars and steal kohl from the eyes.
He had no equal at this kind of thing, but he repented and opened a fish
shop which brought him in two thousand dinars. He put the money in
a purse to which he tied a silk thread and to this he attached brass bells
of various kinds, fixing the other end of it to a peg inside the shop door.
Whenever he opens up the shop, he hangs up the purse and calls out:
"Where are you, knaves of Egypt, rogues of Iraq and skilled thieves of
Persia? Zuraiq the fishmonger has hung up a purse in front of his shop,
and whoever claims to be a subtle operator and can take it by a trick
can keep it." Greedy rogues have come to try their luck, but no one has
been able to take the purse, as Zuraiq keeps lumps of lead under his feet
as he lights his fire and fries his fish, and whenever someone is tempted
to try to surprise him and snatch the purse, he strikes him with a lump
of lead, disabling or killing him. If you want to go up against him, 'Ali,
you will be like a man who beats his breast in a funeral procession with

no idea of who has died. You're no match for him and I'm afraid that he will harm you. There is no need for you to marry Zainab and whoever abandons something can live without it.'

'This is a disgrace, men,' 'Ali said. 'I must take the purse.' He told them to fetch him girl's clothes, and when they brought them, he put them on, dyed himself with henna and veiled his face. He killed a lamb and drained its blood, after which he removed and cleaned its intestine, tying up its rump and filling it with blood. He then fastened this between his thighs underneath his clothes and put on boots. Next he made two false breasts from the crops of birds, filling them with milk, and he put cotton over his stomach, tying cloth over it, and using a starched kerchief as a girdle. Everyone who saw him admired his buttocks.

He gave a dinar to a donkey man who happened to come up, and the man mounted him on his donkey and went off with him in the direction of Zuraiq's shop, where he could clearly see the gold in the purse that was hanging there. Zuraiq was frying fish, and when 'Ali asked the donkey man what the smell was, the man told him that it came from Zuraiq's fish. 'Ali said: 'I'm pregnant and this smell is doing me harm. Fetch me a piece of fish.' The donkey man said to Zuraiq: 'The smell of your fish this morning is affecting pregnant women. I've got with me the pregnant wife of the emir Hasan Sharr al-Tariq and she has smelt it, so give her a piece of fish, as the child is stirring in her womb. May God, the Shelterer, protect us from us the evil of this day!'

Zuraiq took a slice of fish and was about to fry it when he found that his fire had gone out and so he went in to relight it. As 'Ali sat down, he leaned against the intestine, which broke open, spilling the blood out between his legs. 'Oh, my side, oh, my back,' he groaned and the donkey man turned and saw the stream of blood. 'What's wrong with you, my lady?' he asked, and 'Ali, in his character as a woman, said: 'I've miscarried.' Zuraiq looked out and then, alarmed at the sight of the blood, he ran back into the shop. 'God damn you, Zuraiq,' the donkey man said, 'the girl has had a miscarriage, and you won't be able to cope with her husband. Why did you start making smells in the morning, and when I told you to fetch a slice of fish, wouldn't you do it?' He then took his donkey and went on his way.

When Zuraiq ran back into his shop, 'Ali reached out for the purse, but when he touched it, the gold coins in it clinked and the various bells and rings jangled. 'You scum,' cried Zuraiq, 'I can see through your swindle. Are you trying to play a trick on me dressed as a girl? Take what is coming to you,' and he threw a lump of lead at him. This missed him and hit someone else, causing consternation among the bystanders, who said to him: 'Are you a tradesman or a hooligan? If you are a tradesman, take down your purse and give the people a rest from the trouble you cause.' Zuraiq swore that he would do this.

As for 'Ali, he went back to his headquarters, and when Hasan Shuman asked what he had done, he told him the whole story. He then took off his woman's disguise and asked Hasan for the clothes of a groom. When these had been fetched, he put them on and, taking a dish and five dirhams, he went back to Zuraiq. 'What do you want, master?' Zuraiq asked him, at which 'Ali showed him the dirhams he was holding. Zuraiq was about to give him some of the fish that were on his slab, but 'Ali said that he wanted them hot. Zuraiq put them in the frying pan and was about to fry them when the fire again went out. When he went back into the shop to relight it, 'Ali reached out for the purse. He had got hold of the end of it when the bells and rings started to jingle and Zuraiq called out: 'You didn't manage to trick me, for all your disguise as a groom. I recognized you by the way you held the dirhams and the plate.'

Night 715

Morning now dawned and Shahrazad broke off from what she had been allowed to say. Then, when it was the seven hundred and fifteenth night, SHE CONTINUED:

I have heard, O fortunate king, that when 'Ali reached out for the purse, the bells and rings started to jingle and Zuraiq called out: 'You didn't manage to trick me, for all your disguise as a groom. I recognized you by the way you held the dirhams and the plate.' He then threw a lump of lead at 'Ali, but when 'Ali dodged, the lump fell into a pan full of hot meat. The pan broke and its gravy fell on the shoulder of the *qadi* who happened to be passing, pouring down inside his clothes to his private parts. The *qadi* cried out in pain, cursing whatever miserable fellow had done this to him. 'Master,' said the bystanders, 'it was a small boy who threw the stone that landed in the pan and but for God's help things would have been worse.' Then they turned and found the lump of lead, which made them realize that the culprit must have been Zuraiq. They went up to him and protested: 'God does not allow this, Zuraiq. You had better take down your purse.' 'So I shall, God willing,' he told them.

As for 'Ali, he went back to his comrades in their headquarters, and when they asked him where the purse was, he told them everything that had happened to him, to which they replied: 'You have made him use up two-thirds of his cunning.' He then took off the clothes he was wearing, and dressed as a merchant. When he went out, he saw a snake charmer with a sack containing snakes and a satchel in which he kept his equipment. He told the man that he wanted him to entertain his children for a fee, but when he took him to his house, he drugged his food with *banj*, dressed himself in his clothes and set off for Zuraiq's shop. When he got there he played on his flute, but Zuraiq merely said: 'Get your reward from God.' The snakes then came out of the bag and 'Ali threw them down in front of Zuraiq, who was afraid of all snakes and who ran away from them back into his shop. At this, 'Ali picked them up and put them back in their sack. He reached out for the purse, but when he touched the end of it, the rings and bells started to jangle. 'Are you still trying to play tricks on me, this time as a snake charmer?' exclaimed Zuraiq, and he threw a lump of lead at him. A soldier happened to be passing, followed by his groom, and the lead struck the groom on the head, felling him to the ground. 'Who did that?' demanded the soldier, but when the people there told him that a stone had fallen from a roof, he went off. They then turned and, seeing the lump of lead, they went back to Zuraiq again and said: 'Take the purse down.' 'I'll take it down this evening, God willing,' he promised.

'Ali went on trying trick after trick until he had made seven fruitless attempts. After he had returned the clothes and belongings to the snake charmer and made him a present, 'Ali went back to the shop, where he heard Zuraiq saying to himself: 'If I leave the purse here overnight, he will bore through the wall and get it, so I'll take it home with me.' He got up, cleared out his shop and took down the purse, which he stowed away in his cloak. 'Ali followed him, and when Zuraiq got near his house he saw that his neighbour was giving a wedding feast and he said to himself: 'I'll just go home, give the purse to my wife, put on my best clothes and then come back to the feast,' and so he walked on, still followed by 'Ali. He had married a freed slave from the household of the vizier Ja'far, a black girl by whom he had a son called 'Abdallah, and he kept promising his wife that he would use the money in the purse to pay first for his son's circumcision ceremony, and then to get his son a wife and finally to pay for the marriage feast. He now went to his wife with a frown on his face, and when she asked him why this was, he told her:

'God has afflicted me with a sly fellow who has tried to take the purse by trickery seven times but has not succeeded.' 'Hand it over for me to store away for our son's wedding,' his wife told him, and this he did.

'Ali had hidden in a room and was listening and looking. Zuraiq went and removed what he was wearing to put on his best clothes, after which he said: 'Look after the purse, for I'm going to the wedding feast.' 'Have an hour's sleep first,' she told him, and after he had fallen asleep, 'Ali got up and, walking on tiptoe, he managed to take the purse. He then went to the house where the wedding feast was being held and stopped there to look. Meanwhile Zuraiq had dreamt that a bird had taken his purse and, waking up in a panic, he told his wife to get up and take a look at it. When she tried, it was not to be found and, striking herself in the face, she exclaimed: 'You unfortunate woman, the trickster has stolen the purse!' 'By God,' Zuraiq said, 'it can only have been 'Ali and no one else who took it, and I'll have to recover it.' 'If you don't get it, I shall lock the door on you and leave you to spend the night in the street,' she told him.

Zuraiq now went to the wedding feast, where he saw 'Ali looking on. 'This is the man who stole the purse,' he told himself, 'but he's staying in the house of Ahmad al-Danaf.' He got there before 'Ali, climbed the back wall and dropped down into the house, where he found everyone asleep. At that moment, 'Ali arrived and knocked on the door. 'Who's there?' Zuraiq asked, and when 'Ali gave his name he said: 'Have you brought the purse?' 'Ali, thinking that this was Hasan Shuman, said: 'Yes, I have, so open the door.' Zuraiq told him: 'I can't do that until I have seen it, as I have a bet on with your captain.' 'Stretch out your hand,' 'Ali told him and, when Zuraiq reached out through the hole by the pivot at the bottom of the door, 'Ali gave him the purse. He took it and left by the same way that he had come. He then went off to the wedding feast.

As for 'Ali, he went on standing by the door, and when nobody opened it for him he knocked so loudly that the sleepers woke up and said: 'That is the knock of 'Ali al-Zaibaq.' Ahmad's lieutenant opened the door and asked 'Ali if he had brought the purse. 'The joke has gone far enough, Shuman,' 'Ali said. 'Didn't I give it to you through the hole at the bottom of the door, after you told me that you had sworn not to open the door for me until I showed it to you?' 'By God,' said Hasan, 'I didn't take it; it must have been Zuraiq who got it from you.' 'Ali, swearing that he was going to recover it, then went back to the wedding feast. There he heard the jester saying: 'Give me a gift, Zuraiq, and you'll get the benefit of it through your son.' 'I'm in luck,' said 'Ali to himself, and he went to Zuraiq's house, where he climbed in from the back and dropped down. He found Zuraiq's wife sleeping, drugged her with *banj*, dressed himself in her clothes and took the child in his lap, after which, on looking round the house, he discovered in a basket cakes that Zuraiq had meanly saved from 'Id al-Fitr.

It was now that Zuraiq came home, and when he knocked on the door 'Ali answered him, pretending to be his wife and asking who was there. When Zuraiq gave his name, 'Ali said: 'I swore not to open the door until you brought back the purse,' and when Zuraiq said that he had it, 'Ali told him to produce it before he opened the door. 'Lower the basket,' Zuraiq instructed, 'and you can then take the purse up in it.' 'Ali did this; Zuraiq put the purse in the basket and 'Ali took it. He then drugged the child with *banj*, and after having brought the woman back to consciousness, he left by the way that he had come and returned to Ahmad's headquarters. When he went in and showed the others the purse and the child, they thanked him for what he had done and then ate the cakes that he gave them. He told Hasan Shuman that the child was Zuraiq's and asked him to keep him hidden. Hasan did this and then fetched a lamb, and after he had slaughtered it, he gave it to his lieutenant, who roasted it and then wrapped it in a shroud as though it were a dead person.

As for Zuraiq, he went on standing at the door for a while and then knocked loudly. 'Have you brought the purse?' his wife asked, and he said: 'Didn't you take it from the basket which you let down?' 'I never let down any basket,' she replied, 'and I neither saw nor took the purse.' 'By God,' he exclaimed, 'the scoundrel 'Ali has forestalled me and got it!' Then he looked in the house and found that the cakes were gone and that his son was missing. He gave a cry of grief and his wife beat her breast. 'You and I must go to the vizier,' she told him, 'as he can only have been killed by the scoundrel who played those tricks on you, and you're responsible for this.' 'I guarantee to get the child back,' Zuraiq told her, and he tied a kerchief round his neck as a mark of peace and set off for the headquarters of Ahmad al-Danaf. When he knocked on the door, it was opened for him by Ahmad's lieutenant, and when he went in, Hasan Shuman asked him why he had come. 'I want you to intercede for me with 'Ali the Cairene so that he gives me my son back, and in exchange I'll let him have my purse of gold,' Zuraiq told him.

'May God pay you back for this, 'Ali!' Hasan exclaimed. 'Why didn't you tell me that this was Zuraiq's son?' 'What has happened to him?' Zuraiq asked. 'We gave him some raisins to eat, but he had a choking fit and died,' Hasan said, adding, 'and this is his body.'

Zuraiq called out in grief, saying: 'What am I going to tell his mother?' Then he got up and undid the shroud only to find the roasted lamb. 'You have been trying to get a rise from me, 'Ali,' he said, and Ahmad's men then handed over the child. Ahmad said: 'You hung up the purse for any clever thief to take, saying it would then be his by right. So it now belongs to 'Ali the Cairene.' 'I make him a present of it,' Zuraiq told him, but 'Ali said: 'Take it back for the sake of your niece Zainab.' 'I accept it,' said Zuraiq. 'Ali's companions then went on: 'We ask that she be given in marriage to 'Ali,' to which Zuraiq pointed out: 'My only authority over her is a matter of goodwill.' He took his son and the purse, but Hasan asked him: 'Have you accepted this offer of marriage?' 'I shall accept an offer from someone who can pay her bride price,' Zuraiq replied, and when Hasan asked what this was, Zuraiq explained: 'She has sworn not to give herself to anyone unless he can bring her the robe of Qamar, the daughter of 'Adhra the Jew, together with the rest of her finery . . .'

Night 716

Morning now dawned and Shahrazad broke off from what she had been allowed to say. Then, when it was the seven hundred and sixteenth night, SHE CONTINUED:

I have heard, O fortunate king, that Zuraiq told Shuman: 'Zainab has sworn not to give herself to anyone unless he can bring her the robe of Qamar, the daughter of 'Adhra the Jew, together with the crown, the girdle and the golden slippers.' 'If I don't bring the robe tonight, I shall have no right to ask for her hand,' 'Ali agreed, but Zuraiq warned him: 'If you play any of your tricks on Qamar, you are a dead man.' 'Ali asked why and was told: 'The Jew is a wily and treacherous sorcerer who has *jinn* under his command. He has a castle outside the city whose walls are made of alternate bricks of gold and silver. While he is there it is visible, but when he leaves it disappears. He has a daughter named Qamar for whom he brought this robe from a talismanic hoard, and every day he places it on a gold tray, opens the castle windows and calls out: 'Where are you, knaves of Egypt, rogues of Iraq and skilled thieves of Persia? Whoever takes this robe may keep it.' Every young hopeful has tried his tricks, but no one has succeeded and they have then been transformed by magic into apes and donkeys.' 'I have to take the robe,' said 'Ali, 'so that Zainab may wear it at her wedding.'

He went to the Jew's shop, and found him to be a coarse, rough man, with a pair of scales, brass weights, gold, silver and a number of boxes. He also saw that the Jew had a mule there, and when he got up to shut his shop, he put the gold and silver in two purses, which he placed in a pair of saddlebags and loaded them on the mule. He then rode out of the city, followed without his knowledge by 'Ali, until he took some earth from a purse that he had in his pocket, recited a spell over it and scattered it into the air. At that, a castle of unrivalled splendour appeared in front of 'Ali, and the mule carried the Jew up its steps, it being a *jinni* in his service. When the saddlebags had been taken off, it went away and disappeared.

As for the Jew himself, 'Ali watched as he took his seat in the castle. He brought out a rod of gold to which he attached a golden tray by means of golden chains, and in the tray he put the robe. As 'Ali looked from behind the door, he made his proclamation to the knaves, rogues and thieves that whoever was clever enough to take the robe could keep it. He then recited a spell, and a table laden with food appeared in front of him, and after he had finished eating, it removed itself, while a second spell produced wine, which he drank. 'Ali said to himself that the only way in which he could take the robe was if the Jew became drunk.

He crept up behind the Jew and drew his steel sword, but the Jew turned round and uttered a spell that paralysed 'Ali's sword hand, leaving it holding the sword in mid-air. He tried with his left hand, but it too was paralysed, as was his right foot, leaving him balanced on one leg. The spell was then removed and 'Ali returned to normal while the Jew used geomancy to discover his name. He turned to him and said: 'Come here. Who are you and what are you doing?' 'Ali gave him his name and added that he was one of Ahmad al-Danaf's band. 'I have asked for the hand of Zainab, the daughter of Dalila the wily, and by way of bride price they have asked me for the robe of your daughter. If you want to live in safety, let me have it and accept Islam.' 'Not until you are dead,' the Jew told him. 'Many people have tried to trick me out of this, but no one has been able to take it away from me. If you are willing to accept advice, save your own life. The only reason that they asked you for the robe was to get you killed, and had I not seen that your good fortune was greater than mine, I would have cut off your head.' 'Ali was glad to hear what the Jew told him about his good fortune, and insisted: 'I must have the robe and you must accept Islam.' 'This is what you want and what you think you have to have?' asked the Jew, and when 'Ali said yes, he took a cup, filled it with water, recited a spell over it and said: 'Quit your human shape and become a donkey.' He sprinkled some of the water on 'Ali, who was promptly transformed into a donkey, with hooves and long ears. He started to bray and the Jew traced a circle around him, which became a wall keeping him in, and after that the Jew went on drinking until morning.

The next day he told 'Ali: 'I shall give the mule a rest and ride you,' after which he put the robe, the tray, the rod and the chains away in a cupboard. He summoned 'Ali with a spell, put the saddlebags on his back and mounted. The castle vanished from sight as 'Ali moved off with his rider and they got to the shop. Here the Jew dismounted and emptied out the two purses, one containing gold and the other silver, into the box that he kept in front of him. 'Ali, in his donkey shape, was left tethered and, while he could hear and understand, he was unable to speak. Just then, up came the son of a merchant who had fallen on hard times and, in the absence of any other available occupation, had become a water carrier. He had taken his wife's bracelets and had brought them to sell to the Jew so that he could use the money to buy a donkey. 'What are you going to carry on it?' the Jew asked, and the man told him that he proposed to load it with water from the river and make a living by selling this. 'Take this donkey of mine,' said the Jew, and so the man exchanged the bracelets for the donkey and the Jew paid over the difference in price.

The man took 'Ali, still under the spell, back to his house and 'Ali told himself: 'If this fellow puts a wooden pack saddle and a water skin on me, it will only take ten trips to ruin my health and kill me.' So when the man's wife came out to put down his fodder, he butted her with his head, knocking her over on to her back. He then jumped on her and stuck his mouth into her face while lowering his private parts. She shrieked to the neighbours for help and they came and beat 'Ali off her. When her husband, the would-be water carrier, came home, she said: 'Either divorce me or take this donkey back to its owner.' 'What's happened?' he asked, and she told him: 'This is a devil in the shape of a donkey. It jumped on me, and if the neighbours hadn't removed it from

on top of me it would have defiled me.' Her husband took 'Ali back to
the Jew, who asked why he was bringing back his purchase. 'It did
something disgusting to my wife,' the man said, and so the Jew gave him
the money and the man went off.

As for the Jew, he turned to 'Ali and said: 'Are you trying to play
tricks, you miserable creature . . . ?'

Night 717

Morning now dawned and Shahrazad broke off from what she had been
allowed to say. Then, when it was the seven hundred and seventeenth
night, SHE CONTINUED:

I have heard, O fortunate king, that when the water carrier returned
the 'donkey' to the Jew, the latter gave him the money and then turned
to 'Ali and said: 'Are you trying to play tricks, you miserable creature, to
make him return you to me? But since you are happy to be a donkey, I
shall let you be a spectacle for old and young alike.' He took 'Ali the
donkey, mounted him and rode out of the city, before taking some ashes,
reciting a spell over them and then scattering them in the air, at which
the castle reappeared. When he had gone up into it, he unloaded the
saddlebags and took away the purses of gold and silver. He then fetched
out the rod and, after attaching it to the tray with the robe, he made his
proclamation to the rogues of every district, challenging them to take
the robe. As before, he proceeded to conjure up a meal, and after he
had finished eating, another spell produced wine, from which he drank
his fill.

At this point he brought out a cup of water and, when he had recited
a spell over it, he sprinkled it on the donkey and said: 'Change back
from this to your original shape.' When 'Ali had returned to his human
form, the Jew said to him: 'Take my advice, lest I do something worse
to you. There is no need for you to marry Zainab and to take my
daughter's robe, for this is not going to be easy for you. It will be better
for you not to be greedy, or else I shall turn you into a bear or an ape or
hand you over to one of the *jinn*, who will throw you behind Mount
Qaf.' ''Adhra,' replied 'Ali, 'I have undertaken to get the robe and get it
I must, and, unless you accept Islam, I shall kill you.' 'You are like a nut
which cannot be eaten until it has been cracked,' the Jew told him, and
then he took a cup of water, recited a spell over it and sprinkled it over

'Ali, saying: 'Take the shape of a bear.' 'Ali was immediately turned into a bear, and the Jew put a collar round his neck, muzzled him and tethered him to an iron stake. As he ate, he would throw 'Ali some scraps and pour out some of the leftover water.

The next morning he got up and, after removing the tray and the robe, he forced the bear by means of a spell to follow him to his shop, where he emptied out the gold and silver into his box and took his seat. He fastened the chain round the bear's neck inside the shop and, as a bear, 'Ali could hear and understand but was unable to speak. While he was there, a merchant came to visit the Jew in his shop to ask if he would sell him 'the bear', explaining that doctors had advised his wife, who was his cousin, to eat bear meat and to rub herself with bear fat. The delighted Jew said to himself: 'I shall sell him so that this man may kill him and I shall be rid of him,' while 'Ali told himself: 'He wants to kill me, and it is only God who can save me.' 'I shall give you the bear as a present,' the Jew told the merchant, who then took 'Ali and brought him to a butcher, telling the man to fetch his tools and go with him. The butcher followed with his knives, tied up 'Ali and started to sharpen a knife in order to slaughter him. When 'Ali saw the man coming towards him, he found himself free and he then started to fly through the air, not stopping until he came down in front of the Jew in his castle.

The reason for this was that when the Jew had gone home after having given 'the bear' to the merchant, in answer to a question from his daughter he had told her all that had happened. She advised him to summon a *jinni* and ask him whether this really was 'Ali al-Zaibaq or someone else who was trying to play a trick. He used a spell to conjure up a *jinni*, and when he put the question to him the *jinni* snatched up 'Ali and brought him there. 'This is 'Ali the Cairene and no one else,' the *jinni* said. 'The butcher had tied him up, sharpened his knife and was just about to cut his throat when I snatched him away and brought him to you.'

The Jew took a cup of water, recited a spell over it and then sprinkled some of it on 'Ali, saying: 'Return to your human form.' When this happened, the Jew's daughter, Qamar, saw a handsome young man and fell in love with him. 'Unfortunate young man,' she said, 'why do you try to take my robe when my father does this kind of thing to you?' 'I have undertaken to get it for Zainab the trickster, so as to marry her,' 'Ali said. 'Others have tried to trick my father out of it but have failed, so stop coveting it,' she told him, to which he replied: 'I must get it, and if your father does not accept Islam, I shall kill him.' 'See how this wretched fellow does his best to get himself killed,' her father said. 'I shall turn him into a dog.' He took an inscribed cup with water in it, recited a spell and sprinkled some of the water over 'Ali, saying: 'Take the shape of a dog,' and a dog he became.

The Jew caroused with his daughter until morning and then, after taking away the robe and the tray, he mounted the mule and recited a spell over the 'dog', which followed him with all the other dogs barking at it. He passed the shop of a second-hand dealer who got up and drove the other dogs away, after which 'Ali fell asleep in front of him. When the Jew looked round, 'Ali was not to be seen, and when the dealer closed his shop and went home, 'Ali followed him. When the man went into his house and his daughter caught sight of the dog, she covered her face and said: 'Father, are you bringing a strange man in to see me?' 'This is a dog, daughter,' her father said, but she insisted: 'This is 'Ali the Cairene, whom the Jew has bewitched.' Then she turned to the 'dog' and said: 'Are you 'Ali the Cairene?' at which it nodded its head. 'Why did the Jew put a spell on him?' her father asked, and she said: 'Because of the robe of his daughter, Qamar, but I can set him free.' 'This is the time for a good deed,' he told her, and she said: 'I shall free him if he will marry me.' The 'dog' nodded and she took a cup with writing on it, but as she was reciting a spell over it, there was a loud cry and it fell from her hand. She turned and saw that it was her father's slave girl who had cried out, and this girl now said: 'Mistress, is this the arrangement we made? I was the only one who taught you this art, and you agreed to do nothing without my advice, and also that whoever married you should marry me as well and that he should come to us on alternate nights.' Her mistress confirmed that this was so, and when her father asked her who had taught this girl magic, she said: 'It was she who taught me, but you have to ask her yourself who taught her.'

When he did this, the girl told him: 'You must know, master, that I was in service with 'Adhra the Jew, and I used to creep in while he was reciting his spells. Then, when he went off to his shop, I would open his books and read them until I had mastered the art of magic. One day, when he was drunk, he asked me to sleep with him, but I refused and told him: "That cannot be until you become a Muslim." He refused and I insisted that he take me to the sultan's market, which is where he sold me to you. When I came to your house, I taught my mistress on condition that she should do nothing without my advice and that any man who married her should marry me as well, and that we would have him on alternate nights.'

The slave girl then took the cup of water, recited a spell over it and sprinkled some of it over the 'dog', after which 'Ali regained his original human shape. The second-hand dealer greeted him and asked why he had been enchanted, at which 'Ali told him everything that had happened to him.

Night 718

Morning now dawned and Shahrazad broke off from what she had been allowed to say. Then, when it was the seven hundred and eighteenth night, SHE CONTINUED:

I have heard, O fortunate king, that the man greeted 'Ali and asked why he had been enchanted, at which 'Ali told him everything that had happened to him. The man then said: 'Will my daughter and the slave girl not be enough for you?' but 'Ali insisted: 'I must have Zainab as well.' At that moment there was a knock on the door, and when the slave girl asked who was there, a voice answered: 'Qamar, the daughter of the Jew. Is 'Ali the Cairene with you?' The dealer's daughter said: 'If he is, Jew's daughter, what do you want with him?' She then told the slave girl to open the door for her, and when Qamar came in and saw 'Ali and he saw her, he said: 'What has brought you here, daughter of a dog?' She recited the confession of faith, saying: 'I bear witness that there is no god but God and that Muhammad is the Prophet of God,' so becoming a Muslim. Then she asked: 'In Islam do women receive the bride price or do they bring a dowry to their husbands?' 'It is the men who provide the bride price,' 'Ali told her, but she went on: 'I have brought my own bride price, the robe, the rod, the chains and the head of my father, your enemy and the enemy of God,' and, with these words, she threw the head down in front of him.

The reason why she had killed him was that, when he had turned 'Ali into a dog, she saw in a dream a figure who had told her to accept Islam, which she had done. When she woke, she offered conversion to her father, who refused, and she had then drugged him with *banj* and killed him. 'Ali now took what she had brought and said to the dealer: 'We shall meet tomorrow at the caliph's court when I shall marry your daughter and the slave girl.'

'Ali then left full of happiness, but on his way to Ahmad's headquarters with what he had been given he came across a sweet seller who was clapping his hands together and exclaiming: 'There is no might and no power except with God, the Exalted, the Almighty. Hard work has become forbidden and nothing prospers except fraud. I ask you in God's Name to taste this sweet.' 'Ali ate a piece of it and was promptly drugged by the *banj* that it contained. The man took the robe, the rod and the chains and put them inside his sweetmeat box, which he then carried away together with the tray of sweets. As he went, however, a *qadi* shouted at him: 'Come here!' He stopped and put down the box, with the tray on top of it, and asked the *qadi* what he wanted. 'Sweetmeats and sugared nuts,' the *qadi* told him, but when he took some of each of these in his hand the *qadi* said: 'These are adulterated,' after which he himself brought out a sweet from his pocket and said to the man: 'See how well made this is. Taste it, and then try to make another like it.' The sweet seller took it and ate, only to be drugged by the *banj* that was in it. The *qadi* took his paraphernalia, together with the robe and the other things, put the man in a sack and carried everything back to Ahmad's headquarters.

The '*qadi*' was, in fact, Hasan Shuman and this had happened because, when 'Ali had undertaken to fetch the robe and had gone to get it, Ahmad al-Danaf and his band had heard no news of him and as a result he had told them to go and search for him. They looked for him throughout the city and it was then that Hasan Shuman, disguised as a *qadi*, met the sweet seller and recognized him as Ahmad al-Laqit. Having drugged him, he took him off to his quarters, taking the robe with him. Meanwhile, as the forty men of his band were searching the streets, 'Ali Kitf al-Jamal had caught sight of a crowd of people and had gone off to join them. He found that they were standing round the drugged 'Ali al-Zaibaq, who was lying unconscious. He revived him and told him to pull himself together, at which 'Ali, finding himself in the middle of a crowd, said: 'Where am I?' 'Ali Kitf al-Jamal and his companions told him: 'We saw you lying here drugged, but we didn't know who had done this to you.' 'It was a sweet seller who did it,' 'Ali said, 'and he has gone off with my things, but where to?' 'We haven't seen anyone,' the others told him, 'but come back home with us.'

They set off to their base and when they went in they found Ahmad al-Danaf, who greeted them before asking 'Ali the Cairene whether he had brought the robe. 'I got it,' 'Ali said, 'and the other things too, as well as the Jew's head, but I then came across a sweet seller who drugged me and took them from me.' He told Ahmad everything that had happened to him, adding: 'Were I to see that sweet seller again, I'd pay him back for this.' At that point, Hasan Shuman came out of a side room and he too asked 'Ali about the robe and was given the same answer: 'I brought it together with the Jew's head, but a sweet seller whom I met drugged me and took both it and the other things as well. I don't know where he went, but if I could find where he is I would do him an injury.' He then asked Hasan: 'Do you know where he went?' and Hasan said: 'I know where he is now.' He then opened the door of the side room and there 'Ali saw the sweet seller lying drugged. He revived him and when the man opened his eyes he found himself in the presence of 'Ali the Cairene and Ahmad al-Danaf, together with his forty followers. The man jumped up, saying: 'Where am I and who has laid hands on me?' 'I did that,' said Hasan, and 'Ali exclaimed: 'You sly fellow, is this what you get up to?' He was about to cut the man's throat when Hasan stopped him, saying: 'This is a relative of yours by marriage.' 'How is that?' 'Ali asked, and Hasan told him: 'He is Ahmad al-Laqit, the son of Zainab's sister.'

'Ali now asked Ahmad why he had drugged him, and he said: 'My grandmother, Dalila the wily, told me to do it because Zuraiq the fishmonger had met her and told her that 'Ali the Cairene was so skilled a trickster that he was certain to kill the Jew and get the robe. So she got hold of me and asked me whether I could recognize 'Ali. I said that I could as I had directed him to Ahmad al-Danaf's headquarters, and she then told me to prepare a trap for him, so that if he came with the goods I could play a trick on him and take them from him. I went round the streets until I came across a sweet seller, and for ten dinars I got his clothes, his sweets and his equipment, after which you know what happened.'

'Ali told him: 'Go to your grandmother and to Zuraiq the fishmonger and tell them that I have brought the goods, together with the Jew's head, and tell them to meet me tomorrow at the caliph's court where I shall pay over Zainab's bride price.' Ahmad al-Danaf was delighted and exclaimed: 'Your training was not wasted, 'Ali!' The next morning, 'Ali took the robe, the tray, the rod and the golden chains, with the Jew's head mounted on a spear. When he arrived at court with his mentor and his young men, they kissed the ground in front of the caliph . . .

Night 719

Morning now dawned and Shahrazad broke off from what she had been allowed to say. Then, when it was the seven hundred and nineteenth night, SHE CONTINUED:

I have heard, O fortunate king, that when 'Ali arrived at the caliph's court with his uncle, Ahmad al-Danaf, and his young men, they kissed the ground in front of the caliph, who turned to see a young man of unsurpassed bravery. In reply to the caliph's question, Ahmad told him: 'Commander of the Faithful, this is 'Ali al-Zaibaq of Cairo, leader of the young men there, and the first of my pupils.' When the caliph looked at him he felt affection for him, as the signs of courage on 'Ali's face testified in his favour rather than against him. At this point 'Ali threw down the Jew's head in front of him, saying: 'May all your enemies end like this, Commander of the Faithful.' 'Whose head is it?' the caliph asked, and 'Ali told him: 'It is the head of 'Adhra the Jew.' 'Who killed him?' the caliph asked, after which 'Ali told him the whole story from beginning to end. 'I did not think that you could kill him, as he was a sorcerer,' the caliph said, and 'Ali replied: 'It was my Lord Who enabled me to do this, Commander of the Faithful.'

The caliph now sent the *wali* to the castle, where he discovered the Jew's headless body, which he brought in a coffin to the caliph. On the caliph's orders it was burned, and it was then that Qamar arrived and kissed the ground before him. She told him who she was and that she had accepted Islam, after which she renewed her conversion in his presence and asked him to arrange her marriage to 'Ali, nominating him as her guardian. The caliph granted him 'Adhra's castle, with its contents, and allowed him to make a wish. 'I would like to stand on your carpet and eat from your table,' 'Ali told him. 'Have you any followers?' the caliph then asked, and when 'Ali told him that he had forty lads, but that they were in Cairo, the caliph said: 'Send and fetch them.' He went on to ask whether 'Ali had a base, and when he said no, Hasan Shuman said: 'I shall give him mine, Commander of the Faithful.' 'Keep it for yourself,' the caliph told him, and he ordered his treasurer to give ten thousand dinars to his architect to build 'Ali a house with four halls and forty rooms for his followers.

'Do you have any other need that I can satisfy for you?' the caliph asked, and 'Ali replied: 'King of the age, would you approach Dalila the wily on my behalf to ask her to let me marry her daughter Zainab, accepting as a bride price the robe and the other trappings of Qamar, the daughter of the Jew?' Dalila accepted the caliph's approach and took the tray, the robe, the rod and the golden chains. The marriage contract was drawn up, and this was also done for the daughter of the second-hand dealer, her slave girl and for Qamar. The caliph assigned 'Ali a salary, a free meal every morning and evening, allowances, fodder and other favours.

After a thirty-day feast, 'Ali sent a message to his followers in Cairo to tell them of the honours that the caliph had showered on him. He added: 'You must come to celebrate with me as I have married four girls.' It was not long before they had all arrived to attend the wedding feast. 'Ali lodged them in his new house and treated them with the greatest liberality, as well as presenting them to the caliph, who gave them robes of honour. Zainab's attendants displayed her to 'Ali in Qamar's robe, after which he lay with her and discovered her to be an unpierced pearl and a filly whom no one else had mounted. Later he lay with the other three girls, finding them to be perfect in all points of beauty.

As he was talking with the caliph one night, the caliph asked him to tell him the full story of his adventures from start to finish, and when he had detailed all that had happened to him with Dalila, Zainab and Zuraiq, the caliph ordered that the story be written down and stored in his treasury. A full account was written and it became one of the epics of the followers of Muhammad, the best of men. They all then remained enjoying the easiest and pleasantest of lives until they were visited by the destroyer of delights and the parter of companions. The Blessed and Exalted God knows better.

A story is also told, O fortunate king, that in the city of Shiraz there was a great king whose name was al-Saif al-A'zam Shah. He was a childless old man and so he gathered together wise men and doctors and told them: 'I am old and you know my position, the state of my kingdom and how it is governed. I am afraid of what will happen to my subjects when I am dead, as I have no son yet.' 'We shall prepare some drugs to help you, if Almighty God wills it,' they told him, and when he took what they produced and lay with his wife, she conceived with the permission of Almighty God, Who says to something: 'Be' and it is. When the months of her pregnancy had been completed, she gave birth to a boy as beautiful as the moon who was given the name Ardashir. He grew up studying science and literature until he reached the age of fifteen.

In Iraq there was a king called 'Abd al-Qadir who had a daughter as beautiful as the full moon when it rises, named Hayat al-Nufus. This girl had such a hatred of men that no one could mention them in her presence and, although sovereign kings had asked her father for her hand in marriage, when one of them approached her, she would always say: 'I shall never marry and if you force me to do that, I shall kill myself.' Prince Ardashir heard about her and told his father that he would like to marry her. The king was sympathetic when he saw that his son was in love, and every day he would promise to get Hayat al-Nufus for him as a wife. He sent his vizier off to ask her father for her hand, but the request was refused. When the vizier got back and told his master of his failure, the latter was furiously angry and exclaimed: 'Does someone in my position send a request to a king to have it refused?' He ordered a herald to proclaim that his troops were to bring out their tents and equip themselves as best they could, even if they had to borrow the money for their expenses. 'I shall not draw back,' he said, 'until I have ravaged the lands of King 'Abd al-Qadir, killed his men, removed all traces of him and plundered his wealth.'

When Ardashir came to hear of this, he rose from his bed and went to his father. After kissing the ground before him, he said: 'Great king, do not put yourself to any trouble over this . . .'

Glossary

Many of the Arabic terms used in the translation are to be found in *The Oxford English Dictionary*, including 'dinar', 'Ghazi' and 'jinn'. Of these the commonest – 'emir' and 'vizier', for instance – are not entered in italics in the text and, in general, are not glossed here. Equivalents are not given for coins or units of measure as these have varied throughout the Muslim world in accordance with time and place. The prefix 'al-' (equivalent to 'the') is discounted in the alphabetical listing; hence 'al-Mansur' is entered under 'M'. Please note that only the most significant terms and figures, or ones mentioned repeatedly, are covered here.

al-'Abbas *see* 'Abbasids.

'Abbasids the dynasty of Sunni Muslim caliphs who reigned in Baghdad, and for a while in Samarra, over the heartlands of Islam, from 750 until 1258. They took their name from al-'Abbas (d. 653), uncle of the Prophet. From the late ninth century onwards, 'Abbasid rule was nominal as the caliphs were dominated by military protectors.

'Abd Allah ibn Abi Qilaba the discoverer of the legendary city of Iram.

'Abd al-Malik ibn Marwan the fifth of the Umaiyad caliphs (r. 685–705).

'Abd al-Qadir al-Jilani (*c.*1077–1166) a Sufi writer and saint.

Abu Bakr al-Siddiq after the death of the Prophet, Abu Bakr was the first to become caliph (r. 632–4). He was famed for his austere piety.

Abu Hanifa (699–767) a theologian and jurist; founder of the Hanafi school of Sunni religious law.

Abu Hazim an eighth-century preacher and ascetic.

Abu Ja'far al-Mansur *see* al-Mansur.

Abu Muhammad al-Battal a legendary hero of popular tales, in which he plays the part of a master of wiles.

Abu Murra literally, 'the father of bitterness', meaning the devil.

Abu Nuwas Abu Nuwas al-Hasan ibn Hani (*c.*755–*c.*813), a famous, or notorious, poet of the 'Abbasid period, best known for his poems devoted to love, wine and hunting.

Abu Tammam (*c.*805–45) a poet and anthologist of the 'Abbasid period.

'Ad the race of 'Ad were a pre-Islamic tribe who rejected the prophet Hud and who consequently were punished by God for their impiety and arrogance.

'Adi ibn Zaid (d. *c.*600) a Christian poet in Hira.

Ahmad ibn Hanbal (780–855) a *hadith* scholar (student of traditions concerning the Prophet) and a legal authority; founder of the Hanbali school of Sunni religious law.

al-Ahnaf al-Ahnaf Abu Bakr ibn Qais, a *shaikh* of the tribe of Tamim. A leading general in the Arab conquests of Iran and Central Asia in the seventh century, he also had many wise sayings attributed to him.

'A'isha (d. 687) the third and favourite wife of the Prophet.

'Ali 'Ali ibn Abi Talib, cousin of the Prophet and his son-in-law by virtue of his marriage to Fatima. In 656, he became the fourth caliph and in 661 he was assassinated.

'Ali Zain al-'Abidin Zain al-'Abidin meaning 'Ornament of the Believers' (d. 712), the son of Husain and grandson of the caliph 'Ali, he was recognized as one of the Shi'i imams.

alif the first letter of the Arabic alphabet. It takes the shape of a slender vertical line.

Allahu akbar! 'God is the greatest!' A frequently used exclamation of astonishment or pleasure.

aloe aloe was imported from the Orient and the juice of its leaves was used for making a bitter purgative drug.

aloes wood the heartwood of a South-east Asian tree, it is one of the most precious woods, being chiefly prized for its pleasant scent.

al-Amin Muhammad al-Amin ibn Zubaida (d. 813), the son of Harun al-Rashid, succeeding him as caliph and reigning 809–13. He had a reputation as an indolent pleasure lover.

al-Anbari Abu Bakr ibn Muhammad al-Anbari (855–940), *hadith* scholar and philologist.

'Antar 'Antar ibn Shaddad, legendary warrior and poet of the pre-Islamic period who became the hero of a medieval heroic saga bearing his name.

ardabb a dry measure.

Ardashir the name of several pre-Islamic Sasanian kings of Persia. A great deal of early Persian wisdom literature was attributed to Ardashir I (d. 241) and there were many legends about his early years and his reign.

al-Asma'i (740–828?) an expert on the Arabic language and compiler of a famous anthology of Arabic poetry. Harun al-Rashid brought him from Basra to Baghdad in order to tutor his two sons, al-Amin and al-Ma'mun.

'Atiya *see* Jarir ibn 'Atiya.

'aun a powerful *jinni*.

Avicenna the Western version of the Arab name Ibn Sina (980–1037), a Persian physician and philosopher, the most eminent of his time, whose most famous works include *The Book of Healing* and *The Canon of Medicine*.

balila stewed maize or wheat.

ban tree Oriental willow.

banj frequently used as a generic term referring to a narcotic or knock-out drug, but sometimes the word specifically refers to henbane.

banu literally, 'sons of', a term used to identify tribes or clans, e.g. the Banu Quraish.

Barmecides *see* Harun al-Rashid, Ja'far.

Bilal an Ethiopian contemporary of the Prophet and early convert to Islam. The Prophet appointed him to be the first muezzin.

Bishr al-Hafi al-Hafi meaning 'the man who walks barefoot' (767–841), a famous Sufi.

bulbul Eastern song thrush.

Chosroe in Persian 'Khusraw', in Arabic 'Kisra' – the name of several pre-Islamic Sasanian kings of Persia, including Chosroe Anurshirwan – 'the blessed' (r. 531–79).

Dailamis Dailam is a mountainous region to the south of the Caspian Sea whose men were celebrated as warriors.

daniq a medieval Islamic coin equivalent to a sixth of a dirham.

dhikr a religious recitation, particularly a Sufi practice.

dhimmi a non-Muslim subject, usually a Christian or a Jew, living under Muslim rule.

Di'bil al-Khuza'i (765–860) a poet and philologist who lived in Iraq and who was famous for his satirical and invective poetry.

dinar a gold coin. It can also be a measure of weight.

dirham a silver coin, approximately a twentieth of a dinar.

diwan council of state, council hall or reception room.

fals plural *flus*, a low-value copper coin.

faqih a jurisprudent, an expert in Islamic law.

faqir literally, 'a poor man', the term also is used to refer to a Sufi or Muslim ascetic.

al-Fath ibn Khaqan (d. 861) the caliph al-Mutawwakil's adoptive brother, chief scribe and general.

Fatiha literally, the 'opening'; the first *sura* (chapter) of the Quran.

Fatima (d. 633) daughter of the Prophet. She married 'Ali ibn Abi Talib. The Fatimid caliphs of Egypt, whose dynasty lasted from 909 to 1171, claimed descent from her.

fidda silver, a small silver coin.

flus see fals.

ghazi a holy warrior, a slayer of infidels or participant on a raiding expedition.

ghul a cannibalistic monster. A *ghula* is a female *ghul*.

Gog and Magog evil tribes dwelling in a distant region. According to legend, Alexander the Great built a wall to keep them from invading the civilized parts of the earth, but in the Last Days they will break through that wall.

hadith a saying concerning the words or deeds of the Prophet or his companions.

Hafsa daughter of 'Umar ibn al-Khattab, she married the Prophet in 623 and died in 665.

hajj the annual pilgrimage to Mecca.

al-Hajjaj ibn Yusuf al-Thaqafi (*c*.661–714) a governor of Iraq for the Umaiyad caliph 'Abd al-Malik ibn Marwan, he was notorious for his harshness, but famous for his oratory.

al-Hakim bi-amri-'llah Fatimid caliph in Egypt (r. 996–1021), he was notorious for his eccentricities and capricious cruelty. After his murder, he became a focus of Druze devotion.

al-Hariri (1054–1122) a poet, prose writer and government official. He is chiefly famous for his prose masterpiece, the *Maqamat*, a series of sketches involving an eloquently plausible rogue.

Harun al-Rashid (766–809) the fifth of the 'Abbasid caliphs, reigning from 786. In Baghdad, he presided over an efflorescence of literature and science and his court became a magnet for poets, musicians and scholars. Until 803, the administration was largely in the hands of a Persian clan, the Barmecides, but in that year, for reasons that are mysterious, he had them purged. After his death, civil war broke out between his two sons, al-Amin and al-Ma'mun. In retrospect, Harun's caliphate came to be looked upon as a golden age and in the centuries that followed numerous stories were attached to his name.

Harut a fallen angel who, together with another fallen angel, Marut, instructed men in the occult sciences (Quran 2.102).

Hasan of Basra Hasan ibn Abi'l-Hasan of Basra (642–728), a preacher and early Sufi ascetic to whom many moralizing sayings were attributed.

Hatim of Tayy a pre-Islamic poet of the sixth century, famed for his chivalry and his generosity. Many anecdotes and proverbs have been attributed to him.

hijri **calendar** the Muslim calendar, dating from the Hijra, or year of Muhammad's emigration from Mecca to Medina, each year being designated AH – *anno Hegirae* or 'in the year of the Hijra'.

Himyar a pre-Islamic kingdom in southern Arabia.

Hind India.

Hisham ibn 'Abd al-Malik the tenth of the Umaiyad caliphs (r. 724–43).

houri a nymph of the Muslim Paradise. Also a great beauty.

Iblis the devil.

Ibn 'Abbas 'Abd Allah ibn al-'Abbas (625–86 or 688), a cousin of the Prophet and transmitter of many traditions concerning him.

Ibn Zubair 'Abd Allah ibn Zubair (624–92), a grandson of the Prophet and a leading opponent of the Umaiyads. He was besieged by the Umaiyad caliph 'Abd al-Malik in Mecca (where the Ka'ba is situated) and he was eventually killed.

Ibrahim Abu Ishaq al-Mausili (742–804) a famous musician and father of the no less famous musician Ishaq al-Mausili. Like his son, he features in a number of *Nights* stories.

Ibrahim ibn Adham (730–77) a famous Sufi ascetic.

Ibrahim ibn al-Mahdi (779–839) the son of the caliph al-Mahdi and brother of Harun al-Rashid. From 817 to 819, Ibrahim set himself up as the rival of his nephew al-Ma'mun for the caliphate. He was famous as a singer, musician and a poet and as such he features in several *Nights* tales.

'Id al-Adha the Feast of Immolation, also known as Greater Bairam, is celebrated on the 10th of Dhu'l-Hijja (the month of *hajj* or pilgrimage). During this festival those Muslims who can afford it are obliged to sacrifice sheep, cattle or camels.

'Id al-Fitr the Feast of the Fast Breaking, marking the end of Ramadan.

'Ifranja Europe; literally, 'the land of the Franks'.

'ifrit a kind of *jinni*, usually evil; an *'ifrita* is a female *jinni*.

imam the person who leads the prayers in a mosque.

Iram 'Iram, City of the Columns' is referred to in the Quran. Shaddad, king of the Arab tribe of 'Ad, intended Iram to rival Paradise, but God punished him for his pride and ruined his city.

Ishaq ibn Ibrahim al-Mausili (757–850) was the most famous composer and musical performer in the time of Harun al-Rashid. Like his father, Ibrahim al-Mausili, he features in a number of *Nights* stories.

Ja'far the Barmecide a member of a great Iranian clan which served the 'Abbasid caliphs as viziers and other functionaries. In the stories, he features as Harun's vizier, though in reality it was his father, Yahya, who held this post. For reasons that are mysterious, Ja'far and other members of his clan were executed in 803.

Jamil Buthaina Jamil ibn Ma'mar al-'Udhri (d. 701), a Hijazi poet who specialized in eleginc love poetry, famous for his chastely unhappy passion for Buthaina.

Jarir ibn 'Atiya (d. 729) a leading poet of the Umaiyad period, famous for his panegyric and invective verse.

Jawarna Zara, a port on the east coast of the Adriatic.

jinni a (male) spirit in Muslim folklore and theology; *jinniya* is a female spirit.

Jinn (the collective term) assumed various forms: some were servants of Satan, while others were good Muslims and therefore benign.

Joseph features in the Quran as well as the Bible. In the Quran, he is celebrated for his beauty.

jubba a long outer garment, open at the front, with wide sleeves.

Ka'b al-Ahbar (d. *c*.653) a Jew who converted to Islam and a leading transmitter of religious traditions and an expert on biblical lore.

Ka'ba the cube-shaped holy building in Mecca to which Muslims turn when they pray.

kaffryeh a headdress of cloth folded and held by a cord around the head.

khalanj wood tree health (*Erica arborea*), a hard kind of wood.

Khalid ibn Safwan (d. 752) a transmitter of traditions, poems and speeches, famous for his eloquence.

khan an inn, caravanserai or market.

al-Khidr 'the Green Man', features in the Quran as a mysterious guide to Moses as well as appearing in many legends and stories. In some tales, this immortal servant of God is guardian of the Spring of Life, which gives eternal life to those who drink from it.

Khurasan in the medieval period, this designated a large territory that included eastern Persia and Afghanistan.

Kuthayir (660–723) a Hijazi poet who specialized in the theme of unfulfilled love, since the object of his passion, 'Azza, was married to another man.

Luqman a pre-Islamic sage and hero famed for his longevity. Many fables and proverbs were attributed to him.

Magian a Zoroastrian, a fire worshipper. In the *Nights*, the Magians invariably feature as sinister figures.

al-Mahdi (b. *c*.743) the 'Abbasid caliph who reigned from 775 to 785.

mahmal the richly decorated empty litter sent by a Muslim ruler to Mecca during the *hajj* (pilgrimage).

maidan an exercise yard or parade ground; an open space near or in a town.

maisir a pre-Islamic game of chance involving arrows and in which the stakes were designated parts of slaughtered camels.

Majnun Qais ibn Mulawwah al-Majnun ('the mad'), a (probably) legendary Arabian poet of the seventh century, famous for his doomed love for Laila. After she was married to another man, Majnun retired into the wilderness to live among wild beasts.

Malik the angel who is the guardian of hell.

Malik ibn Dinar an eighth-century Basran preacher and moralist.

mamluk slave soldier. Most mamluks were of Turkish origin.

al-Ma'mun (786–833) son of Harun al-Rashid and the 'Abbasid caliph from 813 until his death. He was famous for his patronage of learning and his sponsorship of the translation of Greek and Syriac texts into Arabic.

Ma'n ibn Za'ida (d. 769) a soldier, administrator and patron of poets under the late Umaiyads and early 'Abbasids.

mann a measure of weight.

al-Mansur (r. 754–75) 'Abbasid caliph.

marid a type of *jinni*.

Maslama ibn 'Abd al-Malik (d. 738) son of the Umaiyad caliph 'Abd al-Malik ibn Marwan and a leading general who headed a series of campaigns against the Byzantines.

Masrur the eunuch who was sword-bearer and executioner to Harun al-Rashid.

al-Mausili *see* Ibrahim Abu Ishaq al-Mausili *and* Ishaq ibn Ibrahim al-Mausili.

mithqal a measure of weight.

months of the Muslim year from the first to the twelfth month, these are: (1) al-Muharram, (2) Safar, (3) Rabi' al-awwal, (4) Rabi' al-akhir, (5) Jumada al-ula, (6) Jumada al-akhira, (7) Rajab, (8) Sha'ban, (9) Ramadan, (10) Shawwal, (11) Dhu'l-Qa'da, (12) Dhu'l-Hijja.

Mu'awiya Mu'awiya ibn Abi Sufyan, first of the Umaiyad caliphs (r. 661–80). He came to power after the assassination of 'Ali.

al-Mubarrad Abu al-'Abbas al-Mubarrad (c.815–98), a famous Basran grammarian and philologist.

muezzin the man who gives the call to prayer, usually from the minaret or roof of the mosque.

muhtasib market inspector with duties to enforce trading standards and public morals.

Munkar and Nakir two angels who examine the dead in their tombs and, if necessary, punish them.

al-Muntasir 'Abbasid caliph (r. 861–2).

al-Musta'in 'Abbasid caliph (r. 862–6).

al-Mustansir bi'llah 'Abbasid caliph (r. 1226–42).

al-Mutalammis sixth-century pre-Islamic poet and sage.

al-Mu'tatid bi'llah 'Abbasid caliph (r. 892–902).

al-Mutawakkil (822–61) 'Abbasid caliph, and great cultural patron, who reigned from 847 until he was assassinated by murderers probably hired by his son, who became the caliph al-Muntasir.

muwashshahat strophic poetry, usually recited to a musical accompaniment. This form of verse originated in Spain, but spread throughout the Islamic world.

nadd a type of incense consisting of a mixture of aloes wood with ambergris, musk and frankincense.

Nakir *see* Munkar and Nakir.

naqib an official whose duties varied according to time and place. The term was often used to refer to the chief representative of the *ashraf*, i.e. the descendants of 'Ali.

Al-Nu'man ibn al-Mundhir a fifth-century Arab ruler of the pre-Islamic Christian kingdom of Hira in Iraq.

nusf literally, 'a half'; a small coin.

parasang an old Persian measure of length, somewhere between three and four miles.

qadi a Muslim judge.

Qaf Mount Qaf was a legendary mountain located at the end of the world, or in some versions one that encircles the earth.

qintar a measure of weight, variable from region to region, equivalent to 100 *ratls*.

qirat a dry measure, but the term could also be used of a certain weight; also a coin, equivalent to a twenty-fourth of a dinar.

Quraish the dominant Arab clan in Mecca at the time of the Prophet.

rafidi literally, 'a refuser', a term applied to members of various Shi'i sects.

rak'a in the Muslim prayer ritual, a bowing of the body followed by two prostrations.

Ramadan the ninth month of the Muslim year, in which fasting is observed from sunrise to sunset. *See also* months of the Muslim year.

ratl a measure of weight, varying from region to region.

Ridwan the angel who is the guardian of the gates of Paradise.

Rudaini spear *see* Samhari spear.

rukh a legendary bird of enormous size, strong enough to carry an elephant (in English 'roc').

Rum/Ruman theoretically designates Constantinople and the Byzantine lands more generally, but in some stories the name is merely intended to designate a strange and usually Christian foreign land.

Rumi of Byzantine Greek origin.

Safar *see* months of the Muslim year.

Said ibn Jubair a pious Muslim and Quran reader of the Umaiyad period.

Sakhr an evil *jinni* whose story is related by commentators on the Quran.

Saladin (1138–93), Muslim political and military leader, famed for his chivalry and piety and for opposing the Crusaders. He took over Egypt and abolished the Fatimid caliphate in 1171; in 1174 he also became sultan of most of Syria. In 1187 he invaded the kingdom of Jerusalem, occupying the city and many other places. Thereafter he had to defend his gains from the armies of the Third Crusade.

salam meaning 'peace', the final word at the end of a prayer, similar to the Christian 'amen'.

Samhari spear opinions varied as to whether Samhar was the name of a manufacturer of spears, or whether it was the place where they used to be made. A 'Samhari spear' was a common metaphor for slenderness; likewise 'Rudaini spear', said to be related to Rudaina, the supposed wife of Samhar.

Sasanian the Sasanians were the Persian dynasty who ruled in Persia and Iraq from 224 until 637, when Muslim armies overran their empire.

Serendib the old Arab name for Ceylon or Sri Lanka.

Sha'ban *see* months of the Muslim year.

Shaddad ibn 'Ad legendary king of the tribe of 'Ad who attempted to build the city of Iram as a rival to Paradise and was punished by God for his presumption.

al-Shafi'i Muhammad ibn Idris al-Shafi'i (767–820), jurist and founder of the Shafi'i school of Sunni religious law, whose adherents are know as Shafi'ites.

shaikh a tribal leader, the term also commonly used to refer to an old man or a master of one of the traditional religious sciences or a leader of a dervish order. Similarly, a *shaikha* is an old woman or a woman in authority.

Shaikhs of the Fire Zoroastrian priests or elders.

shari'a shari'a law is the body of Islamic religious law.

sharif meaning 'noble', often used with specific reference to a descendant of the Prophet.

Shi'i an adherent of that branch of Islam that recognizes 'Ali and his descendants as the leaders of the Muslim community after the Prophet.

Sufi a Muslim mystic or ascetic.

Sufyan al-Thauri (716–78) born in Kufa, theologian, ascetic and transmitter of *hadiths* (sayings of the Prophet). He wrote on law and was a leading spokesman of strict Sunnism.

sunna the corpus of practices and teachings of the Prophet as collected and transmitted by later generations of Muslims, the *sunna* served as the guide to the practice of the Sunni Muslims and as one of the pillars of their religious law, supplementing the prescriptions of the Quran.

sura a chapter of the Quran.

sycamore a type of fig; also known as the Egyptian fig.

taghut a term designating pagan idols or idolatry. By extension, the word was used to refer to soothsayers, sorcerers and infidels.

tailasan a shawl-like garment worn over head and shoulders. It was commonly worn by judges and religious high functionaries.

Thamud an impious tribe in pre-Islamic Arabia whom Allah destroyed when they refused to pay heed to his prophet Salih.

'Udhri love this refers to the Banu 'Udhra. Several famous 'Udhri poets were supposed to have died from unconsummated love.

Umaiyads a dynasty of Sunni Muslim caliphs who ruled the Islamic lands from 661 until 750. The Umaiyads descended from the powerful Meccan tribe of the Quraish. In 750, they were overthrown by a revolution in favour of the 'Abbasids. One member of the family succeeded in escaping to Spain, where he set up an Umaiyad empire.

'Umar 'Umar ibn 'Abd al-'Aziz, eighth Umaiyad caliph (r. 717–20), famed for his piety.

'Umar ibn al-Khattab (581–644) the second of the caliphs to succeed the Prophet (r. 634–44).

'umra the minor pilgrimage to Mecca, which, unlike the *hajj*, can be performed at any time of the year.

al-'Utbi (d. 1022) famous author of prose and poetry, worked in the service of the Ghaznavid court. (The Ghaznavids were a Turkish dynasty who ruled in Afghanistan, Khurasan and north-western India from the late tenth till the late twelfth century.)

waiba a dry measure.

wali a local governor.

witr a prayer, performed between the evening and the dawn prayers, which is recommended but not compulsory.

Yahya ibn Khalid the Barmecide a Persian who was a senior government official under the 'Abbasid caliphs al-Mansur and Harun. He was disgraced and executed in 805 for reasons that remain mysterious.

Zaid ibn Aslam a freed slave of 'Umar ibn al-Khattab.

Ziyad ibn Abihi ibn Abihi meaning 'Son of his Father' – the identity of his father being unknown – (d. 676), governor of Iraq under Mu'awiya.

Zubaida (762–831) the granddaughter of the 'Abbasid caliph al-Mansur and famous for her wealth. She became chief wife of the caliph Harun al-Rashid and was mother to al-Amin and al-Ma'mun, both later caliphs.

al-Zuhri Muhammad ibn Muslim al-Zuhri (d. 742), the transmitter of traditions concerning the Prophet and legal authority. He frequented the Umaiyad courts, where, among other things, he was a tutor.

Maps

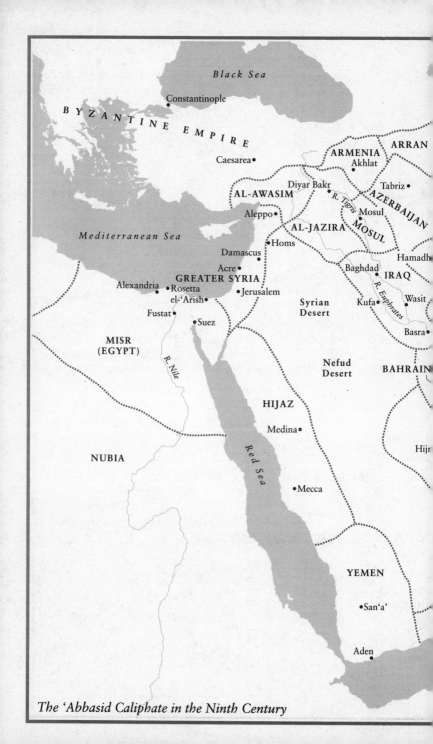

The 'Abbasid Caliphate in the Ninth Century

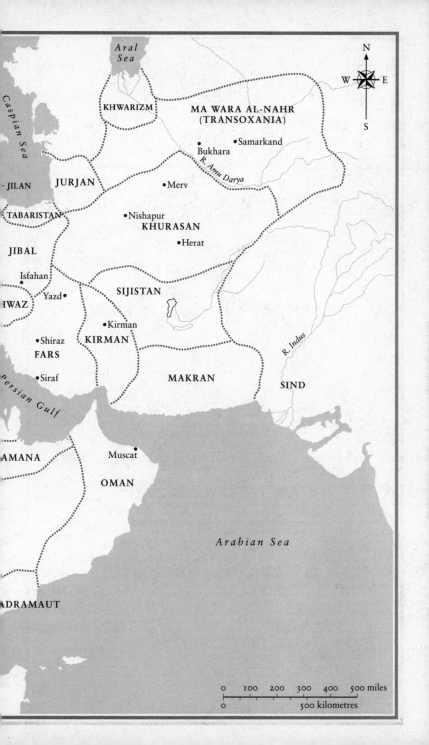

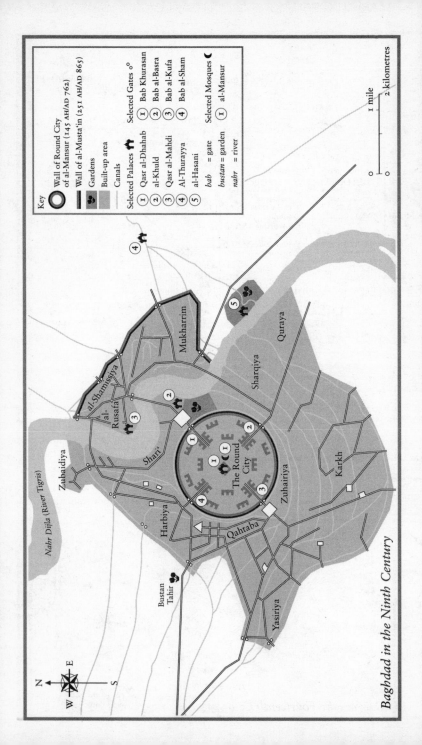

Key

⊙ Wall of Round City of al-Mansur (145 AH/AD 762)

▮ Wall of al-Musta'in (251 AH/AD 865)
🌳 Gardens
▨ Built-up area
— Canals

Selected Palaces 🛕
① Qasr al-Dhahab
② al-Khuld
③ Qasr al-Mahdi
④ Al-Thurayya
⑤ al-Hasani

bab = gate
bustan = garden
nahr = river

Selected Gates ○°
① Bab Khurasan
② Bab al-Basra
③ Bab al-Kufa
④ Bab al-Sham

Selected Mosques ☾
① al-Mansur

Baghdad in the Ninth Century

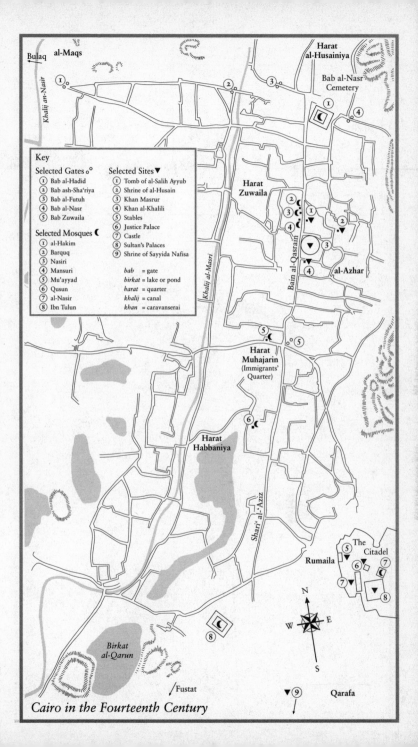

Cairo in the Fourteenth Century

Index of Nights and Stories

Bold *numbers indicate the Night, or series of Nights, over which a story is told.*
Stories told within a story are presented in brackets.

Volume One

Volume Two